CRIME NOVELS

AMERICAN NOIR
OF THE 1950S

CRIME NOVELS

AMERICAN NOIR
OF THE 1950s

The Killer Inside Me
Jim Thompson

The Talented Mr. Ripley
Patricia Highsmith

Pick-Up
Charles Willeford

Down There
David Goodis

The Real Cool Killers
Chester Himes

Robert Polito, *editor*

THE LIBRARY OF AMERICA

The Killer Inside Me copyright 1952 by Jim Thompson. *The Talented
Mr. Ripley* copyright 1955 by Patricia Highsmith. Reprinted by
permission of Alfred A. Knopf, a division of Random House, Inc.
Pick-Up copyright 1967 by Softcover Library, Inc. Reprinted by
permission of the Estate of Charles Willeford. *Down There* copyright
1956 by Fawcett Publications, Inc. Reprinted by permission of the
Estate of David Goodis and Scott Meredith Literary Agency, L.P.
The Real Cool Killers copyright 1959 by Chester Himes. Reprinted by
permission of The Roslyn Targ Literary Agency.

This paper meets the requirements of
ANSI/NISO Z39.48-1992 (Permanence of Paper).

Distributed to the trade in the United States
by Penguin Random House Inc.
and in Canada by Penguin Random House Canada Ltd.

Library of Congress Catalog Number: 97–2487
For cataloging information, see end of Notes.
ISBN 978–1–883011–49–9
ISBN 1–883011–49–3

———

Sixth Printing
The Library of America—95

Manufactured in the United States of America

Contents

THE KILLER INSIDE ME

by Jim Thompson

One

I'D FINISHED my pie and was having a second cup of coffee when I saw him. The midnight freight had come in a few minutes before; and he was peering in one end of the restaurant window, the end nearest the depot, shading his eyes with his hand and blinking against the light. He saw me watching him, and his face faded back into the shadows. But I knew he was still there. I knew he was waiting. The bums always size me up for an easy mark.

I lit a cigar and slid off my stool. The waitress, a new girl from Dallas, watched as I buttoned my coat. "Why, you don't even carry a gun!" she said, as though she was giving me a piece of news.

"No," I smiled. "No gun, no blackjack, nothing like that. Why should I?"

"But you're a cop—a deputy sheriff, I mean. What if some crook should try to shoot you?"

"We don't have many crooks here in Central City, ma'am," I said. "Anyway, people are people, even when they're a little misguided. You don't hurt them, they won't hurt you. They'll listen to reason."

She shook her head, wide-eyed with awe, and I strolled up to the front. The proprietor shoved back my money and laid a couple of cigars on top of it. He thanked me again for taking his son in hand.

"He's a different boy now, Lou," he said, kind of running his words together like foreigners do. "Stays in nights; gets along fine in school. And always he talks about you—what a good man is Deputy Lou Ford."

"I didn't do anything," I said. "Just talked to him. Showed a little interest. Anyone else could have done as much."

"Only you," he said. "Because you are good, you make others so." He was all ready to sign off with that, but I wasn't. I leaned an elbow on the counter, crossed one foot behind the other and took a long slow drag on my cigar. I liked the guy—as much as I like most people, anyway—but he was too good to let go. Polite, intelligent: guys like that are my meat.

"Well, I tell you," I drawled. "I tell you the way I feel,

3

Max. A man doesn't get any more out of life than what he puts into it."

"Umm," he said, fidgeting. "I guess you're right, Lou."

"I was thinking the other day, Max; and all of a sudden I had the doggonedest thought. It came to me out of a clear sky—the boy is father to the man. Just like that. The boy is father to the man."

The smile on his face was getting strained. I could hear his shoes creak as he squirmed. If there's anything worse than a bore, it's a corny bore. But how can you brush off a nice friendly fellow who'd give you his shirt if you asked for it?

"I reckon I should have been a college professor or something like that," I said. "Even when I'm asleep I'm working out problems. Take that heat wave we had a few weeks ago; a lot of people think it's the heat that makes it so hot. But it's not like that, Max. It's not the heat, but the humidity. I'll bet you didn't know that, did you?"

He cleared his throat and muttered something about being wanted in the kitchen. I pretended like I didn't hear him.

"Another thing about the weather," I said. "Everyone talks about it, but no one does anything. But maybe it's better that way. Every cloud has its silver lining, at least that's the way I figure it. I mean, if we didn't have the rain we wouldn't have the rainbows, now would we?"

"Lou . . ."

"Well," I said, "I guess I'd better shove off. I've got quite a bit of getting around to do, and I don't want to rush. Haste makes waste, in my opinion. I like to look before I leap."

That was dragging 'em in by the feet, but I couldn't hold 'em back. Striking at people that way is almost as good as the other, the real way. The way I'd fought to forget—and had almost forgot—until I met her.

I was thinking about her as I stepped out into the cool West Texas night and saw the bum waiting for me.

Two

CENTRAL CITY was founded in 1870, but it never became a city in size until about ten-twelve years ago. It was shipping point for a lot of cattle and a little cotton; and Chester Conway, who was born here, made it headquarters for the Conway Construction Company. But it still wasn't much more than a wide place in a Texas road. Then, the oil boom came, and almost overnight the population jumped to 48,000.

Well, the town had been laid out in a little valley amongst a lot of hills. There just wasn't any room for the newcomers, so they spread out every whichway with their homes and businesses, and now they were scattered across a third of the county. It's not an unusual situation in the oil-boom country—you'll see a lot of cities like ours if you're ever out this way. They don't have any regular city police force, just a constable or two. The sheriff's office handles the policing for both city and county.

We do a pretty good job of it, to our own way of thinking at least. But now and then things get a little out of hand, and we put on a clean-up. It was during a clean-up three months ago that I ran into her.

"Name of Joyce Lakeland," old Bob Maples, the sheriff, told me. "Lives four-five miles out on Derrick Road, just past the old Branch farm house. Got her a nice little cottage up there behind a stand of blackjack trees."

"I think I know the place," I said. "Hustlin' lady, Bob?"

"We-el, I reckon so but she's bein' mighty decent about it. She ain't running it into the ground, and she ain't takin' on no roustabouts or sheepherders. If some of these preachers around town wasn't rompin' on me, I wouldn't bother her a-tall."

I wondered if he was getting some of it, and decided that he wasn't. He wasn't maybe any mental genius, but Bob Maples was straight. "So how shall I handle this Joyce Lakeland?" I said. "Tell her to lay off a while, or to move on?"

"We-el"—he scratched his head, scowling—"I dunno, Lou. Just—well, just go out and size her up, and make your own decision. I know you'll be gentle, as gentle and pleasant as you can be. An' I know you can be firm if you have to. So go on out, an' see how she looks to you. I'll back you up in whatever you want to do."

It was about ten o'clock in the morning when I got there. I pulled the car up into the yard, curving it around so I could swing out easy. The county license plates didn't show, but that wasn't deliberate. It was just the way it had to be.

I eased up on the porch, knocked on the door and stood back, taking off my Stetson.

I was feeling a little uncomfortable. I hardly knew what I was going to say to her. Because maybe we're kind of old-fashioned, but our standards of conduct aren't the same, say, as they are in the east or middle-west. Out here you say yes ma'am and no ma'am to anything with skirts on; anything white, that is. Out here, if you catch a man with his pants down, you apologize . . . even if you have to arrest him af-terwards. Out here you're a man, a man and a gentleman, or you aren't anything. And God help you if you're not.

The door opened an inch or two. Then, it opened all the way and she stood looking at me.

"Yes?" she said coldly.

She was wearing sleeping shorts and a wool pullover; her brown hair was as tousled as a lamb's tail, and her unpainted face was drawn with sleep. But none of that mattered. It wouldn't have mattered if she'd crawled out of a hog-wallow wearing a gunny sack. She had that much.

She yawned openly and said "Yes?" again, but I still couldn't speak. I guess I was staring open-mouthed like a country boy. This was three months ago, remember, and I hadn't had the sickness in almost fifteen years. Not since I was fourteen.

She wasn't much over five feet and a hundred pounds, and she looked a little scrawny around the neck and ankles. But that was all right. It was perfectly all right. The good Lord had known just where to put that flesh where it would *really* do some good.

"Oh, my goodness!" She laughed suddenly. "Come on in. I don't make a practice of it this early in the morning, but . . ." She held the screen open and gestured. I went in and she closed it and locked the door again.

"I'm sorry, ma'am," I said, "but—"

"It's all right. But I'll have to have some coffee first. You go on back."

I went down the little hall to the bedroom, listening uneasily as I heard her drawing water for the coffee. I'd acted like a chump. It was going to be hard to be firm with her after a start like this, and something told me I should be. I didn't know why; I still don't. But I knew it right from the beginning. Here was a little lady who got what she wanted, and to hell with the price tag.

Well, hell, though; it was just a feeling. She'd acted all right, and she had a nice quiet little place here. I decided I'd let her ride, for the time being anyhow. Why not? And then I happened to glance into the dresser mirror and I knew why not. I knew I couldn't. The top dresser drawer was open a little, and the mirror was tilted slightly. And hustling ladies are one thing, and hustling ladies with guns are something else.

I took it out of the drawer, a .32 automatic, just as she came in with the coffee tray. Her eyes flashed and she slammed the tray down on a table. "What," she snapped, "are you doing with that?"

I opened my coat and showed her my badge. "Sheriff's office, ma'am. What are *you* doing with it?"

She didn't say anything. She just took her purse off the dresser, opened it and pulled out a permit. It had been issued in Fort Worth, but it was all legal enough. Those things are usually honored from one town to another.

"Satisfied, copper?" she said.

"I reckon it's all right, miss," I said. "And my name's Ford, not copper." I gave her a big smile, but I didn't get any back. My hunch about her had been dead right. A minute before she'd been all set to lay, and it probably wouldn't have made any difference if I hadn't had a dime. Now she was set for something else, and whether I was a cop or Christ didn't make any difference either.

I wondered how she'd lived so long.

"Jesus!" she jeered. "The nicest looking guy I ever saw and you turn out to be a lousy snooping copper. How much? I don't jazz cops."

I felt my face turning red. "Lady," I said, "that's not very polite. I just came out for a little talk."

"You dumb bastard," she yelled. "I asked you what you wanted."

"Since you put it that way," I said, "I'll tell you. I want you out of Central City by sundown. If I catch you here after that I'll run you in for prostitution."

I slammed on my hat and started for the door. She got in front of me, blocking my way.

"You lousy son-of-a-bitch. You—"

"Don't you call me that," I said. "Don't do it, ma'am."

"I did call you that! And I'll do it again! You're a son-of-a-bitch, bastard, pimp . . ."

I tried to push past her. I had to get out of there. I knew what was going to happen if I didn't get out, and I knew I couldn't let it happen. I might kill her. It might bring *the sickness* back. And even if I didn't and it didn't, I'd be washed up. She'd talk. She'd yell her head off. And people would start thinking, thinking and wondering about that time fifteen years ago.

She slapped me so hard that my ears rang, first on one side then the other. She swung and kept swinging. My hat flew off. I stooped to pick it up, and she slammed her knee under my chin.

I stumbled backward on my heels and sat down on the floor. I heard a mean laugh, then another laugh sort of apologetic. She said, "Gosh, sheriff, I didn't mean to—I—you made me so mad I—I—"

"Sure," I grinned. My vision was clearing and I found my voice again. "Sure, ma'am, I know how it was. Used to get that way myself. Give me a hand, will you?"

"You-you won't hurt me?"

"Me? Aw, now, ma'am."

"No," she said, and she sounded almost disappointed. "I know you won't. Anyone can see you're too easy-going." And she came over to me slowly and gave me her hands.

I pulled myself up. I held her wrists with one hand and swung. It almost stunned her; I didn't want her completely stunned. I wanted her so she would understand what was happening to her.

"No, baby"—my lips drew back from my teeth. "I'm not going to hurt you. I wouldn't think of hurting you. I'm just going to beat the ass plumb off of you."

I said it, and I meant it and I damned near did.

I jerked the jersey up over her face and tied the end in a knot. I threw her down on the bed, yanked off her sleeping shorts and tied her feet together with them.

I took off my belt and raised it over my head . . .

I don't know how long it was before I stopped, before I came to my senses. All I know is that my arm ached like hell and her rear end was one big bruise, and I was scared crazy— as scared as a man can get and go on living.

I freed her feet and hands, and pulled the jersey off her head. I soaked a towel in cold water and bathed her with it. I poured coffee between her lips. And all the time I was talking, begging her to forgive me, telling her how sorry I was.

I got down on my knees by the bed, and begged and apologized. At last her eyelids fluttered and opened.

"D-don't," she whispered.

"I won't," I said. "Honest to God, ma'am, I won't ever—"

"Don't talk." She brushed her lips against mine. "Don't say you're sorry."

She kissed me again. She began fumbling at my tie, my shirt; starting to undress me after I'd almost skinned her alive.

I went back the next day and the day after that. I kept going back. And it was like a wind had been turned on a dying fire. I began needling people in that dead-pan way—needling 'em as a substitute for something else. I began thinking about settling scores with Chester Conway, of the Conway Construction Company.

I won't say that I hadn't thought of it before. Maybe I'd stayed on in Central City all these years, just in the hopes of getting even. But except for her I don't think I'd ever have done anything. She'd made the old fire burn again. She even showed me how to square with Conway.

She didn't know she was doing it, but she gave me the answer. It was one day, one night rather, about six weeks after we'd met.

"Lou," she said, "I don't want to go on like this. Let's pull out of this crummy town together, just you and I."

"Why, you're crazy!" I said. I said it before I could stop myself. "You think I'd—I'd—"

"Go on, Lou. Let me hear you say it. Tell me"—she began to drawl—"what a fine ol' family you-all Fords is. Tell me, we-all Fords, ma'am, we wouldn't think of livin' with one of you mizzable ol' whores, ma'am. Us Fords just ain't built that way, ma'am."

That was part of it, a big part. But it wasn't the main thing. I knew she was making me worse; I knew that if I didn't stop soon I'd never be able to. I'd wind up in a cage or the electric chair.

"Say it, Lou. Say it and I'll say something."

"Don't threaten me, baby," I said. "I don't like threats."

"I'm not threatening you. I'm telling you. You think you're too good for me—I'll—I'll—"

"Go on. It's your turn to do the saying."

"I wouldn't want to, Lou, honey, but I'm not going to give you up. Never, never, never. If you're too good for me now, then I'll make it so you won't be."

I kissed her, a long hard kiss. Because baby didn't know it, but baby was dead, and in a way I couldn't have loved her more.

"Well, now, baby," I said, "you've got your bowels in an uproar and all over nothing. I was thinking about the money problem."

"I've got some money. I can get some more. A lot of it."

"Yeah?"

"I can, Lou. I know I can! He's crazy about me and he's dumb as hell. I'll bet if his old man thought I was going to marry him, he—"

"Who?" I said. "Who are you talking about, Joyce?"

"Elmer Conway. You know who he is, don't you? Old Chester—"

"Yeah," I said. "Yeah, I know the Conways right well. How do you figure on hookin' 'em?"

We talked it over, lying there on her bed together, and off in the night somewhere a voice seemed to whisper to forget it, *forget it, Lou, it's not too late if you stop now.* And I did try, God knows I tried. But right after that, right after the voice, her hand gripped one of mine and kneaded it into her breasts; and she moaned and shivered . . . and so I didn't forget.

"Well," I said, after a time, "I guess we can work it out. The way I see it is, if at first you don't succeed, try, try again."

"Mmm, darling?"

"In other words," I said, "where there's a will there's a way."

She squirmed a little, and then she snickered. "Oh, Lou, you corny so and so! You slay me!"

. . . The street was dark. I was standing a few doors above the cafe, and the bum was standing and looking at me. He was a young fellow, about my age, and he was wearing what must have been a pretty good suit of clothes at one time.

"Well, how about it, bud?" he was saying. "How about it, huh? I've been on a hell of a binge, and by God if I don't get some food pretty soon—"

"Something to warm you up, eh?" I said.

"Yeah, anything at all you can help me with, I'll . . ."

I took the cigar out of my mouth with one hand and made like I was reaching into my pocket with the other. Then, I grabbed his wrist and ground the cigar butt into his palm.

"Jesus, bud!"—He cursed and jerked away from me. "What the hell you tryin' to do?"

I laughed and let him see my badge. "Beat it," I said.

"Sure, bud, sure," he said, and he began backing away. He didn't sound particularly scared or angry; more interested than anything. "But you better watch that stuff, bud. You sure better watch it."

He turned and walked off toward the railroad tracks.

I watched him, feeling sort of sick and shaky; and then I got in my car and headed for the labor temple.

Three

THE Central City Labor Temple was on a side street a couple of blocks off of the courthouse square. It wasn't much of a building, an old two-story brick with the downstairs rented out to a pool hall and the union offices and meeting hall on the second floor. I climbed the stairs, and went down the dark corridor to the end where a door opened into several of the best and largest offices in the place. The sign on the glass read

CENTRAL CITY, TEXAS
Building Trades Council
Joseph Rothman, Pres.

and Rothman opened the door before I could turn the knob.

"Let's go back here in the rear," he said, shaking hands. "Sorry to ask you to come around so late, but you being a public official and all I thought it might be best."

"Yeah," I nodded, wishing I could have ducked seeing him entirely. The law is pretty much on one side of the fence out here; and I already knew what he wanted to talk about.

He was a man of about forty, short and stocky, with sharp black eyes and a head that seemed too big for his body. He had a cigar in his mouth, but he laid it down after he sat down at his desk, and began rolling a cigarette. He lit it and blew smoke over the match, his eyes shying away from mine.

"Lou," the labor leader said, and hesitated. "I've got something to tell you—in the strictest confidence, you understand—but I'd like you to tell me something first. It's probably a pretty touchy subject with you, but . . . well, how did you feel about Mike Dean, Lou?"

"Feel? I'm not sure I know what you mean, Joe," I said.

"He was your foster brother, right? Your father adopted him?"

"Yes. Dad was a doctor, you know—"

"And a very good one, I understand. Excuse me, Lou. Go on."

So that's the way it was going to be. Spar and counter-spar. Each of us feeling the other out, each of us telling things he knows damn well the other fellow has heard a thousand times. Rothman had something important to tell me, and it looked as though he was going to do it the hard—and careful—way. Well, I didn't mind; I'd play along with him.

"He and the Deans were old friends. When they got wiped out in that big flu epidemic, he adopted Mike. My mother was dead—had been dead since I was a baby. Dad figured Mike and me would be company for each other, and the housekeeper could take care of two of us as easily as one."

"Uh-huh. And how did that strike you, Lou? I mean, you're the only son and heir and your dad brings in another son. Didn't that rub you a little the wrong way?"

I laughed. "Hell, Joe, I was four years old at the time, and Mike was six. You're not much concerned with money at that age, and, anyway, Dad never had any. He was too soft-hearted to dun his patients."

"You liked Mike, then?" He sounded like he wasn't quite convinced.

"Like isn't the word for it," I said. "He was the finest, swellest guy that ever lived. I couldn't have loved a real brother more."

"Even after he did what he did?"

"And just what," I drawled, "would that be?"

Rothman raised his eyebrows. "I liked Mike myself, Lou, but facts are facts. The whole town knows that if he'd been a little older he'd have gone to the chair instead of reform school."

"No one *knows* anything. There was never any proof."

"The girl identified him."

"A girl less than three years old! She'd have identified anyone they showed her."

"And Mike admitted it. And they dug up some other cases."

"Mike was scared. He didn't know what he was saying."

Rothman shook his head. "Let it go, Lou. I'm not really interested in that as such; only in your feelings about Mike . . . Weren't you pretty embarrassed when he came back to Central City? Wouldn't you have rather he'd stayed away?"

"No," I said. "Dad and I knew Mike hadn't done it. I mean"—I hesitated—"knowing Mike, we were sure he couldn't be guilty." *Because I was. Mike had taken the blame for me.* "I wanted Mike to come back. So did Dad." *He wanted him here to watch over me.* "My God, Joe, Dad pulled strings for months to get Mike his job as city building inspector. It wasn't easy to do, the way people felt about Mike, as popular and influential as Dad was."

"That all checks," Rothman nodded. "That's my understanding of things. But I have to be sure. You weren't sort of relieved when Mike got killed?"

"The shock killed Dad. He never recovered from it. As for me, well all I can say is that I wish it had been me instead of Mike."

Rothman grinned. "Okay, Lou. Now it's my turn . . . Mike was killed six years ago. He was walking a girder on the eighth floor of the New Texas Apartments, a Conway Construction job, when he apparently stepped on a loose rivet. He threw himself backward so he'd fall inside the building, onto the decking. But the floors hadn't been decked in properly; there were just a few planks scattered here and there. Mike fell all the way through to the basement."

I nodded. "So," I said. "What about it, Joe?"

"What about it!" Rothman's eyes flashed. "You ask me what about it when—"

"As President of the building unions, you know that the Ironworkers are under your jurisdiction, Joe. It's their obligation, and yours, to see that each floor is decked in as a building goes up."

"Now you're talking like a lawyer!" Rothman slapped his desk. "The Ironworkers are weak out here. Conway wouldn't put in the decking, and we couldn't make him."

"You could have struck the job."

"Oh, well," Rothman shrugged. "I guess I made a mistake, Lou. I understood you to say that you—"

"You heard me right," I said. "And let's not kid each other. Conway cut corners to make money. You let him—to make money. I'm not saying you're at fault, but I don't reckon he was either. It was just one of those things."

"Well," Rothman hesitated, "that's a kind of funny attitude for you to take, Lou. It seems to me you're pretty impersonal about it. But since that's the way you feel, perhaps I'd better—"

"Perhaps *I'd* better," I said. "Let me do the talking and then you won't have to feel funny about it. There was a riveter up there with Mike at the time he took his dive. Working after hours. Working by himself. But it takes two men to rivet— one to run the gun and one on the bucking iron. You're going to tell me that he didn't have any rightful business there, but I think you're wrong. He didn't have to be riveting. He could have been gathering up tools or something like that."

"But you don't know the whole story, Lou! This man—"

"I know. The guy was an iron tramp, working on a permit. He blew into town without a dime. Three days after Mike's death he left in a new Chevvy which he paid cash on the line for. That looks bad, but it doesn't really need to mean anything. He might have won the dough in a crap game or—"

"But you still don't know it all, Lou! Conway—"

"Let's see if I don't," I said. "Conway's company was the architect on that job as well as the contractor. And he hadn't allowed enough space for the boilers. To get 'em in, he was going to have to make certain alterations which he knew damned well Mike would never allow. It was either that or lose several hundred thousand dollars."

"Go on, Lou."

"So he took the loss. He hated it like hell, but he went ahead and did it."

Rothman laughed shortly. "He did, huh? I pushed iron on that job, myself, and—and—"

"Well." I gave him a puzzled look. "He did, didn't he? No matter what happened to Mike, your locals couldn't close their eyes to a dangerous situation like that. You're responsible. You can be sued. You could be tried for criminal collusion. You—"

"Lou." Rothman cleared his throat. "You're a hundred per cent right, Lou. Naturally we wouldn't stick our necks out for any amount of money."

"Sure," I smiled stupidly. "You just haven't thought this deal through, Joe. You've been getting along pretty good with Conway, and now he's taken a notion to go non-union, and naturally you're kind of upset about it. I reckon if you thought there'd really been a murder you wouldn't have waited six years to speak up."

"Yeah, I mean certainly not. Certainly, I wouldn't." He began rolling another cigarette. "Uh, how did you find out all these things, Lou, if you don't mind telling me?"

"Well, you know how it is. Mike was a member of the family, and I get around a lot. Any talk that's going around, I'd naturally hear it."

"Mmmm. I didn't realize there'd been so much gossip. In

fact, I didn't know there'd been any. And you never felt inclined to take any action?"

"Why should I?" I said. "It was just gossip. Conway's a
big business man—just about the biggest contractor in West
Texas. He wouldn't get mixed up in a murder any more'n you
people would keep quiet about one."

Rothman gave me another sharp look, and then he looked
down at his desk. "Lou," he said softly, "do you know how
many days a year an ironworker works? Do you know what
his life expectancy is? Did you ever see an old ironworker? Did
you ever stop to figure that there's all kinds of ways of dying,
but only one way of being dead?"

"Well, no. I reckon not," I said. "I guess I don't know
what you're driving at, Joe."

"Let it go. It's not really relevant."

"I suppose the boys don't have it too easy," I said. "But
here's the way I look at it, Joe. There's no law says they have
to stick to one line of work. If they don't like it they can do
something else."

"Yeah," he nodded, "that's right, isn't it? It's funny how
it takes an outsider to see through these problems . . . If they
don't like it let 'em do something else. That's good, that's
very good."

"Aw," I said, "it wasn't anything much."

"I disagree. It's very enlightening. You really surprise me,
Lou. I've been seeing you around town for years and frankly
you hardly struck me as a deep thinker . . . Do you have any
solution for our larger problems, the Negro situation for example?"

"Well, that's pretty simple," I said. "I'd just ship 'em all to
Africa."

"Uh-huh. I see, I see," he said, and he stood up and held
out his hand. "I'm sorry I troubled you for nothing, Lou,
but I've certainly enjoyed our talk. I hope we can get together
again sometime."

"That would be nice," I said.

"Meanwhile, of course, I haven't seen you. Understand?"

"Oh, sure," I said.

We talked for a minute or two more, and then we walked
to the outside door together. He glanced at it sharply,

looked at me. "Say," he said. "Didn't I close that damned thing?"

"I thought you did," I said.

"Well, no harm done, I guess," he said. "Could I make a suggestion to you, Lou, in your own interests?"

"Why, sure you can, Joe. Anything at all."

"Save that bullshit for the birds."

He nodded, grinning at me; and for a minute you could have heard a pin drop. But he wasn't going to say anything. He wasn't ever going to let on. So, finally, I began to grin, too.

"I don't know the why of it, Lou—I don't know a thing, understand? Not a thing. But watch yourself. It's a good act but it's easy to overdo."

"You kind of asked for it, Joe," I said.

"And now you know why. And I'm not very bright or I wouldn't be a labor skate."

"Yeah," I said. "I see what you mean."

We shook hands again and he winked and bobbed his head. And I went down the dark hall and down the stairs.

Four

AFTER Dad died I'd thought about selling our house. I'd had several good offers for it, in fact, since it was right on the edge of the downtown business district; but somehow I couldn't let it go. The taxes were pretty high and there was ten times as much room as I needed, but I couldn't bring myself to sell. Something told me to hold on, to wait.

I drove down the alley to our garage. I drove in and shut off the lights. The garage had been a barn; it still was, for that matter; and I sat there in the doorway, sniffing the musty odors of old oats and hay and straw, dreaming back through the years. Mike and I had kept our ponies in those two front stalls, and back here in the box-stall we'd had an outlaws' cave. We'd hung swings and acting bars from these rafters; and we'd made a swimming pool out of the horse trough. And up overhead in the loft, where the rats now scampered and scurried, Mike had found me with the little gi—

A rat screamed suddenly on a high note.

I got out of the car and hurried out of the big sliding door of the barn, and into the backyard. I wondered if that was why I stayed here: To punish myself.

I went in the back door of the house and went through the house to the front, turning on all the lights, the downstairs lights I mean. Then I came back into the kitchen and made coffee and carried the pot up into Dad's old office. I sat in his big old leather chair, sipping coffee and smoking, and gradually the tension began to leave me.

It had always made me feel better to come here, back from the time I was kneehigh to a grasshopper. It was like coming out of the darkness into sunlight, out of a storm into calm. Like being lost and found again.

I got up and walked along the bookcases, the endless files of psychiatric literature, the bulky volumes of morbid psychology. . . . Krafft-Ebing, Jung, Freud, Bleuler, Adolf Meyer, Kretschmer, Kraepelin . . . All the answers were here, out in the open where you could look at them. And no one was terrified or horrified. I came out of the place I was hiding in—that I always had to hide in—and began to breathe.

I took down a bound volume of one of the German periodicals and read a while. I put it back and took down one in French. I skimmed through an article in Spanish and another in Italian. I couldn't speak any of those languages worth a doggone, but I could understand 'em all. I'd just picked 'em up with Dad's help, just like I'd picked up some higher mathematics and physical chemistry and half a dozen other subjects.

Dad had wanted me to be a doctor, but he was afraid to have me go away to school so he'd done what he could for me at home. It used to irritate him, knowing what I had in my head, to hear me talking and acting like any other rube around town. But, in time, when he realized how bad I had *the sickness*, he even encouraged me to do it. That's what I was going to be; I was going to have to live and get along with rubes. I wasn't ever going to have anything but some safe, small job, and I'd have to act accordingly. If Dad could have swung anything else that paid a living, I wouldn't even have been as much as a deputy sheriff.

I fiddled around Dad's desk, working out a couple of problems in calculus just for the hell of it. Turning away from the desk, I looked at myself in the mirrored door of the laboratory.

I was still wearing my Stetson, shoved a little to the back of my head. I had on a kind of pinkish shirt and a black bow tie, and the pants of my blue serge suit were hitched up so as to catch on the tops of my Justin boots. Lean and wiry; a mouth that looked all set to drawl. A typical Western-country peace officer, that was me. Maybe friendlier looking than the average. Maybe a little cleaner cut. But on the whole typical.

That's what I was, and I couldn't change. Even if it was safe, I doubted if I could change. I'd pretended so long that I no longer had to.

"Lou . . ."

I jumped and whirled.

"Amy!" I gasped. "What in the— You shouldn't be here! Where—"

"Upstairs, waiting for you. Now, don't get excited, Lou. I slipped out after the folks went to sleep and you know them."

"But someone might—"

"No one did. I slipped down the alley. Aren't you glad?"

I wasn't, although I suppose I should have been. She didn't have the shape that Joyce did, but it was a big improvement over anything else around Central City. Except when she stuck her chin out and narrowed her eyes, like she was daring you to cross her, she was a mighty pretty girl.

"Well, sure," I said. "Sure, I'm glad. Let's go back up, huh?"

I followed her up the stairs and into my bedroom. She kicked off her shoes, tossed her coat on a chair with her other clothes, and flopped down backwards on the bed.

"My!" she said, after a moment; and her chin began to edge outward. "Such enthusiasm!"

"Oh," I said, giving my head a shake. "I'm sorry, Amy. I had something on my mind."

"S-something on your mind!" Her voice quavered. "I strip myself for him, I shed my decency and my clothes for him and h-he stands there with 'something' on his m-mind!"

"Aw, now, honey. It's just that I wasn't expecting you, and—"

"No! And why should you? The way you avoid me and make excuses for not seeing me. If I had any pride left I'd—I'd—"

She buried her head in the pillow and began to sob, giving me an A-1 view of what was probably the second prettiest rear end in West Texas. I was pretty sure she was faking; I'd picked up a lot of pointers on women from Joyce. But I didn't dare give her the smacking she deserved. Instead I threw off my own clothes and crawled into bed with her, pulling her around facing me.

"Now, cut it out, honey," I said. "You know I've just been busy as a chigger at a picnic."

"I don't know it! I don't know anything of the kind! You don't want to be with me, that's what!"

"Why, that's plumb crazy, honey. Why wouldn't I want to?"

"B-because. Oh, Lou, darling, I've been so miserable . . ."

"Well, now that's a right foolish way to act, Amy," I said.

She went on whimpering about how miserable she'd been, and I went on holding her, listening—you got to do plenty of listening around Amy—and wondering how it had all started.

To tell the truth, I guess it hadn't started anywhere. We'd just drifted together like straws in a puddle. Our families had grown up together, and we'd grown up together, right here in this same block. We'd walked back and forth to school together, and when we went to parties we were paired off together. We hadn't needed to do anything. It was all done for us.

I suppose half the town, including her own folks, knew we were knocking off a little. But no one said anything or thought anything about it. After all we were going to get married . . . even if we were kind of taking our time.

"Lou!" she nudged me. "You aren't listening to me!"

"Why, sure, I am, honey."

"Well, answer me then."

"Not now," I said. "I've got something else on my mind, now."

"But . . . Oh, *darling* . . ."

I figured she'd been gabbing and nagging about nothing, as usual, and she'd forget about whatever I was supposed to answer. But it didn't work out that way. As soon as it was over and I'd reached her cigarettes for her, taking one for myself, she gave me another one of her looks and another, "Well, Lou?"

"I hardly know what to say," I said, which was exactly the case.

"You want to marry me, don't you?"

"Mar—but, sure," I said.

"I think we've waited long enough, Lou. I can go on teaching school. We'll get by a lot better than most couples."

"But . . . but that's all we'd do, Amy. We'd never get anywhere!"

"What do you mean?"

"Well, I don't want to go on being a deputy sheriff all of my life. I want to—well—be somebody."

"Like what, for example?"

"Oh, I don't know. There's no use in talking about it."

"A doctor, perhaps? I think that would be awfully nice. Is that what you had in mind, Lou?"

"I know it's crazy, Amy. But—"

She laughed. She rolled her head on the pillow, laughing. "Oh, Lou! I never heard of such a thing! You're twenty-nine years old, and y-you don't even speak good English, and—and—oh, ha, ha, ha . . ."

She laughed until she was gasping, and my cigarette burned down between my fingers and I never knew it until I smelled the scorching flesh.

"I'm s-sorry, darling. I didn't mean to hurt your feelings, but— Were you teasing me? Were you joking with your little Amy?"

"You know me," I said. "Lou the laughing boy."

She began to quiet down at the tone of my voice. She turned away from me and lay on her back, picking at the quilt with her fingers. I got up and found a cigar, and sat down on the bed again.

"You don't want to marry me, do you, Lou?"

"I don't think we should marry now, no."

"You don't want to marry me at all."

"I didn't say that."

She was silent for several minutes, but her face talked for her. I saw her eyes narrow and a mean little smile twist her lips, and I knew what she was thinking. I knew almost to a word what she was going to say.

"I'm afraid you'll have to marry me, Lou. You'll have to, do you understand?"

"No," I said, "I won't have to. You're not pregnant, Amy. You've never gone with anyone else, and you're not pregnant by me."

"I'm lying, I suppose?"

"Seems as though," I said. "I couldn't get you pregnant if I wanted to. I'm sterile."

"*You?*"

"Sterile isn't the same thing as impotent. I've had a vasectomy."

"Then why have we always been so—why do you use—?"

I shrugged. "It saved a lot of explanations. Anyway, you're not pregnant, to get back to the subject."

"I just don't understand," she said, frowning. She wasn't at all bothered by my catching her in a lie. "Your father did it? Why, Lou?"

"Oh, I was kind of run down and nervous, and he thought—"

"Why, you were not! You were never that way!"

"Well," I said, "he thought I was."

"He *thought!* He did a terrible thing like that—made you so we can never have children—just because he thought something! Why, it's terrible! It makes me sick! . . . When was it, Lou?"

"What's the difference?" I said. "I don't really remember. A long time ago."

I wished I'd kept my mouth shut about her not being pregnant. Now I couldn't back up on my story. She'd know I was lying and she'd be more suspicious than ever.

I grinned at her and walked my fingers up the curving plane of her belly. I squeezed one of her breasts, and then I moved my hand up until it was resting against her throat.

"What's the matter?" I said. "What have you got that pretty little face all puckered up for?"

She didn't say anything. She didn't smile back. She just lay there, staring, adding me up point by point, and she began to look more puzzled in one way and less in another. The answer was trying to crash through and it couldn't make it— quite. I was standing in the way. It couldn't get around the image she had of gentle, friendly easy-going Lou Ford.

"I think," she said slowly, "I'd better go home now."

"Maybe you'd better," I agreed. "It'll be dawn before long."

"Will I see you tomorrow? Today, I mean."

"Well, Saturday's a pretty busy day for me," I said. "I reckon we might go to church together Sunday or maybe have dinner together, but—"

"But you're busy Sunday night."

"I really am, honey. I promised to do a favor for a fellow, and I don't see how I can get out of it."

"I see. It never occurs to you to think about me when you're making all your plans, does it? Oh, no! I don't matter."

"I won't be tied up too long Sunday," I said. "Maybe until eleven o'clock or so. Why don't you come over and wait for me like you did tonight? I'd be tickled to death to have you."

Her eyes flickered, but she didn't break out with a lecture like she must have wanted to. She motioned for me to move so she could get up; and then she got up and began dressing.

"I'm awfully sorry, honey," I said.

"Are you?" She pulled her dress over her head, patted it down around her hips, and buttoned the collar. Standing first on one foot then the other, she put on her pumps. I got up and held her coat for her, smoothing it around her shoulders as I helped her into it.

She turned inside my arms and faced me. "All right, Lou," she said briskly. "We'll say no more tonight. But Sunday we'll have a good long talk. You're going to tell me why you've acted as you have these last few months, and no lying or evasions. Understand?"

"Ma'am, Miss Stanton," I said. "Yes, ma'am."

"All right," she nodded, "that's settled. Now you'd better put some clothes on or go back to bed before you catch cold."

Five

THAT DAY, Saturday, was a busy one. There were a lot of payday drunks in town, it being the middle of the month, and drunks out here mean fights. All of us deputies and the two constables and Sheriff Maples had our hands full keeping things under control.

I don't have much trouble with drunks. Dad taught me they were touchy as all-hell and twice as jumpy, and if you didn't ruffle 'em or alarm 'em they were the easiest people in the world to get along with. You should never bawl a drunk out, he said, because the guy had already bawled himself out to the breaking point. And you should never pull a gun or swing on a drunk because he was apt to feel that his life was in danger and act accordingly.

So I just moved around, friendly and gentle, taking the guys home wherever I could instead of to jail, and none of them got hurt and neither did I. But it all took time. From the time I went on at noon until eleven o'clock, I didn't so much as stop for a cup of coffee. Then around midnight, when I was already way over shift, I got one of the special jobs Sheriff Maples was always calling me in on.

A Mexican pipeliner had got all hayed up on marijuana and stabbed another Mexican to death. The boys had roughed him up pretty badly bringing him in and now, what with the hay and all, he was a regular wild man. They'd managed to get him off into one of the "quiet" cells, but the way he was cutting up he was going to take it apart or die in the attempt.

"Can't handle the crazy Mex the way we ought to," Sheriff Bob grumbled. "Not in a murder case. I miss my guess, we've already given some shyster defense attorney enough to go yellin' third-degree."

"I'll see what I can do," I said.

I went down to the cell and I stayed there three hours, and I was busy every minute of it. I hardly had time to slam the door before the Mex dived at me. I caught his arms and held him back, letting him struggle and rave; and then I turned him loose and he dived again. I held him back again, turned him loose again. It went on and on.

I never slugged him or kicked him. I never let him struggle hard enough to hurt himself. I just wore him down, little by little, and when he quieted enough to hear me I began talking to him. Practically everyone in this area talks some Mex, but I do it better than most. I talked on and on, feeling him relax; and all the time I was wondering about myself.

This Mex, now, was about as defenseless as a man could be. He was hopped up and crazy. With the booting around he'd had, a little bit more would never have been noticed. I'd taken a lot bigger chance with what I'd done to that bum. The bum could have caused trouble. This Mex, alone in a cell with me, couldn't.

Yet I didn't so much as twist a finger. I'd never hurt a prisoner, someone that I could harm safely. I didn't have the slightest desire to. Maybe I had too much pride in my reputation for not using force. Or maybe I figured subconsciously that the prisoners and I were on the same side. But however it was, I'd never hurt 'em. I didn't want to, and pretty soon I wouldn't want to hurt anyone. I'd get rid of her, and it would all be over for all time.

After three hours, like I say, the Mex was willing to behave. So I got him his clothes back and a blanket for his bunk, and let him smoke a cigarette while I tucked him in. Sheriff Maples peeped in as I was leaving, and shook his head wonderingly.

"Don't see how you do it, Lou," he swore. "Dagnab it, if I see where you get the patience."

"You've just got to keep smiling," I said. "That's the answer."

"Yeah? Do tell," he drawled.

"That's right," I said. "The man with the grin is the man who will win."

He gave me a funny look; and I laughed and slapped him on the back. "Just kidding, Bob," I said.

What the hell? You can't break a habit overnight. And what was the harm in a little kidding?

The sheriff wished me a good Sunday, and I drove on home. I fixed myself a big platter of ham and eggs and French fries, and carried it into Dad's office. I ate at his desk, more at peace with myself than I'd been in a long time.

I'd made up my mind about one thing. Come hell or high water, I wasn't going to marry Amy Stanton. I'd been holding off on her account; I didn't feel I had the right to marry her. Now, though, I just wasn't going to do it. If I had to marry someone, it wouldn't be a bossy little gal with a tongue like barbed-wire and a mind about as narrow.

I carried my dishes into the kitchen, washed them up, and took a long hot bath. Then I turned in and slept like a log until ten in the morning.

While I was having breakfast, I heard gravel crunch in the driveway; and looking out I saw Chester Conway's Cadillac.

He came right in the house without knocking—people had got in the habit of that when Dad was practicing—and back into the kitchen.

"Keep your seat, boy, keep your seat," he said, though I hadn't made any move to get up. "Go right on with your breakfast."

"Thanks," I said.

He sat down, craning his neck so that he could look at the food on my plate. "Is that coffee fresh? I think I'll have some. Hop up and get me a cup, will you?"

"Yes, sir," I drawled. "Right away, Mr. Conway, sir."

That didn't faze him, of course; that was the kind of talk he felt he was entitled to. He took a noisy swill of coffee, then another. The third time he gulped the cup was emptied. He said he wouldn't take any more, without my offering him any, and lighted a cigar. He dropped the match on the floor, puffed, and dusted ashes into his cup.

West Texans as a whole are a pretty high-handed lot, but they don't walk on a man if he stands up; they're quick to respect the other fellow's rights. Chester Conway was an exception. Conway had been *the* big man in town before the oil boom. He'd always been able to deal with others on his own terms. He'd gone without opposition for so many years that, by this time, he hardly knew it when he saw it. I believe I could have cussed him out in church and he wouldn't have turned a hair. He'd have just figured his ears were playing tricks on him.

It had never been hard for me to believe he'd arranged Mike's murder. The fact that *he* did it would automatically make it all right.

"Well," he said, dusting ashes all over the table. "Got everything fixed for tonight, have you? No chance of any slip-ups? You'll wind this thing right on up so it'll stay wound?"

"I'm not doing anything," I said. "I've done all I'm going to."

"Don't think we'd better leave it that way, Lou. 'Member I told you I didn't like the idea? Well, I still don't. That damned crazy Elmer sees her again no telling what'll happen. You take the money yourself, boy. I've got it all ready, ten thousand in small bills, and—"

"No," I said.

"—pay her off. Then bust her around a little, and run her across the county line."

"Mr. Conway," I said.

"That's the way to do it," he chuckled, his big pale jowls jouncing. "Pay her, bust her and chase her . . . You say something?"

I went through it again, real slowly, dealing it out a word at a time. Miss Lakeland insisted on seeing Elmer one more time before she left. She insisted on his bringing the dough, and she didn't want any witnesses along. Those were her terms, and if Conway wanted her to leave quietly he'd have to meet 'em. We could have her pinched, of course, but she was bound to talk if we did and it wouldn't be pretty talk.

Conway nodded irritably. "Understand all that. Can't have a lot of dirty publicity. But I don't see—"

"I'll tell you what you don't see, Mr. Conway," I said. "You don't see that you've got a hell of a lot of gall."

"Huh?" His mouth dropped open. "Wha-at?"

"I'm sorry," I said. "Stop and think a minute. How would it look if it got around that an officer of the law had made a blackmail pay-off—that is, if she was willing to accept it from me? How do you think I feel being mixed up in a dirty affair of this kind? Now, Elmer got into this trouble and he came to me—"

"Only smart thing he ever did."

"—and I came to you. And you asked me to see what could be done about getting her out of town quietly. I did it. That's all I'm going to do. I don't see how you can ask me to do anything more."

"Well, uh"—He cleared his throat—"Maybe not, boy. Reckon you're right. But you will see that she leaves after she gets the money?"

"I'll see to that," I said. "If she's not gone within an hour, I'll move her along myself."

He got up, fidgeting around nervously, so I walked him to the door to get rid of him. I couldn't take him much longer. It would have been bad enough if I hadn't known what he'd done to Mike.

I kept my hands in my pockets, pretending like I didn't see him when he started to shake hands. He opened the screen, then hesitated a moment.

"Better not go off anywhere," he said. "I'm sending Elmer over as soon as I can locate him. Want you to give him a good talking-to; see that he's got everything down straight. Make him know what's what, understand?"

"Yes, sir," I said. "It's mighty nice of you to let me talk to him."

"That's all right. No trouble at all," he said; and the screen slammed behind him.

A couple hours later Elmer showed up.

He was big and flabby-looking like his old man, and he tried to be as overbearing but he didn't quite have the guts for it. Some of our Central City boys had flattened him a few times, and it had done him a world of good. His blotched face was glistening with sweat; his breath would have tested a hundred and eighty proof.

"Getting started pretty early in the day, aren't you?" I said.

"So what?"

"Not a thing," I said. "I've tried to do you a favor. If you ball it up, it's your headache."

He grunted and crossed his legs. "I dunno, Lou," he frowned. "Dunno about all this. What if the old man never cools off? What'll me and Joyce do when the ten thousand runs out?"

"Well, Elmer," I said. "I guess there's some misunderstanding. I understood that you were sure your father would come around in time. If that isn't the case, maybe I'd better tell Miss Lakeland and—"

"No, Lou! Don't do that! . . . Hell, he'll get over it. He always gets over the things I do. But—"

"Why don't you do this?" I said. "Don't let your ten thousand run out. Buy you some kind of business; you and Joyce can run it together. When it's going good, get in touch with your Dad. He'll see that you've made a darned smart move, and you won't have any trouble squaring things."

Elmer brightened a little—doggoned little. Working wasn't Elmer's idea of a good solution to any problem.

"Don't let me talk you into it," I said. "I think Miss Lakeland has been mighty badly misjudged—she convinced me and I'm not easy to convince. I've stuck my neck out a mile to give you and her a fresh start together, but if you don't want to go—"

"Why'd you do it, Lou? Why'd you do all this for me and her?"

"Maybe money," I said, smiling. "I don't make very much. Maybe I figured you'd do something for me in a money way."

His face turned a few shades redder. "Well . . . I could give you a little something out of the ten thousand, I guess."

"Oh, I wouldn't take any of that!" *You're damned right I wouldn't.* "I figured a man like you must have a little dough of his own. What do you do for your cigarettes and gas and whiskey? Does your Dad buy 'em for you?"

"Like hell!" He sat up and jerked out a roll of bills. "I got plenty of money."

He started to peel off a few bills—they were all twenties, it looked like—and then he caught my eye. I gave him a grin. It told him, plain as day, that I expected him to act like a cheapskate.

"Aw, hell," he said, and he wadded the roll together and tossed the whole thing to me. "See you tonight," he said, hoisting himself up.

"At ten o'clock," I nodded.

There were twenty-five twenties in the roll. Five hundred dollars. Now that I had it, it was welcome; I could always use a little extra money. But I hadn't planned on touching Elmer. I'd only done it to shut him up about my motives in helping him.

I didn't feel much like cooking, so I ate dinner in town. Coming home again I listened to the radio a while, read the Sunday papers and went to sleep.

Yes, maybe I was taking things pretty calmly, but I'd gone through the deal so often in my mind that I'd gotten used to it. *Joyce and Elmer were going to die. Joyce had asked for it. The Conways had asked for it. I wasn't any more cold-blooded than the dame who'd have me in hell to get her own way. I wasn't any more cold-blooded than the guy who'd had Mike knocked from an eight-story building.*

Elmer hadn't done it, of course; probably he didn't even know anything about it. But I had to get to the old man through him. It was the only way I could, and it was the way it should be. I'd be doing to him what he'd done to Dad.

. . . It was eight o'clock when I waked up—eight of the dark, moonless night I'd been waiting for. I gulped a cup of coffee, eased the car down the alley and headed for Derrick Road.

Six

HERE in the oil country you see quite a few places like the old Branch house. They were ranch houses or homesteads at one time; but wells were drilled around 'em, right up to their doorsteps sometimes, and everything nearby became a mess of oil and sulphur water and red sun-baked drilling mud. The grease-black grass dies. The creeks and springs disappear. And then the oil is gone and the houses stand black and abandoned, lost and lonely-looking behind the pest growths of sunflowers and sage and Johnson grass.

The Branch place stood back from Derrick Road a few

hundred feet, at the end of a lane so overgrown with weeds that I almost missed it. I turned into the lane, killed the motor after a few yards and got out.

At first I couldn't see a thing; it was that dark. But gradually my eyes became used to it. I could see all I needed to see. I opened the trunk compartment and located a tire tool. Taking a rusty spike from my pocket, I drove it into the right rear tire. There was a *poof!* and a *whish-ss!* The springs squeaked and whined as the car settled rapidly.

I got a jack under the axle, and raised it a foot or so. I rocked the car and slid it off the jack. I left it that way and headed up the lane.

It took maybe five minutes to reach the house and pull a plank from the porch. I leaned it against the gate post where I could find it in a hurry, and headed across the fields to Joyce's house.

"Lou!" She stood back from the door, startled. "I couldn't imagine who—where's your car? Is something wrong?"

"Nothing but a flat tire," I grinned. "I had to leave the car down the road a piece."

I sauntered into the living room, and she came around in front of me, gripping her arms around my back and pressing her face against my shirt. Her negligee fell open, accidentally on purpose I imagine. She moved her body against mine.

"Lou, honey . . ."

"Yeah?" I said.

"It's only about nine and Stupid won't be here for another hour, and I won't see you for two weeks. And . . . well, you know."

I knew. I knew how *that* would look in an autopsy.

"Well, I don't know, baby," I said. "I'm kind of pooped out, and you're all prettied up—"

"Oh, I am not!" She squeezed me. "I'm always prettied up to hear you tell it. Hurry, so I can have my bath."

Bath. That made it okay. "You twisted my arm, baby," I said, and I swept her up and carried her into the bedroom. And, no, it didn't bother me a bit.

Because right in the middle of it, right in the middle of the sweet talk and sighing, she suddenly went still and pushed my head back and looked me in the eye.

"You *will* join me in two weeks, Lou? Just as soon as you sell your house and wind up your affairs?"

"That's the understanding," I said.

"Don't keep me waiting. I want to be sweet to you, but if you won't let me I'll be the other way. I'll come back here and raise hell. I'll follow you around town and tell everyone how you—"

"—robbed you of your bloom and cast you aside?" I said.

"Crazy!" she giggled. "But just the same, Lou . . ."

"I know. I won't keep you waiting, baby."

I lay on the bed while she had her bath. She came back in from it, wiping herself with a big towel, and got some panties and a brassiere out of a suitcase. She stepped into the panties, humming, and brought the brassiere over to me. I helped her put it on, giving her a pinch or two, and she giggled and wiggled.

I'm going to miss you, baby, I thought. You've got to go, but I'm sure going to miss you.

"Lou . . . You suppose Elmer will make any trouble?"

"I already told you," I said. "What can he do? He can't squawk to his Dad. I'll tell him I changed my mind, and we'll have to keep faith with the old man. And that'll be that."

She frowned. "It seems so—oh, so complicated! I mean it looks like we could have got the money without dragging Elmer into it."

"Well. . . ." I glanced at the clock.

Nine-thirty-three. I didn't need to stall any longer. I sat up beside her, swinging my feet to the floor; casually drawing on my gloves.

"Well, I'll tell you, baby," I said. "It *is* kind of complicated, but it has to be that way. You've probably heard the gossip about Mike Dean, my foster brother? Well, Mike didn't do that. He took the blame for me. So if you should do your talking around town, it would be a lot worse than you realized. People would start thinking, and before it was all over . . ."

"But, Lou. I'm not going to say anything. You're going to join me and—"

"Better let me finish," I said. "I told you how Mike fell from that building? Only he didn't fall; he was murdered. Old man Conway arranged it and—"

"Lou"—she didn't get it at all. "I won't let you do anything to Elmer! You mustn't, honey. They'll catch you and you'll go to jail and—oh, honey, don't even think about it!"

"They won't catch me," I said. "They won't even suspect me. They'll think he was half-stiff, like he usually is, and you got to fighting and you both got killed."

She still didn't get it. She laughed, frowning a little at the same time. "But, Lou—that doesn't make sense. How could I be dead when—"

"Easy," I said, and I gave her a slap. And still she didn't get it.

She put a hand to her face and rubbed it slowly. "Y-you'd better not do that, now, Lou. I've got to travel, and—"

"You're not going anywhere, baby," I said, and I hit her again.

And at last she got it.

She jumped up and I jumped with her. I whirled her around and gave her a quick one-two, and she shot backwards across the room and bounced and slumped against the wall. She staggered to her feet, weaving, mumbling, and half-fell toward me. I let her have it again.

I backed her against the wall, slugging, and it was like pounding a pumpkin. Hard, then everything giving away at once. She slumped down, her knees bent under her, her head hanging limp; and then, slowly, an inch at a time, she pushed herself up again.

She couldn't see; I don't know how she could. I don't know how she could stand or go on breathing. But she brought her head up, wobbling, and she raised her arms, raised them and spread them and held them out. And then she staggered toward me, just as a car pulled into the yard.

"Guhguh-guhby . . . kiss guhguh-guh—"

I brought an uppercut up from the floor. There was a sharp *cr-aack!* and her whole body shot upward, and came down in a heap. And that time it stayed down.

I wiped my gloves on her body; it was her blood and it belonged there. I took the gun from the dresser, turned off the light and closed the door.

Elmer was coming up the steps, crossing the porch. I got to the front door and opened it.

"Hiya, Lou, ol' boy, ol' boy, ol' boy," he said. "Right on time, huh? Thass Elmer Conway, always right on time."

"Half-stiff," I said, "that's Elmer Conway. Have you got the money?"

He patted the thick brown folder under his arm. "What's it look like? Where's Joyce?"

"Back in the bedroom. Why don't you go on back? I'll bet she won't say no if you try to slip it to her."

"Aw," he blinked foolishly. "Aw, you shouldn't talk like that, Lou. You know we're gonna get married."

"Suit yourself," I shrugged. "I'd bet money though that she's all stretched out waiting for you."

I wanted to laugh out loud. I wanted to yell. I wanted to leap on him and tear him to pieces.

"Well, maybe . . ."

He turned suddenly and lumbered down the hall. I leaned against the wall, waiting, as he entered the bedroom and turned on the light.

I heard him say, "Hiya, Joyce, ol' kid, ol' ol' k-k-k . . ." I heard a heavy thump, and a gurgling, strangled sound. Then he said, he screamed, "Joyce . . . Joyce . . . *Lou!*"

I sauntered back. He was down on his knees and there was blood on his hands, and a big streak across his chin where he'd wiped it. He looked up at me, his mouth hanging open.

I laughed—I had to laugh or do something worse—and his eyes squeezed shut and he bawled. I yelled with laughter, bending over and slapping my legs. I doubled up, laughing and farting and laughing some more. Until there wasn't a laugh in me or anyone. I'd used up all the laughter in the world.

He got to his feet, smearing his face with his big flabby hands, staring at me stupidly.

"W-who did it, Lou?"

"It was suicide," I said. "A plain case of suicide."

"B-but that d-don't make—"

"It's the only thing that does make sense! It was the way it was, you hear me? Suicide, you hear me? Suicide suicide suicide! I didn't kill her. Don't you say I killed her. SHE KILLED HERSELF!"

I shot him, then, right in his gaping stupid mouth. I emptied the gun into him.

Stooping, I curved Joyce's hand around the gun butt, then dropped the gun at her side. I went out the door and across the fields again, and I didn't look back.

I found the plank and carried it down to my car. If the car had been seen, that plank was my alibi. I'd had to go up and find one to put under the jack.

I ran the jack up on the plank and put on the spare tire. I threw the tools into the car, started the motor and backed toward Derrick Road. Ordinarily, I'd no more back into a highway at night without my lights than I would without my pants. But this wasn't ordinarily. I just didn't think of it.

If Chester Conway's Cadillac had been travelling faster, I wouldn't be writing this.

He swarmed out of his car cursing, saw who I was, and cursed harder than ever. "Goddamit, Lou, you know better'n that! You trying to get killed, for Christ's sake? Huh? What the hell are you doing here, anyhow?"

"I had to pull in there with a flat tire," I said. "Sorry if I—"

"Well, come on. Let's get going. Can't stand here gabbing all night."

"Going?" I said. "It's still early."

"The hell it is! It's a quarter past eleven, and that damned Elmer ain't home yet. Promised to come right back, and he ain't done it. Probably up there working himself into another scrape."

"Maybe we'd better give him a little more time," I said. I had to wait a while. I couldn't go back in that house now. "Why don't you go on home, Mr. Conway, and I'll—"

"I'm going now!" He turned away from the car. "And you follow me!"

The door of the Cadillac slammed. He backed up and pulled around me, yelling again for me to come on. I yelled back that I would and he drove off. Fast.

I got a cigar lit. I started the motor and killed it. I started it and killed it again. Finally, it stayed running, it just wouldn't die, so I drove off.

I drove up the lane at Joyce's house and parked at the end of it. There wasn't room in the yard with Elmer's and the old man's cars there. I shut off the motor and got out. I climbed the steps and crossed the porch.

The door was open and he was in the living room, talking on the telephone. And his face was like a knife had come down it, slicing away all the flabbiness.

He didn't seem very excited. He didn't seem very sad. He was just business-like, and somehow that made it worse.

"Sure, it's too bad," he said. "Don't tell me that again. I know all about how bad it is. He's dead and that's that, and what I'm interested in is her . . . Well, do it then! Get on out here. We ain't going to let her die, get me? Not this way. I'm going to see that she burns."

Seven

IT WAS almost three o'clock in the morning when I got through talking—answering questions, mostly—to Sheriff Maples and the county attorney, Howard Hendricks; and I guess you know I wasn't feeling so good. I was kind of sick to my stomach, and I felt, well, pretty damned sore, angry. Things shouldn't have turned out this way. It was just plumb unreasonable. It wasn't right.

I'd done everything I could to get rid of a couple of undesirable citizens in a neat no-kickbacks way. And here one of 'em was still alive; and purple hell was popping about the other one.

Leaving the courthouse, I drove to the Greek's place and got a cup of coffee that I didn't want. His boy had taken a part-time job in a filling station, and the old man wasn't sure whether it was a good thing or not. I promised to drop by and look in on the lad.

I didn't want to go home and answer a lot more questions from Amy. I hoped that if I stalled long enough, she'd give up and leave.

Johnnie Pappas, the Greek's boy, was working at Slim Murphy's place. He was around at the side of the station when I drove in, doing something to the motor of his hot rod. I got out of my car and he came toward me slowly, sort of watchfully, wiping his hands on a chunk of waste.

"Just heard about your new job, Johnnie," I said. "Congratulations."

"Yeah." He was tall, good-looking; not at all like his father. "Dad send you out here?"

"He told me you'd gone to work here," I said. "Anything wrong with that?"

"Well . . . You're up pretty late."

"Well," I laughed, "so are you. Now how about filling 'er up with gas and checking the oil?"

He got busy, and by the time he was through he'd pretty much lost his suspicions. "I'm sorry if I acted funny, Lou. Dad's been kind of nagging me—he just can't understand that a guy my age needs a little real dough of his own—and I thought he was having you check up on me."

"You know me better than that, Johnnie."

"Sure, I do," he smiled, warmly. "I've got plenty of nagging from people, but no one but you ever really tried to help me. You're the only real friend I've ever had in this lousy town. Why do you do it, Lou? What's the percentage in bothering with a guy that everyone else is down on?"

"Oh, I don't know," I said. And I didn't. I didn't even know how I could stand here talking to him with the terrible load I had on my mind. "Maybe it's because I was a kid myself not so many years ago. Fathers are funny. The best ones get in your hair most."

"Yeah. Well . . ."

"What hours do you work, Johnnie?"

"Just midnight to seven, Saturdays and Sundays. Just enough to keep me in pocket money. Dad thinks I'll be too tired to go to school on Mondays, but I won't, Lou. I'll make it fine."

"Sure, you will," I said. "There's just one thing, Johnnie. Slim Murphy hasn't got a very good reputation. We've never proved that he was mixed up in any of these car-stripping jobs, but . . ."

"I know." He kicked the gravel of the driveway, uncomfortably. "I won't get into any trouble, Lou."

"Good enough," I said. "That's a promise, and I know you don't break your promises."

I paid him with a twenty dollar bill, got my change and headed toward home. Wondering about myself. Shaking my head, as I drove. I hadn't put on an act. I *was* concerned and worried about the kid. Me, worried about *his* troubles.

The house was all dark when I got home, but it would be, whether Amy was there or not. So I didn't get my hopes too high. I figured that my standing her up would probably make her all the more determined to stay; that she was a cinch to crop up at the one time I didn't want any part of her. That's the way I figured it, and that's the way it was.

She was up in my bedroom, in bed. And she'd filled two ash trays with the cigarettes she'd smoked. And mad! I've never seen one little old girl so mad in my life.

I sat down on the edge of the bed and pulled off my boots; and for about the next twenty minutes I didn't say a word. I didn't get a chance. Finally, she began to slow up a little, and I tried to apologize.

"I'm sure sorry, honey, but I couldn't help it. I've had a lot of trouble tonight."

"I'll bet!"

"You want to hear about it or not? If you don't, just say so."

"Oh, go on! I've heard so many of your lies and excuses I may as well hear a few more."

I told her what had happened—that is, what was *supposed* to have happened—and she could hardly hold herself in until I'd finished. The last word was hardly out of my mouth before she'd cut loose on me again.

"How could you be so stupid, Lou? How *could* you do it? Getting yourself mixed up with some wretched prostitute and that awful Elmer Conway! Now, there'll be a big scandal and you'll probably lose your job, and—"

"Why?" I mumbled. "I didn't do anything."

"I want to know why you did it!"

"Well, it was kind of a favor, see? Chester Conway wanted me to see what I could do about getting Elmer out of this scrape, so—"

"Why did he have to come to you? Why do you always

have to be doing favors for other people? You never do any for me!"

I didn't say anything for a minute. But I thought, *That's what you think, honey. I'm doing you a favor by not beating your head off.*

"Answer me, Lou Ford!"

"All right," I said. "I shouldn't have done it."

"You shouldn't have allowed that woman to stay in this county in the first place!"

"No," I nodded. "I shouldn't have."

"Well?"

"I'm not perfect," I snapped. "I make plenty of mistakes. How many times do you want me to say it?"

"Well! All I've got to say is . . ."

All she had to say would take her the rest of her life to finish; and I wasn't even half-way in the mood for it. I reached out and grabbed her by the crotch.

"Lou! You stop that!"

"Why?" I said.

"Y-you stop it!" She shivered. "You s-stop or . . . Oh, *Lou!*"

I lay down beside her with my clothes on. I had to do it, because there was just one way of shutting Amy up.

So I laid down and she swarmed up against me. And there wasn't a thing wrong with Amy when she was like that; you couldn't have asked much more from a woman. But there was plenty wrong with me. Joyce Lakeland was wrong with me.

"Lou . . ." Amy slowed down a little. "What's the matter, dear?"

"All this trouble," I said. "I guess it's thrown me for a loop."

"You poor darling. Just forget everything but me, and I'll pet you and whisper to you, mmm? I'll . . ." She kissed me and whispered what she would do. And she did it. And, hell, she might as well have done it to a fence post.

Baby Joyce had taken care of me, but good.

Amy pulled her hand away, and began brushing it against her hip. Then she snatched up a handful of sheet, and wiped—scrubbed—her hip with it.

"You son-of-a-bitch," she said. "You dirty, filthy bastard."

"Wha-at?" I said. It was like getting a punch in the guts. Amy didn't go in for cussing. At least, I'd never heard her do much.

"You're dirty. I can tell. I can smell it on you. Smell her. You can't wash it off. It'll never come off. You—"

"Jesus Christ!" I grabbed her by the shoulders. "What are you saying, Amy?"

"You screwed her. You've been doing it all along. You've been putting her dirty insides inside of me, smearing me with her. And I'm going to make you pay for it. If it's the l-last thing I ever d-do, I'll—"

She jerked away from me, sobbing, and jumped out of bed. As I got up, she backed around a chair, putting it between me and her.

"K-keep away from me! Don't you dare touch me!"

"Why, sure, honey," I said. "Whatever you say."

She didn't see the meaning yet of what she'd said. All she could think of was herself, the insult to herself. But I knew that, given enough time—and not much time at that— she'd put all the parts of the picture together. She wouldn't have any real proof, of course. All she had to go on was guess-work—intuition—and that operation I'd had; something, thank God, which seemed to have slipped her mind for the moment. Anyway, she'd talk. And the fact that there wasn't any proof for what she said, wouldn't help me much.

You don't need proof, know what I mean? Not from what I've seen of the law in operation. All you need is a tip that a guy is guilty. From then on, unless he's a big shot, it's just a matter of making him admit it.

"Amy," I said. "Amy, honey. Look at me."

"I d-don't want to look at you."

"Look at me . . . This is Lou, honey, Lou Ford, remember? The guy you've known all your life. I ask you, now, would I do what you said I did?"

She hesitated, biting her lips. "You did do it." Her voice was just a shade uncertain. "I know you did."

"You don't know anything," I said. "Just because I'm tired and upset, you jump to a crazy conclusion. Why, why would I fool around with some chippy when I had you? What could a dame like that give me that would make me run the risk of losing a girl like you? Huh? Now, that doesn't make sense, does it, honey."

"Well . . ." That had got to her. It had hit her right in the pride, where she was tenderest. But it wasn't quite enough to jar her loose from her hunch.

She picked up her panties and began putting them on, still standing behind the chair. "There's no use arguing about it, Lou," she said, wearily. "I suppose I can thank my lucky stars that I haven't caught some terrible disease."

"But dammit . . . !" I moved around the chair, suddenly, and got her in my arms. "Dammit, stop talking that way about the girl I'm going to marry! I don't mind for myself, but you can't say it about her, get me? You can't say that the girl I'm going to marry would sleep with a guy who plays around with whores!"

"Let me go, Lou! Let . . ." She stopped struggling, abruptly. "What did you—?"

"You heard me," I said.

"B-but just two days ago—"

"So what?" I said. "No man likes to be yanked into marriage. He wants to do his own proposing, which is just what I'm doing right now. Hell, we've already put it off too long, in my opinion. This crazy business tonight proves it. If we were married we wouldn't have all these quarrels and misunderstandings like we've been having."

"Since that woman came to town, you mean."

"All right," I said. "I've done all I could. If you're willing to believe that about me, I wouldn't want—"

"Wait, Lou!" She hung on to me. "After all, you can't blame me if—" And she let it go at that. She had to give up for her own sake. "I'm sorry, Lou. Of course, I was wrong."

"You certainly were."

"When shall we do it, Lou? Get married, I mean."

"The sooner the better," I lied. I didn't have the slightest intention of marrying her. But I needed time to do some planning, and I had to keep her quiet. "Let's get together in a few days when we're both more ourselves, and talk about it."

"Huh-uh." She shook her head. "Now that you've—we've come to the decision, let's go through with it. Let's talk about it right now."

"But it's getting daylight, honey," I said. "If you're still here even a little while from now, people will see you when you leave."

"I don't care if they do, darling. I don't care a teensy-weensie little bit." She snuggled against me, burrowing her head against my chest. And without seeing her face, I knew she was grinning. She had me on the run, and she was getting a hell of a kick out of it.

"Well, I'm pretty tired," I said. "I think I ought to sleep a little while before—"

"I'll make you some coffee, darling. That'll wake you up."

"But, honey—"

The phone rang. She let go of me, not very hurriedly, and I stepped over to the writing desk and picked up the extension.

"Lou?" It was Sheriff Bob Maples.

"Yeah, Bob," I said. "What's on your mind?"

He told me, and I said, Okay, and hung up the phone again. Amy looked at me, and changed her mind about popping off.

"Your job, Lou? You've got some work to do?"

"Yeah," I nodded. "Sheriff Bob's driving by to pick me up in a few moments."

"You poor dear! And you so tired! I'll get dressed and get right out."

I helped her dress, and walked to the back door with her. She gave me a couple of big kisses and I promised to call her as soon as I got a chance. She left then, a couple of minutes before Sheriff Maples drove up.

Eight

THE county attorney, Howard Hendricks, was with him, sitting in the back seat of the car. I gave him a cold-eyed look and a nod, as I got in the front, and he gave me back the look

without a nod. I'd never had much use for him. He was one
of those professional patriots, always talking about what a
great hero he'd been in the war.

Sheriff Bob put the car in gear, clearing his throat uncomfortably. "Sure hated to bother you, Lou," he said. "Hope I
didn't interrupt anything."

"Nothing that can't wait," I said. "She—I'd already kept
her waiting five-six hours."

"You had a date for last night?" asked Hendricks.

"That's right"—I didn't turn around in the seat.

"For what time?"

"For a little after ten. The time I figured I'd have the Conway business finished."

The county attorney grunted. He sounded more than a
mite disappointed. "Who was the girl?"

"None of your—"

"Wait a minute, Lou!" Bob eased his foot off the gas, and
turned onto Derrick Road. "Howard, you're getting way out
of line. You're kind of a newcomer out this way—been here
eight years now, ain't you?—but you still ought to know better'n to ask a man a question like that."

"What the hell?" said Hendricks. "It's my job. It's an important question. If Ford had himself a date last night, it—
well"—he hesitated—"it shows that he planned on being
there instead of—well, uh—some place else. You see what I
mean, Ford?"

I saw, all right, but I wasn't going to tell him so. I was just
old dumb Lou from Kalamazoo. I wouldn't be thinking about
an alibi, because I hadn't done anything to need an alibi for.

"No," I drawled, "I reckon I don't know what you mean.
To come right down to cases, and no offense meant, I figured
you'd done all the jawing you had to do when I talked to you
an hour or so ago."

"Well, you're dead wrong, brother!" He glared at me, red-
faced, in the rear view mirror. "I've got quite a few more
questions. And I'm still waiting for the answer to the last one
I asked. Who was the—"

"Drop it, Howard!" Bob jerked his head curtly. "Don't ask
Lou that again, or I'm personally going to lose my temper. I
know the girl. I know her folks. She's one of the nicest little

ladies in town, and I ain't got the slightest doubt Lou had a
date with her."

Hendricks scowled, gave out with an irritated laugh. "I
don't get it. She's not too nice to sl—well, skip it—but she's
too nice to have her name mentioned in the strictest confidence. I'm damned if I can understand a deal like that. The
more I'm around you people the less I can understand you."

I turned around, smiling, looking friendly and serious. For
a while, anyway, it wasn't a good idea to have anyone sore at
me. And a guy that's got something on his conscience can't
afford to get riled.

"I guess we're a pretty stiff-necked lot out here, Howard,"
I said. "I suppose it comes from the fact that this country was
never very thickly settled, and a man had to be doggoned
careful of the way he acted or he'd be marked for life. I mean,
there wasn't any crowd for him to sink into—he was always
out where people could see him."

"So?"

"So if a man or woman does something, nothing bad you
understand, but the kind of thing men and women have always been doing, you don't let on that you know anything
about it. You don't, because sooner or later you're going to
need the same kind of favor yourself. You see how it is? It's
the only way we can go on being human, and still hold our
heads up."

He nodded indifferently. "Very interesting. Well, here we
are, Bob."

Sheriff Maples pulled off the pavement and parked on the
shoulder of the road. We got out, and Hendricks nodded toward the weed-grown trail which led up to the old Branch
house. He jerked his head at it, and then turned and looked
at me.

"Do you see that track through there, Ford? Do you know
what caused that?"

"Why, I reckon so," I said. "A flat tire."

"You admit that? You concede that a track of that kind
would have to be there, *if* you had a flat tire?"

I pushed back my Stetson, and scratched my head. I looked
at Bob, frowning a little. "I don't guess I see what you boys
are driving at," I said. "What's this all about, Bob?"

Of course, I did see. I saw that I'd made one hell of a bonehead play. I'd guessed it as soon as I saw the track through the weeds, and I had an answer ready. But I couldn't come out with it too fast. It had to be done easy-like.

"This is Howard's show," said the sheriff. "Maybe you'd better answer him, Lou."

"Okay," I shrugged. "I've already said it once. A flat tire makes that kind of track."

"Do you know," said Hendricks slowly, "when that track was made?"

"I ain't got the slightest idea," I said. "All I know is that my car didn't make it."

"You're a damned li— *Huh?*" Hendricks' mouth dropped open foolishly. "B-but—"

"I didn't have a flat when I turned off the highway."

"Now, wait a minute! You—"

"Maybe you better wait a minute," Sheriff Bob interrupted. "I don't recollect Lou tellin' us his tire went flat here on Derrick Road. Don't recall his sayin' anything of the kind."

"If I did say it," I said, "I sure as heck didn't mean to. I knew I had a puncture, sure; I felt the car sway a little. But I turned off in the lane before the tire could really go down."

Bob nodded and glanced at Hendricks. The county attorney suddenly got busy lighting a cigarette. I don't know which was redder—his face or the sun pushing up over the hills.

I scratched my head again. "Well," I said, "I reckon it's none of my business. But I sure hope you fellows didn't chew up a good tire makin' that track."

Hendricks' mouth was working. Bob's old eyes sparkled. Off in the distance somewhere, maybe three-four miles away, there was a *suck-whush* as a mudhog drilling pump began to growl. Suddenly, the sheriff whuffed and coughed and let out a wild whoop of laughter.

"Haw, haw, haw!" he boomed. "Doggone it, Howard, if this ain't the funniest—haw, haw, haw—"

And then Hendricks started laughing, too. Restrained, uncomfortable, at first; then, plain unashamed laughter. I stood looking on, grinning puzzledly, like a guy who wanted to join in but didn't know the score.

I was glad now that I'd made that bonehead mistake. When a man's rope slides off you once, he's mighty cautious about making a second throw.

Hendricks slapped me on the back. "I'm a damned fool, Lou. I should have known better."

"Say," I said, letting it dawn on me at last. "You don't mean you thought I—"

"Of course, we didn't think so," said Bob, warmly. "Nothing of the kind."

"It was just something that had to be looked into," Hendricks explained. "We had to have an answer for it. Now, you didn't talk much to Conway last night, did you?"

"No," I said. "It didn't seem to me like a very good time to do much talking."

"Well, I talked to him, Bob, I did. Rather he talked to us. And he's really raring and tearing. This woman—what's her name, Lakeland?—is as good as dead. The doctors say she'll never regain consciousness, so Conway isn't going to be able to lay the blame for this mess on her. Naturally, then, he'll want to stick someone else with it; he'll be snatching at straws. That's why we have to head him off on anything that looks— uh—even mildly peculiar."

"But, shucks," I said, "anyone could see what happened. Elmer'd been drinking, and he tried to push her around, and—"

"Sure. But Conway don't want to admit that. And he won't admit it, if there's any way out."

We all rode in the front seat going back to town. I was in the middle, squeezed in between the sheriff and Hendricks; and all of a sudden a crazy notion came over me. Maybe I hadn't fooled 'em. Maybe they were putting on an act, just like I was. Maybe that was why they'd put me in the middle, so I couldn't jump out of the car.

It was a crazy idea, of course, and it was gone in a moment. But I started a little before I could catch myself.

"Feelin' twitchy?" said Bob.

"Just hunger pains," I grinned. "I haven't eaten since yesterday afternoon."

"Wouldn't mind a bite myself," Bob nodded. "How about you, Howard?"

"Might be a good idea. Mind stopping by the courthouse first?"

"Huh-uh," said Bob. "We go by there and we're apt not to get away. You can call from the restaurant—call my office, too, while you're at it."

Word of what had happened was already all over town, and there was a lot of whispering and gawking as we pulled up in front of the restaurant. I mean, there was a lot of whispering and gawking from the newcomers, the oil workers and so on. The old timers just nodded and went on about their business.

Hendricks stopped to use the telephone, and Bob and I sat down in a booth. We ordered ham and eggs all around, and pretty soon Hendricks came back.

"That Conway!" he snapped, sliding in across from us. "Now he wants to fly that woman into Fort Worth. Says she can't get the right kind of medical attention here."

"Yeah?" Bob looked down at the menu, casually. "What time is he takin' her?"

"I'm not at all sure that he is! I'm the man that has the say-so on handling this case. Why, she hasn't even been booked yet, let alone arraigned. We haven't had a chance."

"Can't see that it makes much difference," said Bob, "as long as she's going to die."

"That's not the point! The point is—"

"Yeah, sure," drawled Bob. "You like to take a little trip into Fort Worth, Lou? Maybe I'll go along myself."

"Why, I guess I could," I said.

"I reckon we'll do that, then. Okay, Howard? That'll take care of the technicalities for you."

The waitress set food in front of us, and Bob picked up his knife and fork. I felt his boot kick mine under the table. Hendricks knew how things stood, but he was too much of a phony to admit it. He had to go on playing the big hero— the county attorney that didn't take orders from anyone.

"Now, see here, Bob. Maybe I'm new here, as you see it; maybe I've got a lot to learn. But, by God, I know the law and—"

"So do I," the sheriff nodded. "The one that ain't on the books. Conway wasn't asking you if he could take her to Fort Worth. He was telling you. Did he mention what time?"

"Well"—Hendricks swallowed heavily—"ten this morning," he thought. He wanted to—he's chartering one of the air-line's twin-motor jobs, and they've got to fit it up with oxygen and a—"

"Uh-huh. Well, that ought to be all right. Lou and me'll have time to scrub up a little and pack a bag. I'll drop you off at your place, Lou, as soon as we finish here."

"Fine," I said.

Hendricks didn't say anything.

After a minute or two, Bob glanced at him and raised his eyebrows. "Something wrong with your eggs, son? Better eat 'em before they get cold."

Hendricks heaved a big sigh, and began to eat.

Nine

BOB and I were at the airport quite a bit ahead of time, so we went ahead and got on the plane and made ourselves comfortable. Some workmen were pounding around in the baggage compartment, fixing things up according to the doctor's instructions, but tired as we were it would have taken more than that to keep us awake. Bob began to nod, first. Then I closed my eyes, figuring to just rest them a little. And I guess I must have gone right to sleep. I didn't even know when we took off.

One minute I was closing my eyes. The next, it seemed like, Bob was shaking me and pointing out the window.

"There she is, Lou. There's cow town."

I looked out and down. I felt kind of disappointed. I'd never been out of the county before, and now that I was sure Joyce wasn't going to live I could have enjoyed seeing the sights. As it was I hadn't seen anything. I'd wasted all my time sleeping.

"Where's Mr. Conway?" I asked.

"Back in the baggage compartment. I just went back for a look myself."

"She—she's still unconscious?"

"Uh-huh, and she ain't ever going to be any other way if

you ask me." He shook his head solemnly. "Conway don't know when he's well off. If that no-account Elmer wasn't already dead, he'd be swingin' from a tree about now."

"Yeah," I said. "It's pretty bad all right."

"Don't know what would possess a man to do a thing like that. Dogged if I do! Don't see how he could be drunk enough or mean enough to do it."

"I guess it's my fault," I said. "I shouldn't have ever let her stay in town."

"We-el . . . I told you to use your own judgment, and she was a mighty cute little trick from all I hear. I'd probably have let her stay myself if I'd been in your place."

"I'm sure sorry, Bob," I said. "I sure wish I'd come to you instead of trying to handle this blackmail deal myself."

"Yeah," he nodded slowly, "but I reckon we've been over that ground enough. It's done now, and there's nothing we can do about it. Talking and fretting about might-have-beens won't get us anywhere."

"No," I said. "I guess there's no use crying over spilled milk."

The plane began to circle and lose altitude, and we fastened our seat belts. A couple of minutes later we were skimming along the landing field, and a police car and ambulance were keeping pace with us.

The plane stopped, and the pilot came out of his compartment and unlocked the door. Bob and I got out, and watched while the doctor supervised the unloading of the stretcher. The upper part of it was closed in kind of a little tent, and all I could see was the outline of her body under the sheet. Then I couldn't even see that; they were hustling her off toward the ambulance. And a heavy hand came down on my shoulder.

"Lou," said Chester Conway. "You come with me in the police car."

"Well," I said, glancing at Bob. "I kind of figured on—"

"You come with me," he repeated. "Sheriff, you ride in the ambulance. We'll see you at the hospital."

Bob pushed back his Stetson, and gave him a hard sharp look. Then his face sort of sagged and he turned and walked away, his scuffed boots dragging against the pavement.

I'd been pretty worried about how to act around Conway.

Now, seeing the way he'd pushed old Bob Maples around, I was just plain sore. I jerked away from his hand and got into the police car. I kept my head turned as Conway climbed in and slammed the door.

The ambulance started up, and headed off the field. We followed it. Conway leaned forward and closed the glass partition between our seat and the driver's.

"Didn't like that, did you?" he grunted. "Well, there may be a lot of things you don't like before this is over. I've got the reputation of my dead boy at stake, understand? My own reputation. I'm looking out for that and nothing but that, and I ain't standing on etiquette. I'm not letting someone's tender feelings get in my way."

"I don't suppose you would," I said. "It'd be pretty hard to start in at your time of life."

I wished, immediately, that I hadn't said it; I was giving myself away, you see. But he didn't seem to have heard me. Like always, he wasn't hearing anything he didn't want to hear.

"They're operating on that woman as soon as she gets to the hospital," he went on. "If she pulls through the operation, she'll be able to talk by tonight. I want you there at that time—just as soon as she comes out of the anaesthetic."

"Well?" I said.

"Bob Maples is all right, but he's too old to be on his toes. He's liable to foul up the works right when you need him most. That's why I'm letting him go on now when it don't matter whether anyone's around or not."

"I don't know as I understand you," I said. "You mean—"

"I've got rooms reserved at a hotel. I'll drop you off there, and you stay there until I call you. Get some rest, understand? Get rested up good, so's you'll be on your toes and raring to go when the time comes."

"All right," I shrugged, "but I slept all the way up on the plane."

"Sleep some more, then. You may have to be up all night."

The hotel was on West Seventh Street, a few blocks from the hospital; and Conway had engaged a whole suite of rooms. The assistant manager of the place went up with me and the bellboy, and a couple of minutes after they left a waiter brought in a tray of whiskey and ice. And right behind him came another waiter with a flock of sandwiches and coffee.

I poured myself a nice drink, and took it over by the window. I sat down in a big easy chair, and propped my boots up on the radiator. I leaned back, grinning.

Conway was a big shot, all right. He could push you around and make you like it. He could have places like this, with people jumping sideways to wait on him. He could have everything but what he wanted—his son and a good name.

His son had beaten a whore to death, and she'd killed him; and he'd never be able to live it down. Not if he lived to be a hundred and I damned well hoped he would.

I ate part of a clubhouse sandwich, but it didn't seem to set so well. So I fixed another big drink and took it over to the window. I felt kind of restless and uneasy. I wished I could get out and wander around the town.

Fort Worth is the beginning of West Texas, and I wouldn't have felt conspicuous, dressed as I was, like I would have in Dallas or Houston. I could have had a fine time—seen something new for a change. And instead I had to stay here by myself, doing nothing, seeing nothing, thinking the same old thoughts.

It was like there was a plot against me almost. I'd done something wrong, way back when I was a kid, and I'd never been able to get away from it. I'd had my nose rubbed in it day after day until, like an overtrained dog, I'd started crapping out of pure fright. And, now, here I was—

I poured another drink . . .

—Here I was, now, but it wouldn't be like this much longer. Joyce was bound to die if she wasn't dead already. I'd got rid of her and I'd got rid of *it*—the sickness—when I did it. And just as soon as things quieted down, I'd quit my job and sell the house and Dad's practice and pull out.

Amy Stanton? Well—I shook my head—she wasn't going to stop me. She wasn't going to keep me chained there in Central City. I didn't know just how I'd break away from her, but I knew darned well that I would.

Some way. Somehow.

More or less to kill time, I took a long hot bath; and

afterwards I tried the sandwiches and coffee again. I paced around the room, eating and drinking coffee, moving from window to window. I wished we weren't up so high so's I could see a little something.

I tried taking a nap, and that was no good. I got a shine cloth out of the bathroom and began rubbing at my boots. I'd got one brushed up real good and was starting on the toe of the second when Bob Maples came in.

He said hello, casually, and fixed himself a drink. He sat down, looking into the glass, twirling the ice around and around.

"I was sure sorry about what happened there at the airport, Bob," I said. "I reckon you know I wanted to stick with you."

"Yeah," he said, shortly.

"I let Conway know I didn't like it," I said.

And he said, "Yeah," again. "Forget it. Just drop it, will you?"

"Well, sure," I nodded. "Whatever you say, Bob."

I watched him out of the corner of my eye, as I went ahead rubbing the boot. He acted mad and worried, almost disgusted you might say. But I was pretty sure it wasn't over anything I'd done. In fact, I couldn't see that Conway had done enough to upset him like this.

"Is your rheumatism bothering you again?" I said. "Why don't you face around on that straight chair where I can get at your shoulder muscles, and I'll—"

He raised his head and looked up at me. And his eyes were clear, but somehow there seemed to be tears behind them. Slowly, softly, like he was talking to himself, he began to speak.

"I know what you are, don't I, Lou? Know you backwards and forwards. Known you since you was kneehigh to a grasshopper, and I never knowed a bad thing about you. Know just what you're goin' to say and do, no matter what you're up against. Like there at the airport—seeing Conway order me around. A lot of men in your place would have got a big bang out of that, but I knew you wouldn't. I knew you'd feel a lot more hurt about it than I did. That's the way you are, and you wouldn't know how to be any other way . . ."

"Bob," I said. "You got something on your mind, Bob?"

"It'll keep," he said. "I reckon it'll have to keep for a while. I just wanted you to know that I—I—"

"Yes, Bob?"

"It'll keep," he repeated. "Like I said, it'll have to keep." And he clicked the ice in his glass, staring down at it. "That Howard Hendricks," he went on. "Now, Howard ought to've known better'n to put you through that foolishness this morning. 'Course, he's got his job to do, same as I got mine, and a man can't let friendship stand in the way of duty. But—"

"Oh, hell, Bob," I said. "I didn't think anything of that."

"Well, I did. I got to thinking about it this afternoon after we left the airport. I thought about how you'd have acted if you'd have been in my place and me in yours. Oh, I reckon you'd have been pleasant and friendly, because that's the way you're built. But you wouldn't have left any doubt as to where you stood. You'd have said, 'Look, now, Bob Maples is a friend of mine, and I know he's straight as a string. So if there's something we want to know, let's just up and ask him. Let's don't play no little two-bit sheepherders' tricks on him like he was on one side of the fence and we was on the other.' . . . That's what you'd have done. But me— Well, I don't know, Lou. Maybe I'm behind the times. Maybe I'm getting too old for this job."

It looked to me like he might have something there. He was getting old and unsure of himself, and Conway had probably given him a hell of a riding that I didn't know about.

"You had some trouble at the hospital, Bob?" I said.

"Yeah," he hesitated. "I had some trouble." He got up and poured more whiskey into his glass. Then, he moved over to the window and stood rocking on his heels, his back turned to me. "She's dead, Lou. She never came out of the ether."

"Well," I said. "We all knew she didn't stand a chance. Everyone but Conway, and he was just too stubborn to see reason."

He didn't say anything. I walked over to the window by him and put my arm around his shoulders.

"Look, Bob," I said. "I don't know what Conway said to you, but don't let it get you down. Where the hell does he get off at, anyway? He wasn't even going to have us come along on this trip; we had to deal ourselves in. Then, when we get back here, he wants us to jump whenever he hollers frog, and he raises hell when things don't go to suit him."

He shrugged a little, or maybe he just took a deep breath. I let my arm slide from his shoulders, hesitated a moment, thinking he was about to say something, then went into the bathroom and closed the door. When a man's feeling low, sometimes the best thing to do is leave him alone.

I sat down on the edge of the tub, and lighted a cigar. I sat thinking—standing outside of myself—thinking about myself and Bob Maples. He'd always been pretty decent to me, and I liked him. But no more, I suppose, than I liked a lot of other people. When it came right down to cases, he was just one of hundreds of people I knew and was friendly with. And yet here I was, fretting about his problems instead of my own.

Of course, that might be partly because I'd known my problems were pretty much settled. I'd known that Joyce couldn't live, that she wasn't going to talk. She might have regained consciousness for a while, but she sure as hell wouldn't have talked; not after what had happened to her face . . . But knowing that I was safe couldn't entirely explain my concern for him. Because I'd been damned badly rattled after the murder. I hadn't been able to reason clearly, to accept the fact that I *had* to be safe. Yet I'd tried to help the Greek's boy, Johnnie Pappas.

The door slammed open, and I looked up. Bob grinned at me broadly, his face flushed, whiskey slopping to the floor from his glass.

"Hey," he said, "you runnin' out on me, Lou? Come on in here an' keep me company."

"Sure, Bob," I said. "Sure, I will." And I went back into the living room with him. He flopped down into a chair, and he drained his drink at a gulp.

"Let's do something, Lou. Let's go out and paint old cow town red. Just me'n you, huh?"

"What about Conway?"

"T'hell with him. He's got some business here; stayin' over for a few days. We'll check our bags somewhere, so's we won't have to run into him again, and then we'll have a party."

He made a grab for the bottle, and got it on the second try. I took it away from him, and filled his glass myself.

"That sounds fine, Bob," I said. "I'd sure like to do that. But shouldn't we be getting back to Central City? I mean, with Conway feeling the way he does, it might not look good for us—"

"I said t'hell with him. Said it, an' that's what I meant."

"Well, sure. But—"

"Done enough for Conway. Done too much. Done more'n any white man should. Now, c'mon and slide into them boots an' let's go."

I said, sure, sure I would. I'd do just that. But I had a bad callus, and I'd have to trim it first. So maybe, as long as he'd have to wait, he'd better lie down and take a little nap.

He did it, after a little grumbling and protesting. I called the railroad station, and reserved a bedroom on the eight o'clock train to Central City. It would cost us a few dollars personally, since the county would only pay for first-class Pullman fare. But I figured we were going to need privacy.

I was right. I woke him up at six-thirty, to give him plenty of time to get ready, and he seemed worse off than before his nap. I couldn't get him to take a bath. He wouldn't drink any coffee or eat. Instead, he started hitting the whiskey again; and when we left the hotel he took a full bottle with him. By the time I got him on the train, I was as frazzled as a cow's hide under a branding iron. I wondered what in the name of God Conway had said to him.

I wondered, and, hell, I should have known. Because he'd as good as told me. It was as plain as the nose on my face, and I'd just been too close to it to see it.

Maybe, though, it was a good thing I didn't know. For there was nothing to be done about it, nothing I could do. And I'd have been sweating blood.

Well. That was about the size of my trip to the big town. My first trip outside the county. Straight to the hotel from the plane. Straight to the train from the hotel. Then, the long ride home at night—when there was nothing to see—closed in with a crying drunk.

Once, around midnight, a little while before he went to

sleep, his mind must have wandered. For, all of a sudden, his fist wobbled out and poked me in the chest.

"Hey," I said. "Watch yourself, Bob."

"Wash—watch y'self," he mumbled. "Stop man with grin, smile worthwhile—s-stop all a' stuff spilt milk n' so on. Wha' you do that for, anyway."

"Aw," I said. "I was only kidding, Bob."

"T-tell you somethin'," he said. "T-tell you somethin' I bet you never thought of."

"Yeah?"

"It's—it's always lightest j-just before the dark."

Tired as I was, I laughed. "You got it wrong, Bob," I said. "You mean—"

"Huh-uh," he said. "You got it wrong."

Ten

WE GOT into Central City around six in the morning, and Bob took a taxi straight home. He was sick; really sick, not just hung-over. He was too old a man to pack away the load he'd had.

I stopped by the office, but everything was pretty quiet, according to the night deputy, so I went on home, too. I had a lot more hours in than I'd been paid for. No one could have faulted me if I'd taken a week off. Which, naturally, I didn't intend to do.

I changed into some fresh clothes, and made some scrambled eggs and coffee. As I sat down to eat, the phone rang.

I supposed it was the office, or maybe Amy checking up on me; she'd have to call early or wait until four when her school-day was over. I went to the phone, trying to think of some dodge to get out of seeing her, and when I heard Joe Rothman's voice it kind of threw me.

"Know who it is, Lou?" he said. "Remember our *late* talk."

"Sure," I said. "About the—uh—building situation."

"I'd ask you to drop around tonight, but I have to take a little jaunt to San Angelo. Would you mind if I stopped by your house a few minutes?"

"Well," I said, "I guess you could. Is it something important?"

"A small thing, but important, Lou. A matter of a few words of reassurance."

"Well, maybe I could—"

"I'm sure you could, but I think I'd better *see* you," he said; and he clicked up the receiver.

I hung up my phone, and went back to my breakfast. It was still early. The chances were that no one would see him. Anyway, he wasn't a criminal, opinion in some quarters to the contrary.

He came about five minutes later. I offered him some breakfast, not putting much warmth into the invitation since I didn't want him hanging around; and he said, no, thanks, but sat down at the table with me.

"Well, Lou," he said, starting to roll a cigarette. "I imagine you know what I want to hear."

"I think so," I nodded. "Consider it said."

"The very discreet newspaper stories are correct in their hints? He tried to dish it out and got it thrown back at him?"

"That's the way it looks. I can't think of any other explanation."

"I couldn't help wondering," he said, moistening the paper of his cigarette. "I couldn't help wondering how a woman with her face caved in and her neck broken could score six bull's-eyes on a man, even one as large as the late unlamented Elmer Conway."

He looked up slowly until his eyes met mine. I shrugged. "Probably she didn't fire all the shots at one time. She was shooting him while he was punching her. Hell, she'd hardly stand there and take it until he got through, and then start shooting."

"It doesn't seem that she would, does it?" he nodded. "Yet from the smattering of information I can gather, she must have done exactly that. She was still alive after he died; and almost any one—well, two—of the bullets she put into him was enough to lay him low. Ergo, she must have acquired the broken neck et cetera, before she did her shooting."

I shook my head. I had to do something to get my eyes away from his.

"You said you wanted reassurance," I said. "You—you—"

"The genuine article, Lou; no substitutes accepted. And I'm still waiting to get it."

"I don't know where you get off at questioning me," I said. "The sheriff and the county attorney are satisfied. That's all I care about."

"That's the way you see it, eh?"

"That's the way I see it."

"Well, I'll tell you how I see it. I get off questioning you because I'm involved in the matter. Not directly, perhaps, but—"

"But not indirectly, either."

"Exactly. I knew you had it in for the Conways; in fact, I did everything I could to set you against the old man. Morally—perhaps even legally—I share the responsibility for any untoward action you might take. At any rate, we'll say, I and the unions I head could be placed in a very unfavorable light."

"You said it," I said. "It's your own statement."

"But don't ride that horse too hard, Lou. I don't hold still for murder. Incidentally, what's the score as of to date? One or two?"

"She's dead. She died yesterday afternoon."

"I won't buy it, Lou—if it was murder. Your doing. I can't say offhand what I will do, but I won't let you ride. I couldn't. You'd wind up by getting me into something even worse."

"Oh, hell," I said. "What are we—"

"The girl's dead, and Elmer's dead. So regardless of how funny things look—and this deal should have put the courthouse crowd into hysterics—they can't prove anything. If they knew what I know, about your having a motive—"

"For killing her? Why would I want to do that?"

"Well"—he began to slow down a little—"leave her out of it. Say that she was just an instrument for getting back at Conway. A piece of stage setting."

"You know that doesn't make sense," I said. "About the other, this so-called motive—I'd had it for six years; I'd known about Mike's accident that long. Why would I wait six years, and then all of a sudden decide to pull this? Beat some poor whore to a pulp just to get at Chester Conway's son. Now, tell me if that sounds logical. Just tell me, Joe."

Rothman frowned thoughtfully, his fingers drumming upon the table. "No," he said, slowly. "It doesn't sound logical. That's the trouble. The man who walked away from that job—if he walked away—"

"You know he didn't, Joe."

"So you say."

"So I say," I said. "So everyone says. You'd say so yourself, if you didn't know how I felt about the Conways. Put that out of your mind once, and what do you have? Why, just a double murder—two people getting in a brawl and killing each other—under kind of puzzling circumstances."

He smiled wryly. "I'd call that the understatement of the century, Lou."

"I can't tell you what happened," I said, "because I wasn't there. But I know there are flukes in murder the same as there are in anything else. A man crawls a mile with his brains blown out. A woman calls the police after she's shot through the heart. A man is hanged and poisoned and chopped up and shot, and he goes right on living. Don't ask me why those things are. I don't know. But I do know they happen, and so do you."

Rothman looked at me steadily. Then, his head jerked a little, nodding.

"I guess so, Lou," he said. "I guess you're clean, at least. I've been sitting here watching you, putting together everything I know about you, and I couldn't make it tally with the picture I've got of *that* guy. Screwy as things are, that would be even screwier. You don't fit the part, to coin a phrase."

"What do I say to that?" I said.

"Not a thing, Lou. I should be thanking you for lifting a considerable load from my mind. However, if you don't mind my going into your debt a little further . . . ?"

"Yes?"

"What's the lowdown, just for my own information? I'll concede that you didn't have a killing hate for Conway, but you did hate him. What were you trying to pull off?"

I'd been expecting that question since the night I'd talked to him. I had the answer all ready.

"The money was supposed to be a payoff to get her out of

town. Conway was paying her to go away and leave Elmer alone. Actually—"

"—Elmer was going to leave with her, right?" Rothman got up, and put on his hat. "Well, I can't find it in my heart to chide you for the stunt, despite its unfortunate outcome. I almost wish I'd thought of it."

"Aw," I said, "it wasn't nothing much. Just a matter of a will finding a way."

"Ooof!" he said. "What are Conway's feelings, by the way?"

"Well, I don't think he feels real good," I said.

"Probably something he ate," he nodded. "Don't you imagine? But watch that stuff, Lou. Watch it. Save it for those birds."

He left.

I got the newspapers out of the yard—yesterday afternoon's and this morning's—poured more coffee, and sat back down at the table.

As usual, the papers had given me all of the breaks. Instead of making me look like a boob or a busybody, which they could have done easily enough, they had me down as a kind of combination J. Edgar Hoover-Lombroso, "the shrewd sheriff's sleuth whose unselfish intervention in the affair came to naught, due only to the unpredictable quirks of all-too-human behavior."

I laughed, choking on the coffee I was starting to swallow. In spite of all I'd been through, I was beginning to feel nice and relaxed. Joyce was dead. Not even Rothman suspected me. And when you passed clean with *that* guy, you didn't have anything to worry about. It was sort of an acid test, you might say.

I debated calling up the newspapers and complimenting them on their "accuracy." I often did that, spread a little sunshine, you know, and they ate it up. I could say something— I laughed—I could say something about truth being stranger than fiction. And maybe add something like—well—murder will out. Or crime doesn't pay. Or . . . or the best laid plans of mice and men.

I stopped laughing.

I was supposed to be over that stuff. Rothman had warned me about it, and it'd got Bob Maples' goat. But—

Well, why shouldn't I, if I wanted to? If it helped to take the tension out of me? It was in character. It fitted in with that dull good-natured guy who couldn't do anything bad if he tried. Rothman himself had remarked that no matter how screwy things looked, seeing me as a murderer was even screwier. And my talk was a big part of me—part of the guy that had thrown 'em all off the trail. If I suddenly stopped talking that way, what would people think?

Why, I just about had to keep on whether I wanted to or not. The choice was out of my hand. But, of course, I'd take it kind of easy. Not overdo it.

I reasoned it all out, and wound up still feeling good. But I decided not to call the newspapers, after all. The stories had been more than fair to me, but it hadn't cost 'em anything; they had to fill space some way. And I didn't care too much about a number of the details; what they said about Joyce, for example. She wasn't a "shabby sister of sin." She hadn't, for Christ's sake, "loved not wisely but too well." She was just a cute little ol' gal who'd latched onto the wrong guy, or the right guy in the wrong place; she hadn't wanted anything else, nothing else. And she'd got it. Nothing.

Amy Stanton called a little after eight o'clock, and I asked her to come over that night. The best way to stall, I figured, was not to stall; not to put up any opposition to her. If I didn't hang back, she'd stop pushing me. And, after all, she couldn't get married on an hour's notice. There'd be all sorts of things to attend to, and discuss—God, how they'd have to be discussed! even the size of the douche bag to take along on our honeymoon! And long before she was through, I'd be in shape to pull out of Central City.

After I'd finished talking to her, I went into Dad's laboratory, lighted the Bunsen burner and put an intravenous needle and an ordinary hypodermic on to boil. Then, I looked along the shelves until I found a carton each of male hormone, ACTH, B-complex and sterile water. Dad's stock of drugs was getting old, of course, but the pharmaceutical houses still kept sending us samples. The samples were what I used.

I mixed up an intravenous of the ACTH, B-complex and water and put it into my right arm. (Dad had a theory that shots should never be given on the same side as the heart.) I shot the hormone into my hip . . . and I was set for the night. Amy wouldn't be disappointed again. She wouldn't have anything to wonder about. Whether my trouble had been psychosomatic or real, the result of tension or too much Joyce, I wouldn't have it tonight. Little Amy would be tamed down for a week.

I went up to my bedroom and went to sleep. I woke up at noon, when the refinery whistles began to blow; then, dozed off again and slept until after two. Some times, most of the time, I should say, I can sleep eight-ten hours and still not feel rested. Well, I'm not tired, exactly, but I hate to get up. I just want to stay where I am, and not talk to anyone or see anyone.

Today, though, it was different; just the opposite. I could hardly wait to get cleaned up, and be out and doing something.

I showered and shaved, standing under the cold water a long time because that medicine was really working. I got into a clean tan shirt, and put on a new black bow tie, and took a freshly pressed blue suit out of the closet.

I fixed and ate a bite of lunch, and called Sheriff Maples' house.

His wife answered the phone. She said that Bob was feeling kind of poorly, and that the doctor thought he'd better stay in bed for a day or two. He was asleep, right then, and she kind of hated to wake him up. But if there was anything important . . .

"I just wondered how he was," I said. "Thought I might drop by for a few minutes."

"Well, that's mighty nice of you, Lou. I'll tell him you called when he wakes up. Maybe you can come by tomorrow if he's not up and around by then."

"Fine," I said.

I tried to read a while, but I couldn't concentrate. I wondered what to do with myself, now that I did have a day off. I couldn't shoot pool or bowl. It didn't look good for a cop to hang around pool halls and bowling alleys. It didn't look

good for 'em to go into bars. It didn't look good for them
to be seen in a show in the daytime.

I could drive around. Take a ride by myself. That was about
all.

Gradually, the good feeling began to leave me.

I got the car out, and headed for the courthouse.

Hank Butterby, the office deputy, was reading the paper,
his boots up on the desk, his jaws moving on a cud of tobacco.
He asked me if it was hot enough for me, and why'n hell I
didn't stay home when I had a chance. I said, well, you know
how it is, Hank.

"Nice goin'," he said, nodding at the paper. "Right pretty
little piece they got about you. I was just fixin' to clip it out
and save it for you."

The stupid son-of-a-bitch was always doing that. Not just
stories about me, but everything. He'd clip out cartoons and
weather reports and crappy poems and health columns. Every
goddam thing under the sun. He couldn't read a paper without a pair of scissors.

"I'll tell you what," I said. "I'll autograph it for you, and
you keep it. Maybe it'll be valuable some day."

"Well"—he slanted his eyes at me, and looked quickly away
again—"I wouldn't want to put you to no trouble, Lou."

"No trouble at all," I said. "Here let me have it." I
scrawled my name along the margin, and handed it back to
him. "Just don't let this get around," I said. "If I have to do
the same thing for the other fellows, it'll run the value down."

He stared at the paper, glassy-eyed, like maybe it was going
to bite him. "Uh"—there it went; he'd forgot and swallowed
his spit—"you really think . . . ?"

"Here's what you do," I said, getting my elbows down on
the desk and whispering. "Go out to one of the refineries,
and get 'em to steam you out a steel drum. Then—you know
anyone that'll lend you a welding torch?"

"Yeah"—he was whispering too. "I think I can borry one."

"Well, cut the drum in two, cut it around twice, rather, so's
you'll have kind of a lid. Then put that autographed clipping
inside—the only one in existence, Hank!—and weld it back
together again. Sixty or seventy years from now, you can take
it to some museum and they'll pay you a fortune for it."

"Cripes!" he said. "You keepin' a drum like that, Lou? Want me to pick you up one?"

"Oh, I guess not," I said. "I probably won't live that long."

Eleven

I HESITATED in the corridor in front of Howard Hendricks' office, and he glanced up from his desk and waved to me.

"Hello, there, Lou. Come on in and sit a minute."

I went in, nodding to his secretary, and pulled a chair up to the desk. "Just talked to Bob's wife a little while ago," I said. "He's not feeling so good."

"So I hear." He struck a match for my cigar. "Well, it doesn't matter much. I mean there's nothing more to be done on this Conway case. All we can do is sit tight; just be available in the event that Conway starts tossing his weight around. I imagine he'll become resigned to the situation before too long."

"It was too bad about the girl dying," I said.

"Oh, I don't know, Lou," he shrugged. "I can't see that she'd have been able to tell us anything we don't already know. Frankly, and just between the two of us, I'm rather relieved. Conway wouldn't have been satisfied unless she went to the chair with all the blame pinned on her. I'd have hated to be a party to it."

"Yeah," I said. "That wouldn't have been so good."

"Though of course I would have, Lou, if she'd lived. I mean, I'd have prosecuted her to the hilt."

He was leaning backwards to be friendly since our brush the day before. I was his old pal, and he was letting me know his innermost feelings.

"I wonder, Howard . . ."

"Yes, Lou?"

"Well, I guess I'd better not say it," I said. "Maybe you don't feel like I do about things."

"Oh, I'm sure I do. I've always felt we had a great deal in common. What is it you wanted to tell me?"

THE KILLER INSIDE ME

His eyes strayed a second from mine, and his mouth quirked a little. I knew his secretary had winked at him.

"Well, it's like this," I said. "Now, I've always felt we were one big happy family here. Us people that work for the county . . ."

"Uh-huh. One big happy family, eh?" His eyes strayed again. "Go on, Lou."

"We're kind of brothers under the skin . . ."

"Y-yes."

"We're all in the same boat, and we've got to put our shoulders to the wheel and pull together."

His throat seemed to swell all of a sudden, and he yanked a handkerchief from his pocket. Then he whirled around in his chair, his back to me, coughing and strangling and sputtering. I heard his secretary get up, and hurry out. Her high heels went tap-tapping down the corridor, moving faster and faster toward the woman's john until she was almost running.

I hoped she pissed in her drawers.

I hoped that chunk of shrapnel under his ribs had punctured a lung. That chunk of shrapnel had cost the taxpayers a hell of a pile of dough. He'd got elected to office talking about that shrapnel. Not cleaning up the county and seeing that everyone got a fair shake. Just shrapnel.

He finally straightened up and turned around, and I told him he'd better take care of that cold. "I'll tell you what I always do," I said. "I take the water from a boiled onion, and squeeze a big lemon into it. Well, maybe a middling-size lemon and a small one if—"

"Lou!" he said sharply.

"Yeah?" I said.

"I appreciate your sentiments—your interest—but I'll have to ask you to come to the point. What did you wish to tell me, anyway?"

"Oh, it wasn't any—"

"Please, Lou!"

"Well, here's what I was wondering about," I said. And I told him. The same thing that Rothman had wondered about. I put it into my words, drawling it out, slow and awkward.

That would give him something to worry over. Something

besides flat-tire tracks. And the beauty of it was he couldn't
do much but worry.

"Jesus," he said, slowly. "It's right there, isn't it? Right out
in the open, when you look at it right. It's one of those things
that are so plain and simple you don't see 'em. No matter
how you turn it around, he just about had to kill her after he
was dead. After he couldn't do it!"

"Or vice versa," I said.

He wiped his forehead, excited but kind of sick-looking.
Trying to trap old simple Lou with the tire tracks was one
thing. That was about his speed. But this had him thrown for
a loop.

"You know what this means, Lou?"

"Well, it doesn't necessarily mean that," I said, and I gave
him an out. I rehashed the business about fluke deaths that
I'd given to Rothman. "That's probably the way it was. Just
one of those damned funny things that no one can explain."

"Yeah," he said. "Of course. That's bound to be it. You—
uh—you haven't mentioned this to anyone, Lou?"

I shook my head. "Just popped into my mind a little while
ago. 'Course, if Conway's still riled up when he gets back,
I—"

"I don't believe I would, Lou. I really don't think that'd
be wise, at all."

"You mean I should tell Bob, first? Oh, I intended to do
that. I wouldn't go over Bob's head."

"No, Lou," he said, "that isn't what I mean. Bob isn't well.
He's already taken an awful pounding from Conway. I don't
think we should trouble him with anything else. Something
which, as you point out, is doubtless of no consequence."

"Well," I said, "if it doesn't amount to anything, I don't
see why—"

"Let's just keep it to ourselves, Lou, for the time being, at
least. Just sit tight and see what happens. After all, what else
can we do? What have we got to go on?"

"Nothing much," I said. "Probably nothing at all."

"Exactly! I couldn't have stated it better."

"I tell you what we might do," I said. "It wouldn't be too
hard to round up all the men that visited her. Probably ain't

more than thirty or forty of 'em, her being a kind of high-priced gal. Bob and us, our crowd, we could round 'em up, and you could . . ."

I wish you could have seen him sweat. Rounding up thirty or forty well-to-do citizens wouldn't be any skin off our ass, the sheriff's office. He'd be the one to study the evidence, and ask for indictments. By the time he was through, he'd be *through*. He couldn't be elected dog-catcher, if shrapnel was running out his eyeballs.

Well, though, I didn't really want him to do it any more than he wanted to. The case was closed, right on Elmer Conway's neck, and it was a darned good idea to leave it that way. So, that being the case, and seeing it was about supper time, I allowed him to convince me. I said I didn't have much sense about such things, and I was sure grateful for his setting me straight. And that's the way it ended. Almost.

I gave him my recipe for curing coughs before I left.

I sauntered down to my car, whistling; thinking of what a fine afternoon it had been, after all, and what a hell of a kick there'd be in talking about it.

Ten minutes later I was out on Derrick Road, making a U-turn back toward town.

I don't know why. Well, I do know. She was the only person I could have talked to, who'd have understood what I was talking about. But I knew she wasn't there. I knew she'd never be there again, there or anywhere. She was gone and I knew it. So . . . I don't know why.

I drove back toward town, back toward the rambling old two-story house and the barn where the rats squealed. And once I said, "I'm sorry, baby." I said it out loud. "You'll never know how sorry I am." Then I said, "You understand, don't you? In a few months more I couldn't have stopped. I'd have lost all control and . . ."

A butterfly struck lightly against the wind-screen, and fluttered away again. I went back to my whistling.

It had sure been a fine afternoon.

I was about out of groceries, so I stopped at a grocery and picked up a few, including a steak for my dinner. I went home and fixed myself a whopping big meal, and ate every bite of it. That B-complex was really doing its job. So was the other stuff. I began to actually look forward to seeing Amy. I began to want her bad.

I washed and wiped the dishes. I mopped the kitchen floor, dragging the job out as long as I could. I wrung the mop out and hung it up on the back porch, and came back and looked at the clock. The hands seemed to have been standing still. It would be at least a couple hours yet before she'd dare to come over.

There wasn't any more work I could do, so I filled a big cup with coffee and took it up into Dad's office. I set it on his desk, lighted a cigar and started browsing along the rows of books.

Dad always said that he had enough trouble sorting the fiction out of so-called facts, without reading fiction. He always said that science was already too muddled without trying to make it jibe with religion. He said those things, but he also said that science in itself could be a religion, that a broad mind was always in danger of becoming narrow. So there was quite a bit of fiction on the shelves, and as much Biblical literature, probably, as a lot of ministers had.

I'd read some of the fiction. The other I'd left alone. I went to church and Sunday school, living as I had to live, but that was the end of it. Because kids are kids; and if that sounds pretty obvious, all I can say is that a lot of supposedly deep thinkers have never discovered the fact. A kid hears you cussing all the time, and he's going to cuss, too. He won't understand if you tell him it's wrong. He's loyal, and if you do it, it must be all right.

As I say, then, I'd never looked into any of the religious literature around the house. But I did tonight. I'd already read almost everything else. And I think it was in my mind that, since I was going to sell this place, I'd better be checking things over for value.

So I reached down a big leather-bound concordance to the Bible and blew the dust off of it. And I carried it over to the desk and opened it up; it kind of slid open by itself when I laid it down. And there was a picture in it, a little two-by-four snapshot, and I picked it up.

I turned it around one way, then another. I turned it sideways and upside down—what I thought was upside down. And I kind of grinned like a man will, when he's interested and puzzled.

It was a woman's face, not pretty exactly, but the kind that gets to you without your knowing why. But where the hell it was, what she was doing, I couldn't make out. Offhand, it looked like she was peering through the crotch of a tree, a white maple, say, with two limbs tapering up from the bole. She had her hands clasped around the limbs, and . . . But I knew that couldn't be right. Because the bole was divided at the base, and there were stumps of chopped off limbs almost tangent to the others.

I rubbed the picture against my shirt, and looked at it again. That face was familiar. It was coming back to me from some faraway place, like something coming out of hiding. But it was old, the picture I mean, and there were kind of crisscross blurs—of age, I supposed—scarring whatever she was looking through.

I took a magnifying glass and looked at it. I turned it upside down, as it was supposed to be turned. Then, I kind of dropped the glass and shoved it away from me; and I sat staring into space. At nothing and everything.

She was looking through a crotch, all right. But it was her own.

She was on her knees, peering between them. And those crisscross blurs on her thighs weren't the result of age. They were scars. The woman was Helene, who had been Dad's housekeeper so long ago.

Dad . . .

Twelve

I WAS only like that for a few minutes, sitting there and staring, but a world of things, most of my kid life, came back to me in that time. *She* came back to me, the housekeeper, and she had been so much of that life.

"Want to fight, Helene? Want to learn how to box . . . ?"
And:

"Oh, I'm tired. You just hit me . . ."

And:

"But you'll like it, darling. All the big boys do it . . ."

I lived back through it all, and then I came to the end of it. That last terrible day, with me crouched at the foot of the stairs, sick with fear and shame, terrified, aching with the first and only whipping in my life; listening to the low angry voices, the angry and contemptuous voices, in the library.

"I am not arguing with you, Helene. You're leaving here tonight. Consider yourself lucky that I don't prosecute you."

"Oh, ye-ss? I'd like to see you try it!"

"Why, Helene? How in the world could you do such a thing?"

"Jealous?"

"You—a mere child, and—"

"Yes! That's right! A mere child. Why not remember that? Listen to me, Daniel. I—"

"Don't say it, please. I'm at fault. If I hadn't—"

"Has it hurt you any? Have you harmed anyone? Haven't you, in fact—I should ask!—gradually lost all interest in it?"

"But a child! My child. My only son. If anything should happen—"

"Uh-huh. That's what bothers you, isn't it? Not him, but you. How it would reflect on you."

"Get out! A woman with no more sensibilities than—"

"I'm white trash, that's the term isn't it? Riffraff. I ain't got that ol' quality. All right, and when I see some hypocritical son-of-a-bitch like you, I'm damned glad of it!"

"Get out or I'll kill you!"

"Tsk-tsk! But think of the disgrace, Doctor . . . Now, I'm going to tell you something . . ."

"Get—"

"Something that you above all people should know. This didn't need to mean a thing. Absolutely nothing. But now it will. You've handled it in the worst possible way. You—"

"I . . . please, Helene."

"You'll never kill anyone. Not you. You're too damned smug and self-satisfied and sure of yourself. You like to hurt people, but—"

"No!"

"All right. I'm wrong. You're the great, good Dr. Ford, and I'm white trash, so that makes me wrong . . . I hope."

That was all.

I'd forgotten about it, and now I forgot it again. There are things that have to be forgotten if you want to go on living. And somehow I did want to; I wanted to more than ever. If the Good Lord made a mistake in us people it was in making us want to live when we've got the least excuse for it.

I put the concordance back on the shelf. I took the picture into the laboratory and burned it, and washed the ashes down the sink. But it was a long time burning, it seemed like. And I couldn't help noticing something:

How much she looked like Joyce. How there was even a strong resemblance between her and Amy Stanton.

The phone rang. I wiped my hands against my pants, and answered it, looking at myself in the laboratory-door mirror— at the guy in the black bow tie and the pink-tan shirt, his trouser legs hooked over his boot tops.

"Lou Ford speakin'," I said.

"Howard, Lou. Howard Hendricks. Look. I want you to come right down . . . down to the courthouse, yeah."

"Well, I don't know about that," I said. "I kind of—"

"She'll have to wait, Lou. This is important!" It had to be the way he was sputtering. "Remember what we were talking about this afternoon? About the—you know—the possibility of an outside party being the murderer. Well, you, we were dead right. Our hunch was right!"

"Huh!" I said. "But it couldn't—I mean—"

"We've got him, Lou! We've got the son-of-a-bitch! We've got the bastard cold, and—"

"You mean he's admitted it? Hell, Howard, there's always some crank confessing to—"

"He's not admitting anything! He won't even talk! That's why we need you. We can't, uh, work on him, you know, but you can make him talk. You can soften him up if anyone can. I think you know him, incidentally."

"W-who—yeah?"

"The Greek's kid, Johnnie Pappas. You know him; he's

been in plenty of trouble before. Now, get down here, Lou. I've already called Chester Conway and he's flying out from Fort Worth in the morning. I gave you full credit—told him how we'd worked on this idea together and we'd been sure all along that Elmer wasn't guilty, and . . . and he's pleased as punch, Lou. Boy, if we can just crack this, get a confession right—"

"I'll come down," I said. "I'll be right down, Howard."

I lowered the receiver hook for a moment, figuring out what had happened, what must have happened. Then, I called Amy.

Her folks were still up so she couldn't talk much; and that was a help. I made her understand that I really wanted to see her—and I did—and I shouldn't be gone too long.

I hung up and took out my wallet, and spread all the bills out on the desk.

I hadn't had any twenties of my own, just the twenty-five Elmer'd given me. And when I saw that five of them were gone, I went limp clear down to my toenails. Then I remembered that I'd used four in Fort Worth on my railroad ticket, and that I'd only broken one here in town where it would matter. Only the one . . . with Johnnie Pappas. So . . .

So I got out the car, and drove down to the courthouse.

Office Deputy Hank Butterby gave me a hurt look, and another deputy that was there, Jeff Plummer, winked and said howdy to me. Then Howard bustled in and grabbed me by the elbow, and hustled me into his office.

"What a break, huh, Lou?" He was almost slobbering with excitement. "Now, I'll tell you how to handle it. Here's what you'd better do. Sweet talk him, know what I mean, and get his guard down; then tighten up on him. Tell him if he'll cooperate we'll get him off with manslaughter—we can't do it, of course, but what you say won't be binding on me. Otherwise, tell him, it'll be the chair. He's eighteen years old, past eighteen, and—"

I stared at him. He misread my look.

"Oh, hell," he said, jabbing me in the ribs with his thumb. "Who am I to be telling you what to do? Don't I know how you handle these guys? Haven't I—"

"You haven't told me anything yet," I said. "I know Johnnie's kind of wild, but I can't see him as a murderer. What are you supposed to have on him?"

"Supposed, hell! We've got"—he hesitated—"well, here's the situation, Lou. Elmer took ten thousand bucks out there to that chippy's house. He was supposed to have taken that much. But when we counted it up, five hundred dollars was missing . . ."

"Yeah?" I said. It was like I'd figured. That damned Elmer hadn't wanted to admit that he didn't have any dough of his own.

"Well, we thought, Bob and I did, that Elmer had probably pissed it off in a crap game or something like that. But the bills were all marked, see, and the old man had already tipped off the local banks. If she tried to hang around town after the payoff, he was going to crack down on her for blackmail . . . That Conway! They don't put many past him!"

"It looks like they've put a few past me," I said.

"Now, Lou"—he clapped me on the back. "There's no reason to feel that way at all. We trusted you implicitly. But it was Conway's show, and—well, you *were* there in the vicinity, Lou, and . . ."

"Let it go," I said. "Johnnie spent some of the money?"

"A twenty. He broke it at a drugstore last night and it went to the bank this morning, and it was traced back to him a couple hours ago when we picked him up. Now—"

"How do you know Elmer didn't blow in the dough, and it's just now beginning to circulate?"

"None of it's shown up. Just this one twenty. So— Wait, Lou. Wait just a minute. Let me give you the whole picture, and we'll save time. I was entirely willing to concede that he'd come by the money innocently. He pays himself there at the filling station, and oddly enough that pay comes to exactly twenty dollars for the two nights. It looked all right, see what I mean? He could have taken the twenty in and paid himself with it. But he couldn't say he did—wouldn't say anything— because he damned well couldn't. There's damned few cars stopping at Murphy's between midnight and eight o'clock. He'd have to remember anyone that gave him a twenty. We could have checked the customer or customers, and he'd have been out of here—*if* he was innocent."

"Maybe it was in his cash drawer at the start of his shift?"

"Are you kidding? A twenty-dollar bill to make change with?" Hendricks shook his head. "We'd know he didn't have it, even without Slim Murphy's word. Now, wait! Hold up! We've checked on Murphy, and his alibi's airtight. The kid— huh-uh. From about nine Sunday night until eleven, his time can't be accounted for. We can't account for it, and he won't. . . . Oh, it's a cinch, Lou, anyway you look at it. Take the murders themselves—that dame beaten to a pulp. That's something a crazy kid would lose his head and do. And the money; only five hundred taken out of ten grand. He's overwhelmed by so much dough, so he grabs up a fistful and leaves the rest. A kid stunt again."

"Yeah," I said. "Yeah, I guess you're right, Howard. You think he's got the rest cached somewhere?"

"Either that or he's got scared and thrown it away. He's a set-up, Lou. Man, I've never seen one so pretty. If he dropped dead right now I'd consider it a judgment from heaven, and I'm not a religious man either!"

Well, he'd said it all. He'd proved it in black and white.

"Well, you'd better get busy, now, Lou. We've got him on ice. Haven't booked him yet, and we're not going to until he comes through. I'm not letting some shyster tell him about his rights at this stage of the game."

I hesitated. Then I said, "No, I don't reckon that would be so smart. There's nothing to be gained by that . . . Does Bob know about this?"

"Why bother him? There's nothing he can do."

"Well, I just wondered if we should ask him—if it would be all right for me to—"

"Be all right?" He frowned. "Why wouldn't it be all right? . . . Oh, I know how you feel, Lou. He's just a kid; you know him. But he's a murderer, Lou, and a damned cold-blooded one. Keep that in your mind. Think of how that poor damned woman must have felt while he was beating her face in. You saw her. You saw what her face looked like. Stew meat, hamburger—"

"Don't," I said. "For Christ's sake!"

"Sure, Lou, sure." He dropped an arm around my shoulders. "I'm sorry. I keep forgetting that you've never become hardened to this stuff. Well?"

"Well," I said. "I guess I'd better get it over with."

I walked downstairs to the basement, the jail. The turnkey let me through the gate and closed it again; and we went down past the bullpen and the regular cells to a heavy steel door. There was a small port or peephole in it, and I peered through it. But I couldn't see anything. You couldn't keep a light globe in the place, no matter what kind of guard you put over it; and the basement window, which was two-thirds below the surface of the ground, didn't let in much natural light.

"Want to borrow a flash, Lou?"

"I guess not," I said. "I can see all I need to."

He opened the door a few inches, and I slid inside, and he slammed it behind me. I stood with my back to it a moment, blinking, and there was a squeak and a scrape, and a shadow rose up and faltered toward me.

He fell into my arms, and I held him there, patting him on the back, comforting him.

"It's all right, Johnnie boy. Everything's going to be all right."

"J-jesus, Lou. Jesus Jesus Ca-Christ. I knew—I kn-new you'd come, they'd send for you. But it was so long, so long and I began to think maybe—maybe—you'd—"

"You know me better'n that, Johnnie. You know how much I think of you."

"S-sure." He drew a long breath, and let it out slowly; like a man that's made land after a hard swim. "You got a cigarette, Lou? These dirty bastards took all my—"

"Now, now," I said. "They were just doing their duty, Johnnie. Have a cigar and I'll smoke one with you."

We sat down side-by-side on the bolted-down bunk, and I held a match for our cigars. I shook the match out, and he puffed and I puffed, and the glow came and went from our faces.

"This is going to burn the old man up." He laughed jerkily. "I guess— He'll have to know, won't he?"

"Yes," I said. "I'm afraid he'll have to know, Johnnie."

"How soon can I leave?"

"Very soon. It won't be long now," I said. "Where were you Sunday night?"

"To a picture show." He drew hard on his cigar, and I could see his jaw beginning to set. "What's the difference?"

"You know what I mean, Johnnie. Where'd you go after the show—between the time you left it and started to work?"

"Well"—*puff, puff*—"I don't see what that's got to do with this. I don't ask you"—*puff*—"where you—"

"You can," I said. "I intend to tell you. I guess maybe you don't know me as well as I thought you did, Johnnie. Haven't I always shot square with you?"

"Aw, hell, Lou," he said, shamed. "You know how I feel about you, but— All right. I'd probably tell you sooner or later anyway. It was"—*puff*—"here's the way it was, Lou. I told the old man I had this hot date Wednesday, see, but I was afraid of my tires, and I could pick up a couple good ones cheap an' hand him back something each week until I got 'em paid for. And—"

"Let me sort that out," I said. "You needed tires for your hot-rod and you tried to borrow the money from your father?"

"Sure! Just like I said. And you know what he says, Lou? He tells me I don't need tires, that I gad around too much. He says I should bring this babe to the house and Mom'll make some ice cream, an' we'll all play cards or somethin'! For Christ's sake!" He shook his head bewilderedly. "How stupid can a person get?"

I laughed gently. "You got your two tires anyway, then?" I said. "You stripped a couple off of a parked car?"

"Well—uh—to tell the truth, Lou, I took four. I wasn't meaning to but I knew where I could turn a couple real quick, an'—well—"

"Sure," I said. "This gal was kind of hard to get, and you wanted to be sure of getting over with her. A really hot babe, huh?"

"Mmmph-umph! Wow! You know what I mean, Lou. One of those gals that makes you want to take your shoes off and wade around in her."

I laughed again, and he laughed. Then it was somehow awfully silent, and he shifted uneasily.

"I know who owned the car, Lou. Soon as I get squared away a little I'll send him the money for those tires."

"That's all right," I said. "Don't worry about it."

"Are we—uh—can I—?"

"In just a little," I said. "You'll be leaving in a few minutes, Johnnie. Just a few formalities to take care of first."

"Boy, will I be glad to be out of here! Gosh, Lou, I don't know how people stand it! It'd drive me crazy."

"It'd drive anyone crazy," I said. "It does drive them crazy . . . Maybe you'd better lie down a while, Johnnie. Stretch out on the bunk. I've got a little more talking to do."

"But"—he turned slowly and tried to look at me, to see my face.

"You'd better do that," I said. "The air gets kind of bad with both of us sitting up."

"Oh," he said. "Yeah." And he lay down. He sighed deeply. "Say, this feels pretty good. Ain't it funny, Lou, what a difference it makes? Having someone to talk to, I mean. Someone that likes you and understands you. If you've got that, you can put up with almost anything."

"Yes," I said. "It makes a lot of difference, and— That's that. You didn't tell 'em you got that twenty from me, Johnnie?"

"Hell, no! What do you think I am, anyway? Piss on those guys."

"Why not?" I said. "Why didn't you tell them?"

"Well, uh"—the hard boards of the bunk squeaked—"well, I figured—oh, you know, Lou. Elmer got around in some kind of funny places, an' I thought maybe—well, I know you don't make a hell of a lot of dough, and you're always tossing it around on other people—and if someone should slip you a little tip—"

"I see," I said. "I don't take bribes, Johnnie."

"Who said anything about bribes?" I could feel him shrug. "Who said anything? I just wasn't going to let 'em hit you cold with it until you figured out a—until you remembered where you found it."

I didn't say anything for a minute. I just sat there thinking

about him, this kid that everyone said was no good, and a few
other people I knew. Finally I said, "I wish you hadn't done
it, Johnnie. It was the wrong thing to do."

"You mean they'll be sore?" He grunted. "To hell with
'em. They don't mean anything to me, but you're a square
joe."

"Am I?" I said. "How do you know I am, Johnnie? How
can a man ever really know anything? We're living in a funny
world, kid, a peculiar civilization. The police are playing
crooks in it, and the crooks are doing police duty. The politicians are preachers, and the preachers are politicians. The tax
collectors collect for themselves. The Bad People want us to
have more dough, and the Good People are fighting to keep
it from us. It's not good for us, know what I mean? If we all
had all we wanted to eat, we'd crap too much. We'd have
inflation in the toilet paper industry. That's the way I understand it. That's about the size of some of the arguments I've
heard."

He chuckled and dropped his cigar butt to the floor.
"Gosh, Lou. I sure enjoy hearing you talk—I've never heard
you talk that way before—but it's getting kind of late and—"

"Yeah, Johnnie," I said, "it's a screwed up, bitched up
world, and I'm afraid it's going to stay that way. And I'll tell
you why. Because no one, almost no one, sees anything wrong
with it. They can't see that things are screwed up, so they're
not worried about it. What they're worried about is guys like
you.

"They're worried about guys liking a drink and taking it.
Guys getting a piece of tail without paying a preacher for it.
Guys who know what makes 'em feel good, and aren't going
to be talked out of the notion . . . They don't like you guys,
and they crack down on you. And the way it looks to me
they're going to be cracking down harder and harder as time
goes on. You ask me why I stick around, knowing the score,
and it's hard to explain. I guess I kind of got a foot on both
fences, Johnnie. I planted 'em there early and now they've
taken root, and I can't move either way and I can't jump. All
I can do is wait until I split. Right down the middle. That's
all I can do and . . . But, you, Johnnie. Well, maybe you did

the right thing. Maybe it's best this way. Because it would get harder all the time, kid, and I know how hard it's been in the past."

"I . . . I don't—"

"I killed her, Johnnie. I killed both of them. And don't say I couldn't have, that I'm not that kind of a guy, because you don't know."

"I"— He started to rise up on his elbow, then lay back again. "I'll bet you had a good reason, Lou. I bet they had it coming."

"No one has it coming to them," I said. "But I had a reason, yes."

Dimly in the distance, like a ghost hooting, I heard the refinery whistles blowing for the swing shifts. And I could picture the workmen plodding in to their jobs, and the other shifts plodding out. Tossing their lunch buckets into their cars. Driving home and playing with their kids and drinking beer and watching their television sets and diddling their wives and . . . Just as if nothing was happening. Just as if a kid wasn't dying and a man, part of a man, dying with him.

"Lou . . ."

"Yes, Johnnie." It was a statement, not a question.

"Y-you m-mean I—I should take the rap for you? I—"

"No," I said. "Yes."

"I d-d-don't think—I can't, Lou! Oh, Jesus, I can't! I c-couldn't go through—"

I eased him back on the bunk. I ruffled his hair, chucked him gently under the chin, tilting it back.

" 'There is a time of peace,' " I said, " 'and a time of war. A time to sow and a time to reap. A time to live and a time to die . . .' "

"L-lou . . ."

"This hurts me," I said, "worse than it does you."

And I knifed my hand across his windpipe. Then I reached down for his belt.

. . . I pounded on the door, and after a minute the turnkey came. He cracked the door open a little and I slid out, and he slammed it again.

"Give you any trouble, Lou?"

"No," I said, "he was real peaceful. I think we've broken the case."

"He's gonna talk, huh?"

"They've talked before," I shrugged.

I went back upstairs and told Howard Hendricks I'd had a long talk with Johnnie, and that I thought he'd come through all right. "Just leave him alone for an hour or so," I said. "I've done everything I can. If I haven't made him see the light, then he just ain't going to see it."

"Certainly, Lou, certainly. I know your reputation. You want me to call you after I see him?"

"I wish you would," I said. "I'm kind of curious to know if he talks."

Thirteen

I'VE LOAFED around the streets sometimes, leaned against a store front with my hat pushed back and one boot hooked back around the other—hell, you've probably seen me if you've ever been out this way—I've stood like that, looking nice and friendly and stupid, like I wouldn't piss if my pants were on fire. And all the time I'm laughing myself sick inside. Just watching the people.

You know what I mean—the couples, the men and wives you see walking along together. The tall fat women, and the short scrawny men. The teensy little women, and the big fat guys. The dames with lantern jaws, and the men with no chins. The bowlegged wonders, and the knock-kneed miracles. The . . . I've laughed—inside, that is—until my guts ached. It's almost as good as dropping in on a Chamber of Commerce luncheon where some guy gets up and clears his throat a few times and says, "Gentlemen, we can't expect to get any more out of life than what we put into it . . ." (Where's the percentage in that?) And I guess it—they—the people—those mismatched people—aren't something to laugh about. They're really tragic.

They're not stupid, no more than average anyway. They've not tied up together just to give jokers like me a bang. The truth is, I reckon, that life has played a hell of a trick on 'em. There was a time, just for a few minutes maybe, when all their differences seemed to vanish and they were just what each other wanted; when they looked at each other at exactly the right time in the right place and under the right circumstances. And everything was perfect. They had that time—those few minutes—and they never had any other. But while it lasted . . .

. . . Everything seemed the same as usual. The shades were drawn, and the bathroom door was open a little, just to let in a little light; and she was sprawled out on her stomach asleep. Everything was the same . . . but it wasn't. It was one of those times.

She woke up while I was undressing; some change dropped out of my pocket and rolled against the baseboard. She sat up, rubbing at her eyes, starting to say something sharp. But somehow she smiled, instead, and I smiled back at her. I scooped her up in my arms and sat down on the bed and held her. I kissed her, and her mouth opened a little, and her arms locked around my neck.

That's the way it started. That's the way it went.

Until, finally, we were stretched out close, side by side, her arm around my hips and mine around hers; limp, drained dry, almost breathless. And still we wanted each other—wanted something. It was like the beginning instead of the end.

She burrowed her head against my shoulder, and it was nice. I didn't feel like shoving her away. She whispered into my ear, kind of baby-talking.

"Mad at you. You hurt me."

"I did?" I said. "Gosh, I'm sorry, honey."

"Hurt real bad. 'Iss one. Punch elbow in it."

"Well, gosh—"

She kissed me, let her mouth slide off mine. "Not mad," she whispered.

She was silent then, waiting it looked like for me to say something. Do something. She pushed closer, squirming, still keeping her face hidden.

"Bet I know something . . ."

"Yeah, honey?"

"About that vas—that operation."

"What," I said, "do you think you know?"

"It was after that—after Mike—"

"What about Mike?"

"Darling"—she kissed my shoulder—"I don't care. I don't mind. But it was then, wasn't it? Your father got ex—worried and . . . ?"

I let my breath out slowly. Almost any other night I could have enjoyed wringing her neck, but this was one time when I hadn't felt that way.

"It was about that time, as I recollect," I said. "But I don't know as that had anything to do with it."

"Honey . . ."

"Yeah?"

"Why do you suppose people . . . ?"

"It beats me," I said. "I never have been able to figure it out."

"D-don't some women . . . I'll bet you would think it was awful if—"

"If what?"

She pushed against me, and it felt like she was on fire. She shivered and began to cry. "D-don't, Lou. Don't make me ask. J-just . . ."

So I didn't make her ask.

Later on, when she was still crying but in a different way, the phone rang. It was Howard Hendricks.

"Lou, kid, you really did it! You really softened him up!"

"He signed a confession?" I said.

"Better than that, boy! He hanged himself! Did it with his belt! That proves he was guilty without us having to screw around before a judge and put the taxpayers to a lot of expense, and all that crap! Goddammit, Lou, I wish I was there right now to shake your hand!"

He stopped yelling and tried to get the gloat out of his voice. "Now, Lou, I want you to promise me that you won't take this the wrong way. You mustn't get down about it. A person like that don't deserve to live. He's a lot better off dead than he is alive."

"Yeah," I said. "I guess you're right at that."

I got rid of him and hung up. And right away the phone

rang again. This time it was Chester Conway calling from Fort Worth.

"Great work, Lou. Fine job. Fine! Guess you know what this means to me. Guess I made a mistake about—"

"Yes?" I said.

"Nothing. Don't matter now . . . See you, boy."

I hung up again, and the phone rang a third time. Bob Maples. His voice came over the wire thin and shaky.

"I know how much you thought of that boy, Lou. I know you'd just about as soon it'd happened to yourself."

As soon? "Yeah, Bob," I said. "I just about would have."

"You want to come over and set a spell, Lou? Play a game of checkers or somethin'? I ain't supposed to be up or I'd offer to come over there."

"I—I reckon not, Bob," I said. "But thanks, thanks a heap."

"That's all right, son. You change your mind, come on over. No matter what time it is."

Amy'd been taking in everything; impatient, curious. I hung up and slumped down on the bed, and she sat up beside me.

"For heaven's sake! What was that all about, Lou?"

I told her. Not the truth, of course, but what was supposed to be the truth. She clapped her hands together.

"Oh, darling! That's wonderful. My Lou solving the case! . . . Will you get a reward?"

"Why should I?" I said. "Think of all the fun I had."

"Oh, well . . ." She drew away a little, and I thought she was going to pop off; and I reckon she wanted to. But she wanted something else worse. "I'm sorry, Lou. You have every right to be angry with me."

She lay back down again, turning on her stomach, spreading her arms and legs. She stretched out, waiting, and whispered:

"Very, very angry . . ."

Sure, I know. Tell me something else. Tell a hophead he shouldn't take dope. Tell him it'll kill him, and see if he stops.

She got her money's worth.

It was going to cost her plenty, and I gave her value received. Honest Lou, that was me. Let Lou Titillate Your Tail.

Fourteen

I GUESS I must have got to sweating with all that exercise, and not having any clothes on I caught a hell of a cold. Oh, it wasn't too bad; not enough to really lay me low; but I wasn't fit to do any chasing around. I had to stay in bed for a week. And it was kind of a break for me, you might say.

I didn't have to talk to a lot of people, and have 'em asking damned fool questions and slapping me on the back. I didn't have to go to Johnnie Pappas' funeral. I didn't have to call on his folks, like I'd have felt I had to do ordinarily.

A couple of the boys from the office dropped by to say hello, and Bob Maples came in a time or two. He was still looking pretty peaked, seemed to have aged about ten years. We kept off the subject of Johnnie—just talked about things in general—and the visits went off pretty well. Only one thing came up that kind of worried me for a while. It was on the first—no, I guess the second time he came by.

"Lou," he said, "why in hell don't you get out of this town?"

"Get out?" I was startled. We'd just been sitting there quietly, smoking and passing a word now and then. And suddenly he comes out with this. "Why should I get out?"

"Why've you ever stayed here this long?" he said. "Why'd you ever want to wear a badge? Why didn't you be a doctor like your dad; try to make something of yourself?"

I shook my head, staring down at the bedclothes. "I don't know, Bob. Reckon I'm kind of lazy."

"You got awful funny ways of showin' it, Lou. You ain't never too lazy to take on some extra job. You put in more hours than any man I got. An' if I know anything about you, you don't like the work. You never have liked it."

He wasn't exactly right about that, but I knew what he meant. There was other work I'd have liked a lot better. "I don't know, Bob," I said, "there's a couple of kinds of laziness. The don't-want-to-do-nothin' and the stick-in-the-rut brand. You take a job, figuring you'll just keep it a little while, and that while keeps stretchin' on and on and on. You need a little more money before you can make a jump. You can't quite make up your mind about what you want to jump to. And then maybe you make a stab at it, you send off a few letters, and the people want to know what experience you've had—what you've been doin'. And probably they don't even want to bother with you, and if they do you've got to start right at the bottom, because you don't know anything. So you stay where you are, you just about got to, and you work pretty hard because you know it. You ain't young any more and it's all you've got."

Bob nodded slowly. "Yeah . . . I kinda know how that is. But it didn't need to be that way with you, Lou! Your dad could've sent you off to school. You could've been a practicin' doctor by this time."

"Well," I hesitated, "there'd been that trouble with Mike, and Dad would've been all alone, and . . . well, I guess my mind just didn't run to medicine, Bob. It takes an awful lot of study, you know."

"There's other things you could do, and you lack a lot of bein' broke, son. You could get you a little fortune for this property."

"Yeah, but . . ." I broke off. "Well, to tell the truth, Bob, I have kind of thought about pulling up stakes, but—"

"Amy don't want to?"

"I haven't asked her. The subject never came up. But I don't reckon she would."

"Well," he said slowly, "that's sure too bad. I don't suppose you'd . . . No, you wouldn't do that. I don't expect no man in his right mind would give up Amy."

I nodded a little, like I was acknowledging a compliment; agreeing that I couldn't give her up. And even with the way I felt about her, the nod came easy. On the surface, Amy had everything plus. She was smart and she came from a good family—which was a mighty important consideration with our people. But that was only the beginning. When Amy went down the street with that round little behind twitching, with her chin tucked in and her breasts stuck out, every man under eighty kind of drooled. They'd get sort of red in the face and forget to breathe, and you could hear whispers, *"Man, if I could just have some of that."*

Hating her didn't keep me from being proud of her.

"You trying to get rid of me, Bob?" I said.

"Kind of looks as though, don't it?" he grinned. "Guess I did too much thinkin' while I was laying around the house. Wondering about things that ain't none of my business. I got to thinkin' about how riled I get sometimes, having to give in to things I don't like, and hell, I ain't really fit to do much but what I am doin'; and I thought how much harder it must be on a man like you." He chuckled, wryly. "Fact is, I reckon, you started me thinking that way, Lou. You kind of brought it on yourself."

I looked blank, and then I grinned. "I don't mean anything by it. It's just a way of joking."

"Sure," he said, easily. "We all got our little pe-cul-ye-arities. I just thought maybe you was gettin' kind of saddle-galled, and—"

"Bob," I said, "what did Conway say to you there in Fort Worth?"

"Oh, hell"—he stood up, slapping his hat against his pants—"can't even recollect what it was now. Well, I guess I better be—"

"He said something. He said or did something that you didn't like a little bit."

"You reckon he did, huh?" His eyebrows went up. Then they came down and he chuckled, and put on his hat. "Forget it, Lou. It wasn't nothing important, and it don't matter no more, anyways."

He left; and, like I said, I was kind of worried for a while. But after I'd had time to think, it looked to me like I'd fretted about nothing. It looked like things were working out pretty good.

I was willing to leave Central City; I'd been thinking about leaving. But I thought too much of Amy to go against her wishes. I sure wouldn't do anything that Amy didn't like.

If something should happen to her, though—and something *was* going to happen—why, of course, I wouldn't want to hang around the old familiar scenes any more. It would be more than a soft-hearted guy like me could stand, and there wouldn't be any reason to. So I'd leave, and it'd all seem perfectly natural. No one would think anything of it.

Amy came to see me every day—in the morning for a few

minutes on her way to school, and again at night. She always brought some cake or pie or something, stuff I reckon their dog wouldn't eat (and that hound wasn't high-tone—he'd snatch horseturds on the fly), and she hardly nagged about anything, that I remember. She didn't give me any trouble at all. She was all sort of blushy and shy and shamed like. And she had to take it kind of easy when she sat down.

Two or three nights she drew the bath tub full of warm water and sat in it and soaked; and I'd sit and watch her and think how much she looked like *her*. And afterwards she'd lie in my arms—just lie there because that was about all either of us was up to. And I could almost fool myself into thinking it was *her*.

But it wasn't *her*, and, for that matter, it wouldn't have made any difference if it had been. I'd just been right back where I started. I'd have had to do it all over again.

I'd have had to kill her the second time . . .

I was glad Amy didn't bring up the subject of marriage; she was afraid of starting a quarrel, I guess. I'd already been right in the middle of three deaths, and a fourth coming right on top of 'em might look kind of funny. It was too soon for it. Anyway, I hadn't figured out a good safe way of killing her.

You see why I had to kill her, I reckon. Or do you? It was like this:

There wasn't any evidence against me. And even if there was some, quite a bit, I'd be a mighty hard man to stick. I just wasn't that kind of guy, you see. No one would believe I was. Why, hell, they'd been seeing Lou Ford around for years, and no one could tell them that good ol' Lou would—

But Lou could do it; Lou could convict himself. All he had to do was skip out on a girl who knew just about everything about him there was to know—who, even without that one wild night, could probably have pieced some plenty-ugly stuff together—and that would be the end of Lou. Everything would fall into place, right back to the time when Mike and I were kids.

As things stood now, she wouldn't let herself think things through. She wouldn't even let herself start to think. She'd cut up some pretty cute skylarks herself, and that had put a check on her thinking. And I was going to be her husband,

so everything was all right. Everything had to be all right . . .
But if I ran out on her—well, I knew Amy. That mental block
she'd set up would disappear. She'd have the answer that
quick—and she wouldn't keep it to herself. Because if she
couldn't have me, no one else would.

Yeah, I guess I mentioned that. She and Joyce seemed
pretty much alike.

Well, anyway . . .

Anyway, it had to be done, as soon as it safely could be
done. And knowing that, that there was just no other way
out, kind of made things easier. I stopped worrying, thinking
about it, I should say. I tried to be extra pleasant to her. She
was getting on my nerves, hanging around so much. But she
wouldn't be hanging around long, so I thought I ought to
be as nice as I could.

I'd taken sick on a Wednesday. By the next Wednesday I
was up, so I took Amy to prayer meeting. Being a school
teacher, she kind of had to put in an appearance at those
things, now and then, and I sort of enjoy 'em. I pick up lots
of good lines at prayer meetings. I asked Amy, I whispered to
her, how she'd like to have a little manna on her honey. And
she turned red, and kicked me on the ankle. I whispered to
her again, asked her if I could Mose-y into her Burning Bush.
I told her I was going to take her to my bosom and cleave
unto her, and anoint her with precious oils.

She got redder and redder and her eyes watered, but somehow it made her look cute. And it seemed like I'd never seen
her with her chin stuck out and her eyes narrowed. Then, she
doubled over, burying her face in her songbook; and she shivered and shook and choked, and the minister stood on tiptoe,
frowning, trying to figure out where the racket was coming
from.

It was one of the best prayer meetings I ever went to.

I stopped and bought some ice cream on the way home,
and she was giggling and breaking into snickers all the way.
While I made coffee, she dished up the cream; and I took part
of a spoonful and chased her around and around the kitchen
with it. I finally caught her and put it in her mouth, instead
of down her neck like I'd threatened. A little speck of it got
on her nose and I kissed it away.

Suddenly, she threw her arms around my neck and began to cry.

"Honey," I said, "don't do that, honey. I was just playing. I was just trying to give you a good time."

"Y-you—big—"

"I know," I said, "but don't say it. Let's don't have any more trouble between us."

"D-don't"—her arms tightened around me, and she looked up through the tears, smiling—"don't you understand? I'm j-just so happy, Lou. So h-happy I c-can't s-s-stand it!" And she burst into tears again.

We left the ice cream and coffee unfinished. I picked her up and carried her into Dad's office, and sat down in Dad's big old chair. We sat there in the dark, her on my lap—sat there until she had to go home. And it was all we wanted; it seemed to be enough. It was enough.

It was a good evening, even if we did have one small spat.

She asked me if I'd seen Chester Conway, and I said I hadn't. She said she thought it was darned funny that he didn't so much as come by and say hello, after what I'd done, and that if she were me she'd tell him so.

"I didn't do anything," I said. "Let's not talk about it."

"Well, I don't care, darling! He thought you'd done quite a bit at the time—couldn't wait to call you up long distance! Now, he's been back in town for almost a week, and he's too busy to—I don't care for my own sake, Lou. It certainly means nothing to me. But—"

"That makes two of us, then."

"You're too easy-going, that's the trouble with you. You let people run over you. You're always—"

"I know," I said. "I think I know it all, Amy. I've got it memorized. The whole trouble is that I won't listen to you—and it seems to me like that's about all I ever got done. I've been listening to you almost since you learned how to talk, and I reckon I can do it a while longer. If it'll make you happy. But I don't think it'll change me much."

She sat up very stiff and straight. Then, she settled back again, still holding herself kind of rigid. She was silent for about the time it takes you to count to ten.

"Well, just the same, I—I—"

"Yeah?" I said.

"Oh, be quiet," she said. "Keep still. Don't say anything."
And she laughed. And it was a good evening after all.

But it *was* kind of funny about Conway.

Fifteen

HOW LONG should I wait? that was the question. How long
could I wait? How long was it safe?

Amy wasn't crowding me any. She was still pretty shy and
skittish, trying to keep that barbed-wire tongue of hers in her
mouth—though she wasn't always successful. I figured I could
stall her off on marriage indefinitely, but Amy . . . well, it
wasn't just Amy. There wasn't anything I could put my finger
on, but I had the feeling that things were closing in on me.
And I couldn't talk myself out of it.

Every day that passed, the feeling grew stronger.

Conway hadn't come to see me or spoken to me, but that
didn't necessarily mean anything. It *didn't* mean anything that
I could see. He was busy. He'd never given a whoop in hell
for anyone but himself and Elmer. He was the kind of a guy
that would drop you when he got a favor, then pick you up
again when he needed another one.

He'd gone back to Fort Worth, and he hadn't returned.
But that was all right, too. Conway Construction had big offices in Fort Worth. He'd always spent a lot of time there.

Bob Maples? Well, I couldn't see that he was much different
than ever. I'd study him as the days drifted by, and I couldn't
see anything to fret about. He looked pretty old and sick, but
he *was* old and he had been sick. He didn't have too much
to say to me, but what he did have was polite and friendly—he
seemed hell-bent on being polite and friendly. And he'd never
been what you'd call real talky. He'd always had spells when
you could hardly get a word out of him.

Howard Hendricks? Well . . . Well, something was sure
enough eating on Howard.

I'd run into Howard the first day I was up after my sick
spell; he'd been coming up the steps of the courthouse, just

as I was heading down them to lunch. He nodded, not quite looking at me, and mumbled out a, "H'are you, Lou?" I stopped and said I was feeling a lot better—still felt pretty weak, but couldn't really complain any.

"You know how it is, Howard," I said. "It isn't the flu so much as the after effects."

"So I've heard," he said.

"It's kind of like I always say about auty-mobiles. It's not the original cost so much as the upkeep. But I reckon—"

"Got to run," he mumbled. "See you."

But I wasn't letting him off that easy. I was really in the clear, now, and I could afford to open up a little on him. "As I was sayin'," I said, "I reckon I can't tell you much about sickness, can I, Howard? Not with that shrapnel you got in you. I got an idea about that shrapnel, Howard—what you could do with it. You could get you some X-rays taken and print 'em on the back of your campaign cards. Then on the other side you could have a flag with your name spelled out in thermometers, and maybe a upside down—what do you call them hospital piss-pots? Oh, yeah—urinal for an exclamation mark. Where'd you say that shrapnel was anyway, Howard? Seems like I just can't keep track of it, no matter how hard I try. One time it's in—"

"My ass"—he was looking at me now, all right—"it's in my ass."

I'd been holding him by the lapel to keep him from running off. He took my hand by the wrist, still staring at me, and he pulled it away and let it drop. Then, he turned and went up the steps, his shoulders sagging a little but his feet moving firm and steady. And we hadn't passed a word between us since then. He kept out of my way when he saw me coming, and I did him the same kind of favor.

So there was something wrong there; but what else could I expect? What was there to worry about? I'd given him the works, and it had probably dawned on him that I'd needled him plenty in the past. And that wasn't the only reason he had to act stiff and cold. Elections were coming up in the fall, and he'd be running as usual. Breaking the Conway case would be a big help to him, and he'd want to talk it up. But he'd feel awkward about doing it. He'd have to cut me out of the credit, and he figured I'd be sore. So he was jumping the gun on me.

There was nothing really out of the way, then. Nothing with him or Sheriff Bob or Chester Conway. There wasn't a thing . . . but the feeling kept growing. It got stronger and stronger.

I'd been keeping away from the Greek's. I'd even stayed off the street where his restaurant was. But one day I went there. Something just seemed to pull the wheels of my car in that direction, and I found myself stopping in front of it.

The windows were all soaped over. The doors were closed. But it seemed like I could hear people inside; I heard some banging and clattering.

I got out of my car and stood by the side of it a minute or two. Then, I stepped up on the curb and crossed the walk.

There was a place on one of the double doors where the soap had been scraped away. I sheltered my eyes with my hand and peered through it; rather I started to peer through it. For the door opened suddenly, and the Greek stepped out.

"I am sorry, Officer Ford," he said. "I cannot serve you. We are not open for business."

I stammered that I didn't want anything. "Just thought I'd drop by to—to—"

"Yes?"

"I wanted to see you," I said. "I wanted to see you the night it happened, and it hasn't been off my mind since. But I couldn't bring myself to do it. I couldn't face you. I knew how you'd feel, how you'd be bound to feel, and there wasn't anything I could say. Nothing. Nothing I could say or do. Because if there'd been anything . . . well, it wouldn't have happened in the first place."

It was the truth, and God—God!—what a wonderful thing truth is. He looked at me in a way I didn't like to name; and then he looked kind of baffled; and then he suddenly caught his lip under his teeth and stared down at the sidewalk.

He was a swarthy middle-aged guy in a high-crowned black hat, and a shirt with black sateen protectors pulled over the sleeves; and he stared down at the sidewalk and looked back up again.

"I am glad you did come by, Lou," he said, quietly. "It is

fitting. I have felt, at times, that he regarded you as his one true friend."

"I aimed to be his friend," I said. "There weren't many things I wanted much more. Somehow, I slipped up; I couldn't help him right when he needed help worst. But I want you to know one thing, Max. I—I didn't hurt—"

He laid a hand on my arm. "You need not tell me that, Lou. I do not know why—what—but—"

"He felt lost," I said. "Like he was all alone in the world. Like he was out of step, and he could never get back in again."

"Yes," he said. "But . . . yes. There was always trouble, and he seemed always at fault."

I nodded, and he nodded. He shook his head, and I shook mine. We stood there, shaking our heads and nodding, neither of us really saying anything; and I wished I could leave. But I didn't quite know how to go about it. Finally, I said I was sorry he was closing the restaurant.

"If there's anything I can do . . ."

"I am not closing it," he said. "Why should I close it?"

"Well, I just thought that—"

"I am remodelling it. I am putting in leather booths and an inlaid floor and air-conditioning. Johnnie would have liked those things. Many times he suggested them, and I suggested he was hardly fitted to give me advice. But now we will have them. It will be as he wanted. It is—all that can be done."

I shook my head again. I shook it and nodded.

"I want to ask you a question, Lou. I want you to answer it, and I want the absolute truth."

"The truth?" I hesitated. "Why wouldn't I tell you the truth, Max?"

"Because you might feel that you couldn't. That it would be disloyal to your position and associates. Who else visited Johnnie's cell after you left?"

"Well, there was Howard—the county attorney—"

"I know of that; he made the discovery. And a deputy sheriff and the jailor were with him. Who else?"

My heart gave a little jump. Maybe . . . But, no, it was no good. I couldn't do that. I couldn't bring myself to try it.

"I don't have any idea, Max," I said. "I wasn't there. But

I can tell you you're on the wrong track. I've known all those boys for years. They wouldn't do a thing like that any more than I would."

It was the truth again, and he had to see it. I was looking straight into his eyes.

"Well . . ." he sighed. "Well, we will talk again, Lou."

And I said, "You bet we will, Max," and I got away from him.

I drove out on Derrick Road, five-six miles out. I pulled the car off on the shoulder, up at the crest of a little hill; and I sat there looking down through the blackjacks but I didn't see a thing. I didn't see the blackjacks.

About five minutes after I'd stopped, well, maybe no more than three minutes, a car drew up behind mine. Joe Rothman got out of it, and plodded along the shoulder and looked in at me.

"Nice view here," he said. "Mind if I join you? Thanks, I knew you wouldn't." He said it like that, all run together, without waiting for me to reply. He opened the door and slid into the seat beside me.

"Come out this way often, Lou?"

"Whenever I feel like it," I said.

"Well, it's a nice view all right. Almost unique. I don't suppose you'll find more than forty or fifty thousand billboards like that one in the United States."

I grinned in spite of myself. The billboard had been put up by the Chamber of Commerce; and the words on it were:

> You Are Now Nearing
> CENTRAL CITY, TEX.
> *"Where the hand clasp's a little stronger."*
> Pop. (1932) 4,800   Pop. (1952) 48,000
> WATCH US GROW!!

"Yeah," I said, "that's quite a sign, all right."

"You were looking at it, then? I thought that must be the attraction. After all, what else is there to see aside from those blackjacks and a little white cottage? The murder cottage, I believe they call it."

"What do you want?" I said.

"How many times were you there, Lou? How many times did you lay her?"

"I was there quite a few times," I said. "I had reason to be. And I'm not so hard up for it that I have to lay whores."

"No?" He squinted at me thoughtfully. "No, I don't suppose you would be. Personally, I've always operated on the theory that even in the presence of abundance, it's well to keep an eye out for the future. You never can tell, Lou. You may wake up some morning and find they've passed a law against it. It'll be un-American."

"Maybe they'll put a rider on that law," I said.

"Prohibiting bullshit? I see you don't have a legal type of mind, Lou, or you wouldn't say that. There's a basic contradiction in it. Tail we can do without, as our penal institutions so righteously prove; tail of the orthodox type that is. But what could you substitute for bullshit? Where would we be without it?"

"Well," I said, "I wouldn't be listening to you."

"But you're going to listen to me, Lou. You're going to sit right here and listen, and answer up promptly when the occasion demands. Get me? Get me, Lou?"

"I get you," I said. "I got you right from the beginning."

"I was afraid you hadn't. I wanted you to understand that I can stack it up over your head, and you'll sit there and like it."

He shook tobacco into a paper, twirled it, and ran it across his tongue. He stuck it in the corner of his mouth, and seemed to forget about it.

"You were talking with Max Pappas," he said. "From what I could judge it was a reasonably friendly conversation."

"It was," I said.

"He was resigned to the fact of Johnnie's suicide? He had accepted it as suicide?"

"I can't say that he was resigned to it," I said. "He was wondering whether someone—if someone was in the cell after I left, and . . ."

"And, Lou? And?"

"I told him, no, that it couldn't have been that way. None of the boys would be up to doing such a thing."

"Which settles that," Rothman nodded. "Or does it?"

"What are you driving at?" I snapped. "What—"

"Shut up!" His voice toughened, then went smooth again. "Did you notice the remodelling he's doing? Do you know how much all that will cost? Right around twelve thousand dollars. Where do you suppose he got that kind of money?"

"How the hell do I—"

"Lou."

"Well, maybe he had it saved."

"Max Pappas?"

"Or maybe he borrowed it."

"Without collateral?"

"Well . . . I don't know," I said.

"Let me make a suggestion. Someone gave it to him. A wealthy acquaintance, we'll say. Some man who felt he owed it to him."

I shrugged, and pushed my hat back; because my forehead was sweating. But I was feeling cold inside, so cold inside.

"Conway Construction is handling the job, Lou. Doesn't it strike you as rather odd that he'd do a job for a man whose son killed his son."

"There aren't many jobs that he don't handle," I said. "Anyway, it's the company, not him; he's not in there swinging a hammer himself. More'n likely he doesn't even know about it."

"Well . . ." Rothman hesitated. Then he went on, kind of dogged. "It's a turnkey job. Conway's jobbing all the materials, dealing with the supply houses, paying off the men. No one's seen a nickel coming from Pappas."

"So what?" I said. "Conway takes all the turnkey stuff he can get. He cuts a half a dozen profits instead of one."

"And you think Pappas would hold still for it? You don't see him as the kind of guy who'd insist on bargaining for every item, who'd haggle over everything right down to the last nail? I see him that way, Lou. It's the only way I can see him."

I nodded. "So do I. But he's not in a real good position to have his own way right now. He gets his job like Conway Construction wants to give it to him, or he just don't get it."

"Yeah . . ." He shifted his cigarette from one side of his mouth to the other. He pushed it across with his tongue, his eyes narrowed on my face. "But the money, Lou. That still doesn't explain about the money."

"He lived close," I said. "He could have had it, a big enough part, anyway, so's they'd wait on the rest. It didn't need to be in a bank. He could have had it salted away around his house."

"Yeah," said Rothman, slowly. "Yeah, I suppose so . . ."

He turned back around in the seat, so that he was looking through the windshield instead of me—instead of *at* me. He flicked his cigarette away, fumbled for his tobacco and papers, and began rolling another one.

"Did you get out to the cemetery, Lou? Out to Johnnie's grave?"

"No," I said, "and I've sure got to do that, too. I'm ashamed I haven't done it before."

"Well—dammit, you mean that, don't you? You mean every word of it!"

"Who are you to ask that?" I snapped. "What did you ever do for him? I don't want any credit for it, but I'm the only man in Central City that ever tried to help that kid. I liked him. I understood him. I—"

"I know, I know," he shook his head, dully. "I was just going to say that Johnnie's buried in Sacred Ground . . . You know what that means, Lou?"

"I reckon. The church didn't call it suicide."

"And the answer, Lou? You do have an answer?"

"He was so awful young," I said, "and he hadn't ever had much but trouble. Maybe the church figured he'd been faulted enough, and tried to give him a break. Maybe they figured that it was sort of an accident; that he'd just been fooling around and went too far."

"Maybe," said Rothman. "Maybe, maybe, maybe. One more thing, Lou. The big thing . . . On the Sunday night that Elmer and the late occupant of yon cottage got it, one of my carpenters went to the last show at the Palace. He parked his car around in back at—now get this, Lou—at nine-thirty. When he came out, all four of his tires were gone . . ."

Sixteen

I WAITED and everything got pretty quiet. "Well," I said, finally, "that's sure too bad. All four tires, huh?"

"Too bad? You mean it's funny, don't you, Lou? Plumb funny?"

"Well, it is, kind of," I said. "It's funny I didn't hear anything about it at the office."

"It'd been still funnier if you had, Lou. Because he didn't report the theft. I'd hardly call it the greatest mystery of all time, but, for some reason, you fellas down at the office don't take much interest in us fellas down at the labor temple—unless you find us on a picket line."

"I can't hardly help—"

"Never mind, Lou; it's really not pertinent. The man didn't report the theft, but he did mention it to some of the boys when the carpenters and joiners held their regular Tuesday night meeting. And one of them, as it turned out, had bought two of the tires from Johnnie Pappas. They . . . Do you have a chill, Lou? Are you catching cold?"

I bit down on my cigar. I didn't say anything.

"These lads equipped themselves with a couple of piss-elm clubs, or reasonable facsimiles thereof, and went calling on Johnnie. He wasn't at home and he wasn't at Slim Murphy's filling station. In fact, he wasn't anywhere about that time; he was swinging by his belt from the window-bars of the courthouse cooler. But his hotrod was at the station, and the remaining two stolen tires were on it. They stripped them off—Murphy, of course, isn't confiding in the police either—and that ended the matter. But there's been talk about it, Lou. There's been talk even though—*apparently*—no one has attached any great significance to the event."

I cleared my throat. "I—why should they, Joe?" I said. "I guess I don't get you."

"For the birds, Lou, remember? The starving sparrows. . . . Those tires were stolen after nine-thirty on the night of Elmer's and his lady friend's demise. Assuming that Johnnie didn't go to work on them the moment the owner parked —or even assuming that he did—we are driven to the inevitable conclusion that he was engaged in relatively inno-cent pursuits until well after ten o'clock. He could not, in other words, have had any part in the horrible happenings behind yonder blackjacks."

"I don't see why not," I said.

"You don't?" His eyes widened. "Well, of course, poor old Descartes, Aristotle, Diogenes, Euclid et al are dead, but I think you'll find quite a few people around who'll defend their theories. I'm very much afraid, Lou, that they won't go along with your proposition that a body can be in two places at the same time."

"Johnnie ran with a pretty wild crowd," I said. "I figure that one of his buddies stole those tires and gave 'em to him to peddle."

"I see. I see . . . Lou."

"Why not?" I said. "He was in a good position to get rid of them there at the station. Slim Murphy wouldn't have in-terfered. . . . Why, hell, it's bound to have been that way, Joe. If he'd have had an alibi for the time of the murders, he'd have told me so, wouldn't he? He wouldn't have hanged himself."

"He liked you, Lou. He trusted you."

"For damned good reasons. He knew I was his friend."

Rothman swallowed, and a sort of laughing sound came out of his throat, the kind of sound you make when you don't quite know whether to laugh or cry or get sore.

"Fine, Lou. Perfect. Every brick is laid straight, and the bricklayer is an honest upstanding mechanic. But still I can't help wondering about his handiwork and him. I can't help wondering why he feels the need to defend his structure of perhapses and maybes, his shelter wall of logical alternatives. I can't see why he didn't tell a certain labor skate to get the hell on about his business."

So . . . So there it was. I was. But where was he? He nod-ded as though I'd asked him the question. Nodded, and drew a little bit back in the seat.

"Humpty-Dumpty Ford," he said, "sitting right on top of the labor temple. And how or why he got there doesn't make much difference. You're going to have to move, Lou. Fast. Before someone . . . before you upset yourself."

"I was kind of figuring on leaving town," I said. "I haven't done anything, but—"

"Certainly you haven't. Otherwise, as a staunch Red Fascist Republican, I wouldn't feel free to yank you from the clutches of your detractors and persecutors—your would-be persecutors, I should say."

"You think that—you think maybe—"

He shrugged. "I think so, Lou. I think you just might have a little trouble in leaving. I think it so strongly that I'm getting in touch with a friend of mine, one of the best criminal lawyers in the country. You've probably heard of him—Billy Boy Walker? I did Billy Boy a favor one time, back East, and he has a long memory for favors, regardless of his other faults."

I'd heard of Billy Boy Walker. I reckon almost everyone has. He'd been governor of Alabama or Georgia or one of those states down south. He'd been a United States senator. He'd been a candidate for president on a Divide-the-Dough ticket. He'd started getting shot at quite a bit about that time, so he'd dropped out of politics and stuck to his criminal law practice. And he was plenty good. All the high mucky-mucks cussed and made fun of him for the way he'd cut up in politics. But I noticed that when they or their kin got into trouble, they headed straight for Billy Boy Walker.

It sort of worried me that Rothman thought I needed that kind of help.

It worried me, and it made me wonder all over again why Rothman and his unions would go to all the trouble of getting me a lawyer. Just what did Rothman stand to lose if the Law started asking me questions? Then I realized that if my first conversation with Rothman should ever come out, any jury in the land would figure he'd sicked me on the late Elmer Conway. In other words, Rothman was saving two necks—his and mine—with one lawyer.

"Perhaps you won't need him," he went on. "But it's best to have him alerted. He's not a man who can make himself available on a moment's notice. How soon can you leave town?"

I hesitated. Amy. How was I going to do it? "I'll—I can't do it right away," I said. "I'll have to kind of drop a hint or two around that I've been thinking about leaving, then work up to it gradually. You know, it would look pretty funny—"

"Yeah," he frowned, "but if they know you're getting ready to jump they're apt to close in all the faster . . . Still, I can see your point."

"What can they do?" I said. "If they could close in, they'd be doing it already. Not that I've done—"

"Don't bother. Don't say it again. Just move—start moving as quickly as you can. It shouldn't take you more than a couple of weeks at the outside."

Two weeks. Two weeks more for Amy.

"All right, Joe," I said. "And thanks for—for—"

"For what?" He opened the door. "For you, I haven't done a thing."

"I'm not sure I can make it in two weeks. It may take a little—"

"It hadn't better," he said, "take much longer."

He got out and went back to his own car. I waited until he'd turned around and headed back toward Central City; and then I turned around and started back. I drove slowly, thinking about Amy.

Years ago there was a jeweler here in Central City who had a hell of a good business, and a beautiful wife and two fine kids. And one day, on a business trip over to one of the teachers' college towns he met up with a girl, a real honey, and before long he was sleeping with her. She knew he was married, and she was willing to leave it that way. So everything was perfect. He had her and he had his family and a swell business. But one morning they found him and the girl dead in a motel—he'd shot her and killed himself. And when one of our deputies went to tell his wife about it, he found her and the kids dead, too. This fellow had shot 'em all.

He'd had everything, and somehow nothing was better.

That sounds pretty mixed up, and probably it doesn't have a lot to do with me. I thought it did at first, but now that I look at it—well, I don't know. I just don't know.

I knew I had to kill Amy; I could put the reason into words. But every time I thought about it, I had to stop and think *why* again. I'd be doing something, reading a book or something, or maybe I'd be with her. And all of a sudden it would come over me that I was going to kill her, and the idea seemed so crazy that I'd almost laugh out loud. Then, I'd start thinking and I'd see it, see that it had to be done, and . . .

It was like being asleep when you were awake and awake when you were asleep. I'd pinch myself, figuratively speaking—I had to keep pinching myself. Then I'd wake up kind of in reverse; I'd go back into the nightmare I had to live in. And everything would be clear and reasonable.

But I still didn't know how to go about doing it. I couldn't figure out a way that would leave me in the clear or even reasonably in the clear. And I sure had to be on this one. I was Humpty-Dumpty, like Rothman had said, and I couldn't jiggle around very much.

I couldn't think of a way because it was a real toughie, and I had to keep remembering the *why* of it. But finally it came to me.

I found a way, because I had to. I couldn't stall any longer.

It happened three days after my talk with Rothman. It was a payday Saturday, and I should have been working, but somehow I hadn't been able to bring myself to do it. I'd stayed in the house all day with the shades drawn, pacing back and forth, wandering from room to room. And when night came I was still there. I was sitting in Dad's office, with nothing on but the little desk light; and I heard these footsteps moving lightly across the porch, and the sound of the screen door opening.

It was way too early for Amy; but I wasn't jittered any. I'd had people walk in before like this.

I stepped to the door of the office just as he came into the hall.

"I'm sorry, stranger," I said. "The doctor doesn't practice any more. The sign's just there for sentimental reasons."

"That's okay, bud"—he walked right toward me and I had to move back—"it's just a little burn."

"But I don't—"

"A cigar burn," he said. And he held his hand out, palm up.

And, at last, I recognized him.

He sat down in Dad's big leather chair, grinning at me. He

brushed his hand across the arm, knocking off the coffee cup and saucer I'd left there.

"We got some talking to do, bud, and I'm thirsty. You got some whiskey around? An unopened bottle? I ain't no whiskey hog, understand, but some places I like to see a seal on a bottle."

"I've got a phone around," I said, "and the jail's about six blocks away. Now, drag your ass out of here before you find yourself in it."

"Huh-uh," he said. "You want to use that phone, go right ahead, bud."

I started to. I figured he'd be afraid to go through with it, and if he did, well, my word was still better than any bum's. No one had anything on me, and I was still Lou Ford. And he wouldn't get his mouth open before someone smacked a sap in it.

"Go ahead, bud, but it'll cost you. It'll sure cost you. And it won't be just the price of a burned hand."

I held onto the phone, but I didn't lift the receiver. "Go on," I said, "let's have it."

"I got interested in you, bud. I spent a year stretch on the Houston pea farm, and I seen a couple guys like you there; and I figured it might pay to watch you a little. So I followed you that night. I heard some of the talk you had with that labor fellow . . ."

"And I reckon it meant a hell of a lot to you, didn't it?" I said.

"No, sir," he wagged his head, "hardly meant a thing to me. Fact is, it didn't mean much to me a couple nights later when you came up to that old farm house where I was shacked up, and then cut cross-prairie to that little white house. That didn't mean much neither, *then* . . . You say you had some whiskey, bud? An unopened bottle?"

I went into the laboratory, and got a pint of old prescription liquor from the stores cabinet. I brought it back with a glass; and he opened it and poured the glass half full.

"Have one on the house," he said, and handed it to me.

I drank it; I needed it. I passed the glass back to him, and he dropped it on the floor with the cup and saucer. He took a big swig from the bottle, and smacked his lips.

"No, sir," he went on, "it didn't mean a thing, and I couldn't stick around to figure it out. I hiked out of there early Monday morning, and hit up the pipeline for a job. They put me with a jackhammer crew way the hell over on the Pecos, so far out I couldn't make town my first payday. Just three of us there by ourselves cut off from the whole danged world. But this payday it was different. We'd finished up on the Pecos, and I got to come in. I caught up on the news, bud, and those things you'd done and said meant plenty."

I nodded. I felt kind of glad. It was out of my hands, now, and the pieces were falling into place. I knew I had to do it, and how I was going to do it.

He took another swallow of whiskey and dug a cigarette from his shirt pocket. "I'm an understandin' man, bud, and the law ain't helped me none and I ain't helpin' it none. Unless I have to. What you figure it's worth to you to go on living?"

"I—" I shook my head. I had to go slow. I couldn't give in too easily. "I haven't got much money," I said. "Just what I make on my job."

"You got this place. Must be worth a pretty tidy sum, too."

"Yeah, but, hell," I said. "It's all I've got. If I'm not going to have a window left to throw it out of, there's not much percentage in keeping you quiet."

"You might change your mind about that, bud," he said. But he didn't sound too firm about it.

"Anyway," I said, "it's just not practical to sell it. People would wonder what I'd done with the money. I'd have to account for it to the government and pay a big chunk of taxes on it. For that matter—I reckon you're in kind of a hurry—"

"You reckon right, bud."

"Well, it would take quite a while to get rid of a place like this. I'd want to sell it to a doctor, someone who'd pay for my Dad's practice and equipment. It'd be worth at least a third more that way, but the deal couldn't be swung in a hurry."

He studied me, suspiciously, trying to figure out how much if any I was stringing him. As a matter of fact, I wasn't lying more'n a little bit.

"I don't know," he said slowly. "I don't know much about them things. Maybe—you reckon you could swing a loan on it?"

"Well, I'd sure hate to do that—"

"That ain't what I asked you, bud."

"But, look," I said, making it good, "how would I pay it back out of my job? I just couldn't do it. I probably wouldn't get more than five thousand after they took out interest and brokerage fees. And I'd have to turn right around somewhere and swing another loan to pay off the first one, and—hell, that's no way to do business. Now, if you'll just give me four-five months to find someone who—"

"Huh-uh. How long it take you to swing this loan? A week?"

"Well . . ." I might have to give her a little longer than that. I wanted to give her longer. "I think that'd be a little bit quick. I'd say two weeks; but I'd sure hate—"

"Five thousand," he said, sloshing the whiskey in the bottle. "Five thousand in two weeks. Two weeks from to-night. All right, bud, we'll call that a deal. An' it'll be a deal, understand? I ain't no hog about money or nothin'. I get the five thousand and that's the last we'll see of each other."

I scowled and cussed, but I said, "Well, all right."

He tucked the whiskey into his hip pocket, and stood up. "Okay, bud. I'm goin' back out to the pipeline tonight. This ain't a very friendly place for easy-livin' men, so I'll stay out there another payday. But don't get no notions about runnin' out on me."

"How the hell could I?" I said. "You think I'm crazy?"

"You ask unpleasant questions, bud, and you may get un-pleasant answers. Just be here with that five grand two weeks from tonight and there won't be no trouble."

I gave him a clincher; I still felt I might be giving in too easy. "Maybe you'd better not come here," I said. "Someone might see you and—"

"No one will. I'll watch myself like I did tonight. I ain't no more anxious for trouble than you are."

"Well," I said, "I just thought it might be better if we—"

"Now, bud"—he shook his head—"what happened the last

time you was out wanderin' around old empty farm houses? It didn't turn out so good, did it?"

"All right," I said. "Suit yourself about it."

"That's just what I aim to do." He glanced toward the clock. "We got it all straight, then. Five thousand, two weeks from tonight, nine o'clock. That's it, and don't slip up on it."

"Don't worry. You'll get it," I said.

He stood at the front door a moment, sizing up the situation outside. Then he slipped out and off of the porch, and disappeared in the trees on the lawn.

I grinned, feeling a little sorry for him. It was funny the way these people kept asking for it. Just latching onto you, no matter how you tried to brush them off, and almost telling you how they wanted it done. Why'd they all have to come to me to get killed? Why couldn't they kill themselves?

I cleaned up the broken dishes in the office. I went upstairs and lay down and waited for Amy. I didn't have long to wait.

I didn't have long; and in a way she was the same as always, sort of snappy and trying not to be. But I could sense a difference, the stiffness that comes when you want to say or do something and don't know how to begin. Or maybe she could sense it in me; maybe we sensed it in each other.

I guess that's the way it was, because we both came out with it together. We spoke at the same time:

"Lou, why don't we . . ."
"Amy, why don't we . . .," we said,

We laughed and said "bread and butter," and then she spoke again.

"You do want to, don't you, darling? Honest and truly?"

"Didn't I just start to ask you?" I said.

"How—when do you—"

"Well, I was thinking a couple of weeks would—"

"Darling!" She kissed me. "That was just what I was going to say!"

There was just a little more. That last piece of the picture needed one more little push.

"What are you thinking about, darling?"

"Well, I was thinking we've always had to do kinda like people expected us to. I mean— Well, what were you thinking about?"

"You tell me first, Lou."

"No, you tell me, Amy."

"Well . . ."

"Well . . ."

"Why don't we elope," we said.

We laughed, and she threw her arms around me, snuggled up against me, sort of shivery but warm; so hard but so soft. And she whispered into my ear and I whispered into hers:

"Bread and butter . . .

"Bad luck, stay 'way from my darling."

Seventeen

HE SHOWED UP on, well, I guess it was the following Tuesday. The Tuesday after the Saturday the bum had shown up and Amy and I had decided to elope. He was a tall, stoop-shouldered guy with a face that seemed to be all bone and yellowish tightly drawn skin. He said his name was Dr. John Smith and that he was just passing through, he was just looking around in this section, and he'd heard—he'd thought, perhaps—that the house and the practice might be on the market.

It was around nine o'clock in the morning. By rights, I should have been headed for the courthouse. But I wasn't knocking myself out, these days, to get downtown; and Dad had always laid himself out for any doctors that came around.

"I've thought about selling it, off and on," I said, "but that's about as far as it's gone. I've never taken any steps in that direction. But come in, anyway. Doctors are always welcome in this house."

I sat him down in the office and brought out a box of cigars, and got him some coffee. Then, I sat down with him and tried to visit. I can't say that I liked him much. He kept staring at me out of his big hollow eyes like I was really some sort of curiosity, something to look at instead of to talk to. But—well, doctors get funny mannerisms. They live in an I'm-the-King world, where everyone else is wrong but them.

"You're a general practitioner, Doctor Smith?" I said. "I wouldn't want to discourage you, but I'm afraid the general

practice field is pretty well the monopoly here of long-estab-
lished doctors. Now—I haven't thought too much about dis-
posing of this place, but I might consider it—now, I do think
there's room for a good man in pediatrics or obstetrics . . ."

I let it hang there, and he blinked and came out of his
trance.

"As a matter of fact, I am interested in those fields, Mr.
Ford. I would—uh—hesitate to call myself a specialist, but—
uh—"

"I think you might find an opening here, then," I said.
"What's been your experience in treating nephritis, doctor?
Would you say that inoculation with measles has sufficiently
proven itself as a curative agent to warrant the inherent
danger?"

"Well, uh—uh—" He crossed his legs. "Yes and no."

I nodded seriously. "You feel that there are two sides to the
question?"

"Well—uh—yes."

"I see," I said. "I'd never thought about it quite that way,
but I can see that you're right."

"That's your—uh—specialty, Mr. Ford? Children's diseases?"

"I haven't any specialty, doctor," I laughed. "I'm living
proof of the adage about the shoemaker's son going bare-
footed. But I've always been interested in children, and I suppose the little I do know about medicine is confined to
pediatrics."

"I see. Well, uh, as a matter of fact, most of my work has
been in—uh—geriatrics."

"You should do well here, then," I said. "We have a high
percentage of elderly people in the population. Geriatrics,
eh?"

"Well, uh, as a matter of fact . . ."

"You know *Max Jacobsohn on Degenerative Diseases?* What
do you think of his theorem as to the ratio between deceler-
ated activity and progressive senility? I can understand the basic concept, of course, but my math isn't good enough to
allow me to appreciate his formulae. Perhaps you'll explain
them to me?"

"Well, I—uh—it's pretty complicated . . ."

"I see. You feel, perhaps, that Jacobsohn's approach may be a trifle empirical? Well, I was inclined to that belief myself, for a time, but I'm afraid it may have been because my own approach was too subjective. For instance. Is the condition pathological? Is it psycho-pathological? Is it psycho-patholog-ical-psychosomatic? Yes, yes, yes. It can be one or two or all three—*but* in varying degrees, doctor. Like it or not, we must contemplate an x factor. Now, to strike an equation—and you'll pardon me for oversimplifying—let's say that our cosine is. . . ."

I went on smiling and talking, wishing that Max Jacobsohn was here to see him. From what I'd heard of Dr. Jacobsohn, he'd probably grab this guy by the seat of his pants and boot him out into the street.

"As a matter of fact," he interrupted me, rubbing a big bony hand across his forehead, "I have a very bad headache. What do you do for headaches, Mr. Ford."

"I never have them," I said.

"Uh, oh? I thought perhaps that studying so much, sitting up late nights when you can't—uh—sleep . . ."

"I never have any trouble sleeping," I said.

"You don't worry a lot? I mean that in a town such as this where there is so much gossip—uh—malicious gossip, you don't feel that people are talking about you? It doesn't—uh—seem unbearable at times?"

"You mean," I said, slowly, "do I feel persecuted? Well, as a matter of fact, I do, doctor. But I never worry about it. I can't say that it doesn't bother me, but—"

"Yes? Yes, Mr. Ford?"

"Well, whenever it gets too bad, I just step out and kill a few people. I frig them to death with a barbed-wire cob I have. After that I feel fine."

I'd been trying to place him, and finally it had come to me. It's been several years since I'd seen that big ugly mug in one of the out-of-town papers, and the picture hadn't been too good a resemblance. But I remembered it, now, and some of the story I'd read about him. He'd taken his degree at the University of Edinburgh at a time when we were admitting their graduates to practice. He'd killed half a dozen people before he picked up a jerkwater PhD, and edged into psychiatry.

Out on the West Coast, he'd worked himself into some staff job with the police. And then a big murder case had cropped up, and he'd gotten hog-wild raw with the wrong suspects—people who had the money and influence to fight back. He hadn't lost his license, but he'd had to skip out fast. Now, well, I knew what he'd be doing now. What he'd have to be doing. Lunatics can't vote, so why should the legislature vote a lot of money for them?

"As a matter of fact—uh—" It was just beginning to soak in on him. "I think I'd better—"

"Stick around," I said. "I'll show you that corncob. Or maybe you can show me something from your collection—those Japanese sex goods you used to flash around. What'd you do with that rubber phallus you had? The one you squirted into that high school kid's face? Didn't you have time to pack it when you jumped the Coast?"

"I'm a-afraid you have me confused w-with—"

"As a matter of fact," I said, "I *do*. But you don't have me confused. You wouldn't know how to begin. You wouldn't know shit from wild honey, so go back and sign your report that way. Sign it shitbird. And you'd better add a footnote to the effect, that the next son-of-a-bitch they send out here is going to get kicked so hard he'll be wearing his asshole for a collar."

He backed out into the hall and toward the front door, the bones in his face wobbling and twitching under the tight yellow skin. I followed him grinning.

He stuck a hand out sideways and lifted his hat from the halltree. He put it on backwards; and I laughed and took a quick step toward him. He almost fell out the door; and I picked up his briefcase and threw it into the yard.

"Take care of yourself, doc," I said. "Take good care of your keys. If you ever lose them, you won't be able to get out."

"You—you'll be . . ." The bones were jerking and jumping. He'd got down the steps, and his nerve was coming back. "If I ever get you up—"

"Me, doc? But I sleep swell. I don't have headaches. I'm not worried a bit. The only thing that bothers me is that corncob wearing out."

He snatched up the briefcase and went loping down the walk, his neck stuck out like a buzzard's. I slammed the door, and made more coffee.

I cooked a big second breakfast, and ate it all.

You see, it didn't make a bit of difference. I hadn't lost a thing by telling him off. I'd thought they were closing in on me, and now I knew it. And they'd know that I knew it. But nothing was lost by that, and nothing else had changed.

They could still only guess, suspect. They had no more to go on than they'd ever had. They still wouldn't have anything two weeks—well, ten days from now. They'd have more suspicions, they'd *feel* surer than ever. But they wouldn't have any proof.

They could only find the proof in me—in what I was—and I'd never show it to 'em.

I finished the pot of coffee, smoked a cigar, and washed and wiped the dishes. I tossed some bread scraps into the yard for the sparrows, and watered the sweet potato plant in the kitchen window.

Then, I got out the car and headed for town; and I was thinking how good it had been to talk—even if he had turned out to be a phony—for a while. To talk, really talk, for even a little while.

Eighteen

I KILLED Amy Stanton on Saturday night on the fifth of April, 1952, at a few minutes before nine o'clock.

It had been a bright, crisp spring day, just warm enough so's you'd know that summer was coming, and the night was just tolerably cool. And she fixed her folks an early dinner, and got them off to a picture show about seven. Then, at eight-thirty, she came over to my place, and . . .

Well, I saw them going by my house—her folks, I mean—and I guess she must have been standing at their gate waving to 'em, because they were looking back and waving. Then, I guess, she went back into the house and started getting ready real fast; taking her hair down and bathing, and fixing her face and getting her bags packed. I guess she must have been busy as all-hell, jumping sideways to get ready, because she hadn't been able to do much while her folks were around. I guess she must have been chasing back and forth, turning on the electric iron, shutting off the bathwater, straightening the seams in her stockings, moving her mouth in and out to center the lipstick while she jerked the pins from her hair.

Why, hell, she had dozens of things to do, dozens of 'em, and if she'd just moved a little bit slower, ever so little—but Amy was one of those quick, sure girls. She was ready with time to spare, I guess, and then—I guess—she stood in front of the mirror, frowning and smiling, pouting and tossing her head, tucking her chin in and looking up under her brows; studying herself frontwards and sidewards, turning around and looking over her shoulder and brushing at her bottom, hitching her girdle up a little and down a little and then gripping it by both sides and sort of wiggling her hips in it. Then . . . then, I guess that must have been about all; she was all ready. So she came over where I was, and I . . .

I was ready too. I wasn't fully dressed, but I was ready for her.

I was standing in the kitchen waiting for her, and she was out of breath from hurrying so fast, I guess, and her bags were pretty heavy, I guess, and I guess . . .

I guess I'm not ready to tell about it yet. It's too soon, and it's not necessary yet. Because, hell, we had a whole two weeks before then, before Saturday, April 5th, 1952, at a few minutes before nine p.m.

We had two weeks and they were pretty good ones, because for the first time in I don't remember when my mind was really free. The end was coming up, it was rushing toward me, and everything would be over soon. I could think, well, go ahead and say something, do something, and it won't matter now. I can stall you *that* long; and I don't have to watch myself any more.

I was with her every night. I took her everywhere she

wanted to go, and did everything she wanted to do. And it wasn't any trouble, because she didn't want to go much or do much. One evening we parked by the high school, and watched the baseball team work out. Another time we went down to the depot to see the Tulsa Flyer go through with the people looking out the dining car windows and the people staring back from the observation car.

That's about all we did, things like that, except maybe to drive down to the confectionery for some ice cream. Most of the time we just stayed at home, at my house. Both of us sitting in Dad's big old chair, or both of us stretched out upstairs, face to face, holding each other.

Just holding each other a lot of nights.

We'd lie there for hours, not speaking for an hour at a time sometimes; but the time didn't drag any. It seemed to rush by. I'd lie there listening to the ticking of the clock, listening to her heart beat with it, and I'd wonder why it had to tick so fast; I'd wonder *why*. And it was hard to wake up and go to sleep, to go back into the nightmare where I could remember.

We had a few quarrels but no bad ones. I just wasn't going to have them; I let her have her own way and she tried to do the same with me.

One night she said she was going to the barbershop with me some time, and see that I got a decent haircut for a change. And I said—before I remembered—whenever she felt like doing that, I'd start wearing it in a braid. So we had a little spat, but nothing bad.

Then, one night she asked me how many cigars I smoked in a day, and I said I didn't keep track of 'em. She asked me why I didn't smoke cigarettes like "everyone else" did, and I said I didn't reckon that everyone else did smoke 'em. I said there was two members of my family that never smoked 'em, Dad and me. She said, well, of course, if you thought more of him than you do of me, there's nothing more to be said. And I said, Jesus Christ, how do you figure—what's that got to do with it?

But it was just a little spat. Nothing bad at all. I reckon she forgot about it right away like she did the first one.

I think she must have had a mighty good time those two weeks. Better'n any she'd ever had before.

So the two weeks passed, and the night of April fifth came; and she hustled her folks off to a show, and scampered around getting ready, and she got ready. And at eight-thirty she came over to my place and I was waiting for her. And I . . .

But I guess I'm getting ahead of myself again. There's some other things to tell first.

I went to work every working day of those two weeks; and believe me it wasn't easy. I didn't want to face anyone—I wanted to stay there in the house with the shades drawn, and not see anyone at all, and I knew I couldn't do that. I went to work, I forced myself to, just like always.

They suspected me; and I'd let 'em know that I knew. But there wasn't a thing on my conscience; I wasn't afraid of a thing. And I proved that there wasn't by going down. Because how could a man who'd done what they thought I had, go right on about his business and look people in the eye?

I was sore, sure. My feelings were hurt. But I wasn't afraid and I proved it.

Most of the time, at first, anyway, I wasn't given much to do. And believe me that was hard, standing around with my face hanging out and pretending like I didn't notice or give a damn. And when I did get a little job, serving a warrant or something like that, there was always a reason for another deputy to go along with me. He'd be embarrassed and puzzled, because, of course, they were keeping the secret at the top, between Hendricks and Conway and Bob Maples. He'd wonder what was up but he couldn't ask, because, in our own way, we're the politest people in the world; we'll joke around and talk about everything except what's on our minds. But he'd wonder and he'd be embarrassed, and he'd try to brag me up—maybe talk me up about the Johnnie Pappas deal to make me feel better.

I was coming back from lunch one day when the hall floors had just been oiled. And they didn't make much noise when you stepped on them, and when you kind of had to pick your way along they didn't make any at all. Deputy Jeff Plummer and Sheriff Bob were talking, and they didn't hear me coming. So I stopped just short of the door and listened. I listened and I saw them: I knew them so well I could see 'em without looking.

Bob was at his desk, pretending to thumb through some papers; and his glasses were down on the end of his nose, and he was looking up over them now and then. And he didn't like what he had to say, but you'd never know it the way his eyes came up over those glasses and the way he talked. Jeff Plummer was hunkered down in one of the windows, studying his finger-nails, maybe, his jaws moving on a stick of gum. And he didn't like telling Bob off—and he didn't sound like he was; just easy-going and casual—but he was sure as hell doing it.

"No, sir, Bob," he drawled. "Been kind of studyin' things over, and I reckon I ain't going to do no spying no more. Ain't going to do it a-tall."

"You got your mind made up, huh? You're plumb set?"

"Well, now, it sure looks that way, don't it? Yes, sir, I reckon that's prob'ly the way it is. Can't rightly see it no other way."

"You see how it's possible to do a job if'n you don't follow orders? You reckon you can do that?"

"Now"—Jeff was looking—*looking*—real pleased, like he'd drawn aces to three kings—"now, I'm sure proud you mentioned that, Bob. I plain admire a man that comes square to a point."

There was a second's silence, then a *clink* as Jeff's badge hit the desk. He slid out of the window and sauntered toward the door, smiling but not with his eyes. And Bob cussed and jumped up.

"You ornery coyote! You tryin' to knock my eyes out with that thing? I ever catch you throwin' it around again, I'll whup you down to a nubbin."

Jeff scuffed his boots; he cleared his throat. He said it was a plumb purty day out, and a man'd have to be plain out of his mind to claim different.

"I reckon a man hadn't ought to ask you a question about all the hocus-pocus around here, now had he, Bob? It wouldn't be what you'd call proper."

"Well, now, I don't know as I'd put it that way. Don't reckon I'd even prod him about why he was askin'. I'd just figure he was a man, and a man just does what he has to."

I slipped into the men's john and stayed there a while. And when I went into the office, Jeff Plummer was gone and Bob gave me a warrant to serve. By myself. He didn't exactly meet my eye, but he seemed pretty happy. He had his neck out a mile—he had everything to lose and nothing to gain—and he was happy.

And I didn't know whether I felt better or not.

Bob didn't have much longer to live, and the job was all he had. Jeff Plummer had a wife and four kids, and he was just about standing in the middle of his wardrobe whenever you saw him. People like that, well, they don't make up their mind about a man in a hurry. But once it's made up they hardly ever change it. They can't. They'd almost rather die than do it.

I went on about my business every day, and things were easier for me in a sense, because people acted easier around me, and twice as hard in another way. Because the folks that trust you, that just won't hear no bad about you nor even think it, those are the ones that are hard to fool. You can't put your heart in the job.

I'd think about my—those people, so many of them, and I'd wonder *why* . I'd have to go through it all again, step by step. And just about the time I'd get it settled, I'd start wondering all over again.

I guess I got kind of sore at myself. And at them. All those people. I'd think, why, in the hell did they have to do it—I didn't ask 'em to stick their necks out; I'm not begging for friendship. But they *did* give me their friendship and they *did* stick their necks out. So, along toward the last, I was sticking mine out.

I stopped by the Greek's place every day. I looked over the work and had him explain things to me, and I'd offer him a lift when he had to go some place. I'd say it was sure going to be one up-to-date restaurant and that Johnnie would sure like it—that he did like it. Because there hadn't ever been a better boy, and now he could look on, look down, and admire things the same as we could. I said I knew he could, that Johnnie was really happy now.

And the Greek didn't have much to say for a while—he was polite but he didn't say much. Then, pretty soon, he was taking me out in the kitchen for coffee; and he'd walk me clear out to my car when I had to leave. He'd hang around me, nodding and nodding while I talked about Johnnie. And once in a while he'd remember that maybe he ought to be ashamed, and I knew he wanted to apologize but was afraid of hurting my feelings.

Chester Conway had been staying in Fort Worth, but he came back in town one day for a few hours and I made it my business to hear about it. I was driving by his offices real slow, around two in the afternoon, when he came barging out looking for a taxi. And before he knew what was happening, I had him in charge. I hopped out, took his briefcase away from him, and hustled him into my car.

It was the last thing he'd've expected of me. He was too set back to balk, and he didn't have time to say anything. And after we were headed for the airport, he didn't get a chance. Because I was doing all the talking.

I said, "I've been hoping to run into you, Mr. Conway. I wanted to thank you for the hospitality you showed me in Fort Worth. It was sure thoughtful of you at a time like that, to think of me and Bob's comfort, and I guess I wasn't so thoughtful myself. I was kind of tired, just thinkin' of my own problems instead of yours, how you must feel, and I reckon I was pretty snappy with you there at the airport. But I didn't really mean anything by it, Mr. Conway, and I've been wanting to apologize. I wouldn't blame you a bit if you were put out with me, because I ain't ever had much sense and I guess I've made a hell of a mess of things.

"Now, I knew Elmer was kind of innocent and trusting and I knew a woman like that just couldn't be much good. I shoulda done like you said and gone there with him—I don't rightly see how I could the way she was acting, but I shoulda done that anyway. And don't think I don't know it now, and if cussing me out will help any or if you want to get my job, and I know you can get it, I won't hold any grudge. No matter what you did it wouldn't be enough, it wouldn't bring Elmer back. An' . . . I never got to know him real well, but in a way kinda I felt like I did. I reckon it must've been because he looked so much like you, I'd see him from a distance some times and I'd think it was you. I guess maybe that's one reason I wanted to see you today. It was kinda like seein' Elmer again. I could sorta feel for a minute that he was still here an' nothing had ever happened. An' . . ."

We'd come to the airport.

He got out without speaking or looking at me, and strode off to the plane. Moving fast, never turning around or looking sideways; almost like he was running away from something.

He started up the ramp, but he wasn't moving so fast now. He was walking slower and slower, and halfway up he almost stopped. Then he went on, plodding, dragging his feet; and he reached the top. And he stood there for a second, blocking the door.

He turned around, gave the briefcase a little jerk, and ducked inside the plane.

He'd waved to me.

I drove back to town, and I guess I gave up about then. It was no use. I'd done everything I could. I'd dropped it in their plates, and rubbed their noses in it. And it was no use. They wouldn't see it.

No one would stop me.

So, on Saturday night, April 5th, 1952, at a few minutes before nine o'clock, I . . .

But I guess there's another thing or two to tell you first, and—but I *will* tell you about it. I want to tell you, and I will, exactly how it happened. I won't leave you to figure things out for yourself.

In lots of books I read, the writer seems to go haywire every time he reaches a high point. He'll start leaving out punctuation and running his words together and babble about stars flashing and sinking into a deep dreamless sea. And you can't figure out whether the hero's laying his girl or a cornerstone. I guess that kind of crap is supposed to be pretty deep stuff— a lot of the book reviewers eat it up, I notice. But the way I see it is, the writer is just too goddam lazy to do his job. And I'm not lazy, whatever else I am. I'll tell you everything.

But I want to get everything in the right order.

I want you to understand how it was.

Late Saturday afternoon, I got Bob Maples alone for a minute and told him I wouldn't be able to work that night. I said that Amy and me had something mighty important to do, and maybe I wouldn't be getting in Monday or Tuesday either; and I gave him a wink.

"Well, now"—he hesitated, frowning. "Well, now, you don't think maybe that—" Then, he gripped my hand and wrung it. "That's real good news, Lou. Real good. I know you'll be happy together."

"I'll try not to lay off too long," I said. "I reckon things are, well, kind of up in the air and—"

"No, they ain't," he said, sticking his chin out. "Everything's all right, and it's going to stay that way. Now go on and buss Amy for me, and don't you worry about nothing."

It still wasn't real late in the day, so I drove out on Derrick Road and parked a while.

Then I went home, leaving the car parked out in front, and fixed dinner.

I stretched out on the bed for about an hour, letting my food settle. I drew water in the bath tub and got in.

I lay in the tub for almost an hour, soaking and smoking and thinking. Finally, I got out, looked at the clock and began laying out clothes.

I packed my gladstone, and cinched the straps on it. I put on clean underwear and socks and new-pressed pants, and my Sunday go-to-meetin' boots. I left off my shirt and tie.

I sat on the edge of the bed smoking until eight o'clock. Then, I went downstairs to the kitchen.

I turned the light on in the pantry, moving the door back and forth until I had it like I wanted it. Until there was just enough light in the kitchen. I looked around, making sure that all the blinds were drawn, and went into Dad's office.

I took down the concordance to the Bible and removed the four hundred dollars in marked money, Elmer's money. I dumped the drawers of Dad's desk on the floor. I turned off the light, pulled the door almost shut, and went back into the kitchen.

The evening newspaper was spread out on the table. I slid a butcher knife under it, and— And it was that time. I heard her coming.

She came up the back steps and across the porch, and banged and fumbled around for a minute getting the door open. She came in, out of breath kind of and out of temper, and pushed the door shut behind her. And she saw me standing there, not saying anything because I'd forgotten *why* and I was trying to remember. And, finally, I did remember.

So—or did I mention it already?—on Saturday night, the fifth of April, 1952, at a few minutes before nine o'clock I killed Amy Stanton.

Or maybe you could call it suicide.

Nineteen

SHE SAW me and it startled her for a second. Then she dropped her two traveling cases on the floor and gave one of 'em a kick, and brushed a wisp of hair from her eyes.

"Well!" she snapped. "I don't suppose it would occur to you to give me a little help! Why didn't you leave the car in the garage, anyway?"

I shook my head. I didn't say anything.

"I'll swear, Lou Ford! Sometimes I think— And you're not even ready yet! You're always talking about how slow I am, and here you stand, on your own wedding night of all things, and you haven't—" She stopped suddenly, her mouth shut tight, her breasts rising and falling. And I heard the kitchen clock tick ten times before she spoke again. "I'm sorry, darling," she said softly. "I didn't mean—"

"Don't say anything more, Amy," I said. "Just don't say anything more."

She smiled and came toward me with her arms held out. "I won't, darling. I won't ever say anything like that again. But I do want to tell you how much—"

"Sure," I said. "You want to pour your heart out to me."

And I hit her in the guts as hard as I could.

My fist went back against her spine, and the flesh closed around it to the wrist. I jerked back on it, I had to jerk, and she flopped forward from the waist, like she was hinged.

Her hat fell off, and her head went clear down and touched the floor. And then she toppled over, completely over, like a kid turning a somersault. She lay on her back, eyes bulging, rolling her head from side to side.

She was wearing a white blouse and a light cream-colored suit; a new one, I reckon, because I didn't remember seeing it before. I got my hand in the front of the blouse, and ripped it down to the waist. I jerked the skirt up over her head, and she jerked and shook all over; and there was a funny sound like she was trying to laugh.

And then I saw the puddle spreading out under her.

I sat down and tried to read the paper. I tried to keep my eyes on it. But the light wasn't very good, not good enough to read by, and she kept moving around. It looked like she couldn't lie still.

Once I felt something touch my boot, and I looked down and it was her hand. It was moving back and forth across the toe of my boot. It moved up along the ankle and the leg, and somehow I was afraid to move away. And then her fingers were at the top, clutching down inside; and I almost couldn't move. I stood up and tried to jerk away, and the fingers held on.

I dragged her two-three feet before I could break away.

Her fingers kept on moving, sliding and crawling back and forth, and finally they got ahold of her purse and held on. They dragged it down inside of her skirt, and I couldn't see it or her hands any more.

Well, that was all right. It would look better to have her hanging onto her purse. And I grinned a little, thinking about it. It was so much like her, you know, to latch onto her purse. She'd always been so tight, and . . . and I guess she'd had to be.

There wasn't a better family in town than the Stantons. But both her folks had been ailing for years, and they didn't have much any more aside from their home. She'd had to be tight, like any damned fool ought to have known; because there wasn't any other way of being, and that's all any of us ever are: what we have to be. And I guessed it hadn't been very funny when I'd kidded her dead-pan, and acted surprised when she got mad.

I guess that stuff she'd brought to me when I was sick wasn't really crap. It was as good as she knew how to fix. I guess that dog of theirs didn't have to chase horses unless'n he wanted the exercise. I—

Why the hell didn't he come? Hell, she hadn't had a real breath now in almost thirty minutes, and it was hard as hell on her. I knew how hard it was and I held my own breath a while because we'd always done things together, and . . .

He came.

I'd locked the front screen, so that he couldn't just walk in, and I heard him tugging at it.

I gave her two hard kicks in the head and she rose up off the floor, her skirt falling down off of her face, and I knew there wouldn't be any doubt about her. She was dead on the night of— Then I went and opened the door and let him in.

I pushed the roll of marked twenties on him and said, "Stick this in your pocket. I've got the rest back in the kitchen," and I started back there.

I knew he would put the money in his pocket, and you do too if you can remember back when you were a kid. You'd walk up to a guy and say, "Here, hold this," and probably he'd pulled the same gag himself; he'd know you were handing him a horse turd or a prickly pear or a dead mouse. But if you pulled it fast enough, he'd do just what you told him.

I pulled it fast, and headed right back toward the kitchen. And he was right on my heels, because he didn't want me to get too far away from him.

There was just a little light, like I've said. I was between him and her. He was right behind me, watching me instead of anything else, and we went into the kitchen and I stepped aside quickly.

He almost stepped in her stomach. I guess his foot did touch it for a split second.

He pulled it back, staring down at her like his eyes were steel and she was a magnet. He tried to tug them away, and they'd just roll, going all-white in his head, and finally he got them away.

He looked at me and his lips shook as though he'd been playing a juice-harp, and he said:

"Yeeeeeeee!"

It was a hell of a funny sound, like a siren with a slippy chain that can't quite get started. "Yeeeeee!" he said. "Yeeeeee!" It sounded funny as hell, and he looked funny as hell.

Did you ever see one of these two-bit jazz singers? You know, trying to put something across with their bodies that they haven't got the voice to do? They lean back from the waist a little with their heads hanging forward and their hands held up about even with their ribs and swinging limp. And they sort of wobble and roll on their hips.

That's the way he looked, and he kept making that damned funny noise, his lips quivering ninety to the minute and his eyes rolling all-white.

I laughed and laughed, he looked and sounded so funny I couldn't help it. Then, I remembered what he'd done and I stopped laughing, and got mad—sore all over.

"You son-of-a-bitch," I said. "I was going to marry that poor little girl. We were going to elope and she caught you going through the house and you tried to . . ."

I stopped, because he hadn't done it at all. But he *could* have done it. He could've done it just as easy as not. The son-of-a-bitch could have, but he was just like everyone else. He was too nicey-nice and pretendsy to do anything really hard. But he'd stand back and crack the whip over me, keep moving around me every way I turned so that I couldn't get away no matter what I did, and it was always now-don't-you-do-nothin'-bud; but they kept cracking that old whip all the time they were sayin' it. And they—he'd done it all right; and I wasn't going to take the blame. I could be just as tricky and pretendsy as they were.

I could . . .

I went blind ma—angry seeing him so pretendsy shocked, "Yeeing!" and shivering and doing that screwy dance with his hands—hell, he hadn't had to watch *her* hands!—and white-rolling his eyes. What right did he have to act like that? I was the one that should have been acting that way, but, oh, no, I couldn't. That was their—his right to act that way, and I had to hold in and do all the dirty work.

I was as mad as all-hell.

I snatched the butcher-knife from under the newspaper, and made for him.

And my foot slipped where she'd been lying.

I went sprawling, almost knocking him over backwards if he hadn't moved, and the knife flew out of my hands.

I couldn't have moved a finger for a minute. I was laid out flat, helpless, without any weapon. And I could have maybe rolled a little and put my arms around her, and we'd have been together like we'd always been.

But do you think he'd do it? Do you think he'd pick up that knife and use it, just a little thing like that that wouldn't have been a bit of trouble? Oh, hell, no, oh, God, no, oh, Christ and Mary and all the Saints . . . ?

No.

All he could do was beat it, just like they always did.

I grabbed up the knife and took off after the heartless son-of-a-bitch.

He was out to the street sidewalk by the time I got to the front door; the dirty bastard had sneaked a head start on me. When I got out to the walk, he was better'n a half-block away, heading toward the center of town. I took after him as fast as I could go.

That wasn't very fast on account of the boots. I've seen plenty of men out here that never walked fifty miles altogether in their lives. But he wasn't moving very fast either. He was sort of skipping, jerky, rather than running or walking. He was skipping and tossing his head, and his hair was flying. And he still had his elbows held in at his sides, with his hands doing that funny floppy dance, and he kept saying—it was louder, now—that old siren was warming up—he kept saying, kind of screaming:

"Yeeeee! Yeeeeee! Yeeeeeeeeee. . . . !"

He was skipping and flopping his hands and tossing his head like one of those holy roller preachers at a brushwoods revival meeting. "Yeeeing!" and gone-to-Jesus and all you miserable sinners get right with Gawd like I went and done.

The dirty son-of-a-bitch! How low down can you get?

"MUR-DER!" I yelled. "Stop him, stop him! He killed Amy Stanton! MUR-DER. . . . !"

I yelled at the top of my lungs and I kept yelling. And windows started banging up and doors slammed. And people ran down off their porches. And that snapped him out of that crap—some of it.

He skipped out into the middle of the street, and started moving faster. But I moved faster, too, because it was still dirt in this block, just one short of the business district, and boots are meant for dirt.

He saw that I was gaining a little on him, and he tried to come out of that floppy skippy stuff, but it didn't look like he could quite make it. Maybe he was using too much steam with that "Yeeeeing!"

"MURDER!" I yelled. "MUR-DER! Stop him! He killed Amy Stanton. . . . !"

And everything was happening awful fast. It just sounds like it was a long time, because I'm not leaving out anything. I'm trying to tell you exactly how it was, so's you'll be sure to understand.

Looking up ahead, into the business district, it looked like a whole army of automobiles was bearing down on us. Then, suddenly, it was like a big plough had come down the street, pushing all those cars into the curb.

That's the way people are here in this section. That's the way they get. You don't see them rushing into the middle of a commotion to find out what's happening. There's men that are paid to do that and they do it prompt, without any fuss or feathers. And the folks know that no one's going to feel sorry for 'em if they get in the way of a gun butt or a bullet.

"Yeeeeee! Yeeeeee! Yeeeeeeeeeeeeeee!" he screamed, skipping and flopping.

"MUR-DER! He killed Amy Stanton. . . ."

And up ahead a little old roadster swung crossways with the intersection and stopped, and Jeff Plummer climbed out.

He reached down on the floor and took out a Winchester. Taking his time, easy-like. He leaned back against the fender, one boot heel hooked through the wheel spokes, and brought the gun up to his shoulder.

"Halt!" he called.

He called out the one time and then he fired, because the bum had started to skip toward the side of the street; and a man sure ought to know better than that.

The bum stumbled and went down, grabbing at his knee. But he got up again and he was still jerking and flopping his hands, and it looked like he was reaching into his clothes. And a man *really* hadn't ought to do that. He hadn't even ought to look anything like that.

Jeff fired three times, shifting his aim easy-like with each shot, and the bum was dropping with the first one but all three got him. By the time he hit the dirt he didn't have much left in the way of a head.

I fell down on top of him and began beating him, and they had their hands full dragging me off. I babbled out the story—how I'd been upstairs getting ready and I'd heard some commotion but I hadn't thought much of it. And—

And I didn't have to tell it too good. They all seemed to understand how it was.

A doctor pushed through the crowd, Dr. Zweilman, and he gave me a shot in the arm; and then they took me home.

Twenty

I WOKE UP a little after nine the next morning.

My mouth was sticky and my throat dry from the morphine—I don't know why he hadn't used hyoscin like any damned fool should have—and all I could think of right then was how thirsty I was.

I stood in the bathroom, gulping down glass after glass of water, and pretty soon it began to bounce on me. (I'm telling you almost *anything* is better than morphine.) But after a while it stopped. I drank a couple glasses more, and they stayed down. And I scrubbed my face in hot and cold water, and combed my hair.

Then I went back and sat down on the bed, wondering who'd undressed me; and all at once it hit me. Not about her. I wouldn't think about that. But—well, this.

I shouldn't have been alone. Your friends don't leave you alone at a time like that. I'd lost the girl I was going to marry, and I'd been through a terrible experience. And they'd left me alone. There wasn't anyone around to comfort me, or wait on me or just sit and shake their heads and say it was God's will and she was happy, and I—a man that's been through something like that needs those things. He needs all the help and comfort he can get, and I've never held back when one of my friends was bereaved. Why, hell, I—a man isn't himself when one of these disasters strikes. He might do something to himself, and the least people can do is have a nurse around. And . . .

But there wasn't any nurse around. I got up and looked through the other bedrooms, just to make sure.

And I wasn't doing anything to myself. They'd never done anything for me, and I wasn't doing anything for them.

I went downstairs and . . . and the kitchen had been cleaned up. There was no one there but me. I started to make some coffee, and then I thought I heard someone out in front, someone cough. And I was so all-fired glad I felt the tears come to my eyes. I turned off the coffee and went to the front door and opened it.

Jeff Plummer was sitting on the steps.

He was sitting sideways, his back to a porch post. He slanted a glance at me, then let his eyes go straight again, without turning his head.

"Gosh, Jeff," I said. "How long you been out here? Why didn't you knock?"

"Been here quite a spell," he said. And he fingered a stick of gum from his shirt pocket and began to unwrap it. "Yes, sir, I been here quite a spell."

"Well, come on in! I was just—"

"Kinda like it where I am," he said. "Air smells real good. Been smellin' real good, anyways."

He put the gum in his mouth. He folded the wrapper into a neat little square and tucked it back into his pocket.

"Yes, sir," he said, "it's been smellin' real good, and that's a fact."

I felt like I was nailed there in the doorway. I had to stand there and wait, watch his jaws move on that gum, look at him not looking at me. Never looking at me.

"Has there . . . hasn't anyone been—?"

"Told 'em you wasn't up to it," he said. "Told 'em you was all broke up about Bob Maples."

"Well, I— *Bob?*"

"Shot hisself around midnight last night. Yes, sir, pore ol' Bob killed hisself, and I reckon he had to. I reckon I know just how he felt."

And he still didn't look at me.

I closed the door.

I leaned against it, my eyes aching, my head pounding; and I ticked them off with the pounding that reached from my head to my heart . . . Joyce, Elmer, Johnnie Pappas, Amy, the . . . Him, Bob Maples . . . But he hadn't known anything! He couldn't have known, had any real proof. He'd just jumped to conclusions like they were jumping. He couldn't wait for me to explain like, hell, I'd've been glad to do. Hadn't I always been glad to explain? But he couldn't wait; he'd made up his mind without any proof, like they'd made up theirs.

Just because I'd been around when a few people got killed, just because I happened to be around . . .

They couldn't know anything, because I was the only one who could tell 'em—show 'em—and I never had.

And I sure as hell wasn't going to.

Actually, well, logically, and you can't do away with logic, there *wasn't* anything. Existence and proof are inseparables. You have to have the second to have the first.

I held onto that thought, and I fixed myself a nice big breakfast. But I couldn't eat but a little bit. That damned morphine had taken all my appetite, just like it always does. About all I could get down was part of a piece of toast and two-three cups of coffee.

I went back upstairs and lighted a cigar, and stretched out on the bed. I—a man that'd been through what I had belonged in bed.

About a quarter of eleven, I heard the front door open and close, but I stayed right where I was. I still stayed there, stretched out on the bed, smoking, when Howard Hendricks and Jeff Plummer came in.

Howard gave me a curt nod, and drew up a straight chair near the bed. Jeff sat down, sort of out of the way, in an easy chair. Howard could hardly hold himself in, but he was sure trying. He tried. He did the best he could to be stern and sorrowful, and to hold his voice steady.

"Lou," he said, "we—I'm not at all satisfied. Last night's events—these recent events—I don't like them a bit, Lou."

"Well," I said, "that's natural enough. Don't hardly see how you could like 'em. I know I sure don't."

"You know what I mean!"

"Why, sure I do. I know just how—"

"Now, this alleged robber-rapist—this poor devil you'd have us believe was a robber and rapist. We happen to know he was nothing of the kind! He was a pipeline worker. He had a pocket full of wages. And—and yes, we know he wasn't drunk because he'd just had a big steak dinner! He wouldn't have had the slightest reason to be in this house, so Miss Stanton couldn't have—"

"Are you saying he wasn't here, Howard?" I said. "That should be mighty easy to prove."

"Well—he wasn't prowling, that's a certainty! If—"

"Why is it?" I said. "If he wasn't prowling, what was he doing?"

His eyes began to glitter. "Never mind! Let that go for a minute! But I'll tell you this much. If you think you can get away with planting that money on him and making it look like—"

"What money?" I said. "I thought you said it was his wages?"

You see? The guy didn't have any sense. Otherwise, he'd have waited for me to mention that marked money.

"The money you stole from Elmer Conway! The money you took the night you killed him and that woman!"

"Now, wait a minute, wait a minute," I frowned. "Let's take one thing at a time. Let's take the woman. Why would I kill her?"

"Because—well—because you'd killed Elmer and you had to shut her up."

"But why would I kill Elmer? I'd known him all my life. If I'd wanted to do him any harm, I'd sure had plenty of chances."

"You know—" He stopped abruptly.

"Yeah?" I said, puzzled. "Why would I kill Elmer, Howard?"

And he couldn't say, of course. Chester Conway had given him his orders about that.

"You killed him all right," he said, his face reddening. "You killed her. You hanged Johnnie Pappas."

"You're sure not making much sense, Howard." I shook

my head. "You plumb insisted on me talking to Johnnie because you knew how much I liked him and how much he
liked me. Now you're saying I killed him."

"You had to kill him to protect yourself! You'd given him
that marked twenty-dollar bill!"

"Now you really ain't making sense," I said. "Let's see;
there was five hundred dollars missing, wasn't there? You
claiming that I killed Elmer and that woman for five hundred
dollars? Is that what you're saying, Howard?"

"I'm saying that—that—goddammit, Johnnie wasn't anywhere near the scene of the murders! He was stealing tires at
the time they were committed!"

"Is that a fact?" I drawled. "Someone see him, Howard?"

"Yes! I mean, well—uh—"

See what I mean? Shrapnel.

"Let's say that Johnnie didn't do those killings," I said.
"And you know it was mighty hard for me to believe that he
had, Howard. I said so right along. I always did think he was
just scared and kind of out of his mind when he hanged himself. I'd been his only friend, and now it sort of seemed like
I didn't believe in him any more, an'—"

"His friend! Jesus!"

"So I reckon he didn't do it, after all. Poor little Amy was
killed in pretty much the same way that other woman was.
And this man—you say he had a big part of the missing money
on him. Five hundred dollars would seem like a lot of money
to a man like that, an' seeing that the two killings were so
much alike . . ."

I let my voice trail off, smiling at him; and his mouth
opened and went shut again.

Shrapnel. That's all he had.

"You've got it all figured out, haven't you?" he said, softly.
"Four—five murders; six counting poor Bob Maples who
staked everything he had on you, and you sit there explaining
and smiling. You aren't bothered a bit. How can you do it,
Ford? How can—"

I shrugged. "Somebody has to keep their heads, and it sure
looks like you can't. You got some more questions, Howard?"

"Yes," he nodded, slowly. "I've got one. How did Miss
Stanton get those bruises on her body. Old bruises, not made

last night. The same kind of bruises we found on the body of the Lakeland woman. How did she get them, Ford?"

Shrap—

"Bruises?" I said. "Gosh, you got me there, Howard. How would I know?"

"H-how"—he sputtered—"how would you know?"

"Yeah?" I said, puzzled. "How?"

"Why, goddam you! You'd been screwing that gal for years! You—"

"Don't say that," I said.

"No," said Jeff Plummer, "don't say that."

"But"—Howard turned on him, then turned back to me. "All right, I won't say it! I don't need to say it. That girl had never gone with anyone but you, and only you could have done that to her! You'd been beating on her just like you'd beaten on that whore!"

I laughed, sort of sadly. "And Amy just took it huh, Howard? I bruised her up, and she went right ahead seeing me? She got all ready to marry me? That wouldn't make sense with any woman, and it makes no sense minus about Amy. You sure wouldn't say a thing like that if you'd known Amy Stanton."

He shook his head, staring, like I was some kind of curiosity. That old shrapnel wasn't doing a thing for him.

"Now, maybe Amy did pick up a bruise here and there," I went on. "She had all sorts of work to do, keepin' house and teaching school, and everything there was to be done. It'd been mighty strange if she didn't bang herself up a little, now and—"

"That's not what I mean. You know that's not what I mean."

"—but if you're thinking I did it, and that she put up with it, you're way off base. You sure didn't know Amy Stanton."

"Maybe," he said, "you didn't know her."

"Me? But you just got through sayin' we'd gone together for years—"

"I—" He hesitated, frowning. "I don't know. It isn't all clear to me, and I won't pretend that it is. But I don't think you knew her. Not as well as . . ."

"Yeah?" I said.

He reached into his inside coat pocket, and brought out a square blue envelope. He opened it and removed one of those double sheets of stationery. I could see it was written on both sides, four pages in all. And I recognized that small neat handwriting.

Howard looked up from the paper, and caught my eye.

"This was in her purse." *Her purse.* "She'd written it at home and was planning, apparently, to give it to you after you were out of Central City. As a matter of fact"—he glanced down at the letter—"she intended to have you stop at a restaurant up the road, and have you read it while she was in the restroom. Now, it begins, 'Lou, Darling . . .'"

"Let me have it," I said.

"I'll read—"

"It's his letter," said Jeff. "Let him have it."

"Very well," Howard shrugged; and he tossed me the letter. And I knew he'd planned on having me read it all along. He wanted me to read it while he sat back and watched.

I looked down at the thick double page, holding my eyes on it.

Lou, Darling:

Now you know why I had you stop here, and why I've excused myself from the table. It was to allow you to read this, the things I couldn't somehow otherwise say to you. Please, please read carefully, darling. I'll give you plenty of time. And if I sound confused and rambling, please don't be angry with me. It's only because I love you so much, and I'm a little frightened and worried.

Darling, I wish I could tell you how happy you've made me these last few weeks. I wish I could be sure that you'd been even a tiny fraction as happy. Just a teensy-weensie bit as much. Sometimes I get the crazy, wonderful notion that you have been, that you were even as happy as I was (though I don't see how you could be!) and at others I tell myself . . . Oh, I don't know, Lou!

I suppose the trouble is that it all seemed to come about so suddenly. We'd gone on for years, and you seemed to be growing more and more indifferent; you seemed to keep drawing away from me and taking pleasure in making me follow. (Seemed,

*Lou; I don't say you did do it.) I'm not trying to excuse myself,
darling. I only want to explain, to make you understand that
I'm not going to behave that way any more. I'm not going to
be sharp and demanding and scolding and . . . I may not be
able to change all at once (oh, but I will, darling; I'll watch
myself; I'll do it just as fast as I can) but if you'll just love me,
Lou, just act like you love me, I'm sure—*

*Do you understand how I felt? Just a little? Do you see why
I was that way, then, and why I won't be any more? Everyone
knew I was yours. Almost everyone. I wanted it to be that way;
to have anyone else was unthinkable. But I couldn't have had
anyone else if I'd wished to. I was yours. I'd always be yours if
you dropped me. And it seemed, Lou, that you were slipping
further and further away, still owning me yet not letting yourself belong to me. You were (it seemed, darling, seemed) leaving
me with nothing—and knowing that you were doing it, knowing
I was helpless—and apparently enjoying it. You avoided me. You
made me chase you. You made me question you and beg you,
and—and then you'd act so innocent and puzzled and . . .
Forgive me, darling. I don't want to criticise you ever, ever
again. I only wanted you to understand, and I suppose only
another woman could do that.*

*Lou, I want to ask you something, a few things, and I want
to beg you please, please, please not to take it the wrong way. Are
you—oh, don't be, darling—are you afraid of me? Do you feel
that you have to be nice to me? There I won't say anything more,
but you know what I mean, as well as I do at least. And you
will know . . .*

*I hope and pray I am wrong, darling. I do so hope. But I'm
afraid—are you in trouble? Is something weighing on your
mind? I don't want to ask you more than that, but I do want
you to believe that whatever it is, even if it's what I—whatever
it is, Lou, I'm on your side. I love you (are you tired of my
saying that), and I know you. I know you'd never knowingly do
anything wrong, you just couldn't, and I love you so much and
. . . Let me help you, darling. Whatever it is, whatever help you
need. Even if it should involve being separated for a while, a
long while, let's—let me help you. Because I'll wait for you, however long—and it mightn't be long at all, it might be just a
question of—well, it will be all right, Lou, because you wouldn't*

knowingly do anything. I know that and everyone else knows it, and it will be all right. We'll make it all right, you and I together. If you'll only tell me. If you'll just let me help you.

Now. I asked you not to be afraid of me, but I know how you've felt, how you used to feel, and I know that asking you or telling you might not be enough. That's why I had you stop at this place, here at a bus stop. That's why I'm giving you so much time. To prove to you that you don't need to be afraid.

I hope that when I come back to the table, you'll still be there. But if you aren't, darling, if you feel that you can't . . . then just leave my bags inside the door. I have money with me and I can get a job in some other town, and—do that, Lou. If you feel that you must. I'll understand, and it'll be perfectly all right— honestly it will, Lou—and . . .

Oh, darling, darling, darling, I love you so much. I've always loved you and I always will, whatever happens. Always, darling. Always and always. Forever and forever.

> Always and forever,
> Amy

Twenty-One

WELL. WELL?

What are you going to do? What are you going to say?

What are you going to say when you're drowning in your own dung and they keep booting you back into it, when all the screams in hell wouldn't be as loud as you want to scream, when you're at the bottom of the pit and the whole world's at the top, when it has but one face, a face without eyes or ears, and yet it watches and listens . . .

What are you going to do and say? Why, pardner, that's simple. It's easy as nailing your balls to a stump and falling off backwards. Snow again, pardner, and drift me hard, because that's an easy one.

You're gonna say, they can't keep a good man down. You're gonna say, a winner never quits and a quitter never wins. You're gonna smile, boy, you're gonna show 'em the ol' fightin' smile. And then you're gonna get out there an' hit 'em hard and fast and low, an'—an' Fight!

Rah.

I folded the letter, and tossed it back to Howard.

"She was sure a talky little girl," I said. "Sweet but awful talky. Seems like if she couldn't say it to you, she'd write it down for you."

Howard swallowed. "That—that's all you have to say?"

I lit a cigar, pretending like I hadn't heard him. Jeff Plummer's chair creaked. "I sure liked Miss Amy," he said. "All four of my younguns went to school to her, an' she was just as nice as if they'd had one of these oilmen for a daddy."

"Yes, sir," I said, "I reckon she really had her heart in her work."

I puffed on my cigar, and Jeff's chair creaked again, louder than the first time, and the hate in Howard's eyes seemed to lash out against me. He gulped like a man choking down puke.

"You fellows getting restless?" I said. "I sure appreciate you dropping in at a time like this, but I wouldn't want to keep you from anything important."

"You—y-you!"

"You starting to stutter, Howard? You ought to practice talking with a pebble in your mouth. Or maybe a piece of shrapnel."

"You dirty son-of-a-bitch! You—"

"Don't call me that," I said.

"No," said Jeff, "don't call him that. Don't never say anything about a man's mother."

"To hell with that crap! He—you"—he shook his fist at me—"you killed that little girl. She as good as says so!"

I laughed. "She wrote it down after I killed her, huh? That's quite a trick."

"You know what I mean. She knew you were going to kill her . . ."

"And she was going to marry me, anyway?"

"She knew you'd killed all those other people!"

"Yeah? Funny she didn't mention it."

"She did mention it! She—"

"Don't recall seeing anything like that. Don't see that she said anything much. Just a lot of woman-worry talk."

"You killed Joyce Lakeland and Elmer Conway and Johnnie Pappas and—"

"President McKinley?"

He sagged back in his chair, breathing hard. "You killed them, Ford. You killed them."

"Why don't you arrest me, then? What are you waiting on?"

"Don't worry," he nodded, grimly. "Don't you worry. I'm not waiting much longer."

"And I'm not either," I said.

"What do you mean?"

"I mean you and your courthouse gang are doing spite work. You're pouring it on me because Conway says to, just why I can't figure out. You haven't got a shred of proof but you've tried to smear me—"

"Now, wait a minute! We haven't—"

"You've tried to; you had Jeff out here this morning chasing visitors away. You'd do it, but you can't because you haven't got a shred of proof and people know me too well. You know you can't get a conviction, so you try to ruin my reputation. And with Conway backing you up you may manage it in time. You'll manage it if you have the time, and I guess I can't stop you. But I'm not going to sit back and take it. I'm leaving town, Howard."

"Oh, no you're not. I'm warning you here and now, Ford, don't you even attempt to leave."

"Who's going to stop me?"

"I am."

"On what grounds?"

"Mur—suspicion of murder."

"But who suspects me, Howard, and why? The Stantons? I reckon not. Mike Pappas? Huh-uh. Chester Conway? Well, I've got kind of a funny feeling about Conway, Howard. I've got a feeling that he's going to stay in the background, he's not going to do or say a thing, no matter how bad you need him."

"I see," he said. "I see."

"You see that opening there behind you?" I said. "Well,

that's a door, Howard, in case you were wonderin', and I can't think of a thing to keep you and Mister Plummer from walking through it."

"We're walking through it," said Jeff, "and so are you."

"Huh-uh," I said, "no I ain't. I sure ain't aimin' to do nothing like that, Mister Plummer. And that's a fact."

Howard kept his seat. His face looked like a blob of reddish dough, but he shook his head at Jeff and kept his seat. Howard was really trying hard.

"I—it's to your own interest as well as ours to get this settled, Ford. I'm asking you to place yourself—to remain available until—"

"You mean you want me to cooperate with you?" I said.

"Yes."

"That door," I said. "I wish you'd close it real careful. I'm suffering from shock, and I might have a relapse."

Howard's mouth twisted and opened, and snapped shut. He sighed and reached for his hat.

"I sure liked Bob Maples," said Jeff. "I sure liked that little Miss Amy."

"Sure enough?" I said. "Is that a fact?"

I laid my cigar down on an ashtray, leaned back on the pillow and closed my eyes. A chair creaked and squeaked real loud, and I heard Howard say, "Now, Jeff"—and there was a sound like he'd sort of stumbled.

I opened my eyes again. Jeff Plummer was standing over me.

He was smiling down at me with his lips and there was a .45 in his hand, and the hammer was thumbed back.

"You right sure you ain't coming with us?" he said. "You don't reckon you could change your mind?"

The way he sounded I knew he hoped I wouldn't change it. He was just begging, waiting for me to say no. And I reckoned I wouldn't say all of even a short word like that before I was past saying anything.

I got up and began to dress.

Twenty-Two

IF I'D KNOWN that Rothman's lawyer friend, Billy Boy Walker, was tied up in the East and was having trouble getting away, I might have felt different. I might have cracked up right off. But, on the other hand, I don't think I would have. I had a feeling that I was speeding fast down a one-way trail, that I was almost to the place I had to get to. I was almost there and moving fast, so why hop off and try to run ahead? It wouldn't have made a particle of sense, and you know I don't do things that don't make sense. You know it or you will know it.

That first day and that night, I spent in one of the "quiet" cells, but the next morning they put me on ice, down in the cooler where I'd—where Johnnie Pappas had died. They—

How's that? Well, sure they can do it to you. They can do anything they're big enough to do and you're little enough to take. They don't book you. No one knows where you are, and you've got no one on the outside that can get you out. It's not legal, but I found out long ago that the place where the law is apt to be abused most is right around a courthouse.

Yeah, they can do it all right.

So I was saying. I spent the first day and night in one of the quiet cells, and most of the time I was trying to kid myself. I couldn't face up to the truth yet, so I tried to play like there was a way around it. You know. Those kid games?

You've done something pretty bad or you want something bad, and you think, well, if I can just do such and such I can fix it. If I can count down from a thousand backwards by three and a third or recite the Gettysburg Address in pig-latin while I'm touching my little toes with my big ones, everything will be all right.

I'd play those games and their kin-kind, doing real impossible things in my imagination. I'd trot all the way from Central City to San Angelo without stopping. Or they'd grease the pipeline across the Pecos River, and I'd hop across it on one foot with my eyes blindfolded and an anvil around my neck. I'd really get to sweating and panting sometimes. My feet'd be all achy and blistered from pounding that San

Angelo Highway, and that old anvil would keep swinging and dragging at me, trying to pull me off into the Pecos; and finally I'd win through, just plumb worn out. And—and I'd have to do something still harder.

Well, then they moved me down into the cooler where Johnnie Pappas had died, and pretty soon I saw why they hadn't put me there right away. They'd had a little work to do on it first. I don't know just how they'd rigged the stunt— only that that unused light-socket in the ceiling was part of it. But I was stretched out on the bunk, fixing to shinny up the water tower without using my hands, when all at once I heard Johnnie's voice:

"Hello, you lovely people. I'm certainly having a fine time and I wish you were here. See you soon."

Yes, it was Johnnie, speaking in that sharp smart-alecky way he used a lot. I jumped up from the bunk and started turning around and looking up and down and sideways. And here his voice came again:

"Hello, you lovely people. I'm certainly having a fine time and I wish you were here. See you soon."

He kept saying the same thing over and over, about fifteen seconds between times, and, hell, as soon as I had a couple minutes to think, I knew what it was all about. It was one of those little four-bit voice recordings, like you've just about got time to sneeze on before it's used up. Johnnie'd sent it to his folks the time he visited the Dallas Fair. He'd mentioned it to me when he told me about the trip—and I'd remembered because I liked Johnnie and would remember. He'd mentioned it, apologizing for not sending me some word. But he'd lost all his dough in some kind of wheel game and had to hitch-hike back to Central City.

"Hello, you lovely people . . ."

I wondered what kind of story they'd given the Greek, because I was pretty sure he wouldn't have let 'em have it if he'd known what it was going to be used for. He knew how I felt about Johnnie and how Johnnie'd felt about me.

They kept playing that record over and over, from maybe five in the morning until midnight; I don't know just what the hours were because they'd taken away my watch. It didn't even stop when they brought me food and water twice a day.

I'd lie and listen to it, or sit and listen. And every once in a while, when I could remember to do it, I'd jump up and pace around the cell. I'd pretend like it was bothering the hell out of me, which of course it didn't at all. Why would it? But I wanted 'em to think it did, so they wouldn't turn it off. And I guess I must have pretended pretty good, because they played it for three days and part of a fourth. Until it wore out, I reckon.

After that there wasn't much but silence, nothing but those faraway sounds like the factory whistles which weren't any real company for a man.

They'd taken away my cigars and matches, of course, and I fidgeted around quite a bit the first day, thinking I wanted a smoke. Yeah, *thinking*, because I didn't actually want one. I'd been smoking cigars for—well—around eleven years; ever since my eighteenth birthday when Dad had said I was getting to be a man, so he hoped I'd act like one and smoke cigars and not go around with a coffin-nail in my mouth. So I'd smoked cigars, from then on, never admitting to myself that I didn't like them. But now I could admit it. I had to, and I did.

When life attains a crisis, man's focus narrows. *Nice lines, huh? I could talk that way all the time if I wanted to.* The world becomes a stage of immediate concern, swept free of illusion. *I used to could talk that way all the time.*

No one had pushed me around or even tried to question me since the morning they'd locked me up. No one, at all. And I'd tried to tell myself that that was a good sign. They didn't have any evidence; I'd got their goats, so they'd put me on ice, just like they'd done with plenty of other guys. And pretty soon they'd simmer down and let me go of their own accord, or Billy Boy Walker'd show up and they'd have to let me out . . . That's what I'd told myself and it made sense—all my reasoning does. But it was top-of-the-cliff sense, not the kind you make when you're down near the tag-end of the rope.

They hadn't tried to beat the truth out of me or talk it out of me for a couple of reasons. First of all, they were pretty sure it wouldn't do any good: You can't stamp on a man's corns when he's got his feet cut off. Second—the second reason was—they didn't think they had to.

They *had* evidence.

They'd had it right from the beginning.

Why hadn't they sprung it on me? Well, there were a couple of reasons behind that, too. For one thing, they weren't sure that it was evidence because they weren't sure about me. I'd thrown them off the track with Johnnie Pappas. For another thing, they *couldn't* use it—it wasn't in shape to be used.

But now they were sure of what I'd done, though they probably weren't too clear as to why I'd done it. And that evidence would be ready to be used before long. And I didn't reckon they'd let go of me until it was ready. Conway was determined to get me, and they'd gone too far to back down.

I thought back to the day Bob Maples and I had gone to Fort Worth, and how Conway hadn't invited us on the trip but had got busy ordering us around the minute we'd landed. You see? What could be clearer? He'd tipped his hand on me right there.

Then, Bob had come back to the hotel, and he was all upset about something Conway had said to him, ordered him to do. And he wouldn't tell me what it was. He just talked on and on about how long he'd known me and what a swell guy I was, and . . . Hell, don't you see? Don't you get it?

I'd let it go by me because I had to. I couldn't let myself face the facts. But I reckon you've known the truth all along.

Then, I'd brought Bob home on the train and he'd been babbling drunk, and he'd gotten sore about some of my kidding. So he'd snapped back at me, giving me a tip on where I stood at the same time. He'd said—what was it?—*"It's always lightest just before the dark . . ."*

He'd been sore and drunk so he'd come out with that. He was telling me in so many words that I might not be sitting nearly as pretty as I thought I was. And he was certainly right about that—but I think he'd got his words twisted a little. He was saying 'em to be sarcastic, but they happen to be the truth. At least it seemed so to me.

It *is* lightest just before the dark. Whatever a man is up against, it makes him feel better to know that he *is* up against it. That's the way it seemed to me, anyhow, and I ought to know.

Once I'd admitted the truth about that piece of evidence, it was easy to admit other things. I could stop inventing reasons for what I'd done, stop believing in the reasons I'd invented, and see the truth. And it sure wasn't hard to see. When you're climbing up a cliff or just holding on for dear life, you keep your eyes closed. You know you'll get dizzy and fall if you don't. But after you fall down to the bottom, you open 'em again. And you can see just where you started from, and trace every foot of your trail up that cliff.

Mine had started back with the housekeeper; with Dad finding out about us. All kids pull some pretty sorry stunts, particularly if an older person edges 'em along, so it hadn't needed to mean a thing. But Dad had made it mean something. I'd been made to feel that I'd done something that couldn't ever be forgiven—that would always lie between him and me, the only kin I had. And there wasn't anything I could do or say that would change things. I had a burden of fear and shame put on me that I could never get shed of.

She was gone, and I couldn't strike back at her, yes, kill her, for what I'd been made to feel she'd done to me. But that was all right. She was the first woman I'd ever known; she *was* woman to me; and all womankind bore her face. So I could strike back at any of them, any female, the ones it would be safest to strike at, and it would be the same as striking at her. And I did that, I started striking out . . . and Mike Dean took the blame.

Dad tightened the reins on me after that. I could hardly be out of his sight an hour without his checking up on me. So years passed and I didn't strike out again, and I was able to distinguish between women and *the* woman. Dad slacked off on the reins a little; I seemed to be normal. But every now and then I'd catch myself in that dead-pan kidding, trying to ease the terrific pressure that was building up inside of me. And even without that I knew—though I wouldn't recognize the fact—that I wasn't all right.

If I could have got away somewhere, where I wouldn't have been constantly reminded of what had happened and I'd had something I wanted to do—something to occupy my mind—

it might have been different. But I couldn't get away, and there wasn't anything here I wanted to do. So nothing had changed; I was still looking for *her*. And any woman who'd done what she had would be *her*.

I'd kept pushing Amy away from me down through the years, not because I didn't love her but because I did. I was afraid of what might happen between us. I was afraid of what I'd do . . . what I finally did.

I could admit, now, that I'd never had any real cause to think that Amy would make trouble for me. She had too much pride; she'd have hurt herself too much; and, anyway, she loved me.

I'd never had any real cause, either, to be afraid that Joyce would make trouble. She was too smart to try to, from what I'd seen of her. But if she had been sore enough to try—if she'd been mad enough so's she just didn't give a damn—she wouldn't have got anywhere. After all, she was just a whore and I was old family, quality; and she wouldn't have opened her mouth more than twice before she was run out of town.

No, I hadn't been afraid of her starting talk. I hadn't been afraid that if I kept on with her I'd lose control of myself. I'd never had any control even before I met her. No control—only luck. Because anyone who reminded me of the burden I carried, anyone who did what that first *her* had done, would get killed . . .

Anyone. Amy. Joyce. Any woman who, even for a moment, became *her*.

I'd kill them.

I'd keep trying until I did kill them.

Elmer Conway had had to suffer, too, on *her* account. Mike had taken the blame for me, and then he'd been killed. So, along with the burden, I had a terrible debt to him that I couldn't pay. I could never repay him for what he'd done for me. The only thing I could do was what I did . . . try to settle the score with Chester Conway.

That was my main reason for killing Elmer, but it wasn't the only one. The Conways were part of the circle, the town, that ringed me in; the smug ones, the hypocrites, the holier-than-thou guys—all the stinkers I had to face day in and day out. I had to grin and smile and be pleasant to them; and

maybe there are people like that everywhere, but when you
can't get away from them, when they keep pushing themselves
at you, and you can't get away, never, never, get away . . .

Well.

The bum. The few others I'd struck out at. I don't know—
I'm not really sure about them.

They were all people who didn't have to stay here. People
who took what was handed them because they didn't have
enough pride or guts to strike back. So maybe that was it.
Maybe I think that the guy who won't fight when he can and
should deserves the worst you can toss at him.

Maybe. I'm not sure of all the details. All I can do is give
you the general picture; and not even the experts could do
more than that.

I've read a lot of stuff by a guy—name of Kraepelin, I believe—and I can't remember all of it, of course, or even the
gist of all of it. But I remember the high points of some, the
most important stuff, and I think it goes something like this:

". . . difficult to study because so seldom detected. The
condition usually begins around the period of puberty, and is
often precipitated by a severe shock. The subject suffers from
strong feelings of guilt . . . combined with a sense of frustration and persecution . . . which increase as he grows older;
yet there are rarely if ever any surface signs of . . . disturbance. On the contrary, his behavior appears to be entirely
logical. He reasons soundly, even shrewdly. He is completely
aware of what he does and why he does it . . ."

That was written about a disease, or a condition, rather,
called dementia praecox. Schizophrenia, paranoid type. Acute,
recurrent, advanced.

Incurable.

It was written, you might say, about—

But I reckon you know, don't you?

Twenty-Three

I WAS in jail eight days, but no one questioned me and they
didn't pull any more stunts like that voice recording. I kind

of looked for them to do the last because they couldn't be positive about that piece of evidence they had—about my reaction to it, that is. They weren't certain that it would make me put the finger on myself. And even if they had been certain, I knew they'd a lot rather I cracked up and confessed of my own accord. If I did that they could probably send me to the chair. The other way—if they used their evidence—they couldn't.

But I reckon they weren't set up right at the jail for any more stunts or maybe they couldn't get ahold of the equipment they needed. At any rate, they didn't pull any more. And on the eighth day, around eleven o'clock at night, they transferred me to the insane asylum.

They put me in a pretty good room—better'n any I'd seen the time I'd had to take a poor guy there years before—and left me alone. But I took one look around and I knew I was being watched through those little slots high up on the walls. They wouldn't have left me in a room with cigarette tobacco and matches and a drinking glass and water pitcher unless someone was watching me.

I wondered how far they'd let me go if I started to cut my throat or wrap myself in a sheet and set fire to it, but I didn't wonder very long. It was late, and I was pretty well wornout after sleeping on that bunk in the cooler. I smoked a couple of hand-rolled cigarettes, putting the butts out real careful. Then with the lights still burning—there wasn't any switch for me to turn 'em off—I stretched out on the bed and went to sleep.

About seven in the morning, a husky-looking nurse came in with a couple of young guys in white jackets. And she took my temperature and pulse while they stood and waited. Then, she left and the two attendants took me down the hall to a shower room, and watched while I took a bath. They didn't act particularly tough or unpleasant, but they didn't say a word more than they needed to. I didn't say anything.

I finished my shower and put my short-tailed nightgown back on. We went back to my room, and one of 'em made up my bed while the other went after my breakfast. The scrambled eggs tasted pretty flat, and it didn't help my appetite any to have them cleaning up the room, emptying the enamel night-can and so on. But I ate almost everything and drank all of the weak luke-warm coffee. They were through cleaning, by the time I'd finished. They left, locking me in again.

I smoked a hand-rolled cigarette, and it tasted good.

I wondered—no I didn't, either. I didn't need to wonder what it would be like to spend your whole life like this. Not a tenth as good as this probably, because I was something pretty special right now. Right now I was a hide-out; I'd been kidnapped, actually. And there was always a chance that there'd be a hell of a stink raised. But if that hadn't been the case, if I'd been committed—well, I'd still be something special, in a different way. I'd be worse off than anyone in the place.

Conway would see to that, even if Doc Bony-face didn't have a special sort of interest in me.

I'd kind of figured that the Doc might show up with his hard-rubber playthings, but I guess he had just enough sense to know that he was out of his class. Plenty of pretty smart psychiatrists have been fooled by guys like me, and you can't really fault 'em for it. There's just not much they can put their hands on, know what I mean?

We might have the disease, the condition; or we might just be cold-blooded and smart as hell; or we might be innocent of what we're supposed to have done. We might be any one of those three things, because the symptoms we show would fit any one of the three.

So Bony-face didn't give me any trouble. No one did. The nurse checked on me night and morning, and the two attendants carried on with pretty much the same routine. Bringing my meals, taking me to the shower, cleaning up the room. The second day, and every other day after that, they let me shave with a safety razor while they stood by and watched.

I thought about Rothman and Billy Boy Walker, just thought, wondered, without worrying any. Because, hell, I didn't have anything to worry about, and they were probably doing enough worrying for all three of us. But—

But I'm getting ahead of myself.

They, Conway and the others, still weren't positive about

that piece of evidence they had; and, like I say, they preferred to have me crack up and confess. So, on the evening of my second night in the asylum, there came the stunt.

I was lying on my side in bed, smoking a cigarette, when the lights dimmed way down, down to almost nothing. Then, there was a click and a flash up above me, and Amy Stanton stood looking at me from the far wall of the room.

Oh, sure, it was a picture; one that had been made into a glass slide. I didn't need to do any figuring at all to know that they were using a slide projector to throw her picture against the wall. She was coming down the walk of her house, smiling, but looking kind of fussed like I'd seen her so many times. I could almost hear her saying, *"Well, you finally got here, did you?"* And I knew it was just a picture, but it looked so real, it seemed so real, that I answered her back in my mind. *"Kinda looks that way, don't it?"*

I guess they'd got a whole album of her pictures. Which wouldn't have been any trouble, since the old folks, the Stantons, were awfully innocent and accommodating and not given to asking questions. Anyway, after that first picture, which was a pretty recent one, there was one taken when she was about fifteen years old. And they worked up through the years from that.

They . . . I saw her the day she graduated from high school, she was sixteen that spring, wearing one of those white lacy dresses and flat-heeled slippers, and standing real stiff with her arms held close to her sides.

I saw her sitting on her front steps, laughing in spite of herself . . . *it always seemed hard for Amy to laugh* . . . because that old dog of theirs was trying to lick her on the ear.

I saw her all dressed up, and looking kind of scared, the time she started off for teachers' college. I saw her the day she finished her two-year course, standing very straight with her hand on the back of a chair and trying to look older than she was.

I saw her—and I'd taken a lot of those pictures myself; it seemed just like yesterday—I saw her working in the garden, in a pair of old jeans; walking home from church and kind of frowning up at the little hat she'd made for herself; coming out of the grocery store with both arms around a big sack; sitting in the porch swing with an apple in her hand and a book in her lap.

I saw her with her dress pulled way up high—she'd just slid off the fence where I'd taken a snap of her—and she was bent over, trying to cover herself, and yelling at me, *"Don't you dare, Lou! Don't you dare, now!"* . . . She'd sure been mad about me taking that picture, but she'd saved it.

I saw her . . .

I tried to remember how many pictures there were, to figure out how long they would last. They were sure in a hell of a hurry to get through with them, it looked like to me. They were just racing through 'em, it seemed like. I'd just be starting to enjoy a picture, remembering when it was taken and how old Amy was at the time, when they'd flash it off and put on another one.

It was a pretty sorry way to act, the way I saw it. You know, it was as though she wasn't worth looking at; like, maybe, they'd seen someone that was better to look at. And I'm not prejudiced or anything, but you wouldn't find a girl as pretty and well-built as Amy Stanton in a month of Sundays.

Aside from being a slight on Amy, it was damned stupid to rush through those pictures like they were doing . . . like they seemed to be doing. After all, the whole object of the show was to make me crack up, and how could I do it if they didn't even let me get a good look at her?

I wasn't going to crack up, of course; I felt stronger and better inside every time I saw her. But they didn't know that, and it doesn't excuse them. They were lying down on the job. They had a doggone ticklish job to do, and they were too lazy and stupid to do it right.

Well . . .

They'd started showing the pictures about eight-thirty, and they should have lasted until one or two in the morning. But they had to be in a hell of a hurry, so it was only around eleven when they came to the last one.

It was a picture I'd taken less than three weeks before, and they *did* leave it on long enough—well, not long enough, but they let me get a good look at it. She and I had fixed up a little lunch that evening, and eaten it over in Sam Houston

Park. And I'd taken this picture just as she was stepping back into the car. She was looking over her shoulder at me, wide-eyed, smiling but sort of impatient. Saying:

"Can't you hurry a little, darling?"

Hurry?

"Well, I reckon so, honey. I'll sure try to."

"When, Lou? How soon will I see you, darling?"

"Well, now, honey. I—I . . ."

I was almost glad right then that the lights came back on. I never was real good at lying to Amy.

I got up and paced around the room. I went over by the wall where they'd flashed the pictures, and I rubbed my eyes with my fists and gave the wall a few pats and tugged my hair a little.

I put on a pretty good act, it seemed to me. Just good enough to let 'em think I was bothered, but not enough to mean anything at a sanity hearing.

The nurse and the two attendants didn't have any more to say than usual the next morning. It seemed to me, though, that they acted a little different, more watchful sort of. So I did a lot of frowning and staring down at the floor, and I only ate part of my breakfast.

I passed up most of my lunch and dinner, too, which wasn't much of a chore, hungry as I was. And I did everything else I could to put on just the right kind of act—not too strong, not too weak. But I was too anxious. I had to go and ask the nurse a question when she made the night check on me, and that spoiled everything.

"Will they be showing the pictures tonight?" I said, and I knew doggone well it was the wrong thing to do.

"What pictures? I don't know anything about pictures," she said.

"The pictures of my girl. You know. Will they show 'em, ma'am?"

She shook her head, a kind of mean glint in her eye. "You'll see. You'll find out, mister."

"Well, tell 'em not to do it so fast," I said. "When they do it so fast, I don't get to see her very good. I hardly get to look at her at all before she's gone."

She frowned. She shook her head, staring at me, like

she hadn't heard me right. She edged away from the bed a little.

"You"—she swallowed—"you want to see those pictures?"

"Well—uh—I—"

"You *do* want to see them," she said slowly. "You want to see the pictures of the girl you—you—"

"Sure, I want to see 'em." I began to get sore. "Why shouldn't I want to see them? What's wrong with that? Why the hell wouldn't I want to see them?"

The attendants started to move toward me. I lowered my voice.

"I'm sorry," I said, "I don't want to cause any trouble. If you folks are too busy, maybe you could move the projector in here. I know how to run one, and I'd take good care of it."

That was a pretty bad night for me. There weren't any pictures, and I was so hungry I couldn't go to sleep for hours. I was sure glad when morning came.

So, that was the end of their stunt, and they didn't try any others. I reckon they figured it was a waste of time. They just kept me from then on; just held me without me saying any more than I had to and them doing the same.

That went on for six days, and I was beginning to get puzzled. Because that evidence of theirs should have been about ready to use, by now, if it was ever going to be ready.

The seventh day rolled around, and I was really getting baffled. And, then, right after lunch, Billy Boy Walker showed up.

Twenty-Four

"WHERE is he?" he yelled. "What have you done with the poor man? Have you torn out his tongue? Have you roasted his poor broken body over slow fires? Where is he, I say!"

He was coming down the corridor, yelling at the top of his lungs; and I could hear several people scurrying along with him, trying to shush him up, but no one had ever had much luck at that and they didn't either. I'd never seen him in my life—just heard him a couple of times on the radio—but I knew it was him. I reckon I'd have known he'd come even if I hadn't heard him. You didn't have to see or hear Billy Boy Walker to know he was around. You could just kind of sense it.

They stopped in front of my door, and Billy Boy started beating on it like they didn't have a key and he was going to have to knock it down.

"Mr. Ford! My poor man!" he yelled; and, man, I'll bet they could hear him all the way into Central City. "Can you hear me? Have they punctured your eardrums? Are you too weak to cry out? Be brave, my poor fellow!"

He kept it up, beating on the door and yelling, and it sounds like it must've been funny but somehow it wasn't. Even to me, knowing that they hadn't done a thing to me, really, it didn't sound funny. I could almost believe that they *had* put me through the works.

They managed to get the door unlocked, and he came bounding in. And he looked as funny—he should have looked as funny as he should have sounded—but I didn't feel the slightest call to laugh. He was short and fat and pot-bellied; and a couple of buttons were off his shirt and his belly-button was showing. He was wearing a baggy old black suit and red suspenders; and he had a big floppy black hat sitting kind of crooked on his head. Everything about him was sort of off-size and out-of-shape, as the saying is. But I couldn't see a thing to laugh about. Neither, apparently, could the nurse and the two attendants and old Doc Bony-face.

Billy Boy flung his arms around me and called me a "poor man" and patted me on the head. He had to reach up to do it; but he didn't seem to reach and it didn't seem funny.

He turned around, all at once, and grabbed the nurse by the arm. "Is this the woman, Mr. Ford? Did she beat you with chains? Fie! Fah! Abomination!" And he scrubbed his hand against his pants, glaring at her.

The attendants were helping me into my clothes, and they weren't losing any time about it. But you'd never have known it to hear Billy Boy. "Fiends!" he yelled. "Will your sadistic appetites never be satiated? Must you continue to stare and slaver over your handiwork? Will you not clothe this poor tortured flesh, this broken creature that was once a man built in God's own image?"

The nurse was spluttering and sputtering, her face a half-dozen different colors. The doc's bones were leaping like jumping-jacks. Billy Boy Walker snatched up the night-can, and shoved it under his nose. "You fed him from this, eh? I thought so! Bread and water, served in a slop jar! Shame, shame, fie! You did do it? Answer me, sirrah! You didn't do it? Fie, fah, paah! Perjurer, suborner! Answer, yes or no!"

The doc shook his head, and then nodded. He shook and nodded it at the same time. Billy Boy dropped the can to the floor, and took me by the arm. "Never mind your gold watch, Mr. Ford. Never mind the money and jewelry they have stolen. You have your clothes. Trust me to recover the rest—and more! Much, much more, Mr. Ford."

He pushed me out the door ahead of him, and then he turned around real slow and pointed around the room. "You," he said softly, pointing them out one by one. "You and you and you are through. This is the end for you. The end."

He looked them all in the eye, and no one said a word and none of them moved. He took me by the arm again, and we went down the corridor, and each of the three gates were open for us before we got to 'em.

He squeezed in behind the wheel of the car he'd rented in Central City. He started it up with a roar and a jerk, and we went speeding out through the main gate to the highway where two signs, facing in opposite directions, read:

WARNING! WARNING!
Hitch-hikers May Be Escaped
LUNATICS!

He lifted himself in the seat, reached into his hip pocket, and pulled out a plug of tobacco. He offered it to me and I shook my head, and he took a big chew.

"Dirty habit," he said, in just a quiet conversational voice. "Got it young, though, and I reckon I'll keep it."

He spat out the window, wiped his chin with his hand, and

THE KILLER INSIDE ME 153

wiped his hand on his pants. I found the makings I'd had at the asylum and started rolling a cigarette.

"About Joe Rothman," I said. "I didn't say anything about him, Mr. Walker."

"Why, I didn't think you had, Mr. Ford! It never occurred to me that you would," he said; and whether he meant it or not he sure sounded like it. "You know somethin', Mr. Ford? There wasn't a bit of sense in what I did back there."

"No," I said.

"No, sir, not a bit. I've been snorting and pawing up the earth around here for four days. Couldn't have fought harder getting Christ off the cross. And I reckon it was just habit like this chewing tobacco—I knew it but I kept right on chawing. I didn't get you free, Mr. Ford. I didn't have a thing to do with it. They *let* me have a writ. They *let* me know where you were. That's why you're here, Mr. Ford, instead of back there."

"I know," I said. "I figured it would be that way."

"You understand? They're not letting you go; they've gone too far to start backing water."

"I understand," I said.

"They've got something? Something you can't beat?"

"They've got it."

"Maybe you'd better tell me about it."

I hesitated, thinking, and finally I shook my head. "I don't think so, Mr. Walker. There's nothing you can do. Or I can do. You'd be wasting your time, and you might get Joe and yourself in a fix."

"Well, now, pshaw." He spat out the window again. "I reckon I might be a better judge of some things than you are, Mr. Ford. You—uh—aren't maybe a little distrustful, are you?"

"I think you know I'm not," I said. "I just don't want anyone else to get hurt."

"I see. Put it hypothetically, then. Just say that there are a certain set of circumstances which would have you licked—if they concerned you. Just make me up a situation that doesn't have anything to do with yours."

So I told him what they had and how they planned to use

it, hypothetically. And I stumbled around a lot, because describing my situation, the evidence they had, in a hypothetical way was mighty hard to do. He got it, though, without me having to repeat a word.

"That's the whole thing?" he said. "They haven't got— they can't get, we'll say, anything in the way of actual testimony?"

"I'm pretty sure they can't," I said. "I may be wrong but I'm almost positive they couldn't get anything out of this— evidence."

"Well, then? As long as you're—"

"I know," I nodded. "They're not taking me by surprise, like they figured on. I—I mean this fellow I'm talking about—"

"Go right ahead, Mr. Ford. Just keep on using the first person. It's easier to talk that way."

"Well, I wouldn't cut loose in front of 'em. I don't think I would. But I'd do it sooner or later, with someone. It's best to have it happen now, and get it over with."

He turned his head a moment to glance at me, the big black hat flopping in the wind. "You said you didn't want anyone else to get hurt. You meant it?"

"I meant it. You can't hurt people that are already dead."

"Good enough," he said; and whether he knew what I really meant and was satisfied with it, I don't know. His ideas of right and wrong didn't jibe too close with the books.

"I sure hate to give up, though," he frowned. "Just never got in the habit of giving up, I reckon."

"You can't call it giving up," I said. "Do you see that car way back behind us? And the one up in front, the one that turned in ahead of us, a while back? Those are county cars, Mr. Walker. You're not giving up anything. It's been lost for a long time."

He glanced up into the rear-view mirror, then squinted ahead through the windshield. He spat and rubbed his hand against his pants, wiped it slowly against the soiled black cloth. "Still got quite a little ride ahead of us, Mr. Ford. About thirty miles isn't it?"

"About that. Maybe a little more."

"I wonder if you'd like to tell me about it. You don't need

to, you understand, but it might be helpful, I might be able to help someone else."

"Do you think I could—that I'm able to tell you?"

"Why not?" he said. "I had a client years ago, Mr. Ford, a very able doctor. One of the most pleasant men you'd want to meet, and he had more money than he knew what to do with. But he'd performed about fifty abortions before they moved in on him, and so far as the authorities could find out every one of the abortion patients had died. He'd deliberately seen that they did die of peritonitis about a month after the operation. And he told me why—and he could've told anyone else why, when he finally faced up to the facts—he'd done it. He had a younger brother who was 'unfinished,' a prematurely born monstrosity, as the result of an attempted late-pregnancy abortion. He saw that terrible half-child die in agony for years. He never recovered from the experience—and neither did the women he aborted . . . Insane? Well, the only legal definition we have for insanity is the condition which necessitates the confinement of a person. So, since he hadn't been confined when he killed those women, I reckon he was sane. He made pretty good sense to me, anyhow."

He shifted the cud in his jaw, chewed a moment and went on. "I never had any legal schooling, Mr. Ford; picked up my law by reading in an attorney's office. All I ever had in the way of higher education was a couple years in agricultural college, and that was pretty much a plain waste of time. Crop rotation? Well, how're you going to do it when the banks only make crop loans on cotton? Soil conservation? How're you going to do terracing and draining and contour ploughing when you're cropping on shares? Purebred stock? Sure. Maybe you can trade your razorbacks for Poland Chinas . . . I just learned two things there at that college, Mr. Ford, that was ever of any use to me. One was that I couldn't do any worse than the people that were in the saddle, so maybe I'd better try pulling 'em down and riding myself. The other was a definition I got out of the agronomy books, and I reckon it was even more important than the first. It did more to revise my thinking, if I'd really done any thinking up until that time. Before that I'd seen everything in black and white, good and bad. But after I was set straight I saw that the name you put to a thing depended on where you stood and where it stood. And . . . and here's the definition, right out of the agronomy books: 'A weed is a plant out of place.' Let me repeat that. 'A weed is a plant out of place.' I find a hollyhock in my cornfield, and it's a weed. I find it in my yard, and it's a flower.

"You're in my yard, Mr. Ford."

. . . So I told him how it had been while he nodded and spat and drove, a funny pot-bellied shrimp of a guy who really had just one thing, understanding, but so much of it that you never missed anything else. He understood me better'n I understood myself.

"Yes, yes," he'd say, "you had to like people. You had to keep telling yourself you liked them. You needed to offset the deep, subconscious feelings of guilt." Or, he'd say, he'd interrupt, "And, of course, you knew you'd never leave Central City. Overprotection had made you terrified of the outside world. More important, it was part of the burden you had to carry to stay here and suffer."

He sure understood.

I reckon Billy Boy Walker's been cussed more in high places than any man in the country. But I never met a man I liked more.

I guess the way you felt about him depended on where you stood.

He stopped the car in front of my house, and I'd told him all I had to tell. But he sat there for a few minutes, spitting and sort of studying.

"Would you care to have me come in for a while, Mr. Ford?"

"I don't think it'd be smart," I said. "I got an idea it's not going to be very long, now."

He pulled an old turnip of a watch from his pocket and glanced at it. "Got a couple hours until train time, but—well, maybe you're right. I'm sorry, Mr. Ford. I'd hoped, if I couldn't do any better, to be taking you away from here with me."

"I couldn't have gone, no matter how things were. It's like you say, I'm tied here. I'll never be free as long as I live . . ."

Twenty-Five

YOU'VE GOT no time at all, but it seems like you've got forever. You've got nothing to do, but it seems like you've got everything.

You make coffee and smoke a few cigarettes; and the hands of the clock have gone crazy on you. They haven't moved hardly, they've hardly budged out of the place you last saw them, but they've measured off a half? two-thirds? of your life. You've got forever, but that's no time at all.

You've got forever; and somehow you can't do much with it. You've got forever; and it's a mile wide and an inch deep and full of alligators.

You go into the office and take a book or two from the shelves. You read a few lines, like your life depended on reading 'em right. But you know your life doesn't depend on anything that makes sense, and you wonder where in the hell you got the idea it did; and you begin to get sore.

You go into the laboratory and start pawing along the rows of bottles and boxes, knocking them on the floor, kicking them, stamping them. You find the bottle of one hundred percent pure nitric acid and you jerk out the rubber cork. You take it into the office and swing it along the rows of books. And the leather bindings begin to smoke and curl and wither—and it isn't good enough.

You go back into the laboratory. You come out with a gallon bottle of alcohol and the box of tall candles always kept there for emergencies. For *emergencies.*

You go upstairs, and then on up the little flight of stairs that leads to the attic. You come down from the attic and go through each of the bedrooms. You come back downstairs and go down into the basement. And when you return to the kitchen you are empty-handed. All the candles are gone, all the alcohol.

You shake the coffee pot and set it back on the stove burner. You roll another cigarette. You take a carving knife from a drawer and slide it up the sleeve of your pinkish-tan shirt with the black bow tie.

You sit down at the table with your coffee and cigarette,

and you ease your elbow up and down, seeing how far you can lower your arm without dropping the knife, letting it slide down from your sleeve a time or two.

You think, *"Well how can you? How can you hurt someone that's already dead?"*

You wonder if you've done things right, so's there'll be nothing left of something that shouldn't ever have been, and you know everything has been done right. You know, because you planned this moment before eternity way back yonder someplace.

You look up at the ceiling, listening, up through the ceiling and into the sky beyond. And there isn't the least bit of doubt in your mind. That'll be the plane, all right, coming in from the east, from Fort Worth. It'll be the plane she's on.

You look up at the ceiling, grinning, and you nod and say, "Long time no see. How you been doin' anyway, huh, baby? How are you, Joyce?"

Twenty-Six

JUST FOR the hell of it, I took a peek out the back door, and then I went part way into the living room and stooped down so I could look out the window. It was like I'd thought, of course. They had the house covered from every angle. Men with Winchesters. Deputies, most of 'em, with a few of the "safety inspectors" on Conway's payroll.

It would have been fun to take a real good look, to step to the door and holler howdy to 'em. But it would have been fun for them, too, and I figured they were having far too much as it was. Anyway, some of those "inspectors" were apt to be a mite trigger happy, anxious to show their boss they were on their toes, and I had a little job to do yet.

I had to get everything wrapped up to take with me.

I took one last walk through the house, and I saw that everything—the alcohol and the candles and everything—was going fine. I came back downstairs, closing all the doors behind me—*all the doors behind me*—and sat back down at the kitchen table.

The coffee pot was empty. There was just one cigarette paper left and just enough tobacco to fill it, and, yeah—*yeah!*—I was down to my last match. Things were sure working out fine.

I puffed on the cigarette, watching the red-gray ashes move down toward my fingers. I watched, not needing to, knowing they'd get just so far and no further.

I heard a car pull into the driveway. I heard a couple of its doors slam. I heard them crossing the yard and coming up the steps and across the porch. I heard the front door open; and they came in. And the ashes had burned out, the cigarette had gone dead.

And I laid it in my saucer and looked up.

I looked out the kitchen window, first, at the two guys standing outside. Then I looked at them:

Conway and Hendricks, Hank Butterby and Jeff Plummer. Two or three fellows I didn't know.

They fell back, watching me, letting her move out ahead of them. I looked at her.

Joyce Lakeland.

Her neck was in a cast that came clear up to her chin like a collar, and she walked stiff-backed and jerky. Her face was a white mask of gauze and tape, and nothing much showed of it but her eyes and her lips. And she was trying to say something—her lips were moving—but she didn't really have a voice. She could hardly get out a whisper.

"Lou . . . I didn't . . ."

"Sure," I said. "I didn't figure you had, baby."

She kept coming toward me and I stood up, my right arm raised like I was brushing at my hair.

I could feel my face twisting, my lips pulling back from my teeth. I knew what I must look like, but she didn't seem to mind. She wasn't scared. What did she have to be scared of?

". . . this, Lou. Not like this . . ."

"Sure you can't," I said. "Don't hardly see how you could."

". . . not anyway without . . ."

"Two hearts that beat as one," I said. "T-wo—ha, ha, ha,—two—ha, ha, ha, ha, ha, ha, ha,—two—J-jesus Chri—ha, ha, ha, ha, ha, ha, ha—two Jesus . . ."

And I sprang at her, I made for her just like they'd thought
I would. Almost. And it was like I'd signalled, the way the
smoke suddenly poured up through the floor. And the room
exploded with shots and yells, and I seemed to explode with
it, yelling and laughing and . . . and . . . Because they hadn't
got the point. She'd got that between the ribs and the blade
along with it. And they all lived happily ever after, I guess,
and I guess—that's—all.

Yeah, I reckon that's all unless our kind gets another chance
in the Next Place. Our kind. Us people.

All of us that started the game with a crooked cue, that
wanted so much and got so little, that meant so good and did
so bad. All us folks. Me and Joyce Lakeland, and Johnnie
Pappas and Bob Maples and big ol' Elmer Conway and little
ol' Amy Stanton. All of us.

All of us.

THE TALENTED MR. RIPLEY

by Patricia Highsmith

I.

Tom glanced behind him and saw the man coming out of the Green Cage, heading his way. Tom walked faster. There was no doubt the man was after him. Tom had noticed him five minutes ago, eyeing him carefully from a table, as if he weren't *quite* sure, but almost. He had looked sure enough for Tom to down his drink in a hurry, pay and get out.

At the corner Tom leaned forward and trotted across Fifth Avenue. There was Raoul's. Should he take a chance and go in for another drink? Tempt fate and all that? Or should he beat it over to Park Avenue and try losing him in a few dark doorways? He went into Raoul's.

Automatically, as he strolled to an empty space at the bar, he looked around to see if there was anyone he knew. There was the big man with red hair, whose name he always forgot, sitting at a table with a blond girl. The red-haired man waved a hand, and Tom's hand went up limply in response. He slid one leg over a stool and faced the door challengingly, yet with a flagrant casualness.

"Gin and tonic, please," he said to the barman.

Was this the kind of man they would send after him? Was he, wasn't he, was he? He didn't look like a policeman or a detective at all. He looked like a businessman, somebody's father, well-dressed, well-fed, graying at the temples, an air of uncertainty about him. Was that the kind they sent on a job like this, maybe to start chatting with you in a bar, and then *bang!*—the hand on the shoulder, the other hand displaying a policeman's badge. *Tom Ripley, you're under arrest.* Tom watched the door.

Here he came. The man looked around, saw him, and immediately looked away. He removed his straw hat, and took a place around the curve of the bar.

My God, what did he want? He certainly wasn't a *pervert*, Tom thought for the second time, though now his tortured brain groped and produced the actual word, as if the word could protect him, because he would rather the man be a pervert than a policeman. To a pervert, he could simply say,

163

"No, thank you," and smile and walk away. Tom slid back on the stool, bracing himself.

Tom saw the man make a gesture of postponement to the barman, and come around the bar toward him. Here it was! Tom stared at him, paralyzed. They couldn't give you more than ten years, Tom thought. Maybe fifteen, but with good conduct— In the instant the man's lips parted to speak, Tom had a pang of desperate, agonized regret.

"Pardon me, are you Tom Ripley?"

"Yes."

"My name is Herbert Greenleaf. Richard Greenleaf's father." The expression on his face was more confusing to Tom than if he had focused a gun on him. The face was friendly, smiling and hopeful. "You're a friend of Richard's, aren't you?"

It made a faint connection in his brain. Dickie Greenleaf. A tall blond fellow. He had quite a bit of money, Tom remembered. "Oh, Dickie Greenleaf. Yes."

"At any rate, you know Charles and Marta Schriever. They're the ones who told me about you, that you might— uh— Do you think we could sit down at a table?"

"Yes," Tom said agreeably, and picked up his drink. He followed the man toward an empty table at the back of the little room. Reprieved, he thought. Free! Nobody was going to arrest him. This was about something else. No matter what it was, it wasn't grand larceny or tampering with the mails or whatever they called it. Maybe Richard was in some kind of jam. Maybe Mr. Greenleaf wanted help, or advice. Tom knew just what to say to a father like Mr. Greenleaf.

"I wasn't quite sure you were Tom Ripley," Mr. Greenleaf said. "I've seen you only once before, I think. Didn't you come up to the house once with Richard?"

"I think I did."

"The Schrievers gave me a description of you, too. We've all been trying to reach you, because the Schrievers wanted us to meet at their house. Somebody told them you went to the Green Cage bar now and then. This is the first night I've tried to find you, so I suppose I should consider myself lucky." He smiled. "I wrote you a letter last week, but maybe you didn't get it."

"No, I didn't." Marc wasn't forwarding his mail, Tom thought. Damn him. Maybe there was a check there from Aunt Dottie. "I moved a week or so ago," Tom added.

"Oh, I see. I didn't say much in my letter. Only that I'd like to see you and have a chat with you. The Schrievers seemed to think you knew Richard quite well."

"I remember him, yes."

"But you're not writing to him now?" He looked disappointed.

"No. I don't think I've seen Dickie for a couple of years."

"He's been in Europe for two years. The Schrievers spoke very highly of you, and thought you might have some influence on Richard if you were to write to him. I want him to come home. He has responsibilities here—but just now he ignores anything that I or his mother try to tell him."

Tom was puzzled. "Just what did the Schrievers say?"

"They said—apparently they exaggerated a little—that you and Richard were very good friends. I suppose they took it for granted you were writing him all along. You see, I know so few of Richard's friends any more—" He glanced at Tom's glass, as if he would have liked to offer him a drink, at least, but Tom's glass was nearly full.

Tom remembered going to a cocktail party at the Schrievers' with Dickie Greenleaf. Maybe the Greenleafs were more friendly with the Schrievers than he was, and that was how it had all come about, because he hadn't seen the Schrievers more than three or four times in his life. And the last time, Tom thought, was the night he had worked out Charley Schriever's income tax for him. Charley was a TV director, and he had been in a complete muddle with his free-lance accounts. Charley had thought he was a genius for having doped out his tax and made it lower than the one Charley had arrived at, and perfectly legitimately lower. Maybe that was what had prompted Charley's recommendation of him to Mr. Greenleaf. Judging him from that night, Charley could have told Mr. Greenleaf that he was intelligent, level-headed, scrupulously honest, and very willing to do a favor. It was a slight error.

"I don't suppose you know of anybody else close to

Richard who might be able to wield a little influence?" Mr. Greenleaf asked rather pitifully.

There was Buddy Lankenau, Tom thought, but he didn't want to wish a chore like this on Buddy. "I'm afraid I don't," Tom said, shaking his head. "Why won't Richard come home?"

"He says he prefers living over there. But his mother's quite ill right now— Well, those are family problems. I'm sorry to annoy you like this." He passed a hand in a distraught way over his thin, neatly combed gray hair. "He says he's painting. There's no harm in that, but he hasn't the talent to be a painter. He's got great talent for boat designing, though, if he'd just put his mind to it." He looked up as a waiter spoke to him. "Scotch and soda, please. Dewar's. You're not ready?"

"No, thanks," Tom said.

Mr. Greenleaf looked at Tom apologetically. "You're the first of Richard's friends who's even been willing to listen. They all take the attitude that I'm trying to interfere with his life."

Tom could easily understand that. "I certainly wish I could help," he said politely. He remembered now that Dickie's money came from a shipbuilding company. Small sailing boats. No doubt his father wanted him to come home and take over the family firm. Tom smiled at Mr. Greenleaf, meaninglessly, then finished his drink. Tom was on the edge of his chair, ready to leave, but the disappointment across the table was almost palpable. "Where is he staying in Europe?" Tom asked, not caring a damn where he was staying.

"In a town called Mongibello, south of Naples. There's not even a library there, he tells me. Divides his time between sailing and painting. He's bought a house there. Richard has his own income—nothing huge, but enough to live on in Italy, apparently. Well, every man to his own taste, but I'm sure I can't see the attractions of the place." Mr. Greenleaf smiled bravely. "Can't I offer you a drink, Mr. Ripley?" he asked when the waiter came with his scotch and soda.

Tom wanted to leave. But he hated to leave the man sitting alone with his fresh drink. "Thanks, I think I will," he said, and handed the waiter his glass.

"Charley Schriever told me you were in the insurance business," Mr. Greenleaf said pleasantly.

"That was a little while ago. I—" But he didn't want to say he was working for the Department of Internal Revenue, not now. "I'm in the accounting department of an advertising agency at the moment."

"Oh?"

Neither said anything for a minute. Mr. Greenleaf's eyes were fixed on him with a pathetic, hungry expression. What on earth could he say? Tom was sorry he had accepted the drink. "How old is Dickie now, by the way?" he asked.

"He's twenty-five."

So am I, Tom thought. Dickie was probably having the time of his life over there. An income, a house, a boat. Why should he want to come home? Dickie's face was becoming clearer in his memory: he had a big smile, blondish hair with crisp waves in it, a happy-go-lucky face. Dickie was lucky. What was he himself doing at twenty-five? Living from week to week. No bank account. Dodging cops now for the first time in his life. He had a talent for mathematics. Why in hell didn't they pay him for it, somewhere? Tom realized that all his muscles had tensed, that the matchcover in his fingers was mashed sideways, nearly flat. He was bored, God-damned bloody bored, bored, bored! He wanted to jump up and leave the table without a word. He wanted to be back at the bar, by himself.

Tom took a gulp of his drink. "I'd be very glad to write to Dickie, if you give me his address," he said quickly. "I suppose he'll remember me. We were at a weekend party once out on Long Island, I remember. Dickie and I went out and gathered mussels, and everyone had them for breakfast." Tom smiled. "A couple of us got sick, and it wasn't a very good party. But I remember Dickie talking that weekend about going to Europe. He must have left just—"

"I remember!" Mr. Greenleaf said. "That was the last weekend Richard was here. I think he told me about the mussels." He laughed rather loudly.

"I came up to your apartment a few times, too," Tom went on, getting into the spirit of it. "Dickie showed me some ship models that were sitting on a table in his room."

"Those are only childhood efforts!" Mr. Greenleaf was beaming. "Did he ever show you his frame models? Or his drawings?"

Dickie hadn't, but Tom said brightly, "Yes! Of course he did. Pen-and-ink drawings. Fascinating, some of them." Tom had never seen them, but he could see them now, precise draftsman's drawings with every line and bolt and screw labeled, could see Dickie smiling, holding them up for him to look at, and he could have gone on for several minutes describing details for Mr. Greenleaf's delight, but he checked himself.

"Yes, Richard's got talent along those lines," Mr. Greenleaf said with a satisfied air.

"I think he has," Tom agreed. His boredom had slipped into another gear. Tom knew the sensations. He had them sometimes at parties, but generally when he was having dinner with someone with whom he hadn't wanted to have dinner in the first place, and the evening got longer and longer. Now he could be maniacally polite for perhaps another whole hour, if he had to be, before something in him exploded and sent him running out the door. "I'm sorry I'm not quite free now or I'd be very glad to go over and see if I could persuade Richard myself. Maybe I could have some influence on him," he said, just because Mr. Greenleaf wanted him to say that.

"If you seriously think so—that is, I don't know if you're planning a trip to Europe or not."

"No, I'm not."

"Richard was always so influenced by his friends. If you or somebody like you who knew him could get a leave of absence, I'd even send them over to talk to him. I think it'd be worth more than my going over, anyway. I don't suppose you could possibly get a leave of absence from your present job, could you?"

Tom's heart took a sudden leap. He put on an expression of reflection. It was a possibility. Something in him had smelt it out and leapt at it even before his brain. Present job: nil. He might have to leave town soon, anyway. He wanted to leave New York. "I might," he said carefully, with the same pondering expression, as if he were even now going over the thousands of little ties that could prevent him.

"If you did go, I'd be glad to take care of your expenses, that goes without saying. Do you really think you might be able to arrange it? Say, this fall?"

It was already the middle of September. Tom stared at the gold signet ring with the nearly worn-away crest on Mr. Greenleaf's little finger. "I think I might. I'd be glad to see Richard again—especially if you think I might be of some help."

"I do! I think he'd listen to you. Then the mere fact that you don't know him very well— If you put it to him strongly why you think he ought to come home, he'd know you hadn't any ax to grind." Mr. Greenleaf leaned back in his chair, looking at Tom with approval. "Funny thing is, Jim Burke and his wife—Jim's my partner—they went by Mongibello last year when they were on a cruise. Richard promised he'd come home when the winter began. Last winter. Jim's given him up. What boy of twenty-five listens to an old man sixty or more? You'll probably succeed where the rest of us have failed!"

"I hope so," Tom said modestly.

"How about another drink? How about a nice brandy?"

2.

IT was after midnight when Tom started home. Mr. Greenleaf had offered to drop him off in a taxi, but Tom had not wanted him to see where he lived—in a dingy brownstone between Third and Second with a ROOMS TO LET sign hanging out. For the last two and a half weeks Tom had been living with Bob Delancey, a young man he hardly knew, but Bob had been the only one of Tom's friends and acquaintances in New York who had volunteered to put him up when he had been without a place to stay. Tom had not asked any of his friends up to Bob's, and had not even told anybody where he was living. The main advantage of Bob's place was that he could get his George McAlpin mail there with the minimum chance of detection. But that smelly john down the hall that didn't lock, that grimy single room that looked as if it had been lived in by a thousand different people who had left behind their particular kind of filth and never lifted a hand to clean it, those slithering stacks of *Vogue* and *Harper's Bazaar* and those big chi-chi smoked-glass bowls all over the place, filled with tangles of string and pencils and cigarette butts and decaying fruit! Bob was a free-lance window decorator for shops and department stores, but now the only work he did was occasional jobs for Third Avenue antique shops, and some antique shop had given him the smoked-glass bowls as a payment for something. Tom had been shocked at the sordidness of the place, shocked that he even knew anybody who lived like that, but he had known that he wouldn't live there very long. And now Mr. Greenleaf had turned up. Something always turned up. That was Tom's philosophy.

Just before he climbed the brownstone steps, Tom stopped and looked carefully in both directions. Nothing but an old woman airing her dog, and a weaving old man coming around the corner from Third Avenue. If there was any sensation he hated, it was that of being followed, by *anybody*. And lately he had it all the time. He ran up the steps.

A lot the sordidness mattered now, he thought as he went into the room. As soon as he could get a passport, he'd be sailing for Europe, probably in a first-class cabin. Waiters to bring him things when he pushed a button! Dressing for dinner, strolling into a big dining room, talking with people at his table like a gentleman! He could congratulate himself on tonight, he thought. He had behaved just right. Mr. Greenleaf couldn't possibly have had the impression that he had finagled the invitation to Europe. Just the opposite. He wouldn't let Mr. Greenleaf down. He'd do his very best with Dickie. Mr. Greenleaf was such a decent fellow himself, he took it for granted that everybody else in the world was decent, too. Tom had almost forgotten such people existed.

Slowly he took off his jacket and untied his tie, watching every move he made as if it were somebody else's movements he were watching. Astonishing how much straighter he was standing now, what a different look there was in his face. It was one of the few times in his life that he felt pleased with himself. He put a hand into Bob's glutted closet and thrust the hangers aggressively to right and left to make room for his suit. Then he went into the bathroom. The old rusty showerhead sent a jet against the shower curtain and another jet in an erratic spiral that he could hardly catch to wet himself, but it was better than sitting in the filthy tub.

When he woke up the next morning Bob was not there, and Tom saw from a glance at his bed that he hadn't come home. Tom jumped out of bed, went to the two-ring burner and put on coffee. Just as well Bob wasn't home this morning. He didn't want to tell Bob about the European trip. All that crummy bum would see in it was a free trip. And Ed Martin, too, probably, and Bert Visser, and all the other crumbs he knew. He wouldn't tell any of them, and he wouldn't have anybody seeing him off. Tom began to whistle. He was invited to dinner tonight at the Greenleafs' apartment on Park Avenue.

Fifteen minutes later, showered, shaved, and dressed in a suit and a striped tie that he thought would look well in his passport photo, Tom was strolling up and down the room with a cup of black coffee in his hand, waiting for the morning mail. After the mail, he would go over to Radio City to take care of the passport business. What should he do this afternoon? Go to some art exhibits, so he could chat about them tonight with the Greenleafs? Do some research on Burke-Greenleaf Watercraft, Inc., so Mr. Greenleaf would know that he took an interest in his work?

The whack of the mailbox came faintly through the open window, and Tom went downstairs. He waited until the mailman was down the front steps and out of sight before he took the letter addressed to George McAlpin down from the edge of the mailbox frame where the mailman had stuck it. Tom ripped it open. Out came a check for one hundred and nineteen dollars and fifty-four cents, payable to the Collector of Internal Revenue. Good old Mrs. Edith W. Superaugh! Paid without a whimper, without even a telephone call. It was a good omen. He went upstairs again, tore up Mrs. Superaugh's envelope and dropped it into the garbage bag.

He put her check into a manila envelope in the inside pocket of one of his jackets in the closet. This raised his total in checks to one thousand eight hundred and sixty-three dollars and fourteen cents, he calculated in his head. A pity that he couldn't cash them. Or that some idiot hadn't paid in cash yet, or made out a check to George McAlpin, but so far no one had. Tom had a bank messenger's identification card that he had found somewhere with an old date on it that he could try to alter, but he was afraid he couldn't get away with cashing the checks, even with a forged letter of authorization for whatever the sum was. So it amounted to no more than a practical joke, really. Good clean sport. He wasn't stealing money from anybody. Before he went to Europe, he thought, he'd destroy the checks.

There were seven more prospects on his list. Shouldn't he try just one more in these last ten days before he sailed? Walking home last evening, after seeing Mr. Greenleaf, he had thought that if Mrs. Superaugh and Carlos de Sevilla paid up, he'd call it quits. Mr. de Sevilla hadn't paid up yet—he needed a good scare by telephone to put the fear of God into him, Tom thought—but Mrs. Superaugh had been so easy, he was tempted to try just *one* more.

Tom took a mauve-colored stationery box from his suitcase in the closet. There were a few sheets of stationery in the box, and below them a stack of various forms he had taken from the Internal Revenue office when he had worked there as a stockroom clerk a few weeks ago. On the very bottom was his list of prospects—carefully chosen people who lived in the Bronx or in Brooklyn and would not be too inclined to pay the New York office a personal visit, artists and writers and free-lance people who had no withholding taxes, and who made from seven to twelve thousand a year. In that bracket, Tom figured that people seldom hired professional tax men to compute their taxes, while they earned enough money to be logically accused of having made a two- or three-hundred-dollar error in their tax computations. There was William J. Slatterer, journalist; Philip Robillard, musician; Frieda Hoehn, illustrator; Joseph J. Gennari, photographer; Frederick Reddington, artist; Frances Karnegis— Tom had a hunch about Reddington. He was a comic-book artist. He probably didn't know whether he was coming or going.

He chose two forms headed NOTICE OF ERROR IN COMPUTATION, slipped a carbon between them, and began to copy rapidly the data below Reddington's name on his list. Income:

$11,250. Exemptions: 1. Deductions: $600. Credits: nil. Remittance: nil. Interest: (he hesitated a moment) $2.16. Balance due: $233.76. Then he took a piece of typewriter paper stamped with the Department of Internal Revenue's Lexington Avenue address from his supply in his carbon folder, crossed out the address with one slanting line of his pen, and typed below it:

Dear Sir:

Due to an overflow at our regular Lexington Avenue office, your reply should be sent to:

> Adjustment Department
> Attention of George McAlpin
> 187 E. 51 Street
> New York 22, New York.

Thank you.

> Ralph F. Fischer
> Gen. Dir. Adj. Dept.

Tom signed it with a scrolly, illegible signature. He put the other forms away in case Bob should come in suddenly, and picked up the telephone. He had decided to give Mr. Reddington a preliminary prod. He got Mr. Reddington's number from information and called it. Mr. Reddington was at home. Tom explained the situation briefly, and expressed surprise that Mr. Reddington had not yet received the notice from the Adjustment Department.

"That should have gone out a few days ago," Tom said. "You'll undoubtedly get it tomorrow. We've been a little rushed around here."

"But I've *paid* my tax," said the alarmed voice at the other end. "They were all—"

"These things can happen, you know, when the income's earned on a free-lance basis with no withholding tax. We've been over your return very carefully, Mr. Reddington. There's no mistake. And we wouldn't like to slap a lien on the office you work for or your agent or whatever—" Here he chuckled. A friendly, personal chuckle generally worked wonders. "—but we'll have to do that unless you pay within forty-eight hours. I'm sorry the notice hasn't reached you before now. As I said, we've been pretty—"

"Is there anyone there I can talk to about it if I come in?" Mr. Reddington asked anxiously. "That's a hell of a lot of money!"

"Well, there is, of course." Tom's voice always got folksy at this point. He sounded like a genial old codger of sixty-odd, who might be as patient as could be if Mr. Reddington came in, but who wouldn't yield by so much as a red cent, for all the talking and explaining Mr. Reddington might do. George McAlpin represented the Tax Department of the United States of America, suh. "You can talk to *me*, of course," Tom drawled, "but there's absolutely no mistake about this, Mr. Reddington. I'm just thinking of saving you your time. You can come in if you want to, but I've got all your records right here in my hand."

Silence. Mr. Reddington wasn't going to ask him anything about records, because he probably didn't know what to begin asking. But if Mr. Reddington were to ask him to explain what it was all about, Tom had a lot of hash about net income versus accrued income, balance due versus computation, interest at six per cent per annum accruing from due date of the tax until paid on any balance which represents tax shown on original return, which he could deliver in a slow voice as incapable of interruption as a Sherman tank. So far, no one had insisted on coming in person to hear more of that. Mr. Reddington was backing down, too. Tom could hear it in the silence.

"All right," Mr. Reddington said in a tone of collapse. "I'll read the notice when I get it tomorrow."

"All right, Mr. Reddington," he said, and hung up.

Tom sat there for a moment, giggling, the palms of his thin hands pressed together between his knees. Then he jumped up, put Bob's typewriter away again, combed his light-brown hair neatly in front of the mirror, and set off for Radio City.

3.

"HELLO-O, Tom, my boy!" Mr. Greenleaf said in a voice that promised good martinis, a gourmet's dinner, and a bed for the night in case he got too tired to go home. "Emily, this is Tom Ripley!"

"I'm so happy to meet you!" she said warmly.

"How do you do, Mrs. Greenleaf?"

She was very much what he had expected—blond, rather tall and slender, with enough formality to keep him on his good behavior, yet with the same naïve good-will-toward-all that Mr. Greenleaf had. Mr. Greenleaf led them into the living room. Yes, he had been here before with Dickie.

"Mr. Ripley's in the insurance business," Mr. Greenleaf announced, and Tom thought he must have had a few already, or he was very nervous tonight, because Tom had given him quite a description last night of the advertising agency where he had said he was working.

"Not a very exciting job," Tom said modestly to Mrs. Greenleaf.

A maid came into the room with a tray of martinis and canapés.

"Mr. Ripley's been here before," Mr. Greenleaf said. "He's come here with Richard."

"Oh, has he? I don't believe I met you, though." She smiled. "Are you from New York?"

"No, I'm from Boston," Tom said. That was true.

About thirty minutes later—just the right time later, Tom thought, because the Greenleafs had kept insisting that he drink another and another martini—they went into a dining room off the living room, where a table was set for three with candles, huge dark-blue dinner napkins, and a whole cold chicken in aspic. But first there was céleri rémoulade. Tom was very fond of it. He said so.

"So is Richard!" Mrs. Greenleaf said. "He always liked it the way our cook makes it. A pity you can't take him some."

"I'll put it in with the socks," Tom said, smiling, and Mrs. Greenleaf laughed. She had told him she would like him to take Richard some black woolen socks from Brooks Brothers, the kind Richard always wore.

The conversation was dull, and the dinner superb. In answer to a question of Mrs. Greenleaf's, Tom told her that he was working for an advertising firm called Rothenberg, Fleming and Barter. When he referred to it again, he deliberately called it Reddington, Fleming and Parker. Mr. Greenleaf didn't seem to notice the difference. Tom mentioned the firm's name the second time when he and Mr. Greenleaf were alone in the living room after dinner.

"Did you go to school in Boston?" Mr. Greenleaf asked.

"No, sir. I went to Princeton for a while, then I visited another aunt in Denver and went to college there." Tom waited, hoping Mr. Greenleaf would ask him something about Princeton, but he didn't. Tom could have discussed the system of teaching history, the campus restrictions, the atmosphere at the weekend dances, the political tendencies of the student body, anything. Tom had been very friendly last summer with a Princeton junior who had talked of nothing but Princeton, so that Tom had finally pumped him for more and more, foreseeing a time when he might be able to use the information. Tom had told the Greenleafs that he had been raised by his Aunt Dottie in Boston. She had taken him to Denver when he was sixteen, and actually he had only finished high school there, but there had been a young man named Don Mizell rooming in his Aunt Bea's house in Denver who had been going to the University of Colorado. Tom felt as if he had gone there, too.

"Specialize in anything in particular?" Mr. Greenleaf asked.

"Sort of divided myself between accounting and English composition," Tom replied with a smile, knowing it was such a dull answer that nobody would possibly pursue it.

Mrs. Greenleaf came in with a photograph album, and Tom sat beside her on the sofa while she turned through it. Richard taking his first step, Richard in a ghastly full-page color photograph dressed and posed as the Blue Boy, with long blond curls. The album was not interesting to him until Richard got to be sixteen or so, long-legged, slim, with the wave tightening in his hair. So far as Tom could see, he had hardly changed between sixteen and twenty-three or -four, when the pictures of him stopped, and it was astonishing to Tom how little the bright, naïve smile changed. Tom could not help feeling that Richard was not very intelligent, or else he loved to be photographed and thought he looked best with his mouth spread from ear to ear, which was not very intelligent of him, either.

"I haven't gotten round to pasting these in yet," Mrs. Greenleaf said, handing him a batch of loose pictures. "These are all from Europe."

They were more interesting: Dickie in what looked like a café in Paris, Dickie on a beach. In several of them he was frowning.

"This is Mongibello, by the way," Mrs. Greenleaf said, indicating the picture of Dickie pulling a rowboat up on the sand. The picture was backgrounded by dry, rocky mountains and a fringe of little white houses along the shore. "And here's the girl there, the only other American who lives there."

"Marge Sherwood," Mr. Greenleaf supplied. He sat across the room, but he was leaning forward, following the picture-showing intently.

The girl was in a bathing suit on the beach, her arms around her knees, healthy and unsophisticated-looking, with tousled, short blond hair—the good-egg type. There was a good picture of Richard in shorts, sitting on the parapet of a terrace. He was smiling, but it was not the same smile, Tom saw. Richard looked more poised in the European pictures.

Tom noticed that Mrs. Greenleaf was staring down at the rug in front of her. He remembered the moment at the table when she had said, "I wish I'd never heard of Europe!" and Mr. Greenleaf had given her an anxious glance and then smiled at him, as if such outbursts had occurred before. Now he saw tears in her eyes. Mr. Greenleaf was getting up to come to her.

"Mrs. Greenleaf," Tom said gently, "I want you to know that I'll do everything I can to make Dickie come back."

"Bless you, Tom, bless you." She pressed Tom's hand that rested on his thigh.

"Emily, don't you think it's time you went in to bed?" Mr. Greenleaf asked, bending over her.

Tom stood up as Mrs. Greenleaf did.

"I hope you'll come again to pay us a visit before you go, Tom," she said. "Since Richard's gone, we seldom have any young men to the house. I miss them."

"I'd be delighted to come again," Tom said.

Mr. Greenleaf went out of the room with her. Tom remained standing, his hands at his sides, his head high. In a large mirror on the wall he could see himself: the upright, self-respecting young man again. He looked quickly away. He was doing the right thing, behaving the right way. Yet he had a feeling of guilt. When he had said to Mrs. Greenleaf just now, *I'll do everything I can . . .* Well, he meant it. He wasn't trying to fool anybody.

He felt himself beginning to sweat, and he tried to relax. What was he so worried about? He'd felt so well tonight! When he had said that about Aunt Dottie—

Tom straightened, glancing at the door, but the door had not opened.

That had been the only time tonight when he had felt uncomfortable, unreal, the way he might have felt if he had been lying, yet it had been practically the only thing he had said that *was* true: *My parents died when I was very small. I was raised by my aunt in Boston.*

Mr. Greenleaf came into the room. His figure seemed to pulsate and grow larger and larger. Tom blinked his eyes, feeling a sudden terror of him, an impulse to attack him before he was attacked.

"Suppose we sample some brandy?" Mr. Greenleaf said, opening a panel beside the fireplace.

It's like a movie, Tom thought. In a minute, Mr. Greenleaf or somebody else's voice would say, "Okay, *cut!*" and he would relax again and find himself back in Raoul's with the gin and tonic in front of him. No, back in the Green Cage.

"Had enough?" Mr. Greenleaf asked. "Don't drink this, if you don't want it."

Tom gave a vague nod, and Mr. Greenleaf looked puzzled for an instant, then poured the two brandies.

A cold fear was running over Tom's body. He was thinking of the incident in the drugstore last week, though that was all over and he wasn't *really* afraid, he reminded himself, not now. There was a drugstore on Second Avenue whose phone number he gave out to people who insisted on calling him again about their income tax. He gave it out as the phone number of the Adjustment Department where he could be reached only between three-thirty and four on Wednesday and Friday afternoons. At these times, Tom hung around the booth in the drugstore, waiting for the phone to ring. When the druggist had looked at him suspiciously the second time he had been there, Tom had said that he was waiting for a call from his girl friend. Last Friday when he had answered the telephone, a man's voice had said, "You know what we're talking about, don't you? We know where you live, if you want us to come to your place. . . . We've got the stuff for you, if you've got it for us." An insistent yet evasive voice, so that Tom had thought it was some kind of a trick and hadn't been able to answer anything. Then, "Listen, we're coming right over. To your *house.*" Tom's legs had felt like jelly when he got out of the phone booth, and then he had seen the druggist staring at him, wide-eyed, panicky-looking, and the conversation had suddenly explained itself: the druggist sold dope, and he was afraid that Tom was a police detective who had come to get the goods on *him.* Tom had started laughing, had walked out laughing uproariously, staggering as he went, because his legs were still weak from his own fear.

"Thinking about Europe?" Mr. Greenleaf's voice said.

Tom accepted the glass Mr. Greenleaf was holding out to him. "Yes, I was," Tom said.

"Well, I hope you enjoy your trip, Tom, as well as have some effect on Richard. By the way, Emily likes you a lot. She told me so. I didn't have to ask her." Mr. Greenleaf rolled his brandy glass between his hands. "My wife has leukemia, Tom."

"Oh. That's very serious, isn't it?"

"Yes. She may not live a year."

"I'm sorry to hear that," Tom said.

Mr. Greenleaf pulled a paper out of his pocket. "I've got a list of boats. I think the usual Cherbourg way is quickest, and also the most interesting. You'd take the boat train to Paris, then a sleeper down over the Alps to Rome and Naples."

"That'd be fine." It began to sound exciting to him.

"You'll have to catch a bus from Naples to Richard's village. I'll write him about you—not telling him that you're an emissary from me," he added, smiling, "but I'll tell him we've met. Richard ought to put you up, but if he can't for some reason, there're hotels in the town. I expect you and Richard'll hit it off all right. Now as to money—" Mr. Greenleaf smiled his fatherly smile. "I propose to give you six hundred dollars in traveler's checks apart from your round-trip ticket. Does that suit you? The six hundred should see you through nearly two months, and if you need more, all you have to do is wire me, my boy. You don't look like a young man who'd throw money down the drain."

"That sounds ample, sir."

Mr. Greenleaf got increasingly mellow and jolly on the brandy, and Tom got increasingly close-mouthed and sour. Tom wanted to get out of the apartment. And yet he still wanted to go to Europe, and wanted Mr. Greenleaf to approve of him. The moments on the sofa were more agonizing than the moments in the bar last night when he had been so bored, because now that break into another gear didn't come. Several times Tom got up with his drink and strolled to the fireplace and back, and when he looked into the mirror he saw that his mouth was turned down at the corners.

Mr. Greenleaf was rollicking on about Richard and himself in Paris, when Richard had been ten years old. It was not in the least interesting. If anything happened with the police in the next ten days, Tom thought, Mr. Greenleaf would take him in. He could tell Mr. Greenleaf that he'd sublet his apartment in a hurry, or something like that, and simply hide out here. Tom felt awful, almost physically ill.

"Mr. Greenleaf, I think I should be going."

"Now? But I wanted to show you— Well, never mind. Another time."

Tom knew he should have asked, "Show me what?" and been patient while he showed whatever it was, but he couldn't.

"I want you to visit the yards, of course," Mr. Greenleaf said cheerfully. "When can you come out? Only during your lunch hour, I suppose. I think you should be able to tell Richard what the yards look like these days."

"Yes—I could come in my lunch hour."

"Give me a call any day, Tom. You've got my card with my private number. If you give me half an hour's notice, I'll have a man pick you up at your office and drive you out. We'll have a sandwich as we walk through, and he'll drive you back."

"I'll call you," Tom said. He felt he would faint if he stayed one minute longer in the dimly lighted foyer, but Mr.

Greenleaf was chuckling again, asking him if he had read a certain book by Henry James.

"I'm sorry to say I haven't, sir, not that one," Tom said.

"Well, no matter." Mr. Greenleaf smiled.

Then they shook hands, a long suffocating squeeze from Mr. Greenleaf, and it was over. But the pained, frightened expression was still on his face as he rode down in the elevator, Tom saw. He leaned in the corner of the elevator in an exhausted way, though he knew as soon as he hit the lobby he would fly out the door and keep on running, running, all the way home.

4.

THE atmosphere of the city became stranger as the days went on. It was as if something had gone out of New York—the realness or the importance of it—and the city was putting on a show just for him, a colossal show with its buses, taxis, and hurrying people on the sidewalks, its television shows in all the Third Avenue bars, its movie marquees lighted up in broad daylight, and its sound effects of thousands of honking horns and human voices, talking for no purpose whatsoever. As if when his boat left the pier on Saturday, the whole city of New York would collapse with a *poof* like a lot of cardboard on a stage.

Or maybe he was afraid. He hated water. He had never been anywhere before on water, except to New Orleans from New York and back to New York again, but then he had been working on a banana boat mostly below deck, and he had hardly realized he was on water. The few times he had been on deck the sight of the water had at first frightened him, then made him feel sick, and he had always run below deck again, where, contrary to what people said, he had felt better. His parents had drowned in Boston Harbor, and Tom had always thought that probably had something to do with it, because as long as he could remember he had been afraid of water, and he had never learned how to swim. It gave Tom a sick, empty feeling at the pit of his stomach to think that in less than a

week he would have water below him, miles deep, and that
undoubtedly he would have to look at it most of the time,
because people on ocean liners spent most of their time on
deck. And it was particularly un-chic to be seasick, he felt.
He had never been seasick, but he came very near it several
times in those last days, simply thinking about the voyage to
Cherbourg.

He had told Bob Delancey that he was moving in a week,
but he hadn't said where. Bob did not seem interested, anyway. They saw very little of each other at the Fifty-first Street
place. Tom had gone to Marc Priminger's house in East-
Forty-fifth Street—he still had the keys—to pick up a couple
of things he had forgotten, and he had gone at an hour when
he had thought Marc wouldn't be there, but Marc had come
in with his new housemate, Joel, a thin drip of a young man
who worked for a publishing house, and Marc had put on one
of his suave "Please-do-*just*-as-you-like" acts for Joel's benefit, though if Joel hadn't been there Marc would have cursed
him out in language that even a Portuguese sailor wouldn't
have used. Marc (his given name was, of all things, Marcellus)
was an ugly mug of a man with a private income and a hobby
of helping out young men in temporary financial difficulties
by putting them up in his two-story, three-bedroom house,
and playing God by telling them what they could and couldn't
do around the place and by giving them advice as to their
lives and their jobs, generally rotten advice. Tom had stayed
there three months, though for nearly half that time Marc had
been in Florida and he had had the house all to himself, but
when Marc had come back he had made a big stink about a
few pieces of broken glassware—Marc playing God again, the
Stern Father—and Tom had gotten angry enough, for once,
to stand up for himself and talk back to him. Whereupon Marc
had thrown him out, after collecting sixty-three dollars from
him for the broken glassware. The old tightwad! He should
have been an old maid, Tom thought, at the head of a girls'
school. Tom was bitterly sorry he had ever laid eyes on Marc
Priminger, and the sooner he could forget Marc's stupid, pig-
like eyes, his massive jaw, his ugly hands with the gaudy rings
(waving through the air, ordering this and that from everybody), the happier he would be.

The only one of his friends he felt like telling about his European trip was Cleo, and he went to see her on the Thursday before he sailed. Cleo Dobelle was a tall, slim, dark-haired girl who could have been anything from twenty-three to thirty, Tom didn't know, who lived with her parents in Gracie Square and painted in a small way—a *very* small way, in fact, on little pieces of ivory no bigger than postage stamps that had to be viewed through a magnifying glass, and Cleo used a magnifying glass when she painted them. "But think how convenient it is to be able to carry *all* my paintings in a cigar box! Other painters have to have rooms and rooms to hold their canvases!" Cleo said. Cleo lived in her own suite of rooms with a little bath and kitchen at the back of her parents' section of the apartment, and Cleo's apartment was always rather dark since it had no exposure except to a tiny backyard overgrown with ailanthus trees that blocked out the light. Cleo always had the lights on, dim ones, which gave a nocturnal atmosphere whatever the time of day. Except for the night when he had met her, Tom had seen Cleo only in close-fitting velvet slacks of various colors and gaily striped silk shirts. They had taken to each other from the very first night, when Cleo had asked him to dinner at her apartment on the following evening. Cleo always asked him up to her apartment, and there was somehow never any thought that he might ask her out to dinner or the theatre or do any of the ordinary things that a young man was expected to do with a girl. She didn't expect him to bring her flowers or books or candy when he came for dinner or cocktails, though Tom did bring her a little gift sometimes, because it pleased her so. Cleo was the one person he could tell that he was going to Europe and why. He did.

Cleo was enthralled, as he had known she would be. Her red lips parted in her long, pale face, and she brought her hands down on her velvet thighs and exclaimed, "*Tom*-mie! How too, too marvelous! It's just like out of Shakespeare or something!"

That was just what Tom thought, too. That was just what he had needed someone to say.

Cleo fussed around him all evening, asking him if he had this and that, Kleenexes and cold tablets and woolen socks because it started raining in Europe in the fall, and his vaccinations. Tom said he felt pretty well prepared.

"Just don't come to see me off, Cleo. I don't want to be seen off."

"Of course not!" Cleo said, understanding perfectly. "Oh, Tommie, I think that's such fun! Will you write me everything that happens with Dickie? You're the only person I know who ever went to Europe for a *reason*."

He told her about visiting Mr. Greenleaf's shipyards in Long Island, the miles and miles of tables with machines making shiny metal parts, varnishing and polishing wood, the drydocks with boat skeletons of all sizes, and impressed her with the terms Mr. Greenleaf had used—coamings, inwales, keelsons, and chines. He described the second dinner at Mr. Greenleaf's house, when Mr. Greenleaf had presented him with a wristwatch. He showed the wristwatch to Cleo, not a fabulously expensive wristwatch, but still an excellent one and just the style Tom might have chosen for himself—a plain white face with fine black Roman numerals in a simple gold setting with an alligator strap.

"Just because I happened to say a few days before that I didn't own a watch," Tom said. "He's really adopted me like a son." And Cleo, too, was the only person he knew to whom he could say that.

Cleo sighed. "Men! You have all the luck. Nothing like that could ever happen to a girl. Men're so *free!*"

Tom smiled. It often seemed to him that it was the other way around. "Is that the lamb chops burning?"

Cleo jumped up with a shriek.

After dinner, she showed him five or six of her latest paintings, a couple of romantic portraits of a young man they both knew, in an open-collared white shirt, three imaginary landscapes of a junglelike land, derived from the view of ailanthus trees out her window. The hair of the little monkeys in the paintings was really astoundingly well done, Tom thought. Cleo had a lot of brushes with just one hair in them, and even these varied from comparatively coarse to ultra fine. They drank nearly two bottles of Medoc from her parents' liquor shelf, and Tom got so sleepy he could have spent the night right where he was lying on the floor—they had often slept side by side on the two big bear rugs in front of the fireplace, and it was another of the wonderful things about Cleo that she never wanted or expected him to make a pass at her, and he never had—but Tom hauled himself up at a quarter to twelve and took his leave.

"I won't see you again, will I?" Cleo said dejectedly at the door.

"Oh, I should be back in about six weeks," Tom said, though he didn't think so at all. Suddenly he leaned forward and planted a firm, brotherly kiss on her ivory cheek. "I'll miss you, Cleo."

She squeezed his shoulder, the only physical touch he could recall her ever having given him. "I'll miss you," she said.

The next day he took care of Mrs. Greenleaf's commissions at Brooks Brothers, the dozen pairs of black woolen socks and the bathrobe. Mrs. Greenleaf had not suggested a color for the bathrobe. She would leave that up to him, she had said. Tom chose a dark maroon flannel with a navy-blue belt and lapels. It was not the best-looking robe of the lot, in Tom's opinion, but he felt it was exactly what Richard would have chosen, and that Richard would be delighted with it. He put the socks and the robe on the Greenleafs' charge account. He saw a heavy linen sport shirt with wooden buttons that he liked very much, that would have been easy to put on the Greenleafs' account, too, but he didn't. He bought it with his own money.

5.

THE morning of his sailing, the morning he had looked forward to with such buoyant excitement, got off to a hideous start. Tom followed the steward to his cabin congratulating himself that his firmness with Bob about not wanting to be seen off had taken effect, and had just entered the room when a bloodcurdling whoop went up.

"Where's all the champagne, Tom? We're waiting!"

"Boy, is this a stinking room! Why don't you ask them for something decent?"

"Tommie, take *me?*" from Ed Martin's girl friend, whom Tom couldn't bear to look at.

There they all were, mostly Bob's lousy friends, sprawled on his bed, on the floor, everywhere. Bob had found out he was sailing, but Tom had never thought he would do a thing like this. It took self-control for Tom not to say in an icy voice, "There *isn't* any champagne." He tried to greet them all, tried to smile, though he could have burst into tears like a child. He gave Bob a long, withering look, but Bob was already high, on something. There were very few things that got under his skin, Tom thought self-justifyingly, but this was one of them: noisy surprises like this, the riffraff, the vulgarians, the slobs he had thought he had left behind when he crossed the gangplank, littering the very stateroom where he was to spend the next five days!

Tom went over to Paul Hubbard, the only respectable person in the room, and sat down beside him on the short, built-in sofa. "Hello, Paul," he said quietly. "I'm sorry about all this."

"Oh!" Paul scoffed. "How long'll you be gone?—What's the matter, Tom? Are you sick?"

It was awful. It went on, the noise and the laughter and the girls feeling the bed and looking in the john. Thank God the Greenleafs hadn't come to see him off! Mr. Greenleaf had had to go to New Orleans on business, and Mrs. Greenleaf, when Tom had called this morning to say good-bye, had said that she didn't feel quite up to coming down to the boat.

Finally, Bob or somebody produced a bottle of whisky, and they all began to drink out of the two glasses from the bathroom, and then a steward came in with a tray of glasses. Tom refused to have a drink. He was sweating so heavily, he took off his jacket so as not to soil it. Bob came over and rammed a glass in his hand, and Bob was not exactly joking, Tom saw, and he knew why—because he had accepted Bob's hospitality for a month, and he might at least put on a pleasant face, but Tom could not put on a pleasant face any more than if his face had been made of granite. So what if they all hated him after this, he thought, what had he lost?

"I can fit in here, Tommie," said the girl who was determined to fit in somewhere and go with him. She had wedged herself sideways into a narrow closet about the size of a broom closet.

"I'd like to see Tom caught with a girl in his room!" Ed Martin said, laughing.

Tom glared at him. "Let's get out of here and get some air," he murmured to Paul.

The others were making so much noise, nobody noticed their leaving. They stood at the rail near the stern. It was a sunless day, and the city on their right was already like some gray, distant land that he might be looking at from mid-ocean—except for those bastards inside his stateroom.

"Where've you been keeping yourself?" Paul asked. "Ed called up to tell me you were leaving. I haven't seen you in weeks."

Paul was one of the people who thought he worked for the Associated Press. Tom made up a fine story about an assignment he had been sent on. Possibly the Middle East, Tom said. He made it sound rather secret. "I've been doing quite a lot of night work lately, too," Tom said, "which is why I haven't been around much. It's awfully nice of you to come down and see me off."

"I hadn't any classes this morning." Paul took the pipe out of his mouth and smiled. "Not that I wouldn't have come anyway, probably. Any old excuse!"

Tom smiled. Paul taught music at a girls' school in New York to earn his living, but he preferred to compose music on his own time. Tom could not remember how he had met Paul, but he remembered going to his Riverside Drive apartment for Sunday brunch once with some other people, and Paul had played some of his own compositions on the piano, and Tom had enjoyed it immensely. "Can't I offer you a drink? Let's see if we can find the bar," Tom said.

But just then a steward came out, hitting a gong and shouting, "Visitors ashore, please! All visitors ashore!"

"That's me," Paul said.

They shook hands, patted shoulders, promised to write postcards to each other. Then Paul was gone.

Bob's gang would stay till the last minute, he thought, probably have to be blasted out. Tom turned suddenly and ran up a narrow, ladderlike flight of stairs. At the top of it he was confronted by a CABIN CLASS ONLY sign hanging from a chain, but he threw a leg over the chain and stepped onto the deck. They surely wouldn't object to a first-class passenger going into second-class, he thought. He couldn't bear to look at Bob's gang again. He had paid Bob half a month's rent and given him a good-bye present of a good shirt and tie. What more did Bob want?

The ship was moving before Tom dared to go down to his room again. He went into the room cautiously. Empty. The neat blue bedcover was smooth again. The ashtrays were clean. There was no sign they had ever been here. Tom relaxed and smiled. This was service! The fine old tradition of the Cunard Line, British seamanship and all that! He saw a big basket of fruit on the floor by his bed. He seized the little white envelope eagerly. The card inside said:

> Bon voyage and bless you, Tom. All our good wishes go with you.
> Emily and Herbert Greenleaf

The basket had a tall handle and it was entirely under yellow cellophane—apples and pears and grapes and a couple of candy bars and several little bottles of liqueurs. Tom had never received a bon voyage basket. To him, they had always been something you saw in florists' windows for fantastic prices and laughed at. Now he found himself with tears in his eyes, and he put his face down in his hands suddenly and began to sob.

6.

HIS mood was tranquil and benevolent, but not at all sociable. He wanted his time for thinking, and he did not care to meet any of the people on the ship, not any of them, though when he encountered the people with whom he sat at his table, he greeted them pleasantly and smiled. He began to play a role on the ship, that of a serious young man with a serious job ahead of him. He was courteous, poised, civilized and preoccupied.

He had a sudden whim for a cap and bought one in the haberdashery, a conservative bluish-gray cap of soft English wool. He could pull its visor down over nearly his whole face when he wanted to nap in his deckchair, or wanted to look as if he were napping. A cap was the most versatile of head-gears, he thought, and he wondered why he had never thought of wearing one before? He could look like a country gentleman, a thug, an Englishman, a Frenchman, or a plain American eccentric, depending on how he wore it. Tom amused himself with it in his room in front of the mirror. He had always thought he had the world's dullest face, a thoroughly forgettable face with a look of docility that he could not understand, and a look also of vague fright that he had never been able to erase. A real conformist's face, he thought. The cap changed all that. It gave him a country air, Greenwich, Connecticut, country. Now he was a young man with a private income, not long out of Princeton, perhaps. He bought a pipe to go with the cap.

He was starting a new life. Good-bye to all the second-rate people he had hung around and had let hang around him in the last three years in New York. He felt as he imagined immigrants felt when they left everything behind them in some foreign country, left their friends and relations and their past mistakes, and sailed for America. A clean slate! Whatever happened with Dickie, he would acquit himself well, and Mr. Greenleaf would know that he had, and would respect him for it. When Mr. Greenleaf's money was used up, he might not come back to America. He might get an interesting job in a hotel, for instance, where they needed somebody bright and personable who spoke English. Or he might become a representative for some European firm and travel everywhere in the world. Or somebody might come along who needed a young man exactly like himself, who could drive a car, who was quick at figures, who could entertain an old grandmother or squire somebody's daughter to a dance. He was versatile, and the world was wide! He swore to himself he would stick to a job once he got it. Patience and perseverance! Upward and onward!

"Have you Henry James' *The Ambassadors*?" Tom asked the officer in charge of the first-class library. The book was not on the shelf.

"I'm sorry, we haven't, sir," said the officer.

Tom was disappointed. It was the book Mr. Greenleaf had asked him if he had read. Tom felt he ought to read it. He went to the cabin-class library. He found the book on the shelf, but when he started to check it out and gave his cabin number, the attendant told him sorry, that first-class passengers were not allowed to take books from the cabin-class library. Tom had been afraid of that. He put the book back docilely, though it would have been easy, so easy, to make a pass at the shelf and slip the book under his jacket.

In the mornings he strolled several times round the deck, but very slowly, so that the people puffing around on their morning constitutionals always passed him two or three times before he had been around once, then settled down in his deckchair for bouillon and more thought on his own destiny. After lunch, he pottered around in his cabin, basking in its privacy and comfort, doing absolutely nothing. Sometimes he sat in the writing room, thoughtfully penning letters on the ship's stationery to Marc Priminger, to Cleo, to the Greenleafs. The letter to the Greenleafs began as a polite greeting and a thank-you for the bon voyage basket and the comfortable accommodations, but he amused himself by adding an imaginary postdated paragraph about finding Dickie and living with him in his Mongibello house, about the slow but steady progress he was making in persuading Dickie to come home, about the swimming, the fishing, the café life, and he got so carried away that it went on for eight or ten pages and he knew he would never mail any of it, so he wrote on about Dickie's not being romantically interested in Marge (he gave a complete character analysis of Marge) so it was not Marge who was holding Dickie, though Mrs. Greenleaf had thought it might be, etc., etc., until the table was covered with sheets of paper and the first call came for dinner.

On another afternoon, he wrote a polite note to Aunt Dottie:

Dear Auntie [which he rarely called her in a letter and never to her face],

As you see by the stationery, I am on the high seas. An unexpected business offer which I cannot explain now. I had to leave rather suddenly, so I was not able to get up to Boston and I'm sorry, because it may be months or even years before I come back.

I just wanted you not to worry and not to send me any more checks, thank you. Thank you very much for the last one of a month or so ago. I don't suppose you have sent any more since then. I am well and extremely happy.

Love,
Tom

No use sending any good wishes about her health. She was as strong as an ox. He added:

P.S. I have no idea what my address will be, so I cannot give you any.

That made him feel better, because it definitely cut him off from her. He needn't ever tell her where he was. No more of the snidely digging letters, the sly comparisons of him to his father, the piddling checks for the strange sums of six dollars and forty-eight cents and twelve dollars and ninety-five, as if she had had a bit left over from her latest bill-paying, or taken something back to a store and had tossed the money to him, like a crumb. Considering what Aunt Dottie might have sent him, with her income, the checks were an insult. Aunt Dottie insisted that his upbringing had cost her more than his father had left in insurance, and maybe it had, but did she have to keep rubbing it in his face? Did anybody human keep rubbing a thing like that in a child's face? Lots of aunts and even strangers raised a child for nothing and were delighted to do it.

After his letter to Aunt Dottie, he got up and strode around the deck, walking it off. Writing her always made him feel angry. He resented the courtesy to her. Yet until now he had always wanted her to know where he was, because he had always needed her piddling checks. He had had to write a score of letters about his changes of address to Aunt Dottie. But he didn't need her money now. He would hold himself independent of it, forever.

He thought suddenly of one summer day when he had been about twelve, when he had been on a cross-country trip with Aunt Dottie and a woman friend of hers, and they had gotten stuck in a bumper-to-bumper traffic jam somewhere. It had been a hot summer day, and Aunt Dottie had sent him out with the thermos to get some ice water at a filling station, and suddenly the traffic had started moving. He remembered running between huge, inching cars, always about to touch the door of Aunt Dottie's car and never being quite able to, because she had kept inching along as fast as she could go, not willing to wait for him a minute, and yelling, "Come on, come on, slowpoke!" out the window all the time. When he had finally made it to the car and gotten in, with tears of frustration and anger running down his cheeks, she had said gaily to her friend, "Sissy! He's a sissy from the ground up. Just like his father!" It was a wonder he had emerged from such treatment as well as he had. And just what, he wondered, made Aunt Dottie think his father had been a sissy? Could she, had she, ever cited a single thing? No.

Lying in his deckchair, fortified morally by the luxurious surroundings and inwardly by the abundance of well-prepared food, he tried to take an objective look at his past life. The last four years had been for the most part a waste, there was no denying that. A series of haphazard jobs, long perilous intervals with no job at all and consequent demoralization because of having no money, and then taking up with stupid, silly people in order not to be lonely, or because they could offer him something for a while, as Marc Priminger had. It was not a record to be proud of, considering he had come to New York with such high aspirations. He had wanted to be an actor, though at twenty he had not had the faintest idea of the difficulties, the necessary training, or even the necessary talent. He had thought he had the necessary talent, and that all he would have to do was show a producer a few of his original one-man skits—Mrs. Roosevelt writing "My Day" after a visit to a clinic for unmarried mothers, for instance—but his first three rebuffs had killed all his courage and his hope. He had had no reserve of money, so he had taken the job on the banana boat, which at least had removed him from New York. He had been afraid that Aunt Dottie had called the police to look for him in New York, though he hadn't done anything wrong in Boston, just run off to make his own way in the world as millions of young men had done before him.

His main mistake had been that he had never stuck to anything, he thought, like the accounting job in the department store that might have worked into something, if he had not been so completely discouraged by the slowness of department-store promotions. Well, he blamed Aunt Dottie to some extent for his lack of perseverance, never giving him credit when he was younger for anything he had stuck to—like his paper route when he was thirteen. He had won a silver medal from the newspaper for "Courtesy, Service, and Reliability." It was like looking back at another person to remember himself then, a skinny, sniveling wretch with an eternal cold in the nose, who had still managed to win a medal for courtesy, service, and reliability. Aunt Dottie had hated him when he had a cold; she used to take her handkerchief and nearly wrench his nose off, wiping it.

Tom writhed in his deckchair as he thought of it, but he writhed elegantly, adjusting the crease of his trousers.

He remembered the vows he had made, even at the age of eight, to run away from Aunt Dottie, the violent scenes he had imagined—Aunt Dottie trying to hold him in the house, and he hitting her with his fists, flinging her to the ground and throttling her, and finally tearing the big brooch off her dress and stabbing her a million times in the throat with it. He had run away at seventeen and been brought back, and he had done it again at twenty and succeeded. And it was astounding and pitiful how naïve he had been, how little he had known about the way the world worked, as if he had spent so much of his time hating Aunt Dottie and scheming how to escape her, that he had not had enough time to learn and grow. He remembered the way he had felt when he had been fired from the warehouse job during his first month in New York. He had held the job less than two weeks, because he hadn't been strong enough to lift orange crates eight hours a day, but he had done his best and knocked himself out trying to hold the job, and when they had fired him, he remembered how horribly unjust he had thought it. He remembered deciding then that the world was full of Simon Legrees, and that you had to be an animal, as tough as the gorillas who worked with him at the warehouse, or starve. He remembered that right after that, he had stolen a loaf of bread from a delicatessen counter and had taken it home and devoured it, feeling that the world owed a loaf of bread to him, and more.

"Mr. Ripley?" One of the Englishwomen who had sat on

the sofa with him in the lounge the other day during tea was bending over him. "We were wondering if you'd care to join us in a rubber of bridge in the game room? We're going to start in about fifteen minutes."

Tom sat up politely in his chair. "Thank you very much, but I think I prefer to stay outside. Besides, I'm not too good at bridge."

"Oh, neither are we! All right, another time." She smiled and went away.

Tom sank back in his chair again, pulled his cap down over his eyes and folded his hands over his waist. His aloofness, he knew, was causing a little comment among the passengers. He had not danced with either of the silly girls who kept looking at him hopefully and giggling during the after-dinner dancing every night. He imagined the speculations of the passengers: Is he an American? I *think* so, but he doesn't act like an American, does he? Most Americans are so *noisy*. He's terribly serious, isn't he, and he can't be more than twenty-three. He must have something very important on his mind.

Yes, he had. The present and the future of Tom Ripley.

7.

PARIS was no more than a glimpse out a railroad station window of a lighted café front, complete with rain-streaked awning, sidewalk tables, and boxes of hedges, like a tourist poster illustration, and otherwise a series of long station platforms down which he followed dumpy little blue-clad porters with his luggage, and at last the sleeper that would take him all the way to Rome. He could come back to Paris at some other time, he thought. He was eager to get to Mongibello.

When he woke up the next morning, he was in Italy. Something very pleasant happened that morning. Tom was watching the landscape out the window, when he heard some Italians in the corridor outside his compartment say something with the word "Pisa" in it. A city was gliding by on the other side of the train. Tom went into the corridor to get a better look at it, looking automatically for the Leaning Tower, though he was not at all sure that the city was Pisa or that the tower would even be visible from here, but there it was!— a thick white column sticking up out of the low chalky houses that formed the rest of the town, and *leaning*, leaning at an angle that he wouldn't have thought possible! He had always taken it for granted that the leaning of the Leaning Tower of Pisa was exaggerated. It seemed to him a good omen, a sign that Italy was going to be everything that he expected, and that everything would go well with him and Dickie.

He arrived in Naples late that afternoon, and there was no bus to Mongibello until tomorrow morning at eleven. A boy of about sixteen in dirty shirt and trousers and G.I. shoes latched onto him at the railroad station when he was changing some money, offering him God knew what, maybe girls, maybe dope, and in spite of Tom's protestations actually got into the taxi with him and instructed the driver where to go, jabbering on and holding a finger up as if he were going to fix him up fine, wait and see. Tom gave up and sulked in a corner with his arms folded, and finally the taxi stopped in front of a big hotel that faced the bay. Tom would have been afraid of the imposing hotel if Mr. Greenleaf had not been paying the bill.

"Santa Lucia!" the boy said triumphantly, pointing seaward.

Tom nodded. After all, the boy seemed to mean well. Tom paid the driver and gave the boy a hundred-lire bill, which he estimated to be sixteen and a fraction cents and appropriate as a tip in Italy, according to an article on Italy he had read on the ship, and when the boy looked outraged, gave him another hundred, and when he still looked outraged, waved a hand at him and went into the hotel behind the bellboys who had already gathered up his luggage.

Tom had dinner that evening at a restaurant down on the water called Zi' Teresa, which had been recommended to him by the English-speaking manager of the hotel. He had a difficult time ordering, and he found himself with a first course of miniature octopuses, as virulently purple as if they had been cooked in the ink in which the menu had been written. He tasted the tip of one tentacle, and it had a disgusting consistency like cartilage. The second course was also a mistake, a

platter of fried fish of various kinds. The third course—which
he had been sure was a kind of dessert—was a couple of small
reddish fish. Ah, Naples! The food didn't matter. He was feeling mellow on the wine. Far over on his left, a three-quarter
moon drifted above the jagged hump of Mount Vesuvius.
Tom gazed at it calmly, as if he had seen it a thousand times
before. Around the corner of land there, beyond Vesuvius, lay
Richard's village.

He boarded the bus the next morning at eleven. The road
followed the shore and went through little towns where they
made brief stops—Torre del Greco, Torre Annunciata, Cas-
tellammare, Sorrento. Tom listened eagerly to the names of
the towns that the driver called out. From Sorrento, the road
was a narrow ridge cut into the side of the rock cliffs that
Tom had seen in the photographs at the Greenleafs'. Now
and then he caught glimpses of little villages down at the water's edge, houses like white crumbs of bread, specks that were
the heads of people swimming near the shore. Tom saw a
boulder-sized rock in the middle of the road that had evidently broken off of a cliff. The driver dodged it with a
nonchalant swerve.

"Mongibello!"

Tom sprang up and yanked his suitcase down from the rack.
He had another suitcase on the roof, which the bus boy took
down for him. Then the bus went on, and Tom was alone at
the side of the road, his suitcases at his feet. There were houses
above him, straggling up the mountain, and houses below,
their tile roofs silhouetted against the blue sea. Keeping an
eye on his suitcases, Tom went into a little house across the
road marked POSTA, and inquired of the man behind the window where Richard Greenleaf's house was. Without thinking,
he spoke in English, but the man seemed to understand, because he came out and pointed from the door up the road
Tom had come on the bus, and gave in Italian what seemed
to be explicit directions how to get there.

"Sempre seeneestra, seeneestra!"

Tom thanked him, and asked if he could leave his two suitcases in the post office for a while, and the man seemed to
understand this, too, and helped Tom carry them into the
post office.

He had to ask two more people where Richard Greenleaf's house was, but everybody seemed to know it, and the third person was able to point it out to him—a large two-story house with an iron gate on the road, and a terrace that projected over the cliff's edge. Tom rang the metal bell beside the gate. An Italian woman came out of the house, wiping her hands on her apron.

"Mr. Greenleaf?" Tom asked hopefully.

The woman gave him a long, smiling answer in Italian and pointed downward toward the sea. "Jew," she seemed to keep saying. "Jew."

Tom nodded. "Grazie."

Should he go down to the beach as he was, or be more casual about it and get into a bathing suit? Or should he wait until the tea or cocktail hour? Or should he try to telephone him first? He hadn't brought a bathing suit with him, and he'd certainly have to have one here. Tom went into one of the little shops near the post office that had shirts and bathing shorts in its tiny front window, and after trying on several pairs of shorts that did not fit him, or at least not adequately enough to serve as a bathing suit, he bought a black-and-yellow thing hardly bigger than a G-string. He made a neat bundle of his clothing inside his raincoat, and started out the door barefoot. He leapt back inside. The cobblestones were hot as coals.

"Shoes? Sandals?" he asked the man in the shop.

The man didn't sell shoes.

Tom put on his own shoes again and walked across the road to the post office, intending to leave his clothes with his suitcases, but the post office door was locked. He had heard of this in Europe, places closing from noon to four sometimes. He turned and walked down a cobbled lane which he supposed led toward the beach. He went down a dozen steep stone steps, down another cobbled slope past shops and houses, down more steps, and finally he came to a level length of broad sidewalk slightly raised from the beach, where there were a couple of cafés and a restaurant with outdoor tables. Some bronzed adolescent Italian boys sitting on wooden benches at the edge of the pavement inspected him thoroughly as he walked by. He felt mortified at the big brown

shoes on his feet and at his ghost-white skin. He had not been
to a beach all summer. He hated beaches. There was a wooden
walk that led half across the beach, which Tom knew must be
hot as hell to walk on, because everybody was lying on a towel
or something else, but he took his shoes off anyway and stood
for a moment on the hot wood, calmly surveying the groups
of people near him. None of the people looked like Richard,
and the shimmering heat waves kept him from making out
the people very far away. Tom put one foot out on the sand
and drew it back. Then he took a deep breath, raced down
the rest of the walk, sprinted across the sand, and sank his feet
into the blissfully cool inches of water at the sea's edge. He
began to walk.

Tom saw him from a distance of about a block—unmistakably Dickie, though he was burnt a dark brown and his crinkly
blond hair looked lighter than Tom remembered it. He was
with Marge.

"Dickie Greenleaf?" Tom asked, smiling.

Dickie looked up. "Yes?"

"I'm Tom Ripley. I met you in the States several years ago.
Remember?"

Dickie looked blank.

"I think your father said he was going to write you about
me."

"Oh, yes!" Dickie said, touching his forehead as if it was
stupid of him to have forgotten. He stood up. "Tom *what* is
it?"

"Ripley."

"This is Marge Sherwood," he said. "Marge, Tom Ripley."

"How do you do?" Tom said.

"How do you do?"

"How long are you here for?" Dickie asked.

"I don't know yet," Tom said. "I just got here. I'll have
to look the place over."

Dickie was looking him over, not entirely with approval,
Tom felt. Dickie's arms were folded, his lean brown feet
planted in the hot sand that didn't seem to bother him at all.
Tom had crushed his feet into his shoes again.

"Taking a house?" Dickie asked.

"I don't know," Tom said undecidedly, as if he had been considering it.

"It's a good time to get a house, if you're looking for one for the winter," the girl said. "The summer tourists have practically all gone. We could use a few more Americans around here in winter."

Dickie said nothing. He had reseated himself on the big towel beside the girl, and Tom felt that he was waiting for him to say good-bye and move on. Tom stood there, feeling pale and naked as the day he was born. He hated bathing suits. This one was very revealing. Tom managed to extract his pack of cigarettes from his jacket inside the raincoat, and offered it to Dickie and the girl. Dickie accepted one, and Tom lighted it with his lighter.

"You don't seem to remember me from New York," Tom said.

"I can't really say I do," Dickie said. "Where did I meet you?"

"I think— Wasn't it at Buddy Lankenau's?" It wasn't, but he knew Dickie knew Buddy Lankenau, and Buddy was a very respectable fellow.

"Oh," said Dickie, vaguely. "I hope you'll excuse me. My memory's rotten for America these days."

"It certainly is," Marge said, coming to Tom's rescue. "It's getting worse and worse. When did you get here, Tom?"

"Just about an hour ago. I've just parked my suitcases at the post office." He laughed.

"Don't you want to sit down? Here's another towel." She spread a smaller white towel beside her on the sand.

Tom accepted it gratefully.

"I'm going down for a dip to cool off," Dickie said, getting up.

"Me, too!" Marge said. "Coming in, Tom?"

Tom followed them. Dickie and the girl went out quite far—both seemed to be excellent swimmers—and Tom stayed near the shore and came in much sooner. When Dickie and the girl came back to the towels, Dickie said, as if he had been prompted by the girl, "We're leaving. Would you like to come up to the house and have lunch with us?"

"Why, yes. Thanks very much." Tom helped them gather up the towels, the sunglasses, the Italian newspapers.

Tom thought they would never get there. Dickie and Marge went in front of him, taking the endless flights of stone steps slowly and steadily, two at a time. The sun had enervated Tom. The muscles of his legs trembled on the level stretches. His shoulders were already pink, and he had put on his shirt against the sun's rays, but he could feel the sun burning through his hair, making him dizzy and nauseous.

"Having a hard time?" Marge asked, not out of breath at all. "You'll get used to it, if you stay here. You should have seen this place during the heat wave in July."

Tom hadn't breath to reply anything.

Fifteen minutes later he was feeling better. He had had a cool shower, and he was sitting in a comfortable wicker chair on Dickie's terrace with a martini in his hand. At Marge's suggestion, he had put his swimming outfit on again, with his shirt over it. The table on the terrace had been set for three while he was in the shower, and Marge was in the kitchen now, talking in Italian to the maid. Tom wondered if Marge lived here. The house was certainly big enough. It was sparsely furnished, as far as Tom could see, in a pleasant mixture of Italian antique and American bohemian. He had seen two original Picasso drawings in the hall.

Marge came out on the terrace with her martini. "That's my house over there." She pointed. "See it? The square-looking white one with the darker red roof than the houses just beside it."

It was hopeless to pick it out from the other houses, but Tom pretended he saw it. "Have you been here long?"

"A year. All last winter, and it was quite a winter. Rain every day except one for three whole months!"

"Really!"

"Um-hm." Marge sipped her martini and gazed out contentedly at her little village. She was back in her bathing suit, too, a tomato-colored bathing suit, and she wore a striped shirt over it. She wasn't bad-looking, Tom supposed, and she even had a good figure, if one liked the rather solid type. Tom didn't, himself.

"I understand Dickie has a boat," Tom said.

"Yes, the *Pipi*. Short for *Pipistrello*. Want to see it?"

She pointed at another indiscernible something down at the little pier that they could see from the corner of the terrace. The boats looked very much alike, but Marge said Dickie's boat was larger than most of them and had two masts.

Dickie came out and poured himself a cocktail from the pitcher on the table. He wore badly ironed white duck trousers and a terra cotta linen shirt the color of his skin. "Sorry there's no ice. I haven't got a refrigerator."

Tom smiled. "I brought a bathrobe for you. Your mother said you'd asked for one. Also some socks."

"Do you know my mother?"

"I happened to meet your father just before I left New York, and he asked me to dinner at his house."

"Oh? How was my mother?"

"She was up and around that evening. I'd say she gets tired easily."

Dickie nodded. "I had a letter this week saying she was a little better. At least there's no particular crisis right now, is there?"

"I don't think so. I think your father was more worried a few weeks ago." Tom hesitated. "He's also a little worried because you won't come home."

"Herbert's always worried about something," Dickie said.

Marge and the maid came out of the kitchen carrying a steaming platter of spaghetti, a big bowl of salad, and a plate of bread. Dickie and Marge began to talk about the enlargement of some restaurant down on the beach. The proprietor was widening the terrace so there would be room for people to dance. They discussed it in detail, slowly, like people in a small town who take an interest in the most minute changes in the neighborhood. There was nothing Tom could contribute. He spent the time examining Dickie's rings. He liked them both: a large rectangular green stone set in gold on the third finger of his right hand, and on the little finger of the other hand a signet ring, larger and more ornate than the signet Mr. Greenleaf had worn. Dickie had long, bony hands, a little like his own hands, Tom thought.

"By the way, your father showed me around the Burke-Greenleaf yards before I left," Tom said. "He told me he'd made a lot of changes since you've seen it last. I was quite impressed."

"I suppose he offered you a job, too. Always on the lookout for promising young men." Dickie turned his fork round and round, and thrust a neat mass of spaghetti into his mouth.

"No, he didn't." Tom felt the luncheon couldn't have been going worse. Had Mr. Greenleaf told Dickie that he was coming to give him a lecture on why he should go home? Or was Dickie just in a foul mood? Dickie had certainly changed since Tom had seen him last.

Dickie brought out a shiny espresso machine about two feet high, and plugged it into an outlet on the terrace. In a few moments there were four little cups of coffee, one of which Marge took into the kitchen to the maid.

"What hotel are you staying at?" Marge asked Tom.

Tom smiled. "I haven't found one yet. What do you recommend?"

"The Miramare's the best. It's just this side of Giorgio's. The only other hotel is Giorgio's, but—"

"They say Giorgio's got pulci in his beds," Dickie interrupted.

"That's fleas. Giorgio's is cheap," Marge said earnestly, "but the service is—"

"Nonexistent," Dickie supplied.

"You're in a fine mood today, aren't you?" Marge said to Dickie, flicking a crumb of gorgonzola at him.

"In that case, I'll try the Miramare," Tom said, standing up. "I must be going."

Neither of them urged him to stay. Dickie walked with him to the front gate. Marge was staying on. Tom wondered if Dickie and Marge were having an affair, one of those old, faute de mieux affairs that wouldn't necessarily be obvious from the outside, because neither was very enthusiastic. Marge was in love with Dickie, Tom thought, but Dickie couldn't have been more indifferent to her if she had been the fifty-year-old Italian maid sitting there.

"I'd like to see some of your paintings sometime," Tom said to Dickie.

"Fine. Well, I suppose we'll see you again if you're

around," and Tom thought he added it only because he remembered that he had brought him the bathrobe and the socks.

"I enjoyed the lunch. Good-bye, Dickie."

"Good-bye."

The iron gate clanged.

8.

TOM took a room at the Miramare. It was four o'clock by the time he got his suitcases up from the post office, and he had barely the energy to hang up his best suit before he fell down on the bed. The voices of some Italian boys who were talking under his window drifted up as distinctly as if they had been in the room with him, and the insolent, cackling laugh of one of them, bursting again and again through the pattering syllables, made Tom twitch and writhe. He imagined them discussing his expedition to Signor Greenleaf, and making unflattering speculations as to what might happen next.

What was he doing here? He had no friends here and he didn't speak the language. Suppose he got sick? Who would take care of him?

Tom got up, knowing he was going to be sick, yet moving slowly because he knew just when he was going to be sick and that there would be time for him to get to the bathroom. In the bathroom he lost his lunch, and also the fish from Naples, he thought. He went back to his bed and fell instantly asleep.

When he awoke, groggy and weak, the sun was still shining and it was five-thirty by his new watch. He went to a window and looked out, looking automatically for Dickie's big house and projecting terrace among the pink and white houses that dotted the climbing ground in front of him. He found the sturdy reddish balustrade of the terrace. Was Marge still there? Were they talking about him? He heard a laugh rising over the little din of street noises, tense and resonant, and as

American as if it had been a sentence in American. For an instant he saw Dickie and Marge as they crossed a space between houses on the main road. They turned the corner, and Tom went to his side window for a better view. There was an alley by the side of the hotel just below his window, and Dickie and Marge came down it, Dickie in the white trousers and terra cotta shirt, Marge in a skirt and blouse. She must have gone home, Tom thought. Or else she had clothes at Dickie's house. Dickie talked with an Italian on the little wooden pier, gave him some money, and the Italian touched his cap, then untied the boat from the pier. Tom watched Dickie help Marge into the boat. The white sail began to climb. Behind them, to the left, the orange sun was sinking into the water. Tom could hear Marge's laugh, and a shout from Dickie in Italian toward the pier. Tom realized he was seeing them on a typical day—a siesta after the late lunch, probably, then the sail in Dickie's boat at sundown. Then apéritifs at one of the cafés on the beach. They were enjoying a perfectly ordinary day, as if he did not exist. Why should Dickie want to come back to subways and taxis and starched collars and a nine-to-five job? Or even a chauffeured car and vacations in Florida and Maine? It wasn't as much fun as sailing a boat in old clothes and being answerable to nobody for the way he spent his time, and having his own house with a good-natured maid who probably took care of everything for him. And money besides to take trips, if he wanted to. Tom envied him with a heartbreaking surge of envy and of self-pity.

Dickie's father had probably said in his letter the very things that would set Dickie against him, Tom thought. How much better it would have been if he had just sat down in one of the cafés down at the beach and struck up an acquaintance with Dickie out of the blue! He probably could have persuaded Dickie to come home eventually, if he had begun like that, but this way it was useless. Tom cursed himself for having been so heavy-handed and so humorless today. Nothing he took desperately seriously ever worked out. He'd found that out years ago.

He'd let a few days go by, he thought. The first step, anyway, was to make Dickie like him. That he wanted more than anything else in the world.

9.

Tom let three days go by. Then he went down to the beach on the fourth morning around noon, and found Dickie alone, in the same spot Tom had seen him first, in front of the gray rocks that extended across the beach from the land.

"Morning!" Tom called. "Where's Marge?"

"Good morning. She's probably working a little late. She'll be down."

"Working?"

"She's a writer."

"Oh."

Dickie puffed on the Italian cigarette in the corner of his mouth. "Where've you been keeping yourself? I thought you'd gone."

"Sick," Tom said casually, tossing his rolled towel down on the sand, but not too near Dickie's towel.

"Oh, the usual upset stomach?"

"Hovering between life and the bathroom," Tom said, smiling. "But I'm all right now." He actually had been too weak even to leave the hotel, but he had crawled around on the floor of his room, following the patches of sunlight that came through his windows, so that he wouldn't look so white the next time he came down to the beach. And he had spent the remainder of his feeble strength studying an Italian conversation book that he had bought in the hotel lobby.

Tom went down to the water, went confidently up to his waist and stopped there, splashing the water over his shoulders. He lowered himself until the water reached his chin, floated around a little, then came slowly in.

"Can I invite you for a drink at the hotel before you go up to your house?" Tom asked Dickie. "And Marge, too, if she comes. I wanted to give you your bathrobe and socks, you know."

"Oh, yes. Thanks very much, I'd like to have a drink." He went back to his Italian newspaper.

Tom stretched out on his towel. He heard the village clock strike one.

"Doesn't look as if Marge is coming down," Dickie said. "I think I'll be going along."

Tom got up. They walked up to the Miramare, saying practically nothing to each other, except that Tom invited Dickie to lunch with him, and Dickie declined because the maid had his lunch ready at the house, he said. They went up to Tom's room, and Dickie tried the bathrobe on and held the socks up to his bare feet. Both the bathrobe and the socks were the right size, and, as Tom had anticipated, Dickie was extremely pleased with the bathrobe.

"And this," Tom said, taking a square package wrapped in drugstore paper from a bureau drawer. "Your mother sent you some nosedrops, too."

Dickie smiled. "I don't need them any more. That was sinus. But I'll take them off your hands."

Now Dickie had everything, Tom thought, everything he had to offer. He was going to refuse the invitation for a drink, too, Tom knew. Tom followed him toward the door. "You know, your father's very concerned about your coming home. He asked me to give you a good talking to, which of course I won't, but I'll still have to tell him something. I promised to write him."

Dickie turned with his hand on the doorknob. "I don't know what my father thinks I'm doing over here—drinking myself to death or what. I'll probably fly home this winter for a few days, but I don't intend to stay over there. I'm happier here. If I went back there to live, my father would be after me to work in Burke-Greenleaf. I couldn't possibly paint. I happen to like painting, and I think it's my business how I spend my life."

"I understand. But he said he wouldn't try to make you work in his firm if you came back, unless you wanted to work in the designing department, and he said you liked that."

"Well—my father and I have been over that. Thanks, anyway, Tom, for delivering the message and the clothes. It was very nice of you." Dickie held out his hand.

Tom couldn't have made himself take the hand. This was the very edge of failure, failure as far as Mr. Greenleaf was concerned, and failure with Dickie. "I think I ought to tell you something else," Tom said with a smile. "Your father sent me over here especially to ask you to come home."

"What do you mean?" Dickie frowned. "Paid your way?"

"Yes." It was his one last chance to amuse Dickie or to repel him, to make Dickie burst out laughing or go out and slam the door in disgust. But the smile was coming, the long corners of his mouth going up, the way Tom remembered Dickie's smile.

"Paid your way! What do you know! He's getting desperate, isn't he?" Dickie closed the door again.

"He approached me in a bar in New York," Tom said. "I told him I wasn't a close friend of yours, but he insisted I could help if I came over. I told him I'd try."

"How did he ever meet you?"

"Through the Schrievers. I hardly know the Schrievers, but there it was! I was your friend and I could do you a lot of good."

They laughed.

"I don't want you to think I'm someone who tried to take advantage of your father," Tom said. "I expect to find a job somewhere in Europe soon, and I'll be able to pay him back my passage money eventually. He bought me a round-trip ticket."

"Oh, don't bother! It goes on the Burke-Greenleaf expense list. I can just see Dad approaching you in a bar! Which bar was it?"

"Raoul's. Matter of fact, he followed me from the Green Cage." Tom watched Dickie's face for a sign of recognition of the Green Cage, a very popular bar, but there was no recognition.

They had a drink downstairs in the hotel bar. They drank to Herbert Richard Greenleaf.

"I just realized today's Sunday," Dickie said. "Marge went to church. You'd better come up and have lunch with us. We always have chicken on Sunday. You know it's an old American custom, chicken on Sunday."

Dickie wanted to go by Marge's house to see if she was still there. They climbed some steps from the main road up the side of a stone wall, crossed part of somebody's garden, and

climbed more steps. Marge's house was a rather sloppy-look-
ing one-story affair with a messy garden at one end, a couple
of buckets and a garden hose cluttering the path to the door,
and the feminine touch represented by her tomato-colored
bathing suit and a bra hanging over a windowsill. Through
an open window, Tom had a glimpse of a disorderly table with
a typewriter on it.

"Hi!" she said, opening the door. "Hello, Tom! Where've
you been all this time?"

She offered them a drink, but discovered there was only
half an inch of gin in her bottle of Gilbey's.

"It doesn't matter, we're going to my house," Dickie said.
He strolled around Marge's bedroom–living room with an air
of familiarity, as if he lived half the time here himself. He bent
over a flower pot in which a tiny plant of some sort was growing, and touched its leaf delicately with his forefinger. "Tom
has something funny to tell you," he said. "Tell her, Tom."

Tom took a breath and began. He made it very funny, and
Marge laughed like someone who hadn't had anything funny
to laugh at in years. "When I saw him coming in Raoul's after
me, I was ready to climb out a back window!" His tongue
rattled on almost independently of his brain. His brain was
estimating how high his stock was shooting up with Dickie
and Marge. He could see it in their faces.

The climb up the hill to Dickie's house didn't seem half so
long as before. Delicious smells of roasting chicken drifted out
on the terrace. Dickie made some martinis. Tom showered
and then Dickie showered, and came out and poured himself
a drink, just like the first time, but the atmosphere now was
totally changed.

Dickie sat down in a wicker chair and swung his legs over
one of the arms. "Tell me more," he said, smiling. "What
kind of work do you do? You said you might take a job."

"Why? Do you have a job for me?"

"Can't say that I have."

"Oh, I can do a number of things—valeting, baby-sitting,
accounting—I've got an unfortunate talent for figures. No
matter how drunk I get, I can always tell when a waiter's
cheating me on a bill. I can forge a signature, fly a helicopter,
handle dice, impersonate practically anybody, cook—and do a

one-man show in a nightclub in case the regular entertainer's sick. Shall I go on?" Tom was leaning forward, counting them off on his fingers. He could have gone on.

"What kind of a one-man show?" Dickie asked.

"Well—" Tom sprang up. "This, for example." He struck a pose with one hand on his hip, one foot extended. "This is Lady Assburden sampling the American subway. She's never even been in the underground in London, but she wants to take back some American experiences." Tom did it all in pantomime, searching for a coin, finding it didn't go into the slot, buying a token, puzzling over which stairs to go down, registering alarm at the noise and the long express ride, puzzling again as to how to get out of the place—here Marge came out, and Dickie told her it was an Englishwoman in the subway, but Marge didn't seem to get it and asked, "What?"—walking through a door which could only be the door of the men's room from her twitching horror of this and that, which augmented until she fainted. Tom fainted gracefully onto the terrace glider.

"Wonderful!" Dickie yelled, clapping.

Marge wasn't laughing. She stood there looking a little blank. Neither of them bothered to explain it to her. She didn't look as if she had that kind of sense of humor, anyway, Tom thought.

Tom took a gulp of his martini, terribly pleased with himself. "I'll do another for you sometime," he said to Marge, but mostly to indicate to Dickie that he had another one to do.

"Dinner ready?" Dickie asked her. "I'm starving."

"I'm waiting for the darned artichokes to get done. You know that front hole. It'll barely make anything come to a boil." She smiled at Tom. "Dickie's very old-fashioned about some things, Tom, the things *he* doesn't have to fool with. There's still only a wood stove here, and he refuses to buy a refrigerator or even an icebox."

"One of the reasons I fled America," Dickie said. "Those things are a waste of money in a country with so many servants. What'd Ermelinda do with herself, if she could cook a meal in half an hour?" He stood up. "Come on in, Tom, I'll show you some of my paintings."

Dickie led the way into the big room Tom had looked into a couple of times on his way to and from the shower, the room with a long couch under the two windows and the big easel in the middle of the floor. "This is one of Marge I'm working on now." He gestured to the picture on the easel.

"Oh," Tom said with interest. It wasn't good in his opinion, probably in anybody's opinion. The wild enthusiasm of her smile was a bit off. Her skin was as red as an Indian's. If Marge hadn't been the only girl around with blond hair, he wouldn't have noticed any resemblance at all.

"And these—a lot of landscapes," Dickie said with a deprecatory laugh, though obviously he wanted Tom to say something complimentary about them, because obviously he was proud of them. They were all wild and hasty and monotonously similar. The combination of terra cotta and electric blue was in nearly every one, terra cotta roofs and mountains and bright electric-blue seas. It was the blue he had put in Marge's eyes, too.

"My surrealist effort," Dickie said, bracing another canvas against his knee.

Tom winced with almost a personal shame. It was Marge again, undoubtedly, though with long snakelike hair, and worst of all two horizons in her eyes, with a miniature landscape of Mongibello's houses and mountains in one eye, and the beach in the other full of little red people. "Yes, I like that," Tom said. Mr. Greenleaf had been right. Yet it gave Dickie something to do, kept him out of trouble, Tom supposed, just as it gave thousands of lousy amateur painters all over America something to do. He was only sorry that Dickie fell into this category as a painter, because he wanted Dickie to be much more.

"I won't ever set the world on fire as a painter," Dickie said, "but I get a great deal of pleasure out of it."

"Yes." Tom wanted to forget all about the paintings and forget that Dickie painted. "Can I see the rest of the house?"

"Absolutely! You haven't seen the salon, have you?"

Dickie opened a door in the hall that led into a very large room with a fireplace, sofas, bookshelves, and three exposures—to the terrace, to the land on the other side of the house, and to the front garden. Dickie said that in summer he did not use the room, because he liked to save it as a change of scene for the winter. It was more of a bookish den than a living room, Tom thought. It surprised him. He had Dickie figured out as a young man who was not particularly brainy, and who probably spent most of his time playing. Perhaps he was wrong. But he didn't think he was wrong in feeling that Dickie was bored at the moment and needed someone to show him how to have fun.

"What's upstairs?" Tom asked.

The upstairs was disappointing: Dickie's bedroom in the corner of the house above the terrace was stark and empty— a bed, a chest of drawers, and a rocking chair, looking lost and unrelated in all the space—a narrow bed, too, hardly wider than a single bed. The other three rooms of the second floor were not even furnished, or at least not completely. One of them held only firewood and a pile of canvas scraps. There was certainly no sign of Marge anywhere, least of all in Dickie's bedroom.

"How about going to Naples with me sometime?" Tom asked. "I didn't have much of a chance to see it on my way down."

"All right," Dickie said. "Marge and I are going Saturday afternoon. We have dinner there nearly every Saturday night and treat ourselves to a taxi or a carrozza ride back. Come along."

"I meant in the daytime or some weekday so I could see a little more," Tom said, hoping to avoid Marge in the excursion. "Or do you paint all day?"

"No. There's a twelve o'clock bus Mondays, Wednesdays, and Fridays. I suppose we could go tomorrow, if you feel like it."

"Fine," Tom said, though he still wasn't sure that Marge wouldn't be asked along. "Marge is a Catholic?" he asked as they went down the stairs.

"With a vengeance! She was converted about six months ago by an Italian she had a mad crush on. Could that man talk! He was here for a few months, resting up after a ski accident. Marge consoles herself for the loss of Eduardo by embracing his religion."

"I had the idea she was in love with you."

"With me? Don't be silly!"

The dinner was ready when they went out on the terrace. There were even hot biscuits with butter, made by Marge.

"Do you know Vic Simmons in New York?" Tom asked Dickie.

Vic had quite a salon of artists, writers, and dancers in New York, but Dickie didn't know of him. Tom asked him about two or three other people, also without success.

Tom hoped Marge would leave after the coffee, but she didn't. When she left the terrace for a moment Tom said, "Can I invite you for dinner at my hotel tonight?"

"Thank you. At what time?"

"Seven-thirty? So we'll have a little time for cocktails?— After all, it's your father's money," Tom added with a smile.

Dickie laughed. "All right, cocktails and a good bottle of wine. Marge!" Marge was just coming back. "We're dining tonight at the Miramare, compliments of Greenleaf père!"

So Marge was coming, too, and there was nothing Tom could do about it. After all, it was Dickie's father's money.

The dinner that evening was pleasant, but Marge's presence kept Tom from talking about anything he would have liked to talk about, and he did not feel even like being witty in Marge's presence. Marge knew some of the people in the dining room, and after dinner she excused herself and took her coffee over to another table and sat down.

"How long are you going to be here?" Dickie asked.

"Oh, at least a week, I'd say," Tom replied.

"Because—" Dickie's face had flushed a little over the cheekbones. The chianti had put him into a good mood. "If you're going to be here a little longer, why don't you stay with me? There's no use staying in a hotel, unless you really prefer it."

"Thank you very much," Tom said.

"There's a bed in the maid's room, which you didn't see. Ermelinda doesn't sleep in. I'm sure we can make out with the furniture that's scattered around, if you think you'd like to."

"I'm sure I'd like to. By the way, your father gave me six hundred dollars for expenses, and I've still got about five hundred of it. I think we both ought to have a little fun on it, don't you?"

"Five hundred!" Dickie said, as if he'd never seen that much money in one lump in his life. "We could pick up a little car for that!"

Tom didn't contribute to the car idea. That wasn't his idea of having fun. He wanted to fly to Paris. Marge was coming back, he saw.

The next morning he moved in.

Dickie and Ermelinda had installed an armoire and a couple of chairs in one of the upstairs rooms, and Dickie had thumb-tacked a few reproductions of mosaic portraits from St. Mark's Cathedral on the walls. Tom helped Dickie carry up the nar-row iron bed from the maid's room. They were finished be-fore twelve, a little lightheaded from the frascati they had been sipping as they worked.

"Are we still going to Naples?" Tom asked.

"Certainly." Dickie looked at his watch. "It's only a quarter to twelve. We can make the twelve o'clock bus."

They took nothing with them but their jackets and Tom's book of traveler's checks. The bus was just arriving as they reached the post office. Tom and Dickie stood by the door, waiting for people to get off; then Dickie pulled himself up, right into the face of a young man with red hair and a loud sports shirt, an American.

"Dickie!"

"Freddie!" Dickie yelled. "What're you doing here?"

"Came to see you! And the Cecchis. They're putting me up for a few days."

"Ch'elegante! I'm off to Naples with a friend. Tom?" Dickie beckoned Tom over and introduced them.

The American's name was Freddie Miles. Tom thought he was hideous. Tom hated red hair, especially this kind of carrot-red hair with white skin and freckles. Freddie had large red-brown eyes that seemed to wobble in his head as if he were cockeyed, or perhaps he was only one of those people who never looked at anyone they were talking to. He was also overweight. Tom turned away from him, waiting for Dickie to finish his conversation. They were holding up the bus, Tom noticed. Dickie and Freddie were talking about skiing, making a date for some time in December in a town Tom had never heard of.

"There'll be about fifteen of us at Cortina by the second," Freddie said. "A real bang-up party like last year! Three weeks, if our money holds out!"

"If we hold out!" Dickie said. "See you tonight, Fred!"

Tom boarded the bus after Dickie. There were no seats, and they were wedged between a skinny, sweating man who smelled, and a couple of old peasant women who smelled worse. Just as they were leaving the village Dickie remembered that Marge was coming for lunch as usual, because they had thought yesterday that Tom's moving would cancel the Naples trip. Dickie shouted for the driver to stop. The bus stopped with a squeal of brakes and a lurch that threw everybody who was standing off balance, and Dickie put his head through a window and called, "Gino! Gino!"

A little boy on the road came running up to take the hundred-lire bill that Dickie was holding out to him. Dickie said something in Italian, and the boy said, "Subito, signor!" and flew up the road.

Dickie thanked the driver, and the bus started again. "I told him to tell Marge we'd be back tonight, but probably late," Dickie said.

"Good."

The bus spilled them into a big, cluttered square in Naples, and they were suddenly surrounded by pushcarts of grapes, figs, pastry, and watermelon, and screamed at by adolescent boys with fountain pens and mechanical toys. The people made way for Dickie.

"I know a good place for lunch," Dickie said. "A real Neapolitan pizzeria. Do you like pizza?"

"Yes."

The pizzeria was up a street too narrow and steep for cars. Strings of beads hanging in the doorway, a decanter of wine on every table, and there were only six tables in the whole place, the kind of place you could sit in for hours and drink wine and not be disturbed. They sat there until five o'clock, when Dickie said it was time to move on to the Galleria. Dickie apologized for not taking him to the art museum, which had original da Vincis and El Grecos, he said, but they could see that at another time. Dickie had spent most of the afternoon talking about Freddie Miles, and Tom had found it as uninteresting as Freddie's face. Freddie was the son of an American hotel-chain owner, and a playwright—self-styled, Tom gathered, because he had written only two plays, and neither had seen Broadway. Freddie had a house in Cagnes-sur-Mer, and Dickie had stayed with him several weeks before he came to Italy.

"This is what I like," Dickie said expansively in the Galleria, "sitting at a table and watching the people go by. It does something to your outlook on life. The Anglo-Saxons make a great mistake not staring at people from a sidewalk table."

Tom nodded. He had heard it before. He was waiting for something profound and original from Dickie. Dickie was handsome. He looked unusual with his long, finely cut face, his quick, intelligent eyes, the proud way he carried himself regardless of what he was wearing. He was wearing broken-down sandals and rather soiled white pants now, but he sat there as if he owned the Galleria, chatting in Italian with the waiter when he brought their espressos.

"Ciao!" he called to an Italian boy who was passing by.

"Ciao, Dickie!"

"He changes Marge's traveler's checks on Saturdays," Dickie explained to Tom.

A well-dressed Italian greeted Dickie with a warm hand-shake and sat down at the table with them. Tom listened to their conversation in Italian, making out a word here and there. Tom was beginning to feel tired.

"Want to go to Rome?" Dickie asked him suddenly.

"Sure," Tom said. "Now?" He stood up, reaching for money to pay the little tabs that the waiter had stuck under their coffee cups.

The Italian had a long gray Cadillac equipped with venetian blinds, a four-toned horn, and a blaring radio that he and Dickie seemed content to shout over. They reached the out-skirts of Rome in about two hours. Tom sat up as they drove along the Appian Way, especially for his benefit, the Italian told Tom, because Tom had not seen it before. The road was bumpy in spots. These were stretches of original Roman brick left bare to show people how Roman roads felt, the Italian said. The flat fields to left and right looked desolate in the twilight, like an ancient graveyard, Tom thought, with just a few tombs and remains of tombs still standing. The Italian dropped them in the middle of a street in Rome and said an abrupt good-bye.

"He's in a hurry," Dickie said. "Got to see his girl friend and get away before the husband comes home at eleven. There's the music hall I was looking for. Come on."

They bought tickets for the music-hall show that evening. There was still an hour before the performance, and they went to the Via Veneto, took a sidewalk table at one of the cafés, and ordered americanos. Dickie didn't know anybody in Rome, Tom noticed, or at least none who passed by, and they watched hundreds of Italians and Americans pass by their table. Tom got very little out of the music-hall show, but he tried his very best. Dickie proposed leaving before the show was over. Then they caught a carrozza and drove around the city, past fountain after fountain, through the Forum and around the Colosseum. The moon had come out. Tom was still a little sleepy, but the sleepiness, underlaid with excitement at being in Rome for the first time, put him into a receptive, mellow mood. They sat slumped in the carrozza, each with a sandaled foot propped on a knee, and it seemed to Tom that he was looking in a mirror when he looked at Dickie's leg and his propped foot beside him. They were the same height, and very much the same weight, Dickie perhaps a bit heavier, and they wore the same size bathrobe, socks, and probably shirts.

Dickie even said, "Thank you, Mr. Greenleaf," when Tom paid the carrozza driver. Tom felt a little weird.

They were in even finer mood by one in the morning, after a bottle and a half of wine between them at dinner. They walked with their arms around each other's shoulders, singing, and around a dark corner they somehow bumped into a girl and knocked her down. They lifted her up, apologizing, and offered to escort her home. She protested, they insisted, one on either side of her. She had to catch a certain trolley, she said. Dickie wouldn't hear of it. Dickie got a taxi. Dickie and

Tom sat very properly on the jump seats with their arms folded like a couple of footmen, and Dickie talked to her and made her laugh. Tom could understand nearly everything Dickie said. They helped the girl out in a little street that looked like Naples again, and she said, "Grazie tante!" and shook hands with both of them, then vanished into an absolutely black doorway.

"Did you hear that?" Dickie said. "She said we were the nicest Americans she'd ever met!"

"You know what most crummy Americans would do in a case like that—rape her," Tom said.

"Now where are we?" Dickie asked, turning completely around.

Neither had the slightest idea where they were. They walked for several blocks without finding a landmark or a familiar street name. They urinated against a dark wall, then drifted on.

"When the dawn comes up, we can see where we are," Dickie said cheerfully. He looked at his watch. "'S only a couple of more hours."

"Fine."

"It's worth it to see a nice girl home, isn't it?" Dickie asked, staggering a little.

"Sure it is. I like girls," Tom said protestingly. "But it's just as well Marge isn't here tonight. We never could have seen that girl home with Marge with us."

"Oh, I don't know," Dickie said thoughtfully, looking down at his weaving feet. "Marge isn't—"

"I only mean, if Marge was here, we'd be worrying about a hotel for the night. We'd be *in* the damned hotel, probably. We wouldn't be seeing half of Rome!"

"That's right!" Dickie swung an arm around his shoulder.

Dickie shook his shoulder, roughly. Tom tried to roll out from under it and grab his hand. "Dickie-e!" Tom opened his eyes and looked into the face of a policeman.

Tom sat up. He was in a park. It was dawn. Dickie was sitting on the grass beside him, talking very calmly to the policeman in Italian. Tom felt for the rectangular lump of his traveler's checks. They were still in his pocket.

"Passaporti!" the policeman hurled at them again, and again Dickie launched into his calm explanation.

Tom knew exactly what Dickie was saying. He was saying that they were Americans, and they didn't have their passports because they had only gone out for a little walk to look at the stars. Tom had an impulse to laugh. He stood up and staggered, dusting his clothing. Dickie was up, too, and they began to walk away, though the policeman was still yelling at them. Dickie said something back to him in a courteous, explanatory tone. At least the policeman was not following them.

"We do look pretty cruddy," Dickie said.

Tom nodded. There was a long rip in his trouser knee where he had probably fallen. Their clothes were crumpled and grass-stained and filthy with dust and sweat, but now they were shivering with cold. They went into the first café they came to, and had caffe latte and sweet rolls, then several Italian brandies that tasted awful but warmed them. Then they began to laugh. They were still drunk.

By eleven o'clock they were in Naples, just in time to catch the bus for Mongibello. It was wonderful to think of going back to Rome when they were more presentably dressed and seeing all the museums they had missed, and it was wonderful to think of lying on the beach at Mongibello this afternoon, baking in the sun. But they never got to the beach. They had showers at Dickie's house, then fell down on their respective beds and slept until Marge woke them up around four. Marge was annoyed because Dickie hadn't sent her a telegram saying he was spending the night in Rome.

"Not that I minded your spending the night, but I thought you were in Naples and anything can happen in Naples."

"Oh-h," Dickie drawled with a glance at Tom. He was making Bloody Marys for all of them.

Tom kept his mouth mysteriously shut. He wasn't going to tell Marge anything they had done. Let her imagine what she pleased. Dickie had made it evident that they had had a very good time. Tom noticed that she looked Dickie over with disapproval of his hangover, his unshaven face, and the drink he was taking now. There was something in Marge's eyes when she was very serious that made her look wise and old in spite of the naïve clothes she wore and her windblown hair and her general air of a Girl Scout. She had the look of a mother or an older sister now—the old feminine disapproval of the destructive play of little boys and men. La dee da! Or was it jealousy? She seemed to know that Dickie had formed a closer bond with him in twenty-four hours, just because he was another man, than she could ever have with Dickie, whether he loved her or not, and he didn't. After a few moments she loosened up, however, and the look went out of her eyes. Dickie left him with Marge on the terrace. Tom asked her about the book she was writing. It was a book about Mongibello, she said, with her own photographs. She told him she was from Ohio and showed him a picture, which she carried in her wallet, of her family's house. It was just a plain clapboard house, but it was home, Marge said with a smile. She pronounced the adjective "Clabbered," which amused Tom, because that was the word she used to describe people who were drunk, and just a few minutes before she had said to Dickie, "You look absolutely clabbered!" Her speech, Tom thought, was abominable, both her choice of words and her pronunciation. He tried to be especially pleasant to her. He felt he could afford to be. He walked with her to the gate, and they said a friendly good-bye to each other, but neither said anything about their all getting together later that day or tomorrow. There was no doubt about it, Marge was a little angry with Dickie.

IO.

FOR three or four days they saw very little of Marge except down at the beach, and she was noticeably cooler toward both of them on the beach. She smiled and talked just as much or maybe more, but there was an element of politeness now, which made for the coolness. Tom noticed that Dickie was concerned, though not concerned enough to talk to Marge alone, apparently, because he hadn't seen her alone since Tom had moved into the house. Tom had been with Dickie every moment since he had moved into Dickie's house.

Finally Tom, to show that he was not obtuse about Marge, mentioned to Dickie that he thought she was acting strangely.

"Oh, she has moods," Dickie said. "Maybe she's working well. She doesn't like to see people when she's in a streak of work."

The Dickie–Marge relationship was evidently just what he had supposed it to be at first, Tom thought. Marge was much fonder of Dickie than Dickie was of her.

Tom, at any rate, kept Dickie amused. He had lots of funny stories to tell Dickie about people he knew in New York, some of them true, some of them made up. They went for a sail in Dickie's boat every day. There was no mention of any date when Tom might be leaving. Obviously Dickie was enjoying his company. Tom kept out of Dickie's way when Dickie wanted to paint, and he was always ready to drop whatever he was doing and go with Dickie for a walk or a sail or simply sit and talk. Dickie also seemed pleased that Tom was taking his study of Italian seriously. Tom spent a couple of hours a day with his grammar and conversation books.

Tom wrote to Mr. Greenleaf that he was staying with Dickie now for a few days, and said that Dickie had mentioned flying home for a while in the winter, and that probably he could by that time persuade him to stay longer. This letter sounded much better now that he was staying at Dickie's house than his first letter in which he had said he was staying at a hotel in Mongibello. Tom also said that when his money gave out he intended to try to get himself a job, perhaps at one of the hotels in the village, a casual statement that served the double purpose of reminding Mr. Greenleaf that six hundred dollars could run out, and also that he was a young man ready and willing to work for a living. Tom wanted to convey the same good impression to Dickie, so he gave Dickie the letter to read before he sealed it.

Another week went by, of ideally pleasant weather, ideally lazy days in which Tom's greatest physical exertion was climbing the stone steps from the beach every afternoon and his greatest mental effort trying to chat in Italian with Fausto, the twenty-three-year-old Italian boy whom Dickie had found in the village and had engaged to come three times a week to give Tom Italian lessons.

They went to Capri one day in Dickie's sailboat. Capri was just far enough away not to be visible from Mongibello. Tom was filled with anticipation, but Dickie was in one of his pre-occupied moods and refused to be enthusiastic about anything. He argued with the keeper of the dock where they tied the *Pipistrello*. Dickie didn't even want to take a walk through the wonderful-looking little streets that went off in every direction from the plaza. They sat in a café on the plaza and drank a couple of Fernet-Brancas, and then Dickie wanted to start home before it became dark, though Tom would have willingly paid their hotel bill if Dickie had agreed to stay over-night. Tom supposed they would come again to Capri, so he wrote that day off and tried to forget it.

A letter came from Mr. Greenleaf, which had crossed Tom's letter, in which Mr. Greenleaf reiterated his arguments for Dickie's coming home, wished Tom success, and asked for a prompt reply as to his results. Once more Tom dutifully took up the pen and replied. Mr. Greenleaf's letter had been in such a shockingly businesslike tone—really as if he had been checking on a shipment of boat parts, Tom thought—that he found it very easy to reply in the same style. Tom was a little high when he wrote the letter, because it was just after lunch and they were always slightly high on wine just after lunch, a delicious sensation that could be corrected at once with a couple of espressos and a short walk, or prolonged with another glass of wine, sipped as they went about their leisurely afternoon routine. Tom amused himself by injecting a faint hope in this letter. He wrote in Mr. Greenleaf's own style:

". . . If I am not mistaken, Richard is wavering in his decision to spend another winter here. As I promised you, I shall do everything in my power to dissuade him from spending another winter here, and in time—though it may be as long as Christmas—I may be able to get him to stay in the States when he goes over."

Tom had to smile as he wrote it, because he and Dickie were talking of cruising around the Greek islands this winter, and Dickie had given up the idea of flying home even for a few days, unless his mother should be really seriously ill by then. They had talked also of spending January and February, Mongibello's worst months, in Majorca. And Marge would

not be going with them, Tom was sure. Both he and Dickie
excluded her from their travel plans whenever they discussed
them, though Dickie had made the mistake of dropping to
her that they might be taking a winter cruise somewhere.
Dickie was so damned open about everything! And now,
though Tom knew Dickie was still firm about their going
alone, Dickie was being more than usually attentive to Marge,
just because he realized that she would be lonely here by herself, and that it was essentially unkind of them not to ask her
along. Dickie and Tom both tried to cover it up by impressing
on her that they would be traveling in the cheapest and worst
possible way around Greece, cattleboats, sleeping with peas-
ants on the decks and all that, no way for a girl to travel. But
Marge still looked dejected, and Dickie still tried to make it
up by asking her often to the house now for lunch and dinner.
Dickie took Marge's hand sometimes as they walked up from
the beach, though Marge didn't always let him keep it. Sometimes she extricated her hand after a few seconds in a way that
looked to Tom as if she were dying for her hand to be held.

And when they asked her to go along with them to Her-
culaneum, she refused.

"I think I'll stay home. You boys enjoy yourselves," she
said with an effort at a cheerful smile.

"Well, if she won't, she won't," Tom said to Dickie, and
drifted tactfully into the house so that she and Dickie could
talk alone on the terrace if they wanted to.

Tom sat on the broad windowsill in Dickie's studio and
looked out at the sea, his brown arms folded on his chest. He
loved to look out at the blue Mediterranean and think of himself and Dickie sailing where they pleased. Tangiers, Sofia,
Cairo, Sevastopol . . . By the time his money ran out, Tom
thought, Dickie would probably be so fond of him and so
used to him that he would take it for granted they would go
on living together. He and Dickie could easily live on Dickie's
five hundred a month income. From the terrace he could hear
a pleading tone in Dickie's voice, and Marge's monosyllabic
answers. Then he heard the gate clang. Marge had left. She
had been going to stay for lunch. Tom shoved himself off the
windowsill and went out to Dickie on the terrace.

"Was she angry about something?" Tom asked.

"No. She feels kind of left out, I suppose."

"We certainly tried to include her."

"It isn't just this." Dickie was walking slowly up and down the terrace. "Now she says she doesn't even want to go to Cortina with me."

"Oh, she'll probably come around about Cortina before December."

"I doubt it," Dickie said.

Tom supposed it was because he was going to Cortina, too. Dickie had asked him last week. Freddie Miles had been gone when they got back from their Rome trip: he had had to go to London suddenly, Marge had told them. But Dickie had said he would write Freddie that he was bringing a friend along. "Do you want me to leave, Dickie?" Tom asked, sure that Dickie didn't want him to leave. "I feel I'm intruding on you and Marge."

"Of course not! Intruding on what?"

"Well, from her point of view."

"No. It's just that I owe her something. And I haven't been particularly nice to her lately. *We* haven't."

Tom knew he meant that he and Marge had kept each other company over the long, dreary last winter, when they had been the only Americans in the village, and that he shouldn't neglect her now because somebody else was here. "Suppose I talk to her about going to Cortina," Tom suggested.

"Then she surely won't go," Dickie said tersely, and went into the house.

Tom heard him telling Ermelinda to hold the lunch because he wasn't ready to eat yet. Even in Italian, Tom could hear that Dickie said *he* wasn't ready for lunch, in the master-of-the-house tone. Dickie came out on the terrace, sheltering his lighter as he tried to light his cigarette. Dickie had a beautiful silver lighter, but it didn't work well in the slightest breeze. Tom finally produced his ugly, flaring lighter, as ugly and efficient as a piece of military equipment, and lighted it for him. Tom checked himself from proposing a drink: it wasn't his house, though as it happened he had bought the three bottles of Gilbey's that now stood in the kitchen.

"It's after two," Tom said. "Want to take a little walk and go by the post office?" Sometimes Luigi opened the post office at two-thirty, sometimes not until four, they could never tell.

They walked down the hill in silence. What *had* Marge said about him, Tom wondered. The sudden weight of guilt made sweat come out on Tom's forehead, an amorphous yet very strong sense of guilt, as if Marge had told Dickie specifically that he had stolen something or had done some other shameful thing. Dickie wouldn't be acting like this only because Marge had behaved coolly, Tom thought. Dickie walked in his slouching, downhill gait that made his bony knees jut out in front of him, a gait that Tom had unconsciously adopted, too. But now Dickie's chin was sunk down on his chest and his hands were rammed into the pockets of his shorts. He came out of the silence only to greet Luigi and thank him for his letter. Tom had no mail. Dickie's letter was from a Naples bank, a form slip on which Tom saw typewritten in a blank space: $500.00. Dickie pushed the slip carelessly into a pocket and dropped the envelope into a wastebasket. The monthly announcement that Dickie's money had arrived in Naples, Tom supposed. Dickie had said that his trust company sent his money to a Naples bank. They walked on down the hill, and Tom assumed that they would walk up the main road to where it curved around a cliff on the other side of the village, as they had done before, but Dickie stopped at the steps that led up to Marge's house.

"I think I'll go up to see Marge," Dickie said. "I won't be long, but there's no use in your waiting."

"All right," Tom said, feeling suddenly desolate. He watched Dickie climb a little way up the steep steps cut into the wall, then he turned abruptly and started back toward the house.

About halfway up the hill he stopped with an impulse to go down to Giorgio's for a drink (but Giorgio's martinis were terrible), and with another impulse to go up to Marge's house, and, on a pretense of apologizing to her, vent his anger by surprising them and annoying them. He suddenly felt that Dickie was embracing her, or at least touching her, at this minute, and partly he wanted to see it, and partly he loathed the idea of seeing it. He turned and walked back to Marge's gate. He closed the gate carefully behind him, though her house was so far above she could not possibly have heard it, then ran up the steps two at a time. He slowed as he climbed the last flight of steps. He would say, "Look here, Marge, I'm sorry if *I've* been causing the strain around here. We asked you to go today, and we mean it. *I* mean it."

Tom stopped as Marge's window came into view: Dickie's arm was around her waist. Dickie was kissing her, little pecks on her cheek, smiling at her. They were only about fifteen feet from him, but the room was shadowed compared to the bright sunlight he stood in, and he had to strain to see. Now Marge's face was tipped straight up to Dickie's, as if she were fairly lost in ecstasy, and what disgusted Tom was that he knew Dickie didn't mean it, that Dickie was only using this cheap, obvious, easy way to hold onto her friendship. What disgusted him was the big bulge of her behind in the peasant skirt below Dickie's arm that circled her waist. And Dickie—! Tom really wouldn't have believed it possible of Dickie!

Tom turned away and ran down the steps, wanting to scream. He banged the gate shut. He ran all the way up the road home, and arrived gasping, supporting himself on the parapet after he entered Dickie's gate. He sat on the couch in Dickie's studio for a few moments, his mind stunned and blank. That kiss—it hadn't looked like a first kiss. He walked to Dickie's easel, unconsciously avoiding looking at the bad painting that was on it, picked up the kneaded eraser that lay on the palette and flung it violently out the window, saw it arc down and disappear toward the sea. He picked up more erasers from Dickie's table, pen points, smudge sticks, charcoal and pastel fragments, and threw them one by one into corners or out the windows. He had a curious feeling that his brain remained calm and logical and that his body was out of control. He ran out on the terrace with an idea of jumping onto the parapet and doing a dance or standing on his head, but the empty space on the other side of the parapet stopped him.

He went up to Dickie's room and paced around for a few moments, his hands in his pockets. He wondered when Dickie was coming back? Or was he going to stay and make an afternoon of it, really take her to bed with him? He jerked Dickie's closet door open and looked in. There was a freshly pressed, new-looking gray flannel suit that he had never seen Dickie wearing. Tom took it out. He took off his knee-length shorts and put on the gray flannel trousers. He put on a pair of Dickie's shoes. Then he opened the bottom drawer of the chest and took out a clean blue-and-white striped shirt.

He chose a dark-blue silk tie and knotted it carefully. The suit fitted him. He reparted his hair and put the part a little more to one side, the way Dickie wore his.

"Marge, you must understand that I don't *love* you," Tom said into the mirror in Dickie's voice, with Dickie's higher pitch on the emphasized words, with the little growl in his throat at the end of the phrase that could be pleasant or unpleasant, intimate or cool, according to Dickie's mood. "Marge, stop it!" Tom turned suddenly and made a grab in the air as if he were seizing Marge's throat. He shook her, twisted her, while she sank lower and lower, until at last he left her, limp, on the floor. He was panting. He wiped his forehead the way Dickie did, reached for a handkerchief and, not finding any, got one from Dickie's top drawer, then resumed in front of the mirror. Even his parted lips looked like Dickie's lips when he was out of breath from swimming, drawn down a little from his lower teeth. "You know why I had to do that," he said, still breathlessly, addressing Marge, though he watched himself in the mirror. "You were interfering between Tom and me.—No, not that! But there *is* a bond between us!"

He turned, stepped over the imaginary body, and went stealthily to the window. He could see, beyond the bend of the road, the blurred slant of the steps that went up to Marge's house level. Dickie was not on the steps or on the parts of the road that he could see. Maybe they were sleeping together, Tom thought with a tighter twist of disgust in his throat. He imagined it, awkward, clumsy, unsatisfactory for Dickie, and Marge loving it. She'd love it even if he tortured her! Tom darted back to the closet again and took a hat from the top shelf. It was a little gray Tyrolian hat with a green-and-white feather in the brim. He put it on rakishly. It surprised him how much he looked like Dickie with the top part of his head covered. Really it was only his darker hair that was very different from Dickie. Otherwise, his nose—or at least its general form—his narrow jaw, his eyebrows if he held them right—

"What're you *doing?*"

Tom whirled around. Dickie was in the doorway. Tom realized that he must have been right below at the gate when he had looked out. "Oh—just amusing myself," Tom said in the deep voice he always used when he was embarrassed. "Sorry, Dickie."

Dickie's mouth opened a little, then closed, as if anger churned his words too much for them to be uttered. To Tom, it was just as bad as if he had spoken. Dickie advanced into the room.

"Dickie, I'm sorry if it—"

The violent slam of the door cut him off. Dickie began opening his shirt, scowling, just as he would have if Tom had not been there, because this was his room, and what was Tom doing in it? Tom stood petrified with fear.

"I wish you'd get out of my clothes," Dickie said.

Tom started undressing, his fingers clumsy with his mortification, his shock, because up until now Dickie had always said wear this and wear that that belonged to him. Dickie would never say it again.

Dickie looked at Tom's feet. "Shoes, too? Are you crazy?"

"No." Tom tried to pull himself together as he hung up the suit, then he asked, "Did you make it up with Marge?"

"Marge and I are fine," Dickie snapped in a way that shut Tom out from them. "Another thing I want to say, but clearly," he said, looking at Tom, "I'm not queer. I don't know if you have the idea that I am or not."

"Queer?" Tom smiled faintly. "I never thought you were queer."

Dickie started to say something else, and didn't. He straightened up, the ribs showing in his dark chest. "Well, Marge thinks you are."

"Why?" Tom felt the blood go out of his face. He kicked off Dickie's second shoe feebly, and set the pair in the closet. "Why should she? What've I ever done?" He felt faint. Nobody had ever said it outright to him, not in this way.

"It's just the way you act," Dickie said in a growling tone, and went out the door.

Tom hurried back into his shorts. He had been half concealing himself from Dickie behind the closet door, though
he had his underwear on. Just because Dickie liked him, Tom
thought, Marge had launched her filthy accusations of him at
Dickie. And Dickie hadn't had the guts to stand up and deny
it to her! He went downstairs and found Dickie fixing himself
a drink at the bar shelf on the terrace. "Dickie, I want to get
this straight," Tom began. "I'm not queer either, and I don't
want anybody thinking I am."

"All right," Dickie growled.

The tone reminded Tom of the answers Dickie had given
him when he had asked Dickie if he knew this person and that
in New York. Some of the people he had asked Dickie about
were queer, it was true, and he had often suspected Dickie of
deliberately denying knowing them when he did know them.
All right! Who was making an issue of it, anyway? Dickie was.
Tom hesitated while his mind tossed in a welter of things he
might have said, bitter things, conciliatory things, grateful and
hostile. His mind went back to certain groups of people he
had known in New York, known and dropped finally, all of
them, but he regretted now having ever known them. They
had taken him up because he amused them, but *he* had never
had anything to do with any of them! When a couple of them
had made a pass at him, he had rejected them—though he
remembered how he had tried to make it up to them later by
getting ice for their drinks, dropping them off in taxis when
it was out of his way, because he had been afraid they would
start to dislike him. He'd been an ass! And he remembered,
too, the humiliating moment when Vic Simmons had said,
Oh, for Christ sake, Tommie, shut up! when he had said to a
group of people, for perhaps the third or fourth time in Vic's
presence, "I can't make up my mind whether I like men or
women, so I'm thinking of giving them *both* up." Tom had
used to pretend he was going to an analyst, because everybody
else was going to an analyst, and he had used to spin wildly
funny stories about his sessions with his analyst to amuse people at parties, and the line about giving up men and women
both had always been good for a laugh, the way he delivered
it, until Vic had told him for Christ sake to shut up, and after
that Tom had never said it again and never mentioned his

analyst again, either. As a matter of fact, there was a lot of truth in it, Tom thought. As people went, he was one of the most innocent and clean-minded he had ever known. That was the irony of this situation with Dickie.

"I feel as if I've—" Tom began, but Dickie was not even listening. Dickie turned away with a grim look around his mouth and carried his drink to the corner of the terrace. Tom advanced toward him, a little fearfully, not knowing whether Dickie would hurl him off the terrace, or simply turn around and tell him to get the hell out of the house. Tom asked quietly, "Are you in love with Marge, Dickie?"

"No, but I feel sorry for her. I care about her. She's been very nice to me. We've had some good times together. You don't seem to be able to understand that."

"I do understand. That was my original feeling about you and her—that it was a platonic thing as far as you were concerned, and that she was probably in love with you."

"She is. You go out of your way not to hurt people who're in love with you, you know."

"Of course." He hesitated again, trying to choose his words. He was still in a state of trembling apprehension, though Dickie was not angry with him any more. Dickie was not going to throw him out. Tom said in a more self-possessed tone, "I can imagine that if you both were in New York, you wouldn't have seen her nearly so often—or at all—but this village being so lonely—"

"That's exactly right. I haven't been to bed with her and I don't intend to, but I do intend to keep her friendship."

"Well, have I done anything to prevent you? I told you, Dickie, I'd rather leave than do anything to break up your friendship with Marge."

Dickie gave him a glance. "No, you haven't done anything, specifically, but it's obvious you don't like her around. Whenever you make an effort to say anything nice to her, it's so obviously an effort."

"I'm sorry," Tom said contritely. He was sorry he hadn't made more of an effort, that he had done a bad job when he might have done a good one.

"Well, let's let it go. Marge and I are okay," Dickie said defiantly. He turned away and stared off at the water.

Tom went into the kitchen to make himself a little boiled coffee. He didn't want to use the espresso machine, because Dickie was very particular about it and didn't like anyone using it but himself. He'd take the coffee up to his room and study some Italian before Fausto came, Tom thought. This wasn't the time to make it up with Dickie. Dickie had his pride. He would be silent for most of the afternoon, then come around by about five o'clock after he had been painting for a while, and it would be as if the episode with the clothes had never happened. One thing Tom was sure of: Dickie was glad to have him here. Dickie was bored with living by himself, and bored with Marge, too. Tom still had three hundred dollars of the money Mr. Greenleaf had given him, and he and Dickie were going to use it on a spree in Paris. Without Marge. Dickie had been amazed when Tom had told him he hadn't had more than a glimpse of Paris through a railroad station window.

While he waited for his coffee, Tom put away the food that was to have been their lunch. He set a couple of pots of food in bigger pots of water to keep the ants away from them. There was also the little paper of fresh butter, the pair of eggs, the paper of four rolls that Ermelinda had brought for their breakfast tomorrow. They had to buy small quantities of everything every day, because there was no refrigerator. Dickie wanted to buy a refrigerator with part of his father's money. He had mentioned it a couple of times. Tom hoped he changed his mind, because a refrigerator would cut down their traveling money, and Dickie had a very definite budget for his own five hundred dollars every month. Dickie was cautious about money, in a way, yet down at the wharf, and in the village bars, he gave generous tips right and left, and gave five-hundred-lire bills to any beggar who approached him.

Dickie was back to normal by five o'clock. He had had a good afternoon of painting, Tom supposed, because he had been whistling for the last hour in his studio. Dickie came out on the terrace where Tom was scanning his Italian grammar, and gave him some pointers on his pronunciation.

"They don't always say 'voglio' so clearly," Dickie said. "They say 'io vo' presentare mia amica Marge,' per esempio." Dickie drew his long hand backward through the air. He always made gestures when he spoke Italian, graceful gestures as if he were leading an orchestra in a legato. "You'd better listen to Fausto more and read that grammar less. I picked my Italian up off the streets." Dickie smiled and walked away down the garden path. Fausto was just coming in the gate.

Tom listened carefully to their laughing exchanges in Italian, straining to understand every word.

Fausto came out on the terrace smiling, sank into a chair, and put his bare feet up on the parapet. His face was either smiling or frowning, and it could change from instant to instant. He was one of the few people in the village, Dickie said, who didn't speak in a southern dialect. Fausto lived in Milan, and he was visiting an aunt in Mongibello for a few months. He came, dependably and punctually, three times a week between five and five-thirty, and they sat on the terrace and sipped wine or coffee and chatted for about an hour. Tom tried his utmost to memorize everything Fausto said about the rocks, the water, politics (Fausto was a Communist, a card-carrying Communist, and he showed his card to Americans at the drop of a hat, Dickie said, because he was amused by their astonishment at his having it), and about the frenzied, catlike sex-life of some of the village inhabitants. Fausto found it hard to think of things to talk about sometimes, and then he would stare at Tom and burst out laughing. But Tom was making great progress. Italian was the only thing he had ever studied that he enjoyed and felt he could stick to. Tom wanted his Italian to be as good as Dickie's, and he thought he could make it that good in another month, if he kept on working hard at it.

II.

TOM walked briskly across the terrace and into Dickie's studio. "Want to go to Paris in a coffin?" he asked.

"*What?*" Dickie looked up from his watercolor.

"I've been talking to an Italian in Giorgio's. We'd start out from Trieste, ride in coffins in the baggage car escorted by some Frenchman, and we'd get a hundred thousand lire apiece. I have the idea it concerns dope."

"Dope in the coffins? Isn't that an old stunt?"

"We talked in Italian, so I didn't understand everything, but he said there'd be three coffins, and maybe the third has a real corpse in it and they've put the dope into the corpse. Anyway, we'd get the trip plus the experience." He emptied his pockets of the packs of ship's store Lucky Strikes that he had just bought from a street peddler for Dickie. "What do you say?"

"I think it's a marvelous idea. To Paris in a coffin!"

There was a funny smile on Dickie's face, as if Dickie were pulling his leg by pretending to fall in with it, when he hadn't the least intention of falling in with it. "I'm serious," Tom said. "He really is on the lookout for a couple of willing young men. The coffins are supposed to contain the bodies of French casualties from Indo-China. The French escort is supposed to be the relative of one of them, or maybe all of them." It wasn't exactly what the man had said to him, but it was near enough. And two hundred thousand lire was over three hundred dollars, after all, plenty for a spree in Paris. Dickie was still hedging about Paris.

Dickie looked at him sharply, put out the bent wisp of the Nazionale he was smoking, and opened one of the packs of Luckies. "Are you sure the guy you were talking to wasn't under the influence of dope himself?"

"You're so damned cautious these days!" Tom said with a laugh. "Where's your spirit? You look as if you don't even believe me! Come with me and I'll show you the man. He's still down there waiting for me. His name's Carlo."

Dickie showed no sign of moving. "Anybody with an offer like that doesn't explain all the particulars to you. They get a couple of toughs to ride from Trieste to Paris, maybe, but even that doesn't make sense to me."

"Will you come with me and talk to him? If you don't believe me, at least look at him."

"Sure." Dickie got up suddenly. "I might even do it for a hundred thousand lire." Dickie closed a book of poems that had been lying face down on his studio couch before he followed Tom out of the room. Marge had a lot of books of poetry. Lately Dickie had been borrowing them.

The man was still sitting at the corner table in Giorgio's when they came in. Tom smiled at him and nodded.

"Hello, Carlo," Tom said. "Posso sedermi?"

"Si, si," the man said, gesturing to the chairs at his table.

"This is my friend," Tom said carefully in Italian. "He wants to know if the work with the railroad journey is correct." Tom watched Carlo looking Dickie over, sizing him up, and it was wonderful to Tom how the man's dark, tough, callous-looking eyes betrayed nothing but a polite interest, how in a split second he seemed to take in and evaluate Dickie's faintly smiling but suspicious expression, Dickie's tan that could not have been acquired except by months of lying in the sun, his worn, Italian-made clothes and his American rings.

A smile spread slowly across the man's pale, flat lips, and he glanced at Tom.

"Allora?" Tom prompted, impatient.

The man lifted his sweet martini and drank. "The job is real, but I do not think your friend is the right man."

Tom looked at Dickie. Dickie was watching the man alertly, with the same neutral smile that suddenly struck Tom as contemptuous. "Well, at least it's true, you see!" Tom said to Dickie.

"Mm-m," Dickie said, still gazing at the man as if he were some kind of animal which interested him, and which he could kill if he decided to.

Dickie could have talked Italian to the man. Dickie didn't say a word. Three weeks ago, Tom thought, Dickie would have taken the man up on his offer. Did he have to sit there looking like a stool pigeon or a police detective waiting for reinforcements so he could arrest the man? "Well," Tom said finally, "you believe me, don't you?"

Dickie glanced at him. "About the job? How do I know?"

Tom looked at the Italian expectantly.

The Italian shrugged. "There is no need to discuss it, is there?" he asked in Italian.

"No," Tom said. A crazy, directionless fury boiled in his blood and made him tremble. He was furious at Dickie. Dickie was looking over the man's dirty nails, dirty shirt collar, his ugly dark face that had been recently shaven though not recently washed, so that where the beard had been was much lighter than the skin above and below it. But the Italian's dark eyes were cool and amiable, and stronger than Dickie's. Tom felt stifled. He was conscious that he could not express himself in Italian. He wanted to speak both to Dickie and to the man.

"Niente, grazie, Berto," Dickie said calmly to the waiter who had come over to ask what they wanted. Dickie looked at Tom. "Ready to go?"

Tom jumped up so suddenly his straight chair upset behind him. He set it up again, and bowed a good-bye to the Italian. He felt he owed the Italian an apology, yet he could not open his mouth to say even a conventional good-bye. The Italian nodded good-bye and smiled. Tom followed Dickie's long white-clad legs out of the bar.

Outside, Tom said, "I just wanted you to see that it's true at least. I hope you see."

"All right, it's true," Dickie said, smiling. "What's the matter with you?"

"What's the matter with *you*?" Tom demanded.

"The man's a crook. Is that what you want me to admit? Okay!"

"Do you have to be so damned superior about it? Did he do anything to you?"

"Am I supposed to get down on my knees to him? I've seen crooks before. This village gets a lot of them." Dickie's blond eyebrows frowned. "What the hell *is* the matter with you? Do you want to take him up on his crazy proposition? Go ahead!"

"I couldn't now if I wanted to. Not after the way you acted."

Dickie stopped in the road, looking at him. They were arguing so loudly, a few people around them were looking, watching.

"It could have been fun," Tom said, "but not the way you chose to take it. A month ago when we went to Rome, you'd have thought something like this was fun."

"Oh, no," Dickie said, shaking his head. "I doubt it."

The sense of frustration and inarticulateness was agony to

Tom. And the fact that they were being looked at. He forced himself to walk on, in tense little steps at first, until he was sure that Dickie was coming with him. The puzzlement, the suspicion, was still in Dickie's face, and Tom knew Dickie was puzzled about his reaction. Tom wanted to explain it, wanted to break through to Dickie so he would understand and they would feel the same way. Dickie had felt the same way he had a month ago. "It's the way you acted," Tom said. "You didn't have to act that way. The fellow wasn't doing you any harm."

"He looked like a dirty crook!" Dickie retorted. "For Christ sake, go back if you like him so much. You're under no obligation to do what I do!"

Now Tom stopped. He had an impulse to go back, not necessarily to go back to the Italian, but to leave Dickie. Then his tension snapped suddenly. His shoulders relaxed, aching, and his breath began to come fast, through his mouth. He wanted to say at least, "All right, Dickie," to make it up, to make Dickie forget it. He felt tongue-tied. He stared at Dickie's blue eyes that were still frowning, the sun-bleached eyebrows white and the eyes themselves shining and empty, nothing but little pieces of blue jelly with a black dot in them, meaningless, without relation to him. You were supposed to see the soul through the eyes, to see love through the eyes, the one place you could look at another human being and see what really went on inside, and in Dickie's eyes Tom saw nothing more now than he would have seen if he had looked at the hard, bloodless surface of a mirror. Tom felt a painful wrench in his breast, and he covered his face with his hands. It was as if Dickie had been suddenly snatched away from him. They were not friends. They didn't know each other. It struck Tom like a horrible truth, true for all time, true for the people he had known in the past and for those he would know in the future: each had stood and would stand before him, and he would know time and time again that he would never know them, and the worst was that there would always be the il- lusion, for a time, that he did know them, and that he and they were completely in harmony and alike. For an instant the wordless shock of his realization seemed more than he could bear. He felt in the grip of a fit, as if he would fall to the ground. It was too much: the foreignness around him, the different language, his failure, and the fact that Dickie hated him. He felt surrounded by strangeness, by hostility. He felt Dickie yank his hands down from his eyes.

"What's the matter with you?" Dickie asked. "Did that guy give you a shot of something?"

"No."

"Are you sure? In your drink?"

"No." The first drops of the evening rain fell on his head. There was a rumble of thunder. Hostility from above, too. "I want to die," Tom said in a small voice.

Dickie yanked him by the arm. Tom tripped over a doorstep. They were in the little bar opposite the post office. Tom heard Dickie ordering a brandy, specifying Italian brandy because he wasn't good enough for French, Tom supposed. Tom drank it off, slightly sweetish, medicinal-tasting, drank three of them, like a magic medicine to bring him back to what his mind knew was usually called reality: the smell of the Nazionale in Dickie's hand, the curlycued grain in the wood of the bar under his fingers, the fact that his stomach had a hard pressure in it as if someone were holding a fist against his navel, the vivid anticipation of the long steep walk from here up to the house, the faint ache that would come in his thighs from it.

"I'm okay," Tom said in a quiet, deep voice. "I don't know what was the matter. Must have been the heat that got me for a minute." He laughed a little. That was reality, laughing it off, making it silly, something that was more important than anything that had happened to him in the five weeks since he had met Dickie, maybe that had ever happened to him.

Dickie said nothing, only put the cigarette in his mouth and took a couple of hundred-lire bills from his black alligator wallet and laid them on the bar. Tom was hurt that he said nothing, hurt like a child who has been sick and probably a nuisance, but who expects at least a friendly word when the sickness is over. But Dickie was indifferent. Dickie had bought him the brandies as coldly as he might have bought them for a stranger he had encountered who felt ill and had no money. Tom thought suddenly, *Dickie doesn't want me to go to Cortina.* It was not the first time Tom had thought that. Marge was going to Cortina now. She and Dickie had bought a new giant-sized thermos to take to Cortina the last time they had been in Naples. They hadn't asked him if he had liked the thermos, or anything else. They were just quietly and gradually leaving him out of their preparations. Tom felt that Dickie expected him to take off, in fact, just before the Cortina trip. A couple of weeks ago, Dickie had said he would show him some of the ski trails around Cortina that were marked on a map that he had. Dickie had looked at the map one evening, but he had not talked to him.

"Ready?" Dickie asked.

Tom followed him out of the bar like a dog.

"If you can get home all right by yourself, I thought I'd run up and see Marge for a while," Dickie said on the road.

"I feel fine," Tom said.

"Good." Then he said over his shoulder as he walked away, "Want to pick up the mail? I might forget."

Tom nodded. He went into the post office. There were two letters, one to him from Dickie's father, one to Dickie from someone in New York whom Tom didn't know. He stood in the doorway and opened Mr. Greenleaf's letter, unfolded the typewritten sheet respectfully. It had the impressive pale green letterhead of Burke-Greenleaf Watercraft, Inc., with the ship's-wheel trademark in the center.

Nov. 10, 19——

My dear Tom,

In view of the fact you have been with Dickie over a month and that he shows no more sign of coming home than before you went, I can only conclude that you haven't been successful. I realize that with the best of intentions you reported that he is considering returning, but frankly I don't see it anywhere in his letter of October 26th. As a matter of fact, he seems more determined than ever to stay where he is.

I want you to know that I and my wife appreciate whatever efforts you have made on our behalf, and his. You need no longer consider yourself obligated to me in any way. I trust you have not inconvenienced yourself greatly by your efforts of the past month, and I sincerely hope the trip has afforded you some pleasure despite the failure of its main objective.

Both my wife and I send you greetings and our thanks.

Sincerely,
H. R. Greenleaf

It was the final blow. With the cool tone—even cooler than his usual businesslike coolness, because this was a dismissal and he had injected a note of courteous thanks in it—Mr. Greenleaf had simply cut him off. He had failed. "I trust you have not inconvenienced yourself greatly . . ." Wasn't that sarcastic? Mr. Greenleaf didn't even say that he would like to see him again when he returned to America.

Tom walked mechanically up the hill. He imagined Dickie in Marge's house now, narrating to her the story of Carlo in the bar, and his peculiar behavior on the road afterward. Tom knew what Marge would say: "Why don't you get *rid* of him, Dickie?" Should he go back and explain to them, he wondered, force them to listen? Tom turned around, looking at the inscrutable square front of Marge's house up on the hill, at its empty, dark-looking window. His denim jacket was getting wet from the rain. He turned its collar up. Then he walked on quickly up the hill toward Dickie's house. At least, he thought proudly, he hadn't tried to wheedle any more money out of Mr. Greenleaf, and he might have. He might have, even with Dickie's cooperation, if he had ever approached Dickie about it when Dickie had been in a good mood. Anybody else would have, Tom thought, anybody, but he hadn't, and that counted for *something*.

He stood at the corner of the terrace, staring out at the vague empty line of the horizon and thinking of nothing, feeling nothing except a faint, dreamlike lostness and aloneness. Even Dickie and Marge seemed far away, and what they might be talking about seemed unimportant. He was alone. That was the only important thing. He began to feel a tingling fear at the end of his spine, tingling over his buttocks.

He turned as he heard the gate open. Dickie walked up the path, smiling, but it struck Tom as a forced, polite smile.

"What're you doing standing there in the rain?" Dickie asked, ducking into the hall door.

"It's very refreshing," Tom said pleasantly. "Here's a letter for you." He handed Dickie his letter and stuffed the one from Mr. Greenleaf into his pocket.

Tom hung his jacket in the hall closet. When Dickie had finished reading his letter—a letter that had made him laugh out loud as he read it—Tom said, "Do you think Marge would like to go up to Paris with us when we go?"

Dickie looked surprised. "I think she would."

"Well, ask her," Tom said cheerfully.

"I don't know if I should go up to Paris," Dickie said. "I wouldn't mind getting away somewhere for a few days, but Paris—" He lighted a cigarette. "I'd just as soon go up to San Remo or even Genoa. That's quite a town."

"But Paris—Genoa can't compare with Paris, can it?"

"No, of course not, but it's a lot closer."

"But when *will* we get to Paris?"

"I don't know. Any old time. Paris'll still be there."

Tom listened to the echo of the words in his ears, searching their tone. The day before yesterday, Dickie had received a letter from his father. He had read a few sentences aloud and they had laughed about something, but he had not read the whole letter as he had a couple of times before. Tom had no doubt that Mr. Greenleaf had told Dickie that he was fed up with Tom Ripley, and probably that he suspected him of using his money for his own entertainment. A month ago Dickie would have laughed at something like that, too, but not now, Tom thought. "I just thought while I have a little money left, we ought to make our Paris trip," Tom persisted.

"You go up. I'm not in the mood right now. Got to save my strength for Cortina."

"Well—I suppose we'll make it San Remo then," Tom said, trying to sound agreeable, though he could have wept.

"All right."

Tom darted from the hall into the kitchen. The huge white form of the refrigerator sprang out of the corner at him. He had wanted a drink, with ice in it. Now he didn't want to touch the thing. He had spent a whole day in Naples with Dickie and Marge, looking at refrigerators, inspecting ice trays, counting the number of gadgets, until Tom hadn't been able to tell one refrigerator from another, but Dickie and Marge had kept at it with the enthusiasm of newlyweds. Then they had spent a few more hours in a café discussing the respective merits of all the refrigerators they had looked at before they decided on the one they wanted. And now Marge

was popping in and out more often than ever, because she
stored some of her own food in it, and she often wanted to
borrow ice. Tom realized suddenly why he hated the refrigerator so much. It meant that Dickie was staying put. It finished not only their Greek trip this winter, but it meant Dickie
probably never would move to Paris or Rome to live, as he
and Tom had talked of doing in Tom's first weeks here. Not
with a refrigerator that had the distinction of being one of
only about four in the village, a refrigerator with six ice trays
and so many shelves on the door that it looked like a super-
market swinging out at you every time you opened it.

Tom fixed himself an iceless drink. His hands were shaking.
Only yesterday Dickie had said, "Are you going home for
Christmas?" very casually in the middle of some conversation,
but Dickie knew damned well he wasn't going home for
Christmas. He didn't have a home, and Dickie knew it. He
had told Dickie all about Aunt Dottie in Boston. It had simply
been a big hint, that was all. Marge was full of plans about
Christmas. She had a can of English plum pudding she was
saving, and she was going to get a turkey from some conta-
dino. Tom could imagine how she would slop it up with her
saccharine sentimentality. A Christmas tree, of course, probably cut out of cardboard. "Silent Night." Eggnog. Gooey
presents for Dickie. Marge knitted. She took Dickie's socks
home to darn all the time. And they'd both slightly, politely,
leave him out. Every friendly thing they would say to him
would be a painful effort. Tom couldn't bear to imagine it.
All right, he'd leave. He'd do something rather than endure
Christmas with them.

12.

MARGE said she didn't care to go with them to San Remo.
She was in the middle of a "streak" on her book. Marge
worked in fits and starts, always cheerfully, though it seemed
to Tom that she was bogged down, as she called it, about
seventy-five per cent of the time, a condition that she always
announced with a merry little laugh. The book must stink,

Tom thought. He had known writers. You didn't write a book with your little finger, lolling on a beach half the day, wondering what to eat for dinner. But he was glad she was having a "streak" at the time he and Dickie wanted to go to San Remo.

"I'd appreciate it if you'd try to find that cologne, Dickie," she said. "You know, the Stradivari I couldn't find in Naples. San Remo's bound to have it, they have so many shops with French stuff."

Tom could see them spending a whole day looking for it in San Remo, just as they had spent hours looking for it in Naples one Saturday.

They took only one suitcase of Dickie's between them, because they planned to be away only three nights and four days. Dickie was in a slightly more cheerful mood, but the awful finality was still there, the feeling that this was the last trip they would make together anywhere. To Tom, Dickie's polite cheerfulness on the train was like the cheerfulness of a host who has loathed his guest and is afraid the guest realizes it, and who tries to make it up at the last minute. Tom had never before in his life felt like an unwelcome, boring guest. On the train, Dickie told Tom about San Remo and the week he had spent there with Freddie Miles when he first arrived in Italy. San Remo was tiny, but it had a famous name as an international shopping center, Dickie said, and people came across the French border to buy things there. It occurred to Tom that Dickie was trying to sell him on the town and might try to persuade him to stay there alone instead of coming back to Mongibello. Tom began to feel an aversion to the place before they got there.

Then, almost as the train was sliding into the San Remo station, Dickie said, "By the way, Tom—I hate to say this to you, if you're going to mind terribly, but I really would prefer to go to Cortina d'Ampezzo alone with Marge. I think she'd prefer it, and after all I owe something to her, a pleasant holiday at least. You don't seem to be too enthusiastic about skiing."

Tom went rigid and cold, but he tried not to move a muscle. Blaming it on Marge! "All right," he said. "Of course." Nervously he looked at the map in his hands, looking des-

perately around San Remo for somewhere else to go, though
Dickie was already swinging their suitcase down from the rack.
"We're not far from Nice, are we?" Tom asked.

"No."

"And Cannes. I'd like to see Cannes as long as I'm this far.
At least Cannes is France," he added on a reproachful note.

"Well, I suppose we could. You brought your passport,
didn't you?"

Tom had brought his passport. They boarded a train for
Cannes, and arrived around eleven o'clock that night.

Tom thought it beautiful—the sweep of curving harbor extended by little lights to long thin crescent tips, the elegant
yet tropical-looking main boulevard along the water with its
rows of palm trees, its row of expensive hotels. France! It was
more sedate than Italy, and more chic, he could feel that even
in the dark. They went to a hotel on the first back street, the
Gray d'Albion, which was chic enough but wouldn't cost
them their shirts, Dickie said, though Tom would gladly have
paid whatever it cost at the best hotel on the ocean front.
They left their suitcase at the hotel, and went to the bar of
the Hotel Carlton, which Dickie said was the most fashionable
bar in Cannes. As he had predicted, there were not many
people in the bar, because there were not many people in
Cannes at this time of year. Tom proposed a second round of
drinks, but Dickie declined.

They breakfasted at a café the next morning, then strolled
down to the beach. They had their swimming trunks on under
their trousers. The day was cool, but not impossibly cool for
swimming. They had been swimming in Mongibello on colder
days. The beach was practically empty—a few isolated pairs of
people, a group of men playing some kind of game up near
the embankment. The waves curved over and broke on the
sand with a wintry violence. Now Tom saw that the group of
men were doing acrobatics.

"They must be professionals," Tom said. "They're all in
the same yellow G-strings."

Tom watched with interest as a human pyramid began
building, feet braced on bulging thighs, hands gripping forearms. He could hear their "Allez!" and their "Un—deux!"

"Look!" Tom said. "There goes the top!" He stood still to watch the smallest one, a boy of about seventeen, as he was boosted to the shoulders of the center man in the three top men. He stood poised, his arms open, as if receiving applause. "Bravo!" Tom shouted.

The boy smiled at Tom before he leapt down, lithe as a tiger.

Tom looked at Dickie. Dickie was looking at a couple of men sitting nearby on the beach.

"Ten thousand saw I at a glance, nodding their heads in sprightly dance," Dickie said sourly to Tom.

It startled Tom, then he felt that sharp thrust of shame, the same shame he had felt in Mongibello when Dickie had said, *Marge thinks you are.* All right, Tom thought, the acrobats were fairies. Maybe Cannes was full of fairies. So what? Tom's fists were clenched tight in his trousers pockets. He remembered Aunt Dottie's taunt: *Sissy! He's a sissy from the ground up. Just like his father!* Dickie stood with his arms folded, looking out at the ocean. Tom deliberately kept himself from even glancing at the acrobats again, though they were certainly more amusing to watch than the ocean. "Are you going in?" Tom asked, boldly unbuttoning his shirt, though the water suddenly looked cold as hell.

"I don't think so," Dickie said. "Why don't you stay here and watch the acrobats? I'm going back." He turned and started back before Tom could answer.

Tom buttoned his clothes hastily, watching Dickie as he walked diagonally away, away from the acrobats, though the next stairs up to the sidewalk were twice as far as the stairs nearer the acrobats. Damn him anyway, Tom thought. Did he have to act so damned aloof and superior all the time? You'd think he'd never seen a pansy! Obvious what was the matter with Dickie, all right! Why didn't he break down, just for once? What did he have that was so important to lose? A half-dozen taunts sprang to his mind as he ran after Dickie. Then Dickie glanced around at him coldly, with distaste, and the first taunt died in his mouth.

They left for San Remo that afternoon, just before three o'clock, so there would not be another day to pay on the hotel bill. Dickie had proposed leaving by three, though it was Tom who paid the 3,430-franc bill, ten dollars and eight cents American, for one night. Tom also bought their railroad tickets to San Remo, though Dickie was loaded with francs. Dickie had brought his monthly remittance check from Italy and cashed it in francs, figuring that he would come out better converting the francs back into lire later, because of a sudden recent strengthening of the franc.

Dickie said absolutely nothing on the train. Under a pretense of being sleepy, he folded his arms and closed his eyes. Tom sat opposite him, staring at his bony, arrogant, handsome face, at his hands with the green ring and the gold signet ring. It crossed Tom's mind to steal the green ring when he left. It would be easy: Dickie took it off when he swam. Sometimes he took it off even when he showered at the house. He would do it the very last day, Tom thought. Tom stared at Dickie's closed eyelids. A crazy emotion of hate, of affection, of impatience and frustration was swelling in him, hampering his breathing. He wanted to kill Dickie. It was not the first time he had thought of it. Before, once or twice or three times, it had been an impulse caused by anger or disappointment, an impulse that vanished immediately and left him with a feeling of shame. Now he thought about it for an entire minute, two minutes, because he was leaving Dickie anyway, and what was there to be ashamed of any more? He had failed with Dickie, in every way. He hated Dickie, because, however he looked at what had happened, his failing had not been his own fault, not due to anything he had done, but due to Dickie's inhuman stubbornness. And his blatant rudeness! He had offered Dickie friendship, companionship, and respect, everything he had to offer, and Dickie had replied with ingratitude and now hostility. Dickie was just shoving him out in the cold. If he killed him on this trip, Tom thought, he could simply say that some accident had happened. He could— He had just thought of something brilliant: he could become Dickie Greenleaf himself. He could do everything that Dickie did. He could go back to Mongibello first and collect Dickie's things, tell Marge any damned story, set up an apartment in Rome or Paris, receive Dickie's check every month and forge Dickie's signature on it. He could step right into Dickie's shoes. He could have Mr. Greenleaf, Sr., eating out of his hand. The danger of it, even the inevitable temporariness of it which he vaguely realized, only made him more enthusiastic. He began to think of *how*.

The water. But Dickie was such a good swimmer. The cliffs. It would be easy to push Dickie off some cliff when they took a walk, but he imagined Dickie grabbing at him and pulling *him* off with him, and he tensed in his seat until his thighs ached and his nails cut red scallops in his thumbs. He would have to get the other ring off, too. He would have to tint his hair a little lighter. But he wouldn't live in a place, of course, where anybody who knew Dickie lived. He had only to look enough like Dickie to be able to use his passport. Well, he did. If he—

Dickie opened his eyes, looking right at him, and Tom relaxed, slumped into the corner with his head back and his eyes shut, as quickly as if he had passed out.

"Tom, are you okay?" Dickie asked, shaking Tom's knee.

"Okay," Tom said, smiling a little. He saw Dickie sit back with an air of irritation, and Tom knew why: because Dickie had hated giving him even that much attention. Tom smiled to himself, amused at his own quick reflex in pretending to collapse, because that had been the only way to keep Dickie from seeing what must have been a very strange expression on his face.

San Remo. Flowers. A main drag along the beach again, shops and stores and French and English and Italian tourists. Another hotel, with flowers in the balconies. Where? In one of these little streets tonight? The town would be dark and silent by one in the morning, if he could keep Dickie up that long. In the water? It was slightly cloudy, though not cold. Tom racked his brain. It would be easy in the hotel room, too, but how would he get rid of the body? The body had to *disappear*, absolutely. That left only the water, and the water was Dickie's element. There were boats, rowboats and little motorboats, that people could rent down at the beach. In each motorboat, Tom noticed, was a round weight of cement attached to a line, for anchoring the boat.

"What do you say we take a boat, Dickie?" Tom asked, trying not to sound eager, though he did, and Dickie looked at him, because he had not been eager about anything since they had arrived here.

They were little blue-and-white and green-and-white motorboats, about ten of them, lined up at the wooden pier, and the Italian was anxious for customers because it was a chilly and rather gloomy morning. Dickie looked out at the Mediterranean, which was slightly hazy though not with a presage of rain. This was the kind of grayness that would not disappear all day, and there would be no sun. It was about ten-thirty, that lazy hour after breakfast, when the whole long Italian morning lay before them.

"Well, all right. For an hour around the port," Dickie said, almost immediately jumping into a boat, and Tom could see from his little smile that he had done it before, that he was looking forward to remembering, sentimentally, other mornings or some other morning here, perhaps with Freddie, or Marge. Marge's cologne bottle bulged the pocket of Dickie's corduroy jacket. They had bought it a few minutes ago at a store very much like an American drugstore on the main drag.

The Italian boatkeeper started the motor with a yanked string, asking Dickie if he knew how to work it, and Dickie said yes. And there was an oar, a single oar in the bottom of the boat, Tom saw. Dickie took the tiller. They headed straight out from the town.

"Cool!" Dickie yelled, smiling. His hair was blowing.

Tom looked to right and left. A vertical cliff on one side, very much like Mongibello, and on the other a flattish length of land fuzzing out in the mist that hovered over the water. Offhand he couldn't say in which direction it was better to go.

"Do you know the land around here?" Tom shouted over the roar of the motor.

"Nope!" Dickie said cheerfully. He was enjoying the ride.

"Is that thing hard to steer?"

"Not a bit! Want to try it?"

Tom hesitated. Dickie was still steering straight out to the open sea. "No, thanks." He looked to right and left. There was a sailboat off to the left. "Where're you going?" Tom shouted.

"Does it matter?" Dickie smiled.

No, it didn't.

Dickie swerved suddenly to the right, so suddenly that they both had to duck and lean to keep the boat righted. A wall of white spray rose up on Tom's left, then gradually fell to show the empty horizon. They were streaking across the empty water again, toward nothing. Dickie was trying the speed, smiling, his blue eyes smiling at the emptiness.

"In a little boat it always feels so much faster than it is!" Dickie yelled.

Tom nodded, letting his understanding smile speak for him. Actually, he was terrified. God only knew how deep the water was here. If something happened to the boat suddenly, there wasn't a chance in the world that they could get back to shore, or at least that *he* could. But neither was there a chance that anybody could see anything that they did here. Dickie was swerving very slightly toward the right again, toward the long spit of fuzzy gray land, but he could have hit Dickie, sprung on him, or kissed him, or thrown him overboard, and nobody could have seen him at this distance. Tom was sweating, hot under his clothes, cold on his forehead. He felt afraid, but it was not of the water, it was of Dickie. He knew that he was going to do it, that he would not stop himself now, maybe *couldn't* stop himself, and that he might not succeed.

"You dare me to jump in?" Tom yelled, beginning to unbutton his jacket.

Dickie only laughed at this proposal from him, opening his mouth wide, keeping his eyes fixed on the distance in front of the boat.

Tom kept on undressing. He had his shoes and socks off. Under his trousers he wore his swimming trunks, like Dickie. "I'll go in if you will!" Tom shouted. "Will you?" He wanted Dickie to slow down.

"Will I? Sure!" Dickie slowed the motor abruptly. He released the tiller and took off his jacket. The boat bobbed, losing its momentum. "Come on," Dickie said, nodding at Tom's trousers that were still on.

Tom glanced at the land. San Remo was a blur of chalky white and pink. He picked up the oar, as casually as if he were

playing with it between his knees, and when Dickie was shoving his trousers down, Tom lifted the oar and came down with
it on the top of Dickie's head.

"Hey!" Dickie yelled, scowling, sliding half off the wooden
seat. His pale brows lifted in groggy surprise.

Tom stood up and brought the oar down again, sharply, all
his strength released like the snap of a rubber band.

"For God's sake!" Dickie mumbled, glowering, fierce,
though the blue eyes wobbled, losing consciousness.

Tom swung a left-handed blow with the oar against the side
of Dickie's head. The edge of the oar cut a dull gash that
filled with a line of blood as Tom watched. Dickie was on the
bottom of the boat, twisted, twisting. Dickie gave a groaning
roar of protest that frightened Tom with its loudness and its
strength. Tom hit him in the side of the neck, three times,
chopping strokes with the edge of the oar, as if the oar were
an ax and Dickie's neck a tree. The boat rocked, and water
splashed over his foot that was braced on the gunwale. He
sliced at Dickie's forehead, and a broad patch of blood came
slowly where the oar had scraped. For an instant Tom was
aware of tiring as he raised and swung, and still Dickie's hands
slid toward him on the bottom of the boat, Dickie's long legs
straightened to thrust him forward. Tom got a bayonet grip
on the oar and plunged its handle into Dickie's side. Then
the prostrate body relaxed, limp and still. Tom straightened,
getting his breath back painfully. He looked around him.
There were no boats, nothing, except far, far away a little
white spot creeping from right to left, a speeding motorboat
heading for the shore.

He stooped and yanked at Dickie's green ring. He pocketed
it. The other ring was tighter, but it came off, over the bleeding scuffed knuckle. He looked in the trousers pockets.
French and Italian coins. He left them. He took a keychain
with three keys. Then he picked up Dickie's jacket and took
Marge's cologne package out of the pocket. Cigarettes and
Dickie's silver lighter, a pencil stub, the alligator wallet and
several little cards in the inside breast pocket. Tom stuffed it
all into his own corduroy jacket. Then he reached for the rope
that was tumbled over the white cement weight. The end of

the rope was tied to the metal ring at the prow. Tom tried to untie it. It was a hellish, water-soaked, immovable knot that must have been there for years. He banged at it with his fist. He had to have a knife.

He looked at Dickie. Was he dead? Tom crouched in the narrowing prow of the boat watching Dickie for a sign of life. He was afraid to touch him, afraid to touch his chest or his wrist to feel a pulse. Tom turned and yanked at the rope frenziedly, until he realized that he was only making it tighter.

His cigarette lighter. He fumbled for it in the pocket of his trousers on the bottom of the boat. He lighted it, then held a dry portion of the rope over its flame. The rope was about an inch and a half thick. It was slow, very slow, and Tom used the minutes to look all around him again. Would the Italian with the boats be able to see him at this distance? The hard gray rope refused to catch fire, only glowed and smoked a little, slowly parting, strand by strand. Tom yanked it, and his lighter went out. He lighted it again, and kept on pulling at the rope. When it parted, he looped it four times around Dickie's bare ankles before he had time to feel afraid, and tied a huge, clumsy knot, overdoing it to make sure it would not come undone, because he was not very good at tying knots. He estimated the rope to be about thirty-five or forty feet long. He began to feel cooler, and smooth and methodical. The cement weight should be just enough to hold a body down, he thought. The body might drift a little, but it would not come up to the surface.

Tom threw the weight over. It made a *ker-plung* and sank through the transparent water with a wake of bubbles, disappeared, and sank and sank until the rope drew taut on Dickie's ankles, and by that time Tom had lifted the ankles over the side and was pulling now at an arm to lift the heaviest part, the shoulders, over the gunwale. Dickie's limp hand was warm and clumsy. The shoulders stayed on the bottom of the boat, and when he pulled, the arm seemed to stretch like rubber, and the body not to rise at all. Tom got down on one knee and tried to heave him out over the side. It made the boat rock. He had forgotten the water. It was the only thing that scared him. He would have to get him out over the stern, he thought, because the stern was lower in the water. He pulled the limp body toward the stern, sliding the rope around the gunwale. He could tell from the buoyancy of the weight in the water that the weight had not touched bottom. Now he began with Dickie's head and shoulders, turned Dickie's body on its belly and pushed him out little by little. Dickie's head was in the water, the gunwale cutting across his waist, and now the legs were a dead weight, resisting Tom's strength with their amazing weight, as his shoulders had done, as if they were magnetized to the boat bottom. Tom took a deep breath and heaved. Dickie went over, but Tom lost his balance and fell against the tiller. The idling motor roared suddenly.

Tom made a lunge for the control lever, but the boat swerved at the same time in a crazy arc. For an instant he saw water underneath him and his own hand outstretched toward it, because he had been trying to grab the gunwale and the gunwale was no longer there.

He was in the water.

He gasped, contracting his body in an upward leap, grabbing at the boat. He missed. The boat had gone into a spin. Tom leapt again, then sank lower, so low the water closed over his head again with a deadly, fatal slowness, yet too fast for him to get a breath, and he inhaled a noseful of water just as his eyes sank below the surface. The boat was farther away. He had seen such spins before: they never stopped until somebody climbed in and stopped the motor, and now in the deadly emptiness of the water he suffered in advance the sensations of dying, sank threshing below the surface again, and the crazy motor faded as the water *thugged* into his ears, blotting out all sound except the frantic sounds that he made inside himself, breathing, struggling, the desperate pounding of his blood. He was up again and fighting automatically toward the boat, because it was the only thing that floated, though it was spinning and impossible to touch, and its sharp prow whipped past him twice, three times, four, while he caught one breath of air.

He shouted for help. He got nothing but a mouthful of water.

His hand touched the boat beneath the water and was

pushed aside by the animal-like thrust of the prow. He reached out wildly for the end of the boat, heedless of the propeller's blades. His fingers felt the rudder. He ducked, but not in time. The keel hit the top of his head, passing over him. Now the stern was close again, and he tried for it, fingers slipping down off the rudder. His other hand caught the stern gunwale. He kept an arm straight, holding his body away from the propeller. With an unpremeditated energy, he hurled himself toward a stern corner, and caught an arm over the side. Then he reached up and touched the lever.

The motor began to slow.

Tom clung to the gunwale with both hands, and his mind went blank with relief, with disbelief, until he became aware of the flaming ache in his throat, the stab in his chest with every breath. He rested for what could have been two or ten minutes, thinking of nothing at all but the gathering of strength enough to haul himself into the boat, and finally he made slow jumps up and down in the water and threw his weight over and lay face down in the boat, his feet dangling over the gunwale. He rested, faintly conscious of the slipperiness of Dickie's blood under his fingers, a wetness mingled with the water that ran out of his own nose and mouth. He began to think before he could move, about the boat that was all bloody and could not be returned, about the motor that he would have to get up and start in a moment. About the direction.

About Dickie's rings. He felt for them in his jacket pocket. They were still there, and after all what could have happened to them? He had a fit of coughing, and tears blurred his vision as he tried to look all around him to see if any boat was near, or coming toward him. He rubbed his eyes. There was no boat, except the gay little motorboat in the distance, still dashing around in wide arcs, oblivious of him. Tom looked at the boat bottom. *Could* he wash it all out? But blood was hell to get out, he had always heard. He had been going to return the boat, and say, if he were asked by the boatkeeper where his friend was, that he had set him ashore at some other point. Now that couldn't be.

Tom moved the lever cautiously. The idling motor picked up and he was afraid even of that, but the motor seemed more human and manageable than the sea, and therefore less frightening. He headed obliquely toward the shore, north of San Remo. Maybe he could find some place, some little deserted cove in the shore where he could beach the boat and get out. But if they found the boat? The problem seemed immense. He tried to reason himself back to coolness. His mind seemed blocked as to how to get rid of the boat.

Now he could see pine trees, a dry empty-looking stretch of tan beach and the green fuzz of a field of olive trees. Tom cruised slowly to right and left of the place, looking for people. There were none. He headed in for the shallow, short beach, handling the throttle respectfully, because he was not sure it wouldn't flare up again. Then he felt the scrape and jolt of earth under the prow. He turned the lever to FERMA, and moved another lever that cut the motor. He got out cautiously into about ten inches of water, pulled the boat up as far as he could, then transferred the two jackets, his sandals, and Marge's cologne box from the boat to the beach. The little cove where he was—not more than fifteen feet wide— gave him a feeling of safety and privacy. There was not a sign anywhere that a human foot had ever touched the place. Tom decided to try to scuttle the boat.

He began to gather stones, all about the size of a human head because that was all he had the strength to carry, and to drop them one by one into the boat, but finally he had to use smaller stones because there were no more big ones near enough by. He worked without a halt, afraid that he would drop in a faint of exhaustion if he allowed himself to relax even for an instant, and that he might lie there until he was found by somebody. When the stones were nearly level with the gunwale, he shoved the boat off and rocked it, more and more, until water slopped in at the sides. As the boat began to sink, he gave it a shove toward deeper water, shoved and walked with it until the water was up to his waist, and the boat sank below his reach. Then he plowed his way back to the shore and lay down for a while, face down on the sand. He began to plan his return to the hotel, and his story, and his next moves: leaving San Remo before nightfall, getting back to Mongibello. And the story there.

13.

AT sundown, just the hour when the Italians and everybody else in the village had gathered at the sidewalk tables of the cafés, freshly showered and dressed, staring at everybody and everything that passed by, eager for whatever entertainment the town could offer, Tom walked into the village wearing only his swimming shorts and sandals and Dickie's corduroy jacket, and carrying his slightly bloodstained trousers and jacket under his arm. He walked with a languid casualness because he was exhausted, though he kept his head up for the benefit of the hundreds of people who stared at him as he walked past the cafés, the only route to his beachfront hotel. He had fortified himself with five espressos full of sugar and three brandies at a bar on the road just outside of San Remo. Now he was playing the role of an athletic young man who had spent the afternoon in and out of the water because it was his peculiar taste, being a good swimmer and impervious to cold, to swim until late afternoon on a chilly day. He made it to the hotel, collected the key at the desk, went up to his room and collapsed on the bed. He would allow himself an hour to rest, he thought, but he must not fall asleep lest he sleep longer. He rested, and when he felt himself falling asleep, got up and went to the basin and wet his face, took a wet towel back to his bed simply to waggle in his hand to keep from falling asleep.

Finally he got up and went to work on the blood smear on one leg of his corduroy trousers. He scrubbed it over and over with soap and a nailbrush, got tired and stopped for a while to pack the suitcase. He packed Dickie's things just as Dickie had always packed them, toothpaste and toothbrush in the back left pocket. Then he went back to finish the trouser leg. His own jacket had too much blood on it ever to be worn again, and he would have to get rid of it, but he could wear Dickie's jacket, because it was the same beige color and almost identical in size. Tom had had his suit copied from Dickie's, and it had been made by the same tailor in Mongibello. He put his own jacket into the suitcase. Then he went down with the suitcase and asked for his bill.

The man behind the desk asked where his friend was, and Tom said he was meeting him at the railroad station. The clerk was pleasant and smiling, and wished Tom "Buon' viaggio."

Tom stopped in at a restaurant two streets away and forced himself to eat a bowl of minestrone for the strength it would give him. He kept an eye out for the Italian who owned the boats. The main thing, he thought, was to leave San Remo tonight, take a taxi to the next town, if there was no train or bus.

There was a train south at ten twenty-four, Tom learned at the railroad station. A sleeper. Wake up tomorrow in Rome, and change trains for Naples. It seemed absurdly simple and easy suddenly, and in a burst of self-assurance he thought of going to Paris for a few days.

" 'Spetta un momento," he said to the clerk who was ready to hand him his ticket. Tom walked around his suitcase, thinking of Paris. Overnight. Just to see it, for two days, for instance. It wouldn't matter whether he told Marge or not. He decided abruptly against Paris. He wouldn't be able to relax. He was too eager to get to Mongibello and see about Dickie's belongings.

The white, taut sheets of his berth on the train seemed the most wonderful luxury he had ever known. He caressed them with his hands before he turned the light out. And the clean blue-gray blankets, the spanking efficiency of the little black net over his head—Tom had an ecstatic moment when he thought of all the pleasures that lay before him now with Dickie's money, other beds, tables, seas, ships, suitcases, shirts, years of freedom, years of pleasure. Then he turned the light out and put his head down and almost at once fell asleep, happy, content, and utterly, utterly confident, as he had never been before in his life.

In Naples he stopped in the men's room of the railway station and removed Dickie's toothbrush and hairbrush from the suitcase, and rolled them up in Dickie's raincoat together with his own corduroy jacket and Dickie's blood-spotted trousers. He took the bundle across the street from the station and pressed it into a huge burlap bag of garbage that leaned against an alley wall. Then he breakfasted on caffe latte and a sweet roll at a café on the bus-stop square, and boarded the old eleven o'clock bus for Mongibello.

He stepped off the bus almost squarely in front of Marge, who was in her bathing suit and the loose white jacket she always wore to the beach.

"Where's Dickie?" she asked.

"He's in Rome." Tom smiled easily, absolutely prepared. "He's staying up there for a few days. I came down to get some of his stuff to take up to him."

"Is he staying with somebody?"

"No, just in a hotel." With another smile that was half a good-bye, Tom started up the hill with his suitcase. A moment later he heard Marge's cork-soled sandals trotting after him. Tom waited. "How's everything been in our home sweet home?" he asked.

"Oh, dull. As usual." Marge smiled. She was ill at ease with him. But she followed him into the house—the gate was unlocked, and Tom got the big iron key to the terrace door from its usual place, back of a rotting wooden tub that held earth and a half-dead shrub—and they went onto the terrace together. The table had been moved a little. There was a book on the glider. Marge had been here since they left, Tom thought. He had been gone only three days and nights. It seemed to him that he had been away for a month.

"How's Skippy?" Tom asked brightly, opening the refrigerator, getting out an ice tray. Skippy was a stray dog Marge had acquired a few days ago, an ugly black-and-white bastard that Marge pampered and fed like a doting old maid.

"He went off. I didn't expect him to stay."

"Oh."

"You look like you've had a good time," Marge said, a little wistfully.

"We did." Tom smiled. "Can I fix you a drink?"

"No, thanks. How long do you think Dickie's going to be away?"

"Well—" Tom frowned thoughtfully. "I don't really know. He says he wants to see a lot of art shows up there. I think he's just enjoying a change of scene." Tom poured himself a generous gin and added soda and a lemon slice. "I suppose he'll be back in a week. By the way!" Tom reached for the suitcase, and took out the box of cologne. He had removed the shop's wrapping paper, because it had had blood smears on it. "Your Stradivari. We got it in San Remo."

"Oh, thanks—very much." Marge took it, smiling, and began to open it, carefully, dreamily.

Tom strolled tensely around the terrace with his drink, not saying a word to Marge, waiting for her to go.

"Well—" Marge said finally, coming out on the terrace. "How long are you staying?"

"Where?"

"Here."

"Just overnight. I'll be going up to Rome tomorrow. Probably in the afternoon," he added, because he couldn't get the mail tomorrow until perhaps after two.

"I don't suppose I'll see you again, unless you're at the beach," Marge said with an effort at friendliness. "Have a good time in case I don't see you. And tell Dickie to write a postcard. What hotel is he staying at?"

"Oh—uh—what's the name of it? Near the Piazza di Spagna?"

"The Inghilterra?"

"That's it. But I think he said to use the American Express as a mailing address." She wouldn't try to telephone Dickie, Tom thought. And he could be at the hotel tomorrow to pick up a letter if she wrote. "I'll probably go down to the beach tomorrow morning," Tom said.

"All right. Thanks for the cologne."

"Don't mention it!"

She walked down the path to the iron gate, and out.

Tom picked up the suitcase and ran upstairs to Dickie's bedroom. He slid Dickie's top drawer out: letters, two address books, a couple of little notebooks, a watchchain, loose keys, and some kind of insurance policy. He slid the other drawers out, one by one, and left them open. Shirts, shorts, folded sweaters and disordered socks. In the corner of the room a sloppy mountain of portfolios and old drawing pads. There was a lot to be done. Tom took off all his clothes, ran downstairs naked and took a quick, cool shower, then put on

Dickie's old white duck trousers that were hanging on a nail in the closet.

He started with the top drawer, for two reasons: the recent letters were important in case there were current situations that had to be taken care of immediately, and also because, in case Marge happened to come back this afternoon, it wouldn't look as if he were dismantling the entire house so soon. But at least he could begin, even this afternoon, packing Dickie's biggest suitcases with his best clothes, Tom thought.

Tom was still pottering about the house at midnight. Dickie's suitcases were packed, and now he was assessing how much the house furnishings were worth, what he would bequeath to Marge, and how he would dispose of the rest. Marge could have the damned refrigerator. That ought to please her. The heavy carved chest in the foyer, which Dickie used for his linens, ought to be worth several hundred dollars, Tom thought. Dickie had said it was four hundred years old, when Tom had asked him about it. Cinquecento. He intended to speak to Signor Pucci, the assistant manager of the Miramare, and ask him to act as agent for the sale of the house and the furniture. And the boat, too. Dickie had told him that Signor Pucci did jobs like that for residents of the village.

He had wanted to take all of Dickie's possessions straight away to Rome, but in view of what Marge might think about his taking so much for presumably such a short time, he decided it would be better to pretend that Dickie had later made a decision to move to Rome.

Accordingly, Tom went down to the post office around three the next afternoon, claimed one uninteresting letter for Dickie from a friend in America and nothing for himself, but as he walked slowly back to the house again he imagined that he was reading a letter from Dickie. He imagined the exact words, so that he could quote them to Marge, if he had to, and he even made himself feel the slight surprise he would have felt at Dickie's change of mind.

As soon as he got home he began packing Dickie's best drawings and best linens into the big cardboard box he had gotten from Aldo at the grocery store on the way up the hill. He worked calmly and methodically, expecting Marge to drop in at any minute, but it was after four before she came.

"Still here?" she asked as she came into Dickie's room.

"Yes. I had a letter from Dickie today. He's decided he's going to move to Rome." Tom straightened up and smiled a little, as if it were a surprise to him, too. "He wants me to pick up all his things, all I can handle."

"*Move* to Rome? For how long?"

"I don't know. The rest of the winter apparently, anyway." Tom went on tying canvases.

"He's not coming back all winter?" Marge's voice sounded lost already.

"No. He said he might even sell the house. He said he hadn't decided yet."

"Gosh!—What happened?"

Tom shrugged. "He apparently wants to spend the winter in Rome. He said he was going to write to you. I thought you might have gotten a letter this afternoon, too."

"No."

Silence. Tom kept on working. It occurred to him that he hadn't packed up his own things at all. He hadn't even been into his room.

"He's still going to Cortina, isn't he?" Marge asked.

"No, he's not. He said he was going to write to Freddie and cancel it. But that shouldn't prevent your going." Tom watched her. "By the way, Dickie said he wants you to take the refrigerator. You can probably get somebody to help you move it."

The present of the refrigerator had no effect at all on Marge's stunned face. Tom knew she was wondering whether he was going to live with Dickie or not, and that she was probably concluding, because of his cheerful manner, that he was going to live with him. Tom felt the question creeping up to her lips—she was as transparent as a child to him—then she asked: "Are you going to stay with him in Rome?"

"Maybe for a while. I'll help him get settled. I want to go to Paris this month, then I suppose around the middle of December I'll be going back to the States."

Marge looked crestfallen. Tom knew she was imagining the lonely weeks ahead—even if Dickie did make periodic little visits to Mongibello to see her—the empty Sunday mornings, the lonely dinners. "What's he going to do about Christmas? Do you think he wants to have it here or in Rome?"

Tom said with a trace of irritation, "Well, I don't think here. I have the feeling he wants to be alone."

Now she was shocked to silence, shocked and hurt. Wait till she got the letter he was going to write from Rome, Tom thought. He'd be gentle with her, of course, as gentle as Dickie, but there would be no mistaking that Dickie didn't want to see her again.

A few minutes later, Marge stood up and said good-bye in an absent-minded way. Tom suddenly felt that she might be going to telephone Dickie today. Or maybe even go up to Rome. But what if she did? Dickie could have changed his hotel. And there were enough hotels in Rome to keep her busy for days, even if she came to Rome to find him. When she didn't find him, by telephone or by coming to Rome, she would suppose that he had gone to Paris or to some other city with Tom Ripley.

Tom glanced over the newspaper from Naples for an item about a scuttled boat's having been found near San Remo. *Barca affondata vicino San Remo,* the caption would probably say. And they would make a great to-do over the bloodstains in the boat, if the bloodstains were still there. It was the kind of thing the Italian newspapers loved to write up in their melodramatic journalese: "Giorgio di Stefani, a young fisherman of San Remo, yesterday at three o'clock in the afternoon made a most terrible discovery in two meters of water. A little motorboat, its interior covered with horrible bloodstains . . ." But Tom did not see anything in the paper. Nor had there been anything yesterday. It might take months for the boat to be found, he thought. It might never be found. And if they did find it, how could they know that Dickie Greenleaf and Tom Ripley had taken the boat out together? They had not told their names to the Italian boatkeeper at San Remo. The boatkeeper had given them only a little orange ticket which Tom had had in his pocket, and had later found and destroyed.

Tom left Mongibello by taxi around six o'clock, after an espresso at Giorgio's, where he said good-bye to Giorgio,

Fausto, and several other village acquaintances of his and Dickie's. To all of them he told the same story, that Signor Greenleaf was staying in Rome for the winter, and that he sent his greetings until he saw them again. Tom said that undoubtedly Dickie would be down for a visit before long.

He had had Dickie's linens and paintings crated by the American Express that afternoon, and the boxes sent to Rome along with Dickie's trunk and two heavier suitcases, to be claimed in Rome by Dickie Greenleaf. Tom took his own two suitcases and one other of Dickie's in the taxi with him. He had spoken to Signor Pucci at the Miramare, and had said that there was a possibility that Signor Greenleaf would want to sell his house and furniture, and could Signor Pucci handle it? Signor Pucci had said he would be glad to. Tom had also spoken to Pietro, the dockkeeper, and asked him to be on the lookout for someone who might want to buy the *Pipistrello*, because there was a good chance that Signor Greenleaf would want to get rid of it this winter. Tom said that Signor Green-leaf would let it go for five hundred thousand lire, hardly eight hundred dollars, which was such a bargain for a boat that slept two people, Pietro thought he could sell it in a matter of weeks.

On the train to Rome Tom composed the letter to Marge so carefully that he memorized it in the process, and when he got to the Hotel Hassler he sat down at Dickie's Hermes Baby, which he had brought in one of Dickie's suitcases, and wrote the letter straight off.

Rome
November 28, 19——

Dear Marge,

I've decided to take an apartment in Rome for the winter, just to have a change of scene and get away from old Mongy for a while. I feel a terrific urge to be by myself. I'm sorry it was so sudden and that I didn't get a chance to say good-bye, but actually I'm not far away, and I hope I'll be seeing you now and then. I just didn't feel like going back to pack my stuff, so I threw the burden on Tom.

As to us, it can't harm anything and possibly may improve every-thing if we don't see each other for a while. I had a terrible feeling I was boring you, though you weren't boring *me*, and please don't think I am running away from anything. On the contrary, Rome should bring me closer to reality. Mongy certainly didn't. Part of my discontent was you. My going away doesn't solve anything, of course, but it will help me to discover how I really feel about you. For this reason, I prefer not to see you for a while, darling, and I hope you'll understand. If you don't—well, you don't, and that's the risk I run. I may go up to Paris for a couple of weeks with Tom, as he's dying to go. That is, unless I start painting right away. Met a painter named Di Massimo whose work I like very much, an old fellow without much money who seems to be very glad to have me as a student if I pay him a little bit. I am going to paint with him in his studio.

The city looks marvelous with its fountains going all night and everybody up all night, contrary to old Mongy. You were on the wrong track about Tom. He's going back to the States soon and I don't care when, though he's really not a bad guy and I don't dislike him. He has nothing to do with us, anyway, and I hope you realize that.

Write me c/o American Express, Rome until I know where I am. Shall let you know when I find an apartment. Meanwhile keep the home fires burning, the refrigerators working and your typewriter also. I'm terribly sorry about Xmas, darling, but I don't think I should see you that soon, and you can hate me or not for that.

All my love,
Dickie

Tom had kept his cap on since entering the hotel, and he had given Dickie's passport in at the desk instead of his own, though hotels, he had noticed, never looked at the passport photo, only copied the passport number which was on the front cover. He had signed the register with Dickie's hasty and rather flamboyant signature with the big looping capitals R and G. When he went out to mail the letter he walked to a drugstore several streets away and bought a few items of make-up that he thought he might need. He had fun with the Italian salesgirl, making her think that he was buying them for his wife who had lost her make-up kit, and who was in-disposed in the hotel with the usual upset stomach.

He spent that evening practicing Dickie's signature for the bank checks. Dickie's monthly remittance was going to arrive from America in less than ten days.

14.

HE moved the next day to the Hotel Europa, a moderately priced hotel near the Via Veneto, because the Hassler was a trifle flashy, he thought, the kind of hotel that was patronized by visiting movie people, and where Freddie Miles, or people like him who knew Dickie, might choose to stay if they came to Rome.

Tom held imaginary conversations with Marge and Fausto and Freddie in his hotel room. Marge was the most likely to come to Rome, he thought. He spoke to her as Dickie, if he imagined it on the telephone, and as Tom, if he imagined her face to face with him. She might, for instance, pop up to Rome and find his hotel and insist on coming up to his room, in which case he would have to remove Dickie's rings and change his clothing.

"I don't know," he would say to her in Tom's voice. "You know how he is—likes to feel he's getting away from everything. He said I could use his hotel room for a few days, because mine happens to be so badly heated. . . . Oh, he'll be back in a couple of days, or there'll be a postcard from him saying he's all right. He went to some little town with Di Massimo to look at some paintings in a church."

("But you don't know whether he went north or south?")

"I really don't. I guess south. But what good does that do us?"

("It's just my bad luck to miss him, isn't it? Why couldn't he at least have said where he was going?")

"I know. I asked him, too. Looked the room over for a map or anything else that might have shown where he was going. He just called me up three days ago and said I could use his room if I cared to."

It was a good idea to practice jumping into his own character again, because the time might come when he would need to in a matter of seconds, and it was strangely easy to forget the exact timbre of Tom Ripley's voice. He conversed with Marge until the sound of his own voice in his ears was exactly the same as he remembered it.

But mostly he was Dickie, discoursing in a low tone with

Freddie and Marge, and by long distance with Dickie's mother, and with Fausto, and with a stranger at a dinner party, conversing in English and Italian, with Dickie's portable radio turned on so that if a hotel employee passed by in the hall and happened to know that Signor Greenleaf was alone he would not think him an eccentric. Sometimes, if the song on the radio was one that Tom liked, he merely danced by himself, but he danced as Dickie would have with a girl—he had seen Dickie once on Giorgio's terrace, dancing with Marge, and also in the Giardino degli Orangi in Naples—in long strides yet rather stiffly, not what could be called exactly good dancing. Every moment to Tom was a pleasure, alone in his room or walking the streets of Rome, when he combined sightseeing with looking around for an apartment. It was impossible ever to be lonely or bored, he thought, so long as he was Dickie Greenleaf.

They greeted him as Signor Greenleaf at the American Express, where he called for his mail. Marge's first letter said:

Dickie,

Well, it was a bit of a surprise. I wonder what came over you so suddenly in Rome or San Remo or wherever it was? Tom was most mysterious except to say that he would be staying with you. I'll believe he's leaving for America when I see it. At the risk of sticking my neck out, old boy, may I say that *I* don't like that guy? From my point of view or anybody else's he is using you for what you are worth. If you want to make some changes for your own good, for gosh sakes get *him* away from you. All right, he may not be queer. He's just a nothing, which is worse. He isn't normal enough to have *any* kind of sex life, if you know what I mean. However I'm not interested in Tom but in you. Yes, I can bear the few weeks without you, darling, and even Christmas, though I prefer not to think of Christmas. I prefer not to think about you and—as you said—let the feelings come or not. But it's impossible not to think of you here because every inch of the village is haunted with you as far as I'm concerned, and in this house, everywhere I look there is some sign of you, the hedge we planted, the fence we started repairing and never finished, the books I borrowed from you and never returned. And your chair at the table, that's the worst.

To continue with the neck-sticking, I don't say that Tom is going to do anything actively bad to you, but I know that he has a subtly bad influence on you. You act vaguely ashamed of being around him when you *are* around him, do you know that? Did you ever try to analyze it? I thought you were beginning to realize all this in the last few weeks, but now you're with him again and frankly, dear boy, I don't know what to make of it. If you really "don't care when" he takes off, for God's sake send him packing! He'll never help you or anybody else to get straightened out about anything. In fact it's greatly to his interest to keep you muddled and string you along and your father, too.

Thanks loads for the cologne, darling. I'll save it—or most of it—for when I see you next. I haven't got the refrigerator over to my house yet. You can have it, of course, any time you want it back.

Maybe Tom told you that Skippy skipped out. Should I capture a gecko and tie a string around its neck? I have to get to work on the house wall right away before it mildews completely and collapses on me. Wish you were here, darling—of course.

Lots of love and *write*,

XX
Marge

c/o American Express
Rome
Dec. 12, 19——

Dear Mother and Dad,

I'm in Rome looking for an apartment, though I haven't found exactly what I want yet. Apartments here are either too big or too small, and if too big you have to shut off every room but one in winter in order to heat it properly anyway. I'm trying to get a medium-sized, medium-priced place that I can heat completely without spending a fortune for it.

Sorry I've been so bad about letters lately. I hope to do better with the quieter life I'm leading here. I felt I needed a change from Mongibello—as you've both been saying for a long time—so I've moved bag and baggage and may even sell the house and the boat. I've met a wonderful painter called Di Massimo who is willing to give me instruction in his studio. I'm going to work like blazes for a few months and see what happens. A kind of trial period. I realize this doesn't interest you, Dad, but since you're always asking how I spend my time, this is how. I'll be leading a very quiet, studious life until next summer.

Apropos of that, could you send me the latest folders from Burke-Greenleaf? I like to keep up with what you're doing, too, and it's been a long time since I've seen anything.

Mother, I hope you haven't gone to great trouble for my Christmas. I don't really need anything I can think of. How are you feeling? Are you able to get out very much? To the theatre, etc.? How is Uncle Edward now? Send him my regards and keep me posted.

With love,
Dickie

Tom read it over, decided there were probably too many commas, and retyped it patiently and signed it. He had once seen a half-finished letter of Dickie's to his parents in Dickie's typewriter, and he knew Dickie's general style. He knew that Dickie had never taken more than ten minutes writing any letter. If this letter was different, Tom thought, it could be different only in being a little more personal and enthusiastic than usual. He felt rather pleased with the letter when he read it over for the second time. Uncle Edward was a brother of Mrs. Greenleaf, who was ill in an Illinois hospital with some kind of cancer, Tom had learned from the latest letter to Dickie from his mother.

A few days later he was off to Paris by plane. He had called the Inghilterra before he left Rome: no letters or phone calls for Richard Greenleaf. He landed at Orly at five in the afternoon. The passport inspector stamped his passport after only a quick glance at him, though Tom had lightened his hair slightly with a peroxide wash and had forced some waves into it, aided by hair oil, and for the inspector's benefit he had put on the rather tense, rather frowning expression of Dickie's passport photograph. Tom checked in at the Hôtel du Quai-Voltaire, which had been recommended to him by some Americans with whom he had struck up an acquaintance at a Rome café, as being conveniently located and not too full of Americans. Then he went out for a stroll in the raw, foggy December evening. He walked with his head up and a smile on his face. It was the atmosphere of the city that he loved, the atmosphere that he had always heard about, crooked streets, gray-fronted houses with skylights, noisy car horns, and everywhere public urinals and columns with brightly colored theatre notices on them. He wanted to let the atmosphere seep in slowly, perhaps for several days, before he visited the Louvre or went up in the Eiffel Tower or anything like that. He bought a *Figaro*, sat down at a table in the Dôme, and ordered a fine à l'eau, because Dickie had once said that fine à l'eau was his usual drink in France. Tom's French was limited, but so was Dickie's, Tom knew. Some interesting people stared at him through the glass-enclosed front of the café, but no one came in to speak to him. Tom was prepared for someone to get up from one of the tables at any moment, and come over and say, "Dickie Greenleaf! Is it really you?"

He had done so little artificially to change his appearance, but his very expression, Tom thought, was like Dickie's now. He wore a smile that was dangerously welcoming to a stranger, a smile more fit to greet an old friend or a lover. It was Dickie's best and most typical smile when he was in a good humor. Tom was in a good humor. It was Paris. *Wonderful* to sit in a famous café, and to think of tomorrow and tomorrow and tomorrow being Dickie Greenleaf! The cuff links, the white silk shirts, even the old clothes—the worn brown belt with the brass buckle, the old brown grain-leather shoes, the kind advertised in *Punch* as lasting a lifetime, the old mustard-colored coat sweater with the sagging pockets, they were all his and he loved them all. And the black fountain pen with little gold initials. And the wallet, a well-worn alligator wallet from Gucci's. And there was plenty of money to go in it.

By the next afternoon he had been invited to a party in the Avenue Kléber by some people—a French girl and an American young man—with whom he had started a conversation in a large café-restaurant on the Boulevard Saint-Germain. The party consisted of thirty or forty people, most of them middle-aged, standing around rather frigidly in a huge, chilly, formal apartment. In Europe, Tom gathered, inadequate heating was a hallmark of chic in winter, like the iceless martini in summer. He had moved to a more expensive hotel in Rome, finally, in order to be warmer, and had found that the more expensive hotel was even colder. In a gloomy, old-fashioned way the house was chic, Tom supposed. There were a butler and a maid, a vast table of pâtés en croûte, sliced turkey, and petits fours, and quantities of champagne, although the upholstery of the sofa and the long drapes at the windows were threadbare and rotting with age, and he had seen mouseholes in the hall by the elevator. At least half a dozen of the guests he had been presented to were counts and countesses. An

American informed Tom that the young man and the girl who had invited him were going to be married, and that her parents were not enthusiastic. There was an atmosphere of strain in the big room, and Tom made an effort to be as pleasant as possible to everyone, even the severer-looking French people, to whom he could say little more than "C'est très agréable, n'est-ce pas?" He did his very best, and won at least a smile from the French girl who had invited him. He considered himself lucky to be there. How many Americans alone in Paris could get themselves invited to a French home after only a week or so in the city? The French were especially slow in inviting strangers to their homes, Tom had always heard. Not a single one of the Americans seemed to know his name. Tom felt completely comfortable, as he had never felt before at any party that he could remember. He behaved as he had always wanted to behave at a party. This was the clean slate he had thought about on the boat coming over from America. This was the real annihilation of his past and of himself, Tom Ripley, who was made up of that past, and his rebirth as a completely new person. One Frenchwoman and two of the Americans invited him to parties, but Tom declined with the same reply to all of them: "Thank you very much, but I'm leaving Paris tomorrow."

It wouldn't do to become too friendly with any of these, Tom thought. One of them might know somebody who knew Dickie very well, someone who might be at the next party.

At eleven-fifteen, when he said good-bye to his hostess and to her parents, they looked very sorry to see him go. But he wanted to be at Notre Dame by midnight. It was Christmas Eve.

The girl's mother asked his name again.

"Monsieur Granelafe," the girl repeated for her. "Deekie Granelafe. Correct?"

"Correct," Tom said, smiling.

Just as he reached the downstairs hall he remembered Freddie Miles' party at Cortina. December second. Nearly a month ago! He had meant to write to Freddie to say that he wasn't coming. Had Marge gone, he wondered? Freddie would think it very strange that he hadn't written to say he wasn't coming, and Tom hoped Marge had told Freddie, at least. He must write Freddie at once. There was a Florence address for Freddie in Dickie's address book. It was a slip, but nothing serious, Tom thought. He just mustn't let such a thing happen again.

He walked out into the darkness and turned in the direction of the illuminated, bone-white Arc de Triomphe. It was strange to feel so alone, and yet so much a part of things, as he had felt at the party. He felt it again, standing on the outskirts of the crowd that filled the square in front of Notre Dame. There was such a crowd he couldn't possibly have got into the cathedral, but the amplifiers carried the music clearly to all parts of the square. French Christmas carols whose names he didn't know. "Silent Night." A solemn carol, and then a lively, babbling one. The chanting of male voices. Frenchmen near him removed their hats. Tom removed his. He stood tall and straight, sober-faced, yet ready to smile if anyone had addressed him. He felt as he had felt on the ship, only more intensely, full of good will, a gentleman, with nothing in his past to blemish his character. He was Dickie, good-natured, naïve Dickie, with a smile for everyone and a thousand francs for anyone who asked him. An old man did ask him for money as Tom was leaving the cathedral square, and he gave him a crisp blue thousand-franc bill. The old man's face exploded in a smile, and he tipped his hat.

Tom felt a little hungry, though he rather liked the idea of going to bed hungry tonight. He would spend an hour or so with his Italian conversation book, he thought, then go to bed. Then he remembered that he had decided to try to gain about five pounds, because Dickie's clothes were just a trifle loose on him and Dickie looked heavier than he in the face, so he stopped at a bar-tabac and ordered a ham sandwich on long crusty bread and a glass of hot milk, because a man next to him at the counter was drinking hot milk. The milk was almost tasteless, pure and chastening, as Tom imagined a wafer tasted in church.

He came down in a leisurely way from Paris, stopping overnight in Lyon and also in Arles to see the places that Van Gogh had painted there. He maintained his cheerful equanimity in the face of atrociously bad weather. In Arles, the rain borne on the violent mistral soaked him through as he tried to discover the exact spots where Van Gogh had stood to paint from. He had bought a beautiful book of Van Gogh reproductions in Paris, but he could not take the book out in the rain, and he had to make a dozen trips back to his hotel to verify the scenes. He looked over Marseille, found it drab except for the Cannebière, and moved on eastward by train, stopping for a day in St. Tropez, Cannes, Nice, Monte Carlo, all the places he had heard of and felt such affinity for when he saw them, though in the month of December they were overcast by gray winter clouds, and the gay crowds were not there, even on New Year's Eve in Menton. Tom put the people there in his imagination, men and women in evening clothes descending the broad steps of the gambling palace in Monte Carlo, people in bright bathing costumes, light and brilliant as a Dufy watercolor, walking under the palms of the Boulevard des Anglais at Nice. People—American, English, French, German, Swedish, Italian. Romance, disappointment, quarrels, reconciliations, murder. The Côte d'Azur excited him as no other place he had yet seen in the world excited him. And it was so tiny, really, this curve in the Mediterranean coastline with the wonderful names strung like beads— Toulon, Fréjus, St. Rafaël, Cannes, Nice, Menton, and then San Remo.

There were two letters from Marge when he got back to Rome on the fourth of January. She was giving up her house on the first of March, she said. She had not quite finished the first draft of her book, but she was sending three-quarters of it with all the photographs to the American publisher who had been interested in her idea when she wrote him about it last summer. She wrote:

When am I going to see you? I hate passing up a summer in Europe after I've weathered another awful winter, but I think I'll go home early in March. Yes, I'm *homesick*, finally, *really*. Darling, it would be so wonderful if we could go home on the same boat together. Is there a possibility? I don't suppose there *is*. You're not going back to the U.S. even for a short visit this winter?

I was thinking of sending all my stuff (eight pieces of luggage, two trunks, three boxes of books and miscellaneous!) by slow boat from Naples and coming up through Rome and if you were in the mood we could at least go up the coast again and see Forte dei Marmi and

Viareggio and the other spots we like—a last look. I'm not in the
mood to care about the weather, which I know will be *horrid*. I
wouldn't ask you to accompany me to Marseille, where I catch the
boat, but from *Genoa*??? What do you think? . . .

The other letter was more reserved. Tom knew why: he had
not sent her even a postcard for nearly a month. She said:

Have changed my mind about the Riviera. Maybe this damp
weather has taken away my enterprise or my book has. Anyway, I'm
leaving from Naples on an earlier boat—the *Constitution* on Feb.
28th. Imagine—back to America as soon as I step aboard. American
food, Americans, dollars for drinks and the horseraces— Darling, I'm
sorry not to be seeing you, as I gather from your silence you still
don't want to see me, so don't give it a thought. Consider me off
your hands.

Of course I do hope I see you again, in the States or anywhere
else. Should you possibly be inspired to make a trip down to Mongy
before the 28th, you know damned well you are welcome.

As ever,

Marge

P.S. I don't even know if you're still in Rome.

Tom could see her in tears as she wrote it. He had an impulse to write her a very considerate letter, saying he had just
come back from Greece, and had she gotten his two post-
cards? But it was safer, Tom thought, to let her leave without
being sure where he was. He wrote her nothing.

The only thing that made him uneasy, and that was not
very uneasy, was the possibility of Marge's coming up to see
him in Rome before he could get settled in an apartment. If
she combed the hotels she could find him, but she could never
find him in an apartment. Well-to-do Americans didn't have
to report their places of residence at the questura, though,
according to the stipulations of the Permesso di Soggiorno,
one was supposed to register every change of address with the
police. Tom had talked with an American resident of Rome
who had an apartment and who had said he never bothered
with the questura, and it never bothered him. If Marge did
come up to Rome suddenly, Tom had a lot of his own

clothing hanging ready in the closet. The only thing he had changed about himself, physically, was his hair, but that could always be explained as being the effect of the sun. He wasn't really worried. Tom had at first amused himself with an eyebrow pencil—Dickie's eyebrows were longer and turned up a little at the outer edges—and with a touch of putty at the end of his nose to make it longer and more pointed, but he abandoned these as too likely to be noticed. The main thing about impersonation, Tom thought, was to maintain the mood and temperament of the person one was impersonating, and to assume the facial expressions that went with them. The rest fell into place.

On the tenth of January Tom wrote Marge that he was back in Rome after three weeks in Paris alone, that Tom had left Rome a month ago, saying he was going up to Paris and from there to America though he hadn't run into Tom in Paris, and that he had not yet found an apartment in Rome but he was looking and would let her know his address as soon as he had one. He thanked her extravagantly for the Christmas package: she had sent the white sweater with the red V stripes that she had been knitting and trying on Dickie for size since October, as well as an art book of quattrocento painting and a leather shaving kit with his initials, H.R.G., on the lid. The package had arrived only on January sixth, which was the main reason for Tom's letter: he didn't want her to think he hadn't claimed it, imagine that he had vanished into thin air, and then start a search for him. He asked if she had received a package from him? He had mailed it from Paris, and he supposed it was late. He apologized. He wrote:

I'm painting again with Di Massimo and am reasonably pleased. I miss you, too, but if you can still bear with my experiment, I'd prefer not to see you for several more weeks (unless you do suddenly go home in February, which I still doubt!) by which time you may not care to see me again. Regards to Giorgio and wife and Fausto if he's still there and Pietro down at the dock . . .

It was a letter in the absent-minded and faintly lugubrious tone of all Dickie's letters, a letter that could not be called warm or unwarm, and that said essentially nothing.

Actually he had found an apartment in a large apartment

house in the Via Imperiale near the Pincian Gate, and had signed a year's lease for it, though he did not intend to spend most of his time in Rome, much less the winter. He only wanted a home, a base somewhere, after years of not having any. And Rome was chic. Rome was part of his new life. He wanted to be able to say in Majorca or Athens or Cairo or wherever he was: "Yes, I live in Rome. I keep an apartment there." "Keep" was the word for apartments among the international set. You kept an apartment in Europe the way you kept a garage in America. He also wanted his apartment to be elegant, though he intended to have the minimum of people up to see him, and he hated the idea of having a telephone, even an unlisted telephone, but he decided it was more of a safety measure than a menace, so he had one installed. The apartment had a large living room, a bedroom, a kind of sitting room, kitchen, and bath. It was furnished somewhat ornately, but it suited the respectable neighborhood and the respectable life he intended to lead. The rent was the equivalent of a hundred and seventy-five dollars a month in winter including heat, and a hundred and twenty-five in summer.

Marge replied with an ecstatic letter saying she had just received the beautiful silk blouse from Paris which she hadn't expected *at all* and it fitted to perfection. She said she had had Fausto and the Cecchis for Christmas dinner at her house and the turkey had been divine, with marrons and giblet gravy and plum pudding and blah blah blah and everything but *him*. And what was he doing and thinking about? And was he happier? And that Fausto would look him up on his way to Milan if he sent an address in the next few days, otherwise leave a message for Fausto at the American Express, saying where Fausto could find him.

Tom supposed her good humor was due mostly to the fact that she now thought Tom had departed for America via Paris. Along with Marge's letter came one from Signor Pucci, saying that he had sold three pieces of his furniture for a hundred and fifty thousand lire in Naples, and that he had a prospective buyer for the boat, a certain Anastasio Martino of Mongibello, who had promised to pay the first down payment within a week, but that the house probably couldn't be sold until summer when the Americans began coming in again. Less fifteen per cent for Signor Pucci's commission, the furniture sale amounted to two hundred and ten dollars, and Tom celebrated that night by going to a Roman nightclub and ordering a superb dinner which he ate in elegant solitude at a candlelit table for two. He did not at all mind dining and going to the theatre alone. It gave him the opportunity to concentrate on being Dickie Greenleaf. He broke his bread as Dickie did, thrust his fork into his mouth with his left hand as Dickie did, gazed off at the other tables and at the dancers in such a profound and benevolent trance that the waiter had to speak to him a couple of times to get his attention. Some people waved to him from a table, and Tom recognized them as one of the American couples he had met at the Christmas Eve party in Paris. He made a sign of greeting in return. He even remembered their name, Souders. He did not look at them again during the evening, but they left before he did and stopped by his table to say hello.

"All by yourself?" the man asked. He looked a little tipsy.

"Yes. I have a yearly date here with myself," Tom replied. "I celebrate a certain anniversary."

The American nodded a little blankly, and Tom could see that he was stymied for anything intelligent to say, as uneasy as any small-town American in the presence of cosmopolitan poise and sobriety, money and good clothes, even if the clothes were on another American.

"You said you were living in Rome, didn't you?" his wife asked. "You know, I think we've forgotten your name, but we remember you very well from Christmas Eve."

"Greenleaf," Tom replied. "Richard Greenleaf."

"*Oh*, yes!" she said, relieved. "Do you have an apartment here?"

She was all ready to take down his address in her memory. "I'm staying at a hotel at the moment, but I'm planning to move into an apartment any day, as soon as the decorating's finished. I'm at the Elisio. Why don't you give me a ring?"

"We'd love to. We're on our way to Majorca in three more days, but that's plenty of time!"

"Love to see you," Tom said. "Buona sera!"

Alone again, Tom returned to his private reveries. He ought to open a bank account for Tom Ripley, he thought, and from

time to time put a hundred dollars or so into it. Dickie Greenleaf had two banks, one in Naples and one in New York, with
about five thousand dollars in each account. He might open
the Ripley account with a couple of thousand, and put into it
the hundred and fifty thousand lire from the Mongibello furniture. After all, he had two people to take care of.

15.

HE visited the Capitoline and the Villa Borghese, explored
the Forum thoroughly, and took six Italian lessons from an
old man in his neighborhood who had a tutoring sign in his
window, and to whom Tom gave a false name. After the sixth
lesson, Tom thought that his Italian was on a par with
Dickie's. He remembered verbatim several sentences that
Dickie had said at one time or another which he now knew
were incorrect. For example, "Ho paura che non c'e arrivata,
Giorgio," one evening in Giorgio's, when they had been waiting for Marge and she had been late. It should have been "sia
arrivata" in the subjunctive after an expression of fearing.
Dickie had never used the subjunctive as often as it should be
used in Italian. Tom studiously kept himself from learning the
proper uses of the subjunctive.

Tom bought dark red velvet for the drapes in his living
room, because the drapes that had come with the apartment
offended him. When he had asked Signora Buffi, the wife of
the house superintendent, if she knew of a seamstress who
could make them up, Signora Buffi had offered to make them
herself. Her price was two thousand lire, hardly more than
three dollars. Tom forced her to take five thousand. He
bought several minor items to embellish his apartment,
though he never asked anyone up—with the exception of one
attractive but not very bright young man, an American, whom
he had met in the Café Greco when the young man had asked
him how to get to the Hotel Excelsior from there. The
Excelsior was on the way to Tom's house, so Tom asked him
to come up for a drink. Tom had only wanted to impress him
for an hour and then say good-bye to him forever, which he

did, after serving him his best brandy and strolling about his apartment discoursing on the pleasures of life in Rome. The young man was leaving for Munich the following day.

Tom carefully avoided the American residents of Rome who might expect him to come to their parties and ask them to his in return, though he loved to chat with Americans and Italians in the Café Greco and in the students' restaurants in the Via Margutta. He told his name only to an Italian painter named Carlino, whom he met in a Via Margutta tavern, told him also that he painted and was studying with a painter called Di Massimo. If the police ever investigated Dickie's activities in Rome, perhaps long after Dickie had disappeared and become Tom Ripley again, this one Italian painter could be relied upon to say that he knew Dickie Greenleaf had been painting in Rome in January. Carlino had never heard of Di Massimo, but Tom described him so vividly that Carlino would probably never forget him.

He felt alone, yet not at all lonely. It was very much like the feeling on Christmas Eve in Paris, a feeling that everyone was watching him, as if he had an audience made up of the entire world, a feeling that kept him on his mettle, because to make a mistake would be catastrophic. Yet he felt absolutely confident he would not make a mistake. It gave his existence a peculiar, delicious atmosphere of purity, like that, Tom thought, which a fine actor probably feels when he plays an important role on a stage with the conviction that the role he is playing could not be played better by anyone else. He was himself and yet not himself. He felt blameless and free, despite the fact that he consciously controlled every move he made. But he no longer felt tired after several hours of it, as he had at first. He had no need to relax when he was alone. Now, from the moment when he got out of bed and went to brush his teeth, he was Dickie, brushing his teeth with his right elbow jutted out, Dickie rotating the eggshell on his spoon for the last bite, Dickie invariably putting back the first tie he pulled off the rack and selecting a second. He had even produced a painting in Dickie's manner.

By the end of January Tom thought that Fausto must have come and gone through Rome, though Marge's last letters had not mentioned him. Marge wrote, care of the American

Express, about once a week. She asked if he needed any socks or a muffler, because she had plenty of time to knit, besides working on her book. She always put in a funny anecdote about somebody they knew in the village, just so Dickie wouldn't think she was eating her heart out for him, though obviously she was, and obviously she wasn't going to leave for the States in February without making another desperate try for him in person, Tom thought, hence the investments of the long letters and the knitted socks and muffler which Tom knew were coming, even though he hadn't replied to her letters. Her letters repelled him. He disliked even touching them, and after he glanced through them he tore them up and dropped them into the garbage.

He wrote finally:

I'm giving up the idea of an apartment in Rome for the time being. Di Massimo is going to Sicily for several months, and I may go with him and go on somewhere from there. My plans are vague, but they have the virtue of freedom and they suit my present mood.

Don't send me any socks, Marge. I really don't need a thing. Wish you much luck with "Mongibello."

He had a ticket for Majorca—by train to Naples, then the boat from Naples to Palma over the night of January thirty-first and February first. He had bought two new suitcases from Gucci's, the best leather goods store in Rome, one a large, soft suitcase of antelope hide, the other a neat tan canvas with brown leather straps. Both bore Dickie's initials. He had thrown the shabbier of his own two suitcases away, and the remaining one he kept in a closet of his apartment, full of his own clothes, in case of an emergency. But Tom was not expecting any emergencies. The scuttled boat in San Remo had never been found. Tom looked through the papers every day for something about it.

While Tom was packing his suitcases one morning his doorbell rang. He supposed it was a solicitor of some kind, or a mistake. He had no name on his doorbell, and had told the superintendent that he did not want his name on the doorbell because he didn't like people to drop in on him. It rang for the second time, and Tom still ignored it, and went on with his lackadaisical packing. He loved to pack, and he took a long time about it, a whole day or two days, laying Dickie's clothes affectionately into suitcases, now and then trying on a good-looking shirt or a jacket in front of the mirror. He was standing in front of the mirror, buttoning a blue-and-white seahorse-patterned sport shirt of Dickie's that he had never worn, when there came a knock at his door.

It crossed his mind that it might be Fausto, that it would be just like Fausto to hunt him down in Rome and try to surprise him.

That was silly, he told himself. But his hands were cool with sweat as he went to the door. He felt faint, and the absurdity of his faintness, plus the danger of keeling over and being found prostrate on the floor, made him wrench the door open with both hands, though he opened it only a few inches.

"Hello!" the American voice said out of the semidarkness of the hall. "Dickie? It's Freddie!"

Tom took a step back, holding the door open. "He's— Won't you come in? He's not here right now. He should be back a little later."

Freddie Miles came in, looking around. His ugly, freckled face gawked in every direction. How in hell had he found the place, Tom wondered. Tom slipped his rings off quickly and pocketed them. And what else? He glanced around the room.

"You're staying with him?" Freddie asked with that wall-eyed stare that made his face look idiotic and rather scared.

"Oh, no. I'm just staying here for a few hours," Tom said, casually removing the seahorse shirt. He had another shirt on under it. "Dickie's out for lunch. Otello's, I think he said. He should be back around three at the latest." One of the Buffis must have let Freddie in, Tom thought, and told him which bell to press, and told him Signor Greenleaf was in, too. Freddie had probably said he was an old friend of Dickie's. Now he would have to get Freddie out of the house without running into Signora Buffi downstairs, because she always sang out, "Buon' giorno, Signor Greenleaf!"

"I met you in Mongibello, didn't I?" Freddie asked. "Aren't you Tom? I thought you were coming to Cortina."

"I couldn't make it, thanks. How was Cortina?"

"Oh, fine. What happened to Dickie?"

"Didn't he write to you? He decided to spend the winter in Rome. He told me he'd written to you."

"Not a word—unless he wrote to Florence. But I was in Salzburg, and he had my address." Freddie half sat on Tom's long table, rumpling the green silk runner. He smiled. "Marge told me he'd moved to Rome, but she didn't have any address except the American Express. It was only by the damnedest luck I found his apartment. I ran into somebody at the Greco last night who just happened to know his address. What's his idea of—"

"Who?" Tom asked. "An American?"

"No, an Italian fellow. Just a young kid." Freddie was looking at Tom's shoes. "You've got the same kind of shoes Dickie and I have. They wear like iron, don't they? I bought my pair in London eight years ago."

They were Dickie's grain-leather shoes. "These came from America," Tom said. "Can I offer you a drink or would you rather try to catch Dickie at Otello's? Do you know where it is? There's not much use in your waiting, because he generally takes till three with his lunches. I'm going out soon myself."

Freddie had strolled toward the bedroom and stopped, looking at the suitcases on the bed. "Is Dickie leaving for somewhere or did he just get here?" Freddie asked, turning.

"He's leaving. Didn't Marge tell you? He's going to Sicily for a while."

"When?"

"Tomorrow. Or late tonight, I'm not quite sure."

"Say, what's the matter with Dickie lately?" Freddie asked, frowning. "What's the idea of all the seclusion?"

"He says he's been working pretty hard this winter," Tom said in an offhand tone. "He seems to want privacy, but as far as I know he's still on good terms with everybody, including Marge."

Freddie smiled again, unbuttoning his big polo coat. "He's not going to stay on good terms with me if he stands me up a few more times. Are you sure he's on good terms with Marge? I got the idea from her that they'd had a quarrel. I thought maybe that was why they didn't go to Cortina." Freddie looked at him expectantly.

"Not that I know of." Tom went to the closet to get his jacket, so that Freddie would know he wanted to leave, then realized just in time that the gray flannel jacket that matched his trousers might be recognizable as Dickie's, if Freddie knew Dickie's suit. Tom reached for a jacket of his own and for his own overcoat that were hanging at the extreme left of the closet. The shoulders of the overcoat looked as if the coat had been on a hanger for weeks, which it had. Tom turned around and saw Freddie staring at the silver identification bracelet on his left wrist. It was Dickie's bracelet, which Tom had never seen him wearing, but had found in Dickie's stud box. Freddie was looking at it as if he had seen it before. Tom put on his overcoat casually.

Freddie was looking at him now with a different expression, with a little surprise. Tom knew what Freddie was thinking. He stiffened, sensing danger. You're not out of the woods yet, he told himself. You're not out of the house yet.

"Ready to go?" Tom asked.

"You do live here, don't you?"

"No!" Tom protested, smiling. The ugly, freckle-blotched face stared at him from under the garish thatch of red hair. If they could only get out without running into Signora Buffi downstairs, Tom thought. "Let's go."

"Dickie's loaded you up with all his jewelry, I see."

Tom couldn't think of a single thing to say, a single joke to make. "Oh, it's a loan," Tom said in his deepest voice. "Dickie got tired of wearing it, so he told me to wear it for a while." He meant the identification bracelet, but there was also the silver clip on his tie, he realized, with the G on it. Tom had bought the tieclip himself. He could feel the belligerence growing in Freddie Miles as surely as if his huge body were generating a heat that he could feel across the room. Freddie was the kind of ox who might beat up somebody he thought was a pansy, especially if the conditions were as propitious as these. Tom was afraid of his eyes.

"Yes, I'm ready to go," Freddie said grimly, getting up. He walked to the door and turned with a swing of his broad shoulders. "That's the Otello not far from the Inghilterra?"

"Yes," Tom said. "He's supposed to be there by one o'clock."

Freddie nodded. "Nice to see you again," he said unpleasantly, and closed the door.

Tom whispered a curse. He opened the door slightly and listened to the quick *tap-tap—tap-tap* of Freddie's shoes descending the stairs. He wanted to make sure Freddie got out without speaking to one of the Buffis again. Then he heard Freddie's "Buon' giorno, signora." Tom leaned over the stairwell. Three stories down, he could see part of Freddie's coatsleeve. He was talking in Italian with Signora Buffi. The woman's voice came more clearly.

". . . only Signor Greenleaf," she was saying. "No, only one. . . . Signor Chi? . . . No, signor. . . . I do not think he has gone out today at all, but I could be wrong!" She laughed.

Tom twisted the stair rail in his hands as if it were Freddie's neck. Then Tom heard Freddie's footsteps running up the stairs. Tom stepped back into the apartment and closed the door. He could go on insisting that he didn't live here, that Dickie was at Otello's, or that he didn't know where Dickie was, but Freddie wouldn't stop now until he had found Dickie. Or Freddie would drag him downstairs and ask Signora Buffi who he was.

Freddie knocked on the door. The knob turned. It was locked.

Tom picked up a heavy glass ashtray. He couldn't get his hand across it, and he had to hold it by the edge. He tried to think just for two seconds more: wasn't there another way out? What would he do with the body? He couldn't think. This was the only way out. He opened the door with his left hand. His right hand with the ashtray was drawn back and down.

Freddie came into the room. "Listen, would you mind telling—"

The curved edge of the ashtray hit the middle of his forehead. Freddie looked dazed. Then his knees bent and he went down like a bull hit between the eyes with a hammer. Tom kicked the door shut. He slammed the edge of the ashtray into the back of Freddie's neck. He hit the neck again and again, terrified that Freddie might be only pretending and that one of his huge arms might suddenly circle his legs and pull him down. Tom struck his head a glancing blow, and blood came. Tom cursed himself. He ran and got a towel from the bathroom and put it under Freddie's head. Then he felt Freddie's wrist for a pulse. There was one, faint, and it seemed to flutter away as he touched it as if the pressure of his own fingers stilled it. In the next second it was gone. Tom listened for any sound behind the door. He imagined Signora Buffi standing behind the door with the hesitant smile she always had when she felt she was interrupting. But there wasn't any sound. There hadn't been any loud sound, he thought, either from the ashtray or when Freddie fell. Tom looked down at Freddie's mountainous form on the floor and felt a sudden disgust and a sense of helplessness.

It was only twelve-forty, hours until dark. He wondered if Freddie had people waiting for him anywhere? Maybe in a car downstairs? He searched Freddie's pockets. A wallet. The American passport in the inside breast pocket of the overcoat. Mixed Italian and some other kind of coins. A keycase. There were two car keys on a ring that said FIAT. He searched the wallet for a license. There it was, with all the particulars: FIAT 1400 nero–convertible–1955. He could find it if it was in the neighborhood. He searched every pocket, and the pockets in the buff-colored vest, for a garage ticket, but he found none. He went to the front window, then nearly smiled because it was so simple: there stood the black convertible across the street almost directly in front of the house. He could not be sure, but he thought there was no one in it.

He suddenly knew what he was going to do. He set about arranging the room, bringing out the gin and vermouth bottles from his liquor cabinet, and on second thought the pernod because it smelled so much stronger. He set the bottles on the long table and mixed a martini in a tall glass with a couple of ice cubes in it, drank a little of it so that the glass would be soiled, then poured some of it into another glass, took it over to Freddie and crushed his limp fingers around it and carried it back to the table. He looked at the wound, and found that it had stopped bleeding or was stopping and had not run through the towel onto the floor. He propped Freddie up against the wall, and poured some straight gin from the bottle down his throat. It didn't go down very well, most of it went onto his shirtfront, but Tom didn't think the Italian police would actually make a blood test to see how drunk Freddie had been. Tom let his eyes rest absently on Freddie's limp, messy face for a moment, and his stomach contracted sickeningly and he quickly looked away. He mustn't do that again. His head had begun ringing as if he were going to faint.

That'd be a fine thing, Tom thought as he wobbled across the room toward the window, to faint now! He frowned at the black car down below, and breathed the fresh air in deeply. He wasn't going to faint, he told himself. He knew exactly what he was going to do. At the last minute, the pernod, for both of them. Two other glasses with their fingerprints and pernod. And the ashtrays must be full. Freddie smoked Chesterfields. Then the Appian Way. One of those dark places behind the tombs. There weren't any street lights for long stretches on the Appian Way. Freddie's wallet would be missing. Objective: robbery.

He had hours of time, but he didn't stop until the room was ready, the dozen lighted Chesterfields and the dozen or so Lucky Strikes burnt down and stabbed out in the ashtrays, and a glass of pernod broken and only half cleaned up from the bathroom tiles, and the curious thing was that as he set his scene so carefully, he pictured having hours more time to clean it up—say between nine this evening when the body might be found, and midnight, when the police just might decide he was worth questioning, because somebody just might have known that Freddie Miles was going to call on Dickie Greenleaf today—and he knew that he *would* have it all cleaned up by eight o'clock, probably, because according to the story he was going to tell, Freddie would have left his house by seven (as indeed Freddie was going to leave his house by seven), and Dickie Greenleaf was a fairly tidy young man, even with a few drinks in him. But the point of the messy house was that the messiness substantiated merely for his own benefit the story that he was going to tell, and that therefore he had to believe himself.

And he would still leave for Naples and Palma at ten-thirty tomorrow morning, unless for some reason the police detained him. If he saw in the newspaper tomorrow morning that the body had been found, and the police did not try to contact him, it was only decent that he should volunteer to tell them that Freddie Miles had been at his house until late afternoon, Tom thought. But it suddenly occurred to him that a doctor might be able to tell that Freddie had been dead since noon. And he couldn't get Freddie out now, not in broad daylight. No, his only hope was that the body wouldn't be found for so many hours that a doctor couldn't tell exactly how long he had been dead. And he must try to get out of the house without *anybody* seeing him—whether he could carry Freddie down with a fair amount of ease like a passed-out drunk or not—so that if he had to make any statement, he could say that Freddie left the house around four or five in the afternoon.

He dreaded the five- or six-hour wait until nightfall so much that for a few moments he thought he *couldn't* wait. That mountain on the floor! And he hadn't wanted to kill him at all. It had been so unnecessary. Freddie and his stinking, filthy suspicions. Tom was trembling, sitting on the edge of a chair cracking his knuckles. He wanted to go out and take a walk, but he was afraid to leave the body lying here. There had to be noise, of course, if he and Freddie were supposed to be talking and drinking all afternoon. Tom turned the radio on to a station that played dance music. He could have a drink, at least. That was part of the act. He made another couple of martinis with ice in the glass. He didn't even want it, but he drank it.

The gin only intensified the same thoughts he had had. He stood looking down at Freddie's long, heavy body in the polo coat that was crumpled under him, that he hadn't the energy or the heart to straighten out, though it annoyed him, and thinking how sad, stupid, clumsy, dangerous and unnecessary his death had been, and how brutally unfair to Freddie. Of course, one could loathe Freddie, too. A selfish, stupid bastard, who had sneered at one of his best friends—Dickie certainly was one of his best friends—just because he suspected him of sexual deviation. Tom laughed at that phrase "sexual deviation." Where was the sex? Where was the deviation? He looked at Freddie and said low and bitterly: "Freddie Miles, you're a victim of your own dirty mind."

16.

HE waited after all until nearly eight, because around seven there were always more people coming in and out of the house than at other times. At ten to eight, he strolled downstairs to make sure that Signora Buffi was not pottering around in the hall and that her door was not open, and to make sure there really was no one in Freddie's car, though he had gone down in the middle of the afternoon to look at the car and see if it was Freddie's. He tossed Freddie's polo coat into the back seat. He came back upstairs, knelt down and pulled Freddie's arm around his neck, set his teeth, and lifted. He staggered, jerking the flaccid weight higher on his shoulder. He had lifted Freddie earlier that afternoon, just to see if he could, and he had seemed barely able to walk two steps in the room with Freddie's pounds pressing his own feet against the floor, and Freddie was exactly as heavy now, but the difference was that he knew he had to get him out now. He let Freddie's feet drag to relieve some of his weight, managed to pull his door shut with his elbow, then began to descend the stairs. Halfway down the first flight, he stopped, hearing someone come out of an apartment on the second floor. He waited until the person had gone down the stairs and out the front door, then recommenced his slow, bumping descent. He had pulled a hat of Dickie's well down over Freddie's head so that the bloodstained hair would not show. On a mixture of gin and pernod, which he had been drinking for the last hour, Tom had gotten himself to a precisely calculated state of intoxication in which he thought he could move with a certain nonchalance and smoothness and at the same time be courageous and even foolhardy enough to take chances without flinching. The first chance, the worst thing that could happen, was that he might simply collapse under Freddie's weight before he got him to the car. He had sworn that he would not stop to rest going down the stairs. He didn't. And nobody else came out of any of the apartments, and nobody came in the front door. During the hours upstairs, Tom had imagined so tortuously everything that might happen—Signora Buffi or her husband coming out of their apartment just as he reached

the bottom of the stairs, or himself fainting so that both he
and Freddie would be discovered sprawled on the stairs together, or being unable to pick Freddie up again if he had to
put him down to rest—imagined it all with such intensity,
writhing upstairs in his apartment, that to have descended all
the stairs without a single one of his imaginings happening
made him feel he was gliding down under a magical protection of some kind, with ease in spite of the mass on his
shoulder.

He looked out the glass of the two front doors. The street
looked normal: a man was walking on the opposite sidewalk,
but there was always someone walking on one sidewalk or the
other. He opened the first door with one hand, kicked it aside
and dragged Freddie's feet through. Between the doors, he
shifted Freddie to the other shoulder, rolling his head under
Freddie's body, and for a second a certain pride went through
him at his own strength, until the ache in his relaxing arm
staggered him with its pain. The arm was too tired even to
circle Freddie's body. He set his teeth harder and staggered
down the four front steps, banging his hip against the stone
newel post.

A man approaching him on the sidewalk slowed his steps
as if he were going to stop, but he went on.

If anyone came over, Tom thought, he would blow such a
breath of pernod in his face there wouldn't be any reason to
ask what was the matter. Damn them, damn them, damn
them, he said to himself as he jolted down the curb. Passersby,
innocent passersby. Four of them now. But only two of them
so much as glanced at him, he thought. He paused a moment
for a car to pass. Then with a few quick steps and a heave he
thrust Freddie's head and one shoulder through the open
window of the car, far enough in that he could brace Freddie's
body with his own body while he got his breath. He looked
around, under the glow of light from the street lamp across
the street, into the shadows in front of his own apartment
house. At that instant the Buffis' youngest boy ran out the
door and down the sidewalk without looking in Tom's direction. Then a man crossing the street walked within a yard of
the car with only a brief and faintly surprised look at Freddie's
bent figure, which did look almost natural now, Tom thought,

practically as if Freddie were only leaning into the car talking to someone, only he really *didn't* look quite natural, Tom knew. But that was the advantage of Europe, he thought. Nobody helped anybody, nobody meddled. If this had been America—

"Can I help you?" a voice asked in Italian.

"Ah, no, no, grazie," Tom replied with drunken good cheer. "I know where he lives," he added in mumbled English.

The man nodded, smiling a little, too, and walked on. A tall thin man in a thin overcoat, hatless, with a mustache. Tom hoped he wouldn't remember. Or remember the car.

Tom swung Freddie out on the door, pulled him around the door and onto the car seat, came around the car and pulled Freddie into the seat beside the driver's seat. Then he put on the pair of brown leather gloves he had stuck into his overcoat pocket. He put Freddie's key into the dashboard. The car started obediently. They were off. Down the hill to the Via Veneto, past the American Library, over to the Piazza Venezia, past the balcony on which Mussolini used to stand to make his speeches, past the gargantuan Victor Emmanuel Monument and through the Forum, past the Colosseum, a grand tour of Rome that Freddie could not appreciate at all. It was just as if Freddie were sleeping beside him, as sometimes people did sleep when you wanted to show them scenery.

The Via Appia Antica stretched out before him, gray and ancient in the soft lights of its infrequent lamps. Black fragments of tombs rose up on either side of the road, silhouetted against the still not quite dark sky. There was more darkness than light. And only a single car ahead, coming this way. Not many people chose to take a ride on such a bumpy, gloomy road after dark in the month of January. Except perhaps lovers. The approaching car passed him. Tom began to look around for the right spot. Freddie ought to have a handsome tomb to lie behind, he thought. There was a spot ahead with three or four trees near the edge of the road and doubtless a tomb behind them, or part of a tomb. Tom pulled off the road by the trees and shut off his lights. He waited a moment, looking at both ends of the straight, empty road.

THE TALENTED MR. RIPLEY   287

Freddie was still as limp as a rubber doll. What was all this about rigor mortis? He dragged the limp body roughly now, scraping the face in the dirt, behind the last tree and behind the little remnant of tomb that was only a four-feet-high, jagged arc of wall, but which was probably a remnant of the tomb of a patrician, Tom thought, and quite good enough for this pig. Tom cursed his ugly weight and kicked him suddenly in the chin. He was tired, tired to the point of crying, sick of the sight of Freddie Miles, and the moment when he could turn his back on him for the last time seemed never to come. There was still the God-damned coat! Tom went back to the car to get it. The ground was hard and dry, he noticed as he walked back, and should not leave any traces of his steps. He flung the coat down beside the body and turned away quickly and walked back to the car on his numb, staggering legs, and turned the car around toward Rome again.

As he drove, he wiped the outside of the car door with his gloved hand to get the fingerprints off, the only place he had touched the car before he put his gloves on, he thought. On the street that curved up to the American Express, opposite the Florida nightclub, he parked the car and got out and left it with the keys in the dashboard. He still had Freddie's wallet in his pocket, though he had transferred the Italian money to his own billfold and had burnt a Swiss twenty-frank note and some Austrian schilling notes in his apartment. Now he took the wallet out of his pocket, and as he passed a sewer grate he leaned down and dropped it in.

There were only two things wrong, he thought as he walked toward his house: robbers would logically have taken the polo coat, because it was a good one, and also the passport, which was still in the overcoat pocket. But not every robber was logical, he thought, maybe especially an Italian robber. And not every murderer was logical, either. His mind drifted back to the conversation with Freddie. *". . . an Italian fellow. Just a young kid . . ."* Somebody had followed him home at some time, Tom thought, because he hadn't told *anybody* where he lived. It shamed him. Maybe two or three delivery boys might know where he lived, but a delivery boy wouldn't be sitting in a place like the Café Greco. It shamed him and made him shrink inside his overcoat. He imagined a dark, panting young face following him home, staring up to see which window had lighted up after he had gone in. Tom hunched in his overcoat and walked faster, as if he were fleeing a sick, passionate pursuer.

17.

TOM went out before eight in the morning to buy the papers. There was nothing. They might not find him for days, Tom thought. Nobody was likely to walk around an unimportant tomb like the one he had put Freddie behind. Tom felt quite confident of his safety, but physically he felt awful. He had a hangover, the terrible, jumpy kind that made him stop halfway in everything he began doing, even stop halfway in brushing his teeth to go and see if his train really left at ten-thirty or at ten-forty-five. It left at ten-thirty.

He was completely ready by nine, dressed and with his overcoat and raincoat out on the bed. He had even spoken to Signora Buffi to tell her he would be gone for at least three weeks and possibly longer. Signora Buffi had behaved just as usual, Tom thought, and had not mentioned his American visitor yesterday. Tom tried to think of something to ask her, something quite normal in view of Freddie's questions yesterday, that would show him what Signora Buffi really thought about the questions, but he couldn't think of anything, and decided to let well enough alone. Everything was fine. Tom tried to reason himself out of the hangover, because he had had only the equivalent of three martinis and three pernods at most. He knew it was a matter of mental suggestion, and that he had a hangover because he had intended to pretend that he had been drinking a great deal with Freddie. And now when there was no need of it, he was still pretending, uncontrollably.

The telephone rang, and Tom picked it up and said "Pronto" sullenly.

"Signor Greenleaf?" asked the Italian voice.

"Si."

"Qui parla la stazione polizia numero ottantatre. Lei e un amico di un' americano chi se chiama Fred-derick Mee-lays?"

"Frederick Miles? Si," Tom said.

The quick, tense voice stated that the corpse of Fred-derick Mee-lays had been found that morning on the Via Appia Antica, and that Signor Mee-lays had visited him at some time yesterday, was that not so?

"Yes, that is so."

"At what time exactly?"

"From about noon to—perhaps five or six in the afternoon, I am not quite sure."

"Would you be kind enough to answer some questions? . . . No, it is not necessary that you trouble yourself to come to the station. The interrogator will come to you. Will eleven o'clock this morning be convenient?"

"I'll be very glad to help if I can," Tom said in a properly excited voice, "but can't the interrogator come now? It is necessary for me to leave the house at ten o'clock."

The voice made a little moan and said it was doubtful, but they would try it. If they could not come before ten o'clock, it was very important that he should not leave the house.

"Va bene," Tom said acquiescently, and hung up.

Damn them! He'd miss his train *and* boat now. All he wanted to do was get out, leave Rome and leave his apartment. He started to go over what he would tell the police. It was all so simple, it bored him. It was the absolute truth. They had had drinks, Freddie had told him about Cortina, they had talked a lot, and then Freddie had left, maybe a little high but in a very good mood. No, he didn't know where Freddie had been going. He had supposed Freddie had a date for the evening.

Tom went into the bedroom and put a canvas, which he had begun a few days ago, on the easel. The paint on the palette was still moist because he had kept it under water in a pan in the kitchen. He mixed some more blue and white and began to add to the grayish-blue sky. The picture was still in Dickie's bright reddish-browns and clear whites—the roofs and walls of Rome out his window. The sky was the only departure, because the winter sky of Rome was so gloomy, even Dickie would have painted it grayish-blue instead of blue, Tom thought. Tom frowned, just as Dickie frowned when he painted.

The telephone rang again.

"God damn it!" Tom muttered, and went to answer it. "Pronto!"

"Pronto! Fausto!" the voice said. "Come sta?" And the familiar bubbling, juvenile laugh.

"Oh-h! Fausto! Bene, grazie! Excuse me," Tom continued in Italian in Dickie's laughing, absent voice, "I've been trying to paint—trying." It was calculated to be possibly the voice of Dickie after having lost a friend like Freddie, and also the voice of Dickie on an ordinary morning of absorbing work.

"Can you have lunch?" Fausto asked. "My train leaves at four-fifteen for Milano."

Tom groaned, like Dickie. "I'm just taking off for Naples. Yes, immediately, in twenty minutes!" If he could escape Fausto now, he thought, he needn't let Fausto know that the police had called him at all. The news about Freddie wouldn't be in the papers until noon or later.

"But I'm here! In Roma! Where's your house? I'm at the railroad station!" Fausto said cheerfully, laughing.

"Where'd you get my telephone number?"

"Ah! allora, I called up information. They told me you didn't give the number out, but I told the girl a long story about a lottery you won in Mongibello. I don't know if she believed me, but I made it sound very important. A house and a cow and a well and even a refrigerator! I had to call her back three times, but finally she gave it to me. Allora, Deekie, where are you?"

"That's not the point. I'd have lunch with you if I didn't have this train, but—"

"Va bene, I'll help you carry your bags! Tell me where you are and I'll come over with a taxi for you!"

"The time's too short. Why don't I see you at the railroad station in about half an hour? It's the ten-thirty train for Naples."

"Okay!"

"How is Marge?"

"Ah—inamorata di te," Fausto said, laughing. "Are you going to see her in Naples?"

"I don't think so. I'll see you in a few minutes, Fausto. Got to hurry. Arrividerch."

" 'Rividerch, Deekie! Addio!" He hung up.

When Fausto saw the papers this afternoon, he would un-derstand why he hadn't come to the railroad station, other-wise Fausto would just think they had missed each other somehow. But Fausto probably would see the papers by noon, Tom thought, because the Italian papers would play it up big—the murder of an American on the Appian Way. After the interview with the police, he would take another train to Naples—after four o'clock, so Fausto wouldn't be still around the station—and wait in Naples for the next boat to Majorca.

He only hoped that Fausto wouldn't worm the address out of information, too, and decide to come over before four o'clock. He hoped Fausto wouldn't land here just when the police were here.

Tom shoved a couple of suitcases under the bed, and carried the other to a closet and shut the door. He didn't want the police to think he was just about to leave town. But what was he so nervous about? They probably hadn't any clues. Maybe a friend of Freddie's had known that Freddie was going to try to see him yesterday, that was all. Tom picked up a brush and moistened it in the turpentine cup. For the benefit of the police, he wanted to look as if he was not too upset by the news of Freddie's death to do a little painting while he waited for them, though he was dressed to go out, because he had said he intended to go out. He was going to be a friend of Freddie's, but not too close a friend.

Signora Buffi let the police in at ten-thirty. Tom looked down the stairwell and saw them. They did not stop to ask her any questions. Tom went back into his apartment. The spicy smell of turpentine was in the room.

There were two: an older man in the uniform of an officer, and a younger man in an ordinary police uniform. The older man greeted him politely and asked to see his passport. Tom produced it, and the officer looked sharply from Tom to the picture of Dickie, more sharply than anyone had ever looked at it before, and Tom braced himself for a challenge, but there was none. The officer handed him the passport with a little bow and a smile. He was a short, middle-aged man who looked like thousands of other middle-aged Italians, with heavy gray-and-black eyebrows and a short, bushy gray-and-black mustache. He looked neither particularly bright nor stupid.

"How was he killed?" Tom asked.

"He was struck on the head and in the neck by some heavy instrument," the officer replied, "and robbed. We think he was drunk. Was he drunk when he left your apartment yesterday afternoon?"

"Well—somewhat. We had both been drinking. We were drinking martinis and pernod."

The officer wrote it down in his tablet, and also the time that Tom said Freddie had been there, from about twelve until about six.

The younger policeman, handsome and blank of face, was strolling around the apartment with his hands behind him, bending close to the easel with a relaxed air as if he were alone in a museum.

"Do you know where he was going when he left?" the officer asked.

"No, I don't."

"But you thought he was able to drive?"

"Oh, yes. He was not too drunk to drive or I would have gone with him."

The officer asked another question that Tom pretended not quite to grasp. The officer asked it a second time, choosing different words, and exchanged a smile with the younger officer. Tom glanced from one to the other of them, a little resentfully. The officer wanted to know what his relationship to Freddie had been.

"A friend," Tom said. "Not a very close friend. I had not seen or heard from him in about two months. I was terribly upset to hear about the disaster this morning." Tom let his anxious expression make up for his rather primitive vocabulary. He thought it did. He thought the questioning was very perfunctory, and that they were going to leave in another minute or so. "At exactly what time was he killed?" Tom asked.

The officer was still writing. He raised his bushy eyebrows. "Evidently just after the signor left your house, because the doctors believe that he had been dead at least twelve hours, perhaps longer."

"At what time was he found?"

"At dawn this morning. By some workmen who were walking along the road."

"Dio mio!" Tom murmured.

"He said nothing about making an excursion yesterday to the Via Appia when he left your apartment?"

"No," Tom said.

"What did you do yesterday after Signor Mee-lays left?"

"I stayed here," Tom said, gesturing with open hands as Dickie would have done, "and then I had a little sleep, and later I went out for a walk around eight or eight-thirty." A man who lived in the house, whose name Tom didn't know, had seen him come in last night at about a quarter to nine, and they had said good evening to each other.

"You took a walk alone?"

"Yes."

"And Signor Mee-lays left here alone? He was not going to meet anybody that you know of?"

"No. He didn't say so." Tom wondered if Freddie had had friends with him at his hotel, or wherever he had been staying? Tom hoped that the police wouldn't confront him with any of Freddie's friends who might know Dickie. Now his name—Richard Greenleaf—would be in the Italian newspapers, Tom thought, and also his address. He'd have to move. It was hell. He cursed to himself. The police officer saw him, but it looked like a muttered curse against the sad fate that had befallen Freddie, Tom thought.

"So—" the officer said, smiling, and closed his tablet.

"You think it was—" Tom tried to think of the word for hoodlum "—violent boys, don't you? Are there any clues?"

"We are searching the car for fingerprints now. The murderer may have been somebody he picked up to give a ride to. The car was found this morning in the vicinity of the Piazza di Spagna. We should have some clues before tonight. Thank you very much, Signor Greenleaf."

"Di niente! If I can be of any further assistance—"

The officer turned at the door. "Shall we be able to reach you here for the next few days, in case there are any more questions?"

Tom hesitated. "I was planning to leave for Majorca tomorrow."

"But the questions may be, who is such-and-such a person who is a suspect," the officer explained. "You may be able to tell us who the person is in relation to the deceased." He gestured.

"All right. But I do not think I knew Signor Miles that well. He probably had closer friends in the city."

"Who?" The officer closed the door and took out his tablet.

"I don't know," Tom said. "I only know he must have had several friends here, people who knew him better than I did."

"I am sorry, but we still must expect you to be in reach for the next couple of days," he repeated quietly, as if there were no question of Tom's arguing about it, even if he was an American. "We shall inform you as soon as you may go. I am sorry if you have made travel plans. Perhaps there is still time to cancel them. Good day, Signor Greenleaf."

"Good day." Tom stood there after they had closed the door. He could move to a hotel, he thought, if he told the police what hotel it was. He didn't want Freddie's friends or any friends of Dickie's calling on him after they saw his address in the newspapers. He tried to assess his behavior from the polizia's point of view. They hadn't challenged him on anything. He had not acted horrified at the news of Freddie's death, but that jibed with the fact that he was not an especially close friend of Freddie's, either. No, it wasn't bad, except that he had to be on tap.

The telephone rang, and Tom didn't answer it, because he had a feeling that it was Fausto calling from the railroad station. It was eleven-five, and the train for Naples would have departed. When the phone stopped ringing, Tom picked it up and called the Inghilterra. He reserved a room, and said he would be there in about an hour. Then he called the police station—he remembered that it was number eighty-three—and after nearly ten minutes of difficulties because he couldn't find anyone who knew or cared who Richard Greenleaf was, he succeeded in leaving a message that Signor Richard Greenleaf could be found at the Albergo Inghilterra, in case the police wanted to speak to him.

He was at the Inghilterra before an hour was up. His three suitcases, two of them Dickie's and one his own, depressed him: he had packed them for such a different purpose. And now this!

He went out at noon to buy the papers. Every one of the papers had it: AMERICANO MURDERED ON THE VIA APPIA ANTICA . . . SHOCKING MURDER OF RICCISSIMO AMERICANO FREDERICK MILES LAST NIGHT ON THE VIA APPIA . . . VIA APPIA MURDER OF AMERICANO WITHOUT CLUES . . . Tom read every word. There really were no clues, at least not yet, no tracks, no fingerprints, no suspects. But every paper carried the name Herbert Richard Greenleaf and gave his address as the place where Freddie had last been seen by anybody. Not one of the papers implied that Herbert Richard Greenleaf was under suspicion, however. The papers said that Miles had apparently had a few drinks and the drinks, in typical Italian journalistic style, were all enumerated and ran from americanos through Scotch whisky, brandy, champagne, even grappa. Only gin and pernod were omitted.

Tom stayed in his hotel room over the lunch hour, walking the floor and feeling depressed and trapped. He telephoned the travel office in Rome that had sold him his ticket to Palma, and tried to cancel it. He could have twenty per cent of his money back, they said. There was not another boat to Palma for about five days.

Around two o'clock his telephone rang urgently.

"Hello," Tom said in Dickie's nervous, irritable tone.

"Hello, Dick. This is Van Houston."

"Oh-h," Tom said, as if he knew him, yet the single word conveyed no excess of surprise or warmth.

"How've you been? It's been a long time, hasn't it?" the hoarse, strained voice asked.

"Certainly has. Where are you?"

"At the Hassler. I've been going over Freddie's suitcases with the police. Listen, I want to see you. What was the matter with Freddie yesterday? I tried to find you all last evening, you know, because Freddie was supposed to be back at the hotel by six. I didn't have your address. What happened yesterday?"

"I wish I knew! Freddie left the house around six. We both had taken on quite a lot of martinis, but he looked capable of driving or naturally I wouldn't have let him go off. He said he had his car downstairs. I can't imagine what happened, except that he picked up somebody to give them a lift, and they pulled a gun on him or something."

"But he wasn't killed by a gun. I agree with you somebody must have forced him to drive out there, or he blotted out, because he'd have had to get clear across town to get to the Appian Way. The Hassler's only a few blocks from where you live."

"Did he ever black out before? At the wheel of a car?"

"Listen, Dickie, can I see you? I'm free now, except that I'm not supposed to leave the hotel today."

"Neither am I."

"Oh, come on. Leave a message where you are and come over."

"I can't, Van. The police are coming over in about an hour and I'm supposed to be here. Why don't you call me later? Maybe I can see you tonight."

"All right. What time?"

"Call me around six."

"Right. Keep your chin up, Dickie."

"You too."

"See you," the voice said weakly.

Tom hung up. Van had sounded as if he were about to cry at the last. "Pronto?" Tom said, clicking the telephone to get the hotel operator. He left a message that he was not in to anybody except the police, and that they were to let nobody up to see him. Positively no one.

After that the telephone did not ring all afternoon. At about eight, when it was dark, Tom went downstairs to buy the evening papers. He looked around the little lobby and into the hotel bar whose door was off the main hall, looking for anybody who might be Van. He was ready for anything, ready even to see Marge sitting there waiting for him, but he saw no one who looked even like a police agent. He bought the evening papers and sat in a little restaurant a few streets away, reading them. Still no clues. He learned that Van Houston was a close friend of Freddie's, aged twenty-eight, traveling with him from Austria to Rome on a holiday that was to have ended in Florence, where both Miles and Houston had residences, the papers said. They had questioned three Italian youths, two of them eighteen and one sixteen, on suspicion of having done the "horrible deed," but the youths had been later released. Tom was relieved to read that no fingerprints that could be considered fresh or usable had been found on Miles' "bellissimo Fiat 1400 convertibile."

Tom ate his costoletta di vitello slowly, sipped his wine, and glanced through every column of the papers for the last-minute items that were sometimes put into Italian papers just before they went to press. He found nothing more on the Miles case. But on the last page of the last newspaper he read:

BARCA AFFONDATA CON MACCHIE DI SANGUE TROVATA NELL' ACQUA POCO FONDO VICINO SAN REMO

He read it rapidly, with more terror in his heart than he had felt when he had carried Freddie's body down the stairs, or when the police had come to question him. This was like a nemesis, like a nightmare come true, even the wording of the headline. The boat was described in detail and it brought the scene back to him, Dickie sitting in the stern at the throttle, Dickie smiling at him, Dickie's body sinking through the water with its wake of bubbles. The text said that the stains were believed to be bloodstains, not that they were. It did not say what the police or anybody else intended to do about them. But the police would do something, Tom thought. The boat-keeper could probably tell the police the very day the boat was lost. The police could then check the hotels for that day. The Italian boatkeeper might even remember that it was two Americans who had not come back with the boat. If the police bothered to check the hotel registers around that time, the name Richard Greenleaf would stand out like a red flag. In which case, of course, it would be Tom Ripley who would be missing, who might have been murdered that day. Tom's imagination went in several directions: suppose they searched for Dickie's body and found it? It would be assumed to be Tom Ripley's now. Dickie would be suspected of murder. Ergo, Dickie would be suspected of Freddie's murder, too. Dickie would become overnight "a murderous type." On the other hand, the Italian boatkeeper might not remember the day that one of his boats had not been brought back. Even if he did remember, the hotels might not be checked. The Italian police just might not be that interested. Might, might, *might* not.

Tom folded up his papers, paid his check, and went out.

He asked at the hotel desk if there were any messages for him.

"Si, signor. Questo e questo e questo—" The clerk laid them out on the desk before him like a card player laying down a winning straight.

Two from Van. One from Robert Gilbertson. (Wasn't there a Robert Gilbertson in Dickie's address book? Check on that.) One from Marge. Tom picked it up and read its Italian carefully: Signorina Sherwood had called at three-thirty-five P.M. and would call again. The call was long distance from Mongibello.

Tom nodded, and picked them up. "Thanks very much." He didn't like the looks of the clerk behind the desk. Italians were so damned curious!

Upstairs he sat hunched forward in an armchair, smoking and thinking. He was trying to figure out what would logically happen if he did nothing, and what he could make happen by his own actions. Marge would very likely come up to Rome. She had evidently called the Rome police to get his address. If she came up, he would have to see her as Tom, and try to convince her that Dickie was out for a while, as he had with Freddie. And if he failed— Tom rubbed his palms together nervously. He mustn't see Marge, that was all. Not now with the boat affair brewing. Everything would go haywire if he saw her. It'd be the end of everything! But if he could only sit tight, nothing at all would happen. It was just this moment, he thought, just this little crisis with the boat story and the unsolved Freddie Miles murder, that made things so difficult. But absolutely nothing would happen to him, if he could keep on doing and saying the right things to everybody. Afterwards it could be smooth sailing again. Greece, or India. Ceylon. Some place far, far away, where no old friend could possibly come knocking on his door. What a fool he had been to think he could stay in Rome! Might as well have picked Grand Central Station, or put himself on exhibition in the Louvre!

He called the Stazione Termini, and asked about the trains for Naples tomorrow. There were four or five. He wrote down the times for all of them. It would be five days before a boat left from Naples for Majorca, and he would sit the time out in Naples, he thought. All he needed was a release from the police, and if nothing happened tomorrow he should get it. They couldn't hold a man forever, without even any grounds for suspicion, just in order to throw an occasional question at him! He began to feel he would be released tomorrow, that it was absolutely logical that he should be released.

He picked up the telephone again, and told the clerk that if Miss Marjorie Sherwood called again, he would accept the call. If she called again, he thought, he could convince her in two minutes that everything was all right, that Freddie's murder didn't concern him at all, that he had moved to a hotel just to avoid annoying telephone calls from total strangers and yet still be within reach of the police in case they wanted him to identify any suspects they picked up. He would tell her that he was flying to Greece tomorrow or the next day, so there was no use in her coming to Rome. As a matter of fact, he thought, he could fly to Palma from Rome. He hadn't even thought of that before.

He lay down on the bed, tired, but not ready to undress, because he felt that something else was going to happen tonight. He tried to concentrate on Marge. He imagined her at this moment sitting in Giorgio's, or treating herself to a long, slow Tom Collins in the Miramare bar, and debating whether to call him up again. He could see her troubled eyebrows, her tousled hair as she sat brooding about what might be happening in Rome. She would be alone at the table, not talking to anyone. He saw her getting up and going home, taking a suitcase and catching the noon bus tomorrow. He was there on the road in front of the post office, shouting to her not to go, trying to stop the bus, but it pulled away . . .

The scene dissolved in swirling yellow-grayness, the color of the sand in Mongibello. Tom saw Dickie smiling at him, dressed in the corduroy suit that he had worn in San Remo.

The suit was soaking wet, the tie a dripping string. Dickie bent over him, shaking him. "I swam!" he said. "Tom, wake up! I'm all right! I swam! I'm alive!" Tom squirmed away from his touch. He heard Dickie laugh at him, Dickie's happy, deep laugh. *"Tom!"* The timbre of the voice was deeper, richer, *better* than Tom had ever been able to make it in his imitations. Tom pushed himself up. His body felt leaden and slow, as if he were trying to raise himself out of deep water.

"I swam!" Dickie's voice shouted, ringing and ringing in Tom's ears as if he heard it through a long tunnel.

Tom looked around the room, looking for Dickie in the yellow light under the bridge lamp, in the dark corner by the tall wardrobe. Tom felt his own eyes stretched wide, terrified, and though he knew his fear was senseless, he kept looking everywhere for Dickie, below the half-drawn shades at the window, and on the floor on the other side of the bed. He hauled himself up from the bed, staggered across the room, and opened a window. Then the other window. He felt drugged. *Somebody put something in my wine,* he thought suddenly. He knelt below the window, breathing the cold air in, fighting the grogginess as if it were something that was going to overcome him if he didn't exert himself to the utmost. Finally he went into the bathroom and wet his face at the basin. The grogginess was going away. He knew he hadn't been drugged. He had let his imagination run away with him. He had been out of control.

He drew himself up and calmly took off his tie. He moved as Dickie would have done, undressed himself, bathed, put his pajamas on and lay down in bed. He tried to think about what Dickie would be thinking about. His mother. Her last letter had enclosed a couple of snapshots of herself and Mr. Greenleaf sitting in the living room having coffee, the scene he remembered from the evening he had had coffee with them after dinner. Mrs. Greenleaf had said that Herbert had taken the pictures himself by squeezing a bulb. Tom began to compose his next letter to them. They were pleased that he was writing more often. He must set their minds at rest about the Freddie affair, because they knew of Freddie. Mrs. Greenleaf had asked about Freddie Miles in one of her letters. But Tom was listening for the telephone while he tried to compose the letter, and he couldn't really concentrate.

18.

THE first thing he thought of when he woke up was Marge. He reached for the telephone and asked if she had called during the night. She had not. He had a horrible premonition that she was coming up to Rome. It shot him out of bed, and then as he moved in his routine of shaving and bathing, his feeling changed. Why should he worry so much about Marge? He had always been able to handle her. She couldn't be here before five or six, anyway, because the first bus left Mongibello at noon, and she wasn't likely to take a taxi to Naples.

Maybe he would be able to leave Rome this morning. At ten o'clock he would call the police and find out.

He ordered caffe latte and rolls sent up to his room, and also the morning papers. Very strangely, there was not a thing in any of the papers about either the Miles case or the San Remo boat. It made him feel odd and frightened, with the same fear he had had last night when he had imagined Dickie standing in the room. He threw the newspapers away from him into a chair.

The telephone rang and he jumped for it obediently. It was either Marge or the police. "Pronto?"

"Pronto. There are two signori of the police downstairs to see you, signor."

"Very well. Will you tell them to come up?"

A minute later he heard their footsteps in the carpeted hall. It was the same older officer as yesterday, with a different younger policeman.

"Buon' giorno," said the officer politely, with his little bow.

"Buon' giorno," Tom said. "Have you found anything new?"

"No," said the officer on a questioning note. He took the chair that Tom offered him, and opened his brown leather briefcase. "Another matter has come up. You are also a friend of the American Thomas Reepley?"

"Yes," Tom said.

"Do you know where he is?"

"I think he went back to America about a month ago."

The officer consulted his paper. "I see. That will have to be confirmed by the United States Immigration Department. You see, we are trying to find Thomas Reepley. We think he may be dead."

"Dead? Why?"

The officer's lips under his bushy iron-gray mustache compressed softly between each statement so that they seemed to be smiling. The smile had thrown Tom off a little yesterday, too. "You were with him on a trip to San Remo in November, were you not?"

They had checked the hotels. "Yes."

"Where did you last see him? In San Remo?"

"No. I saw him again in Rome." Tom remembered that Marge knew he had gone back to Rome after Mongibello, because he had said he was going to help Dickie get settled in Rome.

"When did you last see him?"

"I don't know if I can give you the exact date. Something like two months ago, I think. I think I had a postcard from— from Genoa from him, saying that he was going to go back to America."

"You think?"

"I know I had," Tom said. "Why do you think he is dead?"

The officer looked at his form paper dubiously. Tom glanced at the younger policeman, who was leaning against the bureau with his arms folded, staring impersonally at him.

"Did you take a boat ride with Thomas Reepley in San Remo?"

"A boat ride? Where?"

"In a little boat? Around the port?" the officer asked quietly, looking at Tom.

"I think we did. Yes, I remember. Why?"

"Because a little boat has been found sunken with some kind of stains on it that may be blood. It was lost on November twenty-fifth. That is, it was not returned to the dock from which it was rented. November twenty-fifth was the day you were in San Remo with Signor Reepley." The officer's eyes rested on him without moving.

The very mildness of the look offended Tom. It was dishonest, he felt. But Tom made a tremendous effort to behave in the proper way. He saw himself as if he were standing apart from himself and watching the scene. He corrected even his stance, and made it more relaxed by resting a hand on the end post of the bed. "But nothing happened to us on that boat ride. There was no accident."

"Did you bring the boat back?"

"Of course."

The officer continued to eye him. "We cannot find Signor Reepley registered in any hotel after November twenty-fifth."

"Really?—How long have you been looking?"

"Not long enough to search every little village in Italy, but we have checked the hotels in the major cities. We find you registered at the Hassler on November twenty-eighth to thirtieth, and then—"

"Tom didn't stay with me in Rome—Signor Ripley. He went to Mongibello around that time and stayed for a couple of days."

"Where did he stay when he came up to Rome?"

"At some small hotel. I don't remember which it was. I didn't visit him."

"And where were you?"

"When?"

"On November twenty-sixth and twenty-seventh. That is, just after San Remo."

"In Forte dei Marmi," Tom replied. "I stopped off there on the way down. I stayed at a pension."

"Which one?"

Tom shook his head. "I don't recall the name. A very small place." After all, he thought, through Marge he could prove that Tom was in Mongibello, alive, after San Remo, so why should the police investigate what pension Dickie Greenleaf had stayed at on the twenty-sixth and twenty-seventh? Tom sat down on the side of his bed. "I do not understand yet why you think Tom Ripley is dead."

"We think *somebody* is dead," the officer replied, "in San

Remo. Somebody was killed in that boat. That was why the
boat was sunk—to hide the bloodstains."

Tom frowned. "They are sure they are bloodstains?"

The officer shrugged.

Tom shrugged, too. "There must have been a couple of
hundred people renting boats that day in San Remo."

"Not so many. About thirty. It's quite true, it could have
been any one of the thirty—or any pair of the fifteen," he
added with a smile. "We don't even know all their names. But
we are beginning to think Thomas Reepley is missing." Now
he looked off at a corner of the room, and he might have
been thinking of something else, Tom thought, judging from
his expression. Or was he enjoying the warmth of the radiator
beside his chair?

Tom recrossed his legs impatiently. What was going on in
the Italian's head was obvious: Dickie Greenleaf had twice
been on the scene of a murder, or near enough. The missing
Thomas Ripley had taken a boat ride November twenty-fifth
with Dickie Greenleaf. Ergo— Tom straightened up, frowning. "Are you saying that you do not believe me when I tell
you that I saw Tom Ripley in Rome around the first of
December?"

"Oh, no, I didn't say that, no, indeed!" The officer gestured placatingly. "I wanted to hear what you would say about
your—your traveling with Signor Ripley after San Remo, because we cannot find him." He smiled again, a broad, conciliatory smile that showed yellowish teeth.

Tom relaxed with an exasperated shrug. Obvious that the
Italian police didn't want to accuse an American citizen outright of murder. "I'm sorry that I can't tell you exactly where
he is right now. Why don't you try Paris? Or Genoa? He'd
always stay in a small hotel, because he prefers them."

"Have you got the postcard that he sent you from Genoa?"

"No, I haven't," Tom said. He ran his fingers through his
hair, as Dickie sometimes did when he was irritated. He felt
better, concentrating on being Dickie Greenleaf for a few seconds, pacing the floor once or twice.

"Do you know any friends of Thomas Reepley?"

Tom shook his head. "No, I don't even know him very
well, at least not for a very long time. I don't know if he has

many friends in Europe. I think he said he knew someone in Faenza. Also in Florence. But I don't remember their names." If the Italian thought he was protecting Tom's friends from a lot of police questioning by not giving their names, then let him, Tom thought.

"Va bene, we shall inquire," the officer said. He put his papers away. He had made at least a dozen notations on them.

"Before you go," Tom said in the same nervous, frank tone, "I want to ask when I can leave the city. I was planning to go to Sicily. I should like very much to leave today if it is possible. I intend to stay at the Hotel Palma in Palermo. It will be very simple for you to reach me if I am needed."

"Palermo," the officer repeated. "Ebbene, that may be possible. May I use the telephone?"

Tom lighted an Italian cigarette and listened to the officer asking for Capitano Aulicino, and then stating quite impassively that Signor Greenleaf did not know where Signor Reepley was, and that he might have gone back to America, or he might be in Florence or Faenza in the opinion of Signor Greenleaf. "Faenza," he repeated carefully, "vicino Bologna." When the man had that, the officer said that Signor Greenleaf wished to go to Palermo today. "Va bene. Benone." The officer turned to Tom, smiling. "Yes, you may go to Palermo today."

"Benone. Grazie." He walked with the two to the door. "If you find where Tom Ripley is, I wish you would let me know, too," he said ingenuously.

"Of course! We shall keep you informed, signor. Buon' giorno!"

Alone, Tom began to whistle as he repacked the few things he had taken from his suitcases. He felt proud of himself for having proposed Sicily instead of Majorca, because Sicily was still Italy and Majorca wasn't, and naturally the Italian police would be more willing to let him leave if he stayed in their territory. He had thought of that when it had occurred to him that Tom Ripley's passport did not show that he had been to France again after the San Remo–Cannes trip. He remembered he had told Marge that Tom Ripley had said he was going up to Paris and from there back to America. If they ever questioned Marge as to whether Tom Ripley was in Mongi-

bello after San Remo, she might also add that he later went
to Paris. And if he ever had to become Tom Ripley again, and
show his passport to the police, they would see that he hadn't
been to France again after the Cannes trip. He would just
have to say that he had changed his mind after he told Dickie
that, and had decided to stay in Italy. That wasn't important.

Tom straightened up suddenly from a suitcase. Could it all
be a trick, really? Were they just letting him have a little more
rope in letting him go to Sicily, apparently unsuspected? A sly
little bastard, that officer. He'd said his name once. What was
it? Ravini? Roverini? Well, what could be the advantage of
letting him have a little more rope? He'd told them exactly
where he was going. He had no intention of trying to run
away from anything. All he wanted was to get out of Rome.
He was frantic to get out! He threw the last items into his
suitcase and slammed the lid down and locked it.

The phone again!

Tom snatched it up. "Pronto?"

"Oh, Dickie—!" breathlessly.

It was Marge and she was downstairs, he could tell from
the sound. Flustered, he said in Tom's voice, "Who's this?"

"Is this Tom?"

"Marge! Well, hello! Where are you?"

"I'm downstairs. Is Dickie there? Can I come up?"

"You can come up in about five minutes," Tom said with
a laugh. "I'm not quite dressed yet." The clerks always sent
people to a booth downstairs, he thought. The clerks
wouldn't be able to overhear them.

"Is Dickie there?"

"Not at the moment. He went out about half an hour ago,
but he'll be back any minute. I know where he is, if you want
to find him."

"Where?"

"At the eighty-third police station. No, excuse me, it's the
eighty-seventh."

"Is he in any trouble?"

"No, just answering questions. He was supposed to be
there at ten. Want me to give you the address?" He wished
he hadn't started talking in Tom's voice: he could so easily

have pretended to be a servant, some friend of Dickie's, any-body, and told her that Dickie was out for hours.

Marge was groaning. "No-o. I'll wait for him."

"Here it is!" Tom said as if he had found it. "Twenty-one Via Perugia. Do you know where that is?" Tom didn't, but he was going to send her in the opposite direction from the American Express, where he wanted to go for his mail before he left town.

"I don't want to go," Marge said. "I'll come up and wait with you, if it's all right."

"Well, it's—" He laughed, his own unmistakable laugh that Marge knew well. "The thing is, I'm expecting somebody any minute. It's a business interview. About a job. Believe it or not, old believe-it-or-not Ripley's trying to put himself to work."

"Oh," said Marge, not in the least interested. "Well, how is Dickie? Why does he have to talk to the police?"

"Oh, just because he had some drinks with Freddie that day. You saw the papers, didn't you? The papers make it ten times more important than it was for the simple reason that the dopes haven't got any clues at all about anything."

"How long has Dickie been living here?"

"Here? Oh, just overnight. I've been up north. When I heard about Freddie, I came down to Rome to see him. If it hadn't been for the police, I'd never have found him!"

"You're telling me! I went to the police in desperation! I've been so worried, Tom. He might at least have phoned me—at Giorgio's or somewhere—"

"I'm awfully glad you're in town, Marge. Dickie'll be tick-led pink to see you. He's been worried about what you might think of all this in the papers."

"Oh, has he?" Marge said disbelievingly, but she sounded pleased.

"Why don't you wait for me in Angelo's? It's that bar right down the street in front of the hotel going toward the Piazza di Spagna steps. I'll see if I can sneak out and have a drink or a coffee with you in about five minutes, okay?"

"Okay. But there's a bar right here in the hotel."

"I don't want to be seen by my future boss in a bar."

"Oh, all right. Angelo's?"

"You can't miss it. On the street straight in front of the hotel. Bye-bye."

He whirled around to finish his packing. He really was finished except for the coats in the closet. He picked up the telephone and asked for his bill to be prepared, and for somebody to carry his luggage. Then he put his luggage in a neat heap for the bellboys and went down via the stairs. He wanted to see if Marge was still in the lobby, waiting there for him, or possibly still there making another telephone call. She couldn't have been downstairs waiting when the police were here, Tom thought. About five minutes had passed between the time the police left and Marge called up. He had put on a hat to conceal his blonder hair, a raincoat which was new, and he wore Tom Ripley's shy, slightly frightened expression.

She wasn't in the lobby. Tom paid his bill. The clerk handed him another message: Van Houston had been here. The message was in his own writing, dated ten minutes ago.

Waited for you half an hour. Don't you ever go out for a walk? They won't let me up. Call me at the Hassler.

Van

Maybe Van and Marge had run into each other, if they knew each other, and were sitting together in Angelo's now.

"If anybody else asks for me, would you say that I've left the city?" Tom said to the clerk.

"Va bene, signor."

Tom went out to his waiting taxi. "Would you stop at the American Express, please?" he asked the driver.

The driver did not take the street that Angelo's was on. Tom relaxed and congratulated himself. He congratulated himself above all on the fact that he had been too nervous to stay in his apartment yesterday and had taken a hotel room. He never could have evaded Marge in his apartment. She had the address from the newspapers. If he had tried the same trick, she would have insisted on coming up and waiting for Dickie in the apartment. Luck was with him!

He had mail at the American Express—three letters, one from Mr. Greenleaf.

"How are you today?" asked the young Italian girl who had handed him his mail.

She'd read the papers, too, Tom thought. He smiled back at her naïvely curious face. Her name was Maria. "Very well, thanks, and you?"

As he turned away, it crossed his mind that he could never use the Rome American Express as an address for Tom Ripley. Two or three of the clerks knew him by sight. He was using the Naples American Express for Tom Ripley's mail now, though he hadn't claimed anything there or written them to forward anything, because he wasn't expecting anything important for Tom Ripley, not even another blast from Mr. Greenleaf. When things cooled off a little, he would just walk into the Naples American Express some day and claim it with Tom Ripley's passport, he thought.

He couldn't use the Rome American Express as Tom Ripley, but he had to keep Tom Ripley with him, his passport and his clothes in order for emergencies like Marge's telephone call this morning. Marge had come damned close to being right in the room with him. As long as the innocence of Dickie Greenleaf was debatable in the opinion of the police, it was suicidal to think of leaving the country as Dickie, because if he had to switch back suddenly to Tom Ripley, Ripley's passport would not show that he had left Italy. If he wanted to leave Italy—to take Dickie Greenleaf entirely away from the police—he would have to leave as Tom Ripley, and re-enter later as Tom Ripley and become Dickie again once the police investigations were over. That was a possibility.

It seemed simple and safe. All he had to do was weather the next few days.

19.

THE boat approached Palermo harbor slowly and tentatively, nosing its white prow gently through the floating orange peels, the straw and the pieces of broken fruit crates. It was the way Tom felt, too, approaching Palermo. He had spent two days in Naples, and there had been nothing of any interest in the papers about the Miles case and nothing at all about the San Remo boat, and the police had made no attempt to reach him that he knew of. But maybe they had just not bothered to look for him in Naples, he thought, and were waiting for him in Palermo at the hotel.

There were no police waiting for him on the dock, anyway. Tom looked for them. He bought a couple of newspapers, then took a taxi with his luggage to the Hotel Palma. There were no police in the hotel lobby, either. It was an ornate old lobby with great marble supporting columns and big pots of palms standing around. A clerk told him the number of his reserved room, and handed a bellboy the key. Tom felt so much relieved that he went over to the mail counter and asked boldly if there was any message for Signor Richard Greenleaf.

The clerk told him there was not.

Then he began to relax. That meant there was not even a message from Marge. Marge would undoubtedly have gone to the police by now to find out where Dickie was. Tom had imagined horrible things during the boat trip: Marge beating him to Palermo by plane, Marge leaving a message for him at the Hotel Palma that she would arrive on the next boat. He had even looked for Marge on the boat when he got aboard in Naples.

Now he began to think that perhaps Marge had given Dickie up after this episode. Maybe she'd caught onto the idea that Dickie was running away from her and that he wanted to be with Tom, alone. Maybe that had even penetrated *her* thick skull. Tom debated sending her a letter to that effect as he sat in his deep warm bath that evening, spreading soapsuds luxuriously up and down his arms. Tom Ripley ought to write the letter, he thought. It was about time. He would say that he'd wanted to be tactful all this while, that he hadn't wanted to come right out with it on the telephone in Rome, but that by now he had the feeling she understood, anyway. He and Dickie were very happy together, and that was that. Tom began to giggle merrily, uncontrollably, and squelched himself by slipping all the way under the water, holding his nose.

Dear Marge, he would say. I'm writing this because I don't think Dickie ever will, though I've asked him to many times.

You're much too fine a person to be strung along like this for so long . . .

He giggled again, then sobered himself by deliberately concentrating on the little problem that he hadn't solved yet: Marge had also probably told the Italian police that she had talked to Tom Ripley at the Inghilterra. The police were going to wonder where the hell he went to. The police might be looking for him in Rome now. The police would certainly look for Tom Ripley around Dickie Greenleaf. It was an added danger—if they were, for instance, to think that he was Tom Ripley now, just from Marge's description of him, and strip him and search him and find both his and Dickie's passports. But what had he said about risks? Risks were what made the whole thing fun. He burst out singing:

> *Papa non vuole, Mama ne meno,*
> *Come faremo far' l'amor'?*

He boomed it out in the bathroom as he dried himself. He sang it in Dickie's loud baritone that he had never heard, but he felt sure Dickie would have been pleased with his ringing tone.

He dressed, put on one of his new nonwrinkling traveling suits, and strolled out into the Palermo dusk. There across the plaza was the great Norman-influenced cathedral he had read about, built by the English archbishop Walter-of-the-Mill, he remembered from a guidebook. Then there was Siracusa to the south, scene of a mighty naval battle between the Latins and the Greeks. And Dionysius' Ear. And Taormina. And Etna! It was a big island and brand-new to him. Sicilia! Stronghold of Giuliano! Colonized by the ancient Greeks, invaded by Norman and Saracen! Tomorrow he would commence his tourism properly, but this moment was glorious, he thought as he stopped to stare at the tall, towered cathedral in front of him. Wonderful to look at the dusty arches of its façade and to think of going inside tomorrow, to imagine its musty, sweetish smell, composed of the uncounted candles and incense-burnings of hundreds and hundreds of years. Anticipation! It occurred to him that his anticipation was more pleasant to him than his experiencing. Was it always going to be like that? When he spent evenings alone, handling Dickie's possessions, simply looking at his rings on his own fingers, or his woolen ties, or his black alligator wallet, was that experiencing or anticipation?

Beyond Sicily came Greece. He definitely wanted to see Greece. He wanted to see Greece as Dickie Greenleaf with Dickie's money, Dickie's clothes, Dickie's way of behaving with strangers. But would it happen that he couldn't see Greece as Dickie Greenleaf? Would one thing after another come up to thwart him—murder, suspicion, *people?* He hadn't wanted to murder, it had been a necessity. The idea of going to Greece, trudging over the Acropolis as Tom Ripley, American tourist, held no charm for him at all. He would as soon not go. Tears came in his eyes as he stared up at the campanile of the cathedral, and then he turned away and began to walk down a new street.

There was a letter for him the next morning, a fat letter from Marge. Tom squeezed it between his fingers and smiled. It was what he had expected, he felt sure, otherwise it wouldn't have been so fat. He read it at breakfast. He savored every line of it along with his fresh warm rolls and his cinnamon-flavored coffee. It was all he could have expected, and more.

. . . If you really *didn't* know that I had been by your hotel, that only means that Tom didn't tell you, which leaves the same conclusion to be drawn. It's pretty obvious now that you're running out and can't face me. Why don't you admit that you can't live without your little chum? I'm only sorry, old boy, that you didn't have the courage to tell me this before and *outright*. What do you think I am, a small-town hick who doesn't know about such things? *You're* the only one who's acting small-town! At any rate, I hope my telling you what you hadn't the courage to tell me relieves your conscience a little bit and lets you hold your head up. There's nothing like being proud of the person you love, is there? Didn't we once talk about this?

Accomplishment Number Two of my Roman holiday is informing the police that Tom Ripley is with you. They seemed in a perfect tizzy to find him. (I wonder why? What's he done now?) I also informed the police in my best Italian that you and Tom are inseparable and how they could have found you and still missed *Tom*, I could not imagine.

Changed my boat and I'll be leaving for the States around the end of March, after a short visit to Kate in Munich, after which I presume our paths will never cross again. No hard feelings, Dickie boy. I'd just given you credit for a lot more guts.

Thanks for all the wonderful memories. They're like something in a museum already or something preserved in amber, a little unreal, as you must have felt yourself always to me.

Best wishes for the future,
Marge

Ugh! That corn at the end! Ah, Clabber Girl! Tom folded the letter and stuck it into his jacket pocket. He glanced at the two doors of the hotel restaurant, automatically looking for police. If the police thought that Dickie Greenleaf and Tom Ripley were traveling together, they must have checked the Palermo hotels already for Tom Ripley, he thought. But he hadn't noticed any police watching him, or following him. Or maybe they'd given the whole boat scare up, since they were sure Tom Ripley was alive. Why on earth should they go on with it? Maybe the suspicion against Dickie in San Remo and in the Miles murder, too, had already blown over. Maybe.

He went up to his room and began a letter to Mr. Greenleaf on Dickie's portable Hermes. He began by explaining the Miles affair very soberly and logically, because Mr. Greenleaf would probably be pretty alarmed by now. He said that the police had finished their questioning, and that all they conceivably might want now was for him to try to identify any suspects they might find, because the suspect might be a mutual acquaintance of his and Freddie's.

The telephone rang while he was typing. A man's voice said that he was a Tenente Somebody of the Palermo police force.

"We are looking for Thomas Phelps Ripley. Is he with you in your hotel?" he asked courteously.

"No, he is not," Tom replied.

"Do you know where he is?"

"I think he is in Rome. I saw him just three or four days ago in Rome."

"He has not been found in Rome. You do not know where he might have been going from Rome?"

"I'm sorry, I haven't the slightest idea," Tom said.

"Peccato," sighed the voice, with disappointment. "Grazie tante, signor."

"Di niente." Tom hung up and went back to his letter.

The dull yards of Dickie's prose came out more fluently now than Tom's own letters ever had. He addressed most of the letter to Dickie's mother, told her the state of his wardrobe, which was good, and his health, which was also good, and asked if she had received the enamel triptych he had sent her from an antique store in Rome a couple of weeks ago. While he wrote, he was thinking of what he had to do about Thomas Ripley. The quest was apparently very courteous and lukewarm, but it wouldn't do to take wild chances. He shouldn't have Tom's passport lying right in a pocket of his suitcase, even if it was wrapped up in a lot of old income tax papers of Dickie's so that it wasn't visible to a custom inspector's eyes. He should hide it in the lining of the new antelope suitcase, for instance, where it couldn't be seen even if the suitcase were emptied, yet where he could get at it on a few minutes' notice if he had to. Because some day he might have to. There might come a time when it would be more dangerous to be Dickie Greenleaf than to be Tom Ripley.

Tom spent half the morning on the letter to the Greenleafs. He had a feeling that Mr. Greenleaf was getting restless and impatient with Dickie, not in the same way that he had been impatient when Tom had seen him in New York, but in a much more serious way. Mr. Greenleaf thought his removal from Mongibello to Rome had been merely an erratic whim, Tom knew. Tom's attempt to make his painting and studying in Rome sound constructive had really been a failure. Mr. Greenleaf had dismissed it with a withering remark: something about his being sorry that he was still torturing himself with painting at all, because he should have learned by now that it took more than beautiful scenery or a change of scene to make a painter. Mr. Greenleaf had also not been much impressed by the interest Tom had shown in the Burke-Greenleaf folders that Mr. Greenleaf had sent him. It was a far cry from what Tom had expected by this time: that he would have Mr. Greenleaf eating out of his hand, that he would have made up for all Dickie's negligence and unconcern for his parents in the past, and that he could ask Mr. Greenleaf for some extra money and get it. He couldn't possibly ask Mr. Greenleaf for money now.

Take care of yourself, moms [he wrote]. Watch out for those colds. [She had said she'd had four colds this winter, and had spent Christmas propped up in bed, wearing the pink woolen shawl he had sent her as one of his Christmas presents.] If you'd been wearing a pair of those wonderful woolen socks you sent me, you never would have caught the colds. I haven't had a cold this winter, which is something to boast about in a European winter. . . . Moms, can I send you anything from here? I enjoy buying things for you . . .

20.

FIVE days passed, calm, solitary but very agreeable days in which he rambled about Palermo, stopping here and there to sit for an hour or so in a café or a restaurant and read his guidebooks and the newspapers. He took a carrozza one gloomy day and rode all the way to Monte Pelligrino to visit the fantastic tomb of Santa Rosalia, the patron saint of Palermo, depicted in a famous statue, which Tom had seen pictures of in Rome, in one of those states of frozen ecstasy that are given other names by psychiatrists. Tom found the tomb vastly amusing. He could hardly keep from giggling when he saw the statue: the lush, reclining female body, the groping hands, the dazed eyes, the parted lips. It was all there but the actual sound of the panting. He thought of Marge. He visited a Byzantine palace, the Palermo library with its paintings and old cracked manuscripts in glass cases, and studied the formation of the harbor, which was carefully diagrammed in his guidebook. He made a sketch of a painting by Guido Reni, for no particular purpose, and memorized a long inscription by Tasso on one of the public buildings. He wrote letters to Bob Delancey and to Cleo in New York, a long letter to Cleo describing his travels, his pleasures, and his multifarious acquaintances with the convincing ardor of Marco Polo describing China.

But he was lonely. It was not like the sensation in Paris of being alone yet not alone. He had imagined himself acquiring a bright new circle of friends with whom he would start a new life with new attitudes, standards, and habits that would be far better and clearer than those he had had all his life. Now he realized that it couldn't be. He would have to keep a distance from people, always. He might acquire the different standards and habits, but he could never acquire the circle of friends—not unless he went to Istanbul or Ceylon, and what was the use of acquiring the kind of people he would meet in those places? He was alone, and it was a lonely game he was playing. The friends he might make were most of the danger, of course. If he had to drift about the world entirely alone, so much the better: there was that much less chance that he would be found out. That was one cheerful aspect of it, anyway, and he felt better having thought of it.

He altered his behavior slightly, to accord with the role of a more detached observer of life. He was still courteous and smiling to everyone, to people who wanted to borrow his newspaper in restaurants and to clerks he spoke to in the hotel, but he carried his head even higher and he spoke a little less when he spoke. There was a faint air of sadness about him now. He enjoyed the change. He imagined that he looked like a young man who had had an unhappy love affair or some kind of emotional disaster, and was trying to recuperate in a civilized way, by visiting some of the more beautiful places on the earth.

That reminded him of Capri. The weather was still bad, but Capri was Italy. That glimpse he had had of Capri with Dickie had only whetted his appetite. Christ, had Dickie been a bore *that* day! Maybe he should hold out until summer, he thought, hold the police off until then. But even more than Greece and the Acropolis, he wanted one happy holiday in Capri, and to hell with culture for a while. He had read about Capri in winter—wind, rain, and solitude. But still Capri! There was Tiberius' Leap and the Blue Grotto, the plaza without people but still the plaza, and not a cobblestone changed. He might even go today. He quickened his steps toward his hotel. The lack of tourists hadn't detracted from the Côte

d'Azur. Maybe he could fly to Capri. He had heard of a seaplane service from Naples to Capri. If the seaplane wasn't running in February, he could charter it. What was money for?

"Buon' giorno! Come sta?" He greeted the clerk behind
the desk with a smile.

"A letter for you, signor. Urgentissimo," the clerk said,
smiling, too.

It was from Dickie's bank in Naples. Inside the envelope
was another envelope from Dickie's trust company in New
York. Tom read the letter from the Naples bank first.

Feb. 10, 19——

Most esteemed signor:

It has been called to our attention by the Wendell Trust Company
of New York, that there exists a doubt whether your signature of
receipt of your remittance of five hundred dollars of January last is
actually your own. We hasten to inform you so that we may take the
necessary action.

We have already deemed it proper to inform the police, but we
await your confirmation of the opinion of our Inspector of Signatures
and of the Inspector of Signatures of the Wendell Trust Company of
New York. Any information you may be able to give will be most
appreciated, and we urge you to communicate with us at your earliest
possible convenience.

Most respectfully and obediently yours,
Emilio di Braganzi
Segretario Generale della Banca di Napoli

P.S. In the case that your signature is in fact valid, we urge you despite
this to visit our offices in Naples as soon as possible in order to sign
your name again for our permanent records. We enclose a letter to
you sent in our care from the Wendell Trust Company.

Tom ripped open the trust company's letter.

Feb. 5, 19——

Dear Mr. Greenleaf:

Our Department of Signatures has reported to us that in its opinion your signature of January on your regular monthly remittance,
No. 8747, is invalid. Believing this may for some reason have escaped
your notice, we are hastening to inform you, so that you may confirm
the signing of the said check or confirm our opinion that the said

check has been forged. We have called this to the attention of the Bank of Naples also.

Enclosed is a card for our permanent signature file which we request you to sign and return to us.

Please let us hear from you as soon as possible.

> Sincerely,
> Edward T. Cavanach
> Secretary

Tom wet his lips. He'd write to both banks that he was not missing any money at all. But would that hold them off for long? He had signed three remittances, beginning in December. Were they going to go back and check on all his signatures now? Would an expert be able to tell that all three signatures were forged?

Tom went upstairs and immediately sat down at the typewriter. He put a sheet of hotel stationery into the roller and sat there for a moment, staring at it. They wouldn't rest with this, he thought. If they had a board of experts looking at the signatures with magnifying glasses and all that, they probably would be able to tell that the three signatures were forgeries. But they were such damned good forgeries, Tom knew. He'd signed the January remittance a little fast, he remembered, but it wasn't a bad job or he never would have sent it off. He would have told the bank he lost the remittance and would have had them send him another. Most forgeries took months to be discovered, he thought. Why had they spotted this one in four weeks? Wasn't it because they were checking on him in every department of his life, since the Freddie Miles murder and the San Remo boat story? They wanted to see him personally in the Naples bank. Maybe some of the men there knew Dickie by sight. A terrible, tingling panic went over his shoulders and down his legs. For a moment he felt weak and helpless, too weak to move. He saw himself confronted by a dozen policemen, Italian and American, asking him where Dickie Greenleaf was, and being unable to produce Dickie Greenleaf or tell them where he was or prove that he existed. He imagined himself trying to sign H. Richard Greenleaf under the eyes of a dozen handwriting experts, and going to pieces suddenly and not being able to write at all. He brought his hands up to the typewriter keys and forced himself to begin. He addressed the letter to the Wendell Trust Company of New York.

Feb. 12, 19——

Dear Sirs:

In regard to your letter concerning my January remittance:

I signed the check in question myself and received the money in full. If I had missed the check, I should of course have informed you at once.

I am enclosing the card with my signature for your permanent record as you requested.

Sincerely,
H. Richard Greenleaf

He signed Dickie's signature several times on the back of the trust company's envelope before he signed his letter and then the card. Then he wrote a similar letter to the Naples bank, and promised to call at the bank within the next few days and sign his name again for their permanent record. He marked both envelopes "Urgentissimo," went downstairs and bought stamps from the porter and posted them.

Then he went out for a walk. His desire to go to Capri had vanished. It was four-fifteen in the afternoon. He kept walking, aimlessly. Finally, he stopped in front of an antique shop window and stared for several minutes at a gloomy oil painting of two bearded saints descending a dark hill in moonlight. He went into the shop and bought it for the first price the man quoted to him. It was not even framed, and he carried it rolled up under his arm back to his hotel.

21.

83 Stazione Polizia
Roma
Feb. 14, 19——

Most esteemed Signor Greenleaf:

You are urgently requested to come to Rome to answer some important questions concerning Thomas Ripley. Your presence would be most appreciated and would greatly expedite our investigations.

Failure to present yourself within a week will cause us to take certain measures which will be inconvenient both to us and to you.

Most respectfully yours,

Cap. Enrico Farrara

So they were still looking for Tom. But maybe it meant
that something had happened on the Miles case, too, Tom
thought. The Italians didn't summon an American in words
like these. That last paragraph was a plain threat. And of
course they knew about the forged check by now.

He stood with the letter in his hand, looking blankly
around the room. He caught sight of himself in the mirror,
the corners of his mouth turned down, his eyes anxious and
scared. He looked as if he were trying to convey the emotions
of fear and shock by his posture and his expression, and because the way he looked was involuntary and real, he became
suddenly twice as frightened. He folded the letter and pocketed it, then took it out of his pocket and tore it to bits.

He began to pack rapidly, snatching his robe and pajamas
from the bathroom door, throwing his toilet articles into the
leather kit with Dickie's initials that Marge had given him for
Christmas. He stopped suddenly. He had to get rid of Dickie's
belongings, all of them. Here? Now? Should he throw them
overboard on the way back to Naples?

The question didn't answer itself, but he suddenly knew
what he had to do, what he was going to do when he got
back to Italy. He would not go anywhere near Rome. He
could go straight up to Milan or Turin, or maybe somewhere
near Venice, and buy a car, secondhand, with a lot of mileage
on it. He'd say he'd been roaming around Italy for the last
two or three months. He hadn't heard anything about the
search for Thomas Ripley. Thomas Reepley.

He went on packing. This was the end of Dickie Greenleaf,
he knew. He hated becoming Thomas Ripley again, hated being nobody, hated putting on his old set of habits again, and
feeling that people looked down on him and were bored with
him unless he put on an act for them like a clown, feeling
incompetent and incapable of doing anything with himself
except entertaining people for minutes at a time. He hated
going back to himself as he would have hated putting on a
shabby suit of clothes, a grease-spotted, unpressed suit of

clothes that had not been very good even when it was new. His tears fell on Dickie's blue-and-white-striped shirt that lay uppermost in the suitcase, starched and clean and still as new-looking as when he had first taken it out of Dickie's drawer in Mongibello. But it had Dickie's initials on the pocket in little red letters. As he packed he began to reckon up defiantly the things of Dickie's that he could still keep because they had no initials, or because no one would remember that they were Dickie's and not his own. Except maybe Marge would remember a few, like the new blue leather address book that Dickie had written only a couple of addresses in, and that Marge had very likely given to him. But he wasn't planning to see Marge again.

Tom paid his bill at the Palma, but he had to wait until the next day for a boat to the mainland. He reserved the boat ticket in the name of Greenleaf, thinking that this was the last time he would ever reserve a ticket in the name of Greenleaf, but that maybe it wouldn't be, either. He couldn't give up the idea that it might all blow over. Just might. And for that reason it was senseless to be despondent. It was senseless to be despondent, anyway, even as Tom Ripley. Tom Ripley had never really been despondent, though he had often looked it. Hadn't he learned something from these last months? If you wanted to be cheerful, or melancholic, or wistful, or thoughtful, or courteous, you simply had to *act* those things with every gesture.

A very cheerful thought came to him when he awoke on the last morning in Palermo: he could check all Dickie's clothes at the American Express in Venice under a different name and reclaim them at some future time, if he wanted to or had to, or else never claim them at all. It made him feel much better to know that Dickie's good shirts, his studbox with all the cuff links and the identification bracelet and his wristwatch would be safely in storage somewhere, instead of at the bottom of the Tyrrhenian Sea or in some ashcan in Sicily.

So, after scraping the initials off Dickie's two suitcases, he sent them, locked, from Naples to the American Express Company, Venice, together with two canvases he had begun painting in Palermo, in the name of Robert S. Fanshaw, to be stored until called for. The only things, the only revealing things, he kept with him were Dickie's rings, which he put into the bottom of an ugly little brown leather box belonging to Thomas Ripley, that he had somehow kept with him for years everywhere he traveled or moved to, and which was otherwise filled with his own uninteresting collection of cuff links, collar pins, odd buttons, a couple of fountain-pen points, and a spool of white thread with a needle stuck in it.

Tom took a train from Naples up through Rome, Florence, Bologna, and Verona, where he got out and went by bus to the town of Trento about forty miles away. He did not want to buy a car in a town as big as Verona, because the police might notice his name when he applied for his license plates, he thought. In Trento he bought a secondhand cream-colored Lancia for the equivalent of about eight hundred dollars. He bought it in the name of Thomas Phelps Ripley, as his passport read, and took a hotel room in that name to wait the twenty-four hours until his license plates should be ready. Six hours later nothing had happened. Tom had been afraid that even this small hotel might recognize his name, that the office that took care of the applications for plates might also notice his name, but by noon the next day he had his plates on his car and nothing had happened. Neither was there anything in the papers about the quest for Thomas Ripley, or the Miles case, or the San Remo boat affair. It made him feel rather strange, rather safe and happy, and as if perhaps all of it were unreal. He began to feel happy even in his dreary role as Thomas Ripley. He took a pleasure in it, overdoing almost the old Tom Ripley reticence with strangers, the inferiority in every duck of his head and wistful, sidelong glance. After all, would anyone, *anyone*, believe that such a character had ever done a murder? And the only murder he could possibly be suspected of was Dickie's in San Remo, and they didn't seem to be getting very far on that. Being Tom Ripley had one compensation, at least: it relieved his mind of guilt for the stupid, unnecessary murder of Freddie Miles.

He wanted to go straight to Venice, but he thought he should spend one night doing what he intended to tell the police he had been doing for several months: sleeping in his car on a country road. He spent one night in the back seat of the Lancia, cramped and miserable, somewhere in the neighborhood of Brescia. He crawled into the front seat at dawn with such a painful crick in his neck he could hardly turn his head sufficiently to drive, but that made it authentic, he thought, that would make him tell the story better. He bought a guidebook of Northern Italy, marked it up appropriately with dates, turned down corners of its pages, stepped on its covers and broke its binding so that it fell open at Pisa.

The next night he spent in Venice. In a childish way Tom had avoided Venice simply because he expected to be disappointed in it. He had thought only sentimentalists and American tourists raved over Venice, and that at best it was only a town for honeymooners who enjoyed the inconvenience of not being able to go anywhere except by a gondola moving at two miles an hour. He found Venice much bigger than he had supposed, full of Italians who looked like Italians anywhere else. He found he could walk across the entire city via the narrow streets and bridges without setting foot in a gondola, and that the major canals had a transportation system of motor launches just as fast and efficient as the subway system, and that the canals did not smell bad, either. There was a tremendous choice of hotels, from the Gritti and the Danieli, which he had heard of, down to crummy little hotels and pensions in back alleys so off the beaten track, so removed from the world of police and American tourists, that Tom could imagine living in one of them for months without being noticed by anybody. He chose a hotel called the Costanza, very near the Rialto bridge, which struck the middle between the famous luxury hotels and the obscure little hostelries on the back streets. It was clean, inexpensive, and convenient to points of interest. It was just the hotel for Tom Ripley.

Tom spent a couple of hours pottering around in his room, slowly unpacking his old familiar clothes, and dreaming out the window at the dusk falling over the Canale Grande. He imagined the conversation he was going to have with the police before long. . . . Why, I haven't any idea. I saw him in Rome. If you've any doubt of that, you can verify it with Miss Marjorie Sherwood. . . . Of course I'm Tom Ripley! (He would give a laugh.) I can't understand what all the fuss is about! . . . San Remo? Yes, I remember. We brought the boat back after an hour. . . . Yes, I came back to Rome after Mongibello, but I didn't stay more than a couple of nights. I've been roaming around the north of Italy. . . . I'm afraid I haven't any idea where he is, but I saw him about three weeks ago. . . . Tom got up from the windowsill smiling, changed his shirt and tie for the evening, and went out to find a pleasant restaurant for dinner. A good restaurant, he thought. Tom Ripley could treat himself to something expensive for once. His billfold was so full of long ten- and twenty-thousand-lire notes it wouldn't bend. He had cashed a thousand dollars' worth of traveler's checks in Dickie's name before he left Palermo.

He bought two evening newspapers, tucked them under his arm and walked on, over a little arched bridge, through a long street hardly six feet wide full of leather shops and men's shirt shops, past windows glittering with jeweled boxes that spilled out necklaces and rings like the boxes Tom had always imagined that treasures spilled out of in fairy tales. He liked the fact that Venice had no cars. It made the city human. The streets were like veins, he thought, and the people were the blood, circulating everywhere. He took another street back and crossed the great quadrangle of San Marco's for the second time. Pigeons everywhere, in the air, in the light of shops—even at night, pigeons walking along under people's feet like sightseers themselves in their own home town! The chairs and tables of the cafés spread across the arcade into the plaza itself, so that people and pigeons had to look for little aisles through them to get by. From either end of the plaza blaring phonographs played in disharmony. Tom tried to imagine the place in summer, in sunlight, full of people tossing handfuls of grain up into the air for the pigeons that fluttered down for it. He entered another little lighted tunnel of a street. It was full of restaurants, and he chose a very substantial and respectable-looking place with white tablecloths and brown wooden walls, the kind of restaurant which experience had taught him by now concentrated on food and not the passing tourist. He took a table and opened one of his newspapers.

And there it was, a little item on the second page:

POLICE SEARCH FOR MISSING AMERICAN
Dickie Greenleaf, Friend of the Murdered Freddie Miles,
Missing After Sicilian Holiday

Tom bent close over the paper, giving it his full attention, yet he was conscious of a certain sense of annoyance as he read it, because in a strange way it seemed silly, silly of the police to be so stupid and ineffectual, and silly of the newspaper to waste space printing it. The text stated that H. Richard ("Dickie") Greenleaf, a close friend of the late Frederick Miles, the American murdered three weeks ago in Rome, had disappeared after presumably taking a boat from Palermo to Naples. Both the Sicilian and Roman police had been alerted and were keeping a vigilantissimo watch for him. A final paragraph said that Greenleaf had just been requested by the Rome police to answer questions concerning the disappearance of Thomas Ripley, also a close friend of Greenleaf. Ripley had been missing for about three months, the paper said.

Tom put the paper down, unconsciously feigning so well the astonishment that anybody might feel on reading in a newspaper that he was "missing," that he didn't notice the waiter trying to hand him the menu until the menu touched his hand. This was the time, he thought, when he ought to go straight to the police and present himself. If they had nothing against him—and what could they have against Tom Ripley?—they wouldn't likely check as to when he had bought the car. The newspaper item was quite a relief to him, because it meant that the police really had not picked up his name at the bureau of automobile registration in Trento.

He ate his meal slowly and with pleasure, ordered an espresso afterward, and smoked a couple of cigarettes as he thumbed through his guidebook on Northern Italy. By then he had had some different thoughts. For example, why should he have seen an item this small in the newspaper? And it was in only one newspaper. No, he oughtn't to present himself until he had seen two or three such items, or one big one that would logically catch his attention. They probably would come out with a big item before long: when a few days passed

and Dickie Greenleaf still had not appeared, they would begin
to suspect that he was hiding away because he had killed
Freddie Miles and possibly Tom Ripley, too. Marge might
have told the police she spoke with Tom Ripley two weeks
ago in Rome, but the police hadn't seen him yet. He leafed
through the guidebook, letting his eyes run over the colorless
prose and statistics while he did some more thinking.

He thought of Marge, who was probably winding up her
house in Mongibello now, packing for America. She'd see in
the papers about Dickie's being missing, and Marge would
blame him, Tom knew. She'd write to Dickie's father and say
that Tom Ripley was a vile influence, at very least. Mr. Greenleaf might decide to come over.

What a pity he couldn't present himself as Tom Ripley and
quiet them down about that, then present himself as Dickie
Greenleaf, hale and hearty, and clear up that little mystery,
too!

He might play up Tom a little more, he thought. He could
stoop a little more, he could be shyer than ever, he could even
wear horn-rimmed glasses and hold his mouth in an even sadder, droopier manner to contrast with Dickie's tenseness. Because some of the police he might talk to might be the ones
who had seen him as Dickie Greenleaf. What was the name
of that one in Rome? Rovassini? Tom decided to rinse his hair
again in a stronger solution of henna, so that it would be even
darker than his normal hair.

He looked through all the papers a third time for anything
about the Miles case. Nothing.

22.

THE next morning there was a long account in the most important newspaper, saying in only a small paragraph that
Thomas Ripley was missing, but saying very boldly that Richard
Greenleaf was "exposing himself to suspicion of participation"
in the murder of Miles, and that he must be considered as
evading the "problem," unless he presented himself to be

cleared of suspicion. The paper also mentioned the forged check. It said that the last communication from Richard Greenleaf had been his letter to the Bank of Naples, attesting that no forgeries had been committed against him. But two experts out of three in Naples said that they believed Signor Greenleaf's January and February checks were forgeries, concurring with the opinion of Signor Greenleaf's American bank, which had sent photostats of his signatures back to Naples. The newspaper ended on a slightly facetious note: "Can anybody commit a forgery against himself? Or is the wealthy American shielding one of his friends?"

To hell with them, Tom thought. Dickie's own handwriting changed often enough: he had seen it on an insurance policy among Dickie's papers, and he had seen it in Mongibello, right in front of his eyes. Let them drag out everything he had signed in the last three months, and see where it got them! They apparently hadn't noticed that the signature on his letter from Palermo was a forgery, too.

The only thing that really interested him was whether the police had found anything that actually incriminated Dickie in the murder of Freddie Miles. And he could hardly say that that really interested him, personally. He bought *Oggi* and *Epoca* at a news stand in the corner of San Marco's. They were tabloid-sized weeklies full of photographs, full of anything from murder to flagpole-sitting, anything spectacular that was happening anywhere. There was nothing in them yet about the missing Dickie Greenleaf. Maybe next week, he thought. But they wouldn't have any photographs of him in them, anyway. Marge had taken pictures of Dickie in Mongibello, but she had never taken one of him.

On his ramble around the city that morning he bought some rimmed glasses at a shop that sold toys and gadgets for practical jokers. The lenses were of plain glass. He visited San Marco's cathedral and looked all around inside it without seeing anything, but it was not the fault of the glasses. He was thinking that he had to identify himself, immediately. It would look worse for him, whatever happened, the longer he put it off. When he left the cathedral he inquired of a policeman where the nearest police station was. He asked it sadly. He felt sad. He was not afraid, but he felt that identifying himself as Thomas Phelps Ripley was going to be one of the saddest things he had ever done in his life.

"*You* are Thomas Reepley?" the captain of police asked, with no more interest than if Tom had been a dog that had been lost and was now found. "May I see your passport?"

Tom handed it to him. "I don't know what the trouble is, but when I saw in the papers that I am believed missing—" It was all dreary, dreary, just as he had anticipated. Policemen standing around blank-faced, staring at him. "What happens now?" Tom asked the officer.

"I shall telephone to Rome," the officer answered calmly, and picked up the telephone on his desk.

There was a few minutes' wait for the Rome line, and then, in an impersonal voice, the officer announced to someone in Rome that the American, Thomas Reepley, was in Venice. More inconsequential exchanges, then the officer said to Tom, "They would like to see you in Rome. Can you go to Rome today?"

Tom frowned. "I wasn't planning to go to Rome."

"I shall tell them," the officer said mildly, and spoke into the telephone again.

Now he was arranging for the Rome police to come to him. Being an American citizen still commanded certain privileges, Tom supposed.

"At what hotel are you staying?" the officer asked.

"At the Costanza."

The officer gave this piece of information to Rome. Then he hung up and informed Tom politely that a representative of the Rome police would be in Venice that evening after eight o'clock to speak to him.

"Thank you," Tom said, and turned his back on the dismal figure of the officer writing on his form sheet. It had been a very boring little scene.

Tom spent the rest of the day in his room, quietly thinking, reading, and making further small alterations in his appearance. He thought it quite possible that they would send the same man who had spoken to him in Rome, Tenente Rovassini or whatever his name was. He made his eyebrows a trifle darker with a lead pencil. He lay around all afternoon in his brown tweed suit, and even pulled a button off the jacket. Dickie had been rather on the neat side, so Tom Ripley was going to be notably sloppy by contrast. He ate no lunch, not that he wanted any, anyway, but he wanted to continue losing the few pounds he had added for the role of Dickie Greenleaf. He would make himself thinner than he had even been before as Tom Ripley. His weight on his own passport was one hundred and fifty-five. Dickie's was a hundred and sixty-eight, though they were the same height, six feet one and one-half.

At eight-thirty that evening his telephone rang, and the switchboard operator announced that Tenente Roverini was downstairs.

"Would you have him come up, please?" Tom said.

Tom went to the chair that he intended to sit in, and drew it still farther back from the circle of light cast by the standing lamp. The room was arranged to look as if he had been reading and killing time for the last few hours—the standing lamp and a tiny reading lamp were on, the counterpane was not smooth, a couple of books lay open face down, and he had even begun a letter on the writing table, a letter to Aunt Dottie.

The tenente knocked.

Tom opened the door in a languid way. "Buona sera."

"Buona sera. Tenente Roverini della Polizia Romana." The tenente's homely, smiling face did not look the least surprised or suspicious. Behind him came another tall, silent young police officer—not another, Tom realized suddenly, but the one who had been with the tenente when Tom had first met Roverini in the apartment in Rome. The officer sat down in the chair Tom offered him, under the light. "You are a friend of Signor Richard Greenleaf?" he asked.

"Yes." Tom sat down in the other chair, an armchair that he could slouch in.

"When did you last see him and where?"

"I saw him briefly in Rome, just before he went to Sicily."

"And did you hear from him when he was in Sicily?" The tenente was writing it all down in the notebook that he had taken from his brown briefcase.

"No, I didn't hear from him."

"Ah-hah," the tenente said. He was spending more time

looking at his papers than at Tom. Finally, he looked up with
a friendly, interested expression. "You did not know when you
were in Rome that the police wanted to see you?"

"No, I did not know that. I cannot understand why I am
said to be missing." He adjusted his glasses, and peered at the
man.

"I shall explain later. Signor Greenleaf did not tell you in
Rome that the police wanted to speak to you?"

"No."

"Strange," he remarked quietly, making another notation.
"Signor Greenleaf knew that we wanted to speak to you. Signor Greenleaf is not very cooperative." He smiled at Tom.

Tom kept his face serious and attentive.

"Signor Reepley, where have you been since the end of
November?"

"I have been traveling. I have been mostly in the north of
Italy." Tom made his Italian clumsy, with a mistake here and
there, and with quite a different rhythm from Dickie's Italian.

"Where?" The tenente gripped his pen again.

"Milano, Torino, Faenza—Pisa—"

"We have inquired at the hotels in Milano and Faenza, for
example. Did you stay all the time with friends?"

"No, I—slept quite often in my car." It was obvious that
he hadn't a great deal of money, Tom thought, and also that
he was the kind of young man who would prefer to rough it
with a guidebook and a volume of Silone or Dante, than to
stay in a fancy hotel. "I am sorry that I did not renew my
permiso di soggiorno," Tom said contritely. "I did not
know that it was such a serious matter." But he knew that
tourists in Italy almost never took the trouble to renew their
soggiorno, and stayed for months after stating on entering
the country that they intended to be here for only a few
weeks.

"*Permesso* di soggiorno," the tenente said in a tone of
gentle, almost paternal correction.

"Grazie."

"May I see your passport?"

Tom produced it from his inside jacket pocket. The tenente
studied the picture closely, while Tom assumed the faintly
anxious expression, the faintly parted lips, of the passport

photograph. The glasses were missing from the photograph, but his hair was parted in the same manner, and his tie was tied in the same loose, triangular knot. The tenente glanced at the few stamped entries that only partially filled the first two pages of the passport.

"You have been in Italy since October second, except for the short trip to France with Signor Greenleaf?"

"Yes."

The tenente smiled, a pleasant Italian smile now, and leaned forward on his knees. "Ebbene, this settles one important matter—the mystery of the San Remo boat."

Tom frowned. "What is that?"

"A boat was found sunken there with some stains that were believed to be bloodstains. Naturally, when you were missing, so far as we knew, immediately after San Remo—" He threw his hands out and laughed. "We thought it might be advisable to ask Signor Greenleaf what had happened to you. Which we did. The boat was missed the same day that you two were in San Remo!" He laughed again.

Tom pretended not to see the joke. "But did not Signor Greenleaf tell you that I went to Mongibello after San Remo? I did some—" he groped for a word "—little labors for him."

"Benone!" Tenente Roverini said, smiling. He loosened his brass-buttoned overcoat comfortably, and rubbed a finger back and forth across the crisp, bushy mustache. "Did you also know Fred-erick Mee-lays?" he asked.

Tom gave an involuntary sigh, because the boat incident was apparently closed. "No. I only met him once when he was getting off the bus in Mongibello. I never saw him again."

"Ah-hah," said the tenente, taking this in. He was silent a minute, as if he had run out of questions, then he smiled. "Ah, Mongibello! A beautiful village, is it not? My wife comes from Mongibello."

"Ah, indeed!" Tom said pleasantly.

"Si. My wife and I went there on our honeymoon."

"A most beautiful village," Tom said. "Grazie." He accepted the Nazionale that the tenente offered him. Tom felt that this was perhaps a polite Italian interlude, a rest between rounds. They were surely going to get into Dickie's private life, the forged checks and all the rest. Tom said seriously in his plodding Italian, "I have read in a newspaper that the police think that Signor Greenleaf may be guilty of the murder of Freddie Miles, if he does not present himself. Is it true that they think he is guilty?"

"Ah, no, no, no!" the tenente protested. "But it is imperative that he present himself! Why is he hiding from us?"

"I don't know. As you say—he is not very cooperative," Tom commented solemnly. "He was not enough cooperative to tell me in Rome that the police wanted to speak with me. But at the same time—I cannot believe it is possible that he killed Freddie Miles."

"*But*—you see, a man has said in Rome that he saw two men standing beside the car of Signor Mee-lays across the street from the house of Signor Greenleaf, and that they were both drunk or—" he paused for effect, looking at Tom "—perhaps one man was dead, because the other was holding him up beside the car! Of course, we cannot say that the man who was being supported was Signor Mee-lays or Signor Greenleaf," he added, "but if we could find Signor Greenleaf, we could at least ask him if he was so drunk that Signor Mee-lays had to hold him up!" He laughed. "Yes."

"It is a very serious matter."

"Yes, I can see that."

"You have absolutely no idea where Signor Greenleaf might be at this moment?"

"No. Absolutely no."

The tenente mused. "Signor Greenleaf and Signor Mee-lays had no quarrel that you know of?"

"No, but—"

"But?"

Tom continued slowly, doing it just right. "I know that Dickie did not go to a ski party that Freddie Miles had invited him to. I remember that I was surprised that he had not gone. He did not tell me why."

"I know about the ski party. In Cortina d'Ampezzo. Are you sure there was no woman involved?"

Tom's sense of humor tugged at him, but he pretended to think this one over carefully. "I do not think so."

"What about the girl, Marjorie Sherwood?"

"I suppose it is *possible*," Tom said, "but I do not think so. I am perhaps not the person to answer questions about Signor Greenleaf's personal life."

"Signor Greenleaf never talked to you about his affairs of the heart?" the tenente asked with a Latin astonishment.

He could lead them on indefinitely, Tom thought. Marge would back it up, just by the emotional way she would react to questions about Dickie, and the Italian police could never get to the bottom of Signor Greenleaf's emotional involvements. He hadn't been able to himself! "No," Tom said. "I cannot say that Dickie ever talked to me about his most personal life. I know he is very fond of Marjorie." He added, "She also knew Freddie Miles."

"How well did she know him?"

"Well—" Tom acted as if he might say more if he chose.

The tenente leaned forward. "Since you lived for a time with Signor Greenleaf in Mongibello, you are perhaps in a position to tell us about Signor Greenleaf's attachments in general. They are most important."

"Why don't you speak to Signorina Sherwood?" Tom suggested.

"We have spoken to her in Rome—before Signor Greenleaf disappeared. I have arranged to speak to her again when she comes to Genoa to embark for America. She is now in Munich."

Tom waited, silent. The tenente was waiting for him to contribute something more. Tom felt quite comfortable now. It was going just as he had hoped in his most optimistic moments: the police held nothing against him at all, and they suspected him of nothing. Tom felt suddenly innocent and strong, as free of guilt as his old suitcase from which he had carefully scrubbed the *Deponimento* sticker from the Palermo baggage room. He said in his earnest, careful, Ripley-like way, "I remember that Marjorie said for a while in Mongibello that she would *not* go to Cortina, and later she changed her mind. But I do not know why. If that could mean anything—"

"But she never went to Cortina."

"No, but only because Signor Greenleaf did not go, I think. At least, Signorina Sherwood likes him so much that she would not go alone on a holiday after she expected to go on the holiday with him."

"Do you think they had a quarrel, Signors Mee-lays and Greenleaf, about Signorina Sherwood?"

"I cannot say. It is possible. I know that Signor Miles was very fond of her, too."

"Ah-hah." The tenente frowned, trying to figure all that out. He glanced up at the younger policeman, who was evidently listening, though, from his immobile face, he had nothing to contribute.

What he had said gave a picture of Dickie as a sulking lover, Tom thought, unwilling to let Marge go to Cortina to have some fun, because she liked Freddie Miles too much. The idea of anybody, Marge especially, liking that wall-eyed ox in preference to Dickie made Tom smile. He turned the smile into an expression of noncomprehension. "Do you actually think Dickie is running away from something, or do you think it is an accident that you cannot find him?"

"Oh, no. This is too much. First, the matter of the checks. You perhaps know about that from the newspapers."

"I do not completely understand about the checks."

The officer explained. He knew the dates of the checks and the number of people who believed they were forged. He explained that Signor Greenleaf had denied the forgeries. "But when the bank wishes to see him again about a forgery against himself, and also the police in Rome wish to see him again about the murder of his friend, and he suddenly vanishes—" The tenente threw out his hands. "That can only mean that he is running away from us."

"You don't think someone may have murdered *him?*" Tom said softly.

The officer shrugged, holding his shoulders up under his ears for at least a quarter of a minute. "I do not think so. The facts are not like that. Not quite. Ebbene—we have checked by radio every boat of any size with passengers which has left from Italy. He has either taken a small boat, and it must have been as small as a fishing boat, or else he is hiding in Italy. Or of course, anywhere else in Europe, because we do not ordinarily take the names of people leaving our country, and Signor Greenleaf had several days in which to leave. In any case, he is hiding. In any case, he acts guilty. *Something* is the matter."

Tom stared gravely at the man.

"Did you ever *see* Signor Greenleaf sign any of those remittances? In particular, the remittances of January and February?"

"I saw him sign one of them," Tom said. "But I am afraid it was in December. I was not with him in January and February. —Do you seriously suspect that he might have killed Signor Miles?" Tom asked again, incredulously.

"He has no actual alibi," the officer replied. "He says he was taking a walk after Signor Mee-lays departed, but nobody saw him taking the walk." He pointed a finger at Tom suddenly. "*And*—we have learned from the friend of Signor Mee-lays, Signor Van Houston, that Signor Mee-lays had a difficult time finding Signor Greenleaf in Rome—as if Signor Greenleaf were trying to hide from him. Signor Greenleaf might have been angry with Signor Mee-lays, though, according to Signor Van Houston, Signor Mee-lays was not at all angry with Signor Greenleaf!"

"I see," Tom said.

"Ecco," the tenente said conclusively. He was staring at Tom's hands.

Or at least Tom imagined that he was staring at his hands. Tom had his own ring on again, but did the tenente possibly notice some resemblance? Tom boldly thrust his hand forward to the ashtray and put out his cigarette.

"Ebbene," the tenente said, standing up. "Thank you so much for your help, Signor Reepley. You are one of the very few people from whom we can find out about Signor Greenleaf's personal life. In Mongibello, the people he knew are extremely quiet. An Italian trait, alas! You know, afraid of the police." He chuckled. "I hope we can reach you more easily the next time we have questions to ask you. Stay in the cities a little more and in the country a little less. Unless, of course, you are addicted to our countryside."

"I am!" Tom said heartily. "In my opinion, Italy is the most beautiful country of Europe. But if you like, I shall keep in touch with you in Rome so you will always know where I am. I am as much interested as you in finding my friend." He said it as if his innocent mind had already forgotten the possibility that Dickie could be a murderer.

The tenente handed him a card with his name and the address of his headquarters in Rome. He bowed. "Grazie tante, Signor Reepley. Buona sera!"

"Buona sera," Tom said.

The younger policeman saluted him as he went out, and Tom gave him a nod and closed the door.

He could have flown—like a bird, out the window, with spread arms! The idiots! All around the thing and never guessing it! Never guessing that Dickie was running from the forgery questions because he wasn't Dickie Greenleaf in the first place! The one thing they were bright about was that Dickie Greenleaf might have killed Freddie Miles. But Dickie Greenleaf was dead, dead, deader than a doornail and he, Tom Ripley, was safe! He picked up the telephone.

"Would you give me the Grand Hotel, please," he said in Tom Ripley's Italian. "Il ristorante, per piacere. —Would you reserve a table for one for nine-thirty? Thank you. The name is Ripley. R-i-p-l-e-y."

Tonight he was going to have a dinner. And look out at the moonlight on the Grand Canal. And watch the gondolas drifting as lazily as they ever drifted for any honeymooner, with the gondoliers and their oars silhouetted against the moonlit water. He was suddenly ravenous. He was going to have something luscious and expensive to eat—whatever the Grand Hotel's specialty was, breast of pheasant or petto di pollo, and perhaps cannelloni to begin with, creamy sauce over delicate pasta, and a good valpolicella to sip while he dreamed about his future and planned where he went from here.

He had a bright idea while he was changing his clothes: he ought to have an envelope in his possession, on which should be written that it was not to be opened for several months to come. Inside it should be a will signed by Dickie, bequeathing him his money and his income. Now that was an idea.

23.

Venice
Feb. 28, 19—

Dear Mr. Greenleaf,

I thought under the circumstances you would not take it amiss if I wrote you whatever personal information I have in regard to Richard—I being one of the last people, it seems, who saw him.

I saw him in Rome around February 2nd at the Inghilterra Hotel. As you know, this was only two or three days after the death of Freddie Miles. I found Dickie upset and nervous. He said he was going to Palermo as soon as the police finished their questioning him in regard to Freddie's death, and he seemed eager to get away, which was understandable, but I wanted to tell you that there was a certain depression underlying all this that troubled me much more than his obvious nervousness. I had the feeling he would try to do something violent—perhaps to himself. I knew also that he didn't want to see his friend Marjorie Sherwood again, and he said he would try to avoid her if she came up from Mongibello to see him because of the Miles affair. I tried to persuade him to see her. I don't know if he did. Marge has a soothing effect on people, as perhaps you know.

What I am trying to say is that I feel Richard may have killed himself. At the time of this writing he has not been found. I certainly hope he will be before this reaches you. It goes without saying that I am sure Richard had nothing to do, directly or indirectly, with Freddie's death, but I think the shock of it and the questioning that followed did do something to upset his equilibrium. This is a depressing message to send to you and I regret it. It may be all completely unnecessary and Dickie may be (again understandably, according to his temperament) simply in hiding until these unpleasantnesses blow over. But as the time goes on, I begin to feel more uneasy myself. I thought it my duty to write you this, simply by way of letting you know. . . .

Munich
March 3, 19—

Dear Tom,

Thanks for your letter. It was very kind of you. I've answered the police in writing, and one came up to see me. I won't be coming by Venice, but thanks for your invitation. I am going to Rome day after tomorrow to meet Dickie's father, who is flying over. Yes, I agree with you that it was a good idea for you to write to him.

I am so bowled over by all this, I have come down with something resembling undulant fever, or maybe what the Germans call Foehn, but with some kind of virus thrown in. Literally unable to get out of bed for four days, otherwise I'd have gone to Rome before now. So please excuse this disjointed and probably feeble-minded letter which is such a bad answer to your very nice one. But I did want to say I don't agree with you at all that Dickie might have committed suicide. He just isn't the type, though I know all you're going to say about people never acting like they're going to do it, etc. No, anything else but this for Dickie. He might have been murdered in some back alley of Naples—or even Rome, because who knows whether he got up to Rome or not after he left Sicily? I can also imagine him running out on obligations to such an extent that he'd be *hiding* now. I think that's what he's doing.

I'm glad you think the forgeries are a mistake. Of the bank, I mean. So do I. Dickie has changed so much since November, it could easily have changed his handwriting, too. Let's hope something's happened by the time you get this. Had a wire from Mr. Greenleaf about Rome—so must save all my energy for that.

Nice to know your address finally. Thanks again for your letter, your advice, and invitations.

Best,
Marge

P.S. I didn't tell you my *good* news. I've got a publisher interested in "Mongibello"! Says he wants to see the whole thing before he can give me a contract, but it really sounds hopeful! Now if I can only finish the damn thing!

M.

She had decided to be on good terms with him, Tom supposed. She'd probably changed her tune about him to the police, too.

Dickie's disappearance was stirring up a great deal of excitement in the Italian press. Marge, or somebody, had provided the reporters with photographs. There were pictures in *Epoca* of Dickie sailing his boat in Mongibello, pictures of Dickie in *Oggi* sitting on the beach in Mongibello and also on Giorgio's terrace, and a picture of Dickie and Marge—"girl friend of both il sparito Dickie and il assassinato Freddie"— smiling, with their arms around each other's shoulders, and there was even a businesslike portrait of Herbert Greenleaf, Sr. Tom had gotten Marge's Munich address right out of a newspaper. *Oggi* had been running a life story of Dickie for the past two weeks, describing his school years as "rebellious" and embroidering his social life in America and his flight to Europe for the sake of his art to such an extent that he emerged as a combination of Errol Flynn and Paul Gauguin. The illustrated weeklies always gave the latest police reports, which were practically nil, padded with whatever theorizing the writers happened to feel like concocting that week. A favorite theory was that he had run off with another girl—a girl who might have been signing his remittances—and was having a good time, incognito, in Tahiti or South America or Mexico. The police were still combing Rome and Naples and Paris, that was all. No clues as to Freddie Miles' killer, and nothing about Dickie Greenleaf's having been seen carrying Freddie Miles, or vice versa, in front of Dickie's house. Tom wondered why they were holding that back from the newspapers. Probably because they couldn't write it up without subjecting themselves to charges of libel by Dickie. Tom was gratified to find himself described as "a loyal friend" of the missing Dickie Greenleaf, who had volunteered everything he knew as to Dickie's character and habits, and who was as bewildered by his disappearance as anybody else. "Signor Ripley, one of the young well-to-do American visitors in Italy," said *Oggi*, "now lives in a palazzo overlooking San Marco in Venice." That pleased Tom most of all. He cut out that write-up.

Tom had not thought of it as a "palace" before, but of course it was what the Italians called a palazzo—a two-story house of formal design more than two hundred years old, with a main entrance on the Grand Canal approachable only by gondola, with broad stone steps descending into the water, and iron doors that had to be opened by an eight-inch-long key, besides the regular doors behind the iron doors which also took an enormous key. Tom used the less formal "back door" usually, which was on the Viale San Spiridione, except when he wanted to impress his guests by bringing them to his home in a gondola. The back door—itself fourteen feet high like the stone wall that enclosed the house from the street—led into a garden that was somewhat neglected but still green, and which boasted two gnarled olive trees and a birdbath made of an ancient-looking statue of a naked boy holding a wide shallow bowl. It was just the garden for a Venetian palace, slightly run down, in need of some restoration which it was not going to get, but indelibly beautiful because it had sprung into the world so beautiful more than two hundred years ago. The inside of the house was Tom's ideal of what a civilized bachelor's home should look like, in Venice, at least: a checkerboard black-and-white marble floor downstairs extending from the formal foyer into each room, pink-and-white marble floor upstairs, furniture that did not resemble furniture at all but an embodiment of cinquecento music played on hautboys, recorders, and violas da gamba. He had his servants—Anna and Ugo, a young Italian couple who had worked for an American in Venice before, so that they knew the difference between a Bloody Mary and a crème de menthe frappé—polish the carved fronts of the armoires and chests and chairs until they seemed alive with dim lustrous lights that moved as one moved around them. The only thing faintly modern was the bathroom. In Tom's bedroom stood a gargantuan bed, broader than it was long. Tom decorated his bedroom with a series of panoramic pictures of Naples from 1540 to about 1880, which he found at an antique store. He had given his undivided attention to decorating his house for more than a week. There was a sureness in his taste now that he had not felt in Rome, and that his Rome apartment had not hinted at. He felt surer of himself now in every way.

His self-confidence had even inspired him to write to Aunt Dottie in a calm, affectionate and forbearing tone that he had never wanted to use before, or had never before been able to use. He had inquired about her flamboyant health, about her little circle of vicious friends in Boston, and had explained to her why he liked Europe and intended to live here for a while, explained so eloquently that he had copied that section of his letter and put it into his desk. He had written this inspired letter one morning after breakfast, sitting in his bedroom in a new silk dressing gown made to order for him in Venice, gazing out the window now and then at the Grand Canal and the Clock Tower of the Piazza San Marco across the water. After he had finished the letter he had made some more coffee and on Dickie's own Hermes he had written Dickie's will, bequeathing him his income and the money he had in various

banks, and had signed it Herbert Richard Greenleaf, Jr. Tom
thought it better not to add a witness, lest the banks or Mr.
Greenleaf challenge him to the extent of demanding to know
who the witness was, though Tom had thought of making up
an Italian name, presumably someone Dickie might have
called into his apartment in Rome for the purpose of wit-
nessing the will. He would just have to take his chances on
an unwitnessed will, he thought, but Dickie's typewriter was
so in need of repair that its quirks were as recognizable as a
particular handwriting, and he had heard that holograph wills
required no witnesses. But the signature was perfect, exactly
like the slim, tangled signature on Dickie's passport. Tom
practiced for half an hour before he signed the will, relaxed
his hands, then signed a piece of scrap paper, then the will, in
rapid succession. And he would defy anybody to prove that
the signature on the will wasn't Dickie's. Tom put an envelope
into the typewriter and addressed it To Whom It May Concern, with a notation that it was not to be opened until June
of this year. He tucked it into a side pocket of his suitcase, as
if he had been carrying it there for some time and hadn't
bothered unpacking it when he moved into the house. Then
he took the Hermes Baby in its case downstairs and dropped
it into the little inlet of the canal, too narrow for a boat, which
ran from the front corner of his house to the garden wall. He
was glad to be rid of the typewriter, though he had been
unwilling to part with it until now. He must have known,
subconsciously, he thought, that he was going to write the
will or something else of great importance on it, and that was
the reason why he had kept it.

Tom followed the Italian newspapers and the Paris edition
of the *Herald-Tribune* on the Greenleaf and Miles cases with
the anxious concern befitting a friend of both Dickie and
Freddie. The papers were suggesting by the end of March that
Dickie might be dead, murdered by the same man or men
who had been profiting by forging his signature. A Rome paper said that one man in Naples now held that the signature
on the letter from Palermo, stating that no forgeries had been
committed against him, was also a forgery. Others, however,
did not concur. Some man on the police force, not Roverini,
thought that the culprit or culprits had been "intimo" with

Greenleaf, that they had had access to the bank's letter and had had the audacity to reply to it themselves. "The mystery is," the officer was quoted, "not only who the forger was but how he gained access to the letter, because the porter of the hotel remembers putting the registered bank letter into Greenleaf's hands. The hotel porter also recalls that Greenleaf was always alone in Palermo. . . ."

More hitting around the answer without ever hitting it. But Tom was shaken for several minutes after he read it. There remained only one more step for them to take, and wasn't somebody going to take it today or tomorrow or the next day? Or did they really already know the answer, and were they just trying to put him off guard—Tenente Roverini sending him personal messages every few days to keep him abreast of what was happening in the search for Dickie—and were they going to pounce on him one day soon with every bit of evidence they needed?

It gave Tom the feeling that he was being followed, especially when he walked through the long, narrow street to his house door. The Viale San Spiridione was nothing but a functional slit between vertical walls of houses, without a shop in it and with hardly enough light for him to see where he was going, nothing but unbroken housefronts and the tall, firmly locked doors of the Italian house gates that were flush with the walls. Nowhere to run to if he were attacked, no house door to duck into. Tom did not know who would attack him, if he were attacked. He did not imagine police, necessarily. He was afraid of nameless, formless things that haunted his brain like the Furies. He could go through San Spiridione comfortably only when a few cocktails had knocked out his fear. Then he walked through swaggering and whistling.

He had his pick of cocktail parties, though in his first two weeks in his house he went to only two. He had his choice of people because of a little incident that had happened the first day he had started looking for a house. A rental agent, armed with three huge keys, had taken him to see a certain house in San Stefano parish, thinking it would be vacant. It had not only been occupied but a cocktail party had been in progress, and the hostess had insisted on Tom and the rental agent, too, having a cocktail by way of making amends for their inconvenience and her remissness. She had put the house up for rent a month ago, had changed her mind about leaving, and had neglected to inform the rental agency. Tom stayed for a drink, acted his reserved, courteous self, and met all her guests, who he supposed were most of the winter colony of Venice and rather hungry for new blood, judging from the way they welcomed him and offered their assistance in finding a house. They recognized his name, of course, and the fact that he knew Dickie Greenleaf raised his social value to a degree that surprised even Tom. Obviously they were going to invite him everywhere and quiz him and drain him of every last little detail to add some spice to their dull lives. Tom behaved in a reserved but friendly manner appropriate for a young man in his position—a sensitive young man, unused to garish publicity, whose primary emotion in regard to Dickie was anxiety as to what had happened to him.

He left that first party with the addresses of three other houses he might look at (one being the one he took) and invitations to two other parties. He went to the party whose hostess had a title, the Condessa Roberta (Titi) della Latta-Cacciaguerra. He was not at all in the mood for parties. He seemed to see people through a mist, and communication was slow and difficult. He often asked people to repeat what they had said. He was terribly bored. But he could use them, he thought, to practice on. The naïve questions they asked him ("Did Dickie drink a lot?" and "But he *was* in love with Marge, wasn't he?" and "Where do you *really* think he went?") were good practice for the more specific questions Mr. Greenleaf was going to ask him when he saw him, if he ever saw him. Tom began to be uneasy about ten days after Marge's letter, because Mr. Greenleaf had not written or telephoned him from Rome. In certain frightened moments, Tom imagined that the police had told Mr. Greenleaf that they were playing a game with Tom Ripley, and had asked Mr. Greenleaf not to talk to him.

Each day he looked eagerly in his mailbox for a letter from Marge or Mr. Greenleaf. His house was ready for their arrival. His answers to their questions were ready in his head. It was like waiting interminably for a show to begin, for a curtain to rise. Or maybe Mr. Greenleaf was so resentful of him (not to

mention possibly being actually suspicious) that he was going
to ignore him entirely. Maybe Marge was abetting him in that.
At any rate, he couldn't take a trip until *something* happened.
Tom wanted to take a trip, the famous trip to Greece. He had
bought a guidebook of Greece, and he had already planned
his itinerary over the islands.

Then, on the morning of April fourth, he got a telephone
call from Marge. She was in Venice, at the railroad station.

"I'll come and pick you up!" Tom said cheerfully. "Is Mr.
Greenleaf with you?"

"No, he's in Rome. I'm alone. You don't have to pick me
up. I've only got an overnight bag."

"Nonsense!" Tom said, dying to do something. "You'll
never find the house by yourself."

"Yes, I will. It's next to della Salute, isn't it? I take the
motoscafo to San Marco's, then take a gondola across."

She knew, all right. "Well, if you insist." He had just
thought that he had better take one more good look around
the house before she got here. "Have you had lunch?"

"No."

"Good! We'll lunch together somewhere. Watch your step
on the motoscafo!"

They hung up. He walked soberly and slowly through the
house, into both large rooms upstairs, down the stairs and
through his living room. Nothing, anywhere, that belonged
to Dickie. He hoped the house didn't look too plush. He took
a silver cigarette box, which he had bought only two days ago
and had had initialed, from the living-room table and put it
in the bottom drawer of a chest in the dining room.

Anna was in the kitchen, preparing lunch.

"Anna, there'll be one more for lunch," Tom said. "A
young lady."

Anna's face broke into a smile at the prospect of a guest.
"A young American lady?"

"Yes. An old friend. When the lunch is ready, you and Ugo
can have the rest of the afternoon off. We can serve ourselves."

"Va bene," Anna said.

Anna and Ugo came at ten and stayed until two, ordinarily.
Tom didn't want them here when he talked with Marge. They

understood a little English, not enough to follow a conversation perfectly, but he knew both of them would have their ears out if he and Marge talked about Dickie, and it irritated him.

Tom made a batch of martinis, and arranged the glasses and a plate of canapés on a tray in the living room. When he heard the door knocker, he went to the door and swung it open.

"Marge! Good to see you! Come in!" He took the suitcase from her hand.

"How are you, Tom? My! —Is all this yours?" She looked around her, and up at the high coffered ceiling.

"I rented it. For a song," Tom said modestly. "Come and have a drink. Tell me what's new. You've been talking to the police in Rome?" He carried her topcoat and her transparent raincoat to a chair.

"Yes, and to Mr. Greenleaf. He's very upset—naturally." She sat down on the sofa.

Tom settled himself in a chair opposite her. "Have they found anything new? One of the police officers there has been keeping me posted, but he hasn't told me anything that really matters."

"Well, they found out that Dickie cashed over a thousand dollars' worth of traveler's checks before he left Palermo. *Just* before. So he must have gone off somewhere with it, like Greece or Africa. He couldn't have gone off to kill himself after just cashing a thousand dollars, anyway."

"No," Tom agreed. "Well, that sounds hopeful. I didn't see that in the papers."

"I don't think they put it in."

"No. Just a lot of nonsense about what Dickie used to eat for breakfast in Mongibello," Tom said as he poured the martinis.

"Isn't it awful! It's getting a little better now, but when Mr. Greenleaf arrived, the papers were at their worst. Oh, thanks!" She accepted the martini gratefully.

"How is he?"

Marge shook her head. "I feel so sorry for him. He keeps saying the American police could do a better job and all that, and he doesn't know any Italian, so that makes it twice as bad."

"What's he doing in Rome?"

"Waiting. What can any of us do? I've postponed my boat again. —Mr. Greenleaf and I went to Mongibello, and I questioned everyone there, mostly for Mr. Greenleaf's benefit, of course, but they can't tell us anything. Dickie hasn't been back there since November."

"No." Tom sipped his martini thoughtfully. Marge was optimistic, he could see that. Even now she had that energetic buoyance that made Tom think of the typical Girl Scout, that look of taking up a lot of space, of possibly knocking something over with a wild movement, of rugged health and vague untidiness. She irritated him intensely suddenly, but he put on a big act, got up and patted her on the shoulder, and gave her an affectionate peck on the cheek. "Maybe he's sitting in Tangiers or somewhere living the life of Riley and waiting for all this to blow over."

"Well, it's damned inconsiderate of him if he is!" Marge said, laughing.

"I certainly didn't mean to alarm anybody when I said what I did about his depression. I felt it was a kind of duty to tell you and Mr. Greenleaf."

"I understand. No, I think you were right to tell us. I just don't think it's true." She smiled her broad smile, her eyes glowing with an optimism that struck Tom as completely insane.

He began asking her sensible, practical questions about the opinions of the Rome police, about the leads that they had (they had none worth mentioning), and what she had heard on the Miles case. There was nothing new on the Miles case, either, but Marge did know about Freddie and Dickie's having been seen in front of Dickie's house around eight o'clock that night. She thought the story was exaggerated.

"Maybe Freddie was drunk, or maybe Dickie just had an arm around him. How could anybody tell in the dark? Don't tell me Dickie murdered him!"

"Have they any concrete clues at all that would make them think Dickie killed him?"

"Of course not!"

"Then why don't the so-and-so's get down to the business

of finding out who really did kill him? And also where Dickie is?"

"Ecco!" Marge said emphatically. "Anyway, the police are sure now that Dickie at least got from Palermo to Naples. A steward remembers carrying his bags from his cabin to the Naples dock."

"Really," Tom said. He remembered the steward, too, a clumsy little oaf who had dropped his canvas suitcase, trying to carry it under one arm. "Wasn't Freddie killed hours after he left Dickie's house?" Tom asked suddenly.

"No. The doctors can't say exactly. And it seems Dickie didn't have an alibi, of course, because he was undoubtedly alone. Just more of Dickie's bad luck."

"They don't actually *believe* Dickie killed him, do they?"

"They don't say it, no. It's just in the air. Naturally, they can't make rash statements right and left about an American citizen, but as long as they haven't any suspects and Dickie's disappeared— Then also his landlady in Rome said that Freddie came down to ask her who was living in Dickie's apartment or something like that. She said Freddie looked angry, as if they'd been quarreling. She said he asked if Dickie was living alone."

Tom frowned. "I wonder why?"

"I can't imagine. Freddie's Italian wasn't the best in the world, and maybe the landlady got it wrong. Anyway, the mere fact that Freddie was angry about something looks bad for Dickie."

Tom raised his eyebrows. "I'd say it looked bad for Freddie. Maybe Dickie wasn't angry at all." He felt perfectly calm, because he could see that Marge hadn't smelled out anything about it. "I wouldn't worry about that unless something concrete comes out of it. Sounds like nothing at all to me." He refilled her glass. "Speaking of Africa, have they inquired around Tangiers yet? Dickie used to talk about going to Tangiers."

"I think they've alerted the police everywhere. I think they ought to get the French police down here. The French are terribly good at things like this. But of course they can't. This is Italy," she said with the first nervous tremor in her voice.

"Shall we have lunch here?" Tom asked. "The maid is functioning over the lunch hour and we might as well take advantage of it." He said it just as Anna was coming in to announce that the lunch was ready.

"Wonderful!" Marge said. "It's raining a little, anyway."

"Pronta la collazione, signor," Anna said with a smile, staring at Marge.

Anna recognized her from the newspaper pictures, Tom saw. "You and Ugo can go now if you like, Anna. Thanks."

Anna went back into the kitchen—there was a door from the kitchen to a little alley at the side of the house, which the servants used—but Tom heard her pottering around with the coffee maker, stalling for another glimpse, no doubt.

"And Ugo?" Marge said. "Two servants, no less?"

"Oh, they come in couples around here. You may not believe it, but I got this place for fifty dollars a month, not counting heat."

"I don't believe it! That's practically like Mongibello rates!"

"It's true. The heating's fantastic, of course, but I'm not going to heat any room except my bedroom."

"It's certainly comfortable here."

"Oh, I opened the whole furnace for your benefit," Tom said, smiling.

"What happened? Did one of your aunts die and leave you a fortune?" Marge asked, still pretending to be dazzled.

"No, just a decision of my own. I'm going to enjoy what I've got as long as it lasts. I told you that job I was after in Rome didn't pan out, and here I was in Europe with only about two thousand dollars to my name, so I decided to live it up and go home—broke—and start over again." Tom had explained to her in his letter that the job he had applied for had been selling hearing aids in Europe for an American company, and he hadn't been able to face it, and the man who had interviewed him, he said, hadn't thought him the right type, either. Tom had also told her that the man had appeared one minute after he spoke to her, which was why he had been unable to keep his appointment with her in Angelo's that day in Rome.

"Two thousand dollars won't last you long at this rate."

She was probing to see if Dickie had given him anything, Tom knew. "It will last till summer," Tom said matter-of-factly. "Anyway, I feel I deserve it. I spent most of the winter going around Italy like a gypsy on practically no money, and I've had about enough of that."

"Where *were* you this winter?"

"Well, not with Tom. I mean, not with Dickie," he said laughing, flustered at his slip of the tongue. "I know you probably thought so. I saw about as much of Dickie as you did."

"Oh, come on now," Marge drawled. She sounded as if she were feeling her drinks.

Tom made two or three more martinis in the pitcher. "Except for the trip to Cannes and the two days in Rome in February, I haven't seen Dickie at all." It wasn't quite true, because he had written her that "Tom was staying" with Dickie in Rome for several days after the Cannes trip, but now that he was face to face with Marge he found he was ashamed of her knowing, or thinking, that he had spent so much time with Dickie, and that he and Dickie might be guilty of what she had accused Dickie of in her letter. He bit his tongue as he poured their drinks, hating himself for his cowardice.

During lunch—Tom regretted very much that the main dish was cold roast beef, a fabulously expensive item on the Italian market—Marge quizzed him more acutely than any police officer on Dickie's state of mind while he was in Rome. Tom was pinned down to ten days spent in Rome with Dickie after the Cannes trip, and was questioned about everything from Di Massimo, the painter Dickie had worked with, to Dickie's appetite and the hour he got up in the morning.

"How do you think he felt about *me*? Tell me honestly. I can take it."

"I think he was worried about you," Tom said earnestly. "I think—well, it was one of those situations that turn up quite often, a man who's terrified of marriage to begin with—"

"But I never asked him to marry me!" Marge protested.

"I know, but—" Tom forced himself to go on, though the subject was like vinegar in his mouth. "Let's say he couldn't face the responsibility of your caring so much about him. I think he wanted a more casual relationship with you." That told her everything and nothing.

Marge stared at him in that old, lost way for a moment, then rallied bravely and said, "Well, all that's water under the bridge by now. I'm only interested in what Dickie might have done with himself."

Her fury at his apparently having been with Dickie all winter was water under the bridge, too, Tom thought, because she hadn't wanted to believe it in the first place, and now she didn't have to. Tom asked carefully, "He didn't happen to write to you when he was in Palermo?"

Marge shook her head. "No. Why?"

"I wanted to know what kind of state you thought he was in then. Did you write to him?"

She hesitated. "Yes—matter of fact, I did."

"What kind of a letter? I only ask because an unfriendly letter might have had a bad effect on him just then."

"Oh—it's hard to say what kind. A fairly friendly letter. I told him I was going back to the States." She looked at him with wide eyes.

Tom enjoyed watching her face, watching somebody else squirm as they lied. That had been the filthy letter in which she said she had told the police that he and Dickie were always together. "I don't suppose it matters then," Tom said, with sweet gentleness, sitting back.

They were silent a few moments, then Tom asked her about her book, who the publisher was, and how much more work she had to do. Marge answered everything enthusiastically. Tom had the feeling that if she had Dickie back and her book published by next winter, she would probably just explode with happiness, make a loud, unattractive *ploop!* and that would be the end of her.

"Do you think I should offer to talk to Mr. Greenleaf, too?" Tom asked. "I'd be glad to go to Rome—" Only he wouldn't be so glad, he remembered, because Rome had simply too many people in it who had seen him as Dickie Greenleaf. "Or do you think he would like to come here? I could put him up. Where's he staying in Rome?"

"He's staying with some American friends who have a big apartment. Somebody called Northup in Via Quattro Novembre. I think it'd be nice if you called him. I'll write the address down for you."

"That's a good idea. He doesn't like me, does he?"

Marge smiled a little. "Well, frankly, no. I think he's a little hard on you, considering. He probably thinks you sponged off Dickie."

"Well, I didn't. I'm sorry the idea didn't work out about my getting Dickie back home, but I explained all that. I wrote him the nicest letter I could about Dickie when I heard he was missing. Didn't that help any?"

"I think it did, but— Oh, I'm terribly sorry, Tom! All over this wonderful tablecloth!" Marge had turned her martini over. She daubed at the crocheted tablecloth awkwardly with her napkin.

Tom came running back from the kitchen with a wet cloth. "Perfectly all right," he said, watching the wood of the table turn white in spite of his wiping. It wasn't the tablecloth he cared about, it was the beautiful table.

"I'm so sorry," Marge went on protesting.

Tom hated her. He suddenly remembered her bra hanging over the windowsill in Mongibello. Her underwear would be draped over his chairs tonight, if he invited her to stay here. The idea repelled him. He deliberately hurled a smile across the table at her. "I hope you'll honor me by accepting a bed for the night. Not mine," he added, laughing, "but I've got two rooms upstairs and you're welcome to one of them."

"Thanks a lot. All right, I will." She beamed at him.

Tom installed her in his own room—the bed in the other room being only an outsized couch and not so comfortable as his double bed—and Marge closed her door to take a nap after lunch. Tom wandered restlessly through the rest of the house, wondering whether there was anything in his room that he ought to remove. Dickie's passport was in the lining of a suitcase in his closet. He couldn't think of anything else. But women had sharp eyes, Tom thought, even Marge. She might snoop around. Finally he went into the room while she was still asleep and took the suitcase from the closet. The floor squeaked, and Marge's eyes fluttered open.

"Just want to get something out of here," Tom whispered. "Sorry." He continued tiptoeing out of the room. Marge probably wouldn't even remember, he thought, because she hadn't completely waked up.

Later he showed Marge all around the house, showed her the shelf of leather-bound books in the room next to his bedroom, books that he said had come with the house, though they were his own, bought in Rome and Palermo and Venice. He realized that he had had about ten of them in Rome, and that one of the young police officers with Roverini had bent close to them, apparently studying their titles. But it was nothing really to worry about, he thought, even if the same police officer were to come back. He showed Marge the front entrance of the house, with its broad stone steps. The tide was low and four steps were bared now, the lower two covered with thick wet moss. The moss was a slippery, long-filament variety, and hung over the edges of the steps like messy darkgreen hair. The steps were repellent to Tom, but Marge thought them very romantic. She bent over them, staring at the deep water of the canal. Tom had an impulse to push her in.

"Can we take a gondola and come in this way tonight?" she asked.

"Oh, sure." They were going out to dinner tonight, of course. Tom dreaded the long Italian evening ahead of them, because they wouldn't eat until ten, and then she'd probably want to sit in San Marco's over espressos until two in the morning.

Tom looked up at the hazy, sunless Venetian sky, and watched a gull glide down and settle on somebody else's front steps across the canal. He was trying to decide which of his new Venetian friends he would telephone and ask if he could bring Marge over for a drink around five o'clock. They would all be delighted to meet her, of course. He decided on the Englishman Peter Smith-Kingsley. Peter had an Afghan, a piano, and a well-equipped bar. Tom thought Peter would be best because Peter never wanted anybody to leave. They could stay there until it was time for them to go to dinner.

24.

Tom called Mr. Greenleaf from Peter Smith-Kingsley's house at about seven o'clock. Mr. Greenleaf sounded friendlier than Tom had expected, and sounded pitifully hungry for the little crumbs Tom gave him about Dickie. Peter and Marge and the Franchettis—an attractive pair of brothers from Trieste whom Tom had recently met—were in the next room and able to hear almost every word he said, so Tom did it better than he would have done it completely alone, he felt.

"I've told Marge all I know," he said, "so she'll be able to tell you anything I've forgotten. I'm only sorry that I can't contribute anything of real importance for the police to work on."

"These police!" Mr. Greenleaf said gruffly. "I'm beginning to think Richard is dead. For some reason the Italians are reluctant to admit he might be. They act like amateurs or— or old ladies playing at being detectives."

Tom was shocked at Mr. Greenleaf's bluntness about Dickie's possibly being dead. "Do *you* think Dickie might have killed himself, Mr. Greenleaf?" Tom asked quietly.

Mr. Greenleaf sighed. "I don't know. I think it's possible, yes. I never thought much of my son's stability, Tom."

"I'm afraid I agree with you," Tom said. "Would you like to talk to Marge? She's in the next room."

"No, no, thanks. When's she coming back?"

"I think she said she'd be going back to Rome tomorrow. If you'd possibly like to come to Venice, just for a slight rest, Mr. Greenleaf, you're very welcome to stay at my house."

But Mr. Greenleaf declined the invitation. It wasn't necessary to bend over backwards, Tom realized. It was as if he were really inviting trouble, and couldn't stop himself. Mr. Greenleaf thanked him for his telephone call and said a very courteous good night.

Tom went back into the other room. "There's no more news from Rome," he said dejectedly to the group.

"Oh." Peter looked disappointed.

"Here's for the phone call, Peter," Tom said, laying twelve hundred lire on top of Peter's piano. "Thanks very much."

"I have an idea," Pietro Franchetti began in his English-accented English. "Dickie Greenleaf has traded passports with a Neapolitan fisherman or maybe a Roman cigarette peddler, so that he can lead the quiet life he always wanted to. It so happens that the bearer of the Dickie Greenleaf passport is not so good a forger as he thought he was, and he had to disappear suddenly. The police should find a man who can't produce his proper carta d'identità, find out who he is, then look for a man with his name, who will turn out to be Dickie Greenleaf!"

Everybody laughed, and Tom loudest of all.

"The trouble with that idea," Tom said, "is that lots of people who knew Dickie saw him in January and February—"

"*Who?*" Pietro interrupted with that irritating Italian belligerence in conversation that was doubly irritating in English.

"Well, I did, for one. Anyway, as I was going to say, the forgeries now date from December, according to the bank."

"Still, it's an idea," Marge chirruped, feeling very good on her third drink, lolling back on Peter's big chaise-longue. "A very Dickie-like idea. He probably would have done it right after Palermo, when he had the bank forgery business on top of everything else. I don't believe those forgeries for one minute. I think Dickie'd changed so much that his handwriting changed."

"I think so, too," Tom said. "The bank isn't unanimous, anyway, in saying they're all forged. America's divided about it, and Naples fell right in with America. Naples never would have noticed a forgery if the U.S. hadn't told them about it."

"I wonder what's in the papers tonight?" Peter asked brightly, pulling on the slipperlike shoe that he had half taken off because it probably hurt. "Shall I go out and get them?"

But one of the Franchettis volunteered to go, and dashed out of the room. Lorenzo Franchetti was wearing a pink embroidered waistcoat, all' inglese, and an English-made suit and heavy-soled English shoes, and his brother was dressed in much the same way. Peter, on the other hand, was dressed in Italian clothes from head to foot. Tom had noticed, at parties and at the theatre, that if a man was dressed in English clothes he was bound to be an Italian, and vice versa.

Some more people arrived just as Lorenzo came back with the papers—two Italians and two Americans. The papers were passed around. More discussion, more exchanges of stupid speculation, more excitement over today's news: Dickie's house in Mongibello had been sold to an American for twice the price he originally asked for it. The money was going to be held by a Naples bank until Greenleaf claimed it.

The same paper had a cartoon of a man on his knees, looking under his bureau. His wife asked, "Collar button?" And his answer was, "No, I'm looking for Dickie Greenleaf."

Tom had heard that the Rome music halls were taking off the search in skits, too.

One of the Americans who had just come in, whose name was Rudy something, invited Tom and Marge to a cocktail party at his hotel the following day. Tom started to decline, but Marge said she would be delighted to come. Tom hadn't thought she would be here tomorrow, because she had said something at lunch about leaving. The party would be deadly, Tom thought. Rudy was a loud-mouthed, crude man in flashy clothes who said he was an antique dealer. Tom maneuvered himself and Marge out of the house before she accepted any more invitations that might be further into the future.

Marge was in a giddy mood that irritated Tom throughout their long five-course dinner, but he made the supreme effort and responded in kind—like a helpless frog twitching from an electric needle, he thought—and when she dropped the ball, he picked it up and dribbled it a while. He said things like, "Maybe Dickie's suddenly found himself in his painting, and he's gone away like Gauguin to one of the South Sea Islands." It made him ill. Then Marge would spin a fantasy about Dickie and the South Sea Islands, making lazy gestures with her hands. The worst was yet to come, Tom thought: the gondola ride. If she dangled those hands in the water, he hoped a shark bit them off. He ordered a dessert that he hadn't room for, but Marge ate it.

Marge wanted a private gondola, of course, not the regular ferry-service gondola that took people over ten at a time from San Marco's to the steps of Santa Maria della Salute, so they engaged a private gondola. It was one-thirty in the morning. Tom had a dark-brown taste in his mouth from too many espressos, his heart was fluttering like bird wings, and he did not expect to be able to sleep until dawn. He felt exhausted, and lay back in the gondola's seat about as languidly as Marge, careful to keep his thigh from touching hers. Marge was still in ebullient spirits, entertaining herself now with a monologue about the sunrise in Venice, which she had apparently seen on some other visit. The gentle rocking of the boat and the rhythmic thrusts of the gondolier's oar made Tom feel slightly sickish. The expanse of water between the San Marco boat stop and his steps seemed interminable.

The steps were covered now except for the upper two, and the water swept just over the surface of the third step, stirring its moss in a disgusting way. Tom paid the gondolier mechanically, and was standing in front of the big doors when he realized he hadn't brought the keys. He glanced around to see if he could climb in anywhere, but he couldn't even reach a window ledge from the steps. Before he even said anything, Marge burst out laughing.

"You didn't bring the key! Of all things, stuck on the doorstep with the raging waters around us, and no key!"

Tom tried to smile. Why the hell should he have thought to bring two keys nearly a foot long that weighed as much as a couple of revolvers? He turned and yelled to the gondolier to come back.

"Ah!" the gondolier chuckled across the water. "Mi dispiace, signor! Deb' ritornare a San Marco! Ho un appuntamento!" He kept on rowing.

"We have no keys!" Tom yelled in Italian.

"Mi dispiace, signor!" replied the gondolier. "Mandarò un altro gondoliere!"

Marge laughed again. "Oh, some other gondolier'll pick us up. Isn't it beautiful?" She stood on tiptoe.

It was not at all a beautiful night. It was chilly, and a slimy little rain had started falling. He might get the ferry gondola to come over, Tom thought, but he didn't see it. The only boat he saw was the motoscafo approaching the San Marco pier. There was hardly a chance that the motoscafo would trouble to pick them up, but Tom yelled to it, anyway. The motoscafo, full of lights and people, went blindly on and nosed in at the wooden pier across the canal. Marge was sitting on the top step with her arms around her knees, doing nothing. Finally, a lowslung motorboat that looked like a fishing boat of some sort slowed down, and someone yelled in Italian: "Locked out?"

"We forgot the keys!" Marge explained cheerfully.

But she didn't want to get into the boat. She said she would wait on the steps while Tom went around and opened the street door. Tom said it might take fifteen minutes or more, and she would probably catch a cold there, so she finally got in. The Italian took them to the nearest landing at the steps of the Santa Maria della Salute church. He refused to take any money for his trouble, but he accepted the rest of Tom's pack of American cigarettes. Tom did not know why, but he felt more frightened that night, walking through San Spiridione with Marge, than if he had been alone. Marge, of course, was not affected at all by the street, and talked the whole way.

25.

TOM was awakened very early the next morning by the banging of his door knocker. He grabbed his robe and went down. It was a telegram, and he had to run back upstairs to get a tip for the man. He stood in the cold living room and read it.

CHANGED MY MIND. WOULD LIKE TO SEE YE. ARRIVING 11:45 AM.
                                          H. GREENLEAF

Tom shivered. Well, he had expected it, he thought. But he hadn't really. He dreaded it. Or was it just the hour? It was barely dawn. The living room looked gray and horrible. That "YE" gave the telegram such a creepy, archaic touch. Generally Italian telegrams had much funnier typographical errors. And what if they'd put "R." or "D." instead of the "H."? How would he be feeling then?

He ran upstairs and got back into his warm bed to try to catch some more sleep. He kept wondering if Marge would come in or knock on his door because she had heard that loud knocker, but he finally decided she had slept through it. He imagined greeting Mr. Greenleaf at the door, shaking his hand firmly, and he tried to imagine his questions, but his mind blurred tiredly and it made him feel frightened and uncomfortable. He was too sleepy to form specific questions and answers, and too tense to get to sleep. He wanted to make coffee and wake Marge up, so he would have someone to talk to, but he couldn't face going into that room and seeing the underwear and garter belts strewn all over the place, he absolutely *couldn't*.

It was Marge who woke him up, and she had already made coffee downstairs, she said.

"What do you think?" Tom said with a big smile. "I got a telegram from Mr. Greenleaf this morning and he's coming at noon."

"He *is*? When did you get the telegram?"

"This morning early. If I wasn't dreaming." Tom looked for it. "Here it is."

Marge read it. " 'Would like to see ye,' " she said, laughing a little. "Well, that's nice. It'll do him good. I hope. Are you coming down or shall I bring the coffee up?"

"I'll come down," Tom said, putting on his robe.

Marge was already dressed in slacks and a sweater, black corduroy slacks, well-cut and made to order, Tom supposed, because they fitted her gourdlike figure as well as pants possibly could. They prolonged their coffee drinking until Anna and Ugo arrived at ten with milk and rolls and the morning papers. Then they made more coffee and hot milk and sat in the living room. It was one of the mornings when there was nothing in the papers about Dickie or the Miles case. Some mornings were like that, and then the evening papers would have something about them again, even if there was no real news to report, just by way of reminding people that Dickie was still missing and the Miles murder was still unsolved.

Marge and Tom went to the railroad station to meet Mr. Greenleaf at eleven forty-five. It was raining again, and so windy and cold that the rain felt like sleet on their faces. They stood in the shelter of the railroad station, watching the people come through the gate, and finally there was Mr. Greenleaf, solemn and ashen. Marge rushed forward to kiss him on the cheek, and he smiled at her.

"Hello, Tom!" he said heartily, extending his hand. "How're you?"

"Very well, sir. And you?"

Mr. Greenleaf had only a small suitcase, but a porter was carrying it and the porter rode with them on the motoscafo, though Tom said he could easily carry the suitcase himself. Tom suggested they go straight to his house, but Mr. Greenleaf wanted to install himself in a hotel first. He insisted.

"I'll come over as soon as I register. I thought I'd try the Gritti. Is that anywhere near your place?" Mr. Greenleaf asked.

"Not too close, but you can walk to San Marco's and take a gondola over," Tom said. "We'll come with you, if you just want to check in. I thought we might all have lunch together—unless you'd rather see Marge by yourself for a while." He was the old self-effacing Ripley again.

"Came here primarily to talk to you!" Mr. Greenleaf said.

"Is there any news?" Marge asked.

Mr. Greenleaf shook his head. He was casting nervous, absent-minded glances out the windows of the motoscafo, as if the strangeness of the city compelled him to look at it, though nothing of it was registering. He had not answered Tom's question about lunch. Tom folded his arms, put a pleasant expression on his face, and did not try to talk any more. The boat's motor made quite a roar, anyway. Mr. Greenleaf and Marge were talking very casually about some people they knew in Rome. Tom gathered that Marge and Mr. Greenleaf got along very well, though Marge had said she had not known him before she met him in Rome.

They went to lunch at a modest restaurant between the Gritti and the Rialto, which specialized in seafoods that were always displayed raw on a long counter inside. One of the plates held varieties of the little purple octopuses that Dickie had liked so much, and Tom said to Marge, nodding toward the plates as they passed, "Too bad Dickie isn't here to enjoy some of those."

Marge smiled gaily. She was always in a good mood when they were about to eat.

Mr. Greenleaf talked a little more at lunch, but his face kept its stony expression, and he still glanced around as he spoke, as if he hoped that Dickie would come walking in at any moment. No, the police hadn't found a blessed thing that could be called a clue, he said, and he had just arranged for an American private detective to come over and try to clear the mystery up.

It made Tom swallow thoughtfully—he, too, must have a lurking suspicion, or illusion, perhaps, that American detectives were better than the Italian—but then the evident futility of it struck him as it was apparently striking Marge, because her face had gone long and blank suddenly.

"That may be a very good idea," Tom said.

"Do you think much of the Italian police?" Mr. Greenleaf asked him.

"Well—actually, I do," Tom replied. "There's also the advantage that they speak Italian and they can get around everywhere and investigate all kinds of suspects. I suppose the man you sent for speaks Italian?"

"I really don't know. I don't know," Mr. Greenleaf said in a flustered way, as if he realized he should have demanded that, and hadn't. "The man's name is McCarron. He's said to be very good."

He probably didn't speak Italian, Tom thought. "When is he arriving?"

"Tomorrow or the next day. I'll be in Rome tomorrow to meet him if he's there." Mr. Greenleaf had finished his vitello alla parmigiana. He had not eaten much.

"Tom has the most beautiful house!" Marge said, starting in on her seven-layer rum cake.

Tom turned his glare at her into a faint smile.

The quizzing, Tom thought, would come at the house, probably when he and Mr. Greenleaf were alone. He knew Mr. Greenleaf wanted to talk to him alone, and therefore he proposed coffee at the restaurant where they were before Marge could suggest having it at home. Marge liked the coffee that his filter pot made. Even so, Marge sat around with them in the living room for half an hour after they got home. Marge was incapable of sensing anything, Tom thought. Finally Tom frowned at her facetiously and glanced at the stairs, and she got the hint, clapped her hand over her mouth and announced that she was going up to have a wee nap. She was

in her usual invincibly merry mood, and she had been talking
to Mr. Greenleaf all during lunch as if of *course* Dickie wasn't
dead, and he mustn't, mustn't worry so much because it
wasn't good for his digestion. As if she still had hopes of being
his daughter-in-law one day, Tom thought.

Mr. Greenleaf stood up and paced the floor with his hands
in his jacket pockets, like an executive about to dictate a letter
to his stenographer. He hadn't commented on the plushness
of the house, or even much looked at it, Tom had noticed.

"Well, Tom," he began with a sigh, "this is a strange end,
isn't it?"

"End?"

"Well, you living in Europe now, and Richard—"

"None of us has suggested yet that he might have gone
back to America," Tom said pleasantly.

"No. That couldn't be. The immigration authorities in
America are much too well alerted for that." Mr. Greenleaf
continued to pace, not looking at him. "What's your real
opinion as to where he may be?"

"Well, sir, he could be hiding out in Italy—very easily if he
doesn't use a hotel where he has to register."

"Are there any hotels in Italy where one doesn't have to
register?"

"No, not officially. But anyone who knows Italian as well
as Dickie might get away with it. Matter of fact, if he bribed
some little innkeeper in the south of Italy not to say anything, he could stay there even if the man knew his name was
Richard Greenleaf."

"And is that your idea of what he may be doing?" Mr.
Greenleaf looked at him suddenly, and Tom saw that pitiful
expression he had noticed the first evening he had met him.

"No, I— It's possible. That's all I can say about it." He
paused. "I'm sorry to say it, Mr. Greenleaf, but I think there's
a possibility that Dickie is dead."

Mr. Greenleaf's expression did not change. "Because of
that depression you mentioned in Rome? What exactly did he
say to you?"

"It was his general mood." Tom frowned. "The Miles
thing had obviously shaken him. He's the sort of man— He
really does hate publicity of any kind, violence of any kind."

Tom licked his lips. His agony in trying to express himself was genuine. "He did say if one more thing happened, he would blow his top—or he didn't know what he would do. Also for the first time, I felt he wasn't interested in his painting. Maybe it was only temporary, but up until then I'd always thought Dickie had his painting to go to, whatever happened to him."

"Does he really take his painting so seriously?"

"Yes, he does," Tom said firmly.

Mr. Greenleaf looked off at the ceiling again, his hands behind him. "A pity we can't find this Di Massimo. He might know something. I understand Richard and he were going to go together to Sicily."

"I didn't know that," Tom said. Mr. Greenleaf had got that from Marge, he knew.

"Di Massimo's disappeared, too, if he ever existed. I'm inclined to think Richard made him up to try to convince me he was painting. The police can't find a painter called Di Massimo on their—their identity lists or whatever it is."

"I never met him," Tom said. "Dickie mentioned him a couple of times. I never doubted his identity—or his actuality." He laughed a little.

"What did you say before about 'if one more thing happened to him'? What else had happened to him?"

"Well, I didn't know then, in Rome, but I think I know what he meant now. They'd questioned him about the sunken boat in San Remo. Did they tell you about that?"

"No."

"They found a boat in San Remo, scuttled. It seems the boat was missed on the day or around the day Dickie and I were there, and we'd taken a ride in the same kind of boat. They were the little motorboats people rented there. At any rate, the boat was scuttled, and there were stains on it that they thought were bloodstains. They happened to find the boat just after the Miles murder, and they couldn't find *me* at that time, because I was traveling around the country, so they asked Dickie where I was. I think for a while, Dickie must have thought they suspected him of having murdered me!" Tom laughed.

"Good lord!"

"I only know this, because a police inspector questioned

me about it in Venice just a few weeks ago. He said he'd questioned Dickie about it before. The strange thing is that I didn't know I was being looked for—not very seriously, but still being looked for—until I saw it in the newspaper in Venice. I went to the police station here and presented myself." Tom was still smiling. He had decided days ago that he had better narrate all this to Mr. Greenleaf, if he ever saw him, whether Mr. Greenleaf had heard about the San Remo boat incident or not. It was better than having Mr. Greenleaf learn about it from the police, and be told that he had been in Rome with Dickie at a time when he should have known that the police were looking for him. Besides, it fitted in with what he was saying about Dickie's depressed mood at that time.

"I don't quite understand all this," Mr. Greenleaf said. He was sitting on the sofa, listening attentively.

"It's blown over now, since Dickie and I are both alive. The reason I mention it at all is that Dickie knew I was being looked for by the police, because they had asked him where I was. He may not have known exactly where I was at the first interview with the police, but he did know at least that I was still in the country. But even when I came to Rome and saw him, he didn't tell the police he'd seen me. He wasn't going to be that cooperative, he wasn't in the mood. I know this because at the very time Marge talked to me in Rome at the hotel, Dickie was out talking to the police. His attitude was, let the police find me themselves, he wasn't going to tell them where I was."

Mr. Greenleaf shook his head, a kind of fatherly, mildly impatient shake of the head, as if he could easily believe it of Dickie.

"I think that was the night he said, if one more thing happened to him— It caused me a little embarrassment when I was in Venice. The police probably thought I was a moron for not knowing before that I was being looked for, but the fact remains I didn't."

"Hm-m," Mr. Greenleaf said uninterestedly.

Tom got up to get some brandy.

"I'm afraid I don't agree with you that Richard committed suicide," Mr. Greenleaf said.

"Well, neither does Marge. I just said it's a possibility. I don't even think it's the most likely thing that's happened."

"You don't? What do you think is?"

"That he's hiding out," Tom said. "May I offer you some brandy, sir? I imagine this house feels pretty chilly after America."

"It does, frankly." Mr. Greenleaf accepted his glass.

"You know, he could be in several other countries besides Italy, too," Tom said. "He could have gone to Greece or France or anywhere else after he got back to Naples, because no one was looking for him until days later."

"I know, I know," Mr. Greenleaf said tiredly.

26.

Tom had hoped Marge would forget about the cocktail party invitation of the antique dealer at the Danieli, but she didn't. Mr. Greenleaf had gone back to his hotel to rest around four o'clock, and as soon as he had gone Marge reminded Tom of the party at five o'clock.

"Do you really want to go?" Tom asked. "I can't even remember the man's name."

"Maloof. M-a-l-o-o-f," Marge said. "I'd like to go. We don't have to stay long."

So that was that. What Tom hated about it was the spectacle they made of themselves, not one but two of the principals in the Greenleaf case, conspicuous as a couple of spotlighted acrobats at a circus. He felt—he knew—they were nothing but a pair of names that Mr. Maloof had bagged, guests of honor that had actually turned up, because certainly Mr. Maloof would have told everybody today that Marge Sherwood and Tom Ripley were attending his party. It was unbecoming, Tom felt. And Marge couldn't excuse her giddiness simply by saying that she wasn't worried a bit about Dickie's being missing. It even seemed to Tom that Marge guzzled the martinis because they were free, as if she couldn't get all she wanted at his house, or as if he wasn't going to buy her several more when they met Mr. Greenleaf for dinner.

Tom sipped one drink slowly and managed to stay on the other side of the room from Marge. He was the friend of Dickie Greenleaf, when anybody began a conversation by asking him if he was, but he knew Marge only slightly.

"Miss Sherwood is my house guest," he said with a troubled smile.

"Where's Mr. Greenleaf? Too bad you didn't bring him," Mr. Maloof said, sidling up like an elephant with a huge Manhattan in a champagne glass. He wore a checked suit of loud English tweed, the kind of pattern, Tom supposed, the English made, reluctantly, especially for such Americans as Rudy Maloof.

"I think Mr. Greenleaf is resting," Tom said. "We're going to see him later for dinner."

"Oh," said Mr. Maloof. "Did you see the papers tonight?" This last politely, with a respectfully solemn face.

"Yes, I did," Tom replied.

Mr. Maloof nodded, without saying anything more. Tom wondered what inconsequential item he could have been going to report if he had said he hadn't read the papers. The papers tonight said that Mr. Greenleaf had arrived in Venice and was staying at the Gritti Palace. There was no mention of a private detective from America arriving in Rome today, or that one was coming at all, which made Tom question Mr. Greenleaf's story about the private detective. It was like one of those stories told by someone else, or one of his own imaginary fears, which were never based on the least fragment of fact and which, a couple of weeks later, he was ashamed that he *could* have believed. Such as that Marge and Dickie were having an affair in Mongibello, or were even on the brink of having an affair. Or that the forgery scare in February was going to ruin him and expose him if he continued in the role of Dickie Greenleaf. The forgery scare had blown over, actually. The latest was that seven out of ten experts in America had said that they did not believe the checks were forged. He could have signed another remittance from the American bank, and gone on forever as Dickie Greenleaf, if he hadn't let his imaginary fears get the better of him. Tom set his jaw. He was still listening with a fraction of his brain to Mr. Maloof, who was trying to sound intelligent and serious by describing his expedition to the islands of Murano and Burano that morning. Tom set his jaw, frowning, listening, and concentrating doggedly on his own life. Perhaps he should believe Mr. Greenleaf's story about the private detective coming over, until it was disproven, but he would not let it rattle him or cause him to betray fear by so much as the blink of an eye.

Tom made an absent-minded reply to something Mr. Maloof had said, and Mr. Maloof laughed with inane good cheer and drifted off. Tom followed his broad back scornfully with his eyes, realizing that he had been rude, was being rude, and that he ought to pull himself together, because behaving courteously even to this handful of second-rate antique dealers and bric-a-brac and ashtray buyers—Tom had seen the samples of their wares spread out on the bed in the room where they had put their coats—was part of the business of being a gentleman. But they reminded him too much of the people he had said good-bye to in New York, he thought, that was why they got under his skin like an itch and made him want to run. Marge was the reason he was here, after all, the only reason. He blamed *her*. Tom took a sip of his martini, looked up at the ceiling, and thought that in another few months his nerves, his patience, would be able to bear even people like this, if he ever found himself with people like this again. He had improved, at least, since he left New York, and he would improve still more. He stared up at the ceiling and thought of sailing to Greece, down the Adriatic from Venice, into the Ionian Sea to Crete. That was what he would do this summer. June. *June.* How sweet and soft the word was, clear and lazy and full of sunshine! His reverie lasted only a few seconds, however. The loud, grating American voices forced their way into his ears again, and sank like claws into the nerves of his shoulders and his back. He moved involuntarily from where he stood, moved toward Marge. There were only two other women in the room, the horrible wives of a couple of the horrible businessmen, and Marge, he had to admit, was better-looking than either of them, but her voice, he thought, was worse, like theirs only worse.

He had something on the tip of his tongue to say about their leaving, but, since it was unthinkable for a man to propose leaving, he said nothing at all, only joined Marge's group and smiled. Somebody refilled his glass. Marge was talking about Mongibello, telling them about her book, and the three gray-templed, seamy-faced, bald-headed men seemed to be entranced with her.

When Marge herself proposed leaving a few minutes later, they had a ghastly time getting clear of Maloof and his co-horts, who were a little drunker now and insistent that they *all* get together for dinner, and Mr. Greenleaf, too.

"That's what Venice is for—a good time!" Mr. Maloof kept saying idiotically, taking the opportunity to put his arm around Marge and maul her a little as he tried to make her stay, and Tom thought it was a good thing that he hadn't eaten yet because he would have lost it right then. "What's Mr. Greenleaf's number? Let's call him up!" Mr. Maloof weaved his way to the telephone.

"I think we'd better get out of here!" Tom said grimly into Marge's ear. He took a hard, functional grip on her elbow and steered her toward the door, both of them nodding and smiling good-byes as they went.

"What's the *matter*?" Marge asked when they were in the corridor.

"Nothing. I just thought the party was getting out of hand," Tom said, trying to make light of it with a smile. Marge was a little high, but not too high to see that some-thing was the matter with him. He was perspiring. It showed on his forehead, and he wiped it. "People like that get me down," he said, "talking about Dickie all the time, and we don't even know them and I don't want to. They make me ill."

"Funny. Not a soul talked to me about Dickie or even men-tioned his name. I thought it was much better than yesterday at Peter's house."

Tom lifted his head as he walked and said nothing. It was the class of people he despised, and why say that to Marge, who was of the same class?

They called for Mr. Greenleaf at his hotel. It was still early for dinner, so they had apéritifs at a café in a street near the Gritti. Tom tried to make up for his explosion at the party by being pleasant and talkative during dinner. Mr. Greenleaf was in a good mood, because he had just telephoned his wife and found her in very good spirits and feeling much better. Her doctor had been trying a new system of injections for the past ten days, Mr. Greenleaf said, and she seemed to be responding better than to anything they had tried before.

It was a quiet dinner. Tom told a clean, mildly funny joke, and Marge laughed hilariously. Mr. Greenleaf insisted on paying for the dinner, and then said he was going back to his hotel because he didn't feel quite up to par. From the fact that he carefully chose a pasta dish and ate no salad, Tom thought that he might be suffering from the tourist's complaint, and he wanted to suggest an excellent remedy, obtainable in every drugstore, but Mr. Greenleaf was not quite the person one could say a thing like that to, even if they had been alone.

Mr. Greenleaf said he was going back to Rome tomorrow, and Tom promised to give him a ring around nine o'clock the next morning to find out which train he had decided on. Marge was going back to Rome with Mr. Greenleaf, and she was agreeable to either train. They walked back to the Gritti— Mr. Greenleaf with his taut face-of-an-industrialist under his gray homburg looking like a piece of Madison Avenue walking through the narrow, zigzagging streets—and they said good night.

"I'm terribly sorry I didn't get to spend more time with you," Tom said.

"So am I, my boy. Maybe some other time." Mr. Greenleaf patted his shoulder.

Tom walked back home with Marge in a kind of glow. It had all gone awfully well, Tom thought. Marge chattered to him as they walked, giggling because she had broken a strap of her bra and had to hold it up with one hand, she said. Tom was thinking of the letter he had received from Bob Delancey this afternoon, the first word he'd gotten from Bob except one postcard ages ago, in which Bob had said that the police had questioned everybody in his house about an income tax fraud of a few months ago. The defrauder, it seemed, had used the address of Bob's house to receive his checks, and had gotten the checks by the simple means of taking the letters down from the letter-box edge where the postman had stuck them. The postman had been questioned, too, Bob had said, and remembered the name George McAlpin on the letters. Bob seemed to think it was rather funny. He described the reactions of some of the people in the house when they were questioned by the police. The mystery was, who took the letters addressed to George McAlpin? It was very reassuring. That income tax episode had been hanging over his head in a vague way, because he had known there would be an investigation at some time. He was glad it had gone this far and no further. He couldn't imagine how the police would ever, could ever, connect Tom Ripley with George McAlpin. Besides, as Bob had remarked, the defrauder had not even tried to cash the checks.

He sat down in the living room to read Bob's letter again when he got home. Marge had gone upstairs to pack her things and to go to bed. Tom was tired too, but the anticipation of freedom tomorrow, when Marge and Mr. Greenleaf would be gone, was so pleasant to relish he would not have minded staying up all night. He took his shoes off so he could put his feet up on the sofa, lay back on a pillow, and continued reading Bob's letter. "The police think it's some outsider who dropped by occasionally to pick up his mail, because none of the dopes in this house look like criminal types. . . ." It was strange to read about the people he knew in New York, Ed and Lorraine, the newt-brained girl who had tried to stow herself away in his cabin the day he sailed from New York. It was strange and not at all attractive. What a dismal life they led, creeping around New York, in and out of subways, standing in some dingy bar on Third Avenue for their entertainment, watching television, or even if they had enough money for a Madison Avenue bar or a good restaurant now and then, how dull it all was compared to the worst little trattoria in Venice with its tables of green salads, trays of wonderful cheeses, and its friendly waiters bringing you the best wine in the world! "I certainly do envy you sitting there in Venice in an old palazzo!" Bob wrote. "Do you take a lot of gondola rides? How are the girls? Are you getting so cultured you won't speak to any of us when you come back? How long are you staying, anyway?"

Forever, Tom thought. Maybe he'd never go back to the States. It was not so much Europe itself as the evenings he had spent alone, here and in Rome, that made him feel that way. Evenings by himself simply looking at maps, or lying around on sofas thumbing through guidebooks. Evenings looking at his clothes—his clothes and Dickie's—and feeling Dickie's rings between his palms, and running his fingers over the antelope suitcase he had bought at Gucci's. He had polished the suitcase with a special English leather dressing, not that it needed polishing, because he took such good care of it, but for its protection. He loved possessions, not masses of them, but a select few that he did not part with. They gave a man self-respect. Not ostentation but quality, and the love that cherished the quality. Possessions reminded him that he existed, and made him enjoy his existence. It was as simple as that. And wasn't that worth something? He existed. Not many people appreciated existence as he did. Not many people in the world knew how to, even if they had the money. It really didn't take money, masses of money, it took a certain security. He had been on the road to it, even with Marc Priminger. He had appreciated Marc's possessions, and they were what had attracted him to the house, but they were not his own, and it had been impossible to make a beginning at acquiring anything of his own on forty dollars a week. It would have taken him the best years of his life, even if he had economized stringently, to buy the things he wanted. Dickie's money had given him only an added momentum on the road he had been traveling. The money gave him the leisure to see Greece, to collect Etruscan pottery if he wanted to (he had recently read an interesting book on that subject by an American living in Rome), to join art societies if he cared to and to donate to their work. It gave him the leisure, for instance, to read his Malraux tonight as late as he pleased, because he did not have to go to a job in the morning. He had just bought a two-volume edition of Malraux's *Psychologie de l'Art* which he was now reading, with great pleasure, in French with the aid of a dictionary. He thought he might nap for a while, then read some in it, whatever the hour. He felt cozy and drowsy, in spite of the espressos. The curve of the sofa corner fitted his shoulders like somebody's arm, or rather fitted it better than somebody's arm. He decided he would spend the night here.

It was more comfortable than the sofa upstairs. In a few minutes he might go up and get a blanket.

"Tom?"

He opened his eyes. Marge was coming down the stairs, barefoot. Tom sat up. She had his brown leather box in her hand.

"I just found Dickie's rings in here," she said rather breathlessly.

"Oh. He gave them to me. To take care of." Tom stood up.

"When?"

"In Rome, I think." He took a step back, struck one of his shoes and picked it up, mostly in an effort to seem calm.

"What was he going to do? Why'd he give them to you?"

She'd been looking for thread to sew her bra, Tom thought. Why in hell hadn't he put the rings somewhere else, like in the lining of that suitcase? "I don't really know," Tom said. "A whim or something. You know how he is. He said if anything ever happened to him, he wanted me to have his rings."

Marge looked puzzled. "Where was he going?"

"To Palermo. Sicily." He was holding the shoe in both hands, in a position to use the wooden heel of it as a weapon. And how he would do it went quickly through his head: hit her with the shoe, then haul her out by the front door and drop her into the canal. He'd say she'd fallen, slipped on the moss. And she was such a good swimmer, he'd thought she could keep afloat.

Marge stared down at the box. "Then he *was* going to kill himself."

"Yes—if you want to look at it that way, the rings— They make it look more likely that he did."

"Why didn't you say anything about it before?"

"I think I absolutely forgot them. I put them away so they wouldn't get lost and I never thought of looking at them since the day he gave them to me."

"He either killed himself or changed his identity—didn't he?"

"Yes." Tom said it sadly and firmly.

"You'd better tell Mr. Greenleaf."

"Yes, I will. Mr. Greenleaf and the police."

"This practically *settles* it," Marge said.

Tom was wringing the shoe in his hands like a pair of gloves now, yet still keeping the shoe in position, because Marge was staring at him in a funny way. She was still thinking. Was she kidding him? Did she know now?

Marge said earnestly, "I just can't imagine Dickie ever being without his rings," and Tom knew then that she hadn't guessed the answer, that her mind was miles up some other road.

He relaxed then, limply, sank down on the sofa and pretended to busy himself with putting on his shoes. "No," he agreed, automatically.

"If it weren't so late, I'd call Mr. Greenleaf now. He's probably in bed, and he wouldn't sleep all night if I told him, I know."

Tom tried to push a foot into the second shoe. Even his fingers were limp, without strength. He racked his brain for something sensible to say. "I'm sorry I didn't mention it sooner," he brought out in a deep voice. "It was just one of those—"

"Yes, it makes it kind of silly at this point for Mr. Greenleaf to bring a private detective over, doesn't it?" Her voice shook.

Tom looked at her. She was about to cry. This was the very first moment, Tom realized, that she was admitting to herself that Dickie could be dead, that he probably was dead. Tom went toward her slowly. "I'm sorry, Marge. I'm sorry above all that I didn't tell you sooner about the rings." He put his arm around her. He fairly had to, because she was leaning against him. He smelled her perfume. The Stradivari, probably. "That's one of the reasons I felt so sure he'd killed himself—at least that he might have."

"Yes," she said in a miserable, wailing tone.

She was not crying, actually, only leaning against him with her head rigidly bent down. Like someone who has just heard the news of a death, Tom thought. Which she had.

"How about a brandy?" he said tenderly.

"No."

"Come over and sit on the sofa." He led her toward it.

She sat down, and he crossed the room to get the brandy. He poured brandy into two inhalers. When he turned around, she was gone. He had just time to see the edge of her robe and her bare feet disappear at the top of the stairs.

She preferred to be by herself, he thought. He started to take a brandy up to her, then decided against it. She was probably beyond the help of brandy. He knew how she felt. He carried the brandies solemnly back to the liquor cabinet. He had meant to pour only one back, but he poured them both back, and then let it go and replaced the bottle among the other bottles.

He sank down on the sofa again, stretched a leg out with his foot dangling, too exhausted now even to remove his shoes. As tired as after he had killed Freddie Miles, he thought suddenly, or as after Dickie in San Remo. He had come so close! He remembered his cool thoughts of beating her senseless with his shoe heel, yet not roughly enough to break the skin anywhere, of dragging her through the front hall and out the doors with the lights turned off so that no one would see them, and his quickly invented story, that she had evidently slipped, and thinking she could surely swim back to the steps, he hadn't jumped in or shouted for help until— In a way, he had even imagined the exact words that he and Mr. Greenleaf would say to each other afterward, Mr. Greenleaf shocked and astounded, and he himself just as apparently shaken, but only apparently. Underneath he would be as calm and sure of himself as he had been after Freddie's murder, because his story would be unassailable. Like the San Remo story. His stories were good because he imagined them intensely, so intensely that he came to believe them.

For a moment he heard his own voice saying: ". . . I stood there on the steps calling to her, thinking she'd come up any second, or even that she might be playing a trick on me. . . . But I wasn't *sure* she'd hurt herself, and she'd been in such good humor standing there a moment before. . . ." He tensed himself. It was like a phonograph playing in his head, a little drama taking place right in the living room that he was unable to stop. He could see himself standing with the Italian police and Mr. Greenleaf by the big doors that opened to the front hall. He could see and hear himself talking earnestly. And being believed.

But what seemed to terrify him was not the dialogue or his

hallucinatory belief that he had done it (he knew he hadn't), but the memory of himself standing in front of Marge with the shoe in his hand, imagining all this in a cool, methodical way. And the fact that he had done it twice before. Those two other times were *facts*, not imagination. He could say he hadn't wanted to do them, but he had done them. He didn't want to be a murderer. Sometimes he could absolutely forget that he had murdered, he realized. But sometimes—like now—he couldn't. He had surely forgotten for a while tonight, when he had been thinking about the meaning of possessions, and why he liked to live in Europe.

He twisted onto his side, his feet drawn up on the sofa. He was sweating and shaking. What was happening to him? What had happened? Was he going to blurt out a lot of nonsense tomorrow when he saw Mr. Greenleaf, about Marge falling into the canal, and his screaming for help and jumping in and not finding her? Even with Marge standing there with them, would he go berserk and spill the story out and betray himself as a maniac?

He had to face Mr. Greenleaf with the rings tomorrow. He would have to repeat the story he had told to Marge. He would have to give it details to make it better. He began to invent. His mind steadied. He was imagining a Roman hotel room, Dickie and he standing there talking, and Dickie taking off both his rings and handing them to him. Dickie said: "It's just as well you don't tell anybody about this. . . ."

27.

MARGE called Mr. Greenleaf at eight-thirty the next morning to ask how soon they could come over to his hotel, she had told Tom. But Mr. Greenleaf must have noticed that she was upset. Tom heard her starting to tell him the story of the rings. Marge used the same words that Tom had used to her about the rings—evidently Marge had believed him—but Tom could not tell what Mr. Greenleaf's reaction was. He was afraid this piece of news might be just the one that would bring the whole picture into focus, and that when they saw

Mr. Greenleaf this morning he might be in the company of a policeman, ready to arrest Tom Ripley. This possibility rather offset the advantage of his not being on the scene when Mr. Greenleaf heard about the rings.

"What did he say?" Tom asked when Marge had hung up.

Marge sat down tiredly on a chair across the room. "He seems to feel the way I do. He said it himself. It looks as if Dickie meant to kill himself."

But Mr. Greenleaf would have a little time to think about it before they got there, Tom thought. "What time are we due?" Tom asked.

"I told him about nine-thirty or before. As soon as we've had some coffee. The coffee's on now." Marge got up and went into the kitchen. She was already dressed. She had on the traveling suit that she had worn when she arrived.

Tom sat up indecisively on the edge of the sofa and loosened his tie. He had slept in his clothes on the sofa, and Marge had awakened him when she had come down a few minutes ago. How he had possibly slept all night in the chilly room he didn't know. It embarrassed him. Marge had been amazed to find him there. There was a crick in his neck, his back, and his right shoulder. He felt wretched. He stood up suddenly. "I'm going upstairs to wash," he called to Marge.

He glanced into his room upstairs and saw that Marge had packed her suitcase. It was lying in the middle of the floor, closed. Tom hoped that she and Mr. Greenleaf were still leaving on one of the morning trains. Probably they would, because Mr. Greenleaf was supposed to meet the American detective in Rome today.

Tom undressed in the room next to Marge's, then went into the bathroom and turned on the shower. After a look at himself in the mirror he decided to shave first, and he went back to the room to get his electric razor which he had removed from the bathroom, for no particular reason, when Marge arrived. On the way back he heard the telephone ring. Marge answered it. Tom leaned over the stairwell, listening.

"Oh, that's fine," she said. "Oh, that doesn't matter if we don't. . . . Yes, I'll tell him. . . . All right, we'll hurry. Tom's just washing up. . . . Oh, less than an hour. Byebye."

He heard her walking toward the stairs, and he stepped back because he was naked.

"Tom?" she yelled up. "The detective from America just got here! He just called Mr. Greenleaf and he's coming from the airport!"

"Fine!" Tom called back, and angrily went into the bedroom. He turned the shower off, and plugged his razor into the wall outlet. Suppose he'd been under the shower? Marge would have yelled up, anyway, simply assuming that he would be able to hear her. He would be glad when she was gone, and he hoped she left this morning. Unless she and Mr. Greenleaf decided to stay to see what the detective was going to do with him. Tom knew that the detective had come to Venice especially to see him, otherwise he would have waited to see Mr. Greenleaf in Rome. Tom wondered if Marge realized that too. Probably she didn't. That took a minimum of deduction.

Tom put on a quiet suit and tie, and went down to have coffee with Marge. He had taken his shower as hot as he could bear it, and he felt much better. Marge said nothing during the coffee except that the rings should make a great difference both to Mr. Greenleaf and the detective, and she meant that it should look to the detective, too, as if Dickie had killed himself. Tom hoped she was right. Everything depended on what kind of man the detective would be. Everything depended on the first impression he made on the detective.

It was another gray, clammy day, not quite raining at nine o'clock, but it had rained, and it would rain again, probably toward noon. Tom and Marge caught the gondola from the church steps to San Marco, and walked from there to the Gritti. They telephoned up to Mr. Greenleaf's room. Mr. Greenleaf said that Mr. McCarron was there, and asked them to come up.

Mr. Greenleaf opened his door for them. "Good morning," he said. He pressed Marge's arm in a fatherly way. "Tom—"

Tom came in behind Marge. The detective was standing by the window, a short, chunky man of about thirty-five. His face looked friendly and alert. Moderately bright, but only moderately, was Tom's first impression.

"This is Alvin McCarron," Mr. Greenleaf said. "Miss Sherwood and Mr. Tom Ripley."

They all said, "How do you do?"

Tom noticed a brand-new briefcase on the bed with some papers and photographs lying around it. McCarron was looking him over.

"I understand you're a friend of Richard's?" he asked.

"We both are," Tom said.

They were interrupted for a minute while Mr. Greenleaf saw that they were all seated. It was a good-sized, heavily furnished room with windows on the canal. Tom sat down in an armless chair upholstered in red. McCarron had installed himself on the bed, and was looking through his sheaf of papers. There were a few photostated papers, Tom saw, that looked like pictures of Dickie's checks. There were also several loose photographs of Dickie.

"Do you have the rings?" McCarron asked, looking from Tom to Marge.

"Yes," Marge said solemnly, getting up. She took the rings from her handbag and gave them to McCarron.

McCarron held them out on his palm to Mr. Greenleaf. "These are his rings?" he asked, and Mr. Greenleaf nodded after only a glance at them, while Marge's face took on a slightly affronted expression as if she were about to say, "*I* know his rings just as well as Mr. Greenleaf and probably better." McCarron turned to Tom. "When did he give them to you?" he asked.

"In Rome. As nearly as I can remember, around February third, just a few days after the murder of Freddie Miles," Tom answered.

The detective was studying him with his inquisitive, mild brown eyes. His lifted eyebrows put a couple of wrinkles in the thick-looking skin of his forehead. He had wavy brown hair, cut very short on the sides, with a high curl above his forehead, in a rather cute college-boy style. One couldn't tell a thing from that face, Tom thought; it was trained. "What did he say when he gave them to you?"

"He said that if anything happened to him he wanted me to have them. I asked him what he thought was going to happen to him. He said he didn't know, but something might." Tom paused deliberately. "He didn't seem more depressed at that particular moment than a lot of other times I'd talked to him, so it didn't cross my mind that he was going to kill himself. I knew he intended to go away, that was all."

"Where?" asked the detective.

"To Palermo, he said." Tom looked at Marge. "He must have given them to me the day you spoke to me in Rome—at the Inghilterra. That day or the day before. Do you remember the date?"

"February second," Marge said in a subdued voice.

McCarron was making notes. "What else?" he asked Tom. "What time of day was it? Had he been drinking?"

"No. He drinks very little. I think it was early afternoon. He said it would be just as well if I didn't mention the rings to anybody, and of course I agreed. I put the rings away and completely forgot about them, as I told Miss Sherwood—I suppose because I'd so impressed on myself that he didn't want me to say anything about them." Tom spoke straightforwardly, stammering a little, inadvertently, just as anybody might stammer under the circumstances, Tom thought.

"What did you do with the rings?"

"I put them in an old box that I have—just a little box I keep odd buttons in."

McCarron regarded him for a moment in silence, and Tom took the moment to brace himself. Out of that placid yet alert Irish face could come anything, a challenging question, a flat statement that he was lying. Tom clung harder in his mind to his own facts, determined to defend them unto death. In the silence, Tom could almost hear Marge's breathing, and a cough from Mr. Greenleaf made him start. Mr. Greenleaf looked remarkably calm, almost bored. Tom wondered if he had fixed up some scheme with McCarron against him, based on the rings story?

"Is he the kind of man to lend you the rings for luck for a short time? Had he ever done anything else like that?" McCarron asked.

"No," Marge said before Tom could answer.

Tom began to breathe more easily. He could see that

McCarron didn't know yet what he should make out of it. McCarron was waiting for him to answer. "He had lent me certain things before," Tom said. "He'd told me to help myself to his ties and jackets now and then. But that's quite a different matter from the rings, of course." He had felt a compulsion to say that, because Marge undoubtedly knew about the time Dickie had found him in his clothes.

"I can't imagine Dickie without his rings," Marge said to McCarron. "He took the green one off when he went swimming, but he always put it right on again. They were just like part of his dressing. That's why I think he was either intending to kill himself or he meant to change his identity."

McCarron nodded. "Had he any enemies that you know of?"

"Absolutely none," Tom said. "I've thought of that."

"Any reason you can think of why he might have wanted to disguise himself, or assume another identity?"

Tom said carefully, twisting his aching neck, "*Possibly*—but it's next to impossible in Europe. He'd have had to have a different passport. Any country he'd have entered, he would have had to have a passport. He'd have had to have a passport even to get into a hotel."

"You told me he might not have had to have a passport," Mr. Greenleaf said.

"Yes, I said that about small hotels in Italy. It's a remote possibility, of course. But after all this publicity about his disappearance, I don't see how he could still be keeping it up," Tom said. "Somebody would surely have betrayed him by this time."

"Well, he left with his passport, obviously," McCarron said, "because he got into Sicily with it and registered at a big hotel."

"Yes," Tom said.

McCarron made notes for a moment, then looked up at Tom. "Well, how do you see it, Mr. Ripley?"

McCarron wasn't nearly finished, Tom thought. McCarron was going to see him alone, later. "I'm afraid I agree with Miss Sherwood that it looks as if he's killed himself, and it looks as if he intended to all along. I've said that before to Mr. Greenleaf."

McCarron looked at Mr. Greenleaf, but Mr. Greenleaf said nothing, only looked expectantly at McCarron. Tom had the feeling that McCarron was now inclined to think that Dickie was dead, too, and that it was a waste of time and money for him to have come over.

"I just want to check these facts again," McCarron said, still plodding on, going back to his papers. "The last time Richard was seen by anyone is February fifteenth, when he got off the boat in Naples, coming from Palermo."

"That's correct," Mr. Greenleaf said. "A steward remembers seeing him."

"But no sign of him at any hotel after that, and no communications from him since." McCarron looked from Mr. Greenleaf to Tom.

"No," Tom said.

McCarron looked at Marge.

"No," Marge said.

"And when was the last time you saw him, Miss Sherwood?"

"On November twenty-third, when he left for San Remo," Marge said promptly.

"You were then in Mongibello?" McCarron asked, pronouncing the town's name with a hard "g," as if he had no knowledge of Italian, or at least no relationship to the spoken language.

"Yes," Marge said. "I just missed seeing him in Rome in February, but the last time I saw him was in Mongibello."

Good old Marge! Tom felt almost affectionate toward her—underneath everything. He had begun to feel affectionate this morning, even though she had irritated him. "He was trying to avoid everyone in Rome," Tom put in. "That's why, when he first gave me the rings, I thought he was on some tack of getting away from everyone he had known, living in another city, and just vanishing for a while."

"Why, do you think?"

Tom elaborated, mentioning the murder of his friend Freddie Miles, and its effect on Dickie.

"Do you think Richard knew who killed Freddie Miles?"

"No. I certainly don't."

McCarron waited for Marge's opinion.

"No," Marge said, shaking her head.

"Think a minute," McCarron said to Tom. "Do you think that might have explained his behavior? Do you think he's avoiding answering the police by hiding out now?"

Tom thought for a minute. "He didn't give me a single clue in that direction."

"Do you think Dickie was afraid of something?"

"I can't imagine of what," Tom said.

McCarron asked Tom how close a friend Dickie had been of Freddie Miles, whom else he knew who was a friend of both Dickie and Freddie, if he knew of any debts between them, any girl friends— "Only Marge that I know of," Tom replied, and Marge protested that she wasn't a *girl* friend of Freddie's, so there couldn't possibly have been any *rivalry* over her—and could Tom say that he was Dickie's best friend in Europe?

"I wouldn't say that," Tom answered. "I think Marge Sherwood is. I hardly know any of Dickie's friends in Europe."

McCarron studied Tom's face again. "What's your opinion about these forgeries?"

"Are they forgeries? I didn't think anybody was sure."

"I don't think they are," Marge said.

"Opinion seems to be divided," McCarron said. "The experts don't think the letter he wrote to the bank in Naples is a forgery, which can only mean that if there is a forgery somewhere, he's covering up for someone. Assuming there is a forgery, do you have any idea who he might be trying to cover up for?"

Tom hesitated a moment, and Marge said, "Knowing him, I can't imagine him covering up for anyone. Why should he?"

McCarron was staring at Tom, but whether he was debating his honesty or mulling over all they had said to him, Tom couldn't tell. McCarron looked like a typical American automobile salesman, or any other kind of salesman, Tom thought—cheerful, presentable, average in intellect, able to talk baseball with a man or pay a stupid compliment to a woman. Tom didn't think too much of him, but, on the other hand, it was not wise to underestimate one's opponent. McCarron's small, soft mouth opened as Tom watched him, and he said, "Would you mind coming downstairs with me for a few minutes, Mr. Ripley, if you've still got a few minutes?"

"Certainly," Tom said, standing up.

"We won't be long," McCarron said to Mr. Greenleaf and Marge.

Tom looked back from the door, because Mr. Greenleaf had gotten up and was starting to say something, though Tom didn't listen. Tom was suddenly aware that it was raining, that thin, gray sheets of rain were slapping against the window-panes. It was like a last glimpse, blurred and hasty—Marge's figure looking small and huddled across the big room, Mr. Greenleaf doddering forward like an old man, protesting. But the comfortable room was the thing, and the view across the canal to where his house stood—invisible now because of the rain—which he might never see again.

Mr. Greenleaf was asking, "Are you—you are coming back in a few minutes?"

"Oh, yes," McCarron answered with the impersonal firm-ness of an executioner.

They walked toward the elevator. Was this the way they did it? Tom wondered. A quiet word in the lobby. He would be handed over to the Italian police, and then McCarron would return to the room just as he had promised. McCarron had brought a couple of the papers from his briefcase with him. Tom stared at an ornamental vertical molding beside the floor numbers panel in the elevator: an egg-shaped design framed by four raised dots, egg-shape, dots, all the way down. *Think of some sensible, ordinary remark to make about Mr. Greenleaf, for instance*, Tom said to himself. He ground his teeth. If he only wouldn't start sweating now. He hadn't started yet, but maybe it would break out all over his face when they reached the lobby. McCarron was hardly as tall as his shoulder. Tom turned to him just as the elevator stopped, and said grimly, baring his teeth in a smile, "Is this your first trip to Venice?"

"Yes," said McCarron. He was crossing the lobby. "Shall we go in here?" He indicated the coffee bar. His tone was polite.

"All right," Tom said agreeably. The bar was not crowded, but there was not a single table that would be out of earshot of some other table. Would McCarron accuse him in a place like this, quietly laying down fact after fact on the table? He took the chair that McCarron pulled out for him. McCarron sat with his back to the wall.

A waiter came up. "Signori?"

"Coffee," McCarron said.

"Cappuccino," Tom said. "Would you like a cappuccino or an espresso?"

"Which is the one with milk? Cappuccino?"

"Yes."

"I'll have that."

Tom gave the order.

McCarron looked at him. His small mouth smiled on one side. Tom imagined three or four different beginnings: "You killed Richard, didn't you? The rings are just too much, aren't they?" Or "Tell me about the San Remo boat, Mr. Ripley, in detail." Or simply, leading up quietly, "Where were you on February fifteenth, when Richard landed in Naples? . . . All right, but where were you living then? Where were you living in January, for instance? . . . Can you prove it?"

McCarron was saying nothing at all, only looking down at his plump hands now, and smiling faintly. As if it had been so absurdly simple for him to unravel, Tom thought, that he could hardly force himself to put it into words.

At a table next to them four Italian men were babbling away like a madhouse, screeching with wild laughter. Tom wanted to edge away from them. He sat motionless.

Tom had braced himself until his body felt like iron, until sheer tension created defiance. He heard himself asking, in an incredibly calm voice, "Did you have time to speak to Tenente Roverini when you came through Rome?" and at the same time he asked it, he realized that he had even an objective in the question: to find out if McCarron had heard about the San Remo boat.

"No, I didn't," McCarron said. "There was a message for me that Mr. Greenleaf would be in Rome today, but I'd landed in Rome so early, I thought I'd fly over and catch him—and also talk to you." McCarron looked down at his papers. "What kind of a man is Richard? How would you describe him as far as his personality goes?"

Was McCarron going to lead up to it like this? Pick out

more little clues from the words he chose to describe him? Or did he only want the objective opinion that he couldn't get from Dickie's parents? "He wanted to be a painter," Tom began, "but he knew he'd never be a very good painter. He tried to act as if he didn't care, and as if he were perfectly happy and leading exactly the kind of life he wanted to lead over here in Europe." Tom moistened his lips. "But I think the life was beginning to get him down. His father disapproved, as you probably know. And Dickie had got himself into an awkward spot with Marge."

"How do you mean?"

"Marge was in love with him, and he wasn't with her, and at the same time he was seeing her so much in Mongibello, she kept on hoping—" Tom began to feel on safer ground, but he pretended to have difficulty in expressing himself. "He never actually discussed it with me. He always spoke very highly of Marge. He was very fond of her, but it was obvious to everybody—Marge too—that he never would marry her. But Marge never quite gave up. I think that's the main reason Dickie left Mongibello."

McCarron listened patiently and sympathetically, Tom thought. "What do you mean never gave up? What did she do?"

Tom waited until the waiter had set down the two frothy cups of cappuccino and stuck the tab between them under the sugar bowl. "She kept writing to him, wanting to see him, and at the same time being very tactful, I'm sure, about not intruding on him when he wanted to be by himself. He told me all this in Rome when I saw him. He said, after the Miles murder, that he certainly wasn't in the mood to see Marge, and he was afraid that she'd come up to Rome from Mongibello when she heard of all the trouble he was in."

"Why do you think he was nervous after the Miles murder?" McCarron took a sip of the coffee, winced from the heat or the bitterness, and stirred it with the spoon.

Tom explained. They'd been quite good friends, and Freddie had been killed just a few minutes after leaving his house.

"Do you think Richard might have killed Freddie?" McCarron asked quietly.

"No, I don't."

"Why?"

"Because there was no reason for him to kill him—at least no reason that I happen to know of."

"People usually say, because so-and-so wasn't the type to kill anybody," McCarron said. "Do you think Richard was the type who could have killed anyone?"

Tom hesitated, seeking earnestly for the truth. "I never thought of it. I don't know what kind of people are apt to kill somebody. I've seen him angry—"

"When?"

Tom described the two days in Rome, when Dickie, he said, had been angry and frustrated because of the police questioning, and had actually moved out of his apartment to avoid phone calls from friends and strangers. Tom tied this in with a growing frustration in Dickie, because he had not been progressing as he had wanted to in his painting. He depicted Dickie as a stubborn, proud young man, in awe of his father and therefore determined to defy his father's wishes, a rather erratic fellow who was generous to strangers as well as to his friends, but who was subject to changes of mood—from sociability to sullen withdrawal. He summed it up by saying that Dickie was a very ordinary young man who liked to think he was extraordinary. "If he killed himself," Tom concluded, "I think it was because he realized certain failures in himself—inadequacies. It's much easier for me to imagine him a suicide than a murderer."

"But I'm not so sure that he didn't kill Freddie Miles. Are you?"

McCarron was perfectly sincere. Tom was sure of that. McCarron was even expecting him to defend Dickie now, because they had been friends. Tom felt some of his terror leaving him, but only some of it, like something melting very slowly inside him. "I'm not sure," Tom said, "but I just don't believe that he did."

"I'm not sure either. But it would explain a lot, wouldn't it?"

"Yes," Tom said. "Everything."

"Well, this is only the first day of work," McCarron said with an optimistic smile. "I haven't even looked over the report in Rome. I'll probably want to talk to you again after I've been to Rome."

Tom stared at him. It seemed to be over. "Do you speak Italian?"

"No, not very well, but I can read it. I do better in French, but I'll get along," McCarron said, as if it were not a matter of much importance.

It was very important, Tom thought. He couldn't imagine McCarron extracting everything that Roverini knew about the Greenleaf case solely through an interpreter. Neither would McCarron be able to get around and chat with people like Dickie Greenleaf's landlady in Rome. It was most important. "I talked with Roverini here in Venice a few weeks ago," Tom said. "Give him my regards."

"I'll do that." McCarron finished his coffee. "Knowing Dickie, what places do you think he would be likely to go if he wanted to hide out?"

Tom squirmed back a little on his chair. This was getting down to the bottom of the barrel, he thought. "Well, I know he likes Italy best. I wouldn't bet on France. He also likes Greece. He talked about going to Majorca at some time. All of Spain is a possibility, I suppose."

"I see," McCarron said, sighing.

"Are you going back to Rome today?"

McCarron raised his eyebrows. "I imagine so, if I can catch a few hours' sleep here. I haven't been to bed in two days."

He held up very well, Tom thought. "I think Mr. Greenleaf was wondering about the trains. There are two this morning and probably some more in the afternoon. He was planning to leave today."

"We can leave today." McCarron reached for the check. "Thanks very much for your help, Mr. Ripley. I have your address and phone number, in case I have to see you again."

They stood up.

"Mind if I go up and say good-bye to Marge and Mr. Greenleaf?"

McCarron didn't mind. They rode up in the elevator again. Tom had to check himself from whistling. *Papa non vuole* was going around in his head.

Tom looked closely at Marge as they went in, looking for

signs of enmity. Marge only looked a little tragic, he thought. As if she had recently been made a widow.

"I'd like to ask you a few questions alone, too, Miss Sherwood," McCarron said. "If you don't mind," he said to Mr. Greenleaf.

"Certainly not. I was just going down to the lobby to buy some newspapers," Mr. Greenleaf said.

McCarron was carrying on. Tom said good-bye to Marge and to Mr. Greenleaf, in case they were going to Rome today and he did not see them again. He said to McCarron, "I'd be very glad to come to Rome at any time, if I can be of any help. I expect to be here until the end of May, anyway."

"We'll have something before then," McCarron said with his confident Irish smile.

Tom went down to the lobby with Mr. Greenleaf.

"He asked me the same questions all over again," Tom told Mr. Greenleaf, "and also my opinion of Richard's character."

"Well, what is your opinion?" Mr. Greenleaf asked in a hopeless tone.

Whether he was a suicide or had run away to hide himself would be conduct equally reprehensible in Mr. Greenleaf's eyes, Tom knew. "I told him what I think is the truth," Tom said, "that he's capable of running away and also capable of committing suicide."

Mr. Greenleaf made no comment, only patted Tom's arm. "Good-bye, Tom."

"Good-bye," Tom said. "Let me hear from you."

Everything was all right between him and Mr. Greenleaf, Tom thought. And everything would be all right with Marge, too. She had swallowed the suicide explanation, and that was the direction her mind would run in from now on, he knew.

Tom spent the afternoon at home, expecting a telephone call, one telephone call at least from McCarron, even if it was not about anything important, but none came. There was only a call from Titi, the resident countess, inviting him for cocktails that afternoon. Tom accepted.

Why should he expect any trouble from Marge, he thought. She never had given him any. The suicide was an idée fixe, and she would arrange everything in her dull imagination to fit it.

28.

McCarron called Tom the next day from Rome, wanting the names of everyone Dickie had known in Mongibello. That was apparently all that McCarron wanted to know, because he took a leisurely time getting them all, and checking them off against the list that Marge had given him. Most of the names Marge had already given him, but Tom went through them all, with their difficult addresses—Giorgio, of course, Pietro the boatkeeper, Fausto's Aunt Maria whose last name he didn't know though he told McCarron in a complicated way how to get to her house, Aldo the grocer, the Cecchis, and even old Stevenson, the recluse painter who lived just outside the village and whom Tom had never even met. It took Tom several minutes to list them all, and it would take McCarron several days to check on them, probably. He mentioned everybody but Signor Pucci, who had handled the sale of Dickie's house and boat, and who would undoubtedly tell McCarron, if he hadn't learned it through Marge, that Tom Ripley had come to Mongibello to arrange Dickie's affairs. Tom did not think it very serious, one way or the other, if McCarron did know that he had taken care of Dickie's affairs. And as to people like Aldo and Stevenson, McCarron was welcome to all he could get out of them.

"Anyone in Naples?" McCarron asked.

"Not that I know of."

"Rome?"

"I'm sorry, I never saw him with any friends in Rome."

"Never met this painter—uh—Di Massimo?"

"No. I saw him once," Tom said, "but I never met him."

"What does he look like?"

"Well, it was just on a street corner. I left Dickie as he was going to meet him, so I wasn't very close to him. He looked about five feet nine, about fifty, grayish-black hair—that's about all I remember. He looked rather solidly built. He was wearing a light-gray suit, I remember."

"Hm-m—okay," McCarron said absently, as if he were writing all that down. "Well, I guess that's about all. Thanks very much, Mr. Ripley."

"You're very welcome. Good luck."

Then Tom waited quietly in his house for several days, just as anybody would do, if the search for a missing friend had reached its intensest point. He declined three or four invitations to parties. The newspapers had renewed their interest in Dickie's disappearance, inspired by the presence in Italy of an American private detective who had been hired by Dickie's father. When some photographers from *Europeo* and *Oggi* came to take pictures of him and his house, he told them firmly to leave, and actually took one insistent young man by the elbow and propelled him across the living room toward the door. But nothing of any importance happened for five days—no telephone calls, no letters, even from Tenente Roverini. Tom imagined the worst sometimes, especially at dusk when he felt more depressed than at any other time of day. He imagined Roverini and McCarron getting together and developing the theory that Dickie could have disappeared in November, imagined McCarron checking on the time he had bought his car, imagined him picking up a scent when he found out that Dickie had not come back after the San Remo trip and that Tom Ripley had come down to arrange for the disposal of Dickie's things. He measured and remeasured Mr. Greenleaf's tired, indifferent good-bye that last morning in Venice, interpreted it as unfriendly, and imagined Mr. Greenleaf flying into a rage in Rome when no results came of all the efforts to find Dickie, and suddenly demanding a thorough investigation of Tom Ripley, that scoundrel he had sent over with his own money to try to get his son home.

But each morning Tom was optimistic again. On the good side was the fact that Marge unquestioningly believed that Dickie had spent those months sulking in Rome, and she would have kept all his letters and she would probably bring them all out to show to McCarron. Excellent letters they were, too. Tom was glad he had spent so much thought on them. Marge was an asset rather than a liability. It was really a very good thing that he had put down his shoe that night that she had found the rings.

Every morning he watched the sun, from his bedroom window, rising through the winter mists, struggling upward over the peaceful-looking city, breaking through finally to give a couple of hours of actual sunshine before noon, and the quiet beginning of each day was like a promise of peace in the future. The days were growing warmer. There was more light, and less rain. Spring was almost here, and one of these mornings, one morning finer than these, he would leave the house and board a ship for Greece.

On the evening of the sixth day after Mr. Greenleaf and McCarron had left, Tom called him in Rome. Mr. Greenleaf had nothing new to report, but Tom had not expected anything. Marge had gone home. As long as Mr. Greenleaf was in Italy, Tom thought, the papers would carry something about the case every day. But the newspapers were running out of sensational things to say about the Greenleaf case.

"And how is your wife?" Tom asked.

"Fair. I think the strain is telling on her, however. I spoke to her again last night."

"I'm sorry," Tom said. He ought to write her a nice letter, he thought, just a friendly word while Mr. Greenleaf was away and she was by herself. He wished he had thought of it before.

Mr. Greenleaf said he would be leaving at the end of the week, via Paris, where the French police were also carrying on the search. McCarron was going with him, and if nothing happened in Paris they were both going home. "It's obvious to me or to anybody," Mr. Greenleaf said, "that he's either dead or deliberately hiding. There's not a corner of the world where the search for him hasn't been publicized. Short of Russia, maybe. My God, he never showed any liking for that place, did he?"

"Russia? No, not that I know of."

Apparently Mr. Greenleaf's attitude was that Dickie was either dead or to hell with him. During that telephone call, the to-hell-with-him attitude seemed to be uppermost.

Tom went over to Peter Smith-Kingsley's house that same evening. Peter had a couple of English newspapers that his friends had sent him, one with a picture of Tom ejecting the *Oggi* photographer from his house. Tom had seen it in the Italian newspapers too. Pictures of him on the streets of Venice and pictures of his house had also gotten to America. Bob and Cleo both had airmailed him photographs and write-ups from New York tabloids. They thought it was all terribly exciting.

"I'm good and sick of it," Tom said. "I'm only hanging around here to be polite and to help if I can. If any more reporters try to crash my house, they're going to get it with a shotgun as soon as they walk in the door." He really was irritated and disgusted, and it sounded in his voice.

"I quite understand," Peter said. "I'm going home at the end of May, you know. If you'd like to come along and stay at my place in Ireland, you're more than welcome. It's deadly quiet there, I can assure you."

Tom glanced at him. Peter had told him about his old Irish castle and had shown him pictures of it. Some quality of his relationship with Dickie flashed across his mind like the memory of a nightmare, like a pale and evil ghost. It was because the same thing could happen with Peter, he thought, Peter the upright, unsuspecting, naive, generous good fellow—except that he didn't look enough like Peter. But one evening, for Peter's amusement, he had put on an English accent and had imitated Peter's mannerisms and his way of jerking his head to one side as he talked, and Peter had thought it hilariously funny. He shouldn't have done that, Tom thought now. It made Tom bitterly ashamed, that evening and the fact that he had thought even for an instant that the same thing that had happened with Dickie could happen with Peter.

"Thanks," Tom said. "I'd better stay by myself for a while longer. I miss my friend Dickie, you know. I miss him terribly." He was suddenly near tears. He could remember Dickie's smiles that first day they began to get along, when he had confessed to Dickie that his father had sent him. He remembered their crazy first trip to Rome. He remembered with affection even that half-hour in the Carlton Bar in Cannes, when Dickie had been so bored and silent, but there had been a reason why Dickie had been bored, after all: he had dragged Dickie there, and Dickie didn't care for the Côte d'Azur. If he'd only gotten his sightseeing done all by himself, Tom thought, if he only hadn't been in such a hurry and so greedy, if he only hadn't misjudged the relationship between Dickie and Marge so stupidly, or had simply waited for them to separate of their own volition, then none of this would have happened, and he *could* have lived with Dickie for the rest of his life, traveled and lived and enjoyed living for the rest of his life. If he only hadn't put on Dickie's clothes that day—

"I understand, Tommie boy, I really do," Peter said, patting his shoulder.

Tom looked up at him through distorting tears. He was imagining traveling with Dickie on some liner back to America for Christmas holidays, imagining being on as good terms with Dickie's parents as if he and Dickie had been brothers. "Thanks," Tom said. It came out a childlike "blub."

"I'd really think something was the matter with you if you didn't break down like this," Peter said sympathetically.

29.

Venice
June 3, 19——

Dear Mr. Greenleaf,

While packing a suitcase today, I came across an envelope that Richard gave me in Rome, and which for some unaccountable reason I had forgotten until now. On the envelope was written "Not to be opened until June" and, as it happens, it is June. The envelope contained Richard's will, and he leaves his income and possessions to me. I am as astounded by this as you probably are, yet from the wording of the will (it is typewritten) he seems to have been in possession of his senses.

I am only bitterly sorry I did not remember having the envelope, because it would have proven much earlier that Dickie intended to take his own life. I put it into a suitcase pocket, and then I forgot it. He gave it to me on the last occasion I saw him, in Rome, when he was so depressed.

On second thought, I am enclosing a photostat copy of the will so that you may see it for yourself. This is the first will I have ever seen in my life, and I am absolutely unfamiliar with the usual procedure. What should I do?

Please give my kindest regards to Mrs. Greenleaf and realize that I sympathize deeply with you both, and regret the necessity of writing this letter. Please let me hear from you as soon as possible. My next address will be:

> c/o American Express
> Athens, Greece
>> Most sincerely yours,
>> Tom Ripley

In a way it was asking for trouble, Tom thought. It might start a new investigation of the signatures, on the will and also the remittances, one of the relentless investigations that insurance companies and probably trust companies also launched when it was a matter of money out of their own pockets. But that was the mood he was in. He had bought his ticket for Greece in the middle of May, and the days had grown finer and finer, making him more and more restless. He had taken his car out of the Fiat garage in Venice and had driven over the Brenner to Salzburg and Munich, down to Trieste and over to Bolzano, and the weather had held everywhere, except for the mildest, most springlike shower in Munich when he had been walking in the Englischer Garten, and he had not even tried to get under cover from it but had simply kept on walking, thrilled as a child at the thought that this was the first German rain that had ever fallen on him. He had only two thousand dollars in his own name, transferred from Dickie's bank account and saved out of Dickie's income, because he hadn't dared to withdraw any more in so short a time as three months. The very chanciness of trying for all of Dickie's money, the peril of it, was irresistible to him. He was so bored after the dreary, eventless weeks in Venice, when each day that went by had seemed to confirm his personal safety and to emphasize the dullness of his existence. Roverini had stopped writing to him. Alvin McCarron had gone back to America (after nothing more than another inconsequential telephone call to him from Rome), and Tom supposed that he and Mr. Greenleaf had concluded that Dickie was either dead or hiding of his own will, and that further search was useless. The newspapers had stopped printing anything about Dickie for want of anything to print. Tom had a feeling of emptiness and abeyance that had driven him nearly mad until he made the trip to Munich in his car. When he came back to Venice to pack for Greece and to close his house, the sensation had been worse: he was about to go to Greece, to those ancient heroic islands, as little Tom Ripley, shy and meek, with a dwindling two-thousand-odd in his bank, so that he would practically have to think twice before he bought himself even a book on Greek art. It was intolerable.

He had decided in Venice to make his voyage to Greece an heroic one. He would see the islands, swimming for the first time into his view, as a living, breathing, courageous individual—not as a cringing little nobody from Boston. If he sailed right into the arms of the police in Piraeus, he would at least have known the days just before, standing in the wind at the prow of a ship, crossing the wine-dark sea like Jason or Ulysses returning. So he had written the letter to Mr. Greenleaf and mailed it three days before he was to sail from Venice. Mr. Greenleaf would probably not get the letter for four or five days, so there would be no time for Mr. Greenleaf to hold him in Venice with a telegram and make him miss his ship. Besides, it looked better from every point of view to be casual about the thing, not to be reachable for another two weeks until he got to Greece, as if he were so unconcerned as to whether he got the money or not, he had not let the fact of the will postpone even a little trip he had planned to make.

Two days before his sailing, he went to tea at the house of Titi della Latta-Cacciaguerra, the countess he had met the day he had started looking for a house in Venice. The maid showed him into the living room, and Titi greeted him with the phrase he had not heard for many weeks: "Ah, ciao, Tomaso! Have you seen the afternoon paper? They have found Deekie's suitcases! And his paintings! Right here in the American Express in Venice!" Her gold earrings trembled with her excitement.

"What?" Tom hadn't seen the papers. He had been too busy packing that afternoon.

"Read it! Here! All his clothes deposited only in February! They were sent from Naples. Perhaps he is here in Venice!"

Tom was reading it. The cord around the canvases had come undone, the paper said, and in wrapping them again a clerk had discovered the signature R. Greenleaf on the paintings. Tom's hands began to shake so that he had to grip the sides of the paper to hold it steady. The paper said that the police were now examining everything carefully for fingerprints.

"Perhaps he is alive!" Titi shouted.

"I don't think—I don't see why this proves he is alive. He could have been murdered or killed himself after he sent the suitcases. The fact that it's under another name—Fanshaw—" He had the feeling the countess, who was sitting rigidly on the sofa staring at him, was startled by his nervousness, so he pulled himself together abruptly, summoned all his courage and said, "You see? They're looking through everything for fingerprints. They wouldn't be doing that if they were sure Dickie sent the suitcases himself. Why should he deposit them under Fanshaw, if he expected to claim them again himself? His passport's even here. He packed his passport."

"Perhaps he is hiding himself under the name of Fanshaw! Oh, caro mio, you need some tea!" Titi stood up. "Giustina! Il te, per piacere, subitissimo!"

Tom sank down weakly on the sofa, still holding the newspaper in front of him. What about the knot on Dickie's body? Wouldn't it be just his luck to have that come undone now?

"Ah, carissimo, you are so pessimistic," Titi said, patting his knee. "This is good news! Suppose all the fingerprints are his? Wouldn't you be happy then? Suppose tomorrow, when you are walking in some little street of Venice, you will come face to face with Deekie Greenleaf, alias Signor Fanshaw!" She let out her shrill, pleasant laugh that was as natural to her as breathing.

"It says here that the suitcases contained everything—shaving kit, toothbrush, shoes, overcoat, complete equipment," Tom said, hiding his terror in gloom. "He couldn't be alive and leave all that. The murderer must have stripped his body and deposited his clothes there because it was the easiest way of getting rid of them."

This gave even Titi pause. Then she said, "Will you not be so downhearted until you know what the fingerprints are? You are supposed to be off on a pleasure trip tomorrow. Ecco il te!"

The day after tomorrow, Tom thought. Plenty of time for Roverini to get his fingerprints and compare them with those

on the canvases and in the suitcases. He tried to remember
any flat surfaces on the canvas frames and on things in the
suitcases from which fingerprints could be taken. There was
not much, except the articles in the shaving kit, but they could
find enough, in fragments and smears, to assemble ten perfect
prints if they tried. His only reason for optimism was that they
didn't have his fingerprints yet, and that they might not ask
for them, because he was not yet under suspicion. But if they
already had Dickie's fingerprints from somewhere? Wouldn't
Mr. Greenleaf send Dickie's fingerprints from America the
very first thing, by way of checking? There could be any number of places they could find Dickie's fingerprints: on certain
possessions of his in America, in the house in Mongibello—

"Tomaso! Take your tea!" Titi said, with another gentle
press of his knee.

"Thank you."

"You will see. At least this is a step toward the truth, what
really happened. Now let us talk about something else, if it
makes you so unhappy! Where do you go from Athens?"

He tried to turn his thoughts to Greece. For him, Greece
was gilded, with the gold of warriors' armor and with its own
famous sunlight. He saw stone statues with calm, strong faces,
like the women on the porch of the Erechtheum. He didn't
want to go to Greece with the threat of the fingerprints in
Venice hanging over him. It would debase him. He would feel
as low as the lowest rat that scurried in the gutters of Athens,
lower than the dirtiest beggar who would accost him in the
streets of Salonika. Tom put his face in his hands and wept.
Greece was finished, exploded like a golden balloon.

Titi put her firm, plump arm around him. "Tomaso, cheer
up! Wait until you have reason to feel so downcast!"

"I can't see why you don't see that this is a bad sign!" Tom
said desperately. "I really don't!"

30.

THE worst sign of all was that Roverini, whose messages had
been so friendly and explicit up to now, sent him nothing at

all in regard to the suitcases and canvases having been found in Venice. Tom spent a sleepless night and then a day of pacing his house while he tried to finish the endless little chores pertaining to his departure, paying Anna and Ugo, paying various tradesmen. Tom expected the police to come knocking on his door at any hour of the day or night. The contrast between his tranquil self-confidence of five days ago and his present apprehension almost tore him apart. He could neither sleep nor eat nor sit still. The irony of Anna's and Ugo's commiseration with him, and also of the telephone calls from his friends, asking him if he had any ideas as to what might have happened in view of the finding of the suitcases, seemed more than he could bear. Ironic, too, that he could let them know that he was upset, pessimistic, desperate even, and they thought nothing of it. They thought it was perfectly normal, because Dickie after all might have been murdered: everybody considered it very significant that all Dickie's possessions had been in the suitcases in Venice, down to his shaving kit and comb.

Then there was the matter of the will. Mr. Greenleaf would get it day after tomorrow. By that time they might know that the fingerprints were not Dickie's. By that time they might have intercepted the *Hellenes*, and taken his own fingerprints. If they discovered that the will was a forgery, too, they would have no mercy on him. All three murders would come out, as naturally as ABC.

By the time he boarded the *Hellenes* Tom felt like a walking ghost. He was sleepless, foodless, full of espressos, carried along only by his twitching nerves. He wanted to ask if there was a radio, but he was positive there was a radio. It was a good-sized, triple-deck ship with forty-eight passengers. He collapsed about five minutes after the stewards had brought his luggage into his cabin. He remembered lying face down on his bunk with one arm twisted under him, and being too tired to change his position, and when he awakened the ship was moving, not only moving but rolling gently with a pleasant rhythm that suggested a tremendous reserve of power and a promise of unending, unobstructable forward movement that would sweep aside anything in its way. He felt better, except that the arm he had been lying on hung limply at his side like a dead member, and flopped against him when he walked through the corridor so that he had to grip it with the other hand to hold it in place. It was a quarter of ten by his watch, and utterly dark outside.

There was some kind of land on his extreme left, probably part of Yugoslavia, five or six little dim white lights, and otherwise nothing but black sea and black sky, so black that there was no trace of an horizon and they might have been sailing against a black screen, except that he felt no resistance to the steadily plowing ship, and the wind blew freely on his forehead as if out of infinite space. There was no one around him on the deck. They were all below, eating their late dinner, he supposed. He was glad to be alone. His arm was coming back to life. He gripped the prow where it separated in a narrow V and took a deep breath. A defiant courage rose in him. What if the radioman were receiving at this very minute a message to arrest Tom Ripley? He would stand up just as bravely as he was standing now. Or he might hurl himself over the ship's gunwale—which for him would be the supreme act of courage as well as escape. Well, what if? Even from where he stood, he could hear the faint *beep—beep-beep* from the radio room at the top of the superstructure. He was not afraid. This was it. This was the way he had hoped he would feel, sailing to Greece. To look out at the black water all around him and not be afraid was almost as good as seeing the islands of Greece coming into view. In the soft June darkness ahead of him he could construct in imagination the little islands, the hills of Athens dotted with buildings, and the Acropolis.

There was an elderly Englishwoman on board the ship, traveling with her daughter who herself was forty, unmarried, and so wildly nervous she could not even enjoy the sun for fifteen minutes in her deckchair without leaping up and announcing in a loud voice that she was "off for a walk." Her mother, by contrast, was extremely calm and slow—she had some kind of paralysis in her right leg, which was shorter than the other so that she had to wear a thick heel on her right shoe and could not walk except with a cane—the kind of person who would have driven Tom insane in New York with her slowness and

her unvarying graciousness of manner, but now Tom was inspired to spend hours with her in the deckchairs, talking to
her and listening to her talk about her life in England and
about Greece, when she had last seen Greece in 1926. He took
her for slow walks around the deck, she leaning on his arm
and apologizing constantly for the trouble she was giving him,
but obviously she loved the attention. And the daughter was
obviously delighted that someone was taking her mother off
her hands.

Maybe Mrs. Cartwright had been a hellcat in her youth,
Tom thought, maybe she was responsible for every one of her
daughter's neuroses, maybe she had clutched her daughter so
closely to her that it had been impossible for the daughter to
lead a normal life and marry, and maybe she deserved to be
kicked overboard instead of walked around the deck and listened to for hours while she talked, but what did it matter?
Did the world always mete out just deserts? Had the world
meted his out to him? He considered that he had been lucky
beyond reason in escaping detection for two murders, lucky
from the time he had assumed Dickie's identity until now. In
the first part of his life fate had been grossly unfair, he
thought, but the period with Dickie and afterward had more
than compensated for it. But something was going to happen
now in Greece, he felt, and it couldn't be good. His luck had
held just too long. But supposing they got him on the fingerprints, and on the will, and they gave him the electric
chair—could that death in the electric chair equal in pain, or
could death itself, at twenty-five, be so tragic, that he could
not say that the months from November until now had not
been worth it? Certainly not.

The only thing he regretted was that he had not seen all
the world yet. He wanted to see Australia. And India. He
wanted to see Japan. Then there was South America. Merely
to look at the art of those countries would be a pleasant,
rewarding life's work, he thought. He had learned a lot about
painting, even in trying to copy Dickie's mediocre paintings.
At the art galleries in Paris and Rome he had discovered an
interest in paintings that he had never realized before, or perhaps that had not been in him before. He did not want to be

a painter himself, but if he had money, he thought, his greatest pleasure would be to collect paintings that he liked, and to help young painters with talent who needed money.

His mind went off on such tangents as he walked with Mrs. Cartwright around the deck, or listened to her monologues that were not always interesting. Mrs. Cartwright thought him charming. She told him several times, days before they got to Greece, how much he had contributed to her enjoyment of the voyage, and they made plans as to how they would meet at a certain hotel in Crete on the second of July, Crete being the only place their itineraries crossed. Mrs. Cartwright was traveling by bus on a special tour. Tom acquiesced to all her suggestions, though he never expected to see her again once they got off the ship. He imagined himself seized at once and taken on board another ship, or perhaps a plane, back to Italy. No radio messages had come about him—that he knew of— but would they necessarily inform him if any had come? The ship's paper, a little one-page mimeographed sheet that appeared every evening at each place on the dinner tables, was entirely concerned with international political news, and would not have contained anything about the Greenleaf case even if something important had happened. During the ten-day voyage Tom lived in a peculiar atmosphere of doom and of heroic, unselfish courage. He imagined strange things: Mrs. Cartwright's daughter falling overboard and he jumping after her and saving her. Or fighting through the waters of a ruptured bulkhead to close the breach with his own body. He felt possessed of a preternatural strength and fearlessness.

When the boat approached the mainland of Greece Tom was standing at the rail with Mrs. Cartwright. She was telling him how the port of Piraeus had changed in appearance since she had seen it last, and Tom was not interested at all in the changes. It existed, that was all that mattered to him. It wasn't a mirage ahead of him, it was a solid hill that he could walk on, with buildings that he could touch—if he got that far.

The police were waiting on the dock. He saw four of them, standing with folded arms, looking up at the ship. Tom helped Mrs. Cartwright to the very last, boosted her gently over the curb at the end of the gangplank, and said a smiling good-bye to her and her daughter. He had to wait under the R's and they under the C's to receive their luggage, and the two Cartwrights were leaving right away for Athens on their special bus.

With Mrs. Cartwright's kiss still warm and slightly moist on his cheek, Tom turned and walked slowly toward the policemen. No fuss, he thought, he'd just tell them himself who he was. There was a big newsstand behind the policemen, and he thought of buying a paper. Perhaps they would let him. The policemen stared back at him from over their folded arms as he approached them. They wore black uniforms with visored caps. Tom smiled at them faintly. One of them touched his cap and stepped aside. But the others did not close in. Now Tom was practically between two of them, right in front of the newsstand, and the policemen were staring forward again, paying no attention to him at all.

Tom looked over the array of papers in front of him, feeling dazed and faint. His hand moved automatically to take a familiar paper of Rome. It was only three days old. He pulled some lire out of his pocket, realized suddenly that he had no Greek money, but the newsdealer accepted the lire as readily as if he were in Italy, and even gave him back change in lire.

"I'll take these, too," Tom said in Italian, choosing three more Italian papers and the Paris *Herald-Tribune*. He glanced at the police officers. They were not looking at him.

Then he walked back to the shed on the dock where the ship's passengers were awaiting their luggage. He heard Mrs. Cartwright's cheerful halloo to him as he went by, but he pretended not to have heard. Under the R's he stopped and opened the oldest Italian paper, which was four days old.

NO ONE NAMED ROBERT S. FANSHAW FOUND,
DEPOSITOR OF GREENLEAF BAGGAGE

said the awkward caption on the second page. Tom read the long column below it, but only the fifth paragraph interested him:

The police ascertained a few days ago that the fingerprints on the suitcases and paintings are the same as the fingerprints found in Greenleaf's abandoned apartment in Rome. Therefore, it has been assumed that Greenleaf deposited the suitcases and the paintings himself. . . .

Tom fumbled open another paper. Here it was again:

. . . In view of the fact that the fingerprints on the articles in the suitcases are identical with those in Signor Greenleaf's apartment in Rome, the police have concluded that Signor Greenleaf packed and dispatched the suitcases to Venice, and there is speculation that he may have committed suicide, perhaps in the water in a state of total nudity. An alternative speculation is that he exists at present under the alias of Robert S. Fanshaw or another alias. Still another possibility is that he was murdered, after packing or being made to pack his own baggage—perhaps for the express purpose of confusing police inquiries through fingerprints. . . .

In any case, it is futile to search for "Richard Greenleaf" any longer, because, even if he is alive, he has not his "Richard Greenleaf" passport. . . .

Tom felt shaky and lightheaded. The glare of sunlight under the edge of the roof hurt his eyes. Automatically he followed the porter with his luggage toward the customs counter, and tried to realize, as he stared down at his open suitcase that the inspector was hastily examining, exactly what the news meant. It meant he was not suspected at all. It meant that the fingerprints really had guaranteed his innocence. It meant not only that he was not going to jail, and not going to die, but that he was not suspected at all. He was free. Except for the will.

Tom boarded the bus for Athens. One of his table companions was sitting next to him, but he gave no sign of greeting, and couldn't have answered anything if the man had spoken to him. There would be a letter concerning the will at the American Express in Athens, Tom was sure. Mr. Greenleaf had had plenty of time to reply. Perhaps he had put his lawyers onto it right away, and there would be only a polite negative reply in Athens from a lawyer, and maybe the next message would come from the American police, saying that he was answerable for forgery. Maybe both messages were awaiting him at the American Express. The will could undo it all. Tom looked out the window at the primitive, dry landscape. Nothing was registering on him. Maybe the Greek police were waiting for him at the American Express. Maybe the four men he had seen had not been police but some kind of soldiers.

The bus stopped. Tom got out, corraled his luggage, and found a taxi.

"Would you stop at the American Express, please?" he asked the driver in Italian, but the driver apparently understood "American Express" at least, and drove off. Tom remembered when he had said the same words to the taxi driver in Rome, the day he had been on his way to Palermo. How sure of himself he'd been that day, just after he had given Marge the slip at the Inghilterra!

He sat up when he saw the American Express sign, and looked around the building for policemen. Perhaps the police were inside. In Italian, he asked the driver to wait, and the driver seemed to understand this too, and touched his cap. There was a specious ease about everything, like the moment just before something was going to explode. Tom looked around inside the American Express lobby. Nothing seemed unusual. Maybe the minute he mentioned his name—

"Have you any letters for Thomas Ripley?" he asked in a low voice in English.

"Reepley? Spell it, if you please."

He spelt it.

She turned and got some letters from a cubbyhole.

Nothing was happening.

"Three letters," she said in English, smiling.

One from Mr. Greenleaf. One from Titi in Venice. One from Cleo, forwarded. He opened the letter from Mr. Greenleaf.

June 9, 19——

Dear Tom,

Your letter of June 3rd received yesterday.

It was not so much of a surprise to my wife and me as you may have imagined. We were both aware that Richard was very fond of you, in spite of the fact he never went out of his way to tell us this in any of his letters. As you pointed out, this will does, unhappily, seem to indicate that Richard has taken his own life. It is a conclusion that we here have at last accepted—the only other chance being that Richard has assumed another name and for reasons of his own has chosen to turn his back on his family.

My wife concurs with me in the opinion that we should carry out Richard's preferences and the spirit of them, whatever he may have done with himself. So you have, insofar as the will is concerned, my personal support. I have put your photostat copy into the hands of my lawyers, who will keep you informed as to their progress in making over Richard's trust fund and other properties to you.

Once more, thank you for your assistance when I was overseas. Let us hear from you.

With best wishes,
Herbert Greenleaf

Was it a joke? But the Burke-Greenleaf letterpaper in his hand felt authentic—thick and slightly pebbled and the letterhead engraved—and besides, Mr. Greenleaf wouldn't joke like this, not in a million years. Tom walked on to the waiting taxi. It was no joke. It was his! Dickie's money and his freedom. And the freedom, like everything else, seemed combined, his and Dickie's combined. He could have a house in Europe and a house in America too, if he chose. The money for the house in Mongibello was still waiting to be claimed, he thought suddenly, and he supposed he should send that to the Greenleafs, since Dickie put it up for sale before he wrote the will. He smiled, thinking of Mrs. Cartwright. He must take her a big box of orchids when he met her in Crete, if they had any orchids in Crete.

He tried to imagine landing in Crete—the long island, peaked with the dry, jagged lips of craters, the little bustle of excitement on the pier as his boat moved into the harbor, the small-boy porters, avid for his luggage and his tips, and he would have plenty to tip them with, plenty for everything and everybody. He saw four motionless figures standing on the imaginary pier, the figures of Cretan policemen waiting for him, patiently waiting with folded arms. He grew suddenly tense, and his vision vanished. Was he going to see policemen waiting for him on every pier that he ever approached? In Alexandria? Istanbul? Bombay? Rio? No use thinking about that. He pulled his shoulders back. No use spoiling his trip worrying about imaginary policemen. Even if there *were* policemen on the pier, it wouldn't necessarily mean—

"A donda, a donda?" the taxi driver was saying, trying to speak Italian for him.

"To a hotel, please," Tom said. "Il meglio albergo. Il meglio, il meglio!"

PICK-UP

by Charles Willeford

ONE

Enter Madame

IT MUST have been around a quarter to eleven. A sailor came in and ordered a chile dog and coffee. I sliced a bun, jerked a frank out of the boiling water, nested it, poured a half-dipper of chile over the frank and sprinkled it liberally with chopped onions. I scribbled a check and put it by his plate. I wouldn't have recommended the unpalatable mess to a starving animal. The sailor was the only customer, and after he ate his dog he left.

That was the exact moment she entered.

A small woman, hardly more than five feet.

She had the figure of a teen-age girl. Her suit was a blue tweed, smartly cut, and over her thin shoulders she wore a fur jacket, bolero length. Tiny gold circular earrings clung to her small pierced ears. Her hands and feet were small, and when she seated herself at the counter I noticed she wasn't wearing any rings. She was pretty drunk.

"What'll it be?" I asked her.

"I believe I need coffee." She steadied herself on the stool by bracing her hands against the edge of the counter.

"Yes, you do," I agreed, "and you need it black."

I drew a cupful and set it before her. The coffee was too hot for her to drink and she bent her head down and blew on it with comical little puffs. I stood behind the counter watching her. I couldn't help it; she was beautiful. Even Benny, from his seat behind the cash register, was staring at her, and his only real interest is money. She wasn't nearly as young as I had first thought her to be. She was about twenty-six or -seven. Her fine blonde hair was combed straight back. Slightly to the right of a well-defined widow's-peak, an inch-wide strip of silver hair glistened, like a moonlit river flowing through night fields. Her oval face was unlined and very white. The only make-up she had on was lipstick; a dark shade of red, so dark it was almost black. She looked up from her coffee and noticed that I was staring at her. Her eyes were a charred sienna-brown, flecked with dancing particles of shining gold.

"This coffee is too hot." She smiled good-humoredly.

"Sure it is," I replied, "but if you want to sober up you should drink it hot as you can."

"My goodness! Who wants to sober up?"

Benny was signaling me from the cash register. I dropped my conversation with the girl to see what he wanted. Benny was a flat, bald, hook-nosed little man with a shaggy horseshoe of gray hair circling his head. I didn't particularly like him, but he never pushed or tried to boss me and I'd stuck it out as his counterman for more than two months. For me, this was a record. His dirty eyes were gleaming behind his gold-rimmed glasses.

"There's your chance, Harry!" He laughed a throaty, phlegmy laugh.

I knew exactly what he meant. About two weeks before a girl had entered the cafe at closing time and she had been pretty well down on her luck. She'd been actually hungry and Benny had had me fix her up with a steak and french fries. Afterwards, he had made her pay him for the meal by letting him take it out in trade in the kitchen.

"I don't need any advice from you," I said angrily.

He laughed again, deep in his chest. "It's quitting time. Better take advantage." He climbed down from his stool and walked stiffly to the door. He shot the bolt and hung the CLOSED sign from the hook. I started toward the kitchen and as I passed the woman she shook her empty cup at me.

"See? All finished. May I have another?"

I filled her cup, set it in front of her and went into the back room and slipped into my tweed jacket. The jacket was getting ratty. It was my only outer garment, with the exception of my trenchcoat, and I'd worn it for more than two years. The elbows were thin and the buttons, except one, were missing. The good button was the top one and a coat looks funny buttoned at the top. I resolved to move it to the middle in the morning. My blue gabardine trousers hadn't been cleaned for three weeks and they were spotted here and there with grease. I had another pair of trousers in my room, but they were tuxedo trousers, and I used them on waiter and busboy jobs. Sober, I was always embarrassed about my appearance, but I didn't intend to stay sober very long. I combed my hair and I was ready for the street, a bar and a drink.

She was still sitting at the counter and her cup was empty again.

"Just one more and I'll go," she said with a drunken little laugh. "I promise."

For the third time I gave her a cup of coffee. Benny was counting on his fingers and busily going over his receipts for the day. I tapped him on the shoulder.

"Benny, I need a ten until payday," I told him.

"Not again? I let you have ten last night and today's only Tuesday. By Saturday you won't have nothing coming."

"You don't have to worry about it."

He took his copy-book from under the counter and turned to my page. After he entered the advance in the book he reluctantly gave me a ten dollar bill. I folded the bill and put it in my watch pocket. I felt a hand timidly tugging at my sleeve and I turned around. The little woman was looking up at me with her big blue innocent eyes.

"I haven't any money," she said bitterly.

"Is that right?"

"Not a penny. Are you going to call a policeman?"

"Ask Mr. Freeman. He's the owner; I just work here."

"What's that?" Benny asked, at the mention of his name. He was in the middle of his count and didn't like to be disturbed.

"This young lady is unable to pay for her coffee."

"Coffee is ten cents," he said firmly.

"I'll tell you what, Benny. Just take it out of my pay."

"Don't think I won't!" He returned to his counting.

I unlocked the door, and the woman and I went outside.

"You're a free woman," I said to the girl. "You're lucky that Benny didn't notice you were without a purse when you came in. Where is your purse, by the way?"

"I think it's in my suitcase."

"All right. Where's your suitcase?"

"It's in a locker. I've got the key." She took a numbered key out of the pocket of her fur jacket. "The main trouble is that I can't seem to remember whether the locker's in the railroad station or the bus station." She was genuinely puzzled.

"If I were you I'd look in the bus station first. You're quite a ways from the railroad station. Do you know where it is?"

"The bus station?"

"Yes. It's seven blocks that way and one block that way." I pointed down Market Street. "You can't miss it. I'm going to have a drink."

"Would you mind buying me one too?"

"Sure. Come on."

She took my arm and we walked down Market. It was rather pleasant having a beautiful woman in tow and I was glad she had asked me to buy her a drink. I would never have asked her, but as long as she didn't mind, I certainly didn't mind. I shortened my stride so she could keep up with me and from time to time I looked down at her. Gin was my weakness, not women, but with a creature like her . . . well, it was enough to make a man think. We were nearing the bar where I always had my first drink after work and my mind returned to more practical things. We entered, found seats at the end of the bar.

"Say," she said brightly. "I remember being in here tonight!"

"That's fine. It's a cinch you were in some bar." The bartender knew me well, but his eyebrows lifted when he saw the girl with me.

"What'll you have, Harry?" he asked.

"Double gin and tonic." I turned to the girl.

"I'd better not have a double. Give me a little shot of bourbon and a beer chaser." She smiled at me. "I'm being smart, aren't I?"

"You bet." I lit two cigarettes and passed her one. She sucked it deeply.

"My name is Harry Jordan," I said solemnly. "I'm thirty-two years of age and when I'm not working, I drink."

Her laugh closely resembled a tinkling bell. "My name is Helen Meredith. I'm thirty-three years old and I don't work at all. I drink all of the time."

"You're not thirty-three, are you? I took you for about twenty-six, maybe less."

"I'm thirty-three all right, and I can't forget it."

"Well, you've got an advantage on me then. Married?"

"Uh huh. I'm married, but I don't work at that either."
She shrugged comically. I stared at her delicate fingers as she handled the cigarette.

The bartender arrived with our drinks. Mine was good and cold and the gin taste was strong. The way I like it. I love the first drink best of all.

"Two more of the same," I told the bartender, "and see if Mrs. Meredith's purse was left here, will you?"

"I haven't seen a purse laying around. Are you sure you left it in here, miss?" he asked Helen worriedly.

"I'm not sure of anything," she replied.

"Well, I'll take a look around. Maybe you left it in a booth."

"Helen Meredith," I said, when the bartender left. "Here's to you!" We clicked our glasses together and drained them down. Helen choked a bit and followed her shot down with the short beer chaser.

"Ahhh," she sighed. "Harry, I'm going to tell you something while I'm still able to tell you. I haven't lived with my husband for more than ten years, and even though I don't wear a ring, I'm still married."

"You don't have to convince me."

"But I want to tell you. I live with my mother in San Sienna. Do you know where that is?"

"Sure. It's a couple of hundred miles down the coast. Noted for tourists, beaches, a mission and money. Nothing else."

"That's right. Well as I told you, I drink. In the past two years I've managed to embarrass Mother many times. It's a small community and we're both well-known, so I decided the best thing to do was get out. This morning I was half-drunk, half-hungover, and I bought a bottle and I left. For good. But I hit the bottle so hard I'm not sure whether I came to San Francisco on the bus or on the train."

"I'm willing to lay odds of two to one it was the bus."

"You're probably right. I really don't remember."

The bartender brought us our second drink. He shook his head emphatically. "You didn't leave no purse in here, miss. You might've thought you did, but you didn't."

"Thanks for looking," I told him. "After we finish this one," I said to Helen, "we'll go back down to the bus station and I'll find your purse for you. Then you'd better head back for San Sienna and Mother."

Helen shook her head back and forth slowly. "No. I'm not going back. Never."

"That's your business. Not mine."

We finished our second drink and left the bar. It was a long walk to the bus station. Market Street blocks are long and crowded. Helen hung on to my arm possessively, and by the time we reached the station she had sobered considerably. The place was jampacked with servicemen of all kinds and a liberal sprinkling of civilians. The Greyhound station is the jumping-off place for servicemen. San Francisco is the hub for all the spokes leading to air bases, navy bases and army posts that dot the bay area.

"Does the bus station look familiar to you?"

"Of course!" She laughed. "I've been to San Francisco many times. I always come up on the bus for my Christmas shopping."

I felt a little foolish. "Let's start looking then." She handed me the numbered key. There are a lot of parcel lockers inside the Greyhound station and many more out on the waiting ramp, but in a few minutes we were able to locate the locker. It was in the first row to the left of the Ladies' Room. I inserted the key and opened the locker. I took the suitcase out of the locker and handed it to Helen. She unsnapped the two catches on the aluminum over-nighter and raised the lid. Her tiny hands ruffled deftly through the clothing. There wasn't any purse. I looked. No purse. I felt around inside the locker. No purse.

"Do you suppose I could have left it in some other bar, Harry?" she asked me worriedly. "Somewhere between here and the cafe?"

"That's probably what you did, all right. And if you did, you can kiss it goodbye. How much money did you have?"

"I don't know, but drunk or sober I wouldn't have left San Sienna broke. I know I had some traveler's checks."

I took my money out of my watch pocket. There were eight dollars and seventy cents. I gave the five dollar bill to Helen.

"This five'll get you a ticket back to San Sienna. You'd better get one."

Helen shook her head vigorously this time and firmly set her mouth. "I'm not going back, Harry. I told you I wasn't and I meant it!" She held the bill out to me. "Take it back; I don't want it."

"No, you go ahead and keep it. We'll consider it a loan. But I'm going to take you to a hotel. If I turned you loose you'd drink it up."

"It didn't take you long to get to know me, did it?" She giggled.

"I don't know you. It's just that I know what I'd do. Come on, we'll find a hotel."

I picked up the light suitcase and we left the station. We crossed Market Street and at Powell we turned and entered the first hotel that looked satisfactory to me. There are more than a dozen hotels on Powell Street, all of them adequate, and it was our best bet to find a vacancy. The hotel we entered was furnished in cheap modern furniture and the floor was covered with a rose wall-to-wall carpet. There were several green plants scattered about, all of them set in white pots with wrought-iron legs, and by each foam-cushioned lobby chair, there were skinny, black wrought-iron ash-stands. We crossed the empty lobby to the desk and I set the bag on the floor. The desk clerk was a fairly young man with sleek black hair. He looked up from his comic book with surly gray eyes.

"Sorry," he said flatly. "No doubles left. Just singles."

"That's fine," I said. "That's what I want."

Helen signed the register card. Her handwriting was cramped and it slanted to the left, almost microscopic in size. She put the pen back into the holder and folded her arms across her chest.

"The lady will pay in advance," I said to the clerk, without looking at Helen. She frowned fiercely for a second, then in spite of herself, she giggled and gave the clerk the five dollar bill. He gave her two ones in return. The night clerk also doubled as a bell boy and he came out from behind the desk with Helen's key in his hand.

"You want to go up now?" he asked Helen, pointedly ignoring me.

"I've still got two dollars," Helen said to me. "I'll buy you a drink!"

"No. You go to bed. You've had enough for one day."

"I'll buy you one tomorrow then."

"Tomorrow will be time enough," I said.

Helen's eyes were glassy and her eyelids were heavy. It was difficult for her to hold them open. In the warmth of the lobby she was beginning to stagger a little bit. The night clerk opened the door to the self-operated elevator and helped her in, holding her by the arm. I selected a comfortable chair near the desk and waited in the lobby until he returned. He didn't like it when he saw me sitting there.

"Do you think she'll manage all right?" I asked him.

"She managed to lock her door after I left," he replied dryly.

"Fine. Good night."

I left the hotel and walked up Powell as far as Lefty's, ordered a drink at the bar. It was dull, drinking alone, after drinking with Helen. She was the most attractive woman I had met in years. There was a quality about her that appealed to me. The fact that she was an alcoholic didn't make any difference to me. In a way, I was an alcoholic myself. She wasn't afraid to admit that she was a drunk; she was well aware of it, and she didn't have any intention to stop drinking. It wasn't necessary for her to tell me she was a drunk. I can spot an alcoholic in two minutes. Helen was still a good-looking woman, and she'd been drinking for a long time. I never expected to see her again. If I wanted to, I suppose it would have been easy enough. All I had to do was go down to her hotel in the morning, and . . .

I finished my drink quickly and left the bar. I didn't feel like drinking any more. I crossed the street and waited for my cable car. In a few minutes it dragged up the hill, slowed down at the corner, and I jumped on. I gave the conductor my fare and went inside where it was warmer. Usually, I sat in the outside section where I could smoke, but I was cold that night, my entire body was chilled.

On the long ride home I decided it would be best to steer clear of a woman like Helen.

TWO

Finder's Keepers

I GOT OUT of bed the next morning at ten, and still half-asleep, put the coffee pot on the two-ring gas burner. I padded next door to the bathroom, stood under the hot water of the shower for fifteen minutes, shaved, and returned to my room. It was the last one on the left, downstairs in Mrs. Frances McQuade's roominghouse. The house was on a fairly quiet street and my room was well separated from the other rooms and roomers. This enabled me to drink in my room without bothering anybody, and nobody could bother me.

I sat down at the table, poured a cup of black coffee, and let my mind think about Helen. I tried to define what there was about her that attracted me. Class. That was it. I didn't intend to do anything about the way I felt, but it was pleasant to let my mind explore the possibilities. I finished my coffee and looked around the room. Not only was it an ugly room; it was a filthy room. The walls were covered with a dull gray paper spotted with small crimson flowers. There was a sink in one corner, and next to it the gas burner in a small alcove. My bed was a double, and the head and footboard were made of brass rods, ornately twisted and tortured into circular designs. The dresser was metal, painted to look like maple or walnut, some kind of wood, and each leg rested in a small can of water. I kept my food in the bottom drawer and the cans of water kept the ants away. There were no pictures on the walls and no rug upon the floor, just a square piece of tangerine linoleum under the sink.

The room was in foul shape. Dirty shirts and dirty socks were scattered around, the dresser was messy with newspapers, book matches, my set of oil paints; and the floor was covered with gently moving dust motes. Lined up beneath the sink were seven empty gin bottles and an overflowing paper sack full of empty beer cans. The window was dirty and the sleazy cotton curtains were dusty. Dust was on everything . . .

Suppose, by some chance, I had brought Helen home with

me the night before? I sadly shook my head. Here was a project for me; I'd clean my room. A momentous decision.

I slipped into my shoes and blue gabardine slacks and walked down the hall to Mrs. McQuade's room.

"Good morning," I said, when she opened the door. "I want to borrow your broom and mop."

"The broom and mop are in the closet," she said, and closed the door again.

Mrs. McQuade had a few eccentricities, but she was a kind, motherly type of woman. Her hair was always freshly blued and whenever I thought about it I would comment on how nice it looked. Why women with beautiful white hair doctor it with bluing has always been a mystery to me.

I found the broom and a rag mop and returned to my room.

I spent the rest of the morning cleaning the room, even going so far as to wash my window inside and out. The curtains needed washing, but I shook the dust out of them and hung them back on the rod. Dusted and cleaned, the room looked fairly presentable, even with its ancient, battered furniture. I was dirty again so I took another shower before I dressed. I put my bundle of laundry under my arm, dragged the mop and broom behind me, and leaned them up against Mrs. McQuade's door.

I left the house and dumped my dirty laundry off at the Spotless Cleaner on my way to the corner and Big Mike's Bar and Grill. This was my real home, Big Mike's, and I spent more time in his bar than anywhere else. It was a friendly place, old-fashioned, with sawdust on the floor, and the walls paneled in dark oak. The bar was long and narrow, extending the length of the room, and it had a section with cushioned stools and another section with a rail for those who preferred to stand. There were a few booths along the wall, but there was also a dining-room next door that could be entered either from the street outside or from the barroom. The food was good, reasonable, and there was plenty of it. I seldom ate anything at Mike's. Food costs money and money spent for food is money wasted. When I got hungry, which was seldom, I ate at Benny's.

I took my regular seat at the end of the bar and ordered a

draught beer. It was lunch hour and very busy, but both of
the bartenders knew me well and when my stein was emptied
one of them would quickly fill it again. After one-thirty, the
bar was clear of the lunch crowd and Big Mike joined me in
a beer.

"You're a little late today, Harry," Mike said jokingly. He
had a deep pleasant voice.

"Couldn't be helped."

Mike was an enormous man; everything about him was
large, especially his head and hands. The habitual white shirt
and full-sized apron he wore added to his look of massiveness.
His face was badly scarred, but it didn't make him look hard
or tough; it gave him a kindly, mellowed expression. He could
be tough when it was necessary, however, and he was his own
bouncer. The bar and grill belonged to him alone, and it had
been purchased by his savings after ten years of professional
football—all of it on the line, as a right tackle.

"How does my tab stand these days, Mike?" I asked him.

"I'll check." He looked in the credit book hanging by a
string next to the cash register. "Not too bad," he smiled.
"Twelve twenty-five. Worried about it?"

"When it gets to fifteen, cut me off, will you, Mike?"

"If I do you'll give me an argument."

"Don't pay any attention to me. Cut me off just the same."

"Okay." He shrugged his heavy shoulders. "We've gone
through this before, we might as well go through it again."

"I'm not that bad, Mike."

"I honestly believe you don't know how bad you really are
when you're loaded." He laughed to show he was joking,
finished his beer, and lumbered back to the kitchen. I drank
several beers, nursing them along, and at two-thirty I left the
bar to go to work.

We picked up a little business from the theatre crowd when
the afternoon show at the Bijou got out at three-thirty, and
after that the cafe was fairly quiet until five. When things were
busy, there was too much work for only one counterman, and
I met myself coming and going. Benny was of no help at all. He
never stirred all day from his seat behind the register. I don't
know how he had the patience to sit like that from seven in the
morning until eleven at night. His only enjoyment in life was

obtained by eating orange gum-drops and counting his money at night. Once that day, during a lull, when no one was in the cafe, he tried to kid me about Helen. I didn't like it.

"Come on, Harry, where'd you take her last night?"

"Just forget about it, Benny. There's nothing to tell." I went into the kitchen to get away from him. I don't like that kind of talk. It's dirty. All of a sudden, all ten seats at the counter were filled, and I was too busy to think of anything except what I was doing. In addition to taking the orders, I had to prepare the food and serve it myself. It was quite a job to handle alone, even though Benny didn't run a regular lunch or dinner menu. Just when things are running well and the orders are simple things like sandwiches, bowls of chile, and coffee, a damned aesthete will come in and order soft-boiled eggs, wanting them two-and-one-half minutes in the water or something like that. But I like to work and the busier I am the better I like it. When I'm busy I don't have time to think about when I'll get my next drink.

Ten o'clock rolled around at last, the hour I liked the best of all. The traffic was always thin about this time and I only had another hour to go before I could have a drink. I felt a little hungry—I hadn't eaten anything all day—and I made myself a bacon and tomato sandwich. I walked around the counter and sat down to eat it. Benny eyed my sandwich hungrily.

"How about fixing me one of those, Harry?" he asked.

"Sure. Soon as I finish."

"Fix me one too," a feminine voice said lightly. I glanced to the left and there was Helen, standing in the doorway.

"You came back." My voice sounded flat and strained. No longer interested in food, I pushed my sandwich away from me.

"I told you I would. I owe you a drink. Remember?" She had a black patent leather purse in her hand. "See?" She shook the purse in the air. "I found it."

"Do you really want a sandwich?" I asked her, getting to my feet.

"No." She shook her head. "I was just talking."

"Wait right there," I said firmly, pointing my finger at Helen. "I'll be back in one second."

I went into the back room, and feverishly removed the dirty white jacket and leather tie. I changed into my own tie and sport jacket. Benny was ringing up thirty-one cents on the register when I came back. Helen had paid him for the coffee she had drunk the night before. Trust Benny to get his money.

I took Helen's arm, and Benny looked at us both with some surprise.

"Now just where in the hell do you think you're going?" he asked acidly.

"I quit. Come on, Helen." We walked through the open door.

"Hey!" he shouted after us, and I know that he said something else, but by that time we were walking down the street and well out of range.

THREE

First Night

"DID YOU really quit just like that?" Helen asked me as we walked down the street. Her voice was more amused than incredulous.

"Sure. You said you were going to buy me a drink. That's much more important than working."

"Here we are then." Helen pointed to the entrance door of the bar where we'd had our drinks the night before. "Is this all right?"

I smiled. "It's the nearest." We went inside and sat down at the bar. The bartender recognized Helen right away. He nodded pleasantly to me and then asked Helen: "Find your purse all right?"

"Sure did," Helen said happily.

"Now I'm glad to hear that," the bartender said. "I was afraid somebody might have picked it up and gone south with it. You know how these things happen sometimes. What'll you have?"

"Double gin and tonic for me," I said.

"Don't change it," Helen ordered, stringing along.

As soon as the bartender left to fix our drinks I took a sideways look at Helen. She wasn't tight, not even mellow, but barely under the influence; just enough under to give her a warm, rosy-cheeked color.

"Where did you find your purse, by the way?" I asked Helen.

"It was easy," she laughed merrily. "But I didn't think so this morning." She opened her purse, put enough change down on the bar to pay for the check and handed me a five dollar bill. "Now we're even, Harry."

"Thanks," I said, folding the bill and shoving it into my watch pocket, "I can use it."

"This morning," she began slowly, "I woke up in that miserable little hotel room with a hangover to end them all. God, I felt rotten! I could remember everything pretty well—you going down to the bus station with me, getting the room and so on, but the rest of the day was nothing. Did you ever get like that?"

"I recall a similar experience," I admitted.

"All I had was two dollars, as you know, so after I showered and dressed I checked out of the hotel, leaving my bag at the desk. I was hungry, so I ate breakfast and had four cups of coffee, black, and tried to figure out what to do next.

"Without money, I was in a bad way—" She quickly finished her drink and shook the ice in her glass at the bartender for another. I downed mine fast in order to join her for the next round.

"So I returned to the bus station after breakfast and started from there." She smiled slyly and sipped her drink. "Now where would you have looked for the purse, Harry?"

I thought the question over for a moment. "The nearest bar?"

"Correct!" She laughed appreciatively. "That's where I found it. The first bar to the left of the station. There was a different bartender on duty—about eleven this morning—and he didn't know me, of course, but I described my bag and it was there, under the shelf by the cash register. At first he wouldn't give it to me because there wasn't any identification inside. Like a driver's license, something like that, but my traveler's checks were in the bag and after I wrote my name

on a piece of paper and he compared the signatures on the
checks he gave it to me. The first thing I did was cash a check
and buy him a drink, joining him, of course."

"No money at all?"

"Just the traveler's checks. I'm satisfied. Two hundred dollars in traveler's checks is better than money."

"Cash a couple then and let's get out of here," I said happily. "This isn't the only bar in San Francisco."

We went to several places that night and knowing where to
go is a mighty tricky business. Having lived in San Francisco
for more than a year I could just about tell and I was very
careful about the places I took her to. I didn't want to embarrass Helen any—not that she would have given a damn—
but I wanted to have a good time, and I wanted her to have
a good time too.

The last night club we were in was The Dolphin. I had been
there once before, when I was in the chips, and I knew Helen
would like it. It's a club you have to know about or you can't
find it. It's down an alley off Divisadero Street and I had to
explain to the taxicab driver how to get there. There isn't any
lettered sign over the door; just a large, blue neon fish blinking intermittently, and the fish itself doesn't look like a
dolphin. But once inside you know you're in The Dolphin,
because the name is in blue letters on the menu, and the prices
won't let you forget where you are. We entered and luckily
found a booth well away from the bar. The club is designed
with a South Seas effect, and the drinks are served in tall, thick
glasses, the size and shape of a vase. The booth we sat in was
very soft, padded thickly with foam rubber, and both of us had
had enough to drink to appreciate the atmosphere and the
deep, gloomy lighting that made it almost impossible to see
across the room. The waiter appeared at our table out of the
darkness and handed each of us a menu. He was a Mexican,
naked except for a grass skirt, and made up to look like an is-
lander of some sort: there were blue and yellow streaks of
paint on his brown face, and he wore a shark's-teeth necklace.

"Do you still have the Dolphin Special?" I asked him.

"Certainly," he said politely. "And something to eat? Poi,
dried squid, bird's-nest soup, breadfruit au gratin, sago palm
salad—"

Helen's laugh startled the waiter. "No thanks," she said. "I guess I'm not hungry."

"Just bring us two of the Dolphin Specials," I told him. He nodded solemnly and left for the bar. The Special is a good drink; it contains five varieties of rum, mint, plenty of snow-ice, and it's decorated with orange slices, pineapple slices and cherries with a sprinkling of sugar cane gratings floating on top. I needed at least two of them. I had to build up my nerve.

After the waiter brought our drinks I lighted cigarettes and we smoked silently, dumping the ashes into the large abalone shell on the table that served as an ash-tray. The trio hummed into action and the music floating our way gave me a wistful feeling of nostalgia. The trio consisted of chimes, theremin and electric guitar and the unusual quality of the theremin prevented me from recognizing the melody of the song although I was certain I knew what it was.

With sudden impulsive boldness I put my hand on Helen's knee. Her knee jumped under the touch of my hand, quivered and was still again. She didn't knock my hand away. I drank my drink, outwardly calm, bringing my glass up to my lips with my free hand, and wondering vaguely what to do next.

"Helen," I said, my voice a little hoarse, "I've been hoping and dreading to see you all day. I didn't really expect to see you, and yet, when I thought I wouldn't, my heart would sort of knot up."

"Why, Harry, you're a poet!"

"No, I'm serious. I'm trying to tell you how I feel about you."

"I didn't mean to be rude or flippant, Harry. I feel very close to you, and trying to talk about it isn't any good."

"I've had terrible luck with women, Helen," I said, "and for the last two years I've kept away from them. I didn't want to go through it all again—you know, the bickering, the jealousy, nagging, that sort of thing. Am I scaring you off?"

"You couldn't if you tried, Harry. You're my kind of man and it isn't hard to say so. What I mean is—you're somebody, underneath, a person, and not just another man. See?" She shook her head impatiently. "I told you I couldn't talk about it."

"One thing I want to get straight is this," I said. "I'll never tell you that I love you."

"That word doesn't mean anything anyway."

"I never thought I'd hear a woman say that. But it's the truth. Love is in what you do, not in what you say. Couples work themselves into a hypnotic state daily by repeating to each other over and over again that they love each other. And they don't know the meaning of the word. They also say they love a certain brand of toothpaste and a certain brand of cereal in the same tone of voice."

Cautiously, I gathered the material of her skirt with my fingers until the hem was above her knee. My hand squeezed the warm flesh above her stocking. It was soft as only a woman's thigh is soft. She spread her legs at the touch of my hand and calmly sipped her drink. I tried to go a little higher and she clamped her legs on my hand.

"After all, Harry," she chided me, "we're not alone, you know."

I took my hand away from the softness of her thigh and she pulled her skirt down, smiling at me sympathetically. With trembling hands I lighted a cigarette. I didn't know what to do or what to say next. I felt as immature and inept as a teenager on his first date. And Helen wasn't helping me at all. I couldn't imagine what she was thinking about my crude and foolish passes.

"Helen," I blurted out like a schoolboy, "will you sleep with me tonight?" I felt like I had staked my life on the turn of a card.

"Why, Harry! What a thing to say." Her eyes didn't twinkle, that is impossible, but they came close to it. Very close. "Where else did you think I was going if I didn't go home with you?"

"I don't know," I said honestly.

"You didn't have to ask me like that. I thought there was an understanding between us, that it was understood."

"I don't like to take people for granted."

"In that case then, I'll tell you. I'm going home with you."

"I hope we're compatible," I said. "Then everything will be perfect."

"We are. I know it."

"I'm pretty much of a failure in life, Helen. Does it matter to you?"

"No. Nothing matters to me." Her voice had a resigned quality and yet it was quietly confident. There was a tragic look in her brown eyes, but her mouth was smiling. It was the smile of a little girl who knows a secret and isn't going to tell it. I held her hand in mine. It was a tiny, almost pudgy hand, soft and warm and trusting. We finished our drinks.

"Do you want another?" I asked her.

"Not really. After I go to the potty I want you to take me home." I helped her out of the booth. It wasn't easy for her to hold her feet, and she had had more to drink than I'd had. I watched her affectionately as she picked her way across the dimly lighted room. She was everything I ever wanted in a woman.

When she returned to the table I took the twenty she gave me and paid for the drinks. We walked to the mouth of the alley and I hailed a taxi. I gave my address to the driver and we settled back on the seat. I took Helen in my arms and kissed her.

"It makes me dizzy," she said. "Roll the windows down."

I had to laugh, but I rolled the windows down. The night air was cold and it was a long ride to my neighborhood. By the time we reached the roominghouse I knew she would be all right. I lit two cigarettes, passed one to Helen. She took one deep drag, tossed it out the window.

"I'm a little nervous, Harry."

"Why?"

"It's been a long time. Years, in fact."

"It doesn't change."

"Please don't say that! Be gentle with me, Harry."

"How could I be otherwise? You're just a little girl."

"I trust you, Harry."

The taxi pulled up in front of my roominghouse and we got out. We climbed the stairs quietly and walked down the long, dark hall to my room. There was only a single 40-watt bulb above the bathroom door to light the entire length of the hall. I unlocked my door and guided Helen inside. It took me a while to find the dangling string to the overhead light in the ceiling. Finding it at last, I flooded the room with light. I pulled the shade down and Helen looked the shabby room over with an amused smile.

"You're a good housekeeper," she said.

"Today anyway. I must have expected company," I said nervously.

Slowly, we started to undress. The more clothes we took off, the slower we got.

"Hadn't you better turn the light off?" Helen asked, timidly.

"No," I said firmly, "I don't want it that way."

We didn't hesitate any longer. Both of us undressed hurriedly. Helen crawled to the center of the bed, rolled over on her back and put her hands behind her head. She kept her eyes on the ceiling. Her breasts were small and the slenderness of her hips made her legs look longer than they were. Her skin was pale, almost like living mother-of-pearl, except for the flush that lay on her face like a delicately tinted rose. I stood in the center of the room and I could have watched her forever. I pulled the light cord and got into bed.

At first I just held her hot body against mine, she was trembling so hard. I covered her face with soft little kisses, her throat, her breasts. When my lips touched the tiny nipples of her breasts she sighed and relaxed somewhat. Her body still trembled, but it wasn't from fear. As soon as the nipples hardened I kissed her roughly on the mouth and she whimpered, dug her fingernails into my shoulders. She bit my lower lip with her sharp little teeth and I felt the blood spurt into my mouth.

"Now, Harry! Now!" she murmured softly.

It was even better than I'd thought it would be.

FOUR

Nude Model

WHEN I awoke the next morning Helen was curled up beside me. Her face was flushed with sleep and her nice hair curled all over her head. If it hadn't been for the single strand of pure silver hair she wouldn't have looked more than thirteen years old. I kissed her on the mouth and she opened her eyes. She sat up and stretched luxuriously, immediately awake, like a cat.

"I've never slept better in my entire life," she said.

"I'll fix some coffee. Then while you're in the bathroom, I'd better go down the hall and tell Mrs. McQuade you're here."

"Who is she?"

"The landlady. You'll meet her later on."

"Oh. What're you going to tell her?"

"I'll tell her we're married. We had a long, trial separation and now we've decided to try it again. It's a pretty thin story, but it'll hold."

"I feel married to you, Harry."

"For all practical purposes, we are married."

I got out of bed, crossed to the dresser, and tossed a clean, white shirt to Helen. She put it on and the shirt tail came to her knees. After she rolled up the sleeves she left the room. I put on my slacks and a T-shirt, fixed the coffee and lighted the gas burner under it, walked down the hall and knocked on Mrs. McQuade's door.

"Good morning, Mrs. McQuade," I said, when she opened the door.

"You're not going to clean your room again?" she asked with mock surprise in her voice.

"No." I laughed. "Two days in a row would be overdoing it. I just wanted to tell you my wife was back."

"I didn't even know you were married!" She raised her eyebrows.

"Oh, yes! I've been married a good many years. We were separated, but we've decided to try it again. I'll bring Helen down after a while. I want you to meet her."

"I'm very happy for you, Mr. Jordan."

"I think it'll work this time."

"Would you like a larger room?" she asked eagerly. "The front upstairs room is vacant, and if you want me to—"

"No, thanks," I said quickly, "we'll be all right where we are."

I knew Mrs. McQuade didn't believe me, but a woman running a roominghouse doesn't get surprised at anything.

She didn't mention it right then, but by the end of the week I could expect an increase in rent. That is the way those things go.

The coffee was ready and when Helen returned I finished my cup quickly and poured one for her.

"We've only got one cup," I said apologetically.

"We'll have to get another one."

After I shaved, and both of us were dressed, we finished the pot of coffee, taking turns with the cup. Helen borrowed my comb, painted her dark lipstick on with a tiny brush, and she was ready for the street.

"Don't you even use powder?" I asked her curiously.

"Uh uh. Just lipstick."

"We'd better go down and get your suitcase."

"I'm ready."

Mrs. McQuade and Miss Foxhall, a retired schoolteacher, were standing by the front door when we came down the hall. Mrs. McQuade had a broom in her hand, and Miss Foxhall held an armful of books; she was either going to or returning from the neighborhood branch public library. They both eyed Helen curiously, Mrs. McQuade with a smile, Miss Foxhall with hostility. I introduced Helen to the two older women. Mrs. McQuade wiped her hands on her apron and shook Helen's hand. Miss Foxhall snorted audibly, pushed roughly between us and hurried up the stairs without a word. I noticed that the top book in the stack she carried was *Ivanhoe*, by Sir Walter Scott.

"You're a very pretty girl, Mrs. Jordan," Mrs. McQuade said sincerely. All three of us pretended to ignore the rudeness of Miss Foxhall.

We walked down the block to Big Mike's, Helen holding my arm. The sun was shining and despite a slight persisting hangover I was a proud and happy man. Everyone who passed stared at Helen, and to know that she was mine made me straighten my back and hold my head erect. We entered Mike's and sat down at the bar. Big Mike joined us at once.

"You're on time today, Harry." He smiled.

"Mike, I want you to meet my wife. Helen Jordan, Big Mike."

"How do you do, Mrs. Jordan? This calls for one on the house. Now what'll it be?"

"Since it's on the house, Mike," Helen smiled, "I'll have a double bourbon and water."

"Double gin and tonic for me," I added.

Mike set up our drinks, drew a short beer for himself, and we raised our glasses in salute. He returned to his work table where he was slicing oranges, sticking toothpicks into cherries, and preparing generally for the noon-hour rush period. It was quite early to be drinking and Helen and I were the only people sitting at the bar. Rodney, the crippled newsboy, was eating breakfast in one of the booths along the wall. He waved to me with his fork and I winked at him.

After we finished our drinks we caught the cable car to the hotel on Powell Street and picked up Helen's suitcase. It only took a minute and we were able to catch the same car back, after it was ready to climb the hill again and turned on the Market Street turnaround. The round trip took more than an hour.

"I'm disgustingly sober," Helen said, as we stood on the curb, waiting for the light to change.

"What do you want to do? I'll give you two choices. We can drink in Big Mike's or we can get a bottle and go back to the room."

"Let's get a bottle, by all means."

At Mr. Watson's delicatessen I bought a fifth of gin, a fifth of whiskey and a cardboard carrier of six small bottles of soda. To nibble on, in case we happened to get hungry, I added a box of cheese crackers to the stack. We returned to our room and I removed my jacket and shirt. Helen took off her suit and hung it carefully in the closet. While I fixed the drinks Helen explored the room, digging into everything. She pulled out all of the dresser drawers, then examined the accumulation of junk above the sink. It was pleasant to watch her walking around the room in her slip. She discovered my box of oil paints on the shelf, brought it to the table and opened it.

"Do you paint, Harry?"

"At one time I did. That's the first time that box has been opened in three years." I handed her a drink. "There isn't any ice."

"All ice does is take up room. Why don't you paint any more?"

I looked into the opened paint box. The caps were tightly screwed on all of the tubes and most of the colors were there, all except yellow ochre and zinc white. I fingered the brushes, ran a finger over the edges of the bristles. They were in good shape, still usable, and there was a full package of charcoal sticks.

"I discovered I couldn't paint, that's why. It took me a long time to accept it, but after I found out I gave it up."

"Who told you you couldn't paint?"

"Did you ever do any painting?"

"Some. I graduated from Mills College, where they taught us something about everything. I even learned how to shoot a bow and arrow."

"I'll tell you how it is about painting, Helen, the way it was with me. It was a love affair. I used painting as a substitute for love. All painters do; it's their nature. When you're painting, the pain in your stomach drives you on to a climax of pure feeling, and if you're any good the feeling is transmitted to the canvas. In color, in form, in line and they blend together in a perfect design that delights your eye and makes your heart beat a little faster. That's what painting meant to me, and then it turned into an unsuccessful love affair, and we broke it off. I'm over it now, as much as I'll ever be, and certainly the world of art hasn't suffered."

"Who told you to give it up? Some critic?"

"Nobody had to tell me. I found it out for myself, the hard way. Before the war I went to the Art Institute in Chicago for two years, and after the war I took advantage of the GI Bill and studied another year in Los Angeles."

"Wouldn't anybody buy your work? Was that it?"

"No, that isn't it. I never could finish anything I started. I'd get an idea, block it out, start on it, and then when I'd get about halfway through I'd discover the idea was terrible. And I couldn't finish a picture when I knew it wasn't going to be any good. I taught for a while, but that wasn't any good either."

Helen wasn't looking at me. She had walked to the window and appeared to be studying the littered backyard next door with great interest. I knew exactly what she had on her mind. The Great American Tradition: *You can do anything you think you can do!* All Americans believe in it. What a joke that is! Can a jockey last ten rounds with Rocky Marciano? Can Marciano ride in the Kentucky Derby? Can a poet make his living by writing poetry? The entire premise was so false it was stupid to contemplate. Helen finished her drink, turned around, and set the empty glass on the table.

"Harry," she said seriously, "I want you to do something for me."

"I'll do anything for you."

"No, not just like that. I want you to hear what it is first."

"It sounds serious."

"It is. I want you to paint my portrait."

"I don't think I could do it." I shrugged, looked into my empty glass. "It's been more than three years since I tried to paint anything, and portraits are hard. To do a good one, anyway, and if I were to paint you, I'd want it to be perfect. It would have to be, and I'm not capable of it."

"I want you to paint it anyway."

"How about a sketch? If you want a picture of yourself, I can draw a charcoal likeness in five minutes."

"No. I want you to paint an honest-to-God oil painting of me."

"You really want me to; this isn't just a whim?"

"I really want you to." Her face was as deadly serious as her voice.

I thought it over and it made me feel a little sick to my stomach. The mere thought of painting again made me tremble. It was like asking a pilot to take an airplane up again after a bad crash; a crash that has left him horribly disfigured and frightened. Helen meant well. She wanted me to prove to myself that I was wrong . . . that I could do anything I really wanted to do. That is, as long as she was there to help me along by her inspiration and encouragement. More than anything else in the world, I wanted to please her.

"It takes time to paint a portrait," I said.

"We've got the time. We've got forever."

"Give me some money then."

"How much do you need?"

"I don't know. I'll need a canvas, an easel, linseed oil, tur-pentine, I don't know what all. I'll have to look around when I get to the art store."

"I'm going with you." She began to dress.

Once again, we made the long trip downtown by cable car. We went to an art store on Polk Street and I picked out a cheap metal easel, in addition to the regular supplies, and a large canvas, thirty by thirty-four inches. As long as I had decided to paint Helen's portrait, I was going to do it right. We left the store, both of us loaded down with bundles and I searched the streets for a taxi. Helen didn't want to return home immediately.

"You're doing something for me," she said, "and I want to do something for you. Before we go home I'm going to buy you a new pair of pants and a new sport coat."

"You can't do it, Helen," I protested. "We've spent too much already."

She had her way, but I didn't let her spend too much money on my new clothes. I insisted on buying a pair of gray cor-duroy trousers, and a dark blue corduroy jacket at the nearest Army and Navy surplus store. These were cheap clothes, but they satisfied Helen's desire to do something nice for me. I certainly needed them. Wearing my new clothes in the taxi, on the way home, and looking at all of the new art supplies piled on the floor, gave me a warm feeling inside and a plea-sant tingling of anticipation.

The minute we entered our room I removed my new jacket and set up the easel. While I opened the paints and arranged the materials on a straight backed chair next to the easel, Helen fixed fresh drinks. She held up her glass and posed, a haughty expression on her face.

"Look, Harry. Woman of Distinction." We both laughed. "Do you want me to pose like this?"

The pose I wanted Helen to take wasn't difficult. The hard part was to paint her in the way I wanted to express my feel-ings for her. I wanted to capture the mother-of-pearl of her body, the secret of her smile, the strand of silver in her hair, the jet, arched brows, the tragedy in her brown, gold-flecked eyes. I wasn't capable of it; I knew that in advance. I placed two pillows on the floor, close to the bed, so she could lean back against the bed to support her back. The light from the window would fall across her body and create sharp and difficult shadows. The hard way, like always, I took the hard way.

"Take off your clothes, Helen, and sit down on the pillows."

After Helen had removed her clothes and settled herself comfortably I rearranged her arms, her right hand in her lap, her left arm stretched full length on the bed. Her legs were straight out, with the right ankle crossed over the other. The similarity between Helen and the woman in the *Olympia* almost took my breath away with the awesomeness of it.

"Is that comfortable?" I asked her.

"It feels all right. How long do you want me to stay like this?"

"Just remember it, that's all. When I tell you to pose, get into it, otherwise, sit any way you like. As I told you, this is going to take a long time. Drink your drink, talk, or smile that smile of yours. Okay?"

"I'm ready."

I started with the charcoal, blocking in Helen's figure. She was sitting too stiffly, eyes straight ahead, tense. To me, the drawing is everything and I wanted her to talk, to get animation in her face.

"Talk to me, Helen," I told her.

"Is it all right?"

"Sure. I want you to talk. Tell me about Mills College. What did you major in?"

"Geology."

"That's a strange subject for a woman to take. What made you major in geology?"

"I was romantic in those days, Harry. I liked rocks and I thought geology was fascinating, but secretly, I thought if I could learn geology I could get away from Mother. I used to dream about going to Tibet or South America with some archeological expedition. Mother was never in the dream, but she was with me all the way through college. I had a miserable college education. She came with me and we took an apartment together. While the other girls lived in sororities and had a good time I studied. She stood right over me, just like she did all the way through high school. My grades were fine, the highest in my class. Not that I was a brilliant student, but because I didn't do anything except study.

"In the summers we went back to San Sienna. One summer we went to Honolulu, and once to Mexico City so I could look at ruins. The trips weren't any fun, because Mother was along. No night life, no dates, no romance."

"It sounds terrible."

"It was, believe me." She lapsed into silence, brooding.

It was a pleasant day. Helen made a drink for herself once in awhile, but I didn't join her; I was much too busy. The outline shaped well and I was satisfied with the progress I had made. By the time the light failed Helen had finished the bottle of whiskey and was more than a little tight. We were both extremely tired from the unaccustomed activity. Helen would find that modeling was one of the toughest professions in the world before we were through.

We dressed and walked down the street to Big Mike's for dinner. I ordered steaks from Tommy the waiter, and while we waited we sat at the end of the bar and had a drink. There were three workmen in overalls occupying the booth opposite from where we were sitting and their table was completely covered with beer cans. They made a few choice nasty remarks about Helen and me, but I ignored them. Big Mike was a friend of mine and I didn't want to cause any trouble in his bar.

"Look at that," the man wearing white overalls said. "Ain't that the limit?" His voice was loud, coarse, and it carried the length of the barroom.

"By God," the man on the inside said, "I believe I've seen it *all* now!" He nodded his head solemnly. "Yes, sir, I've seen it *all!*" His voice had a forced quality of comic seriousness and his companions laughed.

Helen's face had changed from pale to chalky white. She quickly finished her drink, set the glass on the bar and took my arm. "Come on, Harry," she said anxiously, "let's go inside the dining room and find a table."

"All right." My voice sounded as though it belonged to someone else.

We climbed down from the stools and crossed to the dining room entrance. We paused in the doorway and I searched the room for a table. One of the men shouldered us apart and stared insolently at Helen.

"Why don't you try me for size, baby?"

His two friends were standing behind me and they snickered.

Without a word I viciously kicked the man in front of me in the crotch. The insolent smile left his face in a hurry. His puffy red face lost its color and he clutched his groin with both hands and sank to his knees. I kicked him in the mouth and blood bubbled out of his ripped cheek from the corner of his torn mouth all the way to his ear. I whirled around quickly, expecting an attack from the two men behind me, but Big Mike was holding both of them by the collar. There was a wide grin on his multi-scarred face.

"Go ahead, Harry," he said gruffly, "finish the job. These lice won't interfere."

The man was on his feet again; some of the color was back in his mutilated face. He snatched a bread knife from the waiter's work table and backed slowly across the room.

Many of the diners had left their tables and were crowded against the far wall near the kitchen. I advanced on the man cautiously, my arms widely spread. He lunged forward in a desperate attempt to disembowel me, bringing the knife up fast, aiming for my stomach. At the last moment I twisted sideways and brought my right fist up from below my knee. His jaw was wide open and my blow caught him flush below the chin. He fell forward on the floor, like a slugged ox.

My entire body was shaking with fear and excitement. I looked wildly around the room for Helen. She was standing, back to the wall, frozen with fear. She ran to my side, hugged me around the waist.

"Come on, Harry!" she said tearfully. "Let's get out of here!"

"Nothing doing," I said stubbornly. "We ordered steaks and we're going to eat them."

I guided Helen to an empty table against the wall. Big Mike had bounced the other two workmen out and now he was back in the dining-room. Two waiters, at his nod, dragged the unconscious man out of the room through the kitchen exit. Mike came over to our table.

"I saw the whole thing, Harry," Tommy said, "and if it goes to court or anything like that, I'll swear that he started the fight by pulling a knife on you!" He was so sincere I found it difficult to keep from laughing.

"Thanks, Tommy," I told him, "but I think that's the end of it."

I couldn't eat my steak and neither could Helen although both of us made a valiant try.

"The hell with it, Harry," Helen smiled. "Let's get a bottle and go home."

We left the grill, bought another fifth of whiskey at the delicatessen and returned to our room. My bottle of gin was scarcely tapped. I held it up to my lips, and drinking in short swallows, I drank until I almost passed out.

Helen had to undress me and put me to bed.

FIVE

Celebration

IF THERE was anything I didn't want to do the next morning, it was paint. My head was vibrating like a struck gong and my stomach was full of fluttering, little winged creatures. Every muscle of my body ached and all I wanted to do was stay in bed and quietly nurse my hangover.

Helen was one of those rare persons who seldom get a hangover. She felt fine. She showered, dressed, left the house and returned with a fifth of whiskey and a paper sack filled with cold bottles of beer.

"Drink this beer," she ordered, "and let's get started. You can't let a little thing like a fight and a hangover stop you." She handed me an opened bottle of beer. I sat up in bed, groaning, and let the icy beer flow down my throat. It tasted marvelous, tangy, refreshing, and I could feel its coldness all the way down. I drank some coffee, two more beers and started to work.

I had to draw slowly at first. There was still a slight tremor in my fingers, caused partly by the hangover, but the unexpected fight the night before had a lot to do with it. I've never been a fighter and when I thought about my vicious assault on the man in Mike's, I could hardly believe it had happened. Within a short time, Helen's beauty pushed the ugly memory out of my head and I was more interested in the development of her picture.

Painting or drawing from a nude model had never been an exciting experience before, but Helen was something else . . . I didn't have the feeling of detachment an artist is supposed to have toward his model. I was definitely aware of Helen's body as an instrument of love, and as my hangover gradually disappeared I couldn't work any longer unless I did something about it . . .

Helen talked about the dullness of San Sienna as I worked and from time to time she would take a shot from the bottle of whiskey resting on the floor, following it down with a sip of water. As she began to feel the drinks her voice became animated. And so did I. Unable to stand it any longer I tossed my charcoal stick down, scooped Helen from the floor and dropped her sideways on the bed. She laughed softly.

"It's about time," she said.

I dropped to my knees beside the bed, pressed my face into her warm, soft belly and kissed her navel. She clutched my hair with both hands and shoved my head down hard.

"Oh, yes, Harry! Make love to me! Make love to me . . ."

And I did. She didn't have to coax me.

It took all of the will power I could muster to work on the picture again, but I managed, and surprisingly enough it was much easier than it had been. With my body relaxed I could now approach my work with the proper, necessary detachment an artist must have if he is to get anywhere. The drawing was beginning to look very well, and by four in the afternoon, when I couldn't stick it out any longer and quit for the day, I was exhilarated by my efforts and Helen was pleasantly tight from the whiskey.

After we were dressed I took a last look at the picture before leaving for Mike's.

"This is my first portrait," I told Helen as I opened the door for her. "And probably my last."

"I didn't know that, Harry," she said, somewhat surprised. "What kind of painting did you do? Landscapes?"

"No," I laughed. "Non-objective, or as you understand it, abstract."

"You mean these weird things with the lines going every which way, and the limp watches and stuff—"

"That's close enough." I couldn't explain what is impossible to explain. We went to Big Mike's, had dinner, and drank at the bar until closing time.

This was the pattern of our days for the next week and a half, except for one thing: I quit drinking. Not completely; I still drank beer, but I laid off whiskey and gin completely. I didn't need it any more. Painting and love were all I needed to make me happy. Helen continued to drink, and during the day, whether drunk or sober, if I told her to pose she assumed it without any trouble, and held it until I told her to relax.

For me, this was a fairly happy period. I hadn't realized how much I had missed painting. And with Helen for a model it was pure enjoyment. I seldom said anything. I was contented to merely paint and look at Helen. Often there were long silences between us when all we did was look at each other. These long periods usually ended up in bed without a word being spoken. It was as though our bodies had their own methods of communication. More relaxed, more sure of myself, I would take up my brush again and Helen would sit, very much at ease, on the two pillows beside the bed, and assume the pose I had given her. My Helen! *My Olympia!*

When I finished the drawing in charcoal I made a complete underpainting in tints and shades of burnt sienna, lightening the browns carefully with white and turpentine. The underpainting always makes me nervous. The all-important drawing which takes so many tedious hours is destroyed with the first stroke of the brush and replaced with shades of brown oil paint. The completed drawing, which is a picture worthy of framing by itself, is now a memory as the turpentine and oil soaks up the charcoal and replaces it with a tone in a different medium. But it is a base that will last through the years when the colors are applied over it. I had Helen look at the completed brown-tone painting.

"It looks wonderful, Harry! Is my figure that perfect?"

"It's the way it looks to me. Don't worry about your face. It's just drawn in a general way . . . the effects of the shadows."

"I'm not worried. It looks like me already."

"When I'm finished, it will be you," I said determinedly.

I started with the colors, boldly but slowly, in my old style. I didn't pay any attention to background, but concentrated on Helen's figure. At the time I felt that I shouldn't neglect the background, but no ideas came to me and I let it go. The painting was turning out far better than I had expected it to; it was good, very good. My confidence in my ability soared. I could paint, really paint. All I had to do was work at it, boldly but slowly.

Along with the ninth day, Helen, cramped by a long session, got up and walked around the room shaking her arms and kicking her legs. I lit two cigarettes and handed her one. She put an arm around my waist and studied the painting for several minutes.

"This is me, Harry, only it looks like me when I was a little girl."

"I'm not finished yet. I've been working on the hands. I figure a good two days to finish your face. If possible I want to paint your lips the same shade as your lipstick, but if I do I'm afraid it'll look out of place. It's a tricky business."

"What about the background?"

"I'm letting that go. It isn't important."

"But the picture won't be complete without a background."

"I'm not going to fill the empty places with that gray wallpaper and its weird pattern of pink flowers!"

"You don't have to. Can't you paint in an open sky, or the ocean and clouds behind me?"

"No. That would look lousy. Wrong light, anyway."

"You can't leave it blank!"

"I can until I get an idea. If I have to fill it with something I can paint it orange with black spots."

"You can't do that! That would ruin it!"

"Then let's not discuss it any more."

It made me a little sore. A man who's painting a picture doesn't want a layman's advice. At least I didn't. This was the best thing of its kind I had ever done and I was going to do it my way.

That night when we went down to Mike's for dinner I started to drink again. Both of us were well-loaded when we got home and for the first time we went to sleep without making love.

I slept until noon. Helen didn't wake me when she went to the delicatessen for beer and whiskey. The coffee was perking in the pot and the wonderful odor woke me. I drank two cups of it black and had one shot of whiskey followed by a beer chaser. I felt fine.

"Today and tomorrow and I'll be finished," I told Helen confidently.

"I'm sure tired of that pose."

"You don't have to hold it any longer, baby. All I have to finish is your face."

I had overestimated the time it would take me. By three-thirty there was nothing more to do. Anything else I did to the painting would be plain fiddling. Maybe I hadn't put in a proper background, but I had captured Helen and that was what I had set out to do. Enough of the bed and the two pillows were showing to lend form and solidity to the composition. The girl in the portrait was Helen, a much younger Helen, and if possible, a much prettier and delicate Helen, but it was Helen as she appeared to me. Despite my attempts to create the faint, tiny lines around her eyes and the streak of silver hair, it was the portrait of a young girl.

"It's beautiful," Helen said sincerely and self-consciously.

"It's the best I can do."

"How much could you sell this for, Harry?"

"I wouldn't sell it. It belongs to you."

"But what would it be worth to an art gallery?"

"It's hard to tell. Whatever you could get, I suppose. Twenty dollars, maybe."

"Surely, more than that!"

"It all depends upon how much somebody wants it. That's the way art works. The artist has his asking price, of course, and if a buyer wants the painting he pays the price. If they don't want it he couldn't give the picture away. My price for this picture is one hundred thousand dollars."

"I'd pay that much for it, Harry."

"And so would I." There was a drink apiece left in the bottle of whiskey. We divided it equally and toasted the portrait.

"If I never paint another," I bragged, "I've painted one picture."

"It doesn't really need a background, Harry," Helen said loyally, "it looks better the way it is."

"You're wrong, but the hell with it. Get dressed and we'll go out and celebrate."

"Let's stay in instead," Helen said quietly.

"Why? If you're tired of drinking at Big Mike's we can go some place else. We don't have to go there."

"No, that isn't it," she said hesitantly. "We're all out of money, Harry." The corners of her mouth turned down wryly. "I spent the last cent I had for that bottle."

"Okay. So we're out of money. You didn't expect two hundred dollars to last forever, did you? Our room rent's paid, anyway."

"Do you have any money, Harry?"

After searching through my wallet and my trousers I came up with two dollars and a half dollar in change. Not a large sum, but enough for a few drinks.

"This is enough for a couple at Mike's," I said, "or we can let the drinks go and I can look around for a job. It's up to you."

"I would like to have a drink . . . but while you're looking for work, and even after you find it, there'll still be several days before you get paid."

"We'll worry about that when we come to it. I've got fifteen dollars credit with Mike and it's all paid up. I paid him the other night when you cashed a traveler's check."

"We don't have a worry in the world then, do we?" Helen said brightly.

"Not one." I said it firmly, but with a confidence I didn't feel inside. I had a lot of things to worry about. The smile was back on Helen's lips. She gave me a quick, ardent kiss and dressed hurriedly, so fast I had to laugh.

When we got to Mike's we sat down in an empty booth and ordered hamburgers instead of our usual club steak. It was the only thing we had eaten all day, but it was still too much for me. After two bites I pushed my hamburger aside, left Helen in the booth, and signaled Mike to come down to the end of the bar.

"Mike," I said apprehensively, "I'm back on credit again."

"Okay." He nodded his massive head slowly. "I'm not surprised, though, the way you two been hitting it lately."

"I'm going to find a job tomorrow."

"You've always paid up, Harry. I'm not worried."

"Thanks, Mike." I turned to leave.

"Just a minute, Harry," he said seriously. "That guy you had a fight with the other night was in here earlier and I think he's looking for you. I ran him the hell out, but you'd better be on the lookout for him. His face looks pretty bad. There's about thirty stitches in his face and the way it's sewed up makes him look like he's smiling. Only he ain't smiling."

"I feel sorry for the guy, Mike. I don't know what got into me the other night."

"Well, I thought I'd better mention it."

"Thanks, Mike." I rejoined Helen in the booth. She had finished her sandwich and mine too.

"You didn't want it, did you?" she asked me.

I shook my head. We ordered whiskey with water chasers and stayed where we were, in the last booth against the wall, drinking until ten o'clock. I was in a mighty depressed mood and I unconsciously transmitted it to Helen. I should never have let her talk me into painting her portrait. I should never have tried any type of painting again. There was no use trying to kid myself that I could paint. Of course, the portrait was all right, but any artist with any academic background at all could have done as well. And my temerity in posing Helen as *Olympia* was the crowning height to my folly. Who in the hell did I think I was, anyway? What was I trying to prove? Liquor never helped me when I was in a depressed state of mind; it only made me feel worse. Helen broke the long, dead silence between us.

"This isn't much of a celebration, is it?"

"No. I guess not."

"Do you want to go home, Harry?"

"What do you want to do?"

"If I sit here much longer looking at you, I'll start crying."

"Let's go home, then."

I signed the tab that Tommy the waiter brought and we left. It was a dark, forbidding block to the roominghouse at night. Except for Big Mike's bar and grill on the corner, the light from Mr. Watson's delicatessen across the street was the only bright spot on the way home. We walked slowly, Helen holding onto my arm. Half-way up the street I stopped, fished two cigarettes out of my almost empty package and turned into the wind to light them. Helen accepted the lighted cigarette I handed her and inhaled deeply. We didn't know what to do with ourselves.

"What's ever to become of us, Harry?" Helen sighed.

"I don't know."

"Nothing seems to have much purpose, does it?"

"No, it doesn't."

A man I hadn't noticed in the darkness of the street, detached himself from the shadows of the Spotless Cleaner's storefront and walked toward us. His hat was pulled well down over his eyes and he was wearing a dark-brown topcoat. The faint light from the street lamp on the corner barely revealed a long red scar on his face and neat row of stitches. Like Mike had told me, the left corner of his mouth was pulled up unnaturally, and it made the man look like he was smiling.

With a quick movement he jerked a shiny, nickel-plated pistol out of his topcoat pocket and covered us with it. His hand was shaking violently and the muzzle of the pistol jerked up and down rapidly, as though it was keeping time to wild music.

"I've been waiting for you!" His voice was thick and muffled. His jaws were probably wired together and he was forced to talk through his teeth. I dropped my cigarette to the pavement and put my left arm protectingly around Helen's waist. She stared at the man with a dazed, fixed expression.

"I'm going to kill you," he said through his clenched teeth. "Both of you!"

"I don't blame you," I answered calmly. I felt no fear or anxiety at all, just a morbid feeling of detachment. Helen's body trembled beneath my arm, but it couldn't have been from fear, because the trembling stopped abruptly, and she took another deep drag on her cigarette.

"You may shoot me first, if you prefer," she said quietly.

"God damn the both of you!" the man said through his closed mouth. "Get down on your knees! Beg me! Beg for your lives!"

I shook my head. "No. We don't do that for anybody. Our lives aren't that important."

He stepped forward and jammed the muzzle into my stomach with a hard, vicious thrust.

"Pray, you son-of-a-bitch! Pray!"

I should have been frightened, but I wasn't. I knew that I should have been afraid and I even wondered why I wasn't.

"Go ahead," I told him. "Pull the trigger. I'm ready."

He hesitated and this hesitation, I believe, is what cost him his nerve. He backed slowly away from us, the pistol dancing in his hand, as though it had an independent movement of its own.

"You don't think I'll shoot you, do you?" It was the kind of a question for which there is no answer. We didn't reply.

"All right, bastard," he said softly, "start walking."

We started walking slowly up the sidewalk and he dodged to one side and fell in behind us. He jammed the pistol into the small of my back. I felt its pressure for ten or more steps and then it was withdrawn. Helen held my left arm with a tight grip, but neither one of us looked back as we marched up the hill. At any moment I expected a slug to tear through my body. We didn't look behind us until we reached the steps of the rooming house, and then I turned and looked over my shoulder while Helen kept her eyes straight to the front. There was no one in sight.

We entered the house, walked quietly down the dimly lighted hallway, and went into our room. I closed the door, turned on the light, and Helen sat down on the edge of the bed. Conscious of Helen's eyes on me, I walked across to the painting, and examined it for a long time.

"Did you feel sorry for him, Harry? I did."

"Yes, I did," I replied sincerely. "The poor bastard."

"I don't believe I'd have really cared if he'd killed us both . . ." Helen's voice was reflective, sombre.

"Cared?" I forced a tight smile. "It would have been a favor."

SIX

Suicide Pact

THERE was something bothering me when I got out of bed the next morning. I had a queasy, uneasy feeling in the pit of my stomach and it took me a few minutes to figure out what caused it. It was early in the morning, much too early to be getting out of bed. The sun was just coming up and the light filtering through the window was gray and cold. The sky was matted with low clouds, but an occasional bright spear broke through to stab at the messy backyards and the littered alley extending up the hill. I turned away from the window and the dismal view that looked worse by sunlight than it did by night.

I filled the coffee pot with water and put it on the burner. I took the coffee can down from the shelf above the sink and opened it. The coffee can was empty. I turned the fire out under the pot. No coffee this morning. I searched through my pockets before I put my trousers on and didn't find a dime. I didn't expect to, but I looked anyway. Not only had I spent the two and a half dollars in change, I had signed a chit besides for the drinks we had at Mike's. I opened Helen's purse and searched it thoroughly. There wasn't any money, but the purse contained a fresh, unopened package of cigarettes. After I finished dressing I sat in the straight chair by the window, smoking until Helen awoke.

Helen awoke after three cigarettes, sat up in bed and stretched her arms widely. She never yawned or appeared drowsy when she awoke in the mornings, but always appeared to be alert and fresh, as though she didn't need the sleep at all.

"Good morning, darling," she said. "How about lighting me one of those?"

I lit a fresh cigarette from the end of mine, put it between her lips, and sat down on the edge of the bed.

"No kiss?" she said petulantly, taking the cigarette out of her mouth. I kissed her and then returned to my chair by the window.

"We're out of coffee," I said glumly.

"That isn't such a great calamity, is it?"

"We're out of money too. Remember?"

"We've got credit, haven't we? Let's go down to Big Mike's for coffee. He might put a shot of bourbon in it if we ask him real nice."

"You really feel good, don't you?" I said bitterly.

Helen got out of bed and padded barefoot over to my chair. She put her arms around my neck, sat in my lap and kissed me on the neck.

"Look out," I said. "You'll burn me with your cigarette."

"No, I won't. And I don't feel a bit good. I feel rotten."

She bit me sharply on the ear, dropped her slip over her head and departed for the bathroom next door. I left my chair to examine my painting in the cold light of early morning. I twisted the easel around so the picture would face the window. A good amateur or Sunday painter would be proud of that portrait, I decided. Why wasn't I the one artist in a thousand who could earn his living by painting? Of course, I could always go back to teaching. Few men in the painting world knew as much as I did about color. The coarse thought of teaching made me shudder with revulsion. If you can't do it yourself you tell someone else how to do it. You stand behind them in the role of peer and mentor and watch them get better and better. You watch them overshadow you until you are nothing except a shadow within a shadow and then lost altogether in the unequal merger. Perhaps that was my main trouble? I could bring out talent where there wasn't any talent. Where there wasn't any ability I could bring out the semblance of ability. A fine quality for a man born to teach, but a heartbreaking quality for a man born to be an artist. No, I would never teach again. There were too many art students who thought they were artists who should have been mechanics. But a teacher was never allowed to be honest and tell them to quit. The art schools would have very few students if the teachers were allowed to be honest. But then, didn't the same thing hold true for all schools?

I threw myself across the bed and covered my ears with my hands. I didn't want to think about it any more. I didn't want to think about anything. Helen returned from the bathroom and curled up beside me on the bed.

"What's the matter, darling?" she asked solicitously. "Have you got a headache?"

"No. I was just thinking what a rotten, stinking world this is we live in. This isn't our kind of world, Helen. And we don't have the answer to it either. We aren't going to beat it by drinking and yet, the only way we can possibly face it is by drinking!"

"You're worried because we don't have any money, aren't you?"

"Not particularly."

"I could wire my mother for money if you want me to."

"Do you think she'd send it?"

"She'd probably bring it! She doesn't know where I am and I don't want her to know. But we're going to have to get money someplace."

"Why?"

"You need a cup of coffee and I need a drink. That's why."

"I don't give a damn about the coffee. Why do you have to have a drink? You don't really need it."

"Sure I do. I'm an alcoholic. Alcoholics drink."

"Suppose you were dead? You'd never need another drink. You wouldn't need anything. Everything would be blah. It doesn't make you happy to drink, and when I drink it only makes me unhappier than I am already. All it does in the long run is bring us oblivion."

"I need you when I come out of that oblivion, Harry." Her voice was solemn and barely under control.

"I need you too, Helen." This was as true a statement as I had ever made. Without Helen I was worse than nothing, a dark, faceless shadow, alone in the darkness. I had to take her with me.

"I haven't thought about suicide in a long time, Helen," I said. "Not once since we've been together. I used to think about it all of the time, but I never had the nerve. Together, maybe we could do it. I know I couldn't do it alone."

"I used to think about suicide too." Helen accepted my mood and took it for her own. "Down in San Sienna. It was such a tight, hateful little town. My bedroom overlooked the ocean, and I'd sit there all day, with the door locked, curled up on the window-seat, hiding my empty bottles in my dirty clothes hamper. Sitting there like that, looking at the golden sunshine glistening on the water, watching the breakers as they crashed on the beach . . . It made me depressed as hell. It was all so purposeless!"

"Did you ever attempt it?"

"Suicide?"

"That's what we're considering. Suicide."

"Yes, I tried it once." She smiled wryly. "On my wedding night, Harry. I was still a virgin, believe it or not. Oh, I wasn't ignorant; I knew what was expected of me and I thought I was ready for it. But I wasn't. Not for what happened, anyway. It was a virtual onslaught! My husband was a real estate man, and I'd never seen him in anything except a suit—all dressed up you know, with a clean, respectable look.

"But all of a sudden—I was in bed first, wearing my new nightgown, and shivering with apprehension—he flew out of the bathroom without a stitch on and rushed across the room. He was actually gibbering and drooling at the mouth. He tore the covers off me. He ripped my new, nice nightgown to shreds . . ." Helen's voice broke as she relived this experience and she talked with difficulty. "I fought him. I tore at his face with my nails; I bit him, hit at him, but it didn't make any difference. I'm positive now, that that's what he wanted me to do, you see. He overpowered me easily and completely. Then, in a second, it was all over. I was raped. He walked casually into the bathroom, doctored his scratches with io- dine, put his pajamas on and climbed into bed as though nothing had happened."

Helen smiled grimly, crushed her cigarette in the ashtray.

"It was his first and last chance at me," she continued. "I never gave him another. Lying there beside him in the dark- ness I vowed that he'd never touch me again. After he was

asleep I got out of bed and took the bottle of aspirins out of
my overnight bag and went into the bathroom. There were
twenty-six tablets. I counted them, because I didn't know for
sure whether that was enough or not. But I decided it was
and I took them three at a time until they were gone, washing
each bunch down with a glass of water. Then I climbed back
into bed—"

"That wasn't nearly enough," I said, interested in her story.

"No, it wasn't. But I fell asleep though, and I probably
wouldn't have otherwise. They must have had some kind of
psychological effect. But I awoke the next morning the same
as ever, except for a loud ringing in my ears. The ringing
lasted all day."

"What about your husband? Did he know you attempted
suicide?"

"I didn't give him that satisfaction. We were staying at a
beach motel in Santa Barbara, and after breakfast he went out
to the country club to play golf. I begged off—told him I
wanted to do some shopping—and as soon as he drove away
I packed my bag and caught a bus for San Sienna and Mother.
Mother was glad to have me back."

"And you never went back to him?"

"Never. I told Mother what happened. It was foolish of
me, maybe, but she was determined to find out so I told her
about it. Later on, when he begged me to come back to him,
I was going to, but she wouldn't let me. He didn't know any
better, the poor guy, and he told me so, after he found out
the reason I left him. But it was too late then. I was safe in
Mother's arms."

She finished her story bitterly, and her features assumed the
tragic look I knew so well, the look that entered her face
whenever she mentioned her mother. I kissed her tenderly on
the mouth, got out of bed, and paced the floor restlessly.

"I'm glad you told me about this, Helen. That's when you
started to drink, isn't it?"

"Yes, that's when I started to drink. It was as good an excuse as any other."

We were silent then, deep in our own thoughts. Helen lay
on her back with her eyes closed while I paced the floor. I
understood Helen a little better now. Thanks to me, and I

don't know how many others, she didn't feel the same way
about sex now, but she was so fixed in her drinking habits she
could never change them. Not without some fierce drive from
within, and she wasn't made that way. Before she could ever
stop drinking she would have to have some purpose to her
life, and I couldn't furnish it. Not when I didn't even have a
purpose for my own life. If we continued on, in the direction
we were traveling, the only thing that could possibly happen
would be a gradual lowering of standards, and they were low
enough already. If something happened to me, she would end
up on the streets of San Francisco. The very thought of this
sent a cold chill down my back. And I couldn't take care of
her properly. It was too much of an effort to take care of
myself . . .

"It takes a lot of nerve to commit suicide, Harry," Helen
said suddenly, sitting up in bed, and swinging her feet to the
floor.

"If we did it together I think we could do it," I said confidently. "Right now, we're on the bottom rung of the ladder.
We're dead broke. I haven't got a job, and there's no one we
can turn to for help. No whiskey, no religion, nothing."

"Do you think we'd be together afterwards?"

"Are you talking about the hereafter?"

"That's what I mean. I wouldn't care whether I went to
Heaven or Hell as long as I was with you."

"I don't know anything about those things, Helen. But
here's the way I look at it. If we went together, we'd be together. I'm positive of that."

The thought of death was very attractive to me. I could tell
by the fixed expression in Helen's eyes that she was in the
same mood I was in. She got the cigarettes from the table
and sat down again on the edge of the bed. After she lit the
cigarettes, I took mine and sat down beside her.

"How would we go about it, Harry?" Helen was in earnest,
but her voice quavered at her voiced thought.

"There are lots of ways."

"But how, though? I can't stand being hurt. If it was all
over with like that—" she snapped her fingers— "and I didn't
feel anything, I think I could do it."

"We could cut our wrists with a razor blade."

"Oh, no!" She shuddered. "That would hurt terribly!"

"No it wouldn't," I assured her. "Just for one second, maybe, and then it would all be over."

"I couldn't do it, Harry!" She shook her head emphatically. "If you did it for me I could shut my eyes and—"

"No!" I said sharply. "You'll have to do it yourself. If I cut your wrists, well, then it would be murder. That's what it would be."

"Not if I asked you to."

"No. We'll have to do it together."

When we finished our cigarettes I put the ashtray back on the table. I was serious about committing suicide and determined to go through with it. There wasn't any fight left in me. As far as I was concerned the world we existed on was an overly-large, stinking cinder, a spinning, useless clinker. I didn't want any part of it. My life meant nothing to me and I wanted to go to sleep forever and forget about it. I got my shaving kit down from the shelf above the sink and took the package of razor blades out of it. I unwrapped the waxed paper from two shiny single-edged blades and laid them on the table. Helen joined me at the table and held out her left arm dramatically.

"Go ahead," she said tearfully. "Cut it!"

Her eyes were tightly squeezed shut and she was breathing rapidly. I took her hand in mine and looked at her thin little wrist. I almost broke down and it was an effort to fight back the tears.

"No, sweetheart," I said to her gently, "you'll have to do it yourself. I can't do it for you."

"Which one is mine?" she asked nervously.

"Either one. It doesn't make any difference."

"Are you going to give a signal?" She picked up a blade awkwardly.

"I'll count to three." I picked up the remaining blade.

"I'm ready!" she said bravely, raising her chin.

"One. Two. Three!"

We didn't do anything. We just stood there, looking at each other.

"It's no use, Harry. I can't do it to myself." She threw the blade down angrily on the table and turned away. She covered her face with her hands and sobbed. Her back shook convulsively.

"Do you want me to do it?" I asked her.

She nodded her head almost imperceptibly, but she didn't say anything. I jerked her left hand away from her face and with one quick decisive motion I cut blindly into her wrist. She screamed sharply, then compressed her lips, and held out her other arm. I cut it quickly, close to the heel of her hand, picked her up and carried her to the bed. I arranged a pillow under her head.

"Do they hurt much?"

She shook her head. "They burn a little bit. That's all." Her eyes were closed, but she was still crying noiselessly. The bright blood gushed from her wrists, making crimson pools on the white sheets. I retrieved the bloody blade from the table where I'd dropped it, returned to the bed and sat down. It was much more difficult to cut my own wrists. The skin was tougher, somehow, and I had to saw with the blade to cut through. My heart was beating so loud I could feel it throb through my body. I was afraid to go through with it and afraid not to go through with it. The blood frothed, finally, out of my left wrist and I transferred the blade to my other hand. It was easier to cut my right wrist, even though I was right-handed. It didn't hurt nearly as much as I had expected it to, but there was a searing, burning sensation, as though I had inadvertently touched my wrists to a hot poker. I threw the blade to the floor and got into bed beside Helen. She kissed me passionately. I could feel the life running out of my wrists and it made me happy and excited.

"Harry?"

"Yes?"

"As a woman, I'd like to have the last word. Is it all right?"

"Sure it's all right."

"I. Love. You."

It was the first time she had said the word since we had been living together. I kissed each of her closed eyes tenderly, then buried my face in her neck. I was overwhelmed with emotion and exhaustion.

SEVEN

Return to Life

MY HEAD was like a huge bubble perched on top of my shoulders, and ready for instant flight. I was afraid to move my head or open my eyes for fear it would float away into nothingness. Gradually, as I lay there fearfully, a feeling of solidity returned to my head and I opened my eyes. My arms were entwined around Helen, and she was lying on her side, facing me, her breathing soft and regular, in deep, restful sleep—but she was breathing! We were still alive, very much so! I disentangled my arms and raised my wrists so that I could see them. The blood was coagulated into little black ridges along the lengths of the shallow cuts. The bleeding had completely stopped. Oddly enough, I felt highly exhilarated and happy to be alive. It was as though I was experiencing a "cheap" drunk; I felt the way I had when I had taken a lower lip full of snuff many years before. My head was light and I was a trifle dizzy even though I was still in bed. I awakened Helen by kissing her partly open mouth. For a moment her eyes were startled and then they brightened into alertness the way they always did when she first awakened. She smiled shyly.

"I guess I didn't cut deep enough," I said ruefully. "I must have missed the arteries altogether."

"How do you feel, Harry?" Helen asked me. "I feel kind of wonderful, sort of giddy."

"I feel a little foolish. And at the same time I feel better than I have in months. I'm light-headed as hell and I feel drunk. Not gin-drunk, but drunk with life."

"I feel the same way. I've never been as drunk as I am now and I haven't had a drink. I never expected to wake up at all—not here, anyway."

"Neither did I," I said quietly.

"Are you sorry, Harry?"

"No. I'm not exactly sorry. It's too easy to quit and yet it took me a long time to reach the point when I was ready. But now that I've tried it once I guess I can face things again. It's still a lousy world, but maybe we owe it something."

"Light us a cigarette, Harry."

I got out of bed carefully and staggered dizzily to the table. I picked up the package of cigarettes and a folder of book matches and then noticed the bloody razor blade on the floor. It was unreal and cruel-looking and somehow offended me. I scooped it off the floor with the edge of the cardboard match folder and dropped it into the paper sack where we kept our trash and garbage. I couldn't bear to touch it with my hands. I was so giddy by this time it was difficult to keep my feet. Tumbling back onto the bed I lit Helen's cigarette, then mine.

"You've got a surprise coming when you try to walk," I said.

"You were actually staggering," Helen said, dragging the smoke deeply into her lungs.

"This bed is certainly a mess. Take a look at it."

"We'd better burn these sheets. I don't think the laundry would take them like this." Helen giggled.

"That is, if we could afford to take them to the laundry."

Both of us were in a strange mood, caused mostly by the blood we had lost. It wasn't a gay mood, not exactly, but it wasn't depressed either. All of our problems were still with us, but for a brief moment, out of mind. There was still no money, no job, no liquor and no prospects. I was still a bit light-headed and it was hard for me to think about our many problems. I wished, vaguely, that I had a religion or a God of some sort. It would have been so wonderful and easy to have gone to a priest or a minister and let him solve our problems for us. We could have gone anyway, religious or not, but without faith, any advice we listened to would have been worthless. The pat, standard homilies dished out by the boys in black were easy to predict.

Accept Jesus Christ as your personal Lord and Saviour and you are saved!

Any premise which bases its salvation on blind belief alone is bound to be wrong, I felt. It isn't fair to those who find it impossible to believe, those who have to be convinced, shown, who believe in nothing but the truth. But, all the same, suppose we did go to a church somewhere? What could we lose?

I rejected that false line of reasoning in a hurry.

"Let's bandage each other's wrists," I said quickly to
Helen. It would at least be something to do. I left the bed
and sat down for a moment in the straight chair by the easel.

"I suppose we'd better," Helen agreed, "before they get
infected. If we're going to burn these sheets anyway, why
don't you tear a few strips from the edge? They'll make fine
bandages." Helen got out of bed wearily, and walked in tight
circles, trying her legs. "Boy, am I dizzy!" she exclaimed, sat
down on the foot of the bed.

I tore several strips of sheeting from the top sheet. Helen
did some more circles and then sat down in a chair and fanned
herself with her hands. I patted her bare shoulder reassuringly
on my way to the dresser. My giddiness had all but disappeared, but my feeling of exhilaration remained. I had to dig
through every drawer in the dresser before I could find the
package of band-aids.

"Hold out your arms," I told Helen. The gashes in her
wrists hurt me to look at them. They were much deeper than
my own and the tiny blue veins in her thin wrists were closer
to the surface than they had been before. I was deeply
ashamed, and bound her wrists rapidly with the sheeting. I
used the band-aids to hold the improvised bandages in place
and then we changed places. She bandaged my wrists while I
sat in the chair, but did a much neater job of it.

Without warning Helen rushed into my arms and began to
sob uncontrollably. Her slender back was racked with violent,
shuddering sobs and her hot flush of tears burned on my bare
chest. I tried my best to comfort her.

"There, there, old girl," I said crooningly, "this won't do
at all. Don't cry, baby, everything's going to be all right.
There, there . . ."

She continued to sob piteously for a long time and all I
could do was hold her. I was helpless, confused. It wasn't like
Helen to cry about anything. At last she calmed down, smiled
weakly, and wiped her streaming eyes with her fingers, like a
little girl.

"I know it's childish of me, Harry, to cry like that, but I
couldn't help it. The thought exploded inside my head and
caught me when I wasn't expecting it."

"What did, honey?"

"Well, suppose you had died and I hadn't? And I woke up, and there you were—dead, and there I'd be, alone, still alive, without you, without anything . . ." Her tears started to flow again, but with better restraint. I held her on my lap like a frightened child; her face against my shoulder. I made no attempts to prevent her silent crying. I just patted her gently on her bare back, letting her cry it out. I knew precisely how she felt, because my feelings were exactly the same. Within a few minutes she was calm again and smiling her secret, tragic smile.

"If you'd kept up much longer, I'd have joined you," I said, attempting a smile.

"Do you know what's the matter with us, Harry?"

"Everything. Just name it."

"No." She shook her head. "We've lost our perspective. What we need is help, psychiatric help."

"At fifty bucks an hour, we can't afford one second of help."

"We can go to a hospital."

"That costs even more."

"Not a public hospital."

"Well, there's Saint Paul's, but I'm leery of it."

"Why? Is it free?" she asked eagerly.

"Sure, it's free all right, but what if they decide we're nuts and lock us up in a state institution for a few years? You in a woman's ward, me in a men's ward?"

"Oh, they wouldn't do that, Harry. We aren't crazy. This wholesale depression we're experiencing is caused strictly by alcohol. If we can get a few drugs and a little conversation from a psychiatrist, we'll be just fine again. I'll bet they wouldn't keep us more than a week at the longest."

"That isn't the way it works, baby," I told her. "A psychiatrist isn't a witch doctor with a speedy cure for driving out the devils. It's a long process, as I understand it, and the patient really cures himself. All the psychiatrist can do is help him along by guiding the thinking a little bit. He listens and says nothing. He doesn't even give the patient any sympathy. All he does is listen."

"That doesn't make any sense to me."

"But that's the way it works."

"Well . . ." She thought for a few moments. "They could get us off the liquor couldn't they?"

"If we didn't have any, and couldn't get any, yes. But even there, you have to have a genuine desire to quit drinking."

"I don't want to drink anymore, Harry. Let's take a chance on it, to see what happens. We can't lose anything, and I know they aren't going to lock us up anywhere, because it costs the state too much money for that. Both of us need some kind of help right now, and you know it!"

I caught some of Helen's enthusiasm, but for a different reason. The prospect of a good rest, a chance to sleep at night, some proper food in my stomach appealed to me. It was a place to start from . . .

"A week wouldn't be so bad at that," I said. "I could get straightened around some, maybe do a little thinking. I might come up with an idea."

"I could too, Harry. There are lots of things we could do together! You know all about art. Why, I'll bet we could start an art gallery and make a fortune right here in San Francisco! Did you ever get your G.I. loan?"

"No."

"A veteran can borrow all kinds of money! I think they loan as high as four thousand dollars."

"Maybe so, but an art gallery isn't any good. The dealers are all starving to death, even the well-established ones. People don't buy decent pictures for their homes any more. They buy pictures in the same place they get their new furniture. If the frame matches the davenport, they buy the picture, no matter what it is. No art gallery for me."

"They give business loans too."

"They may not take us in at the hospital." I brought the subject back to the business at hand.

"If we show them our wrists, I'll bet they'll take us in!"

I knew that Helen was right and yet I was afraid to turn in to Saint Paul's Hospital. But I could think of nothing better to do. Maybe a few days of peace and quiet were all we needed. I could use a new outlook on life. It was the smart thing to do, and for once in my life, why couldn't I do the smart thing?

"All right, Helen. Get dressed. We'll try it. If they take us in, fine! If they don't, they can go to hell."

After we were dressed, Helen began to roll up the bloody sheets to take them out to the incinerator. "Just a second," I said, and I tossed my box of oil paints and the rest of my painting equipment into the middle of the pile of sheets. "Burn that junk, too," I told her.

"You don't want to burn your paints!"

"Just do what I tell you. I know what I'm doing."

While Helen took the bundle out to the backyard to burn it in the incinerator, I walked down the hall to Mrs. McQuade's room and knocked on her door.

"Mrs. McQuade," I said, when she answered my insistent rapping. "My wife and I are going out of town for a few days. We're going to visit her mother down in San Sienna."

"How many days will you be gone, Mr. Jordan?" she asked suspiciously.

"I'm not sure yet. About a week, maybe not that long."

"I can't give you any refund, Mr. Jordan. You didn't give me any advance notice."

"I didn't ask for a refund, Mrs. McQuade."

"I know you didn't, but I thought it best to mention it." She fluttered her apron and smiled pleasantly. "Now you go ahead and have a nice time. Your room'll still be here when you get back."

"We will," I said grimly. "We expect to have a grand old time."

I returned to the room. Helen was packing her suitcase with her night things, cold cream, and toothbrush. All I took was my shaving kit. As we left the room she handed me the suitcase and locked the door with her key. At the bottom of the steps, outside in the street, I gave her my leather shaving kit to carry so I could have one hand free.

"How do you feel, baby?" I asked Helen as we paused in front of the house.

"A wee bit dizzy still, but otherwise I'm all right. Why?"

"We've got a long walk ahead of us, that's why." I grinned. "We don't have enough change for carfare."

"Oh!" She lifted her chin bravely. "Then let's get started," she said resolutely, looking into my eyes.

I shrugged my shoulders, Helen took my arm, and we started walking up the hill.

EIGHT

Hospital Case

SAN FRANCISCO is an old city with old buildings, and it is built on seven ancient hills. And long before Helen and I reached the grounds of Saint Paul's Hospital it seemed as though we had climbed every one of them. The narrow, twisted streets, the weathered, brown and crumbling façades of the rotted, huddled buildings frowning upon us as we labored up and down the hills, gave me poignant, bitter memories of my neighborhood in early childhood days: Chicago's sprawling South Side. There was no particular resemblance between the two cities I could put my finger on, but the feeling of similarity persisted. Pausing at the crest of a long, steep hill for rest and breath, I saw the magnificent panorama of the great harbor spreading below us. Angel Island, Alcatraz, several rusty, vagrant ships, a portion of the Golden Gate, and the land mass of Marin County, San Francisco's bedroom, were all within my vision at one time. The water of the bay, a dark and Prussian blue, was the only link with Chicago and my past.

The long walk was good for me. I saw a great many things I had been merely looking at for a long time. It was as though I was seeing the city through new eyes, for the first time.

The late, slanting, afternoon sun made long, fuzzy shadows; dark, colored shadows that dragged from the tops of the buildings like old-fashioned cloaks.

Noisy children were playing in the streets, shouting, screaming, laughing; all of them unaware of money and security and death.

Bright, shiny, new automobiles, chromium-trimmed, two-toned and silent, crept bug-like up and down the steep street.

How long had it been since I had owned an automobile? I couldn't remember.

House-wives in house-dresses, their arms loaded with groceries in brown-paper sacks, on their way home to prepare dinner for their working husbands. How long had it been since I had had a home? I had never had a home.

I saw non-objective designs created with charm and simplicity on every wall, every fence, every puddle of water we passed; the designs of unconscious forms and colors, patterns waiting to be untrapped by an artist's hand. The many-hued spot of oil and water surrounded by blue-black macadam. The tattered, blistered, peeling ochre paint, stripping limply from a redwood wall of an untenanted house. The clean, black spikes of ornamental iron-work fronting a narrow stucco beauty-shop. Arranged for composition and drawn in soft pastels, what delicate pictures these would be for a young girl's bedroom. For Helen's bedroom. For our bedroom. If we had a house and a bedroom and a kitchen and a living-room and a dining-room and maybe another bedroom and I had a job and I was among the living once again and I was painting again and neither one of us was drinking . . .

> *In a dim corner of my room for longer than my*
> *fancy thinks*
> *A beautiful and silent Sphinx has watched me*
> *through the shifting gloom.*

"Let's sit down for a while, Harry," Helen said wearily. There was a bus passenger's waiting bench nearby, and we both sat down. I took the shaving kit out of Helen's lap and put it inside the suitcase. No reason for her to carry it when there was room inside the suitcase. She was more tired than I was. She smiled wanly and patted my hand.

"Do you know what I've been thinking about, Harry?"

"No, but I've been thinking all kinds of things."

"It may be too early to make plans, Harry, but after we get out of the hospital and get some money again I'm going to get a divorce. It didn't make any difference before and it still doesn't—not the way I feel about you, I mean—but I'd like to be married to you. Legally, I mean."

"Why legally?"

"There isn't any real reason. I feel that I'd like it better and so would you."

"I like things better the way they are," I said, trying to discourage her. "Marriage wouldn't make me feel any different. But if it would make you any happier, that's what we'll do. But now is no time to talk about it."

"I know. First off, I'll have to get a divorce."

"That isn't hard. Where's your husband now?"

"Somewhere in San Diego, I think. I could find him. His parents are still living in San Sienna."

"Well, let's not talk about it now, baby. We've got plenty of time. Right now I'm concerned with getting hospital treatment for whatever's the matter with me, if there is such a thing, and there's anything the matter with me. What do you say?"

"I'm rested." Helen got to her feet. "Want me to carry the suitcase a while?"

"Of course not."

Saint Paul's Hospital is a six-story building set well back from the street and surrounded by an eight-foot cyclone wire fence. In front of the hospital a small park of unkempt grass, several rows of geraniums, and a few antlered, unpruned elms are the only greenery to be seen for several blocks. The hospital stands like a red, sore finger in the center of a residential district; a section devoted to four-unit duplexes and a fringe of new ranch-style apartment hotels. Across the street from the entrance-way a new shopping-center and parking lot stretches half-way down the block. As we entered the unraked gravel path leading across the park to the receiving entrance, Helen's tired feet lagged. When we reached the thick, glass double-doors leading into the lobby, she stopped and squeezed my hand.

"Are you sure you want to go through with this, Harry?" she asked me anxiously. "We didn't really have a chance to talk it over much. It was a kind of a spur-of-the-moment decision and we don't have to go through with it. Not if you don't want to," she finished lamely.

"I'm not going to walk the three miles back to the room-inghouse," I said. I could see the tiny cylinders clicking inside her head. "You're scared, aren't you?"

"A little bit," she admitted. Her voice was husky. "Sure I am."

"They won't hurt us. It'll be a nice week's vacation," I assured her.

"Well . . . we've come this far . . ."

I pushed open the door and we timidly entered. The lobby was large and deep and the air was filled with a sharp, antiseptic odor that made my nose burn. There were many well-worn leather chairs scattered over the brown linoleum floor, most of them occupied with in-coming and out-going patients, with their poverty showing in their faces and eyes. In the left corner of the room there was a waist-high circular counter encircling two green, steel desks. Standing behind the desk, instead of the usual bald hotel clerk, was a gray-faced nurse in a white uniform so stiff with starch she couldn't have bent down to tie her shoe-laces. The austere expression on her face was so stern, a man with a broken leg would have denied having it; he would have been afraid she might want to minister to it. We crossed the room to the counter.

"Hello," I said tentatively to her unsmiling face, as I set the suitcase on the floor. "We'd like to see a doctor about admittance to the hospital . . . a psychiatrist, if possible."

"Been here before?"

"No, ma'am."

"Which one of you is entering the hospital?"

"Both of us." I took another look at her gray face. "Maybe we are, I mean. We don't have a dime."

"The money isn't the important thing. If you can pay, we charge, naturally, but if you can't, that's something else again. What seems to be the trouble?"

I looked at Helen, but she looked away, examined the yellowing leaves of a sickly potted plant with great interest. I was embarrassed. It was such a silly thing we had done I hated to blurt it out to the nurse, especially such a practical-minded nurse. I was afraid to tell her for fear she would deliver a lecture of some sort. I forced myself to say it.

"We attempted suicide. We cut our wrists." I stretched my arms over the counter so she could see my bandaged wrists.

"And now you want to see a psychiatrist? Is that right?"

"Yes, ma'am. We thought we would. We need help."

"Come here, dear," the nurse said to Helen, with a sudden change in manner. "Let me see your wrists."

Helen, blushing furiously, pulled the sleeves of her jacket back and held out her wrists to the nurse. At that moment I didn't like myself very well. It was my fault Helen was going through this degrading experience. I had practically forced her into the stupid suicide pact. The nurse deftly unwrapped the clumsy bandages I had affixed to Helen's wrists. She gave me an amused, professional smile.

"Did you fix these?"

"Yes, ma'am. You see, we were in a hurry to get here and I wrapped them rather hastily," I explained.

The nurse puckered her lips and examined the raw wounds on Helen's slender wrists. She clucked sympathetically and handed each of us a three-by-five card and pencils. "Suppose you two sit over there and fill in these cards," she waved us to a decrepit lounge, "and we'll see what we shall see."

We sat down with the cards and Helen asked me in a whisper whether we should use our right names or not. I nodded and we filled in the cards with our names, addresses, etc. The nurse talked on her telephone, so quietly we couldn't hear the conversation from where we were sitting. In a few minutes a young, earnest-faced man, wearing white trousers and a short-sleeved white jacket, got out of the elevator and walked directly to the desk. His feet, much too large for his short, squat body, looked larger than they were in heavy white shoes. He held a whispered conversation with the nurse, nodding his head gravely up and down in agreement. He crossed to our lounge and pulled a straight chair around so it faced us. He sat down on the edge of the chair.

"I am Doctor Davidson," he said briskly, unsmilingly. "We're going to admit you both to the hospital. But first of all you will have to sign some papers. The nurse tells me you have no money. Is that correct?"

"Yes, that is correct," I said. Helen said nothing. She kept her eyes averted from the doctor's face.

"The papers will be a mere formality, then." His face was quite expressionless. I had a hunch that he practiced his blank expression in the mirror whenever he had the chance. He held out his hand for our filled-in cards. "Come with me, please," he ordered. He arose from his chair, dropped the cards on the counter, and marched quickly to the elevator without looking back. We trailed in his wake. At the sixth floor we got out of the elevator, walked to the end of the corridor, and he told us to sit down in two metal folding chairs against the wall. We sat for a solid hour, not talking, and afraid to smoke because there weren't any ashtrays. A young, dark-haired nurse came to Helen, crooked her finger.

"I want you to come with me, dear," she said to Helen.

"Where am I going?" Helen asked nervously.

"To the women's ward." The nurse smiled pleasantly.

"I thought we were going to be together—" Helen tried to protest.

"I'm sorry, dear, but that's impossible."

"What'll I do, Harry?" Helen turned to me helplessly.

"You'd better go with her, I guess. Let me get my shaving kit out of the bag." I opened the suitcase, retrieved my shaving kit, snapped the bag shut. "Go on with her, sweetheart, we've come this far, we might as well go through with it."

The nurse picked up the light over-nighter and Helen followed reluctantly, looking back at me all the way down the corridor. They turned a corner, disappeared from view, and I was alone on my metal folding chair.

In a few minutes Dr. Davidson returned for me and we went down the hall in the opposite direction. We entered his office and he handed me a printed form and told me to sign it. I glanced through the fine print perfunctorily, without reading it in detail. It was a form declaring that I was a pauper. There was no denying that. I signed the paper and shoved it across the desk.

"You're entering the hospital voluntarily, aren't you?" he asked.

"That's about it."

"Fill out these forms then." He handed me three different forms in three different colors. "You can use my office to fill them out." He left the office and I looked at the printed forms. There were questions about everything; my life's history, my health, my relative's health, my schooling, and anything else the hospital would never need to know. For a moment I considered filling them in, but not seriously. I took the desk pen and made a check mark beside each of the numbered questions on all of the forms. That would show that I had read the questions, and if they didn't like it the hell with them. I didn't want to enter the hospital anyway. The doctor returned in about a half an hour and I signed the forms in his presence. Without looking at them he shoved them into a brown manila folder.

"I'm going to be your doctor while you're here," he told me in his well-rehearsed impersonal manner, "but it'll be a couple of days before I can get to you. Let me see your wrists."

I extended my arms and he snipped the bandages loose with a pair of scissors, dropped the soiled sheeting into the wastebasket by his desk.

"What exactly brought this on, Jordan, or do you know?"

"We've been drinking for quite a while and we ran out of money. I suppose that's the main reason. Not that I'm an alcoholic or anything like that, but I'm out of work at present and I got depressed. Helen, more or less—"

"You mean, Mrs. Jordan?"

"No. Mrs. Meredith. Helen Meredith. We don't happen to be married, we're just living together, but we're going to be married later on. As I was saying, Helen takes my moods as hard as I do. If it hadn't been for me—well, this is all strictly my fault."

"We aren't concerned with whose fault it is, Jordan. Our job is to make you well. Do you want a drink now?"

"I could stand one all right."

"Do you feel like you need one?"

"No. I guess not."

"We'll let the drink go then. Hungry?"

"No. Not a bit."

He stood up, patted me on the shoulder, trying to be friendly. "After we take care of those cuts we'll give you some soup, and I'll have the nurse give you a little something that'll make you sleep."

We left his office and I followed him down the corridor to Ward 3-C. There was a heavy, mesh-wire entrance door and a buzzer set into the wall at the right. Dr. Davidson pressed the buzzer and turned me over to an orderly he addressed as Conrad. Conrad dressed my wrists and assigned me to a bed. He issued me a pair of gray flannel pajamas, a blue corduroy robe, and a pair of skivvy slippers. The skivvy slippers were too large for me and the only way I could keep them on was to shuffle my feet without lifting them from the floor. He kept my shaving kit, locked it in a metal cupboard by his desk, which was at the end of the ward.

I sat down on the edge of my bed and looked around the ward. There were twenty-six beds and eleven men including myself. They all looked normal enough to me; none of them looked or acted crazy. The windows were all barred, however, with one-inch bars. I knew I was locked in, but I didn't feel like a prisoner. It was more frightening than jail. A man in jail knows what to expect. Here, I didn't.

Conrad brought me a bowl of weak vegetable soup, a piece of bread and an apple on a tray. He set the tray on my bedside stand.

"See what you can do to this," he said.

I spooned the soup down, not wanting it, but because I thought the doctor wanted me to have it. I ignored the apple and the piece of bread. When he came for the tray, he brought me some foul-tasting lavender medicine in a shot glass and I drank it. He took the tray, and said over his shoulder as he left, "You'd better hop into bed, boy. That stuff'll hit you fast. It's a legitimate Mickey."

I removed my skivvy slippers and robe and climbed into bed. It was soft and high and the sheets were like warm snow. The sun was going down and its softly fading glow came through the windows like a warm good-night kiss. The light bulbs in the ceiling, covered with heavy wire shields, glowed dully, without brightness. I fell asleep almost at once, my head falling down and down into the depths of my pillow.

It was three days before I talked to Dr. Davidson again.

NINE

Shock Treatment

AFTER getting used to it, and it is easy, a neuro-psychiatric ward can be in its own fashion a rather satisfying world within a world. It is the security. Not the security of being locked in, but the security of having everything locked out. The security that comes from the sense of no responsibility for anything. In a way, it is kind of wonderful.

And there is the silence, the peace and the quiet of the ward. The other patients kept to themselves and so did I. One of the orderlies, Conrad or Jones, brought our razors in the morning and watched us while we shaved. I would take a long, hot shower and then make my bed. That left nothing to do but sit in my chair by the side of my bed and wait for breakfast. Breakfast on a cart, was wheeled in and eaten. After breakfast we were left alone until lunch time. Then lunch would be wheeled in.

Near the door to the latrine there was a huge oak table. Spaced around the table there were shiny chromium chairs with colorful, comfortable cushions that whooshed when you first sat down. Along the wall behind the table were stack after stack of old magazines. Except for the brief interruptions for meals and blood-tests I killed the entire first day by going through them. I considered it a pleasant day. I didn't have to think about anything. I didn't have to do anything, and I didn't have anything to worry about. The first night following my admittance I slept like a dead man.

The next morning, after a plain but filling breakfast of mush, buttered toast, orange juice and coffee, I proceeded to the stacks of magazines again. I had a fresh package of king-sized cigarettes furnished by the Red Cross and I was set for another pleasant day. We were not allowed to keep matches and it was inconvenient to get a light from the orderly every time I wanted to smoke, but I knew I couldn't have everything.

Digging deeply into the stacks of magazines I ran across old copies of *Art Digest*, *The American Artist* and *The Modern*

Painter. This was a find that pleased me. It had been a long time since I had done any reading and, although the magazines were old, I hadn't read any of them. One at a time I read them through, cover to cover. I skipped nothing. I read the how-to-do's, the criticism, the personality sketches and the advertisements. It all interested me. I spent considerable time studying the illustrations of the pictures in the recent one-man shows, dissecting pictures in my mind and putting them together again. It was all very nice until after lunch. I was jolted into reality. Really jolted.

There was an article in *The Modern Artist* by one of my old teachers at the Chicago Art Institute. It wasn't an exceptional article: he was deploring at length the plight of the creative artist in America, and filling in with the old standby solution—*Art must have subsidy to survive*—when I read my name in the pages flat before me. It leaped off the pages, filling my eyes. Me. Harry Jordan. A would-be suicide, a resident of a free NP ward, and here was my name in a national magazine! Not that there was so much:

> "... *and what caused Harry Jordan to give up painting? Jordan was an artist who could do more with orange and brown than many painters can do with a full palette*..."

Just that much, but it was enough to dissolve my detached feelings and bring me back to a solid awareness of my true situation. My old teacher was wrong, of course. I hadn't given up painting for economic reasons. No real artist ever does. Van Gogh, Gauguin, Modigliani and a thousand others are the answer to that. But the mention of my name made me realize how far I had dropped from sight, from what I had been, and from what I might have been in my Chicago days. My depression returned full force. A nagging shred of doubt dangled in front of me. Maybe I could paint after all? Didn't my portrait of Helen prove that to me? Certainly, no painter could have captured her as well as I had done. Was I wrong? Had I wasted the years I could have been painting? Wouldn't it have been better to stay close to art, even as a teacher, where at least I would have had the urge to work from time to time? Maybe I would have overcome the block? The four early paintings I had done in orange-and-brown, the non-objective abstractions were still remembered by my old teacher—after all the elapsed time. It shook my convictions. Rocked me. My ruminations were rudely disturbed. My magazine was rudely jerked out of my hands.

"That's my magazine!" I turned in the direction of the high, reedy voice, verging on hysteria. A slight blond man stood by the table, clutching *The Modern Artist* to his pigeon breast. His face was flushed an angry red and his watery blue eyes were tortured with an inner pain.

"Sure," I said noncommittally, "I was just looking at it."

"I'll stick your arm in boiling water!" he informed me shrilly.

"No you won't." I didn't know what else to say to the man.

"I'll stick your arm in boiling water! I'll stick your arm in boiling water! I'll stick your arm in—" He kept repeating it over and over, his voice growing louder and higher, until Conrad was attracted from the end of the ward. Conrad covered the floor in quick strides, took the little man by the arm and led him away from the table.

"I want to show you something," Conrad told the man secretly.

"What are you going to show me?" The feverish face relaxed somewhat and he followed Conrad down the ward to his bed. Conrad showed him his chair and the man sat down wearily and buried his face in his hands. On the walk to his bed and chair, the magazine was forgotten, and it fell to the floor. On his way back to the table, Conrad picked up the magazine, slapped it on the table in front of me, and returned to his desk without a word of explanation. A man who had been watching the scene from the door of the latrine crossed to the table and sat down opposite me.

"Don't worry about him," he said. "He's a Schitzo."

"A what?"

"Schitzo. That's short for schizophrenic. In addition to that, he's a paranoid."

I looked the patient over carefully who was talking to me. Unlike the rest of us, he wore a pair of yellow silk pajamas, and an expensive vermillion brocade robe. His face was lined with crinkly crescents about his eyes and mouth and a light-ning blaze of white shot through his russet hair above each ear. He was smiling broadly; the little scene had amused him.

"My name is Mr. Haas," he told me, reaching out to shake hands.

"Harry Jordan," I said, shaking his hand.

"After a few years," he offered, "you get so you can tell. I've been in and out of these places ever since the war. I'm a Schitzo myself and also paranoid. What's the matter with you?"

"Nothing," I said defensively.

"You're lucky then. Why are your wrists bandaged?"

"I tried suicide, but it didn't work."

"You're a manic-depressive then."

"No, I'm not," I said indignantly. "I'm nothing at all."

"Don't fight it, Jordan." Mr. Haas had a kind, pleasant voice. "It's only a label. It doesn't mean anything. Take my case for instance. I tried to kill my wife this time, and she had me committed. I won't be in here long, I'm being transferred to a V.A. hospital, and this time for good. It isn't so bad being a Schitzo; there are many compensations. Did you ever have hallucinations?"

"No. Never."

"I have them all the time, and the best kind. Most of us hear voices, but my little hallucination comes to me in the night and I can hear him, smell him and feel him. He feels like a rubber balloon filled with warm water, and he smells like Chanel Number Five. We carry on some of the damndest conversations you've ever heard."

"What does he look like?" I was interested.

"The hell with you, Jordan. Get your own hallucination. How about some chess?"

"I haven't played in a long time," I said.

"Neither have I. I'll get my board and chessmen."

For the rest of the day I played chess with Mr. Haas. I didn't win a game.

By supper that night I was my old self again. Playing chess had made me forget the magazine article temporarily. After a supper of liver and new potatoes I crawled into bed. I was a failure and I knew it. The false hopes of the early afternoon were gone. The portrait of Helen was nothing but a lucky accident. My old orange-and-brown abstracts were nothing but experiments. Picasso's *Blue* period. Jordan's *Orange-and-Brown* period. They hadn't sold at my asking price and I'd destroyed them years ago. My name being mentioned, along with a dozen other painters, was no cause for emotion or elation. It was all padding. The prof. had to pad his article some way, and he had probably wracked his brain for enough names to make his point. But seeing my name in *The Modern Artist* had ruined my day.

It took me a long time to fall asleep.

The next morning I awoke with a slight headache and a sharp pain behind my eyeballs. I wasn't hungry, my hands were trembling slightly and my heart had a dull, dead ache. I felt terrible and even the hot water of the shower didn't relieve my depression.

I was back to normal.

At nine-thirty Conrad told me the doctor wanted to see me. He led the way and I sluffed along behind him in my slippers. Dr. Davidson's office was a small bare room, without a window, and lighted by fluorescent tubing the length of the ceiling. Two wooden chairs and a metal desk. The desk was stacked with patients' charts in aluminum covers. I sat down across from Dr. Davidson and Conrad closed the door, leaving us alone.

"Did you think I'd forgotten about you, Jordan?" The doctor tried a thin-lipped smile.

"No, sir." My fists were tightly clenched and I kept my eyes on my bandaged wrists.

"You forgot to fill in the forms I gave you."

"No, I didn't. I read the questions and that was enough."

"We need that information in order to admit you, Jordan."

"You won't get it from me. I'm ready to leave anyway." I got to my feet and half-way to the door.

"Sit down, Jordan." I sat down again. "What's the matter? Don't you want to tell me about it?"

"Not particularly. It all seems silly now. Although it seemed like a good idea at the time."

"Nothing is silly here," he said convincingly, "or strange, or secret. I'd like to hear about it."

"There's nothing really to tell. I was depressed, as I usually am, and I passed my depression on to Helen—Mrs. Meredith. We cut our wrists."

"But why are you depressed?"

"Because I'm a failure. I don't know how else to say it."

"How long had you been drinking?"

"Off and on. Mostly on. Helen drinks more than I do. I don't consider myself an alcoholic, but I suppose she is, or close to it."

"How long have you been drinking?"

"About five years."

"I mean you and Mrs. Meredith."

"Since we've been together. Three weeks, a month. Something like that."

"What have you used for money? Are you employed?"

"Not now. She had a couple of hundred dollars. It's gone now. That's part of this." I held up my arms. "No money."

"What kind of work do you do when you work?"

"Counterman, fry cook, dishwasher."

"Is that all?"

"I used to teach. Painting, drawing and so on. Fine arts."

"Why did you give it up?"

"I don't know."

"By that you mean you won't say."

"Take it any way you want."

"How were your carnal relations with Mrs. Meredith?"

"Carnal? That's a hell of a word to use, and it's none of your business!" I was as high-keyed and ill-strung as a Chinese musical instrument.

"Perhaps the word was unfortunate. How was your sex life, then?"

"How is any sex life? What kind of an answer do you want?"

"As a painter—you did paint, didn't you?" I nodded. "You should have a sharp notice for sensation, then. Where did it feel the best? The tip, the shaft, where?" He held his pencil poised over a sheet of yellow paper.

"I don't remember and it's none of your business!"

"You aren't making it easy for me to help you, Jordan," he said patiently.

"I don't need any help."

"You asked for help when you entered the hospital."

"That was my mistake. I don't need any help. I'm sorry I wasted your time. Just let me out and I'll be all right."

"All right, Jordan. I'll have you released in the morning."

I stood up, anxious to get away from him. "Thanks, Doctor. I'm sorry—"

"Sit down!" I sat down again. "I've already talked to Mrs. Meredith, but I wanted to check with you. Is Mrs. Meredith colored?"

"Helen?" My laugh was hard and brittle. "Of course not. What made you ask that?"

He hesitated for a moment before he answered. "Her expression and eyes, the bone structure of her face. She denied it too, but I thought I'd check with you."

"No," I said emphatically. "She definitely isn't colored."

"I'm going to tell you something, Jordan. I think you need help. As a rule, I don't give advice; people don't take it and it's a waste of time. But in your case I want to mention a thing or two. My own personal opinion. I don't think you and Mrs. Meredith are good for each other. All I can see ahead for you both is tragedy. That is, if you continue to live together."

"Thanks for your opinion. Can I go now?"

"Yes, you can go."

"Will you release Helen tomorrow too?"

"In a few more days."

"Can I see her?"

"No, I don't think so. It would be best for her not to have any visitors for the next few days."

"If you'll call Big Mike's Bar and Grill and ask for me, I'll pick her up when you release her."

"All right." He wrote the address on the sheet of yellow paper. "You can go back to your ward."

Conrad met me outside the office and took me back to the ward. For the rest of the day I played chess with Mr. Haas. I didn't win any games, but my skill improved. I couldn't sleep that night, and finally I got out of bed at eleven and asked the nurse to give me something. She gave me a sleeping pill that worked and I didn't awaken until morning. As soon as

breakfast was over with my clothes were brought to me and
I put them on. Mr. Haas talked with me while I was dressing.

"I'm sorry to see you leave so soon, Jordan. In another day
or so you might have won a game." He laughed pleasantly.
"And then I would have killed you." I didn't know whether
he was kidding or not. "Makes you think, doesn't it?" he
added. We shook hands and I started toward the door. "I'll
be seeing you!" He called after me, and laughed again. This
time rather unpleasantly, I thought. Conrad took me to the
elevator and told me to stop at the desk in the lobby. At the
desk downstairs, the nurse on duty gave me three pieces of
paper to sign, and in a moment I was out on the street.

There wasn't any sun and the fog had closed down heavily
over the city. I walked through the damp mist, up and down
the hills, alone in my own little pocket of isolation. I walked
slowly, but in what seemed like a short length of time I found
myself in front of Big Mike's. I pushed through the swinging
door, sat down at the bar and put my shaving kit on the seat
beside me.

"Hello, Harry," Mike said jovially. "Where you been keeping yourself?"

"Little trip."

"Drink?"

I shook my head. "Mike, I need some money. No, I don't
want a loan," I said when he reached for his hip pocket. "I
want a job. Can you use me for a few days as a busboy or
dishwasher?"

"I've got a dishwasher." Mike rubbed his chin thoughtfully.
"But I don't have a busboy. Maybe the waiters would appreciate a man hustling dishes at noon and dinner. That's a busy
time. But I can't pay you anything, Harry—dollar an hour."

"That's plenty. It would really help out while I look for a
job."

"Want to start now?"

"Sure."

"Pick up a white jacket in the kitchen."

I started to work, grateful for the opportunity. The waiters
were glad to have me clearing dishes and carrying them to
the kitchen. I'm a fast worker and I kept the tables cleared
for them all through the lunch hour, hot-footing it back and

forth to the kitchen with a tray in each hand. By two-thirty the lunch crowd had slowed to a dribble and I was off until five. I took the time to go to my roominghouse for a shower. I straightened the room, dumped trash and beer bottles into the can in the backyard, returned to Mike's. I worked until ten that evening, returned to my room.

I found it was impossible to get to sleep. I quit trying to force it, dressed and went outside. I walked for a while and suddenly started to run. I ran around the block three times and was soon gasping for breath. I kept running. My heart thumped so hard I could feel it beating through my shirt. Bright stars danced in front of my eyes, turned gray, black. I had to stop. I leaned against a building, gasping until I got my breath back. My muscles twitched and ached as I slowly made my way back home. I took a shower and threw myself across the bed. Now I could sleep, and I did until ten the next morning.

It was three days before Dr. Davidson called me. It was in the middle of the noon rush and I was dripping wet when Mike called me to the telephone at the end of the bar. I didn't say anything, but held my hand over the mouthpiece until he walked away.

"Jordan here," I said into the phone.

"This is Doctor Davidson, Jordan. We've decided to re-lease Mrs. Meredith in your custody. As her common-law husband you'll be responsible for her. Do you understand that?"

"What time?" I asked impatiently.

"About three this afternoon. You'll have to sign for her to take her out. Sure you want to do it?"

"Yes, sir. I'll be there." I racked the phone.

Big Mike was in the kitchen eating a salami sandwich and talking with the chef. The chef was complaining about the quality of the pork loin he was getting lately. I broke into the monologue.

"Mike, I have to quit."

"Okay."

"Can I have my money?"

"Okay." He took a roll of bills out of his hip pocket, peeled six ones and handed them to me.

"Only six bucks?"

"I took out for your tab, Harry, but I didn't charge your meals."

"Thanks, Mike. I don't like to leave you in the middle of a rush like this—" I began to apologize.

He waved me away impatiently, bit into his sandwich. "Forget it."

I hung the white mess jacket in the closet and slipped into my corduroy jacket. At the rooming house I showered and shaved for the second time that day. I rubbed my worn shoes with a towel but they were in such bad shape they didn't shine a bit. I caught a trolley, transferred to a bus, transferred to another trolley. It was one-thirty when I reached the entrance to the hospital. I sat down on a bench in the little park and watched the minute hand in the electric clock bounce to each mark, rarely taking my eyes away from it. The clock was set into the center of a Coca-Cola sign above the door of a drug store in the shopping center across the street. At three, on the head, I entered the hospital lobby. Helen was waiting for me by the circular counter, her lower lip quivering. As soon as she saw me she began to cry. I held her tight and kissed her, to the annoyance of the nurse.

"Hey," I said softly. "Cut that out. Everything's going to be all right." Her crying stopped as suddenly as it started. I signed the papers the nurse had ready, picked up Helen's bag and we went outside. We sat down on the bench in the little park.

"How'd they treat you, sweetheart?" I asked her.

"Terrible." Helen shuddered. "Simply terrible, and it was boring as hell."

"What did Dr. Davidson say to you? Anything?"

"He said I should quit drinking. That's about all."

"Anything else?"

"A lot of personal questions. He's got a filthy mind."

"Are you going to quit drinking?"

"Why should I? For him? That bastard!"

"Do you want a drink now?"

"It's all I've thought about all week, Harry," she said sincerely.

"Come on." I took her arm, helping her to her feet. "Let's go across the street."

A few doors down the street from the shopping center we found a small neighborhood bar. We entered and sat down in the last booth. I saved out enough money for carfare and we drank the rest of the six dollars. Helen was unusually quiet and drank nothing but straight shots, holding the glass in both hands, like a child holding a mug. Once in awhile she would almost cry, and then she would smile instead. We didn't talk; there was nothing to talk about. We left the bar and made the long, wearisome trip back to Big Mike's. We sat down in our old seats at the bar and started to drink on a new tab. Mike was glad to see Helen again and he saw that we always had a fresh, full glass in front of us. By midnight Helen was glassy-eyed drunk and I took her home and put her to bed. Despite the many drinks I had had, I was comparatively sober. Before going to bed myself I smoked a cigarette, crushed it savagely in the ashtray.

As far as I could tell, we were no better off than before.

TEN

Mother Love

NEXT MORNING I got out of bed early, and without waking Helen, took a long hot shower and dressed. Helen slept soundly, her lips slightly parted. I raised the blind and the room flooded with bright sunlight. A beautiful day. I shook Helen gently by the shoulder and she opened her eyes quickly, blinked them against the brightness. She was wide awake.

"I hated to wake you out of a sound sleep," I said, "but I'm leaving."

Helen sat up in bed immediately. "Leaving? Where?"

"Job hunting." I grinned at her alarm. "Not a drop of whiskey in the house."

"No money at all, huh?"

"No money, no coffee, nothing at all."

"What time will you be back?"

"I don't know. Depends on whether I can get a job, and if I do, when I get through. But I'll be back as soon as I can."

Helen got out of bed, slid her arms around my neck and kissed me hard on the mouth. "You shouldn't have to work, Harry," she said sincerely and impractically. "You shouldn't have to do anything except paint."

"Yeah," I said, disengaging her arms from my neck, "and make love to you. I'd better get going." I left the room, closing the door behind me.

There was a little change in my pocket, more than enough for carfare, and I caught the cable car downtown to Market Street. I had always been lucky finding jobs on Market, maybe I could again. There are a thousand and one cafes. One of them needed a man like me. From Turk Street I walked toward the Civic Center, looking for signs in windows. I wasn't particular. Waiter, dishwasher, anything, I didn't care. I tried two cafes without success. At last I saw a sign: FRY COOK WANTED, hanging against the inside of a window of a small cafe, attached with scotch tape. I entered the cafe. It was a dark, dingy place with an overpowering smell of fried onions. I reached over the shoulder of the peroxide blonde sitting behind the cash register and jerked the sign out of the window.

"What do you think you're doing?" she said indifferently.

"I'm the new fry cook. Where's the boss?"

"In the kitchen." She jerked her thumb toward the rear of the cafe, appraising me with blue, vacant eyes.

I made my way toward the kitchen. The counter was filled, all twelve stools, and the majority of the customers sitting on them were waiting for their food. There wasn't even a counterman working to give a glass of water or pass out a menu. The boss, a perspiring, overweight Italian, wearing suit pants and a white shirt, was gingerly dishing chile beans into a bowl. Except for the old, slow-moving dishwasher, he was the only one in the kitchen.

"Need a fry cook?" I grinned ingratiatingly, holding up the sign.

"Need one? You from the Alliance?"

"No, but I'm a fry cook."

"I been trying to get a cook from the Alliance for two days, and my waitress quit twenty minutes ago. The hell with the Alliance. Get busy."

"I'm your man." I removed my coat and hung it on a nail.

He wore a greasy, happy smile. "Sixty-five a week, meals and laundry."

"You don't have to convince me," I told him, "I'm working."

I wrapped an apron around my waist and took a look at the stove. The boss left the kitchen, rubbing his hands together, and started to take the orders. Although I was busy, I could handle things easily enough. I can take four or five orders in my head and have four or more working on the stove at the same time. When I try to go over that I sometimes run into trouble. But there was nothing elaborate to prepare. The menu offered nothing but plain food, nothing complicated. The boss was well pleased with my work. I could tell that by the way he smiled at me when he barked in his orders. And I had taken him out of a hole.

At one my relief cook came on duty, a fellow by the name of Tiny Sanders. I told him what was working and he nodded his head and started to break eggs for a Denver with one hand. I put my jacket on, found a brown paper sack, and filled it with food out of the ice-box. I don't believe in buying food when I'm working in a cafe. The boss came into the kitchen and I hit him up for a five spot. He opened his wallet and gave me the five without hesitation.

"I'm giving you the morning shift, Jordan. Five a.m. to one."

"That's the shift I want," I told him. "See you in the morning." It was the best shift to have. It would give me every afternoon and evening with Helen.

I left the cafe and on the corner I bought a dozen red carnations for a dollar from a sidewalk vendor. They were old flowers and I knew they wouldn't last for twenty-four hours, but they would brighten up our room. On the long ride home I sniffed the fragrance of the carnations and felt well-pleased with myself, revelling in my good fortune.

I was humming to myself as I ran up the stairs and down the hall to our room.

I opened my door and jagged tendrils of perfume clawed at my nostrils. Tweed. It was good perfume, but there was too much of a good thing. Helen, fully dressed in her best suit, was sitting nervously on the edge of the unmade bed. Across from her in the strongest chair was a formidable woman in her late fifties. Her hair was a streaked slate-gray and she was at least fifty pounds overweight for her height—about five-nine. Her sharp blue eyes examined me like a bug through a pair of eight-sided gold-rimmed glasses. The glasses were on a thin gold chain that led to a shiny black button pinned to the breast of a rather severe blue taffeta dress.

"Harry," there was a catch in Helen's throat, "this is my mother, Mrs. Mathews."

"How do you do?" I said. I put the carnations and sack of food on the table. "This is a pleasant surprise."

"Is it?" Mrs. Mathews sniffed.

"Well, I didn't expect you—"

"I'll bet you didn't!" She jerked her head to the right.

"The hospital notified Mother I was ill," Helen explained.

"That was very thoughtful of them," I said.

"Yes," Mrs. Mathews said sarcastically, "wasn't it? Yes, it was very thoughtful indeed. They also were thoughtful enough to inform me that my daughter was released from the hospital in the custody of her common-law husband. That was a nice pleasant surprise!"

For a full minute there was a strained silence. I interrupted it. "Helen is all right now," I said, trying a cheery note.

"Is she?" Mrs. Mathews asked.

"Yes, she is."

"Well, I don't think so." Mrs. Mathews jerked her head to the right. "I think she's out of her mind!"

"Please, Mother!" Helen was very close to tears.

"I'm taking good care of Helen," I said.

"Are you?" Mrs. Mathews hefted herself to her feet, clomped heavily across the room to the portrait. "Is this what you call taking good care of her? Forcing her to pose for a filthy, obscene picture?" Her words were like vitriolic drops of acid wrapped in cellophane, and they fell apart when they left her lips, filling the room with poison.

"It's only a portrait," I said defensively. "It isn't for public viewing."

"You bet it isn't! Only a depraved mind could have conceived it; only a depraved beast could execute it; and only a leering, concupiscent goat would look at it!"

"You're too hard on me, Mrs. Mathews. It isn't that bad," I said.

"Where have you been so long, Harry?" Helen asked me, trying to change the subject.

"I got a job, and that sack's full of groceries," I said, pointing.

"What kind of a job?" Mrs. Mathews asked. "Sweeping streets?"

"No. I'm a cook."

"I don't doubt it. Listen, er, ah, Mr. Jordan, if you think anything of Helen at all you'll talk some sense into her. I want her to come home with me, where she belongs. Look at her eyes! They look terrible."

"Now that I've got a job she'll be all right, Mrs. Mathews. Would you like a salami sandwich, Helen?"

"No thanks, Harry," Helen said politely. "Not right now."

"Why not?" Mrs. Mathews asked with mock surprise. "That's exactly what you should eat! Not fresh eggs, milk, orange juice and fruit. That stuff isn't any good for a person right out of a sick bed. Go ahead. Eat a salami sandwich. With pickles!"

"I'm not hungry, Mother!"

"Maybe it's a drink of whiskey you want? Have you got whiskey in that sack, Mr. Jordan, or is it all salami?"

"Just food," I said truthfully. "No whiskey."

"That's something. Are you aware that Helen shouldn't drink anything with alcohol in it? Do you know of her bad heart? Did she tell you she was sick in bed with rheumatic fever for three years when she was a little girl? Did she tell you she couldn't smoke?"

"I'm all right, Mother!" Helen said angrily. "Leave Harry alone!"

Again we suffered a full minute of silence. "I brought you some carnations," I said to Helen; "you'd better put them in water." I crossed to the table, unwrapped the green paper, and gave the flowers to Helen.

"They're lovely, Harry!" Helen exclaimed. She placed the carnations in the water pitcher on the dresser, arranged them quickly, inexpertly, sat down again on the edge of the bed, and stared at her mother. I sat beside her, reached over and took her hand. It was warm, almost feverish.

"Now listen to me, both of you." Mrs. Mathews spoke slowly, as though she were addressing a pair of idiots. "I can perceive that neither one of you has got enough sense to come in out of the rain. Helen has, evidently, made up what little mind she has, to remain under your roof instead of mine. All right. She's over twenty-one and there's nothing I can do about it. If you won't dissuade her and I can see you won't— not that I blame you—will you at least let me in on your plans?"

"We're going to be married soon," Helen said.

"Do you mind if I call to your attention that you're already married?" Mrs. Mathews jerked her head to the right, as though Helen's husband was standing outside the door waiting for her.

"I mean, after I get a divorce," Helen said.

"And meanwhile, while you're waiting, you intend to continue to live here in sin? Is that right?"

Helen didn't answer for a moment and I held my breath. "Yes, Mother, that's what I'm going to do. Only it isn't sin."

"I won't quibble." Mrs. Mathews sniffed, jerked her head to the right and turned her cold blue eyes on me. "How much money do you make per week, Mr. Jordan? Now that you have a job." The way she said it, I don't believe she thought I had a job.

"Sixty-five dollars a week. And I get my meals and laundry."

"That isn't enough. And I doubt in here—" she touched her mammoth left breast with her hand— "whether you can hold a position paying that much for any length of time. Here's what I intend to do. As long as my daughter won't listen to reason, I'll send her a check for twenty-five dollars a week. But under one condition: both of you, stay out of San Sienna!"

"We don't need any money from you, Mother!" Helen said fiercely. "Harry makes more than enough to support me."

"I'm not concerned with that," Mrs. Mathews said self-righteously. "I know where my duty lies. You can save the money if you don't need it, or tear up the check, I don't care. But starting right now, I'm giving you twenty-five dollars a week!"

"You're very generous," I said.

"I'm not doing it for you." Mrs. Mathews jerked her head to the right. "I'm doing it for Helen."

Mrs. Mathews removed a checkbook and ballpoint pen from the depths of a cavernous saddle-leather bag and wrote a check. She crossed the room to the dresser, drying the ink by waving the check in the air, and put the filled-in check beside the pitcher of carnations. She sniffed.

"That's all I have to say, but to repeat it one more time so there'll be no mistake: Stay out of San Sienna!"

"It was nice meeting you, Mrs. Mathews," I said. Helen remained silent.

Mrs. Mathews jerked her head to the right so hard her glasses were pulled off her nose. The little chain spring caught them up and they whirred up to the black button pinned to her dress. She closed the shirred beaver over the glasses, sniffed, and slammed the door in my face.

But the memory lingered on, in the form of a cloud of Tweed perfume.

Helen's face was pale and her upper lip was beaded with tiny drops of perspiration. She wound her arms around my waist tightly and pressed her face into my chest. I patted her on the back, kissed the top of her head.

"Oh, Harry, it was terrible!" Her voice was low and muffled against my chest. "She's been here since ten o'clock this morning. Arguing, arguing, arguing! Trying to break me down. And I almost lost! I was within that much"—she pulled away from me, held thumb and forefinger an inch apart—"of going with her." She looked at me accusingly; her face wore an almost pitiful expression. "Where were you? When I needed you the most, you weren't here!"

"I wasn't lying about the job, Helen. I found a job as a fry cook and had to go to work to get it."

"Why do you have to work? It isn't fair to leave me here all alone."

"We have to have money, sweetheart," I explained patiently. "We were flat broke when I went out this morning, if you remember."

"Can't we live on what money Mother sends us?"

"We could barely exist on twenty-five dollars a week. The room rent's ten dollars, and we'd have to buy food and liquor out of the rest. We just can't do it."

"What are we going to do, Harry? It's so unfair of Mother!" she said angrily. "She could just as easily give us two hundred and fifty a week!"

"Can't you see what she's up to, Helen? She's got it all planned out, she thinks. She doesn't want you to go hungry, but if she gave us more money, she knows damned well you'd never go back to her. This way, she figures she has a chance—"

"Well, she's wrong! I'm never going back to San Sienna!"

"That leaves it up to me then, where it belongs. I'll work this week out, anyway. Maybe another. We'll pay some room rent in advance that way, and the tab at Mike's. And maybe we can get a few loose dollars ahead. Then I'll look for some kind of part time work that'll give me more time with you."

We left it at that.

Helen picked the check up from the dresser and left for the delicatessen. She returned in a few minutes with a bottle of whiskey and a six-pack carton of canned beer. I had one drink with her and I made it last. I didn't want to drink that one. I felt that the situation was getting to be too much for me to handle. Helen drank steadily, pouring them down, one after the other, chasing the raw whiskey with sips of beer. Her mother's visit had upset her badly, and she faced it typically, the way she faced every situation.

By six that evening she sat numbly in the chair by the window. She was in a paralyzed stupor. I undressed her and put her to bed. She lay on her back, breathing with difficulty. Her eyes were like dark bruises, her face a mask of fragile, white tissue paper.

I didn't leave the room; I felt like a sentry standing guard duty. I made a salami sandwich, took one bite, and threw it down on the table. I sat in the chair staring at the wall until well past midnight.

After I went to bed, it was a long time before I fell asleep.

ELEVEN

Bottle Baby

THE LITTLE built-in, automatic alarm clock inside my head waked me at four a.m. and I hadn't even taken the trouble to set it. I tried to fight against it and go back to sleep, but I couldn't. The alarm was too persistent. I reluctantly got out of the warm bed, shiveringly grabbed a towel, and rushed next door to the bathroom. Standing beneath the hot water of the shower almost put me back to sleep. With an involuntary yelp I twisted the faucet to cold and remained under the pelting needles of ice for three minutes. On the way back to my room I dried myself, and then dressed hurriedly against the background of my chattering teeth. The room was much too cold to hang around for coffee to boil and I decided to wait and get a cup when I reached Vitale's Cafe. I got my trenchcoat out of the closet and put it on over my corduroy jacket. The trenchcoat was so filthy dirty I only wore it when I had to, but it was so cold inside the house I knew I would freeze on the street without something to break the wind.

Helen was sleeping on her side facing the wall and I couldn't see her face. Her hip made a minor mountain out of the covers and a long ski slope down to her bare round shoulder. I envied Helen's warm nest, but I pulled the blanket up a little higher and tucked it in all around her neck.

Helen had been so far under the night before when I put her to bed I thought it best to leave a note. I tore a strip of paper from the top of a brown sack and wrote in charcoal:

Dearest Angel,
Your slave has departed for the salt mine. Will be home by
one-thirty at latest. All my love,

Harry

Helen's bottle of whiskey was still a quarter full. I put the note in the center of the table and weighted it with the bottle where I knew she would find it easily when she first got out of bed. I turned out the overhead light and closed the door softly on my way out.

It was colder outside than I had anticipated it to be. A strong, steady wind huffed in from the bay, loaded heavily with salt and mist, and I couldn't make myself stand still on the corner to wait for my car. Cable cars are few and far between at four-twenty in the morning and it was far warmer to run a block, wait, run a block and wait until one came into view. I covered four blocks this way and the exertion warmed me enough to wait on the fourth corner until a car came along and slowed down enough for me to catch it. I paid my fare to the conductor and went inside. I was the only passenger for several blocks and then business picked up for the cable car when several hungry-looking longshoremen boarded it with neatly-lettered placards on their way to the docks to picket. I dismounted at the Powell Street turnaround and walked briskly down Market with my hands shoved deep in my pockets. The wide street was as nearly deserted as it can ever be. There were a few early-cruising cabs and some middle-aged paper boys on the corners waiting for the first morning editions. There was an ugly mechanical monster hugging the curbs and sploshing water and brushing it up behind as it noisily cleaned at the streets. Later on there would be the regular street cleaners with brooms and trash-cans on wheels to pick up what the monster missed. I entered Vitale's Cafe.

"Morning, Mr. Vitale," I said.

"It don't work for me," the boss said ruefully. "I poured hot water through ten times already and it won't turn dark. I have to use fresh coffee grounds after all."

"Did you dry the old grounds on the stove first?"

"No, I been adding hot water."

"That's what's the matter then. If you want to use coffee grounds two days in a row you have to dry them out on the stove in a shallow pan. Add a couple of handfuls of fresh coffee to the dried grounds and the coffee'll be as dark as cheap coffee ever gets."

I took off my jacket and lit the stove and checked on the groceries for breakfast. I wrapped an apron around my waist and stoned the grill while I waited for the coffee to be made, making a mental note to fix my own coffee the next morning before I left my room. By five a.m. I was ready for work and nobody had entered the cafe. I wondered why Vitale opened so early. I soon found out. All of a sudden the counter was jammed with breakfast eaters from the various office buildings and street, most of them ordering the Open Eye Breakfast Special: two ounces of tomato juice, one egg, one strip of bacon, one piece of toast and coffee extra. This breakfast was served for thirty-five cents and although it was meager fare it attracted the low income group. The night elevator operators, the cleaning women, the news-boys, the all-night movie crowd, and some of the policemen going off duty all seemed to go for it. Breakfast was served all day at Vitale's, but at ten-thirty I checked the pale blue menu and began to get ready for the lunch crowd. I was so busy during the noon rush I hated to look up from my full grill when Tiny, my relief, tapped me on the shoulder at one on the head. I told Tiny what was working, wrapped up two one-pound T-bones to take home with me, and left the cafe with a wave at the boss.

On the long ride home I tried to think of ways to bring Helen out of the doldrums, but every idea I thought of was an idea calling for money. By the time I reached my corner my immediate conclusion was that all Helen needed was one of my T-bone steaks, fried medium rare as only I could fry a steak and topped with a pile of french fried onion rings. I bought a dime's worth of onions at the delicatessen and hurried home with my surprise. I opened the door to my room and Helen wasn't there. My note was still under the whiskey bottle, but now the bottle was empty. There was a message from Helen written under mine and I picked it up and studied it.

Dear Harry,
I can't sit here all day waiting for you. If I don't talk to
somebody I'll go nuts. I love you.

Helen

The message was in Helen's unmistakable microscopic handwriting and it was written with the same piece of charcoal I had used and left on the table. It took me several minutes to decipher what she said and I still didn't know what she really meant. Was she leaving me for good? I opened the closet and checked her clothes, the few she had. They were all in the closet and so was her suitcase. That made me feel a little better, knowing she wasn't leaving me. I still didn't like the idea of her running around loose, half-drunk, and with nothing solid in her stomach. She had killed the rest of the whiskey, which was more than a half-pint, and she had the remainder of the twenty-five bucks her mother had given her. She could be anywhere in San Francisco—with anybody. I had to find her before she got into trouble.

I opened the window, put the steaks outside on the sill, and closed the window again. If the sun didn't break through the fog they would keep until that evening before they spoiled. I left the rooming house and walked down the street to Big Mike's Bar and Grill. After I entered the grill I made my way directly to the cash register where Big Mike was standing. By the look in his eyes I could tell he didn't want to talk to me.

"Have you seen Helen, Mike?" I asked him.

"Yeah, I saw her all right. She was in here earlier."

"She left, huh?"

"That's right, Harry. She left." His voice was surly, his expression sour. There was no use to question him any further. How was he supposed to know where she went? It was obvious something was bothering him and I waited for him to tell me about it.

"Listen, Harry," Mike said, after I waited a full minute. "I like you fine, and I suppose Helen's okay too, but from now on I don't want her in here when you ain't with her."

"What happened, Mike. I've been working since five this morning."

"I don't like to say nothing, Harry, but, you might as well know. She was in about eleven and drunker than hell. I wouldn't sell her another drink even, and when I won't sell another drink, they're drunk. She had her load on when she come in, and it was plenty. Anyway, she got nasty with me and I told her to leave. She wouldn't go and I didn't want to toss her out on her ear so I shoved her in a booth and had Tommy take her some coffee. She poured it on the floor, cussing Tommy out and after awhile three Marines took up with her. They sat down in her booth and she quieted down so I let it go. After a while they all left and that was it. I'm sorry as hell, Harry, but that's the way it was. I ain't got time to look after every drunk comes in here."

"I know it, Mike. You don't know where they went, do you?"

"As I said, after a while I looked and they were gone."

"Well, thanks, Mike." I left the bar and went out on the sidewalk. If the Marines and Helen had taken the cable car downtown I'd never find them. But if they took a cab from the hack-stand in the middle of the block, maybe I would be all right. I turned toward the hack-stand. Bud, the young Korean veteran driver for the Vet's Cab Company, was leaning against a telephone pole waiting for his phone to ring, a cigarette glued to the corner of his mouth, when I reached his stand. He had a pinched, fresh face with light beige-colored eyes, and wore his chauffeur's cap so far back on his head it looked like it would fall off. I knew him enough to nod to him, and saw him often around the corner and in Big Mike's, but I had never spoken to him before.

"I guess you're lookin' for your wife, huh, Jordan?" Bud made a flat statement and it seemed to give him great satisfaction.

"Yes, I am, Bud. Have you seen her?"

"Sure did." He ripped the cigarette out of his mouth, leaving a powdering of flaked white paper on his lower lip, and snapped the butt into the street. "She was with three Marines." This statement gave him greater satisfaction.

"Did you take them any place?"

"Sure did."

"Where?"

"Get in." Bud opened the back door of his cab.

"What's the tariff, Bud?" I was thinking of the three one dollar bills in my watch pocket and my small jingle of change.

"It'll run you about a buck and a half." He smiled with the left side of his face. "If you want to go. She was with three Marines." He held up three fingers. "Three," he repeated, "and you are one." He held up one finger. "One."

"We'll see," I said noncommittally and climbed into the back seat.

Bud drove me to The Green Lobster, a bar and grill near Fisherman's Wharf. The bar was too far away from the Wharf for the heavy tourist trade, but it was close enough to catch the overflow on busy days and there was enough fish stink in the air to provide an atmosphere for those who felt they needed it. On the way, Bud gave me a sucker ride in order to run up his buck and a half on the meter. At most the fare should have been six-bits, but I didn't complain. I rode the unnecessary blocks out of the way and paid the fare in full when he stopped at The Green Lobster.

"This is where I left 'em," he said. I waited on the curb until he pulled away. I couldn't understand Bud's attitude. He might have been a friend of the guy I had a fight with in Big Mike's or he might have resented me having a beautiful girl like Helen. I didn't know, but I resented his manner. I like everybody and it's always disconcerting when someone doesn't like me. I entered The Green Lobster and sat down at the end of the bar near the door.

A long, narrow bar hugged the right side of the room for the full length of the dimly lighted room. There were high, wrinkled red-leather stools for the patrons and I perched on one, my feet on the chromium rungs. The left wall had a row of green-curtained booths, and between the booths and the narrow bar, there were many small tables for two covering the rest of the floorspace. Each small table was covered with a green oilcloth cover and held a bud vase with an unidentifiable artificial flower. I surveyed the room in the bar mirror and spotted Helen and the three Marines in the second booth. The four of them leaned across their table, their heads together, and then they sat back and laughed boisterously. I couldn't hear them, but supposed they were taking turns telling dirty jokes. Helen's laugh was loud, clear, and carried across the room above the laughter of the Marines. I hadn't heard her laugh like that since the night I first brought her home with me. After the bartender finished with two other customers at the bar he got around to me.

"Straight shot," I told him.

"It's a dollar a shot," he said quietly, half-apologetically.

"I've got a dollar," and I fished one out of my watch pocket and slapped it on the bar.

He set an empty glass before me and filled it to the brim with bar whiskey. I sipped a little off the top, put the glass back down on the bar. At a dollar a clip the shot would have to last me. I didn't have a plan or course of action, so I sat stupidly, watching Helen and the Marines in the bar mirror, trying to think of what to do next.

If I tried a direct approach and merely asked Helen to leave with me, there would be a little trouble. Not knowing what to do, I did nothing. There was one sergeant and two corporals, all three of them bigger than me. They wore neat, bright-blue Marine uniforms and all had the fresh, well-scrubbed look that servicemen have on the first few hours of leave or pass. But in my mind I didn't see them in uniform. I saw them naked, Helen naked, and all of them cavorting obscenely in a hotel room somewhere, and as this picture formed in my mind my face began to perspire.

Helen inadvertently settled the action for me. She was in the seat against the wall, the sergeant on the outside, with the two corporals facing them across the table. After a while, Helen started out of the booth to go to the ladies' room. The sergeant goosed her as she squeezed by him and she squealed, giggled, and broke clear of the table. As she looked drunkenly around the room for the door to the ladies' room she saw me sitting at the bar.

"Harry!" she screamed joyfully across the room. "Come on over!"

I half-faced her, remaining on my stool, shaking my head. Helen crossed to the bar, weaving recklessly between the tables, and as soon as she reached me, threw her arms around my neck and kissed me wetly on the mouth. The action was swift and blurred from that moment on. An attack of Marines landed on me and I was hit a glancing blow on the jaw, my right arm was twisted cruelly behind my back, and in less than a minute I was next door on the asphalt of the parking lot. A corporal held my arms behind me and another was rounding the building. The sergeant, his white belt wrapped around his fist, the buckle dangling free, waved the man back. "Go back inside, Adams, and watch that bitch! We'll take care of this bastard. She might try and get away and I spent eight bucks on her already." The oncoming corporal nodded grimly and reentered the bar. Under the circumstances I tried to be as calm as possible.

"Before you hit me with that buckle, Sergeant," I said, "why don't you let me explain?"

Businesslike, the sergeant motioned the Marine holding my arms behind my back to stand clear, so he could get a good swing at me with the belt.

"You don't have to hold me," I said over my shoulder. "If you want to beat up a man for kissing his wife, go ahead!" I jerked away and dropped to my knees in front of the sergeant. Hopefully, I prayed loudly, trying to make my voice sound sincere:

"Oh, God above! Let no man tear asunder what You have joined in holy matrimony! Dear sweet God! Deliver this poor sinner from evil, and show these young Christian gentlemen the light of Your love and Your mercy! Sweet Son of the Holy Ghost and—" That was as far as I got.

"Are you and her really married?" the sergeant asked gruffly.

"Yes, sir," I said humbly, remaining on my knees and staring intently at my steepled fingers.

I glanced at the two Marines out of the corner of my eye. The youngest had a disgusted expression on his face, and was tugging at the sergeant's arm.

"Let it go, Sarge," he said, "we were took and the hell with it. I wouldn't get any fun out of hitting him now."

"Neither would I." The sergeant unwrapped the belt from his hand and buckled it around his waist. "I'm not even mad any more." There was a faint gleam of pity in his eyes as he looked at me. "If she's your wife, how come you let her run loose in the bars?"

"I was working, sir," I said, "and I thought she was home with the children." I hung my head lower, kept my eyes on the ground.

"Then it's your tough luck," the sergeant finished grimly. "Both of you got what you deserved." They left the parking lot and reentered the bar. I got off my knees, walked to the curb and waited. The sergeant brought Helen to the door, opened it for her politely, guided her outside, and as he released her arm, he cuffed her roughly across the face. Bright red marks leaped to the surface of her cheek and she reeled across the sidewalk. I caught her under the arms before she fell.

"That evens us up for the eight bucks." The sergeant grinned and shut the door.

Helen spluttered and cursed and then her body went limp in my arms. I lifted her sagging body and carried her down to the corner and the hack-stand. She hadn't really passed out; she was pretending so she wouldn't have to talk to me. I put her into the cab without help from the driver and gave him my address. I paid the eighty-cent fare when he reached my house, and hoped he didn't see the large, wet spot on the back seat until after he pulled away. Helen leaned weakly against me and I half carried her into our room and undressed her. She fell asleep immediately. Looking inside her purse, I found ninety cents in change. No bills.

I thought things over and came to a decision. I couldn't work any more and leave her by herself. Either I'd have to get money from some other source, or do without it. Left to herself, all alone, Helen would only get into serious trouble. Already I noticed things about her that had changed. She let her hair go uncombed. She skipped wearing her stockings. Her voice was slightly louder and she seemed to be getting deaf in one ear.

We never made love any more.

TWELVE

The Dregs

I DIDN'T sleep all night. I sat in the chair by the dark window with the lights out while Helen slept. I didn't try to think about anything, but kept my mind as blank as possible. When I did have a thought it was disquieting and ugly and I would get rid of it by pushing it to the back of my mind like a pack rat trading a rock for a gold nugget.

Vitale would be stuck again for a fry cook when I didn't show up, but it couldn't be helped. To leave Helen to her own devices would be foolish. When I thought about how close I came to losing her my heart would hesitate, skip like a rock on water and then beat faster than ever. I had a day's pay coming from Vitale that I would never collect. It would take more nerve than I possessed to ask him for it. I decided to let it go.

The night passed, somehow, and as soon as the gray light hit the window I left the room and walked down the block to the delicatessen. It wasn't quite six and I had to wait for almost ten minutes before Mr. Watson opened up. I had enough money with some left over for a half-pint of whiskey and Mr. Watson pursed his lips when he put it in a sack for me.

"Most of my customers this early buy milk and eggs, Harry," he said.

"Breakfast is breakfast," I said lightly and the bells above the door tinkled as I closed it behind me.

When I got back to the room, I brought the T-bones inside from the window sill, opened the package and smelled them. They seemed to be all right and I lit the burner and dropped one in the frying pan and sprinkled it with salt. I made coffee on the other burner and watched the steak for the exact moment to turn it. To fry a steak properly it should only be turned one time. Helen awoke after awhile, got out of bed without a word or a glance in my direction and went to the bathroom. The steak was ready when she got back and I had it on a plate at the table.

"How'd you like a nice T-bone for breakfast?" I asked her.

"Ugh!" She put her feet into slippers and wrapped a flow-ered robe around her shoulders. "I'll settle for coffee."

I poured two cups of coffee and Helen joined me at the table. I shoved the half-pint across the table and she poured a quarter of the bottle into her coffee. I started in on the steak. We both carefully avoided any reference to the Marines or the afternoon before.

"This a day off, Harry?" Helen asked after she downed half of her laced coffee.

"No. I quit."

"Good."

"But I'm a little worried."

"What about?" she asked cautiously.

"Damned near everything. Money, for one thing, and I'm worried about you, too."

"I'm all right."

"You're drinking more than you did before, and you aren't eating."

"I'm not hungry."

"Even so, you've got to eat."

"I'm not hungry."

"Suppose . . ." I spoke slowly, choosing my words with care, "all of a sudden, just like that," and I snapped my fin-gers, "we quit drinking? I can pour what's left of that little bottle down the drain and we can start from there. We make a resolution and stick to it, see, stay sober from now on, make a fresh start."

Helen quickly poured another shot into her coffee. "No, Harry. I know what you mean, but I couldn't quit if I wanted to."

"Why not? We aren't getting any place the way we're going."

"Who wants to get any place?" she said sardonically. "Do you? What great pinnacle have you set your eyes on?" She rubbed her cheek gently. It was swollen from the slap the Marine had given her.

"It was just an idea." Helen was right and I was wrong. We were too far down the ladder to climb up now. I was letting my worry about money and Helen lead me into dangerous thinking. The only thing to do was keep the same level without going down any further. If I could do that, we would be all right. "Pass me the bottle," I said.

I took a good swig and I felt better immediately. From now on I wouldn't let worry get me down. I would take things as they came and with any luck at all everything would be all right.

It didn't take much to mellow Helen. After two laced cups of coffee she was feeling the drinks and listening with intent interest to my story about Van Gogh and Gauguin and their partnership at Arles. Fingernails scratched at the door. Irritated by the interruption I jerked the door open. Mrs. McQuade stood in the doorway with a large package in her arms.

"This package came for you, Mrs. Jordan," she said, looking around me at Helen. "I signed for it. It was delivered by American Express."

"Thanks, Mrs. McQuade," I said. "I'll take it." I took the package.

"That's all right. I—" She wanted to talk some more but I closed the door with my shoulder and tossed the package on the bed. Helen untied the package and opened it. It was full of women's clothing.

"It's from Mother," she said happily, "she's sent me some of my things."

"That's fine," I said. Helen started through the package, holding up various items of clothing to show me how they looked. This didn't satisfy her, and she slipped a dress on to show me how well it looked on her, removed it, and started to put another one on. I was bored. But this pre-occupation with a fresh wardrobe would occupy her for quite a while. Long enough for me to look around town for a way to make a few dollars. The half-pint was almost empty.

"Look, sweetheart," I said, "why don't you take your time and go through these things, and I'll go out for a while and look for a part-time job."

"But I want to show them to you—"

"And I've got to pick up a few bucks or we'll be all out of whiskey."

"Oh. How long will you be gone?"

"Not long. An hour or so at the most." I kissed her good-bye and left the house. I caught the cable car downtown and got off at Polk Street. There wasn't any particular plan or idea in my mind and I walked aimlessly down the street. I passed the Continental Garage. It was a five-story building designed solely for the parking of automobiles. At the back of the building I could see two latticed elevators that took the cars up and down to the rest of the building. On impulse, I entered the side office. There were three men in white overalls sitting around on top of the desks. They stopped talking when I entered and I smiled at the man who had MANAGER embroidered in red above the left breast pocket of his spotless overalls. He was a peppery little man with a small red moustache clipped close to his lip. He looked at me for a moment, then closed his eyes. His eyelids were as freckled as the rest of his face.

"What I'm looking for, sir," I said, "is a part-time job. Do you have a rush period from about four to six when you could use another man to park cars?"

He opened his eyes and there was suspicion in them. "Yes and No. How come you aren't looking for an eight-hour day?"

"I am." I smiled. "I'm expecting an overseas job in Iraq," I lied. "It should come through any day now and I have to hang around the union hall all day. That's why I can't take anything permanent. But the job I'm expecting is taking a lot longer to come through than I expected and I'm running short on cash."

"I see." He nodded, compressed his lips. "You a mechanic?"

"No, sir. Petroleum engineer."

"College man, huh?" I nodded, but I didn't say anything. "Can you drive a car?"

I laughed politely. "Of course I can."

"Okay, I'll help you out. You can start this evening from four to six, parking and bringing them down. Buck and a half an hour. Take it or leave it. It's all the same to me."

"I'll take it," I said gratefully, "and thanks."

"Pete," the manager said to a loosed-jointed man with big

knobby hands, "show him how to run the elevator and tell him about the tickets."

Pete left the office for the elevators and I followed him. A push button worked the elevator, but parking the cars was more complicated. The tickets were stamped with a time-stamp and parked in time groups in accordance with time of entry. When the patron brought in his stub, it was checked for the time it was brought in and the serial number of the ticket. Cars brought in early to stay all day were on the top floor and so on down to the main floor. Patrons who said they would only be gone an hour or so had their cars parked downstairs on the main floor. Five minutes after I left Pete I was on the cable car and on my way home. The fears I had in the morning were gone and I was elated. By a lucky break my part time job was solved. With the twenty-five a week coming in from Helen's mother, plus another three dollars a day from the garage, we should be able to get along fine. And counting the half-hour each way to downtown and my two hours of work, Helen would only be alone three hours.

I opened the door to our room and Helen was back in bed fast asleep. Her new clothes were scattered and thrown about the floor. Without waking her I picked them up and hung them in the closet. I wanted a shot but the little half-pint bottle was empty. I pulled the covers over Helen and lay down beside her on top of the bed. I napped fitfully till three and then I left. I started to wake her before I left, but she was sleeping so peacefully I didn't have the heart to do it.

Right after four the rush started and I hustled the cars out until six. It wasn't difficult and after a few minutes I could find the cars easily. I looked up the red-haired manager at six and he gave me three dollars and I left the garage. Going down the hallway I spread the three dollars like a fan before I opened the door to our room.

Helen was gone.

There wasn't any note so I assumed she was at Big Mike's. She had probably forgotten about the ruckus with him the day before and he was the logical man to give her a free drink, or let her sign for one. I left the roominghouse for Big Mike's. He hadn't seen her.

"If you haven't found her by now," he said, "you might as well forget about it, Harry."

"I did find her yesterday, Mike, I was with her till three this afternoon, and then I had to go to work."

"This isn't the only bar in the neighborhood." He grinned. "I wisht it was."

I made the rounds of all the neighborhood bars. She wasn't in any of them and I didn't ask any of the bartenders if she had been in them. I didn't know any of the bartenders that well. At eight-thirty I went back to the roominghouse and checked to see whether she had returned. I didn't want to miss her in case she came back on her own accord. She wasn't there and I started to check the bars outside the neighborhood. I was hoping she hadn't gone downtown, and I knew she didn't have enough carfare to go.

It was ten-thirty before I found her. She was in a little bar on Peacock Street. It was so dark inside I had to stand still for a full minute before my eyes became accustomed to the darkness. There was one customer at the bar and he and the bartender were watching a TV wrestling match. There were two shallow booths opposite the bar and Helen was in the second. A sailor was with her and she was wearing his white sailor hat on the back of her head. His left arm was about her waist, his hand cupping a breast, and his right hand was up under her dress, working furiously. Her legs were spread widely and he was kissing her on the mouth.

I ran directly to the booth, grabbed the sailor by his curly yellow hair and jerked his head back, pulling his mouth away from Helen's. Still keeping a tight grip on his hair I dragged him across her lap to the center of the floor. His body was too heavy to be supported by his hair alone and he slipped heavily to the floor, leaving me with a thick wad of curls in each hand. He mumbled something unintelligible and attempted to sit up. His slack mouth was open and there was a drunken, stupefied expression in his eyes. I wanted to hurt him; not kill him, but hurt him, mutilate his pasty, slack-jawed face. Looking for a handy weapon, I took a beer bottle from the bar and smashed it over his head. The neck of the bottle was still in my hand and the broken section ended in a long, jagged splinter. I carved his face with it, moving the sharp, glass dagger back and forth across his white face with a whipping wrist motion. Each slash opened a spurting channel of bright red blood that ran down his face and neck and splashed on the floor between his knees. My first blow with the bottle had partially stunned him but the pain brought him out of it and the high screams coming from deep inside his throat were what brought me to my senses. I dropped the piece of broken bottle, and in a way, I felt that I had made up somehow for the degradation I had suffered at the hands of the Marines.

Helen had sobered considerably and her eyes were round as saucers as she sat in the booth. I lifted her to her feet and she started for the door, making a wide detour around the screaming sailor. I opened the door for her and looked over my shoulder. The bartender was nowhere in sight, probably flat on the floor behind the bar. The solitary drinker was peering at me nervously from the safety of the doorway to the men's room. The sailor had managed to get to his knees and was crawling under the table to the first booth, the screams still pouring from his throat. I let the door swing shut behind us.

Helen was able to stand by herself, but both of her hands were pressed over her mouth. I released her arm and she staggered to the curb and vomited into the gutter. When she finished I put my arm around her waist and we walked up the hill. A taxi, coming down the hill on the opposite side of the street, made a U-turn when I signaled him and rolled to a stop beside us. I helped Helen into the cab. A block away from our roominghouse I told the driver to stop. When I opened the door to get out I noticed my hand was cut. I wrapped my handkerchief around my bleeding hand and gave a dollar to the hackie. The cold night air had revived Helen considerably, and she scarcely staggered as we walked the block to the house. As soon as we entered our room she made for the bed and curled up on her knees, pressed her arms to her sides, and ducked her head down. In this position it was difficult for me to remove her clothes, but before I finished taking them off she was asleep.

By that time I could have used a drink myself. I heated the leftover coffee and smoked a cigarette to control my uneasy stomach. I looked through Helen's purse and all I found was a crumpled package of cigarettes and a book of paper matches. Not a penny.

What was the use? I couldn't keep her. How could I work and stay home and watch her at the same time? I couldn't make enough money to meet expenses and keep Helen in liquor if I parked a million cars or fried a million eggs or waited on a million tables. I was so beaten down and disgusted with myself my mind wouldn't cope with it any longer. Sitting awake in the chair I had a dream, a strange, merging dream, where everything was unreal and the ordinary turned into the extraordinary. Nothing like it had ever happened to me before. The coffeepot, the cup, and the can of condensed milk on the table turned into a graphic composition, a depth study. It was beautiful. Everything I turned my eyes upon in the room was perfectly grouped. A professional photographer couldn't have arranged the room any better. The unshaded light in the ceiling was like a light above Van Gogh's pool table. Helen's clothing massed upon the chair swirled gracefully to the floor like drapes in a Titian drawing. The faded gray wallpaper with its unknown red flower pattern was suddenly quaint and charming. The gray background fell away from the flowers with a three-dimensional effect. Everything was lovely, lovely . . .

I don't know how long this spell lasted, but it seemed to be a long time and I didn't want it to end. I had no thought at all during this period. I merely sensed the new delights of my quiet, ordinary room. Only Helen's gentle, open-mouthed snoring furnished the hum of life to my introspection. And then, like a blinding flash of headlights striking my eyes, everything was clear to me. Simple. Plain. Clear.

I didn't have to fight any more.

For instance, a man is crossing the street and an automobile almost runs him down. He shakes his fist and curses and says to himself: "That Buick almost hit me!" But it wasn't the Buick that almost hit him; the Buick was merely a vehicle. It was the man or woman *driving* the Buick who almost hit him. Not the Buick. And that was me. I was the automobile, a machine, a well-oiled vehicle now matured to my early thirties. A machine without a driver. The driver was gone. The machine could now relax and run wherever it might, even into a smash. So what? It could function by itself, by habit, reflex, or whatever it was that made it run. Not only didn't I know, I didn't care any more. It might be interesting, for that part of me that used to think things out, to sit somewhere and watch Harry Jordan, the machine, go through the motions. The getting up in the morning, the shaving, the shower, walking, talking, drinking. I. Me. Whatever I was, didn't give a damn any more. Let the body function and the senses sense. The body felt elation. The eyes enjoyed the sudden beauty of the horrible little back bedroom. My mind felt nothing. Nothing at all.

Helen sat up suddenly in bed. She retched, a green streak of fluid burst from her lips and spread over her white breasts. I got a towel from the dresser and wiped her face and chest.

"Use this," and I handed her the towel, "if it hits you again."

"I think I'm all right now," she gasped. I brought her a glass of water and held it to her lips. She shook her head to move her lips away from the glass.

"Oh, Harry, I'm so sick, so sick, so sick, so sick . . ."

"You'll be all right." I set the glass on the table.

"Are you mad at me, Harry?"

"What for?" I was surprised at the question.

"For going out and getting drunk the way I did."

"You were fairly drunk when I left."

"I know, but I shouldn't have gone out like that. That sailor . . . the sailor who was with me didn't mean a thing—"

"Forget it. Go back to sleep."

"Harry, you're the only one I've ever loved. I've never loved anyone but you. And if you got sore at me I don't know what I'd do."

"I'm not angry. Go to sleep."

"You get in bed too."

"Not right now. I'm busy."

"Please, Harry. Please?"

"I'm thinking. You know I'm not going to live very long, Helen. No driver. There isn't any driver, Helen, and the controls are set. And I don't know how long they're going to last."

"What are you talking about?"

"Just that I'm not going to live very long. I quit."

Helen threw the covers back, got out of bed and rushed over to me. I was standing flat-footed by the table. My feet could feel the world pushing up at me from below. Black old cinder. I laughed. Cooling on the outside, fire on the inside and nothing in between. It was easy to feel the world turn beneath my feet. Helen was on her knees, her arms were clasped about my legs. She was talking feverishly, and I put my hand on her head.

"What's the matter, Harry!" she cried. "Are you going to try to kill yourself again? Are you angry with me? Please talk to me! Don't look away like that . . ."

"Yes, Helen," I said calmly. "I'm going to kill myself."

Helen pulled herself up, climbing my body, using my clothes as handholds, pressing her naked body against mine. "Oh, darling, darling," she whimpered. "Let me go first! Don't go away and leave me all alone!"

"All right," I said. I picked her up and carried her to the bed. "I won't leave you behind. I wouldn't do that." I kissed her, stroked her hair. "Go on to sleep, now." Helen closed her eyes and in a moment she was asleep. The tear-streaked lines on her face were drying. I undressed and got into bed beside her. Now I could sleep. The machine would sleep, it would wake, it would do things, and then it would crash, out of control and destroy itself. But first it must run over the little body that slept by its side. The small, pitiful creature with the big sienna eyes and the silver streak in its hair.

As I fell asleep I heard music. I didn't have a radio, but it wasn't the type of music played over the radio anyway. It was wild, cacophonous, and there was an off-beat of drums pounding. My laugh was harsh, rasping. I continued to laugh and the salty taste in my mouth came from the unchecked tears running down my cheeks.

THIRTEEN

Dream World

IN MY DREAM I was running rapidly down an enormous piano keyboard. The white keys made music beneath my hurried feet as I stepped on them, but the black keys were stuck together with glue and didn't play. Trying to escape the discordant music of the white keys I tried to run on the black keys, slipping and sliding to keep my balance. Although I couldn't see the end of the keyboard I felt that I must reach the end and that it was possible if I could only run fast enough and hard enough. My foot slipped on a rounded black key and I fell heavily, sideways, and my sprawled body covered three of the large white keys with a sharp, harsh discord. The notes were loud and ugly. I rolled away from the piano keyboard, unable to stand, and fell into a great mass of silent, swirling, billowing yellow fog and floated down, down, down. The light surrounding my head was like bright, luminous gold. The gloves on my hands were lemon yellow chamois with three black stitches on the back of each hand. I disliked the gloves, but I couldn't take them off no matter how hard I tried. They were glued to my hands; the bright orange glue oozed out of the gloves around my wrists.

I opened my eyes and I was wide awake. My body was drenched with perspiration. I got out of bed without waking Helen, found and lighted a cigarette. My mouth was so dry the smoke choked me and tasted terrible. The perspiration, drying on my body, made me shiver with cold and I put my shirt and trousers on.

What a weird, mixed-up dream to have! I recalled each sequence of the dream vividly and it didn't make any sense at all. Helen, still asleep, turned and squirmed under the covers. She missed the warmth of my body and was trying to get close to me in her sleep. I crushed my foul-tasting cigarette in the ash-tray and tucked the covers in around Helen. I turned on the overhead light and sat down.

I felt calm and contented. It was time for Harry Jordan to have another cigarette. As though I sat in a dark theatre as a spectator somewhere I observed the quiet, studied actions of Harry Jordan. The exacting, unconscious ritual of putting the cigarette in his mouth, the striking of the match on his thumbnail, the slow withdrawal of smoke, the sensuous exhalation and the obvious enjoyment. The man, Harry Jordan, was a very collected individual, a man of the world. Nothing bothered him now. He was about to withdraw his presence from the world and depart on a journey into space, into nothingness. Somewhere, a womb was waiting for him, a dark, warm place where the living was easy, where it was effortless to get by. A wonderful place where a man didn't have to work or think or talk or listen or dream or cavort or play or use artificial stimulation. A kind old gentleman with a long dark cloak was waiting for him. Death. Never had Death appeared so attractive. . . .

I looked at Helen's beautiful face. She slept peacefully, her mouth slightly parted, her pretty hair tousled. I would take Helen with me. This unfeeling world was too much for Helen too, and without me, who would care for her, look after her? And hadn't I promised to take her with me?

I crushed my cigarette decisively and crossed to the bed.

"Helen, baby," I said, shaking her gently by the shoulder. "Wake up."

She stirred under my hand, snapped her eyes open, awake instantly, the perfect animal. She wore a sweet, sleepy smile.

"What time is it?"

"I don't know," I said, "but it's time." My face was as stiff as cardboard and it felt as expressionless as uncarved stone. I didn't know and didn't want to explain what I was going to do and I hoped Helen wouldn't ask me any questions. She didn't question me. Somehow, she knew instinctively. Perhaps she read the thoughts in my eyes, maybe she could see my intentions in the stiffness of my smile.

"We're going away, aren't we, Harry?" Helen's voice was small, childlike, yet completely unafraid.

Not daring to trust my voice, I nodded. Helen's trust affected me deeply. In that instant I loved her more than I had ever loved her before. Such faith and trust were almost enough to take the curse out of the world. Almost.

"All right, Harry. I'm ready." She closed her eyes and the sleepy winsome smile remained on her lips.

I put my hands around her slender neck. My long fingers interlaced behind her neck and my thumbs dug deeply into her throat, probing for a place to stop her breathing. I gradually increased the pressure, choking her with unrelenting firmness of purpose, concentrating. She didn't have an opportunity to make a sound. At first she thrashed about and then her body went limp. Her dark sienna eyes, flecked with tiny spots of gold, stared guilelessly at me and then they didn't see me any more. I closed her eyelids with my thumb, pulled the covers down and put my ear to her chest. No sound came from her heart. I straightened her legs and folded her arms across her chest. They wouldn't stay folded and I had to place a pillow on top of them before they would stay. Later on, I supposed, when her body stiffened with cold, her arms would stay in place without the benefit of the pillow.

My legs were weak at the knees and I had to sit down to stop their trembling. My fingers were cramped and I opened and closed my hands several times to release the tension. I had taken the irrevocable step and had met Death half-way. I could feel his presence in the room. It was now my turn and, with the last tugs of primitive self-preservation, I hesitated, my conscious mind casting about for a way to renege. But I knew that I wouldn't renege; it was unthinkable. It was too late to back out now. However, I didn't have the courage and trust that Helen had possessed. There was no one kind enough to take charge of the operation or do it for me. I had to do it myself, without help from anyone. But I had to have a little something to help me along . . .

I omitted the socks and slipped into my shoes. I couldn't control my hands well enough to tie the laces and I let them hang loose. I put my jacket on and left my room, locked the door, and left for the street. It was dismally cold outside; there were little patches of fog swirling in groups like lost ghosts exploring the night streets. The traffic signals at the corner were turned off for the night; only the intermittent blinking of the yellow caution lights at the four corners of the intersection lighted the lost, drifting tufts of fog. Although it was after one, Mr. Watson's delicatessen was still open. Its brightly colored window was a warm spot on the dark line of buildings. I crossed the street and entered and the tinkling bell above the door announced my entrance. Mrs. Watson was sitting in a comfortable chair by the counter reading a magazine. She was a heavy woman with orange-tinted hair and a faint chestnut moustache. She smiled at me in recognition.

"Hello, Harry," she said. "How are you this evening?"

"Fine, Mrs. Watson, just fine," I replied. I was glad that it was Mrs. Watson instead of her husband in the shop that morning. I wanted to talk to somebody and she was much easier to talk to than her husband. He was a German immigrant and it always seemed to me like he considered it a favor when he waited on me. I fished the two one dollar bills out of my watch pocket and smoothed them out flat on the counter.

"I think I'm getting a slight cold, Mrs. Watson," I said, coughing into my curled fist, "and I thought if I made a little hot gin punch before I went to bed, it might cut the phlegm a little bit."

"Nothing like hot gin for colds." Mrs. Watson smiled and got out of the chair to cross to the liquor shelves. "What kind?"

"Gilbey's is fine—I'd like a pint, but I don't think I have enough here . . ." I pointed to the two one dollar bills.

"I think I can trust you for the rest, Harry. It wouldn't be the first time." She dropped a pint of Gilbey's into a sack, twisted the top and handed it to me. I slipped the bottle into my jacket pocket. My errand was over and I could leave, but I was reluctant to leave the warm room and the friendly, familiar delicatessen smells. Death was waiting for me in my room. I had an appointment with him and I meant to keep it, but he could wait a few minutes longer.

"What are you reading, Mrs. Watson?" I asked politely, when she had returned to her chair after ringing a No Sale on the cash register and putting my money into the drawer.

"Cosmopolitan." Her pleasant laugh was tinged with irony. "Boy meets girl, loses girl, gets girl. They're all the same, but they pass the time."

"That's a mighty fine magazine, Mrs. Watson. I read it all

the time, and so does my wife. Why, Helen can hardly wait for it to come out and we always argue over who gets to read it first and all that. Yes, I guess it's my favorite magazine and I wish it was published every week instead of every month! What month is that, Mrs. Watson? Maybe I haven't read it yet."

"Do you feel all right, Harry?" She looked at me suspiciously.

"Yes, I do." My voice had changed pitch and was much too high.

"You aren't drunk, are you?"

"No, I get a little talkative sometimes. Well, that's a good magazine."

"It's all right." Mrs. Watson's voice was impatient; she wanted to get back to her story.

"Well, good night, Mrs. Watson, and thanks a lot." I opened the door.

"That's all right, Harry. Good night." She had found her place and was reading before I closed the door.

As soon as I was clear of the lighted window I jerked the gin out of the sack, tossed the sack in the gutter, and unscrewed the cap from the bottle. I took a long pull from the bottle, gulping the raw gin down until I choked on it and hot tears leaped to my eyes. It warmed me through and my head cleared immediately. I crossed the street and walked back to the house. Sitting on the outside steps I drank the rest of the gin in little sips, controlling my impulse to down it all at once. I knew that if I tried to let it all go down my throat at once it would be right back up and the effects would be gone. I finished the bottle and tossed it into the hedge by the porch. My stomach had a fire inside it, but I was sorry I hadn't charged a fifth instead of only getting a pint.

I walked down the dimly lighted hall, unlocked my door and entered my room. It rather startled me, in a way, to see Helen in the same position I had left her in. Not that I had expected her to move; I hadn't expected anything, but to see her lying so still, and uncovered in the cold room, unnerved me. Again I wished I had another pint of gin. I started to work.

I locked the door and locked the window. There were three

old newspapers under the sink, and I tore them into strips and stuffed the paper under the crack at the bottom of the door. I opened both jets on the two-ring burner and they hissed full blast. I sniffed the odor and it wasn't unpleasant at all. It was sweet and purifying. By this time the gin had hit me hard, and I found myself humming a little tune. I undressed carefully and hung my clothes neatly in the closet. I lined my shoes up at the end of the bed. Tomorrow we would be found dead and that was that. But there wasn't any note. I staggered to the table and with a piece of charcoal I composed a brief note of farewell. There was no one in particular to address it to, so I headed it:

> *To Who Finds This:*
>   *We did this on purpose. It isn't accidental.*

I couldn't think of anything else to put in the note and I didn't sign it because the charcoal broke between my fingers. Leaving the note on the table I crawled into bed beside Helen and pulled the covers up over us both. I had left the overhead light on purposely and the room seemed gay and cheerful. I took Helen in my arms and kissed her. Her lips were like cold rubber. When I closed my eyes the image of the light bulb remained. I tried to concentrate on other things to induce sleep. The black darkness of the outside street, the inky San Francisco bay, outside space and starless skies. There were other thoughts that tried to force their way into my mind but I fought them off successfully.

The faint hissing of the gas jets grew louder. It filled the room like a faraway waterfall.

I was riding in a barrel and I could hear the falls far away. It was a comfortable barrel, well-padded, and it rocked gently to and fro, comforting me. It floated on a broad stream, drifting along with the current. The roar of the falls was louder in my ears. The barrel was drifting closer to the falls, moving ever faster toward the boiling steam above the lips of the overhang. I wondered how far the drop would be. The barrel hesitated for a second, plunged downward with a sickening drop.

A big, black pair of jaws opened and I dropped inside. They snapped shut.

FOURTEEN

Awakening

THERE was a lot of knocking and some shouting. I don't know whether it was the knocking or the shouting that aroused me from my deep, restful slumbers, but I awoke, and printed in large, wavering red letters on the surface of my returning consciousness was the word for Harry Jordan: *FAILURE.* Somehow, I wasn't surprised. Harry Jordan was a failure in everything he tried. Even suicide.

The sharp little raps still pounded on the door and I could hear Mrs. McQuade's anxious voice calling, "Mr. Jordan! Mr. Jordan! Open the door."

"All right!" I shouted from the bed. "Wait a minute."

I painfully got out of bed, crossed to the window, unlocked it and threw it open. The cold, damp air that rushed in from the alley smelled like old laundry. The gas continued to hiss from the two open burners and I turned them off. Again the rapping and the call from Mrs. McQuade: "Open the door!"

"In a minute!" I replied. The persistent knocking and shouting irritated me. I slipped into my corduroy trousers, buckled my belt as I crossed the room, unlocked and opened the door. Mrs. McQuade and her other two star roomers, Yoshi Endo and Miss Foxhall, were framed in the doorway. It's a composition by Paul Klee, I thought.

I had always thought of Mrs. McQuade as a garrulous old lady with her hand held out, but she took charge of the situation like a television director.

"I smelled the gas," Mrs. McQuade said quietly. "Are you all right?"

"I guess so."

"Go stand by the window and breathe some fresh air."

"Maybe I'd better." I walked to the window and took a few deep breaths which made me cough. After the coughing fit I was giddier than before. I turned and looked at Endo and Miss Foxhall. "Won't you please come in?" I asked them stupidly.

Little Endo, his dark eyes bulging like a toad's in his flat

Oriental face, stared solemnly at Helen's naked figure on the bed. Miss Foxhall had covered her face with both hands and was peering through the lattice-work of her fingers. Mrs. McQuade examined Helen for a moment at the bedside and then she pulled the covers over the body and face. Pursing her lips, she turned and made a flat, quiet statement: "She's dead."

"Yes," I said. Just to be doing something, anything, I put my shirt on, sat down in the straight chair and pulled on my socks. A shrill scream escaped Miss Foxhall and then she stopped herself by shoving all her fingers into her mouth. Her short involuntary scream brought Endo out of his trance-like state and he grabbed the old spinster's arm and began to shake her, saying over and over again in a high, squeaky voice, "No, no! No, no!"

"Leave her alone," Mrs. McQuade ordered sharply. "I'll take care of her." She put an arm around Miss Foxhall's waist. "You go get a policeman." Endo turned and ran down the hall. I heard the outside door slam. As Mrs. McQuade led Miss Foxhall away, she said over her shoulder: "You'd better get dressed, Mr. Jordan."

"Yes, M'am." I was alone with Helen and the room was suddenly, unnaturally quiet. Automatically, I finished dressing, but my hands trembled so much I wasn't able to tie my neck-tie. I let it hang loosely around my neck, sat down in the straight chair after I donned my jacket.

Why had I failed?

I sat facing the door and I looked up and saw the transom. It was open. It wasn't funny but I smiled grimly. No wonder the gas hadn't killed me. The escaping gas was too busy going out over the transom and creeping through the house calling attention to Harry Jordan in the back bedroom. How did I let it happen? To hold the gas in the room I had shoved news-paper under the bottom of the door and yet I had left the transom wide open. Was it a primeval desire to live? plain stupidity? or the effects of the gin? I'll never know.

In a few minutes Endo returned to the room with a po-liceman. The policeman was a slim, nervous young man and he stood in the doorway covering me with his revolver. More than a little startled by the weapon I raised my arms over my

head. The policeman bit his lips while his sharp eyes roved
the room, sizing up the situation. He holstered the pistol and
nodded his head.

"Put your arms down," he ordered. "Little suicide pact,
huh?"

"No," I replied. "I killed her. Choked her to death." I
folded my hand in my lap.

The young policeman uncovered Helen's head and throat
and looked carefully at her neck. Endo was at his side and the
proximity of the little Japanese bothered him. He pushed
Endo roughly toward the door. "Get the hell out of here,"
he told Endo. Leaving the room reluctantly, Endo hovered in
the doorway. Muttering under his breath, the policeman shut
the door in Endo's face and seated himself on the foot of the
bed.

"What's your name?" he asked me, taking a small, black
notebook out of his hip pocket.

"Harry Jordan."

"Her name?" He jerked his thumb over his shoulder.

"Mrs. Helen Meredith."

"You choked her. Right?"

"Yes."

"And then you turned on the gas to kill yourself?"

"Yes."

"She doesn't looked choked."

"There's the note I left," I said pointing to the table. He
crossed to the table and read my charcoaled note without
touching it. He made another notation in his little black book,
returned it to his hip pocket.

"Okay, okay, okay," he said meaninglessly. There was uncertainty in his eyes. "I've got to get my partner," he informed me. Evidently he didn't know whether to take me
along or leave me in the room by myself. He decided on the
latter and handcuffed me to the radiator and hurried out of
the room, closing the door behind him. The radiator was too
low for me to stand and I had to squat down. Squatting nauseated me, and I got down on my knees on the floor. There
was a queasy feeling in the pit of my stomach and it rumbled,
but I didn't get sick enough to throw up.

In a few minutes he was back with his partner. He was a

much older, heavier policeman, with a buff-colored, neatly trimmed mustache and a pair of bright, alert hazel eyes. The older man grinned when he saw me handcuffed to the radiator.

"Take the cuffs off him, for Christ sake!" he told the younger policeman. "He won't get away."

After the first policeman uncuffed me and returned the heavy bracelets to his belt, I sat down in the chair again. By leaning over and sucking in my stomach I could keep the nausea under control. It was much better sitting down. The younger policeman left the room to make a telephone call and the older man took his place at the foot of the bed. He crossed his legs and after he got his cigarettes out he offered me one. He displayed no interest in Helen's body at all. He lit our cigarettes and then smiled kindly at me.

"You're in trouble, boy," he said, letting smoke trickle out through his nose. "Do you know that?"

"I guess I am." I took a long drag and it eased my stomach.

"Relax, boy. I'm not going to ask you any questions. I couldn't care less."

"Would it be all right with you if I kissed her goodbye?" That question slipped out in a rush, but he seemed to be easygoing, and I knew that after the police arrived in force I wouldn't be able to kiss her goodbye. This would be my last chance. He scratched his mustache, got up from the bed and strolled across the room to the window.

"I suppose it's all right," he said thoughtfully. "What do you want to kiss her for?"

"Just kiss her goodbye. That's all." I couldn't explain because I didn't know myself.

"Okay." He shrugged his shoulders and looked out the window. "Go ahead."

Walking bent over I crossed to the bed and kissed Helen's cold lips, her forehead, and on the lips again. "Goodbye, sweetheart," I whispered low enough so the policeman couldn't hear me, "I'll see you soon." I returned to the chair.

For a long time we sat quietly in the silent room. The door opened and the room was filled with people. It was hard to believe so many people could crowd into such a small room. There were the two original uniformed policemen, two more in plainclothes, a couple of hospital attendants or doctors in white—Endo got back into the room somehow—Mrs. McQuade, and a spectator who had crowded in from the group in front of the house. A small man entered the room and removed his hat. He was almost bald and wore a pair of dark glasses. At his entrance the room was quiet again and the noise and activity halted. The young policeman saluted smartly and pointed to me.

"He confessed, Lieutenant," the young man said. "Harry Jordan is his name and she isn't his wife—"

"I'll talk to him," the little man said, holding up a white, manicured hand. He removed the dark glasses and put them in the breast pocket of his jacket, crooked his finger at me and left the room. I followed him out and nobody tried to stop me. We walked down the hall and he paused at the stairway leading to the top floor.

"Want a cigarette, Jordan?"

"No, sir."

"Want to tell me about it, Jordan?" he asked with his quiet voice. "I'm always a little leery of confessions unless I hear them myself."

"Yes, sir. There isn't much to tell. I choked her last night, and then I turned on the gas. It was a suicide pact, in a way, but actually I killed Helen because she didn't have the nerve to do it herself."

"I see. About what time did it happen?"

"Around one, or after. I don't know. By this time I would have been dead myself if I hadn't left the transom open."

"You willing to put all this on paper, Jordan, or are you going to get a shyster and deny everything, or what?"

"I'm guilty, Lieutenant, and I want to die. I'll cooperate in every way I can. I don't want to see a lawyer, I just want to be executed. It'll be easier that way all around."

"Then that's the way it'll be." He raised his hand and a plainclothesman came down the hall, handcuffed me to his wrist, and we left the rooming-house. A sizeable crowd had gathered on the sidewalk and they stared at us curiously as we came down the outside steps and entered the waiting police car. A uniformed policeman drove us to the city jail.

At the desk I was treated impersonally by the booking sergeant. He filled in my name, address, age and height and then asked me to dump my stuff on the desk and remove my belt and shoelaces. There wasn't much to put on the desk. A piece of string, a thin, empty wallet, a parking stub left over from the Continental Garage, a button and a dirty handkerchief were all I had to offer. I put them on the desk and removed my belt and shoelaces, added them to the little pile. The sergeant wrote my name on a large brown manila envelope and started to fill it with my possessions.

"I'd like to keep the wallet, Sergeant," I said. He went through it carefully. All it contained was a small snapshot of Helen taken when she was seven years old. The little snapshot showed a girl in a white dress and Mary Jane slippers standing in the sunlight in front of a concrete bird-bath. Her eyes were squinted against the sun and she stood pigeontoed, with her hands behind her back. Once in a while, I liked to look at it. The sergeant tossed me the wallet with the picture and I shoved it into my pocket.

I was fingerprinted, pictures were taken of my face, profile and full-face, and then I was turned over to the jailer. He was quite old, and walked with an agonized limp. We entered the elevator, were whisked up several floors, and then he led me down a long corridor to the shower room.

After I undressed and folded my clothes neatly on the wooden bench I got under the shower and adjusted the water as hot as I could stand it. The water felt wonderful. I let the needle streams beat into my upturned face. It sluiced down over my body, warming me through and through. I soaped myself roughly with the one-pound cake of dark-brown laundry soap, stood under the hot water again.

I toweled myself with an olive drab towel and dressed in the blue pants and blue work shirt that were laid out on the bench. The trousers were too large around the waist and I had to hold them up with one hand. I followed Mr. Benson the jailer to the special block and he opened the steel door and locked it behind us. We walked down the narrow corridor to the last cell. He unlocked the door, pointed, and I entered. He clanged the door to, locked it with his key. As he turned to leave I hit him up for a smoke. He passed a cigarette through the bars, lighted it for me with his Zippo lighter.

"I suppose you've had breakfast already," he said gruffly.

"No, but I'm not hungry anyway."

"You mean you couldn't stand a cup of coffee?"

"I suppose I could drink a cup of coffee all right."

"I'll get you one then. No use playing coy with me. When you want something you gotta speak up. I ain't no mind-reader."

He limped away and I could hear the slap-and-drag of his feet all the way down the corridor. While I waited for the coffee I investigated my cell. The walls were gray, freshly-painted, but the paint didn't cover all of the obscene drawings and initials beneath the paint where former occupants had scratched their records. I read some of the inscriptions: FRISCO KID '38, H. E., J. D., KILROY WAS HERE, Smoe, DENVER JACK, and others. Along the length of the entire wall, chest high, in two inch letters, someone had cut deeply into the plaster:

UP YOUR RUSTY DUSTY WITH A FLOY FLOY

This was very carefully carved. It must have taken the prisoner a long time to complete it.

A porcelain toilet, without a wooden seat, a washbowl with one spigot of cold water, and a tier of three steel beds with thin cotton pads for mattresses completed the inventory of the cell. No window. I unfastened the chains and let the bottom bunk down. I sat down on it and finished half my cigarette. Instead of throwing the butt away I put it into my shirt pocket. It was all I had. Presently, Mr. Benson came back with my coffee and passed the gray enameled cup through the bars.

"I didn't know whether you liked it with sugar and cream so I brought it black," he said.

"That's fine." I took the cup gratefully and sipped it. It was almost boiling hot and I had to let it cool some before I could finish it, but Mr. Benson waited patiently. When I passed him the empty cup he gave me a fresh sack of tobacco and a sheaf of brown cigarette papers.

"Know how to roll 'em, Jordan?"

"Sure. Thanks a lot." I made a cigarette.

"You get issued a sack every day, but no matches. If you want a light you gotta holler. Okay?"

"Sure." Mr. Benson lit my cigarette and limped away again

down the hollow-sounding corridor. The heavy end door clanged and locked.

The reaction set in quickly, the reaction to Helen's death, my attempt at suicide, the effects of the liquor, all of it. It was the overall cumulation of events that hit me all at once. My knees, my legs, my entire body began to shake violently and I couldn't control any part of it. The wet cigarette fell apart in my hand and I dropped to my knees in a praying position. I started to weep, at first soundlessly, then blubbering, the tears rolled down my cheeks, streamed onto my shirt. Perspiration poured from my body. I prayed:

"Dear God up there! Put me through to Helen! I'm still here, baby! Do you hear me! Please hang on a little while and wait for me! I'll be with you as soon as they send me! I'm all alone now, and it's hard, hard, hard! I'll be with you soon, soon, soon! I love you! Do you you hear me, sweetheart? I love you! I LOVE YOU!"

From one of the cells down the corridor a thick, gutteral voice answered mine: "And I love you, too!" The voice paused, added disgustedly: "Why don't you take a goddam break for Christ's sake!"

I stopped praying, or talking to Helen, whatever I was doing, and stretched out full length on the concrete floor. I stretched my arms out in front of me and pressed my mouth against the cold floor. In that prone position I cried myself out, silently, and it took a long time. I didn't try to pull myself together, because I knew that I would never cry again.

Afterwards, I washed my face with the cold tap water at the washbowl and dried my wet face with my shirt tail. I sat down on the edge of my bunk and carefully tailored another cigarette. It was a good one, nice and fat and round. Getting to my feet I crossed to the barred door.

"Hey! Mr. Benson!" I shouted. "How's about a light?"

FIFTEEN

Confession

LUNCH consisted of beef stew, rice, stewed apricots and coffee. After the delayed-action emotional ordeal I had undergone I was weak physically and I ate every scrap of food on my aluminum tray. With my stomach full, for the first time in weeks, I lay down on the bottom bunk, covered myself with the clean gray blanket and fell asleep immediately.

Mr. Benson aroused me at four-thirty by rattling an empty cup along the bars of my cell. It was time to eat again. The supper was a light one; fried mush, molasses and coffee with a skimpy dessert of three stewed prunes. Again I cleaned the tray, surprised at my hunger. I felt rested, contented, better than I had felt in months. My headache had all but disappeared and the peaceful solitude of my cell was wonderful. Mr. Benson picked up the tray and gave me a book of paper matches before he left. He was tired of walking the length of the corridor to light my cigarettes. I lay on my back on the hard bunk and enjoyed my cigarette. After I stubbed it out on the floor I closed my eyes. When I opened them again it was morning and Mr. Benson was at the bars with my breakfast. Two pieces of bread, a thimble-sized paper cupful of strawberry jam and a cup of coffee.

About an hour after breakfast the old jailer brought a razor and watched me shave with the cold water and the brown laundry soap. In another hour he brought my clothes to the cell. My corduroy slacks and jacket had been sponged and pressed and were fairly presentable.

"Your shirt's in the laundry," he said, "but you can wear your tie with the blue shirt."

"Where am I going?" I asked as I changed clothes.

"The D.A. wants to talk to you. Just leave them blue work pants on the bunk. You gotta change when you get back anyways."

"Okay," I agreed. I tied my necktie as well as I could without a mirror, just as I had shaved without a mirror. I followed Mr. Benson's limping drag down the corridor and this time I took an interest in the other prisoners in the special block, looking into each cell as I passed. There were eight cells, all of them along one side facing the passage wall, but only two others in addition to mine were occupied with prisoners. One held a sober-looking middle-aged man sitting on his bunk staring at his steepled fingers, and the other held a spiky-haired, blond youth with a broken nose and one cocked violet eye. He cocked it at me as I passed the cell and his sullen face was without expression. I quickly concluded that he was the one who had mocked me the day before and I had an over-whelming desire to kick his teeth in.

A plainclothes detective, wearing his hat, met us at the end of the corridor, signed for me, cuffed me to his wrist and we walked down the hall to the elevator. We silently rode the elevator down to the third floor, got out, and walked down a carpeted hallway to a milk-glass door with a block-lettered inscription. Asst District Atty San Francisco. We entered the office and the detective removed the cuff and left the room. The office was small and shabbily furnished. There was a bat-tered, oak desk, a shelf of heavy law books, four straight chairs and a row of hunting prints on the sepia-tinted wall across from the bookshelf. The prints were all of gentlewomen, sit-ting their horses impossibly and following hounds over a field-stone wall. All four prints were exactly the same. I sat down in one of the chairs and a moment later two men entered. The first through the door was a young man with a very white skin and a blue-black beard hovering close to the surface of his chin. It was the kind of beard that shows, because I could tell by the scraped skin on his jaws that he had shaved that morning. He wore a shiny, blue gabardine suit and oversized glasses with imitation tortoise-shell rims. Business-like, he sat behind the desk and studied some papers in a folder. The other man was quite old. He had lank white hair drooping down over his ears and there was a definite tremor in his long, talon-like fingers. His suit coat and trousers didn't match and he carried a shorthand pad and several sharpened pencils. It seemed unusual to me that the city would employ such an old man as a stenographer. His white head nodded rapidly up and down and it never stopped its meaningless bobbing throughout the interview, but his deepset eyes were bright and alert and without glasses.

The younger man closed the folder and shoved it into the top drawer of his desk. His eyes fastened on mine and without taking them away he extracted a king-sized cigarette from the package on the desk, flipped the desk lighter and the flame found the end of the cigarette perfectly. He did this little business without looking away from my eyes at all. A movie gangster couldn't have done it better. After three contemplative drags on the cigarette he crushed it out in the glass ash-tray, rested his elbows on the desk, cradled his square chin in his hands and leaned forward.

"My name is Robert Seely." His voice was deep and resonant with a lot of college speech training behind it. "I'm one of the assistant District Attorneys and your case has been assigned to me." He hesitated, and for a moment I thought he was going to shake hands with me, but he didn't make such an offer. He changed his steady gaze to the old man.

"Are you ready, Timmy?"

The old man, Timmy, held up his pencils and notebook in reply.

"I want to ask you a few questions," Robert Seely said. "Your name is . . . ?"

"Harry Jordan."

"And your residence?"

I gave him my roominghouse address.

"Occupation?"

"Art teacher."

"Place of employment?"

"Unemployed."

"What was the name of the woman you murdered?"

"Helen Meredith. Mrs. Helen Meredith."

"What was she doing in your room?"

"She lived there . . . the past few weeks."

"Where is her husband, Mr. Meredith?"

"I don't know. She said something once about him living in San Diego, but she wasn't sure of it."

"Did Mrs. Meredith have another address here in the city?"

"No. Before she moved to San Francisco she lived with her

mother in San Sienna. I don't know that address either, but her mother's name is Mrs. Mathews. I don't know the first name."

"All right. Take one." He pushed the package of cigarettes across the desk and I removed one and lighted it with the desk lighter. Mr. Seely held the open package out to the ancient stenographer.

"How can I smoke and take this down too?" the old man squeaked peevishly.

"Why did you kill Mrs. Meredith?" Mr. Seely asked me.

"Well, I . . ." I hesitated.

"Before we go any further, Jordan, I think I'd better tell you that anything you say may be held against you. Do you understand that?"

"You should've told him that before," the old man said sarcastically.

"I'm handling this interview, Timmy," Mr. Seely said coldly. "Your job is to take it down. Now, Jordan, are you aware that what you say may be held against you?"

"Of course. I don't care about that."

"Why, then, did you kill Mrs. Meredith?"

"In a way, it's a long story."

"Just tell it in your own words."

"Well, we'd been drinking, and once before we'd tried suicide and it didn't work so we went to the hospital and asked for psychiatric help."

"What hospital was that?"

"Saint Paul's. We stayed for a week, that is, Helen was in a week. I was only kept for three days."

"How did you attempt suicide?"

"With a razor blade." I held my arms over the desk, showing him the thin red scars on my wrists. "The psychiatric help we received was negligible. We started to drink as soon as we were released from the hospital. Anyway, I couldn't work very well and drink too. The small amount of money I made wouldn't stretch and I was despondent all the time."

"And was Mrs. Meredith despondent, too?"

"She always took my moods as her own. If I was happy, she was happy. We were perfectly compatible in every respect—counterparts, rather. So that's how I happened to kill her, you see. She knew all along I was going to kill myself sooner or later and she made me promise to kill her first. So I did. Afterwards I turned on the gas. The next thing I knew, Mrs. McQuade—that's my landlady—was hollering and pounding on the door. My—Helen was dead and I wasn't." With food in my stomach and a good night's sleep and a cigarette in my hand it was easy for me to talk about it.

"I have your suicide note, Jordan, and I notice it's written in charcoal. In the back of your mind, did you have an idea you could rub the charcoal away in case the suicide didn't work? Why did you use charcoal?"

"I didn't have a pencil."

Timmy chuckled at my reply, avoided Mr. Seely's icy stare and bent over his notebook.

"Then the death of Mrs. Meredith was definitely premeditated?"

"Yes, definitely. I plead guilty to everything, anything."

"Approximately what time was it when you choked her?"

"I don't know exactly. Somewhere between one and two a.m. Right afterwards I went out and got a pint of gin at the delicatessen down the street. It must have been before two or it wouldn't have been open."

"What delicatessen?"

"Mr. Watson's. Mrs. Watson sold me the gin, though. I still owe her forty-three cents."

"All right. We'll check the time with her. The police arrested you at ten minutes after eight. If you actually intended to commit suicide, why did you leave your transom open?"

"I don't know. I must have forgot about it, I guess."

"Did you drink the pint of gin?"

"It was a cold night, and I needed something to warm me up."

"I see. Where did you teach art last? You said you were an—"

"Lately I've been working around town as a counterman or fry cook."

"Do you have a particular lawyer in mind? I can get in touch with one for you."

"No. I don't need a lawyer. I'm guilty and that's the way

I plead. I don't like to go through all this red tape. I expected to be dead by now and all these questions are inconvenient. The sooner I get it over with in the gas chamber the happier I'll be."

"Are you willing to sign a confession to that effect?"

"Certainly. I'll sign anything that'll speed things up."

"How did you and Mrs. Meredith get together in the first place?"

I thought the question over and decided it was none of his business.

Timmy's head stopped bobbing up and down and wagged back and forth from side to side for a change. "He doesn't have to answer questions like that, Mr. Seely," he said in his weak whining voice. The two men stared at each other distastefully and Timmy won the battle of the eyes.

"Have you got enough for a confession, Timmy?" Mr. Seely asked the old man, at last.

"Plenty." Timmy nodded his white head up and down.

"That's all I have then, Jordan," Mr. Seely said. "No. One more question. Do you want to complain you were mentally unstable at the time? Or do you think you're mentally ill now?"

"Of course not. I'm perfectly sane and I knew what I was doing at the time. I'd planned it for several weeks."

"You'd better put that in the confession, Timmy." Mr. Seely left the desk and opened the door. The detective was waiting in the hall. "You can return Jordan to his cell now," Mr. Seely told the detective.

I was handcuffed and taken back to the special block and turned over to Mr. Benson. Back in my cell I changed back to my jail clothes and Mr. Benson took my own clothes away on a wire coat hanger. I was alone in my quiet cell.

My mind was much more at ease than it had been before. Thinking back over the interview I felt quite satisfied that the initial step was taken and the ball rolling. Blind justice would filter in and get me sooner or later. It was pleasant to look forward to the gas chamber. What a nice, easy way to die! So painless. Silent and practically odorless and clean! I would sit in a chair, wearing a pair of new black trunks, and stare back at a few rows of spectators staring at me. I would hear nothing and smell nothing. Then I would be dead. When I writhed on the floor and went into convulsions I wouldn't even know about it. Actually, it would be a much more horrible experience for the witnesses than it would be for me. This knowledge gave me a feeling of morbid satisfaction. I had to laugh.

Soon it was time for lunch. Mr. Benson brought a tray to my cell containing boiled cabbage, white meat, bread and margarine, raspberry jello and black coffee. I attacked the food with relish. Food had never tasted better. My mind was relieved now that things were underway and I wasn't eating in a greasy cafe and I hadn't had to cook the food myself. I suppose that is why it all tasted so good. After wiping up the cabbage pot-licker with the last of my bread I rolled and smoked a cigarette. Mr. Benson took the tray away and was back in a few minutes with Old Timmy.

"I've got your confession ready, boy," the old man said.

Timmy signed for me and we left the block for the elevator. After Timmy pushed the button for the third floor, he turned and smiled at me, bobbing his head up and down.

"You aren't sensitive, are you, Jordan?"

"How do you mean," I asked, puzzled.

"Well, it isn't really necessary for me to take you downstairs to sign your confession, and when you aren't in the block you're supposed to wear regular clothes instead of these . . ." He plucked at my blue jail shirt. "And I'm supposed to have a police officer along too." He laughed thinly. "But some of the girls in the office wanted to get a look at you. Funny, the way these young girls go for the *crime passionell*. I didn't think you'd mind."

We walked down the carpeted hallway of the third floor and entered a large office that held five desks, each with telephone and typewriter. Old Timmy winked at me as I nervously looked at the nine women who had crowded into the office. They were all ages, but were still considered girls by Old Timmy.

"This is the steno pool," Timmy said as we crossed to his desk.

"I see it is," I replied.

"I been in charge of this office for thirty-one years." He

had seven neatly typed copies of my confession on his desk and I signed them all with a ball point pen. He called two of the girls over to sign on the witness lines and they came forward timidly and signed where he held his talon-like finger. I had the feeling if I said boo the girls would jump through the window. After they signed their names they rejoined the other women, and the silent group stared at me boldly as we left the office. As Timmy shut the door behind us I heard the foolish giggling begin and so did the old man.

"I hope it didn't bother you, boy," he said. "They're just women."

"Yes, I know," I replied meaninglessly.

We entered the elevator again and Timmy pushed the button and looked at me friendlily.

"What do you think of our brilliant Assistant District Attorney, the eminent Mr. Seely?" There were sharp overtones of sarcasm in his thin, whining voice.

"I don't think anything of him," I said. "That is, one way or the other," I amended.

"He's an ass!" Timmy said convincingly. "I'd like to assign him a case."

"It doesn't make any difference to me," I said.

"You should have read your confession, boy. It's iron-tight, you can bet on that. It's a good habit to get into, reading what you sign."

"I'm not making any more habits, good or bad," I said.

Timmy chuckled deep in his throat. "You're right about that!"

We reached the special block and I returned to the custody of Mr. Benson. He opened the heavy end door and Old Timmy shook hands with me before he left, bobbed his head up and down.

He turned away, head bobbing, hands jerking, and tottered down the corridor, his feet silent on the concrete floor.

I settled down in my cell to wait. I would be tried as a matter of course, convicted, and go to wait some more in the death row at San Quentin. There, after a prescribed period and on a specified date, I would be executed. And that was that.

I wondered how long it all would take.

SIXTEEN

Sanity Test

I DON'T know how long I waited in my quiet cell before I was taken out of it again. It might have been three days, four days or five days. There was no outside light, just the refulgent electric bulbs in my cell and in the corridor, and if it hadn't been for the meals, I wouldn't have known the time of day. I didn't worry about the time; I let it slip by unnoticed. I was fed and I was allowed to take a shower every day. And the forty slim cigarettes that can be rolled from a sack of Bull Durham were just enough to last me one full day. Mr. Benson let me have matches when I ran out, and I got by very well. After breakfast one morning, Mr. Benson brought my clothes down to my cell.

"Get dressed, Jordan," he told me, "you're going on a little trip."

"Where to?"

"Get dressed, I said."

My white shirt, stiffly starched, was back from the laundry. I tore off the cellophane wrapping, put it on, my slacks, tied my necktie. The jailer gave me my belt and shoelaces and I put the laces in my shoes, the belt through the trouser loops, slipped into my sports jacket.

"Don't you know where I'm going?" I asked.

"Of course I know. Hospital. Observation."

I hesitated at the door of my cell. "Hell, I'm all right. I don't want to go to any hospital for observation. I signed a confession; what more do they want?"

"Don't worry about it," Mr. Benson reassured me. "It's routine. They always send murder suspects to the hospital nowadays. It's one of the rules."

"It isn't just me then?"

"No. It's routine. Come on, I ain't got all day."

I followed him down the corridor, but my mind didn't accept his glib explanation. I didn't believe my stay in the hospital would be very long, but I didn't want them to get any ideas that I was insane. That would certainly delay my case and I wanted to get it over with as soon as possible. Right then, I made up my mind to cooperate with the psychiatrist, no matter what it cost me in embarrassment. It wouldn't do at all to be found criminally insane and to spend the rest of my life in an institution.

The detective was the same one who had taken me downstairs for my interview with Mr. Seely. He still had his hat on, and after he signed for me, and we were riding down in the elevator, I took a closer look at him. He was big and tough looking, with the inscrutable look that old time criminals and old time policemen have in common. To be friendly, I tried to start a little conversation with the man.

"Those other two guys, the ones in the special block with me; what are they in for?" I asked him.

"What do you want to know for?"

"Just curious, I suppose."

"You prisoners are all alike. You get in trouble and you want to hear about others in the same fix. If it makes you feel any better, I'll tell you this: they're in a lot worse shape than you are."

We got out of the elevator in the basement and climbed into the back of a white ambulance that was waiting at the loading ramp. The window in back was covered with drawn gray curtains and I couldn't see anything on the way to the hospital. But on the way, the detective told me about the other two prisoners, and like he said, they were in worse shape than I was in. The blond young man had killed his mother with an ax in an argument over the car keys, and the middle-aged man had killed his wife and three children with a shotgun and then had lost his nerve and failed to kill himself. It made me ill to hear about the two men and I was sorry I had asked about them.

A white-jacketed orderly met us at the hospital's receiving entrance and signed the slip the detective gave him. He was a husky, young man in his early thirties and there was a broad smile on his face. His reddish hair was closely cropped in a fresh crew-cut and there was a humorous expression in his blue eyes. The detective uncuffed me, put the slip of paper in his pocket and winked at the orderly.

"He's your baby, Hank," he said.

"We'll take good care of him, don't worry," the orderly said good-naturedly and I followed him inside the hospital. We entered the elevator and rode it up to the sixth floor. Hank had to unlock the elevator door with a key before we could leave the elevator. As soon as we were in the hallway he locked the elevator door again and we left the hallway for a long narrow corridor with locked cells on both sides of it. He unlocked the door marked Number 3, and motioned for me to enter. It was a small windowless room and the walls were of unpainted wood instead of gray plaster. There were no bunks, just a mattress on the floor without sheets, and a white, neatly folded blanket at the foot. The door was made of thick, heavy wood, several layers thick, with a small spy-hole at eye-level, about the size of a silver dollar. Hank started to close the door on me and I was terrified, irrationally so.

"Don't!" I said quickly. "Don't shut me up, please! Leave it open, I won't try to run away."

He nodded, smiling. "All right, I'll leave it open a crack. I'm going to get you some pajamas and I'll be back in a few minutes. You start undressing." He closed the door partially and walked away.

I removed my jacket, shirt and pants, and standing naked except for my shoes I waited apprehensively for Hank's return. It wasn't exactly a padded cell, but it was the next thing to it. I was really frightened. For the first time I knew actual terror. There is a great difference between being locked in a jail cell and being locked in a madman's cell. At the jail I was still an ordinary human being, a murderer, yes, but a normal man locked up in jail with other normal men. Here, in addition to being a murderer, I was under serious suspicion, like a dangerous lunatic, under observation from a tiny spy-hole, not to be trusted. Mr. Benson must have lied to me. Evidently, they thought I was crazy. Why would they lock me away in such a room if they didn't think so? I wanted a cigarette to calm my fears, but I didn't dare call out for one or rap on the door. I was even afraid to look out the open door, afraid they would think I was trying to escape, and then I would be put into a padded cell for sure. From now on I would have to watch out for everything I did, everything I said. Full cooperation. That is what they would get from me. From now on.

The orderly returned with a pair of blue broadcloth pajamas, a thin white cotton robe and a pair of skivvy slippers.

"Shoes too, Harry," he said.

I sat down on the mattress, removed my shoes and socks
and slid my feet into the skivvy slippers. He dropped my
clothes into a blue sack and pulled the cords tight at the top.
He had a kind face and he winked at me.

"Just take it easy, Harry," he said, "I'll be back in a
minute."

It was a little better having something to cover my nakedness. Still, there is a psychological effect to hospital pajamas.
Wearing them, a man is automatically a patient, and a patient
is a sick man or he wouldn't be in a hospital. That was the
way I saw it, the only way I could see it. Hank returned with
a syringe and needle and took a blood sample from my right
arm. When he turned to leave I asked him timidly for a
cigarette.

"Why, shore," he said and reached into his jacket pocket.
He handed me a fresh package of king-sized Chesterfields and
I opened it quickly, stuck a cigarette in my mouth. He flipped
his lighter for me and said: "Keep the pack." I was pleased
to note that my hands had stopped shaking. "I can't give you
any matches," Hank continued, "but anytime you want a
light or want to go to the can, just holler. My name is Hank,
and I'm at the end of the hall."

"Thanks, Hank," I said appreciatively. "It's nice to smoke
tailor-mades again. I've been rolling them at the jail."

"They don't cost me nothing. And when you run out let
me know. I can get all I want from the Red Cross." He started
to leave with the blood sample, turned and smiled. "Don't
worry about the door. I know it's a little rough at first, but
I'm right down the hall and if you holler I can hear you. I'll
shut the door, but I won't latch it. Knowing you aren't locked
in is sometimes as good as an open door."

"Will you do that for me?" I asked eagerly.

"Why shore. This maximum security business is a lotta crap
anyway. The elevator's locked, there's no stairs, and the windows are all barred, and the door to the roof's locked. No
reason to lock your cell." He closed the door behind him,
and he didn't lock it.

I sat down on the mattress, my back to the pine wall and chain-smoked three cigarettes. It gave me something to do. If the rest of the staff was as nice to me as Hank I would be able to survive the ordeal and I knew it would be an ordeal. My short stay at Saint Paul's had given me a sample, but now I would be put through the real thing. At noon, Hank brought me my lunch on a tray. There was no knife or fork and I had to eat the lunch with a spoon. The food was better than the jail food, pork chops, french fries and ice cream, but it almost gagged me to eat it. I forced myself to clean the tray and saved the milk for the last. I gulped the milk down with one long swallow, hoping it would clear away the food that felt caught in my throat. When Hank returned for the tray he gave me a light for my smoke. He was pleased when he saw the empty tray.

"That's the way, Harry," he nodded and smiled good-naturedly. "Eat all you can. A man feels better with a full gut. The doctor'll be back after a while and he'll talk to you then. Don't let him worry you. He's a weirdie. All these psychiatrists are a little nuts themselves."

"I'll try not to let it bother me," I said. "How long are they going to keep me here, anyway?"

"I don't know." He grinned. "That all depends."

"You mean it all depends on me?"

"That's right. And the doctor." He left with the tray, closing the door.

About one-thirty or two Hank returned for me and we left the cell and corridor and entered a small office off the main hallway. The office wasn't much larger than my cell, but it contained a barred window that let in a little sunlight. Through the window I could observe the blue sky and the bright green plot of grass in the park outside the hospital. The doctor was seated behind his desk and he pointed to the chair across from it.

"Sit down, Jordan," he said. "Hank, you can wait outside."

There was a trace of accent in his voice. German, maybe Austrian. It was cultivated, but definitely foreign. That is the way it is in the United States. A native born American can't make a decent living and here was a foreigner all set to tell me what was wrong with me. He had a swarthy sunlamp tan and his black beard was so dark it looked dyed. It was an Imperial beard and it made him resemble the early photographs of Lenin.

"Your beard makes you look like Lenin," I said.

"Why thank you, thank you!" He took it as a compliment. I distrusted the man. There is something about a man with a beard I cannot stand. No particular reason for it. Prejudice, I suppose. I feel the same way about cats.

"I'm Doctor Fischbach," the doctor said unsmilingly. "You're to be here under my observation for a few days." He studied a sheaf of papers, clipped together with large-sized paper clips, for a full five minutes while I sat there under pressure feeling the perspiration rolling freely down my back and under my arms to the elbows. He wagged his bearded chin from side to side, clucked sympathetically.

"Too bad you entered Saint Paul's for help, Jordan." He continued to shake his head. "If you and Mrs. Meredith had come to me in the first place you would have been all right."

"Yeah," I said noncommittally. "You may be right."

"Did Saint Paul's give you any tests of any kind? If so, we could obtain them and save the time of taking them over."

"No, I didn't get any tests—just blood tests."

"Then let us begin with the Rorschach." Dr. Fischbach opened his untidy top desk drawer, dug around in its depths and brought out a stack of cards about six inches by six inches and set them before me, Number One on top. "These are ink blots, Jordan, as you can see. We'll go through the cards one by one and you tell me what they remind you of. Now, how about this one?" He shoved the first card across the desk and I studied it for a moment or so. It looked like nothing.

"It looks like an art student's groping for an idea," I suggested.

"Yes?" he encouraged me.

"It isn't much of anything. Sometimes, Doctor, when an artist is stuck for an idea, he'll doodle around with charcoal to see if he can come up with something. The meaningless lines and mass forms sometimes suggest an idea, and he can develop it into a picture. That's what these ink blots look like to me."

"How about right here?" He pointed with his pencil to

one of the larger blots. "Does this look like a butterfly to
you?"

"Not to me. No."

"What does it look like?"

"It looks like some artist has been doodling around with
black ink trying to get an idea." How many times did he want
me to tell him?

"You don't see a butterfly?" He seemed to be disappointed.

"No butterfly." I wanted to cooperate, but I couldn't see
any point in lying to the man. It was some kind of a trick he
was trying to pull on me. I stared hard at the card again,
trying to see something, some shape, but I couldn't. None of
the blots made a recognizable shape. I shook my head as he
went on to the next card which also had four strangely shaped
blots.

"Do these suggest anything?" he asked hopefully.

"Yeah," I said. If he wanted to trick me I would play one
on him. "I see a chicken in a sack with a man on its back; a
bottle of rum and I'll have some; a red-winged leek, and an
oversized beak; a pail of water and a farmer's daughter; a bottle of gin and a pound of tin; a false-faced friend and days
without end; a big brown bear and he's going everywhere; a
big banjo and a—"

He jerked the cards from the desk and shoved them into
the drawer. He looked at me seriously without any expression
on his dark face and twisted the point of his beard with thumb
and forefinger. My thin cotton robe was oppressively warm. I
smiled, hoping it was ingratiating enough to please the doctor.
Like all doctors, I knew, he didn't have a sense of humor.

"I really want to cooperate with you, Doctor," I said
meekly, "but I actually can't see anything in those ink blots.
I'm an artist, or at least I used to be, and as an artist I can
see anything I want to see in anything."

"That's quite all right, Jordan," he said quietly. "There are
other tests." When he got to his feet I noticed he was slightly
humpbacked and I had a strong desire to rub his hump for
good luck. "Come on with me." I followed him down the
hall, Hank trailing us behind. We entered another small room
that was furnished with a small folding table, typing paper and
a battered, standard Underwood typewriter.

"Do you know how to typewrite, Jordan?" the doctor asked me.

"Some. I haven't typed since I left high school though."

"Sit down."

I sat down at the folding table and the doctor left the room. Hank lit a cigarette for me and before I finished it the doctor was back with another stack of cards. These were about eight by ten inches. He put the stack on the table and picked up the first card to show it to me. "You'll have fun with these."

The first picture was a reproduction of an oil painting in black and white. It was a portrait of a young boy in white blouse and black knickers. His hair was long, with a Dutch bob, and he had a delicate, wistful face. He held a book in his hand. From the side of the portrait a large hand reached out from an unseen body and rested lightly on the boy's shoulder. The background was an ordinary living room with ordinary, old-fashioned furniture. Table, chairs, potted plants and two vases full of flowers made the picture a bit cluttered.

"What I want you to do is this:" Dr. Fischbach explained, "Examine each picture carefully and then write a little story about it. Anything at all, but write a story. You've got plenty of paper and all the time in the world. After you finish with each one, put the story and picture together and start on the next one. Number the story at the top with the same number the picture has and they won't get mixed up. Any questions?"

"No, but I'm not much of a story teller. I don't hardly know the difference between syntax and grammar."

"Don't let that bother you. I'm not looking for polished prose, I merely want to read the stories. Get started now, and if you want to smoke, Hank'll be right outside the door to give you a light. Right, Hank?"

"Yes, sir," Hank replied with his customary smile.

They left the room and I examined the little print for a while and then put a piece of paper into the machine. It wasn't fun, as Dr. Fischbach had suggested, but it passed the time away and I would rather have something to do, anything, rather than sit in the bleak cell they had assigned me. I wrote that the young boy was sitting for his portrait and during the long period of posing he got tired and fidgety. The hand resting on his shoulder was that of his father and it was merely

comforting the boy and telling him the portrait would soon
be over. In a few lines I finished the dull tale.

Each picture I tackled was progressively impressionistic and
it did become fun after all, once I got interested. The last
three reproductions were in color, in a surrealistic vein, and
they bordered on the uncanny and weird. However, I made
up stories on them all, pecking them out on the old machine,
even though some of the stories were quite senseless. When I
finished, I racked stories and cards together and called Hank.
He was down at the end of the hall talking to a nurse. He
dropped the cards and stories off at the doctor's office and
we started back to my cell. I stopped him.

"Just a second, Hank," I said. "Didn't you say something
about a roof?"

"I don't know. We've got a roof," and he pointed toward
a set of stairs leading up, right next to the elevator.

"After being cooped up so long," I said, "I'd like to get
some fresh air. Do you suppose the doc would let me go up
on the roof for a smoke before I go back to that little tomb?
That is, if you go along."

"I'll ask him." Hank left me in the hall and entered the
little office. He was smiling when he came out a moment later.
"Come on," he said, taking my arm. We climbed the short
flight of stairs and Hank unlocked the door to the roof.

The roof was black tar-paper, but near the little building
that housed the elevator machinery and short stairwell to the
sixth floor, there were about twenty feet of duckboards scattered around and a small green bench. It was late in the afternoon and a little chilly that high above the ground, but we
sat and smoked on the bench for about an hour. Hank didn't
mind sitting up there with me, because, as he said, if he was
sitting around he wasn't working. He was an interesting man
to talk to.

"How come you stay with this line of work, Hank?" I asked
him.

"I drifted into it and I haven't drifted out. But it isn't as
bad as it looks. There are a lot of compensations." He winked.
"As a hot-shot male nurse, I rank somewhere between a doctor and an interne. I have to take orders from internes, but
my pay check is about ten times as big as theirs, almost as big

as some of the resident doctors. So the nurses, the lovely frustrated nurses, come flocking around, and I mean the female nurses. An interne doesn't make the dough to take them out and the doctors are married, or else they're too careful to get mixed up with fellow workers, you know, so I do all right. I get my own room right here, my meals, laundry and my money too. Funny thing about these nurses. They all look good in clean white uniforms and nice white shoes, but they look like hell when they dress up to go out. I've never known one yet who knew how to wear clothes on a date. They seem to be self-conscious about it too. But when the clothes come off, they're women, and that's the main thing with me. Did you see that nurse I was talking to in the hall?"

"I caught a glimpse of her."

"She'll be in my room tonight at eleven. So you see, Harry, taking care of nuts like you has its compensations." He slapped me on the knee. "Come on, let's go." He laughed happily and I followed him down the stairs.

For supper that night I ate hamburger patties and boiled potatoes, lime jello and coffee. The mental work of thinking up stories had tired me and I fell asleep easily. As Hank said, having the door unlocked was almost like not being locked in.

The next morning I had another session with Dr. Fischbach. It was an easy one and didn't last very long. He gave me a written intelligence test. The questions were all fairly simple; questions like: "Who wrote *Faust*?", "How do you find the circumference of a circle?", "Who was the thirty-second president?", and so on. In the early afternoon I was given a brainwave test. It was rather painful, but interesting. After I was stretched out on a low operating table, fifty or more needles were stuck into my scalp, each needle attached with a wire to a machine. A man pushed gadgets on the machine and it made flip-flop sounds. It didn't hurt me and I didn't feel any electric shocks, but it was a little painful when the needles were inserted under the skin of my scalp. All of this procedure seemed like a great waste of time and I hated the ascetic loneliness of my wooden cell. Sleeping on the mattress without any springs made my back ache.

The next few boring days were all taken up with more tests.

X-Rays were taken of my chest, head and back.

Urine and feces specimens were taken.

More blood from my arm and from the end of my fore-finger.

My eyes, ears, nose and throat were examined.

My teeth were checked.

At last I began my series of interviews with Dr. Fischbach and these were the most painful experiences of all.

SEVENTEEN

Flashback

DOCTOR Leo Fischbach sat humped behind his desk twirling the point of his beard with thumb and forefinger. I often wondered if his beard was perfumed. It seemed to be the only link or concession between the rest of the world and his personality. If he had a personality. His large brown eyes, fixed and staring, were two dark mirrors that seemed to hold my image without interest, without curiosity, or at most, with an impersonal interest, the way one is interested in a dead, dry starfish, found on the beach. I was tense in my chair as I chain-smoked my free cigarettes and the longer I looked at Dr. Fischbach, the more I hated him. My efforts at total recollection, and he was never satisfied with less, had exhausted me. I began to speak again, my voice harsh and grating to my ears.

"The war, if anything, Doctor, was only another incident in my life. A nice long incident, but all the same, just another. I don't think it affected me at all. I was painting before I was drafted and that's all I did after I got in."

"Tell me about this, er, incident."

"Well, after I was drafted I was assigned to Fort Benning, Georgia. And after basic training I was pulled out of the group to paint murals in the mess-halls there. I was quite happy about this and I was given a free hand. Not literally, but for the army it was a good deal. Naturally, I knew the type of pictures they wanted and that's what I gave them. If I'd attempted a few non-objective pictures I'd have been handed a rifle in a hurry. So I painted army scenes. Stuff like paratroopers dropping out of the sky, a thin line of infantrymen in the field, guns, tank columns and so on."

"Did this type of thing satisfy you? Did you feel you were sacrificing your artistic principles by painting this way?"

"Not particularly. If I thought of it at all I knew I had a damned good deal. I was painting while other soldiers were drilling, running obstacle courses and getting shot at somewhere or other. I missed all that, you see. As a special duty man I was excused from everything except painting."

"You didn't paint murals for the duration of the war, did you?"

"Not at Fort Benning, no. After a year I was transferred to Camp Gordon—that's in Georgia too, at Augusta."

"What did you do there?"

"I painted murals in mess-halls."

"Didn't you have any desire for promotion?"

"No. None at all. But they promoted me anyway. I was made a T/5. Same pay as corporal but no rank or responsibilities."

"How was your reaction to the army? Did you like it?"

"I don't know."

"Did you dislike it then?"

"I don't know. I was in the army. Everybody was in the army."

"How were you treated?"

"In the army everybody is the same. Nobody bothered me, because I was on special duty. Many times the officers would come around and inspect the murals I was working on. They were well pleased, very happy about them. Knowing nothing at all about art was to their advantage. On two different occasions I was given letters of commendation for my murals. Of course, they didn't mean anything. Officers like to give letters like that; they believe it is good for morale. Maybe it is, I don't know."

"What did you do in your off-duty time in Georgia?"

Again I had to think back. What had I done? All I could

remember was a blur of days, distant and hazy days. Pine trees, sand and cobalt skies. And on pay-days, gin and a girl. The rest of the month—days on a scaffolding in a hot wooden building, painting, doing the best I could with regular house paint, finishing up at the end of the day, tired but satisfied, grateful there was no sergeant to make me change what I had done. A shower, a trip to the first movie, bed by nine. Was there nothing else?

"Well, I slept a lot. It was hot in Georgia and I slept. I worked and then I hit the sack."

"When did you get discharged?"

"November, 1945. And then instead of returning to Chicago I decided to come out to California and finish art school out here."

"Why?"

"I must have forgotten to tell you about it. I had a wife and child in Chicago."

"Yes, you did." He made a note on his pad. He made his notes in a bastard mixture of loose German script and Speedwriting. "This is the first time you've mentioned a wife and child."

"It must have slipped my mind. It was some girl I married while I was attending the Chicago Art Institute. She has a child, a boy, that's right, a boy. She named him John, after her father. John Jordan is his name. I've never seen him."

"Why didn't you return to your wife and child? Didn't you want to see your son? Sometimes a son is considered a great event in a man's life."

"Is that right? I considered it an unnecessary expense. I came to California because it was the practical thing to do. If I'd gone to Chicago I wouldn't have been able to continue with my painting. It would have been necessary for me to go to work and support Leonie and the child. And I didn't want to do it."

"Didn't you feel any responsibility for your wife? Or to the child?"

"Of course I did. That's why I didn't go back. I didn't want to live up to the responsibility. It was more important to paint instead. An artist paints and a husband works."

"Where's your family now?"

"I imagine they're still in Chicago. After I left the army I didn't write to her any more."

"Do you have any curiosity about how they're faring?"

"Not particularly."

Curiosity. That was an ill-chosen word for him to use. I could remember my wife well. She was a strong, intelligent, capable young woman. She thought she was a sculptor, but she had as much feeling for form as a steel worker. She didn't like Epstein and her middle-western mind couldn't grasp his purported intentions. If a statue wasn't pretty she didn't like it. But she was good on the pointing-apparatus and a fair copyist. Her drawings were rough but solid, workmanlike. She would get by, anywhere. And my son was only an accident anyway. I certainly didn't want a child, and she hadn't either. But she had one and as long as he was with his mother, as he should be, he was eating. I had no doubt about that, and no curiosity.

"And then you entered the L.A. Art Center," Dr. Fischbach prodded.

"That's right. I attended the Center for almost a year, under the G.I. Bill."

"Did you obtain a degree?"

"Just an A.A. Things didn't go so well for me after the war. I had difficulty returning to my non-objective style and I was unable to finish any picture I started. I still can't understand it. I could visualize, to a certain extent, what my picture would look like on canvas, but I couldn't achieve it. I began and tossed aside painting after painting. The rest of my academic work was way above the average. It was easy to paint academically and I could draw as well as anybody, but that wasn't my purpose in painting."

"So you quit."

"You might say I quit. But actually, I was offered a teaching job at a private school. I weighed things over in my mind and decided to accept it. I thought I'd have more free time to paint and a place to work as an art teacher. The Center was only a place to paint and as a teacher I'd get more money than the G.I. Bill paid."

"What school did you teach at?"

"Mansfield. It's between Oceanside and San Diego. It's a rather conservative little school. There isn't much money in the endowment and the regents wouldn't accept state aid. There were about a hundred and thirty students and most of them were working their way through. It wasn't accredited under the G.I. Bill."

"How did you like teaching?"

"Painting can't be taught, Doctor. Either a man can paint or he can't. I felt that most of the students were being duped, cheated out of their money. It's one thing to study art with money furnished by a grateful government, but it's something else to pay out of your own pocket for something you aren't getting. And every day I was more convinced that I wasn't a painter and never would be one. After a while I quit painting altogether. But I hung onto my job at Mansfield because I didn't know what else to do with myself. Without art as an emotional outlet I turned to drinking as a substitute and I've been drinking ever since."

"Why did you leave Mansfield then?"

"I was fired. After I started to drink I missed a lot of classes. And I never offered any excuses when I didn't show up. In my spare time I talked to some of the more inept students and persuaded them to quit painting and go into something else. Somehow, the school didn't like that. But I was only being honest. I was merely balancing the praise I gave to the students who were good."

"After you were fired, did you come directly to San Francisco?"

"Not directly. It kind of took me by surprise, getting fired, I mean. They thought they had every reason to fire me, but I didn't expect it. I was one of the most popular teachers at the school, that is, with the students. But I suppose drinking had dulled my rational mind to the situation."

"And you felt persecuted?"

"Oh, no, nothing like that. After I got my terminal pay I thought things out. I wanted to get away from the city and things connected with culture, back to the land. Well, not back to it, because I'd never been a farmer or field hand, always in cities, you know. But at the time I felt if I could work in the open, using my muscles, doing really hard labor,

I'd be able to sleep again. So that's what I did. I picked grapes in Fresno, and around Merced. I hit the sugar beet harvests in Chico, drifted in season, over to Utah, and I spent an entire summer in the Soledad lettuce fields."

"Were you happier doing that type of work?"

"I was completely miserable. All my life I had only wanted to paint. There isn't any substitute for painting. Coming to a sudden, brutal stop left me without anything to look forward to. I had nothing. I drank more and more and finally I couldn't hold a field hand's job, not even in the lettuce fields. That's when I came to San Francisco. It was a city and it was close. In a city a man can always live."

"And you've been here ever since?"

"That's right. I've gone from job to job, drinking when I've had the money, working for more when I ran out."

I dropped my head and sat quietly, my hands inert in my lap. I was drained. What possible good did it do the doctor to know these things about me? How could this refugee from Aachen analyze my actions for the drifting into nothingness when I didn't know myself? I was bored with my dull life. I didn't want to remember anything; all I wanted was peace and quiet. The silence that Death brings, an all-enveloping white cloak of everlasting darkness. By my withdrawal from the world I had made my own little niche and it was a dreary little place I didn't want to live in or tell about. But so was Doctor Fischbach's and his world was worse than mine. I wouldn't have traded places with him for anything. He sat across from me silently, fiddling with his idiotic beard, his dark eyes on the ceiling, evaluating my story, probing with his trained mind. I pitied him. The poor bastard thought he was a god.

Did I? This nasty thought hit me below the belt. How else could I have taken Helen's life if I didn't think so? What other justification was there for my brutal murder? I had no right or reason to take her with me into my nothingness. Harry Jordan had played the part of God too. It didn't matter that she had wanted to go with me. I still didn't have the right to kill her. But I had killed her and I had done it as though it was my right, merely because I loved her. Well, it was done now. No use brooding about it. At least I had done it unconsciously and I had been under the influence of gin. Doctor Fischbach was a different case. He was playing god deliberately. This strange, bearded individual had gone to medical school for years, deliberately studied psychiatry for another couple of years. He had been psychoanalyzed himself by some other foreigner who thought he was a god—and now satisfied, with an ego as large as Canada, he sat behind a desk digging for filth into other people's minds. What a miserable bastard he must be behind his implacable beard and face!

"During your employment as a field hand, Jordan, did you have any periods when you felt highly elated, followed by acute depression?"

"No," I said sullenly.

"Did you ever hear voices in the night, a voice talking to you?"

"No."

"As you go about the city, have you ever had the feeling you were being followed?"

"Only once. A man followed me with a gun in his hand, but he didn't shoot me."

"You saw this man with the gun?"

"That's right, but when I looked over my shoulder he was gone."

He made some rapid, scribbling notes on his pad.

"Did you ever see him again?"

"No."

"So far, you've been reluctant to tell me about your sexual relations with Mrs. Meredith. I need this information. It's important that I know about it."

"Not to me it isn't."

"I can't see why you object to telling me about it."

"Naturally, you can't. You think you're above human relationship. To tell you about my intimate life with Helen is indecent. She's dead now, and I have too much respect for her."

"Suppose we talk then about other women in your life. Your wife, for instance. You don't seem to have any attachment for her, of any great strength. Did you enjoy a normal marital relationship?"

"I always enjoy it, but not half as much as you do second-hand."

"How do you mean that?"

I got to my feet. "I'd like to go back to my cell, Doctor," I said, forcing the words through my compressed lips. "I don't feel like talking any more."

"Very well, Jordan. We'll talk some more tomorrow."

"I'd rather not."

"Why not?"

"I don't like to waste the time. I'm not crazy and you know it as well as I do. And I resent your vicarious enjoyment of my life's history and your dirty probing mind."

"You don't really think I enjoy this, Jordan?" he said with surprise.

"You must. If you didn't you'd go into some other kind of work. I can't believe anybody would sink so low just for money. I've gone down the ladder myself, but I haven't hit your level yet."

"I'm trying to help you, Jordan."

"You can help somebody that needs it then. I don't want your help." I turned abruptly and left his office. Hank got up from the bench outside the door and accompanied me to my cell.

My cell didn't frighten me any longer. It was a haven, an escape from Dr. Fischbach. I liked its bareness, the hard mattress on the floor. It no longer mattered that I didn't have a chair to sit down upon. After a while I forced my churning mind into pleasant, happier channels. I wondered what they would have for supper.

I was hungry as hell.

EIGHTEEN

The Big Fixation

WHEN I was about seven or eight years old, somebody gave me a map of the United States that was cut up into a jigsaw

puzzle. Whether I could read or not at the time I don't remember, but I had sense enough to start with the water surrounding the United States. These were the pieces with the
square edges and I realized if I got the outline all around I
could build toward the center a state at a time. This is the
way I worked it and when I came to Kansas it was the last
piece and it fitted into the center in the last remaining space.
This was using my native intelligence and it was the logical
method to put a jigsaw puzzle together. Evidently, Doctor
Fischbach did not possess my native intelligence. He skipped
around with his questions as he daily dug for more revelations
from my past and he reminded me of a door-to-door salesman
avoiding the houses with the BEWARE OF THE DOG signs.
Having started with my relationship with Helen, dropping
back to my art school days, returning to my childhood, then
back to Helen, we were back to my childhood again. I no
longer looked him in the eyes as we talked together, but focused my eyes on my hands or on the floor. I didn't want to
let him see the hate in my eyes.

"Did your mother love you?" he asked me. "Did you feel
that you got all of the attention you had coming to you?"

"Considering the fact that I had two brothers and five sisters I got my share. More than I deserved anyway, and I'm
not counting two other brothers that were stillborn."

"Did you feel left out in any way?"

"Left out of what?"

"Outside of the family. Were you always fairly treated?"

"Well, Doctor, money was always short during the depression, naturally, what with the large family and all, but I always
got my share. More, if anything. My father showed partiality
to me; I know that now. He thought I was more gifted than
my brothers and sisters."

"How did your father support the family? What type of
work did he do? Was he a professional man?"

"No. He didn't have a profession, not even a trade. He
contributed little, if anything, to our support. He worked
once in a while, but never steady. He always said that his boss,
whoever it happened to be at the time, was giving him the
dirty end of the stick. He had a very strong sense of justice
and he'd quit his job at the first sign of what he termed un-

fairness or prejudice. Even though the unfairness happened to someone else, he'd quit in protest."

"How about drinking? Did your father drink?"

"I don't know."

"Please try to remember. There might be some incidents. Surely you know whether he drank or not."

"Listen, Doctor, it was still prohibition when he was alive. I don't remember ever seeing him take a drink. And when he went out at night I was too small to go with him. So if he drank I don't know about it."

"If he didn't support your family, who did?"

"Mother. She was a beauty operator and she must have been a good one, because she always had a job. Ever since I can remember. She had some kind of a new system, and women used to come to our house on Sundays, her off-day, for treatments. It seemed to me that she never had any free time."

"What are your brothers and sisters doing now?"

"I suppose they're working. Father died first and then about a year later my mother died. From that time on we were on our own."

"How old were you then, when your mother died?"

"Sixteen."

"Weren't there any relatives to take you in with them?"

"We had relatives, yes. My mother's brother, Uncle Ralph, gathered us all together in his house about a week after her funeral. He had the insurance money by that time and it was divided equally between us. My share was two hundred and fifty dollars, which was quite a fortune in the depression. My uncle and aunt took my smallest sister to live with them, probably to get her two-fifty, but the rest of us were on our own. I got a room on the South Side, a part time job, and finished high school. I entered the Art Institute as soon as I finished high school. Luckily, I was able to snag a razor-blade-and-condom concession and this supported me and paid my tuition. I studied at the institute until I was drafted, and I've told you about my experiences in the army already."

"Sketchily."

"I told you all I could remember. I wasn't a hero. I was an ordinary soldier like all the draftees. I had a pretty good break, yes, but that was only because I had the skill to paint and also because the army gave me the opportunity to use my skill. Many other soldiers, a hell of a lot more talented than I was, were never given the same breaks."

"Do you have any desire to see your brothers and sisters again?"

"They all live in Chicago, Doctor. We used to have a saying when we were students in L.A.—'A lousy artist doesn't go to heaven or hell when he dies; his soul goes to Chicago.' If that saying turns out to be true, I'll be seeing them soon enough."

"How about sex experiences? Did you ever engage in sex-play with your brothers and sisters?" His well-trained words marched like slugs into the cemetery of my brain. He asked this monstrous question as casually as he asked them all. Appalled, I stared at him unbelievingly.

"You must have a hell of a lot of guts to ask me a filthy question like that!" I said angrily. "What kind of a person do you think I am, anyway? I've confessed to a brutal murder— I'm guilty—I've said I was guilty! Why don't you kill me? Why can't I go to the gas chamber? What you've been doing to me can be classified as cruel and inhuman treatment, and as a citizen I don't have to take it! How much do you think I can stand?" I was on my feet by this time and pounding the doctor's desk with my fists. "You've got everything out of me you're going to get!" I finished decisively. "From now on I'll tell you nothing!"

"What is it you don't want to tell me, Jordan?" he asked quietly, as he calmly twisted the point of his beard.

"Nothing. I've told you everything that ever happened to me. Not once, but time and time again. Why do you insist on asking the same things over and over?"

"Please sit down, Jordan." I sat down. "The reason I ask you these questions is because I haven't much time. I have to return you to the jail tomorrow—"

"Thank God for small favors!" I cut him off.

"So I've taken some unethical short cuts. I know it's most unfair to you and I'm sorry. Now. Tell me about your sex-play with your brothers and sisters."

"My brothers and I all married each other and all my sisters are lesbians. We all slept together in the same bed, including my mother and father and all of us took turns with each other. The relationship was so complicated and the experiences were so varied, all you have to do is attach a medical book of abnormal sex deviations to my file and you'll have it all. Does that satisfy your morbid curiosity?" This falsehood made me feel ashamed.

"You're evading my question. Why? Everything you tell me is strictly confidential. I only ask you these things to enable me to give a correct report—"

"From now on I'm evading you," I said. I got up from my chair and opened the door. Hank, as usual, was waiting for me outside, sitting on the bench. As I started briskly, happily, toward my cell, Hank fell in behind me. My mind was relieved, my step was airy, because I never intended to talk to Dr. Fischbach again. I didn't look back and I've never seen the doctor since.

That afternoon I was so ashamed of myself and so irritable I slammed my fists into the pine wall over and over again. I kept it up until my knuckles hurt me badly enough to get my mind on them instead of the other thoughts that boiled and churned inside my head. After a while, Hank opened the door and looked in on me. There was a wide smile on his lips.

"There's a lot of noise in here. What's going on, Harry?"

"It's that damned doctor, Hank," I said. I smiled in spite of myself. Hank had the most infectious smile I've ever seen.

"Let me tell you something, Harry," Hank said seriously, and he came as close to not smiling as he was able to do, "you've got to keep a cool stool. It don't go for a man to get emotionally disturbed in a place like this. Speaking for myself, I'll tell you this much; you'll be one hell of a lot better off in the gas chamber than you'd ever be in a state institution. Have you ever thought of that?"

I snorted. "Of course I've thought of it. But I'm not insane. You know it and so does the doctor."

"That's right, Harry. But besides working here, I've worked in three different state institutions. And I've seen guys a hell of a lot saner than you in all three of them." This remark made him laugh.

"I'm all right," I told him.

"The way to prove it is to keep a cool stool."

"I guess you're right. Doctor Fischbach says I go back to jail tomorrow. And if he's halfway fair he'll turn in a favorable report on me, Hank. Up till today, anyway, I've cooperated with him all the way."

"I know you have, Harry. Don't spoil it. It must be pretty rough, isn't it?"

"I've never had it any rougher."

He winked at me conspiratorily. "How'd you like to have a drink?" He held up his thumb and forefinger an inch apart.

"Man, I'd love one," I replied sincerely.

Hank reached into his hip-pocket and brought out a half-pint of gin. He unscrewed the cap and offered me the bottle. I didn't take it. Was this some kind of trap? After all, Hank was a hospital employee, when all was said and done. Sure, he had been more than nice to me so far, but maybe there had been a purpose to it, and this might be it. How did I know it was gin in the bottle? It might be some kind of dope, maybe a truth serum of some kind? It might possibly be Fisch-bach's way of getting me into some kind of a jam. I knew he didn't like me.

"No thanks, Hank," I said. "Maybe I'd better not."

Hank shrugged indifferently. "Suit yourself." He took a long swig, screwed the cap back on and returned the bottle to his hip pocket. He left my cell and slammed and locked the door. I was sorry I hadn't taken the drink. It might have made me feel better, and by refusing, I had hurt Hank's feelings. But it didn't make any difference. My problems were almost over. Tomorrow I would be back in jail. It would be almost like going home again.

That night I couldn't sleep. After twisting and turning on the uncomfortable mattress until eleven, I gave up the battle and banged on the door for the nurse. The night nurse gave me a sleeping pill without any argument, but even then it was a long time before I got to sleep. The next morning Hank brought me my breakfast on a tray. If he was still sore at me he didn't give any indication of it.

"This'll be your last meal here, Harry," he said, smiling.

"That's the best news I've had since I got here," I said. "Hank, I'm really sorry about not taking that drink you of-fered me yesterday. I was upset, nervous, and—"

"It doesn't bother me, Harry. I just thought you'd like a little shot."

"After a man's been in this place a while, he gets so he doesn't trust anybody."

"You're telling me!" He opened the door and looked down the corridor, turned and smiled broadly. "I found out something for you, Harry. Last night I managed to get a look at your chart, and Doctor Fischbach is reporting you as absolutely sane. In his report he stated that you were completely in possession of your faculties when you croaked your girl friend."

"That's really good news. Maybe Doctor Fischbach's got a few human qualities after all."

"I thought it would make you happy," Hank said pleasantly.

"What about the Sanity Board you were telling me about the other day? Won't I have to meet that?"

"Not as long as Fischbach says you're okay. He classified you as neurotic depressive, which doesn't mean a damn thing. The Sanity Board is for those guys who have a reasonable doubt. You're all right."

I tore into my breakfast with satisfaction. Now I could go back to the special block safe in the knowledge I would go to the gas chamber instead of the asylum. Hank was in a talkative mood and he chatted about hospital politics while I finished my breakfast, brought me another cup of coffee when I asked for it.

"Now that I'm leaving, Hank," I said, "tell me something. Why is it that I never get a hot cup of coffee? This is barely lukewarm."

He laughed. "I never give patients hot coffee. About two years ago I was taking a pot of hot coffee around the ward giving refills and I asked this guy if he wanted a second cup. 'No,' he says, so I said, 'Not even a half a cup?' and he says, 'Okay.' So I pours about a half-cup and he says, 'A little more.' I pours a little more, and he says, 'More yet.' This time I filled his cup all the way. He reached out then, grabbed my waistband and dumped the whole cupful of hot coffee inside my pants! Liked to have ruined me. I was in bed for three days with second degree burns!"

I joined Hank in laughter, not because it was a funny story, but he told it so well. He finished with the punch line:

"Ever since then I've never given out with hot coffee."

Hank lit my cigarette and we shook hands. He picked up my tray.

"I want to wish you the best of luck, Harry," he said at the door. "You're one of the nicest guys we've had in here in a long time."

"The same goes for you, Hank," I said sincerely. "You've made it bearable for me and I want you to know I appreciate it."

More than a little embarrassed, he turned away with the tray and walked out, leaving the door open. Smitty, another orderly, brought me my clothes and I changed into them quickly. Smitty unlocked the elevator and we rode down to the receiving entrance and I was turned over to a detective in a dark gray suit. I was handcuffed and returned to the jail in a police car instead of an ambulance. I was signed in at the jail and Mr. Benson returned me to my cell, my old cell.

Wearing my blue jail clothes again and stretched out on my bunk, I sighed with contentment. I speculated on how long it would be before the trial. It couldn't be too long, now that the returns were in; all I needed now, I supposed, was an open date on the court calendar. If I could occupy myself somehow, it would make the time pass faster. Maybe, if I asked Mr. Benson, he would get me a drawing pad and some charcoal sticks. I could do a few sketches to pass away the time. It was a better pastime than reading and it would be something to do.

That afternoon, right after lunch, I talked to Mr. Benson, and he said he would see what he could do . . .

NINETEEN

Portrait of a Killer

IT MUST have been about an hour after breakfast. The daily breakfast of two thick slices of bread and the big cup of black coffee didn't always set so well. Scrambled eggs, toast, and a glass of orange juice would have been better. No question about it; I had eaten better at the hospital. The two lumps of dough had absorbed the coffee and the mess felt like a full sponge in my stomach. Somebody was at my door and I looked up. It was Mr. Benson. He had a large drawing pad and a box of colored pencils in his hand. The old man was smiling and it revealed his worn down teeth, uppers and lowers. He stopped smiling the moment I looked at him.

"I bought you this stuff outa my own pocket," he said gruffly. "You can't lay around in here forever doin' nothin'." He passed the pad and pencil box through the bars and I took them.

"Thanks a lot, Mr. Benson," I said. "How'd you like to have me do your portrait? That is, after I practice up a little."

"You pretty good?"

"I used to be, and you've got an interesting face."

"What do you mean by that!" he bridled.

"I mean I'd enjoy trying to draw you."

"Oh." His face flushed. "I guess I wouldn't mind you doin' a picture of me. Maybe some time this afternoon?"

"Any time."

I practiced and experimented with the colored pencils all morning, drawing cones, blocks, trying for perspective. I would rather have had charcoal instead of colored pencils, I like it much better, but maybe the colored pencils gave me more things to do. The morning passed like a shot. I hadn't lost my touch, if anything, my hand was steadier than it had been before.

Mr. Benson held out until mid-afternoon, and then he brought a stool down the corridor and seated himself outside my cell. For some reason, a portrait, whether a plain drawing or a full-scale painting, is the most flattering thing you can do for a person. I've never met a person yet who didn't want an artist to paint his portrait. It is one of the holdovers from the nineteenth century that enables artists who go for that sort of thing to eat. A simple drawing, or a painting should always be done from life to be worthwhile. But this doesn't prevent an organization in New York from making thousands of dollars weekly by having well-known artists paint portraits from photographs that are sent in from all over the United States. If the person has enough money, all he has to do is state what artist he wants and send in his photographs. The artists who do this type of work are a hell of a lot hungrier for money than I ever was.

I didn't spend much time with Mr. Benson. I did a profile view and by doing a profile it is almost impossible not to get a good likeness. By using black, coral, and a white pencil for the highlights, I got the little drawing turned out well and Mr. Benson was more than pleased.

"What do I owe you, Harry?" he asked, after I tore the drawing from the pad and gave it to him.

"Nothing," I laughed. "You're helping me kill time, and besides you bought me the pad and pencils."

"How about a dollar?"

"No." I shook my head. "Nothing."

"Suit yourself." He picked up his stool and left happily with his picture.

Mr. Benson must have spread the word or showed his picture around. In the next three days I did several more drawings. Detectives came up to see me and they would sit belligerently, trying to cover their embarrassment while I whipped out a fast profile. They all offered me money, which I didn't accept, but I never refused a pack of cigarettes. The last portrait I did was that of a young girl. She was one of the stenos from the filing department, well-liked by Mr. Benson, and he let her in. She was very nervous and twitched on the stool while I did a three-quarter view. I suppose she was curious to see what I looked like, more than anything else, but it didn't matter to me. Drawing was a time-killer to me. I gave her the completed drawing and she hesitated outside my cell.

"You haven't been reading the papers have you, ah, Mr. Jordan?" she asked nervously.

"No."

She was about twenty-one or -two with thin blonde hair, glasses, and a green faille suit. Her figure was slim, almost slight, and she twisted her long, slender fingers nervously. "I don't know whether to tell you or not, but seeing you don't read the papers, maybe I'd better . . ."

"Tell me what?" I asked gently.

"Oh, it just makes me sore, that's all!" she said spiritedly. "These detectives! Here you've been decent enough to draw their pictures for nothing, and they've been selling them to the newshawks in the building. All of the papers have been running cuts, and these detectives have been getting ten dollars or more from the reporters."

"The reporters have been getting gypped then," I said, controlling my sudden anger.

"Well I think it's dirty, Mr. Jordan, and I just wanted you to know that I'm going to keep my picture."

"That's fine. Just tell Mr. Benson I'm not doing any more portraits. Tell him on your way out, will you please?"

"All right. Don't tell anybody I told you . . . huh?"

"No, I won't say anything. I'm not sore about them selling the pictures," I told her. "It's just that they aren't good enough for publication."

"*I* think they are." She gave me two packages of Camels and tripped away down the corridor. At first I was angry and then I had to laugh at the irony of the situation. Ten dollars. Nobody had ever paid me ten dollars for a picture. Of course, I had never priced a painting that low. The few I had exhibited, in the Chicago student shows, had all been priced at three hundred or more dollars, and none of them had sold. But anyway, no more portraits from Harry Jordan. The cheap Harry Jordan integrity would be upheld until the last sniff of cyanide gas. . . . Again I laughed.

The following afternoon, Mr. Benson opened the cell door and beckoned to me. He led me through a couple of corridors and into a small room sparsely furnished with a bare scratched desk, a couple of wooden chairs and, surprisingly, a leather couch without arms, but hinged at one end so that the head of it could be raised. It was the kind of a couch you sometimes see in psychiatrists' offices and doctors' examining rooms. "What's this?" I said.

"Examining room," he said, as I'd expected. I started to get angry. He left the room, moving rather furtively, I thought, and he shut the door, locking it on the outside. After a couple of minutes the door opened again. It was that stenographer.

She walked in, her arms full of the drawing stuff I had left in my cell. The door closed behind her and I heard the lock click again, shutting us in. I couldn't figure it out.

She was looking at me, kind of breathlessly. She put the colored pencils and stuff down on the desk. "I want you to draw me again," she said.

"I don't know as I want to do any more drawing."

"Please."

"Why in here?"

"You don't understand. I want you to draw me in the nude."

I looked at her. It was warm in the room, and there was plenty of light streaming in from the high, barred windows. The bars threw interesting shadows across her body. It was a good place to draw or paint, all right. But that wasn't what she wanted. I knew that much.

I sat woodenly. She laughed, kicked off her shoes, lay back on the couch. I could tell she was a little scared of me, but liking it. "I'll be pretty in the nude," she said. "I'll be wonderful to draw." She lifted a long and delicately formed leg and drew off the stocking. She did the same for her other leg. I could see that her thighs were a trifle plump. They were creamy-white, soft-looking, but the rest of her legs, especially around the knees, were faintly rosy.

She flicked a glance at me, to see what my response was. I had not moved. I was just standing there, watching. She stood up, made an eager, ungraceful gesture that unloosed a clasp, or a zipper or something. Her skimpy green skirt fell to the floor. She hesitated then, like a girl about to plunge into a cold shower, but took a deep breath, then quickly undid her blouse. It fell to the floor with the skirt. Another moment and her slip was off, and the wisps of nylon that were her underthings. I smelled their faint perfume in the warm room. She lifted her arms over her head and pirouetted proudly. "See?" she said. "See?"

I had not noticed before, even when I had been drawing her, how pretty she was. Maybe she was the kind of girl whose beauty only awakes when her clothes are off. I examined her thoughtfully, trying to think of her as a problem in art. Long legs. Plump around the hips and thighs. Narrow, long waist.

Jutting bosom, a trifle too soft, too immature. Her face was narrow and bony, but attractive enough. The lips were full and red. Her corn-colored hair fell in a graceful line to her shoulders.

"You fixed this up?" I said.

She was tense and excited. "Me and Mr. Benson," she said. "Nobody will bother us here." She giggled.

This would be the last time, I was thinking. I would never have another chance at a woman. Not on this earth.

"Don't look so surprised," she said. "All kinds of things go on in a place like this. It's just a question of how much money and influence a person has. You don't have money, and neither do I—but I've got the influence—" She giggled again. Like a high school kid. Was this her first adventure with a man, I wondered.

I sat down on the hard leather couch.

"Come here," I said.

She sat down on my lap.

I started by kissing her. First her silky hair. Then her soft parted lips. Then her neck, her shoulders, lower . . .

"Harry," she said. "Harry!"

My arm was around her waist, and her skin felt creamy and smooth. I tilted her back, swinging her off my knees so that she lay supine on the couch. I stroked and kissed and fondled, slowly and easily at first, then faster and harder. Much harder. She began to breathe deeply. She was scared. I kissed her neck, at the same time taking her by the hair and drawing her head back.

"Harry," she said. "What are you going to do to me?"

"You're frightened, aren't you? That's part of the thrill. That's what you want, isn't it? To do it with a freak. A dangerous freak. And a murderer!"

"I want you, Harry!"

She was panting. She threw her arms around me, and her nails clawed my shoulders. It was my head that was pulled down now, and she was smothering me with lipstick and feverish kisses. This was the moment I had been waiting for. The moment when she would be craving ecstasy. I lifted my hand and, as hard as I could, slapped her in the face.

But instead of looking at me with consternation and fear

and disappointment, she giggled. Damn her, in her eyes I was just living up to expectations. This was what she had come for!

In cold disgust, I hit her with my fist, splitting her lip so that the blood ran. The blow rolled her from the couch to the floor. For a moment I pitied her bare, crumpled body, but as soon as the breath got back into her she sprang to her feet. I was standing now, too. She flung her arms around me in a desperate embrace. "I can't bear it. Please, Harry!"

I knocked her down again.

"Please, Harry! Now . . . Now . . . !"

"You slut. I loved a real woman. To her, I was no strange, freakish creature. She didn't come to me for cheap thrills. Get your clothes on!"

I picked up one of the chairs and swung at the door with it.

"Let me out of here," I shouted, pounding the door. "God damn it, let me out!"

Mr. Benson came, and shamefacedly opened the door. The girl, her clothes on, ran sobbing down the corridor. Mr. Benson looked at me.

"I'm sorry, Harry. I thought I was doing you a favor."

I never did find out the girl's name.

The next day was Sunday. After a heavy lunch of baked swordfish and boiled potatoes I fell asleep on my bunk for a little afternoon nap. The jailer aroused me by reaching through the bars and jerking on my foot. It wasn't Mr. Benson; it was the Sunday man, Mr. Paige.

"Come on, Jordan," he said, "wake up. You gotta visitor." Mr. Paige sold men's suits during the week, but he was a member of the Police Reserve, and managed to pick up extra money during the month by getting an active duty day of pay for Sunday work. At least, that is what Mr. Benson told me.

"I'm too sleepy for visitors," I grumbled, still partly asleep. "Who is it anyway?"

"It's a woman," he said softly, "a Mrs. Mathews." I could tell by the expression on his face and his tone of voice he knew Mrs. Mathews was Helen's mother. "Do you want to see her?"

I got off the bed in a hurry. No. Of course I didn't want to see her. But that wasn't the point. She wanted to see me and I couldn't very well refuse. She had every right to see the murderer of her daughter.

"Do you know what she wants to see me about?" I asked Mr. Paige.

He shook his head. "All I know, she's got a pass from the D.A. Even so, if you don't want, you don't have to talk to her."

"I guess it's all right. Give me a light." He lit my cigarette for me and I took several fast drags, hoping the smoke would dissipate my drowsiness. Smoking, I stood close to the barred door, listening nervously for the sound of Mrs. Mathews' footsteps in the corridor. And I heard her long before I saw her. Her step was strong, resolute, purposeful. And she appeared in front of the door, Mr. Paige, the jailer, behind her and slightly to one side.

"Here's Harry Jordan, ma'am. You can't go inside the cell, but you can talk to him for five minutes." I was grateful for the time limit Mr. Paige arbitrarily imposed. He turned away, walked a few steps down the corridor, out of earshot, beyond my range of vision.

Mrs. Mathews was wearing that same beaver coat, black walking shoes, and a green felt, off-the-face hat. Her gray hair was gathered and piled in a knot on the back of her neck. She glared at me through her gold-rimmed glasses. Her full lips curled back, showing her teeth, in a scornful, sneering grimace of disgust. There was a bright gleam of hatred in her eyes, the unreasoning kind of hate one reserves for a dangerous animal, or a loose snake. She made me extremely nervous, looking at me that way. My hands were damp and I took them away from the bars, wiped my palms on my shirt. As tightly as I could, I gripped the bars again.

"It was nice of you to come and visit me, Mrs. Mathews . . ." I said haltingly. She didn't reply to my opening remark and I didn't know what else to say. But I tried.

"I'm sorry things turned out the way they did," I said humbly, "but I want you to know that Helen was in full accord with what I did. It was the way Helen wanted it . . ." My throat was tight, like somebody was holding my windpipe, and

I had to force the words out of my mouth. "If we had it all to do over again, maybe things would have worked out differently . . ."

Mrs. Mathews worked her mouth in and out, pursed her lips.

"I've pleaded guilty, and—" I didn't get to finish my sentence.

Without warning, Mrs. Mathews spat into my face. Involuntarily, I jerked back from the bars. Ordinarily, a woman is quite awkward when she tries to spit. Mrs. Mathews was not. The wet, disgusting spittle struck my forehead, right above my eyebrows. I made no attempt to wipe it off, but came forward again, and tightly gripped the bars. I waited patiently for a stream of invective to follow, but it didn't come. Mrs. Mathews glared at me for another long moment, sniffed, jerked her head to the right, turned and lumbered away.

I sat down on my bunk, wiped off my face with the back of my hand. My legs and hands were trembling and I was as weak as if I had climbed out of a hot Turkish bath.

My mind didn't function very well. Maybe I had it coming to me. At least in her eyes, I did. I didn't know what to think. The viciousness and sudden fury of her pointless action had taken me completely by surprise. But how many times must I be punished before I was put to death? I don't believe I was angry, not even bitter. There was a certain turmoil inside my chest, but it was caused mostly by my reaction to her intense hatred of me. In addition to my disgust and loathing for the woman I also managed to feel sorry for her and I suspected she would suffer later for her impulsive action. After she reflected, perhaps shame would come and she would regret her impulsiveness. It was like kicking an unconscious man in the face. But on the other hand, she had probably planned what she would do for several days. I didn't want to think about it. Mr. Paige was outside the door and there was a contrite expression on his face.

"She didn't stay long," he said.

"No. She didn't."

"I saw what she did," Mr. Paige said indignantly. "If I'd have known what she was up to I wouldn't have let her in, even if she did have a pass from the D.A."

"That's all right, Mr. Paige. I don't blame you; I don't blame anybody. But if she comes back, don't let her in again. I don't want to see her any more. My life is too short."

"Don't worry, Jordan. She won't get in again!" He said this positively. He walked away and I was alone. I washed my face with the brown soap and cold water in my wash basin a dozen times, but my face still felt dirty.

The next day my appetite was off. I tried to draw something, anything, to pass the time away, but I couldn't keep my mind on it. Mr. Paige had told Mr. Benson what had happened and he had tried to talk to me about it, and I cut him off quickly. I didn't feel like talking. I lay on my back all day long, smoking cigarettes, one after another, and looking at the ceiling.

On Tuesday, I had another visitor. Mr. Benson appeared outside my cell with a well-fed man wearing a brown gabardine Brooks Brothers suit and a blue satin vest. His face was lobster red and his larynx gave him trouble when he talked. Mr. Benson opened the door and let the man into my cell.

"This is Mr. Dorrell, Jordan," the old jailer said. "He's an editor from *He-Men Magazine* and he's got an okay from the D.A.'s office so I gotta let him in for ten minutes."

"All right," I said, and I didn't move from my reclining position. There were no stools or chairs and Mr. Dorrell had to stand. "What can I do for you, Mr. Dorrell?" I asked.

"I'm from *He-Men*, Mr. Jordan," he began in his throaty voice. "And our entire editorial staff is interested in your case. To get directly to the point—we want an 'as-told-to' story from you, starting right at the beginning of your, ah, relationship with Mrs. Meredith."

"No. That's impossible."

"No," he smiled, "it isn't impossible. There is a lot of interest for people when a woman as prominent in society as Mrs. Meredith gets, shall we say, involved?"

"Helen wasn't prominent in society."

"Maybe not, not as you and I know it, Mr. Jordan. But certain places, like Biarritz, for instance, Venice, and in California, San Sienna, are very romantic watering places. And the doings of their inhabitants interests our readers very much."

"My answer is no."

"We'll pay you one thousand dollars for such an article."

"I don't want a thousand dollars."

"You might need it."

"What for?"

"Money comes in handy sometimes," he croaked, "and the public has a right to know about your case."

"Why do they?" I asked belligerently. "It's nobody's business but my own!"

"Suppose you consider the offer and let us know later?"

"No. I won't even consider it. I don't blame you, Mr. Dorrell. You've got a job to do. And I suppose your readers would get a certain amount of morbid enjoyment from my unhappy plight, and possibly, more copies of your magazine would be bought. But I can't allow myself to sell such a story. It's impossible."

"Well, I won't say anything more." Mr. Dorrell took a card out of his wallet and handed it to me. "If you happen to change your mind, send me a wire. Send it collect, and I'll send a feature writer to see you and he'll bring you a check, in advance."

At the door he called for Mr. Benson. The jailer let him out of the cell and locked the door again. The two of them chatted as they walked down the corridor and I tore the business card into several small pieces and threw them on the floor. If Mr. Dorrell had been disappointed by my refusal he certainly didn't show it. What kind of a world did I live in, anyway? Everybody seemed to believe that money was everything, that it could buy integrity, brains, art, and now, a man's soul. I had never had a thousand dollars at one time in my entire life. And now, when I had an opportunity to have that much money, I was in a position to turn it down. It made me feel better and I derived a certain satisfaction from the fact that I could turn it down. In my present position, I could afford to turn down ten thousand, a million . . .

I didn't eat any supper that evening. After drinking the black coffee I tried to sleep but all night long I rolled and tossed on my narrow bunk. From time to time I dozed, but I always awakened with a start, and my heart would violently pound. There was a dream after me, a bad dream, and my sleeping mind wouldn't accept it. I was grateful when morning came at last. I knew it was morning, because Mr. Benson brought my breakfast.

After breakfast, when I took my daily shower, I noticed the half-smile on the old jailer's face. He gave me my razor, handing it in to me as I stood under the hot water, and not only did I get a few extra minutes in the shower, I got a better shave with the hot water. As I toweled myself I wondered what was behind the old man's smile.

"What's the joke, Mr. Benson?" I asked.

"I've got news for you, Jordan, but I don't know whether it's good or bad." His smile broadened.

"What news?"

"You're being tried today."

"It's good news."

He brought me my own clothes and I put them on, tied my necktie as carefully as I could without a mirror. I had to wait in my cell for about a half-hour and then I was handcuffed and taken down to the receiving office and checked out. My stuff was returned and I signed the envelope to show that I had gotten it back. All of it. Button, piece of string, handkerchief, and parking stub from the Continental Garage. As the detective and I started toward the parking ramp the desk sergeant called out to the officer. We paused.

"He's minimum security, Jeff."

Jeff removed the handcuffs and we climbed into the waiting police car for the short drive to the Court House.

TWENTY

Trial

I WAITED in a small room adjacent to the courtroom. It was sparsely furnished; just a small chipped wooden table against the wall and four metal chairs. I stood by the window, looking down three stories at the gray haze of fog that palled down over the civic center. A middle-aged uniformed policeman was stationed in the room to stand guard over me, and he leaned against the wall by the door, picking at the loose threads of the buttonholes on his shiny Navy blue serge uniform. There was nothing much to see out of the window, only the fog, the dim outlines of automobiles with their lights on, in the street below, a few walking figures, their sex indistinguishable, but I looked out because it was a window and I hadn't been in a room with a window for a long time. One at a time I pulled at my fingers, cracking the joints. The middle finger of my left hand made the loudest crack.

"Don't do that," the policeman said. "I can't stand it. And besides, cracking your knuckles makes them swell."

I stopped popping my fingers and put my hands in my trousers pockets. That didn't feel right, so I put my hands in my jacket pockets. This was worse. I let my arms hang, swinging them back and forth like useless pendula. I didn't want to smoke because my mouth and throat were too dry, but I got a light from the policeman and inhaled the smoke into my lungs, even though it tasted like scraped bone dust. Before I finished the cigarette there was a hard rapping on the door and the policeman opened it.

A round, overweight man with a shiny bald head bounced into the room. He didn't come into the room, he "came on," like a TV master of ceremonies. There was a hearty falseness to the broad smile on his round face and his eyes were black and glittering, almost hidden by thick, sagging folds of flesh. His white hands were short, white, and puffy, and the scattering of paprika freckles made them look unhealthily pale. I almost expected him to say, "A funny thing happened to me on the way over to the court house today," but instead of saying anything he burst into a contagious, raucous, guffawing laugh that reverberated in the silence of the little room. It was the type of laughter that is usually infectious, but in my solemn frame of mind I didn't feel like joining him. After a moment he stopped abruptly, wiped his dry face with a white handkerchief.

"You are Harry Jordan!" He pointed a blunt fat finger at me.

"Yes, sir," I said.

"I'm Larry Hingen-Bergen." He unbuttoned his double-breasted tweed coat and sat down at the little table. He threw his battered briefcase on the table before him and indicated, by pointing to another chair, that he wanted me to sit down. I pulled up a chair, sat down, and faced him diagonally. "I'm your defense counsel, Jordan, appointed by the court. I suppose you wonder why I haven't been to see you before this?" He closed his eyes, while he waited for my answer.

"No. Not particularly, Mr. Hingen-Bergen. After I told the District Attorney I was guilty, I didn't think I'd need a defense counsel."

His eyes snapped open, glittering. "And you don't!" He guffawed loudly, with false heartiness. "And you don't!" He let the laugh loose again, slapped his heavy thigh with his hand. "You!" he pointed his finger at my nose, "are a very lucky boy! In fact," his expression sobered, "I don't know how to tell you how lucky you are. You're going to be a free man, Jordan."

"What's that?" I asked stupidly.

"Free. Here's the story." He related it in a sober, businesslike manner. "I was assigned to your case about two weeks ago, Jordan. Naturally, the first thing I did was have a little talk with Mr. Seely. You remember him?"

I nodded. "The Assistant D.A."

"My visit happened to coincide with the day the medical report came in. Now get a grip on yourself, boy. Helen Meredith was not choked to death, as you claimed; she died a natural death!" He took a small notebook out of his pocket. It was a long and narrow notebook, fastened at the top, covered with green imitation snakeskin, the kind insurance salesmen give away whether you buy any insurance or not. I sat dazed, tense, leaning forward slightly while he leafed through the little book. "Here it is," he said, smiling. "Coronary thrombosis. Know what that is?"

"It isn't true!" I exclaimed.

He gripped my arm with his right hand, his voice softened. "I'm afraid it is true, Jordan. Of course, there were bruises on her neck and throat where your hands had been, but that's all they were. Bruises. She actually died from a heart attack. Did she ever tell you she had a bad heart?"

I shook my head, scarcely hearing the question. "No. No,

she didn't. Her mother said something about it once, but I didn't pay much attention at the time. And I can't believe this, Mr. Hingen-Bergen. She was always real healthy; why she didn't hardly get a hangover when she drank."

"I'm not making this up, Jordan." He tapped the notebook with the back of his fat fingers. "This was the Medical Examiner's report. Right from the M.E.'s autopsy. There's no case against you at all. Now, the reason the D.A. didn't tell you about this was because he wanted to get a full psychiatrist's report first." Mr. Hingen-Bergen laughed, but it was a softer laugh, kind. "You *might* have been insane, you know. He had to find out before he could release you."

My mind still wouldn't accept the situation. "But if I didn't actually kill her, Mr. Hingen-Bergen, I must have at least hastened her death! And if so, that makes me guilty, doesn't it?"

"No," he replied flatly. "She'd have died anyway. I read the full M.E. report. She was in pretty bad shape. Malnutrition, I don't remember what all. You didn't have anything to do with her death."

The middle-aged policeman had been attentively following the conversation. "By God," he remarked, "this is an interesting case, Mr. Hingen-Bergen!"

"Isn't it?" The fat lawyer smiled at him. He turned to me again. "Now, Jordan, we're going into the court room and Mr. Seely will present the facts to the judge. He'll move for a dismissal of the charges and you'll be free to go."

"Go where?" My mind was in a turmoil.

"Why, anywhere you want to go, naturally. You'll be a free man! Why, this is the easiest case I've ever had. Usually my clients go to jail!" He laughed boisterously and the policeman joined him. "You just sit tight, Jordan, and the bailiff'll call you in a few minutes." He picked his briefcase up from the table and left the room.

I remained in my chair, my mind numb. If this was true, and evidently it was—the lawyer wouldn't lie to me right before the trial—I hadn't done anything! Not only had I fumbled my own suicide, I'd fumbled Helen's death too. I could remember the scene so vividly. I could remember the feel of her throat beneath my thumbs, and the anguish I had under-

gone . . . and all of it for nothing. Nothing. I covered my
face with my hands. I felt a hand on my shoulder. It was the
policeman's hand and he tried to cheer me up.

"Why, hell, boy," he said friendly, "don't take it so hard.
You're lucky as hell. Here . . ." I dropped my hands to my
lap. The policeman held out a package of cigarettes. "Take
one." I took one and he lighted it for me. "You don't want
to let this prey on your mind. You've got a chance to start
your life all over again. Take it. Be grateful for it."

"It was quite a shock. I wasn't ready for it."

"So what? You're out of it, forget it. Better pull yourself
together. You'll be seeing the judge pretty soon."

The bailiff and Mr. Hingen-Bergen came for me and took
me into the court room. I'd never seen a regular trial before.
All I knew about court room procedure was what I had seen
in movies; and movie trials are highly dramatic, loud voices,
screaming accusations, bawling witnesses, things like that.
This was unlike anything I'd ever seen before. Mr. Hingen-
Bergen and I joined the group at the long table. The judge
sat at the end wearing his dark robes. And he was a young
man, not too many years past thirty; he didn't look as old as
Mr. Seely. Mr. Seely sat next to the judge, his face incompliant
behind his glasses. It was a large room, not a regular courtroom, and there were no spectators. A male stenographer, in
his early twenties, made a fifth at the table. The bailiff leaned
against the door, smoking a pipe.

Mr. Seely and the judge carried on what seemed to be a
friendly conversation. I didn't pay any attention to what they
were saying; I was waiting for the trial to get started.

"The Medical Examiner couldn't make it, your honor," Mr.
Seely said quietly to the judge, "but here's his report, if that's
satisfactory."

There was a long period of silence while the judge studied
the typewritten sheets. The judge slid the report across the
desk to Mr. Seely, and the Assistant District Attorney put it
back inside his new cowhide briefcase. The judge pursed his
lips and looked at me for a moment, nodding his head up and
down soberly.

"I believe you're right, Mr. Seely," he said softly. "There's
really no point in holding the defendant any longer. The case

is dismissed." He got to his feet, rested his knuckles on the desk and stared at me. I thought he was going to say something to me, but he didn't. He gathered his robes about him, lifting the hems clear of the floor, and Mr. Hingen-Bergen and I stood up. He left the courtroom by a side door. Mr. Seely walked around the table and shook hands with me.

"I've got some advice for you, Jordan," Mr. Seely said brusquely. "Keep away from liquor, and see if you can find another city to live in."

"Yes, sir," I said.

"That's good advice," Mr. Hingen-Bergen added.

"Of course," Mr. Seely amended gravely, "you don't *have* to leave San Francisco. Larry can tell you that." He looked sideways at my fat defense counsel. "You're free to live any place you want to, but I believe my advice is sound."

"You bet!" Mr. Hingen-Bergen agreed. "Especially, not drinking. You might end up in jail again if you go on a bat."

"Thanks a lot," I said vaguely.

I didn't know what to do with myself. Mr. Seely and the bailiff followed the young stenographer out of the room and I was still standing behind the table with Mr. Hingen-Bergen. He was stuffing some papers into various compartments of his briefcase. I had been told what to do and when to do it for so long I suppose I was waiting for somebody to tell me when to leave.

"Ready to go, Jordan?" Mr. Hingen-Bergen asked me, as he hooked the last strap on his worn leather bag.

"Don't I have to sign something?" It all seemed too unreal to me.

"Nope. That's it. You've had it."

"Then I guess I'm ready to go."

"Fine. I'll buy you a cup of coffee."

I shook my head. "No thanks. I don't believe I want one."

"Suit yourself. What are your plans?"

Again I shook my head bewilderedly. "I don't know. This thing's too much of a surprise. I still can't grasp it or accept it, much less formulate plans."

"You'll be all right." He laughed his coarse hearty laugh. "Come on."

Mr. Hingen-Bergen took my arm and we left the court

room, rode the elevator down to the main floor. We stood on the marble floor of the large entrance way and he pointed to the outside door, the steep flight of stairs leading down to the street level.

"There you are, Jordan," the lawyer smiled. "The city."

I nodded, turned away and started down the steps. Because of the heavy fog I could only see a few feet ahead of me. I heard footsteps behind me and turned as Mr. Hingen-Bergen called out my name.

"Have you got any money?" the lawyer asked me kindly.

"No, sir."

"Here." He handed me a five dollar bill. "This'll help you get started maybe."

I accepted the bill, folded it, put it into my watch pocket.

"I don't know when I'll be able to pay you back . . ." I said lamely.

"Forget it! Next time you get in jail, just look me up!" He laughed boisterously, clapped me on the shoulder and puffed up the stairs into the court house.

I continued slowly down the steps and when I reached the sidewalk, turned left toward Market. I was a free man.

Or was I?

TWENTY-ONE

From Here to Eternity

AFTER I left the Court House I walked for several blocks before I realized I was walking aimlessly and without a destination in mind. So much had happened unexpectedly I was in a daze. The ugly word, "Freedom" overlapped and crowded out any nearly rational thoughts that tried to cope with it. Freedom meant nothing to me. After the time I had spent in jail and in the hospital, not only was I reconciled to the prospect of death, I had eagerly looked forward to it. I wanted to die and I deserved to die. But I was an innocent man. I was free. I was free to wash dishes again, free to smash baggage, carry a waiter's tray, dish up chile beans as a counterman. Free.

The lights on the marquee up ahead advertised two surefire movies. Two old Humphrey Bogart pictures. It was the Bijou Theatre and I had reached Benny's Bijou Beanery. This was where it had started. I looked through the dirty glass of the window. Benny sat in his customary seat behind the cash register and as I watched him he reached into the large jar of orange gum drops on the counter and popped one into his mouth. The cafe was well-filled, most of the stools taken, and two countermen were working behind the counter. Just to see the cafe brought back a vivid memory of Helen and the way she looked and laughed the night she first entered. I turned away and a tear escaped my right eye and rolled down my cheek. A passerby gave me a sharp look. I wiped my eyes with the back of my hand and entered the next bar I came to. Tears in a bar are not unusual.

The clock next to the mouldy deer antlers over the mirror read ten-fifty-five. Except for two soldiers and a B-girl between them, the bar was deserted. I went to the far end and sat down.

"Two ounces of gin and a slice of lemon," I told the bartender.

"No chaser?"

"Better give me a little ice water."

I was in better physical condition than I had enjoyed in two or three years, but after my layoff I expected the first drink to hit me like a sledge hammer. There was no effect. The gin rolled down my throat like a sweet cough syrup with a codeine base. I didn't need the lemon or the water.

"Give me another just like it," I said to the bartender.

After three more my numb feeling disappeared. I wasn't drunk, but my head was clear and I was able to think again. Not that it made any difference, because nothing mattered anymore. I unfolded the five dollar bill Mr. Hingen-Bergen had given me, paid for the drinks and returned to the street. There was a cable car dragging up the hill and it slowed down at my signal. I leaped aboard for the familiar ride to my old neighborhood and the roominghouse. I could no longer think of the ride as going home. Although the trip took a long while it seemed much too short. At my corner, I jumped down.

The well-remembered sign, BIG MIKE'S BAR & GRILL, the twisted red neon tubing, glowed and hummed above the double doors of the saloon. This was really my home, mine and Helen's. This was where we had spent our only really happy hours; hours of plain sitting, drinking, with our shoulders touching. Hours of looking into each other's eyes in the bar mirror. As I stood there, looking at the entrance, the image of Helen's loveliness was vivid in my mind.

Rodney, the crippled newsboy, left his pile of papers and limped toward me. There was surprise in his tired face and eyes.

"Hello, Harry," he said, stretching out his arm. I shook his hand.

"Hello, Rodney."

"You got out of it, huh?"

"Yes."

"Congratulations, Harry. None of us around here really expected you—I mean, well . . ." His voice trailed off.

"That's all right, Rodney. It was all a mistake and I don't want to talk about it."

"Sure, Harry. I'm glad you aren't guilty." Self-conscious, he bobbed his head a couple of times and returned to his newspapers. I pushed through the swinging doors and took the first empty seat at the bar. It was lunch hour and the bar and cafe were both busy; most of the stools were taken and all of the booths. As soon as he saw me, Big Mike left the cash register and waddled toward me.

"The usual, Harry?" he asked me quietly.

"No. I don't want a drink."

Mike's face was unfathomable and I didn't know how he would take the news.

"I didn't kill her, Mike. Helen died a natural death. It was a mistake. That's all."

"I'm glad." His broad face was almost stern. "Let's have one last drink together, Harry," he said, "and then, I think it would be better if you did your drinking somewhere else."

"Sure, Mike. I understand."

He poured a jigger of gin for me and a short draught beer for himself. I downed the shot quickly, nodded briefly and left the bar. So Big Mike was glad. Everybody was glad, everybody was happy, everybody except me.

The overcast had yarded down thickly and now was a dark billowing fog. Soon it would drizzle, and then it would rain. I turned up my coat collar and put my head down. I didn't want to talk to anybody else. On my way to Mrs. McQuade's I had to pass several familiar places. The A & P, the Spotless Cleaners, Mr. Watson's delicatessen; all of these stores held people who knew me well. I pulled my collar up higher and put my head down lower.

When I reached the roominghouse I climbed the front outside steps and walked down the hall to Mrs. McQuade's door. I tapped twice and waited. As soon as she opened the door, Mrs. McQuade recognized me and clapped her hand to her mouth.

"It's quite all right, Mrs. McQuade," I said, "I'm a free man."

"Please come in, Mr. Jordan."

Her room was much too warm for me. I removed my jacket, sat down in a rocker and lighted one of my cigarettes to detract from the musty, close smell of the hot room. The old lady with blue hair sat down across from me in a straight-backed chair and folded her hands in her lap.

"It'll probably be in tonight's paper, Mrs. McQuade, but I didn't kill Helen. She died from a heart attack. A quite natural death. I didn't have anything to do with it."

"I'm not surprised." She nodded knowingly. "You both loved each other too much."

"Yes. We did."

Mrs. McQuade began to cry soundlessly. Her eyes searched the room, found her purse. She opened it and removed a Kleenex and blew her nose with a gentle, refined honk.

"How about Helen's things?" I asked. "Are they still here?"

"No. Her mother, Mrs. Mathews, took them. If I'd known that you . . . well, I didn't know, and she's Helen's mother, so when she wanted them, I helped her pack the things and she took them with her. There wasn't much, you know. That suitcase, now; I didn't know whether it was yours or Helen's, so I let Mrs. Mathews take it."

"How about the portrait?"

"Mr. Endo was keeping it in his room. He wasn't here, but when she asked for it, I got it out of his room. She burned it up . . . in the incinerator. As I say, I didn't—"

"That's all right. I'd have liked to have had it, but it doesn't matter. Is there anything of hers at all?"

"Not a thing, Mr. Jordan. Just a minute." The old lady got out of her chair and opened the closet. She rummaged around in the small, dark room. "These are yours." She brought forth my old trenchcoat and a gray laundry bag. I spread the trenchcoat on the floor and dumped the contents of the bag onto it. There were two dirty white shirts, four dirty T-shirts, four pairs of dirty drawers, six pairs of black sox and two soiled handkerchiefs.

At the bottom of the bag I saw my brushes and tubes of paint, and I could feel the tears coming into my eyes. She hadn't thrown them out after all; she still had had faith in me as an artist!

Mrs. McQuade pretended not to notice my choked emotion.

"If I'd known you were going to be released I'd have had these things laundered, Mr. Jordan."

"That's not important, Mrs. McQuade. I owe you some money, don't I?"

"Not a thing. Mrs. Mathews paid the room rent, and if you want the room you can have it back."

"No, thanks. I'm leaving San Francisco. I think it's best."

"Where are you going?"

"I don't know yet."

"Well, when you get settled, you'd better write me so I can forward your mail."

"There won't be any mail." I got out of the chair, slipped my jacket on, then the trenchcoat.

"You can keep that laundry bag, Mr. Jordan. Seeing I gave away your suitcase I can give you that much, at least."

"Thank you."

"Would you like a cup of coffee? I can make some in a second."

"No, thanks."

I threw the light bag over my shoulder and Mrs. McQuade opened the door for me. We shook hands and she led the way down the hall to the outside door. It was raining.

"Don't you have a hat, Mr. Jordan?"

"No. I never wear a hat."

"That's right. Come to think of it, I've never seen you with a hat."

I walked down the steps to the street and into the rain. A wind came up and the rain slanted sideways, coming down at an angle of almost thirty degrees. Two blocks away I got under the awning of a drug store. It wasn't letting up any; if anything, it was coming down harder. I left the shelter of the awning and walked up the hill in the rain.

Just a tall, lonely Negro.

Walking in the rain.

DOWN THERE

by David Goodis

THERE WERE no street lamps, no lights at all. It was a narrow street in the Port Richmond section of Philadelphia. From the nearby Delaware a cold wind came lancing in, telling all alley cats they'd better find a heated cellar. The late November gusts rattled against midnight-darkened windows, and stabbed at the eyes of the fallen man in the street.

The man was kneeling near the curb, breathing hard and spitting blood and wondering seriously if his skull was fractured. He'd been running blindly, his head down, so of course he hadn't seen the telephone pole. He'd crashed into it face first, bounced away and hit the cobblestones and wanted to call it a night.

But you can't do that, he told himself. You gotta get up and keep running.

He got up slowly, dizzily. There was a big lump on the left side of his head, his left eye and cheekbone were somewhat swollen, and the inside of his cheek was bleeding where he'd bitten it when he'd hit the pole. He thought of what his face must look like, and he managed to grin, saying to himself, You're doing fine, jim. You're really in great shape. But I think you'll make it, he decided, and then he was running again, suddenly running very fast as the headlights rounded a corner, the car picking up speed, the engine noise closing in on him.

The beam of the headlights showed him the entrance to an alley. He veered, went shooting into the alley, went down the alley and came out on another narrow street.

Maybe this is it, he thought. Maybe this is the street you want. No, your luck is running good but not that good, I think you'll hafta do more running before you find that street, before you see that lit-up sign, that drinking joint where Eddie works, that place called Harriet's Hut.

The man kept running. At the end of the block he turned, went on to the next street, peering through the darkness for any hint of the lit-up sign. You gotta get there, he told himself. You gotta get to Eddie before they get to you. But I wish I knew this neighborhood better. I wish it wasn't so cold and dark around here, it sure ain't no night for traveling on foot.

Especially when you're running, he added. When you're running away from a very fast Buick with two professionals in it, two high-grade operators, really experts in their line.

He came to another intersection, looked down the street, and at the end of the street, there it was, the orange glow, the lit-up sign of the tavern on the corner. The sign was very old, separate bulbs instead of neon tubes. Some of the bulbs were missing, the letters unreadable. But enough of it remained so that any wanderer could see it was a place for drinking. It was Harriet's Hut.

The man moved slowly now, more or less staggering as he headed toward the saloon. His head was throbbing, his wind-slashed lungs were either frozen or on fire, he wasn't quite sure what it felt like. And worst of all, his legs were heavy and getting heavier, his knees were giving way. But he staggered on, closer to the lit-up sign, and closer yet, and finally he was at the side entrance.

He opened the door and walked into Harriet's Hut. It was a fairly large place, high-ceilinged, and it was at least thirty years behind the times. There was no juke box, no television set. In places the wallpaper was loose and some of it was ripped away. The chairs and tables had lost their varnish, and the brass of the bar-rail had no shine at all. Above the mirror behind the bar there was a faded and partially torn photograph of a very young aviator wearing his helmet and smiling up at the sky. The photograph was captioned "Lucky Lindy." Near it there was another photograph that showed Dempsey crouched and moving in on a calm and technical Tunney. On the wall adjacent to the left side of the bar there was a framed painting of Kendrick, who'd been mayor of Philadelphia during the Sesqui-Centennial.

At the bar the Friday night crowd was jammed three-and-four-deep. Most of the drinkers wore work pants and heavy-soled work shoes. Some were very old, sitting in groups at the tables, their hair white and their faces wrinkled. But their hands didn't tremble as they lifted beer mugs and shot glasses. They could still lift a drink as well as any Hut regular, and they held their alcohol with a certain straight-seated dignity that gave them the appearance of venerable elders at a town meeting.

The place was really packed. All the tables were taken, and there wasn't a single empty chair for a leg-weary newcomer.

But the leg-weary man wasn't looking for a chair. He was looking for the piano. He could hear the music coming from the piano, but he couldn't see the instrument. A view-blurring fog of tobacco smoke and liquor fumes made everything vague, almost opaque. Or maybe it's me, he thought. Maybe I'm just about done in, and ready to keel over.

He moved. He went staggering past the tables, headed in the direction of the piano music. Nobody paid any attention to him, not even when he stumbled and went down. At twelve-twenty on a Friday night most patrons of Harriet's Hut were either booze-happy or booze-groggy. They were Port Richmond mill workers who'd labored hard all week. They came here to drink and drink some more, to forget all serious business, to ignore each and every problem of the too-real too-dry world beyond the walls of the Hut. They didn't even see the man who was pulling himself up very slowly from the sawdust on the floor, standing there with his bruised face and bleeding mouth, grinning and mumbling, "I can hear the music, all right. But where's the goddam piano?"

Then he was staggering again, bumping into a pile of high-stacked beer cases set up against a wall. It formed a sort of pyramid, and he groped his way along it, his hands feeling the cardboard of the beer cases until finally there was no more cardboard and he almost went down again. What kept him on his feet was the sight of the piano, specifically the sight of the pianist who sat there on the circular stool, slightly bent over, aiming a dim and faraway smile at nothing in particular.

The bruised-faced, leg-weary man, who was fairly tall and very wide across the shoulders and had a thick mop of ruffled yellow hair, moved closer to the piano. He came up behind the musician and put a hand on his shoulder and said, "Hello, Eddie."

There was no response from the musician, not even a twitch of the shoulder on which the man's heavy hand applied more pressure. And the man thought, Like he's far away, he don't even feel it, he's all the way out there with his music, it's a crying shame you gotta bring him in, but that's the way it is, you got no choice.

"Eddie," the man said, louder now. "It's me, Eddie."

The music went on, the rhythm unbroken. It was a soft, easy-going rhythm, somewhat plaintive and dreamy, a stream of pleasant sound that seemed to be saying, Nothing matters.

"It's me," the man said, shaking the musician's shoulder. "It's Turley. Your brother Turley."

The musician went on making the music. Turley sighed and shook his head slowly. He thought, You can't reach this one. It's like he's in a cloud and nothing moves him.

But then the tune was ended. The musician turned slowly and looked at the man and said, "Hello, Turley."

"You're sure a cool proposition," Turley said. "You ain't seen me for six-seven years. You look at me as if I just came back from a walk around the block."

"You bump into something?" the musician inquired mildly, scanning the bruised face, the bloodstained mouth.

Just then a woman got up from a nearby table and made a beeline for a door marked *Girls*. Turley spotted the empty chair, grabbed it, pulled it toward the piano and sat down. A man at the table yelled, "Hey you, that chair is taken," and Turley said to the man, "Easy now, jim. Cantcha see I'm an invalid?" He turned to the musician and grinned again, saying, "Yeah, I bumped into something. The street was too dark and I hit a pole."

"Who you running from?"

"Not the law, if that's what you're thinking."

"I'm not thinking anything," the musician said. He was medium-sized, on the lean side, and in his early thirties. He sat there with no particular expression on his face.

He had a pleasant face. There were no deep lines, no shadows. His eyes were a soft gray and he had a soft, relaxed mouth. His light-brown hair was loosely combed, very loosely, as though he combed it with his fingers. The shirt collar was open and there was no necktie. He wore a wrinkled, patched jacket and patched trousers. The clothes had a timeless look, indifferent to the calendar and the men's fashion columns. The man's full name was Edward Webster Lynn and his sole occupation was here at the Hut where he played the piano six nights a week, between nine and two. His salary was thirty dollars, and with tips his weekly income was anywhere from thirty-five to forty. It more than paid for his requirements. He was unmarried, he didn't own a car, and he had no debts or obligations.

"Well, anyway," Turley was saying, "it ain't the law. If it was the law, I wouldn't be pulling you into it."

"Is that why you came here?" Eddie asked softly. "To pull me into something?"

Turley didn't reply. He turned his head slightly, looking away from the musician. Consternation clouded his face, as though he knew what he wanted to say but couldn't quite manage to say it.

"It's no go," Eddie said.

Turley let out a sigh. As it faded, the grin came back. "Well, anyway, how you doing?"

"I'm doing fine," Eddie said.

"No problems?"

"None at all. Everything's dandy."

"Including the finance?"

"I'm breaking even." Eddie shrugged, but his eyes narrowed slightly.

Turley sighed again.

Eddie said, "I'm sorry, Turl, it's strictly no dice."

"But listen—"

"No," Eddie said softly. "No matter what it is, you can't pull me into it."

"But Jesus Christ, the least you can do is—"

"How's the family?" Eddie asked.

"The family?" Turley was blinking. Then he picked up on it. "We're all in good shape. Mom and Dad are okay—"

"And Clifton?" Eddie said. "How's Clifton?" referring to the other brother, the oldest.

Turley's grin was suddenly wide. "Well, you know how it is with Clifton. He's still in there pitching—"

"Strikes?"

Turley didn't answer. The grin stayed, but it seemed to slacken just a little. Then presently he said, "You've been away a long time. We miss you."

Eddie shrugged.

"We really miss you," Turley said. "We always talk about you."

Eddie gazed past his brother. The far-off smile drifted across his lips. He didn't say anything.

"After all," Turley said, "you're one of the family. We never told you to leave. I mean you're always welcome at the house. What I mean is—"

"How'd you know where to find me?"

"Fact is, I didn't. Not at first. Then I remembered, that last letter we got, you mentioned the name of this place. I figured you'd still be here. Anyway, I hoped so. Well, today I was downtown and I looked up the address in the phone book—"

"Today?"

"I mean tonight. I mean—"

"You mean when things got tight you looked me up. Isn't that it?"

Turley blinked again. "Don't get riled."

"Who's riled?"

"You're plenty riled but you cover it up," Turley said. Then he had the grin working again. "I guess you learned that trick from living here in the city. All us country people, us South Jersey melon-eaters, we can't ever learn that caper. We always gotta show our hole card."

Eddie made no comment. He glanced idly at the keyboard, and hit a few notes.

"I got myself in a jam," Turley said.

Eddie went on playing. The notes were in the higher octaves, the fingers very light on the keyboard, making a cheery, babbling-brook sort of tune.

Turley shifted his position in the chair. He was glancing around, his eyes swiftly checking the front door, the side door, and the door leading to the rear exit.

"Wanna hear something pretty?" Eddie said. "Listen to this—"

Turley's hand came down on the fingers that were hitting the keys. Through the resulting discord, his voice came urgently, somewhat hoarsely. "You gotta help me, Eddie. I'm really in a tight spot. You can't turn me down."

"Can't get myself involved, either."

"Believe me, it won't get you involved. All I'm asking, lemme stay in your room until morning."

"You don't mean stay. You mean hide."

Again Turley sighed heavily. Then he nodded.

"From who?" Eddie asked.

"Two troublemakers."

"Really? You sure they made the trouble? Maybe you made it."

"No, they made it," Turley said. "They been giving me grief since early today."

"Get to it. What kind of grief?"

"Tracing me. They've been on my neck from the time I left Dock Street—"

"Dock Street?" Eddie frowned slightly. "What were you doing on Dock Street?"

"Well, I was—" Turley faltered, swallowed hard, then by-passed Dock Street and blurted, "Damn it all, I ain't askin' for the moon. All you gotta do is put me up for the night—"

"Hold it," Eddie said. "Let's get back to Dock Street."

"For Christ's sake—"

"And another thing," Eddie went on. "What're you doing here in Philadelphia?"

"Business."

"Like what?"

Turley didn't seem to hear the question. He took a deep breath. "Something went haywire. Next thing I know, I got these two on my neck. And then, what fixes me proper, I run clean outta folding money. It happens in a hash house on Delaware Avenue when some joker lifts my wallet. If it hadn't been for that, I coulda bought some transportation, at least a taxi to get past the city limits. As it was, all I had left was nickels and dimes, so every time I'm on a streetcar they're right behind me in a brand-new Buick. I tell you, it's been a mean Friday for me, jim. Of all the goddam days to get my pocket picked—"

"You still haven't told me anything."

"I'll give you the rundown later. Right now I'm pushed for time."

As Turley said it, he was turning his head to have another look at the door leading to the street. Absently he lifted his fingers to the battered left side of his face, and grimaced pain-

fully. The grimace faded as the dizziness came again, and he
weaved from side to side, as though the chair had wheels and
was moving along a bumpy road. "Whatsa matter with the
floor?" he mumbled, his eyes half closed now. "What kinda
dump is this? Can't they even fix the floor? It won't even hold
the chair straight."

He began to slide from the chair. Eddie grabbed his shoulders and steadied him.

"You'll be all right," Eddie said. "Just relax."

"Relax?" It came out vaguely. "Who wantsa relax?" Turley's arm flapped weakly to indicate the jam-packed bar and
the crowded tables. "Look at all the people having fun. Why
can't I have some fun? Why can't I—"

It's bad, Eddie thought. It's worse than I figured it was.
He's got some real damage upstairs. I think what we'll hafta
do is—

"Whatsa matter with him?" a voice said.

Eddie looked up and saw the Hut's owner, Harriet. She
was a very fat woman in her middle forties. She had peroxide-
blonde hair, a huge, jutting bosom and tremendous hips. Despite the excess weight, she had a somewhat narrow waistline.
Her face was on the Slavic side, the nose broad-based and
moderately pugged, the eyes gray-blue with a certain level
look that said, You deal with me, you deal straight. I got no
time for two-bit sharpies, fast-hand slicksters, or any kind of
leeches, fakers, and freebee artists. Get cute or cagey and
you'll wind up buying new teeth.

Turley was slipping off the chair again. Harriet caught him
as he sagged sideways. Her fat hands held him firmly under
his armpits while she leaned closer to examine the lump on
his head.

"He's sorta banged up," Eddie said. "He's really groggy.
I think—"

"He ain't as groggy as he looks," Harriet cut in dryly. "If
he don't stop what he's doing he's gonna get banged up
more."

Turley had sent one arm around her hip, his hand sliding
onto the extra-large, soft-solid bulge. She reached back,
grabbed his wrist and flung his arm aside. "You're either wine-
crazy, punch-crazy, or plain crazy," she informed him. "You

try that again, you'll need a brace on your jaw. Now sit still while I have a look."

"I'll have a look too," Turley said, and while the fat woman bent over him to study his damaged skull, he made a serious study of her forty-four-inch bosom. Again his arm went around her hip, and again she flung it off. "You're askin' for it," she told him, hefting her big fist. "You really want it, don't you?"

Turley grinned past the fist. "I always do, blondie. Ain't no hour of the day when I don't."

"You think he needs a doctor?" Eddie asked.

"I'll settle for a big fat nurse," Turley babbled, the grin very loose, sort of idiotic. And then he looked around, as though trying to figure out where he was. "Hey, somebody tell me somethin'. I'd simply like to know—"

"What year it is?" Harriet said. "It's Nineteen fifty-six, and the city is Philadelphia."

"You'll hafta do better than that." Turley sat up straighter. "What I really wanna know is—" But the fog enveloped him and he sat there gazing vacantly past Harriet, past Eddie, his eyes glazing over.

Harriet and Eddie looked at him, then looked at each other. Eddie said, "Keeps up like this, he'll need a stretcher."

Harriet took another look at Turley. She made a final diagnosis, saying, "He'll be all right. I've seen them like that before. In the ring. A certain nerve gets hit and they lose all track of what's happening. Then first thing you know, they're back in stride, they're doing fine."

Eddie was only half convinced. "You really think he'll be okay?"

"Sure he will," Harriet said. "Just look at him. He's made of rock. I know this kind. They take it and like it and come back for more."

"That's correct," Turley said solemnly. Without looking at Harriet, he reached out to shake her hand. Then he changed his mind and his hand strayed in another direction. Harriet shook her head in motherly disapproval. A wistful smile came onto her blunt features, a smile of understanding. She lowered her hand to Turley's head, her fingers in his mussed-up hair to muss it up some more, to let him know that Harriet's Hut was not as mean-hard as it looked, that it was a place where he could rest a while and pull himself together.

"You know him?" she said to Eddie. "Who is he?"

Before Eddie could answer, Turley was off on another fog-bound ride, saying, "Look at that over there across the room. What's that?"

Harriet spoke soothingly, somewhat clinically. "What is it, johnny? Where?"

Turley's arm came up. He tried to point. It took considerable effort and finally he made it.

"You mean the waitress?" Harriet asked.

Turley couldn't answer. He had his eyes fastened on the face and body of the brunette on the other side of the room. She wore an apron and she carried a tray.

"You really like that?" Harriet asked. Again she mussed his hair. She threw a wink at Eddie.

"Like it?" Turley was saying. "I been lookin' all over for something in that line. That's my kind of material. I wanna get to meet that. What's her name?"

"Lena."

"She's something," Turley said. He rubbed his hands. "She's really something."

"So what are your plans?" Harriet asked quietly, as though she meant it seriously.

"Four bits is all I need." Turley's tone was flat and technical. "A drink for me and a drink for her. And that'll get things going."

"Sure as hell it will," Harriet said, saying it more to herself and with genuine seriousness, her eyes aimed now across the crowded Hut, focused on the waitress. And then, to Turley, "You think you got lumps now, you'll get real lumps if you make a pass at that."

She looked at Eddie, waiting for some comment. Eddie had pulled away from it. He'd turned to face the keyboard. His face showed the dim and far-off smile and nothing more.

Turley stood up to get a better look. "What's her name again?"

"Lena."

"So that's Lena," he said, his lips moving slowly.

"That's sheer aggravation," Harriet said. "Do yourself a favor. Sit down. Stop looking."

He sat down, but he went on looking. "How come it's aggravation?" he wanted to know. "You mean it ain't for sale or rent?"

"It ain't available, period."

"Married?"

"No, she ain't married," Harriet said very slowly. Her eyes were riveted on the waitress.

"Then what's the setup?" Turley insisted on knowing. "She hooked up with someone?"

"No," Harriet said. "She's strictly solo. She wants no part of any man. A man moves in too close, he gets it from the hatpin."

"Hatpin?"

"She's got it stuck there in that apron. Some hungry rooster gets too hungry, she jabs him where it really hurts."

Turley snorted. "Is that all?"

"No," Harriet said. "That ain't all. The hatpin is only the beginning. Next thing the poor devil knows, he's getting it from the bouncer. That's her number-one protection, the bouncer."

"Who's the bouncer? Where is he?"

Harriet pointed toward the bar.

Turley peered through the clouds of tobacco smoke. "Hey, wait now, I've seen a picture somewhere. In the papers—"

"On the sports page, it musta been." Harriet's voice was queerly thick. "They had him tagged as the Harleyville Hugger."

"That's right," Turley said. "The Hugger. I remember. Sure, I remember now."

Harriet looked at Turley. She said, "You really do?"

"Sure," Turley said. "I'm a wrestling fan from way back. Never had the cabbage to buy tickets, but I followed it in the papers." He peered again toward the bar. "That's him, all right. That's the Harleyville Hugger."

"And it wasn't no fake when he hugged them, either," Harriet said. "You know anything about the game, you know what a bear hug can do. I mean the real article. He'd get

them in a bear hug, they were finished." And then, significantly, "He still knows how."

Turley snorted again. He looked from the bouncer to the
waitress and back to the bouncer. "That big-bellied slob?"

"He still has it, regardless. He's a crushing machine."

"He couldn't crush my little finger," Turley said. "I'd hook
one short left to that paunch and he'd scream for help. Why,
he ain't nothing but a worn-out—"

Turley was vaguely aware that he'd lost his listener. He
turned and looked and Harriet wasn't there. She was walking
toward the stairway near the bar. She mounted the stairway,
ascending very slowly, her head lowered.

"Whatsa matter with her?" Turley asked Eddie. "She got a
headache?"

Eddie was half turned away from the keyboard, watching
Harriet as she climbed the stairs. Then he turned fully to the
keyboard and hit a few idle notes. His voice came softly
through the music. "I guess you could call it a headache.
She got a problem with the bouncer. He has it bad for the
waitress—"

"Me, too," Turley grinned.

Eddie went on hitting the notes, working in some chords,
building a melody. "With the bouncer it's real bad. And
Harriet knows."

"So what?" Turley frowned vaguely. "What's the bouncer
to her?"

"They live together," Eddie said. "He's her common-law
husband."

Then Turley sagged again, falling forward, bumping into
Eddie, holding onto him for support. Eddie went on playing
the piano. Turley let go and sat back in the chair. He was
waiting for Eddie to turn around and look at him. And finally
Eddie stopped playing and turned and looked. He saw the
grin on Turley's face. Again it was the idiotic, eyes-glazed
grin.

"You want a drink?" Eddie asked. "Maybe you could use
a drink."

"I don't need no drink." Turley swayed from side to side.
"Tell you what I need. I need some information. Wanna be
straightened out on something. You wanna help me on that?"

"Help you on what?" Eddie murmured. "What is it you wanna know?"

Turley shut his eyes tightly. He opened them, shut them, opened them again. He saw Eddie sitting there. He said, "What you doin' here?"

Eddie shrugged.

Turley had his own answer. "I'll tell you what you're doing. You're wasting away—"

"All right," Eddie said gently. "All right—"

"It ain't all right," Turley said. And then the disjointed phrases spilled from the muddled brain. "Sits there at a second-hand piano. Wearing rags. When what you should be wearing is a full-dress suit. With one of them ties, the really fancy duds. And it should be a grand piano, a great big shiny grand piano, one of them Steinbergs, god-damn it, with every seat taken in the concert hall. That's where you should be, and what I want to know is—why ain't you there?"

"You really need a bracer, Turl. You're away off the groove."

"Don't study my condition, jim. Study your own. Why ain't you there in that concert hall?"

Eddie shrugged and let it slide past.

But Turley banged his hands against his knees. "Why ain't you there?"

"Because I'm here," Eddie said. "I can't be two places at once."

It didn't get across. "Don't make sense," Turley blabbered. "Just don't make sense at all. A knockout of a dame and she ain't got no boy friend. A piano man as good as they come and he don't make enough to buy new shoes."

Eddie laughed.

"It ain't comical," Turley said. "It's a screwed-up state of affairs." He spoke to some invisible third party, pointing a finger at the placid-faced musician. "Here he sits at this wreck of a piano, in this dirty old crummy old joint that oughtta be inspected by the fire marshal, or anyway by the Board of Health. Look at the floor, they still use sawdust on the goddam floor—" He cupped his hands to his mouth and called, "At least buy some new chairs, for Christ's sake—" Then referring again to the soft-eyed musician, "Sits here, night after

night. Sits here wasting away in the bush leagues when he
oughta be way up there in the majors, way up at the top cause
he's got the stuff, he's got it in them ten fingers. He's a star,
I tell you, he's the star of them all—"

"Easy, Turl—"

Turley was feeling it deep. He stood up, shouting again,
"It oughtta be a grand piano, with candlesticks like that
other cat has. Where's the candlesticks? Whatsa matter
here? You cheap or somethin'? You can't afford no candlesticks?"

"Aaah, close yer head," some nearby beer-guzzler offered.

Turley didn't hear the heckler. He went on shouting, tears
streaming down his rough-featured face. The cuts in his
mouth had opened again and the blood was trickling from his
lips. "And there's something wrong somewhere," he proclaimed to the audience that had no idea who he was or what
he was talking about, "—like anyone knows that two and two
adds up to four but this adds up to minus three. It just ain't
right and it calls for some kind of action—"

"You really want action?" a voice inquired pleasantly.

It was the voice of the bouncer, formerly known as the
Harleyville Hugger, known now in the Hut by his real name,
Wally Plyne, although certain admirers still insisted it was
Hugger. He stood there, five feet nine and weighing two-
twenty. There was very little hair on his head, and what remained was clipped short, fuzzy. His left ear was somewhat
out of shape, and his nose was a wreck, fractured so many
times that now it was hardly a nose at all. It was more like a
blob of putty flattened onto the rough-grained face. In Plyne's
mouth there was considerable bridgework, and ribboning
down from his chin and toward the collarbone was a poorly
stitched scar, obviously an emergency job performed by some
intern. Plyne was not pleased with the scar. He wore his shirt
collar buttoned high to conceal it as much as possible. He was
extremely sensitive about his battered face, and when anyone
looked at him too closely he'd stiffen and his neck would swell
and redden. His eyes would plead with the looker not to
laugh. There'd been times when certain lookers had ignored
the plea, and the next thing they knew, their ribs were fractured and they had severe internal injuries. At Harriet's Hut

the first law of self-preservation was never laugh at the bouncer.

The bouncer was forty-three years old.

He stood there looking down at Turley. He was waiting for an answer. Turley looked up at him and said, "Why you buttin' in? Cantcha see I'm talkin'?"

"You're talking too loud," Plyne said. His tone remained pleasant, almost sympathetic. He was looking at the tears rolling down Turley's cheeks.

"If I don't talk loud they won't hear me," Turley said. "I want them to hear me."

"They got other things to do," Plyne said patiently. "They're drinkin' and they don't wanna be bothered."

"That's what's wrong," Turley sobbed. "Nobody wantsa be bothered."

Plyne took a deep breath. He said to Turley, "Now look, whoever messed up your face like that, you go ahead and hit him back. But not here. This here's a quiet place of business—"

"What you sellin' me?" Turley blinked the tears away, his tone changing to a growl. "Who asked you to be sorry for my goddam face? It's my face. The lumps are mine, the cuts are mine. You better worry about your own damn face."

"Worry?" Plyne was giving careful thought to the remark. "How you mean that?"

Turley's eyes and lips started a grin, his mouth started a reply. Before the grin could widen, before the words could come, Eddie moved in quickly, saying to Plyne, "He didn't mean anything, Wally. Cantcha see he's all mixed up?"

"You stay out of this," Plyne said, not looking at Eddie. He was studying Turley's face, waiting for the grin to go away.

The grin remained. At nearby tables there was a waiting quiet. The quiet spread to other tables, then to all the tables, and then to the crowded bar. They were all staring at the big man who stood there grinning at Plyne.

"Get it off," Plyne told Turley. "Get it off your face."

Turley widened the grin.

Plyne took another deep breath. Something came into his eyes, a kind of dull glow. Eddie saw it and knew what it meant.

He was up from the piano stool, saying to Plyne, "Don't, Wally. He's sick."

"Who's sick?" Turley challenged. "I'm in grade-A shape. I'm ready for—"

"He's ready for a brain examination," Eddie said to Plyne, to the staring audience. "He ran into a pole and banged his head. Look at that bump. If it ain't a fracture it's maybe a concussion."

"Call for an ambulance," someone directed.

"Lookit, he's bleeding from the mouth," another voice put in. "Could be that's from the busted head."

Plyne blinked a few times. The glow faded from his eyes.

Turley went on grinning. But now the grin wasn't aimed at Plyne or anyone or anything else. Again it was the idiotic grin.

Plyne looked at Eddie. "You know him?"

Eddie shrugged. "Sort of."

"Who is he?"

Another shrug. "I'll take him outside. Let him get some air—"

Plyne's thick fingers closed on Eddie's sleeve. "I asked you something. Who is he?"

"You hear the man?" It was Turley again, coming out of the brain-battered fog. "The man says he wantsa know. I think he's got a point there."

"Then you tell me," Plyne said to Turley. He stepped closer, peering into the glazed eyes. "Maybe you don't need an ambulance, after all. Maybe you ain't really hurt that bad. Can you tell me who you are?"

"Brother."

"Whose brother?"

"His." Turley pointed to Eddie.

"I didn't know he had a brother," Plyne said.

"Well, that's the way it goes." Turley spoke to all the nearby tables. "You learn something new every day."

"I'm willing to learn," Plyne said. And then, as though Eddie wasn't there, "He never talks about himself. There's a lota things about him I don't know."

"You don't?" Turley had the grin again. "How long has he worked here?"

"Three years."

"That's a long time," Turley said. "You sure oughtta have him down pat by now."

"Nobody's got him down pat. Only thing we know for sure, he plays the piano."

"You pay him wages?"

"Sure we pay him wages."

"To do what?"

"Play the piano."

"And what else?"

"Just that," Plyne said. "We pay him to play the piano, that's all."

"You mean you don't pay him wages to talk about himself?"

Plyne tightened his lips. He didn't reply.

Turley moved in closer. "You want it all for free, don't you? But the thing is, you can't get it for free. You wanna learn about a person, it costs you. And the more you learn, the more it costs. Like digging a well, the deeper you go, the more expenses you got. And sometimes it's a helluva lot more than you can afford."

"What you getting at?" Plyne was frowning now. He turned his head to look at the piano man. He saw the carefree smile and it bothered him, it caused his frown to darken. There was only a moment of that, and then he looked again at Turley. He got rid of the frown and said, "All right, never mind. This talk means nothing. It's jabber, and you're punchy, and I got other things to do. I can't stay here wasting time with you."

The bouncer walked away. The audience at the bar and the tables went back to drinking. Turley and Eddie were seated now, Eddie facing the keyboard, hitting a few chords and starting a tune. It was a placid, soft-sweet tune and the dreamy sounds brought a dreamy smile to Turley's lips. "That's nice," Turley whispered. "That's really nice."

The music went on and Turley nodded slowly, unaware that he was nodding. As his head came up, and started to go down again, he saw the front door open.

Two men came in.

2

"THAT'S them," Turley said.

Eddie went on making the music.

"That's them, all right," Turley said matter-of-factly.

The door closed behind the two men and they stood there turning their heads very slowly, looking from crowded tables to crowded bar, back to the tables, to the bar again, looking everywhere.

Then they spotted Turley. They started forward.

"Here they come," Turley said, still matter-of-factly. "Look at them."

Eddie's eyes stayed on the keyboard. He had his mind on the keyboard. The warm-cool music flowed on and now it was saying to Turley, It's your problem, entirely yours, keep me out of it.

The two men came closer. They moved slowly. The tables were close-packed, blocking their path. They were trying to move faster, to force their way through.

"Here they come," Turley said. "They're really coming now."

Don't look, Eddie said to himself. You take one look and that'll do it, that'll pull you into it. You don't want that, you're here to play the piano, period. But what's this? What's happening? There ain't no music now, your fingers are off the keyboard.

He turned his head and looked and saw the two men coming closer.

They were well-dressed men. The one in front was short and very thin, wearing a pearl-gray felt hat and a white silk muffler and a single-breasted, dark blue overcoat. The man behind him was thin, too, but much taller. He wore a hat of darker gray, a black-and-silver striped muffler, and his overcoat was a dark gray six-button-benny.

Now they were halfway across the room. There was more space here between the tables. They were coming faster.

Eddie jabbed stiffened fingers into Turley's ribs. "Don't sit there. Get up and go."

"Go where?" And there it was again, the idiotic grin.

"Side door," Eddie hissed at him, gave him another finger-stiffened jab, harder this time.

"Hey, quit that," Turley said. "That hurts."

"Does it?" Another jab made it really hurt, pulled the grin off Turley's face, pulled his rump off the chair. Then Turley was using his legs, going past the stacked pyramid of beer cases, walking faster and faster and finally lunging toward the side door.

The two men took a short cut, going diagonally away from the tables. They were running now, streaking to intercept Turley. It looked as though they had it made.

Then Eddie was up from the piano stool, seeing Turley aiming at the side door some fifteen feet away. The two men were closing in on Turley. They'd pivoted off the diagonal path and now they ran parallel to the pyramid of beer cases. Eddie made a short rush that took him into the high-stacked pile of bottle-filled cardboard boxes. He gave the pile a shoulder bump and a box came down and then another box, and more boxes. It caused a traffic jam as the two men collided with the fallen beer cases, tripped over the cardboard hurdles, went down and got up and tripped again. While that happened, Turley opened the side door and ran out.

Some nine beer cases had fallen off the stacked pyramid and several of the bottles had come loose to hit the floor and break. The two men were working hard to get past the blockade of cardboard boxes and broken bottles. One of them, the shorter one, was turning his head to catch a glimpse of whatever funnyman had caused this fiasco. He saw Eddie standing there near the partially crumbled pyramid. Eddie shrugged and lifted his arms in a sheepish gesture, as though to say, An accident, I just bumped into it, that's all. The short thin man didn't say anything. There wasn't time for a remark.

Eddie went back to the piano. He sat down and started to play. He hit a few soft chords, the dim and far-off smile drifting onto his lips while the two thin well-dressed men finally made it to the side door. Through the soft sound of the music he heard the hard sound of the door slamming shut behind them.

He went on playing. There were no wrong notes, no breaks in the rhythm, but he was thinking of Turley, seeing the two men going after Turley along the too-dark streets in the too-cold stillness out there that might be broken any moment now by the sound of a shot.

But I don't think so, he told himself. They didn't have that look, as though they were gunning for meat. It was more of a bargaining look, like all they want is to sit down with Turley and talk some business.

What kind of business? Well, sure, you know what kind. It's something on the shady side. He said it was Clifton's transaction and that puts it on the shady side, with Turl stooging for Clifton like he's always done. So whatever it is, they're in a jam again, your two dear brothers. It's a first-class talent they have for getting into jams, getting out, and getting in again. You think they'll get out this time? Well, we hope so. We really hope so. We wish them luck, and that about says it. So what you do now is get off the trolley. It ain't your ride and you're away from it.

A shadow fell across the keyboard. He tried not to see it, but it was there and it stayed there. He turned his head sideways and saw the bulky legs, the barrel torso and the mashed-nosed face of the bouncer.

He went on playing.

"That's pretty," Plyne said.

Eddie nodded his thanks.

"It's very pretty," Plyne said. "But it just ain't pretty enough. I don't wanna hear any more."

Eddie stopped playing. His arms came down limply at his sides. He sat there and waited.

"Tell me something," the bouncer said. "What is it with you?"

Eddie shrugged.

Plyne took a deep breath. "God damn it," he said to no one in particular. "I've known this party for three years now and I hardly know him at all."

Eddie's soft smile was aimed at the keyboard. He tapped out a few idle notes in the middle octaves.

"That's all you'll ever get from him," Plyne said to invisible listeners. "That same no-score routine. No matter what comes up, it's always I-don't-know-from-nothing."

Eddie's fingers stayed there in the middle octaves.

The bouncer's manner changed. His voice was hard. "I told you to stop playing."

The music stopped. Eddie went on looking at the keyboard. He said, "What is it, Wally? What is it bothers you?"

"You really wanna know?" Plyne said it slowly, as though he'd scored a point. "All right, take a look." His arm stretched out, the forefinger rigid and aiming at the littered floor, the overturned cardboard boxes, the bottles, the scattered glass and the spilled beer foaming on the splintered floor boards.

Eddie shrugged again. "I'll clean it up," he said, and started to rise from the piano stool. Plyne pushed him back onto it.

"Tell me," Plyne said, and pointed again at the beer-stained floor. "What's the deal on that?"

"Deal?" The piano man seemed bewildered. "No deal at all. It was an accident. I didn't see where I was going, and I bumped into—"

But it was no use going on. The bouncer wasn't buying it.

"Wanna bet?" the bouncer asked mildly. "Wanna bet it wasn't no accident?"

Eddie didn't reply.

"You won't tell me, I'll tell you," Plyne said. "A tag-team play, that's what it was."

"Could be." Eddie gave a very slight shrug. "I might have done it without thinking, I mean sort of unconscious-like. I'm really not sure—"

"Not much you ain't." Plyne showed a thick wet smile that widened gradually. "You handled that stunt like you'd planned it on paper. The timing was perfect."

Eddie blinked several times. He told himself to stop it. He said to himself, Something is happening here and you better check it before it goes further.

But there was no way to check it. The bouncer was saying, "First time I ever saw you pull that kind of caper. In all the years you been here, you never butted in, not once. No matter what the issue was, no matter who was in it. So how come you butted in tonight?"

Another slight shrug, and the words coming softly, "I might have figured he could use some help, like I said, I'm not really sure. Or, on the other hand, you see someone in a jam, you remind yourself he's a close relative—I don't know, it's something along those lines."

Plyne's face twisted in a sort of disgusted grimace, as though he knew there was no use digging any deeper. He turned and started away from the piano.

Then something stopped him and caused him to turn and come back. He leaned against the side of the piano. For some moments he said nothing, just listened to the music, his brow creased slightly in a moderately thoughtful frown. Then, quite casually, he moved his heavy hand, brushing Eddie's fingers away from the keyboard.

Eddie looked up, waiting.

"Gimme some more on this transaction," the bouncer said.

"Like what?"

"Them two men you stalled with the beer cases. What's the wire on them?"

"I don't know," Eddie said.

"You don't know why they were chasing him?"

"Ain't got the least idea."

"Come on, come on."

"I can't tell you, Wally. I just don't know."

"You expect me to buy that?"

Eddie shrugged and didn't reply.

"All right," Plyne said. "We'll try it from another angle. This brother of yours. What's his line?"

"Don't know that either. Ain't seen him for years. Last I knew, he was working on Dock Street."

"Doing what?"

"Longshoreman."

"You don't know what he's doing now?"

"If I knew, I'd tell you."

"Yeah, sure." Plyne was folding his thick arms high on his chest. "Spill," he said. "Come on, spill."

Eddie smiled amiably at the bouncer. "What's all this courtroom action?" And then, the smile widening, "You going to law school, Wally? You practicing on me?"

"It ain't like that," Plyne said. He was stumped for a moment. "It's just that I wanna be sure, that's all. I mean—well, the thing of it is, I'm general manager here. Whatever happens in the Hut, I'm sorta responsible. You know that."

Eddie nodded, his eyebrows up. "That's a point."

"You're damn right it is," the bouncer pressed his advantage. "I gotta make sure this place keeps its license. It's a legitimate place of business. If I got anything to say, it's gonna stay legitimate."

"You're absolutely right," Eddie said.

"I'm glad you know it." Plyne's eyes were narrowed again. "Another thing you'd better know, I got more brains than you think. Can't play no music or write poems or anything like that, but sure as hell I can add up a score. Like with this brother of yours and them two engineers who wanted him for more than just a friendly chat."

"That adds," Eddie said.

"It adds perfect," Plyne approved his own arithmetic. "And I'll add it some more. I'll give it to you right down the line. He mighta been a longshoreman then, but it's a cinch he's switched jobs. He's lookin' for a higher income now. Whatever work he's doing, there's heavy cash involved—"

Eddie was puzzled. He was saying to himself, The dumber you play it, the better.

"Them two engineers," the bouncer was saying, "they weren't no small-timers. I gandered the way they were dressed. Them overcoats were hand-stitched; I know that custom quality when I see it. So we take it from there, we do it with arrows—"

"With what?"

"With arrows," Plyne said, his finger tracing an arrow-line on the side of the piano. "From them to your brother. From your brother to you."

"Me?" Eddie laughed lightly. "You're not adding it now. You're stretching it."

"But not too far," Plyne said. "Because it's more than just possible. Because there ain't nothing wrong with my peepers. I seen your brother sitting here and giving you that sales talk. It's like he wants you in on the deal, whatever it is—"

Eddie was laughing again.

"What's funny?" Plyne asked.

Eddie went on laughing. It wasn't loud laughter, but it was real. He was trying to hold it back and he couldn't.

"Is it me?" Plyne spoke very quietly. "You laughing at me?"

"At myself," Eddie managed to say through the laughter. "I got a gilt-framed picture of the setup. The big deal, with me the key man, that final arrow pointing at me. You must be kidding, Wally. Just take a look and see for yourself. Look at the key man."

Plyne looked, seeing the thirty-a-week musician who sat there at the battered piano, the soft-eyed, soft-mouthed no-body whose ambitions and goals aimed at exactly zero, who'd been working here three years without asking or even hinting for a raise. Who never grumbled when the tips were stingy, or griped about anything, for that matter, not even when ordered to help with the chairs and tables at closing time, to sweep the floor, to take out the trash.

Plyne's eyes focused on him and took him in. Three years, and aside from the music he made, his presence at the Hut meant nothing. It was almost as though he wasn't there and the piano was playing all by itself. Regardless of the action at the tables or the bar, the piano man was out of it, not even an observer. He had his back turned and his eyes on the key-board, content to draw his pauper's wages and wear pauper's rags. A gutless wonder, Plyne decided, fascinated with this living example of absolute neutrality. Even the smile was something neutral. It was never aimed at a woman. It was aimed very far out there beyond all tangible targets, really far out there beyond the left-field bleachers. So where does that take it? Plyne asked himself. And of course there was no answer, not even the slightest clue.

But even so, he made a final effort. He squinted hard at the piano man, and said, "Tell me one thing. Where'd you come from?"

"I was born," Eddie said.

The bouncer thought it over for some moments. Then, "Thanks for the tipoff. I had it figured you came from a cloud."

Eddie laughed softly. Plyne was walking away, going toward the bar. At the bar the dark-haired waitress was arranging shot glasses on a tray. Plyne approached her, hesitated, then came in close and said something to her. She didn't reply. She didn't even look at him. She picked up the tray and headed for one of the tables. Plyne stood motionless, staring at her, his mouth tight, his teeth biting hard at the inside of his lip.

The soft-easy music came drifting from the piano.

3

IT was twenty minutes later and the last nightcapper had been ushered out. The bartender was cleaning the last of the glasses, and the bouncer had gone upstairs to bed. The waitress had her overcoat on and was lighting a cigarette as she leaned back against the wall and watched Eddie, who was sweeping the floor.

He finished sweeping, emptied the dust-pan, put the broom away, and took his overcoat off the hanger near the piano. It was a very old overcoat. The collar was torn and two buttons were missing. He didn't have a hat.

The waitress watched him as he walked toward the front door. He turned his head to smile at the bartender and say good night. And then, to the waitress, "See you, Lena."

"Wait," she said, moving toward him as he opened the front door.

He stood there smiling somewhat questioningly. In the four months she'd been working here, they'd never exchanged more than a friendly hello or good night. Never anything much more than that.

Now she was saying, "Can you spare six bits?"

"Sure." Without hesitation he reached into his pants pocket. But the questioning look remained. It even deepened just a little.

"I'm sorta stuck tonight," the waitress explained. "When Harriet pays me tomorrow, you'll get it back."

"No hurry," he said, giving her two quarters, two dimes and a nickel.

"It goes for a meal," Lena explained further, putting the coins into her purse. "I figured Harriet would cook me something, but she went to bed early, and I didn't want to bother her."

"Yeah, I saw her going upstairs," Eddie said. He paused a moment. "I guess she was tired."

"Well, she works hard," Lena said. She took a final puff at the cigarette and tossed it into a cuspidor. "I wonder how she does it. All that weight. I bet she's over two hundred."

"Way over," Eddie said. "But she carries it nice. It's packed in solid."

"Too much of it. She loses a little, she'll feel better."

"She feels all right."

Lena shrugged. She didn't say anything.

Eddie opened the door and stepped aside. She went out, and he followed her. She started across the pavement and he said, "See you tomorrow," and she stopped and turned and faced him. She said, "I think six bits is more than I need. A half is enough," and started to open her purse.

He said, "No, that's all right." But she came toward him, extending the quarter, saying, "At John's I can get a platter for forty. Another dime for coffee and that does it."

He waved away the silver quarter. He said, "You might want a piece of cake or something."

She came closer. "Go on, take it," pushing the coin toward him.

He grinned. "High finance."

"Will you please take it?"

"Who needs it? I won't starve."

"You sure you can spare it?" Her head was slanted, her eyes searching his face.

He went on grinning. "Quit worrying. I won't run short."

"Yeah, I know." She went on searching his face. "Your wallet gets low, you just pick up the phone and call your broker. Who's your broker?"

"It's a big firm on Wall Street. I fly to New York twice a week. Just to have a look at the board."

"When'd you eat last?"

He shrugged. "I had a sandwich—"

"When?"

"I don't know. Around four-thirty, maybe."

"Nothing in between?" And then, not waiting for an answer, "Come on, walk me to John's. You'll have something."

"But—"

"Come on, will you?" She took his arm and pulled him along. "You wanna live, you gotta eat."

It occurred to him that he was really hungry and he could use a bowl of soup and a hot platter. The wet-cold wind was getting through his thin coat and biting into him. The thought of hot food was pleasant. Then another thought came and he winced slightly. He had exactly twelve cents in his pocket.

He shrugged and went on walking with Lena. He decided to settle for a cup of coffee. At least the coffee would warm him up. But you really oughtta have something to eat, he told himself. How come you didn't eat tonight? You always grab a bite at the food counter at the Hut around twelve-thirty. But not tonight. You had nothing tonight. How come you forgot to fill your belly?

Then he remembered. That business with Turley, he told himself. You were busy with Turley and you forgot to eat.

I wonder if Turley made it or not. I wonder if he got away. He knows how to move around and he can take care of himself. Yes, I'd say the chances are he made it. You really think so? He was handicapped, you know. It's a cinch he wasn't in condition to play hare-and-hounds with him the hare. Well, what are you gonna do? You can't do anything. I wish you'd drop it.

And another thing. What is it with this one here, this waitress? What bothers her? You know there's something bothering her. You caught the slightest hint of it when she talked about Harriet. She was sorta fishing then, she had the line out. Well sure, that's what it is. She's worried about Harriet and the bouncer and their domestic difficulties, because the bouncer's got his eyes on someone else these days—this waitress here. Well, it ain't her fault. Only thing she offers Plyne is an ice-cold look whenever he tries to move in. So let him keep trying. What do you care? Say, you wanna do me a favor? Get outta my hair, you're bugging me.

But just then a queer idea came into his brain, a downright

silly notion. He couldn't understand why it was there. He was
wondering how tall the waitress was, whether she was taller
than he was. He tried to discard the thought, but it stayed
there. It nudged him, shoved him, and finally caused him to
turn his head and look at her.

He had to look down a little. He was a few inches taller
than the waitress. He estimated she stood about five-six in
semi-high heels. So what? he asked himself, but he went on
looking as they crossed a narrow street and passed under a
street lamp. The coat she wore fitted rather tightly and it
brought out the lines of her body. She was high-waisted and
with her slimness and her certain way of walking, it made her
look taller. I guess that's it, he thought. I was just curious
about it, that's all.

But he went on looking. He didn't know why he was looking. The glow from the street lamp spread out and lighted
her face and he saw her profiled features that wouldn't make
her a cover girl or a model for cosmetic ads, she didn't have
that kind of face. Except for the skin. Her skin was clear and
it had the kind of texture guaranteed in cosmetic ads, but this
didn't come from cosmetics. This was from inside, and he
thought, Probably she's got a good stomach, or a good set
of glands, it's something along that line. There's nothing fragile about this one. That ain't a fragile nose or mouth or chin,
and yet it's female, more female than them fragile-pretty types
who look more like ornaments than girls. All in all, I'd say
this one could give them cards and spades and still come out
ahead. No wonder the bouncer tries to move in. No wonder
all the roosters at the bar are always looking twice when she
walks past. And still she ain't interested just in anything wears
pants.

It's as though she's all finished with that. Maybe something
happened that made her say, That does it, that ends it. But
now you're guessing. How come you're guessing? Next thing,
you'll want to know how old she is. And merely incidentally,
how old you think she is? I'd say around twenty-seven. Should
we ask her? If you do, she'll ask you why you want to know.
And all you can say is, I just wondered. All right, stop wondering. It ain't as if you're interested. You know you're not
interested.

Then what is it? What put you on this line of thinking? You oughtta get off it, it's like a road with too many turns and first thing you know, you just don't know where you are. But why is it she never has much to say? And hardly ever smiles?

Come to think of it, she's strictly on the solemn side. Not dreary, really. It's just that she's serious-solemn, and yet you've seen her laugh, she'll laugh at something that's comical. That is, when it's really comical.

She was laughing now. She was looking at him and quietly laughing.

"What is it?" he asked.

"Like Charlie Chaplin," she said.

"Like who?"

"Charlie Chaplin. In them silent movies he used to make. When something puzzled him and he wanted to ask about it and couldn't find the words, he'd get a dumb look on his face. You had it perfect just then."

"Did I?"

She nodded. Then she stopped laughing. She said, "What was it? What puzzled you?"

He smiled dimly. "If we're gonna get to John's, we oughtta keep walkin'."

She didn't say anything. They went on walking, turning a corner and coming onto a rutted pavement that bordered a cobblestoned street.

They covered another block and on the corner there was a rectangular structure that had once been a trolley car and was now an eatery that stayed open all night. Some of the windows were cracked, much of the paint was scraped off, and the entrance door slanted on loose hinges. Above the entrance door a sign read, *Best Food in Port Richmond—John's.* They went in and started toward the counter and for some reason she pulled him away from the counter and into a booth. As they sat down he saw she was looking past him, her eyes aimed at the far end of the counter. Her face was expressionless. He knew who it was down there. He knew also why she'd talked him into walking with her when they'd left the Hut. She hadn't wanted him to walk alone. She'd seen his maneuver with the beer cases when the two men had made their try for

Turley, and all that talk about you-gotta-eat was merely so that he shouldn't be on the street alone.

Very considerate of her, he thought. He smiled at her to hide his annoyance. But then it amused him, and he thought, She wants to play nursemaid, let her play nursemaid.

There weren't many people in the diner. He counted four at this section of the counter, and two couples in other booths. Behind the counter the short, chunky Greek named John was breaking eggs above the grill. So with John it comes to nine, he thought. We got nine witnesses in case they try something. I don't think they will. You had a good look at them in the Hut. They didn't look like dunces. No, they won't try anything now.

John served four fried eggs to a fat man at the counter, came out from behind the counter and went over to the booth. The waitress ordered roast pork and mashed potatoes and said she wanted an extra roll. He asked for a cup of coffee with cream. She said, "That all you gonna have?" He nodded and she said, "You know you're hungry. Order something."

He shook his head. John walked away from the booth. They sat there, not saying anything. He hummed a tune and lightly drummed his fingers on the tabletop.

Then she said, "You loaned me seventy-five cents. What you got left for yourself?"

"I'm really not hungry."

"Not much. Come on, tell me. How much change you got?"

He put his hand in his pants pocket. "I hate to break this fifty-dollar bill."

"Now, listen—"

"Forget it," he cut in mildly. Then, his thumb flicking backward, "They still there?"

"Who?"

"You know who."

She looked past him, past the side of the booth, her eyes checking the far end of the counter. Then she looked at him and nodded slowly. She said, "It's my fault. I didn't use my head. I didn't stop to think they might be here—"

"What're they doing now? They still eating?"

"They're finished. They're just sitting there. Smoking."

"Looking?"

"Not at us. They were looking this way a minute ago. I don't think it meant anything. They can't see you."

"Then I guess it's all right," he said. He grinned.

She grinned back at him. "Sure, it's nothing to worry about. Even if they see you, they won't do anything."

"I know they won't." And then, widening the grin, "You won't let them."

"Me?" Her grin faded. She frowned slightly. "What can I do?"

"I guess you can do something." Then, breezily, "You could hold them off while I cut out."

"Is that a joke? Whatcha think I am, Joan of Arc?"

"Well, now that you mention it—"

"Lemme tell you something," she interrupted. "I don't know what's happening between you and them two and I don't care. Whatever it is, I want no part of it. That clear?"

"Sure." And then, with a slight shrug, "If that's the way you really feel about it."

"I said so, didn't I?"

"Yeah. You said so."

"What's that supposed to mean?" Her head was slanted and she was giving him a look. "You think I don't mean what I say?"

He shrugged again. "I don't think anything. You're doing all the arguing."

John arrived with the tray, served the platter and the coffee, figured the price with his fingers and said sixty-five cents. Eddie took the dime and two pennies from his pocket and put the coins on the table. She pushed the coins aside and gave John the seventy-five cents. Eddie smiled at John and pointed to the twelve cents on the table. John said thanks, picked up the coins and went back to the counter. Eddie leaned low over the steaming black coffee, blew on it to cool it, and began sipping it. There was no sound from the other side of the table. He sensed that she wasn't eating, but was just sitting watching him. He didn't look up. He went on sipping the coffee. It was very hot and he sipped it slowly. Then he heard the noise of her knife and fork and he glanced up and saw that she was eating rapidly.

"What's the rush?" he murmured. She didn't reply. The noise of her knife and fork went on and then stopped suddenly and he looked up again. He saw she was looking out and away from the table, focusing again on the far end of the counter.

She frowned and resumed eating. He waited a few moments, and then murmured, "I thought you said it ain't your problem."

She let it slide past. She went on frowning. "They're still sitting there. I wish they'd get up and go out."

"I guess they wanna stay here and get warm. It's nice and warm in here."

"It's getting too warm," she said.

"It is?" He sipped more coffee. "I don't feel it."

"Not much you don't." She gave him another sideways look. "Don't give me that cucumber routine. You're sitting on a hot spot and you know it."

"Got a cigarette?"

"I'm talking to you—"

"I heard what you said." He gestured toward her handbag. "Look, I'm all outa smokes. See if you got a spare."

She opened the handbag and took out a pack of cigarettes. She gave him one, took one for herself, and struck a match. As he leaned forward to get the light, she said, "Who are they?"

"You got me."

"Ever see them before?"

"Nope."

"All right," she said. "We'll drop it."

She finished eating, drank some water, took a final puff at her cigarette and put it out in the ashtray. They got up from the booth and walked out of the eatery. Now the wind came harder and colder and it had started to snow. As the flakes hit the pavement they stayed there white instead of melting. She pulled up her coat collar, and put her hands into her pockets. She looked up and around at the snow coming down, and said she liked the snow, she hoped it would keep on snowing. He said it would probably snow all night and then some tomorrow. She asked him if he liked the snow. He said it didn't really matter to him.

They were walking along on the cobblestoned street and

he wanted to look behind him but he didn't. The wind was coming at them and they had to keep their heads down and push themselves along. She was saying he could walk her home if he wanted to. He said all right, not thinking to ask where she lived. She told him she lived in a rooming house on Kenworth Street. She was telling him the block number but he didn't hear. He was listening to the sound of his footsteps and her footsteps and wondering if that was the only sound. Then he heard the other sound, but it was only some alley cats crying. It was a small sound, and he decided they were kittens wailing for their mother. He wished there was something he could do for them, the motherless kittens. They were somewhere in that alley across the street. He heard the waitress saying, "Where you going?"

He had moved away from her, toward the curb. He was looking at the entrance to the alley across the street. She came up to him and said, "What is it?"

"The kittens," he said.

"Kittens?"

"Listen to them," he said. "Poor little kittens. They're having a sad time."

"You got it twisted," she said. "They ain't no kittens, they're grown-up cats. From what I hear, they're having a damn good time."

He listened again. This time he heard it correctly. He grinned and said, "Guess it needs a new aerial."

"No," she said. "The aerial's all right. You just got your stations mixed, that's all."

He didn't quite get that. He looked at her inquiringly.

She said, "I guess it's a habit you got. Like in the Hut. I've noticed it. You never seem to know or care what's really happening. Always tuned in on some weird kinda wave length that only you can hear. As if you ain't concerned in the least with current events."

He laughed softly.

"Quit that," she cut in. "Quit making it a joke. This ain't no joke, what's happening now. You take a look around, you'll see what I mean."

She was facing him, staring past him. He said, "We got company?"

She nodded slowly.

"I don't hear anything," he said. "Only them cats—"

"Forget the cats. You got your hands full now. You can't afford no side shows."

She's got a point there, he thought. He turned and looked down the street. Far down there the yellow-green glow from a street lamp came dripping off the tops of the parked cars. It formed a faintly lit, yellow-green pool on the cobblestones, a shimmering screen for all moving shadows. He saw two shadows moving on the screen, two creepers crouched down there behind one of the parked cars.

"They're waiting," he said. "They're waiting for us to move."

"If we're gonna move, we'd better do it fast." She spoke technically. "Come on, we'll hafta run—"

"No," he said. "There's no rush. We'll just keep walking."

Again she gave him the searching look. "You been through this sorta thing before?"

He didn't answer. He was concentrating on the distance between here and the street corner ahead. They were walking slowly toward the corner. He estimated the distance was some twenty yards. As they went on walking slowly, he looked at her and smiled and said, "Don't be nervous. There's nothing to be nervous about."

Not much there ain't, he thought.

4

THEY came to the street corner and turned onto a narrow street that had only one lamp. His eyes probed the darkness and found a splintered wooden door, the entrance to an alleyway. He tried the door and it gave, and he went through and she followed him, closing the door behind her. As they stood there, waiting for the sound of approaching footsteps, he heard a rustling noise, as though she was searching for something under her coat.

"What are you doing?" he asked.

"Getting my hatpin," she said. "They come in here, they'll have a five-inch hatpin all ready for them."

"You think it'll bother them?"

"It won't make them happy, that's for sure."

"I guess you're right. That thing goes in deep, it hurts."

"Let them try something." She spoke in a tight whisper. "Just let them try something, and see what happens."

They waited there in the pitch-black darkness behind the alley door. Moments passed, and then they heard the footsteps coming. The footsteps arrived, hesitated, went on and then stopped. Then the footsteps came back toward the alley door. He could feel the rigid stillness of the waitress, close beside him. Then he could hear the voices on the other side of the door.

"Where'd they go?" one of the voices said.

"Maybe into one of these houses."

"We shoulda moved faster."

"We played it right. It's just that they were close to home. They went into one of these houses."

"Well, whaddya want to do?"

"We can't start ringing doorbells."

"You wanna keep walking? Maybe they're somewhere up the street."

"Let's go back to the car. I'm getting cold."

"You wanna call it a night?"

"A loused-up night."

"In spades. God damn it."

The footsteps went away. He said to her, "Let's wait a few minutes," and she said, "I guess I can put the hatpin away."

He grinned and murmured, "Be careful where you put it, I don't wanna get jabbed." They were standing there in the cramped space of the very narrow alley and as her arm moved, her elbow came lightly against his ribs. It wasn't more than a touch, but for some reason he quivered, as though the hatpin had jabbed him. He knew it wasn't the hatpin. And then, moving again, shifting her position in the cramped space, she touched him again and there was more quivering. He breathed in fast through his teeth, feeling something happening. It was happening suddenly and much too fast and he tried to stop it. He said to himself, You gotta stop it. But the thing

of it is, it came on you too quick, you just weren't ready for
it, you had no idea it was on its way. Well, one thing you
know, you can't get rid of it standing here with her so close,
too close, too damn close. You think she knows? Sure she
knows, she's trying not to touch you again. And now she's
moving back so you'll have more room. But it's still too
crowded in here. I guess we can go out now. Come on, open
the door. What are you waiting for?

He opened the alley door and stepped out onto the pavement. She followed him. They walked up the street, not talking, not looking at each other. He started to walk faster,
moving out in front of her. She made no attempt to catch up
with him. It went on like that and he was moving far out in
front of her, not thinking about it, just wanting to walk fast
and get home and go to sleep.

Then presently it occurred to him that he was walking
alone. He'd come to a street crossing and he turned and
waited. He looked for her and didn't see her. Where'd she
go? he asked himself. The answer came from very far down
the street, the sound of her clicking heels, going off in the
other direction.

For a moment he played with the thought of going after
her. So you won't get Z for etiquette, he thought, and took
a few steps. Then he stopped, and shook his head, and said
to himself, You better leave it the way it is. Stay away from
her.

But why? he asked himself, suddenly aware that something
was happening again. It just don't figure, it can't be like that,
like just the thought of her touching you is a little too much
for you to handle and it gets started again. For months she's
been working at the Hut, you've seen her there every night
and she was nothing more than part of the scenery. And now
out of nowhere comes this problem.

You calling it a problem? Come off that, you know it ain't
no problem, you just ain't geared for any problems, for any
issues at all. With you it's everything for kicks, the cool-easy
kicks that ask for no effort at all, the soft-easy style that has
you smiling all the time with your tongue in your cheek. It's
been that way for a long time now and it's worked for you,

it's worked out just fine. You take my advice, you'll keep it that way.

But she said she lived on Kenworth Street. Maybe you better do some scouting, just to make sure she got home all right. Yes, them two operators mighta changed their minds about calling it a night. They coulda decided to have another look around the neighborhood. Maybe they spotted her walking alone and—

Now look, you gotta stop it. You gotta think about something else. Think about what? All right, let's think about Oscar Levant. Is he really talented? Yes, he's really talented. Is Art Tatum talented? Art Tatum is very talented. And what about Walter Gieseking? Well, you never heard him play in person, so you can't say, you just don't know. Another thing you don't know is the house number on Kenworth. You don't even know the block number. Did she tell you the block number? I can't remember.

Oh for Christ's sake go home and go to sleep.

He lived in a rooming house a few blocks away from the Hut. It was a two-story house and his room was on the second floor. The room was small, the rent was five-fifty a week, and it amounted to a bargain because the landlady had a cleanliness phobia; she was always scrubbing or dusting. It was a very old house but all the rooms were spotless.

His room had a bed, a table and a chair. On the floor near the chair there was a pile of magazines. They were all musical publications, most of them dealing with classical music. The magazine on top of the pile was open and as he came into the room he picked it up and leafed through it. Then he started to read an article having to do with some new developments in contrapuntal theory.

The article was very interesting. It was written by a well-known name in the field, someone who really knew what it was all about. He lit a cigarette and stood there under the ceiling light, still wearing his snow-speckled overcoat, focusing on the magazine article. Somewhere in the middle of the third paragraph he lifted his eyes and looked at the window.

The window faced the street; the shade was halfway up. He

walked to the window and looked out. Then he opened the window and leaned out to get a wider look. The street was empty. He stayed there and watched the snow coming down. He felt the wind-whipped flakes taking cold bites at his face. The cold air sliced and chopped at him, and he thought, It's gonna feel good to get into that bed.

He undressed quickly. Then he was naked and climbing in under the sheet and the thick quilt, pulling the cord of the lamp near the bed, pulling the other cord that was a long string attached from the ceiling light to the bedpost. He sat there propped against the pillow, and lit another cigarette and continued with the magazine article.

For a few minutes he went on reading, then he just looked at the printed words without taking them in. It went that way for a while, and finally he let the magazine fall to the floor. He sat there smoking and looking at the wall across the room.

The cigarette burned low and he leaned over to smother it in the ashtray on the table near the bed. As he pressed the stub in the tray, he heard the knock on the door.

The wind whistled in through the open window and mixed with the sound that came from the door. He felt very cold, looking at the door, wondering who it was out there.

Then he smiled at himself, knowing who it was, knowing what he'd hear next because he'd heard it so many times in the three years he'd lived here.

From the other side of the door a female voice whispered. "You in there, Eddie? It's me, Clarice."

He climbed out of bed. He opened the door and the woman came in. He said, "Hello, Clarice," and she looked at him standing there naked and said, "Hey, get under that quilt. You'll catch cold."

Then she closed the door, doing it carefully and quietly. He was in the bed again, sitting there with the quilt up around his middle. He smiled at her and said, "Sit down."

She pulled the chair toward the bed and sat down. She said, "Jesus Christ, it's freezing in here," and got up and lowered the window. Then, seated again, she said, "You cold-air fiends amaze me. It's a wonder you don't get the flu. Or ammonia."

"Fresh air is good for you."

"Not this time of year," she said. "This time of year it's for the birds, and even they don't want it. Them birds got more brains than we got. They go to Florida."

"They can do it. They got wings."

"I wish to hell I had wings," the woman said. "Or at least the cash it needs for bus fare. I'd pack up and head south and get me some of that sunshine."

"You ever been south?"

"Sure, loads of times. On the carnival circuit. One time in Jacksonville I busted an ankle, trying out a new caper. They left me stranded there in the hospital, didn't even leave me my pay. Them carnival people—some of them are dogs, just dogs."

She helped herself to one of his cigarettes. She lit it with a loose, graceful motion of arm and wrist. Then she waved out the flaming match, tossing it from one hand to the other, the flame dying in mid-air, and caught the dead match precisely between her thumb and small finger.

"How's that for timing?" she asked him, as though he'd never seen the trick before.

He'd seen it countless times. She was always performing these little stunts. And sometimes at the Hut she'd clear the tables to give herself room, and do the flips and somersaults that showed she still had some of it left, the timing and the coordination and the extra-fast reflexes. In her late teens and early twenties she'd been a better-than-average acrobatic dancer.

Now, at thirty-two, she was still a professional, but in a different line of endeavor. It was all horizontal acrobatics on a mattress, her body for rent at three dollars a performance. In her room down the hall on the second floor she gave them more than their money's worth. Her contortions on the mattress were strictly circus-stunt variety. Among the barflies at the Hut, the consensus was "—really something, that Clarice. You come outa that room, you're dizzy."

Her abilities in this field, especially the fact that she never slackened the pace, were due mainly to her bent for keeping in condition. As a stunt dancer, she'd adhered faithfully to the strict training rules, the rigid diet and the daily exercises. In this present profession, she was equally devoted to certain laws and regulations of physical culture, maintaining that "it's very important, y'unnerstand. Sure, I drink gin. It's good for me. Keeps me from eating too much. I never overload my belly."

Her body showed it. She still had the acrobat's coiled-spring flexibility, and was double-jointed in so many places that it was as if she had no bones at all. She stood five-five and weighed one-five, but she didn't look skinny, just tightly packed around the frame. There wasn't much of breast or hip or thigh, just about enough to label it female. The female aspect showed mainly in her face, her fragile nose and chin, her wide-set, pale-gray eyes. She wore her hair rather short, and was always having it dyed. Right now it was somewhere between yellow and orange.

She sat there wearing a terry cloth bathrobe, one sleeve ripped halfway up to the elbow. With the cigarette still between the thumb and little finger, she lifted it to her mouth, took a small sip of smoke, let it out and said to him, "How's about it?"

"Not tonight."

"You broke?"

He nodded.

Clarice sipped more smoke. She said, "You want it on credit?"

He shook his head.

"You've had it on credit before," she said. "Your credit's always good with me."

"It ain't that," he said. "It's just that I'm tired. I'm awfully tired."

"You wanna go to sleep?" She started to get up.

"No," he said. "Sit there. Stick around a while. We'll talk."

"Okay." She settled back in the chair. "I need some company, anyway. I get so dragged in that room sometimes. They never wanna sit and talk. As if they're afraid I'll charge them extra."

"How'd you do tonight?"

She shrugged. "So-so." She put her hand in the bathrobe pocket and there was the rustling of paper, the tinkling of coins. "For a Friday night it wasn't bad, I guess. Most Friday nights there ain't much trade. They either spend their last nickel at Harriet's or they're so plastered they gotta be carried home. Or else they're too noisy and I can't chance it. The landlady warned me again last week. She said one more time and out I go." ·

"She's been saying that for years."

"Sometimes I wonder why she lets me stay."

"You really wanna know?" He smiled dimly. "Her room is right under yours. She could take a different room if she wanted to. After all, it's her house. But no, she keeps that room. So it figures she likes the sound it makes."

"The sound? What sound?"

"The bedsprings," he said.

"But look now, that woman is seventy-six years old."

"That's the point," he said. "They get too old for the action, they gotta have something, at least. With her it's the sound."

Clarice pondered it for a few moments. Then she nodded slowly. "Come to think of it, you got something there." And then, with a sigh, "It must be awful to get old like that."

"You think so? I don't think so. It's just a part of the game and it happens, that's all."

"It won't happen to me," she said decisively. "I hit sixty, I'll take gas. What's the point of hanging around doing nothing?"

"There's plenty to do after sixty."

"Not for this one. This one ain't joining a sewing circle, or playing bingo night after night. If I can't do no better than that, I'll just let them put me in a box."

"They put you in, you'd jump right out. You'd come out doing somersaults."

"You think I would? Really?"

"Sure you would." He grinned at her. "Double somersaults and back flips. And getting applause."

Her face lighted up, as though she could see it happening. But then her bare feet felt the solid floor and it brought her back to here and now. She looked at the man in the bed.

And then she was off the chair and onto the side of the bed. She put her hand on the quilt over his knee.

He frowned slightly. "What's the matter, Clarice?"

"I don't know, I just feel like doing something."

"But I told you—"

"That was business. This ain't business. Reminds me of one

night last summer when I came in here and we got to talking, I remember you were flat broke and I said you could have credit and you said no, so I let it drop and we went on talking about this and that and you happened to mention my hairdo. You said it looked real nice, the way I had my hair fixed. I'd fixed it myself earlier that night and I was wondering about how it looked. So of course it gimme a lift when you said that, and I said thanks. I remember saying thanks.

"But I don't know, I guess it needed more than just thanks. I guess I hadda show some real appreciation. Not exactly what you'd call a favor for a favor, but more like an urge, I'd call it. And the windup was I let you have it for free. So now I'll tell you something. I'll tell you the way it went for me. It went all the way up in the sky."

His frown had deepened. And then a grin mixed with the frown and he said, "Whatcha doing? Writing verses?"

She gave a little laugh. "Sounds that way, don't it?" And tried it for sound, mimicking herself, "—way up in the sky." She shook her head, and said, "Jesus Christ, I oughtta put that on tape and sell it to the soap people. But even so, what I'm trying to say, that night last summer was some night, Eddie. I sure remember that night."

He nodded slowly. "Me too."

"You remember?" She leaned toward him. "You really remember?"

"Sure," he said. "It was one of them nights don't come very often."

"And here's something else. If I ain't mistaken, it was a Friday night."

"I don't know," he said.

"Sure it was. It damn sure was a Friday night, cause next day at the Hut you got your pay from Harriet. She always pays you on Saturdays and that's how I remember. She paid you and then you came over to the table where I was sitting with some johns. You tried to give me three dollars. I told you to go to hell. So then you wanted to know what I was sore about, and I said I wasn't sore. And just to prove it, I bought you a drink. A double gin."

"That's right," he said, remembering that he hadn't wanted the gin, he'd accepted it just as a gesture. As they'd raised glasses, she'd been looking through her glass and through his glass, as though trying to tell him something that could only be said through the gin. He remembered that now. He remembered it very clearly.

He said, "I'm really tired, Clarice. If I wasn't—"

Her hand went away from the quilt over his knee. She gave a little shrug and said, "Well, I guess all Friday nights ain't the same."

He winced slightly.

She walked toward the door. At the door she turned and gave him a friendly smile. He started to say something, but he couldn't get it out. He saw that her smile had given way to a look of concern.

"What is it, Eddie?"

He wondered what showed on his face. He was trying to show the soft-easy smile, but he couldn't get it started. Then he blinked several times and made a straining effort and the smile came onto his lips.

But she was looking at his eyes. "You sure you're all right?"

"I'm fine," he said. "Why shouldn't I be? I got no worries."

She winked at him, as though to say, You want me to believe that, I'll believe it. Then she said good night and walked out of the room.

5

HE didn't get much sleep. He thought about Turley. He said to himself, Why think about that? You know they didn't get Turley. If they'd grabbed Turley, they wouldn't need you. They came after you because they're very anxious to have some discussion with Turley. What about? Well, you don't know, and you don't care. So I guess you can go to sleep now.

He thought about the beer cases falling onto the floor at the Hut. When you did that, he thought, you started something. Like telling them you had some connection with Turley. And naturally they snatched at that. They reasoned you could take them to Turley.

But I guess it's all right now. Item one, they don't know you're his brother. Item two, they don't know where you live. We'll skip item three because that item is the waitress and you don't want to think about her. All right, we won't think about her, we'll concentrate on Turley. You know he got away and that's nice to know. It's also nice to know they won't get you. After all, they're not the law, they can't go around asking questions. Not in this neighborhood, anyway. In this neighborhood it sure as hell ain't easy to get information. The citizens here have a closed-mouth policy when it comes to giving out facts and figures, especially someone's address. You've lived here long enough to know that. You know there's a very stiff line of defense against all bill collectors, skip tracers, or any kind of tracers. So no matter who they ask, they'll get nothing. But hold it there. You sure about that?

I'm sure of only one thing, mister. You need sleep and you can't sleep. You've started something and you're making it big, and the truth is it ain't nothing at all. That's just about the size of it, it's way down there at zero.

His eyes were open and he was looking at the window. In the darkness he could see the white dots moving on the black screen, the millions of white dots coming down out there, and he thought, They're gonna have sledding today, the kids. Say, is that window open? Sure it's open, you can see it's open. You opened it after Clarice walked out. Well, let's open it wider. We have more air in here, it might help us to fall asleep.

He got out of bed and went to the window. He opened it all the way. Then he leaned out and looked and the street was empty. In bed again, he closed his eyes and kept them closed and finally fell asleep. He slept for less than an hour and got up and went to the window and looked out. The street was empty. Then he had another couple hours of sleep before he felt the need for one more look. At the window, leaning out, he looked at the street and saw that it was empty. That's final, he told himself. We won't look again.

It was six-fifteen, the numbers yellow-white on the face of the alarm clock. We'll get some sleep now, some real sleep, he decided. We'll sleep till one, or make it one-thirty. He set the clock for one-thirty and climbed into bed and fell asleep. At eight he woke up and went to the window. Then he returned to the bed and slept until ten-twenty, at which time he made another trip to the window. The only action out there was the snow. It came down in thick flurries, and already it looked a few inches deep. He watched it for some moments, then climbed into bed and fell asleep. Two hours later he was up and at the window. There was nothing happening and he went back to sleep. Within thirty minutes he was awake and at the window. The street was empty, except for the Buick.

The Buick was brand-new, a pale green-and-cream hard-top convertible. It was parked across the street and from the angle of the window he could see them in the front seat, the two of them. He recognized the felt hats first, the pearl-gray and the darker gray. It's them, he told himself. And you knew they'd show. You've known it all night long. But how'd they get the address?

Let's find out. Let's get dressed and go out there and find out.

Getting dressed, he didn't hurry. They'll wait, he thought. They're in no rush and they don't mind waiting. But it's cold out there, you shouldn't make them wait too long, it's inconsiderate. After all, they were thoughtful of you, they were really considerate. They didn't come up here and break down the door and drag you out of bed. I think that was very nice of them.

He slipped into the tattered overcoat, went out of the room, down the steps, and out the front door. He walked across the snow-covered street and they saw him coming. He was smiling at them. As he came closer, he gave a little wave of recognition, and the man behind the wheel waved back. It was the short, thin one, the one in the pearl-gray hat.

The car window came down, and the man behind the wheel said, "Hello, Eddie."

"Eddie?"

"That's your name, ain't it?"

"Yes, that's my name." He went on smiling. His eyes were making the mild inquiry, Who told you?

Without sound the short, thin one answered, Let's skip that for now, then said aloud, "They call me Feather. It's sort of a nickname. I'm in that weight division." He indicated the other man, saying, "This is Morris."

"Pleased to meet you," Eddie said.

"Same here," Feather said. "We're very pleased to meet you, Eddie." Then he reached back and opened the rear door. "Why stand out there in the snow? Slide in and get comfortable."

"I'm comfortable," Eddie said.

Feather held the door open. "It's warmer in the car."

"I know it is," Eddie said. "I'd rather stay out here. I like it out here."

Feather and Morris looked at each other. Morris moved his hand toward his lapel, his fingers sliding under and in, and Feather said, "Leave it alone. We don't need that."

"I wanna show it to him," Morris said.

"He knows it's there."

"Maybe he ain't sure. I want him to be sure."

"All right, show it to him."

Morris reached in under his lapel and took out a small black revolver. It was chunky and looked heavy but he handled it as though it were a fountain pen. He twirled it once and it came down flat in his palm. He let it stay there for a few moments, then returned it to the holster under his lapel. Feather was saying to Eddie, "You wanna get in the car?"

"No," Eddie said.

Again Feather and Morris looked at each other. Morris said, "Maybe he thinks we're kidding."

"He knows we're not kidding."

Morris said to Eddie, "Get in the car. You gonna get in the car?"

"If I feel like it." Eddie was smiling again. "Right now I don't feel like it."

Morris frowned. "What's the matter with you? You can't be that stupid. Maybe you're sick in the head, or something." And then, to Feather, "How's he look to you?"

Feather was studying Eddie's face. "I don't know," he murmured slowly and thoughtfully. "He looks like he can't feel anything."

"He can feel metal," Morris said. "He gets a chunk of metal in his face, he'll feel it."

Eddie stood there next to the opened window, his hands going through his pockets and hunting for cigarettes. Feather asked him what he was looking for and he said, "A smoke," but there were no cigarettes and finally Feather gave him one and lit it for him and then said, "I'll give you more if you want. I'll give you an entire pack. If that ain't enough, I'll give you a carton. Or maybe you'd rather have cash."

Eddie didn't say anything.

"How's fifty dollars?" Morris said, smiling genially at Eddie.

"What would that buy me?" He wasn't looking at either of them.

"A new overcoat," Morris said. "You could use a new overcoat."

"I think he wants more than that," Feather said, again studying Eddie's face. He was waiting for Eddie to say something. He waited for some fifteen seconds, then said, "You want to quote a figure?"

Eddie spoke very softly. "For what? What am I selling?"

"You know," Feather said. And then, "A hundred?"

Eddie didn't reply. He was gazing slantwise through the opened window, through the windshield, and past the hood of the Buick.

"Three hundred?" Feather asked.

"That covers a lot of expenses," Morris put in.

"I ain't got much expenses," Eddie said.

"Then why you stalling?" Feather asked mildly.

"I'm not stalling," Eddie said. "I'm just thinking."

"Maybe he thinks we ain't got that kind of money," Morris said.

"Is that what's holding up the deal?" Feather said to Eddie. "You wanna see the roll?"

Eddie shrugged.

"Sure, let him see it," Morris said. "Let him know we're not just talking, we got the solid capital."

Feather reached into the inner pocket of his jacket and took out a shiny lizard billfold. His fingers went in and came out with a sheaf of crisp currency. He counted it aloud, as though counting it for himself, but loud enough for Eddie to hear. There were twenties and fifties and hundreds. The total was well over two thousand dollars. Feather returned the money to the billfold and put it back in his pocket.

"That's a lot of money to carry around," Eddie commented.

"That's chicken feed," Feather said.

"Depends on the annual income," Eddie murmured. "You make a bundle, you can carry a bundle. Or sometimes it ain't yours, they just give it to you to spend."

"They?" Feather narrowed his eyes. "Who you mean by they?"

Eddie shrugged again. "I mean, when you work for big people—"

Feather glanced at Morris. For some moments it was quiet. Then Feather said to Eddie, "You wouldn't be getting cute, would you?"

Eddie smiled at the short, thin man and made no answer.

"Do yourself a favor," Feather said quietly. "Don't be cute with me. I'll only get irritated and then we can't talk business. I'll be too upset." He was looking at the steering wheel. He played his thin fingers around the smooth rim of the steering wheel. "Now let's see. Where were we?"

"It was three," Morris offered. "He wouldn't sell at three. So what I think is, you offer him five—"

"All right," Feather said. He looked at Eddie. "Five hundred dollars."

Eddie glanced down at the cigarette between his fingers. He lifted it to his mouth and took a meditative drag.

"Five hundred," Feather said. "And no more."

"That's final?"

"Capped," Feather said, and reached inside his jacket, going for the billfold.

"Nothing doing," Eddie said.

Feather exchanged another look with Morris. "I don't get this," Feather said. He spoke as though Eddie weren't there. "I've seen all kinds, but this one here is new to me. What gives with him?"

"You're asking me?" Morris made a hopeless gesture, his palms out and up. "I can't reach out that far. He's moon material."

Eddie was wearing the soft-easy smile and gazing at nothing. He stood there taking small drags at the cigarette. His overcoat was unbuttoned, as though he weren't aware of wind and snow. The two men in the car were staring at him, waiting for him to say something, to give some indication that he was actually there.

And finally, from Feather, "All right, let's try it from another angle." His voice was mild. "It's this way, Eddie. All we wanna do is talk to him. We're not out to hurt him."

"Hurt who?"

Feather snapped his fingers, "Come on, let's put it on the table. You know who I'm talking about. Your brother. Your brother Turley."

Eddie's expression didn't change. He didn't even blink. He was saying to himself, Well, there it is. They know you're his brother. So now you're in it, you're pulled in and I wish you could figure a way to slide out.

He heard Feather saying, "We just wanna sit him down and have a little talk. All you gotta do is make the connection."

"I can't do that," he said. "I don't know where he is."

Then, from Morris, "You sure about that? You sure you ain't trying to protect him?"

"Why should I?" Eddie shrugged. "He's only my brother. For half a grand I'd be a fool not to hand him over. After all, what's a brother? A brother means nothing."

"Now he's getting cute again," Feather said.

"A brother, a mother, a father," Eddie said with another shrug, "they ain't important at all. Like merchandise you sell across a counter. That is," and his voice dropped just a little, "according to certain ways of thinking."

"What's he saying now?" Morris wanted to know.

"I think he's telling us to go to hell," Feather said. Then he looked at Morris, and he nodded slowly, and Morris took out the revolver. Then Feather said to Eddie. "Open the door. Get in."

Eddie stood there smiling at them.

"He wants it," Morris said, and then there was the sound of the safety catch.

"That's a pretty noise," Eddie said.

"You wanna hear something really pretty?" Feather murmured.

"First you gotta count to five," Eddie told him. "Go on, count to five. I wanna hear you count."

Feather's thin face was powder-white. "Let's make it three." But as he said it he was looking past Eddie.

Eddie was saying, "All right, we'll count to three. You want me to count for you?"

"Later," Feather said, still looking past him, and smiling now. "That is, when she gets here."

Just then Eddie felt the snow and the wind. The wind was very cold. He heard himself saying, "When who gets here?"

"The skirt," Feather said. "The skirt we saw you with last night. She's coming to pay you a visit."

He turned and saw her coming down the street. She was crossing the street diagonally, coming toward the car. He raised his hand just high enough to make the warning gesture, telling her to stay away, to please stay away. She kept advancing toward the car and he thought, She knows, she knows you're in a situation and she figures she can help. But that gun. She can't see that gun—

He heard the voice of Feather saying, "She your girl friend, Eddie?"

He didn't answer. The waitress came closer. He made another warning gesture but now she was very close and he looked away from her to glance inside the car. He saw Morris sitting slantwise with the gun moving slowly from side to side, to cover two people instead of one. That does it, he thought. That includes her in.

6

THEN she was standing there next to him and they were both looking at the gun. He waited for her to ask him what it was all about, but she didn't say anything. Feather leaned back, smiling at them, giving them plenty of time to study the gun, to think about the gun. It went on that way for perhaps half a minute, and then Feather said to Eddie, "That counting routine. You still want me to count to three?"

"No," Eddie said. "I guess that ain't necessary." He was trying not to frown. He was very much annoyed with the waitress.

"What's the seating arrangement?" Morris wanted to know.

"You in the back," Feather told him, then took the gun from Morris and opened the door and got out of the car. He held the gun close to his side as he walked with Eddie and Lena, staying just a little behind them as they went around to the other side of the car. He told them to get in the front seat. Eddie started to get in first, and Feather said, "No, I want her in the middle." She climbed in and Eddie followed her. Morris was reaching out from the back seat to take the gun from Feather. For just an instant there was a chance for interception, but it wasn't much of a chance and Eddie thought, No matter how quick you are, the gun is quicker. You go for it, it'll go for you. And you know it'll get there first. I guess we'd better face the fact that we're going on a trip somewheres.

He watched Feather climbing in behind the wheel. The waitress sat there looking straight ahead through the windshield. "Sit back," Feather said to her. "You might as well be comfortable." Without looking at Feather, she said, "Thanks," and leaned back, folding her arms. Then Feather started the engine.

The Buick cruised smoothly down the street, turned a corner, went down another narrow street and then moved onto a wider street. Feather switched on the radio. A cool jazz outfit was in the middle of something breezy. It was nicely modulated music, featuring a soft-toned saxophone and someone's light expert touch on the keyboard. That's very fine piano, Eddie said to himself. I think that's Bud Powell.

Then he heard Lena saying, "Where we going?"

"Ask your boy friend," Feather said.

"He's not my boy friend."

"Well, ask him anyway. He's the navigator."

She looked at Eddie. He shrugged and went on listening to the music.

"Come on," Feather said to him. "Start navigating."

"Where you wanna go?"

"Turley."

"Where's that?" Lena asked.

"It ain't a town," Feather said. "It's his brother. We got some business with his brother."

"The man from last night?" She put the question to Eddie. "The one who ran out of the Hut?"

He nodded. "They did some checking," he said. "First they find out he's my brother. Then they get more information. They get my address."

"Who told them?"

"I think I know," he said. "But I'm not sure."

"I'll straighten you," Feather offered. "We went back to that saloon when it opened up this morning. We buy a few drinks and then we get to talking with big-belly, I mean the one who looks like a has-been wrestler—"

"Plyne," the waitress said.

"Is that his name?" Feather hit the horn lightly and two very young sledders jumped back on the curb. "So we're there at the bar and he's getting friendly, he's telling us he's the general manager and he gives us a drink on the house. Then he talks about this and that, staying clear of the point he wants to make. He handles it all right for a while, but finally it's too much for him, and he's getting clumsy with the talk. We just stand there and look at him. Then he makes his pitch. He wants to know what our game is."

"He said it kind of hungry-like," from Morris in the back seat.

"Yeah," Feather said. "Like he has it tabbed we're big time and he's looking for an in. You know how it is with these has-beens, they all want to get right up there again."

"Not all of them," the waitress said. And just for a moment she glanced at Eddie. And then, turning again to Feather, "You were saying?"

"Well, we didn't give him anything, just some nowhere talk that only made him hungrier. And then, just tossing it away, as if it ain't too important, I mention our friend here who knocked down them beer cases. It was a long shot, sure. But it paid off." He smiled congenially at Eddie. "It paid off real nice."

"That Plyne," the waitress said. "That Plyne and his big mouth."

"He got paid off, too," Feather said. "I slipped him a half-C for the info."

"That fifty made his eyes pop," Morris said.

"And made him greedy for more." Feather laughed lightly. "He asked us to come around again. He said if there was anything more he could do, we should call on him and—"

"The pig," she said. "The filthy pig."

Feather went on laughing. He looked over his shoulder, saying to Morris, "Come to think of it, that's what he looked like. I mean, when he went for the fifty. Like a pig going for slop—"

Morris pointed toward the windshield. "Watch where you're going."

Feather stopped laughing. "Who's got the wheel?"

"You got the wheel," Morris said. "But look at all the snow, it's freezing. We don't have chains."

"We don't need chains," Feather said. "We got snow tires."

"Well, even so," Morris said, "you better drive careful."

Again Feather looked at him. "You telling me how to drive?"

"For Christ's sake," Morris said. "I'm only telling you—"

"Don't tell me how to drive. I don't like when they tell me how to drive."

"When it snows, there's always accidents," Morris said. "We wanna get where we're going—"

"That's a sensible statement," Feather said. "Except for one thing. We don't know where we're going yet."

Then he glanced inquiringly at Eddie.

Eddie was listening to the music from the radio.

Feather reached toward the instrument panel and switched off the radio. He said to Eddie, "We'd like to know where we're going. You wanna help us out on that a little?"

Eddie shrugged. "I told you, I don't know where he is."

"You haven't any idea? No idea at all?"

"It's a big city," Eddie said. "It's a very big city."

"Maybe he ain't in the city," Feather murmured.

Eddie blinked a few times. He was looking straight ahead. He sensed that the waitress was watching him.

Feather probed gently. "I said maybe he ain't in the city. Maybe he's in the country."

"What?" Eddie said. All right, he told himself. Easy, now. Maybe he's guessing.

"The country," Feather said. "Like, say, in New Jersey."

That does it, Eddie thought. That wasn't a guess.

"Or let's tighten it a little," Feather said. "Let's make it South Jersey."

Now Eddie looked at Feather. He didn't say anything. The waitress sat there between them, quiet and relaxed, her hands folded in her lap.

Morris said, sort of mockingly, with pretended ignorance, "What's this with South Jersey? What's in South Jersey?"

"Watermelons," Feather said. "That's where they grow them."

"The melons?" Morris was playing straight man. "Who grows them?"

"The farmers, stupid. There's a lotta farmers in South Jersey. There's all these little farms, these watermelon patches."

"Where?"

"Whaddya mean, where? I just told you where. In South Jersey."

"The watermelon trees?"

"Pipe that," Feather said to the two front-seat passengers. "He thinks they grow on trees." And then, to Morris, "They grow in the ground. Like lettuce."

"Well, I've seen them growing lettuce, but never watermelons. How come I ain't seen the watermelons?"

"You didn't look."

"Sure I looked. I always look at the scenery. Especially in South Jersey. I've been to South Jersey loads of times. To Cape May. To Wildwood. All down through there."

"No watermelons?"

"Not a one," Morris said.

"I guess you were driving at night," Feather told him.

"Could be," Morris said. And then, timing it, "Or maybe these farms are far off the road."

"Now, that's an angle." Feather took a quick look at Eddie, then purred, "Some of these farms are way back there in the woods. These watermelon patches, I mean. They're sorta hidden back there—"

"All right, all right," the waitress broke in. She turned to Eddie. "What are they talking about?"

"It's nothing," Eddie said.

"You wish it was nothing," Morris said.

She turned to Feather. "What is it?"

"His folks," Feather said. Again he looked at Eddie. "Go on, tell her. You might as well tell her."

"Tell her what?" Eddie spoke softly. "What's there to tell?"

"There's plenty," Morris said. "That is, if you're in on it." He moved the gun forward just a little, doing it gently, so that the barrel barely touched Eddie's shoulder. "You in on it?"

"Hey, for Christ's sake—" Eddie pulled his shoulder away.

"What's happening there?" Feather asked.

"He's afraid of the rod," Morris said.

"Sure he's afraid. So am I. Put that thing away. We hit a bump it might go off."

"I want him to know—"

"He knows. They both know. They don't have to feel it to know it's there."

"All right." Morris sounded grumpy. "All right, all right."

The waitress was looking at Feather, then at Eddie, then at Feather again. She said, "Well, if he can't tell me, maybe you can—"

"About his folks?" Feather smiled. "Sure, I got some facts. There's the mother and the father and the two brothers. There's this Turley and the other one, his name is Clifton. That right, Eddie?"

Eddie shrugged. "If you say so."

"You know what I think?" Morris said slowly. "I think he's in on it."

"In on what?" the waitress snapped. "At least you could give me some idea—"

"You'll get the idea," Feather told her. "You'll get it when we reach that house."

"What house?"

"In South Jersey," Feather said. "In them woods where it used to be a watermelon patch but the weeds closed in and now it ain't a farm any more. It's just an old wooden house with a lot of weeds around it. And then the woods. There's no other houses around for miles—"

"No roads, either," Morris put in.

"Not cement roads, anyway," Feather said. "Just wagon paths that take you deep in them woods. So all you see is trees and more trees. And finally, there it is, the house. Just that one house far away from everything. It's what I'd call a gloomy layout." He looked at Eddie. "We got no time for fooling around. You know the route, so what you do is, you give the directions."

"How come?" the waitress asked. "Why do you need directions? You pictured that house like you've been there."

"I've never been there," Feather said. He went on looking at Eddie. "I was told about it, that's all. But they left out something. Forgot to tell me how to get there."

"He'll tell you," Morris said.

"Sure he'll tell me. What else can he do?"

Morris nudged Eddie's shoulder. "Give."

"Not yet," Feather said. "Wait'll we cross the bridge into Jersey. Then he'll tell us what roads to take."

"Maybe he don't know," the waitress said.

"You kidding?" Feather flipped it at her. "He was born and raised in that house. For him it's just a trip to the country, to visit the folks."

"Like coming home for Thanksgiving," Morris said. Again he touched Eddie's shoulder. This time it was a friendly pat. "After all, there's no place like home."

"Except it ain't a home," Feather said softly. "It's a hide-out."

7

Now they were on Front Street, headed south toward the Delaware River Bridge. They were coming into heavy traffic, and south of Lehigh Avenue the street was jammed. In addition to cars and trucks, there was a slow-moving swarm of Saturday afternoon shoppers, some of them jay-walkers who kept their heads down against the wind and the snow. The Buick moved very slowly and Feather kept hitting the horn. Morris was cursing the pedestrians. In front of the Buick there was a very old car without chains. It also lacked a windshield wiper. It was traveling at approximately fifteen miles per hour.

"Give him the horn," Morris said. "Give him the horn again."

"He can't hear it," Feather said.

"Give him the goddam horn. Keep blowing it."

Feather pressed the chromed rim, and the horn blasted and kept blasting. In the car ahead the driver turned and scowled and Feather went on blowing the horn.

"Try to pass him," Morris said.

"I can't," Feather muttered. "The street ain't wide enough."

"Try it now. There's no cars coming now."

Feather steered the Buick toward the left and then out a little more. He started to cut past the old car and then a bread truck came riding in for what looked to be a head-on collision. Feather pulled hard at the wheel and got back just in time.

"You shoulda kept on," Morris said. "You had enough room."

Feather didn't say anything.

A group of middle-aged women crossed the street between the Buick and the car in front of it. They seemed utterly oblivious to the existence of the Buick. Feather slammed his foot against the brake pedal.

"What're you stopping for?" Morris yelled. "They wanna get hit, then hit them!"

"That's right," the waitress said. "Smash into them. Grind them to a pulp."

The women passed and the Buick started forward. Then a flock of children darted through and the Buick was stopped again.

Morris opened the window at his side and leaned out and shouted, "What the hell's wrong with you?"

"Drop dead," one of the children said. It was a girl about seven years old.

"I'll break your little neck for you," Morris shouted at her.

"That's all right," the child sang back. "Just stay off my blue suede shoes."

The other children began singing the rock-and-roll tune, "Blue Suede Shoes," twanging on imaginary guitars and imitating various dynamic performers. Morris closed the window, gritting, "Goddam juvenile delinquents."

"Yes, it's quite a problem," the waitress said.

"You shut up," Morris told her.

She turned to Eddie. "The trouble is, there ain't enough playgrounds. We oughtta have more playgrounds. That would get them off the street."

"Yes," Eddie said. "The people ought to do something. It's a very serious problem."

She turned her head and looked back at Morris. "What do you think about it? You got an opinion?"

Morris wasn't listening. He had the window open again and he was leaning out, concentrating on the oncoming traffic. He called to Feather, "It's clear now. Go ahead—"

Feather started to turn the wheel. Then he changed his mind and pulled back in behind the car in front. A moment later a taxicab came whizzing from the other direction. It made a yellow blur as it sped past.

"You coulda made it," Morris complained. "You had plenty of time—"

Feather didn't say anything.

"You gotta cut through while you got the chance," Morris said. "Now if I had that wheel—"

"You want the wheel?" Feather asked.

"All I said was—"

"I'll give you the wheel," Feather said. "I'll wrap it around your neck."

"Don't get excited," Morris said.

"Just leave me alone and let me drive. Is that all right?"

"Sure." Morris shrugged. "You're the driver. You know how to drive."

"Then keep quiet." Feather faced the windshield again. "If there's one thing I can do, it's handle a car. There ain't nobody can tell me about that. I can make a car do anything—"

"Except get through traffic," Morris remarked.

Again Feather's head turned. His eyes were dull-cold, aiming at the tall, thin man. "What are you doing? You trying to irritate me?"

"No," Morris said. "I'm only making talk."

Feather went on looking at him. "I don't need that talk.

You give that talk to someone else. You tell someone else how to drive."

Morris pointed to the windshield. "Keep your eyes on the traffic—"

"You just won't let up, will you?" Feather shifted slightly in his seat, to get a fuller look at the man in the rear of the car. "Now I'm gonna tell you something, Morris. I'm gonna tell you—"

"Watch the light," Morris shouted, and gestured wildly toward the windshield. "You got a red light—"

Feather kept looking at him. "I'm telling you, Morris. I'm telling you for the last time—"

"The light," Morris screeched. "It's red, it's red, it says stop—"

The Buick was some twenty feet from the intersection when Feather took his foot off the gas pedal, then lightly stepped on the brake. The car was coming to a stop and Eddie glanced at the waitress, saw that she was focusing slantwise to the other side of the intersecting street, where a black-and-white police car was double-parked, the two policemen standing out there talking to the driver of a truck parked in a no-parking zone. Eddie had seen the police car and he'd wondered if the waitress would see it and would know what to do about it. He thought, This is the time for it, there won't be another time.

The waitress moved her left leg and her foot came down full force on the accelerator. Pedestrians leaped out of the way as the Buick went shooting past the red light and narrowly missed a westbound car, then stayed southbound going across the trolley tracks and lurching now as Feather hit the brake while the waitress kept her foot on the accelerator. An eastbound trailer made a frantic turn and went up on the pavement. Some women screamed, there was considerable activity on the pavement, brakes screeched, and, finally, a policeman's whistle shrilled through the air.

The Buick was stopped on the south side of the trolley tracks. Feather sat there leaning back, looking sideways at the waitress. Eddie was watching the policeman, who was yelling at the driver of the trailer, telling him to back off the pavement. There was no one hurt, although several of the pedestrians were considerably unnerved. A few women were yelling incoherently, pointing accusingly at the Buick. Then, gradually, a crowd closed in on the Buick. In the Buick there was no talk at all. Around the car the crowd thickened. Feather was still looking at the waitress. Eddie glanced into the rearview mirror and saw Morris with his hat off. Morris had the hat in his hands and was gazing stupidly at the crowd outside the window. Some of the people in the crowd were saying things to Feather. Then the crowd moved to make a path for the policeman from the black-and-white car. Eddie saw that the other policeman was still occupied with the parking violator. He turned his head slowly and the waitress was looking at him. It seemed she was waiting for him to say something or do something. Her eyes said to him, It's your play, from here on in it's up to you. He made a very slight gesture, pointing to himself, as if saying, All right, I'll handle it, I'll do the talking.

The policeman spoke quietly to Feather. "Let's clear this traffic. Get her over there to the curb." The Buick moved slowly across the remainder of the intersection, the policeman walking along with it, guiding the driver to the southeast corner. "Cut the engine," the policeman told Feather. "Get out of the car."

Feather switched off the engine and opened the door and got out. The crowd went on making noise. A man said, "He's stewed. He's gotta be stewed to drive like that." And an elderly woman shouted, "We just ain't safe any more. We venture out we take our lives in our hands—"

The policeman moved in close to Feather and said, "How many?" and Feather answered, "All I had was two, officer. I'll drive you back to the bar, and you can ask the bartender." The policeman looked Feather up and down. "All right, so you're not drunk. Then how do you account for this?" As Feather opened his mouth to reply, Eddie cut in quickly, saying, "He just can't drive, that's all. He's a lousy driver." Feather turned and looked at Eddie. And Eddie went on, "He always gets rattled in traffic." Then he turned to the waitress, saying, "Come on, honey. We don't need this. We'll take a trolley."

"Can't hardly blame you," the policeman said to them as they got out of the car. From the back seat, Morris called out, "See you later, Eddie," and for a moment there was indecision. Eddie glanced toward the policeman, thinking, You wanna tell the cop what's happening? You figure it's better that way? No, he decided. It's probably better this way.

"Later," Morris called to them as they moved off through the crowd. The waitress stopped and looked back at Morris. "Yeah, give us a call," and she waved at the tall, thin man in the Buick, "we'll be waiting—"

They went on moving through the crowd. Then they were walking north on Front Street. The snow had slackened somewhat. It was slightly warmer now, and the sun was trying to come out. But the wind had not lessened, there was still a bite in it, and Eddie thought, There's gonna be more snow, that sky looks strictly from changeable weather. It could be a blizzard coming.

He heard the waitress saying, "Let's get off this street."

"They won't circle back."

"They might."

"I don't think they will," he said. "When that cop gets finished with them, they're gonna be awfully tired. I think they'll go to a movie or a Turkish bath or something. They've had enough for one day."

"He said he'd see us later."

"You gave him a good answer. You said we'd be waiting. That gives them something to think about. They'll really think about that."

"For how long?" She looked at him. "How long until they try again?"

He made an offhand gesture. "Who knows? Why worry?"

She mimicked his gesture, his indifferent tone. "Well, maybe you're right. Except for one little angle. That thing he had wasn't a water pistol. If they come looking for us, it might be something to worry about."

He didn't say anything. They were walking just a little faster now. "Well?" she said, and he didn't answer. She said it again. She was watching his face and waiting for an answer. "How about it?" she asked, and took hold of his arm. They came to a stop and stood facing each other.

"Now look," he said, and smiled dimly. "This ain't your problem."

She shifted her weight onto one leg, put her hand on her hip and said, "I didn't quite get that."

"It's simple enough. I'm only repeating what you said last night. I thought you meant it. Anyway, I was hoping you meant it."

"In other words," and she took a deep breath, "you're telling me to mind my own damn business."

"Well, I wouldn't put it that way—"

"Why not?" She spoke a trifle louder. "Don't be so polite."

He gazed past her, his smile very soft. "Let's not get upset—"

"You're too goddam polite," she said. "You wanna make a point, make it. Don't walk all around it."

His smile fell away. He tried to build it again. It wouldn't build. Don't look at her, he told himself. You look at her, it'll start like it started last night in that alley when she was standing close to you.

She's close now, come to think of it. She's much too close. He took a backward step, went on gazing past her, then heard himself saying, "I don't need this."

"Need what?"

"Nothing," he mumbled. "Let it ride."

"It's riding."

He winced. He took a step toward her. What are you doing? he asked himself. Then he was shaking his head, trying to clear his brain. It was no go. He felt very dizzy.

He heard her saying, "Well, I might as well know who I'm riding with."

"We're not riding now," he said, and tried to make himself believe it. He grinned at her. "We're just standing here and gabbing."

"Is that what it is?"

"Sure," he said. "That's all it is. What else could it be?"

"I wouldn't know." Her face was expressionless. "That is, I wouldn't know unless I was told."

I'll let that pass, he said to himself. I'd better let it pass. But look at her, she's waiting. But it's more than that, she's aching. She's aching for you to say something.

"Let's walk," he said. "It's no use standing here."

"You're right," she said with a little smile. "It sure ain't getting us anywhere. Come on, let's walk."

They resumed walking north on Front Street. Now they were walking slowly and there was no talk. They went on for several blocks without speaking and then she stopped again and said to him, "I'm sorry, Eddie."

"Sorry? About what?"

"Butting in. I shoulda kept my long nose out of it."

"It ain't a long nose. It's just about right."

"Thanks," she said. They were standing outside a five-and-dime. She glanced toward the display window. "I think I'll do some shopping—"

"I'd better go in with you."

"No," she said. "I can make it alone."

"Well, what I mean is, just in case they—"

"Look, you said there was nothing to worry about. You got them going to the movies or a Turkish bath—"

"Or Woolworth's," he cut in. "They might walk into this Woolworth's."

"What if they do?" She gave a little shrug. "It ain't me they want, it's you."

"That cuts it nice." He smiled at her. "Except it don't cut that way at all. They got you tabbed now. Tied up with me. Like as if we're a team—"

"A team?" She looked away from him. "Some team. You won't even tell me the score."

"On what?"

"South Jersey. That house in the woods. Your family—"

"The score on that is zero," he said. "I got no idea what's happening there."

"Not even a hint?" She gave him a side glance.

He didn't reply. He thought, What can you tell her? What the hell can you tell her when you just don't know?

"Well," she said, "whatever it is, you sure kept it away from that cop. I mean the way you played it, not telling the cop about the gun. To keep the law out of this. Or, let's say, to keep your family away from the law. Something along that line?"

"Yes," he said. "It's along that line."

"Anything more?"

"Nothing," he said. "I know from nothing."

"All right," she said. "All right, Edward."

There was a rush of quiet. It was like a valve opening and the quiet rushing in.

"Or is it Eddie?" she asked herself aloud. "Well, now it's Eddie. It's Eddie at the old piano, at the Hut. But years ago it was Edward—"

He waved his hand sideways, begging her to stop it.

She said, "It was Edward Webster Lynn, the concert pianist, performing at Carnegie Hall."

She turned away and walked into the five-and-dime.

8

So there it is, he said to himself. But how did she know? What tipped her off? I think we ought to examine that. Or maybe it don't need examining. It stands to reason she remembered something. It must have hit her all at once. That's it, that's the way it usually happens. It came all at once, the name and the face and the music. Or the music and the name and the face. All mixed in there together from seven years ago.

When did it hit her? She's been working at the Hut for four months, six nights a week. Until last night she hardly knew you were alive. So let's have a look at that. Did something happen last night? Did you pull some fancy caper on that keyboard? Just a bar or two of Bach, maybe? Or Brahms or Schumann or Chopin? No. You know who told her. It was Turley.

Sure as hell it was Turley when he went into that booby-hatch raving, when he jumped up and gave that lecture on musical appreciation and the currently sad state of culture in America, claiming that you didn't belong in the Hut, it was the wrong place, the wrong piano, the wrong audience. He screamed it oughta be a concert hall, with the gleaming grand piano, the diamonds gleaming on the white throats, the full-dress shirt fronts in the seven-fifty orchestra seats. That was what hit her.

But hold it there for just a minute. What's the hookup there? How does she come to Carnegie Hall? She ain't from the classical groove, the way she talks she's from the honky-tonk school. Or no, you don't really know what school she's from. The way a person talks has little or nothing to do with the schooling. You ought to know that. Just listen to the way you talk.

What I mean is, the way Eddie talks. Eddie spills words like "ain't" and says "them there" and "this here" and so forth. You know Edward never talked that way. Edward was educated, and an artist, and had a cultured manner of speaking. I guess it all depends where you're at and what you're doing and the people you hang around with. The Hut is a long way off from Carnegie Hall. *Yes.* And it's a definite fact that Eddie has no connection with Edward. You cut all them wires a long time ago. It was a clean split.

Then why are you drifting back? Why pick it up again? Well, just to look at it. Won't hurt to have a look. Won't hurt? You kidding? You can feel the hurt already, as though it's happening again. The way it happened.

It was deep in the woods of South Jersey, in the wooden house that overlooked the watermelon patch. His early childhood was mostly on the passive side. As the youngest of three brothers, he was more or less a small, puzzled spectator, unable to understand Clifton's knavery or Turley's rowdyism. They were always at it, and when they weren't pulling capers in the house they were out roaming the countryside. Their special meat was chickens. They were experts at stealing chickens. Or sometimes they'd try for a shoat. They were seldom caught. They'd slide out of trouble or fight their way out of it and, on a few occasions, in their middle teens, they shot their way out of it.

The mother called them bad boys, then shrugged and let it go at that. The mother was an habitual shrugger who'd run out of gas in her early twenties, surrendering to farmhouse drudgery, to the weeds and beetles and fungus that lessened the melon crop each year. The father never worried about anything. The father was a slothful, languid, easy-smiling drinker. He had a remarkable capacity for alcohol.

There was another gift the father had. The father could play
the piano. He claimed he'd been a child prodigy. Of course,
no one believed him. But at times, sitting at the ancient upright in the shabby, carpetless parlor, he did some startling
things with the keyboard.

At other times, when he felt in the mood, he'd give music
lessons to five-year-old Edward. It seemed there was nothing
else to do with Edward, who was on the quiet side, who
stayed away from his villainous brothers as though his very
life depended on it. Actually, this was far from the case. They
never bullied him. They'd tease him now and then, but mostly
they left him alone. They didn't even know he was around.
The father felt a little sorry for Edward, who wandered
through the house like some lost creature from the woods
that had gotten in by mistake.

The music lessons increased from once a week to twice a
week and finally to every day. The father became aware that
something was happening here, something really unusual.
When Edward was nine he performed for a gathering of teachers at the schoolhouse six miles away. When he was fourteen,
some people came from Philadelphia to hear him play. They
took him back to Philadelphia, to a scholarship at the Curtis
Institute of Music.

At nineteen, he gave his first concert in a small auditorium.
There wasn't much of an audience, and most of them got in
on complimentary tickets. But one of them was a man from
New York, a concert artists' manager, and his name was
Eugene Alexander.

Alexander had his office on Fifty-seventh Street, not many
doors away from Carnegie Hall. It was a small office and the
list of clients was rather small. But the furnishings of the office
were extremely expensive, and the clients were all big names
or on their way to becoming big names. When Edward signed
with Alexander, he was given to understand that he was just
a tiny drop of water in a very large pool. "And frankly,"
Alexander said, "I must tell you of the obstacles in this field.
In this field the competition is ferocious, downright ferocious.
But if you're willing to—"

He was more than willing. He was bright-eyed and anxious
to get started. He started the very next day, studying under

Gelensky, with Alexander paying for the lessons. Gelensky was
a sweetly-smiling little man, completely bald, his face criss-
crossed with so many wrinkles that he looked like a goblin.
And, as Edward soon learned, the sweet smiles were more on
the order of goblin's smiles, concealing a fiendish tendency to
ignore the fact that the fingers are flesh and bone, that the fingers can get tired. "You must never get tired," the little man
would say, smiling sweetly. "When the hands begin to sweat,
that's good. The flow of sweat is the stream of attainment."

He sweated plenty. There were nights when his fingers were
so stiff that he felt as though he was wearing splints. Nights
when his eyes were seared with the strain of seven and eight
and nine hours at the keyboard, the notes on the music sheets
finally blurring to a gray mist. And nights of self-doubt, of
discouragement. Is it worth all this? he'd ask himself. It's
work, work, and more work. And so much work ahead. So
much to learn. Oh, Christ, this is hard, it's really hard. It's
being cooped up in this room all the time, and even if you
wanted to go out, you couldn't. You're too tired. But you
ought to get out. For some fresh air, at least. Or a walk in
Central Park; it's nice in Central Park. Yes, but there's no
piano in Central Park. The piano is here, in this room.

It was a basement apartment on Seventy-sixth Street between Amsterdam and Columbus Avenues. The rent was fifty
dollars a month and the rent money came from Alexander.
The money for food and clothes and all incidentals also came
from Alexander. And for the piano. And for the radio-
phonograph, along with several albums of concertos and so-
natas. Everything was from Alexander.

Will he get it back? Edward asked himself. Do I have what
he thinks I have? Well, we'll soon find out. Not really soon,
though. Gelensky is certainly taking his time. He hasn't even
mentioned your New York debut. You've been with Gelensky
almost two years now and he hasn't said a word about a concert. Or even a small recital. What does that mean? Well, you
can ask him. That is, if you're not afraid to ask him. But I
think you're afraid. Coming right down to it, I think you're
afraid he'll say yes, and then comes the test, the real test here
in New York.

Because New York is not Philadelphia. These New York

critics are so much tougher. Look what they did last week to
Harbenstein. And Gelensky had Harbenstein for five years.
Another thing, Harbenstein is managed by Alexander. Does
that prove something?

It could. It very well could. It could prove that despite a
superb teacher and a devoted, efficient manager, the per-
former just didn't have it, just couldn't make the grade. Poor
Harbenstein. I wonder what Harbenstein did the next day
when he read the write-ups? Cried, probably. Sure, he cried.
Poor devil. You wait so long for that one chance, you aim
your hopes so high, and next thing you know it's all over and
they've ripped you apart, they've slaughtered you. But what
I think now, you're getting jumpy. And that's absurd, Edward.
There's certainly no reason to be jumpy. Your name is Edward
Webster Lynn and you're a concert pianist, you're an artist.

Three weeks later he was told by Gelensky that he'd soon
be making his New York debut. In the middle of the following
week, in Alexander's office, he signed a contract to give a
recital. It was to be a one-hour recital in the small auditorium
of a small art museum on upper Fifth Avenue. He went back
to the little basement apartment, dizzily excited and elated,
and saw the envelope, and opened it, and stood there staring
at the mimeographed notice. It was from Washington. It ordered him to report to his local draft board.

They classified him 1-A. They were in a hurry and there was
no use preparing for the recital. He went to South Jersey,
spent a day with his parents, who informed him that Clifton
had been wounded in the Pacific and Turley was somewhere
in the Aleutians with the Seabees. His mother gave him a nice
dinner and his father forced him to have a drink "for good
luck." He went back to New York, then to a training camp
in Missouri, and from there he was sent to Burma.

He was with Merrill's Marauders. He got hit three times.
The first time it was shrapnel in the leg. Then it was a bullet
in the shoulder. The last time it was multiple bayonet wounds
in the ribs and abdomen, and in the hospital they doubted
that he'd make it. But he was very anxious to make it. He was
thinking in terms of getting back to New York, to the piano,
to the night when he'd put on a white tie and face the audience at Carnegie Hall.

When he returned to New York, he was informed that Alexander had died of kidney trouble and a university in Chili
had given Gelensky an important professorship. They're really
gone? he asked the Manhattan sky and streets as he walked
alone and felt the ache of knowing it was true, that they were
really gone. It meant he had to start all over.

Well, let's get started. First thing, we find a concert manager.

He couldn't find a manager. Or, rather, the managers didn't
want him. Some were polite, some were kind and said they
wished they could do something but there were so many
pianists, the field was so crowded—

And some were blunt, some were downright brutal. They
didn't even bother to write his name on a card. They made
him acutely aware of the fact that he was unknown, a nobody.

He went on trying. He told himself it couldn't go on this
way, and sooner or later he'd get a chance, there'd be at least
one sufficiently interested to say, "All right, try some Chopin.
Let's hear you play Chopin."

But none of them was interested, not the least bit interested. He wasn't much of a salesman. He couldn't talk about
himself, couldn't get it across that Eugene Alexander had
come to that first recital, had signed him onto a list that included some of the finest, and that Gelensky had said, "No,
they won't applaud. They'll sit there stupefied. The way
you're playing now, you are a master of pianoforte. You think
there are many? In this world, according to my lastest count,
there are nine. Exactly nine."

He couldn't quote Gelensky. There were times when he
tried to describe his own ability, his full awareness of this talent
he had, but the words wouldn't come out. The talent was all
in the fingers and all he could say was, "If you'd let me play
for you—"

They brushed him off.

It went on like that for more than a year while he worked
at various jobs. He was a shipping clerk and truck driver and
construction laborer, and there were other jobs that lasted for
only a few weeks or a couple of months. It wasn't because he
was lazy, or tardy, or lacked the muscle. When they fired
him, they said it was mostly "forgetfulness" or "absent-

mindedness" or some of them, more perceptive, would comment, "you're only half here; you got your thoughts someplace else."

But the Purple Heart with two clusters started paying off and the disability money was enough to get him a larger room, and then an apartment, and finally an apartment just about big enough to label it a studio. He bought a piano on the installment plan, and put out a sign that stated simply, Piano Teacher.

Fifty cents a lesson. They couldn't afford more. They were mostly Puerto Ricans who lived in the surrounding tenements in the West Nineties. One of them was a girl named Teresa Fernandez, who worked nights behind the counter of a tiny fruit-drink enterprise near Times Square. She was nineteen years old, and a war widow. His name had been Luis and he'd been blown to bits on a heavy cruiser during some action in the Coral Sea. There were no children and now she lived alone in a fourth-floor-front on Ninety-third Street. She was a quiet girl, a diligent and persevering music student, and she had no musical talent whatsoever.

After several lessons, he saw the way it was, and he told her to stop wasting the money. She said she didn't care about the money, and if Meester Leen did not mind she would be most grateful to take more lessons. Maybe with some more lessons I will start to learn something. I know I am stupid, but—

"Don't say that," he told her. "You're not stupid at all. It's just—"

"I like dese lessons, Meester Leen. It is a nice way for me to pass the time in dese afternoons."

"You really like the piano?"

"Yes, yes. Very much." A certain eagerness that glowed in her eyes, and he knew what it was, he knew it had nothing to do with music. She looked away, blinking hard and trying to cover it up, and then bit her lip, as though to scold herself for letting it show. She was embarrassed and silently apologetic, her shoulders drooping just a little, her slender throat twitching as she swallowed the words she didn't dare to let out. He told himself that she was something very pleasant, very sweet, and, also, she was lonely. It was apparent that she was terribly lonely.

Her features and her body were on the fragile side, and she had a graceful way of moving. Her looks were more Castilian than Caribbean. Her hair was a soft-hued amber, her eyes were amber, and her complexion was pearl-white, the kind of complexion they try to buy in the expensive salons. Teresa had it from someone down the line a very long time ago, before they'd come over from Spain. There was a trace of deep-rooted nobility in the line of her lips and in the coloring of them. Yes, this is something real, he decided, and wondered why he'd never noticed it before. Until this moment she'd been just another girl who wanted to learn piano.

Three months later they were married. He took her to South Jersey to meet his family, and prepared her for it with a frank briefing, but it turned out to be pleasant in South Jersey. It was especially pleasant because the brothers weren't there to make a lot of noise and lewd remarks. Clifton was presently engaged in some kind of work that required him to do considerable traveling. Turley was a longshoreman on the Philadelphia waterfront. They hadn't been home for more than a year. Once every few months there'd be a post card from Turley, but nothing from Clifton, and the mother said to Teresa, "He ought to write, at least. Don't you think he ought to write?" It was as though Teresa had been a member of the family for years. They were at the table and the mother had roasted a goose. It was a very special dinner and the father made it extra-special by appearing with combed hair, a clean shirt, and scrubbed fingernails. And all day long he'd stayed off the liquor. But after dinner he was at it again and within a few hours he'd consumed the better part of a quart. He winked at Teresa and said, "Say, you're one hell of a pretty girl. Come over here and gimme a kiss." She smiled at her father-in-law and said, "To celebrate the happiness?" and went to him and gave him a kiss. He took another drink from the bottle and winked at Edward and said, "You got yourself a sweet little number here. Now what you wanna do is hold onto her. That New York's a fast town—"

They went back to the basement apartment on Ninety-third Street. He continued giving piano lessons, and Teresa remained at the fruit-drink stand. Some weeks passed, and then he asked her to quit the job. He said he didn't like this night-work routine. It was a locale that worried him, he explained, stating that although she'd never had trouble with Times Square night owls, it was nevertheless a possibility.

"But is always policemen around there," she argued. "The policemen, they protect the women—"

"Even so," he said, "I can think of safer places than Times Square late at night."

"Like what places?"

"Well, like—"

"Like here? With you?"

He mumbled, "Whenever you're not around, it's like— well, it's like I'm blindfolded."

"You like to see me all the time? You need me that much?"

He touched his lips to her forehead. "It's more than that. It's so much more—"

"I know," she breathed, and held him tightly. "I know what you mean. Is same with me. Is more each day—"

She quit the Times Square job, and found nine-to-five employment in a coffee shop on Eighty-sixth Street off Broadway. It was a nice little place, with a generally pleasant atmosphere, and some days he'd go there for lunch. They'd play a game, customer-and-waitress, pretending that they didn't know each other, and he'd try to make a date. Then one day, after she'd worked there for several months, they were playing the customer-waitress game and he was somehow aware of an interruption, a kind of intrusion.

It was a man at a nearby table. The man was watching them, smiling at them. At her? he wondered, and gazed levelly at the man. But then it was all right and he said to himself, It's me, he's smiling at me. As if he knows me—

Then the man stood up and came over and introduced himself. His name was Woodling. He was a concert manager and of course he remembered Edward Webster Lynn. "Yes, of course," Woodling said, as Edward gave his name, "you came to my office about a year ago. I was terribly busy then and couldn't give you much time. I'm sorry if I was rather abrupt—"

"Oh, that's all right. I understand the way it is."

"It shouldn't be that way," Woodling said. "But this is such a frantic town, and there's so much competition."

Teresa said, "Would the gentlemen like to have lunch?"

Her husband smiled at her, took her hand. He introduced her to Woodling, then explained the customer-waitress game. Woodling laughed and said it was a wonderful game, there were always two winners.

"You mean we both get the prize?" Teresa asked.

"Especially the customer," Woodling said, gesturing toward Edward. "He's a very fortunate man. You're really a prize, my dear."

"Thank you," Teresa murmured. "Is very kind of you to say."

Woodling insisted on paying for the lunch. He invited the pianist to visit him at his office. They made an appointment for an afternoon meeting later that week. When Woodling walked out of the coffee shop, the pianist sat there with his mouth open just a little. "What is it?" Teresa asked, and he said, "Can't believe it. Just can't—"

"He gives you a job?"

"Not a job. It's a chance. I never thought it would happen. I'd given up hoping."

"This is something important?"

He nodded very slowly.

Three days later he entered the suite of offices on Fifty-seventh Street. The furnishings were quietly elegant, the rooms large. Woodling's private office was very large, and featured several oil paintings. There was a Matisse and a Picasso and some by Utrillo.

They had a long talk. Then they went into an audition room and Edward seated himself at a mahogany Baldwin. He played some Chopin, some Schumann, and an extremely difficult piece by Stravinsky. He was at the piano for exactly forty-two minutes. Woodling said, "Excuse me a moment," and walked out of the room, and came back with a contract.

It was a form contract and it offered nothing in the way of guarantees. It merely stipulated that for a period of not less than three years the pianist would be managed and represented by Arthur Woodling. But this in itself was like starting the climb up a gem-studded ladder. In the field of classical music, the name Woodling commanded instant attention from coast to coast, from hemisphere to hemisphere. He was one of the biggest.

Woodling was forty-seven. He was of medium height and built leanly and looked as though he took very good care of himself. He had a healthy complexion. His eyes were clear and showed that he didn't go in for overwork or excessively late hours. He had a thick growth of tightly-curled black hair streaked with white and at the temples it was all white. His features were neatly sculptured, except for the left side of his jaw. It was slightly out of line, the souvenir of a romantic interlude some fifteen years before when a colaratura-soprano had ended their relationship during a South American concert tour. She'd used a heavy bronze book-end to fracture his jaw.

On the afternoon of the contract-signing ceremony with Edward Webster Lynn, the concert manager wore a stiffly starched white collar and a gray cravat purchased in Spain. His suit was also from Spain. His cuff links were emphatically Spanish, oblongs of silver engraved with conquistador helmets. The Spanish theme, especially the cuff links, had been selected specifically for this occasion.

Seven months later, Edward Webster Lynn made his New York debut. It was at Carnegie Hall. They shouted for encores. Next it was Chicago, and then New York again. And after his first coast-to-coast tour they wanted him in Europe.

In Europe he had them leaping to their feet, crying "bravo" until their voices cracked. In Rome the women threw flowers onto the stage. When he came back to Carnegie Hall the seats had been sold out three months in advance. During that year when he was twenty-five, he gave four performances at Carnegie Hall.

In November of that year, he played at the Academy of Music in Philadelphia. He performed the Grieg *Concerto* and the audience was somewhat hysterical, some of them were sobbing, and a certain critic became incoherent and finally speechless. Later that night, Woodling gave a party in his suite at the Town-Casa. It was on the fourth floor. At a few minutes past midnight, Woodling came over to the pianist and said, "Where's Teresa?"

"She said she was tired."

"Again?"

"Yes." He said it quietly. "Again."

Woodling shrugged. "Perhaps she doesn't like these parties."

The pianist lit a cigarette. He held it clumsily. A waiter approached with a tray and glasses of champagne. The pianist reached for a glass, changed his mind and pulled tightly at the cigarette. He jetted the smoke from between his teeth, looked down at the floor and said, "It isn't the parties, Arthur. She's tired all the time. She's—"

There was another stretch of quiet. Then Woodling said, "What is it? What's the matter?"

The pianist didn't answer.

"Perhaps the strain of traveling, living in hotels—"

"No." He said it somewhat harshly. "It's me."

"Quarrels?"

"I wish it were quarrels. This is something worse. Much worse."

"You care to talk about it?" Woodling asked.

"That won't help."

Woodling took his arm and led him out of the room, away from the array of white ties and evening gowns. They went into a smaller room. They were alone there, and Woodling said, "I want you to tell me. Tell me all of it."

"It's a personal matter—"

"You need advice, Edward. I can't advise you unless you tell me."

The pianist looked down at the smoking cigarette stub. He felt the fire near his fingers. He moved toward a table, mashed the stub in an ashtray, turned and faced the concert manager. "She doesn't want me."

"Now, really—"

"You don't believe it? I didn't believe it, either. I couldn't believe it."

"Edward, it's impossible."

"Yes, I know. That's what I've been telling myself for months." And then he shut his eyes tightly, gritting it, "For months? It's been more than a year—"

"Sit down."

He fell into a chair. He stared at the floor and said, "It started slowly. At first it was hardly noticeable, as though she were trying to hide it. Like—like fighting something. Then gradually it showed itself. I mean, we'd be talking and she'd turn away and walk out of the room. It got to the point where I'd try to open the door and the door was locked. I'd call to her and she wouldn't answer. And the way it is now—well, it's over with, that's all."

"Has she told you?"

"Not in so many words."

"Then maybe—"

"She's sick? No, she isn't sick. That is, it isn't a sickness they can treat. If you know what I mean."

"I know what you mean, but I still can't believe—"

"She doesn't want me, Arthur. She just doesn't want me, that's all."

Woodling moved toward the door.

"Where are you going?" the pianist asked.

"I'm getting you a drink."

"I don't want a drink."

"You'll have one," Woodling said. "You'll have a double."

The concert manager walked out of the room. The pianist sat bent over, his face cupped in his hands. He stayed that way for some moments. Then he straightened abruptly and got to his feet. He was breathing hard.

He went out of the room, down the hall toward the stairway. Their suite was on the seventh floor. He went up the three flights with a speed that had him breathless as he entered the living room.

He called her name. There was no answer. He crossed the parlor to the bedroom door. He tried it, and it was open.

She was sitting on the edge of the bed, wearing a robe. In her lap was a magazine. It was open but she wasn't looking at it. She was looking at the wall.

"Teresa—"

She went on looking at the wall.

He moved toward her. He said, "Get dressed."

"What for?"

"The party," he said. "I want you there at the party."

She shook her head.

"Teresa, listen—"

"Please go," she said. She was still looking at the wall. She raised a hand and gestured toward the door. "Go—"

"No," he said. "Not this time."

Then she looked at him. "What?" Her eyes were dull. "What did you say?"

"I said not this time. This time we talk it over. We find out what it's all about."

"There is nothing—"

"Stop that," he cut in. He moved closer to her. "I've had enough of that. The least you can do is tell me—"

"Why you shout? You never shout at me. Why you shout now?"

"I'm sorry." He spoke in a heavy whisper. "I didn't mean to—"

"Is all right." She smiled at him. "You have right to shout. You have much right."

"Don't say that." He was turning away, his head lowered.

He heard her saying, "I make you unhappy, no? Is bad for me to do that. Is something I try not to do, but when it is dark you cannot stop the darkness—"

"What's that?" He turned stiffly, staring at her. "What did you mean by that?"

"I mean—I mean—" But then she was shaking her head, again looking at the wall. "All the time is darkness. Gets darker. No way to see where to go, what to do."

She's trying to tell me something, he thought. She's trying so hard, but she can't tell me. Why can't she tell me? She said, "I think there is one thing to do. Only one thing."

He felt coldness in the room.

"I say good-by. I go away—"

"Teresa, please—"

She stood up and moved toward the wall. Then she turned and faced him. She was calm. It was an awful calmness. Her voice was a hollow, toneless semi-whisper as she said, "All right, I tell you—"

"Wait." He was afraid now.

"Is proper that you should know," she said. "Is always proper to give the explanation. To make confession."

"Confession?"

"I did bad thing—"

He winced.

"Was very bad. Was terrible mistake." And then a certain brightness came into her eyes. "But now you are famous pianist, and for that I am glad."

This isn't happening, he told himself. It can't be happening.

"Yes, for that I am glad I did it," she said. "To get you the chance you wanted. Was only one way to get you that chance, to put you in Carnegie Hall."

There was a hissing sound. It was his own breathing.

"Woodling," she said.

He shut his eyes very tightly.

"Was the same week when he signed you to his contract," she went on. "Was a few days later. He comes to the coffee shop. But not for coffee. Not for lunch."

There was another hissing sound. It was louder.

"For business proposition," she said.

I've got to get out of here, he told himself. I can't listen to this.

"At first, when he tells me, is like a puzzle, too much for me. I ask him what he is talking about, and he looks at me as if to say, You don't know? You think about it and you will know. So I think about it. That night I get no sleep. Next day he is there again. You know how a spider works? A spider, he is slow and careful—"

He couldn't look at her.

"—like pulling me away from myself. Like the spirit is one thing and the body is another. Was not Teresa who went with him. Was only Teresa's body. As if I was not there, really. I was with you, I was taking you to Carnegie Hall."

And now it was just a record playing, the narrator's voice giving supplementary details. "—in the afternoons. During my time off. He rented a room near the coffee shop. For weeks, in the afternoons, in that room. And then one night you tell me the news, you have signed the paper to play in Carnegie Hall. When he comes next time to the coffee shop he is just another customer. I hand him the menu and he gives the order. And I think to myself, Is ended, I am me again. Yes, now I can be me.

"But you know, it is a curious thing—what you do yester-

day is always part of what you are today. From others you try
to hide it. For yourself it is no use trying, it is a kind of mirror,
always there. So I look, and what do I see? Do I see Teresa?
Your Teresa?

"Is no Teresa in the mirror. Is no Teresa anywhere now. Is
just a used-up rag, something dirty. And that is why I have
not let you touch me. Or even come close. I could not let
you come close to this dirt."

He tried to look at her. He said to himself, Yes, look at her.
And go to her. And bow, or kneel. It calls for that, it surely
does. But—

His eyes aimed at the door, and beyond the door, and there
was fire in his brain. He clenched his teeth, and his hands
became stone hammerheads. Every fibre in his body was
coiled, braced for the lunge that would take him out of here
and down the winding stairway to the fourth-floor suite.

And then, for just a moment, he groped for a segment of
control, of discretion. He said to himself, Think now, try to
think. If you go out that door she'll see you going away, she'll
be here alone. You mustn't leave her here alone.

It didn't hold him. Nothing could hold him. He moved
slowly toward the door.

"Edward—"

But he didn't hear. All he heard was a low growl from his
own mouth as he opened the door and went out of the bedroom.

Then he was headed across the living room, his arm extended, his fingers clawing at the door leading to the outer
hall. In the instant that his fingers touched the door handle,
he heard the noise from the bedroom.

It was a mechanical noise. It was the rattling of the chain-
pulleys at the sides of the window.

He pivoted and ran across the living room and into the
bedroom. She was climbing out. He leaped, and made a grab,
but there was nothing to grab. There was just the cold empty
air coming in through the wide-open window.

9

ON Front Street, as he stood on the pavement near the red-and-gold entrance to the five-and-dime, the Saturday shoppers swept past him. Some of them bumped him with their shoulders. Others pushed him aside. He was insensible. He wasn't there, really. He was very far away from there.

He was at the funeral seven years ago, and then he was wandering around New York City. It was a time of no direction, no response to traffic signals or changes in the weather. He never knew or cared what hour of the day it was, what day of the week it was. For the sum of everything was a circle, and the circle was labeled Zero.

He had pulled all his savings from the bank. It amounted to about nine thousand dollars. He managed to lose it. He wanted to lose it. The night he lost it, when it was taken from him, he got himself beaten. He wanted that, too. When it happened, when he went down with the blood spilling from his nose and mouth and the gash in his skull, he was glad. He actually enjoyed it.

It happened very late at night, in Hell's Kitchen. Three of them jumped him. One of them had a length of lead pipe. The other two had brass knuckles. The lead pipe came first. It hit him on the side of his head and he walked sideways, then slowly sat down on the curb. Then the others went to work with the brass knuckles. Then something happened. They weren't sure what it was, but it seemed like propeller blades churning the air and coming at them. The one with the lead pipe had made a rapid departure, and they wondered why he wasn't there to help them. They really needed help. One of them went down with four teeth flying out of his mouth. The other was sobbing, "gimme a break, aw, please— gimme a break," and the wild man grinned and whispered, "Fight back—fight back—don't spoil the fun." The thug knew then he had no choice, and did what he could with the brass knuckles and his weight. He had considerable weight. Also, he was quite skilled in the dirtier tactics. He used a knee, he used his thumbs, and he even tried using his teeth. But he just wasn't fast enough. He ended up with both eyes swollen shut, a fractured nose, and a brain concussion. As he lay there on the pavement, flat on his back and unconscious, the wild man whispered, "Thanks for the party."

A few nights later, there was another party. It took place in Central Park when two policemen found the wild man sleeping under a bush. They woke him up, and he told them to go away and leave him alone. They pulled him to his feet, asked him if he had a home. He didn't answer. They started to shoot questions at him. Again he told them to leave him alone. One of them snarled at him and shoved him. The other policeman grabbed his arm. He said, "Let go, please let go." Then they both had hold of him, and they were pulling him along. They were big men and he had to look up at them as he said, "Why don't you leave me alone?" They told him to shut up. He tried to pull loose and one of them hit him on the leg with a night stick. "You hit me," he said. The policeman barked at him, "Sure I hit you. If I want to, I'll hit you again." He shook his head slowly and said, "No, you won't." A few minutes later the two policemen were alone there. One of them was leaning against a tree, breathing hard. The other was sitting on the grass, groaning.

And then, less than a week later, it was in the Bowery and a well-known strong-arm specialist remarked through puffed and bleeding lips, "Like stickin' me face in a concrete mixer."

From someone in the crowd, "You gonna fight him again?"

"Sure I'll fight him again. Just one thing I need."

"What?"

"An automatic rifle," the plug-ugly said, sitting there on the curb and spitting blood. "Buy me one of them rifles and keep him a distance."

He was always on the move, roaming from the Bowery to the Lower East Side and up through Yorkville to Spanish Harlem and down and over to Brooklyn, to the brawling grounds of Greenpoint and Brownsville—to any area where a man who looked for trouble was certain to find it.

Now, looking back on it, he saw the wild man of seven years ago, and thought, What it amounted to, you were crazy, I mean really crazy. Call it horror-crazy. With your fingers, that couldn't touch the keyboard or get anywhere near a keyboard, a set of claws, itching to find the throat of the very dear friend and counselor, that so kind and generous man who took you into Carnegie Hall.

But, of course, you knew you mustn't find him. You had to keep away from him, for to catch even a glimpse of him would mean a killing. But the wildness was there, and it needed an outlet. So let's give a vote of thanks to the hooligans, all the thugs and sluggers and roughnecks who were only too happy to accommodate you, to offer you a target.

What about money? It stands to reason you needed money. You had to put food in your belly. Let's see now, I remember there were certain jobs, like dishwashing and polishing cars and distributing handbills. At times you were out of a job, so the only thing to do was hold out your hand and wait for coins to drop in. Just enough nickels and dimes to get you a bowl of soup and a mattress in a flophouse. Or sometimes a roll of gauze to bandage the bleeding cuts. There were nights when you dripped a lot of blood, especially the nights when you came out second best.

Yes, my good friend, you were in great shape in those days. What I think is, you were a candidate for membership in some high-off-the-ground clubhouse. But it couldn't go on like that. It had to stop somewhere. What stopped it?

Sure, it was that trip you took. The stroll that sent you across the bridge into Jersey, a pleasant little stroll of some hundred-and-forty miles. If I remember correctly, it took you the better part of a week to get there, to the house hidden in the woods of South Jersey.

It was getting on toward Thanksgiving. You were coming home to spend the holiday with the folks. They were all there. Clifton and Turley were home for the holiday, too. At least, they said that was the reason they'd come home. But after a few drinks they kind of got around to the real reason. They said there'd been some complications, and the authorities were looking for them, and this place deep in the woods was far away from all the guideposts.

The way it was, Turley had quit his job on the Philly waterfront and had teamed up with Clifton on a deal involving stolen cars, driving the cars across state lines. They'd been spotted and chased. Not that it worried them. You remember Clifton saying, "Yeah, it's a tight spot, all right. But we'll get

out of it. We always get out of it." And then he laughed, and
Turley laughed, and they went on drinking and started to tell
dirty jokes. . . .

That was quite a holiday. I mean, the way it ended it was
really something. I remember Clifton said something about
your situation, your status as a widower. You asked him not
to talk about it. He went on talking about it. He winked at
Turley and he said to you, "What's it like with a Puerto
Rican?"

You smiled at Clifton, you winked at Turley, and you said
to your father and mother, "It's gonna be crowded in here.
You better go into the next room—"

So then it was you and Clifton, and the table got knocked
over, and a couple chairs got broken. It was Clifton on the
floor, spitting blood and saying, "What goes on here?" Then
he shook his head. He just couldn't believe it. He said to
Turley, "Is that really him?"

Turley couldn't answer. He just stood staring.

Clifton got up and went down and got up again. He was
all right, he could really take it. You went on knocking him
down and he got up and finally he said, "I'm gettin' tired
of this." He looked at Turley and muttered, "Take him off
me—"

I remember Turley moving in and reaching out and then it
was Turley sitting on the floor next to Clifton. It was Clifton
laughing and saying, "You here too?" and Turley nodded solemnly and then he got up. He said, "Tell you what I'll do.
I'll give you fifty to one you can't do that again."

Then he moved in. He came in nice and easy, weaving. You
threw one and missed and then he threw one and his money
was safe. You were out for some twenty minutes. And later
we were gathered at the table again, and Clifton was grinning
and saying, "It figures now, you're slated for the game."

You didn't quite get that. You said, "Game? What game?"

"Our game." He pointed to himself and Turley. "I'm
gonna deal you in."

"No," Turley said. "He ain't for the racket."

"He's perfect for the racket," Clifton said quietly and
thoughtfully. "He's fast as a snake. He's hard as iron—"

"That ain't the point," Turley cut in. "The point is—"

"He's ready for it, that's the point. He's geared for action."

"He is?" Turley's voice was tight now. "Let him say it, then. Let him say what he wants."

Then it was quiet at the table. They were looking at you, waiting. You looked back at them, your brothers—the heist artists, the gunslingers, the all-out trouble-eaters.

And you thought, Is this the answer? Is this what you're slated for? Well, maybe so. Maybe Clifton has you tagged, with your hands that can't make music any more making cash the easy way. With a gun. You know they use guns. You braced for that? You hard enough for that?

Well, you were hard enough in Burma. In Burma you did plenty with a gun.

But this isn't Burma. This is a choice. Between what? The dirty and the clean? The bad and the good?

Let's put it another way. What's the payoff for the clean ones? The good ones? I mean the ones who play it straight. What do they get at the cashier's window?

Well, friends, speaking from experience, I'd say the payoff is anything from a kick in the teeth to the long-bladed scissors slicing in deep and cutting up that pump in your chest. And that's too much, that does it. With all feeling going out and the venom coming in. So then you're saying to the world, All right, you wanna play it dirty, we'll play it dirty.

But no, you were thinking. You don't want that. You join this Clifton-Turley combine, it's strictly on the vicious side and you've had enough of that.

"Well?" Clifton was asking. "What'll it be?"

You were shaking your head. You just didn't know. And then you happened to look up. You saw the other two faces, the older faces. Your mother was shrugging. Your father was wearing the soft-easy smile.

And that was it. That was the answer.

"Well?" from Clifton.

You shrugged. You smiled.

"Come on," Clifton said. "Let's have it."

"He's telling you," from Turley. "Look at his face."

Clifton looked. He took a long look. He said, "It's like— like he's skipped clear outa the picture. As if he just don't care."

"That just about says it," Turley grinned.

Just about. For then and there it was all connections split, it was all issues erased. No venom now, no frenzy, no trace of the wild man in your eyes. The wild man was gone, annihilated by two old hulks who didn't know they were still in there pitching, the dull-eyed, shrugging mother and the easy-smiling, booze-guzzling father.

Without sound you said to them, Much obliged, folks.

And later, when you went away, when you walked down the path that bordered the watermelon patch, you kept thinking it, Much obliged, much obliged.

The path was bumpy, but you didn't feel the bumps. In the woods the narrow, twisting road was deeply rutted, but you sort of floated past the ridges and the chug holes. You remember it was wet-cold in the woods, and there was a blasting wind, but all you felt was a gentle breeze.

You made it through the woods, and onto another road, and still another road, and finally the wide concrete highway that took you into the tiny town and the bus depot. In the depot there was a lush talking loud. He was trying to start something. When he tried with you, it was just no use, he got nowhere. You gave him the shrug, you gave him the smile. It was easy, the way you handled him. Well, sure, it was easy, it was just that nothing look—with your tongue in your cheek.

You took the first bus out. It was headed for Philadelphia. I think it was a few nights later you were in a mid-city ginmill, one of them fifteen-cents-a-shot establishments. It had a kitchen, and you got a job washing dishes and cleaning the floor and so forth. There was an old wreck of a piano, and you'd look at it, and look away, and look at it again. One night you said to the bartender, "Okay if I play it?"

"You?"

"I think I can play it."

"All right, give it a try. But it better be music."

You sat down at the piano. You looked at the keyboard. And then you looked at your hands.

"Come on," the bartender said. "Whatcha waitin' for?"

You lifted your hands. You lowered your hands and your fingers hit the keys.

The sound came out and it was music.

10

A VOICE said, "You still here?"

He looked up. The waitress was coming toward him through the crowd of shoppers. She'd emerged from the five-and-dime with a paper bag in her hand. He saw that it was a small bag. He told himself that she hadn't done much shopping.

"How long were you in there?" he asked.

"Just a few minutes."

"Is that all?"

"I got waited on right away," she asked. "All I bought was some toothpaste and a cake of soap. And a toothbrush."

He didn't say anything.

She said, "I didn't ask you to wait for me."

"I wasn't waiting," he said. "I had no place to go, that's all. I was just hanging around."

"Looking at the people?"

"No," he said. "I wasn't looking at the people."

She pulled him away from an oncoming baby carriage. "Come on," she said. "We're blocking traffic."

They moved along with the crowd. The sky was all gray now and getting darker. It was still early in the afternoon, just a little past two, but it seemed much later. People were looking up at the sky and walking faster, wanting to get home before the storm swept in. The threat of it was in the air.

She looked at him. She said, "Button your overcoat."

"I'm not cold."

"I'm freezing," she said. "How far we gotta walk?"

"To Port Richmond? It's a couple miles."

"That's great."

"We could take a taxi, except I haven't got a cent to my name."

"Likewise," she said. "I borrowed four bits from my landlady and spent it all."

"Well, it ain't too cold for walking."

"The hell it ain't. My toes are coming off."

"We'll walk faster," he said. "That'll keep your feet warm."

They quickened their pace. They were walking with their

heads down against the oncoming wind. It was coming harder, whistling louder. It lifted the snow from pavement and street and there were powdery flurries of the tiny flakes. Then larger snowflakes were falling. The air was thick with snow, and it was getting colder.

"Nice day for a picnic," she said. And just then she slipped on some hard-packed snow and was falling backward and he grabbed her. Then he slipped and they were both falling but she managed to get a foothold and they stayed on their feet. A store owner was standing in the doorway of his dry-goods establishment, saying to them, "Watch your step out there. It's slippery." She glared at the man and said, "Yeah, we know it's slippery. It wouldn't be slippery if you'd clean the pavement." The store owner grinned and said, "So if you fall, you'll sue me."

The man went back into the store. They stood there on the slippery pavement, still holding onto each other to keep from falling. He said to himself, That's all it amounts to, just holding her so she won't slide and slip and go down. But I guess it's all right now, I guess you can let go.

You better let go, damn it. Because it's there again, it's happening again. You'll hafta stop it, that's all. You can't let it get you like this. It's really getting you and she knows it. Of course she knows. She's looking at you and she—

Say, what's the matter with your arms? Why can't you let go of her? Now look, you'll just hafta stop it.

I think the way to stop it is shrug it off. Or take it with your tongue in your cheek. Sure, that's the system. At any rate it's the system that works for you. It's the automatic control board that keeps you way out there where nothing matters, where it's only you and the keyboard and nothing else. Because it's gotta be that way. You gotta stay clear of anything serious.

You wanna know something? The system just ain't working now. I think it's Eddie giving way to Edward Webster Lynn. No, it can't be that way. We won't let it be that way. Oh, Christ, why'd she have to mention that name? Why'd she have to bring it all back? You had it buried and you were getting along fine and having such a high old time not caring about anything. And now this comes along. This hits you and sets a spark and before we know it there's a fire started. A what? You heard me, I said it's a fire. And here's a flash just came in—it's blazing too high and we can't put it out.

We can't? Check the facts, man, check the facts. This is Eddie here. And Eddie can't feel fire. Eddie can't feel anything.

His arms fell away from her. There was nothing at all in his eyes as he gave her the soft-easy smile. He said, "Let's get moving. We got a long way to go."

She looked at him, and took a slow deep breath, and said, "You're telling me?"

Some forty minutes later they entered Harriet's Hut. The place was jammed. It was always busy on Saturday afternoons, but when the weather was bad the crowd was doubled. Against all snow and blasting wind, the Hut was a fortress and a haven. It was also a fueling station. The bartender rushed back and forth, doing his level best to supply the demand for antifreeze.

Harriet was behind the bar, at the cash register. She spotted the waitress and the piano man, and yapped at them, "Where ya been? What the hell ya think it is, a holiday?"

"Sure it's a holiday," the waitress said. "We don't start work till nine tonight. That's the schedule."

"Not today it ain't." Harriet told her. "Not with a mob like this. You shoulda known I'd need you here. And you," she said to Eddie, "you oughta know the score on this kinda weather. They come in off the street, the place gets filled, and they wanna hear music."

Eddie shrugged. "I got up late."

"Yeah, he got up late," Lena said. She spoke very slowly, with a certain deliberation. "Then we went for a ride. And then we took a walk."

Harriet frowned. "Together?"

"Yeah," she said. "Together."

The Hut owner looked at the piano man. "What's the wire on that?"

He didn't answer. The waitress said, "Whatcha want him to do, make a full report?"

"If he wants to," Harriet said, still looking quizzically at the piano man. "It's just that I'm curious, that's all. He usually walks alone."

"Yeah, he's a loner, all right," the waitress murmured. "Even when he's with someone, he's alone."

Harriet scratched the back of her neck. "Say, what goes on here? What's all this who-struck-John routine?"

"You get the answer on page three," the waitress said. "Except there ain't no page three."

"Thanks," Harriet said. "That helps a lot." Then, abruptly, she yelled, "Look, don't stand there giving me puzzles. I don't need puzzles today. Just put on your apron and get to work."

"First we get paid."

"We?" Harriet was frowning again.

"Well, me, anyway," the waitress said. "I want a week's wages and three in advance for this extra time today."

"What's the rush?"

"No rush." Lena pointed to the cash register. "Just take it out nice and slow and hand it to me."

"Later," the fat blonde said. "I'm too busy now."

"Not too busy to gimme my salary. And while you're at it, you can pay him, too. You want him to make music, you pay him."

Eddie shrugged. "I can wait—"

"You'll stay right here and get your money," Lena cut in. And then, to Harriet, "Come on, dish out the greens."

For a long moment Harriet didn't move. She stood there studying the face of the waitress. Then, with a backward gesture of her hand, as though to cast something over her shoulder to get it out of the way, she turned her attention to the cash register.

It's all right now, Eddie thought. It was tight there for a minute but I think it's all right now. He ventured a side glance at the expressionless face of the waitress. If only she leaves it alone, he said to himself. It don't make sense to start with Harriet. With Harriet it's like starting with dynamite. Or maybe that's what she wants. Yes, I think she's all coiled up inside, she's craving some kind of explosion.

Harriet was taking money from the cash register, counting

out the bills and putting them in Lena's palm. She finished
paying Lena and turned to the piano man, putting the money
on the bar in front of him. As she placed some ones on top
of the fives, she was muttering, "Ain't enough I get grief from
the customers. Now the help comes up with labor troubles.
All of a sudden they go and form a union."

"That's the trend," the waitress said.

"Yeah?" Harriet said. "Well, I don't like it."

"Then lump it," Lena said.

The fat blonde stopped counting out the money. She
blinked a few times. Then she straightened slowly, her immense bosom jutting as she inhaled a vast lungful. "What's
that?" she said. "What'd you say?"

"You heard me."

Harriet placed her hands on her huge hips. "Maybe I didn't
hear correct. Because they don't talk to me that way. They
know better. I'll tell you something, girl. Ain't a living cat can
throw that kinda lip at me and get away with it."

"That so?" Lena murmured.

"Yeah, that's so," Harriet said. "And you're lucky. I'm letting you know it the easy way. Next time it won't be so easy.
You sound on me again, you'll get smacked down."

"Is that a warning?"

"Bright red."

"Thanks," Lena said. "Now here's one from me to you.
I've been smacked down before. Somehow I've always managed to get up."

"Jesus." Harriet spoke aloud to herself. "What gives with
this one here? It's like she's lookin' for it. She's really begging
for it."

The waitress stood with her arms loose at her sides. She was
smiling now.

Harriet had a thoughtful look on her face. She spoke softly
to the waitress. "What's the matter, Lena? What bothers
you?"

The waitress didn't answer.

"All right, I'll let it pass," the Hut owner said.

Lena held onto the thin smile. "You don't have to, really."

"I know I don't hafta. But it's better that way. Dontcha
think it's better that way?"

The thin smile was aimed at nothing in particular. The waitress said, "Any way it goes all right with me. But don't do me any favors. I don't need no goddam favors from you."

Harriet frowned and slanted her head and said, "You sure you know what you're saying?"

Lena didn't answer.

"Know what I think?" Harriet murmured. "I think you got your people mixed."

Lena lost the smile. She lowered her head. She nodded, then shook her head, then nodded again.

"Ain't that what it is?" Harriet prodded gently.

Lena went on nodding. She looked up at the fat blonde. She said, "Yeah, I guess so." And then, tonelessly, "I'm sorry, Harriet. It's just that I'm bugged about something—I didn't mean to take it out on you."

"What is it?" Harriet asked. The waitress didn't answer. Harriet looked inquiringly at Eddie. The piano man shrugged and didn't say anything. "Come on, let's have it," Harriet demanded. "What is it with her?" He shrugged again and remained quiet. The fat blonde sighed and said, "All right, I give up," and resumed counting out the money. Then the money was all there on the bar and he picked it up and folded the thin roll and let it fall into his overcoat pocket. He turned away from the bar and took a few steps and heard Lena saying, "Wait, I got something for you."

He came back and she handed him two quarters, two dimes and a nickel. "From last night," she said, not looking at him. "Now we're squared."

He looked down at the coins in his hand. Squared, he thought. All squared away. That makes it quits. That ends it. Well, sure, that's the way you want it. That's fine.

But just then he saw she was stiffening, she was staring at something. He glanced in that direction and saw Wally Plyne coming toward the bar where they stood.

The big-paunched bouncer wore a twisted grin as he approached. His thick shoulders were hunched, weaving in wrestler's style. The grin widened, and Eddie thought, He's forcing it, and what we get next is one of them real friendly hellos, all sugar and syrup.

And then he felt Plyne's big hand on his arm, heard Plyne's

gruff voice saying, "Here he is, the crown prince of the eighty-eights. My boy, Eddie."

"Yeah," the waitress said. "Your boy, Eddie."

Plyne didn't seem to hear her. He said to the piano man, "I was lookin' for you. Where you been hiding?"

"He wasn't hiding," the waitress said.

The bouncer tried to ignore her. He went on grinning at Eddie.

The waitress pushed it further. "How could he hide? He didn't have a chance. They knew his address."

Plyne blinked hard. The grin fell away.

It was quiet for some moments. Then Harriet was saying, "Lemme get in on this." She leaned over from behind the bar. "What's cooking here?"

"Something messy," the waitress said. She indicated the bouncer. "Ask your man there. He knows all about it. He stirred it up."

Harriet squinted at Plyne. "Spill," she said.

"Spill what?" The bouncer backed away. "She's talkin' from nowhere. She's dreamin' or somethin'."

The waitress turned and looked at Harriet. "Look, if you don't wanna hear this—"

The fat blonde took a deep breath. She went on looking at Plyne.

"I hope you can take it," the waitress said to her. "After all, you live with this man."

"Not lately." Harriet's voice was heavy. "Lately I ain't hardly been living at all."

The waitress opened her mouth to speak, and Plyne gritted, "Close your head—"

"Close yours," Harriet told him. And then, to the waitress, "All right, let's have it."

"It's what they call a sellout," Lena said. "I got it straight from the customers. They told me they were here this morning. They bought a few drinks and something else."

Eddie started to move away. The waitress reached out and caught his arm and held him there. He shrugged and smiled. His eyes said to the bouncer, It don't bother me, so don't let it bother you.

The waitress went on, "It was two of them. Two ambassadors, but not the good-will type. These were the ugly kind, the kind that can hurt you. Or make you disappear. You get what I'm talking about?"

Harriet nodded dully.

"They were looking for Eddie," the waitress said.

Harriet frowned, "What for?"

"That ain't the point. The point is, they had a car and they had a gun. What they needed was some information. Like finding out his address."

The frown faded from Harriet's face. She gaped at Plyne. "You didn't tell them—"

"He sure as hell did," Lena said.

Harriet winced.

"They gave him a nice tip, too," the waitress said. "They handed him fifty dollars."

"No." It was a groan. Harriet's mouth twisted. She turned her head to keep from looking at the bouncer.

"I don't wanna work here no more," the waitress said. "I'll just stay a few days, until you get another girl."

"Now wait," the bouncer said. "It ain't that bad."

"It ain't?" Lena faced him. "I'll tell you how bad it is. Ever bait a hook for catfish? They go for the stink. What you do is, you put some worms in a can and leave it out in the sun for a week or so. Then open the can and get a whiff. It'll give you an idea of what this smells like."

Plyne swallowed hard. "Look, you got it all wrong—"

And the waitress said, "Now we get the grease."

"Will ya listen?" Plyne whined. "I'm tellin' you they conned me. I didn't know what they were after. I figured they was—"

"Yeah, we know," Lena murmured. "You thought they were census-takers."

The bouncer turned to Eddie. His arms came up in a pleading gesture. "Ain't I your friend?"

"Sure," Eddie said.

"Would I do anything to hurt you?"

"Of course not."

"You hear that?" The bouncer spoke loudly to the two women. "You hear what he says? He knows I'm on his side."

"I think I'm gonna throw up," Harriet said.

But the bouncer went on, "I'm tellin' you they conned me. If I thought they were out to hurt Eddie, I'da—why for Christ's sake, I'da ripped 'em apart. They come in here again, I'll put them through that plate-glass window, one at a time."

A nearby drinker mumbled, "You tell 'em, Hugger."

And from another guzzler, "When the Hugger tells it, he means it."

"You're goddam right I mean it," Plyne said loudly. "I ain't a man who looks for trouble, but if they want it they'll get it." And then, to Eddie, "Dontcha worry, I can handle them gunpunks. They're little. I'm big."

"How big?" the waitress asked.

Plyne grinned at her. "Take a look."

She looked him up and down. "Yeah, it's there, all right," she murmured. "Really huge."

The bouncer was feeling much better now. He widened the grin. "Huge is correct," he said. "And it's solid, too. It's all man."

"Man?" She stretched the word, her mouth twisted. "What I see is slop."

At the bar the drinkers had stopped drinking. They were staring at the waitress.

"It's just slop," she said. She took a step toward the bouncer. "The only thing big about you is your mouth."

Plyne grunted again. He mumbled, "I don't like that. I ain't gonna take it—"

"You'll take it," she told him. "You'll eat it."

He's eating it, all right, Eddie thought. He's choking on it. Look at him, look what's in the eyes. Because he's getting it from her, that's why. He goes for her so much it's got him all jelly, it's driving him almost loony. And there's nothing he can do about it, except take it. Just stand there and take it. Yes he's getting it, sure enough. I've seen them get it, but not like this.

Now the crowd at the bar was moving in closer. From the tables they were rising and edging forward so as not to miss a word of it. The only sound in the Hut was the voice of the waitress. She spoke quietly, steadily, and what came from her lips was like a blade going into the bouncer.

Really ripping him apart, Eddie thought. Come to think of

it, what's happening here is a certain kind of amputation. And we don't mean the arms or the legs.

And look at Harriet. Look what's happening to her. She's aged some ten years in just a few minutes. Her man is getting slashed and chopped. It's happening right in front of her eyes, and there ain't a word she can say, a move she can make. She knows it's true.

Sure, it's true. No getting away from that. The bouncer played it dirty today. But even so, I think he's getting worse than he deserves. You gotta admit, he's had some hard knocks lately, I mean this problem with the waitress, this night after night of seeing it there and wanting it, and knowing there ain't a chance. And even now, while she tears him to pieces, spits on him in front of all these people, he can't take his hungry eyes off her. You gotta feel sorry for the bouncer, it's a sad matinee for the Harleyville Hugger.

Poor Hugger. He wanted so much to make a comeback, some sort of comeback. He thought if he could make it with the waitress, he'd be proving something. Like proving he still had it, the power, the importance, the stuff and the drive, and whatever it takes to make a woman say yes. What he got from the waitress was a cold, silent no. Not even a look.

Well, he's getting something now. He's getting plenty. It's grief in spades, that's what it is. I wish she'd stop it, I think she's pushing it too far. Does she know what she's doing to him? She can't know. If she knew, she'd stop. If I could only tell her—

Tell her what? That the bouncer ain't as bad as he seems? That he's just another has-been who tried to come back and got himself loused up? Sure, that's the way it is but you can't put it that way. You can't sing the blues for Plyne; you can't sing the blues, period. You're too far away from the scene, that's why. You're high up there and way out there where nothing matters.

Then what are you doing standing here? And looking. And listening. Why ain't you there at the piano?

Or maybe you're waiting for something to happen. It figures, the bouncer can't take much more of this. The waitress keeps it up, something's gonna happen, sure as hell.

Well, so what? It don't involve you. Nothing involves you.

What you do now is, you shove off. You cruise away from here and over there to the piano.

He started to move, and then couldn't move. The waitress was still holding onto his arm. He gave a pull, his arm came loose, and the waitress looked at him. Her eyes said, You can't check out; you're included.

His soft-easy smile said, Not in this. Not in anything.

Then he was headed toward the piano. He heard the voice of the waitress as she went on talking to Plyne. His legs moved faster. He was in a hurry to sit down at the keyboard, to start making music. That'll do it, he thought. That'll drown out the buzzing. He took off his overcoat and tossed it onto a chair.

"Hey, Eddie." It was from a nearby table. He glanced in that direction and saw the yellow-orange dyed hair, the skinny shoulders and the flat chest. The lips of Clarice were gin-wet, and her eyes were gin-shiny. She was sitting there alone, unaware of the situation at the bar.

"C'mere," she said. "C'mere and I'll show you a trick."

"Later," he murmured, and went on toward the piano. But then he thought, That wasn't polite. He turned and smiled at Clarice, and walked over to the table and sat down. "All right," he said. "Let's see it."

She was off her chair and onto the table, attempting a one-armed handstand. She went off the table and landed on the floor.

"Nice try," Eddie said. He reached down and helped her to her feet. She slid back onto the chair. From across the room, from the bar, he could hear the voice of the waitress, still giving it to Plyne. Don't listen, he told himself. Try to concentrate on what Clarice is saying.

Clarice was saying, "You sure fluffed me off last night."

"Well, it just wasn't there."

She shrugged. She reached for a shot glass, picked it up and saw it was empty. With a vague smile at the empty glass she said, "That's the way it goes. If it ain't there, it just ain't there."

"That figures."

"You're damn right it figures." She reached out and gave him an affectionate pat on the shoulder. "Maybe next time—"

"Sure," he said.

"Or maybe—" she lowered the glass to the table and pushed it aside— "maybe there won't be a next time."

"Whatcha mean?" He frowned slightly. "You closing up shop?"

"No," she said. "I'm still in business. I mean you."

"Me? What's with me?"

"Changes," Clarice said. "I gander certain changes."

His frown deepened "Like what?"

"Well, like last night, for instance. And just a little while ago, when you walked in with the waitress. It was—well, I've seen it happen before. I can always tell when it happens."

"When what happens? What're you getting at?"

"The collision," she said. She wasn't looking at him. She was talking to the shot glass and the table top. "That's what it is, a collision. Before they know it, it hits them. They just can't avoid it. Not even this one here, this music man with his real cool style. It was easy-come and easy-go and all of a sudden he gets hit—"

"Say, look, you want another drink?"

"I always want another drink."

He started to get up. "You sure need it now."

She pulled him back onto the chair. "First gimme the low-down. I like to get these facts first hand. Maybe I'll send it to Winchell."

"What is this? You dreaming up something?"

"Could be," Clarice murmured. She looked at him. It was a probing look. "Except it shows. It's scribbled all over your face. It was there when I seen you comin' in with her."

"Her? The waitress?"

"Yeah, the waitress. But she wasn't no cheap-joint waitress then. She was Queen of the Nile and you were that soldier, or something, from Rome."

He laughed. "It's the gin, Clarice. The gin's got you looped."

"You think so? I don't think so." She reached for the empty glass, pulled it toward her on the table. "Let's have a look in the crystal ball," she said.

Her hands were cupped around the shot glass, and she sat there looking intently at the empty jigger.

"I see something," she said.

"Clarice, it's just an empty glass."

"Ain't empty now. There's a cloud. There's shadows—"

"Come off it," he said.

"Quiet," she breathed. "It's comin' closer."

"All right." He grinned. "I'll go along with the gag. Whaddya see in the glass?"

"It's you and the waitress—"

For some reason he closed his eyes. His hands gripped the sides of the chair.

He heard Clarice saying, "—no other people around. Just you and her. It's in the summertime. And there's a beach. There's water—"

"Water?" He opened his eyes, his hands relaxed, and he grinned again. "That ain't water. It's gin. You're swimmin' in it."

Clarice ignored him. She went on gazing at the shot glass. "You both got your clothes on. Then she takes off her clothes. Look what she's doin'. She's all naked."

"Keep it clean," he said.

"You stand there and look at her," Clarice continued. "She runs across the sand. Then she takes a dive in the waves. She tells you to get undressed and come on in, the water's fine. You stand there—"

"That's right," he said. "I just stand there. I don't make a move."

"But she wants you—"

"The hell with her," he said. "That ocean's too deep for me."

Clarice looked at him. Then she looked at the shot glass. Now it was just an empty jigger that needed a refill.

"You see?" he said. And he grinned again. "There ain't nothing happening."

"You leveling? With yourself, I mean."

"Well, if it's proof you need—" He put his hand in his pocket and took out the roll of money, his salary from Harriet. He peeled off three ones and put them on the table. "I'm paying you in advance," he said. "For the next time."

She looked at the three ones.

"Take it," he said. "You might as well take it. You're gonna work for it."

Clarice shrugged and took the money off the table. She slipped the bills under her sleeve. "Well, anyway," she said, "it's nice to know you're still my customer."

"Permanent," he said with the soft-easy smile. "Let's shake on it."

And he put out his hand. Just then he heard the noise from the bar. It was a growl, and then a gasp from the crowd. He turned his head and saw the crowd moving back, shoving and pushing to stay clear of the bouncer. The growl came again, and Harriet was coming out from behind the bar, moving fast as she attempted to step between the bouncer and the waitress. The bouncer shoved her aside. It was a violent shove, and Harriet stumbled and hit the floor sitting down. Then the bouncer let out another growl, and took a slow step toward the waitress. The waitress stood there motionless. Plyne raised his arm. He hesitated, as though he wasn't quite sure what he wanted to do. The waitress smiled thinly, sneeringly, daring him to go through with it. He swung his arm and the flat of his hand cracked hard against her mouth.

Eddie got up from the chair. He walked toward the crowd at the bar.

II

HE was pushing his way through the crowd. They were packed tightly, and he had to use his elbows. As he forced a path, they gasped, for Plyne hit the waitress a second time. This time it was a knuckle smash with the back of the hand.

Eddie kept pushing, making his way through the crowd.

The waitress had not moved. A trickle of red moved slantwise from her lower lip.

"You'll take it back," the bouncer said. He was breathing very hard. "You'll take back every—"

"Kiss my ass," the waitress said.

DAVID GOODIS

Plyne hit her again, with his palm. And then again, with the back of his hand.

Harriet was up from the floor, getting between them. The bouncer grabbed her arm and flung her sideways. She went sailing across the floor, landed heavily on her knees, and then twisted her ankle as she tried to get up. She fell back. She sat there rubbing her ankle, staring at Plyne and the waitress.

The bouncer raised his arm again. "You gonna take it back?"

"No."

His open hand crashed against her face. She reeled against the bar, recovered her balance and stood there, still smiling thinly. Now a thicker stream of blood came from her mouth. One side of her face was welted with fingermarks. The other side was swollen and bruised.

"I'll ruin you," Plyne screamed at her. "I'll make you wish you'd never seen me—"

"I can't see you now," the waitress said. "I can't look down that far."

Plyne hit her again with his palm. Then he clenched his fist.

Eddie was using his arms like scythes, a feeling of desperation on him now.

Plyne said to the waitress, "You're gonna take it back. You'll take it back if I hafta knock all your teeth out."

"That won't do it," the waitress said. She licked at her bleeding lip.

"God damn you." Plyne hissed. He hauled off and swung his fist at her face. His fist was in mid-air when a hand grabbed his arm. He jerked loose and hauled off again. The hand came down on his arm, holding tightly now. He turned his head to see who had interfered.

"Leave her alone," Eddie said.

"You?" the bouncer said again.

Eddie didn't say anything. He was still holding the bouncer's arm. He moved slowly, stepping between Plyne and the waitress.

Plyne's eyes were wide. He was genuinely astonished. "Not Eddie," he said. "Anyone but Eddie."

"All right," the piano man murmured. "Let's break it up."

"Christ," the bouncer said. He turned and gaped at the

gaping crowd. "Look what's happenin' here. Look who's tryin' to break it up."

"I mean it, Wally."

"What? You what?" And then again to the crowd, "Get that? He says he means it."

"It's gone far enough," Eddie said.

"Well I'll be—" The bouncer didn't know what to make of it. Then he looked down and saw the hand still gripping his arm. "Whatcha doin'?" he asked, his voice foggy with amazement. "Whatcha think you're doin'?"

Eddie spoke to the waitress. "Take off."

"What?" from Plyne. And then to the waitress, who hadn't moved, "That's right, stay there. You got more comin'."

"No," Eddie said. "Listen, Wally—"

"To you?" The bouncer ripped out a laugh. He pulled his arm free from Eddie's grasp. "Move, clown. Get outta the way."

Eddie stood there.

"I said move," Plyne barked. "Get back where you belong." He pointed to the piano.

"If you'll leave her alone," Eddie said.

Again Plyne turned to the crowd. "You hear that? Can you believe it? I tell him to move and he won't move. This can't be Eddie."

From someone in the crowd, "It's Eddie, all right."

And from another, "He's still there, Hugger."

Plyne stepped back and looked Eddie up and down. He said, "What goes with you? You really know what you're doin'?"

Eddie spoke again to the waitress. "Take off, will you? Go on, fade."

"Not from this deal," the waitress said. "I like this deal."

"Sure she likes it," Plyne said. "What she got was only a taste. Now I'm gonna give her—"

"No you won't." Eddie's voice was soft, almost a whisper.

"I won't?" The bouncer mimicked Eddie's tone. "What's gonna stop me?"

Eddie didn't say anything.

Plyne laughed again. He reached out and lightly patted Eddie's head, and then he said kindly, almost paternally,

"You're way outa your groove. Somebody musta been feedin' you weeds, or maybe a joker put a capsule in your coffee."

"He ain't high, Hugger," came from someone in the crowd. "He's got both feet on the floor."

From another observer, "He'll have his head on the floor if he don't get outa the way."

"He'll get outa the way," Plyne said. "All I hafta do is snap my fingers—"

Eddie spoke with his eyes. His eyes said to the bouncer, It's gonna take more than that.

Plyne read it, checked it, and decided to test it. He moved toward the waitress. Eddie moved with him, staying in his path. Someone yelled, "Watch out, Eddie—"

The bouncer swiped at him, as though swiping at a fly. He ducked, and the bouncer lunged past him, aiming a fist at the waitress. Eddie pivoted and swung and his right hand made contact with Plyne's head.

"What?" Plyne said heavily. He turned and looked at Eddie.

Eddie was braced, his legs wide apart, his hands low.

"You did that?" Plyne asked.

Did I? Eddie asked himself. Was it really me? Yes, it was. But that can't be. I'm Eddie. Eddie wouldn't do that. The man who would do that is a long-gone drifter, the wild man whose favorite drink was his own blood, whose favorite meat was the Hell's Kitchen maulers, the Bowery sluggers, the Greenpoint uglies. And that was in another city, another world. In this world it's Eddie, who sits at the piano and makes the music and keeps his tongue in his cheek. Then why—

The bouncer moved in and hauled off with his left hand, his right cocked to follow through. As the bouncer swung, Eddie came in low and shot a short right to the belly. Plyne grunted and bent over. Eddie stepped back, then smashed a chopping left to the head.

Plyne went down.

The crowd was silent. The only sound in the Hut was the heavy breathing of the bouncer, who knelt on one knee and shook his head very slowly.

Then someone said, "I'm gonna buy new glasses. I just ain't seein' right."

"You saw what I saw," another said. "It was Eddie did that."

"I'm tellin' ya that can't be Eddie. The way he moved—that's something I ain't seen for years. Not since Henry Armstrong."

"Or Terry McGovern," one of the oldsters remarked.

"That's right, McGovern. That was a McGovern left hand, sure enough."

Then they were quiet again. The bouncer was getting up. He got up very slowly and looked at the crowd. They backed away. On the outer fringe they were pushing chairs and tables aside. "That's right," the bouncer said quietly. "Gimme plenty of room."

Then he turned and looked at the piano man.

"I don't want this," Eddie said. "Let's end it, Wally."

"Sure," the bouncer said. "It's gonna be finished in a jiffy."

Eddie gestured toward the waitress, who had moved toward the far side of the bar. "If you'll only leave her alone—"

"For now," the bouncer agreed. "Now it's you I want."

Plyne rushed to him.

Eddie met him with a whizzing right hand to the mouth. Plyne fell back, started forward, and walked into another right hand that landed on the cheekbone. Then Plyne tried to reach him with both arms flailing and Eddie went very low, grinning widely and happily, coming in to uppercut the bouncer with his left, to follow with a short right that made a crunching sound as it hit the damaged cheekbone. Plyne stepped back again, then came in weaving, somewhat cautiously.

The caution didn't help. Plyne took a right to the head, three lefts to the left eye, and a straight right to the mouth. The bouncer opened his mouth and two teeth fell out.

"Holy Saint Peter!" someone gasped.

Plyne was very careful now. He feinted a left, drew Eddie in, crossed a right that missed and took a series of lefts to the head. He shook them off, drew Eddie in again with another feinting left, then crossed the right. This time it landed. It caught Eddie on the jaw and he went flying. He hit the floor flat on his back. For a few moments his eyes were closed. He heard someone saying, "Get some water—" He opened his eyes. He grinned up at the bouncer.

The bouncer grinned back at him. "How we doin'?"

"We're doin' fine," Eddie said. He got up. The bouncer walked in fast and hit him on the jaw and Eddie went down again. He pulled himself up very slowly, still grinning. He raised his fists, but Plyne was in close and pushed him back. Plyne measured him with a long left, set him up against a table and then hit him with a right that sent him over the table, his legs above his head. He hit the floor and rolled over and got up.

Plyne had circled the table and was waiting for him. Plyne chopped a right to his head, hooked a left to his ribs, then hauled off and swung a roundhouse that caught him on the side of the head. He went to his knees.

"Stay there," someone yelled at him. "For Christ's sake, stay there."

"He won't do that," the bouncer said. "You watch and see. He's gonna get up again."

"Stay there, Eddie—"

"Why should he stay there?" the bouncer asked. "Look at him grinnin'. He's havin' fun."

"Lotsa fun," Eddie said. And then he came up very fast and slugged the bouncer in the mouth, in the cut eye, and in the mouth again. Plyne screamed with agony as his eye was cut again, deeply.

The crowd was backed up against a wall. They saw the bouncer reel from a smashing blow on the mouth. They saw the smaller man lunge and hit the bouncer in the belly. Plyne was wheezing, doubled up, trying to go down. The smaller man came in with a right hand that straightened Plyne. Then he delivered a whistling left that made a sickening sound as it hit the badly damaged eye.

Plyne screamed.

There was another scream and it came from a woman in the crowd.

A man yelled, "Someone stop it—"

Plyne took another left hook to the bad eye, then a sizzling right to the mouth, a left to the eye again, a right to the bruised cheekbone, and two more rights to the same cheekbone. Eddie fractured the bouncer's cheekbone, closed the eye, and knocked four teeth from the bleeding gums. The bouncer opened his mouth to scream again and was hit with a right to the jaw. He crashed into a chair and the chair fell apart. He reached out blindly, his chin on the floor, and his hand closed on a length of splintered wood, the leg from the broken chair. As he got up, he was swinging the club with all his might at the smaller man's head.

The club hit empty air. Plyne swung again and missed. The smaller man was backing away. The bouncer advanced slowly, then lunged and swung and the club grazed the smaller man's shoulder.

Eddie kept backing away. He bumped into a table and threw himself aside as the bouncer aimed again for his skull. The splintered cudgel missed his temple by only a few inches.

Too close, Eddie told himself. Much too close for health and welfare. That thing connects, you're on the critical list. Did you say critical? The shape you're in now, it's critical already. How come you're still on your feet? Look at him. He's gone sheer off his rocker, and that ain't no guess, it ain't no theory. Just look at his eyes. Or make it the one eye, the other's a mess. Look at the one eye that's open. You see what's in that eye? It's slaughter. He's out for slaughter, and you gotta do something.

Whatever it is, you better do it fast. We're in the home stretch now. It's gettin' close to the finish line. Yeah—he nearly got you that time. Another inch or so and that woulda been it. God damn these tables. All these tables in the way. But the door, the back door, I think you're near enough to make a try for it. Sure, that's the only thing you can do. That is, if you wanna get outa here alive.

He turned and made a dash toward the back door. As he neared the door, he heard a loud gasp from the crowd. He whirled, and looked, and saw the bouncer heading toward the waitress.

She was backed up against the bar. She was cornered there, blocked off. On one side it was the overturned tables. On the other side it was the crowd. The bouncer moved forward very slowly, his shoulders hunched, the cudgel raised. A low gurgling noise mixed with the blood dripping from his mouth. It was a macabre noise, like a dirge.

There was a distance of some twenty feet between the bouncer and the waitress. Then it was fifteen feet. The bouncer stepped over a fallen chair, hunched lower now. He reached out to push aside an overturned table. At that moment, Eddie moved.

The crowd saw Eddie running toward the bar, then vaulting over its wooden surface, then was hurling himself toward the food counter at the other end of the bar. They saw him arriving at the food counter and grabbing a bread knife.

He came out from behind the bar and moved between the waitress and the bouncer. It was a large knife. It had a stainless-steel blade and it was very sharp. He thought, The bouncer knows how sharp it is, he's seen Harriet cutting bread with it, cutting meat. I think he'll drop that club now and come to his senses. Look, he's stopped, he's just standing there. If he'll only drop that club.

"Drop it, Wally."

Plyne held onto the cudgel. He stared at the knife, then at the waitress, then at the knife again.

"Drop that stick," Eddie said. He took a slow step forward.

Plyne retreated a few feet. Then he stopped and glanced around, sort of wonderingly. Then he looked at the waitress. He made the gurgling noise again.

Eddie took another step forward. He raised the knife a little. He kicked at the overturned table, clearing the space between himself and the bouncer.

He showed his teeth to the bouncer. He said, "All right, I gave you a chance—"

There was a shriek from a woman in the crowd. It was Harriet. She shrieked again as Eddie kept moving slowly toward the bouncer. She yelled, "No Eddie—please!"

He wanted to look at Harriet, to tell her with his eyes, It's all right, I'm only bluffing. And he thought, You can't do that. You gotta keep your eyes on this one here. Gotta push him with your eyes, push him back—

Plyne was retreating again. He still held the cudgel, but now his grip on it was loose. He didn't seem to realize he had it in his hand. He took a few more backward steps. Then his head turned and he was looking at the back door.

I think it's working, Eddie told himself. If I can get him

outa here, get him running so's he'll be out that door and outa the Hut, away from the waitress—

Look, now, he's dropped the club. All right, that's fine. You're doing fine, Hugger. I think you're gonna make it. Come on, Hugger, work with me. No, don't look at her. Look at me, look at the knife. It's such a sharp knife, Hugger. You wanna get away from it? All you gotta do is go for that door. Please, Wally, go for that door. I'll help you get through, I'll be right with you, right behind you—

He raised the knife higher. He moved in closer and faked a slash at the bouncer's throat.

Plyne turned and ran toward the back door.

Eddie went after him.

"No—" from Harriet.

And from others in the crowd, "No, Eddie. Eddie—"

He chased Plyne through the back rooms of the Hut, through the door leading to the alley. Plyne was going very fast along the wind-whipped, snow-covered alley. Gotta stay with him, Eddie thought, gotta stay with the Hugger who needs a friend now, who sure as hell needs a chummy hand on his shoulder, a soft voice saying, It's all right, Wally. It's all right.

Plyne looked back and saw him coming with the knife. Plyne ran faster. It was a very long alley and Plyne was running against the wind. He'll hafta stop soon, Eddie thought. He's carryin' a lot of weight and a lot of damage and he just can't keep up that pace. And you, you're weighted down yourself. It's a good thing you ain't wearin' your overcoat. Or maybe it ain't so good, because I'll tell you something, bud. It's cold out here.

The bouncer was halfway down the alley, turning again, and looking, then going sideways and bumping into the wooden boards of a high fence. He tried to climb the fence and couldn't obtain a foothold. He went on running down the alley. He slipped in the snow, went down, got up, took another look back, and was running again. He covered another thirty yards and stopped once more, and then he tried a fence door. It was open and he went through.

Eddie ran up to the door. It was still open. It gave way to the small backyard of a two-story dwelling. As he entered the backyard, he saw Plyne trying to climb the wall of the house. Plyne was clawing at the wall, trying to insert his fingers through the tiny gaps between red bricks. It was as though Plyne meant to get up the wall, even if he had to scrape all the flesh off his fingers.

"Wally—"

The bouncer went on trying to climb the wall.

"Wally, listen—"

Plyne leaped up at the wall. His fingernails scraped against the bricks. As he came down, he sagged to his knees. He straightened, looked up along the wall, and then he turned slowly and looked at Eddie.

Eddie smiled at him and dropped the knife. It landed with a soft thud in the snow.

The bouncer stared down at the knife. It was half hidden in the snow. Plyne pointed with a quivering finger.

"The hell with it," Eddie said. He kicked the knife aside.

"You ain't gonna—?"

"Forget it, Wally."

The bouncer lifted his hand to his blood-smeared face. He wiped some blood from his mouth, looked at his red-stained fingers, then looked up at Eddie. "Forget it?" he mumbled, and began to move forward. "How can I forget it?"

Easy now, Eddie thought. Let's take it slow and easy. He went on smiling at the bouncer. He said, "We'll put it this way—I've had enough."

But Plyne kept moving forward. Plyne said, "Not yet. There's gotta be a winner—"

"You're the winner," Eddie said. "You're too big for me, that's all. You're more than I can handle."

"Don't con me," the bouncer said, his pain-battered brain somehow probing through the red haze, somehow seeing it the way it was. "They saw me running away. The bouncer getting bounced. They'll make it a joke—"

"Wally, listen—"

"They'll laugh at me," Plyne said. He was crouched now, his shoulders weaving as he moved in slowly. "I ain't gonna have that. It's one thing I just can't take. I gotta let them know—"

"They know, Wally. It ain't as if they need proof."

"—gotta let them know," Plyne said as though talking to himself. "Gotta cross off all them things she said about me. That I'm just a washed-up nothing, a slob a faker a crawling worm—"

Eddie looked down at the knife in the snow. Too late now, he thought. And much too late for words. Too late for anything. Well, you tried.

"But hear me now," the bouncer appealed to himself. "Them names she called me, it ain't so. I got only one name. I'm the Hugger—" He was sobbing, the huge shoulders shaking, the bleeding mouth twisted grotesquely. "I'm the Hugger, and they ain't gonna laugh at the Hugger."

Plyne leaped, and his massive arms swept out and in and tightened around Eddie's middle. Yes he's the Hugger, Eddie thought, feeling the tremendous crushing power of the bear hug. It felt as though his innards were getting squeezed up into his chest. He couldn't breathe, he couldn't even try to breathe. He had his mouth wide open, his head flung back, his eyes shut tightly as he took the iron-hard pressure of the bouncer's chin applied to his chest bone. He said to himself, You can't take this. Ain't a living thing can take this and live.

The bouncer had him lifted now, his feet several inches off the ground. As the pressure of the bear hug increased, Eddie swung his legs forward, as though he was trying to somersault backwards. His legs went in between the bouncer's knees, and the bouncer went forward stumbling. Then they went down, and he felt the cold wetness of the snow. The bouncer was on top of him, retaining the bear hug, the straddled knees braced hard against the snow as the massive arms applied more force.

Eddie's eyes remained shut. He tried to open them and couldn't. Then he tried to move his left arm, thinking in terms of his fingernails, telling himself it needed claws and if he could reach the bouncer's face—

His left arm came up a few inches and fell back again in the snow. The snow felt very cold against his hand. Then something happened and he couldn't feel the coldness. You're going, he said to himself. You're passing out. As the thought swirled through the fog in his brain, he was trying with his right hand.

Trying what? he asked himself. What can you do now? His

right hand moved feebly in the snow. Then his fingers touched something hard and wooden. At the very moment of contact, he knew what it was. It was the handle of the knife.

He pulled at the knife handle, saying to himself, In the arm, let him have it in the arm. And then he managed to open his eyes, his remaining strength now centered in his eyes and his fingers gripping the knife. He took aim, with the knife pointed at Plyne's left arm. Get in deep, he told himself. Get it in there so he'll really feel it and he'll hafta let go.

The knife came up. Plyne didn't see it coming. At that instant Plyne shifted his position to exert more pressure with the bear hug. Shifting from right to left, Plyne took the blade in his chest. The blade went in very deep.

"What?" Plyne said. "Whatcha do to me?"

Eddie stared at his own hand, still gripping the handle of the knife. The bouncer seemed to be drifting away from him, going back and sideways. He saw the blade glimmering red, and then he saw the bouncer rolling and twitching in the snow.

The bouncer rolled over on his back, on his belly, then again on his back. He stayed there. His mouth opened wide and he started to take a deep breath. Some air went in and came out mixed with bubbles of pink and red and darker red. The bouncer's eyes became very large. Then the bouncer sighed and his eyes remained wide open and he was dead.

12

EDDIE sat there in the snow and looked at the dead man. He said to himself, Who did that? Then he fell back in the snow, gasping and coughing, trying to loosen things up inside. It's so tight in there, he thought, his hands clasped to his abdomen, it's all squashed and outa commission. You feel it? You're damn right you feel it. Another thing you feel is the news coming in on the wire. That thing there in the snow, that's your work, buddy. You wanna look at it again? You wanna admire your work?

No, not now. There's other work we gotta do now. Them sounds you hear in the alley, that's the Hut regulars coming out to see what the score is. How come they waited so long? Well, they musta been scared. Or sorta paralyzed, that's more like it. But now they're in the alley. They're opening the fence doors, the doors that ain't locked. Sure, they figure we're in one of these backyards. So what you gotta do is, you gotta keep them outa this one here. You lock that door.

But wait—let's check that angle. How come you don't want them to see? They're gonna see it sooner or later. And what it amounts to, it's just one of them accidents. It ain't as if you meant to do it. You were aiming for his arm, and then he made that move, he traveled just about four or five inches going from right to left, from right to wrong. Sure, that's what happened, he moved the wrong way and it was an accident.

You say accident. What'll they say? They'll say homicide.

They'll add it up and back it up with their own playback of what happened in the Hut. The way you jugged at him with the knife. The way you went after him when he took off. But hold it there, you know you were bluffing.

Sure, friend. You know. But they don't know. And that's just about the size of it, that bluffing business is the canoe without a paddle. Because that bluff was perfect, too perfect. Quite a sale you made, friend. You know Harriet bought it, they all bought it. They'll say you had homicide written all over your face.

Wanna make a forecast? I think they'll call it second-degree and that makes it five years or seven or ten or maybe more, depending on the emotional condition or the stomach condition of the people on the parole board. You willing to settle for that kinda deal? Well, frankly, no. Quite frankly, no.

You better move now. You better lock that door.

He raised himself on his elbows. He turned his head and looked at the fence door. The distance between himself and the door was somewhat difficult to estimate. There wasn't much daylight. What sun remained was blocked off by the dark-gray curtain, the curtain that was very thick up there, and even thicker down here where it was mottled white with the heavy snowfall. It reminded him again that he wasn't wearing an overcoat. He thought dazedly, stupidly, Oughtta go back and get your overcoat, you'll freeze out here.

It's colder in a cell. Nothing colder than a cell, friend.

He was crawling through the snow, pushing himself toward the fence door some fifteen feet away. Why do it this way? he asked himself. Why not get up and walk over there?

The answer is, you can't get up. You're just about done in. What you need is a warm bed in a white room and some people in white to take care of you. At least give you a shot to make the pain go away. There's so much pain. I wonder if your ribs are busted. All right, let's quit the goddam complaining. Let's keep going toward that door.

As he crawled through the snow toward the fence door, he listened to the sounds coming from the alley. The sounds were closer now. The voices mixed with the clattering of fence doors on both sides of the alley. He heard someone yelling, "Try that one—this one's locked." And another voice, "Maybe they went all the way up the alley—maybe they're out there in the street." A third voice disagreed, "No, they're in one of these backyards—they could'na hit the street that quick."

"Well, they gotta be somewhere around."

"We better call the law—"

"Keep movin' will ya? Keep tryin' them doors."

He crawled just a little faster now. It seemed to him that he hardly moved at all. His open mouth begged the air to come in. As it came in, it was more like someone shoveling hot ashes down his throat. Get there, he said to himself. For Christ's sake, get to that door and lock it. The door.

The voices were closer now. Then one of them yelled, "Hey look, the footprints—"

"What footprints? There's more than two sets of footprints."

"Let's try Spaulding Street—"

"I'm freezin' out here."

"I tell ya, we oughtta call the law—"

He heard them coming closer. He was a few feet away from the fence door. He tried to rise. He made it to his knees, tried to get up higher, and his knees gave way. He was face down in the snow. Get up, he said to himself. Get up, you loafer.

His hands pushed hard at the snow, his arms straightening, his knees gaining leverage as he labored to get up. Then he was up and falling forward, grabbing at the open fence door. His hands hit the door, closed it, and then he fastened the bolt. As it slipped into place, locking the door, he went down again.

I guess we're all right now, he thought. For a while, anyway. But what about later? Well, we'll talk about that when we come to it. I mean, when we get the all-clear, when we're sure they're outa the alley. Then we'll be able to move. And go where? You got me, friend. I can't even give you a hint.

He was resting on his side, feeling the snow under his face, more snow coming down on his head, the wind cutting into his flesh and all the cold getting in there deep, chopping at his bones. He heard the voices in the alley, the footsteps, the fence doors opening and closing, although now the noise was oddly blurred as it came closer. Then the noise was directly outside the door, going past the door, and it was very blurred, it was more like far-off humming. Something like a lullaby, he thought vaguely. His eyes were closed, his head sank deeper into the pillow of snow. He floated down and out, way out.

The voice woke him up. He opened his eyes, wondering if he'd actually heard it.

"Eddie—"

It was the voice of the waitress. He could hear her footsteps in the alley, moving slowly.

He sat up, blinking. He raised his arm to shield his face from the driving wind and the snow.

"Eddie—"

That's her, all right. What's she want?

His arm came away from his face. He looked around, and up, seeing the gray sky, the heavy snowfall coming down on the roof of the dwelling, the swirling gusts falling off the roof into the backyard. Now the snow had arranged itself into a thin white blanket on the bulky thing that was still there in the backyard.

Still there, he thought. What did you expect? That it would get up and walk away?

"Eddie—"

Sorry, I can't talk to you now. I'm sorta busy here. Gotta check some items. First, time element. What time did we go to sleep? Well, I don't think we slept long. Make it about five minutes. Shoulda slept longer. Really need sleep. All right, let's go back to sleep, the other items can wait.

"Eddie—Eddie—"

Is she alone? he asked himself. It sounds that way. It's as though she's saying, It's all clear now, you can come out now.

He heard the waitress calling again. He got up very slowly and unlocked the door and pulled it open.

Footsteps came running toward the door. He stepped back, leaning heavily against the fence as she entered the backyard. She looked at him, started to say something, and then checked it. Her eyes followed in the direction of his pointing finger. She moved slowly in that direction, her face expressionless as she approached the corpse. For some moments she stood there looking down at it. Then her head turned slightly and she focused on the blood-stained knife imbedded in the snow. She turned away from the knife and the corpse, and sighed, and said, "Poor Harriet."

"Yeah," Eddie said. He was slumped against the fence. "It's a raw deal for Harriet. It's—"

He couldn't get the words out. A surge of pain brought a groan from his lips. He sagged to his knees and shook his head slowly. "It goes and it comes," he mumbled.

He heard the waitress saying, "What happened here?"

She was standing over him. He looked up. Through the throbbing pain, the fatigue pressing down on him, he managed to grin. "You'll read about it—"

"Tell me now." She knelt beside him. "I gotta know now."

"What for?" He grinned down at the snow. Then he groaned again, and the grin went away. He said, "It don't matter—"

"The hell it don't." She took hold of his shoulders. "Gimme the details. I gotta know where we stand."

"We?"

"Yeah, we. Come on now, tell me."

"What's there to tell? You can see for yourself—"

"Look at me," she said. She moved in closer as he raised

his head slightly. She spoke quietly, in a clinical tone. "Try not to go under. You gotta stay with it. You gotta let me know what happened here."

"Something went wrong—"

"That's what I figured. The knife, I mean. You're not a knifer. You just wanted to scare him, to get him outa the Hut, away from me. Ain't that the way it was?"

He shrugged. "What difference—"

"Get off that," she cut in harshly. "We hafta get this straight."

He groaned again. He let out a cough. "Can't talk now."

"You gotta." She tightened her grip on his shoulders. "You gotta tell me."

He said, "It's—it's just one of them screwed-up deals. I thought I could reason with him. Nothing doing. He was too far off the track. Strictly section eight. Comes running at me, grabs me, and then I'm gettin' squeezed to jelly."

"And the knife?"

"It was on the ground. I'd tossed it aside so he'd know I wasn't out to carve him. But then he's usin' all his weight, he's got me half dead, and I reach out and there's the knife. I aimed for his arm—"

"Yes? Go on, tell me—"

"Thought if I got him in the arm, he'd let go. But just then he's moving. He moves too fast and I can't stop it in time. It misses the arm and he gets it in the chest."

She stood up. She was frowning thoughtfully. She walked toward the fence door, then turned slowly and stood there looking at him. She said, "You wanna gamble?"

"On what?"

"On the chance they'll buy it."

"They won't buy it," he said. "They only buy evidence."

She didn't say anything. She came away from the fence door and started walking slowly in a small circle, her head down.

He lifted himself from the ground, doing it with a great deal of effort, grunting and wheezing as he came up off his knees. He leaned back against the fence and pointed toward the middle of the yard where the snow was stained red. "There it is," he said. "There's the job, and I did it. That's all they need to know."

"But it wasn't your fault."

"All right, I'll tip them off. I'll write them a letter."

"Yeah. Sure. From where?"

"I don't know yet. All I know is, I'll hafta travel."

"You're in great shape to travel."

He looked down at the snow. "Maybe I'll just dig a hole and hide."

"It ain't right," she said. "It wasn't your fault."

"Say, tell me something. Where can I buy a helicopter?"

"It was his fault. He messed it up."

"Or maybe a balloon," Eddie mumbled. "A nice big balloon to lift me over this fence and get me outa town."

"What a picnic," she said.

"Yeah. Ain't it some picnic?"

She turned her head and looked at the corpse. "You slob," she said to it. "You stupid slob."

"Don't say that."

"You slob. You idiot," talking quietly to the corpse. "Look what you went and done."

"Cut it out," Eddie said. "And for Christ's sake, get outa this yard. If they find you with me—"

"They won't," she said. She beckoned to him, and then gestured toward the fence door.

He hesitated. "Which way they go?"

"Across Spaulding Street," she said. "Then up the next alley. That's why I came back. I knew you hadda be in one of these yards."

She moved toward the fence door, and stood there waiting for him. He came forward very slowly, bent low, his hands clutching his middle.

"Can you make it?" she said.

"I don't know. I don't think so."

"Try," she said. "You gotta try."

"Take a look out there," he said. "I wanna be sure it's clear."

She leaned out past the fence door, looking up and down the alley. "It's all right," she said. "Come on."

He took a few more steps toward her. Then his knees buckled and he started to go down. She moved in quickly and caught hold of him, her hands hooking under his armpits. "Come on," she said. "Come on, now. You're doing fine."

"Yeah. Wonderful."

She held him on his feet, urging him forward, and they went out of the yard and started down the alley. He saw they were moving in the direction of the Hut. He heard her saying, "There's nobody in there now. They're all on the other side of Spaulding Street. I think we got a chance—"

"Quit saying we."

"If we can make it to the Hut—"

"Now look, it ain't we. I don't like this *we* business."

"Don't," she said. "Don't tell me that."

"I'm better off alone."

"Save it," she gritted. "That's corn for the squares."

"Look, Lena—" He made a feeble attempt to pull away from her.

She tightened her hold under his armpits. "Let's keep moving. Come on, we're getting there."

His eyes were closed. He wondered if they were standing still or walking. Or just drifting along through the snow, carried along by the wind. There was no way to be sure. You're fading again, he said to himself. And without sound he said to her, Let go, let go. Cantcha see I wanna sleep? Cantcha leave me alone? Say lady, who are you? What's your game?

"We're almost there," she said.

Almost where? What's she talking about? Where's she taking me? Some dark place, I bet. Sure, that's the dodge. Gonna get rolled. And maybe get your head busted, if it ain't busted already. But why cry the blues? Other people got troubles, too. Sure, everybody got troubles. Except the people in that place where it's always fair weather. It ain't on any map and they call it Nothingtown. I been there, and I know what it's like and I tell you, man, it was sheer delight and the pace never changed, it was you at the piano and you knew from nothing. Until this complication came along. This complication we got here. She comes along with her face and her body and before you know it you're hooked. You tried to wriggle off but it was in deep and it was barbed. So the hooker scored and now you're in the creel and soon it's gonna be frying

time. Well, it's better than freezing. It's really freezing out
here. Out where? Where are we?

He was down in the snow. She pulled him up. He fell
against her, fell away, went sideways across the alley and
bumped into a fence. Then he was down again. She lifted him
to his feet. "Damn it," she said, "come out of it." She bent
over and took some snow in her hand and applied it to his
face.

Who did that? he wondered. Who hit who? Who hit Cy in
the eye with an Eskimo Pie? Was that you, George? Listen
George, you take that attitude, it calls for a swing at your
teeth.

He swung blindly, almost hit her in the face, and then he
was falling again. She caught him. For a few moments he put
up a tussle. Then he was slumped in her arms. She went sliding around him to get behind him, her arms tight around his
chest, lifting him. "Now walk," she said. "Walk, damn you."

"Quit the shovin'," he mumbled. His eyes were closed.
"Why you gotta shove me? I got legs—"

"Then use them," she commanded. She was bumping him
with her knees to push him along. "Worse than a drunk," she
muttered, bumping him harder as he tried to lean back against
her. They went staggering along through the heavily falling
snow. They went past four fence doors. She was measuring
the distance in terms of the fence doors on the left side of the
alley. They were six fence doors away from the Hut when he
fell again. He fell forward, flat in the snow, taking her down
with him. She got up and tried to lift him and this time she
couldn't do it. She stepped back and took a deep breath.

She reached inside her coat. Her hand went under her
apron and came out holding the five-inch hatpin. She jabbed
the long pin into the calf of his leg. Then again, deeper. He
mumbled, "What's bitin' me?" and she said, "You feel it?"
She used the hatpin again. He looked up at her. He said, "You
havin' a good time?"

"A swell time," she said. She showed him the hatpin.
"Want some more?"

"No."

"Then get up."

He made an effort to rise. She tossed the hatpin aside and helped him to his feet. They went on down the alley toward the back door of the Hut.

She managed to keep him on his legs as they entered the Hut, went through the back rooms and then, very slowly, down the cellar steps. In the cellar she half-carried him toward the high-stacked whisky and beer cases. She lowered him to the floor, then dragged him behind the wooden and cardboard boxes. He was resting on his side, mumbling incoherently. She shook his shoulder. He opened his eyes. She said, "Now listen to me," in a whisper. "You'll wait here. You won't move. You won't make a sound. That clear?"

He gave a slight nod.

"I think you'll be all right," she said. "For a while, anyway. They'll search all over the neighborhood, lookin' for you and Plyne. It figures they're gonna find Plyne. They'll try the alley again and they'll find him. Then it's the law and the law starts lookin' for you. But I don't think they'll look here. That is, unless they make a brilliant guess. So maybe there's a chance—"

"Some chance," he murmured. He was smiling wryly. "What am I gonna do, spend the winter here?"

She looked away from him. "I'm hopin' I can getcha out tonight."

"And do what? Take a walk around the block?"

"If we're lucky, we'll ride."

"On some kid's roller coaster? On a sled?"

"A car," she said. "I'll try to borrow a car—"

"From who?" he demanded. "Who's got a car?"

"My landlady." Then she looked away again.

He spoke slowly, watching her face. "You must rate awfully high with your landlady."

She didn't say anything.

He said, "What's the angle?"

"I know where she keeps the key."

"That's great," he said. "That's a great idea. Now do me a favor. Forget it."

"But listen—"

"Forget it," he said. "And thanks anyway."

Then he turned over on his side, his back to her.

"All right," she said very quietly. "You go to sleep now and I'll see you later."

"No you won't." He raised himself on his elbow. He turned his head and looked at her. "I'll make it a polite request. Don't come back."

She smiled at him.

"I mean it," he said.

She went on smiling at him. "See you later, mister."

"I told you, don't come back."

"Later," she said. She moved off toward the steps.

"I won't be here," he called after her. "I'll—"

"You'll wait for me," she said. She turned and looked at him. "You'll stay right there and wait."

He lowered his head to the cellar floor. The floor was cement and it was cold. But the air around him was warm, and the furnace was less than ten feet away. He felt the warmth settling on him as he closed his eyes. He heard her footsteps going up the cellar stairs. It was a pleasant sound that blended with the warmth. It was all very comforting, and he said to himself, She's coming back, she's coming back. Then he fell asleep.

13

HE slept for six hours. Then her hand was on his shoulder, shaking him. He opened his eyes and sat up. He heard her whispering, "Quiet—be very quiet. There's the law upstairs."

It was black in the cellar. He couldn't even see the outlines of her face. He said, "What time is it?"

"Ten-thirty, thereabouts. You had a nice sleep."

"I smell whisky."

"That's me," she said. "I had a few drinks with the law."

"They buy?"

"They never buy. They're just hangin' around the bar. The bartender's stewed and he's been givin' them freebees for hours."

"When'd they find him?"

"Just before it got dark. Some kids came out of the house to have a snowball fight. They saw him there in the yard."

"What's this?" he asked, feeling something heavy on his arm. "What we got here?"

"Your overcoat. Put it on. We're going out."

"Now?"

"Right now. We'll use the ladder and get out through the grating."

"And then what?"

"The car," she said. "I got the car."

"Look, I told you—"

"Shut up," she hissed. "Come on, now. On your feet."

She helped him as he lifted himself from the floor. He did it very slowly and carefully. He was worried he might bump against the wooden boxes, the cardboard beer cases. He murmured, "Need a match."

"I got some," she said. She struck a match. In the orange flare they looked at each other. He smiled at her. She didn't smile back. "Put it on," she said, indicating the overcoat.

He slipped into the overcoat, and followed her as she moved toward the stationary iron ladder that slanted up to the street grating. The match went out and she lit another. They were near the ladder when she stopped and turned and looked at him. She said, "Can you make it up the ladder?"

"I'll try."

"You'll make it," she said. "Hold onto me."

He moved in behind her as she started up the ladder. He held her around the waist. "Tighter," she said. She lit another match and said, "Rest your head against me—stay in close. Whatever you do, don't let go."

They went up a few rungs. They rested. A few more rungs, and they rested again. She said, "How's it going?" and he whispered, "I'm still here."

"Hold me tighter."

"That too tight?"

"No," she said. "Still tighter—like this," and she adjusted his arms around her middle. "Now lock your fingers," she told him. "Press hard against my belly."

"There?"

"Lower."

"How's that?"

"That's fine," she said. "Hold on, now. Hold me real tight."

They went on up the ladder. She lit more matches, striking them against the rusty sides of the ladder. In the glow, he looked up past her head and saw the underside of the grating. It seemed very far away.

When they were halfway up, his foot slipped off the rung. His other foot was slipping but he clung to her as tightly as he could, and managed to steady himself. Then they were climbing again.

But now it wasn't like climbing. It was more like pulling her down. That's what you're doing, he said to himself. You're pulling her down. You're just a goddam burden on her back, and this is only the start. The longer she stays with you, the worse it's gonna be. You can see it coming. You can see her getting nabbed and labeled an accessory. And then they charge her with stealing a car. What do you think they'll give her? I'd say three years, at least. Maybe five. That's a bright future for the lady. But maybe you can stop it before it happens. Maybe you can do something to get her out of this jam and send her on her way.

What can you do?

You can't talk to her, that's for sure. She'll only tell you to shut up. It's a cinch you can't argue with this one. This is one of them iron-heads. She makes up her mind to do something, there ain't no way to swerve her.

Can you pull away from her? Can you let go and drop off the ladder? The noise would bring the law. Would she skip out before they come? You know she wouldn't. She'd stick with you right through to the windup. She's made of that kind of material. It's the kind of material you seldom run across. Maybe once in a lifetime you find one like this. Or no, make it twice in a lifetime. You can't forget the first. You'll never forget the first. But what we're getting now is a certain reissue, except it isn't in the memory, it's something alive. It's alive and it's here, pressing against you. You're holding it very tightly. Can you ever let go?

He heard the waitress saying, "Hold on—"

Then he heard the noise of the grating. She was lifting it.

She was working very quietly, coaxing it up an inch at a time. As it went up, the cold air rushed through and with it came flakes of snow, like needles against his face. Now she had the grating raised high enough for them to get through. She was squirming through the gap, taking him with her. The grating rested on her shoulders, then on her back, and then it was on his shoulders as he followed her over the edge of the opening. She held the grating higher and then they were both on their knees on the pavement and she was closing the grating.

Yellow light came drifting from the side window of the Hut, and glimmered dimly against the darkness of the street. In the glow, he saw the snow coming down, churned by the wind. It's more than just a snowstorm now, he thought. It's a blizzard.

They were on their feet and she held his wrist. They moved along, staying close to the wall of the Hut as they headed west on Fuller Street. He glanced to the side and saw the police cars parked at the curb. He counted five. There were two more parked on the other side of the street. The waitress was saying, "They're all empty. I looked before we climbed out." He said, "If one of them blueboys comes outa the Hut—" and she broke in with, "They'll stay in there. They got all that free booze." But he knew she wasn't sure about that. He knew she was saying it with her fingers crossed.

They crossed a narrow street. The blizzard came at them like a huge swinging door made of ice. They were bent low, pushing themselves against the wind. For another short block they stayed on Fuller, then there was another narrow street and she said, "We turn here."

There were several parked cars, and some old trucks. Half-way up the block there was an ancient Chevvy, a pre-war model. The fenders were battered and much of the paint was chipped off. It was a two-door sedan, but as he looked at it, the impression it gave was that of a sullen weary mule. A real racer, he thought, and wondered how she'd ever managed to start it. She was opening the door, motioning for him to get in.

Then he was leaning back in the front seat and she slid behind the wheel. She hit the starter. The engine gasped, tried to catch, and failed. She hit the starter again. The engine made a wheezing effort, almost caught, then faded and died. The waitress cursed quietly.

"It's cold," he said.

"It didn't gimme trouble before," she muttered. "It started up right away."

"It's much colder now."

"I'll get it started," she said.

She pressed her foot on the starter. The engine worked very hard, almost made it, then gave up.

"Maybe it's just as well," he said.

She looked at him. "Whaddya mean?"

"Even if it moves, it won't get far. They get a report on a stolen car, they work fast."

"Not on this job," she said. "On this one they won't get a report till morning, when my landlady wakes up and takes a look out the window. I made sure she was asleep before I snatched the key."

As she said it, she was pressing the starter again. The engine caught the spark, struggled to hold it, almost lost it, then idled weakly. She fed it gas and it responded. She released the brake and was reaching for the shift when two shafts of bright light came shooting in from Fuller Street. "Get down," she hissed, as the headlights of the other car came closer. "Get your head down—"

They both ducked under the level of the windshield. He heard the engine noise of the other car, coming in closer, very close, then passing them and going away. As he raised his head, there was another sound. It was the waitress, laughing.

He looked at her inquiringly. She was laughing with genuine amusement.

"They just won't give up," she said.

"The law?"

"That wasn't the law. That was a Buick. A pale green Buick. I took a quick look—"

"You sure it was them?"

She nodded, still laughing. "The two ambassadors," she said. "The one named Morris and—what's the other one's name?"

"Feather."

"Yeah, Feather, the little one. And Morris, the back-seat driver. Feather and Morris. Incorporated."

"You think it's funny?"

"It's a scream," she said. "The way they're still mooching around—" She laughed again. "I bet they've circled this block a hundred times. I can hear them beefing about it, fussing at each other. Or maybe now they ain't even on speakin' terms."

He thought, Well, I'm glad she's able to laugh. It's good to know she can take it lightly. But the thing is, you can't take it lightly. You know there's a chance they spotted her when she raised her head. They ain't quite the goofers she thinks they are. They're professionals, you gotta remember that. You gotta remember they were out to get Turley, or let's say a step-by-step production that put them on your trail so they could find Turley, so they could find Clifton, so that finally they'd reach out and grab whatever it is they're after. Whatever it is, it's in South Jersey, in the old homestead deep in the woods. But when you called it a homestead, they gave it another name. They called it the hide-out.

That's what it is, all right. It's a hide-out, a perfect hide-out, not even listed in the post office. You mailed all your letters to a box number in that little town nine miles away. You know, I think we're seeing a certain pattern taking shape. It's sort of in the form of a circle. Like when you take off and move in a certain direction to get you far away, but somehow you're pulled around on that circle, it takes you back to where you started. Well, I guess that's the way it's gotta be. On the city's wanted list right now you're Number One. Hafta get outa the city. Make a run for the place where they'll never find you. The place is in South Jersey, deep in the woods. It's the hiding place of the Clifton-Turley combine, except now it's Clifton-Turley-Eddie, the infamous Lynn brothers.

So there it is, that's the pattern. With a musical background thrown in for good measure. It ain't the soft music now. It ain't the dreamy nothing-matters music that kept you far away from everything. This music here is the buzzing of the hornets. No two ways about that. You hear it getting louder?

It was the noise of the Chevvy's engine. The car was moving now. The waitress glanced at him, as though waiting for him

to say something. His mouth tightened and he stared ahead
through the windshield. They were approaching Fuller Street.

He spoke quietly. "Make a right-hand turn."

"And then?"

"The bridge," he said. "The Delaware River Bridge."

"South Jersey?"

He nodded. "The woods," he said.

14

IN Jersey, twenty miles south of Camden, the Chevvy pulled
into a service station. The waitress reached into her coat
pocket and took out the week's salary she'd received from
Harriet. She told the attendant to fill up the tank, and she
bought some anti-freeze. Then she wanted skid chains. The
attendant gave her a look. He wasn't happy about working
on the skid chains, exposing himself to the freezing wind and
the snow. "It's sure a mean night for driving," he commented. She said it sure was, but it was a nice night for selling
skid chains. He gave her another look. She told him to get
started with the skid chains. While he was working on the
tires, the waitress went into the rest room. When she came
out, she bought a pack of cigarettes from the machine. In the
car, she gave a cigarette to Eddie and lit it for him. He didn't
say thanks. He didn't seem to know he had a cigarette in his
mouth. He was sitting up very straight and staring ahead
through the windshield.

The attendant was finished with the skid chains. He was
breathing hard as he came up to the car window. He cupped
his hands and blew on them. He shivered, stamped his feet,
and then gave the waitress an unfriendly look. He asked her
if there was anything else she wanted. She said yes, she wanted
him to do something about the windshield wipers. The wipers
weren't giving much action, she said. The attendant looked
up at the cold black sky and took a very deep breath. Then
he opened the hood and began to examine the fuel pump and
the lines coming off the pump and connecting with the wipers. He made an adjustment with the lines and said, "Try it

now." She tried the wipers and they worked much faster than before. As she paid him, the attendant muttered, "You sure you got everything you need? Maybe you forgot something." The waitress thought it over for a moment. Then she said, "We could use a bracer." The attendant stamped his feet and shivered again and said, "Me too, lady." She looked down at the paper money in her hand, and murmured, "Got any to spare?" He shook his head somewhat hesitantly. She showed him a five-dollar bill. "Well," he said, "I got a pint bottle of something. But you might not like it. It's that homemade corn—"

"I'll take it," she said. The attendant hurried into the station shack. He came out with the bottle wrapped in some old newspaper. He handed it to the waitress and she handed it to Eddie. She paid for the liquor and the attendant put the money in his pocket and stood there at the car window, waiting for her to start the engine and drive away and go out of his life. She said, "You're welcome," and closed the car window and started the engine.

The skid chains helped considerably, as did the repaired windshield wipers. The Chevvy had been averaging around twenty miles an hour. Now she wasn't worried about skidding or running into something and she pressed harder on the gas pedal. The car did thirty and then thirty-five. It was headed south on Route 47. The wind was coming in from the southeast, from the Atlantic, and the Chevvy went chugging into it sort of pugnaciously, the weary old engine giving loud and defiant back talk to the yowling blizzard. The waitress leaned low over the steering wheel, pressing harder on the gas pedal. The needle of the speedometer climbed to forty.

The waitress was feeling good. She talked to the Chevvy. She said, "You wanna do fifty? Come on, you can do fifty."

"No, she can't," Eddie said. He was taking another drink from the bottle. They'd both had several drinks and the bottle was a third empty.

"I bet she can," the waitress said. The needle of the speedometer climbed toward forty-five.

"Quit that," Eddie said. "You're pushing her too much."

"She can take it. Come on, honeybunch, show him. Move, girl. That's it, move. You keep it up, you'll break a record."

"She'll break a rod, that's what she'll do," Eddie said. He said it tightly, through his teeth.

The waitress looked at him.

"Watch the road," he said. His voice was very tight and low.

"What gives with you?" the waitress asked.

"Watch the road." Now it was a growl. "Watch the goddam road."

She started to say something, held it back, and then focused her attention on the highway. Now her foot was lighter on the gas pedal, and the speed was slackened to thirty-five. It stayed at thirty-five while her hand came off the steering wheel, palm extended for the bottle. He passed it to her. She took a swig and gave it back to him.

He looked at the bottle and wondered if he could use another drink. He decided he could. He put his head back and tipped the bottle to his mouth.

As the liquor went down, he scarcely tasted it. He didn't feel the burning in his throat, the slashing of the alcohol going down through his innards. He was taking a very big drink, unaware of how much he was swallowing.

The waitress glanced at him as he drank. She said, "For Christ's sake—"

He lowered the bottle from his mouth.

She said, "You know what you drank just then? I bet that was two double shots. Maybe three."

He didn't look at her. "You don't mind, do you?"

"No, I don't mind. Why should I mind?"

"You want some?" He offered her the bottle.

"I've had enough," she said.

He smiled tightly at the bottle. "It's good booze."

"How would you know? You ain't no drinker."

"I'll tell you something. This is very good booze."

"You getting high?"

"No," he said. "It's the other way around. That's why I like this juice here." He patted the bottle fondly. "Keeps my feet on the floor. Holds me down to the facts."

"What facts?"

"Tell you later," he said.

"Tell me now."

"Ain't ready yet. Like with cooking. Can't serve the dish until it's ready. This needs a little more cooking."

"You're cooking, all right," the waitress said. "Keep gulping that fire-water and you'll cook your brains to a frazzle."

"Don't worry about it. I can steer the brains. You just steer this car and get me where I'm going."

For some moments she was quiet. And then, "Maybe I'll have that drink, after all."

He handed her the bottle. She took a fast gulp, then quickly opened the car window and tossed the bottle out.

"Why'd you do that?"

She didn't answer. She pressed harder on the gas pedal and the speedometer went up to forty. Now there was no talk between them and they didn't look at each other. Later, at a traffic circle, she glanced at him inquiringly and he told her what road to take. They were quiet again until they approached an intersection. He told her to turn left. It brought them onto a narrow road and they stayed on it for some five miles, the car slowing as they approached a three-pronged fork of narrower roads. He told her to take the road that slanted left, veering acutely into the woods.

It was a bumpy road. There were deep chugholes and she held the Chevvy down to fifteen miles per hour. The snow-drifts were high, resisting the front tires, and there were moments when it seemed the car would stall. She shifted from second gear to first, adjusting the hand throttle to maintain a steady feed of gas. The car went into a very deep chughole, labored to get up and out, came out and ploughed its way through another high snowdrift. There was a wagon path branching off on the right and he told her to take it.

They went ahead at ten miles per hour. The wagon path was very difficult. There were a great many turns and in places the line of route was almost invisible, blanketed under the snow. She was working very hard to keep the car on the path and away from the trees.

The car crawled along. For more than an hour it was on the twisting path going deep into the woods. Then abruptly the path gave way to a clearing. It was a fairly wide clearing, around seventy-five yards in diameter. The headlights beamed across the snow and revealed the very old wooden house in the center of the clearing.

"Stop the car," he said.

"We're not there yet—"

"D'ja hear me?" He spoke louder. "I said stop the car."

The Chevvy was in the clearing, going toward the house. He reached down and pulled up on the hand brake. The car came to a stop thirty yards from the house.

His fingers were on the door handle. He heard the waitress saying, "What are you doing?"

He didn't reply. He was getting out of the car.

The waitress pulled him back. "Answer me—"

"We split," he said. He wasn't looking at her. "You go back to Philly."

"Look at me."

He couldn't do it. He thought, Well, the booze helped a little, but not enough. You shoulda had some more of that liquor. A lot more. Maybe if you'd finished the bottle you'd be able to handle this.

He heard himself saying, "I'll tell you how to get to the bridge. You follow the path to that fork in the road—"

"Don't gimme directions. I know the directions."

"You sure?"

"Yes," she said. "Yes. Don't worry about it."

Again he started to get out of the car, hating himself for doing it. He told himself to do it and get it over with. The quicker it was done, the better.

But it was very difficult to get out of the car.

"Well?" the waitress said quietly. "Whatcha waitin' for?"

He turned his head and looked at her. Something burned into his eyes. Without sound he was saying, I want you with me. You know I want you with me. But the way it is, it's no dice.

"Thanks for the ride," he said, and was out of the car and closing the door.

Then he stood there in the snow and the car pulled away from him and made a turn and headed back toward the path in the woods.

He moved slowly across the clearing. In the darkness he

could barely see the outlines of the house. It seemed to him
that the house was miles away and he'd drop before he got
there. He was trudging through deep snow. The snow was
still coming down and the wind sliced at him, hacking away
at his face, ripping into his chest. He wondered if he ought
to sit down in the snow and rest a while. Just then the beam
of a flashlight hit him in the eyes.

It came from the front of the house. He heard a voice saying, "Hold it there, buddy. Just stay right where you are."

That's Clifton, he thought. Yes, that's Clifton. You know
that voice. It's a cinch he's got a gun. You better do this very
carefully.

He stood motionless. He raised his arms over his head. But
the glare of the flashlight was too much for his eyes and he
had to turn his face aside. He wondered if he was showing
enough of his face to be recognized.

"It's me," he said. "It's Eddie."

"Eddie? What Eddie?"

He kept his eyes open against the glare as he showed his
full face to the flashlight.

"Well, I'll be—"

"Hello, Clifton."

"For Christ's sake," the older brother said. He came in
closer, holding the flashlight so that they could look at each
other. Clifton was tall and very lean. He had black hair and
blue eyes and he was fairly good-looking except for the scars.
There were quite a few scars on the right side of his face. One
of the scars was wide and deep and it ran from a point just
under his eye, slanting down to his jaw. He wore a cream-
colored camel's-hair overcoat with mother-of-pearl buttons.
Under it he wore flannel pajamas. The pajama pants were
tucked into knee-length rubber boots. Clifton was holding the
flashlight in his left hand. In his right hand, resting back over
his forearm, he had a sawed-off shotgun.

As they stood there, Clifton sprayed the ray of the flashlight
across the clearing, spotting the path going into the woods.
He murmured, "You sure you're alone? There was a car—"

"They took off."

"Who was it?"

"A friend. Just a friend."

Clifton kept aiming the flashlight across the clearing. He squinted tightly, checking the area at the edge of the woods. "I hope you weren't traced here," he said. "There's some people lookin' for me and Turley. I guess he told you about it. He said he saw you last night."

"He's here now? When'd he get back?"

"This afternoon," Clifton said. Then he chuckled softly. "Comes in all banged up, half froze, half dead, actually. Claims he hitched a few rides and then walked the rest of the way."

"Through them woods? In that storm?"

Clifton chuckled again. "You know Turley."

"Is he all right now?"

"Sure, he's fine. Fixed himself a dinner, knocked off a pint of whisky, and went to bed."

Eddie frowned slightly. "How come he fixed his own dinner? Where's Mom?"

"She left."

"Whaddya mean she left?"

"With Pop," Clifton said. He shrugged. "A few weeks ago. They just packed their things and shoved."

"Where'd they go?"

"Damned if I know," Clifton said. "We ain't heard from them." He shrugged again. And then, "Hey, I'm freezin' out here. Let's go in the house."

They walked across the snow and entered the house. Then they were in the kitchen and Clifton put a coffee pot on the stove. Eddie took off his overcoat and placed it on a chair. He pulled another chair toward the table and sat down. The chair had weak legs, loose in their sockets, and it sagged under his weight. He looked at the splintered boards of the kitchen floor, and at the chipped and broken plaster of the walls.

There was no sink in the kitchen. The light came from a kerosene lamp. He watched Clifton applying a lit match to the chunks of wood in the old-fashioned stove. No gas lines here, he thought. No water pipes or electric wires in this house. Not a thing to connect it with the outside world. And that makes it foolproof. It's a hide-out, all right.

The stove was lit and Clifton came over to the table and sat down. He took out a pack of cigarettes, flicked it expertly and two cigarettes came up. Eddie took one. They smoked for a while, not saying anything. But Clifton was looking at him questioningly, waiting for him to explain his presence here.

Eddie wasn't quite ready to talk about that. For a while, for a little while anyway, he wanted to forget. He took a long drag at the cigarette and said, "Tell me about Mom and Pop. Why'd they leave?"

"Don't ask me."

"I'm asking you because you know. You were here when they went away."

Clifton leaned back in his chair, puffed at the cigarette, and didn't say anything.

"You sent them away," Eddie said.

The older brother nodded.

"You just put them out the door." Eddie snapped his fingers. "Just like that."

"Not exactly," Clifton said. "I gave them some cash."

"You did? That was nice. That was sure nice of you."

Clifton smiled softly. "You think I wanted to do it?"

"The point is—"

"The point is, I hadda do it."

"Why?"

"Because I like them," Clifton said. "They're nice quiet people. This ain't no place for nice quiet people."

Eddie dragged at the cigarette.

"Another thing," Clifton said. "They ain't bullet-proof." He shifted his position in the chair, sitting sideways and crossing his legs. "Even if they were, it wouldn't help much. They're getting old and they can't take excitement like this."

Eddie glanced at the shiny black sawed-off shotgun on the floor. It rested at Clifton's feet. He looked up, above Clifton's head, to a shelf that showed a similar gun, a few smaller guns, and several boxes of ammunition.

"There's gonna be action here," Clifton said. "I was hoping it wouldn't happen, but I can feel it coming."

Eddie went on looking at the guns and ammunition on the shelf.

"Sooner or later," Clifton was saying. "Sooner or later we're gonna have visitors."

"In a Buick?" Eddie murmured. "A pale green Buick?"

Clifton winced.

"They get around," Eddie said.

Clifton reached across the table and took hold of Eddie's wrist. It wasn't a belligerent move; Clifton had to hold onto something.

Clifton was blinking hard, as though trying to focus on Eddie's face, to understand fully what Eddie was saying. "Who gets around? Who you talking about?"

"Feather and Morris."

Clifton released Eddie's wrist. For the better part of a minute it was quiet. Clifton sucked in smoke, expelled it in a blast, and gritted, "That Turley. That goddam stupid Turley."

"It wasn't Turley's fault."

"Don't gimme that. Don't cover for him. He's a nitwit from way back. There ain't been a time he hasn't screwed things up one way or another. But this deal tops it. This really tops it."

"He was in a fix—"

"He's always in a fix. You know why? He just can't do things right, that's why." Clifton dragged again at the cigarette. "Ain't bad enough he gets them on his tail. He goofs again and drags you into it."

Eddie shrugged. "It couldn't be helped. Just one of them situations."

"Line it up for me," Clifton said. "How come they latched on to you? How come you're here now? Gimme the wire on this."

Eddie gave it to him, making it brief and simple.

"That's it," he finished. "Only thing for me to do was come here. No other place for me to go."

Clifton was gazing off to one side and shaking his head slowly.

"What'll it be?" Eddie asked. "Gonna let me stay?"

The other brother took a deep breath. "Damn it," he muttered to himself. "Damn it to hell."

"Yeah, I know what you mean," Eddie said. "You sure need me here."

"Like rheumatism. You're a white-hot property. Philly wants you, Pennsy wants you, and next thing they do is call

Washington. You crossed a state line and that makes it federal."

"Maybe I'd better—"

"No, you won't," Clifton cut in. "You'll stay. You gotta stay. When you're federal, you can't budge. They're too slick. You make any move at all and they're on you like tweezers."

"That's nice to know," Eddie murmured. He wasn't thinking about himself. He wasn't thinking about Clifton and Turley. His thoughts were centered on the waitress. He was wondering if she'd make it back safely to Philly and return the stolen car to its parking place. If it happened that way, she'd be all right. They wouldn't bother her. They'd have no reason to question her. He kept telling himself it would be all right, but he kept thinking about her and he was worried she'd run into some trouble. Please don't, he said to her. Please stay out of trouble.

He heard Clifton saying, "—sure picked a fine time to come walking in."

He looked up. He shrugged and didn't say anything.

"It's one hell of a situation," Clifton said. "On one side there's this certain outfit lookin' for me and Turley. On the other side it's the law, lookin' for you."

Eddie shrugged again. "Well, anyway, it's nice to be home."

"Yeah," Clifton said wryly. "We oughtta celebrate."

"It's an occasion, all right."

"It's a grief, that's what it is," Clifton said. "It's—" And then he forced it aside. He grinned and reached across the table and hit Eddie on the shoulder. "You know one thing? It's good to see you again."

"Likewise," Eddie said.

"Coffee's boiling," Clifton said. He got up and went to the stove. He came back with the filled cups and set them on the table. "What about grub?" he asked. "Want some grub?"

"No," Eddie said. "I ain't hungry."

They sat there sipping the black sugarless coffee. Clifton said, "You didn't tell me much about the dame. Gimme more on the dame."

"What dame?"

"The one that brought you here. You said she's a waitress—"

"Yeah. Where I worked. We got to know each other."

Clifton looked at him closely, waiting for him to tell more.

For a while it was quiet. They went on sipping the coffee. Then Clifton was saying something that he heard only vaguely, unable to listen attentively because of the waitress. He was looking directly at Clifton and it appeared he was paying close attention to what Clifton was saying. But in his mind he was with the waitress. He was walking with her and they were going somewhere. Then they stopped and he looked at her and told her to leave. She started to walk away. He went after her and she asked him what he wanted. He told her to get away from him. She walked away and he moved quickly and caught up with her. Then again he was telling her to take off, he didn't want her around. He stood there watching her as she departed. But he couldn't bear it and he ran after her. Now very patiently she asked him to decide what they should do. He told her to please go away.

It went on like that while Clifton was telling him about certain events during the past few years, culminating in Turley's trip to Philadelphia, to Dock Street, with Turley trying to make connections along the wharves and piers where he'd once worked as a longshoreman. What Turley had sought was a boat ride for Clifton and himself. They needed the boat ride away from the continent, far away from the people who were looking for them.

The people who were looking for them were members of a certain unchartered and unlicensed corporation. It was a very large corporation that operated along the eastern seaboard, dealing in contraband merchandise such as smuggled perfumes from Europe, furs from Canada, and so forth. Employed by the corporation, Clifton and Turley had been assigned to the department that handled the more physical aspects of the business, the hijacking and the extortion and sometimes the moves that were necessary to eliminate competitors.

Some fourteen months ago, Clifton was saying, he'd decided that he and Turley were not receiving adequate compensation for their efforts. He'd talked it over with certain executives of the corporation and they told him there was no cause for complaint, they didn't have time to hear his complaints. They made it clear that in the future he was to keep away from the front office.

At that time the front office of the corporation was in Savannah, Georgia. They were always changing the location of the front office from one port to another, according to the good will or lack of good will between the executives and certain port authorities. In Savannah, an investigation was taking place and the top people of the corporation were preparing to leave for Boston. It was necessary to leave quickly because the investigators were making rapid strides, and so of course there was some confusion. In the midst of the confusion, Clifton and Turley resigned from the corporation. When they did it, they took something with them. They took a couple of hundred thousand dollars.

They took it from the safe in the warehouse where the front office was located. They did it very late at night, walking in quite casually and chatting with three fellow employees who were playing pinochle. When they showed guns, one of the card players made a move for his own and Turley kicked him in the groin, then hit him on the head with the gun butt sufficiently hard to finish him. The two other card players were Feather and Morris, with Morris perspiring as Turley hefted the gun to use the butt again, with Feather talking very fast and making a proposition.

Feather proposed that it would be better to do this with four than just two. With four walking out, the corporation would be faced with a serious problem. Feather made the point that tracing four men is considerably more difficult than tracing two. And also, Feather said, he and Morris were rather unhappy with the treatment they were getting from the corporation, they'd be grateful for this chance to walk out. Feather went on talking while Clifton thought it over, and while Turley used an acetylene torch to open the safe. Then Clifton decided that Feather was making sense, that it wasn't just a frantic effort to stay alive. Besides, Feather was something of a brain and from here on in it would take considerable brains, much more than Turley had. Another factor, Clifton reasoned, was the potential need for gun-handling, and in that category it would be Morris. He knew what Morris could do with a gun, with anything from a .38 to a Thompson.

When the money was in the suitcase and they walked out of
the warehouse, they took Feather and Morris with them.

On the road going north from Georgia to New Jersey, they
traveled at fairly high speed. In Virginia they were spotted by
some corporation people and there was a chase and an
exchange of bullets and Morris proved himself rather useful.
The other car was stopped with a front tire punctured, and,
later, on a side road in Maryland, another corporation effort
was blocked by Morris, leaning out the rear window to send
bullets seventy yards down the road and through a windshield
and into the face of the driver. There were no further difficulties with the corporation and that night they were crossing
a bridge into South Jersey and Feather was handling the car
very nicely. As Clifton told him what turns to make, he kept
asking where they were going. Morris also asked where they
were going. Clifton said they were going to a place where
they could stay hidden for a while. Feather wanted to know
if the place was sufficiently safe. Clifton said it was, describing
the place, the fact that it was far from the nearest town, that
it was very deep in the woods and extremely difficult to locate.
Feather kept asking questions and presently Clifton decided
there were too many questions and he told Feather to stop
the car. Feather looked at him, and then threw a glance at
Morris who was in the back seat with Turley. As Morris went
for his gun, Turley hauled off and put a fist on his chin and
knocked him out. Feather was trying to get out of the car and
Clifton grabbed him and held him while Turley tagged him
on the jaw, just under his ear. Then Feather and Morris were
asleep in the road and the car was going away.

"—shoulda made a U-turn and came back and run over
them," Clifton was saying. "Shoulda figured what would happen if I let them stay alive. The way it worked out, they musta
played it slick. That Feather's a slick talker. He musta known
just what to tell the corporation. I guess he said it was a
strong-arm deal, that they didn' have no choice and they
hadda come along for the ride. So the corporation takes them
in again. Not all the way in, not yet. First they gotta find me
and Turley. It's like they're on probation. They know they
gotta make good to get in solid again."

Clifton lit another cigarette. He went on talking. He talked about Turley's witless maneuvering and his own mistake in allowing Turley to make the trip to Philadelphia.

"—had a feeling he'd mess things up," Clifton was saying. "But he swore he'd be careful. Kept telling me about his connections on Dock Street, all them boat captains he knew, and how easy it would be to make arrangements. Kept selling me on the idea and finally I bought it. We get in the car and I drive him to Belleville so he can catch a bus to Philly. For that one move alone I oughtta have my head examined."

Eddie was sitting there with his eyes half closed. He was still thinking about the waitress. He told himself to stop it, but he couldn't stop it.

"—so now it's no boat ride," Clifton was saying. "It's just sitting around, wondering what's gonna happen, and when. Some days we go out hunting for rabbits. That's a good one. We're worse off than the rabbits. At least they can run. And the geese, the wild geese. Christ, how I envy them geese.

"I'll tell you something," he went on. "It's really awful when you can't budge. It gets to be a drag and in the morning you hate to wake up because there's just no place to go. We used to joke about it, me and Turley. It actually gave us a laugh. We got two hundred thousand dollars to invest and no way to have fun with it. Not even on a broad. Some nights I crave a broad so bad—

"It ain't no way to live, I'll tell you that. It's the same routine, day after day. Except once a week it's driving the nine miles to Belleville, to buy food. Every time I take that ride, I come near pissing in my pants. A car shows in the rear-view mirror, I keep thinking that's it, that's a corporation car and I'm spotted, they got me now. In Belleville I try to play it cool but I swear it ain't easy. If anyone looks at me twice, I'm ready to go for the rod. Say, that reminds me—"

Clifton got up from the table. He reached to the shelf, to the assortment of guns, and selected a .38 revolver. He checked it, then opened one of the ammunition boxes, loaded the gun and handed it to Eddie. "You'll need this," he said. "Keep it with you. Don't ever be without it."

Eddie looked at the gun in his hand. It had no effect on him. He slipped it under his overcoat, into the side pocket of his jacket.

"Take it out," Clifton said.

"The gun?"

Clifton nodded. "Take it outa your pocket. Let's see you take it out."

He reached under his overcoat, doing it slowly and indifferently. Then the gun was in his hand and he showed it to Clifton.

"Try it again," Clifton said, smiling at him. "Put it back in and take it out."

He did it again. The gun felt heavy and he was awkward with it. Clifton was laughing softly.

"Wanna see something?" Clifton said. "Watch me."

Clifton turned and moved toward the stove. He had his hands at his sides. Then he stood at the stove and reached toward the coffee pot with his right hand. As his fingers touched the handle of the coffee pot, the yellow-tan sleeve of his camel's-hair coat was a flash of caramel color, and almost in the same instant there was a gun in his right hand, held steady there, his finger on the trigger.

"Get the idea?" Clifton murmured.

"I guess it takes practice."

"Every day," Clifton said. "We practice at least an hour a day."

"With shooting?"

"In the woods," Clifton said. "Anything that moves. A weasel, a rat, even the mice. If they ain't showing, we use other targets. Turley throws a stone and I draw and try to hit it. Or sometimes it's tin cans. When it's tin cans it's long range. We do lotsa practicing at long range."

"Is Turley any good?"

"He's awful," Clifton said. "He can't learn."

Eddie looked down at the gun in his hand. It felt less heavy now.

"I hope you can learn," Clifton said. "You think you can?"

Eddie hefted the gun. He was remembering Burma. He said, "I guess so. I've done this before."

"That's right. I forgot. It slipped my mind. You got some medals. You get many Japs?"

"A few."

"How many?"

"Well, it was mostly with a bayonet. Except with the snipers. With the snipers I liked the forty-five."

"You want a forty-five? I got a couple here."

"No, this'll be all right."

"It better be," Clifton said. "This ain't for prizes."

"You think it's coming soon?"

"Who knows? Maybe a month from now. A year from now. Or maybe tomorrow. Who the hell knows?"

"Maybe it won't happen," Eddie said.

"It's gotta happen. It's on the schedule."

"You know, there's a chance you could be wrong," Eddie said. "This place ain't easy to find."

"They'll find it," Clifton muttered. He was staring at the window. The shade was down. He leaned across the table and lifted the shade just a little and looked out. He kept the shade up and stayed there looking out and Eddie turned to see what he was looking at. There was nothing out there except the snow-covered clearing, then the white of the trees in the woods, and then the black sky. The glow from the kitchen showed the woodshed and the privy and the car. It was a gray Packard sedan, expensive-looking, its chromium very bright where the grille showed under the snow-topped hood. Nice car, he thought, but it ain't worth a damn. It ain't armor-plated.

Clifton lowered the shade and moved away from the table. "You sure you ain't hungry?" he asked. "I can fix you something—"

"No," Eddie said. His stomach felt empty but he knew he couldn't eat anything. "I'm sorta done in," he said. "I wanna get some sleep."

Clifton picked up the sawed-off shotgun and put it under his arm, and they went out of the kitchen. In the parlor there was another kerosene lamp and it was lit, the flickering glimmer revealing a scraggly carpet, a very old sofa with some of the stuffing popped out, and two armchairs that were even older than the sofa and looked as though they'd give way if they were sat on.

There was also the piano.

Same piano, he thought, looking at the splintered upright that appeared somewhat ghostly in the dim yellow glow. The time-worn keyboard was like a set of decayed, crooked teeth, the ivory chipped off in places. He stood there looking at it, unaware that Clifton was watching him. He moved toward the keyboard and reached out to touch it. Then something pulled his hand away. His hand went under his overcoat and into the pocket of his jacket and he felt the full weight of the gun.

So what? he asked himself, coming back to now, to the sum of it. They take the piano away and they give you a gun. You wanted to make music and the way it looks from here on in you're finished with that, finished entirely. From here on in it's this—the gun.

He took the .38 from his pocket. It came out easily, smoothly, and he hefted it efficiently.

He heard Clifton saying, "That was nice. You're catching on."

"Maybe it likes me."

"Sure it likes you," Clifton said. "It's your best friend from now on."

The gun felt secure in his hand. He fondled it. Then he put it back into his pocket and followed Clifton toward the rickety stairway. The loose boards creaked as they went up, Clifton holding the kerosene lamp. At the top of the stairs, Clifton turned and handed him the lamp and said, "Wanna wake up Turley? Let him know you're here?"

"No," Eddie said. "Let him sleep. He needs sleep."

"All right." Clifton gestured down the hall. "Use the back room. The bed's made up."

"Same bed?" Eddie murmured. "The one with the busted springs?"

Clifton gazed past him. "He remembers."

"I oughtta remember. I was born in that room."

Clifton nodded slowly. "You had that room for twelve-thirteen years."

"Fourteen," Eddie said. "I was fourteen when they took me off to Curtis."

"What Curtis?"

"The Institute," Eddie said. "The Curtis Institute of Music."

Clifton looked at him and started to say something and held it back.

He grinned at Clifton. He said, "Remember the slingshots?"

"Slingshots?"

"And the limousine. They came for me in a limousine, them people from Curtis. Then in the woods it was you and Turley, with slingshots, shooting at the car. The people didn't know who you were. One of the women, she says to me, 'Who are they?' and I say, 'The boys, ma'am? The two boys?' She says 'They ain't boys, they're wild animals.' "

"And what did you say?"

"I said, 'They're my brothers, ma'am.' So then of course she tries to smooth it over, starts talking about the Institute and what a wonderful place it is. But the stones kept hitting the car, and it was like you were telling me something. That I couldn't really get away. That it was just a matter of time. That some day I'd come back to stay."

"With the wild animals," Clifton said, smiling thinly at him.

"You knew all along?"

Clifton nodded very slowly. "You hadda come back. You're one of the same, Eddie. The same as me and Turley. It's in the blood."

That says it, Eddie thought. That nails it down for sure. Any questions? Well yes, there's one. The wildness, I mean. Where'd we get it from? We didn't get it from Mom and Pop. I guess it skipped past them. It happens that way sometimes. Skips maybe a hundred years or a couple hundred or maybe three and then it shows again. If you look way back you'll find some Lynns or Websters raising hell and running wild and hiding out the way we're hiding now. If we wanted to, we could make it a ballad. For laughs, that is. Only for laughs.

He was laughing softly as he moved past Clifton and went on down the hall to the back room. Then he was undressed and standing at the window and looking out. The snow had stopped falling. He opened the window and the wind came in, not blasting now. It was more like a slow stream. But it was still very cold. Nice when it's cold, he thought. It's good for sleeping.

He climbed into the sagging bed, slid between a torn sheet and a scraggly quilt, and put the gun under the pillow. Then he closed his eyes and started to fall asleep, but something tugged at his brain and it was happening again, he was thinking about the waitress.

Go away, he said to her. Let me sleep.

Then it was like a tunnel and she was going away in the darkness and he went after her. The tunnel was endless and he kept telling her to go away, then hearing the departing footsteps and running after her and telling her to go away. Without sound she said to him, Make up your mind, and he said, How can I? This ain't like thinking with the mind. The mind has nothing to do with it.

Please go to sleep, he told himself. But he knew it was no use trying. He opened his eyes and sat up. It was very cold in the room but he didn't feel it. The hours flowed past and he had no awareness of time, not even when the window showed gray and lighter gray and finally the lit-up gray of daylight.

At a few minutes past nine, his brothers came in and saw him sitting there and staring at the window. He talked with them for a while and wasn't sure what the conversation was about. Their voices seemed blurred and through his half-closed eyes he saw them through a curtain. Turley offered him a drink from a pint bottle and he took it and had no idea what it was. Turley said, "You wanna get up?" and he started to climb out of the bed and Clifton said, "It's early yet. Let's all go back to sleep," with Turley agreeing, saying it would be nice to sleep all day. They went out of the room and he sat there on the edge of the bed, looking at the window. He was so tired he wondered how he was able to keep his eyes open. Then later his head was on the pillow and he was trying hard to fall asleep but his eyes remained open and his thoughts kept reaching out, seeking the waitress.

Around eleven, he finally fell asleep. An hour later he opened his eyes and looked at the window. The full glare of noon sunlight, snow-reflected, came in and caused him to blink. He got out of bed and went to the window and stood there looking out. It was very sunny out there, the snow glittering white-yellow and across the clearing the trees, laced with ice, were sparkling like jeweled ornaments. Very pretty, he thought. It's very pretty in the woods in the wintertime.

There was something moving out there, something walking in the woods, coming toward the clearing. It came slowly, hesitantly, with a certain furtiveness. As it edged past the trees, approaching closer to the clearing, a shaft of sunlight found it, lit it up and identified it. He shook his head and rubbed his eyes. He looked again, and it was there. Not a vision, he thought. Not wishful thinking, either. That's real. You see it and you know it's real.

Get out there, he said to himself. Get out there fast and tell her to go away. You gotta keep her away from this house. Because it ain't a house, it's just a den for hunted animals. She stumbles in, she'll never get out. They wouldn't let her. They'd clamp her down and hold her here for security reasons. Maybe they've spotted her already, and you better take the gun. They're your own dear brothers but what we have here is a difference of opinion and you damn well better take the gun.

He was dressed now, pulling the gun from under the pillow, putting it in his jacket pocket, then slipping into the overcoat as he went out of the room. He moved quietly but hastily down the hall, then down the steps and out through the back door. The snow was high, and he churned his way through it, running fast across the clearing, toward the waitress.

15

SHE was leaning against a tree, waiting for him. As he came up, she said, "You ready?"

"For what?"

"Travel," she said. "I'm taking you back to Philly."

He frowned and blinked, his eyes flicking questions.

"You're cleared," she told him. "It's in the file. They're calling it an accident."

The frown deepened. "What're you giving me?"

"A message," she said. "From Harriet. From the crowd at the Hut, the regulars. They're regular, all right."

"They're backing me?"

"All the way."

"And the law?"

"The law bought it."

"Bought what? They don't buy hearsay evidence. This needs a witness. I don't have a witness—"

"You got three."

He stared at her.

"Three," she said. "From the Hut."

"They saw it happen?"

She smiled thinly. "Not exactly."

"You told them what to say?"

She nodded.

Then he began to see it. He saw the waitress in there pitching, first talking to Harriet, then going out to round up the others, ringing doorbells very early in the morning. He saw them all assembled at the Hut, the waitress telling them the way it was and what had to be done. Like a company commander, he thought.

"Who was it?" he asked. "Who volunteered?"

"All of them."

He took a deep breath. It quivered somewhat, going in. His throat felt thick and he couldn't talk.

"We figured three was enough," the waitress said. "More than three, it would seem sorta phony. We hadda make sure it would hold together. What we did was, we picked three with police records. For gambling, that is. They're on the list as well-known crapshooters."

"Why crapshooters?"

"To make it look honest. First thing, they hadda explain why they didn't tell the law right away. Reason is, they didn't wanna get pinched for gambling. Another thing, the way we lined it up they were upstairs, in the back room. The law wantsa know what they're doing up there, they got a perfect answer, they're having a private session with the dice."

"You briefed them on that?"

"We went over it I don't know how many times. At seven-thirty this morning I figured they were ready. So they go to the law and spill it and then they're signing the statements."

"Like what? What was the pitch?"

"The window in the back room was the angle we needed. From the window you look down on a slant and you can see that backyard."

"Close enough?"

"Just about. So the way they tell it to the law, they're on the floor shooting crap and they hear the commotion from downstairs. At first they don't pay it no mind, the dice are hot and they're betting heavy. But later it sounds bad from downstairs, and then they hear the door slamming when you chase him out to the alley. They go to the window and look out. You getting it now?"

"It checks," he nodded.

"They give it to the law like a play-by-play, exactly the way you told it to me. They said they saw you throwing the knife away and trying to talk to him but he won't listen, he's sort of off his rocker and he comes leaping in. Then he's got you in the bear hug and the way it looks, you won't come outa there alive. They said you made a grab for the knife, tried to stick him in the arm to get him off you, and just then he shifts around and the blade goes into his chest."

He gazed past her. "And that's it? I'm really cleared?"

"Entirely," she said. "They dropped all charges."

"They hold the crapshooters?"

"No, just called them names. Called them goddam liars and kicked them outa the station house. You know how it is with the law. If they can't make it stick, they drop it."

He looked at her. "How'd you get here?"

"The car."

"The Chevvy?" frowning again. "Your landlady's gonna—"

"It's all right," she said. "This time it's rented. I slipped her a few bucks and she's satisfied."

"That's good to know." But he was still frowning. He turned and looked across the clearing, at the house. He was focusing on the upstairs windows. He murmured, "Where's the car?"

"Back there," she said. "In the woods. I didn't want your people to see. I thought if they spotted me, it might get complicated."

He went on looking at the house. "It's complicated already. I can't go away without telling them."

"Why not?"

"Well, after all—"

She took hold of his arm. "Come on."

"I really oughtta tell them."

"The hell with them," she said. She tugged at his arm. "Come on, will you? Let's get outa here."

"No," he murmured, still looking at the house. "First I gotta tell them."

She kept tugging at his arm. "You can't go back there. That's a hide-out. We'll both be dragged in—"

"Not you," he said. "You'll wait here."

"You'll come back?"

He turned his head and looked at her. "You know I'll come back."

She let go of his arm. He started walking across the clearing. It won't take long, he thought. I'll just tell them the way it is, and they'll understand, they'll know they got nothing to worry about, it stays a hide-out. But on the other hand, you know Clifton. You know the way he thinks, the way he operates. He's strictly a professional. A professional takes no chances. With Turley it's different. Turley's more on the easy side and you know he'll see it your way. I hope you can bring Clifton around. Not with pleading, though. Whatever you do, don't plead with him. Just let him know you're checking out with the waitress and give him assurance she'll keep her mouth shut. And what if he says no? What if he goes out and brings her into the house and says she's gotta stay? If it comes to that, we'll hafta do something. Maybe it won't come to that. Let's hope so, anyway. Let's see if we can keep it on the bright side. Sure, that's better. It's nice to think along the cheery lines, to tell yourself it's gonna work out fine and you won't be needing the gun.

He was a little more than halfway across the clearing, moving fast through the snow. He was headed toward the back door of the house, the door some sixty feet away and then fifty feet when he heard the sound of an automobile.

And even before he turned and looked, he was thinking, That ain't the Chevvy going away. That's a Buick coming in.

He pivoted, his eyes aiming at the edge of the woods where the wagon path showed a pale green Buick. The car came slowly, impeded by the snow. Then it gave a lurch, the snow spraying as the tires screeched, and it was coming faster now.

They followed her, he thought. They followed her from Philly. Kept their distance so it wouldn't give them away in the rear-view mirror. Score one for them. It's quite a score that's for sure. Maybe it's a grand slam.

He saw Feather and Morris getting out of the car. Morris circled the car and came up to Feather and they stood there talking. Morris was pointing toward the house and Feather was shaking his head. They were focused on the front of the house and he knew they hadn't seen him. But they will, he thought. You make another move and you're spotted. And this time it's no discussions, no preliminaries. This time you're on the check-off list and they'll try to put you outa the way.

What you need, of course, is a fox-hole. It would sure come in handy right now. Or a sprinter's legs. Or better yet, a pair of wings. But I think you'll hafta settle for the snow. The snow looks deep enough.

He was crouched, then flattened on his belly in the snow. In front of his face it was a white wall. He brushed at it, his fingers creating a gap, and he looked through it and saw Feather and Morris still standing beside the car and arguing. Morris kept gesturing toward the house and Feather was shaking his head. Morris started walking toward the house and Feather pulled him back. They were talking loudly now but he couldn't make out what they were saying. He estimated they were some sixty yards away.

And you're some fifteen yards from the back door, he told himself. Wanna try it? There's a chance you can make it, but not much of a chance, considering Morris. You remember what Clifton said about Morris and his ability with a gun. I think we better wait a little longer and see what they're gonna do.

But what about her? You forgetting her? No, it ain't that, you know damn well it ain't that. It's just that you're sure she'll use her head and stay right there where she is. She stays there, she'll be all right.

Then he saw Feather and Morris taking things from the car. The things were Tommy guns. Feather and Morris moved toward the house.

But that's no way to do it, he said to them. That's like betting everything on one card, hoping to fill an inside straight. Or it could be you're too anxious, you've waited a long time and you just can't wait any more. Whatever the reason, it's a tactical error, it's actually a boner and you'll soon find out.

You sure? he asked himself. You really sure they'll come out losers? Better give it another look and line it up the way it is. I think it's Clifton and Turley in bed asleep and of course you're hoping they heard the car when it came outa the woods and they ain't asleep. But that's only hoping, and hoping ain't enough. If they're still asleep, you gotta wake them up.

You gotta do it now. Right now. After all, it's only fifteen yards to the back door. Maybe if you crawl it— No, you can't crawl it. You don't have time for that. You'll hafta run. All right let's run.

He was up and racing toward the back door. He'd made less than five yards when he heard the blast of a Tommy and saw punctures in the snow in front of him, a few feet off to the side.

Nothing doing, he told himself. You'll never make it. You'll hafta pretend you're hit. And as the thought flashed through his brain he was already going down in simulated collapse. He hit the snow and rolled over and then rested on his side, motionless.

Then he heard the other guns, the shots coming from an upstairs window. He looked up and saw Clifton, with the sawed-off shotgun. A moment later it was Turley showing at another window. Turley was using two revolvers.

He grinned and thought, Well, anyway, you did it. You managed to wake them up. They're really awake now. They're wide awake and very busy.

Feather and Morris were running back to the car. Feather seemed to be hit in the leg. He was limping. Morris turned and let go a short blast at Turley's window. Turley dropped one of the revolvers and grabbed at his shoulder and ducked out of sight. Then Morris took aim at Clifton, started a volley and Clifton quickly took cover. It was all happening very fast and now Feather was on his knees, crawling behind the Buick to use it as a shield. Morris moved closer to the house and sent another blast at the upstairs windows, swinging the Tommy to get as many bullets up there as he could. Now from the house there was no shooting at all. Morris kept blasting at the upstairs windows. Feather yelled at him and he lowered the gun and walked backward toward the Buick. He stood at the side of the Buick, the Tommy still lowered but appearing ready as he looked up at the windows.

Some moments later the back door opened and Clifton came running out. He was carrying a small black suitcase. He was running toward the gray Packard parked near the woodshed. As he neared the car, he stumbled and the suitcase fell open and some paper money dropped out. Clifton bent over to pick it up. Morris didn't see this happening. Morris was still watching the upstairs windows. Now Clifton had the suitcase closed again and was climbing into the Packard. Then Turley, holding a sawed-off shotgun and a revolver with one hand while his other hand clutched his shoulder, came out of the back door and joined Clifton in the Packard.

The motor started and the Packard accelerated very fast, coming out from the rear of the house and sweeping in a wide circle, cutting through the snow with the skid-chained tires getting full traction, the car now moving at high speed across the clearing, aiming at the wagon path leading into the woods. Morris was using the Tommy again but he was somewhat disconcerted and his shooting was off. He shot for the tire and he was short. Then he shot for the front side window and hit the rear side window. Feather was yelling at him and he kept shooting at the Packard, now running toward the Packard as it went galloping away from him. He was screaming at the Packard, his voice cracked and twisted, with the Thompson still blasting but no longer useful because he couldn't aim it, he was much too upset.

Feather was crawling along the side of the Buick, opening the door and climbing in behind the wheel. Morris had stopped running but was still shooting at the Packard. From the Packard there was a return of fire as Turley leaned out and used the sawed-off shotgun. Morris let out a yowl and dropped the Thompson and began to hop around, his left arm dangling, his wrist and hand bright red, the redness dripping. He kept hopping around and making loud noises. Then with

his right hand he pulled out a revolver and shot at the Packard
as it cut across the clearing headed for the wagon path. The
shot went very wide and then the Packard was on the wagon
path and going away.

Feather opened the rear door of the Buick and Morris
climbed in. The Buick leaped into a turn and aimed at the
wagon path to chase after the Packard.

Eddie sat up. He looked to the side and saw the waitress
running out from the edge of the woods. She was coming fast
across the clearing and he waved at her to get back, to stay
in the woods until the Buick was gone. Now the Buick had
slowed just a little and he knew they'd seen the waitress.

He reached into his jacket pocket and pulled out the .38.
With his other hand he kept waving at her to get back.

The Buick came to a stop. Feather was using the Tommy,
shooting at the waitress. Eddie fired blindly at the Buick, unable to aim because he wasn't thinking in terms of hitting
anything. He kept pulling the trigger, hoping it would get the
Tommy off the waitress. With his fourth shot he lured the
Tommy to point in his direction. He felt the swish of slugs
going past his head and he fired a fifth shot to keep the
Tommy on him and away from her.

He couldn't see her now, he was concentrating on the
Buick. The Tommy had stopped firing and the Buick was
moving again. It picked up speed going toward the wagon
path and he thought, It's the Packard they want, they're going
away to go after the Packard. Will they get it? It really doesn't
matter. You don't even want to think about it. You got her
to think about. Because you can't see her now. You're looking
and you can't see her.

Where is she? Did she make it back to the woods? Sure,
that's what happened. She ran back and she's waiting there.
So it's all right. You can go to her now. The hornets are gone
and it's nice to know you can drop the gun and go to her.

He dropped the .38 and started walking through the snow.
At first he walked fast, but then he slowed, and then he walked
very slowly. Finally he stopped and looked at something half
hidden in the deep snow.

She was resting face down. He knelt beside her and said
something and she didn't answer. Then very carefully he

turned her onto her side and looked at her face. There were two bullet holes in her forehead and very quickly he looked away. Then his eyes were shut tightly and he was shaking his head. There was a sound from somewhere but he didn't hear it. He didn't know he was moaning.

He stayed there for a while, kneeling beside Lena. Then he got up and walked across the clearing and went into the woods to look for the Chevvy. He found it parked between some trees near the wagon path. The key was in the ignition lock and he drove the Chevvy into the clearing. He placed the body in the back seat. It's gotta be delivered, he thought. It's just a package gotta be delivered.

He took her to Belleville. In Belleville the authorities held him for thirty-two hours. During that time they offered him food but he couldn't eat. There was an interval of getting into an official car with some men in plain clothes, and he guided them to the house in the woods. He was vaguely aware of answering their questions, although his answers seemed to satisfy them. When they found Tommy slugs in the clearing it confirmed what he'd told them in Belleville. But then they wanted to know more about the battle, the reason for it, and he said he couldn't tell them much about that. He said it was some kind of a dispute between these people and his brothers and he wasn't sure what it was about. They grilled him and he kept saying. "Can't help you there," and it wasn't an evasion. He really couldn't tell them because it wasn't clear in his mind. He was far away from it and it didn't matter to him, it had no importance at all.

Then, in Belleville again, they asked if he could help in establishing the identity of the victim. They said they'd done some checking but they couldn't find any relatives or records of past employment. He repeated what he'd told them previously, that she was a waitress and her first name was Lena and he didn't know her last name. They wanted to know if there was anything more. He said that was all he knew, that she'd never told him about herself. They shrugged and told him to sign a few papers, and when he'd done that, they let him go. Just before he walked out, he asked if they'd found where she lived in Philadelphia. They gave him the address of the rooming house. They were somewhat perplexed that he hadn't even known the address. After he walked out, one of them commented, "Claimed he hardly knew her. Then why's he taking it so hard? That man's been hit so hard he's goofy."

Later that day, in Philadelphia, he returned the Chevvy to its owner. Then he went to his room. Without thinking about it, he pulled down the shade and then he locked the door. At the wash basin he brushed his teeth and shaved and combed his hair. It was as though he expected company and wanted to make a presentable appearance. He put on a clean shirt and a necktie and seated himself on the edge of the bed, waiting for a visitor.

He waited there a long time. At intervals he slept, pulled from sleep whenever he heard footsteps in the hall. But the footsteps never approached the door.

Very late that night there was a knock on the door. He opened the door and Clarice came in with some sandwiches and a carton of coffee. He thanked her and said he wasn't hungry. She unwrapped the sandwiches and forced them into his hands. She sat there and watched him while he ate. The food had no taste but he managed to eat it, washing it down with the coffee. Then she gave him a cigarette, lit one for herself, and after taking a few puffs she suggested they go out for a walk. She said the air would do him good.

He shook his head.

She told him to get some sleep and then she went out of the room. The next day she was there again with more food. For several days she kept bringing him food and urging him to eat. On the fifth day he was able to eat without being coaxed. But he refused to go out of the room. Each night she asked him to go for a walk and told him he needed fresh air and some exercise and he shook his head. His lips smiled at her, but with his eyes he was begging her to leave him alone.

Night after night she kept asking him to go for a walk. Then it was the ninth night and instead of shaking his head, he shrugged, put on his overcoat and they went out.

They were on the street and walking slowly and he had no idea where they were going. But suddenly, through the darkness, he saw the orange glow of the lit-up sign with some of the bulbs missing.

He stopped. He said, "Not there. We ain't going there."

"Why not?"

"Nothing there for me," he said. "Nothing I can do there."

Clarice took hold of his arm. She pulled him along toward the lit-up sign.

Then they were walking into the Hut. The place was jammed. Every table was taken and they were three-deep and four-deep all along the bar. It was the same crowd, the same noisy regulars, except that now there was very little noise. Just a low murmuring.

He wondered why it was so quiet in the Hut. Then he saw Harriet behind the bar. She was looking directly at him. Her face was expressionless.

Now heads were turning and others were looking at him and he told himself to get out of here, get out fast. But Clarice had tightened her hold on his arm. She was pulling him forward, taking him past the tables and toward the piano.

"No," he said. "I can't—"

"The hell you can't," Clarice said, and kept pulling him toward the piano.

She pushed him onto the revolving stool. He sat there staring at the keyboard.

And then, from Harriet, "Come on, give us a tune."

But I can't, he said without sound. Just can't.

"Play it," Harriet yelled at him. "Whatcha think I'm payin' you for? We wanna hear some music."

From the bar someone shouted, "Do it, Eddie. Hit them keys. Put some life in this joint."

Others chimed in, coaxing him to get started.

He heard Clarice saying, "Give, man. You got an audience."

And they're waiting, he thought. They've been coming here every night and waiting.

But there's nothing you can give them. You just don't have it to give.

His eyes were closed. A whisper came from somewhere, saying, You can try. The least you can do is try.

Then he heard the sound. It was warm and sweet and it

came from a piano. That's fine piano, he thought. Who's playing that?

He opened his eyes. He saw his fingers caressing the keyboard.

THE REAL COOL KILLERS

by Chester Himes

I.

I'm gwine down to de river,
Set down on de ground;
If de blues overtake me,
I'll jump overboard an' drown . . .

Big Joe Turner was singing a rock-and-roll adaptation of *Dink's Blues.*

The loud licking rhythm blasted from the juke box with enough heat to melt bones.

A woman leapt from her seat in a booth as though the music had stuck her full of tacks. She was a lean black woman clad in a pink cotton jersey dress and red silk stockings. She pulled up her skirt and began doing a shake dance as though trying to throw off the tacks one by one.

Her mood was contagious. Other women jumped down from their high stools and shook themselves into the act. The customers laughed and shouted and began shaking too. The aisle between the bar and the booths became stormy with shaking bodies.

Big Smiley, the giant-size bartender, began doing a flat-footed locomotive shuffle up and down behind the bar.

The colored patrons of Harlem's Dew Drop Inn on 129th Street and Lenox Avenue were having the time of their lives that crisp October night.

A white man standing near the middle of the bar watched them with cynical amusement. He was the only white person present.

He was a big man, over six feet tall, dressed in a dark gray flannel suit, white shirt and blood red tie. He had a big featured sallow face with the blotched skin of dissipation. His thick black hair was shot with gray. He held a dead cigar butt between the first two fingers of his left hand. On the third finger was a signet ring. He looked to be about forty.

The colored women seemed to be dancing for his exclusive entertainment. A slight flush spread over his sallow face.

The music stopped.

A loud grating voice said dangerously above the panting

laughter: "Ah feels like cutting me some white mother-raper's throat."

The laughter stopped. The room became suddenly silent.

The man who had spoken was a scrawny little chicken-neck bantam-weight, twenty years past his fist fighting days, with gray stubble tinging his rough black skin. He wore a battered black derby green with age, a ragged plaid mackinaw and blue denim overalls.

His small enraged eyes were as red as live coals. He stalked toward the big white man stifflegged, holding an open spring-blade knife in his right hand with the blade pressed flat against his overalled leg.

The big white man turned to face him, looking as though he were caught in a situation where he didn't know whether to laugh or get angry. His hand strayed casually to the heavy glass ashtray on the bar.

"Take it easy, little man, and no one will get hurt," he said.

The little knifeman stopped two paces in front of him and said, "Ef'n Ah finds me some white mother-raper up here on my side of town trying to diddle my little gals Ah'm gonna cut his throat."

"What an idea," the white man said. "I'm a salesman. I sell that fine King Cola you folks like so much up here. I just dropped in here to patronize my customers."

Big Smiley came down and leaned his ham-size fists on the bar.

"Looka here, big bad and burly," he said to the little knife-man. "Don't try to scare my customers just 'cause you're big-ger than they is."

"He doesn't want to hurt anyone," the big white man said. "He just wants some King Cola to soothe his mind. Give him a bottle of King Cola."

The little knifeman slashed at his throat and severed his red tie neatly just below the knot.

The big white man jumped back. His elbow struck the edge of the bar and the ash tray he'd been gripping flew from his hand and crashed into the shelf of ornamental wine glasses behind the bar.

The crashing sound caused him to jump back again. His second reflex action followed so closely on his first that he

avoided the second slashing of the knife blade without even
seeing it either. The knot that had remained of his tie was split
through the middle and blossomed like a bloody wound over
his white collar.

". . . throat cut!" a voice shouted excitedly as though yelling *Home Run!*

Big Smiley leaned across the bar and grabbed the red-eyed
knifeman by the lapels of his mackinaw and lifted him from
the floor.

"Gimme that chiv, shorty, 'fore I makes you eat it," he said
lazily, smiling as though it were a joke.

The knifeman twisted in his grip and slashed him across the
arm. The white fabric of his jacket sleeve parted like a bursted
balloon and his black-skinned muscles opened like the Red
Sea.

Blood spurted.

Big Smiley looked at his cut arm. He was still holding the
knifeman off the floor by the mackinaw collar. His eyes had a
surprised look. His nostrils flared.

"You cut me, didn't you," he said. His voice sounded unbelieving.

"Ah'll cut you again," the little knifeman said, wriggling in
his grip.

Big Smiley dropped him as though he'd turned red hot.

The little knifeman bounced on his feet and slashed at Big
Smiley's face.

Big Smiley drew back and reached beneath the bar counter
with his right hand. He came up with a short handled fireman's axe. It had a red handle and a honed, razor-sharp blade.

The little knifeman jumped into the air and slashed at Big
Smiley again, matching his knife against Big Smiley's axe.

Big Smiley countered with a right cross with the red-
handled axe. The axe blade met the knifeman's arm in the
middle of its stroke and cut it off just below the elbow as
though it had been guillotined.

The severed coat-sleeved short-arm, still clutching the knife,
sailed through the air, sprinkling the nearby spectators with
drops of blood, landed on the linoleum tile floor, and skidded
beneath the table of a booth.

The little knifeman landed on his feet, still making cutting motions with his half-an-arm. He was too drunk to feel the full impact of the shock. He saw that the lower part of his arm had been chopped off; he saw Big Smiley drawing back the red-handled axe. He thought Big Smiley was going to chop at him again.

"Wait a minute, you big mother-raper, 'til Ah find my arm!" he yelled. "It got my knife in his hand."

He dropped to his knees and began scrabbling about the floor with his one hand, searching for his severed arm. Blood spouted from his jerking stub as though from the nozzle of a hose.

Then he lost consciousness and flopped on his face.

Two customers turned him over; one wrapped a neck-tie about the bleeding arm for a tourniquet; the other inserted a chair leg to tighten it.

A waitress and another customer were twisting a knotted towel about Big Smiley's arm for a tourniquet. He was still holding the fireman's axe in his right hand and looking surprised.

The white manager stood atop the bar and shouted, "Please remain seated, folks. Everybody go back to his seat and pay his bill. The police have been called and everything will be taken care of."

As though he'd fired a starting gun, there was a race for the door.

When Sonny Pickens came out on the sidewalk he saw the big white man looking inside through one of the small front windows.

Sonny had been smoking two marijuana cigarets and he was tree top high. Seen from his drugged eyes, the dark night-sky looked bright purple and the dingy smoke-blackened tenements looked like brand new skyscrapers made of strawberry colored bricks. The neon signs of the bars and pool rooms and greasy spoons burned like phosphorescent fires.

He drew a blue-steel revolver from his inside coat pocket, spun the cylinder and aimed it at the big white man.

His two friends, Rubberlips Wilson and Lowtop Brown, looked at him in popeyed amazement. But before either could restrain him, Sonny advanced on the white man, walking on the balls of his feet.

"You there!" he shouted. "You the man what's been messing around with my wife."

The big white man jerked his head about and saw the pistol. His eyes stretched and the blood drained from his sallow face.

"My God, wait a minute!" he cried. "You're making a mistake. All of you folks are confusing me with some one else."

"Ain't going to be no waiting now," Sonny said and pulled the trigger.

Orange flame lanced toward the big white man's chest. Sound shattered the night.

Sonny and the white man both leapt straight up into the air simultaneously. Both began running before their feet touched the ground. Both ran straight ahead. They ran head on into one another at full speed. The white man's superior weight knocked Sonny down and he ran over him.

He plowed through the crowd of colored spectators, scattering them like nine pins, and cut across the street through the traffic, running in front of cars as though he didn't see them.

Sonny jumped to his feet and took out after him. He ran over the people the big white man had knocked down. Muscles rolled on bones beneath his feet. He staggered drunkenly. Screams followed him and car lights came down on him like shooting stars.

The big white man was going between two parked cars across the street when Sonny shot at him again. He gained the sidewalk unhit and began running south along the inner edge.

Sonny followed between the cars and kept after him.

People in the line of fire did acrobatics diving for safety. People up ahead crowded into the doorways to see what was happening. They saw a big white man with wild blue eyes and a stubble of red tie which looked as though his throat were cut, being chased by a slim black man with a big blue pistol. They drew back out of range.

But the people behind who were safely out of range joined the chase.

The white man was in front. Sonny was next. Rubberlips and Lowtop were running at Sonny's heels. Behind them the spectators stretched out in a ragged line.

The white man ran past a group of eight Arabs at the corner of 127th Street. All of the Arabs had heavy black grizzly beards. All wore bright green turbans, smoked glasses, and ankle-length white robes. Their complexions ranged from stove-pipe black to mustard tan. They were jabbering and gesticulating like a cage of frenzied monkeys. The air was redolent with the pungent scent of marijuana.

"An infidel!" one yelled.

The jabbering stopped abruptly. They wheeled after the white man in a group.

The white man heard the ejaculation. He saw the sudden movement through the corner of his eyes. He leaped forward from the curb.

A car coming fast down 127th Street burnt rubber in an earsplitting shriek to keep from running him down.

Seen in the car's headlights, his sweating face was bright red and muscle-ridged; his blue eyes were black with panic; his grayshot hair in wild disorder.

Instinctively he leaped high and sideways from the on-coming car. His arms and legs flew out in grotesque silhouette.

At that instant Sonny came abreast of the Arabs and shot at the leaping white man while he was still in the air.

The orange blast lit up Sonny's distorted face and the roar of the gunshot sounded like a fusillade.

The big white man shuddered and came down limp. He landed face downward in a spread-eagle posture. He didn't get up.

Sonny ran up to him with the smoking pistol dangling from his hand. He was starkly spotlighted by the car's headlights. He looked at the white man lying face downward in the middle of the street and started laughing. He doubled over laughing, his arms jerking and his body rocking.

Lowtop and Rubberlips caught up. The eight Arabs joined them in the beams of light.

"Man, Jesus Christ, what happened?" Lowtop asked.

The Arabs looked at him and began to laugh.

Rubberlips began to laugh too, then Lowtop.

All of them stood in the stark white light, swaying and rocking and doubling over with laughter.

Sonny was trying to say something but he was laughing so hard he couldn't get it out.

A police siren sounded nearby.

2.

THE TELEPHONE rang in the captain's office at the 126th Street precinct station.

The uniformed officer behind the desk reached for the outside phone without looking up from the record sheet he was filling out.

"Harlem precinct. Lieutenant Anderson," he said.

A high-pitched proper-speaking voice said, "Are you the man in charge?"

"Yes, lady," Lieutenant Anderson said patiently and went on writing with his free hand.

"I want to report that a white man is being chased down Lenox Avenue by a colored man with a gun," the voice said with the smug sanctimoniousness of a saved sister.

Lieutenant Anderson pushed aside the record sheet and pulled forward a report pad.

When he had finished taking down the essential details of her incoherent account, he said, "Thank you, Mrs. Collins," hung up and reached for the closed line to central police on Centre Street.

"Give me the radio dispatcher," he said.

Two colored men were driving east on 135th Street in the wake of a crosstown bus. Shapeless dark hats sat squarely on their clipped kinky heads and their big frames filled up the front seat of a small battered black sedan.

Static crackled from the shortwave radio and a metallic voice said:

Calling all cars. Riot threatens in Harlem. White man running South on Lenox Avenue at 128th Street. Chased by drunken Negro with gun. Danger of murder.

"Better goose it," the one on the inside said in a grating voice.

"I reckon so," the driver replied laconically.

He gave a short sharp blast on the siren and gunned the small sedan in a crying U-turn in the middle of the block, cutting in front of a taxi coming fast from the direction of the Bronx.

The taxi tore its brakes to keep from ramming it. Seeing the private license plates, the taxi driver thought they were two smalltime hustlers trying to play bigshots with the siren on their car. He was an Italian from the Bronx who had grown up with bigtime gangsters and Harlem hoodlums didn't scare him.

He leaned out of his window and yelled, "You ain't plowing cotton in Mississippi, you black son of a bitch. This is New York City, the Big Apple, where people drive—"

The colored man riding with his girl friend in the back seat leaned quickly forward and yanked at his sleeve.

"Man, come back in here and shut yo' mouth," he warned anxiously. "Them is Grave Digger Jones and Coffin Ed Johnson you is talking to. Can't you see that police antenna stuck up from their tail."

"Oh, that's them," the driver said, cooling off as quickly as a showgirl on a broke stud. "I didn't recognize 'em."

Grave Digger had heard him but he mashed the gas without looking around.

Coffin Ed drew his pistol from its shoulder sling and spun the cylinder. Passing street lights glinted from the long nickel-plated barrel of the special-made .38 calibre revolver, and the five brass-jacketed bullets looked deadly in the six chambers. The one beneath the trigger was empty, but he kept an extra box of shells along with his report book and handcuffs in his greased-leather lined right coat pocket.

"Lieutenant Anderson asked me last night why we stuck to these old-fashioned rods when the new ones were so much better. He was trying to sell me on the idea of one of those new hydraulic automatics that shoot fifteen times; said they were faster, lighter and just as accurate. But I told him we'd stick to these."

"Did you tell him how fast you could reload?"

Grave Digger carried its mate beneath his left arm.

"Naw, I told him he didn't know how hard these Negroes' heads were in Harlem," Coffin Ed said.

His acid-scarred face looked sinister in the dim panel light.

Grave Digger chuckled. "You should have told him that these people don't have any respect for a gun that doesn't have a shiny barrel a half a mile long. They want to see what they're being shot at with."

"Or else hear it, otherwise they figure it can't do any more damage than their knives."

When they came into Lenox, Grave Digger wheeled southward through the red light with the siren open, passing in front of an eastbound trailer truck, and slowed down behind a sky blue Cadillac Coupe de Ville trimmed in yellow metal, hogging the southbound lane between a bus and a fleet of northbound refrigerator trucks.

It had a New York State license plate numbered B-H-21. It belonged to Big Henry who ran the "21" numbers house. Big Henry was driving. His bodyguard, Cousin Cuts, was sitting beside him on the front seat. Two other rugged looking men occupied the back seat.

Big Henry took the cigar from his thick-lipped mouth with his right hand, tapped ash in the tray sticking from the instrument panel and kept on talking to Cuts as though he hadn't heard the siren. The flash of a diamond from his cigar hand lit up the rear window.

"Get him over," Grave Digger said in a flat voice.

Coffin Ed leaned out of the right side window and shot the rear view mirror off the door hinge of the big Cadillac.

The cigar hand of Big Henry became rigid and the back of his fat black neck began to swell as he looked at his shattered mirror. Cuts rose up in his seat, twisting about threateningly, and reached for his pistol. But when he saw Coffin Ed's sinister face staring at him from behind the long nickel-plated barrel of the .38 he ducked like an artful dodger from a hard-thrown ball.

Coffin Ed planted a hole in the Cadillac's left front fender.

Grave Digger chuckled. "That'll hurt Big Henry more than a hole in Cousin Cuts' head."

Big Henry turned about with a look of pop-eyed indignation on his puffed black face, but it sunk in like a burst balloon when he recognized the detectives. He wheeled the car frantically toward the curb without looking and crumpled his right front fender into the side of the bus.

Grave Digger had space enough to squeeze through. As they passed, Coffin Ed lowered his aim and shot Big Henry's gold lettered initials from the Cadillac's door.

"And stay over!" he yelled in a grating voice.

They left Big Henry giving them a how-could-you-do-this-to-me look with tears in his eyes.

When they came abreast the Dew Drop Inn they saw the deserted ambulance with the crowd running on ahead. Without slowing down they wormed between the cars parked haphazardly in the street and pushed through the dense jam of people with the siren open. They dragged to a stop when their headlights focused on the macabre scene.

"Split!" one of the Arabs hissed. "Here's the Things."

"The monsters," another chimed.

"Keep cool, fool," the third admonished. "They got nothing on us."

The two tall lanky loose-jointed detectives hit the pavement in unison, their nickel-plated .38 specials gripped in their hands. They looked like big-shouldered plow-hands in Sunday suits at a Saturday night jamboree.

"Straighten up!" Grave Digger yelled at the top of his voice.

"Count off!" Coffin Ed echoed.

There was movement in the crowd. The morbid and the innocent moved in closer. Suspicious characters began to blow.

Sonny and his two friends turned startled popeyed faces.

"Where they come from?" Sonny mumbled in a daze.

"I'll take him," Grave Digger said.

"Covered," Coffin Ed replied.

Their big flat feet made slapping sounds as they converged on Sonny and the Arabs. Coffin Ed halted at an angle that put them all in line of fire.

Without a break in motion, Grave Digger closed on Sonny and slapped him on the elbow with the barrel of his pistol.

With his free hand he caught Sonny's pistol when it flew from his nerveless fingers.

"Got it," he said as Sonny yelped in pain and grabbed his numb arm.

"I ain't—" Sonny was trying to say but Grave Digger shouted, "Shut up!"

"Line up and reach!" Coffin Ed ordered in a threatening voice, menacing them with his pistol. He sounded as though his teeth were on edge.

"Tell the man, Sonny!" Lowtop urged in a trembling voice, but it was drowned by Grave Digger thundering at the crowd, "Back up!" He lined a shot overhead.

They backed up.

Sonny's good arm shot up and his two friends reached. He was still trying to say something. His Adam's apple bobbed helplessly in his dry wordless throat.

But the Arabs were defiant. They dangled their arms and shuffled about.

"Reach where, man?" one of them said in a husky voice.

Coffin Ed grabbed him by the neck, lifted him off his feet.

"Easy, Ed," Grave Digger cautioned in a strangely anxious voice. "Easy does it."

Coffin Ed halted his pistol on the verge of shattering the Arab's teeth and shook his head like a dog coming out of water. Releasing the Arab's neck, he backed up one step and said in his grating voice,

"One for the money . . . and two for the show . . ."

It was the first line of a jingle chanted in the game of hide-and-seek as a warning from the "seeker" to the "hiders" that he was going after them.

Grave Digger took the next line, "Three to get ready . . ."

But before he could finish it with "And here we go," the Arabs had fallen into line with Sonny and had raised their hands high into the air.

"Now keep them up," Coffin Ed said.

"Or you'll be the next ones lying on the ground," Grave Digger added.

Sonny finally got out the words, "He ain't dead. He's just fainted."

"That's right," Rubberlips confirmed. "He ain't been hit. It just scared him so he fell unconscious."

"Just shake him and he'll come to," Sonny added.

The Arabs started to laugh again, but Coffin Ed's sinister face silenced them.

Grave Digger stuck Sonny's revolver into his own belt, holstered his own revolver, and bent down and lifted the white man's face. Blue eyes looked off at nowhere with a fixed stare. He lowered the head gently and picked up a limp warm hand, feeling for a pulse.

"He ain't dead," Sonny repeated. But his voice had grown weaker. "He's just fainted, that's all."

He and his two friends watched Grave Digger as though he were Jesus Christ bending over the body of Lazarus.

Grave Digger's eyes explored the white man's back. Coffin Ed stood without moving, his scarred face like a bronze mask cast with trembling hands. Grave Digger saw a black wet spot in the white man's thick black grayshot hair, low down at the base of the skull. He put his fingertips to it and they came off stained. He straightened up slowly, held his wet fingertips in the white headlights, and they showed red. He said nothing.

The spectators crowded nearer. Coffin Ed didn't notice; he was looking at Grave Digger's bloody fingertips.

"Is that blood?" Sonny asked in a breaking whisper. His body began trembling, coming slowly upward from his grasshopper legs.

Grave Digger and Coffin Ed stared at him, saying nothing.

"Is he dead?" Sonny asked in a terrorstricken whisper. His trembling lips were dust dry and his eyes were turning white in a black face gone gray.

"Dead as he'll ever be," Grave Digger said in a flat toneless voice.

"I didn't do it," Sonny whispered. "I swear 'fore God in heaven."

"He didn't do it," Rubberlips and Lowtop echoed in unison.

"How does it figure?" Coffin Ed asked.

"It figures for itself," Grave Digger said.

"So help me, God, boss, I couldn't have done it," Sonny said in a terrified whisper.

Grave Digger stared at him from agate hard eyes in a petrified face, and said nothing.

"You gotta believe him, boss, he couldn't have done it," Rubberlips vouched.

"Nawsuh," Lowtop echoed.

"I wasn't trying to hurt him, I just wanted to scare him," Sonny said. Tears were trickling from his eyes.

"It were that crazy drunk man with the knife that started it," Rubberlips said. "Back there in the Dew Drop Inn."

"Then afterwards the big white man kept looking in the window," Lowtop said. "That made Sonny mad."

"But I was just playing a joke," Sonny said.

The detectives stared at him from blank eyes. The Arabs were motionless.

"He's a comedian," Coffin Ed said finally.

"How could I be mad about my old lady," Sonny argued. "I ain't even got any old lady."

"Don't tell me," Grave Digger said in a hard flat unrelenting voice, and handcuffed Sonny. "Save it for the judge."

"Boss, listen, I beg you, I swear 'fore God—"

"Shut up, you're under arrest," Coffin Ed said.

3.

A POLICE CAR siren sounded from the distance. It came from the east; it started like the wail of an anguished banshee and grew into a scream. Another sounded from the west; it was joined by others from the north and south, one sounding after another like jets taking off from an aircraft carrier.

"Let's see what these real cool Moslems are carrying," Grave Digger said.

"Count off, you sheiks," Coffin Ed said.

They had the case wrapped up before the prowl cars arrived and the pressure was off. They felt cocky.

"Praise Allah," the tallest of the Arabs said.

As though performing a ritual, the others said, "Mecca," and all bowed low with outstretched arms.

"Cut the comedy and straighten up," Grave Digger said. "We're holding you for witnesses."

"Who's got the prayer?" the leader asked with bowed head.

"I've got the prayer," another replied.

"Pray to the great monster," the leader commanded.

The one who had the prayer turned slowly and presented his white-robed backside to Coffin Ed. A sound like a hound dog baying issued from his rear end.

"Allah be praised," the leader said, and the loose white sleeves of their robes fluttered in response.

Coffin Ed didn't get it until Sonny and his friends laughed in amazement. Then his face contorted in black rage.

"Punks!" he grated harshly, kicked the bowed Arab somersaulting, and leveled on him with his pistol as though to shoot him.

"Easy man, easy," Grave Digger said, trying to keep a straight face. "You can't shoot a man for aiming a fart at you."

"Hold it, monster," a third Arab cried, and flung liquid from a glass bottle toward Coffin Ed's face. "Sweeten thyself."

Coffin Ed saw the flash of the bottle and the liquid flying and ducked as he swung his pistol barrel.

"It's just perfume," the Arab cried in alarm.

But Coffin Ed didn't hear him through the roar of blood in his head. All he could think of was a con man called Hank throwing a glass of acid into his face. And this looked like another acid thrower. Quick scalding rage turned his acid burnt face into a hideous mask and his scarred lips drew back from his clenched teeth.

He wired two shots together and the Arab holding the half-filled perfume bottle said, "Oh," softly and folded slowly to the pavement. Behind, in the crowd, a woman screamed as her leg gave away beneath her.

The other Arabs broke in wild flight. Sonny broke with them. A split second later his friends took off in his wake.

"Goddammit, Ed!" Grave Digger shouted and lunged for the gun.

He made a grab for the barrel, deflecting the aim as it went off again. The bullet cut a telephone cable in two overhead and it fell into the crowd, setting off a cacophony of screams.

Everybody ran.

The panicstricken crowd stampeded for the nearest doorways, trampling the woman who was shot and two others who fell.

Grave Digger grappled with Coffin Ed and they crashed down on top of the dead white man. Grave Digger had Coffin Ed's pistol by the barrel and was trying to wrest it from his grip.

"It's me, Digger, Ed," he kept saying. "Let go the gun."

"Turn me loose, Digger, turn me loose. Let me kill 'im," Coffin Ed mouthed insanely, tears streaming from his hideous face. "They tried it again, Digger."

They rolled over the corpse and rolled back.

"That wasn't acid, that was perfume," Grave Digger said, gasping for breath.

"Turn me loose, Digger, I'm warning you," Coffin Ed mumbled.

While they threshed back and forth over the corpse, two of the Arabs followed Sonny into the doorway of a tenement. The other people crowding into the doorway got aside and let them pass. Sonny saw the stairs crowded and kept on through, looking for a back exit. He came out in a small back courtyard, enclosed with stone walls. The Arabs followed him. One put a noose over his head, knocking off his hat, and drew it tight. The other pulled a switchblade knife and pressed the point against his side.

"If you holler you're dead," the first one said.

The Arab leader joined them.

"Let's get him away from here," he said.

At that moment the patrol cars began to unload. Two harness cops and Detective Haggerty hit the deck and were the first on the murder scene.

"Holy mother!" Haggerty exclaimed.

The cops stared aghast.

It looked to them as though the two colored detectives had the big white man locked in a death struggle.

"Just don't stand there," Grave Digger panted. "Give me a hand."

"They'll kill him," Haggerty said, wrapping his arms about

Grave Digger and trying to pull him away. "You grab the other one," he said to the cops.

"To hell with that," the cop said, swinging his blackjack across Coffin Ed's head, knocking him unconscious.

The other cop drew his pistol and took aim at the corpse. "One move out of you and I'll shoot," he said.

"He won't move, he's dead," Grave Digger said.

The cop looked sheepish. "I thought it was him you were fighting," he said.

"Turn me loose, goddammit," Grave Digger said to Haggerty.

"Well, hell," Haggerty said indignantly, releasing him. "You asked me to help. How the hell do I know what's going on?"

Grave Digger shook himself and looked at the third cop. "You didn't have to slug him," he said.

"I wasn't taking no chances," the cop said.

"Shut up and watch the Arab," Haggerty said.

The cop moved over and looked at the Arab. "He's dead too."

"Holy Mary, the plague," Haggerty said. "Look after that woman then."

Four more cops came running. At Haggerty's order, two turned toward the woman who'd been shot. She was lying deserted in the street.

"She's alive, just unconscious," the cop said.

"Leave her for the ambulance," Haggerty said.

"Who're you ordering about," the cop said. "We know our business."

"To hell with you," Haggerty said.

Grave Digger bent over Coffin Ed, lifted his head and put an open bottle of ammonia to his nose. Coffin Ed groaned.

A redfaced uniformed sergeant built like a General Sherman tank loomed above him.

"What happened here?" he asked.

Grave Digger looked up. "A rumpus broke and we lost our prisoner."

"Who shot your partner?"

"He's not shot, he's just knocked out."

"That's all right then. What's your prisoner look like?"

"Black man, about five-eleven, twenty-five to thirty years, one-seventy to one-eighty pounds, narrow face sloping down to chin, wearing light gray hat, dark gray hickory striped suit, white tab collar, red striped tie, beige chukker boots. He's handcuffed."

The sergeant's small china blue eyes went from the big white corpse to the bearded Arab corpse.

"What one did he kill?" he asked.

"The white man," Grave Digger said.

"That's all right, we'll get him," he said. Raising his voice, he called, "Professor!"

The corporal who'd stopped to light a cigaret said, "Yeah."

"Rope off this whole goddamned area," the sergeant said. "Don't let anybody out. We want a Harlem-dressed zulu. Killed a white man. Can't have gotten far 'cause he's hand-cuffed."

"We'll get 'im," the corporal said.

"Pick up all suspicious persons," the sergeant said.

"Right," the corporal said, taking the cops and hurrying off toward the other cops that were arriving.

"Who shot the Arab?" the sergeant asked.

"Ed shot him," Grave Digger said.

"That's all right then," the sergeant said. "We'll get your prisoner. I'm sending for the lieutenant and the medical examiner. Save the rest for them."

He turned and followed the corporal.

Coffin Ed stood up shakily. "You should have let me killed that son of a bitch, Digger," he said.

"Look at him," Grave Digger said, nodding toward the Arab's corpse.

Coffin Ed stared.

"I didn't even know I hit him," he said as though coming out of a daze. After a moment he added, "I can't feel sorry for him. I tell you, Digger, death is on any son of a bitch who tries to throw acid into my eyes again."

"Smell yourself, man," Grave Digger said.

Coffin Ed bent his head. The front of his dark wrinkled suit reeked with the scent of dime store perfume.

"That's what he threw. Just perfume," Grave Digger said. "I tried to warn you."

"I must not have heard you."

Grave Digger took a deep breath. "Goddammit, man, you got to control yourself."

"Well, Digger, a burnt child fears fire. Anybody who tries to throw anything at me when they're under arrest is apt to get shot."

Grave Digger said nothing.

"What happened to our prisoner?" Coffin Ed asked.

"He got away," Grave Digger said.

They turned in unison and surveyed the scene.

Patrol cars were arriving by the minute, erupting cops like an invasion. Others had formed blockades across Lenox Avenue at 128th and 126th Streets, and had blocked off 127th Street on both sides.

Most of the people had gotten off the street. Those that stayed were being arrested as suspicious persons. Several drivers trying to move their cars were protesting their innocence loudly.

The packed bars in the area were being rapidly sealed by the police. The windows of tenements were jammed with black faces and the exits blocked by police.

"They'll have to go through this jungle with a fine tooth comb," Grave Digger said. "With all these white cops about, any colored family might hide him."

"I want those gangster punks too," Coffin Ed said.

"Well, we'll just have to wait now for the men from homicide."

But Lieutenant Anderson arrived first, with the harness sergeant and Detective Haggerty latched on to him. The five of them stood in a circle in the car's headlights between the two corpses.

"All right, just give me the essential points first," Anderson said. "I put out the flash so I know the start. The man hadn't been killed when I got the first report."

"He was dead when we got here," Grave Digger said in a flat toneless voice. "We were the first here. The suspect was standing over the victim with the pistol in his hand—"

"Hold it," a new voice said.

A plainclothes lieutenant and sergeant from downtown homicide bureau came into the circle.

"These are the arresting officers," Anderson said.

"Where's the prisoner?" the homicide lieutenant asked.

"He got away," Grave Digger said.

"Okay, start over," the homicide lieutenant said.

Grave Digger gave him the first part, then went on:

"There were two friends with him and a group of teenage gangsters standing around the corpse. We disarmed the suspect and handcuffed him. When we started to frisk the gangster punks we had a rumble. Coffin Ed shot one. In the rumble the suspect got away."

"Now let's get this straight," said the lieutenant. "Were the teenagers implicated too?"

"No, we just wanted them as witnesses," Grave Digger said. "There's no doubt about the suspect."

"Right."

"When I got here Jones and Johnson were fighting, rolling all over the corpse," Haggerty said. "Jones was trying to disarm Johnson."

Lieutenant Anderson and the men from homicide looked at him, then turned to look at Grave Digger and Coffin Ed in turn.

"It was like this," Coffin Ed said. "One of the punks turned up his ass and farted toward me and—"

Anderson said, "Huh!" and the lieutenant said incredulously, "You killed a man for farting?"

"No, it was another punk he shot," Grave Digger said in his toneless voice. "One who threw perfume on him from a bottle. He thought it was acid the punk was throwing."

They looked at Coffin Ed's acid burnt face and looked away embarrassedly.

"The fellow who was killed is an A-rab," the sergeant said.

"That's just a disguise," Grave Digger said. "They belong to a group of teenage gangsters who call themselves Real Cool Moslems."

"Hah!" the homicide lieutenant said.

"Mostly they fight a teenage gang of Jews from the Bronx," Grave Digger elaborated. "We leave that to the welfare people."

The homicide sergeant stepped over to the Arab corpse and removed the turban and peeled off the artificial beard. The face of a colored youth with slick conked hair and beardless cheeks stared up. He dropped the disguises beside the corpse and sighed.

"Just a baby," he said.

For a moment no one spoke.

Then the homicide lieutenant asked, "You have the gun?"

Grave Digger took it from his pocket, holding the barrel by the thumb and first finger, and gave it to him.

The lieutenant took it in a handkerchief and examined it for some moments curiously. Then he wrapped it in his handkerchief and slipped it into his coat pocket.

"Had you questioned the suspect?" he asked.

"We hadn't got to it," Grave Digger said. "All we know is the homicide grew out of a rumpus at the Dew Drop Inn."

"That's a bistro a couple of blocks up the street," Anderson said. "They had a cutting there a short time earlier."

"It's been a hot time in the old town tonight," Haggerty said.

The lieutenant raised his brows enquiringly at Lieutenant Anderson.

"Suppose you go to work on that angle, Haggerty," Anderson said. "Look into that cutting. Find out how it ties in."

"We figure on doing that ourselves," Grave Digger said.

"Let him go on and get started," Anderson said.

"Right-o," Haggerty said. "I'm the man for the cutting."

Everybody looked at him. He left.

The homicide lieutenant said, "Well, let's take a look at the stiffs."

He gave each a cursory examination. The teenager was shot once in the heart.

"Nothing to do with them but wait for the coroner," he said.

They looked at the unconscious woman.

"Shot in the thigh, high up," the homicide sergeant said. "Loss of blood but not fatal—I don't think."

"The ambulance will be here any minute," Anderson said.

"How did she get shot?" the homicide lieutenant asked.

"Ed shot at the gangster twice," Grave Digger said. "It must have been then."

"Right."

No one looked at Coffin Ed. Instead, they made a pretence of examining the area.

Anderson shook his head. "It's going to be a hell of a job finding your prisoner in this dense slum," he said.

"There isn't any need," the homicide lieutenant said. "If this was the pistol he had, he's as innocent as you and me. This pistol won't kill anyone." He took the pistol from his pocket and unwrapped it. "This is a .37 calibre blank pistol. The only bullets made to fit it are blanks and they can't be tampered with enough to kill a man. And it hasn't been made over into a zip gun."

They stared at him as though stupefied.

"Well," Lieutenant Anderson said at last. "That tears it."

4.

THERE WAS a rusty sheet-iron gate in the concrete wall between the small back courts. The gang leader unlocked it with his own key. The gate opened silently on oiled hinges.

He went ahead.

"March!" the henchman with the knife ordered, prodding Sonny.

Sonny marched.

The other henchman kept the noose around his neck like a dog chain.

When they'd passed through, the leader closed and locked the gate.

One of the henchmen said, "You reckon Caleb is bad hurt?"

"Shut up talking in front of the captive," the leader said. "Ain't you got no better sense than that."

The broken concrete paving was strewn with broken glass, bottles, rags and divers objects thrown from the back windows; a rusty bed spring, a cotton mattress with a big hole burnt in the middle, several worn out automobile tires, and the half dried carcass of a black cat with its left hind foot missing and its eyes eaten out by rats.

They picked their way through the debris carefully. Sonny

bumped into a loose stack of garbage cans. One fell with a loud clatter. A sudden putrid stink arose.

"Goddammit, look out!" the leader said. "Watch where you're going."

"Aw, man, ain't nobody thinking about us back here," Choo-Choo said.

"Don't call me *man*," the leader said.

"Sheik then."

"What you jokers gonna do with me?" Sonny asked.

His weed jag was gone; he felt weak-kneed and hungry; his mouth tasted brackish and his stomach was knotted with fear.

"We're going to sell you to the Jews," Choo-Choo said.

"You ain't fooling me, I know you ain't no A-rabs," Sonny said.

"We're going to hide you from the police," Sheik said.

"I ain't done nothing," Sonny said.

Sheik stopped still and they all turned and looked at Sonny. His eyes were white halfmoons in the dark.

"All right then, if you ain't done nothing we'll turn you back to the cops," Sheik said.

"Naw, wait a minute, I just want to know where you're taking me."

"We're taking you home with us."

"Well that's all right then."

There was no back door from the hall as in the other tenement. Decayed concrete stairs led down to a basement door. Sheik produced a key on his ring for that one also. They entered a dark passage. Foul water stood on the broken pavement. The air smelled like molded rags and stale sewer pipes. They had to remove their smoked glasses in order to see.

Halfway along, feeble yellow light slanted from an open door. They entered a small filthy room.

A sick man clad in long cotton drawers lay beneath a ragged horse blanket on a filthy pallet with burlap sacks.

"You got anything for old Badeye," he said in a whining voice.

"We got you a fine black gal," Choo-Choo said.

The old man raised up on his elbows. "Whar she at?"

"Don't tease him," Inky said.

"Lie down and shut," Sheik said. "I told you before we

wouldn't have nothing for you tonight." Then to his hench-men, "Come on, you jokers, hurry up."

They began stripping off their disguises. Beneath their white robes they wore sweat shirts and black slacks. The beards were put on with makeup gum.

Without their disguises they looked like three high school students.

Sheik was a tall yellow boy with strange yellow eyes and reddish kinky hair. He had the broad-shouldered, trim-waisted figure of an athlete. His face was broad, his nose flat with wide, flaring nostrils, and his skin freckled. He looked disagreeable.

Choo-Choo was shorter, thicker and darker, with the short-cropped egg-shaped head and flat, mobile face of the natural born joker. He was bowlegged and pigeon-toed but fast on his feet.

Inky was an inconspicuous boy of medium size, with a mild, submissive manner, and black as the ace of spades.

"Where's the gun?" Choo-Choo asked when he didn't see it stuck in Sheik's belt.

"I slipped it to Bones."

"What's he going to do with it?"

"Shut up and quit questioning what I do."

"Where you reckon they all went to, Sheik?" Inky asked, trying to be peacemaker.

"They went home if they got sense," Sheik said.

The old man on the pallet watched them fold their disguises into small packages.

"Not even a little taste of King Kong," he whined.

"Naw, nothing!" Sheik said.

The old man raised up on his elbows. "What do you mean, naw? I'll throw you out of here. I'se the janitor. I'll take my keys away from you. I'll—"

"Shut your mouth before I shut it and if any cops come messing around down here you'd better keep it shut too. I'll have something for you tomorrow."

"Tomorrow? A bottle?"

"Yeah, a whole bottle."

The old man lay back, mollified.

"Come on," Sheik said to the others.

As they were leaving he snatched a ragged army overcoat from a nail on the door without the janitor noticing. He stopped Sonny in the passage and took the noose from about his neck, then looped the over coat overtop the handcuffs. It looked as though Sonny were merely carrying an overcoat with both hands.

"Now nobody'll see those cuffs," Sheik said. Turning to Inky, he said, "You go up first and see how it looks. If you think we can get by the cops without being stopped, give us the high sign."

Inky went up the rotten wooden stairs and through the doorway to the ground floor hall. After a minute he opened the door and beckoned.

They went up in single file.

Strangers who'd ducked into the building to escape the shooting were held there by two uniformed cops blocking the outside doorway. No one paid any attention to Sonny and the three gangsters. They kept on up to the top floor.

Sheik unlocked a door with another key on his ring, and led the way into a kitchen.

An old colored woman clad in a faded blue Mother Hub-bard with darker blue patches sat in a rocking chair by a coal burning kitchen stove, darning a threadbare man's woolen sock on a wooden egg and smoking a corn cob pipe.

"Is that you, Caleb?" she asked, looking over a pair of ancient steel-rimmed spectacles.

"It's just me and Choo-Choo and Inky," Sheik said.

"Oh, it's you, Samson." The note of expectancy in her voice died to disappointment. "Whar's Caleb?"

"He went to work downtown in a bowling alley, Granny. Setting up pins," Sheik said.

"Lord, that chile is always out working at night," she said with a sigh. "I sho hope God he ain't getting into no trouble with all this night work, 'cause his old Granny is too old to watch over him as a mammy would."

She was so old the color had faded from her dark brown skin in spots like the skin of a dried speckled pea, and her once-brown eyes had turned milky blue. Her bony cranium was bald at the front and over the ears and the speckled skin was taut against the skull. What remained of her short gray hair was gathered into a small tight ball at back. The outline of each fingerbone plying the darning needle was plainly visible through the transparent parchment-like skin.

"He ain't getting in to no trouble," Sheik said.

Inky and Choo-Choo pushed Sonny into the kitchen and closed the door.

Granny peered over her spectacles at Sonny. "I don't know this boy. Is he a friend of Caleb's too."

"He's the fellow Caleb is taking his place," Sheik said. "He hurt his hands."

She pursed her lips. "There's so many of you boys coming and going in here all the time I sho hope you ain't getting into no mischief. And this new boy looks older than you others is."

"You worry too much," Sheik said harshly.

"Hannh?"

"We're going on to our room," Sheik said. "Don't wait up for Caleb. He's going to be late."

"Hannh?"

"Come on," Sheik said. "She ain't hearing no more."

It was a shotgun flat, one room opening to the other. The next room contained two small white enameled iron beds where Caleb and his grandmother slept, and a small potbellied stove on a tin mat in one corner. A table held a pitcher and washbowl; there was a small dimestore mirror atop a chest of drawers. Like in the kitchen, everything was spotlessly clean.

"Give me your things and watch out for Granny," Sheik said, taking their bundled-up disguises.

Choo-Choo bent his head to the keyhole.

Sheik unlocked a large old cedar chest with another key from his ring and stored their bundles beneath layers of old blankets and house furnishings. It was Granny's hope chest where she stored things given her by the white folks she worked for to give to Caleb when he got married. Sheik locked the chest and unlocked the door to the next room. They followed him and he locked the door behind them.

It was the room he and Choo-Choo rented. There was a double bed where he and Choo-Choo slept, chest of drawers and mirror, pitcher and bowl on the table, as in the other room. The corner was curtained off with calico for a closet. But a lot of junk lay around and it wasn't as clean.

A narrow window opened to the platform of the red-painted iron fire escape that ran down the front of the building. It was protected by an iron grill closed by a padlock.

Sheik unlocked the grill and stepped out on the fire escape. "Look at this," he said.

Choo-Choo joined him; Inky and Sonny squeezed into the window.

"Watch the captive, Inky," Sheik said.

"I ain't no captive," Sonny said.

"Just look," Sheik said, pointing toward the street.

Below, on the broad avenue, red-eyed prowl cars were scattered thickly like monster ants about an anthill. Three ambulances were threading through the maze, two police hearses, and cars from the police commissioner's office and the medical examiner's office. Uniformed cops and men in plain clothes were coming and going in every direction.

"The men from Mars," Sheik said. "The big dragnet. What you think about that, Choo-Choo?"

Choo-Choo was busy counting.

The lower landings and stairs of the fire escape were packed with other colored people watching the show. Every front window on both sides of the street as far as the eye could see was jammed with black heads.

"I counted thirty-one prowl cars," Choo-Choo said. "That's more than was up on Eighth Avenue when Coffin Ed got that acid throwed in his eyes."

"They're shaking down the buildings one by one," Sheik said.

"What we're going to do with our captive?" Choo-Choo asked.

"We got to get the cuffs off first. Maybe we can hide him up in the pigeon's roost."

"Leave the cuffs on him."

"Can't do that. We got to get ready for the shakedown."

He and Choo-Choo stepped back into the room. He took Sonny by the arm, and pointed toward the street.

"They're looking for you, man."

Sonny's black face began graying again.

"I ain't done nothing. That wasn't a real pistol I had. That was a blank gun."

The three of them stared at him disbelievingly.

"Yeah, that ain't what they think," Choo-Choo said.

Sheik was staring at Sonny with a strange expression. "You sure, man?" he asked tensely.

"Sure I'm sure. It wouldn't shoot nothing but .37 calibre blanks."

"Then it wasn't you who shot the big gray stud?"

"That's what I been telling you. I couldn't have shot him."

A change came over Sheik. His flat freckled yellow face took on a brutal look. He hunched his shoulders, trying to look dangerous and important.

"The cops are trying to frame you, man," he said. "We got to hide you now for sure."

"What you doing with a gun that don't shoot bullets?" Choo-Choo asked.

"I keep it in my shine parlor as a gag is all," Sonny said.

Choo-Choo snapped his fingers. "I know you. You're the joker what works in that shoe shine parlor beside the Savoy."

"It's my own shoe shine parlor."

"How much marijuana you got stashed there?"

"I don't handle it."

"Sheik, this joker's a square."

"Cut the gab," Sheik said. "Let's get these handcuffs off the captive."

He tried keys and lockpicks but he couldn't get them open. So he gave Inky a triangle file and said, "Try filing the chain in two. You and him sit on the bed." Then to Sonny, "What's your name, man?"

"Aesop Pickens but people mostly call me Sonny."

"All right then, Sonny."

They heard a girl's voice talking to Granny and listened silently to rubbersoled shoes crossing the other room.

A single rap, then three quickly, then another single rap sounded on the door.

"Gaza," Sheik said with his mouth against the panel.

"Suez," a girl's voice replied.

Sheik unlocked the door.

A girl entered and he locked the door behind her.

She was a tall sepia-colored girl with short black curls, wearing a black turtleneck sweater, plaid skirt, bobby sox, and white buckskin shoes. She had a snub nose, wide mouth, full lips, even white teeth, and wide-set brown eyes fringed with long black lashes.

She looked about sixteen years old, and was breathless with excitement.

Sonny stared at her.

"Hell, it's just Sissie. I thought it was Bones with the gun," Choo-Choo said.

"Stop beefing about the gun. It's safe with Bones. The cops ain't going to shake down no garbage collector's house. His old man works for the city same as they do."

"What's this about Bones and the gun?" Sissie asked.

"Sheik's got—"

"It's none of Sissie's business," Sheik cut him off.

"Somebody said an Arab had been shot and at first I thought it was you," Sissie said.

"You hoped it was me," Sheik said.

She turned away, blushing.

"Don't look at me," Choo-Choo said to Sheik. "You tell her. She's your girl."

"It was Caleb," Sheik said.

"Caleb! Jesus!" Sissie dropped onto the bed beside Sonny. She looked stunned. "Jesus! Poor little Caleb. What will Granny do?"

"What the hell can she do," Sheik said brutally. "Raise him from the dead?"

"Does she know?"

"Does it look like she knows?"

"Jesus! Poor little Caleb. What did he do?"

"I gave old Coffin Ed the stink gun and—" Choo-Choo began.

"You didn't!" she exclaimed.

"The hell I didn't."

"What did Caleb do?"

"He threw perfume over the monster. It's the Moslem salute for cops. I told you about it before. But the monster must have thought Cal was throwing some more acid into his eyes. He blasted so fast we couldn't tell him any better."

"Jesus!"

"Where's Sugartit?" Sheik asked.

"At home. She didn't come in to town tonight. I phoned her and she said she was sick."

"Yeah. Did you have any trouble getting in here?"

"No. I told the cops at the door that I lived here."

They heard the signal rapped on the door.

Sissie gasped.

Sheik looked at her suspiciously. "What the hell's the matter with you?" he asked.

"Nothing."

He hesitated before opening the door. "You ain't expecting nobody?"

"Me? No. Who could I expect?"

"You're acting mighty funny."

"I'm just nervous."

The signal was rapped again.

Sheik stepped to the door and said, "Gaza."

"Suez," a girl's lilting voice replied.

Sheik gave Sissie a threatening look as he unlocked the door.

A small-boned chocolate-brown girl dressed like Sissie slipped hurriedly into the room.

At sight of Sissie she stopped and said, "Oh!" in a guilty tone of voice.

Sheik looked from one to the other. "I thought you said she was at home," he accused Sissie.

"I thought she was," Sissie said.

He turned his gaze on Sugartit. "What the hell's the matter with you? What the hell's going on here?"

"A Moslem's been killed and I thought it was you," she said.

"All you little bitches were hoping it was me," he said.

She had sloe eyes with long black lashes which looked secretive. She threw a quick defiant look at Sissie and said, "Don't include me in that."

"Did you tell Granny?" Sheik asked.

"Of course not."

"It was your lover, Caleb," Sheik said brutally.

She gave a shriek and charged at Sheik, clawing and kicking.

"You dirty bastard!" she cried. "You're always picking at me."

Sissie pulled her off. "Shut up and keep your mouth shut," she said tightly.

"You tell her," Sheik said.

"It was Caleb all right," Sissie said.

"Caleb!" Sugartit screamed and flung herself face-downward across the bed. She was up in a flash, hurling accusations at Sheik. "You did it. You got him killed. On account of me. 'Cause he had the best go and you couldn't get me to do what you made Sissie do."

"That's a lie," Sissie said.

"Caleb!" Sugartit screamed at the top of her voice.

"Shut up, Granny will hear you," Choo-Choo said.

"Granny! Caleb's dead! Sheik killed him!" she screamed again.

"Stop her," Sheik commanded Sissie. "She's getting hysterical and I don't want to have to hurt her."

Sissie clutched her from behind, put one hand over her mouth and twisted her arm behind her back with the other.

Sugartit looked furiously at Sheik overtop Sissie's hand.

"Granny can't hear," Inky said.

"The hell she can't," Choo-Choo said. "She can hear when she wants to."

"Let me go!" Sugartit mumbled and bit Sissie's hand.

"Stop that!" Sissie said.

"I'm going to him," Sugartit mumbled. "I love him. You can't stop me. I'm going to find out who shot him."

"Your old man shot him," Sheik said brutally. "The monster, Coffin Ed."

"Did I hear some one calling Caleb?" Granny asked from the other side of the door.

Sheik closed his hands quickly about Sugartit's throat and choked her into silence.

"Naw, Granny," he called. "It's just these silly girls arguing about their cubebs."

"Hannh?"

"Cubebs!" Sheik shouted.

"You chillen make so much racket a body can't hear herself think," she muttered.

They heard her shuffling back to the kitchen.

"Jesus, she's sitting up waiting for him," Sissie said.

Sheik and Choo-Choo exchanged glances.

"She don't even know what's happening in the street," Choo-Choo said.

Sheik took his hands from about Sugartit's throat.

5.

"How soon can you find out what he was killed with?" the chief of police asked.

"He was killed with a bullet, naturally," the assistant Medical Examiner said.

"You're not funny," the chief said. "I mean what calibre bullet."

His brogue had begun thickening and the cops who knew him best began getting nervous.

The assistant M.E. snapped his bag shut with a gesture of coyness and peered at the chief through magnified eyeballs encircled by black gutta-percha.

"That can't be known until after the autopsy. The bullet will have to be removed from the corpse's brain and subjected to tests—"

The chief listened in red-faced silence.

"I don't perform the autopsy. I'm the night man. I just pass on whether they're dead. I marked this one down as D.O.A. That means dead on arrival—my arrival, not his. You know more about whether he was dead on his arrival than I do, and more about how he was killed too."

"I asked you a civil question."

"I'm giving you a civil answer. Or, I should say, a civil service answer. The men who do the autopsy come on duty at nine o'clock. You ought to get your report by ten."

"That's all I asked you. Thanks. And damn little good that'll do me tonight. And by ten o'clock tomorrow morning the killer ought to be hell and gone to another part of the United States if he's got any sense."

"That's your affair, not mine. You can send the stiffs to the morgue when you've finished with them. I'm finished with them now. Good night, everyone."

No one answered. He left.

"I never knew why we needed a goddamned doctor to tell us whether a stiff was dead or not," the chief grumbled.

He was a big weatherbeaten man dressed in a lot of gold braid. He'd come up from the ranks. Everything about him from the arm full of gold hash stripes to the box-toed special made shoes said, "Flat foot." Behind his back the cops on Centre Street called him Spark Plug after the tender-footed nag in the comic strip, *Barney Google*.

He formed the hub of the group near the white man's corpse, which, by then, had grown to include, in addition to the principals, two deputy police commissioners, an inspector from homicide, and nameless uniformed lieutenants from adjoining precincts.

The deputy commissioners kept quiet. Only the commissioner himself had any authority over the chief, and he was at home in bed.

"This thing's hot as hell," the chief said at large. "Have we got our stories synchronized?"

Heads nodded.

"Come on then, Anderson, we'll meet the press," he said to the lieutenant in charge of the 126th Street precinct station.

They walked across the street to where a group of newsmen were being held in leash.

"Okay, men, you can get your pictures," he said.

Flashlights exploded in his face. Then the photographers converged on the corpses and left him facing the reporters.

"Here it is, men, the dead man has been identified by his papers as Ulysses Galen of New York City. He lives alone in a two-room suite at Hotel Lexington. We've checked that. They think his wife is dead. He's a sales manager for the King Cola Company. We've contacted their main office in Jersey City and learned that Harlem is in his district."

His thick brogue dripped like milk and honey through the

noisy night. Stylos scratched on pads. Flashbulbs went off around the corpses like an anti-aircraft barrage.

"A letter in his pocket from a Mrs. Helen Kruger, Wading River, Long Island, begins with, *Dear Dad*—. There's an unposted letter addressed to Homer Galen in the sixteen hundred block on Michigan Avenue in Chicago. That's a business district. We don't know whether Homer Galen is his son or another relation—"

"What about how he was killed?" a reporter interrupted.

"We know that he was shot in the back of the head by a Negro man named Sonny Pickens who operates a shoe shine parlor at 134th Street and Lenox Avenue. Several Negroes resented the victim drinking in a bar at 129th Street and Lenox—"

"What was he doing at a crumby bar up here in Harlem?"

"We haven't found that out yet. Probably just slumming. We know that the barman was cut trying to protect him from another colored assailant—"

"How did the shine assail him?"

"This is not funny, men. The first Negro attacked him with a knife—tried to attack him; the bartender saved him. After he left the bar Pickens followed him down the street and shot him in the back."

"You expect him to shoot a white man in the front."

"Two colored detectives from the 126th Street precinct station arrived on the scene in time to arrest Pickens virtually in the act of homicide. He still had the gun in his hand," the chief continued. "They handcuffed the prisoner and were in the act of bringing him in when he was snatched by a teenage Harlem gang who call themselves Real Cool Moslems."

Laughter burst from the reporters.

"What, no Mau-Maus?"

"It's not funny, men," the chief said. "One of them tried to throw acid in one of the detective's eyes."

The reporters were silenced.

"Another gangster threw acid in an officer's face up here about a year ago, wasn't it?" a reporter said. "He was a colored cop too. Johnson, Coffin Ed Johnson, they called him."

"It's the same officer," Anderson said, speaking for the first time.

"He must be a magnet," the reporter said.

"He's just tough and they're scared of him," Anderson said. "You've got to be tough to be a colored cop in Harlem. Unfortunately, colored people don't respect colored cops unless they're tough."

"He shot and killed the acid thrower," the chief said.

"You mean the first one or this one?" the reporter asked.

"This one, the Moslem," Anderson said.

"During the excitement, Pickens and the others escaped into the crowd," the chief said.

He turned and pointed toward a tenement building across the street. It looked stark naked and indescribably ugly in the glare of a dozen powerful spotlights. Uniformed police stood on the roof; others were coming and going through the entrance; still others stuck their heads from front windows to shout to other cops in the street. The other front windows were jammed with colored faces, looking like clusters of strange purple fruit in the stark white light.

"You can see for yourselves we're looking for the killer," the chief said. "We're going through those buildings with a fine tooth comb, one by one, flat by flat, room by room. We have the killer's description. He's wearing toolproof handcuffs. We should have him in custody before morning. He'll never get out of that dragnet."

"If he isn't already out," a reporter said.

"He's not out. We got here too soon for that."

The reporters began then to question him.

"Is Pickens one of the Real Cool Moslems?"

"We know he was rescued by seven of them. The eighth was killed."

"Was there any indication of robbery?"

"Not unless the victim had valuables we don't know anything about. His wallet, watch and rings are intact."

"Then what was the motive? A woman?"

"Well, hardly. He was an important man, well off financially. He didn't have to chase up here."

"It's been done before."

The chief spread his hands. "That's right. But in this case both negroes who attacked him did so because they resented his presence in a colored bar. They expressed their resentment in so many words. We have colored witnesses who heard them. Both negroes were intoxicated. The first had been drinking all evening. And Pickens had been smoking marijuana also."

"Okay, chief, it's your story," the dean of the police reporters said, calling a halt.

The chief and Anderson recrossed the street to the silent group.

"Did you get away with it?" one of the deputy commissioners asked.

"Goddammit, I had to tell them something," the chief said defensively. "Did you want me to tell them that a $15,000.00 a year white executive was shot to death on a Harlem street by a weedhead negro with a blank pistol who was immediately rescued by a gang of Harlem juvenile delinquents while all we got to show for the efforts of the whole goddamned police force is a dead adolescent calling himself a Real Cool Moslem?"

"Sho nuff cool now," Haggerty slipped in soto voce.

"You want us to become the laughing stock of the whole goddamned world," the chief continued, warming up to his subject. "You want it said the New York City police stood by helpless while a white man got himself killed in the middle of a crowded nigger street?"

"Well, didn't he?" the homicide lieutenant said.

"I wasn't accusing you," the deputy commissioner said apologetically.

"Pickens is the one it's rough on," Anderson said. "We've got him branded as a killer when we know he didn't do it."

"We don't know any such a goddamned thing," the chief said, turning purple with rage. "He might have rigged the blanks with bullets. It's been done, goddammit. And even if he didn't shoot him, he hadn't ought have been chasing him with a goddamned pistol that sounded as if it was firing bullets. We haven't got anybody to work on but him and it's just his black ass."

"Somebody shot him, and it wasn't with any blank gun," the homicide lieutenant said.

"Well, goddammit, go ahead and find out who did it!" the chief roared. "You're on homicide; that's your job."

"Why not one of the Moslems," the deputy commissioner offered helpfully. "They were on the scene, and these teenage gangsters always carry guns."

There was a moment of silence while they considered this.

"What do you think, Jones?" the chief asked Grave Digger. "Do you think there was any connection between Pickens and the Moslems."

"It's like I said before," Grave Digger said. "It didn't look to me like it. The way I figure it, those teenagers gathered about the corpse directly after the shooting, like everybody else was doing. And when Ed began shooting, they all ran together, like everybody else. I see no reason to believe that Pickens even knows them."

"That's what I gathered too," the chief said disappointedly.

"But this is Harlem," Grave Digger amended. "Nobody knows all the connections here."

"Futhermore, we don't have but one of them and that one isn't carrying any gun," Anderson said. "And you've heard Haggerty's report on the statement he took from the bartender and the manager of the Dew Drop Inn. Both Pickens and the other man resented Galen making passes at the colored women. And none of the Moslem gang were even there at the time."

"It could have been some other man feeling the same way," Grave Digger said. "He might have seen Pickens shooting at Galen and thought he'd get in a shot too."

"These people," the chief said. "Okay, Jones, you begin work on that angle and see what you can dig up. But keep it from the press."

As Grave Digger started to walk away, Coffin Ed fell in beside him.

"Not you, Johnson," the chief said. "You go home."

Both Grave Digger and Coffin Ed turned and faced the silence.

"Am I under suspension?" Coffin Ed asked in a grating voice.

"For the rest of the night anyway," the chief said. "I want you both to report to the commissioner's office at nine o'clock tomorrow morning. Jones, you go ahead with your investigation. You know Harlem, you know where to go, who to see." He turned to Anderson. "Have you got a man to work with him?"

"Haggerty," Anderson offered.

"I'll work alone," Grave Digger said.

"Don't take any chances," the chief said. "If you need help, just holler. Bear down hard. I don't give a goddamn how many heads you crack; I'll back you up. Just don't kill any more juveniles."

Grave Digger turned and walked with Coffin Ed to their car.

"Drop me at the Independent Subway," Coffin Ed said.

Both of them lived in Jamaica and rode the E-train when they didn't use the car.

"I saw it coming," Grave Digger said.

"If it had happened earlier I could have taken my daughter to a movie," Coffin Ed said. "I see so little of her it's getting so I hardly know her."

6.

"Let her loose now," Sheik said.

Sissie let her go.

"I'll kill him!" Sugartit raved in a choked voice. "I'll kill him for that!"

"Kill who?" Sheik asked, scowling at her.

"My father. I hate him. The ugly bastard. I'll steal his pistol and shoot him."

"Don't talk like that," Sissie said. "That's no way to talk about your father."

"I hate him, the dirty cop!"

Inky looked up from filing the handcuffs. Sonny stared at her.

"Shut up," Sissie said.

"Let her go ahead and croak him," Sheik said.

"Stop picking on her," Sissie said.

Choo-Choo said, "They won't do nothing to her for it. All she's got to say is her old man beat her all the time and they'll start crying and talking 'bout what a poor mistreated girl she is. They'll take one look at Coffin Ed and believe her."

"They'll give her a medal," Sheik said.

"Those old welfare biddies will find her a fine family to live with. She'll have everything she wants. She won't have to do nothing but eat and sleep and go to the movies and ride around in a big car," Choo-Choo elaborated.

Sugartit flung herself across the foot of the bed and burst into loud sobbing.

"It'll save us the trouble," Sheik said.

Sissie's eyes widened. "You wouldn't!" she said.

"You want to bet we wouldn't."

"If you keep on talking like that I'm going to quit."

Sheik gave her a threatening look. "Quit what?"

"Quit the Moslems."

"The only way you can quit the Moslems is like Caleb quit," Sheik said.

"If I'd ever thought that poor little Caleb—"

Sheik cut her off. "I'll kill you myself."

"Aw, Sheik, she don't mean nothing," Choo-Choo said nervously. "Why don't you light up a couple of sticks and let us Islamites fly to Mecca."

"And let the cops smell it when they shake us down and take us all in. Where are your brains at?"

"We can go up on the roof."

"There're cops on the roof too."

"On the fire escape then. We can close the window."

Sheik gave it grave consideration. "Okay, on the fire escape. I ain't got but two left and we got to get rid of them anyway."

"I'm going to look and see where the cops is at by now," Choo-Choo said, putting on his smoked glasses.

"Take those cheaters off," Sheik said. "You want the cops to identify you?"

"Aw hell, Sheik, they couldn't tell me from nobody else. Half the cats in Harlem wear their smoke cheaters all night long."

"Go 'head and take a gander at the avenue. We ain't got all night," Sheik said.

Choo-Choo started climbing out the window.

At that moment the links joining the handcuffs separated beneath Inky's file with a small clinking sound.

"Sheik, I've got 'em filed in two," Inky said triumphantly. "Let's see."

Sonny stood up and stretched his arms apart.

"Who's he?" Sissie asked as though she'd noticed him for the first time.

"He's our captive," Sheik said.

"I ain't no captive," Sonny said. "I just come with you 'cause you said you was gonna hide me."

Sissie looked bigeyed at the severed handcuffs dangling from his wrists.

"What did he do?" she asked.

"He's the gangster who killed the syndicate boss," Sheik said.

Sugartit stopped sobbing abruptly and rolled over and looked up at Sonny through wide wet eyes.

"Was that who he is?" Sissie asked in an awed tone. "The man who was killed, I mean."

"Sure, didn't you know," Sheik said.

"I done told you I didn't kill him," Sonny said.

"He claims he had a blank gun," Sheik said. "He's just trying to build up his defense. But the cops know better."

"It was a blank gun," Sonny said.

"What did he kill him for?" Sissie asked.

"They're having a gang war and he got assigned by the Brooklyn mob to make the hit."

"Oh, go to hell," Sissie said.

"I ain't killed nobody," Sonny said.

"Shut up," Sheik said. "Captives ain't allowed to talk."

"I'm getting tired of that stuff," Sonny said.

Sheik looked at him threateningly. "You want us to turn you over to the cops."

Sonny back-tracked quickly. "Naw, Sheik, but hell, ain't no need of taking advantage of me—"

Choo-Choo stuck his head in the window and cut him off, "Cops is out here like white on rice. Ain't nothing but cops."

"Where they at now?" Sheik asked.

"They're everywhere, but right now they's taking the house

two doors down. They got all kinds of spotlights turned on the front of the house and cops is walking around down in the street with machine guns. We better hurry if we're going to move the prisoner."

"Keep cool, fool," Sheik said. "Take a look at the roof."

"Praise Allah," Choo-Choo said, backing away on his hands and knees.

"Get off that coat and shirt," Sheik ordered Sonny.

When Sonny had stripped to his underwear shirt, Sheik looked at him and said, "Nigger, you sure are black. When you was a baby your mama must'a had to chalk your mouth to tell where to stick it."

"I ain't no blacker than Inky," Sonny said defensively.

"I ain't in that," Inky said.

Sheik grinned at him derisively. "You didn't have no trouble, did you, Inky? Your mama used luminous paint on you."

"Come on, man, I'm getting cold," Sonny said.

"Keep your pants on," Sheik said. "Ladies present."

He hung Sonny's coat with his own clothes on the wire line behind the curtain and threw the shirt in the corner. Then he tossed Sonny an old faded red shaker knit turtle-neck sweater.

"Pull the sleeve down over the irons and put on that there overcoat," he directed, indicating the old army coat he'd taken from the janitor.

"It's too hot," Sonny protested.

"You gonna do what I say, or do I have to slug you?"

Sonny put on the coat.

Sheik then took a pair of leather driving gauntlets from his pasteboard suitcase beneath the bed and handed them to Sonny too.

"What am I gonna do with these?" Sonny asked.

"Just put them on and shut up, fool," Sheik said.

He then took a long bamboo pole from behind the bed and began passing it through the window. On one end was attached a frayed felt pennant of the New York Giants baseball team.

Choo-Choo came down the fire escape in time to take the pole and lean it against the ladder.

"Ain't no cops on this roof yet but the roof down where they's shaking down is lousy with 'em," he reported.

His face was shiny with sweat and the whites of his eyes had begun to grow.

"Don't you chicken out on me now," Sheik said.

"I just needs some pot to steady my nerves."

"Okay, we're going to blow two now." Sheik turned to Sonny and said, "Outside, boy."

Sonny gave him a look, hesitated, then climbed out on the fire escape landing.

"Let me come too," Sissie said.

Sugartit sat up with sudden interest and pulled down her skirt.

"I want both you little jailbaits to stay right here in this room and don't move," Sheik ordered in a hard voice, then turned to Inky, "You come on, Inky, I'm gonna need you."

Inky joined the others on the fire escape. Sheik came last and closed the window. They squatted in a circle. The landing was crowded.

Sheik took two limp cigarets from the roll of his sweatshirt and stuck them into his mouth.

"Bombers!" Choo-Choo exclaimed. "You've been holding out on us."

"Give me some fire and less of your lip," Sheik said.

Choo-Choo flipped a dollar lighter and lit both cigarets. Sheik sucked the smoke deep into his lungs, then he passed one of the sticks to Inky.

"You and Choo-Choo take halvers and me and the captive will split this one."

Sonny raised both gloved hands in a pushing gesture. "Pass me. That gage done got me into more trouble now than I can get out of."

"You're chicken," Sheik said contemptuously, sucking another puff. He swallowed back the smoke each time it started up from his lungs. His face swelled and began darkening with blood as the drug took hold. His eyes became dilated and his nostrils flared.

"Man, if I had my heater I bet I could shoot that sergeant down there dead between the eyes," he said.

The marijuana cigaret was stuck to his bottom lip and dangled up and down when he talked.

"What I'd rather have me is one of those hard-shooting

long barrelled thirty-eights like Grave Digger and Coffin Ed have got," Choo-Choo said. "Them heaters can kill a rock. Only I'd want me a silencer on it and I could sit here and pick off any mother-raper I wanted. But I wouldn't shoot nobody unless he was a big shot or the chief of police or somebody like that."

"You're talking about rathers, what you'd rather have; me, I'm talking about facts," Sheik said, the cigaret dangling from his lips.

"What you're talking about will get you burnt up in Sing-Sing if you don't watch out," Choo-Choo said.

"What you mean!" Sheik said, jumping to his feet threateningly. "You're going to make me throw your ass off this fire escape."

Choo-Choo jumped to his feet too and backed against the rail. "Throw whose ass off where. This ain't Inky you're talking to. My ass ain't made of chicken feathers."

Inky scrambled to his feet in between them. "What about the captive, Sheik," he asked in alarm.

"Damn the captive!" Sheik raved and whipped out a bone-handled knife, shaking open the six inch blade with the same motion.

"Don't cut 'im!" Inky cried.

He knocked Inky into the iron steps with a backhanded slap and grabbed a handful of Choo-Choo's sweatshirt collar.

"You blab and I'll cut your mother-raping throat," he said.

Violence surged through him like runaway blood.

Choo-Choo's eyes turned three-quarters white and sweat popped out on his dark brown skin like a fever breaking.

"I didn't mean nothing, Sheik," he whined desperately, talking low. "You know I didn't mean nothing. A man can talk 'bout his rathers, can't he?"

The violence receded but Sheik was still gripped in a murderous compulsion.

"If I thought you'd pigeon I'd kill you."

"You know I ain't gonna pigeon, Sheik. You know me better than that."

Sheik let go his collar. Choo-Choo took a deep sighing breath.

Inky straightened up and rubbed his bruised shin. "You done made me lose the stick," he complained.

"Hell with the stick," Sheik said.

"That's what I mean," Sonny said. "This here gage they sells now will make you cut your own mama's throat. They must be mixing it with loco weed or somethin'."

"Shut up!" Sheik said, still holding the open knife in his hand. "I ain't gonna tell you no more."

Sonny cast a look at the knife and said, "I ain't saying nothing."

"You better not," Sheik said. Then he turned to Inky and said, "Inky, you take the captive up on the roof and you and him start flying Caleb's pigeons. You, Sonny, when the cops come you tell them your name is Caleb Bowee and you're just trying to teach your pigeons how to fly at night. You got that."

"Yeah," Sonny said skeptically.

"You know how to make pigeons fly?"

Sonny hesitated. "Chunk rocks at 'em?"

"Hell, nigger, your brain ain't big as a mustard seed. You can't chunk no rocks up there with all these cops about. What you got to do is take this pole and wave the end with the flag at 'em every time they try to light."

Sonny looked at the bamboo pole skeptically. "S'posen they fly away and don't come back."

"They ain't going nowhere. They just fly in circles trying all the time to get back into the coop." Sheik doubled over suddenly and started laughing. "Pigeons ain't got no sense, man."

The rest of them just looked at him.

Finally Inky asked, "What you want me to do?"

Sheik straightened up quickly and stopped laughing. "You guard the captive and see that he don't escape."

"Oh!" Inky said. After a moment he asked, "What I'm gonna tell the cops when they ask me what I'm doin'."

"Hell, you tell the cops Caleb is teaching you how to train pigeons."

Inky bent over and started rubbing his shins again. Without looking up he said, "You reckon the cops gonna fall for that,

Sheik? You reckon they gonna be crazy enough to believe anybody's gonna be flying pigeons with all this going on all around here?"

"Hell, these is white cops," Sheik said contemptuously. "They believe spooks are crazy anyway. You and Sonny just act kind of simpleminded. They going to swallow it like it's chocolate ice cream. They ain't going to do nothing but kick you in the ass and laugh like hell about how crazy spooks are. They gonna go home and tell their old ladies and everybody they see about two simpleminded spooks up on the roof teaching pigeons how to fly at night all during the biggest dragnet they ever had in Harlem. You see if they don't."

Inky kept on rubbing his shin. "It ain't that I doubt you, Sheik, but s'posen they don't believe it."

"Goddammit, go ahead and do what I told you and don't stand there arguing with me," Sheik said, hit by another squall of fury. "I'd take me one look at you and this nigger here and I'd believe it myself, and I ain't even no gray cop."

Inky turned reluctantly and started up the stairs toward the roof. Sonny gave another sidelong look at Sheik's open knife and started to follow.

"Wait a minute, simple, don't forget the pole," Sheik said. "I've told you not to try chunking rocks at those pigeons. You might kill one and then you'd have to eat it." He doubled over laughing at his joke.

Sonny picked up the pole with a sober face and climbed slowly after Inky.

"Come on," Sheik said to Choo-Choo, "open the window and let's get back inside."

Before turning his back and bending to open the window, Choo-Choo said, "Listen, Sheik, I didn't mean nothing by that."

"Forget it," Sheik said.

Sissie and Sugartit were sitting silently side by side on the bed, looking frightened and dejected. Sugartit had stopped crying but her eyes were red and her cheeks stained.

"Jesus Christ, you'd think this is a funeral," Sheik said.

No one replied. Choo-Choo fidgeted from one foot to the other.

"I want you chicks to wipe those sad looks off your face,"

Sheik said. "We got to look like we're balling and ain't got a thing to worry about when the cops get here."

"You go ahead and ball by yourself," Sissie said.

Sheik lunged forward and slapped her over on her side.

She got up without a word and walked to the window.

"If you go out that window I'll throw you down on the street," Sheik threatened.

She stood looking out the window with her back turned and didn't answer.

Sugartit sat quietly on the edge of the bed and trembled.

"Hell," Sheik said disgustedly and flopped lengthwise on the bed behind Sugartit.

She got up and went to stand in the window beside Sissie.

"Come on, Choo-Choo, to hell with those bitches," Sheik said. "Let's decide what to do with the captive."

"Now you're getting down to the gritty," Choo-Choo said enthusiastically, straddling a chair. "You got any plans?"

"Sure. Give me a butt."

Choo-Choo fished two Camels from a squashed package in his sweatshirt roll and lit them, passing one to Sheik.

"This square weed on top of gage makes you crazy," he said.

"Man, my head already feels like it's going to pop open, it's so full of ideas," Sheik said. "If I had me a real mob like Dutch Schultz I could take over Harlem with the ideas I got. All I need is just the mob."

"Hell, you and me could do it alone," Choo-Choo said.

"We'd need some arms and stuff, some real factory-made heaters and a couple of machine guns and maybe some pineapples."

"If we croaked Grave Digger and the Monster we'd have two real cool heaters to start off with," Choo-Choo suggested.

"We ain't going to mess with those studs until after we're organized," Sheik said. "Then maybe we can import some talent to make the hit. But we'd need some dough."

"Hell, we can hold the prisoner for ransom," Choo-Choo said.

"Who'd ransom that chickenshit nigger," Sheik said. "I bet his own mama wouldn't even pay to get him back."

"He can ransom hisself," Choo-Choo said. "He got a shine parlor, ain't he. Shine parlors make good dough. Maybe he's got a chariot too."

"Hell, I knew all along he was valuable," Sheik said. "That's why I had us snatch him."

"We can take over his shine parlor," Choo-Choo said.

"I got some other plans too," Sheik said. "Maybe we can sell him to the Stars of David for some zip guns. They got lots of zip guns and they're scared to use them."

"We could do that or we could swap him to the Porto Rican Bandits for Burrhead. We promised Burrhead we'd pay his ransom and they been saying if we don't hurry up and get 'im they're gonna cut his throat."

"Let 'em cut the black mother-raper's throat," Sheik said. "That chicken-hearted bastard ain't no good to us."

"I tell you what, Sheik," Choo-Choo said exuberantly. "We could put him in a sack like them ancient cats like the Dutchman and them used to do and throw him into the Harlem River. I've always wanted to put some bastard into a sack."

"You know how to put a mother-raper into a sack?" Sheik asked.

"Sure, you—"

"Shut up, I'm gonna tell you how. You knock the mother-raper unconscious first; that's to keep him from jumping about. Then you put a noose with a slipknot 'round his neck. Then you double him up into a Z and tie the other end of the wire around his knees. Then when you put him in the gunny sack you got to be sure it's big enough to give him some space to move around in. When the mother-raper wakes up and tries to straighten out he chokes himself to death. Ain't nobody killed 'im. The mother-raper has just committed suicide." Sheik rolled over on the bed laughing.

"You got to tie his hands behind his back first," Choo-Choo said.

Sheik stopped laughing and his face became livid with fury. "Who don't know that, fool!" he shouted. " 'Course you got to tie his hands behind his back. You trying to tell me I don't know how to put a mother-raper into a sack. I'll put you into a sack."

"I know you know how, Sheik," Choo-Choo said hastily.

"I just didn't want you to forget nothing when we put the captive in a sack."

"I ain't going to forget nothing," Sheik said.

"When we gonna put him in a sack?" Choo-Choo asked. "I know where to find a sack."

"Okay, we'll put him in a sack just soon as the police finish here, then we take him down and leave him in the basement," Sheik said.

7.

GRAVE DIGGER flashed his badge at the two harness bulls guarding the door and pushed inside the Dew Drop Inn.

The joint was jammed with colored people who'd seen the big white man die, but nobody seemed to be worrying about it.

The juke box was giving out with a stomp version of *Big Legged Woman*. Saxophones were pleading; the horns were teasing; the bass was patting; the drums were chatting; the piano was catting, laying and playing the jive, and a husky female voice was shouting:

> *". . . you can feel my thigh*
> *but don't you feel up high."*

Happy-tail women were bouncing out their dresses on the high bar stools.

Grave Digger trod on the sawdust sprinkled over the bloodstains that wouldn't wash off and parked on the stool at the end of the bar.

Big Smiley was serving drinks with his left arm in a sling.

The white manager, with the sleeves of his tan silk shirt rolled up, was helping.

Big Smiley shuffled down the wet footing and showed Grave Digger most of his big yellow teeth.

"Is you drinking, chief, or just sitting and thinking?"

"How's the wing?" Grave Digger asked.

"Favorable. It wasn't cut deep enough to do no real damage."

The manager came down and said, "If I'd thought there was going to be any trouble I'd have called the police right away."

"What do you calculate as trouble in this joint?" Grave Digger asked.

The manager reddened. "I meant about the white man getting killed."

"Just what started all the trouble in here?"

"It wasn't exactly what you'd call trouble, chief," Big Smiley said. "It was only a drunk attacked one of my white customers with his chiv and naturally I had to protect my customer."

"What did he have against the white man?"

"Nothing, chief. Not a single thing. He was setting over there drinking one shot of rye after another and looking at the white man standing here tending to his own business. Then he gets red-eyed drunk and his evil tells him to get up and cut the man. That's all. And naturally I couldn't let him do that."

"He must have had some reason. You're not trying to tell me he got up and attacked the man without any reason whatever."

"Nawsuh, chief, I'll bet my life he ain't had no reason at all to wanta cut the man. You know how our folks is, chief; he was just one of those evil niggers that when they get drunk they start hating white folks and get to remembering all the bad things white folks have ever done to them. That's all. More than likely he was mad at some white man that done something bad to him twenty years ago down South and he just wanted to take it out on this white man in here. It's like I told that white detective who was in here, this white man was standing here at the bar by hisself and that nigger just figgered with all these colored folks in here he could cut him and get away with it."

"Maybe. What's his name?"

"I ain't never seen that nigger before tonight, chief; I don't know what is his name."

A customer called from up the bar, "Hey, boss, how about a little service up here."

"If you want me, Jones, just holler," the manager said, moving off to serve the customer.

"Yeah," Grave Digger said, then asked Big Smiley, "Who was the woman?"

"There she is," Big Smiley said, nodding toward a booth.

Grave Digger turned his head and scanned her.

The black lady in the pink jersey dress and red silk stockings was back in her original seat in a booth surrounded by three workers.

"It wasn't on account of her," Big Smiley added.

Grave Digger slid from his stool and went over to her booth and flashed his badge. "I want to talk to you."

She looked at the gold badge and complained, "Why don't you folks leave me alone. I done already told a white cop everything I know about that shooting, which ain't nothing."

"Come on, I'll buy you a drink," Grave Digger said.

"Well, in that case," she said and went with him to the bar.

At Grave Digger's order Big Smiley poured her a shot of gin grudgingly and Grave Digger said, "Fill it up."

Big Smiley filled the glass and stayed there to listen.

"How well did you know the white man?" Grave Digger asked the lady.

"I didn't know him at all. I'd just seen him around here once or twice."

"Doing what?"

"Just chasing."

"Alone?"

"Yeah."

"Did you see him pick up anyone?"

"Naw, he was one of those particular kind. He never saw nothing he liked."

"Who was the colored man who tried to cut him?"

"How the hell should I know?"

"He wasn't a relative of yours?"

"A relation of mine. I should hope not."

"Just exactly what did he say to the white man when he started to attack him?"

"I don't remember exactly; he just said something 'bout him messing around with his gal."

"That's the same thing the other man, Sonny Pickens, accused him of."

"I don't know nothing about that."

He thanked her and wrote down her name and address.

She went back to her seat.

He turned back to Big Smiley. "What did Pickens and the white man argue about?"

"They ain't had no argument, chief. Not in here. It wasn't on account of nothing that happened in here that he was shot."

"It was on account of something," Grave Digger said. "Robbery doesn't figure, and people in Harlem don't kill for revenge."

"Nawsuh, leastwise they don't shoot."

"More than likely they'll throw acid or hot lye," Grave Digger said.

"Nawsuh, not on no white gennelman."

"So what else is there left but a woman," Grave Digger said.

"Nawsuh," Big Smiley contradicted flatly. "You know better'n that, chief. A colored woman don't consider diddling with a white man as being unfaithful. They don't consider it no more than just working in service, only they is getting better paid and the work is less straining. 'Sides which, the hours is shorter. And they old men don't neither. Both she and her old man figger it's like finding money in the street. And I don't mean no cruisers neither; I means church people and christians and all the rest."

"How old are you, Smiley?" Grave Digger asked.

"I be forty-nine come December seventh."

"You're talking about old times, son. These young colored men don't go for that slavery time deal anymore."

"Shucks, chief, you just kidding. This is old Smiley. I got dirt on these women in Harlem ain't never been plowed. Shucks, you and me both can put our finger on high society colored ladies here who got their whole rep just by going with some big important white man. And their old men is cashing in on it too; makes them important too to have their old ladies going with some bigshot gray. Shucks, even a hard working nigger wouldn't shoot a white man if he come home and found him in bed with his old lady with his pants down. He might whup his old lady just to show her who was boss, after he done took the money 'way from her, but he wouldn't sure 'nough hurt her like he'd do if he caught her screwing some other nigger."

"I wouldn't bet on it," Grave Digger said.

"Have it your own way, chief, but I still think you're barking up the wrong tree. Lissen, the only way I figger a colored man in Harlem gonna kill a white man is in a fight. He'll draw his chiv if he getting his ass whupped and maybe stab him to death. But I'll bet my life ain't no nigger up here gonna shoot down no white man in cold blood—no important white gennelman like him."

"Would the killer have to know he was important?"

"He'd know it," Big Smiley said positively.

"You knew him," Grave Digger said.

"Nawsuh, not to say knew him. He come in here two or three times before but I didn't know his name."

"You expect me to believe he came in here two or three times and you didn't find out who he was?"

"I didn't mean exactly I didn't know his name," Big Smiley hemmed. "But I'se telling you, chief, ain't no leads 'round here, that's for sure."

"You're going to have to tell me more than that, son," Grave Digger said in a flat, toneless voice.

Big Smiley looked at him; then suddenly he leaned across the bar and said in a low voice, "Try at Bucky's, chief."

"Why Bucky's?"

"I seen him come in here once with a pimp what hangs 'round in Bucky's."

"What's his name?"

"I don't recollect his name, chief. They driv up in his car and just stopped for a minute like they was looking for somebody and went out and driv away."

"Don't play with me," Grave Digger said with a sudden show of anger. "This ain't the movies; this is real. A white man has been killed in Harlem and Harlem is my beat. I'll take you down to the station and turn a dozen white cops loose on you and they'll work you over until the black comes off."

"Name's Ready Belcher, chief, but I don't want nobody to know I told you," Big Smiley said in a whisper. "I don't want no trouble with that starker."

"Ready," Grave Digger said and got down from his stool.

He didn't know much about Ready other than he operated uptown on the swank side of Harlem above 145th Street which the residents called Washington Heights.

He drove up to the 154th Street precinct station at the corner of Amsterdam Avenue and asked for his friend, Bill Cresus. Bill was a colored detective on the vice squad. No one knew where Bill was at the time. He left word for Bill to contact him at Bucky's if he called within the hour. Then he got into his car and coasted down the sharp incline to St. Nicholas Avenue and turned south down the lesser incline past 149th Street.

Outwardly it was a quiet neighborhood of private houses and five and six story apartment buildings flanking the wide black paved street. But the houses had been split up into bed-size one room kitchenettes, renting for $25 weekly, at the disposal of frantic couples who wished to shack up for a season. And behind the respectable looking façades of the apartment buildings were the plush flesh cribs and poppy pads and circus tents of Harlem.

The excitement of the dragnet hadn't reached this far and the street was comparatively empty.

He coasted to a stop before a sedate basement entrance. Four steps below street level was a black door with a shiny brass knocker in the shape of three musical notes. Above it red neon lights spelled out the word B U C K Y ' S.

He felt strange to be alone. The last time had been when Coffin Ed was in the hospital after the acid throwing. The memory of it made his head tight with anger and it took a special effort to keep his temper under wraps.

He pushed and the door opened.

People sat at white-clothed tables beneath pink-shaded wall lights in a long narrow room, eating fried chicken daintily with their fingers. There was a white party of six, several colored couples, and two colored men with white women. They looked well-dressed and reasonably clean.

The walls behind them were covered with innumerable

pink-stained small pencil portraits of all the great and the near-great who had ever lived in Harlem. Musicians led nine to one.

The hat check girl stationed in a cubicle beside the entrance stuck out her hand with a supercilious look.

Grave Digger kept on his hat and strode down the narrow aisle between the tables.

A chubby pianist with shining black skin and a golden smile dressed in a tan tweed sport jacket and white silk sport shirt open at the throat sat at a baby grand piano wedged between the last table and the circular bar. Soft white light spilled on his partly bald head while he played nocturnes with a bedroom touch.

He gave Grave Digger an apprehensive look and got up and followed him to the semi-darkness of the bar.

"I hope you're not on business, Digger, I pay to keep this place off-limits for cops," he said in a fluttery voice.

Grave Digger's gaze circled the bar. Its high stools were inhabited by a big dark-haired white man; two slim young colored men; a short heavy-set white man with blond crew cut hair; two dark brown women dressed in white silk evening gowns, flanking a chocolate dandy in a box back double-breasted tuxedo sporting a shoe-string dubonet bow; and a high yellow waitress with a tin tray waiting to be served. It was presided over by another tall slim ebony young man.

"I'm just looking around, Bucky," Grave Digger said. "Just looking for a break."

"Many folks have found a break in here," Bucky said suggestively.

"I don't doubt it."

"But maybe that's not the kind of break you're looking for."

"I'm looking for a break on a case. An important white man was shot to death over on Lenox Avenue a short time ago."

Bucky gestured with lotioned hands. His manicured nails flashed in the dim light.

"What has that to do with us here? Nobody ever gets hurt in here. Everything is smooth and quiet. You can see for yourself. Genteel people dining in leisure. Fine food. Soft music.

Low lights and laughter. Doesn't look like business for the police in this respectable atmosphere."

In the pause following, one of the marcelled ebonies was heard saying in a lilting voice, "I positively did not even look at her man, and she upped and knocked me over the head with a whiskey bottle."

"These black bitches are so violent," his companion said.

"And strong, honey."

Grave Digger smiled sourly.

"The man who was killed was a patron of yours," he said. "Name of Ulysses Galen."

"My God, Digger, I don't know the names of all the ofays who come into my place," Bucky said. "I just play for them and try to make them happy."

"I believe you," Grave Digger said. "Galen was seen about town with Ready. Does that stir your memory?"

"Ready!" Bucky exclaimed innocently. "He hardly ever comes in here. Who gave you that notion?"

"The hell he doesn't," Grave Digger said. "He panders out of here."

"You hear that!" Bucky appealed to the barman in a shrill horrified voice, then caught himself as the silence from the diners reached his sensitive ears. With hushed indignation he added, "This flatfoot comes in here and accuses me of harboring panderers."

"A little bit of that goes a long way, son," Grave Digger said in his flat toneless voice.

"Oh, that man's an ogre, Bucky," the barman said. "You go back to your entertaining and I'll see what he wants." He switched over to the bar, put his hands on his hips and looked down at Grave Digger with a haughty air. "And just what can we do for you, you mean rude grumpy man."

The white men at the bar laughed.

Bucky turned and started off.

Grave Digger caught him by the arm and pulled him back. "Don't make me get rough, son," he warned.

"Don't you dare manhandle me," Bucky said in a low tense whisper, his whole chubby body quivering with indignation. "I don't have to take that from you. I'm covered."

The bartender backed away, shaking himself. "Don't let

him hurt Bucky," he appealed to the white men in a frightened voice.

"Maybe I can help you," the white man with the blond crew cut said to Grave Digger. "You're a detective, aren't you?"

"Yeah," Grave Digger said, holding on to Bucky. "A white man was killed in Harlem tonight and I'm looking for the killer."

The white man's eyebrows went up an inch.

"Do you expect to find him in here?"

"I'm following a lead, is all. The man has been seen with a pimp called Ready Belcher who hangs out here."

The white man's eyebrows subsided.

"Oh, Ready. I know him. But he's merely—"

Bucky cut him off, "You don't have to tell him anything, you're protected in here."

"Sure," the white man said. "That's what the officer is trying to do, protect us all."

"He's right," one of the evening gowned colored women said. "If Ready has killed some trick he was steering to Reba's the chair's too good for him."

"Shut your mouth, woman," the barman whispered fiercely.

The muscles in Grave Digger's face began to jump as he let go of Bucky and stood up with his heels hooked into the rungs of the barstool and leaned over the bar. He caught the barman by the front of his red silk shirt as he was trying to dance away. The shirt ripped down the seam with a ragged sound but enough held for him to jerk the barman close to the bar.

"You got too goddamned much to say, Tarbelle," he said in a thick cottony voice, and slapped the barman spinning across the circular enclosure with the palm of his open hand.

"He didn't have to do that," the first woman said.

Grave Digger turned on her and said thickly, "And you, little sister, you and me are going to see Reba."

"Reba!" the woman said. "Who's she?" Turning to her companion, she asked, "You know any Reba."

"Reba?" her companion replied. "Do I know anybody named Reba. Lord no."

Grave Digger stepped down from his high stool.

"Cut that Aunt Jemima routine and get up off your ass," he said thickly. "Or I'll take my pistol and break off your teeth."

The two white men stared at him as though at a dangerous animal escaped from the zoo.

"You mean that?" the woman said.

"I mean it," he said.

She scrunched from the stool and said, "Gimme my coat, Jule."

The chocolate dandy took a coat from the top of the juke box behind them.

"That's putting it on rather thick," the blond white man protested in a reasonable voice.

"I'm just a cop," Grave Digger said thickly. "If you white people insist on coming up to Harlem where you force colored people to live in vice-and-crime ridden slums, it's my job to see that you are safe."

The white man turned bright red.

8.

THE SERGEANT knocked at the door. He was flanked by two uniformed cops and a corporal.

There was another searching party led by another sergeant at the door across the hall.

Other cops were in the corridors all the way down. They were starting at the bottom, working up, and sealing off the area they'd covered.

"Come in," Granny called in a querulous voice. "The door ain't locked." She bit the stem of her corncob pipe with toothless gums.

The sergeant and his party entered the small kitchen. It was crowded.

At sight of the very old woman working innocently at her darning, the sergeant started to remove his cap, then remembered he was on duty and kept it on.

"You don't lock your door, grandma?" he observed.

Granny looked at the cops over the rims of her ancient spectacles and her old fingers went lax on the darning egg.

"Nawsuh, Ah ain't got nuthin' for nobody to steal and ain't nobody want nuthin' else from an old 'oman like me."

The sergeant's beady blue eyes scanned the kitchen.

"You keep this place mighty clean, grandma," he remarked in surprise.

"Yessuh, it don't kill a body to keep clean and my old missy used to always say de cleaness is next to the Goddess."

Her old milky eyes held a terrified question she couldn't ask and her thin old body began to tremble.

"You mean goodness," the sergeant said.

"Nawsuh, Ah means Goddess; Ah know what she said."

"She means cleanliness is next to Godliness," the corporal interposed.

"The professor," one of the cops said.

Granny pursed her lips. "Ah know what my missy said; Goddess she said."

"Were you in slavery?" the sergeant asked as though struck suddenly by the thought.

The others stared at her with sudden interest.

"Ah don't rightly know, suh. Ah 'spect so though."

"How old are you?"

Her lips moved soundlessly; she seemed to be trying to remember.

"She must be all of a hundred," the professor said.

She couldn't stop her body from trembling and slowly it got worse.

"What for you white 'licemen wants with me, suh?" she finally asked.

The sergeant noticed that she was trembling and said reassuringly, "We ain't after you, grandma; we're looking for an escaped prisoner and some teenage gangsters."

"Gangsters!"

Her spectacles slipped down on her nose and her hands shook as though she had the palsy.

"They belong to a gang in this neighborhood that calls itself Real Cool Moslems."

She went from terrified to scandalized. "We ain't no heathen in here, suh," she said indignantly. "We be Godfearing Christians."

The cops laughed.

"They're not real Moslems," the sergeant said. "They just call themselves that. One of them who's older than the rest, named Sonny Pickens, killed a white man outside on the street."

The darning dropped unnoticed from Granny's nerveless fingers. The corncob pipe wobbled in her puckered mouth; the professor looked at it with morbid fascination.

"A white man! Merciful hebens!" she exclaimed in a quavering voice. "What's this wicked world coming to?"

"Nobody knows," the sergeant said, then his manner changed abruptly. "Well, let's get down to business, grandma. What's your name?"

"Bowee, suh, but e'body calls me Granny."

"Bowee. How you spell that, grandma?"

"Ah don't rightly know, suh. Hit's just short for boll weevil. My old missy name me that. They say the boll weevil was mighty bad the year Ah was born."

"What about your husband, didn't he have a name?"

"Ah neber had no regular 'usban, suh. Just whosoever was thar."

"You got any children?"

"Jesus Christ, sarge," the professor said. "Her youngest child would be sixty years old."

The two cops laughed; the sergeant reddened sheepishly.

"Who lives here with you, Granny?" the sergeant continued.

Her bony frame stiffened beneath her faded Mother Hubbard. The corncob pipe fell into her lap and rolled unnoticed to the floor. The cops came to attention.

"Just me and mah grandchile, Caleb, suh," she said in a forced voice. "And Ah rents a room to two workin' boys; but they be good boys and don't neber bother nobody."

The cops grew sudden speculative looks.

"Now this grandchild, Caleb, grandma—" the sergeant began cunningly.

"He might be mah great-grandchile, suh," she interrupted. He frowned. "Great, then. Where is he now?"

"You mean right now, suh?"

"Yeah, grandma, right this minute."

"He at work in a bowling alley downtown, suh."

"How long has he been at work?"

"He left right after supper, suh. We gennally eats supper at six 'clock."

"And he has a regular job in this bowling alley?"

"Nawsuh, hit's just for t'night, suh. He goes to school— Ah don't rightly 'member the number of his new P.S."

"Where is this bowling alley where he's working tonight?"

"Ah don't know, suh. Ah guess youall 'ill have to ast Samson. He one of mah roomers."

"Samson, yeah." The sergeant stored it in his memory. "And you haven't seen Caleb since supper—about seven o'clock, say?"

"Ah don't know what time it was but it war right after supper."

"And when he left here he went directly to work?"

"Yassuh, you find him right dar on the job. He a good boy and always mind me what Ah say."

"And your roomers, where are they?"

"They is in they room, suh. Hit's in the front. They got visitors with 'em."

"Visitors?"

"Gals."

"Oh!" Then to his assistants he said, "Come on."

They went through the middle room like hounds on a hot scent. The sergeant tried the handle to the front room door without knocking, found it locked and hammered angrily.

"Who's that?" Sheik asked.

"The police."

Sheik unlocked the door. The cops rushed in. Sheik's eyes glittered at them.

"What the hell you keep your door locked for?" the sergeant asked.

"We didn't want to be disturbed."

Four pairs of eyes quickly scanned the room.

Two teenage colored girls sat side by side on the bed, leafing through a colored picture magazine. Another youth stood looking out the open window at the excitement on the street.

"Who the hell you think you're kidding with this phony stage setting?" the sergeant roared.

"Not you, Ace," Sheik said flippantly.

The sergeant's hand flicked out like a whip, passing inches in front of Sheik's eyes.

Sheik jumped back as though he'd been scalded.

"Jagged to the gills," the sergeant said, looking minutely about the room. His eyes lit on Choo-Choo's half-smoked package of Camel's on the table. "Dump out those fags," he ordered a cop, watching Sheik's reaction. "Never mind," he added. "The bastard's got rid of them."

He closed in on Sheik like a prizefighter and stuck his red sweaty face within a few inches of Sheik's dry freckled face. His veined blue eyes bored into Sheik's pale yellow eyes.

"Where's that A-rab costume?" he asked in a browbeating voice.

"What Arab costume? Do I look like an A-rab to you?"

"You look like a two-bit punk to me. You got the eyes of a yellow cur."

"You ain't got no prizewinning eyes yourself."

"Don't give me none of your lip, punk; I'll knock out your teeth."

"I could knock out your teeth too if I had on a sergeant's uniform and three big flatfeet backing me up."

The cops stared at him from blank shuttered faces.

"What do they call you, Mo-hammed or Nasser?" the sergeant hammered.

"They call me by my name, Samson."

"Samson what?"

"Samson Hyers."

"Don't give me that crap; we know you're one of those Moslems."

"I ain't no Moslem, I'm a cannibal."

"Oh, so you think you're a comedian."

"You the one asking the funny questions."

"What's that other punk's name?"

"Ask him."

The sergeant slapped him with his open palm with such force it sounded like a .22 calibre shot.

Sheik reeled back from the impact of the slap but kept his

feet. Blood darkened his face to the color of beef liver, on which the imprint of the sergeant's hand glowed purple red. His pale yellow eyes looked wildcat crazy. But he kept his lip buttoned.

"When I ask you a question I want you to answer it," the sergeant said.

He didn't answer.

"You hear me?"

He still didn't answer.

The sergeant loomed in front of him with both fists cocked like red meataxes.

"I want an answer."

"Yeah, I hear you," Sheik muttered sullenly.

"Frisk him," the sergeant ordered the professor, then to the other two cops said, "You and Price start shaking down this room."

The professor set to work on Sheik methodically, as though searching for lice, while the other cops started dumping dresser drawers onto the table.

The sergeant left them and turned his attention to Choo-Choo.

"What kind of Moslem are you?"

Choo-Choo started grinning and fawning like the original Uncle Tom.

"I ain't no Moslem, boss, I'se just a plain old unholy roller."

"I guess your name is Delilah."

"He-he, nawsuh, boss, but you're warm. It's Justis Broome."

All three cops looked about and grinned, and the sergeant had to clamp his jaws to keep from grinning too.

"You know these Moslems?"

"What Moslems, boss?"

"These Harlem Moslems in this neighborhood."

"Nawsuh, boss, I don't know no Moslems in Harlem."

"You think I was born yesterday? They're a neighborhood gang. Every black son of a bitch in this neighborhood knows who they are."

"Everybody 'cept me, boss."

The sergeant's palm flew out and caught Choo-Choo unexpectedly on the mouth while it was still open in a grin. It didn't rock his short thick body but his eyes rolled back whitely in their sockets. He spit blood on the floor.

"Boss, suh, please be careful with my chops, they're tender."

"I'm getting damn tired of your lying."

"Boss, I swear 'fore God, if I knowed anything 'bout them Moslems you'd be the first one I'd tell it to."

"What do you do?"

"I works, boss, yessuh."

"Doing what?"

"I helps out."

"Helps out what? You want to lose some of your pearly teeth?"

"I helps out a man who writes numbers."

"What's his name?"

"His name?"

The sergeant cocked his fists.

"Oh, you mean his name, boss. Hit's Four-Four Row."

"You call that a name?"

"Yessuh, that's what they calls him."

"What does your buddy do?"

"The same thing," Sheik said.

The sergeant wheeled on him. "You keep quiet; when I want you I'll call you." Then he said to the professor, "Can't you keep that punk quiet?"

The professor unhooked his sap. "I'll quiet him."

"I don't want you to quiet him; just keep him quiet. I got some more questions for him." Then he turned back to Choo-Choo. "When do you punks work?"

"In the morning, boss. We got to get the numbers in by noon."

"What do you do the rest of the day?"

"Go 'round and pay off."

"What if there isn't any payoff?"

"Just go 'round."

"Where's your beat?"

" 'Round here."

"Goddammit, you mean to tell me you write numbers in

this neighborhood and you don't know anything about the Moslems?"

"I swear on my mother's grave, boss, I ain't never heard of no Moslems 'round here. They must not be in this neighborhood, boss."

"What time did you leave the house tonight?"

"I ain't never left it, boss. We come here right after we et supper and ain't been out since."

"Stop lying, I saw you both when you slipped back in here a half hour ago."

"Nawsuh, boss, you musta seen somebody what looks like us 'cause we been here all the time."

The sergeant crossed to the door and flung it open. "Hey, grandma!" he called.

"Hannh?" she answered querulously from the kitchen.

"How long have these boys been in their room?"

"Hannh?"

"You have to talk louder, she can't hear you," Sissie volunteered.

Sheik and Choo-Choo gave her threatening looks.

The sergeant crossed the middle room to the kitchen door.

"How long have your roomers been back from supper?" he roared.

She looked at him from uncomprehending eyes.

"Hannh?"

"She can't hear no more," Sissie called. "She gets that way sometime."

"Hell," the sergeant said disgustedly and stormed back to Choo-Choo. "Where'd you pick up these girls?"

"We didn't pick 'em up, boss; they come here by themselves."

"You're too Goddamned innocent to be alive," the sergeant said frustratedly, then turned to the professor. "What did you find on that punk?"

"This knife."

"Hell," the sergeant said. He took it and dropped it into his pocket without a glance. "Okay, fan this other punk—Justice."

"I'll do Justice," the professor punned.

The two cops crossed glances suggestively.

They had dumped out all the drawers and turned out all the boxes and pasteboard suitcases and now they were ready for the bed.

"You gals rise and shine," one said.

The girls got up and stood uncomfortably in the center of the room.

"Find anything?" the sergeant asked.

"Nothing that I'd care even to have in my dog house," the cop said.

The sergeant began on the girls. "What's your name?" he asked Sissie.

"Sissieratta Hamilton."

"Sissie-what?"

"Sissieratta."

"Where do you live, Sissie?"

"At 2702 Seventh Avenue with my aunt and uncle, Mr. and Mrs. Coolie Dunbar."

"Ummm," he said. "And yours?" he asked Sugartit.

"Evelyn Johnson."

"Where do you live, Eve?"

"In Jamaica with my parents, Mr. and Mrs. Edward Johnson."

"It's mighty late for you to be so far from home."

"I'm going to spend the night with Sissieratta."

"How long have you girls been here?" he asked of both.

"About half an hour, more or less," Sissie replied.

"Then you saw the shooting down on the street?"

"It was over when we got here."

"Where did you come from?"

"From my house."

"You don't know if these punks have been in all evening or not."

"They were here when we got here and they said they'd been waiting here since supper. We promised to come at eight but we had to stay help my aunty and we got here late."

"Sounds too good to be true," the sergeant commented.

The girls didn't reply.

The cops finished with the bed and the talkative one said, "Nothing but stink."

"Can that talk," the sergeant said. "Grandma's clean."

"These punks aren't."

The sergeant turned to the professor. "What's on Justice besides the blindfold?"

His joke laid an egg.

"Nothing but his black," the professor said.

His joke drew a laugh.

"What do you say, shall we run 'em in?" the sergeant asked.

"Why not," the professor said. "If we haven't got space in the bullpen for everybody we can put up tents."

The sergeant wheeled suddenly on Sheik as though he'd forgotten something.

"Where's Caleb?"

"Up on the roof tending his pigeons."

All four cops froze. They stared at Sheik with those blank shuttered looks.

Finally the sergeant said carefully, "His grandma said you told her he was working in a bowling alley downtown."

"We just told her that to keep her from worrying. She don't like for him to go up on the roof at night."

"If I find you punks are holding out on me, God help you," the sergeant said in a slow sincere voice.

"Go look then," Sheik said.

The sergeant nodded to the professor. The professor climbed out of the window into the bright glare of the spotlights and began ascending the fire escape.

"What's he doing with them at night?" the sergeant asked Sheik.

"I don't know. Trying to make them lay black eggs, I suppose."

"I'm going to take you down to the station and have a private talk with you, punk," the sergeant said. "You're one punk who needs talking to privately."

The professor came down from the roof and called through the window, "They're holding two coons up here beside a pigeon loft. They're waiting on you."

"Okay, I'm coming. You and Price hold these punks on ice," he directed the other cops and climbed out of the window behind the professor.

9.

"GET IN," Grave Digger said.

She pulled up the skirt of her evening gown, drew the black coat tight, and eased her jumbo hams onto the seat usually occupied by Coffin Ed.

Grave Digger went around on the other side and climbed beneath the wheel and waited.

"Does I just have to go along, honey," the woman said in a wheedling voice. "I can just as well tell you where she's at."

"That's what I'm waiting for."

"Well, why didn't you say so. She's in the Knickerbocker Apartments on 145th Street—the old Knickerbocker I mean. She on the sixth story, 669."

"Who is she?" Grave Digger asked, probing a little.

"Who she is? Just a landprop is all."

"That ain't what I mean."

"Oh, I know what you means. You means who is she. You means you don't know who Reba is, Digger?" She tried to sound jocular but unsuccessfully. "She the landprop what used to be old Cap Murphy's go-between 'fore he got sent up for taking all them bribes. It was in all the papers."

"That was ten years ago and they called her Sheba then," he said.

"Yare, that's right, but she changed her name after she got in that last shooting scrape. You musta 'member that. She caught the nigger with some chippie or 'nother and made him jump buck naked out the third story window. That wouldn't 'ave been so bad but she shot 'im through the head as he was going down. That was when she lived in the Valley. Since then she done come up here on the hill. 'Course it warn't nobody but her husband and she didn't get a day. But Reba always has been lucky that way."

He took a shot in the dark. "What would anybody shoot Galen for?"

She grew stiff with caution. "Who he?"

"You know damn well who he was. He's the man who was shot tonight."

"Nawsuh, I didn't know nothing 'bout that gennelman. I don't know why nobody would want to shoot him."

"You people give me a pain in the seat with all that ducking and dodging every time some one asks you a question. You act like you belong to a race of artful dodgers."

"You is asking me something I don't know nothing 'bout."

"Okay, get out."

She got out faster than she got in.

He drove down the hill of St. Nicholas Avenue and turned up the hill of 145th Street toward Convent Avenue.

On the lefthand corner, next to a new fourteen story apartment building erected by a white insurance company, was the *Brown Bomber Bar*, across from it *Big Crip's Bar*, on the righthand corner *Cohen's Drug Store* with its iron-grilled windows crammed with electric hair straightening irons, Hi-Life hair cream, Black & White bleaching cream, SSS and 666 blood tonics, Dr. Scholl's corn pads, men's and women's nylon head caps with chin straps to press the hair while sleeping, a bowl of blue stone good for body lice, tins of Sterno canned heat good for burning or drinking, Halloween post cards and all of the latest in enamelware hygiene utensils; across from it *Zazully's Delicatessen* with a white-lettered announcement on the plate glass window: WE HAVE FROZEN CHITTERLINGS AND OTHER HARD-TO-FIND DELICACIES.

Going up the hill from *Cohen's* was a green fronted Chinese restaurant with fly-specked yellow curtains called *The New Manchu*; the *Alabama-Georgia Bar*; a small wooden shack built out from a crumbling brick house bearing a wooden sign reading *Slam's Real Cool Shoe Shine Parlor* above the front window which was filled with glossy portraits of blues singers, band leaders and prize fighters; and a green basement door with the plaque, *S. Zucker, M.D.*

Grave Digger parked in front of a big frame house with peeling yellow paint which had been converted into offices, got out and walked next door to a six story rotten-brick tenement long overdue at the wreckers.

Three cars were parked at the curb in front; two with upstate New York plates and the other from Mid-Manhattan.

He pushed open a scaly door beneath the arch of a concrete block on which the word KNICKERBOCKER was embossed.

An old grayhaired man with a looselipped mouth in a splotched brown face sat in a motheaten red plush chair just inside the doorway to the semi-dark corridor. He drew back gnarled feet in felt bedroom slippers to keep them from being trodden on and looked Grave Digger over with dull satiated eyes.

"Evenin'," he said.

Grave Digger flung him a glance. "Evenin'."

"Fourth story on de right. Number 421," the old man informed him.

Grave Digger stopped. "That Reba's?"

"You don't want Reba's. You want Topsy's. Dat's 421."

"What's happening at Topsy's?"

"What always happen. Dat's where the trouble is."

"What kind of trouble?"

"Just general trouble. Fightin' an' cuttin'."

"I'm not looking for trouble. I'm looking for Reba's."

"You're the man, ain't you?"

"Yeah, I'm the man."

"Then you wants 421. I'se de janitor."

"If you're the janitor then you know Mr. Galen."

A veil fell over the old man's face. "Who he?"

"He's the big Greek man who goes up to Reba's."

"I don't know no Greeks, boss. Don't no white folks come in here. Nothin' but cullud folks. You'll find 'em all at Topsy's."

"He was killed over on Lenox tonight."

"Sho nuff?"

Grave Digger started off.

The old man called to him, "I guess you wonderin' why we got them big numbers on de doors."

Grave Digger paused. "All right, why?"

"They sounds good." The old man cackled.

Grave Digger walked up five flights of shaky wooden stairs, knocked on a red-painted door with a round glass peephole in the upper panel.

After an interval a heavy woman's voice asked, "Who's you?"

"I'm the Digger."

Bolts clicked and the door cracked a few inches on the

chain. A big dark silhouette loomed in the crack, outlined by blue light from behind.

"I didn't recognize you, Digger," a pleasant bass voice said. "Your hat shades your face. Long time no see."

"Unchain the door, Reba, before I shoot it off."

A deep bass laugh accompanied chain rattling and the door swung inward.

"Same old Digger, shoot first and talk later. Come on in, we're all colored folks in here."

He stepped into a blue-lit carpeted hall reeking with the smell of incense.

"You're sure."

She laughed again as she closed and bolted the door.

"Those are not folks, those are clients."

Then she turned casually to face him. "What's on your mind, honey?"

She was as tall as his six feet two, but half again as heavy, with snow white hair cut short as a man's and brushed straight back from her forehead. Her lips were painted carnation red and her eyelids silver but her smooth unlined jet black skin was untouched. She wore a black sequined evening gown with a red rose in the V of her mammoth bosom which was a lighter brown than her face. She looked like the last of the Amazons blackened by time.

"Where can we talk," Grave Digger said. "I don't want to strain you."

"You don't strain me, honey," she said, opening the first door to the right. "Come into the kitchen."

She put a bottle of bourbon and a siphon beside two tall glasses on the table and sat in a kitchen chair.

"Say when," she said as she started to pour.

"By me," Grave Digger said, pushing his hat to the back of his head and planting a foot on the adjoining chair.

She stopped pouring and put down the bottle.

"You go ahead," he said.

"I don't drink no more," she said. "I quit after I killed Sam."

He crossed his arms on his raised knee and leaned forward on them, looking at her.

"You used to wear a rosary," he said.

She smiled, showing gold crowns on her outside incisors.

"When I got religion I quit that too," she said.

"What religion did you get?"

"Just the faith, Digger, just the spirit."

"It lets you run this joint?"

"Why not. It's nature, just like eating. Nothing in my faith 'gainst eating. I just make it convenient and charge 'em for it."

"You'd better get a new steerer, the one downstairs is simpleminded."

Her big bass laugh rang out again. "He don't work for us; he does that on his own."

"Don't make this hard on yourself," he said. "This can be easy for us both."

She looked at him calmly. "I ain't got nothing to fear."

"When was the last time you saw Galen?"

"The big Greek? Been some time now, Digger. Three or four months. He don't come here no more."

"Why?"

"I don't let him."

"How come?"

"Be your age, Digger. This is a sporting house. If I don't let a white John with money come here, I must have good reasons. And if I want to keep my other white clients I'd better not say what they are. You can't close me up and you can't make me talk, so why don't you let it go at that."

"The Greek was shot to death tonight over on Lenox."

"I just heard it over the radio," she said.

"I'm trying to find who did it."

She looked at him in surprise. "It said on the radio the killer was known. A Sonny Pickens. Said a teenage gang called the something-or-nother Moslems snatched him."

"He didn't do it. That's why I'm here."

"Well, if he didn't do it, you got your job cut out," she said. "I wish I could help you but I can't."

"Maybe," he said. "Maybe not."

She raised her eyebrows slightly. "By the way, where's your sidekick, Coffin Ed. The radio said he shot one of the gang."

"Yeah, he got suspended."

She went still, like an animal alert to danger.

"Don't take it out on me, Digger."

"I just want to know why you stopped the Greek from coming here."

She stared long into his eyes. She had dark brown eyes with clear whites and long black lashes faintly seen.

"I'll let you talk to Ready. He knows."

"Is he here now?"

"He got a little chippie whore here he can't stay 'way from for five minutes. I'm going to throw 'em both out soon. Would have before now but my clients like her."

"Was the Greek her client?"

She got up slowly, sighing slightly from the effort.

"I'll send him out here."

"Bring him out."

"All right. But take him away, Digger. I don't want him talking in here. I don't want no more trouble. I've had trouble all my days."

"I'll take him away," he said.

She went out and Grave Digger heard doors being discreetly opened and shut and then her controlled bass voice saying, "How do I know. He said he was a friend."

A tall evil-faced man with pockmarked skin a dirty shade of black stepped into the kitchen. An old razor scar cut a purple ridge from the lobe of his left ear to the tip of his chin. There was a cast in one eye, the other was reddish brown. Thin conked hair stuck to a doublejointed head shaped like a peanut. He was flashily dressed in a light tan suit. Glass glittered from two goldplated rings. His pointed tan shoes were shined to mirror brilliance.

At sight of Grave Digger he drew up short and turned a murderous look on Reba.

"You tole me hit was a friend," he accused in a rough, dangerous sounding voice.

She didn't let it bother her. She pushed him into the kitchen and closed the door.

"Well, ain't he?" she asked.

"What's this, some kind of frameup?" he began to shout.

Grave Digger chuckled at the look of outrage on his face.

"How can a buck as ugly as you be a pimp?" he asked.

"You're gonna make me talk about you mama," Ready said, digging his right hand into his pants pocket.

With nothing moving but his arm, Grave Digger back-handed him in the solar plexus, knocking out his wind, then pivoted on his left foot and followed with a right cross to the same spot, and with the same motion raised his knee and sunk it into Ready's belly as the pimp's slim frame jackknifed forward. Spit showered from Ready's fish-like mouth, and the sense was already gone from his eyes when Grave Digger grabbed him by the back of the coat collar, jerked him erect, and started to slap him in the face with his open palm.

Reba grabbed his arm, saying, "Not in here, Digger, I beg you; don't make him bleed. You said you'd take him out."

"I'm taking him out now," he said in a cottony voice, shaking off her hold.

"Then finish him without bleeding him; I don't want nobody coming in here finding blood on the floor."

Grave Digger grunted and eased off. He propped Ready against the wall, holding him up on his rubbery legs with one hand while he took the knife and frisked him quickly with the other.

The sense came back into Ready's good eye and Grave Digger stepped back and said, "All right, let's go quietly, son."

Ready fussed about without looking at him, straightening his coat and tie, then fished a greasy comb from his pocket and combed his rumpled conk. He was bent over in the middle from pain and breathing in gasps and a white froth had collected in both corners of his mouth.

Finally he mumbled, "You can't take me outa here without no warrant."

"Go ahead with the man and shut up," Reba said quickly.

He gave her a pleading look. "You gonna let him take me outa here?"

"If he don't I'm going to throw you out myself," she said. "I don't want any hollering and screaming in here scaring my white clients."

"That's gonna cost you," Ready threatened.

"Don't threaten me, nigger," she said dangerously. "And don't set your foot in my door again."

"Okay, Reba, that's the lick that killed Dick," Ready said slowly. "You and him got me outnumbered." He gave her a last sullen look and turned to go.

Reba walked to the door and let them out.

"I hope I get what I want," Grave Digger said. "If I don't I'll be back."

"If you don't it's your own fault," she said.

He marched Ready ahead of him down the shaky stairs.

The old man in the ragged red chair looked up in surprise.

"You got the wrong nigger," he said. "Hit ain't him what's makin' all the trouble."

"Who is it?" Grave Digger asked.

"Hit's Cocky. He the one what's always pulling his chiv."

Grave Digger filed the information for future reference.

"I'll keep this one since I got him," he said.

"Shit," the old man said disgustedly. "He's just a halfass pimp."

10.

STARK white light, coming from the street as though from a carnival midway, slanted upward past the edge of the roof and made a milky wall in the dark.

Beyond the wall of light the flat tar roof was shrouded in semi-darkness.

The sergeant emerged from the edge of light like a hammerhead turtle rising from the deep. He took one look at Sonny beating frantically at a flock of panicstricken pigeons with a long bamboo pole and Inky standing motionless as though he'd sprouted from the tar.

"By God, now I know why they're called tarbabies!" he exclaimed.

Gripping the pole for dear life with both gauntleted hands, Sonny speared desperately at the pigeons. His eyes rolled whitely at the red-faced sergeant. His ragged overcoat flapped in the wind. The pigeons ducked and dodged and flew in lopsided circles. Their heads were cocked on one side as they observed Sonny's gymnastics with one-eyed beady apprehension.

Inky stood like a silhouette cut from black paper, looking at nothing. The whites of his eyes gleamed phosphorescently in the dark.

The pigeon loft was a rickety coop about six feet high, made of scraps of chicken wire, discarded screen windows and assorted rags tacked to a frame of rotten boards propped against the low brick wall separating the roofs. It had a tarpaulin top and was equipped with precarious roosts, tin cans of rusty water, and a rusty tin dishpan for feeding.

Blue uniformed white cops formed a jagged semi-circle in front of it, staring at Sonny in silent and bemused amazement.

The sergeant climbed onto the roof, puffing, and paused for a moment to mop his brow.

"What's he doing, voodoo?" he asked.

"It's only Don Quixote in blackface dueling a windmill," the professor said.

"That ain't funny," the sergeant said. "I like Don Quixote."

The professor let it go.

"Is he a halfwit?" the sergeant asked.

"If he's got that much," the professor said.

The sergeant pushed to the center of the stage, but once there hesitated as though he didn't know how to begin.

Sonny looked at him through the corners of his eyes and kept working the pole. Inky stared at nothing with silent intensity.

"All right, all right, so your feet don't stink," the sergeant said. "What one of you punks are Caleb?"

"Dass me," Sonny said, without for an instant neglecting the pigeons.

"What the hell you call yourself doing?"

"I'se teaching my pigeons how to fly."

The sergeant's jowls began to swell. "You trying to be funny?"

"Nawsuh, I didn' mean they didn' know how to fly. They can fly all right at day but they don't know how to night fly."

The sergeant looked at the professor. "Don't pigeons fly at night?"

"Search me," the professor said.

"Nawsuh, not unless you makes 'em," Inky said.

Everybody looked at him.

"Hell, he can talk," the professor said.

"They sleeps," Sonny added.

"Roosts," Inky corrected.

"We're going to make some pigeons fly too," the sergeant said. "Stool pigeons."

"If they don't fly, they'll fry," the professor said.

The sergeant turned to Inky. "What do they call you, boy?"

"Inky," Inky said. "But my name's Rufus Tree."

"So you're Inky," the sergeant said.

"They're both Inky," the professor said.

The cops laughed.

The sergeant smiled into his hand. Then he wheeled abruptly on Sonny and shouted, *"Sonny! Drop that pole!"*

Sonny gave a violent start and speared a pigeon in the craw, but he hung on to the pole. The pigeon flew crazily into the light and kept on going. Sonny watched it until he got control of himself, then he turned slowly and looked at the sergeant with big white innocent eyes.

"You talking to me, boss?" His black face shone with sweat.

"Yeah, I'm talking to you, Sonny."

"They don't calls me, Sonny, boss; they calls me Cal."

"You look like a boy called Sonny."

"Lots of folks is called Sonny, boss."

"What did you jump for if your name isn't Sonny. You jumped halfway out of your skin."

"Most anybody'd jump with you hollerin' at 'em like that, boss."

The sergeant wiped off another smile. "You told your grandma you were going downtown to work."

"She don't want me messin' round these pigeons at night. She think I might fall off'n the roof."

"Where have you been since supper?"

"Right up here, boss."

"He's just been up here about a half an hour," one of the cops volunteered.

"Nawsuh, I been here all the time," Sonny contradicted. "I been inside the coop."

"Ain't nobody in heah but us pigeons, boss," the professor cracked.

"Did you look in the coop?" the sergeant asked the cop.

The cop reddened. "No I didn't; I wasn't looking for a screwball."

The sergeant glanced at the coop. "By God, boy, your pigeons lead a hard life," he said. Then turning suddenly to the other cops, he asked, "Have these punks been frisked?"

"We were waiting for you," another cop replied.

The sergeant sighed theatrically. "Well, who are you waiting for now."

Two cops converged on Inky with alacrity; the professor and a third cop took on Sonny.

"Put that damn pole down!" the sergeant shouted at Sonny.

"No, let him hold it," the professor said. "It keeps his hands up."

"What the hell are you wearing that heavy overcoat for?" The sergeant kept on picking at Sonny in a frustrated manner.

"I'se cold," Sonny said. Sweat was running down his face in rivers.

"You look it," the sergeant said.

"Jesus Christ, this coat stinks," the professor complained, working Sonny over fast to get away from it.

"Nothing?" the sergeant asked when he'd finished.

"Nothing," the professor said. In his haste he hadn't thought to make Sonny put down the pole and take off his gauntlets.

The sergeant looked at the cops frisking Inky.

They shook their heads.

"What's Harlem coming to," the sergeant complained.

The cops grinned.

"All right, you punks, get downstairs," the sergeant ordered.

"I got to get my pigeons in," Sonny said.

The sergeant looked at him.

Sonny leaned the pole against the coop and began moving. Inky opened the door of the coop and began moving too. The pigeons took one look at the open door and began rushing to get inside.

"IRT subway at Times Square," the professor remarked.

The cops laughed and moved off to the next roof, laughing and talking.

The sergeant and the professor followed Inky and Sonny through the window and into the room below.

Sissie and Sugartit sat side by side on the bed again. Choo-Choo sat in the straight-back chair. Sheik stood in the center of the floor with his feet wide apart, looking defiant. The two cops stood with their buttocks propped against the edge of the table, looking bored.

With the addition of the four others, the room became crowded.

Everybody looked at the sergeant, waiting his next move.

"Get grandma in here," he said.

The professor went after her.

They heard him saying, "Grandma, you're needed."

There was no reply.

"Grandma!" they heard him shout.

"She's asleep," Sissie called to him. "She's hard to wake once she gets to sleep."

"She's not asleep," the professor called back in an angry tone of voice.

"All right, let her alone," the sergeant said.

The professor returned, red-faced with vexation. "She sat there looking at me without saying a word," he said.

"She gets like that," Sissie said. "She just sort of shuts out the world and quits seeing and hearing anything."

"No wonder her grandson's a halfwit," the professor said, giving Sonny a malicious look.

"Well, what the hell are we going to do with them?" the sergeant said in a frustrated tone of voice.

The cops had no suggestions.

"Let's run them all in," the professor said.

The sergeant looked at him reflectively. "If we take in all the punks who look like them in this block, we'll have a thousand prisoners," he said.

"So what," the professor said. "We can't afford to risk losing Pickens because of a few hundred shines."

"Well, maybe we'd better," the sergeant said.

"Are you going to take her in too," Sheik said, nodding toward Sugartit on the bed. "She's Coffin Ed's daughter."

The sergeant wheeled on him. "What! What's that about Coffin Ed?"

"Evelyn Johnson there is his daughter," Sheik said evenly.

The cops turned as though their heads were synchronized and stared at her. None spoke.

"Ask her," Sheik said.

The sergeant's face turned bright red.

It was the professor who spoke. "Well, girl? Are you Detective Johnson's daughter?"

Sugartit hesitated.

"Go on and tell 'em," Sheik said.

The red started crawling up the back of the sergeant's neck and engulfed his ears.

"I don't like you," he said to Sheik in a constricted tone of voice.

Sheik threw him a careless look, started to say something, then bit it off.

"Yes I am," Sugartit said finally.

"We can soon check on that," the professor said, moving toward the window. "He and his partner must be in the vicinity."

"No, Jones might be but Johnson was sent home," the sergeant said.

"What! Suspended?" the professor asked in surprise.

Sugartit looked startled; Sheik grinned smugly; the others remained impassive.

"Yeah, for killing the Moslem punk."

"For that!" the professor exclaimed indignantly. "Since when did they start penalizing policemen for shooting in self defense?"

"I don't blame the chief," the sergeant said. "He's protecting himself. The punk was underage and the newspapers are sure to put up a squawk."

"Anyway, Jones ought to know her," the professor said, going out on the fire escape and shouting to the cops below.

He couldn't make himself understood so he started down.

The sergeant asked Sugartit, "Have you got any identification?"

She drew a red leather card case from her skirt pocket and handed it to him without speaking.

It held a black, white-lettered identification card with her photograph and thumb print, similar to the ones issued to policemen. It had been given to her as a souvenir for her sixteenth birthday and was signed by the chief of police.

The sergeant studied it for a moment and handed it back. He had seen others like it; his own daughter had one.

"Does your father know you're here visiting these hoodlums?" he asked.

"Certainly," Sugartit said. "They're friends of mine."

"You're lying," the sergeant said wearily.

"He doesn't know she's over here," Sissie put in.

"I know damn well he doesn't," the sergeant said.

"She's supposed to be visiting me."

"Well, do your folks know you're here?"

She dropped her gaze. "No."

"Eve and I are engaged," Sheik said with a smirk.

The sergeant wheeled toward him with his right cocked high. Sheik ducked automatically, his guard coming up. The sergeant hooked a left to his stomach underneath his guard, and when Sheik's guard dropped, he crossed his right to the side of Sheik's head, knocking him into a spinning stagger. Then he kicked him in the side of the stomach as he spun and when he doubled over, the sergeant chopped him across the back of the neck with the meaty edge of his right hand. Sheik shuddered as though poleaxed and crashed to the floor. The sergeant took dead aim and kicked him in the valley of the buttocks with all his force.

The professor returned just in time to see the sergeant spit on him.

"Hey, what's happened to him?" he asked, climbing hastily through the window.

The sergeant took off his hat and wiped his perspiring forehead with a soiled white handkerchief.

"His mouth did it," he said.

Sheik groaned feebly in unconsciousness.

The professor chuckled. "He's still trying to talk." Then he said, "They couldn't find Jones. Lieutenant Anderson says he's working on another angle."

"It's okay, she's got an ID card," the sergeant said, then asked, "Is the chief still there?"

"Yeah, he's still hanging around."

"Well, that's his job."

The professor looked about at the silent group. "What's the verdict?"

"Let's get on to the next house," the sergeant said. "If I'm here when this punk comes to I'll probably be the next one to get suspended."

"Can we leave the building now?" Sissie asked.

"You two girls can come with us," the sergeant offered.

Sheik groaned and rolled over.

"We can't leave him like that," she said.

The sergeant shrugged. The cops passed into the next room. The sergeant started to follow, then hesitated.

"All right, I'll fix it up," he said.

He took the girls out on the fire escape and got the attention of the cops guarding the entrance below.

"Let these two girls pass!" he shouted.

The cops looked at the girls standing in the spotlight glare. "Okay."

The sergeant followed them back into the room.

"If I were you I'd get the hell away from this punk fast," he advised, prodding Sheik with his toe. "He's headed straight for trouble, big trouble."

Neither replied.

He followed the professor from the flat.

Granny sat unmoving in the rocking chair where they'd left her, tightly gripping the arms. She stared at them with an expression of fierce disapproval on her puckered old face and in her dim milky eyes.

"It's our job, grandma," the sergeant said apologetically.

She didn't reply.

They passed on sheepishly.

Back in the front room, Sheik groaned and sat up.

Everyone moved at once. The girls moved away from him. Sonny began taking off the heavy overcoat. Inky and Choo-Choo bent over Sheik and each taking an arm began helping him to his feet.

"How you feel, Sheik?" Choo-Choo asked.

Sheik looked dazed. "Can't no copper hurt me," he muttered thickly, wobbling on his legs.

"Does it hurt?"

"Naw, it don't hurt," he said with a grimace of pain. Then he looked about stupidly. "They gone?"

"Yeah," Choo-Choo said jubilantly and cut a jig step. "We done beat 'em, Sheik. We done fooled 'em two ways sides and flat."

Sheik's confidence came back in a rush. "I told you we was going to do it."

Sonny grinned and raised his clasped hands in the prize-fight salute. "They had me sweating in the crotch," he confessed.

A look of crazed triumph distorted Sheik's flat freckled yellow face. "I'm the Sheik, Jack," he said. His yellow eyes were getting wild again.

Sissie looked at him and said apprehensively, "Me and Sugartit got to go. We were just waiting to see if you were all right."

"You can't go now, we got to celebrate," Sheik said.

"We ain't got nothing to celebrate with," Choo-Choo said.

"The hell we ain't," Sheik said. "Cops ain't so smart. You go up on the roof and get the pole."

"Who, me, Sheik?"

"Sonny then."

"Me!" Sonny said. "I done got enough of that roof."

"Go on," Sheik said. "You're a Moslem now and I command you in the name of Allah."

"Praise Allah," Choo-Choo said.

"I don't want to be no Moslem," Sonny said.

"All right, you're still our captive then," Sheik decreed. "You go get the pole, Inky. I got five sticks stashed in the end."

"Hell, I'll go," Choo-Choo said.

"No, let Inky go, he's been up there before and they won't think it's funny."

When Inky left for the pole, Sheik said to Choo-Choo, "Our captive's getting biggety since we saved him from the cops."

"I ain't gettin' biggety," Sonny denied. "I just want to get the hell outen here and get these cuffs off'n me without havin' to become no Moslem."

"You know too much for us to let you go now," Sheik said, exchanging a look with Choo-Choo.

Then Inky returned with the pole and he let up on Sonny. Pulling the plug out of the end joint, he shook five marijuana cigarets onto the table top.

"A feast!" Choo-Choo exclaimed. He grabbed one, opened the end with his thumb, and lit up.

Sheik lit another.

"Take one, Inky," he said.

Inky took one.

Everybody put on smoked glasses.

"Granny will smell it if you smoke in here," Sissie said.

"She thinks they're cubebs," Choo-Choo said, then mimicked Granny saying, "Ah wish you chillens would stop smokin' them coo-bebs 'cause they make a body feel moughty funny in de head."

He and Sheik doubled over laughing.

The room stunk with the pungent smoke.

Sugartit picked up a stick, sat on the bed and lit it.

"Come on, baby, strip," Sheik urged her. "Celebrate your old man's flop by getting up off of some of it."

Sugartit stood up and undid her skirt zipper and began going into a slow striptease routine.

Sissie clutched her by the arms. "You stop that," she said. "You'd better go on home before your old man gets there first and comes out looking for you."

In a sudden rage, Sheik snatched Sissie's hands away from Sugartit and flung her across the bed.

"Leave her alone," he raved. "She's going to entertain the Sheik."

"If her old man's really Coffin Ed you oughta let her go on home," Sonny said soberly. "You just beggin' for trouble messin' round with his kinfolks."

"Choo-Choo, go to the kitchen and get Granny's wire clothesline," Sheik ordered.

Choo-Choo went out grinning.

When he saw Granny staring at him with such fierce disapproval, he said guiltily, "Pay no tenshion to me, Granny," and began clowning.

She didn't answer.

He tiptoed with elaborate pantomime to the closet and took out her coil of clothesline.

"Just wanna hang out the wash," he said.

Still she didn't answer.

He tiptoed close to the chair and passed his hand slowly in front of her face. She didn't bat an eye. His grin widened.

Returning to the front room, he said, "Granny's dead asleep with her eyes wide open."

"Leave her to Gabriel," Sheik said, taking the line and beginning to uncoil it.

"What you gonna do with that?" Sonny asked apprehensively.

Sheik made a running loop in one end. "We going to play cowboy," he said. "Look."

Suddenly he threw the loop over Sonny's head and pulled on the line with all his strength. The loop tightened about Sonny's neck and jerked him off his feet.

"Grab him, men!" Sheik ordered.

They both jumped straddle him at once; Choo-Choo grabbed his arms and Inky his feet.

Sissie ran toward Sheik and tried to pull the wire from his hands. "You're choking him," she said.

Sheik knocked her down with a backhanded blow.

"You can let up on him now," Choo-Choo said. "We got 'im."

"Now I'm gonna show you how to tie up a mother-raper to put him in a sack," Sheik said.

II.

GRAVE DIGGER halted on the sidewalk in front of the yellow frame house next door to the Knickerbocker. It had been partitioned into offices and all of the front windows were lettered with business announcements.

"Can you read that writing on those windows?" Grave Digger asked Ready Belcher.

Ready glanced at him suspiciously. "'Course I can read that writing."

"Read it then," Grave Digger said.

Ready stole another look. "Read what one?"

"Take your choice."

Ready squinted his good eye against the dark and read aloud, "*Joseph C. Clapp, Real Estate and Notary Public.*" He looked at Grave Digger like a dog that's retrieved a stick. "That one?"

"Try another."

He hesitated. Passing car lights played over his pockmarked black face, brought out the white cast in his bad eye and lit up his flashy tan suit.

"I haven't got much time," Grave Digger warned.

He read, "*Amazing 100 year old Gypsy Bait Oil—MAKES CAT FISH GO CRAZY.*" He looked at Grave Digger again like the same dog with another stick.

"Not that one," Grave Digger said.

"What the hell is this, a gag," he muttered.

"Just read."

"*JOSEPH, The Only and Original Skin Lightener. I guarantee to lighten the darkest skin by twelve shades in six months.*"

"You don't want your skin lightened?"

"My skin suit me," he said sullenly.

"Then read on."

"*MAGIC FORMULA FOR SUCCESSFUL PRAYER . . .* That it?"

"Yeah, that's it. Read what it says underneath."

"*Here are some of the amazing things it tells you about: When to pray; Where to pray; How to pray; The Magic Formulas for Health and Success through prayer; for conquering fear through prayer; for obtaining work through prayer; for money through prayer; for influencing others through prayer; and—*"

"That's enough." Grave Digger took a deep breath and said in a voice gone thick and cottony again, "Ready, if you don't tell me what I want to know, you'd better get yourself one of those prayers. Because I'm going to take you over on 129th Street beside the Harlem River in that deserted jungle of warehouses and junk yards underneath the New York Central railroad bridge. You know where that is?"

"Yare, I know where it's at."

"And I'm going to pistol whip you until your own whore

won't recognize you again. And if you try to run, I'm going to let you run fifty feet and then shoot you through the head for attempting to escape. You understand me?"

"Yare, I understand you."

"You believe me?"

Ready took a quick look at Grave Digger's rage-swollen face and said quickly, "Yare, I believes you."

"My partner got suspended tonight for killing a criminal rat like you and I'd just as soon they suspended me too."

"You ain't asted me yet what you want to know."

"Get into the car."

The car was parked at the curb. Ready got into Coffin Ed's seat. Grave Digger went around and climbed beneath the wheel.

"This is as good a spot as any," he said. "Start talking."

" 'Bout what?"

"About the Big Greek. I want to know who killed him."

Ready jumped as though he'd been stung. "Digger, I swear 'fore God—"

"Don't call me Digger, you lousy pimp."

"Mista Jones, lissen—"

"I'm listening."

"Lots of folks mighta killed him if they'd knowed—" he broke off. The pockmarks in his skin began filling with sweat.

"Known what? I haven't got all night."

Ready gulped and said, "He was a whipper."

"What?"

"He liked to whip 'em."

"Whores?"

"Not 'specially. If they was regular whores he wanted them to be big black mannish looking bitches like what might cut a mother-raper's throat. But what he liked most was liddle colored school gals."

"That's it? That's why Reba barred him?"

"Yassuh. He proposition her once. She got so mad she drew her pistol on him."

"Did she shoot him?"

"Nawsuh, she just scared him."

"I mean tonight. Was she the one?"

Ready's eyes started rolling slowly in their sockets and the sweat began to trickle down his mean black face.

"You mean the one what killed him? Nawsuh, she was home all evening."

"Where were you?"

"I was there too."

"Do you live there?"

"Nawsuh, I just drops by for a visit now and then."

"Where did he find the girls?"

"You mean the school girls?"

"What other girls would I mean?"

"He picked 'em up in his car. He had a little Mexican bull whip with nine tails he kept in his car. He whipped 'em with that."

"Where did he take them?"

"He brung 'em to Reba's 'til she got suspicious 'bout all the screaming and carrying on. She didn't think nothing of it at first; these little chippies likes to make lots of noise for a white man. But they was making more noise than seemed natural and she went in and caught 'im. That's when he proposition her."

"How did he get 'em to take it?"

"Get 'em to take what?"

"The whipping."

"Oh, he paid 'em a hundred bucks. They was glad to take it for that."

"You're certain of that, that he paid them a hundred dollars?"

"Yassuh. Not only me but lots of chippies all over Harlem knew about him. A hundred bucks didn't mean nothing to him. They boyfriends knew too. Lots of times they boyfriends made 'em. There was chippies all over town on the lookout for him. 'Course one time was enough for most of 'em."

"He hurt them?"

"He got his money's worth. Sometime he whale hell out of 'em. I s'pect he hurt more'n one of 'em bad. 'Member that kid they picked up in Broadhurst Park. It were all in the paper. She was in the hospital three or four days. She said she'd been attacked but the police thought she was beat up by a gang. I believes she was one of 'em."

"What was her name?"

"I don't recollect."

"Where'd he take them after Reba barred him from her place?"

"I don't know."

"Do you know the names of any of them?"

"Nawsuh, he brung 'em and took 'em away by hisself. I never even seen any of 'em."

"You're lying."

"Nawsuh, I swear 'fore God."

"How did you know they were school girls if you never saw any of them?"

"He tole me."

"What else did he tell you?"

"Nuthin' else. He just talk to me 'bout gals."

"How old is your girl?"

"My gal?"

"The one you have at Reba's."

"Oh, she twenty-five or more."

"One more lie and off we go."

"She sixteen, boss."

"She had him too?"

"Yassuh. Once."

The sweat was coming in streamers down Ready's face.

"Once. Why only once?"

"She got scared."

"You tried to fix it up for another time?"

"Nawsuh, boss, she didn't need to. Hit cost her more'n it was worth."

"What were you doing with him in the Dew Drop Inn?"

"He was looking for a little gal he knew and he ast me to come 'long, that's all, boss."

"When was that?"

" 'Bout a month ago."

"You said you didn't know where he took them after he was barred from Reba's."

"I don't, boss, I swear 'fore—"

"Can that uncle toming crap. Reba said she barred him three or four months ago."

"Yassuh, but I didn't say I hadn't seed him since."

"Did Reba know you were seeing him?"

"I only seed him that once, boss. I was in the Alabama-Georgia bar and he just happen in."

Grave Digger nodded toward the three alien cars parked ahead, in front of the Knickerbocker.

"One of those cars his?"

"Them struggle buggies!" Scorn pushed the fear from Ready's voice. "Nawsuh, he had a dream boat, a big green Caddy Coupe de Ville."

"Who was the girl he and you were looking for?"

"I wasn't looking for her; I just went 'long with him to look for her."

"Who was she, I asked."

"I didn't know her. Some little chippie what hung 'round in that section."

"How did he come to know her?"

"He said he'd done whipped her girl friend once. That's how come he knew her. Said Sissie's boyfriend brought her to 'im."

"Sissie! You said you didn't know the names of any of them."

"I'd forgotten her, boss. He didn't bring her to Reba's. I didn't know nuthin' 'bout her but just what he said."

"What did he say exactly?"

"He just say Sissie's boyfriend, some boy they call Sheik, arrange it for him and he pay Sheik. Then he wanted Sheik to arrange for the other one but Sheik couldn't do it."

"What was the other one called? The one he and you were looking for?"

"He call her Sugartit. She was Sissie's girl friend. He'd seen 'em walking together down Seventh Avenue one time after he'd whipped Sissie."

"Where did you find her?"

"We didn't find her, I swear 'fore—"

"Does your girl know them?"

"I didn' hear you."

"Your girl, does she know them?"

"Know who, boss?"

"Either Sissie or Sugartit."

"Nawsuh. My gal's a pro and them is just chippies. I recollect him saying one time they all belonged to a kid gang over in that section. I means them two chippies and Sheik. He say Sheik was the chief."

"What's the name of the gang?"

"He say they call themselves the Real Cool Moslems. He thought it were funny."

"Did you listen to the news on the radio tonight?"

"You mean what it say 'bout him getting croaked? Nawsuh, I was lissening to the 1280 Club. Reba tole me 'bout it. She were lissening. That were just 'fore you come. She were telling me when the doorbell rang. She say the big Greek's been croaked over on Lenox Avenue and I say so what."

"You said before that lots of people might have killed him if they'd known about him. Who?"

"All I meant was some of those gal's pas. Like Sissie's or some of 'em. He might have been hanging 'round over there looking for Sugartit again and her pa might have got hep to it some kind of way and been layin' for him and when he seed him coming down the street might have lowered the boom on 'im."

"You mean slipped up behind him?"

"He were in his car, warn't he?"

"How about the Moslems—the kid gang?"

"Them! What they'd wanta do it for? He was money in the street for them."

"Who's Sugartit's father?"

"You mean her old man?"

"I mean her father."

"How am I gonna know that, boss? I ain't never heard of her 'fore he talk 'bout her."

"What did he say about her?"

"Just say she was the gal for him."

"Did he say where she lived?"

"Nawsuh, he just say what I say, boss. I swear 'fore God."

"You stink. What are you sweating so much for?"

"I'se just nervous, that's all."

"You stink with fear. What are you scared of?"

"Just naturally scared, boss. You got that big pistol and you mad at everybody and talkin' 'bout killin' me and all that. Enough to make anybody scared."

"You're scared of something else, something in particular. What are you holding out?"

"I ain't holding nothing out. I done tole you everything I know, I swear, boss, I swears on everything that's holy in this whole green world."

"I know you're lying. I can hear it in your voice. What are you lying about?"

"I ain't lying, boss. If I'm lying I hope God'll strike me dead on the spot."

"You know who her father is, don't you?"

"Nawsuh, boss. I swear. I done tole you everything I know. You could whup me 'til my head is soft as clabber but I couldn't tell you no more than I'se already tole you."

"You know who her father is and you're scared to tell me."

"Nawsuh, I swear—"

"Is he a politician?"

"Boss, I—"

"A numbers banker?"

"I swear, boss—"

"Shut up before I knock out your goddamned teeth."

He mashed the starter as though tromping on Ready's head. The motor purred into life. But he didn't slip in the clutch. He sat there listening to the softly purring motor in the small black nondescript car, trying to get his temper under control.

Finally he said, "If I find out that you're lying I'm going to kill you like a dog. I'm not going to shoot you, I'm going to break all your bones. I'm going to try to find out who killed Galen because that's what I'm paid for and that was my oath when I took this job. But if I had my way I'd pin a medal on him and I'd string up every goddamned one of you who were up with Galen. You've turned my stomach and it's all I can do right now to keep from beating out your brains."

12.

THE reception room of the Harlem Hospital, ten blocks south on Lenox Avenue from the scene of the murder, was wrapped in a midnight hush.

It was called an interracial hospital; more than half of its staff of doctors and nurses were colored people.

A graduate nurse sat behind the reception desk. A bronze shaded desk lamp spilled light on the hospital register before her while leaving her brownskin face in shadow. She looked up enquiringly as Grave Digger and Ready Belcher approached, walking side by side.

"May I help you," she said in a trained courteous voice.

"I'm Detective Jones," Grave Digger said, exhibiting his badge.

She looked at it but didn't touch it.

"You received an emergency patient here about two hours ago; a man with his right arm cut off."

"Yes?"

"I would like to question him."

"I will call Dr. Banks. You may talk to him. Please be seated."

Grave Digger prodded Ready in the direction of chairs surrounding a table with magazines. They sat silently like relatives awaiting word of a critical case.

Dr. Banks came in silently, crossing the linoleum tile floor on rubber-soled shoes. He was a tall, athletic-looking young colored man dressed in white.

"I'm sorry to have kept you waiting, Mr. Jones," he said to Grave Digger whom he knew by sight. "You want to know about the case with the severed arm." He had a quick smile and a pleasant voice.

"I want to talk to him," Grave Digger said.

Dr. Banks pulled up a chair and sat down. "He's dead. I've just come from him. He had a rare type of blood—type O—which we don't have in our blood bank. You realize transfusions were imperative. We had to contact the Red Cross blood bank. They located the type in Brooklyn, but it arrived too late. Is there anything I can tell you?"

"I want to know who he was."

"So do we. He died without revealing his identity."

"Didn't he make a statement of any kind before he died?"

"There was another detective here earlier, but the patient was unconscious at the time. The patient regained consciousness later, but the detective had left. Before leaving he examined the patient's effects, however, but found nothing to establish his identity."

"He didn't talk at all, didn't say anything?"

"Oh yes. He cried a great deal. One moment he was cursing and the next he was praying. Most of what he said was incoherent. I gathered he regretted not killing the man whom he had attacked—the white man who was killed later."

"He didn't mention any names?"

"No. Once he said 'the little one' but mostly he used the word *mother-raper* which Harlemites apply to everybody, enemies, friends and strangers."

"Well, that's that," Grave Digger said. "Whatever he knew he took it with him. Still I'd like to examine his effects too, whatever they are."

"Certainly; they're just the clothes he wore and the contents of his pockets when he arrived here." He stood up. "Come this way."

Grave Digger got to his feet and motioned his head for Ready to walk ahead of him.

"Are you an officer too?" Dr. Banks asked Ready.

"No, he's my prisoner," Grave Digger said. "We're not that hard up for cops as yet."

Dr. Banks smiled. He led them down a corridor smelling strongly of ether to a room at the far end where the clothes and personal effects of the emergency and ward patients were stored in neatly wrapped bundles on shelves against the walls. He took down a bundle bearing a metal tag and placed it on the bare wooden table.

"Here you are."

From the room adjoining an anguished male voice was heard reciting the Lord's Prayer.

Ready stared as though fascinated at the number "219" on the metal tag fastened to the bundle of clothes and whispered, "Death row."

Dr. Banks flicked a glance at him and said to Grave Digger, "Most of the attendants play the numbers. When an emergency patient arrives they put this tag with the death number on his bundle and if he dies they play it."

Grave Digger grunted and began untying the bundle.

"If you discover anything leading to his identity, let us

know," Dr. Banks said. "We'd like to notify his relatives." He left them.

Grave Digger spread the blood-caked mackinaw and overalls on the table. Ready's face turned gray at sight of the black clots of dried blood.

The contents of the pockets had been put into a cellophane bag. Grave Digger dumped it onto the table. It contained two incredibly filthy one dollar bills, some loose change, a small brown paper sack of dried roots, two Yale keys and a skeleton key on a rusty key ring, a dried rabbit's foot, a dirty piece of resin, a cheese-cloth rag that had served as a handkerchief, a putty knife, a small piece of pumice stone, and a scrap of writing paper folded into a small dirty square. The putty knife and pumice stone indicated that the man had worked somewhere as a porter, the putty knife being used to scrape chewing gum from the floor and the pumice stone for cleaning his hands. That didn't help much.

He unfolded the square of paper and found a note on cheap school paper written in a childish hand.

> *"GB, you want to know something. The Big John hangs out in the Inn. How about that. Just like those old Romans. Bee."*

Grave Digger folded it again and slipped it into his pocket. "Is your girl called Bee?" he asked Ready.

"Nawsuh, she called Doe."

"Do you know any girl called Bee—school girl?"

"Nawsuh."

"GB?"

"Nawsuh."

Grave Digger turned out the pockets of the clothes but found nothing more. He wrapped the bundle and attached the tag. He noticed Ready staring at the number on the tag again.

"Don't let that number catch up with you," he said. "Don't you end up with that tag on your fine clothes."

Ready licked his dry lips.

They didn't see Dr. Banks on their way out. Grave Digger stopped at the reception desk to tell the nurse he hadn't found anything to identify the corpse.

"Now we're going to look for the Greek's car," he said to Ready.

They found the big green Cadillac beneath a street lamp in the middle of the block on 130th Street between Lenox and Seventh Avenues. It had an Empire State license number UG-16 and it was parked beside a fire hydrant. It was as conspicuous as a fire truck.

He pulled up behind it and parked.

"Who covered for him in Harlem?" he asked Ready.

"I don't know, Mista Jones."

"Was it the precinct captain?"

"Mista Jones, I—"

"One of our councilmen?"

"Honest to God, Mista Jones—"

He got out and walked forward to the big car.

The doors were locked. He broke the glass of the left side windscreen with the butt of his pistol and reached inside past the wheel and unlocked the door. The interior lights came on.

A quick search revealed the usual paraphernalia of a motorist: gloves, handkerchiefs, Kleenex, half-used packages of different brands of cigarettes, insurance papers, a woman's plastic overshoes and compact. A felt monkey dangled from the rear view mirror and two medium sized dolls, a black-faced Topsy and a blonde Little Eva, sat in opposite corners on the back seat.

He found the miniature bull whip and a manila envelope of postcard size photos in the right hand glove compartment. He studied the photos in the light. They were pornographic pictures of nude colored girls in various postures, revealing a well developed technique of sadism. On most of the pictures the faces of the girls were distinct although distorted by pain and shame.

He put the whip in his leather-lined coat pocket, kept the photos in his hand, slammed the door, walked back to his own car and climbed beneath the wheel.

"Was he a photographer?" he asked Ready.

"Yassuh, sometime he carried a camera."

"Did he show you the pictures he took?"

"Nawsuh, he never said nothing about any pictures. I just seen him with the camera."

He snapped on the top light and showed Ready the photos. "Do you recognize any of them?"

Ready whistled softly and his eyes popped as he turned over one photo after another.

"Nawsuh, I don't know none of them," he said, handing them back.

"Your girl's not one of them?"

"Nawsuh."

Grave Digger pocketed the envelope and mashed the starter.

"Ready, don't let me catch you in a lie," he said again, letting out the clutch.

13.

HE PARKED directly in front of the Dew Drop Inn and pushed Ready through the door ahead of him. On first sight it looked just as he had left it: the two white cops guarding the door and the colored patrons celebrating noisily. He ushered Ready between the bar and the booths, toward the rear. The vari-colored faces turned toward them curiously as they passed.

But in the last booth he noticed an addition. It was crowded with teenagers, three schoolboys and four school-girls, who hadn't been there before. They stopped talking and looked at him intently as he and Ready approached. Then at sight of the bull whip all four girls gave a start and their young dark faces tightened with sudden fear. He wondered how they'd got past the white cops on the door.

All the places at the bar were taken.

Big Smiley came down and asked two men to move.

One of them began to complain. "What for I got to give up my seat for some other niggers."

Big Smiley thumbed toward Grave Digger. "He's the man."

"Oh, one of them two."

Both of the men rose with alacrity, picked up their glasses

and vacated the stools, grinning at Grave Digger obse-
quiously.

"Don't show me your teeth," Grave Digger snarled. "I'm no
dentist. I don't fix teeth. I'm a cop. I'll knock your teeth out."

The men doused their grins and slunk away.

Grave Digger threw the bull whip on top of the bar and sat
on the high bar stool.

"Sit down," he ordered Ready who stood by hesitantly. "Sit
down, goddammit."

Ready sat down as though the stool were covered with cake
icing.

Big Smiley looked from one to another, smiling warily.

"You held out on me," Grave Digger said in his thick cottony voice of smoldering rage. "And I don't like that."

Big Smiley's smile got a sudden case of constipation. He
threw a quick look at Ready's impassive face, found nothing
there to reassure him, then fell back on his cut arm which he
carried in a sling.

"Guess I must be runnin' some fever, Chief, 'cause I don't
remember what I told you."

"You told me you didn't know who Galen was looking for
in here," Grave Digger said thickly.

Big Smiley stole another look at Ready, but all he got was
a picture of a black pockmarked face and two blank reddish
brown eyes with a cast in one which told him nothing. He
sighed heavily.

"Who he were looking for? Is dat what you ast me?" he
stalled, trying to meet Grave Digger's smoldering hot gaze.
"I dunno who he were looking for, Chief."

Grave Digger rose up on the bar stool rungs as though his
feet were in stirrups, snatched the bullwhip from the bar and
slashed Big Smiley across one cheek after another before Big
Smiley could get his good hand moving.

Big Smiley stopped smiling. Talk stopped suddenly the
length of the bar, petered out in the booths. In the vacuum
left by the cessation of talk, Lil Green's whining voice issued
from the juke box at front:

> *Why don't you do right*
> *Like other mens do . . .*

Grave Digger sat back on the stool, breathing hard, struggling to control his rage. Arteries stood out in his temples,
growing out of his short cropped kinky hair like strange roots
climbing toward the brim of his kicked back misshapen hat.
His brown eyes laced with red veins generated a steady white
heat.

The white manager who'd been working the front end of
the bar hastened down toward them with a face full of outrage.

"Get back," Grave Digger said thickly.

The manager got back.

Grave Digger stabbed at Big Smiley with his left forefinger
and said in a voice so thick it was hard to understand, "Smiley,
all I want from you is the truth. And I ain't got long to get
it."

Big Smiley didn't look at Ready any more. He didn't touch
his cheeks on which welts rose beneath his greasy black skin
like tunnels of psychopathic moles. He didn't smile. He didn't
whine.

He said, "Just ast the questions, Chief, and I'll answer 'em
to the best of my knowledge."

Grave Digger looked around at the teenagers in the booth.
They were listening with open mouths, staring at him with
popping eyes. His breath burned from his flaring nostrils. He
turned back to Big Smiley. But he sat quietly for a moment
to give the blood time to recede from his head.

"Who killed him?" he finally asked.

"I don't know, Chief."

"He was killed on your street."

"Yassuh, but I don't know who done it."

"Do Sissie and Sugartit come in here?"

"Yassuh, sometimes."

Out of the corners of his eyes Grave Digger noticed
Ready's shoulders begin to sag as though his spine were
melting.

"Sit up straight, goddammit," he said. "You'll have plenty
of time to lie down if I find out you've been lying."

Ready sat up straight.

Grave Digger addressed Big Smiley. "Galen met them in
here?"

"Nawsuh, he met Sissie in here once but I never seen him with Sugartit."

"What was she doing in here then?"

"She come in here twice with Sissie."

"How'd you know her name?"

"I heard Sissie call her that."

"Was Sheik with her when he met her?"

"You mean with Sissie, when she met the big man? Yassuh."

"He paid Sheik the money?"

"I couldn't be sure, Chief, but I seen money being passed. I don't know who got it."

"He got it. Did they both leave with him?"

"You mean both Sheik and Sissie?"

"That's what I mean."

Big Smiley took out a blue bandana handkerchief and mopped his sweating black face.

The four schoolgirls in the booth began going through the motions of leaving. Grave Digger wheeled toward them.

"Sit down, I want to talk to you later," he ordered.

They began a shrill cacophony of protest: "We got to get home . . . got to be at school tomorrow at nine o'clock . . . haven't finished homework . . . can't stay out this late . . . get into trouble . . ."

He got up and went over and showed them his gold badge. "You're already in trouble. Now I want you to sit down and keep quiet."

He took hold of the two girls who were standing and forced them back into their seats.

"He can't hold you 'less he's got a warrant," the boy in the aisle seat said.

Grave Digger slapped him out of his seat, reached down and lifted him from the floor by his coat lapels and slammed him back into his seat.

"Now say that again," he suggested.

The boy didn't speak.

Grave Digger waited for a moment until they had settled down and got quiet, then he returned to his bar stool.

Neither Big Smiley nor Ready had moved; neither had looked at the other.

"You didn't answer my question," Grave Digger said.

"When he took Sissie off Sheik stayed in his seat," Big Smiley said.

"What kind of a goddamned answer is that?"

"That's the way it was, Chief."

"Where did he take her?"

Rivers of sweat poured from Big Smiley's face. He sighed. "Downstairs," he said.

"Downstairs! In here?"

"Yassuh. They's stairs in the back room."

"What's downstairs?"

"Just a cellar like any other bar's got. It's full of bottles an' old bar fixtures and beer barrels. The compression unit for the draught beer is down there and the refrigeration unit for the ice boxes. That's all. Some rats and we keeps a cat."

"No bed or bedroom?"

"Nawsuh."

"He whipped them down there in that kind of place?"

"I don't know what he done."

"Couldn't you hear them?"

"Nawsuh. You can't hear nothin' through this floor. You could shoot off your pistol down there and you couldn't hear it up here."

Grave Digger turned a look on Ready. "Did you know that?"

Ready began to wilt again. "Nawsuh, I swear 'fore—"

"Sit up straight, goddammit! I don't want to have to tell you again."

He turned back to Big Smiley. "Did he know it?"

"Not as far as I know, unless he told him."

"Is Sissie or Sugartit among those girls over there?"

"Nawsuh," Big Smiley said without looking.

Grave Digger showed him the pornographic photos.

"Know any of these?"

Big Smiley leafed through them slowly without a change of expression. Three he laid aside from the others.

"I've seen them," he said.

"What's their names?"

"I don't know only two of 'em." He separated them gin-

gerly with his fingertips as though they were coated with external poison. "Them two. This here one is called Good
Booty, t'other one is called Honey Bee. This one here, I never
heard her name called."

"What are their family names?"

"I don't know none of 'em's square monickers."

"He took these downstairs?"

"Just them two."

"Who came here with them?"

"They came by theyself, most of 'em did."

"Did he have appointments with them?"

"Nawsuh, not with most of 'em anyway. They just come in
here and laid for him."

"Did they come together?"

"Sometime, sometime not."

"You just said they came by themselves."

"I meant they didn't bring no boyfriends."

"Did he know them before?"

"I couldn't say. When he come in if he seed any of 'em he
just made his choice."

"He knew they hung around here looking for him?"

"Yassuh. When he started comin' here he was already
known."

"When was that?"

"Three or four months ago. I don't remember 'zactly."

"When did he start taking them downstairs?"

"'Bout two months ago."

"Did you suggest it?"

"Nawsuh, he propositioned me."

"How much did he pay you?"

"Twenty-five bucks."

"You're talking yourself into Sing-Sing."

"Maybe."

Grave Digger examined the note addressed to GB and
signed Bee he'd taken from the dead man's effects; then
passed it over to Big Smiley.

"That came from the pocket of the man you cut," he said.

Big Smiley read the note carefully, his lips spelling out each
word. His breath came out in a sighing sound.

"Then he must be a relation of her," he said.

"You didn't know that?"

"Nawsuh, I swear 'fore God. If I'd knowed that I wouldn't 'ave chopped him with the axe."

"What exactly did he say to Galen when he started toward him with the knife?"

Big Smiley wrinkled his forehead. "I don't remember exactly. Something 'bout if he found a white mother-raper trying to diddle his little gals he'd cut his throat. But I just took that to mean colored women in general. You know how our folks talk. I didn't figure he meant his own kin."

"Maybe some other girl's father had the same idea with a pistol," Grave Digger suggested.

"Could be," Big Smiley said cautiously.

"So evidently he's the father and he's got more girls than one."

"Looks like it."

"He's dead," Grave Digger informed him.

Big Smiley's expression didn't change. "I'm sorry to hear it."

"You look like it. Who went your bail?"

"My boss."

Grave Digger looked at him soberly.

"Who's covering for you?" he asked.

"Nobody."

"I know that's a lie but I'm going to pass it. Who was covering for Galen?"

"I don't know."

"I'm going to pass that lie too. What was he doing here tonight?"

"He was looking for Sugartit."

"Did he have a date with her?"

"I don't know. He said she was coming by with Sissie."

"Did they come by after he'd left?"

"Nawsuh."

"Okay, Smiley, this one is for keeps. Who was Sugartit's father?"

"I don't know none of 'em's kinfolks nor neither where they lives, Chief, like I told you before. It didn't make no difference."

"You must have some idea."

"Nawsuh, it's just like I say, I never thought about it. You don't never think 'bout where a gal live in Harlem, 'less you goin' home with her. What do anybody's address mean up here."

"Don't let me catch you in a lie, Smiley."

"I ain't lying, Chief. I went with a woman for a whole year once and never did know where she lived. Didn't care neither."

"Who are the Real Cool Moslems?"

"Them punks! Just a kid gang around here."

"Where do they hang out?"

"I don't know 'zactly. Somewhere down the street."

"Do they come in here?"

"Only three of 'em sometime. Sheik, I think he's they leader; and a boy called Choo-Choo and the one they call Bones."

"Where do they live?"

"Somewhere near here, but I don't know 'zactly. The boy down the street on t'other side. I don't know his name but he got a pigeon coop on the roof."

"Is he one of 'em?"

"I don't know for sure but you can see a gang of boys on the roof when he's flying his pigeons."

"I'll find him. Do you know the ages of those girls in the booth?"

"Nawsuh, when I ask 'em they say they're eighteen."

"You know they're underage."

"I s'pect so but all I can do is ast 'em."

"Did he have any of them?"

"Only one I knows of."

Grave Digger turned and looked at the girls again.

"What one?" he asked.

"The dark one in the green tam." Big Smiley pushed forward one of the three photos. "She's this one here, the one called Good Booty."

"Okay, son, that's all for the moment," Grave Digger said.

He got down from the stool and walked forward to talk to the manager.

As soon as he left, without saying a word or giving a warning, Big Smiley leaned forward and hit Ready in the face with his big ham-size fist. Ready sailed backward from his stool, crashed into the wall and crumpled to the floor.

Grave Digger looked down in time to see his head disappearing beneath the edge of the bar then turned his attention to the white manager across from him.

"Collect your tabs and shut the bar; I'm closing up this joint and you're under arrest," he said.

"For what?" the manager challenged hotly.

"For contributing to the delinquency of minors."

The manager sputtered, "I'll be open again by tomorrow night."

"Don't say another goddamned word," Grave Digger said and kept looking at him until the manager closed his mouth and turned away.

Then he beckoned one of the white cops on the door and told him, "I'm putting the manager and the bartender under arrest and closing the joint. I want you to hold the manager and some teenagers I'll turn over to you. I'm going to leave in a minute and I'll send back the wagon. I'll take the bartender with me."

"Right, Jones," the cop said, as happy as a kid with a new toy.

Grave Digger walked back to the rear.

Ready was down on the floor on his hands and knees, spitting out blood and teeth.

Grave Digger looked at him and smiled grimly. Then he looked up at Big Smiley who was licking his bruised knuckles with a big red tongue.

"You're under arrest, Smiley," he said. "If you try to escape, I'm going to shoot you through the back of the head."

"Yassuh," Big Smiley said.

Grave Digger shook a customer loose from a plastic covered chair and sat astride it at the end of the table in the booth, facing the scared, silent teenagers. He took out his notebook and stylo and wrote down their names, addresses, numbers of the public schools they attended, and their ages as they replied in turn to his questions. The oldest was a boy of seventeen.

None of them admitted knowing either Sissie, Sugartit, the big white man, Galen, or anyone connected with the gang of Real Cool Moslems.

He called the second cop down from the door and said, "Hold these kids for the wagon."

Then he said to the girl in the green tam who'd given her name as Gertrude B. Richardson, "Gertrude, I want you to come with me."

One of the girls tittered. "You might have known he'd take Good Booty," she said.

"My name is Beauty," Good Booty said, tossing her head disdainfully.

On sudden impulse Grave Digger stopped her as she was about to get up.

"What's your father's name, Gertrude?"

"Charlie."

"What does he do?"

"He's a porter."

"Is that so? Do you have any sisters?"

"One. She's a year younger than me."

"What does your mother do?"

"I don't know. She don't live with us."

"I see. You two girls live with your father."

"Where else we going to live."

"That's a good question, Gertrude, but I can't answer it. Did you know a man got his arm cut off in here earlier tonight?"

"I heard about it. So what? People are always getting cut around here."

"This man tried to knife the white man because of his daughters."

"He did." She giggled. "He was a square."

"No doubt. The bartender chopped off his arm with an axe to protect the white man. What do you think about that?"

She giggled again, nervously. "Maybe he figured the white man was more important than some colored drunk."

"He must have. The man died in Harlem Hospital less than an hour ago."

Her eyes got big and frightened. "What are you trying to say, Mister."

"I'm trying to tell you that he was your father."

Grave Digger hadn't anticipated her reaction. She came up

out of her seat so fast that she was past him before he could grab her.

"Stop her!" he shouted.

A customer wheeled from his bar stool into her path and she stuck her fingers into his eye. The man yelped and tried to hold her. She wrenched from his grip and sprang toward the door. The white cop headed her off and wrapped his arms about her. She twisted in his grip like a panicstricken cat and clawed at his pistol. She had gotten it out the holster when a colored man rushed in and wrenched it from her grip. The white cop threw her onto the floor on her back and sat straddle her, pinning down her arms. The colored man grabbed her by the feet. She writhed on her back and spat in the cop's face.

Grave Digger came up and looked down at her from sad brown eyes. "It's too late now, Gertrude," he said. "They're both dead."

Suddenly she began crying hysterically.

"What did he have to mess in it for?" she sobbed. "Oh, pa, what did you have to mess in it for?"

14.

Two uniformed white cops standing guard on a dark rooftop were talking.

"Do you think we'll find him?"

"Do I think we'll find him? Do you know who we're looking for? Have you stopped to think for a moment that we're looking for one colored man who supposedly is handcuffed and seven other colored men who were wearing green turbans and false beards when last seen. Have you turned that over in your mind? By this time they've long since got rid of those phony disguises and maybe Pickens has got rid of his handcuffs too. And then what does that make them, I ask you. That makes them just like eighteen thousand or one hundred and eighty thousand other colored men, all looking alike. Have you ever stopped to think there are five hundred thousand colored people in Harlem—one half of a million people with black skin. All looking alike. And we're trying to pick eight out of them. It's like trying to find a cinder in a coal bin. It ain't possible."

"Do you think all these colored people in this neighborhood know who Pickens and the Moslems are?"

"Sure they know. Every last one of them. Unless some other colored person turns Pickens in he'll never be found. They're laughing at us."

"As much as the chief wants that coon, whoever finds him is sure to get a promotion," the first cop said.

"Yeah, I know, but it ain't possible," the second cop said. "If that coon's got any sense at all he would at least have filed those cuffs in two a long time ago."

"What good would that do him if he couldn't get them off?"

"Well, he could wear heavy gloves with gauntlets like— Hey! Didn't we see some coon wearing driving gauntlets?"

"Yeah, that halfwit coon with the pigeons."

"Wearing gauntlets and an old ragged overcoat. And a coal black coon at that. He certainly fits the description."

"That halfwitted coon. You think it's possible that he's the one."

"Come on! What are we waiting for?"

Sheik said, "Now all we've got to do is get this mother-raper past the police lines and throw him into the river."

"Doan do that to me, please, Sheik," Sonny's muffled voice pleaded from inside the sack.

"Shhhh," Choo-Choo cautioned. "Chalk the walking Jeffs."

The two cops leaned over head by head and peered in through the open window.

"Where's that boy who was wearing gloves?" the first cop asked.

"Gloves!" Choo-Choo echoed, going into his clowning act like a chameleon changing color. "You means boxing gloves?"

The second cop sniffed.

"A weed pad!" he exclaimed.

They climbed inside. Their gazes swept quickly over the room.

The room reeked with the scent of marijuana smoke. Everyone in it was high. The ones who hadn't smoked were high from inhaling the smoke and watching the eccentric motions of the ones who had smoked.

"Who's got the sticks?" the first cop demanded in a bullying tone of voice.

"Come on, come on, who's got the sticks?" the second cop echoed, looking from one to the other. He passed over Sheik who stood in the center of the floor where he'd been arrested in motion by Choo-Choo's warning and stared at them as though trying to make out what they were; then over Inky who was caught in the act of ducking behind the curtains in the corner and stood there half in and half out like a billboard advertisement for a movie about bad girls; and landed on Choo-Choo who seemed the most vulnerable because he was grinning like an idiot. "You got the sticks, boy?"

"Sticks! You mean that there pigeon stick," Choo-Choo said, pointing at the bamboo pole on the floor beside the bed.

"Don't get funny with me, boy!"

"I just don't know what you means, boss."

"Forget the sticks," the first cop said. "Let's find the boy with the gloves."

He looked about. His gaze lit on Sugartit who was sitting in the straightbacked chair and staring with a fixed popeyed expression at what appeared to be a gunny sack filled with huge lumps of coal lying in the middle of the bed.

"What's in that sack?" he asked suspiciously.

For an instant no one replied.

Then Choo-Choo said, "Just some coal."

"On the bed?"

"It's clean coal."

The cop pinned a threatening look on him.

"It's my bed," Sheik said. "I can put what I want on it."

Both cops went suddenly still and stared at him.

"You're a kind of a lippy bastard," the first cop said. "What's your name?"

"Samson."

"You live here?"

"Right here."

"Then you're the boy we're looking for. That's your pigeon loft on the roof."

"No, that's not him," the second cop said. "The boy we want is blacker than he is and has another name."

"What's a name to these coons?" the first cop said. "They're always changing about."

"No, the one we want is called Inky. He was the one wearing the gloves."

"Now I remember. He was called Caleb. He was the one wearing the gloves. The other one was Inky, the one who couldn't talk."

The second cop wheeled on Sheik. "Where's Caleb?"

"I don't know anybody named Caleb."

"The hell you don't! He lives here with you."

"Nawsuh, you means that boy what lives down on the first floor," Choo-Choo said.

"Don't tell me what I mean. I mean the boy who lives here on this floor. He's the boy who's got the pigeon loft."

"Nawsuh, boss, if you means the Caleb what's got the pigeon roost, he lives on the first floor."

"Don't lie to me, boy. I saw the sergeant bring him down the fire escape to this floor."

"Nawsuh, boss, the sergeant taken him on by this floor and carried him down on the fire escape to the first floor. We seen 'em when they came by the window. Didn't we, Amos?" he called on Inky.

"That's right, suh," Inky said. "They went right past that window there."

"What other window could they go by?"

"None other window, suh."

"They had another boy with 'em called Inky," Choo-Choo said. "It looked like they had 'em both arrested."

The second cop was staring at Inky. "This boy here looks like Inky to me," he said. "Aren't you Inky, boy?"

"Nawsuh—" Inky began, but Choo-Choo quickly cut him off, "They calls him Smokey. Inky is the other one."

"Let him talk for himself," the first cop said.

The second cop pinned another threatening look on Choo-Choo. "Are you trying to make a fool out of me, boy?"

"Nawsuh, boss, I'se just tryna help."

"Leave up off him," the first cop said. "These coons are jagged on weed; they're not strictly responsible."

"Responsible or not, they'd better be careful before they get some lumps on their heads."

The first cop noticed Sissie standing quietly in the corner, holding her hand to her bruised cheek.

"You know them, Caleb and Inky, don't you, girl?" he asked her.

"No sir, I just know Smokey," she said.

Suddenly Sonny sneezed.

Sugartit giggled.

The cop wheeled toward the bed, looked at the sack and then looked at her.

"Who was that sneezed?"

She put her hand to her mouth and tried to stop laughing.

The cop turned slightly pinkish and drew his pistol.

"Some one's underneath the bed," he said. "Keep the others covered while I look."

The second cop drew his pistol.

"Just relax and won't anybody get hurt," he said calmly.

The first cop got down on his hands and knees, holding his cocked pistol ready to shoot, and looked underneath the bed.

Sugartit put both hands over her mouth and bit into her palm. Her face swelled with suppressed laughter and tears overflowed her eyes.

The cop straightened to his knees and braced himself on the edge of the bed. There was a perplexed look on his blood red face.

"There's something funny going on in here," he said. "There's someone else in this room."

"Ain't nobody here but us ghosts, boss," Choo-Choo said.

The cop threw him a look of frustrated fury, and started to his feet.

"By God I'll—" His voice was dried up by choking sounds issuing from inside the sack.

He jumped upward and backward as though one of the ghosts had sure enough groaned. Leveling his pistol, he said in a quaking voice, "What's in that sack?"

Sugartit burst into hysterical laughter.

For an instant no one spoke.

Then Choo-Choo said hastily, "Hit's just Joe."

"What!"

"Hit's just Joe in the sack."

"Joe!"

Gingerly the cop leaned over, holding his cocked pistol in his right hand, and untied the cord closing the sack with his left. He drew the top of the sack open.

A gray-black face containing a protruding purple-red tongue stared up at him from white-walled popping eyes.

The cop drew back in horror. His face turned white and a shudder passed over his big solid frame.

"It's a body," he said in a choked voice. "All trussed up."

"Hit ain't no body, hit's just Joe," Choo-Choo said with no intention whatsoever of sounding funny.

The second cop hastened over to look.

"It's still alive," he said.

"He's choking!" Sissie cried and ran over and began loosening the noose about Sonny's neck.

Sonny sucked in breath with a gasp.

"My God, what's he doing in there?" the first cop asked in amazement.

"He's just studying magic," Choo-Choo said. He was beginning to sweat from the strain.

"Magic!"

The second cop noticed Sheik inching toward the window and aimed his pistol at him.

"Oh no you don't," he said. "You come over here."

Sheik turned and came closer.

"Studying magic!" the first cop said. "In a sack?"

"Yassuh, he's trying to learn how to get out, like Houdini."

Color flooded back into the cop's face.

"I ought to take him in for indecent exposure," he said.

"Hell, he's wearing a sack, ain't he," the second cop said, amused by his own wit.

Both of them grinned at Sonny as though he were a harmless halfwit.

Then the second cop said suddenly, "It ain't possible! There can't be two such halfwits in the whole world."

The first cop looked closely at Sonny and said slowly, "I

believe you're right." Then to the others at large, "Get that boy out of that sack."

Sheik didn't move, but Choo-Choo and Inky hastened over and pulled Sonny out while Sissie held the bottom of the sack.

The cops stared at Sonny with awe.

"Looks like barbecued coon, don't he," the first cop said.

Sugartit burst into renewed laughter.

Sonny was buck naked. His heels were pulled tight against his buttocks and his knees were jackknifed up to his chin. The wire clothesline ran from a noose about his neck out between his legs, was looped loosely about each knee with a slipknot between the loops, then down to his ankles, binding them tightly, and finally up his back where the remainder was wrapped several times about his wrists. His black skin had a gray pallor as though dusted over lightly with wood ashes. He was shaking like a leaf.

The second cop reached out and turned him around.

Everyone stared at the handcuff bracelets clamped about each wrist.

"That's our boy," the first cop said.

"Lawd, suh, I wish I'd gone home and gone to bed," Sonny said in a moaning voice.

"I'll bet you do," the cop said.

Sugartit couldn't stop laughing.

15.

THE BODIES had been taken to the morgue. All that remained were chalk outlines on the pavement where they had lain.

The street had been cleared of private cars. Police tow trucks had come and carried away those that had been abandoned in the middle of the street. Most of the patrol cars had returned to duty. Only those remained that were blockading the area.

The chief of police's car occupied the center of the stage. It was parked in the middle of the intersection of 127th Street and Lenox Avenue.

To one side of it the chief, Lieutenant Anderson, the lieutenant from homicide and the precinct sergeant who'd led one
of the searching parties were grouped about the boy called
Bones.

The lieutenant from homicide had a zip gun in his hand.

"All right then, it isn't yours," he said to Bones in a voice
of tried patience. "Whose is it then? Who were you hiding it
for?"

Bones stole a glance at the lieutenant's face and his gaze
dropped quickly to the street. It crawled over the four pairs
of big black copper's boots. They looked like the 6th Fleet at
anchor. He didn't answer.

He was a slim black boy of medium height with girlish features and short hair almost straight at the roots parted on one
side. He wore a natty shot topcoat over his sweat shirt and
tight fitting black pants above shiny tan pointed-toed shoes.

An elderly man, a head taller, with a black face grizzled from
hard outdoor work, stood beside him. Kinky hair grew like
burdock weeds about his shiny black dome; and worried
brown eyes looked down at Bones from behind steel-rimmed
spectacles.

"Go 'head, tell 'em, son, don't be no fool," he said; then
he looked up and saw Grave Digger approaching with his prisoners. "Here comes Digger Jones," he said. "You can tell
him, cain't you?"

Everybody looked about.

Grave Digger had Big Smiley and Ready Belcher handcuffed together walking in front of him; and he held Good
Booty by the arm.

He looked at Anderson and said, "I closed up the Dew
Drop Inn and gave the manager and some juvenile delinquents to the officers on duty to hold. You'd better send a
wagon up there."

Anderson whistled for a patrol car team and gave them the
order.

"What did you find out on Galen?" the chief asked.

"I found out he was a pervert," Grave Digger said.

"It figures," the homicide lieutenant said.

The chief turned red. "I don't give a goddamn what he
was," he said. "Have you found out who killed him?"

"No, right now I'm still guessing at it," Grave Digger said.

"Well, guess fast then. I'm getting goddamned tired of standing up here watching this comedy of errors."

"I'll give you a quick fill-in and let you guess too," Grave Digger said.

"Well, make it short and sweet and I damn sure ain't going to guess," the chief said.

"Lissen, Digger," the colored civilian interposed. "You and me is both city workers. Tell 'em my boy ain't done no harm."

"He's broken the Sullivan law concerning concealed weapons by having this gun in his possession," the homicide lieutenant said.

"That little thing," Bones' father said scornfully. "I don't b'lieve that'll even shoot."

"Get these people away from here and let Jones report," the chief said testily.

"Well, do something with them, sergeant," Lieutenant Anderson said.

"Come on, both of you," the sergeant said, taking the man by the arm.

"Digger—" the man appealed.

"It'll keep," Grave Digger said harshly. "Your boy belonged to the Moslem gang."

"Naw-naw, Digger—"

"Do I have to slug you," the sergeant said.

The man allowed himself to be taken along with his son across the street.

The sergeant turned them over to a corporal and hurried back. Before he'd gone three steps the corporal was already summoning two cops to take charge of them.

"What kind of city work does he do?" the chief asked.

"He's in the sanitation department," the sergeant said. "He's a garbage collector."

"All right, get on, Jones," the chief ordered.

"Galen picked up colored school girls, teenagers, and took them to a crib on 145th Street," Grave Digger said in a flat toneless voice.

"Did you close it?" the chief asked.

"It'll keep; I'm looking for a murderer now," Grave Digger

said. Taking the miniature bullwhip from his pocket, he went on, "He whipped them with this."

The chief reached out silently and took it from his hand.

"He paid them $100 for each whipping," Grave Digger said.

"You're sure he didn't pay to get whipped," the homicide lieutenant said.

"No, he whipped them. He was a sadist."

"At that price, it's usually the other way around," the homicide lieutenant said. "Sadists are usually cheap."

"He hurt some of them pretty bad," Grave Digger said.

The chief hefted the bull whip and tested it against his leg.

"It's got a sting all right," he said. "Have you got a list of them, Jones?"

"What for?"

"There might be a connection."

"I'm coming to that—"

"Well, get to it then."

"The landprop, a woman named Reba—used to call herself Sheba, the one who testified against Captain Murphy—"

"Ah, that one," the chief said softly. "She won't slip out of this."

"She'll take somebody with her," Grave Digger warned. "She's covered and Galen was too."

The chief looked at Lieutenant Anderson reflectively.

The silence ran on until the sergeant blurted, "That's not in this precinct."

Anderson looked at the sergeant. "No one's charging you with it."

"Get on, Jones," the chief said.

"Reba got scared of the deal and barred him. Her story will be that she barred him when she found out what he was doing. But that's neither here nor there. After she barred him Galen started meeting them in the Dew Drop Inn. He arranged with the bartender so he could whip them in the cellar."

Everyone except Grave Digger appeared embarrassed.

"He ran into a girl named Sissie," Grave Digger said. "How doesn't matter at the moment. She's the girl friend of a boy called Sheik, who is the leader of the Real Cool Moslems."

Sudden tension took hold of the group.

"Sheik sold Sissie to him. Then Galen wanted Sissie's girl-friend, Sugartit. Sheik couldn't get Sugartit, but Galen kept looking for her in the neighborhood. I have the bartender here and a two-bit pimp who has a girl at Reba's who steered for Galen. I got this much from them."

The officers stared appraisingly at the two handcuffed prisoners.

"If they know that much, they know who killed him," the chief said.

"It's going to be their asses if they do," Grave Digger said. "But I think they're leveling. The way I figure it is the whole thing hinges on Sugartit. I think he was killed because of her."

"By who?"

"That's the jackpot question."

The chief looked at Good Booty. "Is this girl Sugartit?"

The others stared at her too.

"No, she's another one."

"Who is Sugartit then?"

"I haven't found out yet. This girl knows but she doesn't want to tell."

"Make her tell."

"How?"

The chief appeared embarrassed by the question. "Well, what the hell do you want with her if you can't make her talk?" he growled.

"I think she'll talk when we get close enough. The Moslem gang hangs out somewhere near here. The bartender here thinks it might be in the flat of a boy who has a pigeon loft."

"I know where that is!" the sergeant exclaimed. "I searched there."

Everyone, including the prisoners, stared at him.

His face reddened. "Now I remember," he said. "There were several boys in the flat. The boy who kept the pigeons, Caleb Bowee is his name, lives there with his grandma; and two of the others roomed there."

"Why in the hell didn't you bring them in?" the chief asked.

"I didn't find anything on them to connect them with the Moslem gang or the escaped prisoner," the sergeant said, defending himself. "The boy with the pigeons is a halfwit—he's harmless; and I'm sure the grandma wouldn't put up with a gang in there."

"How in the hell do you know he's harmless?" the chief stormed. "Half the murderers in Sing-Sing look like you and me."

The homicide lieutenant and Anderson exchanged smiles.

"They had two girls with them and—" the sergeant began to explain but the chief wouldn't let him.

"Why in the hell didn't you bring them in too?"

"What were the girls' names?" Grave Digger asked.

"One was called Sissieratta and—"

"That must be Sissie," Grave Digger said. "It fits. One was Sissie and the other was Sugartit. And one of the boys was Sheik." Turning to Big Smiley, he asked, "What does Sheik look like?"

"Freckled-faced boy the color of a bay horse with yellow cat eyes," Big Smiley said impassively.

"You're right," the sergeant admitted sheepishly. "He was one of them. I should have trusted my instinct; I started to haul that punk in."

"Well, for God's sake get the lead out of your ass now," the chief roared. "If you still consider yourself working for the police department."

"Well, Jesus Christ, the other girl, the one Jones calls Sugartit, was Ed Johnson's daughter," the sergeant exploded. "She had one of those souvenir police ID cards signed by yourself and I thought—"

He was interrupted by the flat whacking sound of metal striking against a human skull.

No one had seen Grave Digger move.

What they saw now was Ready Belcher sagging forward with his eyes rolled back into his head and a white cut two inches wide in the black pockmarked skin of his forehead, not yet beginning to bleed; and Big Smiley rearing back on the other end of the handcuffs like a dray horse shying from a rattlesnake.

Grave Digger had his nickel-plated thirty eight gripped by

the long barrel, making a club out of the butt. The muscles were corded in his rage swollen neck like rigging ropes and his face was distorted like a maniac's. An effluvium of violence came out of him like the sudden smell of death.

Looking at him, the others were caught up and suspended in motion as though turned to stone.

Before their startled eyes had time to blink, he struck again. Beneath the pistol butt the top of Ready's four dollar conked head caved in like a softboiled egg. A small gush of breath slipped from Ready's slack mouth and he sunk like a stone.

Big Smiley shied again and Grave Digger struck him across his injured arm hard enough to break it, mouthing out the words like cotton spewing from the gin, "Keep still, you're moving him!"

The irises of Big Smiley's eyes disappeared, leaving slits of dirty whites barely visible between his half-closed eyelids.

"Stop him, goddammit!" the chief roared. "He'll kill them."

Grave Digger kicked at Ready's prone head, missed and clubbed Big Smiley in the middle of the spine as he went off balance.

The sculptured figures of the police officers came to life. The sergeant grabbed Grave Digger from behind in a bear hug. Grave Digger doubled over forward and sent the sergeant flying over his head toward the chief, who ducked in turn and let the sergeant sail on by.

Lieutenant Anderson and the homicide lieutenant converged on Grave Digger from opposite directions and each grabbed an arm while he was still in a crouch and lifted him upward and backward.

Ready was lying prone on the pavement, blood tricking from the two dents in his skull, a slack arm drawn tight by the handcuffs attached to Big Smiley's wrist. He looked already dead.

Big Smiley gave the appearance of a terrified blind beggar caught in a bombing raid; his giant frame trembled from head to foot.

Grave Digger had just time enough to kick Ready in the face before the officers jerked him out of range.

Ready's jawbone broke with a stomach retching sound and his lower jaw swung out at an angle that exposed one whole row of his bottom teeth and the edge of his white coated tongue swimming in blood.

"Get him to the hospital quick!" the chief shouted; and in the next breath added, "Rap him on the head!"

Grave Digger had carried the lieutenants to the ground and it was more than either could do to rap him on the head.

The sergeant had already picked himself up and at the chief's order set off at a gallop.

"Goddammit, phone for it, don't run after it!" the chief yelled. "Where the hell is my chauffeur anyway."

Cops came running from all directions.

"Give the lieutenants a hand," the chief said. "They have got a wild man."

Four cops jumped into the fray. Finally they pinned Grave Digger to the ground.

The sergeant climbed into the chief's car and began talking into the telephone.

Coffin Ed appeared suddenly. No one had noticed him approaching from his parked car down the street.

"Great God, what's happening, Digger!" he exclaimed.

Everybody got quiet. Their embarrassment was noticeable.

"What the hell!" he said, looking from one to the other. "What the hell's going on."

Grave Digger's muscles relaxed as though he'd lost consciousness.

"It's just me, Ed," he said, looking up from the ground at his friend. "I just lost my head is all."

"Let him go," Anderson ordered his helpers. "He's back to normal now."

The cops released Grave Digger and he got to his feet.

"Cooled off now?" the homicide lieutenant asked.

"Yeah, give me my gun," Grave Digger said.

"Give it to him," the chief said.

The lieutenant gave him back his gun.

Coffin Ed looked down at Ready Belcher's mangled head.

"You too, eh, partner," he said. "What did this rebel do?"

"I told him if I caught him holding out on me I'd kill him."

"You told him no lie," Coffin Ed said. Then asked, "Is it that bad?"

"It's dirty, Ed. Galen was a rotten son of a bitch."

"That doesn't surprise me. Have you got anything on it so far?"

"A little, not much."

"What the hell do you want here?" the chief said testily. "I suppose you want to help your buddy kill some more of your folks."

Grave Digger knew the chief was trying to steer the conversation away from Coffin Ed's daughter, but he didn't know how to help him.

"You two men act as if you want to kill off the whole population of Harlem," the chief kept on.

"You told me to crack down," Grave Digger reminded him.

"Yeah, but I didn't mean in front of my eyes where I would have to be a witness to it."

"It's our beat," Coffin Ed spoke up for his friend. "If you don't like the way we handle it why don't you take us off."

"You're already off," the chief said. "What in the hell did you come back for anyway?"

"Strictly on private business."

The chief snorted.

"My little daughter hasn't come home and I'm worried about her," Coffin Ed explained. "It's not like her to stay out this late and not let us know where she is."

The chief looked away to hide his embarrassment.

Grave Digger swallowed audibly.

"Hell, Ed, you don't have to worry about Eve," he said in a tone of voice he hoped sounded reassuring. "She'll be home soon. You know nothing can happen to her. She's got that police ID card you got for her on her last birthday, hasn't she?"

"I know, but she always phones her mother if she's going to stay out."

"While you're out here looking for her she's probably gone home. Why don't you go back home and go to bed. She'll be all right."

"Jones is telling you right, Ed," the chief said brusquely.

"Go home and relax. You're off duty and you're in our way here. Nothing is going to happen to your daughter. You're just having nightmares."

A siren sounded in the distance.

"Here comes the ambulance," Lieutenant Anderson said.

"I'll go and phone home again," Coffin Ed said. "Take it easy, Digger, don't get yourself docked too."

As he turned and started off a fusillade of shots sounded from the upper floor of some nearby tenement. Ten shots from regulation .38 calibre police specials were fired so fast that by the time the sound had reached the street it was chained together.

Every cop within hearing distance froze to alert attention. They strained their ears in almost superhuman effort to place the direction from which the shots had come. Their eyes scanned the fronts of the tenements until not a spot escaped their observation.

But no more shots were fired.

The only signs of life left were the lights going out. With the rapidity of the gun shots, one light after another went out until only one lighted window remained in all the totally dark dingy buildings. It was on the top floor behind a fire escape landing of the tenement a half block up the street.

All eyes focused on that spot.

The grotesque silhouette of something crawling over the window sill appeared in the glare of light. Slowly it straightened and took the shape of a short husky man. It staggered slowly the three foot width of the grilled iron footing and leaned against the low outer rail. For a moment it swayed back and forth in a macabre pantomime and then slowly, like a roulette ball climbing the last hurdle before the final slot, it fell over the railing, turning slowly in the air, missing the second landing by a breath, but turned sufficiently for the head to strike the railing of the third, which started it to spinning faster. It landed with a resounding thud on top of a parked car and lay there with one hand hanging down beside the driver's window as though signaling for a stop.

"Well, goddammit, get going!" the chief shouted in a stentorian voice, then on second thought added quickly, "Not you, Jones, not you!" and ran toward his car to get his megaphone.

Already motion had broken out. Cops were heading toward the tenement like the Marines landing.

The two cops guarding the entrance ran out into the street to locate the scene of the disturbance.

The chief grabbed his megaphone and shouted, "Get the lights on that building."

Two spotlights that had been extinguished were turned back on immediately and beamed on the tenement's top floor.

A patrolman stepped from the window onto the fire escape landing and raised his hands in the light.

"Hold it, everybody!" he shouted. "I want the chief! Is the chief there?"

"Lower the lights," the chief megaphoned. "I'm here. What is it?"

"Send for an ambulance, Petersen is shot—"

"An ambulance is coming."

"Yes sir, but don't let anybody in here yet—"

Grave Digger took hold of Coffin Ed's arm.

"Hang on tight, Ed," he said. "Your daughter's up there."

He felt Coffin Ed's muscles tighten beneath his grip as the cop went on,

"We found Pickens but one of the Moslem gangsters grabbed Pete's pistol and shot him. He used his buddy as a shield and I got his buddy but he snatched one of the girls here and escaped into the back room. He's locked himself in there and there's no other way out of this shotgun shack. He says the girl is detective Ed Johnson's daughter. He threatening to cut her throat if he can't talk to you and Grave Digger Jones. Whatcha want me to do?"

The ambulance approached and the chief had to wait until the siren had died away to make himself heard.

"Has he still got Petersen's pistol?"

"Yes sir, but he emptied it."

"All right, officer, sit pat," the chief megaphoned. "We'll get Petersen down the fire escape and I'll go up and see what it's about."

Coffin Ed's acid burnt face was hideous with fear.

16.

"You stay down here, Johnson," the chief ordered. "I'll take Anderson and Jones."

"Not unless you shoot me," Coffin Ed said.

The chief looked at him.

"Let him come," Grave Digger said in his thick cottony voice.

"I ought to come too, I know the flat," the sergeant said.

"It's my job to come," the lieutenant from homicide said.

"Who the hell's running this police department," the chief said.

"We haven't got any time," Grave Digger said.

All of them went quickly and quietly as possible. No one spoke again until the chief said through the kitchen door,

"All right, I'm the chief. Come out and give yourself up and you won't get hurt."

"How do I know you're the chief?" asked a fuzzy voice from within.

"If you open the door and come out you'll see."

"Don't get so mother-raping smart. You're the chief but I'm the Sheik."

"Well, all right, you're a big shot gang boss. What do you want?"

"Keep him talking," Coffin Ed whispered. "I'm going up on the roof."

"Who's that with you?" Sheik asked sharply.

Grave Digger pointed to the sergeant and Lieutenant Anderson.

"The precinct lieutenant and a sergeant," the chief said.

"Where's Grave Digger?"

"He's not here yet. I had to send for him."

"Send these other mother-rapers away. Let's you and me settle this, the Sheik and the Chief."

"How would you know if they'd gone if you're scared to come out and look?"

"Let 'em stay then. I don't give a good goddamn. And don't think I'm scared. I don't need to take any chances. I got Coffin Ed's daughter by the hair with my left hand and

I'm holding a razor-edged butcher knife against her throat with my right hand. If you try to take me I'll cut her mother-raping head off before you can get through the door."

"All right, Sheik, you got us by the balls, but you know you can't get away. Why don't you come out peaceably and give yourself up like a man. I give you my word that no one will abuse you. The officer you shot ain't seriously hurt. There's no other charge against you. You ought to get off with five years. With time off for good behavior, you'll be back in the big town in three years. Why risk sudden death or the hot seat just for a moment of playing the big shot?"

"Don't hand me that mother-raping crap. You'll hang a kidnapping charge on me for snatching your prisoner."

"What the hell! You can keep him. We don't want him anymore. We found out he didn't kill the man. All he had was a blank pistol."

"So he didn't kill the man?"

"No."

"Who killed him?"

"We don't know yet."

"So you don't know who killed the Big Greek, do you?"

"All right, all right, what's that to you? What do you want to get mixed up in something that don't concern you?"

"You're one of those smart mother-rapers, ain't you? You're going to be so smart you're going to make me cut her mother-raping throat just to show you."

"Please don't argue with him, Mr. Chief, please," said a small scared voice from within. "He'll kill me. I know he will."

"Shut up!" Sheik said roughly. "I don't need you to tell 'im I'm going to kill you."

Beads of sweat formed on the ridge of the chief's red nose and about the blue bags beneath his eyes.

"Why don't you be a man," he urged, filling his voice with contempt. "Don't be a mad dog like Vincent Coll. Be a man like Dillinger was. You won't get much. Three years and no more. Don't hide behind an innocent little girl."

"Who the hell do you think you're kidding with that stale crap. This is the Sheik. Can't no dumb cop like you make a fool out of the Sheik. You got the chair waiting for me and you think you're going to kid me into walking out there and sitting in it."

"Don't play yourself too big, punk," the chief said, losing his temper for a moment. "You shot an officer but you didn't kill him. You snatched a prisoner but we don't want him. Now you want to take it out on a little girl who can't defend herself. And you call yourself the Sheik, the big gang leader. You're just a cheap tin horn punk, yellow to the core."

"Keep on, just keep on. You ain't kidding me with that mother-raping sucker bait. You know mother-raping well it was me killed him. You've had me tabbed ever since you found out that chickenshit nigger was shooting blanks."

"What!" The chief was startled. Forgetting himself, he asked Grave Digger, "What the hell's he talking about?"

"Galen," Grave Digger said with his lips.

"Galen!" the chief exclaimed. "You're trying to tell me you killed the white man, you chicken-livered punk?" he roared.

"Keep on, just keep on. You know mother-raping well it was me lowered the boom on the Big Greek." He sounded as though he bitterly resented an oversight. "Who do you think you're kidding? You're talking to the Sheik. You think 'cause I'm colored I'm dumb enough to fall for that rock-a-bye baby crap you're putting down."

The chief had to readjust his train of thought.

"So it was you who killed Galen?"

"He was just the Greek to me," Sheik said scornfully. "Just another gray sucker up here trying to get his kicks. Yeah, I killed him." There was pride in his voice.

"Yeah, it figures," the chief said thoughtfully. "You saw him running down the street and you took advantage of that and shot him in the back. Just what a yellow son of a bitch like you would do. You were probably laying for him and were scared to go out and face him like a man."

"I wasn't laying for the mother-raper no such a goddamn thing," Sheik said. "I didn't even know he was anywhere about."

"You were nursing a grudge against him."

"I didn't have nothing against the mother-raper. You must

be having pipe dreams. He was just another gray sucker to me."

"Then why the hell did you shoot him?"

"I was just trying out my new zip gun. I saw the mother-raper running by where I was standing so I just blasted at him to see how good my gun would shoot."

"You goddamned little rat," the chief said, but there was more sorrow in his voice than anger. "You sick little bastard. What the goddamned hell can be done with somebody like you?"

"I just want you to quit trying to kid me, 'cause I'd just as soon cut this girl's throat right now as not."

"All right, *Mister* Sheik," the chief said in a cold quiet voice. "What do you want me to do?"

"Is Grave Digger come yet?"

Grave Digger nodded.

"Yeah, he's here, *Mister* Sheik."

"Let him say something then, and you better can that *Mister* crap."

"Eve, this is me, Digger Jones," Grave Digger said, spurning Sheik.

"Answer him," Sheik said.

"Yes, Mr. Jones," she said in a voice so weightless it floated out to the tense group listening like quivering eiderdown.

"Is Sissie in there with you?"

"No sir, just Granny Bowee and she's sitting in her chair asleep."

"Where's Sissie?"

"She and Inky are in the front room."

"Has he hurt you?"

"Quit stalling," Sheik said dangerously. "I'm going to give you until I count to three."

"Please, Mr. Jones, do what he says. He's going to kill me if you don't."

"Don't worry, child, we're going to do what he says," he reassured her and then said, "What do you want, boy?"

"These are my terms: I want the street cleared of cops; all the police blockades moved—"

"What the hell!" the chief exploded.

"We'll do it," Grave Digger said.

"I want to hear the chief say it," Sheik demanded.

"I'll be damned if I will," the chief said.

"Please," came a tiny voice no bigger than a little prayer.

"What if she was your daughter," Grave Digger said.

"I'm going to give you until I count three," Sheik said.

"All right, I'll do it," the chief said, sweating blood.

"On your word of honor as a great white man," Sheik persisted.

The chief's red sweating face drained of color.

"All right, all right, on my word of honor," he said.

"Then I want an ambulance driven up to the door downstairs. I want all its doors left open so I can see inside, the back doors and both the side doors, and I want the motor left running."

"All right, all right, what else? The Statue of Liberty?"

"I want this house cleared—"

"All right, all right, I said I'd do that."

"I don't want any mother-raping alarm put out. I don't want anybody to try to stop me. If anybody messes with me before I get away you're going to have a dead girl to bury. I'll put her out somewhere safe when I get clear away, clear out of the state."

The chief looked at Grave Digger.

"Don't cross him," Grave Digger whispered tensely. "He's teaed to the eyes."

"All right, all right," the chief said. "We'll give you safe passage. If you don't hurt the girl. If you hurt her don't think that we're going to kill you. But you'll beg for us to. Now take five minutes and come out and we'll let you drive away."

"Who you think you're kidding?" Sheik said. "I ain't that big a fool. I want Grave Digger to come inside of here and put his pistol down on the table, then I'm going to come out."

"You're crazy if you think we're going to give you a pistol," the chief roared.

"Then I'm going to kill her now."

"I'll give it to you," Grave Digger said.

"You're under suspension as of now," the chief said.

"All right," Grave Digger said; then to Sheik, "What do you want me to do?"

"I want you to stand outside the door with the pistol held by the barrel. When I open the door I want you to stick it forward and walk into the room so the first thing I see is the butt. Then I want you to walk straight ahead and put it on the kitchen table. You got that?"

"Yeah, I got it."

"The rest of you mother-rapers get downstairs," Sheik said.

The two lieutenants and the sergeant looked at the chief for orders.

"All right, Jones, it's your show," the chief said, adding on second thought, "I wish you luck."

He turned and started down the stairs.

The others hesitated. Grave Digger motioned violently for them to leave too. Reluctantly they followed the chief.

Silence came from the kitchen until the sound of the officers' feet had diminished into silence below.

Grave Digger stood facing the kitchen door, holding the pistol as instructed. Sweat poured down his lumpy cordovan colored face and collected in the collar about his rage swollen neck.

Finally the sound of movement came from the kitchen. The bolt of the Yale lock clicked open, a hand bolt was pulled back with a grating snap, a chain was unfastened. The door swung slowly inward.

Only Granny was visible from the doorway. She sat bolt upright in the immobile rocking chair with her hands gripping the arms and her old milky eyes wide open and staring at Grave Digger with a fixed look of fierce disapproval.

Sheik spoke from behind the door, "Turn the butt this way so I can see if it's loaded."

Without looking around, Grave Digger turned the pistol so that Sheik could see the shells in the chambers of the cylinder.

"Go ahead, keep walking," Sheik ordered.

Still without looking around, Grave Digger advanced slowly across the room. When he came to the table he looked swiftly toward the small window at the far end of the back wall. It was on the other side of an old-fashioned home-made cupboard which partially blocked the view of the kitchen from the outside, so that only the half between the table and the side wall was visible.

He saw what he was looking for. He then leaned slowly forward and placed the pistol on the far side of the table.

"There," he said.

Raising his hands high above his head, he turned slowly away from the table and faced the back wall. He stood so that Sheik had either to pass in front of him to reach the pistol or go around on the other side of the table.

Sheik kicked the door shut, revealing himself and Sugartit, but Grave Digger didn't turn his head or even move his eyes to look at them.

Sheik gripped Sugartit's pony tail tightly in his left hand, pulling her head back hard to make her slender brown throat taut beneath the blade of the butcher knife. They began a slow shuffling walk, like a weird Apache dance staged in a Montmartre night club.

Sugartit's eyes had the huge liquid fatalistic look of a dying doe's, and her small brown face looked as fragile as toasted meringue. Her upper lip was sweating copiously.

Sheik kept his gaze pinned on Grave Digger's back while slowly skirting the opposite walls of the room and approaching the table from the far side. When he came within reach of the pistol he released his hold on Sugartit's pony tail, pressed the knife blade tighter against her throat and reached out with his left hand for the pistol.

Coffin Ed was hanging head downward from the roof with just his head and shoulders visible below the top edge of the kitchen window. He had been hanging there for twenty minutes waiting for Sheik to come into view. He took careful aim at a spot just above Sheik's left ear.

Some sixth sense caused Sheik to jerk his head around at the exact instant Coffin Ed fired.

A third eye, small and black and sightless, appeared suddenly in the exact center of Sheik's forehead between his two startled yellow cat eyes.

The high powered bullet had only cut a small round hole in the window glass, but the sound of the shot shattered the whole pane and blasted a shower of glass into the room.

Grave Digger wheeled to catch the fainting girl as the knife clattered harmlessly onto the table top.

Sheik was dead when he started going down. He went straight down in total collapse and landed crumpled up beside Granny's immobile rocking chair.

The room was full of cops.

"That was too much of a risk, too much of a risk," Lieutenant Anderson said, shaking his head with a dazed expression.

"What isn't risky on this job," the chief said authoritatively. "We cops got to take risks."

No one disputed him.

"This is a violent city," he added belligerently.

"There wasn't that much risk," Coffin Ed said. He had his arm about his daughter's trembling shoulders. "They don't have any reflexes when you shoot them in the head."

Sugartit winced.

"Take Eve and go home," Grave Digger said harshly.

"I guess I'd better," Coffin Ed said, limping painfully as he guided Sugartit gently toward the door.

"Geeze," a young patrol car rookie was saying. "Geeze. He hung there all that time on just some wire tied around his ankles. I don't know how he stood the pain."

"You'd have stood it too if she'd been your daughter," Grave Digger said.

"Forget what I said to you about being under suspension, Jones," the chief said.

"I didn't hear you," Grave Digger said.

"Jesus Christ, look at that!" the sergeant exclaimed in amazement. "All that noise and it hasn't even waked up grandma."

Everybody turned and looked at him. They were solemn for a moment.

"Nothing's ever going to wake her up again," the lieutenant from homicide said. "She must have been dead for hours."

"All right, all right, all right," the chief shouted. "Let's clean up here and get away. We've got this case tied up tighter than Dick's hat band." Then he added in a pleased tone of voice, "That wasn't too difficult, was it."

17.

IT WAS eleven o'clock the next morning.

Inky and Bones had spilled their guts.

It had gone hard for them and when the cops got through with them they were as knotty as fat pine.

The remaining members of the Real Cool Moslems—Camel Mouth, Beau Baby, Punkin Head and Slow Motion—had been rounded up and questioned and were now being held along with Inky and Bones.

Their statements had been practically identical:

They had been standing on the corner of 127th Street and Lenox Avenue.

Q. What for?

A. Just having a dress rehearsal.

Q. What? Dress rehearsal?

A. Yassuh. Like they do on Broadway. We was practising wearing our new A-rab costumes.

Q. And you saw Mr. Galen when he ran past.

A. Yassuh, that's when we seed him.

Q. Did you recognize him?

A. Nawsuh, we didn't know him.

Q. Sheik knew him.

A. Yassuh, but he didn't say he knew 'im and we'd never seen him before.

Q. Choo-Choo must have known him too.

A. Yassuh, must 'ave. Him and Sheik usta room together.

Q. But you saw Sheik shoot him?

A. Yassuh. He said, "Watch this," and pulled out his new zip gun and shot at him.

Q. How many times did he shoot?

A. Just once. That's all a zip gun will shoot.

Q. Yes, these zip guns are single shots. But you knew he had the gun?

A. Yassuh, he'd been working on it for 'most a week.

Q. He made it himself?

A. Yassuh.

Q. Had you ever seen him shoot it previously?

A.   Nawsuh. It were just finished. He hadn't tried it out.

Q.   But you knew he had it on his person?

A.   Yassuh, he were going to try it out that night.

Q.   And after he shot the white man, what did you do?

A.   The man fell down and we went up to see if he'd hit him.

Q.   Were you acquainted with the first suspect, Sonny Pickens?

A.   Nawsuh, we seed him for the first time too when he come past there shootin'.

Q.   When you saw the white man had been killed, did you know Sheik had shot him?

A.   Nawsuh, we thought the other fellow had did it.

Q.   What one of you, er, ah, passed the wind?

A.   Suh?

Q.   What one of you broke wind?

A.   Oh, that were Choo-Choo, suh, he the one farted.

Q.   Was there any special significance in that?

A.   Suh?

Q.   Why did he do it?

A.   That were just a salute we give to the cops.

Q.   Oh! Was the perfume throwing part of it?

A.   Yassuh, when they got mad Caleb threw the perfume on them.

Q.   To allay their anger, er, ah, make them jolly?

A.   Nawsuh, to make them madder.

Q.   Oh! Well, why did Sheik kidnap, snatch, the other suspect, Pickens?

A.   Just to put something over on the cops. He hated cops.

Q.   Why?

A.   Suh?

Q.   Why did he hate cops? Did he have any special reason to hate cops?

A.   Special reason? To hate cops? Nawsuh. He didn't need none. Just they was cops is all.

Q.   Ah, yes, just they was cops. Is this the zip gun Sheik had?

A.   Yassuh. Leastwise it looks like it.

Q.   How did Bones come to be in possession of it?

A.   He give it to Bones when we was running off. Bones's old man work for the city and he figgered it was safe with Bones.

Q.   That's all for you, boy. You had better be scared.

A.   Ah is.

That was the case. Open and shut.

No complicity was established linking Sonny Pickens with the murder. He was being temporarily held on a charge of disturbing the peace while a district attorney's assistant was studying the New York State criminal code to see what other charge could be lodged against him for shooting at a citizen with a blank gun.

His friends, Lowtop Brown and Rubberlips Wilson, had been hauled in as suspicious persons.

The cases of the two girls had been referred to the probation officers, but as yet nothing had been done. Both were supposedly at their respective homes, suffering from shock.

The bullet had been removed from the victim's brain and given to the ballistics bureau. No further autopsy was required. Mr. Galen's daughter, Mrs. Helen Kruger of Wading River, Long Island, had claimed the body for burial.

The bodies of the others, Granny and Caleb, Choo-Choo and Sheik, lay unclaimed in the morgue. Perhaps the Baptist church in Harlem, of which Granny was a member, would give her a decent Christian burial. She had no life insurance and it would be financially inconvenient for the church, unless the members contributed to defray the costs.

Caleb would be buried along with Sheik and Choo-Choo in potter's field, unless the medical college of one of the universities obtained their bodies for dissection. No college would want Choo-Choo's, however, because it had been too badly damaged.

Ready Belcher was under an oxygen tent in Harlem Hospital, in the same ward where Charlie Richardson whose arm had been chopped off had died earlier. His condition was critical, but the staff was doing everything possible to keep him alive at the request of the police. He would never look the same, however, and should his teenage whore ever see him again she wouldn't recognize him.

Big Smiley and Reba were being held on charges of contributing to the deliquency of minors, manslaughter, operating a house of prostitution, and sundry other charges collectively.

The woman who was shot in the leg by Coffin Ed was in Knickerbocker Hospital. Two ambulance chasing shysters were vying with each other for her consent to sue Coffin Ed and the New York City police department on a fifty-fifty split of the judgement, but her husband was holding out for a 60% cut.

That was the story; the second and corrected story. The late editions of the morning newspapers had gone hog wild with it:

The prominent New York Citizen hadn't been shot, as first reported, by a drunken Negro who had resented his presence in a Harlem bar. No, not a little bit. He had been shot to death by a teenage Harlem gangster, called Sheik, leader of a Harlem teenage gang, called the Real Cool Moslems. Why? Well, Sheik had wanted to find out if his zip gun would actually shoot.

The copy writers threw the book of adjectives at the bizarre and Harlemistic aspects of the three ring murder; and meanwhile tossed a bone of commendation to the police department, the brave policemen who had worked through the small hours of the morning, tracked down the killer in the Harlem jungle and shot him to death in his lair within less than six hours after the fatal shot had been fired.

The headlines read:

POLICE PUT THE HEAT TO REAL COOL MOSLEMS
DEATH IS THE KISSOFF FOR THRILL KILL
HARLEM MANIAC RUNS AMUCK
PANDEMONIUM UPTOWN

The hawkers cried:

"Read allabawt really cool muslims and zip gun murder . . . allabawt cops kill three to one . . . allabawt ex-po-say of Harlem vice . . . allabawt bloody nightmare . . ."

But already the story was a thing of the past, as dead as the four main characters.

"Kill it," the city editor of an afternoon paper ordered the composing room. "Someone else is already being murdered somewhere else."

Uptown in Harlem the sun shone on the same drab scenes it shone on every other morning at eleven o'clock, when it shone.

No one missed the few expendable colored people being held on their sundry charges in the big new granite skyscraper jail on Centre Street that had replaced the old New York City Tombs.

Not far off in the same building, in a room high up on the southwest corner with a fine clear view of the Battery and North River, all that remained of the case was being polished off.

Earlier the police commissioner and the chief of police had had a heart-to-heart talk about possible corruption in the Harlem branch of the police department.

"There are strong indications that Galen was protected by some influential person up there, either in the police department or in the city government," the police commissioner said.

"Not in the department," the chief maintained. "In the first place, that low license number of his—UG-16—tells me he had friends higher up than a precinct captain, because that kind of a license number is only issued to the specially privileged, and that don't even include me."

"Did you find any connections with politicians in that area?"

"Not connecting Galen; but the woman, Reba, telephoned a colored councilman this morning and ordered him to get down here and get her out on bail."

The commissioner sighed. "Perhaps we'll never know the extent of Galen's activities up there."

"Maybe not, but one thing we know," the chief said. "The son of a bitch is dead, and his money won't corrupt anybody else."

Afterwards the police commissioner reviewed the suspension of Coffin Ed which the chief had clamped on him the night before.

Grave Digger and Lieutenant Anderson were present along with the chief at this conference.

Coffin Ed had exercised his privilege to be absent.

"In the light of subsequent developments in this case, I am inclined to be lenient towards Detective Johnson," the commissioner said. "His compulsion to fire at the youth is understandable, if not justifiable, in view of his previous unfortunate experience with an acid thrower." The commissioner had come into office by way of a law practice and could handle those jawbreaking words with much greater ease than the cops who learned their trade pounding beats.

"What's your opinion, Jones?" he asked.

Grave Digger turned from his customary seat, one ham propped on the window ledge and one foot planted on the floor, and said, "Yes sir, he's been touchy and on edge ever since that con-man threw the acid in his eyes, but he was never rough on anybody in the right."

"Hell, I wasn't disciplining Johnson so much as I was just taking the weight off the whole goddamned police department," the chief said in defense of his action. "We'd have caught holy hell from all the sob sisters, male and female, in this town if those punks had turned out to be innocent pranksters."

"So you are in favor of his reinstatement?" the commissioner asked.

"Why not," the chief said. "If he's got the jumps let him work them off on those hoodlums up in Harlem who gave them to him."

"Right ho," the commissioner said, then turned to Grave Digger again: "Perhaps you can tell me, Jones; this aspect of the case has me puzzled. All of the reports state that there was a huge crowd of people present at the victim's death, and witnessed the actual shooting. One report states—" He fumbled among the papers on his desk until he found the page he wanted. " 'The street was packed with people for a distance of two blocks when deceased met death by gunfire.' Why is this? Why do the people up in Harlem congregate about a killing as though it were a three ring circus?"

"It is," Grave Digger said tersely. "It's the greatest show on earth."

"That happens everywhere," Anderson said. "People will congregate at a killing wherever it takes place."

"Yes, of course, out of morbid curiosity. But I don't mean that exactly. According to reports, not only the reports on this case, but all reports that have come into my office, this, er, phenomenon let us say, is more evident in Harlem than any place else. What do you think, Jones?"

"Well, it's like this, Mister Commissioner," Grave Digger said. "Every day in Harlem, two and three times a day, the colored people see some colored man being chased by another colored man with a knife or an axe or a club. Or else being chased by a white cop with a gun, or by a white man with his fists. But it's only once in a blue moon they get to see a white man being chased by one of them. A big white man at that. That was an event. A chance to see some white blood spilled for a change, and spilled by a black man at that. That was greater than Emancipation Day. As they say up in Harlem, that was the greatest. That's what Ed and I are always up against when we try to make Harlem safe for white people."

"Perhaps I can explain it," the commissioner said.

"Not to me," the chief said drily. "I ain't got the time to listen. If the folks up there want to see blood, they're going to see all the blood they want if they kill another white man."

"Jones is right," Anderson said. "But it makes for trouble."

"Trouble!" Grave Digger echoed. "All they know up there is trouble. If trouble was money, everybody in Harlem would be a millionaire."

The telephone rang. The commissioner picked up the receiver.

"Yes? . . . Yes, send him up." He replaced the receiver and said, "It's the ballistics report. It's coming up."

"Fine," the chief said. "Let's write it in the record and close this case up. It was a dirty business from start to finish and I'm sick and goddamned tired of it."

"Right ho," the commissioner said.

Some one knocked.

"Come in," he said.

The lieutenant from homicide who had worked on the case

came in and placed the zip gun and the battered lead pellet taken from the murdered man's brain on the commissioner's desk.

The commissioner picked up the gun and examined it curiously.

"So this is a zip gun?"

"Yes sir. It's made from an ordinary toy cap pistol. The barrel of the toy pistol is sawed off and this four inch section of heavy brass pipe is fitted in its place. See, it's soldered to the frame, then for greater stability it's bound with adjustable clamps of the kind used to hold small pipe or electrical cables in place. The shell goes directly into the barrel, then this clip is inserted to prevent it from backfiring. The firing pin is soldered to the original hammer. On this one it's made from the head and a quarter-inch section of an ordinary no. 6 nail, filed down to a point."

"It is more primitive than I had imagined, but it is certainly ingenious."

The others looked at it with bored indifference; they had seen zip guns before.

"And this will project a bullet with sufficient force to kill a man, to penetrate his skull?"

"Yes sir."

"Well, well, so this is the gun which killed Galen and led the boy who made it to be killed in turn."

"No sir, not this gun."

"What!"

Everybody sat bolt upright with stretched eyes and open mouths. Had the lieutenant said the Empire State Building had been stolen and smuggled out of town, he couldn't have caused greater stupefaction.

"What do you mean, not that gun!" the chief roared.

"That's what I came up to tell you," the lieutenant said. "This gun fires a .22 calibre bullet. It contained the case of a .22 calibre shell when the sergeant found it. Galen was killed with a .32 calibre bullet fired from a more powerful pistol."

"This is where we came in," Anderson said.

"I'll be goddamned if it is!" the chief bellowed like an enraged bull. "The papers have already gotten the story that he was killed with this gun and have gone crazy with it. We'll be the laughing stock of the world."

"No," the commissioner said quietly but firmly. "We have made a mistake, that is all."

"I'll be goddamned if we have," the chief said, his face turning blood red with passion. "I say the son of a bitch was killed with that gun and that punk lying in the morgue killed him, and I don't give a goddamned what ballistics show."

The commissioner looked solemnly from face to face. There was no question in his eyes, but he waited for some one else to speak.

"I don't think it's worth re-opening the case," Lieutenant Anderson said. "Galen wasn't a particularly lovable character."

"Lovable or not, we got the killer and that's the gun and that's that," the chief said.

"Can we afford to let a murderer go free?" the commissioner asked quietly.

"Who said anything about letting a murderer go free," the chief said.

The commissioner looked again from face to face.

"This one," Grave Digger said harshly. "He did a public service."

"That's not for us to determine, is it?" the commissioner said.

"You'll have to decide that, sir," Grave Digger said. "But if you assign me to look for the killer, I resign."

"Er, what? Resign from the force?"

"Yes sir. I say the killer will never kill again and I'm not going to track him down to pay for this killing even if it costs me my job."

"Who killed him, Jones?"

"I couldn't say, sir."

The commissioner looked grave. "Was he as bad as that?"

"Yes sir."

The commissioner looked at the lieutenant from homicide. "But this zip gun was fired, wasn't it?"

"Yes sir. But I've checked with all the hospitals and the precinct stations in Harlem and there has been no gunshot injury reported."

"Some one could have been injured who would be afraid to report it."

"Yes sir. Or the bullet might have landed harmlessly against a building or an automobile."

"Yes. But there are the other boys who are involved. They might be indicted for complicity. If it is proved that they were his accomplices, they face the maximum penalty for murder."

"Yes sir," Anderson said. "But it's been pretty well established that the murder—or rather the action of the boy firing the zip gun—was not premeditated. And the others knew nothing of his intention to fire at Galen until it was too late to prevent him."

"According to their statements."

"Well, yes sir. But it's up to us to accept their statements or have them bound over to the grand jury for indictment. If we don't charge complicity when they go up for arraignment the court will only fine them for disturbing the peace."

The commissioner looked back at the lieutenant from homicide. "Who else knows about this?"

"No one outside of this office, sir. They never had the gun in ballistics; they only had the bullet."

"Shall we put it to a vote?" the commissioner asked.

No one said anything.

"The ayes have it," the commissioner said. He picked up the small lead pellet that had murdered a man. "Jones, there is a flat roof on a building across the park. Do you think you can throw this so it will land there?"

"If I can't, sir, my name ain't Don Newcombe," Grave Digger said.

18.

2702 Seventh Avenue was an old stone apartment house with pseudo-Greek trimmings left over from the days when Harlem was a fashionable white neighborhood and the Negro slums centered about San Juan Hill on West 42nd Street.

Grave Digger pushed open the cracked glass door and searched for the name of Coolie Dunbar among the row of mail boxes nailed to the front hall wall. He found the name on a flyspecked card, followed by the apartment number, 3-B.

The automatic elevator, one of the first made, was out of order.

He climbed the dark ancient stairs to the third floor and knocked on the left hand door at the front.

A middle-aged brownskin woman with a worried expression opened the door and said, "Coolie's at work and we've told the people already we'll come in and pay our rent in the office when—"

"I'm not the rent collector, I'm a detective," Grave Digger said, flashing his badge.

"Oh!" The worried expression turned to one of apprehension. "You're Mr. Johnson's partner. I thought you were finished with her."

"Almost. May I talk to her."

"I don't see why you got to keep on bothering her if you ain't got nothing on Mr. Johnson's daughter," she complained as she guarded the entrance. "They were both in it together."

"I'm not going to arrest her. I would just like to ask her a few questions to clear up the last details."

"She's in bed now."

"I don't mind."

"All right," she consented grudgingly. "Come on in. But if you've got to arrest her, then keep her. Me and Coolie have been disgraced enough by that girl. We're respectable church people—"

"I'm sure of it," he cut her off. "But she's your niece, isn't she?"

"She's Coolie's niece. I haven't got any wild ones in my family."

"You're lucky," he said.

She pursed her lips and opened a door next to the kitchen.

"Here's a policeman to see you, Sissie," she said.

Grave Digger entered the small bedroom and closed the door behind him.

Sissie lay in a narrow single bed with the covers pulled up to her chin. At sight of Grave Digger her red, tear-swollen eyes grew wide with terror.

He drew up the single hard-back chair and sat down.

"You're a very lucky little girl," he said. "You have just missed being a murderer."

"I don't know what you mean," she said in a terrified whisper.

"Listen," he said. "Don't lie to me. I'm dogtired and you children have already made me as depressed as I've ever been. You don't know what kind of hell it is sometimes to be a cop."

She watched him like a half-wild kitten poised for flight.

"I didn't kill him. Sheik killed him," she whispered.

"We know Sheik killed him," he said in a flat voice. He looked weary beyond words. "Listen, I'm not here as a cop. I'm here as a friend. Ed Johnson is my closest friend and his daughter is your closest friend. That ought to make us friends too. As a friend I tell you we've got to get rid of the gun."

She hesitated, debating with herself, then said quickly before she could change her mind, "I threw it down a water drain on 128th Street near Fifth Avenue."

He sighed. "That's good enough. What kind of gun was it?"

"It was a thirty-two. It had the picture of an owl's head on the handle and Uncle Coolie called it an Owls Head."

"Has he missed it?"

"He missed it out of the drawer this morning when he started for work and asked Aunt Cora if she'd moved it. But he ain't said nothing to me yet. He was late for work and I think he wanted to give me all day to put it back."

"Does he need it in his work?"

"Oh no, he works in a garage in the Bronx."

"Good. Does he have a permit for it?"

"No sir. That's what he's so worried about."

"Okay. Now listen. When he asks you about it tonight, you tell him you took it to protect yourself against Mr. Galen and that during the excitement you left it in Sheik's room. Tell him that I found it there but I don't know whom it belongs to. He won't say any more about it."

"Yes sir. But he's going to be awfully mad."

"Well, Sissie, you can't escape all punishment."

"No sir."

"Why did you shoot at Mr. Galen anyway? You can tell me now since it doesn't matter."

"It wasn't on account of myself," she said. "It was on account of Sugartit—Evelyn Johnson. He was after her all the time and I was afraid he was going to get her. She tries to be wild and does crazy things sometimes and I was afraid he was going to get her and do to her what he did to me. That would ruin her. She ain't an orphan like me with nobody to really care what happens to her; she's from a good family with a father and a mother and a good home and I wasn't going to let him ruin her."

He sat there listening to her, a big tough lumpy-faced cop, looking as though he might cry.

"How'd you plan to do it?" he asked.

"Oh, I was just going to shoot him. I'd made a date with him at the Inn for me and Sugartit, but I wasn't going to take her. I was going to make him drive me out somewhere in his car by telling him we were going to pick her up; and then I was going to shoot him and run away. I took Uncle Coolie's pistol and hid it downstairs in the hall in a hole in the plaster so I could get it when I went out. But before time came for me to go, Sugartit came by here. I wasn't expecting her and I couldn't tell her I wanted to go out so it was late before I could get rid of her. I left her at the subway at 125th Street, thinking she was going home, then I ran all the way over to Lenox to meet Mr. Galen; but when I got over on Lenox I saw all the commotion going on. Then I saw him come running down the street and Sonny chasing him with a gun shooting at him. It looked like half the people in Harlem were running after him. I got in the crowd and followed and when I caught up with him at 127th Street I saw that Sonny was going to shoot at him again, so I shot at him too. I don't think anyone even saw me shoot; everybody was looking at Sonny. But when I saw him fall and all the Moslems in their costumes run up and gang around him I was scared one of them was going to see me, so I ran around the block and threw the gun in a drain then came back to Caleb's from the other way and made out like I didn't know what had happened. I didn't know then that Caleb had been shot."

"Have you told anyone else about this?"

"No sir. When I saw Sugartit come sneaking into Caleb's, I was going to tell her I'd shot him because I knew she'd come back looking for him. But Choo-Choo had let it slip out that Sheik was carrying his zip gun, and then after Sonny said his gun wouldn't shoot anything but blanks I knew right away it was Sheik who'd shot him; and I was scared to say anything."

"Good. Now listen to me. Don't tell anybody else. I won't tell anybody either. We'll just keep it to ourselves, our own private secret. Okay?"

"Yes sir. You can bet I won't tell anybody else. I just want to forget about it—if I ever can."

"Good. I don't suppose there's any need of me telling you to keep away from bad company; you ought to have learned your lesson by now."

"I'm going to do that, I promise."

"Good. Well, Sissie," Grave Digger said, getting slowly to his feet. "You made your bed hard, if it hurts lying on it, don't complain."

It was the visiting hour next day in the Centre Street jail.

Sissie said, "I brought you some cigarettes, Sonny. I didn't know whether you had a girl to bring you any."

"Thanks," Sonny said. "I ain't got no girl."

"How long do you think they'll give you?"

"Six months, I suppose."

"That much. Just for what you did."

"They don't like for people to shoot at anybody, even if you don't hit them, or even if they ain't shooting nothing but blanks like what I did."

"I know," she said sympathetically. "Maybe you're getting off easy at that."

"I ain't complaining," Sonny said.

"What are you going to do when you get out?"

"Go back to shining shoes, I suppose."

"What's going to happen to your shine parlor?"

"Oh, I'll lose that one, but I'll get me another one."

"You got a car?"

"I had one but I couldn't keep up the payments and the man took it back."

"You need a girl to look after you."

"Yeah, who don't? What you going to do yourself, now that your boyfriend's dead?"

"I don't know. I just want to get married."

"That shouldn't be hard for you."

"I don't know anybody who'll have me."

"Why not?"

"I've done a lot of bad things."

"Like what?"

"I'd be ashamed to tell you everything I've done."

"Listen, to show you I ain't scared of nothing you might have done, I want you to be my girl."

"I don't want to play around anymore."

"Who's talking about playing around. I'm talking about for keeps."

"I don't mind. But there's something I've got to tell you first. It's about me and Sheik."

"What about you and Sheik?"

"I'm going to have a baby by the time you get out of jail."

"Well, that makes it different," he said. "We'd better get married right away. I'll talk to the man and ask him to see if he can't arrange it."

BIOGRAPHICAL NOTES

NOTE ON THE TEXTS

NOTES

Biographical Notes

JIM THOMPSON   Born September 27, 1906, in Anadarko, Oklahoma Territory. Father was a peace officer, later a lawyer, accountant, and oil man; mother was a teacher. Raised in Oklahoma, Nebraska, and Texas. Worked as bellboy at the Hotel Texas, Fort Worth, while in high school; suffered nervous collapse partly precipitated by heavy drinking (in later life suffered from alcoholism). As an itinerant worker in the West Texas oil fields, joined the Wobblies in 1926. Enrolled in the College of Agriculture of the University of Nebraska in 1929. Published folklore, sketches, stories, and poems in *Texas Monthly*, *Prairie Schooner*, and *Cornhusker Countryman*. Married Alberta Hesse in September 1931; daughter Patricia born in 1932. Returned to Fort Worth and worked as night doorman at the Worth Hotel; wrote for *True Detective*, *Master Detective*, *Daring Detective*, and other true crime magazines. Moved to Oklahoma City in 1936, and joined the Oklahoma Federal Writers' Project. Second daughter, Sharon, born in 1936, and son Michael in 1938. Appointed director of the Writers' Project in 1938. Contracted with Viking to write *Always To Be Blest* (novel was never published). Left Writers' Project; received fellowship from Rockefeller Foundation General Education Board to write book about southwestern building trades, *We Talked About Labor* (never published). Moved to San Diego in 1940, and joined Ryan Aeronautical Company as stockroom clerk and book-keeper. Published novel *Now and On Earth*, based closely on his experiences at Ryan, in 1942. Took job as timekeeper at Solar Aircraft Company in San Diego. Published *Heed the Thunder*, agrarian novel based on history of mother's family, in 1946. Worked as reporter for *San Diego Journal* and rewrite man for *Los Angeles Mirror*, 1947–48. First crime novel, *Nothing More Than Murder*, published in 1949. Moved to New York City in 1950 and worked as editor at *Saga* (1950–51) and *Police Gazette* (1951–52). Wrote series of paperback originals for Lion Books with strong encouragement of Lion editor Arnold Hano: *The Killer Inside Me* (1952), *Cropper's Cabin* (1952), *Recoil* (1953), *The Alcoholics* (1953), *Savage Night* (1953), *The Criminal* (1953), *The Golden Gizmo* (1954), *A Swell-Looking Babe* (1954), *A Hell of a Woman* (1954), *The Kill-Off* (1957), and two ostensible autobiographies, *Bad Boy* (1953) and *Roughneck* (1954); during same period also published *The Nothing Man* (1954) with Dell and *After Dark, My Sweet* (1955) with Popular Library. Worked on screenplays for two films directed by Stanley Kubrick, *The Killing* (1955) and *Paths of Glory* (1957). Published *Wild Town* (1957) with New American Library and moved to Hollywood, where during the late 1950s and early 1960s he wrote teleplays for *Mackenzie's Raiders*, *Cain's Hundred*, and *Doctor Kildare*. Published *The Getaway* (1959), *The Transgressors* (1961), *The Grifters* (1963), *Pop. 1280* (1964), *Texas by the Tail* (1965), and *South of Heaven* (1967) as paperback originals. Was involved in various unproduced film projects, including hobo screenplays written for Tony Bill and Robert Redford; hired to write novelizations of television series *Ironside* (1967) and films *The Undefeated* (1969) and *Nothing But a Man* (1969). Published *Child of Rage* (1972) and *King Blood* (1973). *The Getaway* filmed by Sam Peckinpah in 1973; *The Killer Inside Me* filmed by Burt Kennedy in 1975. Played small role in *Farewell, My Lovely* (1975, directed by Dick Richards). Died in Los Angeles on April 7, 1977.

PATRICIA HIGHSMITH   Born Patricia Plangman in January 19, 1921, in Fort Worth, Texas; parents divorced shortly after her birth, and she moved to New York City with mother and stepfather Stanley Highsmith; grew up mostly under care of maternal grandmother. Graduated Barnard College in 1942. In 1948 stayed at Yaddo, writers' colony in Saratoga, New York, along with Chester Himes, Truman Capote, and Katherine Anne Porter. Published first novel, *Strangers on a Train*, in 1950 (rights purchased for small amount by Alfred Hitchcock, whose film version, starring Farley Granger and Robert Walker, was released the following year). *The Price of Salt*, a novel with a lesbian theme, published under pseudonym Claire Morgan in 1952. Moved to Europe, living in Italy, England, and France; settled in a small village near Locarno, Switzerland, in 1981. Published series of novels including *The Blunderer* (1954), *The Talented Mr. Ripley* (1955), *Deep Water* (1957), *A Game for the Living* (1958), *This Sweet Sickness* (1960), *The Cry of the Owl* (1962), *The Two Faces of January* (1964), *The Glass Cell* (1964), *The Story-Teller* (1965), *Those Who Walk Away* (1967), *The Tremor of Forgery* (1969), *Ripley Under Ground* (1970), *A Dog's Ransom* (1972), *Ripley's Game* (1974), *Edith's Diary* (1977), *The Boy Who Followed Ripley* (1980), *People Who Knock on the Door* (1982), *Found in the Street* (1986), and *Ripley Under Water* (1992); also published a number of collections of short stories and a guide for writers, *Plotting and Writing Suspense Fiction* (1966). Her work was frequently adapted by European filmmakers including Rene Clement (*Purple Noon*, based on *The Talented Mr. Ripley*), Wim Wenders (*The American Friend*, based on *Ripley's Game*), Claude Chabrol (*The Cry of the Owl*), and Claude Miller (*This Sweet Sickness*). Besides writing she occupied herself with drawing, sculpture, and gardening. Died February 4, 1995, in Locarno, Switzerland. A final novel, *Small g: A Summer Idyll*, was published posthumously in 1995.

CHARLES WILLEFORD Born January 2, 1919, in Little Rock, Arkansas. Joined U.S. Army in 1936. Served as tank commander in Europe during World War II, earning Silver Star, Bronze Star, Purple Heart, and Luxembourg Croix de Guerre. Wrote radio serial "The Saga of Mary Miller" for Armed Forces Radio Service in 1948. First book, poetry collection *Proletarian Laughter*, published 1948. Married Mary Jo Norton in 1951 (divorced, 1976). First novel, paperback original *High Priest of California* (1953), followed by other novels written for small paperback imprints: *Pick-Up* (1955), *Wild Wives* (1954, also known as *Until I Am Dead*), *Lust Is a Woman* (1956), *Soldier's Wife* (1958), *Honey Gal* (1958, also known as *The Black Mass of Brother Springer*), and *The Woman Chaser* (1958, also known as *The Director*). Television play *The Basic Approach* broadcast by Canadian Broadcasting Corporation, 1956. Retired from military in 1956 with rank of master sergeant. After leaving military attended Palm Beach Junior College; obtained B.A. (1962) and M.A. (1964) from University of Miami, where he worked as instructor in humanities department, 1964–67. From 1967 served as English professor, and later chairman of English and philosophy departments, at Miami-Dade Junior College. Published further fiction including *Understudy for Love* (1961), *No Experience Necessary* (1962, in a version drastically revised by publisher), *The Machine in Ward Eleven* (1962), *The Burnt Orange Heresy* (1971), *Hombre from Sonora* (1972), *Cockfighter* (1962, revised 1972), and *Off the Wall* (1980). Also published *Poontang and Other Poems* (1967) and critical study *New Forms of Ugly: The Immobilized Man in Modern Literature* (1967). Achieved wider success with series of novels about Miami police detective Hoke Mosley: *Miami Blues* (1984), *New Hope for the Dead* (1985), and *Sideswipe* (1987). Also published memoir *Something About a Soldier* (1986). Died in Miami of a heart attack on March 27, 1988. The final Hoke Mosley book, *The Way We Die Now* (1988), the memoir *I Was Looking for a Street* (1988), and another novel, *The Shark-Infested Custard* (1990), were published posthumously.

DAVID GOODIS Born 1917 in Philadelphia. Attended University of Indiana in 1936 and Temple University, 1937–38; had already begun writing for the pulps and other magazines. First novel, *Retreat from Oblivion*, published 1938. Moved to New York in 1939; worked for advertising agencies and wrote for radio and the pulps. Married in 1942; his wife, Elaine, left him the following year. Became associate producer of radio program *Hap Harrigan of the Airwaves* in 1945. Second novel, *Dark Passage*, published in 1946 after being serialized in *The Saturday Evening Post*. Signed contract with Warner Brothers; worked on screenplays of *The Unfaithful* (1947, directed by Vincent

Sherman) and *Dark Passage* (1947, directed by Delmer Daves and starring Humphrey Bogart and Lauren Bacall); published novels *Behold This Woman* and *Nightfall* in 1947. *Dark Passage* appeared in French translation in 1949, and Goodis's books thereafter enjoyed great popularity and literary respect in France. After gradual decline of his screenwriting career, left Hollywood in 1950 and returned to his family home in Philadelphia, where he lived for the rest of his life. Published first paperback original, *Cassidy's Girl*, for Gold Medal in 1951; last hardcover novel, *Of Missing Persons*, published the same year. Continued to write novels for Gold Medal (*Street of the Lost*, 1952; *Of Tender Sin*, 1952; *The Moon in the Gutter*, 1953; *Street of No Return*, 1954; *The Wounded and the Slain*, 1955; *Down There*, 1956; *Fire in the Flesh*, 1957) and for Lion Books (*The Burglar*, 1953; *The Blonde on the Street Corner*, 1954; *Black Friday*, 1954). Film version of *Nightfall*, directed by Jacques Tourneur and starring Aldo Ray and Anne Bancroft, released in 1956. Collaborated with director Paul Wendkos, an old friend from Philadelphia, on film adaptation of *The Burglar*, starring Jayne Mansfield and Dan Duryea, that was released in 1957. Film version of *Down There*, directed by François Truffaut under title *Tirez sur le pianiste* (*Shoot the Piano Player*), starring Charles Aznavour, released 1960. Final Gold Medal novel, *Night Squad*, appeared in 1961. Met Truffaut in New York at American opening of *Shoot the Piano Player*. Sued producers of the television series *The Fugitive* in 1965, claiming it appropriated elements from *Dark Passage* (suit was settled out of court after Goodis's death). Died January 7, 1967, in Philadelphia. Last novel, *Somebody's Done For*, published later that year.

CHESTER HIMES   Born July 29, 1909, in Jefferson City, Missouri. Moved with family in 1914 to Cleveland, Ohio, where father was chairman of Mechanical Arts Department of Alcorn College; family later lived in Georgia and Arkansas before returning to Cleveland in 1925. Attended Ohio State University, 1926–28. Left university and worked as bellhop. Arrested twice for armed robbery during 1928, and sentenced in December to 20–25 years of hard labor in Ohio State Penitentiary. Survived fire that killed over 300 inmates in 1930. While in prison, began publishing short stories in *Atlanta Daily World*, *Esquire*, and other periodicals. Paroled in April 1936; returned to Cleveland. Married Jean Johnson in August 1937. Worked at a variety of jobs, including writing assignments for the Federal Writers' Project and the CIO; wrote first version of prison novel later published as *Cast the First Stone*. Hired by novelist Louis Bromfield to work on his farm (Bromfield subsequently attempted to promote his literary career); formed friendship with novelist Richard Wright and his wife,

Ellen. Moved to Los Angeles and between 1940 and 1943 worked in war industries there and in San Francisco. Moved to New York City. First novel, *If He Hollers Let Him Go*, published in 1945, followed by *Lonely Crusade* (1947). Separated from wife in 1950. Published *Cast the First Stone* (1952), a novel based on his prison experience, before moving to France in 1953. Published *The Third Generation* (1954). *The End of a Primitive* published by New American Library in censored form in 1956 as *The Primitive*. Marcel Duhamel, editor of the Série Noire (crime fiction series published by Gallimard), asked Himes in 1956 to write a detective novel for the series. The novel was published in French as *La Reine des pommes* and in English as *For Love of Imabelle* and *A Rage in Harlem* (Himes's title, never used, was *The Five Cornered Square*); it won an important French prize, the Grand Prix de la Littérature Policière. It was the first of a series of novels featuring Harlem detectives Coffin Ed Johnson and Grave Digger Jones, a number of which appeared in French before they were published in America as paperback originals: *The Real Cool Killers* (1959), *The Crazy Kill* (1960), *The Big Gold Dream* (1960), *All Shot Up* (1960), *Cotton Comes to Harlem* (1965), *The Heat's On* (1966), and *Blind Man with a Pistol* (1969). Also published non-series novels: *A Case of Rape* (1963 in French only; first English-language publication 1984), *Pinktoes* (1965), and *Run Man Run* (1966). Met Malcolm X in Paris in 1962. Married Lesley Packard in 1965, and moved with her to Alicante, Spain, in 1968. Film version of *Cotton Comes to Harlem*, directed by Ossie Davis and starring Godfrey Cambridge and Raymond St. Jacques, released in 1970, followed by *Come Back Charleston Blue* (1972, based on *The Heat's On*), directed by Mark Warren with the same leading actors. Visited New York in 1972 and was honored by Carnegie Endowment for International Peace. His autobiography was published in two volumes as *The Quality of Hurt* (1972) and *My Life of Absurdity* (1976). Novel *Plan B* published in French in 1983 (English-language publication 1993). Died November 12, 1984, in Moraira, Spain.

Note on the Texts

This volume collects five American novels of the 1950s that have come to be identified with the "noir" genre of crime fiction: *The Killer Inside Me* by Jim Thompson (1952); *The Talented Mr. Ripley* by Patricia Highsmith (1955); *Pick-Up* by Charles Willeford (1955); *Down There* by David Goodis (1956); and *The Real Cool Killers* by Chester Himes (1959).

In the summer of 1952 Jim Thompson was introduced by Ingrid Hallen, his literary agent, to Arnold Hano, editor-in-chief of Lion Books, a paperback line begun in 1949 by Magazine Management Company, which also published Marvel Comics and a variety of pulp magazines. Lion Books issued original fiction in softcover as well as paperback reprints of hardcover titles; the firm often commissioned writers to develop novels from short synopses, usually about two-thirds of a page in length, that were prepared by Lion editors. Hano showed Thompson several of these story ideas, and Thompson chose to work from a synopsis, written by Lion editor Jim Bryans, for a novel about a New York City policeman who murders a prostitute he is involved with. Working at his home in Astoria, Queens, Thompson wrote the first twelve chapters of *The Killer Inside Me* in two weeks. After submitting them to Lion, he went to stay with Maxine and Joseph Kouba, his sister and brother-in-law, at their home on the marine base at Quantico, Virginia, where he completed the novel in another two weeks. *The Killer Inside Me*, Thompson's fourth published novel and the first of eleven books that he would publish with Lion between 1952 and 1954, was brought out by Lion Books in September 1952. Thompson did not revise the book after its initial publication. This volume prints the text of the first edition.

Patricia Highsmith recalled in an interview published in 1993 that she began to imagine the character of Tom Ripley when she saw a man walking along a beach in Positano, Italy. "I wondered why he was there alone at 6 A.M. Later I thought of a story about a man sent to Positano on a mission, and maybe he failed." *The Talented Mr. Ripley*, Highsmith's fourth novel, was published in 1955 by Coward-McCann, Inc. Highsmith did not revise the book after its initial publication. This volume prints the text of the first edition.

Charles Willeford wrote *Pick-Up*, his second novel, while serving as a sergeant in the United States Air Force. He sold the novel to Beacon Books, a paperback line established in 1954 by Universal Publishing and Distribution Corporation. (This corporation also owned

Royal Books, the paperback line that had published Willeford's first novel, *High Priest of California*, in 1953, after it had been rejected by Fawcett Gold Medal.) *Pick-Up* was published in 1955 as a "Beacon First Award Original Novel" and was the first of five Willeford novels, including a reissue of *High Priest of California*, to appear as a Beacon Book between 1955 and 1957. Willeford made no changes in the novel after its initial publication. This volume prints the text of the first edition.

David Goodis published five novels in hardcover between 1938, the year he graduated from Temple University, and 1950, when he left Hollywood and returned to Philadelphia to live with his parents. Goodis then began writing fiction for original paperback publication, and between 1951 and 1955 he published six novels with Gold Medal Books, a paperback line founded by Fawcett Publications in 1949, and three novels with Lion Books. *Down There*, his seventh novel for Fawcett Gold Medal, was published as a "Gold Medal Original" in November 1956. Goodis did not revise *Down There* after its initial publication. This volume prints the text of the first edition.

Chester Himes was living in Paris in 1956 when he met poet Marcel Duhamel while visiting Editions Gallimard, the publishing house. Duhamel had translated Himes's first novel, *If He Hollers Let Him Go*, into French; he was also the founder and editor of the Série Noire, a series of crime novels (established in 1945 and published by Gallimard) that presented work by French, British, and American writers. During their meeting, Duhamel asked Himes to write a crime novel for the Série Noire and suggested that he study the novels of Peter Cheyney (the British writer who created the series character Lemmy Caution), Raymond Chandler, and Dashiell Hammett. Himes agreed and began writing a story about a confidence game. He showed the first 80 pages of the manuscript to Duhamel, who told him that a crime novel should have police characters in it; Himes then introduced two detectives, Coffin Ed Johnson and Grave Digger Jones, into the story. Himes completed the novel, which he called *The Five Cornered Square*, early in 1957. It was published in France by Gallimard in 1958 as *La Reine des pommes* and in the United States by Fawcett Gold Medal in 1957 as *For Love of Imabelle* (a new American edition was published by Avon in 1965 under the title *A Rage in Harlem*).

Using the title *If Trouble Was Money*, Himes wrote his third novel for the Série Noire, and his third to feature the team of Coffin Ed and Grave Digger, in the summer of 1957 while staying in Hørsholm, a village outside of Copenhagen, Denmark. The novel was translated into French by Chantel Wourgraft and published by Gallimard in 1958 as *Il pleut des coups durs*. An American edition was published in paperback as an Avon Original by Avon Publications, Inc., in 1959 under the title *The Real Cool Killers*. Two typescripts of *The Real Cool Killers* are in the James Weldon Johnson Memorial Collection of the Beinecke Library at Yale University. One typescript, 205 pages in length, is complete; the other, 203 pages long, is missing the last two pages of the novel. Except for the retyping of the first page of the 205-page version, and the cancellation by overtyping in the 205-page version of passages cancelled by hand in the 203-page version, the typing of the two documents is identical. Both typescripts are titled "If Trouble Was Money"; the 205-page version has been re-titled "The Real Cool Killers," while the 203-page version has "Real Cool Killers" written above the original title.

The 203-page typescript contains handwritten revisions by Himes not found in the 205-page version, while the 205-page typescript, which was used as setting copy for the 1959 Avon edition, contains extensive handwritten revisions, not found in the 203-page version, that were made by someone other than Himes—most probably, by an editor working for Avon Publications. These editorial revisions, which were made throughout the novel and substantively alter the wording of many passages, were incorporated in the 1959 edition and in all subsequent American editions. For example, at 734.13–15 of this volume, where Himes wrote, "The big white man turned to face him, looking as though he were caught in a situation where he didn't know whether to laugh or to get angry," the Avon text reads, "The big white man turned to face him, looking as though he didn't know whether to laugh or to get angry"; at 735.36, where Himes wrote, "The severed coat-sleeved short-arm, still clutching the knife," the Avon text reads, "The severed arm in its coat sleeve, still clutching the knife"; and at 803.5–6 the passage "She stared long into his eyes. She had dark brown eyes with clear whites and long black lashes faintly seen" was changed to "She stared into his eyes. She had dark brown eyes with clear whites and long black lashes."

The second volume of Himes's autobiography, *My Life of Absurdity* (1976), contains evidence that these revisions were made in the 1959 Avon edition without the knowledge or approval of Himes. Regarding the publication of his detective novels in the United States in the early 1960s, Himes wrote, "By that time my books were published in America in paperback, but the American publishers didn't pay any more than Série Noire and they scrambled the books up in what they call editing and they were practically senseless." Himes also printed in his autobiography a letter written to him from the United States by his friend Herbert Hill on August 14, 1961; in this letter, Hill reports on his efforts to find and send to Himes a copy of *The Real Cool Killers*, suggesting that at the time Himes had not yet seen the

1959 Avon edition. Therefore, the text of *The Real Cool Killers* presented in this volume is taken from the two typescripts in the James Weldon Johnson Memorial Collection of the Beinecke Library: the text of the 203-page typescript is printed on pp. 733.1–875.26 of this volume, and the text of the last two pages of the 205-page typescript, which do not contain any editorial alterations, are printed on pp. 875.27–876.22. (These typescripts are reprinted by permission of the Yale Collection of American Literature, Beinecke Rare Book and Manuscript Library, Yale University.) In presenting the text of these typescripts, this volume accepts Himes's handwritten and typed revisions and corrects unmistakable typing errors.

This volume presents the texts of the original printings and typescripts chosen for inclusion here, but it does not attempt to reproduce features of their typographic design, such as display capitalization of chapter openings. The texts are printed without change, except for the correction of typographical errors. Spelling, punctuation, and capitalization are often expressive features, and they are not altered, even when inconsistent or irregular. The following is a list of typographical errors corrected, cited by page and line number: 57.26, bulls-eyes; 61.4, If fitted; 80.11, him.; 80.28, The. . . . ; 82.7, and. . . . ?; 98.18, They. . . . ; 100.31, he's; 120.18, here to; 144.3, as you; 189.37, *Ambassador*; 195.40, cartilege; 200.34, UM-hm; 202.19, Georgio's; 202.20, Georgio's; 362.6, him.; 380.13, at at; 383.25, screaching; 412.33, She; 419.12, He; 432.16, anyway; 434.32, She; 441.30, acadamic; 460.19, hospital; 468.12, He; 468.32, latrine,; 469.16, Jordan,; 470.23, patient's; 473.28, dishwasher,; 476.3, on,; 477.21, window,; 477.27, She; 478.32, See; 479.33, so,; 481.37, hand—" whether; 482.11, you,; 488.22, Company; 490.27, seregant; 490.34, She; 491.27, The; 494.14, She; 494.34, She; 502.11, She; 505.26, However;; 506.8, said,; 506.21, colds,; 509.31, winow; 511.16, He; 513.19, He; 520.8, The; 520.21, Why; 522.13, He; 524.10, said,; 527.7, side; 528.5, tne; 530.31, idea.; 530.33, He; 531.16, He; 532.1, The; 534.16, it's; 538.19, Center.; 541.18, city;; 543.20, He; 545.27, He; 545.31, in; 548.18, your; 548.35, litttle; 550.18, He; 551.13, Nothing.; 551.34, nevously; 552.2, She; 552.24, then; 558.34, Meredith,; 562.13, He; 578.36, mens'; 634.35, reply.; 651.22, tuned; 651.23, that"; 651.24, mean"; 654.7, years,; 671.18, an; 682.5, fingers."; 683.33, face—"; 769.13, Jamacia.

Notes

In the notes below, the reference numbers denote page and line of this volume (the line count includes headings). No note is made for material included in standard desk-reference books such as Webster's *Collegiate*, *Biographical*, and *Geographical* dictionaries. For references to other studies and further biographical background than is contained in the Biographical Notes, see Robert Polito, *Savage Art: A Biography of Jim Thompson* (New York: Alfred A. Knopf, 1995); *Fireworks: The Lost Writings of Jim Thompson* (New York: Donald I. Fine, 1988), edited by Robert Polito and Michael McCauley; Philippe Garnier, *Goodis: La Vie en Noir et Blanc* (Paris: Editions du Seuil, 1984); Richard Gehr, "The Pope of Psychopulp: Charles Ray Willeford's Unholy Rites," *Voice Literary Supplement*, March 1989; Lou Stathis, "Charles Willeford: New Hope for the Living," in Charles Willeford, *High Priest of California/Wild Wives* (San Francisco: Re/Search Publications, 1987); Joan Dupont, "Patricia Highsmith: Criminal Pursuits," *New York Times Magazine*, June 12, 1988; Chester Himes, *The Quality of Hurt: The Autobiography of Chester Himes, Volume I* (New York: Doubleday & Co., 1972); Chester Himes, *My Life of Absurdity: The Autobiography of Chester Himes, Volume II* (New York: Doubleday & Co., 1976); *Conversations with Chester Himes* (Jackson: University of Mississippi Press, 1995), edited by Michel Fabre and Robert E. Skinner; Gilbert H. Muller, *Chester Himes* (Boston: Twayne Publishers, 1989); Geoffrey O'Brien, *Hardboiled America: Lurid Paperbacks and the Masters of Noir* (revised edition, New York: Da Capo Press, 1997); and Lee Server, *Over My Dead Body, The Sensational Age of the American Paperback: 1945–1955* (San Francisco: Chronicle Books, 1994).

THE KILLER INSIDE ME

61.37   ACTH]   Adrenocorticotropic hormone, a cortisone derivative.

108.34   *Max Jacobsohn on Degenerative Diseases*]   The New York physician Max Jacobson over a period of years prescribed Thompson injections of vitamins, amphetamines, and animal glands; Thompson had dedicated his novel *Nothing More Than Murder* (1949) to him. Jacobson, whose other patients included John F. Kennedy, Jacqueline Kennedy, Judy Garland, and Truman Capote, had his medical license revoked in 1975.

THE TALENTED MR. RIPLEY

192.29   "My Day"] Syndicated newspaper column by Eleanor Roosevelt which began publication in 1935.

196.36   "Sempre seeneestra, seeneestra!"] *Sempre sinistra*, Italian: Keep left, left!

214.20   "Subito, signor!"] Italian: Right away, sir!

216.14   americanos] Cocktails made with Campari and sweet vermouth, garnished with an orange slice.

217.5   "Grazie tante!"] Italian: Thank you very much!

230.38–39   'voglio' . . . per esempio] Italian: 'I want' . . . 'I want to present my friend Marge,' for example.

233.3   "Posso sedermi?"] Italian: May I sit down?

234.8   "Niente, grazie] Italian: Nothing, thank you.

252.14   FERMA] Italian: Close.

254.15   "'Spetta un momento,"] Italian: Wait a moment.

270.31–32   questura . . . Permesso di Soggiorno] Italian: Police head-quarters. . . . Residency Permit.

274.15   "Ho . . . c'e arrivata] Italian: I'm afraid he hasn't arrived.

289.1–2   "Qui parla . . . Fred-derick Mee-lays?"] Italian: This is police station number 83. Are you a friend of an American named Fred-derick Mee-lays?

290.39   inamorata di te] Italian: in love with you.

293.37   "Di niente!] Italian: Not at all!

297.14–15   BARCA AFFONDATA . . . SAN REMO] Italian: Sunken boat with traces of blood found in shallow water near San Remo.

298.9   Questo e questo e questo] Italian: This and this and this.

311.15–16   *Papa non vuole . . . far' l'amor'*?] Italian: Papa doesn't want it, Mama doesn't either, / So how can we ever make love?

311.29   Giuliano] Salvatore Giuliano, notorious Sicilian bandit leader of the late 1940s, who gave interviews with the press and met with politicians while being sought by the police. He is believed to have been responsible for the murder of 11 left-wing demonstrators in Portella della Ginestra on May 1, 1947. Giuliano was assassinated by the Sicilian Mafia in 1950.

314.2–3   "Peccato . . . Grazie tante, signor."] Italian: My mistake . . . Thank you so much, sir.

331.23   "Benone!"] Italian: Very well!

338.38   il sparito . . . il assassinato] Italian: the vanished . . . the murdered.

348.6   "Pronta la collazione, signor,"] Italian: Lunch will be ready right away, sir.

356.25–30   "Mi dispiace, signor! . . . altro gondoliere!"] Italian: "I'm sorry, sir! I have to return to San Marco! I have an appointment! . . . I will call another gondolier!"

395.18   Il te, per piacere, subitissimo!] Italian: Tea, please, right away!

404.37–40   "A donda . . . il meglio!"] Italian: "Where, where?" . . . "The best hotel. The best, the best!"

PICK-UP

430.4   Rocky Marciano] Boxer (1923–69) who held the heavyweight title from 1952 to 1955, when he retired undefeated.

432.10   *Olympia*] Painting (1863) by Edouard Manet.

459.22–25   *In a dim corner . . . the shifting gloom.*] First stanza of "The Sphinx" by Oscar Wilde.

500.17–18   Van Gogh's pool table] In *The Night Cafe* (1888).

536.21   T/5] Rank of corporal in the U.S. army technical services.

DOWN THERE

611.10–13   Oscar Levant . . . Art Tatum . . . Walter Gieseking] Levant (1906–72), composer and pianist; Tatum (1909–56), jazz pianist; Gieseking (1895–1956), French-born concert pianist.

625.28   Bud Powell] Jazz pianist and composer (1924–66), a leading innovator in the bebop era whose compositions included "Un Poco Loco," "Parisian Thoroughfare," and "52nd Street Theme."

631.38   "Blue Suede Shoes,"] Rock and roll hit (1956) written and performed by Carl Perkins.

642.33   Merrill's Marauders] Popular name for the 5307th Provisional Regiment, an all-volunteer American infantry unit that fought the Japanese in northern Burma in 1944.

677.4–6   Henry Armstrong . . . Terry McGovern] Armstrong (1912–88) who in the late 1930s held simultaneously the featherweight, welterweight, and lightweight titles; McGovern (1880–1918), boxer known as "Terrible Terry."

THE REAL COOL KILLERS

733.6   Joe Turner]   Blues singer (1911–85) who performed in his youth with Kansas City musicians such as Bennie Moten and Count Basie, and later recorded a series of hits including "Shake, Rattle and Roll" (1954) and "Corrine Corrina" (1956).

777.25   Dutch Schultz]   Born Arthur Flegenheimer (1902–35); racketeer and bootlegger assassinated by other underworld figures.

855.35–36   Vincent Coll . . . Dillinger]   Vincent "Mad Dog" Coll, New York gangster murdered in 1932; John Dillinger (1902–34), bank robber killed by FBI agents.

871.28   Don Newcombe]   Baseball player (b. 1926), star pitcher with the Brooklyn Dodgers (1949–57).

Library of Congress Cataloging-in-Publication Data

Crime novels: American noir of the fifties.
    p.   cm. — (The library of America: 95)
    Contents: The killer inside me / Jim Thompson — The
talented Mr. Ripley / Patricia Highsmith — Pick-up /
Charles Willeford — Down there / Davis Goodis — The real
cool killers / Chester Himes.
    ISBN 1-883011-49-3 (alk. paper)
    1. Detective and mystery stories, American.   2. American
fiction—20th century.   3. Crime—Fiction.   I. Thompson,
Jim, 1905–1977. Killer inside me. II. Highsmith, Patricia, 1921–
1995. Talented Mr. Ripley.   III. Willeford, Charles, 1919–1988.
Pick-up. IV. Goodis, David, 1917–1967. Down there.
V. Himes, Chester, 1909–1984. Real cool killers.   VI. Series.
PS648.D4C697   1997
813'.087208054—dc21   97-2487
                                                    CIP

THE LIBRARY OF AMERICA SERIES

The Library of America fosters appreciation and pride in America's literary heritage by publishing, and keeping permanently in print, authoritative editions of America's best and most significant writing. An independent nonprofit organization, it was founded in 1979 with seed funding from the National Endowment for the Humanities and the Ford Foundation.

To subscribe to the series or to order individual copies, please visit www.loa.org or call (800) 964-5778.

This book is set in 10 point Linotron Galliard,
a face designed for photocomposition by Matthew Carter
and based on the sixteenth-century face Granjon. The paper
is acid-free lightweight opaque and meets the requirements
for permanence of the American National Standards Institute.
The binding material is Brillianta, a woven rayon cloth made
by Van Heek–Scholco Textielfabrieken, Holland. Composition
by The Clarinda Company. Printing and binding
by Edwards Brothers Malloy, Ann Arbor.
Designed by Bruce Campbell.

CRIME NOVELS

AMERICAN NOIR
OF THE 1930S AND 40S

CRIME NOVELS

AMERICAN NOIR
OF THE 1930S AND 40S

The Postman Always Rings Twice
James M. Cain

They Shoot Horses, Don't They?
Horace McCoy

Thieves Like Us
Edward Anderson

The Big Clock
Kenneth Fearing

Nightmare Alley
William Lindsay Gresham

I Married a Dead Man
Cornell Woolrich

Robert Polito, *editor*

THE LIBRARY OF AMERICA

Visit our website at www.loa.org.

The Postman Always Rings Twice copyright 1934 by James M. Cain;
copyright renewed 1962 by James M. Cain. Published by
arrangement with Alfred A. Knopf, Inc. *They Shoot Horses, Don't
They?* copyright 1935 by Horace McCoy. Published by arrangement
with the Estate of Horace McCoy. *Thieves Like Us* copyright 1937 by
Edward Anderson. *The Big Clock* copyright 1946 by Kenneth
Fearing, copyright renewed in 1973 by Bruce Fearing. Reprinted by
the permission of Russell & Volkening as agents for the author.
Nightmare Alley copyright 1946 by William Lindsay Gresham.
Reprinted by permission of Renee Gresham, David Gresham, and
Douglas H. Gresham. *I Married a Dead Man* copyright 1948 by
William Irish. Copyright assigned to Sheldon Abend D/B/A
Author's Research Company, 1982. Published by arrangement with
Viking Penguin, a division of Penguin Books USA, Inc.

This paper meets the requirements of
ANSI/NISO Z39.48–1992 (Permanence of Paper).

Distributed to the trade in the United States
by Penguin Random House Inc.
and in Canada by Penguin Random House Canada Ltd.

Library of Congress Catalog Number: 97-2485
For cataloging information, see end of Notes.
ISBN 978-1-883011-46-8
ISBN 1-883011-46-9

———

Seventh Printing
The Library of America—94

Contents

THE POSTMAN
ALWAYS RINGS TWICE

by James M. Cain

To
Vincent Lawrence

T HEY threw me off the hay truck about noon. I had swung on the night before, down at the border, and as soon as I got up there under the canvas, I went to sleep. I needed plenty of that, after three weeks in Tia Juana, and I was still getting it when they pulled off to one side to let the engine cool. Then they saw a foot sticking out and threw me off. I tried some comical stuff, but all I got was a dead pan, so that gag was out. They gave me a cigarette, though, and I hiked down the road to find something to eat.

That was when I hit this Twin Oaks Tavern. It was nothing but a roadside sandwich joint, like a million others in California. There was a lunchroom part, and over that the house part, where they lived, and off to one side a filling station, and out back a half dozen shacks that they called an auto court. I blew in there in a hurry and began looking down the road. When the Greek showed, I asked if a guy had been by in a Cadillac. He was to pick me up here, I said, and we were to have lunch. Not today, said the Greek. He layed a place at one of the tables and asked me what I was going to have. I said orange juice, corn flakes, fried eggs and bacon, enchilada, flapjacks, and coffee. Pretty soon he came out with the orange juice and the corn flakes.

"Hold on, now. One thing I got to tell you. If this guy don't show up, you'll have to trust me for it. This was to be on him, and I'm kind of short, myself."

"Hokay, fill'm up."

I saw he was on, and quit talking about the guy in the Cadillac. Pretty soon I saw he wanted something.

"What you do, what kind of work, hey?"

"Oh, one thing and another, one thing and another. Why?"

"How old you?"

"Twenty four."

"Young fellow, hey. I could use young fellow right now. In my business."

"Nice place you got here."

"Air. Is a nice. No fog, like in a Los Angeles. No fog at all. Nice, a clear, all a time nice a clear."

3

"Must be swell at night. I can smell it now."

"Sleep fine. You understand automobile? Fix'm up?"

"Sure. I'm a born mechanic."

He gave me some more about the air, and how healthy he's been since he bought this place, and how he can't figure it out, why his help won't stay with him. I can figure it out, but I stay with the grub.

"Hey? You think you like it here?"

By that time I had put down the rest of the coffee, and lit the cigar he gave me. "I tell you how it is. I got a couple of other propositions, that's my trouble. But I'll think about it. I sure will do that all right."

Then I saw her. She had been out back, in the kitchen, but she came in to gather up my dishes. Except for the shape, she really wasn't any raving beauty, but she had a sulky look to her, and her lips stuck out in a way that made me want to mash them in for her.

"Meet my wife."

She didn't look at me. I nodded at the Greek, gave my cigar a kind of wave, and that was all. She went out with the dishes, and so far as he and I were concerned, she hadn't even been there. I left, then, but in five minutes I was back, to leave a message for the guy in the Cadillac. It took me a half hour to get sold on the job, but at the end of it I was in the filling station, fixing flats.

"What's your name, hey?"

"Frank Chambers."

"Nick Papadakis, mine."

We shook hands, and he went. In a minute I heard him singing. He had a swell voice. From the filling station I could just get a good view of the kitchen.

2

About three o'clock a guy came along that was all burned up because somebody had pasted a sticker on his wind wing. I had to go in the kitchen to steam it off for him.

"Enchiladas? Well, you people sure know how to make them."

"What do you mean, you people?"

"Why, you and Mr. Papadakis. You and Nick. That one I had for lunch, it was a peach."

"Oh."

"You got a cloth? That I can hold on to this thing with?"

"That's not what you meant."

"Sure it is."

"You think I'm Mex."

"Nothing like it."

"Yes you do. You're not the first one. Well, get this. I'm just as white as you are, see? I may have dark hair and look a little that way, but I'm just as white as you are. You want to get along good around here, you won't forget that."

"Why, you don't look Mex."

"I'm telling you. I'm just as white as you are."

"No, you don't look even a little bit Mex. Those Mexican women, they all got big hips and bum legs and breasts up under their chin and yellow skin and hair that looks like it had bacon fat on it. You don't look like that. You're small, and got nice white skin, and your hair is soft and curly, even if it is black. Only thing you've got that's Mex is your teeth. They all got white teeth, you've got to hand that to them."

"My name was Smith before I was married. That don't sound much like a Mex, does it?"

"Not much."

"What's more, I don't even come from around here. I come from Iowa."

"Smith, hey. What's your first name?"

"Cora. You can call me that, if you want to."

I knew for certain, then, what I had just taken a chance on when I went in there. It wasn't those enchiladas that she had to cook, and it wasn't having black hair. It was being married to that Greek that made her feel she wasn't white, and she was even afraid I would begin calling her Mrs. Papadakis.

"Cora. Sure. And how about calling me Frank?"

She came over and began helping me with the wind wing. She was so close I could smell her. I shot it right close to her ear, almost in a whisper. "How come you married this Greek, anyway?"

She jumped like I had cut her with a whip. "Is that any of your business?"

"Yeah. Plenty."

"Here's your wind wing."

"Thanks."

I went out. I had what I wanted. I had socked one in under her guard, and socked it in deep, so it hurt. From now on, it would be business between her and me. She might not say yes, but she wouldn't stall me. She knew what I meant, and she knew I had her number.

That night at supper, the Greek got sore at her for not giving me more fried potatoes. He wanted me to like it there, and not walk out on him like the others had.

"Give a man something to eat."

"They're right on the stove. Can't he help himself?"

"It's all right. I'm not ready yet."

He kept at it. If he had had any brains, he would have known there was something back of it, because she wasn't one to let a guy help himself, I'll say that for her. But he was dumb, and kept crabbing. It was just the kitchen table, he at one end, she at the other, and me in the middle. I didn't look at her. But I could see her dress. It was one of these white nurse uniforms, like they all wear, whether they work in a dentist's office or a bakeshop. It had been clean in the morning, but it was a little bit rumpled now, and mussy. I could smell her.

"Well for heaven's sake."

She got up to get the potatoes. Her dress fell open for a second, so I could see her leg. When she gave me the potatoes, I couldn't eat. "Well there now. After all that, and now he doesn't want them."

"Hokay. But he have'm, *if* he want'm."

"I'm not hungry. I ate a big lunch."

He acted like he had won a great victory, and now he would forgive her, like the big guy he was. "She is a all right. She is my little white bird. She is my little white dove."

He winked and went upstairs. She and I sat there, and didn't say a word. When he came down he had a big bottle and a guitar. He poured some out of the bottle, but it was sweet Greek wine, and made me sick to my stomach. He started to sing. He had a tenor voice, not one of these little tenors like you hear on the radio, but a big tenor, and on the high notes he would put in a sob like on a Caruso record. But I couldn't listen to him now. I was feeling worse by the minute.

He saw my face and took me outside. "Out in a air, you feel better."

" 'S all right. I'll be all right."

"Sit down. Keep quiet."

"Go ahead in. I just ate too much lunch. I'll be all right."

He went in, and I let everything come up. It was like hell the lunch, or the potatoes, or the wine. I wanted that woman so bad I couldn't even keep anything on my stomach.

Next morning the sign was blown down. About the middle of the night it had started to blow, and by morning it was a windstorm that took the sign with it.

"It's awful. Look at that."

"Was a very big wind. I could no sleep. No sleep all night."

"Big wind all right. But look at the sign."

"Is busted."

I kept tinkering with the sign, and he would come out and watch me. "How did you get this sign anyway?"

"Was here when I buy the place. Why?"

"It's lousy all right. I wonder you do any business at all."

I went to gas up a car, and left him to think that over. When I got back he was still blinking at it, where it was leaning against the front of the lunchroom. Three of the lights were busted. I plugged in the wire, and half the others didn't light.

"Put in new lights, hang'm up, will be all right."

"You're the boss."

"What's a matter with it?"

"Well, it's out of date. Nobody has bulb signs any more. They got Neon signs. They show up better, and they don't burn as much juice. Then, what does it say? Twin Oaks, that's all. The Tavern part, it's not in lights. Well, Twin Oaks don't make me hungry. It don't make me want to stop and get something to eat. It's costing you money, that sign is, only you don't know it."

"Fix'm up, will be hokay."

"Why don't you get a new sign?"

"I'm busy."

But pretty soon he was back, with a piece of paper. He had drew a new sign for himself, and colored it up with red, white, and blue crayon. It said Twin Oaks Tavern, and Eat, and Bar-B-Q, and Sanitary Rest Rooms, and N. Papadakis, Prop.

"Swell. That'll knock them for a loop."

I fixed up the words, so they were spelled right, and he put some more curley cues on the letters.

"Nick, why do we hang up the old sign at all? Why don't you go to the city today and get this new sign made? It's a beauty, believe me it is. And it's important. A place is no better than its sign, is it?"

"I do it. By golly, I go."

Los Angeles wasn't but twenty miles away, but he shined himself up like he was going to Paris, and right after lunch, he went. Soon as he was gone, I locked the front door. I picked up a plate that a guy had left, and went on back in the kitchen with it. She was there.

"Here's a plate that was out there."

"Oh, thanks."

I set it down. The fork was rattling like a tambourine.

"I was going to go, but I started some things cooking and I thought I better not."

"I got plenty to do, myself."

"You feeling better?"

"I'm all right."

"Sometimes just some little thing will do it. Like a change of water, something like that."

"Probably too much lunch."

"What's that?"

Somebody was out front, rattling the door. "Sounds like somebody trying to get in."

"Is the door locked, Frank?"

"I must have locked it."

She looked at me, and got pale. She went to the swinging

door, and peeped through. Then she went into the lunch-room, but in a minute she was back.

"They went away."

"I don't know why I locked it."

"I forgot to unlock it."

She started for the lunchroom again, but I stopped her. "Let's—leave it locked."

"Nobody can get in if it's locked. I got some cooking to do. I'll wash up this plate."

I took her in my arms and mashed my mouth up against hers. . . . "Bite me! Bite me!"

I bit her. I sunk my teeth into her lips so deep I could feel the blood spurt into my mouth. It was running down her neck when I carried her upstairs.

3

For two days after that I was dead, but the Greek was sore at me, so I got by all right. He was sore at me because I hadn't fixed the swing door that led from the lunchroom into the kitchen. She told him it swung back and hit her in the mouth. She had to tell him something. Her mouth was all swelled up where I had bit it. So he said it was my fault, that I hadn't fixed it. I stretched the spring, so it was weaker, and that fixed it.

But the real reason he was sore at me was over the sign. He had fallen for it so hard he was afraid I would say it was my idea, stead of his. It was such a hell of a sign they couldn't get it done for him that afternoon. It took them three days, and when it was ready I went in and got it and hung it up. It had on it all that he had drew on the paper, and a couple of other things besides. It had a Greek flag and an American flag, and hands shaking hands, and Satisfaction Guaranteed. It was all in red, white, and blue Neon letters, and I waited until dark to turn on the juice. When I snapped the switch, it lit up like a Christmas tree.

"Well, I've seen many a sign in my time, but never one like that. I got to hand it to you, Nick."

"By golly. By golly."
We shook hands. We were friends again.

Next day I was alone with her for a minute, and swung my
fist up against her leg so hard it nearly knocked her over.
"How do you get that way?" She was snarling like a cougar.
I liked her like that.
"How are you, Cora?"
"Lousy."
From then on, I began to smell her again.

One day the Greek heard there was a guy up the road un-
dercutting him on gas. He jumped in the car to go see about
it. I was in my room when he drove off, and I turned around
to dive down in the kitchen. But she was already there, standing in the door.
I went over and looked at her mouth. It was the first chance
I had had to see how it was. The swelling was all gone, but
you could still see the tooth marks, little blue creases on both
lips. I touched them with my fingers. They were soft and
damp. I kissed them, but not hard. They were little soft kisses.
I had never thought about them before. She stayed until the
Greek came back, about an hour. We didn't do anything. We
just lay on the bed. She kept rumpling my hair, and looking
up at the ceiling, like she was thinking.
"You like blueberry pie?"
"I don't know. Yeah. I guess so."
"I'll make you some."

"Look out, Frank. You'll break a spring leaf."
"To hell with the spring leaf."
We were crashing into a little eucalyptus grove beside the
road. The Greek had sent us down to the market to take back
some T-bone steaks he said were lousy, and on the way back
it had got dark. I slammed the car in there, and it bucked and
bounced, but when I was in among the trees I stopped. Her
arms were around me before I even cut the lights. We did
plenty. After a while we just sat there. "I can't go on like this,
Frank."
"Me neither."

"I can't stand it. And I've got to get drunk with you, Frank. You know what I mean? Drunk."

"I know."

"And I hate that Greek."

"Why did you marry him? You never did tell me that."

"I haven't told you anything."

"We haven't wasted any time on talk."

"I was working in a hash house. You spend two years in a Los Angeles hash house and you'll take the first guy that's got a gold watch."

"When did you leave Iowa?"

"Three years ago. I won a beauty contest. I won a high school beauty contest, in Des Moines. That's where I lived. The prize was a trip to Hollywood. I got off the Chief with fifteen guys taking my picture, and two weeks later I was in the hash house."

"Didn't you go back?"

"I wouldn't give them the satisfaction."

"Did you get in movies?"

"They gave me a test. It was all right in the face. But they talk, now. The pictures, I mean. And when I began to talk, up there on the screen, they knew me for what I was, and so did I. A cheap Des Moines trollop, that had as much chance in pictures as a monkey has. Not as much. A monkey, anyway, can make you laugh. All I did was make you sick."

"And then?"

"Then two years of guys pinching your leg and leaving nickel tips and asking how about a little party tonight. I went on some of them parties, Frank."

"And then?"

"You know what I mean about them parties?"

"I know."

"Then he came along. I took him, and so help me, I meant to stick by him. But I can't stand it any more. God, do I look like a little white bird?"

"To me, you look more like a hell cat."

"You know, don't you. That's one thing about you. I don't have to fool you all the time. And you're clean. You're not greasy. Frank, do you have any idea what that means? You're not greasy."

"I can kind of imagine."

"I don't think so. No man can know what that means to a woman. To have to be around somebody that's greasy and makes you sick at the stomach when he touches you. I'm not really such a hell cat, Frank. I just can't stand it any more."

"What you trying to do? Kid me?"

"Oh, all right. I'm a hell cat, then. But I don't think I would be so bad. With somebody that wasn't greasy."

"Cora, how about you and me going away?"

"I've thought about it. I've thought about it a lot."

"We'll ditch this Greek and blow. Just blow."

"Where to?"

"Anywhere. What do we care?"

"Anywhere. Anywhere. You know where that is?"

"All over. Anywhere we choose."

"No it's not. It's the hash house."

"I'm not talking about the hash house. I'm talking about the road. It's fun, Cora. And nobody knows it better than I do. I know every twist and turn it's got. And I know how to work it, too. Isn't that what we want? Just to be a pair of tramps, like we really are?"

"You were a fine tramp. You didn't even have socks."

"You liked me."

"I loved you. I would love you without even a shirt. I would love you specially without a shirt, so I could feel how nice and hard your shoulders are."

"Socking railroad detectives developed the muscles."

"And you're hard all over. Big and tall and hard. And your hair is light. You're not a little soft greasy guy with black kinky hair that he puts bay rum on every night."

"That must be a nice smell."

"But it won't do, Frank. That road, it don't lead anywhere but to the hash house. The hash house for me, and some job like it for you. A lousy parking lot job, where you wear a smock. I'd cry if I saw you in a smock, Frank."

"Well?"

She sat there a long time, twisting my hand in both of hers. "Frank, do you love me?"

"Yes."

"Do you love me so much that not anything matters?"

"Yes."

"There's one way."

"Did you say you weren't really a hell cat?"

"I said it, and I mean it. I'm not what you think I am, Frank. I want to work and be something, that's all. But you can't do it without love. Do you know that, Frank? Anyway, a woman can't. Well, I've made one mistake. And I've got to be a hell cat, just once, to fix it. But I'm not really a hell cat, Frank."

"They hang you for that."

"Not if you do it right. You're smart, Frank. I never fooled you for a minute. You'll think of a way. Plenty of them have. Don't worry. I'm not the first woman that had to turn hell cat to get out of a mess."

"He never did anything to me. He's all right."

"The hell he's all right. He stinks, I tell you. He's greasy and he stinks. And do you think I'm going to let you wear a smock, with Service Auto Parks printed on the back, Thank-U Call Again, while he has four suits and a dozen silk shirts? Isn't that business half mine? Don't I cook? Don't I cook good? Don't you do your part?"

"You talk like it was all right."

"Who's going to know if it's all right or not, but you and me?"

"You and me."

"That's it, Frank. That's all that matters, isn't it? Not you and me and the road, or anything else but you and me."

"You must be a hell cat, though. You couldn't make me feel like this if you weren't."

"That's what we're going to do. Kiss me, Frank. On the mouth."

I kissed her. Her eyes were shining up at me like two blue stars. It was like being in church.

4

"Got any hot water?"

"What's the matter with the bathroom?"

"Nick's in there."

"Oh. I'll give you some out of the kettle. He likes the whole heater full for his bath."

We played it just like we would tell it. It was about ten o'clock at night, and we had closed up, and the Greek was in the bathroom, putting on his Saturday night wash. I was to take the water up to my room, get ready to shave, and then remember I had left the car out. I was to go outside, and stand by to give her one on the horn if somebody came. She was to wait till she heard him in the tub, go in for a towel, and clip him from behind with a blackjack I had made for her out of a sugar bag with ball bearings wadded down in the end. At first, I was to do it, but we figured he wouldn't pay any attention to her if she went in there, where if I said I was after my razor, he might get out of the tub or something and help me look. Then she was to hold him under until he drowned. Then she was to leave the water running a little bit, and step out the window to the porch roof, and come down the stepladder I had put there, to the ground. She was to hand me the blackjack, and go back to the kitchen. I was to put the ball bearings back in the box, throw the bag away, put the car in, and go up to my room and start to shave. She would wait till the water began dripping down in the kitchen, and call me. We would break the door down, find him, and call the doctor. In the end, we figured it would look like he had slipped in the tub, knocked himself out, and then drowned. I got the idea from a piece in the paper where a guy had said that most accidents happen right in people's own bathtubs.

"Be careful of it. It's hot."

"Thanks."

It was in a saucepan, and I took it up in my room and set it on the bureau, and laid my shaving stuff out. I went down and out to the car, and took a seat in it so I could see the road and the bathroom window, both. The Greek was singing. It came to me I better take note what the song was. It was Mother Machree. He sang it once, and then sang it over again. I looked in the kitchen. She was still there.

A truck and a trailer swung around the bend. I fingered the horn. Sometimes those truckmen stopped for something to

eat, and they were the kind that would beat on the door till
you opened up. But they went on. A couple more cars went
by. They didn't stop. I looked in the kitchen again, and she
wasn't there. A light went on in the bedroom.

Then, all of a sudden, I saw something move, back by the
porch. I almost hit the horn, but then I saw it was a cat. It
was just a gray cat, but it shook me up. A cat was the last
thing I wanted to see then. I couldn't see it for a minute, and
then there it was again, smelling around the stepladder. I
didn't want to blow the horn, because it wasn't anything but
a cat, but I didn't want it around that stepladder. I got out
of the car, went back there, and shooed it away.

I got halfway back to the car, when it came back, and
started up the ladder. I shooed it away again, and ran it clear
back to the shacks. I started back to the car, and then stood
there for a little bit, looking to see if it was coming back. A
state cop came around the bend. He saw me standing there,
cut his motor, and came wheeling in, before I could move.
When he stopped he was between me and the car. I couldn't
blow the horn.

"Taking it easy?"

"Just came out to put the car away."

"That your car?"

"Belongs to this guy I work for."

"O.K. Just checking up."

He looked around, and then he saw something. "I'll be
damned. Look at that."

"Look at what?"

"Goddam cat, going up that stepladder."

"Ha."

"I love a cat. They're always up to something."

He pulled on his gloves, took a look at the night, kicked
his pedal a couple of times, and went. Soon as he was out of
sight I dove for the horn. I was too late. There was a flash of
fire from the porch, and every light in the place went out.
Inside, Cora was screaming with an awful sound in her voice.
"Frank! Frank! Something has happened!"

I ran in the kitchen, but it was black dark in there and I

didn't have any matches in my pocket, and I had to feel my way. We met on the stairs, she going down, me going up. She screamed again.

"Keep quiet, for God's sake keep quiet! Did you do it?"

"Yes, but the lights went out, and I haven't held him under yet!"

"We got to bring him to! There was a state cop out there, and he saw that stepladder!"

"Phone for the doctor!"

"You phone, and I'll get him out of there!"

She went down, and I kept on up. I went in the bathroom, and over to the tub. He was laying there in the water, but his head wasn't under. I tried to lift him. I had a hell of a time. He was slippery with soap, and I had to stand in the water before I could raise him at all. All the time I could hear her down there, talking to the operator. They didn't give her a doctor. They gave her the police.

I got him up, and laid him over the edge of the tub, and then got out myself, and dragged him in the bedroom and laid him on the bed. She came up, then, and we found matches, and got a candle lit. Then we went to work on him. I packed his head in wet towels, while she rubbed his wrists and feet.

"They're sending an ambulance."

"All right. Did he see you do it?"

"I don't know."

"Were you behind him?"

"I think so. But then the lights went out, and I don't know what happened. What did you do to the lights?"

"Nothing. The fuse popped."

"Frank. He'd better not come to."

"He's got to come to. If he dies, we're sunk. I tell you, that cop saw the stepladder. If he dies, then they'll know. If he dies, they've got us."

"But suppose he saw me? What's he going to say when he comes to?"

"Maybe he didn't. We just got to sell him a story, that's all. You were in here, and the lights popped, and you heard him slip and fall, and he didn't answer when you spoke to him. Then you called me, that's all. No matter what he says, you got to stick to it. If he saw anything, it was just his imagination, that's all."

"Why don't they hurry with that ambulance?"

"It'll be here."

Soon as the ambulance came, they put him on a stretcher and shoved him in. She rode with him. I followed along in the car. Halfway to Glendale, a state cop picked us up and rode on ahead. They went seventy miles an hour, and I couldn't keep up. They were lifting him out when I got to the hospital, and the state cop was bossing the job. When he saw me he gave a start and stared at me. It was the same cop.

They took him in, put him on a table, and wheeled him in an operating room. Cora and myself sat out in the hall. Pretty soon a nurse came and sat down with us. Then the cop came, and he had a sergeant with him. They kept looking at me. Cora was telling the nurse how it happened. "I was in there, in the bathroom I mean, getting a towel, and then the lights went out just like somebody had shot a gun off. Oh my, they made a terrible noise. I heard him fall. He had been standing up, getting ready to turn on the shower. I spoke to him, and he didn't say anything, and it was all dark, and I couldn't see anything, and I didn't know what had happened. I mean I thought he had been electrocuted or something. So then Frank heard me screaming, and he came, and got him out, and then I called up for the ambulance, and I don't know what I would have done if they hadn't come quick like they did."

"They always hurry on a late call."

"I'm so afraid he's hurt bad."

"I don't think so. They're taking X-Rays in there now. They can always tell from X-Rays. But I don't think he's hurt bad."

"Oh my, I hope not."

The cops never said a word. They just sat there and looked at us.

They wheeled him out, and his head was covered with bandages. They put him on an elevator, and Cora, and me, and the nurse, and the cops all got on, and they took him up and put him in a room. We all went in there. There weren't

enough chairs, and while they were putting him to bed the
nurse went and got some extra ones. We all sat down. Somebody said something, and the nurse made them keep quiet. A
doctor came in and took a look, and went out. We sat there
a hell of a while. Then the nurse went over and looked at him.

"I think he's coming to now."

Cora looked at me, and I looked away quick. The cops
leaned forward, to hear what he said. He opened his eyes.

"You feel better now?"

He didn't say anything, and neither did anybody else. It
was so still I could hear my heart pounding in my ears. "Don't
you know your wife? Here she is. Aren't you ashamed of yourself, falling in the bathtub like a little boy, just because the
lights went out. Your wife is mad at you. Aren't you going to
speak to her?"

He strained to say something, but couldn't say it. The nurse
went over and fanned him. Cora took hold of his hand and
patted it. He lay back for a few minutes, with his eyes closed,
and then his mouth began to move again and he looked at
the nurse.

"Was a all go dark."

When the nurse said he had to be quiet, I took Cora down,
and put her in the car. We no sooner started out than the cop
was back there, following us on his motorcycle.

"He suspicions us, Frank."

"It's the same one. He knew there was something wrong,
soon as he saw me standing there, keeping watch. He still
thinks so."

"What are we going to do?"

"I don't know. It all depends on that stepladder, whether
he tumbles what it's there for. What did you do with that
slungshot?"

"I still got it here, in the pocket of my dress."

"God Almighty, if they had arrested you back there, and
searched you, we'd have been sunk."

I gave her my knife, made her cut the string off the bag,
and take the bearings out. Then I made her climb back, raise
the back seat, and put the bag under it. It would look like a
rag, like anybody keeps with the tools.

"You stay back there, now, and keep an eye on that cop. I'm going to snap these bearings into the bushes one at a time, and you've got to watch if he notices anything."

She watched, and I drove with my left hand, and leaned my right hand on the wheel. I let one go. I shot it like a marble, out the window and across the road.

"Did he turn his head?"

"No."

I let the rest go, one every couple of minutes. He never noticed it.

We got out to the place, and it was still dark. I hadn't had time to find the fuses, let alone put a new one in. When I pulled in, the cop went past, and was there ahead of me. "I'm taking a look at that fuse box, buddy."

"Sure. I'm taking a look myself."

We all three went back there, and he snapped on a flashlight. Right away, he gave a funny grunt and stooped down. There was the cat, laying on its back with all four feet in the air.

"Ain't that a shame? Killed her deader than hell."

He shot the flashlight up under the porch roof, and along the stepladder. "That's it, all right. Remember? We were looking at her. She stepped off the ladder on to your fuse box, and it killed her deader than hell."

"That's it all right. You were hardly gone when it happened. Went off like a pistol shot. I hadn't even had time to move the car."

"They caught me down the road."

"You were hardly out of sight."

"Stepped right off the ladder on to the fuse box. Well, that's the way it goes. Them poor dumb things, they can't get it through their head about electricity, can they? No sir, it's too much for them."

"Tough, all right."

"That's what it is, it's tough. Killed her deader than hell. Pretty cat, too. Remember, how she looked when she was creeping up that ladder? I never seen a cuter cat than she was."

"And pretty color."

"And killed her deader than hell. Well, I'll be going along. I guess that straightens us out. Had to check up, you know."

"That's right."

"So long. So long, Miss."

"So long."

5

We didn't do anything about the cat, the fuse box, or anything else. We crept into bed, and she cracked up. She cried, and then got a chill so she was trembling all over, and it was a couple of hours before I could get her quiet. She lay in my arms a while, then, and we began to talk.

"Never again, Frank."

"That's right. Never again."

"We must have been crazy. Just plain crazy."

"Just our dumb luck that pulled us through."

"It was my fault."

"Mine too."

"No, it was my fault. I was the one that thought it up. You didn't want to. Next time I'll listen to you, Frank. You're smart. You're not dumb like I am."

"Except there won't be any next time."

"That's right. Never again."

"Even if we had gone through with it they would have guessed it. They *always* guess it. They guess it anyway, just from habit. Because look how quick that cop knew something was wrong. That's what makes my blood run cold. Soon as he saw me standing there he knew it. If he could tumble to it all that easy, how much chance would we have had if the Greek had died?"

"I guess I'm not really a hell cat, Frank."

"I'm telling you."

"If I was, I wouldn't have got scared so easy. I was *so* scared, Frank."

"I was scared plenty, myself."

"You know what I wanted when the lights went out? Just

you, Frank. I wasn't any hell cat at all, then. I was just a little girl, afraid of the dark."

"I was there, wasn't I?"

"I loved you for it. If it hadn't been for you, I don't know what would have happened to us."

"Pretty good, wasn't it? About how he slipped?"

"And he believed it."

"Give me half a chance, I got it on the cops, every time. You got to have something to tell, that's it. You got to fill in all those places, and yet have it as near the truth as you can get it. I know them. I've tangled with them, plenty."

"You fixed it. You're always going to fix it for me, aren't you, Frank?"

"You're the only one ever meant anything to me."

"I guess I really don't want to be a hell cat."

"You're my baby."

"That's it, just your dumb baby. All right, Frank. I'll listen to you, from now on. You be the brains, and I'll work. I can work, Frank. And I work good. We'll get along."

"Sure we will."

"Now shall we go to sleep?"

"You think you can sleep all right?"

"It's the first time we ever slept together, Frank."

"You like it?"

"It's grand, just grand."

"Kiss me goodnight."

"It's so sweet to be able to kiss you goodnight."

Next morning, the telephone waked us up. She answered it, and when she came up her eyes were shining. "Frank, guess what?"

"What?"

"His skull is fractured."

"Bad?"

"No, but they're keeping him there. They want him there for a week, maybe. We can sleep together again, tonight."

"Come here."

"Not now. We've got to get up. We've got to open the place up."

"Come here, before I sock you."

"You nut."

It was a happy week, all right. In the afternoon, she would drive in to the hospital, but the rest of the time we were together. We gave him a break, too. We kept the place open all the time, and went after the business, and got it. Of course it helped, that day when a hundred Sunday school kids showed up in three busses, and wanted a bunch of stuff to take out in the woods with them, but even without that we would have made plenty. The cash register didn't know anything to tell on us, believe me it didn't.

Then one day, stead of her going in alone, we both went in, and after she came out of the hospital, we cut for the beach. They gave her a yellow suit and a red cap, and when she came out I didn't know her at first. She looked like a little girl. It was the first time I ever really saw how young she was. We played in the sand, and then we went way out and let the swells rock us. I like my head to the waves, she liked her feet. We lay there, face to face, and held hands under water. I looked up at the sky. It was all you could see. I thought about God.

"Frank."

"Yes?"

"He's coming home tomorrow. You know what that means?"

"I know."

"I got to sleep with him, stead of you."

"You would, except that when he gets here we're going to be gone."

"I was hoping you'd say that."

"Just you and me and the road, Cora."

"Just you and me and the road."

"Just a couple of tramps."

"Just a couple of gypsies, but we'll be together."

"That's it. We'll be together."

Next morning, we packed up. Anyway, she packed. I had bought a suit, and I put that on, and it seemed to be about all. She put her things in a hatbox. When she got done with it, she handed it to me. "Put that in the car, will you?"

"The car?"

"Aren't we taking the car?"

"Not unless you want to spend the first night in jail, we're not. Stealing a man's wife, that's nothing, but stealing his car, that's larceny."

"Oh."

We started out. It was two miles to the bus stop, and we had to hike it. Every time a car went by, we would stand there with our hand stuck out, like a cigar store Indian, but none of them stopped. A man alone can get a ride, and a woman alone, if she's fool enough to take it, but a man and a woman together don't have much luck. After about twenty had gone by, she stopped. We had gone about a quarter of a mile.

"Frank, I can't."

"What's the matter?"

"This is it."

"This is what?"

"The road."

"You're crazy. You're tired, that's all. Look. You wait here, and I'll get somebody down the road to drive us in to the city. That's what we ought to done anyhow. Then we'll be all right."

"No, it's not that. I'm not tired. I can't, that's all. At all."

"Don't you want to be with me, Cora?"

"You know I do."

"We can't go back, you know. We can't start up again, like it was before. You know that. You've got to come."

"I told you I wasn't really a bum, Frank. I don't feel like no gypsy. I don't feel like nothing, only ashamed, that I'm out here asking for a ride."

"I told you. We're getting a car in to the city."

"And then what?"

"Then we're there. Then we get going."

"No we don't. We spend one night in a hotel, and then we start looking for a job. And living in a dump."

"Isn't that a dump? What you just left?"

"It's different."

"Cora, you going to let it get your goat?"

"It's got it, Frank. I can't go on. Goodbye."

"Will you listen to me a minute?"

"Goodbye, Frank. I'm going back."

She kept tugging at the hatbox. I tried to hold on to it, anyway to carry it back for her, but she got it. She started back with it. She had looked nice when she started out, with a little blue suit and blue hat, but now she looked all battered, and her shoes were dusty, and she couldn't even walk right, from crying. All of a sudden, I found out I was crying too.

6

I caught a ride to San Bernardino. It's a railroad town, and I was going to hop a freight east. But I didn't do it. I ran into a guy in a poolroom, and began playing him one ball in the side. He was the greatest job in the way of a sucker that God ever turned out, because he had a friend that could really play. The only trouble with him was, he couldn't play good enough. I hung around with the pair of them a couple of weeks, and took $250 off them, all they had, and then I had to beat it out of town quick.

I caught a truck for Mexicali, and then I got to thinking about my $250, and how with that much money we could go to the beach and sell hot dogs or something until we got a stake to take a crack at something bigger. So I dropped off, and caught a ride back to Glendale. I began hanging around the market where they bought their stuff, hoping I would bump into her. I even called her up a couple of times, but the Greek answered and I had to make out it was a wrong number.

In between walking around the market, I hung around a poolroom, about a block down the street. One day a guy was practicing shots alone on one of the tables. You could tell he was new at it from the way he held his cue. I began practicing shots on the next table. I figured if $250 was enough for a hot dog stand, $350 would leave us sitting pretty.

"How you say to a little one ball in the side?"

"I never played that game much."

"Nothing to it. Just the one ball in the side pocket."

"Anyhow, you look too good for me."

"Me? I'm just a punk."

"Oh well. If it's just a friendly game."

We started to play, and I let him take three or four, just to feel good. I kept shaking my head, like I couldn't understand it.

"Too good for you hey. Well, that's a joke. But I swear, I'm really better than this. I can't seem to get going. How you say we put $1 on it, just to make it lively?"

"Oh well. I can't lose much at a dollar."

We made it $1 a game, and I let him take four or five, maybe more. I shot like I was pretty nervous, and in between shots I would wipe off the palm of my hand with a handkerchief, like I must be sweating.

"Well, it looks like I'm not doing so good. How about making it $5, so I can get my money back, and then we'll go have a drink?"

"Oh well. It's just a friendly game, and I don't want your money. Sure. We'll make it $5, and then we'll quit."

I let him take four or five more, and from the way I was acting, you would have thought I had heart failure and a couple more things besides. I was plenty blue around the gills.

"Look. I got sense enough to know when I'm out of my class all right, but let's make it $25, so I can break even, and then we'll go have that drink."

"That's pretty high for me."

"What the hell? You're playing on my money, aren't you?"

"Oh well. All right. Make it $25."

Then was when I really started to shoot. I made shots that Hoppe couldn't make. I banked them in from three cushions, I made billiard shots, I had my english working so the ball just floated around the table, I even called a jump shot and made it. He never made a shot that Blind Tom the Sightless Piano Player couldn't have made. He miscued, he got himself all tangled up on position, he scratched, he put the one ball in the wrong pocket, he never even called a bank shot. And when I walked out of there, he had my $250 and a $3 watch that I had bought to keep track of when Cora might be driving in to the market. Oh, I was good all right. The only trouble was I wasn't quite good enough.

"Hey, Frank!"

It was the Greek, running across the street at me before I had really got out the door.

"Well Frank, you old son a gun, where you been, put her there, why you run away from me just a time I hurt my head I need you most?"

We shook hands. He still had a bandage around his head and a funny look in his eyes, but he was all dressed up in a new suit, and had a black hat cocked over on the side of his head, and a purple necktie, and brown shoes, and his gold watch chain looped across his vest, and a big cigar in his hand.

"Well Nick! How you feeling, boy?"

"Me, I feel fine, couldn't feel better if was right out a the can, but why you run out on me? I sore as hell at you, you old son a gun."

"Well, you know me, Nick. I stay put a while, and then I got to ramble."

"You pick one hell of a time to ramble. What you do, hey? Come on, you don't do nothing, you old son a gun, I know you, come on over while I buy'm steaks I tell you all about it."

"You alone?"

"Don't talk so dumb, who the hell you think keep a place open now you run out on me, hey? Sure I'm alone. Me a Cora never get to go out together now, one go, other have to stay."

"Well then, let's walk over."

It took him an hour to buy the steaks, he was so busy telling me how his skull was fractured, how the docs never saw a fracture like it, what a hell of a time he's had with his help, how he's had two guys since I left and he fired one the day after he hired him, and the other one skipped after three days and took the inside of the cash register with him, and how he'd give anything to have me back.

"Frank, I tell you what. We go to Santa Barbara tomorrow, me a Cora. Hell boy, we got to step out a little, hey? We go

see a fiesta there, and you come with us. You like that, Frank?
You come with us, we talk about you come back a work for
me. You like a fiesta a Santa Barbara?"

"Well, I hear it's good."

"Is a girls, is a music, is a dance in streets, is swell. Come
on, Frank, what you say?"

"Well, I don't know."

"Cora be sore as hell at me if I see you and no bring you
out. Maybe she treat you snotty, but she think you fine fellow,
Frank. Come on, we all three go. We have a hell of a time."

"O.K. If she's willing, it's a go."

There were eight or ten people in the lunchroom when we
got there, and she was back in the kitchen, washing dishes as
fast as she could, to get enough plates to serve them.

"Hey. Hey Cora, look. Look who I bring."

"Well for heaven's sake. Where did he come from?"

"I see'm today a Glendale. He go to Santa Barbara with
us."

"Hello, Cora. How you been?"

"You're quite a stranger around here."

She wiped her hands quick, and shook hands, but her hand
was soapy. She went out front with an order, and me and the
Greek sat down. He generally helped her with the orders, but
he was all hot to show me something, and he let her do it all
alone. It was a big scrapbook, and in the front of it he had
pasted his naturalization certificate, and then his wedding certificate, and then his license to do business in Los Angeles
County, and then a picture of himself in the Greek Army, and
then a picture of him and Cora the day they got married, and
then all the clippings about his accident. Those clippings in
the regular papers, if you ask me, were more about the cat
than they were about him, but anyway they had his name in
them, and how he had been brought to the Glendale Hospital, and was expected to recover. The one in the Los Angeles
Greek paper, though, was more about him than about the cat,
and had a picture of him in it, in the dress suit he had when
he was a waiter, and the story of his life. Then came the X-
Rays. There were about a half dozen of them, because they
took a new picture every day to see how he was getting along.
How he had them fixed up was to paste two pages together,

along the edges, and then cut out a square place in the middle, where the X-Ray was slipped in so you could hold it up to the light and look through it. After the X-Rays came the receipted hospital bills, the receipted doctors' bills, and the receipted nurses' bills. That rap on the conk cost him $322, believe it or not.

"Is a nice, hey?"

"Swell. It's all there, right on the line."

"Of course, is a not done yet. I fix'm up red, a white, a blue, fix'm up fine. Look."

He showed me where he had put the fancy stuff on a couple of the pages. He had inked in the curley cues, and then colored it with red, white, and blue. Over the naturalization certificate, he had a couple of American flags, and a eagle, and over the Greek Army picture he had crossed Greek flags, and another eagle, and over his wedding certificate he had a couple of turtle doves on a twig. He hadn't figured out yet what to put over the other stuff, but I said over the clippings he could put a cat with red, white, and blue fire coming out of its tail, and he thought that was pretty good. He didn't get it, though, when I said he could have a buzzard over the Los Angeles County license, holding a couple of auctioneer's flags that said Sale Today, and it didn't look like it would really be worth while to try to explain it to him. But I got it, at last, why he was all dressed up, and not carrying out the chow like he used to, and acted so important. This Greek had had a fracture of the skull, and a thing like that don't happen to a dumb cluck like him every day. He was like a wop that opens a drug store. Soon as he gets that thing that says Pharmacist, with a red seal on it, a wop puts on a gray suit, with black edges on the vest, and is so important he can't even take time to mix the pills, and wouldn't even touch a chocolate icecream soda. This Greek was all dressed up for the same reason. A big thing had happened in his life.

It was pretty near supper time when I got her alone. He went up to wash, and the two of us were left in the kitchen.

"You been thinking about me, Cora?"

"Sure. I wouldn't forget you all that quick."

"I thought about you a lot. How are you?"

"Me? I'm all right."

"I called you up a couple of times, but he answered and I was afraid to talk to him. I made some money."

"Well, gee, I'm glad you're getting along good."

"I made it, but then I lost it. I thought we could use it to get started with, but then I lost it."

"I declare, I don't know where the money goes."

"You sure you think about me, Cora?"

"Sure I do."

"You don't act like it."

"Seems to me I'm acting all right."

"Have you got a kiss for me?"

"We'll be having supper pretty soon. You better get ready, if you've got any washing to do."

That's the way it went. That's the way it went all evening. The Greek got out some of his sweet wine, and sang a bunch of songs, and we sat around, and so far as she was concerned, I might just as well have been just a guy that used to work there, only she couldn't quite remember his name. It was the worst flop of a home-coming you ever saw in your life.

When it came time to go to bed, I let them go up, and then I went outside to try and figure out whether to stay there and see if I couldn't get going with her again, or blow and try to forget her. I walked quite a way off, and I don't know how long it was, or how far away I was, but after a while I could hear a row going on in the place. I went back, and when I got close I could hear some of what they were saying. She was yelling like hell and saying I had to leave. He was mumbling something, probably that he wanted me to stay and go back to work. He was trying to shut her up, but I could tell she was yelling so I would hear it. If I had been in my room, where she thought I was, I could have heard it plain enough, and even where I was I could hear plenty.

Then all of a sudden it stopped. I slipped in the kitchen, and stood there listening. But I couldn't hear anything, because I was all shook up, and all I could get was the sound of my own heart, going bump-bump, bump-bump, bump-bump, like that. I thought that was a funny way for my heart to sound, and then all of a sudden I knew there was two hearts in that kitchen, and that was why it sounded so funny.

I snapped on the light.

She was standing there, in a red kimono, as pale as milk, staring at me, with a long thin knife in her hand. I reached out and took it away from her. When she spoke, it was in a whisper that sounded like a snake licking its tongue in and out.

"Why did you have to come back?"

"I had to, that's all."

"No you didn't. I could have gone through with it. I was getting so I could forget you. And now you have to come back. God damn you, you have to come back!"

"Go through with what?"

"What he's making that scrapbook for. *It's to show to his children!* And now he wants one. He wants one right away."

"Well, why didn't you come with me?"

"Come with you for what? To sleep in box cars? Why would I come with you? Tell me that."

I couldn't say anything. I thought about my $250, but what good was it telling her that I had some money yesterday, but today I lost it playing one ball in the side?

"You're no good. I know that. You're just no good. Then why don't you go away and let me alone instead of coming back here again? Why don't you leave me be?"

"Listen. Stall him on this kid stuff just a little while. Stall him, and we'll see if we can't figure something out. I'm not much good, but I love you, Cora. I swear it."

"You swear it, and what do you do? He's taking me to Santa Barbara, so I'll say I'll have the child, and you—you're going right along with us. You're going to stay at the same hotel with us! You're going right along in the car. You're—"

She stopped, and we stood there looking at each other. The three of us in the car, we knew what that meant. Little by little we were nearer, until we were touching.

"Oh, my God, Frank, isn't there any other way out for us than that?"

"Well. You were going to stick a knife in him just now."

"No. That was for me, Frank. Not him."

"Cora, it's in the cards. We've tried every other way out."

"I can't have no greasy Greek child, Frank. I can't, that's all. The only one I can have a child by is you. I wish you were some good. You're smart, but you're no good."

"I'm no good, but I love you."

"Yes, and I love you."

"Stall him. Just this one night."

"All right, Frank. Just this one night."

7

"There's a long, long trail a-winding
Into the land of my dreams,
Where the nightingale is singing
And the white moon beams.

"There's a long, long night of waiting
Until my dreams all come true,
Till the day when I'll be going down
That long, long trail with you."

"Feeling good, ain't they?"

"Too good to suit me."

"So you don't let them get hold of that wheel, Miss. They'll be all right."

"I hope so. I've got no business out with a pair of drunks, I know that. But what could I do? I told them I wouldn't go with them, but then they started to go off by themselves."

"They'd break their necks."

"That's it. So I drove myself. It was all *I* knew to do."

"It keeps you guessing, sometimes, to know what to do. One sixty for the gas. Is the oil O.K.?"

"I think so."

"Thanks, Miss. Goodnight."

She got in, and took the wheel again, and me and the Greek kept on singing, and we went on. It was all part of the play.

I had to be drunk, because that other time had cured me of this idea we could pull a perfect murder. This was going to be such a lousy murder it wouldn't even be a murder. It was going to be just a regular road accident, with guys drunk, and booze in the car, and all the rest of it. Of course, when I started to put it down, the Greek had to have some too, so he was just like I wanted him. We stopped for gas so there would be a witness that she was sober, and didn't want to be with us anyhow, because she was driving, and it wouldn't do for her to be drunk. Before that, we had had a piece of luck. Just before we closed up, about nine o'clock, a guy stopped by for something to eat, and stood there in the road and watched us when we shoved off. He saw the whole show. He saw me try to start, and stall a couple of times. He heard the argument between me and Cora, about how I was too drunk to drive. He saw her get out, and heard her say she wasn't going. He saw me try to drive off, just me and the Greek. He saw her when she made us get out, and switched the seats, so I was behind, and the Greek up front, and then he saw her take the wheel and do the driving herself. His name was Jeff Parker and he raised rabbits at Encino. Cora got his card when she said she might try rabbits in the lunchroom, to see how they'd go. We knew right where to find him, whenever we'd need him.

Me and the Greek sang Mother Machree, and Smile, Smile, Smile, and Down by the Old Mill Stream, and pretty soon we came to this sign that said To Malibu Beach. She turned off there. By rights, she ought to have kept on like she was going. There's two main roads that lead up the coast. One, about ten miles inland, was the one we were on. The other, right alongside the ocean, was off to our left. At Ventura they meet, and follow the sea right on up to Santa Barbara, San Francisco, and wherever you're going. But the idea was, she had never seen Malibu Beach, where the movie stars live, and she wanted to cut over on this road to the ocean, so she could drop down a couple of miles and look at it, and then turn around and keep right on up to Santa Barbara. The real idea was that this connection is about the worst piece of road in Los Angeles County, and an accident there wouldn't surprise anybody, not even a cop. It's dark, and has no traffic on it hardly, and no houses or anything, and suited us for what we had to do.

The Greek never noticed anything for a while. We passed a little summer colony that they call Malibu Lake up in the hills, and there was a dance going on at the clubhouse, with couples out on the lake in canoes. I yelled at them. So did the Greek. "Give a one f' me." It didn't make much difference, but it was one more mark on our trail, if somebody took the trouble to find it.

We started up the first long up-grade, into the mountains. There were three miles of it. I had told her how to run it. Most of the time she was in second. That was partly because there were sharp curves every fifty feet, and the car would lose speed so quick going around them that she would have to shift up to second to keep going. But it was partly because the motor had to heat. Everything had to check up. We had to have plenty to tell.

And then, when he looked out and saw how dark it was, and what a hell of a looking country those mountains were, with no light, or house, or filling station, or anything else in sight, the Greek came to life and started an argument.

"Hold on, hold on. Turn around. By golly, we off the road."

"No we're not. I know where I am. It takes us to Malibu Beach. Don't you remember? I told you I wanted to see it."

"You go slow."

"I'm going slow."

"You go plenty slow. Maybe all get killed."

We got to the top and started into the down-grade. She cut the motor. They heat fast for a few minutes, when the fan stops. Down at the bottom she started the motor again. I looked at the temp gauge. It was 200. She started into the next up-grade and the temp gauge kept climbing.

"Yes sir, yes sir."

It was our signal. It was one of those dumb things a guy can say any time, and nobody will pay any attention to it. She pulled off to one side. Under us was a drop so deep you couldn't see the bottom of it. It must have been 500 feet.

"I think I'll let it cool off a bit."

"By golly, you bet. Frank, look a that. Look what it says."

"Whassit say?"

"Two hundred a five. Would be boiling in minute."

"Letta boil."

I picked up the wrench. I had it between my feet. But just then, away up the grade, I saw the lights of a car. I had to stall. I had to stall for a minute, until that car went by.

"C'me on, Nick. Sing's a song."

He looked out on those bad lands, but he didn't seem to feel like singing. Then he opened the door and got out. We could hear him back there, sick. That was where he was when the car went by. I looked at the number to burn it in my brain. Then I burst out laughing. She looked back at me.

" 'S all right. Give them something to remember. Both guys alive when they went by."

"Did you get the number?"

"2R-58-01."

"2R-58-01. 2R-58-01. All right. I've got it too."

"O.K."

He came around from behind, and looked like he felt better. "You hear that?"

"Hear what?"

"When you laugh. Is a echo. Is a fine echo."

He tossed off a high note. It wasn't any song, just a high note, like on a Caruso record. He cut it off quick and listened. Sure enough, here it came back, clear as anything, and stopped, just like he had.

"Is a sound like me?"

"Jus' like you, kid. Jussa same ol' toot."

"By golly. Is swell."

He stood there for five minutes, tossing off high notes and listening to them come back. It was the first time he ever heard what his voice sounded like. He was as pleased as a gorilla that seen his face in the mirror. She kept looking at me. We had to get busy. I began to act sore. "Wot th' hell? You think we got noth'n t' do but lis'n at you yod'l at y'self all night? C'me on, get in. Le's get going."

"It's getting late, Nick."

"Hokay, hokay."

He got in, but shoved his face out to the window and let go one. I braced my feet, and while he still had his chin on the window sill I brought down the wrench. His head cracked, and I felt it crush. He crumpled up and curled on the seat like a cat on a sofa. It seemed a year before he was still. Then Cora, she gave a funny kind of gulp that ended in a moan. Because here came the echo of his voice. It took the high note, like he did, and swelled, and stopped, and waited.

8

We didn't say anything. She knew what to do. She climbed back, and I climbed front. I looked at the wrench under the dash light. It had a few drops of blood on it. I uncorked a bottle of wine, and poured it on there till the blood was gone. I poured so the wine went over him. Then I wiped the wrench on a dry part of his clothes, and passed it back to her. She put it under the seat. I poured more wine over where I had wiped the wrench, cracked the bottle against the door, and laid it on top of him. Then I started the car. The wine bottle gave a gurgle, where a little of it was running out the crack.

I went a little way, and then shifted up to second. I couldn't tip it down that 500-foot drop, where we were. We had to get down to it afterward, and besides, if it plunged that far, how would we be alive? I drove slow, in second, up to a place where the ravine came to a point, and it was only a 50-foot drop. When I got there, I drove over to the edge, put my foot on the brake, and fed with the hand throttle. As soon as the right front wheel went off, I stepped hard on the brake. It stalled. That was how I wanted it. The car had to be in gear, with the ignition on, but that dead motor would hold it for the rest of what we had to do.

We got out. We stepped on the road, not the shoulder, so there wouldn't be footprints. She handed me a rock, and a piece of 2 × 4 I had back there. I put the rock under the rear axle. It fitted, because I had picked one that would fit. I slipped the 2 × 4 over the rock and under the axle. I heaved down on it. The car tipped, but it hung there. I heaved again.

It tipped a little more. I began to sweat. Here we were, with a dead man in the car, and suppose we couldn't tip it over?

I heaved again, but this time she was beside me. We both heaved. We heaved again. And then all of a sudden, there we were, sprawled down on the road, and the car was rolling over and over, down the gully, and banging so loud you could hear it a mile.

It stopped. The lights were still on, but it wasn't on fire. That was the big danger. With that ignition on, if the car burned up, why weren't we burned too? I snatched up the rock, and gave it a heave down the ravine. I picked up the 2 × 4, ran up the road with it a way, and slung it down, right in the roadway. It didn't bother me any. All over the road, wherever you go, are pieces of wood that have dropped off trucks, and they get all splintered up from cars running over them, and this was one of them. I had left it out all day, and it had tire marks on it, and the edges were all chewed up.

I ran back, picked her up, and slid down the ravine with her. Why I did that was on account of the tracks. My tracks, they didn't worry me any. I figured there would be plenty of men piling down there pretty soon, but those sharp heels of hers, they had to be pointed in the right direction, if anybody took the trouble to look.

I set her down. The car was hanging there, on two wheels, about halfway down the ravine. He was still in there, but now he was down on the floor. The wine bottle was wedged between him and the seat, and while we were looking it gave a gurgle. The top was all broken in, and both fenders were bent. I tried the doors. That was important, because I had to get in there, and be cut up with glass, while she went up on the road to get help. They opened all right.

I began to fool with her blouse, to bust the buttons, so she would look banged up. She was looking at me, and her eyes didn't look blue, they looked black. I could feel her breath coming fast. Then it stopped, and she leaned real close to me.

"Rip me! Rip me!"

I ripped her. I shoved my hand in her blouse and jerked. She was wide open, from her throat to her belly.

"You got that climbing out. You caught it in the door handle."

My voice sounded queer, like it was coming out of a tin phonograph.

"And this you don't know how you got."

I hauled off and hit her in the eye as hard as I could. She went down. She was right down there at my feet, her eyes shining, her breasts trembling, drawn up in tight points, and pointing right up at me. She was down there, and the breath was roaring in the back of my throat like I was some kind of a animal, and my tongue was all swelled up in my mouth, and blood pounding in it.

"Yes! Yes, Frank, yes!"

Next thing I knew, I was down there with her, and we were staring in each other's eyes, and locked in each other's arms, and straining to get closer. Hell could have opened for me then, and it wouldn't have made any difference. I had to have her, if I hung for it.

I had her.

9

We lay there a few minutes, then, like we were doped. It was so still that all you could hear was this gurgle from the inside of the car.

"What now, Frank?"

"Tough road ahead, Cora. You've got to be good, from now on. You sure you can go through it?"

"After that, I can go through anything."

"They'll come at you, those cops. They'll try to break you down. You ready for them?"

"I think so."

"Maybe they'll pin something on you. I don't think they can, with those witnesses we got. But maybe they do it. Maybe they pin it on you for manslaughter, and you spend a year in jail. Maybe it's as bad as that. You think you can take it on the chin?"

"So you're waiting for me when I come out."

"I'll be there."

"Then I can do it."

"Don't pay any attention to me. I'm a drunk. They got tests that'll show that. I'll say stuff that's cock-eyed. That's to cross them up, so when I'm sober and tell it my way, they'll believe it."

"I'll remember."

"And you're pretty sore at me. For being drunk. For being the cause of it all."

"Yes. I know."

"Then we're set."

"Frank."

"Yes?"

"There's just one thing. We've got to be in love. If we love each other, then nothing matters."

"Well, do we?"

"I'll be the first one to say it. I love you, Frank."

"I love you, Cora."

"Kiss me."

I kissed her, and held her close, and then I saw a flicker of light on the hill across the ravine.

"Up on the road, now. You're going through with it."

"I'm going through with it."

"Just ask for help. You don't know he's dead yet."

"I know."

"You fell down, after you climbed out. That's how you got the sand on your clothes."

"Yes. Goodbye."

"Goodbye."

She started up to the road, and I dived for the car. But all of a sudden, I found I didn't have my hat. I had to be in the car, and my hat had to be with me. I began clawing around for it. The car was coming closer and closer. It was only two or three bends away, and I didn't have my hat yet, and I didn't have a mark on me. I gave up, and started for the car. Then I fell down. I had hooked my foot in it. I grabbed it, and jumped in. My weight no sooner went on the floor than it sank and I felt the car turning over on me. That was the last I knew for a while.

Next, I was on the ground, and there was a lot of yelling

and talking going on around me. My left arm was shooting pain so bad I would yell every time I felt it, and so was my back. Inside my head was a bellow that would get big and go away again. When it did that the ground would fall away, and this stuff I had drunk would come up. I was there and I wasn't there, but I had sense enough to roll around and kick. There was sand on my clothes too, and there had to be a reason.

Next there was a screech in my ears, and I was in an ambulance. A state cop was at my feet, and a doctor was working on my arm. I went out again as soon as I saw it. It was running blood, and between the wrist and the elbow it was bent like a snapped twig. It was broke. When I came out of it again the doctor was still working on it, and I thought about my back. I wiggled my foot and looked at it to see if I was paralyzed. It moved.

The screech kept bringing me out of it, and I looked around, and saw the Greek. He was on the other bunk.

"Yay Nick."

Nobody said anything. I looked around some more, but I couldn't see anything of Cora.

After a while they stopped, and lifted out the Greek. I waited for them to lift me out, but they didn't. I knew he was really dead, then, and there wouldn't be any cock-eyed stuff this time, selling him a story about a cat. If they had taken us both out, it would be a hospital. But when they just took him out, it was a mortuary.

We went on, then, and when they stopped they lifted me out. They carried me in, and set the stretcher on a wheel table, and rolled me in a white room. Then they got ready to set my arm. They wheeled up a machine to give me gas for that, but then they had an argument. There was another doctor there by that time that said he was the jail physician, and the hospital doctors got pretty sore. I knew what it was about. It was those tests for being drunk. If they gave me the gas first, that would ball up the breath test, the most important one. The jail doctor won out, and made me blow through a glass pipe into some stuff that looked like water but turned yellow when I blew in it. Then he took some blood, and some other samples that he poured in bottles through a funnel. Then they gave me the gas.

When I began to come out of it I was in a room, in bed, and my head was all covered with bandages, and so was my arm, with a sling besides, and my back was all strapped up with adhesive tape so I could hardly move. A state cop was there, reading the morning paper. My head ached like hell, and so did my back, and my arm had shooting pains in it. After a while a nurse came in and gave me a pill, and I went to sleep.

When I woke up it was about noon, and they gave me something to eat. Then two more cops came in, and they put me on a stretcher again, and took me down and put me in another ambulance.

"Where we going?"

"Inquest."

"Inquest. That's what they have when somebody's dead, ain't it."

"That's right."

"I was afraid they'd got it."

"Only one."

"Which?"

"The man."

"Oh. Was the woman bad hurt?"

"Not bad."

"Looks pretty bad for me, don't it?"

"Watch out there, buddy. It's O.K. with us if you want to talk, but anything you say may fall back in your lap when you get to court."

"That's right. Thanks."

When we stopped it was in front of a undertaker shop in Hollywood, and they carried me in. Cora was there, pretty battered up. She had on a blouse that the police matron had lent her, and it puffed out around her belly like it was stuffed with hay. Her suit and her shoes were dusty, and her eye was all swelled up where I had hit it. She had the police matron with her. The coroner was back of a table, with some kind of a secretary guy beside him. Off to one side were a half dozen guys that acted pretty sore, with cops standing guard over them. They were the jury. There was a bunch of other people, with cops pushing them around to the place where they ought to stand. The undertaker was tip-toeing around, and every now and then he would shove a chair under somebody. He brought a couple for Cora and the matron. Off to one side, on a table, was something under a sheet.

Soon as they had me parked the way they wanted me, on a table, the coroner rapped with his pencil and they started. First thing, was a legal identification. She began to cry when they lifted the sheet off, and I didn't like it much myself. After she looked, and I looked, and the jury looked, they dropped the sheet again.

"Do you know this man?"

"He was my husband."

"His name?"

"Nick Papadakis."

Next came the witnesses. The sergeant told how he got the call and went up there with two officers after he phoned for an ambulance, and how he sent Cora in by a car he took charge of, and me and the Greek in by ambulance, and how the Greek died on the way in, and was dropped off at the mortuary. Next, a hick by the name of Wright told how he was coming around the bend, and heard a woman scream, and heard a crash, and saw the car going over and over, the lights still on, down the gully. He saw Cora in the road, waving at him for help, and went down to the car with her and tried to get me and the Greek out. He couldn't do it, because the car was on top of us, so he sent his brother, that was in the car with him, for help. After a while more people came, and the cops, and when the cops took charge they got the car off us and put us in the ambulance. Then Wright's brother told about the same thing, only he went back for the cops.

Then the jail doctor told how I was drunk, and how examination of the stomach showed the Greek was drunk, but Cora wasn't drunk. Then he told which cracked bone it was that the Greek died of. Then the coroner turned to me and asked me if I wanted to testify.

"Yes sir, I guess so."

"I warn you that any statement you make may be used against you, and that you are under no compulsion to testify unless you so wish."

"I got nothing to hold back."

"All right, then. What do you know about this?"

"All I know is that first I was going along. Then I felt the car sink under me, and something hit me, and that's all I can remember until I come to in the hospital."

"*You* were going along?"

"Yes sir."

"You mean you were driving the car?"

"Yes sir, I was driving it."

That was just a cock-eyed story I was going to take back later on, when we got in a place where it really meant something, which this inquest didn't. I figured if I told a bum story first, and then turned around and told another story, it would sound like the second story was really true, where if I had a pat story right from the beginning, it would sound like what it was, pat. I was doing this one different from the first time. I meant to look bad, right from the start. But if I wasn't driving the car, it didn't make any difference how bad I looked, they couldn't do anything to me. What I was afraid of was that perfect murder stuff that we cracked up on last time. Just one little thing, and we were sunk. But here, if I looked bad, there could be quite a few things and still I wouldn't look much worse. The worse I looked on account of being drunk, the less the whole thing would look like a murder.

The cops looked at each other, and the coroner studied me like he thought I was crazy. They had already heard it all, how I was pulled out from under the back seat.

"You're sure of that? That you were driving?"

"Absolutely sure."

"You had been drinking?"

"No sir."

"You heard the results of the tests that were given you?"

"I don't know nothing about the tests. All I know is I didn't have no drink."

He turned to Cora. She said she would tell what she could.

"Who was driving this car?"

"I was."

"Where was this man?"

"On the back seat."

"Had he been drinking?"

She kind of looked away, and swallowed, and cried a little bit. "Do I have to answer that?"

"You don't have to answer any question unless you so wish."

"I don't want to answer."

"Very well, then. Tell in your own words what happened."

"I was driving along. There was a long up-grade, and the car got hot. My husband said I had better stop to let it cool off."

"How hot?"

"Over 200."

"Go on."

"So after we started the down-grade, I cut the motor, and when we got to the bottom it was still hot, and before we started up again we stopped. We were there maybe ten minutes. Then I started up again. And I don't know what happened. I went into high, and didn't get enough power, and I went into second, right quick, and the men were talking, or maybe it was on account of making the quick shift, but anyhow, I felt one side of the car go down. I yelled to them to jump, but it was too late. I felt the car going over and over, and next thing I knew I was trying to get out, and then I was out, and then I was up on the road."

The coroner turned to me again. "What are you trying to do, shield this woman?"

"I don't notice her shielding me any."

The jury went out, and then came in and gave a verdict that the said Nick Papadakis came to his death as the result of an automobile accident on the Malibu Lake Road, caused in whole or in part by criminal conduct on the part of me and Cora, and recommended that we be held for the action of the grand jury.

There was another cop with me that night, in the hospital, and next morning he told me that Mr. Sackett was coming over to see me, and I better get ready. I could hardly move yet, but I had the hospital barber shave me up and make me look as good as he could. I knew who Sackett was. He was the District Attorney. About half past ten he showed up, and the cop went out, and there was nobody there but him and me. He was a big guy with a bald head and a breezy manner.

"Well, well, well. How do you feel?"

"I feel O.K., judge. Kind of shook me up a little, but I'll be all right."

"As the fellow said when he fell out of the airplane, it was a swell ride but we lit kind of hard."

"That's it."

"Now Chambers, you don't have to talk to me if you don't want to, but I've come over here, partly to see what you look like, and partly because it's been my experience that a frank talk saves a lot of breath afterwards, and sometimes paves the way to the disposition of a whole case with a proper plea, and anyway, as the fellow says, after it's over we understand each other."

"Why sure, judge. What was it you wanted to know?"

I made it sound pretty shifty, and he sat there looking me over. "Suppose we start at the beginning."

"About this trip?"

"That's it. I want to hear all about it."

He got up and began to walk around. The door was right by my bed, and I jerked it open. The cop was halfway down the hall, chinning a nurse. Sackett burst out laughing. "No, no dictaphones in this. They don't use them anyway, except in movies."

I let a sheepish grin come over my face. I had him like I wanted him. I had pulled a dumb trick on him, and he had got the better of me. "O.K., judge. I guess it was pretty silly, at that. All right, I'll begin at the beginning and tell it all. I'm in dutch all right, but I guess lying about it won't do any good."

"That's the right attitude, Chambers."

I told him how I walked out on the Greek, and how I bumped into him on the street one day, and he wanted me back, and then asked me to go on this Santa Barbara trip with them to talk it over. I told about how we put down the wine, and how we started out, with me at the wheel. He stopped me then.

"So you *were* driving the car?"

"Judge, suppose *you* tell *me* that."

"What do you mean, Chambers?"

"I mean I heard what she said, at the inquest. I heard what those cops said. I know where they found me. So I know who was driving, all right. She was. But if I tell it like I remember it, I got to say I was driving it. I didn't tell that coroner any lie, judge. *It still seems to me I was driving it.*"

"You lied about being drunk."

"That's right. I was all full of booze, and ether, and dope that they give you, and I lied all right. But I'm all right now, and I got sense enough to know the truth is all that can get me out of this, if anything can. Sure, I was drunk. I was stinko. And all I could think of was, I mustn't let them know I was drunk, because I was driving the car, and if they find out I was drunk, I'm sunk."

"Is that what you'd tell a jury?"

"I'd have to, judge. But what I can't understand is how she came to be driving it. I started out with it. I know that. I can even remember a guy standing there laughing at me. Then how come she was driving when it went over?"

"You drove it about two feet."

"You mean two miles."

"I mean two feet. Then she took the wheel away from you."

"Gee, I *must* have been stewed."

"Well, it's one of those things that a jury might believe. It's just got that cock-eyed look to it that generally goes with the truth. Yes, they might believe it."

He sat there looking at his nails, and I had a hard time to keep the grin from creeping over my face. I was glad when he started asking me more questions, so I could get my mind on something else, besides how easy I had fooled him.

"When did you go to work for Papadakis, Chambers?"

"Last winter."

"How long did you stay with him?"

"Till a month ago. Maybe six weeks."

"You worked for him six months, then?"

"About that."

"What did you do before that?"

"Oh, knocked around."

"Hitch-hiked? Rode freights? Bummed your meals wherever you could?"

"Yes sir."

He unstrapped a briefcase, put a pile of papers on the table, and began looking through them. "Ever been in Frisco?"

"Born there."

"Kansas City? New York? New Orleans? Chicago?"

"I've seen them all."

"Ever been in jail?"

"I have, judge. You knock around, you get in trouble with the cops now and then. Yes sir, I've been in jail."

"Ever been in jail in Tucson?"

"Yes sir. I think it was ten days I got there. It was for trespassing on railroad property."

"Salt Lake City? San Diego? Wichita?"

"Yes sir. All those places."

"Oakland?"

"I got three months there, judge. I got in a fight with a railroad detective."

"You beat him up pretty bad, didn't you?"

"Well, as the fellow says, he was beat up pretty bad, but you ought to seen the other one. I was beat up pretty bad, myself."

"Los Angeles?"

"Once. But that was only three days."

"Chambers, how did you come to go to work for Papadakis, anyhow?"

"Just a kind of an accident. I was broke, and he needed somebody. I blew in there to get something to eat, and he offered me a job, and I took it."

"Chambers, does that strike you as funny?"

"I don't know how you mean, judge."

"That after knocking around all these years, and never doing any work, or even trying to do any, so far as I can see, you suddenly settled down, and went to work, and held a job steady?"

"I didn't like it much, I'll own up to that."

"But you stuck."

"Nick, he was one of the nicest guys I ever knew. After I got a stake, I tried to tell him I was through, but I just didn't have the heart, much trouble as he had had with his help. Then when he had the accident, and wasn't there, I blew. I just blew, that's all. I guess I ought to treated him better, but I got rambling feet, judge. When they say go, I got to go with them. I just took a quiet way out."

"And then, the day after you came back, he got killed."

"You kind of make me feel bad now, judge. Because maybe I tell the jury different, but I'm telling you now I feel that was a hell of a lot my fault. If I hadn't been there, and begun promoting him for something to drink that afternoon, maybe he'd be here now. Understand, maybe that didn't have anything to do with it at all. I don't know. I was stinko, and I don't know what happened. Just the same, if she hadn't had two drunks in the car, maybe she could have drove better, couldn't she? Anyway, that's how I feel about it."

I looked at him, to see how he was taking it. He wasn't even looking at me. All of a sudden he jumped up and came over to the bed and took me by the shoulder. "Out with it, Chambers. Why did you stick with Papadakis for six months?"

"Judge, I don't get you."

"Yes you do. I've seen her, Chambers, and I can guess why you did it. She was in my office yesterday, and she had a black eye, and was pretty well banged up, but even with that she looked pretty good. For something like that, plenty of guys have said goodbye to the road, rambling feet or not."

"Anyhow they rambled. No, judge, you're wrong."

"They didn't ramble long. It's too good, Chambers. Here's an automobile accident that yesterday was a dead open-and-shut case of manslaughter, and today it's just evaporated into nothing at all. Every place I touch it, up pops a witness to tell me something, and when I fit all they have to say together, I haven't got any case. Come on, Chambers. You and that woman murdered this Greek, and the sooner you own up to it the better it'll be for you."

There wasn't any grin creeping over my face then, I'm here to tell you. I could feel my lips getting numb, and I tried to speak, but nothing would come out of my mouth.

"Well, why don't you say something?"

"You're coming at me. You're coming at me for something pretty bad. I don't know anything to say, judge."

"You were gabby enough a few minutes ago, when you were handing me that stuff about the truth being all that would get you out of this. Why can't you talk now?"

"You got me all mixed up."

"All right, we'll take it one thing at a time, so you won't be mixed up. In the first place, you've been sleeping with that woman, haven't you?"

"Nothing like it."

"How about the week Papadakis was in the hospital? Where did you sleep then?"

"In my own room."

"And she slept in hers? Come on, I've seen her, I tell you. I'd have been in there if I had to kick the door down and hang for rape. So would you. So *were* you."

"I never even thought of it."

"How about all those trips you took with her to Hasselman's Market in Glendale? What did you do with her on the way back?"

"Nick told me to go on those trips himself."

"I didn't ask you who told you to go. I asked you what you did."

I was so groggy I had to do something about it quick. All I could think of was to get sore. "All right, suppose we did. We didn't, but you say we did, and we'll let it go at that. Well, if it was all that easy, what would we be knocking him off for? Holy smoke, judge, I hear tell of guys that would commit murder for what you say I was getting, when they weren't getting it, but I never hear tell of a guy that would commit murder for it when he already had it."

"No? Well I'll tell you what you were knocking him off for. A piece of property out there, for one thing, that Papadakis paid $14,000 for, cash on the nail. And for that other little Christmas present you and she thought you would get on the boat with, and see what the wild waves looked like. *That little $10,000 accident policy that Papadakis carried on his life.*"

I could still see his face, but all around it was getting black and I was trying to keep myself from keeling over in bed. Next thing, he was holding a glass of water to my mouth. "Have a drink. You'll feel better."

I drank some of it. I had to.

"Chambers, I think this is the last murder you'll have a hand in for some time, but if you ever try another, for God's sake leave insurance companies out of it. They'll spend five times as much as Los Angeles County will let me put into a case. They've got detectives five times as good as any I'll be able to hire. They know their stuff from A to izzard, and they're right on your tail now. It means money to them. That's where you and she made your big mistake."

"Judge, I hope Christ may kill me, I never heard of an insurance policy until just this minute."

"You turned white as a sheet."

"Wouldn't you?"

"Well, how about getting me on your side, right from the start? How about a full confession, a quick plea of guilty, and I'll do what I can for you with the court? Ask for clemency for you both."

"Nothing doing."

"How about all that stuff you were telling me just now? About the truth, and how you'd have to come clean with the jury, and all that? You think you can get away with lies now? You think I'm going to stand for that?"

"I don't know what you're going to stand for. To hell with that. You stand for your side of it and I'll stand for mine. I didn't do it, and that's all I stand for. You got that?"

"The hell you say. Getting tough with me, hey? All right, now you get it. You're going to find out what that jury's really going to hear. First, you were sleeping with her, weren't you? Then Papadakis had a little accident, and you and she had a swell time. In bed together at night, down to the beach by day, holding hands and looking at each other in between. Then you both had a swell idea. Now that he's had an accident, make him take out an accident policy, and then knock him off. So you blew, to give her a chance to put it over. She worked at it, and pretty soon she had him. He took out a policy, a real good policy, that covered accidents, and health, and all the rest of it, and cost $46.72. Then you were ready. Two days after that, Frank Chambers accidentally on purpose

ran into Nick Papadakis on the street, and Nick tries to get
him to go back to work for him. And what do you know
about that, he and his wife had it already fixed up they were
going to Santa Barbara, had the hotel reservations and everything, so of course there was nothing to it but Frank Chambers had to come with them, just for old times' sake. And you
went. You got the Greek a little bit drunk, and did the same
for yourself. You stuck a couple of wine bottles in the car, just
to get the cops good and sore. Then you had to take that
Malibu Lake Road, so she could see Malibu Beach. Wasn't
that an idea, now. Eleven o'clock at night, and she was going
to drive down there to look at a bunch of houses with waves
in front of them. But you didn't get there. You stopped. And
while you were stopped, you crowned the Greek with one of
the wine bottles. A beautiful thing to crown a man with,
Chambers, and nobody knew it better than you, because that
was what you crowned that railroad dick with, over in Oakland. You crowned him, and then she started the car. And
while she was climbing out on the running board, you leaned
over from behind, and held the wheel, and fed with the hand
throttle. It didn't need much gas, because it was in second
gear. And after she got on the running board, she took the
wheel and fed with the hand throttle, and it was your turn to
climb out. But you were just a little drunk, weren't you? You
were too slow, and she was a little too quick to shoot the car
over the edge. So she jumped and you were caught. You think
a jury won't believe that, do you? It'll believe it, because I'll
prove every word of it, from the beach trip to the hand throttle, and when I do, there won't be any clemency for you, boy.
It'll be the rope, with you hanging on the end of it, and when
they cut you down they'll bury you out there with all the
others that were too goddam dumb to make a deal when they
had the chance to keep their neck from being broke."

"Nothing like that happened. Not that I know of."

"What are you trying to tell me? That *she* did it?"

"I'm not trying to tell you that anybody did it. Leave me
alone! Nothing like that happened."

"How do you know? I thought you were stinko."

"It didn't happen that I know of."

THE POSTMAN ALWAYS RINGS TWICE

"Then you mean she did it?"

"I don't mean no such a goddam thing. I mean what I say and that's all I mean."

"Listen, Chambers. There were three people in the car, you, and she, and the Greek. Well, it's a cinch the Greek didn't do it. If you didn't do it, that leaves her, doesn't it?"

"Who the hell says anybody did it?"

"I do. Now we're getting somewhere, Chambers. Because maybe you didn't do it. You say you're telling the truth, and maybe you are. But if you are telling the truth, and didn't have any interest in this woman except as the wife of a friend, then you've got to do something about it, haven't you? You've got to sign a complaint against her."

"What do you mean complaint?"

"If she killed the Greek, she tried to kill you too, didn't she? You can't let her get away with that. Somebody might think it was pretty funny if you did. Sure, you'd be a sucker to let her get away with it. She knocks off her husband for the insurance, and she tries to knock off you too. You've got to do something about that, haven't you?"

"I might, if she did it. But I don't know she did it."

"If I prove it to you, you'll have to sign the complaint, won't you?"

"Sure. *If* you can prove it."

"All right, I'll prove it. When you stopped, you got out of the car, didn't you?"

"No."

"What? I thought you were so stinko you didn't remember anything. That's the second time you've remembered something now. I'm surprised at you."

"Not that I know of."

"But you did. Listen to this man's statement: 'I didn't notice much about the car, except that a woman was at the wheel and one man was inside laughing when we went by, and another man was out back, sick.' So you were out back a few minutes, sick. That was when she crowned Papadakis with the bottle. And when you got back you never noticed anything, because you were stinko, and Papadakis had passed out anyhow, and there was hardly anything to notice. You sat back and passed out, and that was when she slid up into second, kept her hand on the hand throttle, fed with that, and as soon as she had slid out on the running board, shot the car over."

"That don't prove it."

"Yes it does. The witness Wright says that the car was rolling over and over, down the gully, when he came around the bend, *but the woman was up on the road, waving to him for help!*"

"Maybe she jumped."

"If she jumped, it's funny she took her handbag with her, isn't it? Chambers, can a woman drive with a handbag in her hand? When she jumps, has she got time to pick it up? Chambers, it can't be done. It's impossible to jump from a sedan car that's turning over into a gully. She wasn't in the car when it went over! That proves it, doesn't it?"

"I don't know."

"What do you mean you don't know? Are you going to sign that complaint or not?"

"No."

"Listen, Chambers, it was no accident that car went over a second too soon. It was you or her, and she didn't mean it would be you."

"Let me alone. I don't know what you're talking about."

"Boy, it's still you or her. If you didn't have anything to do with this, you better sign this thing. Because if you don't, then I'll know. And so will the jury. And so will the judge. And so will the guy that springs the trap."

He looked at me a minute, then went out, and came back with another guy. The guy sat down and made out a form with a fountain pen. Sackett brought it over to me. "Right here, Chambers."

I signed. There was so much sweat on my hand the guy had to blot it off the paper.

10

After he went, the cop came back and mumbled something about blackjack. We played a few rounds, but I couldn't get

my mind on it. I made out it got on my nerves to deal with
one hand, and quit.

"He kind of got to you, hey?"

"Little bit."

"He's tough, he is. He gets to them all. He looks like a
preacher, all full of love for the human race, but he's got a
heart like a stone."

"Stone is right."

"Only one guy in this town has got it on him."

"Yeah?"

"Guy named Katz. You've heard of him."

"Sure, I heard of him."

"Friend of mine."

"It's the kind of a friend to have."

"Say. You ain't supposed to have no lawyer yet. You ain't
been arraigned, and you can't send for nobody. They can hold
you forty eight hours incommunicado, they call it. But if he
shows up here, I got to let him see you, you get it? He might
show up here, if I happened to be talking to him."

"You mean you get a cut."

"I mean he's a friend of mine. Well, if he didn't give me
no cut, he wouldn't be no friend, would he? He's a great guy.
He's the only one in this town can throw the headlock on
Sackett."

"You're on, kid. And the sooner the better."

"I'll be back."

He went out for a little while, and when he came back he
gave me a wink. And pretty soon, sure enough, there came a
knock on the door, and in came Katz. He was a little guy,
about forty years old, with a leathery face and a black moustache, and the first thing he did when he came in was take
out a bag of Bull Durham smoking tobacco and a pack of
brown papers and roll himself a cigarette. When he lit it, it
burned halfway up one side, and that was the last he did about
it. It just hung there, out the side of his mouth, and if it was
lit or out, or whether he was asleep or awake, I never found
out. He just sat there, with his eyes half shut and one leg
hung over the arm of the chair, and his hat on the back of his
head, and that was all. You might think that was a poor sight
to see, for a guy in my spot, but it wasn't. He might be asleep,

but even asleep he looked like he knew more than most guys awake, and a kind of a lump came up in my throat. It was like the sweet chariot had swung low and was going to pick me up.

The cop watched him roll the cigarette like it was Cadona doing the triple somersault, and he hated to go, but he had to. After he was out, Katz motioned to me to get going. I told him about how we had an accident, and how Sackett was trying to say we murdered the Greek for the insurance, and how he made me sign that complaint paper that said she had tried to murder me too. He listened, and after I had run down he sat there a while without saying anything. Then he got up.

"He's got you in a spot all right."

"I ought not to signed it. I don't believe she did any such a goddam thing. But he had me going. And now I don't know where the hell I'm at."

"Well, anyhow, you ought not to have signed it."

"Mr. Katz, will you do one thing for me? Will you see her, and tell her—"

"I'll see her. And I'll tell her what's good for her to know. For the rest of it, I'm handling this, and that means I'm handling it. You got that?"

"Yes sir, I've got it."

"I'll be with you at the arraignment. Or anyhow, somebody that I pick will be with you. As Sackett has made a complainant out of you, I may not be able to appear for you both, but I'll be handling it. And once more, that means that whatever I do, I'm handling it."

"Whatever you do, Mr. Katz."

"I'll be seeing you."

That night they put me on a stretcher again, and took me over to court for the arraignment. It was a magistrate's court, not a regular court. There wasn't any jury box, or witness stand, or any of that stuff. The magistrate sat on a platform, with some cops beside him, and in front of him was a long desk that ran clear across the room, and whoever had something to say hooked his chin over the desk and said it. There was a big crowd there, and photographers were snapping flashlights at me when they carried me in, and you could tell from the buzz that something big was going on. I couldn't see much, from down there on the stretcher, but I got a flash at Cora, sitting on the front bench with Katz, and Sackett, off to one side talking to some guys with briefcases, and some of the cops and witnesses that had been at the inquest. They set me down in front of the desk, on a couple of tables they had shoved together, and they hadn't much more than got the blankets spread over me right than they wound up a case about a Chinese woman, and a cop began rapping for quiet. While he was doing that, a young guy leaned down over me, and said his name was White, and Katz had asked him to represent me. I nodded my head, but he kept whispering that Mr. Katz had sent him, and the cop got sore and began banging hard.

"Cora Papadakis."

She stood up, and Katz took her up to the desk. She almost touched me as she went by, and it seemed funny to smell her, the same smell that had always set me wild, in the middle of all this stuff. She looked a little better than she had yesterday. She had on another blouse, that fitted her right, and her suit had been cleaned and pressed, and her shoes had been polished, and her eye was black, but not swelled. All the other people went up with her, and after they had spread out in a line, the cop told them to raise their right hand, and began to mumble about the truth, the whole truth, and nothing but the truth. He stopped in the middle of it to look down and see if I had my right hand raised. I didn't. I shoved it up, and he mumbled all over again. We all mumbled back.

The magistrate took off his glasses, and told Cora she was charged with the murder of Nick Papadakis, and with assault against Frank Chambers, with intent to kill, that she could make a statement if she wanted to, but any statement she made could be used against her, that she had the right to be represented by counsel, that she had eight days to plead, and the court would hear her plea at any time during that period. It was a long spiel, and you could hear them coughing before he got done.

Then Sackett started up, and told what he was going to prove. It was about the same as he had told me that morning, only he made it sound solemn as hell. When he got through, he began putting on his witnesses. First there was the ambulance doctor, that told when the Greek had died, and where. Then came the jail doctor, that had made the autopsy, and then came the coroner's secretary, that identified the minutes of the inquest, and left them with the magistrate, and then came a couple of more guys, but I forget what they said. When they got done, all that the whole bunch had proved was that the Greek was dead, and as I knew that anyway, I didn't pay much attention. Katz never asked any of them anything. Every time the magistrate would look at him, he would wave his hand and the guy would step aside.

After they had the Greek dead enough to suit them, Sackett really straightened out, and put some stuff in that meant something. He called a guy that said he represented the Pacific States Accident Assurance Corporation of America, and he told how the Greek had taken out a policy just five days before. He told what it covered, how the Greek would get $25 a week for 52 weeks if he got sick, and the same if he got hurt in an accident so he couldn't work, and how he would get $5,000 if he lost one limb, and $10,000 if he lost two limbs, and how his widow would get $10,000 if he was killed in an accident, and $20,000 if the accident was on a railroad train. When he got that far it began to sound like a sales talk, and the magistrate held up his hand.

"I've got all the insurance I need."

Everybody laughed at the magistrate's gag. Even I laughed. You'd be surprised how funny it sounded.

Sackett asked a few more questions, and then the magistrate turned to Katz. Katz thought a minute, and when he talked to the guy, he did it slow, like he wanted to make sure he had every word straight.

"You are an interested party to this proceeding?"

"In a sense I am, Mr. Katz."

"You wish to escape payment of this indemnity, on the ground that a crime has been committed, is that correct?"

"That is correct."

"You really believe that a crime has been committed, that this woman killed her husband to obtain this indemnity, and either tried to kill this man, or else deliberately placed him in jeopardy that might cause his death, all as part of a plan to obtain this indemnity?"

The guy kind of smiled, and thought a minute, like he would return the compliment and get every word straight too. "Answering that question, Mr. Katz, I would say I've handled thousands of such cases, cases of fraud that go over my desk every day, and I think I have an unusual experience in that kind of investigation. I may say that I have never seen a clearer case in all my years' work for this and other companies. I don't only believe a crime has been committed, Mr. Katz. I practically know it."

"That is all. Your honor, I plead her guilty on both charges."

If he had dropped a bomb in that courtroom, he couldn't have stirred it up quicker. Reporters rushed out, and photographers rushed up to the desk to get pictures. They kept bumping into each other, and the magistrate got sore and began banging for order. Sackett looked like he had been shot, and all over the place there was a roar like somebody had all of a sudden shoved a seashell up against your ear. I kept trying to see Cora's face. But all I could get of it was the corner of her mouth. It kept twitching, like somebody was jabbing a needle into it about once every second.

Next thing I knew, the guys on the stretcher picked me up, and followed the young guy, White, out of the courtroom. Then they went with me on the double across a couple of halls into a room with three or four cops in it. White said something about Katz, and the cops cleared out. They set me down on the desk, and then the guys on the stretcher went out. White walked around a little, and then the door opened and a matron came in with Cora. Then White and the matron went out, and the door closed, and we were alone. I tried to think of something to say, and couldn't. She walked around, and didn't look at me. Her mouth was still twitching. I kept swallowing, and after a while I thought of something.

"We've been flim-flammed, Cora."

She didn't say anything. She just kept walking around.

"That guy Katz, he's nothing but a cop's stool. A cop sent

him to me. I thought he was on the up-and-up. But we've been flim-flammed."

"Oh no, we ain't been flim-flammed."

"We been flim-flammed. I ought to have known, when the cop tried to sell him to me. But I didn't. I thought he was on the level."

"I've been flim-flammed, but you haven't."

"Yes I have. He fooled me too."

"I see it all now. I see why I had to drive the car. I see it, that other time, why it was me that had to do it, not you. Oh yes. I fell for you because you were smart. And now I find out you're smart. Ain't that funny? You fall for a guy because he's smart and then you find out he's smart."

"What are you trying to tell me, Cora?"

"Flim-flammed! I'll say I was. You and that lawyer. You fixed it up all right. You fixed it up so I tried to kill you too. That was so it would look like you couldn't have had anything to do with it. Then you have me plead guilty in court. So you're not in it at all. All right. I guess I'm pretty dumb. But I'm not that dumb. Listen, Mr. Frank Chambers. When I get through, just see how smart you are. There's just such a thing as being too smart."

I tried to talk to her, but it wasn't any use. When she had got so that even her lips were white, under the lipstick, the door opened and Katz came in. I tried to jump for him, off the stretcher. I couldn't move. They had me strapped so I couldn't move.

"Get out of here, you goddam stool. *You* were handling it. I'll say you were. But now I know you for what you are. Do you hear that? Get out of here!"

"Why, what's the matter, Chambers?"

You would have thought he was a Sunday school teacher, talking to some kid that was crying for his chewing gum that had been taken away. "Why, what's the matter? I *am* handling it. I told you that."

"That's right. Only God help you if I ever get you so I got my hands on you."

He looked at her, like it was something he just couldn't understand, and maybe she could help him out. She came over to him.

"This man here, this man and you, you ganged up on me so I would get it and he would go free. Well, he was in this as much as I was, and he's not going to get away with it. I'm going to tell it. I'm going to tell it all, and I'm going to tell it right now."

He looked at her, and shook his head, and it was the phoniest look I ever saw on a man's face. "Now my dear. I wouldn't do that. If you'll just let me handle this—"

"You handled it. Now I'll handle it."

He got up, shrugged his shoulders, and went out. He was hardly gone before a guy with big feet and a red neck came in with a little portable typewriter, set it on a chair with a couple of books under it, hitched up to it, and looked at her.

"Mr. Katz said you wanted to make a statement?"

He had a little squeaky voice, and a kind of a grin when he talked.

"That's right. A statement."

She began to speak jerky, two or three words at a time, and as fast as she said it, he rattled it off on the typewriter. She told it all. She went back to the beginning, and told how she met me, how we first began going together, how we tried to knock off the Greek once, but missed. A couple of times, a cop put his head in at the door, but the guy at the typewriter held up his hand.

"Just a few minutes, sarge."

"O.K."

When she got to the end, she said she didn't know anything about the insurance, we hadn't done it for that at all, but just to get rid of him.

"That's all."

He gathered his sheets together, and she signed them. "Will you just initial these pages?" She initialed them. He got out a notary stamp, and made her hold up her right hand, and put the stamp on, and signed it. Then he put the papers in his pocket, closed his typewriter, and went out.

She went to the door and called the matron. "I'm ready now." The matron came in and took her out. The guys on the stretcher came in and carried me out. They went on the double, but on the way they got jammed in with the crowd that was watching her, where she was standing in front of the elevators with the matron, waiting to go up to the jail. It's on the top floor of the Hall of Justice. They pushed on through, and my blanket got pulled so it was trailing on the floor. She picked it up and tucked it around me, then turned away quick.

II

They took me back to the hospital, but instead of the state cop watching me, it was this guy that had taken the confession. He lay down on the other bed. I tried to sleep, and after a while I did. I dreamed she was looking at me, and I was trying to say something to her, but couldn't. Then she would go down, and I would wake up, and that crack would be in my ears, that awful crack that the Greek's head made when I hit it. Then I would sleep again, and dream I was falling. And I would wake up again, holding on to my neck, and that same crack would be in my ears. One time when I woke up I was yelling. He leaned up on his elbow.

"Yay."

"Yay."

"What's the matter?"

"Nothing's the matter. Just had a dream."

"O.K."

He never left me for a minute. In the morning, he made them bring him a basin of water, and took out a razor from his pocket, and shaved. Then he washed himself. They brought in breakfast, and he ate his at the table. We didn't say anything.

They brought me a paper, then, and there it was, with a big picture of Cora on the front page, and a smaller picture of me on the stretcher underneath it. It called her the bottle killer. It told how she had pleaded guilty at the arraignment, and would come up for sentence today. On one of the inside pages, it had a story that it was believed the case would set a record for speed in its disposition, and another story about a preacher that said if all cases were railroaded through that quick, it would do more to prevent crime than passing a hundred laws. I looked all through the paper for something about the confession. It wasn't in there.

About twelve o'clock a young doctor came in and went to work on my back with alcohol, sopping off some of the adhesive tape. He was supposed to sop it off, but most of the time he just peeled it, and it hurt like hell. After he got part of it off, I found I could move. He left the rest on, and a nurse brought me my clothes. I put them on. The guys on the stretcher came in and helped me to the elevator and out of the hospital. There was a car waiting there, with a chauffeur. The guy that had spent the night with me put me in, and we drove about two blocks. Then he took me out, and we went in an office building, and up to an office. And there was Katz with his hand stuck out and a grin all over his face.

"It's all over."

"Swell. When do they hang her?"

"They don't hang her. She's out, free. Free as a bird. She'll be over in a little while, soon as they fix up some things in court. Come in. I'll tell you about it."

He took me in a private office and closed the door. Soon as he rolled a cigarette, and half burned it up, and got it pasted on his mouth, he started to talk. I hardly knew him. It didn't seem that a man that had looked so sleepy the day before could be as excited as he was.

"Chambers, this is the greatest case I ever had in my life. I'm in it, and out of it, in less than twenty four hours, and yet I tell you I never had anything like it. Well, the Dempsey-Firpo fight lasted less than two rounds, didn't it? It's not how long it lasts. It's what you do while you're in there.

"This wasn't really a fight, though. It was a four-handed card game, where every player has been dealt a perfect hand. Beat that, if you can. You think it takes a card player to play a bum hand, don't you. To hell with that. I get those bum hands every day. Give me one like this, where they've all got cards, *where they've all got cards that'll win if they play them right,* and then watch me. Oh, Chambers, you did me a favor all right when you called me in on this. I'll never get another one like it."

"You haven't said anything yet."

"I'll say it, don't worry about that. But you won't get it, you won't know how the hand was played, until I get the cards straightened out for you. Now first. There were you and the woman. You each held a perfect hand. Because that was a perfect murder, Chambers. Maybe you don't even know how good it was. All that stuff Sackett tried to scare you with, about her not being in the car when it went over, and having her handbag with her, and all that, that didn't amount to a goddam thing. A car can teeter before it goes over, can't it? And a woman can grab her handbag before she jumps, can't she? That don't prove any crime. That just proves she's a woman."

"How'd you find out about that stuff?"

"I got it from Sackett. I had dinner with him last night, and he was crowing over me. He was pitying me, the sap. Sackett and I are enemies. We're the friendliest enemies that ever were. He'd sell his soul to the devil to put something over on me, and I'd do the same for him. We even put up a bet on it. We bet $100. He was giving me the razz, because he had a perfect case, where he could just play the cards and let the hangman do his stuff."

That was swell, two guys betting $100 on what the hangman would do to me and Cora, but I wanted to get it straight, just the same.

"If we had a perfect hand, where did his hand come in?"

"I'm getting to that. You had a perfect hand, but Sackett knows that no man and no woman that ever lived could play that hand, not if the prosecutor plays his hand right. He knows that all he's got to do is get one of you working against the other, and it's in the bag. That's the first thing. Next thing, he doesn't even have to work the case up. He's got an insurance company to do that for him, so he doesn't have to lift a finger. That's what Sackett loved about it. All he had to do was play the cards, and the pot would fall right in his lap. So what does he do? He takes this stuff the insurance company dug up for him, and scares the hell out of you with it, and gets you to sign a complaint against her. He takes the best card you've got, which is how bad you were hurt yourself, and makes you trump your own ace with it. If you were hurt that bad, it had to be an accident, and yet Sackett uses that to make you sign a complaint against her. And you sign it, because you're afraid if you don't sign it he'll know goddam well you did it."

"I turned yellow, that's all."

"Yellow is a color you figure on in murder, and nobody figures on it better than Sackett. All right. He's got you where he wants you. He's going to make you testify against her, and he knows that once you do that, no power on earth can keep her from ratting on you. So that's where he's sitting when he has dinner with me. He razzes me. He pities me. He bets me $100. And all the time I'm sitting there with a hand that I know I can beat him with, if I only play the cards right. All right, Chambers. You're looking in my hand. What do you see in it?"

"Not much."

"Well, what?"

"Nothing, to tell you the truth."

"Neither did Sackett. But now watch. After I left you yesterday, I went to see her, and got an authorization from her to open Papadakis's safe deposit box. And I found what I expected. There were some other policies in that box, and I went to see the agent that wrote them, and this is what I found out:

"That accident policy didn't have anything to do with that accident that Papadakis had a few weeks ago. The agent had turned up on his calendar that Papadakis's automobile insurance had pretty near run out, and he went out there to see him. She wasn't there. They fixed it up pretty quick for the automobile insurance, fire, theft, collision, public liability, the regular line. Then the agent showed Papadakis where he was covered on everything but injury to himself, and asked him how about a personal accident policy. Papadakis got interested right away. Maybe that other accident was the reason for that, but if it was the agent didn't know anything about it. He signed up for the whole works, and gave the agent his check, and next day the policies were mailed out to him. You understand, an agent works for a lot of companies, and not all these policies were written by the same company. That's No. 1 point that Sackett forgot. But the main thing to remember is that Papadakis didn't only have the new insurance. He had the old policies too, *and they still had a week to run.*

"All right, now, get this set-up. The Pacific States Accident is on a $10,000 personal accident policy. The Guaranty of California is on a $10,000 new public liability bond, and the Rocky Mountain Fidelity is on an old $10,000 public liability bond. So that's my first card. He had an insurance company working for him up to $10,000. I had two insurance companies working for me up to $20,000, whenever I wanted to call them in. Do you get it?"

"No, I don't."

"Look. Sackett stole your big card off you, didn't he? Well, I stole the same card off him. You were hurt, weren't you? You were hurt bad. Well, if Sackett convicts her of murder, and you bring suit against her for injuries sustained as a result of that murder, then a jury will give you whatever you ask for. And those two bonding companies are liable for every cent of their policies to satisfy that judgment."

"Now I get it."

"Pretty, Chambers, pretty. I found that card in my mitt, but you didn't find it, and Sackett didn't find it, and the Pacific States Accident didn't find it, because they were so busy playing Sackett's game for him, and so sure his game would win, that they didn't even think of it."

He walked around the room a few times, falling for himself every time he passed a little mirror that was in the corner, and then he went on.

"All right, there it was, but the next thing was how to play it. I had to play it quick, because Sackett had already played his, and that confession was due any minute. It might even come at the arraignment, as soon as she heard you testify against her. I had to move fast. So what did I do? I waited till the Pacific States Accident man had testified, and then got him on record that he really believed a crime had been committed. That was just in case I had a false arrest action against him later on. And then, wham, I pleaded her guilty. That ended the arraignment, and for that night, blocked off Sackett. Then I rushed her in a counsel room, claimed a half hour before she was locked up for the night, and sent you in there with her. Five minutes with you was all she needed.

When I got in there she was ready to spill it. Then I sent Kennedy in."

"The dick that was with me last night?"

"He used to be a dick, but he's not a dick any more. He's my gum-shoe man now. She thought she was talking to a dick, but she was really talking to a dummy. But it did the work. After she got it off her chest, she kept quiet till today, and that was long enough. The next thing was you. What you would do was blow. There was no charge against you, so you weren't under arrest any more, even if you thought you were. Soon as you tumbled to that, I knew no tape, or sore back, or hospital orderly, or anything else would hold you, so after he got done with her I sent Kennedy over to keep an eye on you. The next thing was a little midnight conference between the Pacific States Accident, the Guaranty of California, and the Rocky Mountain Fidelity. And when I laid it in front of them, they did business awful quick."

"What do you mean, they did business?"

"First, I read them the law. I read them the guest clause, Section 141¾, California Vehicle Act. That says if a guest in an automobile gets hurt, he has no right of recovery, *provided*, that if his injury resulted from intoxication or willful misconduct on the part of the driver, then he can recover. You see, you were a guest, and I had pleaded her guilty to murder and assault. Plenty of willful misconduct there, wasn't there? And they couldn't be sure, you know. Maybe she did do it alone. So those two companies on the liability policies, the ones that had their chin hanging out for a wallop from you, they chipped in $5,000 apiece to pay the Pacific States Accident policy, and the Pacific States Accident agreed to pay up and shut up, and the whole thing didn't take over a half hour."

He stopped and grinned at himself some more.

"What then?"

"I'm still thinking about it. I can still see Sackett's face just now when that Pacific States Accident fellow went on the stand today and said his investigation had convinced him that no crime had been committed, and his company was paying the accident claim in full. Chambers, do you know what that feels like? To feint a guy open and then let him have it, right on the chin? There's no feeling like it in the world."

"I still don't get it. What was this guy testifying again for?"

"She was up for sentence. And after a plea of guilty, a court usually wants to hear some testimony to find out what the case is really about. To determine the sentence. And Sackett had started in howling for blood. He wanted the death penalty. Oh, he's a blood-thirsty lad, Sackett is. That's why it stimulates me to work against him. He really believes hanging them does some good. You're playing for stakes when you're playing against Sackett. So he put his insurance man on the stand again. But instead of it being *his* son of a bitch, after that little midnight session it was *my* son of a bitch, only Sackett didn't know it. He roared plenty when he found it out. But it was too late. If an insurance company didn't believe she was guilty, a jury would never believe it, would it? There wasn't a chance in the world of convicting her after that. And that was when I burned Sackett. I got up and made a speech to the court. I took my time about it. I told how my client had protested her innocence from the beginning. I told how I didn't believe it. I told how I knew there existed what I regarded as overwhelming evidence against her, enough to convict her in any court, and that I believed I was acting in her best interest when I decided to plead her guilty and throw her on the mercy of the court. But, Chambers, do you know how I rolled that *but* under my tongue? But, in the light of the testimony just given, there was no course open to me but to withdraw the pleas of guilty and allow the cases to proceed. Sackett couldn't do a thing, because I was still within the limit of eight days for a plea. He knew he was sunk. He consented to a plea for manslaughter, the court examined the other witnesses itself, gave her six months, suspended sentence, and practically apologized even for that. We quashed the assault charge. That was the key to the whole thing, and we almost forgot it."

There came a rap on the door. Kennedy brought Cora in, put some papers down in front of Katz, and left. "There you are, Chambers. Just sign that, will you? It's a waiver of damages for any injuries sustained by you. It's what they get out of it for being so nice."

I signed.

"You want me to take you home, Cora?"

"I guess so."

"One minute, one minute, you two. Not so fast. There's one other little thing. That ten thousand dollars you get for knocking off the Greek."

She looked at me and I looked at her. He sat there looking at the check. "You see, it wouldn't be a perfect hand if there hadn't been some money in it for Katz. I forgot to tell you about that. Well. Oh, well. I won't be a hog. I generally take it all, but on this, I'll just make it half. Mrs. Papadakis, you make out your check for $5,000, and I'll make this over to you and go over to the bank and fix up the deposits. Here. Here's a blank check."

She sat down, and picked up the pen, and started to write, and then stopped, like she couldn't quite figure out what it was all about. All of a sudden, he went over and picked up the blank check and tore it up.

"What the hell. Once in a lifetime, isn't it? Here. You keep it all. I don't care about the ten grand. I've got ten grand. This is what I want!"

He opened his pocketbook, took out a slip, and showed it to us. It was Sackett's check for $100. "You think I'm going to cash that? I am like hell. I'm going to frame it. It goes up there, right over my desk."

12

We went out of there, and got a cab, because I was so crippled up, and first we went to the bank, and put the check in, and then we went to a flower shop, and got two big bunches of flowers, and then we went to the funeral of the Greek. It seemed funny he was only dead two days, and they were just burying him. The funeral was at a little Greek church, and a big crowd of people was there, some of them Greeks I had seen out to the place now and then. They gave her a dead pan when we came in, and put her in a seat about three rows from the front. I could see them looking at us, and I wondered what I would do if they tried to pull some rough stuff later. They were his friends, not ours. But pretty soon I saw an afternoon paper being passed around, that had big headlines in it that she was innocent, and an usher took a look at it, and came running over and moved us up on the front bench. The guy that did the preaching started out with some dirty cracks about how the Greek died, but a guy went up and whispered to him, and pointed at the paper that had got up near the front by that time, and he turned around and said it all over again, without any dirty cracks, and put in about the sorrowing widow and friends, and they all nodded their head it was O.K. When we went out in the churchyard, where the grave was, a couple of them took her by the arm, and helped her out, and a couple more helped me. I got to blubbering while they were letting him down. Singing those hymns will do it to you every time, and specially when it's about a guy you like as well as I liked the Greek. At the end they sang some song I had heard him sing a hundred times, and that finished me. It was all I could do to lay our flowers out the way they were supposed to go.

The taxi driver found a guy that would rent us a Ford for $15 a week, and we took it, and started out. She drove. When we got out of the city we passed a house that was being built, and all the way out we talked about how not many of them have gone up lately, but the whole section is going to be built up as soon as things get better. When we got out to the place she let me out, put the car away, and then we went inside. It was all just like we left it, even to the glasses in the sink that we had drunk the wine out of, and the Greek's guitar, that hadn't been put away yet because he was so drunk. She put the guitar in the case, and washed the glasses, and then went upstairs. After a minute I went up after her.

She was in their bedroom, sitting by the window, looking out at the road.
"Well?"
She didn't say anything. I started to leave.
"I didn't ask you to leave."
I sat down again. It was a long while before she snapped out of it.

"You turned on me, Frank."

"No I didn't. He had me, Cora. I had to sign his paper. If I didn't, then he would tumble to everything. I didn't turn on you. I just went along with him, till I could find out where I was at."

"You turned on me. I could see it in your eye."

"All right, Cora, I did. I just turned yellow, that's all. I didn't want to do it. I tried not to do it. But he beat me down. I cracked up, that's all."

"I know."

"I went through hell about it."

"And I turned on you, Frank."

"They made you do it. You didn't want to. They set a trap for you."

"I wanted to do it. I hated you then."

"That's all right. It was for something I didn't really do. You know how it was, now."

"No. I hated you for something you really did."

"I never hated you, Cora. I hated myself."

"I don't hate you now. I hate that Sackett. And Katz. Why couldn't they leave us alone? Why couldn't they let us fight it out together? I wouldn't have minded that. I wouldn't have minded it even if it meant—you know. We would have had our love. And that's all we ever had. But the very first time they started their meanness, you turned on me."

"And you turned on me, don't forget that."

"That's the awful part. I turned on you. We both turned on each other."

"Well, that makes it even, don't it?"

"It makes it even, but look at us now. We were up on a mountain. We were up so high, Frank. We had it all, out there, that night. I didn't know I could feel anything like that. And we kissed and sealed it so it would be there forever, no matter what happened. We had more than any two people in the world. And then we fell down. First you, and then me. Yes, it makes it even. We're down here together. But we're not up high any more. Our beautiful mountain is gone."

"Well what the hell? We're together, ain't we?"

"I guess so. But I thought an awful lot, Frank. Last night. About you and me, and the movies, and why I flopped, and the hashhouse, and the road, and why you like it. We're just two punks, Frank. God kissed us on the brow that night. He gave us all that two people can ever have. And we just weren't the kind that could have it. We had all that love, and we just cracked up under it. It's a big airplane engine, that takes you through the sky, right up to the top of the mountain. But when you put it in a Ford, it just shakes it to pieces. That's what we are, Frank, a couple of Fords. God is up there laughing at us."

"The hell he is. Well we're laughing at him too, aren't we? He put up a red stop sign for us, and we went past it. And then what? Did we get shoved off the deep end? We did like hell. We got away clean, and got $10,000 for doing the job. So God kissed us on the brow, did he? Then the devil went to bed with us, and believe you me, kid, he sleeps pretty good."

"Don't talk that way, Frank."

"Did we get that ten grand, or didn't we?"

"I don't want to think about the ten grand. It's a lot, but it couldn't buy our mountain."

"Mountain, hell, we got the mountain and ten thousand smackers to pile on top of that yet. If you want to go up high, take a look around from that pile."

"You nut. I wish you could see yourself, yelling with that bandage on your head."

"You forgot something. We got something to celebrate. We ain't never had that drunk yet."

"I wasn't talking about that kind of a drunk."

"A drunk's a drunk. Where's that liquor I had before I left?"

I went to my room and got the liquor. It was a quart of Bourbon, three quarters full. I went down, got some Coca Cola glasses, and ice cubes, and White Rock, and came back upstairs. She had taken her hat off and let her hair down. I fixed two drinks. They had some White Rock in them, and a couple of pieces of ice, but the rest was out of the bottle.

"Have a drink. You'll feel better. That's what Sackett said when he put the spot on me, the louse."

"My, but that's strong."

"You bet it is. Here, you got too many clothes on."

I pushed her over to the bed. She held on to her glass, and some of it spilled. "The hell with it. Plenty more where that came from."

I began slipping off her blouse. "Rip me, Frank. Rip me like you did that night."

I ripped all her clothes off. She twisted and turned, slow, so they would slip out from under her. Then she closed her eyes and lay back on the pillow. Her hair was falling over her shoulders in snaky curls. Her eye was all black, and her breasts weren't drawn up and pointing up at me, but soft, and spread out in two big pink splotches. She looked like the great grandmother of every whore in the world. The devil got his money's worth that night.

13

We kept that up for six months. We kept it up, and it was always the same way. We'd have a fight, and I'd reach for the bottle. What we had the fights about was going away. We couldn't leave the state until the suspended sentence was up, but after that I meant we should blow. I didn't tell her, but I wanted her a long way from Sackett. I was afraid if she got sore at me for something, she'd go off her nut and spill it like she had that other time, after the arraignment. I didn't trust her for a minute. At first, she was all hot for going too, specially when I got talking about Hawaii and the South Seas, but then the money began to roll in. When we opened up, about a week after the funeral, people flocked out there to see what she looked like, and then they came back because they had a good time. And she got all excited about here was our chance to make some more money.

"Frank, all these roadside joints around here are lousy. They're run by people that used to have a farm back in Kansas or somewhere, and got as much idea how to entertain people as a pig has. I believe if somebody came along that knew the business like I do, and tried to make it nice for them, they'd come and bring all their friends."

"To hell with them. We're selling out anyhow."

"We could sell easier if we were making money."

"We're making money."

"I mean good money. Listen, Frank. I've got an idea people would be glad of the chance to sit out under the trees. Think of that. All this nice weather in California, and what do they do with it? Bring people inside of a joint that's set up ready-made by the Acme Lunch Room Fixture Company, and stinks so it makes you sick to your stomach, and feed them awful stuff that's the same from Fresno down to the border, and never give them any chance to feel good at all."

"Look. We're selling out, aren't we? Then the less we got to sell the quicker we get rid of it. Sure, they'd like to sit under the trees. Anybody but a California Bar-B-Q slinger would know that. But if we put them under the trees we've got to get tables, and wire up a lot of lights out there, and all that stuff, and maybe the next guy don't want it that way at all."

"We've got to stay six months. Whether we like it or not."

"Then we use that six months finding a buyer."

"I want to try it."

"All right, then try it. But I'm telling you."

"I could use some of our inside tables."

"I said try it, didn't I? Come on. We'll have a drink."

What we had the big blow-off over was the beer license, and then I tumbled to what she was really up to. She put the tables out under the trees, on a little platform she had built, with a striped awning over them and lanterns at night, and it went pretty good. She was right about it. Those people really enjoyed a chance to sit out under the trees for a half hour, and listen to a little radio music, before they got in their cars and went on. And then beer came back. She saw a chance to leave it just like it was, put beer in, and call it a beer garden.

"I don't want any beer garden, I tell you. All I want is a guy that'll buy the whole works and pay cash."

"But it seems a shame."

"Not to me it don't."

"But look, Frank. The license is only twelve dollars for six months. My goodness, we can afford twelve dollars, can't we?"

"We get the license and then we're in the beer business. We're in the gasoline business already, and the hot dog business, and now we got to go in the beer business. The hell with it. I want to get out of it, not get in deeper."

"Everybody's got one."

"And welcome, so far as I'm concerned."

"People wanting to come, and the place all fixed up under the trees, and now I have to tell them we don't have beer because we haven't any license."

"Why do you have to tell them anything?"

"All we've got to do is put in coils and then we can have draught beer. It's better than bottled beer, and there's more money in it. I saw some lovely glasses in Los Angeles the other day. Nice tall ones. The kind people like to drink beer out of."

"So we got to get coils and glasses now, have we? I tell you I don't *want* any beer garden."

"Frank, don't you ever want to *be* something?"

"Listen, get this. I want to get away from this place. I want to go somewhere else, where every time I look around I don't see the ghost of a goddam Greek jumping out at me, and hear his echo in my dreams, and jump every time the radio comes out with a guitar. I've got to go away, do you hear me? I've got to get out of here, or I go nuts."

"You're lying to me."

"Oh no, I'm not lying. I never meant anything more in my life."

"You don't see the ghost of any Greek, that's not it. Somebody else might see it, but not Mr. Frank Chambers. No, you want to go away just because you're a bum, that's all. That's what you were when you came here, and that's what you are now. When we go away, and our money's all gone, then what?"

"What do I care? We go away, don't we?"

"That's it, you don't care. We could stay here—"

"I knew it. That's what you really mean. That's what you've meant all along. That we stay here."

"And why not? We've got it good. Why wouldn't we stay here? Listen, Frank. You've been trying to make a bum out of me ever since you've known me, but you're not going to do it. I told you, I'm not a bum. I want to *be* something. We stay here. We're not going away. We take out the beer license. We amount to something."

It was late at night, and we were upstairs, half undressed. She was walking around like she had that time after the arraignment, and talking in the same funny jerks.

"Sure we stay. We do whatever you say, Cora. Here, have a drink."

"I don't want a drink."

"Sure you want a drink. We got to laugh some more about getting the money, haven't we?"

"We already laughed about it."

"But we're going to make more money, aren't we? On the beer garden? We got to put down a couple on that, just for luck."

"You nut. All right. Just for luck."

That's the way it went, two or three times a week. And the tip-off was that every time I would come out of a hangover, I would be having those dreams. I would be falling, and that crack would be in my ears.

Right after the sentence ran out, she got the telegram her mother was sick. She got some clothes in a hurry, and I put her on the train, and going back to the parking lot I felt funny, like I was made of gas and would float off somewhere. I felt free. For a week, anyway, I wouldn't have to wrangle, or fight off dreams, or nurse a woman back to a good humor with a bottle of liquor.

On the parking lot a girl was trying to start her car. It wouldn't do anything. She stepped on everything and it was just plain dead.

"What's the matter? Won't it go?"

"They left the ignition on when they parked it, and now the battery's run out."

"Then it's up to them. They've got to charge it for you."

"Yes, but I've got to get home."

"I'll take you home."

"You're awfully friendly."

"I'm the friendliest guy in the world."

"You don't even know where I live."

"I don't care."

"It's pretty far. It's in the country."

"The further the better. Wherever it is, it's right on my way."

"You make it hard for a nice girl to say no."

"Well then, if it's so hard, don't say it."

She was a light-haired girl, maybe a little older than I was, and not bad on looks. But what got me was how friendly she was, and how she wasn't any more afraid of what I might do to her than if I was a kid or something. She knew her way around all right, you could see that. And what finished it was when I found out she didn't know who I was. We told our names on the way out, and to her mine didn't mean a thing. Boy oh boy what a relief that was. One person in the world that wasn't asking me to sit down to the table a minute, and then telling me to give them the low-down on that case where they said the Greek was murdered. I looked at her, and I felt the same way I had walking away from the train, like I was made of gas, and would float out from behind the wheel.

"So your name is Madge Allen, hey?"

"Well, it's really Kramer, but I took my own name again after my husband died."

"Well listen Madge Allen, or Kramer, or whatever you want to call it, I've got a little proposition to make you."

"Yes?"

"What do you say we turn this thing around, point her south, and you and me take a little trip for about a week?"

"Oh, I couldn't do that."

"Why not?"

"Oh, I just couldn't, that's all."

"You like me?"

"Sure I like you."

"Well, I like you. What's stopping us?"

She started to say something, didn't say it, and then laughed. "I own up. I'd like to, all right. And if it's something

I'm supposed not to do, why that don't mean a thing to me. But I can't. It's on account of the cats."

"Cats?"

"We've got a lot of cats. And I'm the one that takes care of them. That's why I had to get home."

"Well, they got pet farms, haven't they? We'll call one up, and tell them to come over and get them."

That struck her funny. "I'd like to see a pet farm's face when it saw them. They're not that kind."

"Cats are cats, ain't they?"

"Not exactly. Some are big and some are little. Mine are big. I don't think a pet farm would do very well with that lion we've got. Or the tigers. Or the puma. Or the three jaguars. They're the worst. A jaguar is an awful cat."

"Holy smoke. What do you do with those things?"

"Oh, work them in movies. Sell the cubs. People have private zoos. Keep them around. They draw trade."

"They wouldn't draw my trade."

"We've got a restaurant. People look at them."

"Restaurant, hey. That's what I've got. Whole goddam country lives selling hot dogs to each other."

"Well, anyway, I couldn't walk out on my cats. They've got to eat."

"The hell we can't. We'll call up Goebel and tell him to come get them. He'll board the whole bunch while we're gone for a hundred bucks."

"Is it worth a hundred bucks to you to take a trip with me?"

"It's worth exactly a hundred bucks."

"Oh my. I can't say no to that. I guess you better call up Goebel."

I dropped her off at her place, found a pay station, called up Goebel, went back home, and closed up. Then I went back after her. It was about dark. Goebel had sent a truck over, and I met it coming back, full of stripes and spots. I parked about a hundred yards down the road, and in a minute she showed up with a little grip, and I helped her in, and we started off.

"You like it?"

"I love it."

We went down to Caliente, and next day we kept on down the line to Ensenada, a little Mexican town about seventy miles down the coast. We went to a little hotel there, and spent three or four days. It was pretty nice. Ensenada is all Mex, and you feel like you left the U.S.A. a million miles away. Our room had a little balcony in front of it, and in the afternoon we would just lay out there, look at the sea, and let the time go by.

"Cats, hey. What do you do, train them?"

"Not the stuff we've got. They're no good. All but the tigers are outlaws. But I do train them."

"You like it?"

"Not much, the real big ones. But I like pumas. I'm going to get an act together with them some time. But I'll need a lot of them. Jungle pumas. Not these outlaws you see in the zoos."

"What's an outlaw?"

"He'd kill you."

"Wouldn't they all?"

"They might, but an outlaw does anyhow. If it was people, he would be a crazy person. It comes from being bred in captivity. These cats you see, they look like cats, but they're really cat lunatics."

"How can you tell it's a jungle cat?"

"I catch him in a jungle."

"You mean you catch them *alive*?"

"Sure. They're no good to me dead."

"Holy smoke. How do you do that?"

"Well, first I get on a boat and go down to Nicaragua. All the really fine pumas come from Nicaragua. These California and Mexican things are just scrubs compared to them. Then I hire me some Indian boys and go up in the mountains. Then I catch my pumas. Then I bring them back. But this time, I stay down there with them a while, to train them. Goat meat is cheaper there than horse meat is here."

"You sound like you're all ready to start."

"I am."

She squirted a little wine in her mouth, and gave me a long look. They give it to you in a bottle with a long thin spout

on it, and you squirt it in your mouth with the spout. That's
to cool it. She did that two or three times, and every time she
did it she would look at me.

"I am if you are."

"What the hell? You think I'm going with you to catch
them goddam things?"

"Frank, I brought quite a lot of money with me. Let's let
Goebel keep those bughouse cats for their board, sell your car
for whatever we can get, and hunt cats."

"You're on."

"You mean you will?"

"When do we start?"

"There's a freight boat out of here tomorrow and it puts
in at Balboa. We'll wire Goebel from there. And we can leave
your car with the hotel here. They'll sell it and send us whatever they get. That's one thing about a Mexican. He's slow,
but he's honest."

"O.K."

"Gee I'm glad."

"Me too. I'm so sick of hot dogs and beer and apple pie
with cheese on the side I could heave it all in the river."

"You'll love it, Frank. We'll get a place up in the mountains,
where it's cool, and then, after I get my act ready, we can go
all over the world with it. Go as we please, do as we please,
and have plenty of money to spend. Have you got a little bit
of gypsy in you?"

"Gypsy? I had rings in my ears when I was born."

I didn't sleep so good that night. When it was beginning
to get light, I opened my eyes, wide awake. It came to me,
then, that Nicaragua wouldn't be quite far enough.

14

When she got off the train she had on a black dress, that
made her look tall, and a black hat, and black shoes and stockings, and didn't act like herself while the guy was loading the
trunk in the car. We started out, and neither one of us had
much to say for a few miles.

"Why didn't you let me know she died?"

"I didn't want to bother you with it. Anyhow, I had a lot to do."

"I feel plenty bad now, Cora."

"Why?"

"I took a trip while you were away. I went up to Frisco."

"Why do you feel bad about that?"

"I don't know. You back there in Iowa, your mother dying and all, and me up in Frisco having a good time."

"I don't know why you should feel bad. I'm glad you went. If I'd have thought about it, I'd have told you to before I left."

"We lost some business. I closed down."

"It's all right. We'll get it back."

"I felt kind of restless, after you left."

"Well my goodness, I don't mind."

"I guess you had a bad time of it, hey?"

"It wasn't very pleasant. But anyhow, it's over."

"I'll shoot a drink in you when we get home. I got some nice stuff out there I brought back to you."

"I don't want any."

"It'll pick you up."

"I'm not drinking any more."

"No?"

"I'll tell you about it. It's a long story."

"You sound like plenty happened out there."

"No, nothing happened. Only the funeral. But I've got a lot to tell you. I think we're going to have a better time of it from now on."

"Well for God's sake. What is it?"

"Not now. Did you see your family?"

"What for?"

"Well anyway, did you have a good time?"

"Fair. Good as I could have alone."

"I bet it was a swell time. But I'm glad you said it."

When we got out there, a car was parked in front, and a guy was sitting in it. He got a silly kind of grin on his face and climbed out. It was Kennedy, the guy in Katz's office.

"You remember me?"

"Sure I remember you. Come on in."

We took him inside, and she gave me a pull into the kitchen.

"This is bad, Frank."

"What do you mean, bad?"

"I don't know, but I can feel it."

"Better let me talk to him."

I went back with him, and she brought us some beer, and left us, and pretty soon I got down to cases.

"You still with Katz?"

"No, I left him. We had a little argument and I walked out."

"What are you doing now?"

"Not a thing. Fact of the matter, that's what I came out to see you about. I was out a couple of times before, but there was nobody home. This time, though, I heard you were back, so I stuck around."

"Anything I can do, just say the word."

"I was wondering if you could let me have a little money."

"Anything you want. Of course, I don't keep much around, but if fifty or sixty dollars will help, I'll be glad to let you have it."

"I was hoping you could make it more."

He still had this grin on his face, and I figured it was time to quit the feinting and jabbing, and find out what he meant.

"Come on, Kennedy. What is it?"

"I tell you how it is. I left Katz. And that paper, the one I wrote up for Mrs. Papadakis, was still in the files, see? And on account of being a friend of yours and all that, I knew you wouldn't want nothing like that laying around. So I took it. I thought maybe you would like to get it back."

"You mean that hop dream she called a confession?"

"That's it. Of course, I know there wasn't anything to it, but I thought you might like to get it back."

"How much do you want for it?"

"Well, how much would you pay?"

"Oh, I don't know. As you say, there's nothing to it, but I might give a hundred for it. Sure. I'd pay that."

"I was thinking it was worth more."

"Yeah?"

"I figured on twenty five grand."

"Are you crazy?"

"No, I ain't crazy. You got ten grand from Katz. The place has been making money, I figure about five grand. Then on the property, you could get ten grand from the bank. Papadakis gave fourteen for it, so it looks like you could get ten. Well, that makes twenty five."

"You would strip me clean, just for that?"

"It's worth it."

I didn't move, but I must have had a flicker in my eye, because he jerked an automatic out of his pocket and leveled it at me. "Don't start anything, Chambers. In the first place, I haven't got it with me. In the second place, if you start anything I let you have it."

"I'm not starting anything."

"Well, see you don't."

He kept the gun pointed at me, and I kept looking at him. "I guess you got me."

"I don't guess it. I know it."

"But you're figuring too high."

"Keep talking, Chambers."

"We got ten from Katz, that's right. And we've still got it. We made five off the place, but we spent a grand in the last couple weeks. She took a trip to bury her mother, and I took one. That's why we been closed up."

"Go on, keep talking."

"And we can't get ten on the property. With things like they are now, we couldn't even get five. Maybe we could get four."

"Keep talking."

"All right, ten, four, and four. That makes eighteen."

He grinned down the gun barrel a while, and then he got up. "All right. Eighteen. I'll phone you tomorrow, to see if you've got it. If you've got it, I'll tell you what to do. If you haven't got it, that thing goes to Sackett."

"It's tough, but you got me."

"Tomorrow at twelve, then, I phone you. That'll give you time to go to the bank and get back."

"O.K."

He backed to the door and still held the gun on me. It was late afternoon, just beginning to get dark. While he was backing away, I leaned up against the wall, like I was pretty down in the mouth. When he was half out the door I cut the juice in the sign, and it blazed down in his eyes. He wheeled, and I let him have it. He went down and I was on him. I twisted the gun out of his hand, threw it in the lunchroom, and socked him again. Then I dragged him inside and kicked the door shut. She was standing there. She had been at the door, listening, all the time.

"Get the gun."

She picked it up and stood there. I pulled him to his feet, threw him over one of the tables, and bent him back. Then I beat him up. When he passed out, I got a glass of water and poured it on him. Soon as he came to, I beat him up again. When his face looked like raw beef, and he was blubbering like a kid in the last quarter of a football game, I quit.

"Snap out of it, Kennedy. You're talking to your friends over the telephone."

"I got no friends, Chambers. I swear, I'm the only one that knows about—"

I let him have it, and we did it all over again. He kept saying he didn't have any friends, so I threw an arm lock on him and shoved up on it. "All right, Kennedy. If you've got no friends, then I break it."

He stood it longer than I thought he could. He stood it till I was straining on his arm with all I had, wondering if I really could break it. My left arm was still weak where it had been broke. If you ever tried to break the second joint of a tough turkey, maybe you know how hard it is to break a guy's arm with a hammerlock. But all of a sudden he said he would call. I let him loose and told him what he was to say. Then I put him at the kitchen phone, and pulled the lunchroom extension through the swing door, so I could watch him and hear what he said and they said. She came back there with us, with the gun.

"If I give you the sign, he gets it."

She leaned back and an awful smile flickered around the corner of her mouth. I think that smile scared Kennedy worse than anything I had done.

"He gets it."

He called, and a guy answered. "Is that you, Willie?"

"Pat?"

"This is me. Listen. It's all fixed. How soon can you get out here with it?"

"Tomorrow, like we said."

"Can't you make it tonight?"

"How can I get in a safe deposit box when the bank is closed?"

"All right, then do like I tell you. Get it, first thing in the morning, and come out here with it. I'm out to his place."

"His *place*?"

"Listen, get this, Willie. He knows we got him, see? But he's afraid if she finds out he's got to pay all that dough, she won't let him, you get it? If he leaves, she knows something is up, and maybe she takes a notion to go with him. So we do it all here. I'm just a guy that's spending the night in their auto camp, and she don't know nothing. Tomorrow, you're just a friend of mine, and we fix it all up."

"How does he get the money if he don't leave?"

"That's all fixed up."

"And what in the hell are you spending the night there for?"

"I got a reason for that, Willie. Because maybe it's a stall, what he says about her, and maybe it's not, see? But if I'm here, neither one of them can skip, you get it?"

"Can he hear you, what you're saying?"

He looked at me, and I nodded my head yes. "He's right here with me, in the phone booth. I want him to hear me, you get it, Willie? I want him to know we mean business."

"It's a funny way to do, Pat."

"Listen, Willie. You don't know, and I don't know, and none of us don't know if he's on the level with it or not. But maybe he is, and I'm giving him a chance. What the hell, if a guy's willing to pay, we got to go along with him, haven't we? That's it. You do like I tell you. You get it out here soon as you can in the morning. Soon as you can, you get it? Because I don't want her to get to wondering what the hell I'm doing hanging around here all day."

"O.K."

He hung up. I walked over and gave him a sock. "That's just so you talk right when he calls back. You got it, Kennedy?"

"I got it."

I waited a few minutes, and pretty soon here came the call back. I answered, and when Kennedy picked up the phone he gave Willie some more of the same. He said he was alone that time. Willie didn't like it much, but he had to take it. Then I took him back to the No. 1 shack. She came with us, and I took the gun. Soon as I had Kennedy inside, I stepped out the door with her and gave her a kiss.

"That's for being able to step on it when the pinch comes. Now get this. I'm not leaving him for a minute. I'm staying out here the whole night. There'll be other calls, and we'll bring him in to talk. I think you better open the place up. The beer garden. Don't bring anybody inside. That's so if his friends do some spying, you're right on deck and it's business as usual."

"All right. And Frank."

"Yes?"

"Next time I try to act smart, will you hang one on my jaw?"

"What do you mean?"

"We ought to have gone away. Now I know it."

"Like hell we ought. Not till we get this."

She gave me a kiss, then. "I guess I like you pretty well, Frank."

"We'll get it. Don't worry."

"I'm not."

I stayed out there with him all night. I didn't give him any food, and I didn't give him any sleep. Three or four times he had to talk to Willie, and once Willie wanted to talk to me. Near as I could tell, we got away with it. In between, I would beat him up. It was hard work, but I meant he should want that paper to get there, bad. While he was wiping the blood off his face, on a towel, you could hear the radio going, out in the beer garden, and the people laughing and talking.

About ten o'clock the next morning she came out there. "They're here, I think. There are three of them."

"Bring them back."

She picked up the gun, stuck it in her belt so you couldn't see it from in front, and went. In a minute, I heard something fall. It was one of his gorillas. She was marching them in front of her, making them walk backwards with their hands up, and one of them fell when his heel hit the concrete walk. I opened the door. "This way, gents."

They came in, still holding their hands up, and she came in after them and handed me the gun. "They all had guns, but I took them off them in the lunchroom."

"Better get them. Maybe they got friends."

She went, and in a minute came back with the guns. She took out the clips, and laid them on the bed, beside me. Then she went through their pockets. Pretty soon she had it. And the funny part was that in another envelope were photostats of it, six positives and one negative. They had meant to keep on blackmailing us, and then hadn't had any more sense than to have the photostats on them when they showed up. I took them all, with the original, outside, crumpled them up on the ground, and touched a match to them. When they were burned I stamped the ashes into the dirt and went back.

"All right, boys. I'll show you out. We'll keep the artillery here."

After I had marched them out to their cars, and they left, and I went back inside, she wasn't there. I went out back, and she wasn't there. I went upstairs. She was in our room. "Well, we did it, didn't we? That's the last of it, photostats and all. It's been worrying me, too."

She didn't say anything, and her eyes looked funny. "What's the matter, Cora?"

"So that's the last of it, is it? Photostats and all. It isn't the last of me, though. I've got a million photostats of it, just as good as they were. Jimmy Durante. I've got a million of them. Am I mortified?"

She burst out laughing, and flopped down on the bed.

"All right. If you're sucker enough to put your neck in the

noose, just to get me, you've got a million of them. You sure
have. A million of them."

"Oh no, that's the beautiful part. I don't have to put my
neck in the noose at all. Didn't Mr. Katz tell you? Once they
just made it manslaughter, they can't do any more to me. It's
in the Constitution or something. Oh no, Mr. Frank Chambers. It don't cost me a thing to make you dance on air. And
that's what you're going to do. Dance, dance, dance."

"What ails you, anyhow?"

"Don't you know? Your friend was out last night. She
didn't know about me, and she spent the night here."

"What friend?"

"The one you went to Mexico with. She told me all about
it. We're good friends now. She thought we better be good
friends. After she found out who I was she thought I might
kill her."

"I haven't been to Mexico for a year."

"Oh yes you have."

She went out, and I heard her go in my room. When she
came back she had a kitten with her, but a kitten that was
bigger than a cat. It was gray, with spots on it. She put it on
the table in front of me and it began to meow. "The puma
had little ones while you were gone, and she brought you one
to remember her by."

She leaned back against the wall and began to laugh again,
a wild, crazy laugh. "And the cat came back! It stepped on
the fuse box and got killed, but here it is back! Ha, ha, ha,
ha, ha, ha! Ain't that funny, how unlucky cats are for you?"

15

She cracked up, then, and cried, and after she got quiet she
went downstairs. I was down there, right after her. She was
tearing the top flaps off a big carton.

"Just making a nest for our little pet, dearie."

"Nice of you."

"What did you think I was doing?"

"I didn't."

"Don't worry. When the time comes to call up Mr. Sackett, I'll let you know. Just take it easy. You'll need all your strength."

She lined it with excelsior, and on top of that put some woolen cloths. She took it upstairs and put the puma in it. It meowed a while and then went to sleep. I went downstairs to fix myself a coke. I hadn't any more than squirted the ammonia in it than she was at the door.

"Just taking something to keep my strength up, dearie."

"Nice of you."

"What did you think I was doing?"

"I didn't."

"Don't worry. When I get ready to skip I'll let you know. Just take it easy. You may need all your strength."

She gave me a funny look and went upstairs. It kept up all day, me following her around for fear she'd call up Sackett, her following me around for fear I'd skip. We never opened the place up at all. In between the tip-toeing around, we would sit upstairs in the room. We didn't look at each other. We looked at the puma. It would meow and she would go down to get it some milk. I would go with her. After it lapped up the milk it would go to sleep. It was too young to play much. Most of the time it meowed or slept.

That night we lay side by side, not saying a word. I must have slept, because I had those dreams. Then, all of a sudden, I woke up, and before I was even really awake I was running downstairs. What had waked me was the sound of that telephone dial. She was at the extension in the lunchroom, all dressed, with her hat on, and a packed hat box on the floor beside her. I grabbed the receiver and slammed it on the hook. I took her by the shoulders, jerked her through the swing door, and shoved her upstairs. "Get up there! Get up there, or I'll—"

"Or you'll what?"

The telephone rang, and I answered it.

"Here's your party, go ahead."

"Yellow Cab."

"Oh. Oh. I called you, Yellow Cab, but I've changed my mind. I won't need you."

"O.K."

When I got upstairs she was taking off her clothes. When we got back in bed we lay there a long time again without saying a word. Then she started up.

"Or you'll what?"

"What's it to you? Sock you in the jaw, maybe. Maybe something else."

"Something else, wasn't it?"

"What are you getting at now?"

"Frank, I know what you've been doing. You've been lying there, trying to think of a way to kill me."

"I've been asleep."

"Don't lie to me, Frank. Because I'm not going to lie to you, and I've got something to say to you."

I thought that over a long time. Because that was just what I had been doing. Lying there beside her, just straining to think of a way I could kill her.

"All right, then. I was."

"I knew it."

"Were you any better? Weren't you going to hand me over to Sackett? Wasn't that the same thing?"

"Yes."

"Then we're even. Even again. Right back where we started."

"Not quite."

"Oh yes we are." I cracked up a little, then, myself, and put my head on her shoulder. "That's just where we are. We can kid ourself all we want to, and laugh about the money, and whoop about what a swell guy the devil is to be in bed with, but that's just where we are. I was going off with that woman, Cora. We were going to Nicaragua to catch cats. And why I didn't go away, I knew I had to come back. We're chained to each other, Cora. We thought we were on top of a mountain. That wasn't it. It's on top of us, and that's where it's been ever since that night."

"Is that the only reason you came back?"

"No. It's you and me. There's nobody else. I love you, Cora. But love, when you get fear in it, it's not love any more. It's hate."

"So you hate me?"

"I don't know. But we're telling the truth, for once in our life. That's part of it. You got to know it. And what I was lying here thinking, that's the reason. Now you know it."

"I told you I had something to tell you, Frank."

"Oh."

"I'm going to have a baby."

"What?"

"I suspicioned it before I went away, and right after my mother died I was sure."

"The hell you say. The hell you say. Come here. Give me a kiss."

"No. Please. I've got to tell you about it."

"Haven't you told it?"

"Not what I mean. Now listen to me, Frank. All that time I was out there, waiting for the funeral to be over, I thought about it. What it would mean to us. Because we took a life, didn't we? And now we're going to give one back."

"That's right."

"It was all mixed up, what I thought. But now, after what happened with that woman, it's not mixed up any more. I couldn't call up Sackett, Frank. I couldn't call him up, because I couldn't have this baby, and then have it find out I let its father hang for murder."

"You were going to see Sackett."

"No I wasn't. I was going away."

"Was that the only reason you weren't going to see Sackett?"

She took a long time before she answered that. "No. I love you, Frank. I think you know that. But maybe, if it hadn't been for this, I would have gone to see him. Just *because* I love you."

"She didn't mean anything to me, Cora. I told you why I did it. I was running away."

"I know that. I knew it all along. I knew why you wanted to take me away, and what I said about you being a bum, I didn't believe that. I believed it, but it wasn't why you wanted to go. You being a bum, I love you for it. And I hated her for the way she turned on you just for not telling her about something that wasn't any of her business. And yet, I wanted to ruin you for it."

"Well?"

"I'm trying to say it, Frank. This is what I'm trying to say. I wanted to ruin you, and yet I couldn't go to see Sackett. It wasn't because you kept watching me. I could have run out of the house and got to him. It was because, like I told you. Well then, I'm rid of the devil, Frank. I know I'll never call up Sackett, because I had my chance, and I had my reason, and I didn't do it. So the devil has left me. But has he left you?"

"If he's left you, then what more have I got to do with him?"

"We wouldn't be sure. We couldn't ever be sure unless you had your chance. The same chance I had."

"I tell you, he's gone."

"While you were thinking about a way to kill me, Frank, I was thinking the same thing. Of a way you could kill me. You can kill me swimming. We'll go way out, the way we did last time, and if you don't want me to come back, you don't have to let me. Nobody'll ever know. It'll be just one of those things that happen at the beach. Tomorrow morning we'll go."

"Tomorrow morning, what we do is get married."

"We can get married if you want, but before we come back we go swimming."

"To hell with swimming. Come on with that kiss."

"Tomorrow night, if I come back, there'll be kisses. Lovely ones, Frank. Not drunken kisses. Kisses with dreams in them. Kisses that come from life, not death."

"It's a date."

We got married at the City Hall, and then we went to the beach. She looked so pretty I just wanted to play in the sand with her, but she had this little smile on her face, and after a while she got up and went down to the surf.

"I'm going out."

She went ahead, and I swam after her. She kept on going, and went a lot further out than she had before. Then she stopped, and I caught up with her. She swung up beside me, and took hold of my hand, and we looked at each other. She knew, then, that the devil was gone, that I loved her.

"Did I ever tell you why I like my feet to the swells?"

"No."

"It's so they'll lift them."

A big one raised us up, and she put her hand to her breasts, to show how it lifted them. "I love it. Are they big, Frank?"

"I'll tell you tonight."

"They feel big. I didn't tell you about that. It's not only knowing you're going to make another life. It's what it does to you. My breasts feel so big, and I want you to kiss them. Pretty soon my belly is going to get big, and I'll love that, and want everybody to see it. It's life. I can feel it in me. It's a new life for us both, Frank."

We started back, and on the way in I swam down. I went down nine feet. I could tell it was nine feet, by the pressure. Most of these pools are nine feet, and it was that deep. I whipped my legs together and shot down further. It drove in on my ears so I thought they would pop. But I didn't have to come up. The pressure on your lungs drives the oxygen in your blood, so for a few seconds you don't think about breath. I looked at the green water. And with my ears ringing and that weight on my back and chest, it seemed to me that all the devilment, and meanness, and shiftlessness, and no-account stuff in my life had been pressed out and washed off, and I was all ready to start out with her again clean, and do like she said, have a new life.

When I came up she was coughing. "Just one of those sick spells, like you have."

"Are you all right?"

"I think so. It comes over you, and then it goes."

"Did you swallow any water?"

"No."

We went a little way, and then she stopped. "Frank, I feel funny inside."

"Here, hold on to me."

"Oh, Frank. Maybe I strained myself, just then. Trying to keep my head up. So I wouldn't gulp down the salt water."

"Take it easy."

"Wouldn't that be awful? I've heard of women that had a miscarriage. From straining theirself."

"Take it easy. Lie right out in the water. Don't try to swim. I'll tow you in."

"Hadn't you better call a guard?"

"Christ no. That egg will want to pump your legs up and down. Just lay there now. I'll get you in quicker than he can."

She lay there, and I towed her by the shoulder strap of her bathing suit. I began to give out. I could have towed her a mile, but I kept thinking I had to get her to a hospital, and I hurried. When you hurry in the water you're sunk. I got bottom, though, after a while, and then I took her in my arms and rushed her through the surf. "Don't move. Let me do it."

"I won't."

I ran with her up to the place where our sweaters were, and set her down. I got the car key out of mine, then wrapped both of them around her and carried her up to the car. It was up beside the road, and I had to climb the high bank the road was on, above the beach. My legs were so tired I could hardly lift one after the other, but I didn't drop her. I put her in the car, started up, and began burning the road.

We had gone in swimming a couple of miles above Santa Monica, and there was a hospital down there. I overtook a big truck. It had a sign on the back, Sound Your Horn, the Road Is Yours. I banged on the horn, and it kept right down the middle. I couldn't pass on the left, because a whole line of cars was coming toward me. I pulled out to the right and stepped on it. She screamed. I never saw the culvert wall. There was a crash, and everything went black.

When I came out of it I was wedged down beside the wheel, with my back to the front of the car, but I began to moan from the awfulness of what I heard. It was like rain on a tin roof, but that wasn't it. It was her blood, pouring down on the hood, where she went through the windshield. Horns were blowing, and people were jumping out of cars and running to her. I got her up, and tried to stop the blood, and in between I was talking to her, and crying, and kissing her. Those kisses never reached her. She was dead.

16

They got me for it. Katz took it all this time, the $10,000 he had got for us, and the money we had made, and a deed for the place. He did his best for me, but he was licked from the start. Sackett said I was a mad dog, that had to be put out of the way before life would be safe. He had it all figured out. We murdered the Greek to get the money, and then I married her, and murdered her so I could have it all myself. When she found out about the Mexican trip, that hurried it up a little, that was all. He had the autopsy report, that showed she was going to have a baby, and he said that was part of it. He put Madge on the stand, and she told about the Mexican trip. She didn't want to, but she had to. He even had the puma in court. It had grown, but it hadn't been taken care of right, so it was mangy and sick looking, and yowled, and tried to bite him. It was an awful looking thing, and it didn't do me any good, believe me. But what really sunk me was the note she wrote before she called up the cab, and put in the cash register so I would get it in the morning, and then forgot about. I never saw it, because we didn't open the place before we went swimming, and I never even looked in the cash register. It was the sweetest note in the world, but it had in it about us killing the Greek, and that did the work. They argued about it three days, and Katz fought them with every law book in Los Angeles County, but the judge let it in, and that let in all about us murdering the Greek. Sackett said that fixed me up with a motive. That and just being a mad dog. Katz never even let me take the stand. What could I say? That I didn't do it, because we had just fixed it up, all the trouble we had had over killing the Greek? That would have been swell. The jury was out five minutes. The judge said he would give me exactly the same consideration he would show any other mad dog.

So I'm in the death house, now, writing the last of this, so Father McConnell can look it over and show me the places where maybe it ought to be fixed up a little, for punctuation and all that. If I get a stay, he's to hold on to it and wait for what happens. If I get a commutation, then, he's to burn it, and they'll never know whether there really was any murder or not, from anything I tell them. But if they get me, he's to take it and see if he can find somebody to print it. There won't be any stay, and there won't be any commutation, I know that. I never kidded myself. But in this place, you hope anyhow, just because you can't help it. I never confessed anything, that's one thing. I heard a guy say they never hang you without you confess. I don't know. Unless Father McConnell crosses me, they'll never know anything from me. Maybe I'll get a stay.

I'm getting up tight now, and I've been thinking about Cora. Do you think she knows I didn't do it? After what we said in the water, you would think she would know it. But that's the awful part, when you monkey with murder. Maybe it went through her head, when the car hit, that I did it anyhow. That's why I hope I've got another life after this one. Father McConnell says I have, and I want to see her. I want her to know that it was all so, what we said to each other, and that I didn't do it. What did she have that makes me feel that way about her? I don't know. She wanted something, and she tried to get it. She tried all the wrong ways, but she tried. I don't know what made her feel that way about me, because she knew me. She called it on me plenty of times, that I wasn't any good. I never really wanted anything, but her. But that's a lot. I guess it's not often that a woman even has that.

There's a guy in No. 7 that murdered his brother, and says he didn't really do it, his subconscious did it. I asked him what that meant, and he says you got two selves, one that you know about and the other that you don't know about, because it's subconscious. It shook me up. Did I really do it, and not know it? God Almighty, I can't believe that! I didn't do it! I loved her so, then, I tell you, that I would have died for her! To hell with the sub-conscious. I don't believe it. It's just a lot of hooey, that this guy thought up so he could fool the judge. You know what you're doing, and you do it. I didn't do it, I know that. That's what I'm going to tell her, if I ever see her again.

*

I'm up awful tight, now. I think they give you dope in the grub, so you don't think about it. I try not to think. Whenever I can make it, I'm out there with Cora, with the sky above us, and the water around us, talking about how happy we're going to be, and how it's going to last forever. I guess I'm over the big river, when I'm there with her. That's when it seems real, about another life, not with all this stuff how Father McConnell has got it figured out. When I'm with her I believe it. When I start to figure, it all goes blooey.

No stay.

Here they come. Father McConnell says prayers help. If you've got this far, send up one for me, and Cora, and make it that we're together, wherever it is.

THEY SHOOT HORSES, DON'T THEY?

by Horace McCoy

To
Michael Fessier
and
Harry Clay Withers

THE
PRISONER
WILL
STAND.

I

I STOOD UP. *For a moment I saw Gloria again, sitting on that bench on the pier. The bullet had just struck her in the side of the head; the blood had not even started to flow. The flash from the pistol still lighted her face. Everything was plain as day. She was completely relaxed, was completely comfortable. The impact of the bullet had turned her head a little away from me; I did not have a perfect profile view but I could see enough of her face and her lips to know she was smiling. The Prosecuting Attorney was wrong when he told the jury she died in agony, friendless, alone except for her brutal murderer, out there in that black night on the edge of the Pacific. He was as wrong as a man can be. She did not die in agony. She was relaxed and comfortable and she was smiling. It was the first time I had ever seen her smile. How could she have been in agony then? And she wasn't friendless.*

I was her very best friend. I was her only friend. So how could she have been friendless?

IS THERE

ANY LEGAL CAUSE

WHY

SENTENCE

SHOULD NOT NOW

BE PRONOUNCED?

2

WHAT could I say? . . . All those people knew I had killed her; the only other person who could have helped me at all was dead too. So I just stood there, looking at the judge and shaking my head. I didn't have a leg to stand on.

"Ask the mercy of the court," said Epstein, the lawyer they had assigned to defend me.

"What was that?" the judge said.

"Your Honor," Epstein said, "—we throw ourselves on the mercy of the court. This boy admits killing the girl, but he was only doing her a personal favor——"

The judge banged on the desk, looking at me.

THERE BEING

NO LEGAL CAUSE

WHY SENTENCE

SHOULD NOT NOW

BE PRONOUNCED . . .

3

I<small>T WAS</small> funny the way I met Gloria. She was trying to get into pictures too, but I didn't know that until later. I was walking down Melrose one day from the Paramount studios when I heard somebody hollering, "Hey! Hey!" and I turned around and there she was running towards me and waving. I stopped, waving back. When she got up to me she was all out of breath and excited and I saw I didn't know her.

"Damn that bus," she said.

I looked around and there was the bus half a block down the street going towards Western.

"Oh," I said, "I thought you were waving at me. . . ."

"What would I be waving at you for?" she asked.

I laughed. "I don't know," I said. "You going my way?"

"I may as well walk on down to Western," she said; and we began to walk on down towards Western.

That was how it all started and it seems very strange to me now. I don't understand it at all. I've thought and thought and still I don't understand it. This wasn't murder. I try to do somebody a favor and I wind up getting killed myself. *They are going to kill me. I know exactly what the judge is going to say. I can tell by the look of him that he is going to be glad to say it and I can tell by the feel of the people behind me that they are going to be glad to hear him say it.*

Take that morning I met Gloria. I wasn't feeling very good; I was still a little sick, but I went over to Paramount because von Sternberg was making a Russian picture and I thought maybe I could get a job. I used to ask myself what could be nicer than working for von Sternberg, or Mamoulian or Boleslawsky either, getting paid to watch him direct, learning about composition and tempo and angles . . . so I went over to Paramount.

I couldn't get inside, so I hung around the front until noon when one of his assistants came out for lunch. I caught up with him and asked what was the chance to get some atmosphere.

"None," he said, telling me that von Sternberg was very careful about his atmospheric people.

I thought that was a lousy thing to say but I knew what he was thinking, that my clothes didn't look any too good. "Isn't this a costume picture?" I asked.

"All our extras come through Central," he said, leaving me. . . .

I wasn't going anywhere in particular; I was just riding along in my Rolls-Royce, having people point me out as the greatest director in the world, when I heard Gloria hollering. You see how those things happen? . . .

So we walked on down Melrose to Western, getting acquainted all the time; and when we got to Western I knew she was Gloria Beatty, an extra who wasn't doing well either, and she knew a little about me. I liked her very much.

She had a small room with some people over near Beverly and I lived only a few blocks from there, so I saw her again that night. That first night was really what did it but even now I can't honestly say I regret going to see her. I had about seven dollars I had made squirting soda in a drug store (subbing for a friend of mine. He had got a girl in a jam and had to take her to Santa Barbara for the operation.) and I asked her if she'd rather go to a movie or sit in the park.

"What park?" she asked.

"It's right over here a little way," I said.

"All right," she said. "I got a bellyful of moving pictures anyway. If I'm not a better actress than most of those dames I'll eat your hat— Let's go sit and hate a bunch of people. . . ."

I was glad she wanted to go to the park. It was always nice there. It was a fine place to sit. It was very small, only one block square, but it was very dark and very quiet and filled with dense shrubbery. All around it palm trees grew up, fifty, sixty feet tall, suddenly tufted at the top. Once you entered the park you had the illusion of security. I often imagined they were sentries wearing grotesque helmets: my own private sentries, standing guard over my own private island. . . .

The park was a fine place to sit. Through the palms you could see many buildings, the thick, square silhouettes of apartment houses, with their red signs on the roofs, reddening the sky above and everything and everybody below. But if you wanted to get rid of these things you had only to sit and stare at them with a fixed gaze . . . and they would begin receding. That way you could drive them as far into the distance as you wanted to. . . .

"I never paid much attention to this place before," Gloria said.

. . . "I like it," I said, taking off my coat and spreading it on the grass for her. "I come here three or four times a week."

"You do like it," she said, sitting down.

"How long you been in Hollywood?" I asked.

"About a year. I been in four pictures already. I'd have been in more," she said, "but I can't get registered by Central."

"Neither can I," I said.

Unless you were registered by Central Casting Bureau you didn't have much chance. The big studios call up Central and say they want four Swedes or six Greeks or two Bohemian peasant types or six Grand Duchesses and Central takes care of it. I could see why Gloria didn't get registered by Central. She was too blonde and too small and looked too old. With a nice wardrobe she might have looked attractive, but even then I wouldn't have called her pretty.

"Have you met anybody who can help you?" I asked.

"In this business how can you tell who'll help you?" she said. "One day you're an electrician and the next day you're a producer. The only way I could ever get to a big shot would be to jump on the running board of his car as it passed by. Anyway, I don't know whether the men stars can help me as much as the women stars. From what I've seen lately I've about made up my mind that I've been letting the wrong sex try to make me. . . ."

"How'd you happen to come to Hollywood?" I asked.

"Oh, I don't know," she said in a moment—"but anything is an improvement over the life I led back home." I asked her where that was. "Texas," she said. "West Texas. Ever been there?"

"No," I said, "I come from Arkansas."

"Well, West Texas is a hell of a place," she said. "I lived with my aunt and uncle. He was a brakeman on a railroad. I only saw him once or twice a week, thank God. . . ."

She stopped, not saying anything, looking at the red, va-porish glow above the apartment buildings.

"At least," I said, "you had a home——"

"That's what you call it," she said. "Me, I got another name for it. When my uncle was home he was always making passes at me and when he was on the road my aunt and I were always fighting. She was afraid I'd tattle on her——"

"Nice people," I said to myself.

"So I finally ran away," she said, "to Dallas. Ever been there?"

"I've never been in Texas at all," I said.

"You haven't missed anything," she said. "I couldn't get a job, so I decided to steal something in a store and make the cops take care of me."

"That was a good idea," I said.

"It was a swell idea," she said, "only it didn't work. I got arrested all right but the detectives felt sorry for me and turned me loose. To keep from starving to death I moved in with a Syrian who had a hot-dog place around the corner from the City Hall. He chewed tobacco. He chewed tobacco all the time . . . Have you ever been in bed with a man who chewed tobacco?"

"I don't believe I have," I said.

"I guess I might even have stood that," she said, "but when he wanted to make me between customers, on the kitchen table, I gave up. A couple of nights later I took poison."

"Jesus," I said to myself.

"I didn't take enough," she said. "I only got sick. Ugh, I can still taste the stuff. I stayed in the hospital a week. That was where I got the idea of coming to Hollywood."

"It was?" I said.

"From the movie magazines," she said. "After I got dis-charged I started hitch-hiking. Is that a laugh or not? . . ."

"That's a good laugh," I said, trying to laugh. . . . "Haven't you got any parents?"

"Not any more," she said. "My old man got killed in the war in France. I wish I could get killed in a war."

"Why don't you quit the movies?" I asked.

"Why should I?" she said. "I may get to be a star overnight. Look at Hepburn and Margaret Sullavan and Josephine

Hutchinson . . . but I'll tell you what I would do if I had the guts: I'd walk out of a window or throw myself in front of a street car or something."

"I know how you feel," I said; "I know exactly how you feel."

"It's peculiar to me," she said, "that everybody pays so much attention to living and so little to dying. Why are these high-powered scientists always screwing around trying to prolong life instead of finding pleasant ways to end it? There must be a hell of a lot of people in the world like me—who want to die but haven't got the guts——"

"I know what you mean," I said; "I know exactly what you mean."

Neither of us said anything for a couple of seconds.

"A girl friend of mine has been trying to get me to enter a marathon dance down at the beach," she said. "Free food and free bed as long as you last and a thousand dollars if you win."

"The free food part of it sounds good," I said.

"That's not the big thing," she said. "A lot of producers and directors go to those marathon dances. There's always the chance they might pick you out and give you a part in a picture. . . . What do you say?"

"Me?" I said . . . "Oh, I don't dance very well. . . ."

"You don't have to. All you have to do is keep moving."

"I don't think I better try it," I said. "I been pretty sick. I just got over the intestinal flu. I almost died. I was so weak I used to have to crawl to the john on my hands and knees. I don't think I better try it," I said, shaking my head.

"When was all this?"

"A week ago," I said.

"You're all right now," she said.

"I don't think so—I better not try it. I'm liable to have a relapse."

"I'll take care of that," she said.

". . . Maybe in a week—" I said.

"It'll be too late then. You're strong enough now," she said. . . .

. . . IT IS

THE JUDGMENT

AND SENTENCE

OF THIS COURT . . .

4

The marathon dance was held on the amusement pier at the beach in an enormous old building that once had been a public dance hall. It was built out over the ocean on pilings, and beneath our feet, beneath the floor, the ocean pounded night and day. I could feel it surging through the balls of my feet, as if they had been stethoscopes.

Inside there was a dance space for the contestants, thirty feet wide and two hundred feet long, and around this on three sides were loge seats, behind these were the circus seats, the general admission. At the end of the dance space was a raised platform for the orchestra. It played only at night and was not a very good orchestra. During the day we had what music we could pick up with the radio, made loud by the amplifiers. Most of the time it was too loud, filling the hall with noise. We had a master of ceremonies, whose duty it was to make the customers feel at home; two floor judges who moved around on the floor all the time with the contestants to see that everything went all right, two male and female nurses, and a house doctor for emergencies. The doctor didn't look like a doctor at all. He was much too young.

One hundred and forty-four couples entered the marathon dance but sixty-one dropped out the first week. The rules were you danced for an hour and fifty minutes, then you had a ten-minute rest period in which you could sleep if you wanted to. But in those ten minutes you also had to shave or bathe or get your feet fixed or whatever was necessary.

The first week was the hardest. Everybody's feet and legs swelled—and down beneath the ocean kept pounding, pounding against the pilings all the time. Before I went into this marathon dance I used to love the Pacific Ocean: its name, its size, its color, its smell—I used to sit for hours look- ing at it, wondering about the ships that had sailed it and never returned, about China and the South Seas, wondering all sorts of things . . . But not any more. I've had enough of the Pacific. I don't care whether I ever see it again or not. *I probably won't. The judge is going to take care of that.*

Gloria and I had been tipped off by some old-timers that
the way to beat a marathon dance was to perfect a system for
those ten-minute rest periods: learning to eat your sandwich
while you shaved, learning to eat when you went to the john,
when you had your feet fixed, learning to read newspapers
while you danced, learning to sleep on your partner's shoulder
while you were dancing; but these were all tricks of the trade
you had to practice. They were very difficult for Gloria and
me at first.

I found out that about half of the people in this contest
were professionals. They made a business of going in marathon dances all over the country, some of them even hitch-
hiking from town to town. The others were just girls and boys
who came in like Gloria and me.

Couple No. 13 were our best friends in the dance. This was
James and Ruby Bates, from some little town in northern
Pennsylvania. It was their eighth marathon dance; they had
won a $1500 prize in Oklahoma, going 1253 hours in contin-
uous motion. There were several other teams in this dance
who claimed championships of some kind, but I knew James
and Ruby would be right in there for the finish. That is, if
Ruby's baby didn't come first. She expected a baby in four
months.

"What's the matter with Gloria?" James asked me one day
as we came back to the floor from the sleeping quarters.

"Nothing. What do you mean?" I asked. But I knew what
he meant. Gloria had been singing the blues again.

"She keeps telling Ruby what a chump she would be to
have the baby," he said. "Gloria wants her to have an abortion."

"I can't understand Gloria talking like that," I said, trying
to smooth things over.

"You tell her to lay off Ruby," he said.

When the whistle started us off on the 216th hour I told
Gloria what James had said.

"Nuts to him," she said. "What does he know about it?"

"I don't see why they can't have a baby if they want
to. It's their business," I said. "I don't want to make James
sore. He's been through a lot of these dances and he's al-

ready given us some good tips. Where would we be if he got sore?"

"It's a shame for that girl to have a baby," Gloria said. "What's the sense of having a baby unless you got dough enough to take care of it?"

"How do you know they haven't?" I asked.

"If they have what're they doing here? . . . That's the trouble now," she said. "Everybody is having babies——"

"Oh, not everybody," I said.

"A hell of a lot you know about it. You'd been better off if you'd never been born——"

"Maybe not," I said. "How do you feel?" I asked, trying to get her mind off her troubles.

"I always feel lousy," she said. "God, the hand on that clock moves slow." There was a big strip of canvas on the master of ceremonies' platform, painted in the shape of a clock, up to 2500 hours. The hand now pointed to 216. Above it was a sign: ELAPSED HOURS—216. COUPLES REMAINING —83.

"How are your legs?"

"Still pretty weak," I said. "That flu is awful stuff. . . ."

"Some of the girls think it'll take 2000 hours to win," Gloria said.

"I hope not," I said. "I don't believe I can hold out that long."

"My shoes are wearing out," Gloria said. "If we don't hurry up and get a sponsor I'll be bare-footed." A sponsor was a company or a firm that gave you sweaters and advertised their names or products on the backs. Then they took care of your necessities.

James and Ruby danced over beside us. "Did you tell her?" he asked, looking at me. I nodded.

"Wait a minute," Gloria said, as they started to dance away. "What's the big idea of talking behind my back?"

"Tell that twist to lay off me," James said, still speaking directly to me.

Gloria started to say something else but before she could get it out I danced her away from there. I didn't want any scenes.

"The son of a bitch," she said.

"He's sore," I said. "Now where are we?"

"Come on," she said, "I'll tell him where he gets off——"

"Gloria," I said, "will you please mind your own business?"

"Soft pedal that loud cussing," a voice said. I looked around. It was Rollo Peters, the floor judge.

"Nuts to you," Gloria said. Through my fingers I could feel the muscles twitching in her back, just like I could feel the ocean surging through the balls of my feet.

"Pipe down," Rollo said. "The people in the box can hear you. What do you think this is—a joint?"

"Joint is right," Gloria said.

"All right, all right," I said.

"I told you once already about that cussing," Rollo said. "I better not have to tell you again. It sounds bad to the customers."

"Customers? Where are they?" Gloria said.

"You let us worry about that," Rollo said, glaring at me.

"All right, all right," I said.

He blew his whistle, stopping everybody from moving. Some of them were barely moving, just enough to keep from being disqualified. "All right, kids," he said, "a little sprint."

"A little sprint, kids," the master of ceremonies, Rocky Gravo, said into the microphone. The noise of his voice in the amplifiers filled the hall, shutting out the pounding of the ocean. "A little sprint—around the track you go— Give," he said to the orchestra, and the orchestra began playing. The contestants started dancing with a little more animation.

The sprint lasted about two minutes and when it was finished Rocky led the applause, and then said into the microphone:

"Look at these kids, ladies and gentlemen—after 216 hours they are as fresh as a daisy in the world's championship marathon dance—a contest of endurance and skill. These kids are fed seven times a day—three big meals and four light lunches. Some of them have even gained weight while in the contest— and we have doctors and nurses constantly in attendance to see that they are in the best of physical condition. Now I'm going to call on Couple No. 4, Mario Petrone and Jackie Miller, for a specialty. Come on, Couple No. 4—there they are, ladies and gentlemen. Isn't that a cute pair? . . ."

Mario Petrone, a husky Italian, and Jackie Miller, a little blonde, went up to the platform to some applause. They spoke to Rocky and then began a tap dance that was very bad. Neither Mario nor Jackie seemed conscious that it was bad. When it was over a few people pitched money onto the floor.

"Give, people," Rocky said. "A silver shower. Give."

A few more coins hit the floor. Mario and Jackie picked them up, moving over near us.

"How much?" Gloria asked them.

"Feels like about six-bits," Jackie said.

"Where you from, kid?" Gloria asked.

"Alabama."

"I thought so," Gloria said.

"You and I ought to learn a specialty," I said to Gloria. "We could make some extra money."

"You're better off without knowing any," Mario said. "It only means extra work and it don't do your legs any good."

"Did you all hear about the derbies?" Jackie asked.

"What are they?" I asked.

"Some kind of a race," she said. "I think they're going to explain them at the next rest period."

"The cheese is beginning to bind," Gloria said.

. . . THAT

FOR THE CRIME

OF MURDER

IN

THE FIRST DEGREE . . .

5

I

N THE dressing room Rocky Gravo introduced Vincent (Socks) Donald, one of the promoters.

"Lissen, kids," Socks said, "don't none of you be discouraged because people ain't coming to the marathon dance. It takes time to get these things going, so we have decided to start a little novelty guaranteed to pack 'em in. Now here's what we're gonna do. We're gonna have a derby race every night. We're going to paint an oval on the floor and every night everybody will race around the track for fifteen minutes and the last couple every night is disqualified. I guarantee that'll bring in the crowds."

"It'll bring in the undertaker too," somebody said.

"We'll move some cots out in the middle of the track," the promoter said, "and have the doctor and nurses on hand during the derby. When a contestant falls out and has to go to the pit, the partner will have to make two laps to make up for it. You kids will get more kick out of it because the crowds will be bigger. Say, when that Hollywood bunch starts coming here, we'll be standing 'em up. . . . Now, how's the food? Anybody got any kicks about anything? All right, kids, that's fine. You play ball with us and we'll play ball with you."

We went out to the floor. None of the contestants had anything to say about the derbies. They seemed to think that anything was a good idea if it would only start the crowds to coming. Rollo came up to me as I sat down on the railing. I had about two minutes more of rest before the next two-hour grind.

"Don't get me wrong about what I said a few minutes ago," he said. "It's not you, it's Gloria."

"I know," I said. "She's all right. She's just sore on the world, that's all."

"Try to keep her piped down," he said.

"That's a hard job, but I'll do the best I can," I said.

In a moment I looked up to the runway from the girls' dressing room and I was surprised to see Gloria and Ruby coming to the floor together. I went over to meet her.

"What do you think about the derbies?" I asked her.

"It's one good way to kill us off," she said.

The whistle started us away again.

"There's not more than a hundred people here tonight," I said. Gloria and I weren't dancing. I had my arm around her shoulder and she had hers around my waist, walking. That was all right. For the first week we had to dance, but after that you didn't. All you had to do was keep moving. I saw James and Ruby coming over to us and I could tell by the expression on his face that something was wrong. I wanted to get away, but there was no place to go.

"I told you to lay off my wife, didn't I?" he said to Gloria.

"You go to hell, you big ape," Gloria said.

"Wait a minute," I said. "What's the matter?"

"She's been after Ruby again," James said. "Every time I turn my back she's after her again."

"Forget it, Jim," Ruby said, trying to steer him away.

"Naw, I won't forget it. I told you to keep your mouth shut, didn't I?" he said to Gloria.

"You take a flying——"

Before Gloria could get the words finished he slapped her hard on the side of the face, knocking her head against my shoulder. It was a hard wallop. I couldn't stand for that. I reached up and hit him in the mouth. He hit me in the jaw with his left hand, knocking me back against some of the dancers. That kept me from falling to the floor. He rushed at me and I grabbed him, wrestling with him, trying to jerk my knee up between his legs to foul him. It was the only chance I had.

A whistle blew in my ear and somebody grabbed us. It was Rollo Peters. He shoved us apart.

"Cut it out," he said. "What's coming off here?"

"Nothing," I said.

"Nothing," Ruby said.

Rollo raised his hand, waving to Rocky on the platform.

"Give," said Rocky, and the orchestra started to play.

"Scatter out," Rollo said to the contestants, who started to move away. "Come on," he said, leading them around the floor.

"Next time I'm going to cut your throat," James said to Gloria.

"F— you," Gloria said.

"Shut up," I said.

I walked away with her, down into a corner, where we slowed up, barely moving along.

"Are you crazy?" I said. "Why don't you let Ruby alone?"

"Don't worry, I'm through wasting my breath on her. If she wants to have a deformed baby, that's okay by me."

"Hello, Gloria," a voice said.

We looked around. It was an old woman in a front row box seat by the railing. I didn't know her name but she was quite a character. She had been there every night, bringing her blanket and her lunch. One night she wrapped up in her blanket and stayed all night. She was about sixty-five years old.

"Hello," Gloria said.

"What was the matter down there?" the old woman asked.

"Nothing," Gloria said. "Just a little argument."

"How do you feel?" the old woman asked.

"All right, I guess," Gloria replied.

"I'm Mrs. Layden," the old woman said. "You're my favorite couple."

"Well, thanks," I said.

"I tried to enter this," Mrs. Layden said, "but they wouldn't let me. They said I was too old. But I'm only sixty."

"Well, that's fine," I said.

Gloria and I had stopped, our arms around each other, swaying our bodies. You had to keep moving all the time. A couple of men moved into the loge behind the old woman. Both of them were chewing unlighted cigars.

"They're dicks," Gloria said under her breath.

". . . How do you like the contest?" I asked Mrs. Layden.

"I enjoy it very much," she said. "Very much. Such nice boys and girls . . ."

"Move along, kids," Rollo said, walking by.

I nodded to Mrs. Layden, moving along. "Can you feature that?" Gloria asked. "She ought to be home putting a diaper on the baby. Christ, I hope I never live to be that old."

"How do you know those fellows are detectives?" I asked.

"I'm psychic," Gloria replied. "My God, can you feature that old lady? She's a nut about these things. They ought to charge her room rent." She shook her head. "I hope I never live to be that old," she said again.

The meeting with the old lady depressed Gloria very much. She said it reminded her of the women in the little town in West Texas where she had lived.

"Alice Faye's just come in," one of the girls said. "See her? Sitting right over there."

It was Alice Faye all right, with a couple of men I didn't recognize.

"See her?" I asked Gloria.

"I don't want to see her," Gloria said.

"Ladies and gentlemen," Rocky said into the microphone, "we are honored tonight to have with us that beautiful moving picture star, Miss Alice Faye. Give Miss Faye a big hand, ladies and gentlemen."

Everybody applauded and Miss Faye nodded her head, smiling. Socks Donald, sitting in a box seat by the orchestra platform, was smiling too. The Hollywood crowd had started coming.

"Come on," I said to Gloria, "clap your hands."

"Why should I applaud for her?" Gloria said. "What's she got I haven't? . . ."

"You're jealous," I said.

"You're goddam right I'm jealous. As long as I am a failure I'm jealous of anybody who's a success. Aren't you?"

"Certainly not," I said.

"You're a fool," she said.

"Hey, look," I said.

The two detectives had left the box with Mrs. Layden and were sitting with Socks Donald. They had their heads together, looking at a sheet of paper one of them was holding.

"All right, kids," Rocky said into the microphone. "A little sprint before the rest period. . . . Give," he said to the orchestra, clapping his hands together and stamping on the platform, keeping time to the music. In a moment the customers were clapping their hands together and stamping too.

We were all milling around in the middle of the floor, all of us watching the minute hand of the clock, when suddenly

Kid Kamm of couple No. 18 began slapping his partner on the cheek. He was holding her up with his left hand, slapping her backwards and forwards with his right hand. But she did not respond. She was dead to the world. She gurgled a couple of times and then slid to the floor, unconscious.

The floor judge blew his whistle and all the customers jumped to their feet, excited. Customers at a marathon dance do not have to be prepared for their excitement. When anything happens they get excited all at once. In that respect a marathon dance is like a bull fight.

The floor judge and a couple of nurses picked up the girl and carried her off, her toes dragging, to the dressing room.

"Mattie Barnes, of Couple No. 18, has fainted," Rocky announced to the crowd. "She has been taken to the dressing room, ladies and gentlemen, where she will have the best of medical attention. Nothing serious, ladies and gentlemen—nothing serious. It just proves that there's always something happening at the world's championship marathon dance."

"She was complaining last rest period," Gloria said.

"What's the matter with her?" I asked.

"It's that time of the month," Gloria said. "And she'll never be able to come back either. She's the type that has to go to bed for three or four days when she gets it."

"Can I pick 'em?" said Kid Kamm. He shook his head, disgusted. "Boy, am I hoodooed! I been in nine of these things and I ain't finished one yet. My partner always caves in on me."

"She'll probably be all right," I said, trying to cheer him up.

"Nope," he said, "she's finished. She can go back to the farm now."

The siren blew, meaning it was the end of another grind. Everybody ran for the dressing rooms. I kicked off my shoes, piling on my cot. I felt the ocean surge once—just once. Then I was asleep.

I woke up, my nose full of ammonia. One of the trainers was moving a bottle across my chin letting me inhale it. (This was the best way to arouse one of us from a deep sleep, the doctor said. If they had tried to wake you up by shaking you, they never would have done it.)

"All right," I said to the trainer. "I'm all right."

I sat up, reaching for my shoes. Then I saw those two detectives and Socks Donald standing near me, by Mario's cot. They were waiting for the other trainer to wake him up. Finally Mario rolled over, looking up at them.

"Hello, buddy," said one of the detectives. "Know who this is?" He handed him a sheet of paper. Now I was close enough to see what it was. It was a page torn out of a detective magazine, containing several pictures.

Mario looked at it, then handed it back. "Yeah, I know who it is," he said, sitting up.

"You ain't changed much," said the other detective.

"You wop son of a bitch," Socks said, doubling his fist. "What're you trying to pull on me?"

"Nix, Socks," the first detective said. Then he spoke to Mario. "Well, Giuseppe, get your things together."

Mario started tying his shoes. "I ain't got nothing but a coat and a toothbrush," he said. "But I would like to say good-bye to my partner."

"You dirty wop son of a bitch," Socks said. "This'll look good in the newspapers, won't it?"

"Never mind your partner, Giuseppe," the second detective said. "Hey son," he said to me, "you tell Giuseppe's partner good-bye for him. Come on, Giuseppe," he said to Mario.

"Take that wop son of a bitch out the back way, boys," said Socks Donald.

"Everybody on the floor," yelled the floor judge. "Everybody on the floor."

"So long, Mario," I said.

Mario did not say anything. It had all been very quiet, very matter-of-fact. These detectives acted as if this kind of thing happened every day.

. . . OF WHICH
YOU HAVE BEEN
CONVICTED
BY VERDICT
OF THE JURY . . .

6

So Mario went to jail and Mattie went back to the farm. *I remember how surprised I was when they arrested Mario for murder. I couldn't believe it. He was one of the nicest boys I'd ever met. But that was then that I couldn't believe it. Now I know you can be nice and be a murderer too. Nobody was ever any nicer to a girl than I was to Gloria, but there came the time when I shot and killed her. So you see being nice doesn't mean a thing. . . .*

Mattie was automatically disqualified when the doctor refused to let her continue in the contest. He said if she did go on with the dance she would injure some of her organs and never be able to have a baby. She raised hell about it, Gloria said, calling the doctor a lot of names and absolutely refusing to quit. But she did quit. She had to. They had the axe over her.

That teamed her partner, Kid Kamm, with Jackie. Under the rules you could do that. You could solo for twenty-four hours but if you didn't get a partner by then you were disqualified. Both the Kid and Jackie seemed well satisfied with the new arrangement. Jackie had nothing to say about losing Mario. Her attitude was that a partner was a partner. But the Kid was all smiles. He seemed to think that at last he had broken his hoodoo.

"They're liable to win," Gloria said. "They're strong as mules. That Alabama is corn-fed. Look at that beam. I bet she can go six months."

"I'll string along with James and Ruby," I said.

"After the way they've treated us?"

"What's that got to do with it? Besides, what's the matter with us? We've got a chance to win, haven't we?"

"Have we?"

"Well, you don't seem to think so," I said.

She shook her head, not saying anything to that. "More and more and more I wish I was dead," she said.

There it was again. No matter what I talked about she al-

ways got back to that. "Isn't there something I can talk about
that won't remind you that you wish you were dead?" I asked.

"No," she said.

"I give up," I said.

Somebody on the platform turned the radio down. The
music sounded like music now. (We used the radio all the time
the orchestra wasn't there. This was in the afternoon. The
orchestra came only at night.) "Ladies and gentlemen,"
Rocky said into the microphone, "I have the honor to announce that two sponsors have come forward to sponsor two
couples. The Pompadour Beauty Shop, of 415 Avenue B, will
sponsor Couple No. 13—James and Ruby Bates. Let's give the
Pompadour Beauty Shop, of 415 Avenue B, a big hand for
this, ladies and gentlemen—you too, kids. . . ."

Everybody applauded.

"The second couple to be sponsored," Rocky said, "is No.
34, Pedro Ortega and Lillian Bacon. They are sponsored by
the Oceanic Garage. All right, now, a big hand for the Oceanic
Garage, located at 11,341 Ocean Walkway in Santa Monica."

Everybody applauded again.

"Ladies and gentlemen," Rocky said, "there ought to be
more sponsors for these marvelous kids. Tell your friends,
ladies and gentlemen, and let's get sponsors for all the kids.
Look at them, ladies and gentlemen, after 242 hours of continuous motion they are as fresh as daisies . . . a big hand for
these marvelous kids, ladies and gentlemen."

There was some more applause.

"And don't forget, ladies and gentlemen," Rocky said,
"there's the Palm Garden right down there at the end of the
hall where you can get delicious beverages—all kinds of beer
and sandwiches. Visit the Palm Garden, ladies and gentlemen. . . . Give," he said to the radio, turning the knob and
filling the hall with noise again.

Gloria and I walked over to Pedro and Lillian. Pedro limped
from a game leg. The story was that he had been gored in a
bull ring in Mexico City. Lillian was a brunette. She too had
been trying to get in the movies when she heard about the
marathon dance.

"Congratulations," I said.

"It proves somebody is for us," Pedro said.

"As long as it couldn't be Metro-Goldwyn-Mayer it might as well be a garage," Lillian said. "Only it seems a little queer for a garage to be buying me underclothes."

"Where do you get that underclothes stuff?" Gloria said. "You don't get underclothes. You get a sweatshirt with the garage's name across the back of it."

"I get underclothes, too," Lillian said.

"Hey, Lillian," said Rollo, the floor judge, "the woman from the Oceanic Garage wants to talk to you."

"The what? . . ." asked Lillian.

"Your sponsor, Mrs. Yeargan——"

"For crying out loud," said Lillian. "Pedro, it looks like you get the underclothes."

Gloria and I walked down by the master of ceremonies' platform. It was nice down there about this time of the afternoon. There was a big triangle of sunshine that came through the double window above the bar in the Palm Garden. It only lasted about ten minutes but during those ten minutes I moved slowly about in it (I had to move to keep from being disqualified) letting it cover me completely. It was the first time I had ever appreciated the sun. "When this marathon is over," I told myself, "I'm going to spend the rest of my life in the sun. I can't wait to go to the Sahara desert to make a picture." *Of course, that won't ever happen now.*

I watched the triangle on the floor get smaller and smaller. Finally it closed altogether and started up my legs. It crawled up my body like a living thing. When it got to my chin I stood on my toes, to keep my head in it as long as possible. I did not close my eyes. I kept them wide open, looking straight into the sun. It did not blind me at all. In a moment it was gone.

I looked around for Gloria. She was standing at the platform, swaying from side to side, talking to Rocky, who was sitting on his haunches. Rocky was swaying too. (All the employes—the doctor, the nurses, the floor judges, the master of ceremonies, even the boys who sold soda pop—had been given orders to keep moving when they talked to one of the contestants. The management was very strict about this.)

"You looked very funny standing out there on your toes," Gloria said. "You looked like a ballet dancer."

"You practice up on that and I'll let you do a solo," Rocky said, laughing.

"Yes," Gloria said. "How was the sun today?"

"Don't let 'em kid you," Mack Aston, of Couple No. 5, said as he passed by.

"Rocky!" a voice called. It was Socks Donald. Rocky got down from the platform and went to him.

"I don't think it's very nice of you to razz me," I said to Gloria. "I don't ever razz you."

"You don't have to," she said. "I get razzed by an expert. God razzes me. . . . You know what Socks Donald wants with Rocky? You want some inside information?"

"What?" I asked.

"You know No. 6—Freddy and that Manski girl. Her mother is going to prefer charges against him and Socks. She ran away from home."

"I don't see what that's got to do with it," I said.

"She's jail bait," Gloria said. "She's only about fifteen. God, with all of it running around loose it does look like a guy would have better sense."

"Why blame Freddy? It may not be his fault."

"According to the law it's his fault," Gloria said. "That's what counts."

I steered Gloria back to where Socks and Rocky were standing, trying to overhear what was being said; but they were talking too low. Rather, Socks was doing all the talking. Rocky was listening, nodding his head.

"Right now," I heard Socks say, and Rocky nodded that he understood and came back on the floor, winking wisely to Gloria as he passed. He went to Rollo Peters and called him aside, whispering earnestly for a few seconds. Then Rollo left, looking around as if he were trying to find somebody, and Rocky went back to the platform.

"The kids only have a few more minutes left before they retire for their well-earned rest period," Rocky announced into the microphone. "And while they are off the floor, ladies and gentlemen, the painters will paint the big oval on the floor for the derby tonight. The derby tonight, ladies and gentlemen: don't forget the derby. Positively the most thrilling thing you ever saw—all right, kids, two minutes to go before you retire—a little sprint, kids—show the ladies and gentlemen how fresh you are— You, too, ladies and gentlemen, show these marvelous kids you're behind them with a rally——"

He turned up the radio a little and began clapping his hands and stamping his foot. The audience joined in the rally. All of us stepped a little more lively, but it was not because of the rally. It was because within a minute or two we got a rest period and directly after that we were to be fed.

Gloria nudged me and I looked up to see Rollo Peters walking between Freddy and the Manski girl. I thought the Manski girl was crying, but before Gloria and I could catch up with them the siren blew and everybody made a dash for the dressing rooms.

Freddy was standing over his cot, stuffing an extra pair of shoes into a small zipper bag.

"I heard about it," I said. "I'm very sorry."

"It's all right," he said. "Only she's the one who did the raping. . . . I'll be all right if I can get out of town before the cops pick me up. It's a lucky thing for me that Socks was tipped off."

"Where are you going?" I asked.

"South, I guess. I've always had a yen to see Mexico. So long. . . ."

"So long," I said.

He was gone before anybody knew it. As he went through the back door I had a glimpse of the sun glinting on the ocean. For a moment I was so astounded I could not move. I do not know whether I was the more surprised at really seeing the sun for the first time in almost three weeks or discovering the door. I went over to it, hoping the sun would not be gone when I got there. *The only other time I ever was this eager was one Christmas when I was a kid, the first year I was big enough to really know what Christmas was, and I went into the front room and saw the tree all lighted up.*

I opened the door. At the end of the world the sun was sinking into the ocean. It was so red and bright and hot I wondered why there was no steam. *I once saw steam come out of the ocean. It was on the highway at the beach and some men were working with gunpowder. Suddenly, it exploded, setting*

them on fire. They ran and dived into the ocean. That was when
I saw the steam.

The color of the sun had shot up into some thin clouds,
reddening them. Out there where the sun was sinking the
ocean was very calm, not looking like an ocean at all. It was
lovely, lovely, lovely, lovely, lovely, lovely. Several people were
fishing off the pier, not paying any attention to the sunset.
They were fools. "You need that sunset worse than you do
fish," I told them in my mind.

The door flew out of my hands, slamming shut with a bang
like that of a cannon going off.

"Are you deaf?" a voice yelled in my ear. It was one of the
trainers. "Keep that door closed! You wanna be disqualified?"

"I was only watching the sun set," I said.

"Are you nuts? You ought to be asleep. You need your
sleep," he said.

"I don't need any sleep," I said. "I feel fine. I feel better
than I ever felt in my life."

"You need your rest anyway," he said. "You only got a few
minutes left. Get off your feet."

He followed me across the floor to my cot. Now I could
notice the dressing room didn't smell so good. I am very
susceptible to unpleasant odors and I wondered why I hadn't
noticed this smell before, the smell of too many men in a
room. I kicked off my shoes and stretched out on my back.

"You want your legs rubbed?" he asked.

"I'm all right," I said. "My legs feel fine."

He said something to himself and went away. I lay there,
thinking about the sunset, trying to remember what color it
was. I don't mean the red, I mean the other shades. Once or
twice I almost remembered; it was like a name you once had
known but now had forgotten, whose size and letters and
cadence you remembered but could not quite assemble.

Through the legs of my cot I could feel the ocean quivering
against the pilings below. It rose and fell, rose and fell, went
out and came back, went out and came back. . . .

I was glad when the siren blew, waking us up, calling us
back to the floor.

. . . CARRYING
WITH IT
THE EXTREME PENALTY
OF THE LAW . . .

7

THE PAINTERS had finished. They had painted a thick white line around the floor in the shape of an oval. This was the track for the derby.

"Freddy's gone," I said to Gloria, as we walked to the table where the sandwiches and coffee had been set up. (This was called a light lunch. We had our big meal at ten o'clock at night.)

"So is the Manski girl," Gloria said. "Two welfare workers came and got her. I bet her old lady burns her cute little bottom."

"I hate to say it," I said, "but Freddy's leaving was the brightest spot of my life."

"What had he ever done to you?" she asked.

"Oh, I don't mean that," I said. "But if he hadn't left I wouldn't have got to see the sunset."

"My God," Gloria said, looking at her sandwich. "Ain't there nothing in the world but ham?"

"To you that's turkey," said Mack Aston, who was in line behind me. He was kidding.

"Here's a beef," said the nurse. "Would you rather have a beef?"

Gloria took the beef sandwich, but kept the ham too. "Put four lumps in mine," she said to Rollo, who was pouring the coffee. "And lots of cream."

"She's got a little horse in her," said Mack Aston.

"Black," I said to Rollo.

Gloria took her food over to the master of ceremonies' platform where the musicians were tuning up their instruments. When Rocky Gravo saw her he jumped down on the floor and began talking to her. There wasn't room there for me, so I went around to the opposite side.

"Hello," said a girl. The shield on her back said: 7. She had black hair and black eyes and was rather pretty. I didn't know her name.

"Hello," I said, looking around, trying to see whose partner she was. He was talking to a couple of women in a front row box.

"How are you making out?" No. 7 asked. Her voice sounded as if she had been well educated.

"What is she doing in this thing?" I asked myself. "I guess I'm doing all right," I replied. "Only I wish it was all over and I was the winner."

"What would you do with the money if you won?" she asked, laughing.

"I'd make a picture," I said.

"You couldn't make much of a picture for a thousand dollars, could you?" she asked, taking a bite of her sandwich.

"Oh, I don't mean a big picture," I explained. "I mean a short. I could make a two-reeler for that, maybe three."

"You interest me," she said. "I've been watching you for two weeks."

"You have?" I said, surprised.

"Yes, I've seen you stand over there in the sun every afternoon and I've seen you with a thousand different expressions on your face. Sometimes I got the idea you were badly frightened."

"You must be wrong," I said. "What's there to be frightened about?"

"I overheard what you said to your partner about seeing the sunset this afternoon," she said, smiling.

"That doesn't prove anything," I said.

"Suppose . . ." she said, glancing around. She looked at the clock, frowning. "We've still got four minutes. Would you like to do something for me?"

"Well . . . sure," I said.

She motioned with her head and I followed her behind the master of ceremonies' platform. This platform was about four feet high, draped with heavy, decorated canvas that fell to the floor. We were standing alone in a sort of cave that was formed by the back of the platform and a lot of signs. Except for the noise she and I might have been the only people left in the world. We were both a little excited.

"Come on," she said. She dropped to the floor and lifted the canvas, crawling under the platform. My heart was beating rapidly and I felt the blood leave my face. Through the balls of my feet I could feel the ocean surging against the pilings below.

"Come on," she whispered, pulling at my ankle. Suddenly I knew what she meant. *There is no new experience in life. Something may happen to you that you think has never happened before, that you think is brand new, but you are mistaken. You have only to see or smell or hear or feel a certain something and you will discover that this experience you thought was new has happened before. When she pulled at my ankle, trying to get me beneath the platform, I remembered the time when another girl had done exactly the same thing. Only it was a front porch in-stead of a platform. I was thirteen or fourteen years old then and the girl was about the same age. Her name was Mabel and she lived next door. After school we used to play under the front porch, imagining it was a cove and we were robbers and pris-oners. Later on we used it to play papa and mama, imagining it was a house. But on this day I am speaking of I stood by the front porch, not thinking of Mabel or games at all, and I felt something pulling at my ankle. I looked down and there was Mabel. "Come on," she said.*

It was very dark under the platform and while I crouched there on my hands and knees trying to see through the gloom No. 7 suddenly grabbed me around the neck.

"Hurry . . ." she whispered.

"What's coming off here?" growled a man's voice. He was so close I could feel his breath against my hair. "Who is that?"

I recognized the voice now. It was Rocky Gravo's. My stomach turned over. No. 7 let go my neck and slid out from under the platform. I was afraid if I tried to apologize or say anything Rocky would recognize my voice, so I quickly rolled under the curtain. No. 7 was already on her feet moving away, looking back over her shoulder at me. Her face was white as chalk. Neither of us spoke. We strolled onto the dance floor, trying to look very innocent. The nurse was collecting our dirty coffee cups in a basket. Then I discovered my hands and clothes were filthy with dust. I had a couple of minutes before the whistle blew, so I hurried into the dressing room to clean up. When that was done I felt better.

"What a close shave that was," I told myself. "I'll never do anything like that again."

I got back on the floor as the whistle blew and the orchestra began to play. This was not a very good orchestra; but it was better than the radio because you didn't have to listen to a lot of announcers begging and pleading with you to buy something. Since I've been in this marathon I've had enough radio to last me the rest of my life. *There is a radio going now, in a building across the street from the court room. It is very distinct. "Do you need money? . . . Are you in trouble? . . ."*

"Where've you been?" Gloria asked, taking my arm.

"I haven't been anywhere," I said. "Feel like dancing?"

"All right," she said. We danced once around the floor and then she stopped. "That's too much like work," she said.

As I took my hand from around her waist I noticed my fingers were dirty again. "That's funny," I thought. "I just washed them a minute ago."

"Turn around," I said to Gloria.

"What's the matter?" she asked.

"Turn around," I said.

She hesitated, biting her lip, so I stepped behind her. She was wearing a white woolen skirt and a thin white woolen sweater. Her back was covered with thick dust and I knew where it had come from.

"What's the matter?" she said.

"Stand still," I said. I brushed her off with my hand, knocking most of the dust and lint loose from her sweater and skirt. She did not speak for a moment or two. "I must have got that when I was wrestling in the dressing room with Lillian," she said finally.

"I'm not as big a sap as she thinks I am," I told myself. "I guess you did," I said.

Rollo Peters fell in with us as we walked around the floor.

"Who is that girl?" I asked, pointing to No. 7.

"That's Guy Duke's partner. Her name is Rosemary Loftus."

"All your taste is in your mouth," Gloria said.

"I merely asked who she was," I said. "I haven't got a crush on her."

"You don't need one," Gloria said. "You tell him, Rollo."

"Leave me out of this," Rollo said, shaking his head. "I don't know a thing about her."

"What about her?" I asked Gloria, as Rollo walked away, joining James and Ruby Bates.

"Are you that innocent?" she said. "On the level—are you?" She laughed, shaking her head. "You certainly are a card."

"All right, forget it," I said.

"Why, that dame is the biggest bitch west of the Mississippi River," she said. "She's a bitch with an exclusive education and when you get that kind of bitch you've got the worst bitch of all. Why not even the girls can go to the can when she's around——"

"Hello, there, Gloria," called out Mrs. Layden. She was sitting in her usual seat in the front row box the far end of the hall, away from the master of ceremonies' platform. Gloria and I walked over to the railing. . . .

"How's my favorite couple?" she asked.

"Fine," I said. "How are you, Mrs. Layden?"

"I'm fine too," she said. "I'm going to stay a long time tonight. See?" She pointed to her blanket and her lunch basket on the chair beside her. "I'll be here to cheer you on."

"We'll need it," Gloria said.

"Why don't you take one of those boxes down there away from the Palm Garden?" I asked. "It gets pretty rowdy at the bar later on when everybody starts drinking——"

"This is fine for me," she said, smiling. "I like to be here for the derby. I want to watch them make the turns. Would you like to see the afternoon paper?" she asked, pulling the paper out from under the blanket.

"Thank you," I said. "I would like to know what's going on in the world. How is the weather outside? Has the world changed much?"

"You're poking fun at me," she said.

"No, I'm not . . . it just seems like I've been in this hall a million years . . . Thanks for the paper, Mrs. Layden. . . ."

As we moved away I unfolded the paper. Big, black headlines hit me in the face.

NAB YOUTHFUL MURDERER
IN MARATHON DANCE

Escaped Criminal Was Taking
Part in Beach Contest

Detectives yesterday picked a murderer from the marathon dance now in progress on the amusement pier at Santa Monica. He was Giuseppe Lodi, 26-year-old Italian, who escaped eight months ago from the Illinois state prison at Joliet after serving four years of a fifty-year sentence for the conviction of the hold-up slaying of an aged druggist in Chicago.

Lodi, entered in the marathon dance under the alias of Mario Petrone, offered no resistance when he was arrested by Detectives Bliss and Voight, of the Robbery Detail. The officers had dropped into the marathon dance seeking diversion from their duties, they said, and recognized Lodi through a picture they had seen in "The Line-Up," a department of a popular detective monthly which contains pictures and measurements of badly wanted criminals . . .

"Can you beat that?" I said. "I was right beside him when all that happened. I certainly feel sorry for Mario now."

"Why," said Gloria, "what's the difference between us?"

Pedro Ortega, Mack Aston and a few others gathered around us, talking excitedly. I handed the paper to Gloria and walked on alone.

"That's a hell of a thing," I thought. "Fifty years! Poor Mario . . ." *And when Mario hears the news about me, if he ever does, he will think: 'Poor guy! wasting his sympathy on me and him getting the rope. . . .'*

At the next rest period Socks Donald had a surprise for us. He issued the uniforms we were to wear in the derby races; tennis shoes, white shorts, white sweatshirts. All the boys were given thick leather belts to wear around their waists, and on either side of the belt were little handles, like those on luggage. These were for our partners to hold on when we went around the curves. It seemed very silly to me then, but later on I discovered Socks Donald knew what he was doing.

"Lissen, kids," Socks said. "Tonight we start on our first million. There'll be a lot of movie stars here for the derby and wherever they go the crowds will follow. Some team will lose tonight—some team will lose every night. I don't want no squawks about this because it's on the level. Everybody has the same chance. You'll get some extra time to get on your uniforms and some extra time to take them off. And by the way, I talked to Mario Petrone this afternoon. He told me to say good-bye to all his pals. Now, don't forget to give the customers a run for their money in the derby, kids——"

I was surprised to hear him mention Mario's name because the night before, when Mario was arrested, Socks had wanted to beat him up.

"I thought he was sore at Mario," I said to Rollo.

"Not any more," Rollo said. "That was the best break we ever had. If it hadn't been for that nobody ever would have known there was a marathon dance. That newspaper publicity was just what the doctor ordered. Reservations have been coming in all afternoon."

. . . YOU,
ROBERT SYVERTEN,
BE DELIVERED . . .

8

T HAT NIGHT, for the first time since the contest started, the hall was crowded and practically every seat was taken. The Palm Garden was crowded too and there was a lot of boisterous laughing and talking at the bar. "Rollo was right," I said to myself. "Mario's arrest was the best break Socks ever had." (But not all those people had been attracted by the newspaper publicity. I found out later that Socks was having us advertised over several radio stations.)

We walked around in our track suits while the trainers and nurses set up the floor for the derby.

"I feel naked," I said to Gloria.

"You look naked," she said. "You ought to have on a jock-strap."

"They didn't give me one," I said. "Does it show that much?"

"It's not only that," she said. "You're liable to get ruptured. Get Rollo to buy you one tomorrow. They come in three sizes: small, medium and large. You take a small."

"I'm not by myself," I said, looking around at some of the other boys.

"They're bragging," Gloria said.

Most of the contestants looked very funny in their track suits. I never saw such an odd assortment of arms and legs in my life.

"Look," Gloria said, nodding to James and Ruby Bates. "Ain't that something?"

You could see Ruby was going to have a baby. It looked as if she had stuffed a pillow under her sweatshirt.

"It certainly is noticeable," I said. "But remember it's none of your business."

"Ladies and gentlemen," Rocky said into the microphone, "before this sensational derby starts I want to call your attention to the rules and regulations. Because of the number of contestants the derby will be run in two sections—forty couples in the first and forty in the second. The second derby will be run a few minutes after the first one and the entries in each one will be decided by drawing the numbers out of a hat.

"We'll run these derbies in two sections for a week, the couple in each one making the least number of laps to be eliminated. After the first week there will be only one derby. The kids will race around the track for fifteen minutes, the boys heeling and toeing, the girls trotting or running as they see fit. There is no prize for the winner, but if some of you ladies and gentlemen want to send up some prize money to encourage the kids, I know they will appreciate it.

"You will notice the cots in the middle of the floor, the nurses and trainers standing by with sliced oranges, wet towels, smelling salts—and the doctor in charge to see that none of these kids carry on unless they're in good physical condition."

The young doctor was standing in the middle of the floor, his stethoscope hanging from his neck, looking very important.

"Just a minute, ladies and gentlemen—just a minute," Rocky said. "I have in my hand a ten-dollar bill for the winner of tonight's derby, contributed by that marvelous little screen star, none other than Miss Ruby Keeler. A hand for Miss Keeler, ladies and gentlemen——"

Ruby Keeler stood up, bowing to the applause.

"That's the spirit, ladies and gentlemen," Rocky said. "And now we need some judges, ladies and gentlemen, to check the laps each couple makes." He stopped to wipe the perspiration off his face. "All right now, ladies and gentlemen, I want these judges out of the audience—forty of them. Step right up here—don't be afraid——"

Nobody in the audience moved for a moment, and then Mrs. Layden crawled under the railing and started across the floor. As she passed Gloria and me she smiled and winked.

"Maybe she'll turn out to be useful after all," Gloria said.

Soon others followed Mrs. Layden until all the judges had been selected. Rollo gave each of them a card and a pencil and seated them on the floor around the platform.

"All right, ladies and gentlemen," Rocky said. "We've got enough judges. Now we'll have the drawing for the first derby. There are eighty numbers in this hat and we'll draw forty of them. The other couples will be in the second derby. Now we need somebody to draw the numbers. How about you, lady?" he asked Mrs. Layden, holding out the hat. Mrs. Layden smiled and nodded her head.

"This is a big moment in her life," Gloria said sarcastically.

"I think she is a very sweet old lady," I said.

"Nuts," Gloria said.

Mrs. Layden began drawing out the numbers, passing them to Rocky who announced them into the microphone.

"The first one," he said, "is couple No. 105. Right over here, kids—all you couples who are drawn stand over here on this side of the platform."

As fast as Mrs. Layden would draw the numbers Rocky would announce them, then pass them to one of the judges. That was the couple he checked, counting the number of laps they made.

". . . Couple No. 22," Rocky said, handing the number to a young man who wore spectacles.

"Come on," I said to Gloria. That was our number.

"I'd like that one," I heard Mrs. Layden say to Rocky. "That's my favorite couple."

"Sorry, lady," Rocky said. "You have to take them in order."

When the drawing was finished and we were all together near the starting line, Rocky said, "All right, ladies and gentlemen, we're almost ready. Now, kids, all you boys remember heel and toe. If one of you has to go to the pit for any reason whatsoever, your partner has to make two laps of the track to count for one. Will you start 'em off, Miss Keeler?"

She nodded and Rocky handed Rollo the pistol. He took it to Miss Keeler, who was sitting in a front-row box with another girl I didn't recognize. Jolson was not there.

"All right, ladies and gentlemen, hold your hats," Rocky said. "All right, Miss Keeler. . . ." He signaled to her with his hand.

Gloria and I had edged along the side of the platform towards the starting line and when Miss Keeler pulled the trigger we jumped away, pushing and shoving to get in front. Gloria had me by the arm.

"Hold on to the belt," I yelled, struggling to get through

the crowd. Everybody was stumbling over everybody else, trying to get in front . . . but in a minute we spread out and
began pounding around the track. I was taking such long
steps Gloria had to trot to keep up with me.

"Heel and toe there," Rollo said. "You're running."

"I'm doing the best I can," I said.

"Heel and toe," he said. "Like this——"

He stepped in front of me, illustrating what he meant. I
had no trouble at all in learning. The trick was to keep your
shoulders and arms properly timed. I had no trouble at all in
figuring that. It seemed to come to me naturally. It was so
simple I thought for a moment I must have done some heel-
and-toe walking before. I couldn't remember it, so evidently
I hadn't. I've got a marvelous memory.

We had been going about five minutes and were well up
towards the front when I felt Gloria stop propelling herself;
that is, she stopped traveling under her own power. I was
dragging her. I felt as if she were trying to pull the belt
through my stomach.

"Too fast?" I asked, slowing down.

"Yes," she replied, almost out of breath.

One of the nurses slammed a wet bath towel around my
neck, almost knocking me off balance. "Rub your face with
it," I said to Gloria. . . . Just then couple No. 35 cut in front
of us, trying to get into the turn first. The spurt was too much
for the girl. She began to stagger, loosening her hold on his
belt.

"Stand by No. 35," yelled Rocky Gravo, but before a nurse
or trainer could reach her she had fallen on her face, sliding
a couple of feet across the floor. If I had been alone I could
have side-stepped the body, but with Gloria hanging on me I
was afraid if I dodged I would sling her off. (Making these
turns with a girl hanging on you was like playing pop-the-
whip.)

"Look out!" I yelled, but the warning was too late to do
any good. Gloria stumbled over the body pulling me down
with her, and the next thing I knew four or five couples were
piled together on the floor, struggling to get up. Rocky said
something into the microphone and the crowd gasped.

I picked myself up. I wasn't hurt, only I knew from the way

my knees were burning that all the skin was rubbed off. The nurses and trainers rushed over and began tugging at the girls, carrying Gloria and Ruby to the cots in the pit.

"Nothing serious, ladies and gentlemen," Rocky said. "Just a little spill . . . something happens every minute in the derbies . . . while the girls are in the pit the boys have to make two laps to count as one full lap for the team. All right, kids, give those solos the inside track."

I began walking very fast so as not to lose our position in the race. Now that Gloria wasn't hanging on to the strap any more I felt light as a feather. A nurse and a trainer began working over her while the doctor listened to her heart with his stethoscope. The nurse was holding smelling salts at her nose and the trainer was massaging her legs. Another trainer and nurse were doing the same thing to Ruby. I made four laps before Gloria came back to the floor. She was very pale.

"Can you hold out?" I asked, slowing down. She said yes with her head. The people were applauding and stamping their feet and Rocky was speaking words into the microphone. Ruby came back into the race, looking all in too.

"Take it easy," Rollo said, moving beside me. "You're in no danger——"

Then I felt a sharp pain in my left leg that shot up through my body and almost blew off the top of my head. "My God," I told myself; "I'm paralyzed!"

"Kick it out, kick it out," Rollo said.

I couldn't bend my leg. It simply wouldn't work. It was stiff as a board. Every time I took a step the pain went through the top of my head.

"There's a charley horse on Couple 22," Rocky said into the microphone. "Stand by there, trainers——"

"Kick it out, kick it out," Rollo said.

I kicked my leg against the floor but that was more painful than ever.

"Kick it out, kick it out——"

"You son of a bitch," I said; "my leg hurts——"

Two of the trainers grabbed me by the arms and helped me to the pit.

"There goes the brave little girl of No. 22," Rocky announced, "little Gloria Beatty. What a brave kid she is!

She's soloing while her partner is in the pit with a charley horse——look at her burn up that track! Give her the inside, kids——"

One of the trainers held my shoulders down while the other one worked my leg up and down, beating the muscles with the heels of his fists.

"That hurts," I said.

"Take it easy," said the trainer who was holding my shoulders. "Didn't you ever have one of those things before?"

Then I felt something snap in my leg and the pain was suddenly gone.

"Okay," the trainer said.

I got up, feeling fine, and went back on the track, standing there waiting for Gloria. She was on the opposite side from me, trotting, her head bobbing up and down every time she took a step. I had to wait for her to come around. (The rules were you had to come out of the pit at the point where you went in.) As Gloria neared me I started walking and in a moment she had coupled on to the belt.

"Two minutes to go," Rocky announced. "A little rally, ladies and gentlemen—" They began clapping their hands and stamping their feet, much louder than before.

Other couples began to sprint past us and I put on a little more steam. I was pretty sure Gloria and I weren't in last place, but we had both been in the pit and I didn't want to take a chance on being eliminated. When the pistol sounded for the finish half the teams collapsed on the floor. I turned around to Gloria and saw her eyes were glassy. I knew she was going to faint.

"Hey . . ." I yelled to one of the nurses, but just then Gloria sagged and I had to catch her myself. It was all I could do to carry her to the pit. "Hey!" I yelled to one of the trainers. "Doctor."

Nobody paid any attention to me. They were too busy picking up the bodies. The customers were standing on their seats, screaming in excitement.

I began rubbing Gloria's face with a wet towel. Mrs. Layden suddenly appeared beside me and took a bottle of smelling salts off the table by the cot.

"You go on to your dressing room," she said. "Gloria'll be all right in a minute. She's not used to the strain."

I was on a boat going to Port Said. I was on my way to the Sahara Desert to make that picture. I was famous and I had plenty of money. I was the most important motion picture director in the world. I was more important than Sergei Eisenstein. The critics of *Vanity Fair* and *Esquire* had agreed that I was a genius. I was walking around the deck, thinking of that marathon dance I once had been in, wondering what had become of all those girls and boys, when something hit me a terrific blow in the back of the head, knocking me unconscious. I had a feeling I was falling.

When I struck the water I began lashing out with my arms and legs because I was afraid of sharks. Something brushed my body and I screamed in fright.

I woke up swimming in water that was freezing cold. Instantly I knew where I was. "I've had a nightmare," I told myself. The thing that had brushed my body was a hundred-pound block of ice. I was in a small tank of water in the dressing room. I was still wearing my track suit. I climbed out, shivering, and one of the trainers handed me a towel.

Two other trainers came in, carrying one of the contestants who was unconscious. It was Pedro Ortega. They carried him to the tank and dumped him in.

"Is that what happened to me?" I asked.

"That's right," the trainer said. "You passed out just as you left the dance floor—" Pedro whimpered something in Spanish and splashed the water, fighting to get out. The trainer laughed. "I'll say Socks knew what he was doing when he brought that tank in here," he said. "That ice water fixes 'em right up. Get off those wet pants and shoes."

. . . BY THE
SHERIFF OF
LOS ANGELES
COUNTY
TO THE
WARDEN OF
STATE PRISON . . .

> HOURS ELAPSED 752
> Couples Remaining 26

THE DERBY races were killing them off. Fifty-odd couples had been eliminated in two weeks. Gloria and I had come close to the finish once or twice, but by the skin of our teeth we managed to hang on. After we changed our technique we had no more trouble: we had stopped trying to win, not caring where we finished so long as it wasn't last.

We had got a sponsor too: Jonathan Beer, Non-Fattening. This came just in time. Our shoes were worn out and our clothes were ragged. Mrs. Layden sold Jonathan Beer on the idea of sponsoring us. *Sell St. Peter on the idea of letting me in, Mrs. Layden. I think I'm on my way.* They gave Gloria and me three pairs of shoes, three pairs of gray flannel trousers and three sweaters each with their product advertised on the backs of them.

I had gained five pounds since the contest started and was beginning to think that maybe we had some chance to win that thousand dollar first prize after all. But Gloria was very pessimistic.

"What are you going to do after this thing is over?" she asked.

"Why worry about that?" I said. "It's not over yet. I don't see what you're kicking about," I told her. "We're better off than we've ever been—at least we know where our next meal is coming from."

"I wish I was dead," she said. "I wish God would strike me dead."

She kept saying that over and over again. It was beginning to get on my nerves.

"Some day God is going to do that little thing," I said.

"I wish He would . . . I wish I had the guts to do it for Him."

"If we win this thing you can take your five-hundred dollars and go away somewhere," I said. "You can get married. There are always plenty of guys willing to get married. Haven't you ever thought about that?"

"I've thought about it plenty," she said. "But I couldn't ever marry the kind of man I want. The only kind that would marry me would be the kind I wouldn't have. A thief or a pimp or something."

"I know why you're so morbid," I said. "You'll be all right in a couple of days. You'll feel better about it then."

"That hasn't got anything to do with it," she said. "I don't even get a backache from that. That's not it. This whole business is a merry-go-round. When we get out of here we're right back where we started."

"We've been eating and sleeping," I said.

"Well, what's the good of that when you're just postponing something that's bound to happen?"

"Hey, Jonathan Beer," Rocky Gravo called out. "Come over here——"

He was standing by the platform with Socks Donald. Gloria and I went over.

"How'd you kids like to pick up a hundred bucks?" Rocky asked.

"Doing what?" Gloria asked.

"Well, kids," Socks Donald said, "I've got a swell idea only I need a bit of some help——"

"That's the Ben Bernie influence," Gloria said to me.

"What?" Socks said.

"Nothing," Gloria said. "Go on—you need a bit of some help——"

"Yeah," Socks said. "I want you two kids to get married here. A public wedding."

"Married?" I said.

"Now, wait a minute," Socks said. "It's not that bad. I'll give you fifty dollars apiece and after the marathon is over you can get divorced if you want to. It don't have to be permanent. It's just a showmanship angle. What do you say?"

"I say you're nuts," Gloria said.

"She doesn't mean that, Mr. Donald—" I said.

"The hell I don't," she said. "I've got no objections to

getting married," she said to Socks, "but why don't you pick out Gary Cooper or some big-shot producer or director? I don't want to marry this guy. I got enough trouble looking out for myself——"

"It don't have to be permanent," Rocky said. "It's just showmanship."

"That's right," Socks said. "Of course, the ceremony'll have to be on the square—we'll have to do that to get the crowd. But——"

"You don't need a wedding to get a crowd," Gloria said. "You're hanging 'em off the rafters now. Ain't it enough of a show to see these poor bastards falling all over the floor every night?"

"You don't get the angle," Socks said, frowning.

"The hell I don't," Gloria said. "I'm way ahead of you."

"You want to get in pictures and here's your chance," Socks said. "I already got some stores lined up to give you your wedding dress and your shoes and a beauty shop that'll fix you up—there'll be a lot of directors and supervisors here and they'll all be looking at nobody but you. It's the chance of a lifetime. What do you say, kid?" he asked me.

"I don't know—" I said, not wanting to make him sore. After all, he was the promoter. I knew if he got sore at us we were as good as disqualified.

"He says no," Gloria said.

"She does his thinking for him," Rocky said sarcastically.

"Okay," Socks said, shrugging his shoulders. "If you can't use a hundred dollars maybe some of these other kids can. At least," he said to me, "you know who wears the drawers in your family." He and Rocky both laughed.

"You just can't be polite to anybody, can you?" I said to Gloria when we had walked away. "We'll be out in the street any minute now."

"Might as well be now as tomorrow," she said.

"You're the gloomiest person I ever met," I said. "Sometimes I think you would be better off dead."

"I know it," she said.

When we came around by the platform again I saw Socks and Rocky talking earnestly to Vee Lovell and Mary Hawley, Couple No. 71.

"Looks like Socks is selling her a bill of goods," Gloria said. "That Hawley horse couldn't get in out of the rain."

James and Ruby Bates joined up and we walked four abreast. We were on friendly terms again since Gloria had stopped trying to talk Ruby into having an abortion performed. "Did Socks proposition you to get married?" Ruby asked.

"Yes," I said. "How did you know?"

"He's propositioned everybody," she said.

"We turned him down cold," Gloria said.

"A public wedding isn't so bad," Ruby said. "We had one——"

"You did?" I said, surprised. James and Ruby were so dignified and quiet and so much in love with each other I couldn't imagine them being married in a public ceremony.

"We were married in a marathon dance in Oklahoma," she said. "We got about three hundred dollars worth of stuff too. . . ."

"Her old man gave us the shotgun for a wedding present——" James said, laughing.

Suddenly a girl screamed behind us. We turned around. It was Lillian Bacon, Pedro Ortega's partner. She was walking backwards, trying to get away from him. Pedro caught up with her, slamming her in the face with his fist. She sat down on the floor, screaming again. Pedro grabbed her by the throat with both hands, choking her and trying to lift her up. His face was the face of a maniac. There was no doubt he was trying to kill her.

Everybody started running for him at the same time. There was a lot of confusion.

James and I reached him first, grabbing him and breaking his hold on Lillian's neck. She was sitting on the floor, her body rigid, her arms behind her, her head thrown back, her mouth open—like a patient in a dentist's chair.

Pedro was muttering to himself and did not seem to recognize any of us. James shoved him and he staggered backward. I put my hands under Lillian's armpits, helping her to her feet. She was shaking like a muscle dancer.

Socks and Rocky rushed up and took Pedro by either arm.

"What's the big idea?" Socks roared.

Pedro looked at Socks, moving his lips but not saying anything. Then he saw Rocky and the expression on his face changed, becoming one of ferocious resentment. He suddenly twisted his arms free, stepping backward and reaching into his pocket.

"Look out—" somebody cried.

Pedro lunged forward, a knife in his hand. Rocky tried to dodge, but it all happened so quickly he never had a chance. The knife caught him across the left arm two inches below the shoulder. He yelled and started running. Pedro turned around to follow but before he could take a step Socks hit him in the back of the head with a leather blackjack. You could hear the plunk above the music of the radio. It sounded exactly like somebody thumping their finger against a watermelon. Pedro stood there, an idiotic grin on his face and Socks hit him again with the blackjack.

Pedro's arms fell and the knife dropped to the floor. He wobbled on his legs and then he went down.

"Get him out of here," Socks said, picking up the knife.

James Bates, Mack Aston and Vee Lovell lifted Pedro, carrying him off to the dressing room.

"Keep your seats, ladies and gentlemen—" Socks said to the audience. "Please——"

I was bracing Lillian from behind. She was still shaking.

"What happened?" Socks asked her.

"He accused me of cheating—" she said. "Then he hit me and started choking me——"

"Go on, kids," Socks said. "Act like nothing has happened. Hey, nurse—help this girl to the dressing room—" Socks signaled to Rollo on the platform and the siren blew for a rest period. It was a few minutes early. The nurse took Lillian out of my arms and all the girls gathered around them, going into the dressing room.

As I went off I could hear Rollo making some kind of casual announcement over the loud speakers.

Rocky was standing at the wash basin, his coat and shirt off, dabbing at his shoulder with a handful of paper towels. The blood was streaming down his arm, running off his fingers.

"You better get the doctor on that," Socks said. "Where the hell is that doctor?" he bellowed.

"Here—" the doctor said, coming out of the lavatory.

"The only time we need you you're sitting on your ass," Socks said. "See what's the matter with Rocky."

Pedro was lying on the floor with Mack Aston straddling him, working on his stomach like a life guard with a man who has been drowning.

"Watch it—" Vee Lovell said, coming up with a bucket of water. Mack stepped back and Vee dumped the water in Pedro's face. It had no effect on him. He lay there like a log.

James Bates brought another bucket of water and doused him with that. Now Pedro began to show signs of life. He stirred, opening his eyes.

"He's coming to," Vee Lovell said.

"I better get Rocky to the hospital in my car," the doctor said, taking off his linen coat. "He's got a deep cut—almost to the bone. It'll have to be sutured. Who did it?"

"That bastard—" Socks said, pointing to Pedro with his leg.

"He must have used a razor," the doctor said.

"Here—" Socks said, handing him the knife. Socks had the leather blackjack in his other hand, the thong still around his wrist.

"Same thing," the doctor said, handing back the knife.

Pedro sat up, rubbing his jaw, a dazed look on his face.

"It wasn't your jaw," I said to him in my mind, "it was the back of your head."

"For Christ's sake, let's get going," Rocky said to the doctor. "I'm bleeding like a stuck pig. And you, you son of a bitch," he said to Pedro; "I'm going to prefer charges against you——"

Pedro looked at him fiercely, saying nothing.

"There won't be any charges filed," Socks said. "I'm having enough trouble keeping open now. Next time be careful who you cheat with."

"I wasn't cheating with anybody," Rocky said.

"Balls—" Socks said. "Take him out the back way, Doc."

"All right, Rocky," the doctor said. Rocky started out. The temporary gauze bandage on his arm was soaked already. The doctor draped a coat around Rocky's shoulders and they went out.

"Are you trying to bust up this contest?" Socks asked, turning his full attention to Pedro. "Whyn't you wait till this was over to get him?"

"I tried to cut his throat," Pedro stated calmly, in precise English. "He seduced my fiancée——"

"If he seduced your fiancée around here he's a magician," Socks said. "There's no place to seduce anybody."

"I know a place," I said in my mind.

Rollo Peters came in to the dressing room. "You guys ought to be getting your sleep," he said. "Where's Rocky?" he asked, looking around.

"The doc took him to the hospital," Socks told him. "How are they out there?"

"They're calmed down," Rollo said. "I told 'em we were rehearsing a novelty act. What was the matter with Rocky?"

"Nothing much," Socks said. "He just damn near had his arm cut off by this greaseball, that's all." He handed him Pedro's knife. "Here, take this thing and get rid of it. You do the announcing till we find out about Rocky."

Pedro got up off the floor. "I am very sorry this happened before the audience," he said. "I am very sorry I have a very quick temper——"

"I guess it could have been worse," Socks said. "It could have happened at night when we had a full house. How's your head?"

"It is sore," Pedro said. "I am very sorry this happened. I wanted to win the thousand dollars——"

"You still got a chance," Socks said.

"You mean I am not disqualified? You mean you forgive me?"

"I forgive you——" Socks said, dropping the blackjack into his pocket.

. . . TO BE
BY SAID
WARDEN . . .

```
HOURS ELAPSED . . . . . . 783
Couples Remaining . . . . . . 26
```

L ADIES and gentlemen," Rocky announced, "before the derby starts the management has asked me to tell you that there will be a public wedding here one week from to-night—a real, bona-fide wedding right here on the floor be-tween Couple No. 71, Vee Lovell and Mary Hawley. Step out there, Vee and Mary, and let the ladies and gentlemen see what a cute couple you are——"

Vee and Mary, in track suits, went to the center of the floor, bowing to the applause. The hall was packed again.

"—That is," Rocky said, "if they are not eliminated in the derby by then. We hope not, anyway. This public wedding is in line with the management's policy to give you nothing but high-class amusement——"

Mrs. Layden tugged at the back of my sweatshirt.

"What's the matter with Rocky's arm?" she asked in a whis-per. You could see Rocky had had some kind of an accident. His right arm was through his coat sleeve in the usual way, but his left arm was in a sling and on that side he wore his coat like a cape.

"He sprained it," I said.

"They only took nine stitches in it," Gloria said, under her breath.

"That's why he wasn't here last night," Mrs. Layden said. "He had an accident——"

"Yes'm——"

"Did he fall?"

"Yes'm, I think so——"

"—introducing that beautiful screen star Miss Mary Brian. Will you take a bow, Miss Brian?"

Miss Brian took a bow. The audience applauded.

"—and that master comedian, Mr. Charley Chase——"

There was more applause as Charley Chase stood up in a box seat and took a bow.

"I hate these introductions," Gloria said.

"It would be all right if you were being introduced though, wouldn't it?" I said.

"Good luck——" Mrs. Layden said as we moved towards the platform.

"I'm sick of this," Gloria said. "I'm sick of looking at celebrities and I'm sick of doing the same thing over and over again——"

"Sometimes I'm sorry I ever met you," I said. "I don't like to say a thing like that, but it's the truth. Before I met you I didn't know what it was to be around gloomy people. . . ."

We crowded behind the starting line with the other couples.

"I'm tired of living and I'm afraid of dying," Gloria said.

"Say, that's a swell idea for a song," said James Bates, who had overheard her. "You could write a song about an old nigger down on the levee who was tired of living and afraid of dying. He could be heaving cotton and singing a song to the Mississippi River. Say, that's a good title—you could call it Old Man River——"

Gloria looked daggers at him, thumbing her nose.

"Hello, there——" Rocky called out to Mrs. Layden, who had arrived at the platform. "Ladies and gentlemen——" he said into the microphone, "I want to introduce to you the champion marathon dance fan of the world—a woman who hasn't missed a single night since this contest started. This is Mrs. Layden, and the management has issued a season pass to her—good any time, good all the time. A big hand for Mrs. Layden, ladies and gentlemen.—Will you take a bow, Mrs. Layden——"

Mrs. Layden hesitated a moment, badly rattled, not knowing exactly what she should do or say. But as the audience applauded she took a couple of steps forward, bowing awkwardly. You could see this was one of the biggest surprises of her life.

"You people who are dance fans have seen her here before," Rocky said. "She is a judge in the derby every night—we couldn't have a derby unless she was here. How do you like the marathon dance, Mrs. Layden?" he asked, stooping down on his haunches and moving the microphone so she could talk into it.

"She hates it," Gloria said under her breath. "She wouldn't come to one on a bet, you dumb bastard——"

"I like it," Mrs. Layden said. She was so nervous she could hardly speak.

"Who's your favorite couple, Mrs. Layden?"

"My favorite couple is No. 22—Robert Syverten and Gloria Beatty."

"Her favorite couple is No. 22, ladies and gentlemen, sponsored by Jonathan Non-Fattening Beer— You're pulling for them to win, are you Mrs. Layden?"

"Yes, I am and if I were younger, I'd be in this contest myself."

"That's fine. Thank you very much, Mrs. Layden. All right—and now it gives me pleasure to present you with a season pass, Mrs. Layden—the gift of the management. You can come in any time without paying——"

Mrs. Layden took the pass. She was so overwhelmed with gratitude and emotion that she was smiling and crying and nodding her head at the same time.

"That's another big moment," Gloria said.

"Shut up!" I said.

"All right—are the judges ready?" Rocky asked straightening up.

"All ready," said Rollo, helping Mrs. Layden to a chair in the judges' row.

"Ladies and gentlemen," Rocky announced, "most of you are familiar with the rules and regulations of the derby—but for the benefit of those who are seeing their first contest of this kind, I will explain so they will know what is going on. The kids race around the track for fifteen minutes, the boys heeling-and-toeing, the girls running or trotting as they so desire. If for any reason whatsoever one of them goes in the pit—the pit is in the center of the floor where the iron cots are—if for any reason one of them goes in the pit, the partner has to make two laps of the track to count for one. Is that clear?"

"Get going," somebody in the audience yelled.

"Are the nurses and trainers ready? Is the doctor standing by? All right—" He handed the starter's pistol down to Rollo. "Will you start the kids off, Miss Delmar?" Rocky asked into the microphone. "Ladies and gentlemen, Miss Delmar is a famous Hollywood author and novelist——"

Rollo took the pistol to Miss Delmar.

"Hold your hats, ladies and gentlemen," Rocky sang out. "Orchestra, get ready to give. All right, Miss Delmar——"

She shot the pistol and we were off.

Gloria and I let the racehorses set the pace. We made no effort to get up in front. Our system was to set a steady clip and hold it. There was no special prize money tonight. Even if there had been it would have made no difference to us.

The audience applauded and stamped their feet, begging for thrills, but this was one night they didn't get them. Only one girl, Ruby Bates, went into the pit and that was only for two laps. And for the first time in weeks nobody collapsed on the floor when the race was over.

But something had happened that frightened me. Gloria had pulled on my belt harder and longer than she ever had before. For the last five minutes of the derby it seemed she had no power of her own. I had practically dragged her around the track. I had a feeling we had just missed being eliminated ourselves. *We had just missed. Later that night Mrs. Layden told me she had spoken to the man who had checked us. We had made only two more laps than the losers. That chilled me. I made up my mind then that from now on I had better forget my system and open up.*

The losers were Basil Gerard and Geneva Tomblin, Couple No. 16. They were automatically disqualified. I knew Geneva was glad it was over. Now she could get married to the Captain of that live bait boat she had met during the first week of the contest.

Geneva came back on the floor while we were eating. She was dressed for the street and carried a small grip.

"Ladies and gentlemen—" Rocky said into the microphone "—there's that marvelous kid who was eliminated tonight. Doesn't she look pretty? A big hand, ladies and gentlemen——"

The audience applauded and Geneva bowed from side to side as she walked towards the platform.

"That's sportsmanship, ladies and gentlemen—she and her partner lost a hard-fought derby, but she is smiling— I'll let you in on a little secret, ladies and gentlemen—" he moved his face closer to the microphone and whispered loudly: "She's in love—she's going to get married. Yes, sir, ladies and gentlemen, the old marathon dance is the original home of romance, because Geneva is marrying a man she met right here in this hall. Is he in the house, Geneva? Is he here?"

Geneva nodded, smiling.

"Where is the lucky man?" Rocky asked. "Where is he? Stand up, skipper, and take a bow——"

Everybody in the audience craned their necks, looking around.

"There he is—" Rocky shouted, pointing to the opposite end of the hall. A man had stepped over the railing from the box and was walking down the floor towards Geneva. He had the peculiar walk of a sailor.

"Say a word, skipper—" Rocky said, tilting the microphone stand over.

"I fell in love with Geneva the first time I saw her," the skipper said to the audience, "and a couple of days later I asked her to quit the marathon dance and marry me. But she said no, she didn't want to let her partner down; and there wasn't nothing for me to do but stick around. Now I'm glad she's disqualified and I can hardly wait for the honey-moon——"

The audience rocked with laughter. Rocky pulled the microphone stand upright again. "A silver shower for the new bride, ladies and gentlemen——"

The skipper grabbed the stand, yanked the microphone down to his mouth. "Never mind any contributions, folks," he said. "I guess I'm plenty able to take care of her——"

"The original Popeye," Gloria said.

There was no silver shower. Not a single coin hit the floor.

"You see how modest he is," Rocky said. "But I guess it's all right for me to tell you he is the captain of the Pacific Queen, an old four-master that's now a live-bait barge anchored three miles off the pier. There are water taxies every hour during the day—and if any of you folks want some good deep-sea fishing go out with the skipper——"

"Kiss her, you chump," somebody in the audience yelled.

The skipper kissed Geneva, then steered her off the floor while the audience howled and applauded.

"That's the second wedding the marathon dance has arranged, ladies and gentlemen," Rocky announced. "Don't forget our big public ceremony here next week when Couple No. 71, Vee Lovell and Mary Hawley, will get married right before your very eyes. Give——" he said to the orchestra.

Basil Gerard came out of the dressing room in his street clothes and went to the table to get his last meal on the house.

Rocky sat down on the platform, swinging his legs off.

"Look out for my coffee——" Gloria said.

"Okay, okay," Rocky said, moving the cup a little. "How's the food?"

"All right," I said.

Two middle-aged women came up to us. I had seen them several times before, sitting in box seats. "Are you the manager?" one of them asked Rocky.

"Not exactly," Rocky said. "I'm the assistant manager. What was it you wanted?"

"I'm Mrs. Higby," the woman said. "This is Mrs. Witcher. Could we talk to you in private?"

"This is private as any place I got," Rocky said. "What was it you wanted?"

"We are the president and the vice-president——"

"What's the matter?" asked Socks Donald, coming around behind me.

"This is the manager," Rocky said, looking relieved.

The two women looked at Socks. "We are Mrs. Higby and Mrs. Witcher," Mrs. Higby said. "We are the president and the vice-president of the Mothers' League for Good Morals——"

"Aw-aw," Gloria said, under her breath.

"Yes?"

"We have a resolution for you," Mrs. Higby said, thrusting a folded paper into his hand.

"What's this all about?" Socks asked.

"Simply this," Mrs. Higby said. "Our Good Morals League has condemned your contest——"

"Wait a minute," Socks said. "Let's go to my office and talk this thing over——"

Mrs. Higby looked at Mrs. Witcher, who nodded. "Very well," she said.

"You kids come along—you too, Rocky. Hey nurse—take these cups and plates away—" He smiled at the two women. "You see," he said, "we don't let the kids do anything that would waste their energy. This way, ladies——"

He led the way off the floor behind the platform to his office, in a corner of the building. As we walked along Gloria pretended to stumble, falling heavily against Mrs. Higby, grabbing her around the head with her arms.

"Oh, I beg your pardon—I'm sorry—" Gloria said, looking on the floor to see what she had stumbled over.

Mrs. Higby said nothing, looking fiercely at Gloria, straightening her hat. Gloria nudged me, winking behind Mrs. Higby's back.

"Remember, you kids are witnesses—" Socks whispered as we went into his office. This office had formerly been a lounge and was very small. I noticed there had been very little change in it since the day Gloria and I had come here to make entries for the marathon. The only change was two more pictures of nude women Socks had tacked on the wall. Mrs. Higby and Mrs. Witcher spotted these instantly, exchanging significant looks.

"Sit down, ladies," Socks said. "What is it, now?"

"The Mothers' League for Good Morals has condemned your contest," Mrs. Higby said. "We have decided it is low and degrading and a pernicious influence in the community. We have decided you must close it——"

"Close it?"

"At once. If you refuse we shall go to the City Council. This contest is low and degrading——"

"You got me all wrong, ladies," Socks said. "There's nothing degrading about this contest. Why, these kids love it. Every one of them has gained weight since it started——"

"You have a girl in this contest who is about to become a

mother," Mrs. Higby said, "one Ruby Bates. It is criminal to have that girl running and walking all day when her baby is about to be born. Moreover, it is shocking to see her exhibiting herself to the world in that half-dressed condition. I should think she at least would have the decency to wear a coat——"

"Well, ladies," Socks said, "I never looked at that angle before. Ruby always seemed to know what she was doing— and I never paid no attention to her stomach. But I can see your point. You want me to put her out of the contest?"

"Most certainly," Mrs. Higby said. Mrs. Witcher nodded her head.

"All right, ladies," Socks said, "anything you say. I'm not hard to do business with. I'll even pay her hospital bills. . . . Thanks for telling me about it. I'll take care of that right away——"

"That isn't all," Mrs. Higby said. "Do you plan to have a public wedding next week or was that merely an announcement to draw a crowd of morons?"

"I never pulled nothing phony in my life," Socks said. "That wedding is on the level. I wouldn't double-cross my customers like that. You can ask anybody I do business with what kind of a guy I am——"

"We are familiar with your reputation," Mrs. Higby said. "But even at that I can hardly believe you intend to sponsor a sacrilege like that——"

"The kids who are going to get married are very much in love with each other," Rocky said.

"We won't permit such mockery," Mrs. Higby said. "We demand that you close this contest immediately!"

"What'll happen to these kids if he does?" Gloria asked. "They'll go right back on the streets——"

"Don't try to justify this thing, young woman," Mrs. Higby said. "This contest is vicious. It attracts the bad element. One of your participants was an escaped murderer— that Chicago Italian——"

"Well, ladies, you surely don't blame me for that," Socks said.

"We certainly do. We are here because it is our duty to keep our city clean and free from all such influences——"

"Do you mind if me and my assistant go outside to talk this over?" Socks asked. "Maybe we can figure this out——"

". . . Very well," Mrs. Higby said.

Socks motioned to Rocky and they went outside.

"Do you ladies have children of your own?" Gloria asked, when the door had closed.

"We both have grown daughters," Mrs. Higby said.

"Do you know where they are tonight and what they're doing?"

Neither woman said anything.

"Maybe I can give you a rough idea," Gloria said. "While you two noble characters are here doing your duty by some people you don't know, your daughters are probably in some guy's apartment, their clothes off, getting drunk."

Mrs. Higby and Mrs. Witcher gasped in unison.

"That's generally what happens to the daughters of reformers," Gloria said. "Sooner or later they all get laid and most of 'em don't know enough to keep from getting knocked up. You drive 'em away from home with your goddam lectures on purity and decency, and you're too busy meddling around to teach 'em the facts of life——"

"Why—" said Mrs. Higby, getting red in the face.

"I—" Mrs. Witcher said.

"Gloria—" I said.

"It's time somebody got women like you told," Gloria said, moving over and standing with her back to the door, as if to keep them in, "and I'm just the baby to do it. You're the kind of bitches who sneak in the toilet to read dirty books and tell filthy stories and then go out and try to spoil somebody else's fun——"

"You move away from that door, young woman, and let us out of here!" Mrs. Higby shrieked. "I refuse to listen to you. I'm a respectable woman. I'm a Sunday School teacher——"

"I don't move a f — — inch until I finish," Gloria said.

"Gloria——"

"Your Morals League and your goddam women's clubs," she said, ignoring me completely, "—filled with meddlesome old bitches who haven't had a lay in twenty years. Why don't you old dames go out and buy a lay once in a while? That's all that's wrong with you. . . ."

Mrs. Higby advanced on Gloria, her arm raised as if to strike her.

"Go on—hit me," Gloria said, not moving. "Hit me!—You even touch me and I'll kick your f — — head off!"

"You—goddam—whore!" Mrs. Higby said, furious with passion.

The door opened, bumping Gloria away from it. Socks and Rocky came in.

"This—this—" Mrs. Higby said, shaking her finger at Gloria.

"Don't stutter," Gloria said, "—say it. You know how to say the word. Whore. W-h-o——"

"Pipe down!" Socks said. "Ladies, me and my assistant have decided to take any suggestions you have to offer——"

"Our suggestion is you close this place at once!" Mrs. Higby said. "Else we shall go to the City Council in the morning——"

She started out, followed by Mrs. Witcher.

"Young woman," Mrs. Higby said to Gloria, "you ought to be in a reform school!"

"I was in one once," Gloria said. "There was a dame just like you in charge. She was a lesbian. . . ."

Mrs. Higby gasped again and went out, followed by Mrs. Witcher.

Gloria slammed the door behind them, then sat down in a chair and began sobbing. She covered her face with her hands and tried to fight it off, but it was no use. She slowly leaned forward in the chair, bending double, shaking and twitching with emotion, as if she had completely lost control of the upper half of her body. For a full moment the only sounds in the room were her sobs and the rise and fall of the ocean which came through the half-raised window.

Then Socks went over and laid his hand tenderly on Gloria's head. "Nix, kid, nix—" he said.

"Keep all this under your hat," Rocky said to me. "Don't say anything to the others——"

"I won't," I said. "Does this mean we'll have to close up?"

"I don't think so," Socks said. "It just means we'll have to try to grease somebody. I'll talk to my lawyer in the morning. In the meantime, Rocky—break the news to Ruby. She's got

to quit. A lot of women have been squawking about her—"
He looked at the door. "I should have stuck to my own
racket," he said. "Goddam bastard women . . ."

. . . EXECUTED AND PUT TO DEATH . . .

II

```
HOURS ELAPSED . . . . . . 855
Couples Remaining . . . . . . 21
```

MARATHON DANCE WAR STILL RAGES

Mothers' League Threatens
Mass Meeting Unless City
Council Will Close Contest

IS THIRD DAY OF CONTROVERSY

The Mothers' League for Good Morals continued their war on the marathon dance today, threatening to take the issue directly to the citizens themselves unless the City Council closes the contest. The marathon dance has been in progress at a beach resort for the past 36 days.

Mrs. J. Franklin Higby and Mrs. William Wallace Witcher, president and first vice-president of the Morals League, appeared before the City Council again this afternoon, protesting the continuance of the dance. They were told by the Council that the City Attorney was making a thorough study of the law to determine what legal steps could be taken.

"We can't take any action until we know how the law reads," Tom Hinsdell, Council chief, said. "So far we have failed to find any specific statute that covers this case, but the City Attorney is examining all the codes."

"Would the City Council hesitate if a plague threatened our city?" Mrs. Higby said. "Certainly it wouldn't. If there are no specific laws to fit this situation let them pass emergency laws. The marathon dance is a plague—it is low and degrading and in the same hall there is a public bar that is a rendezvous for gangsters, racketeers and notorious criminals. Surely this is not the proper atmosphere for children . . ."

I handed the newspaper back to Mrs. Layden. "Mr. Donald told us his lawyer said the city couldn't do anything," I said.

"That doesn't make much difference," Mrs. Layden said. "Those women are out to close it and law or no law, they'll do it."

"I don't see any harm in the marathon," I said, "but they're right about the bar. I've seen a lot of tough characters in the Palm Garden. . . . How long do you think it'll take them to close us up?"

"I don't know," she said. "But they'll close it. What are you going to do then?"

"The first thing I'm going to do is get a lot of sun," I said. "I used to love the rain and hate the sun, but now it's the other way around. You don't get much sun in here——"

"After that what are you going to do?"

"I haven't made any plans," I said.

"I see. Where's Gloria?"

"She's putting on her track suit. She'll be out in a minute."

"She's beginning to weaken, isn't she? The doctor said he had to look at her heart several times a day."

"That doesn't mean anything," I said. "He looks at all of them. Gloria's all right."

Gloria wasn't all right and I knew it. We were having a lot of trouble with the derbies. I never will know how we got by the last two nights. Gloria was in and out of the pit a dozen times in the two races. But I didn't jump at conclusions simply because the doctor examined her heart six or seven times a day. I knew he could never locate her trouble with a stethoscope.

"Lean over here, Robert," Mrs. Layden said. It was the first time she had ever used my given name and I was a little embarrassed. I leaned over the railing, swaying my body so nobody could say I was violating the rules of the contest by not being in motion. The hall was packed and jammed. "You know I'm your friend, don't you?" Mrs. Layden said.

"Yes'm, I know that."

"You know I got you your sponsor, don't you?"

"Yes'm, I know that."

"You trust me, don't you?"

"Yes'm, I trust you."

"Robert—Gloria's not the right kind of girl for you."

I didn't say anything, wondering what was coming next. I had never been able to understand why Mrs. Layden had taken such an interest in me unless . . . But it couldn't be that. She was old enough to be my grandmother.

"She'll never be any good," Mrs. Layden said. "She's an evil person and she'll wreck your life. You don't want your life wrecked, do you?"

"She's not going to wreck my life," I said.

"Promise me when you get out of this you'll never see her again."

"Oh, I'm not going to marry her or anything like that," I said. "I'm not in love with her. She's all right. She just gets a little depressed sometimes."

"She's not depressed," Mrs. Layden said. "She's bitter. She hates everything and everybody. She's cruel and she's dangerous."

"I didn't know you felt that way about her, Mrs. Layden."

"I'm an old woman," she said. "I'm a very, very—old, old woman. I know what I'm talking about. When this thing is over— Robert," she said suddenly, "I'm not as poor as you think I am. I look poor but I'm not poor at all. I'm rich. I'm very rich. I'm very eccentric. When you get out of here——"

"Hello—" Gloria said, coming from nowhere.

"——Hello," Mrs. Layden said.

"What's the matter?" Gloria asked quickly. "Am I interrupting something?"

"You're not interrupting anything," I told her.

Mrs. Layden opened the newspaper and started reading it. Gloria and I walked towards the platform.

"What was she saying about me?" Gloria asked.

"Nothing," I said. "We were just talking about the marathon closing——"

"You were talking about something else too. Why did she shut up like a clam when I got there?"

"You're imagining things—" I said.

"Ladies and gentlemen—" Rocky said into the microphone, "—or maybe after reading the newspapers," he went on when the crowd had quieted down, "I should say—Fellow Morons." There was a big laugh at this; the crowd knew what

he meant. "You can see we're still going in the world's champion marathon dance," he said, "and we'll keep on going
until only one contestant is left—the final winner. I want to
thank you very much for coming out tonight and I'd like to
remind you that tomorrow night is the night you can't afford
to miss—our big public wedding, when Couple No. 71—Vee
Lovell and Mary Hawley—will be married right here before
your very eyes by a well-known minister of the city. If you
haven't made your reservations you better do so at once——

"And now, before the derby starts, I'd like to introduce a
few of our celebrities—" He looked at a piece of paper. "Ladies and gentlemen, one of our honor guests is none other
than that handsome screen star, Bill Boyd. Will you take a
bow, Mr. Boyd?——"

Bill (Screen) Boyd stood up, taking a bow, while the audience applauded.

"Next, another screen and stage star—Ken Murray. Mr.
Murray has a party of distinguished guests with him. I wonder
if he'd come up to the platform and introduce them himself?——"

The audience applauded loudly. Murray hesitated, but finally stepped over the railing and went to the platform.

"All right, folks—" he said, taking the microphone. "First
a young featured player, Miss Anita Louise——"

Miss Louise stood.

"——and now Miss June Clyde——"

Miss Clyde stood.

"——Miss Sue Carol——"

Miss Carol stood.

"——Tom Brown——"

Tom Brown stood.

"——Thornton Freeland——"

Thornton Freeland stood.

"——and that's all, folks——"

Murray shook hands with Rocky and went back to his party.

"Ladies and gentlemen—" Rocky said.

"There's a big director over there he didn't introduce," I
said to Gloria. "There's Frank Borzage. Let's go speak to
him——"

"For what?" Gloria said.

"He's a director, isn't he? He might help you get in pictures——"

"The hell with pictures," Gloria said. "I wish I was dead——"

"I'm going," I said.

I strolled down the floor in front of the boxes, feeling very self-conscious. Two or three times I almost lost my nerve and turned back.

"It's worth it," I told myself. "He's one of the finest directors in the world. Some day I'll be as famous as he is and then I'll remind him of this——"

"Hello, Mr. Borzage," I said.

"Hello, son," he said. "Are you going to win tonight?"

"I hope so . . . I saw 'No Greater Glory.' I thought it was swell," I said.

"I'm glad you liked it——"

"That's what I want to be some day," I said. "A director like you——"

"I hope you are," he said.

"Well——" I said, "good-bye——"

I went back to the platform.

"That was Frank Borzage," I said to Kid Kamm.

"Yeah?——"

"He's a big director," I explained.

"Oh—," the Kid said.

"All right—" Rocky said. "Are the judges ready? Have they got their score sheets, Rollo? —All right, kids——"

We moved out to the starting line.

"Let's not take any chances tonight," I whispered to Gloria. "We can't fool around——"

"On your marks, there, kids," Rocky said. "Stand by nurses and trainers— Hold your hats, ladies and gentlemen— Orchestra, get ready to give——"

He shot the pistol himself.

Gloria and I jumped away, pushing through into second place, directly behind Kid Kamm and Jackie Miller. They were in front, the position usually held by James and Ruby Bates. As I went into the first turn I thought about James and Ruby, wondering where they were. It didn't seem like a derby without them.

At the finish of the first lap Mack Aston and Bess Cartwright sprinted in front of us and went into second place. I began to heel-and-toe faster than I ever had before. I knew I had to. All the weaklings had been eliminated. All these couples were fast.

I stayed in third place for six or seven laps and the audience began howling and yelling for us to move up. I was afraid to try that. You can pass a fast team only on the turn and that takes a lot of energy. So far Gloria was holding up fine and I didn't want to put too much pressure on her. I wasn't worried as long as she could keep propelling herself.

After eight minutes I commenced to get hot. I yanked off my sweatshirt and tossed it to a trainer. Gloria did likewise. Most of the girls were out of their sweatshirts now and the audience was howling. When the girls removed their sweatshirts they wore only small brassieres, and as they trotted around the track their breasts bounced up and down.

"Everything is fine now unless somebody challenges us," I told myself.

Just then we were challenged. Pedro Ortega and Lillian Bacon sped up alongside, trying to get inside at the turn. This was about the only way to pass a couple but it was not as easy as it sounds. You had to get at least two paces ahead on the straightaway and then swing sharply over at the turn. This was what Pedro had in the back of his mind. They collided with us at the turn, but Gloria managed to keep her feet and I dragged her through, holding our place.

I heard the audience gasp and I knew that meant somebody was staggering. In a moment more I heard a body hit the floor. I didn't look around; I kept pounding. This was old stuff to me now. When I got on the straightaway and could look without breaking my stride, I saw it was Mary Hawley, Vee Lovell's partner, who was in the pit. The nurses and trainers were working on her and the doctor was using his stethoscope——

"Give the solo the inside, kids—" Rocky yelled.

I moved over and Vee passed me. Now he had to make two laps to our one. He glanced in the pit as he passed, a look of agony on his face. I knew he was not in pain; he was only wondering when his partner would be out. . . . On his fourth solo lap she got up, coupling on again.

I signaled to the nurse for a wet towel and on the next lap she slammed it around my neck. I stuck the end of it between my teeth.

"Four minutes to go—" Rocky yelled.

This was one of the closest derbies we'd ever had. The Kid and Jackie were setting a terrific pace. I knew Gloria and I were in no danger as long as we held our own, but you never could tell when your partner would collapse. Past a certain point you kept moving automatically, without actually being conscious of moving. One moment you would be traveling at top speed and the next moment you started falling. This was what I was afraid of with Gloria—collapsing. She was beginning to drag on my belt a little.

"Keep going!" I shouted to her in my mind, slowing down a fraction, hoping to relieve the strain on her. Pedro and Lillian evidently had been waiting for this. They shot by us on the turn, taking third place. Directly behind me I could hear the pounding of the others and I realized the entire field was bunched at Gloria's heels. I had absolutely no margin now.

I hitched my hip up high. That was a signal for Gloria to shift her hold on the belt. She did, changing to the right hand.

"Thank God," I said to myself. That was a good sign. That proved she was thinking all right.

"One minute to go—" Rocky announced.

I put on the steam now. Kid Kamm and Jackie had slowed the pace somewhat, thus slowing Mack and Bess and Pedro and Lillian. Gloria and I were between them and the others. It was a bad position. I prayed that nobody behind us had the energy for a spurt because I realized that the slightest bump would break Gloria's stride and put her on the floor. And if anybody hit the floor now . . .

I used every ounce of my strength to move up, to get just one step ahead, to remove that threat from behind. . . . When the gun sounded for the finish I turned around to catch Gloria. But she didn't faint. She staggered into my arms, shiny with perspiration, fighting to get air.

"Want a nurse?" Rocky yelled from the platform.

"She's all right," I said. "Let her rest a minute——"

Most of the girls were being helped into the dressing room, but the boys crowded around the platform to see who had been disqualified. The judges had handed their tally sheets to Rollo and Rocky, who were checking them.

"Ladies and gentlemen—" Rocky announced in a minute or two. "Here are the results of the most sensational derby you have ever seen. First place—Couple No. 18, Kid Kamm and Jackie Miller. Second place—Mack Aston and Bess Cartwright. Third place—Pedro Ortega and Lillian Bacon. Fourth place—Robert Syverten and Gloria Beatty. Those were the winners—and now, the losers—the last team to finish—the couple that, under the rules and regulations, is disqualified and out of the marathon dance. That is Couple No. 11—Jere Flint and Vera Rosenfield——"

"You're crazy!" Jere Flint shouted, loud enough for everybody in the hall to hear. "That's wrong—" he said, moving closer to the platform.

"Look at 'em yourself," Rocky said, handing him the tally sheets.

"I wish it had been us," Gloria said, lifting her head. "I wish I had thrown the race——"

"Sh-h-h—" I said.

"I don't give a damn what these score cards say; they're wrong," Jere Flint said, handing them back to Rocky. "I know they're wrong. How the hell could we get eliminated when we weren't last?"

"Are you able to keep track of the laps while you're racing?" Rocky asked. He was trying to show Jere up. He knew it wasn't possible for anybody to do that.

"I can't do that," Jere said. "But I know we didn't go into the pit and Mary did. We started ahead of Vee and Mary and we finished ahead of 'em——"

"How about that, mister?" Rocky said to a man standing near-by. "You checked Couple No. 11——"

"You're mistaken, fellow," the man said to Jere. "I checked you carefully——"

"It's too bad, son," Socks Donald said, coming through the crowd of judges. "You had tough luck——"

"It wasn't tough luck; it was a goddam frame-up," Jere

said. "You ain't kidding anybody. If Vee and Mary had been eliminated you wouldn't have a wedding tomorrow——"

"Now—now—" Socks said. "You run on to the dressing room——"

"Okay," Jere said. He walked over to the man who had kept check on him and Vera. "How much is Socks giving you for this?" he asked.

"I don't know what you're talking about——"

Jere turned sidewise, slamming the man in the mouth with his fist, knocking him down.

Socks ran over to Jere, squaring off, glaring at him his hand in his hip pocket.

"If you pull that blackjack on me I'll make you eat it," Jere told him. Then he walked away, going across the floor towards the dressing room.

The audience was standing, jabbering, trying to see what was going on.

"Let's get dressed," I said to Gloria.

. . . UPON
THE 19TH DAY
OF THE MONTH
OF SEPTEMBER,
IN THE YEAR
OF OUR LORD,
1935 . . .

> HOURS ELAPSED 879
> Couples Remaining 20

A LL DAY Gloria had been very morbid. I asked her a hundred times what she was thinking about. "Nothing,"
she would reply. *I realize now how stupid I was. I should have
known what she was thinking. Now that I look back on that last
night I don't see how I possibly could have been so stupid. But
in those days I was dumb about a lot of things . . . The judge
is sitting up there, making his speech, looking through his glasses
at me, but his words are doing the same thing to my body that
his eyesight is doing to his glasses—going right through without
stopping, rushing out of the way of each succeeding look and
each succeeding word. I am not hearing the judge with my ears
and my brain any more than the lenses of his glasses are catching
and imprisoning each look that comes through them. I hear him
with my feet and my legs and torso and arms, with everything
but my ears and brain. With my ears and brain I hear a newsboy in the street shouting something about King Alexander, I
hear the rolling of the street cars, I hear automobiles, I hear the
warning bells of the traffic semaphores; in the courtroom I hear
people breathing and moving their feet, I hear the wood squeak-
ing in a bench, I hear the light splash as someone spits in the
cuspidor. All these things I hear with my ears and my brain, but
I hear the judge with my body only. If you ever hear a judge say
to you what this one is saying to me, you will know what I mean.*

This was one day Gloria had no reason to be morbid. The
crowds had been coming and going all day, since noon the
place had been packed, and now, just before the wedding,
there were very few vacant seats left and most of them had
been reserved. The entire hall had been decorated with so
many flags and so much red, white and blue bunting that you
expected any moment to hear firecrackers go off and the band

play the national anthem. The whole day had been full of excitement: the workmen decorating the interior, the big crowds, the rehearsals for the wedding, the rumors that the Morals League women were coming down to set fire to the hall—and the two complete new outfits the Jonathan Beer people had sent Gloria and me.

This was one day Gloria had no reason to be morbid, but she was more morbid than ever.

"Son—" a man called from a box. I had never seen him before. He was motioning for me to come over.

"You won't be in that seat long," I told him in my mind. "That's Mrs. Layden's regular seat. When she comes you'll have to move."

"Aren't you the boy of Couple 22?" he asked.

"Yessir," I said.

"Where's your partner?"

"She's down there—" I replied, pointing towards the platform where Gloria stood with the other girls.

"Get her," the man said. "I want to meet her."

"All right," I said, going to get Gloria. "Now who can that be?" I asked myself.

"There's a man down here who wants to meet you," I said to Gloria.

"I don't want to meet anybody."

"This man's no bum," I said. "He's well-dressed. He looks like somebody."

"I don't care what he looks like," she said.

"He may be a producer," I said. "Maybe you've made a hit with him. Maybe this is your break."

"The hell with my break," she said.

"Come on," I said. "The man's waiting."

She finally came with me.

"This motion picture business is a lousy business," she said. "You have to meet people you don't want to meet and you have to be nice to people whose guts you hate. I'm glad I'm through with it."

"You're just starting with it," I said, trying to cheer her up. *I never paid any attention to her remark then, but now I realize it was the most significant thing she had ever said.*

"Here she is—" I said to the man.

"You don't know who I am, do you?" the man asked.

"No, sir——"

"My name is Maxwell," he said. "I'm the advertising manager for Jonathan Beer."

"How do you do, Mr. Maxwell," I said, reaching over to shake hands with him. "This is my partner, Gloria Beatty. I want to thank you for sponsoring us."

"Don't thank me," he said. "Thank Mrs. Layden. She brought you to my attention. Did you get your packages today?"

"Yessir," I said, "and they came just in time. We certainly needed clothes. These marathon dances are pretty hard on your clothes— Have you ever been here before?"

"No, and I wouldn't be here now if Mrs. Layden hadn't insisted. She's been telling me about the derbies. Are you having one tonight?"

"A little thing like a wedding couldn't stop the derby," I said. "It goes on right after the ceremony——"

"So long—" Gloria said, walking off.

"Did I say something wrong?" Mr. Maxwell asked.

"No, sir—she's got to go down there and get her final instructions. The wedding starts pretty soon."

He frowned and I could tell he knew I was merely lying to cover Gloria's bad manners. He watched Gloria walking down the floor a minute and then looked back at me. "What chance do you have to win the derby tonight?" he asked.

"We've got a good chance," I said. "Of course, the big thing is not so much to win as it is to keep from losing. If you finish last you're disqualified."

"Suppose Jonathan Beer offered twenty-five dollars to the winner," he said. "You think you'd have a chance to get it?"

"We'll certainly try like the devil," I told him.

"In that case—all right," he said, looking me up and down. "Mrs. Layden tells me you're ambitious to get in the movies?"

"I am," I said. "Not as an actor though. I want to be a director."

"You wouldn't like a job in the brewery business, eh?"

"I don't believe I would——"

"Have you ever directed a picture?"

"No, sir, but I'm not afraid to try it. I know I could make

good," I said. "Oh, I don't mean a big feature like Boles-lawsky or Mamoulian or King Vidor would make—I mean something else at first——"

"For instance——"

"Well, like a two- or three-reel short. What a junkman does all day, or the life of an ordinary man—you know, who makes thirty dollars a week and has to raise kids and buy a home and a car and a radio—the kind of a guy bill collectors are always after. Something different, with camera angles to help tell the story——"

"I see—" he said.

"I didn't mean to bore you," I said, "but it's so seldom I can find anybody who'll listen to me that when I do I never know when to stop talking."

"I'm not bored. As a matter of fact, I'm very much inter-ested," he said. "But maybe I've said too much myself——"

"Good evening—" Mrs. Layden said, entering the box. Mr. Maxwell stood up. "That's my seat, John," Mrs. Layden said. "You sit over here." Mr. Maxwell laughed and took another chair. "My, my, don't you look handsome," Mrs. Layden said to me.

"This is the first time in my life I ever had on a tuxedo," I said blushing. "Mr. Donald rented tuxedoes for all the boys and dresses for the girls. We're all in the wedding march."

"What do you think of him, John?" Mrs. Layden asked Mr. Maxwell.

"He's all right," Mr. Maxwell said.

"I trust John's judgment implicitly," Mrs. Layden said to me. I began to understand now why Mr. Maxwell had asked me all those questions.

"——Down this way, you kids—" Rocky said into the mi-crophone. "Down this way— Ladies and gentlemen. We are about to have the public wedding between Couple No. 71— Vee Lovell and Mary Hawley—and please remember, the en-tertainment for the night is not over when the marriage is finished. That's only the beginnin'—" he said; "—only the beginnin'. After the wedding we have the derby——"

He leaned over while Socks Donald whispered something to him.

"Ladies and gentlemen," Rocky announced, "I take great

pleasure in introducing the minister who will perform the service—a minister you all know, Rev. Oscar Gilder. Will you come up, Mr. Gilder?"

The minister came out on the floor and walked towards the platform while the audience applauded.

"Get your places," Socks said to us. We went to our assigned positions, the girls on one side of the platform and the boys on the other.

"Before the grand march starts," Rocky said, "I want to thank those who have made this feature possible." He looked at a sheet of paper. "The bride's wedding gown," he said, "was donated by Mr. Samuels of the Bon-Ton Shop. Will you stand, Mr. Samuels?"

Mr. Samuels stood, bowing to the applause.

"Her shoes were donated by the Main Street Slipper Shop— Is Mr. Davis here? Stand up, Mr. Davis."

Mr. Davis stood.

"——Her stockings and silken—er—you-know-whats were donated by the Polly-Darling Girls' Bazaar. Mr. Lightfoot, where are you?——"

Mr. Lightfoot stood as the audience howled.

"——and her hair was marcelled by the Pompadour Beauty Shop. Is Miss Smith here?"

Miss Smith stood.

"——And the groom's outfit, from head to foot, was donated by the Tower Outfitting Company. Mr. Tower——"

Mr. Tower stood.

"——All the flowers in the hall and that the girls are wearing are the gift of the Sycamore Ridge Nursery. Mr. Dupré——"

Mr. Dupré stood.

"——And now, ladies and gentlemen, I turn the microphone over to the Rev. Oscar Gilder, who will perform the ceremony for these marvelous kids——"

He handed the microphone stand to Rollo, who stood it on the floor in front of the platform. Rev. Gilder moved behind it, nodding to the orchestra, and the wedding march began.

The procession started, the boys on one side and the girls on the other, going down to the end of the hall and then back to the minister. It was the first time I had seen some of the girls when they weren't in slacks or track suits.

We had rehearsed the march twice that afternoon, being taught to come to a full stop after each step before taking another. When the bride and groom came into view from behind the platform, the audience cheered and applauded.

Mrs. Layden nodded to me as I passed.

At the platform we took our places while Vee and Mary, and Kid Kamm and Jackie Miller, the best man and the maid-of-honor continued to where the minister was standing. He motioned for the orchestra to stop and began the ceremony. All during the ceremony I kept looking at Gloria. I hadn't had a chance to tell her how rude she had been to Mr. Maxwell, so I tried to catch her eye to let her know I had plenty to tell her when we got together.

"——And I now pronounce you man and wife——" Dr. Gilder said. He bowed his head and began to pray:

The Lord is my shepherd; I shall not want. He maketh me to lie down in green pastures: he leadeth me beside the still waters. He restoreth my soul: he leadeth me in the paths of righteousness for his name's sake. Yea, though I walk through the valley of the shadow of death, I will fear no evil: for thou art with me; thy rod and thy staff they comfort me. Thou preparest a table before me in the presence of mine enemies: thou anointest my head with oil; my cup runneth over. Surely goodness and mercy shall follow me all the days of my life; and I will dwell in the house of the Lord for ever.

. . . When the minister had finished Vee kissed Mary timidly on the cheek and we swarmed around. The hall rocked with applause and shouts.

"Just a minute—just a minute—" Rocky yelled into the microphone. "Just a minute, ladies and gentlemen——"

The confusion died down and at that moment, at the opposite end of the hall, in the Palm Garden, there was the clear, distinct sound of glass shattering.

"Don't—" a man screamed. Five shots followed this, so close together they sounded like one solid strip of noise.

Instantly the audience roared.

"Keep your seats—keep your seats—" Rocky yelled. . . .

The other boys and girls were running towards the Palm

Garden to see what had happened, and I joined them. Socks Donald passed me, reaching into his hip pocket.

I jumped over the railing into an empty box and followed Socks into the Palm Garden. A crowd of people were standing in a circle, looking down and jabbering to each other. Socks pushed through and I followed him.

A man was dead on the floor.

"Who did it?" Socks asked.

"A guy over there—" somebody said.

Socks pushed out with me behind him. I was a little surprised to discover Gloria was directly behind me.

The man who had done the shooting was standing at the bar, leaning on his elbow. Blood was streaming down his face. Socks went up to him.

"He started it, Socks," the man said. "—He was trying to kill me with a beer bottle——"

"Monk, you son of a bitch—" Socks said, hitting him in the face with the blackjack. Monk sagged against the bar but did not fall. Socks continued to hit him in the face with the blackjack, again and again and again, splattering blood all over everything and everybody nearby. He literally beat the man to the floor.

"Hey, Socks—" somebody called.

Thirty feet away there was another group of people standing in a circle, looking down and jabbering to each other. We pushed our way through—and there she lay.

"Goddam—" Socks Donald said.

It was Mrs. Layden, a single hole in the front of her forehead. John Maxwell was kneeling beside her, holding her head . . . then he placed the head gently on the floor, and stood up. Mrs. Layden's head slowly turned sidewise and a little pool of blood that had collected in the crater of her eye spilled out on the floor.

John Maxwell saw Gloria and me.

"She was coming around to be a judge in the derby," he said. "She was hit by a stray bullet——"

"I wish it was me—" Gloria said under her breath.

"Goddam—" Socks Donald said.

We were all assembled in the girls' dressing room. There

were very few people outside in the hall, only the police and several reporters.

"I guess you kids know why I got you in here," Socks said slowly, "and I guess you know what I'm going to say. There ain't no use for anybody to feel bad about what's happened—it's just one of those things. It's tough on you kids and it's tough on me. We had just got the marathon started good——

"Rocky and I have been talking it over and we've decided to take the thousand-dollar prize and split it up between all of you—and I'm going to throw in another grand myself. That'll give everybody fifty bucks a piece. Is that fair?"

"Yes—" we said.

"Don't you think there's any chance to keep going?" Kid Kamm asked.

"Not a chance," Socks said, shaking his head. "Not with that Purity League after us——"

"Kids," Rocky said, "we've had a lot of fun and I've enjoyed working with you. Maybe some time we can have another marathon dance——"

"When do we get this dough?" Vee Lovell asked.

"In the morning," Socks said. "Any of you kids that want to can stay here tonight, just like you been doing. But if you want to leave, there's nothing to stop you. I'll have the dough for you in the morning any time after ten. Now, I'll say so-long— I got to go to police headquarters."

...IN
THE MANNER
PROVIDED BY
THE LAWS
OF
THE STATE
OF
CALIFORNIA.
AND...

GLORIA and I walked across the dance floor, my heels making so much noise I couldn't be sure they belonged to me. Rocky was standing at the front door with a policeman.

"Where you kids going?" Rocky asked.

"To get some air," Gloria said.

"Coming back?"

"We'll be back," I told him. "We're just going to get a little air. It's been a long time since we been outside——"

"Don't be long," Rocky said, looking at Gloria and wetting his lips significantly.

"F—— you," Gloria said, going outside.

It was after two o'clock in the morning. The air was damp and thick and clean. It was so thick and so clean I could feel my lungs biting it off in huge chunks.

"I bet you are glad to get that kind of air," I said to my lungs.

I turned around and looked at the building.

"So that's where we've been all the time," I said. "Now I know how Jonah felt when he looked at the whale."

"Come on," Gloria said.

We walked around the side of the building onto the pier. It stretched out over the ocean as far as I could see, rising and falling and groaning and creaking with the movements of the water.

"It's a wonder the waves don't wash this pier away," I said.

"You're hipped on the subject of waves," Gloria said.

"No, I'm not," I said.

"That's all you've been talking about for a month——"

"All right, stand still a minute and you'll see what I mean. You can feel it rising and falling——"

"I can feel it without standing still," she said, "but that's no reason to get yourself in a sweat. It's been going on for a million years."

"Don't think I'm crazy about this ocean," I said. "It'll be all right with me if I never see it again. I've had enough ocean to last me the rest of my life."

We sat down on a bench that was wet with spray. Up towards the end of the pier several men were fishing over the
railing. The night was black; there was no moon, no stars. An
irregular line of white foam marked the shore.

"This air is fine," I said.

Gloria said nothing, staring into the distance. Far down the
shore on a point there were lights.

"That's Malibu," I said. "Where all the movie stars live."

"What are you going to do now?" she finally said.

"I don't know exactly. I thought I'd go see Mr. Maxwell
tomorrow. Maybe I could get him to do something. He certainly seemed interested."

"Always tomorrow," she said. "The big break is always
coming tomorrow."

Two men passed by, carrying deep-sea fishing poles. One
of them was dragging a four-foot hammerhead shark behind
him.

"This baby'll never do any more damage," he said to the
other man. . . .

"What are you going to do?" I asked Gloria.

"I'm going to get off this merry-go-round," she said. "I'm
through with the whole stinking thing."

"What thing?"

"Life," she said.

"Why don't you try to help yourself?" I said. "You got the
wrong attitude about everything."

"Don't lecture to me," she said.

"I'm not lecturing," I said, "but you ought to change your
attitude. On the level. It affects everybody you come in contact with. Take me, for example. Before I met you I didn't
see how I could miss succeeding. I never even thought of
failing. And now——"

"Who taught you that speech?" she asked. "You never
thought that up by yourself."

"Yes, I did," I said.

She looked down the ocean towards Malibu. "Oh, what's
the use in me kidding myself——" she said in a moment. "I
know where I stand . . ."

I did not say anything, looking at the ocean and thinking
about Hollywood, wondering if I'd ever been there or

was I going to wake up in a minute back in Arkansas and have to hurry down and get my newspapers before it got daylight.

"—Sonofabitch," Gloria was saying to herself. "You needn't look at me that way," she said. "I know I'm no good——"

"She's right," I said to myself; "she's exactly right. She's no good——"

"I wish I'd died that time in Dallas," she said. "I always will think that doctor saved my life for just one reason——"

I did not say anything to that, still looking at the ocean and thinking how exactly right she was about being no good and that it was too bad she didn't die that time in Dallas. She certainly would have been better off dead.

"I'm just a misfit. I haven't got anything to give anybody," she was saying. "Stop looking at me that way," she said.

"I'm not looking at you any way," I said. "You can't see my face——"

"Yes, I can," she said.

She was lying. She couldn't see my face. It was too dark.

"Don't you think we ought to go inside?" I said. "Rocky wanted to see you——"

"That p——k," she said. "I know what he wants, but he'll never get it again. Nobody else will, either."

"What?" I said.

"Don't you know?"

"Don't I know what," I said.

"What Rocky wants."

"Oh—" I said. "Sure. It just dawned on me."

"That's all any man wants," she said, "but that's all right. Oh, I didn't mind giving it to Rocky; he was doing me as much of a favor as I did him—but suppose I get caught?"

"You're not just thinking of that, are you?" I asked.

"Yes, I am. Always before this time I was able to take care of myself. Suppose I do have a kid?" she said. "You know what it'll grow up to be, don't you. Just like us."

"She's right," I said to myself; "she's exactly right. It'll grow up to be just like us——"

"I don't want that," she said. "Anyway, I'm finished. I think it's a lousy world and I'm finished. I'd be better off dead and so would everybody else. I ruin everything I get around. You said so yourself."

"When did I say anything like that?"

"A few minutes ago. You said before you met me you never even thought of failing. . . . Well, it isn't my fault. I can't help it. I tried to kill myself once, but I didn't and I've never had the nerve to try again. . . . You want to do the world a favor? . . ." she asked.

I did not say anything, listening to the ocean sloshle against the pilings, feeling the pier rise and fall, and thinking that she was right about everything she had said.

Gloria was fumbling in her purse. When her hand came out it was holding a small pistol. I had never seen the pistol before, but I was not surprised. I was not in the least surprised.

"Here—" she said, offering it to me.

"I don't want it. Put it away," I said. "Come on, let's go back inside. I'm cold——"

"Take it and pinch-hit for God," she said, pressing it into my hand. "Shoot me. It's the only way to get me out of my misery."

"She's right," I said to myself. "It's the only way to get her out of her misery." *When I was a little kid I used to spend the summers on my grandfather's farm in Arkansas. One day I was standing by the smoke-house watching my grandmother making lye soap in a big iron kettle when my grandfather came across the yard, very excited. "Nellie broke her leg," my grandfather said. My grandmother and I went over the stile into the garden where my grandfather had been plowing. Old Nellie was on the ground whimpering, still hitched to the plow. We stood there looking at her, just looking at her. My grandfather came back with the gun he had carried at Chickamauga Ridge. "She stepped in a hole," he said, patting Nellie's head. My grandmother turned me around, facing the other way. I started crying. I heard a shot. I still hear that shot. I ran over and fell down on the ground, hugging her neck. I loved that horse. I hated my grandfather. I got up and went to him, beating his legs with my fists. . . . Later that day he explained that he loved Nellie too, but that he had to shoot her. "It was the kindest thing to do," he said. "She was no more good. It was the only way to get her out of her misery. . . ."*

I had the pistol in my hand.

"All right," I said to Gloria. "Say when."

"I'm ready."

"Where?——"

"Right here. In the side of my head."

The pier jumped as a big wave broke.

"Now?——"

"Now."

I shot her.

The pier moved again, and the water made a sucking noise as it slipped back into the ocean.

I threw the pistol over the railing.

One policeman sat in the rear with me while the other one drove. We were traveling very fast and the siren was blowing. It was the same kind of a siren they had used at the marathon dance when they wanted to wake us up.

"Why did you kill her?" the policeman in the rear seat asked.

"She asked me to," I said.

"You hear that, Ben?"

"Ain't he an obliging bastard?" Ben said, over his shoulder.

"Is that the only reason you got?" the policeman in the rear seat asked.

"They shoot horses, don't they?" I said.

. . .MAY GOD HAVE MERCY ON YOUR SOUL. . .

THIEVES LIKE US

by Edward Anderson

To

MY COUSIN AND MY WIFE

BECAUSE THERE I WAS WITH AN EMPTY GUN
AND YOU, ROY, SUPPLIED THE AMMUNITION
AND YOU, ANNE, DIRECTED MY AIM

"Men do not despise a thief, if he steal to satisfy his soul when he is hungry; but if he be found, he shall restore sevenfold; he shall give all the substance of his house."

—*Proverbs of Solomon.*

Chapter I

THERE was no doubt about it this time: over yonder behind the rise of scrub-oak, the automobile had left the highway and was laboring in low gear over the rutted road to where they waited. Like a saliva-wettened finger scorching across a hot iron, Bowie's insides spitted. He looked at Chicamaw.

Chicamaw's eyes were fixed up the weed-grown road, his thick-soled, convict shoes quiet on the rain-sprinkled earth that he had scarred with pacing. "That's him," he said.

Bowie looked behind him, across the creek's ridge of trees and over the field where the blades of the young corn glimmered like knives in the late-afternoon sun. Above the white-washed walls of Alcatona Penitentiary reared the red-painted water-tank, the big cottonwood tree of the Upper Yard and the guards' towers.

The car was coming on. The jew's-harp twanging of the grasshoppers in the broomweeds seemed to heighten. I can rib myself up to do anything, Bowie thought. Anything. Every day in that place over there is wasted.

The car's springs creaked nearer. Bowie looked at Chicamaw again. "You're not planning on going some place, are you?"

Chicamaw did not move his head. "I'm just waitin' to see a horse about a feller," he said.

The taxicab bumped around the hill and wallowed toward them. Bowie squinted to see better. The figure in the back seat had on a straw hat. It was old T-Dub though. Come on, you cotton-headed old soldier!

The driver was that Kid that had been peddling marihuana to some of the boys. Jasbo they called him.

The cab stopped a few feet away and Bowie and Chicamaw moved toward it.

"Hello, Bowie," Jasbo said.

Bowie did not look at him. "Hi," he said.

T-Dub sat there with a big, paper-wrapped bundle across his knees. The yellow brightness of the new hat made his blond hair look like dry corn-silk.

"Well, what we waitin' on?" Chicamaw said. He opened the door.

T-Dub handed Chicamaw the bundle and then reached inside his blouse and pulled the gun. He scraped the barrel against the driver's cheek. "This is a stick-up, Jasbo," he said.

"Godamighty, Man," Jasbo said. His head quivered on a rigid neck.

Chicamaw ripped at the bundle strings and slapped at the paper. It contained blue denim overalls and white cotton shirts. He began stripping himself of his cotton-sacking prison clothing. Bowie and T-Dub began changing too.

Jasbo said: "Bowie, you know me. You tell these boys I'm all right."

"You just do what you're told," Bowie said.

"All you gotta do is tell me," Jasbo said.

Their clothing changed, Chicamaw pushed Jasbo over and got under the wheel and Bowie and T-Dub got in the back. They turned and went back up the road. On the highway, the wind began beating the speeding car like a hundred fly-swatters.

There was a car under the shed of the filling station on the right. A man in coveralls stood beside the red pump twisting the handle.

"Don't you let me see you throwing no winks, Jasbo," T-Dub said, "or I'll beat your ears down."

"I'll put my head 'tween my legs if you say so," Jasbo said.

They passed the filling station and Bowie looked back. The man was still twisting the pump handle. The empty highway behind looked like a stretching rubber band.

Bowie looked at the revolver in T-Dub's thick grasp. It was a silver-plated gun with a pearl handle. This old soldier knows what he is doing, Bowie thought. "Any rumbles in town?" he said.

T-Dub shook his head.

The highway still stretched emptily. They're finding out things back there now in the Warden's Office, Bowie thought. The Colonel's bowels are gettin' in an uproar now. Get out the stripes for that bunch of no-goods, he is saying. That's what you get for treatin' them like white men. No more baseball and passes to go fishing for that Bowie Bowers and Elmo Mobley. That T. W. Masefeld is not going to work in this prison commissary any more. Get out the dogs and the shot-guns and the .30-30's and run them sons of bitches down. . . .

A car shot up over the rise ahead, hurtled toward them. It passed with a swooshing sound. Cars coming this way don't mean nothing, Bowie thought. No more than them crows flying over yonder. T-Dub shifted the revolver to his left hand, wiped his palm on his thigh and regrasped the gun. Old T-Dub knows what he is doing.

The tendons of Chicamaw's lean neck played into two bony knots behind each ear. That Chicamaw knows what he is do-ing too. A man won't get in with two boys like this just every day. No more Time for any of them. They had shook on it.

The explosion was like the highway had snapped. The es-caping air of the right back tire wailed. The car began to bump. On the left was a sign post: *Alcatona . . . 14 miles.* It was right in the middle of thirteen, Bowie thought. Old un-lucky *thirteen.*

They bumped across the wooden bridge and moved up the dirt side road. When they were out of sight of the highway, Chicamaw stopped. The casing looked like it had been chopped with an ax. The spare was no good either.

Dusk was smoking out the ebbing glow on the horizon. Crickets in the roadside grass sounded like wind in loose tel-ephone wires. Old unlucky *thirteen* is getting us up tight, Bowie thought. Hundred and twenty-two miles to Keota and Chicamaw's cousin, Dee Mobley and our Hole and *thirteen* riding our sore backs.

Chicamaw yanked at the barbed wire of the fence with the pliers and then came back with a strand. He lashed Jasbo to the steering wheel.

They moved now across the field of growing cotton toward the farmhouse light. "This gentleman up here might have a car with some tires on it," T-Dub said.

The earth of the field was soft and the tough stalks whipped their legs. In the distance, back toward the Prison, there was the sound of baying dogs and Bowie stopped. "Man, listen to them dogs," he said. Chicamaw and T-Dub halted. It was a vibrant, sonorous sound like the musical notes of a deep reed instrument.

"Hell, them's possum hounds," Chicamaw said.

They walked faster. The cottonwood stumps squatted in the field like headless toads. The farmhouse light glowed nearer, a fierce orange. T-Dub broke into a lope and Chicamaw and Bowie followed.

The woman with the baby in her arms led T-Dub and Bowie back to the lamp-lighted kitchen and the little man at the table half turned in his chair, a raw, bitten onion in his left hand, and looked up at them, at the gun in T-Dub's hand.

"We need that car out there of yours, Mister," T-Dub said. "Come on up."

Little Man turned and put the onion on the table. There were fried eggs and yellow corn bread on the plate. He got up and pushed the chair against the table. "Where's them keys, Mama?" he said.

The skin about Mama's mouth was twitching and her lower lip looked like it was going to melt on her chin. "I don't know," she said. The baby in her arms began to whimper.

Little Man found the keys in his pocket.

T-Dub looked at Mama. "Lady, if you like this gentleman here and want to see him again and I think you do, you just don't open your mouth after we leave."

"Yessir," Mama said. She began jogging the baby up and down. It began to cry.

Dust was as thick as silk on the car's body and there were chicken droppings on the hood and fenders. Little Man got in front with Chicamaw. "I haven't had this car out in more than a month," he said.

The highway paralleled the high embankment of the Katy railroad now. Bowie watched the rising speedometer needle: *forty-five . . . fifty.* Stomp it, Chicamaw. Two pairs of nines riding our backs now. That kid Jasbo is squawking back yonder now all over the country. Ninety-nine years for highway robbery. Another pair for kidnaping.

The lights of the little highway town ahead spread with their approach and then scattered like flushed prey as they entered its limits. Under the filling-station sheds, swirling insects clouded the naked bulbs. The stores were closed; the depot dark. No Laws jumping us here, Bowie thought. No

Square-Johns with shotguns. He turned toward T-Dub. "How many miles you think we done?"

"Twenty," T-Dub said.

"My woman has been pretty sick," Little Man said. "Been awful torn up lately."

Chicamaw's head went up and down.

Awful sick or scared, Bowie thought. District 'Cuter shouting that all over the Court House won't sound so good, boys. Stomp it, Chicamaw. Fog right up this line. Hour and forty minutes like this and we'll be cooling off with Real People. That Dee Mobley was Real People. Him and Chicamaw had thieved together when they were kids. Chicamaw had been saving this Hole for eight years.

"Hasn't been well since the baby," Little Man said.

The motor coughed, spluttered. Chicamaw yanked out the choke button. The motor fired again, missed; the cylinders pumped with furious emptiness. Loose lugs rasped on the slowing wheels.

"Get her off the highway," T-Dub said. "Goose her. Gentlemen, this wins the fur-lined bathtub."

Bowie, T-Dub and Little Man pushed, their feet clopping on the pavement like horses. At last they reached the crossroads and they pushed the car up over the hump and out of sight of the highway.

Chicamaw started tying Little Man. T-Dub breathed like he had asthma. "I've had plenty of tough teaty in my day, but this is the toughest. I might as well turn this .38 on me and do it up right."

A car was coming; its headlights glowed above the hump. It sped on, its sound diminishing like the roll of a muffled drum.

"Let's get moving," Chicamaw said.

They crossed the highway, crawled through the fence and waded the hip-deep grass of the railroad right-of-way. They climbed the embankment and got down on the railroad bed.

"We could flag a car and throw down on them?" Chicamaw said.

"To hell with them hot cars," T-Dub said. "I'll walk it."

"We can do it by just keeping right down these ties," Chicamaw said.

"Like goddamned hoboes," T-Dub said.

The moon hung in the heavens like a shred of fingernail. There was only the sound of their feet crunching in the gravel. Chicamaw led.

The rails began to murmur. It was a train behind them. After a while, the locomotive's light showed, tiny as a lightning bug. It began to swell.

They climbed up the cut's side, clutching at the grass, and on top lay down. The earth began trembling as if the cut's sides were going to cave in and carry them under the wheels. The pounding wheels of the freight-train thundered and crashed and, after a long time, the twin red lights of the caboose passed.

"I wouldn't of minded holding that down for a while," T-Dub said.

"Why didn't you holler for them to stop, Bowie?" Chicamaw said.

"I didn't want to make them mad at us," Bowie said.

The nail in the heel of Bowie's right shoe was digging now into the flesh. To hell with it, he thought. Bad start is a good ending, boys. You can't throw snake-eyes all day. Box-cars won't jump up in your face every throw. There's a natural for us up this road.

Bowie came out of his sleep with T-Dub's voice, deep as a cistern's echo and Chicamaw's muffled rattle still stroking his ears. His feet felt like the toe-nails had been drawn out and the bits ground in his heels. The sun was piercing the plum thicket like ice picks and when Bowie turned on his back he placed his forearm over his eyes.

"I cased that bank in Zelton four times," T-Dub said. "It was a bird's nest on the ground, but every time something came up. Maybe this time will be different."

"I'm ready for a piece of it myself," Chicamaw said.

"I tell you one thing," T-Dub said. "When I rob my next bank it will be my twenty-eighth."

"I hope it's twenty-nine in a couple of weeks."

Bowie's insides quivered. I can rib myself up to do anything, he thought.

"These kids trying to rob these banks are just ding-bats,"

T-Dub said. "They'll charge a bank with a filling station across the street and a telephone office above and a hardware store next door."

"You got to watch them upstairs offices across the street from a bank too," Chicamaw said. "There's lawyers and doctors and people with shotguns just waiting for a bank to be robbed."

"I'm not going to fool with any of these clodhopper town banks," Chicamaw said. "You got to work just as hard for a thousand out of one of them as you do in a good one for fifty."

"Pick you a bank that's a depository for the county and city and you're going to find a set-up," T-Dub said. "That's why I say it don't hurt to case a bank for a week before you charge it."

Five thousand dollars and I'm backing off, Bowie thought. Five thousand salted away and I'm going back to Alky. I've done so much Time that I can do a couple of more on my ear. Go back there and grin at them from ear to ear. I can twist that Warden around my little finger. He's all right though. He'll close them books on me and my record will be clean in a couple of years. Then I'll buy me a mouthpiece for a couple of thousand that's got friends in the Capital and you'll see me coming out of that Alky squared up and with a stake.

The best way to case the Inside of a bank, T-Dub said, was by going in and cashing twenty-dollar bills. In Florida he had opened up an account in a bank just to big-eye it good.

Bowie sat up.

"The Country Boy is up," Chicamaw said. His teeth were as white as the pearl of a gun butt.

There were tiny lights in T-Dub's eyes, gray as .30-30 bullets. "What do you want for supper, Bowie? Plums or fried chicken?"

Bowie looked at a ripened plum on the stem above his head. "I'll take plums," he said.

Chicamaw had his trousers rolled to his knees and now he was pinching into his hair-matted legs.

"What the hell are you doing?" Bowie said.

"Red bugs," Chicamaw said.

Bowie looked at his blood-crusted feet; at the curled toes and grass-filled wrinkles of his shoes. Just one more night of walking though. Just a half a night. He lay back down.

Chicamaw was talking now about a bank he robbed in Kansas. "I knew I hadn't sacked up no more than two thousand out of that nigger-head and I just happened to pick up that cash slip. You know that one they put in every night to show how much cash they got on hand? . . . Well, it didn't jibe with what I had so I went back up to that Dutchman and I says to him: 'Friend, have I got everything around here?' He says: 'You got every bit of it.' I says: 'Is your cash receipt slip usually right?' He says: 'Why, yes.' I says: 'Well, I haven't got but two thousand here and this slip shows four thousand eight hundred and sixty-two dollars. Now cough it up.' That guy began swearing up and down so I just put the twitch to him. His eyes turned as red as any red you ever did see."

Bowie sat back up. "What's a twitch?" he said.

"Don't worry, you'll see one pretty soon. When I work I always carry myself one. Get you a piece of window cord and make a little stick with a hole in it and fix a loop and just put that around a man's head and give it a twist and he's gonna think his brains are coming out his ears. Anyway, this Dutchman hollers calf rope and he shows me the bottom drawer of a desk there. Sure enough, right there in it, was four little packs of the prettiest *five hundred-* and *one hundred-*dollar bills you ever saw."

A gust of wind combed the thicket and bent the stretch of high Johnston grass that separated them from the railroad. Bowie lay back.

"You know what that banker would have done if you hadn't of got onto that slip," T-Dub said. "He'd of squawked that he had been robbed of it all just the same. There's more of these bankers than you can shake a stick at that's got it stacked around over their banks and just praying every day to be robbed."

"Sure," Chicamaw said.

"They're thieves just like us," T-Dub said.

Bowie flecked an ant off the back of his hand. I'm not going to get in this too deep, gentlemen. You going to see this white child backing off when he's got five thousand.

The feet of T-Dub and Chicamaw scraped in sudden violence and Bowie jerked up like a jackknife. He looked toward
the two. They were looking into the Johnston grass. T-Dub
had the gun in his hand.

Bowie watched. Something was moving in that grass yonder
all right. It wasn't wind either. He picked up his shoes. The
grass parted again!

Chicamaw led the way, plunging through the thicket like a
football half-back; T-Dub behind and Bowie following bare-
footed and carrying his shoes. They did not stop running until
they reached the woods. Then they stopped and looked back
toward the thicket.

"What did you-all see?" Bowie said. "Jesus Christ."

"Something was in that grass," Chicamaw said.

"If there wasn't I left a damned good three-dollar hat over
there," T-Dub said. "I can see your socks hanging from here,
Bowie."

"I thought all the Laws in the county were in that grass the
way you-all tore out," Bowie said.

"I'll bet it was a hog or something," T-Dub said. "Turkey
or something. I'll bet any amount you guys want to name."

"If you think it's just a hog why don't you just trot back
over there and get that hat?" Chicamaw said.

"Ah, I want to go bare-headed anyway. Like these jelly
beans."

Bowie sat down and began putting on his shoes. His feet
were bleeding again.

"Think you going to make it, Bowie?" T-Dub said.

"The way I come across over here looks like I could run
it," Bowie said.

Chapter II

THAT rain-blurred sprinkle of lights yonder was Keota. Before
the rain commenced, Bowie had heard sounds of the town,
but now there was only the smacking of the wind-driven rain
against the shocks of old wheat around him and its clatter on

the stubbled earth. He had been alone now more than two hours and it must be getting along toward three or four o'clock. In the black depths underneath those lights yonder, T-Dub and Chicamaw were looking for Dee Mobley's place. When they found Chicamaw's cousin, they were coming back after him. Three flashes of the headlamps, if they got Dee's car, would be the signal.

Bowie reached down now and pressed his numb feet. They felt like stumps. A man on stumps couldn't do much good if he was jumped and that is why he had stayed here to wait.

The thunder in the east rumbled nearer and then cracked above him in a jagged prong of lightning. The flash bared the sodden stretch to the sagging fence and road.

I won't be hearing any more from my people, Bowie thought. Mama. Aunt Pearl. Cousin Tom. Goodbye to you people. The first thing the Law does is look up the people a man has been writing to and watch them places.

Goodbye, Mama. There's one thing about you. Whatever I ever did was all right with you. This is the only way. Maybe you'll be getting an envelope with three or four hundred dollars in it pretty soon and then you can go off and get that pellagra cured up. Get away from that husband you got for a while.

So long, Cousin Tom. Thanks for them letters and cigarettes. But all the cheering in the world don't help you none, Pal, when you're in a place like that back yonder. You know every day what is going to happen the next.

Aunt Pearl, you're a fine woman, but all the Christian Scientist stuff in the world don't help you none if you haven't got the money to buy a lawyer. And to get a good one you got to have good money.

Approaching car lights bobbed on the road and Bowie got up. The laboring machine plowed the mud of the road right on past. Bowie lowered himself back to the ground.

Them boys will be back here. Takes time to locate a man when you don't know where he lives. Let him stay out here? Them boys weren't made that way. It was getting doggone late though. There wasn't a dozen lights in the town now.

Lightning slashed the swirling heavens. Maybe a man saw something like that when they kicked the switch off on you in the Chair, Bowie thought. It didn't seem like no nine years since that morning when his lawyer came and told him they weren't going to burn him. Maybe though he had died back there in the Chair? This was just his Spirit out here in this rain? In this old world, anything happened. Maybe I'm like a cat with nine lives. I done lost one of them back there in that Alky Chair. Eight more to go. . . . Look here, Bowie, old boy, snap out of it. You're going to go ding-batty out here.

Another car was coming. It sounded like a Model-T; had one twitching feeble light.

Bowie moved toward the fence in a half crouch. The car was a Ford pick-up, its body boards thumping and rattling. That light on it was either just going off and on or signaling. What was it doing? He checked the shout in his throat. The car went on, the sound of its straining motor dying in the night.

He sat now at the side of the road. It couldn't be very long until daybreak. Well, I can't sit out here up into the day. Them boys must have got a rumble over there. They might be in trouble this very minute. They wouldn't leave me out here though. Not them boys. We've had our heads together too long on this business. Take old T-Dub. Him knocking down in that Commissary every day so they would have a stake. A man didn't start out with money that come that hard with two fellows and not intend to go through with it. Not any four hundred and twenty-five dollars. And planning as far ahead as they had? Cooling off at Dee's and then going on down into Texas and getting hold of T-Dub's sister-in-law and getting her to get them a furnished house. Nosir, that boy just wasn't made that way. And Chicamaw? Them white teeth.

The rain slapped his face and crawled on his numb feet. But I can't stay out here forever. If they ain't here by daybreak, I've just got to go on in. I can't help it. I'm going in.

The harnessed mules plowed the road's muck toward Bowie, pulling a wagon with a tarpaulin as gray and soggy as the morning. The driver, his drooping straw sombrero bowed against the drizzle, slopped along at the wagon's side. His overalls were rolled to his calves and hunks of mud leaped from his moving shoes. Now the sombrero raised.

"Good morning, Friend," Bowie said.

Sombrero shifted the wad of tobacco in his jaws. "Mornin'," he said.

Bowie pointed at his shoes. "Mind if I hang on the back of your wagon into town? My feet have plumb played out on me."

Sombrero nodded toward the wagon's rear. "Climb up in it if you want to."

Bowie went around and climbed through the canvas flap and into the wagon. The smell of alfalfa was dry and clean. He saw now the woman and the little boy. They sat on quilt-covered straw against the seat.

"Your man said I could pile in here, Lady?"

The woman nodded.

Bowie leaned back against the sides, stretched his feet in guarded relaxation. The wagon's movement was soothing and its clean dryness began to sponge him like a dry chamois skin. He closed his eyes.

"Who's that man, Ma?"

Bowie opened his eyes, looked at the child and grinned. "You don't mind me riding with you, do you, Son?"

The boy burrowed his face against his mother's bosom and she patted him. "He's a friend of your pappy's, honey."

The hoofs of the mules began clopping and Bowie asked the woman: "We in town?"

The woman nodded. "On the Square."

Bowie edged feet forward to the wagon's end, parted the flap and slid out. The pavement was like a cushion of pins.

In the center of the Square was the Court House, a two-story sandstone building with big basement signs: *Whites . . . Colored.* One- and two-story buildings fenced the Square: *Greenberg's Dry Goods Store . . . Keota State Bank . . . Rexall Drug Store . . . Hamburger's 5 & 10 ¢.*

The rain had stopped and the sun looked like a circle of wet, yellow paper. Bowie walked across the Court House lawn toward the dry goods store on the corner.

The clerk leaned against the doorway with his arms folded across his chest and when Bowie neared he pushed with his shoulder blades and stood erect. "Yessir?" he said.

"I got ten bucks, Pardner," Bowie said, "and I got to have

a pair of pants and a shirt and socks and shoes and some short-handled drawers."

"We'll see," Pardner said.

Bowie followed him back into the gloom and deeper into the smell of damp wool and bolted goods and floor sweep. Pardner turned on a fly-specked bulb above a table of khaki work pants.

In dry clothing now, Bowie sat on a bench while Pardner laced the new shoes on his feet. "You don't know a feller around here by the name of Tobey or Hobby or something like that, do you?" he asked.

Pardner cocked his head. "Don't believe I do."

"I used to know a feller up in Tulsy who settled down here. Been in this town a pretty good while I understand. Mobby or something like that."

"What does he look like?"

Bowie described Chicamaw. "Oh, he's sort of an Indian looking feller. Come up to about my shoulders. Black eyes and pretty skinny."

Pardner shook his head.

"He was working in a filling station up in Tulsy."

"There's a fellow named Mobley out on the Dallas highway that's got a little store and station out there."

"It wasn't Mobley, I'm sure of that."

"Did he have a girl named Keechie, little Indian-looking girl?"

"No. It don't matter. I didn't know him so well."

The new shoes made his feet feel like they were not even sore. It was good to walk. The sun was blotting the puddles and making the dry stretches of the highway glare. He passed the lumber yard with its fence of shredded show posters, the closed cotton gin, the tourist camp: *Kozy Komfort Kamp.*

That was the place yonder all right. That station right yonder with the orange-colored pump. A man sat under the shed in a tilted chair. Back of the station was a smokehouse-looking structure and then woods. Farther up the highway, on the left side, was another station.

Bowie went up under the shed toward the man in the tilted chair. "How you do, Friend?" Bowie said.

"Howdy," the man said. He had a heavy face, rough as oak

bark and long, black sideburns touched with wiry gray. The black cotton shirt had white buttons.

"Got a cold soda?" Bowie said.

The man got up and lifted the lid of the ice-box and Bowie reached in and picked up a bottle.

Bowie saw now the girl standing behind the screened doorway of the store. She was dark and small and her high pointed breasts stretched the blue cotton of the polo shirt.

Bowie looked at the man. "I wonder if I could see you private a minute?"

The man looked toward the girl and she went away.

"You're Dee Mobley, aren't you?"

"That's me."

"You haven't had a couple of visitors lately?"

Mobley looked at Bowie's shoes. "You got on some new shoes there, haven't you? Feet been hurting?"

"You doggone whistling. I just got these up town."

"New pants too?"

Bowie grinned.

"Where in the hell," Mobley said, "have *you* been?"

"Waiting for that Chicamaw and that T-Dub Masefeld."

"I went after you last night myself," Mobley said. "Raining cats and nigger babies."

"In a Model-T truck?"

"That was me."

"Well, I'll be— Can you beat that. And I just sat out there and let you go by."

Mobley made a thumbing motion toward the filling station up the highway. Two figures in uniform coveralls sat on a bench under its shed. "Them Square-Johns up yonder are always big-eyeing this way so you just go on past like you were hitch-hiking and then cut back through the woods. The boys are in that bunk of mine right back of this place."

Bowie dog-trotted through the woods toward the filling station. He could see the place that Dee called his bunk. It had a corrugated iron roof and the limbs of a big pecan tree shaded it. He crawled through the fence and went to the bunk's door and knocked. The springs of a bed inside creaked a little. He knocked again. There was no answer. "Chicamaw," he called.

Feet thumped on the floor inside, stomped toward the door. T-Dub's face was framed in the parted door. "For Christ's sake, come in," he said.

Chicamaw lay on the iron bed in his underwear. "We thought maybe you had gone back to Alky."

"I just been swimming that's all," Bowie said. "And thinking I was a lone wolf."

"I was going to go back out there tonight myself," Chicamaw said.

T-Dub pointed at the bare wooden table. On it was a bowl of pork and beans, a hunk of yellow cheese and a broken loaf of bread. "You want to glom?"

"Man, I'll say."

"We didn't get holed up here until five o'clock this morning," Chicamaw said. "I was going to go back after you tonight. I don't see how Dee missed you."

"It was my fault," Bowie said. He poured beans on a hunk of the bread and pressed it into a sandwich. He took a bite and chewed and grinned.

Chapter III

UP until a year ago, Dee Mobley had been bootlegging corn whisky, but the new Sheriff in Keota had it in for him, he said. He squatted now against the wall of the Bunk, his breath as strong as rubbing-alcohol fumes, a finger-rolled cigarette wagging on his lower lip. "The Sheriff likes these druggist boys here," Dee said. "They're doing all the booze business here now."

"Them Laws and druggists are thieves just like us," T-Dub said. He drew his hand across his sweat-beaded forehead and his fingers made a clicking sound as he slung it on the floor. "It's getting so a man has to have a gun to make a piece of money."

The afternoon sun was packing heat into the low-ceilinged, crowded room. Chicamaw sat on an up-turned bucket filing on the barrels of the 12-gauge shotgun with a hack saw. Bowie lay on the bed, a wet towel across his face.

The druggists were fixing up the cheap trade with jake and orange peel and hair tonics, Dee said, and the Indians were buying their canned heat at the five & ten. Doctors were getting the good business with prescriptions.

Dee said he had been running the grocery and filling station since fall. His daughter Keechie helped him. She stayed up in town with his sister Mara, and he stayed in the Bunk here at nights.

"That girl of yours sure mean-eyed me this morning when she brought that grub out here," T-Dub said. "I don't think she likes us around here worth a doggone."

"She don't have much to do with nobody," Dee said.

Bowie took the towel off his face so he could see Dee.

"She'll take care of you while I'm up in Tulsy," Dee said. "Just you boys don't go around in front of the station and be careful about lights at night."

T-Dub counted out three hundred and twenty-five dollars and gave it to Dee. This was to buy a second-hand car in Tulsa, cover ten dollars for the shotgun and twenty-five for Dee's trouble.

"I might be able to make it back by tomorrow night," Dee said. "But if I see I'm going to get in here after daylight I'll just wait until the next night."

"We'd like to shell out of here about eight o'clock at night," T-Dub said.

"We don't forget our friends, Dee," Chicamaw said. "You do the best you can for us and when we get in some real money, you're liable to see a piece of it."

After Dee left, T-Dub said they had ninety-five dollars left. It had to take them to Texas and pay a month's rent on a furnished house.

Chicamaw put the shotgun down and went over and picked up a road map on the bed.

T-Dub said the best way to leave a Hole was early in the evening when the traffic was heaviest. Stay off the main highways as much as you could and follow timbered country. Keep a couple of five-gallon cans filled with gasoline and circle cities like Dallas and Fort Worth where the Laws had them scout cars and radios.

The wheels of a truck ground in the gravel of the station's

driveway and they listened. Bottles rattled. "Soda-pop truck," Bowie said.

"I can run these roads all day and night through," T-Dub said. "Just keep your car clean and not let it look like it was being run hard and everybody stay shaved up and looking like you were just a fellow about town. I can count it on my hand the times I been jumped on the road."

"Just give me one man driving and me sitting in the back with a .30-30 and I can hold off any carload of Laws that ever took out after anybody," Chicamaw said.

"You can do it with a nigger-shooter," T-Dub said. "I don't see where these fellows they call G-men, them Big Shots, get that stuff about thieves not having no guts. I don't see how they get that."

"Me neither," Bowie said. "They don't do anything unless they got ten carloads and when they jump anybody they use about fourteen hundred rounds of ammunition."

"Laws never did worry me," T-Dub said. "It's the fellers you thought were your friends that beats you. And a woman mad at you. They are what beat you."

"Liquor too," Bowie said. "Some guys have to be stewed to the gills before they can work. Me, I want my head clear when I start out."

"Whiss will do it all right," T-Dub said. "But a woman mad at you can get you in a rank quicker than anything. Yessir, the Laws would be up tight if it wasn't for sore women and snitches."

"They're full of rabbit all right, them Laws," Chicamaw said.

"I wouldn't trust Jesus Christ," Bowie said.

"Listen to old Country Boy," Chicamaw said.

"Even if I saw Jesus Christ walking right in this place I wouldn't trust him," Bowie said.

The heat was getting more intense. It stuffed Bowie's nostrils and seared high up in his nose. He took the towel and soaked it again in the bucket of water.

Chicamaw started taking off his overalls.

"You ought not to do that," Bowie said. "No tellin' when that girl might come out here."

Chicamaw resnapped the overall straps.

"I'd sure like to let that sister-in-law of mine know I'm coming," T-Dub said. "But that's a good way to get a rumble. Writing letters. We'll just go on to MacMasters and I'll get her on the phone."

Chicamaw looked up from the road map. "It's three hundred and twenty-five miles from here. That country is sure bald out in there. Nothing but oil-wells and mesquite trees."

"Plenty of roads though," T-Dub said. "Man, I was raised in that West Texas country."

"I guess you know that sister-in-law of yours pretty good?" Chicamaw said.

"She's Real People," T-Dub said. "A woman that has stuck by that bud of mine like she has isn't going to turn down a chance to make some money. That bud of mine can be sprung out of Texas with a couple of thousand. He's just doing five years. On a two-for-one job now. And that woman of his is going to do all she can."

"Zelton is forty miles from MacMasters," Chicamaw said. "That's where we going to get the house, uh?"

"There's mighty nice banks in both of those towns, but Zelton, I think, takes my eye first."

Chicamaw folded the map. "I know a mouthpiece in MacMasters," he said. "Name Hawkins. Archibald J. Hawkins. Old Windy we called him. Him and me were holed up together in Mexico for a year. There's one old boy that sure beat the Law."

"What did he do?" Bowie said.

"He was a county treasurer right there in MacMasters and he sacked himself up twenty or twenty-five thousand just knocking down every month and then things started gettin' hot and he rabbited to Mexico."

"Unlatched a vault?" Bowie asked.

"Oh, no. Just knocking down. He bought all the County's stuff, see. Gravel and machinery and things like that. He would make out a voucher for five loads of gravel when he had bought only one and then go down to the bank and cash it and pocket the other four. He was in Mexico for fourteen years. All the witnesses died or forgot and then he went back just as big as you please. And on top of that took the bar examination and is practising law right there now."

"Them politicians are thieves just like us," T-Dub said. "Only they got more sense and use their damned tongues instead of a gun."

"If you ever need a mouthpiece," Chicamaw said, "Old Windy wouldn't be bad."

"I'm not needing any more lawyers myself," T-Dub said. "The way I figure is that when they get me again I won't be in any shape for a lawyer or anything else in this world to do me any good."

"That's me," Bowie said. "I mean to get me out of any new trouble."

"Well, the way I figure it," Chicamaw said, "is that two and two make five and if at first you don't suck seed, keep on sucking 'til you do suck seed."

"Aw, you damned Indian," Bowie said.

The voice of the girl, Keechie, made Bowie's veins distend and there was a velvety, fluttering sensation in his spine. She was squatting over there now by the Bunk's kerosene heater, the brown flannel of her skirt stretched tight across her bottom, showing T-Dub how to keep the wick from smoking. T-Dub had tried to boil coffee on it this morning and had only succeeded in filling everybody's noses full of soot and blacking the underwear Bowie had washed.

"Just wipe it off with a match like this," Keechie said.

"That's one thing old T-Dub don't know nothing about," Chicamaw said.

Keechie got up, holding her blackened hands out. Bowie snatched the towel off the bed post and held it toward her. "It's pretty dirty," he said.

Keechie took the towel. "Thank you."

"That big Country Boy is some gallant, ain't he, Keechie?" Chicamaw said.

Bowie's ears felt like the velvet was being pressed against them now. "Don't pay no attention to that ignoramus," he said.

"Were you raised in the country?" Keechie said.

Bowie shook his head. "Don't pay no attention to them two."

"He's just hard-headed, Miss Keechie," T-Dub said. "That's all."

"Soft-headed," Chicamaw said.

"His head looks all right to me," Keechie said.

Bowie tried hard not to swallow. "All right, you guys, that's enough."

Keechie pointed at the bed. On it was a filled paper sack and two folded newspapers. "There's some canned soup in that sack and you can heat it on that stove now." She turned toward the door.

"Thanks for the grub and papers, Miss Keechie," T-Dub said.

Bowie looked at her, the black hair, cut like a boy's; the short, strong neck and compact shoulders. "Sure thank you," he said.

"Forget it," Keechie said. She went out the door.

"That little girl don't think any too much of us, I'm here to tell you," T-Dub said. He went over to the bed and picked up a newspaper.

"She's all right," Chicamaw said. "Just stuck up."

"She acts like a little soldier to me," Bowie said.

"Old Dee just lets her do him anyway," Chicamaw said. "He won't never go on a real toot around here any more. If he wants to get boiled, he'll go clear up to Muskogee. That man's got a right to drink though. Wife leaving him like she did."

"Keechie's mother?" Bowie said.

"She run off with some damned guy. Running a medicine show."

"That little girl hasn't got no business around a bunch of criminals like us," Bowie said.

"Man, lookee here," T-Dub said. He had the Oklahoma City newspaper spread out on the bed and was tapping the left top column. "Just lookee here."

Bowie went over and he and Chicamaw looked:

ALCATONA, Okla., Sept. 15—The escape of three life-term prisoners who kidnaped a taxicab driver and a farmer in their desperate flight was announced here tonight by Warden Everett Gaylord of the State Penitentiary. Combined forces of prison, County and City officers were looking for the trio. The fugitives are:

Elmo (Three-Toed) Mobley, 35, bank robbery; T. W. (Tommy Gun) Masefeld, 44, bank robbery and Bowie A. Bowers, 27, murder.

"Pulling that toe stuff again on me," Chicamaw said. "All right, you sons of bitches."

Mobley and Bowers, Warden Gaylord disclosed, took advantage of permits allowing them to go fishing on prison property and Masefeld of a pass to town. All three were privileged trusties.

Jed Miracle, 21, Alcatona taxi driver, was bound in his own taxi which the fugitives abandoned after a tire blew out. E. T. Waters, farmer living at the edge of Akota, twelve miles south of here, gave descriptions of three men who commandeered his car at the point of a gun. After traveling with the trio for more than an hour, the fuel of the car was exhausted and Waters was tied and abandoned in his own car like Miracle.

The desperate trio are believed to be headed for the hills of Eastern Oklahoma where so many criminals have found refuge in the past few years.

Bowers, youngest of the escaped men, was serving a life sentence that had been commuted from the death penalty. He was convicted in the murder of a storekeeper in Selpa County when he was 18 years old. The killing took place during an attempted robbery. He was a member of the prison baseball team.

All of the men had good prison records, Warden Gaylord said. Masefeld had charge of the prison commissary, selling cigarettes and candies to the inmates. He had been in the prison six years. Mobley, also a member of the prison ball team, had served five years of a 99 year sentence from Larval County.

Miracle, the cab driver, described tonight how he was lured to the creek a mile from the prison by Masefeld and forced at the point of a gun to surrender his cab and accompany them.

"Masefeld told me in town he wanted to take some sandwiches and soda pop out to some friends of his who were fishing," Miracle declared. "I had done that plenty of times for some of the trusty boys and I did not think anything about it. When we reached the place, Masefeld jabbed the gun in my back and said he would kill me if I did not obey him," Miracle asserted.

"A tire blew out," Miracle went on, "and the extra was down too, so they tied me up and went on across a cotton field toward the highway. I managed to work myself loose and drove the car back to town."

The shouts of Waters, the farmer kidnaped by the men, attracted coon hunters who freed him. He declared the men treated him courteously.

"That toe stuff," Chicamaw said.

"It tickles me," T-Dub said, "about this Tommy Gun they're putting on me. I never did have but one machine gun in my life and I never did even try it out. I'll take an automatic pump gun any old day."

"It's not a very long piece about us though, is it?" Chicamaw said.

"Brother, I wish it was just two lines," Bowie said.

"Nothing at all you mean," T-Dub said. "Papers can raise more heat than anything. These Laws work like hell to get their names in the papers."

They lolled on the ground in front of the Bunk, unrecognizable bundles in the darkness, only their slapping and blowing at mosquitoes interrupting the quiet. This was the second night they had waited on Dee Mobley. The lights of the station had not been turned on this evening. Everything was set to take off. Chicamaw had the shotgun sawed off so he could carry it underneath the old lumberjacket Dee had given him. Keechie had two five-gallon cans of gasoline filled up in front of the station, two sacks of groceries and three cotton-picking sacks.

"I just hope it's not the car that's holding him up," T-Dub said. "I'll be damned if I start out in a wreck."

"He's probably drinking a little," Chicamaw said.

Bowie got up and stretched. "I wish he had picked some other time to drink if that's it." He walked over to the edge of the tree's inky shadow and stood there, looking at the back of the station. Then he came back and stood above Chicamaw and T-Dub. They were quiet again.

Bowie moved up the side of the station and peered around under the shed. He saw the figure sitting in the chair by the ice-box and his shoes rasped in the gravel with his start.

"My goodness," he said. "I didn't know that was you."

"That's all right," Keechie said.

He cleared his throat. "I didn't know anybody was around here."

"That's all right."

He looked at the Model-T pick-up parked just off the driveway. "I was thinking though that I hadn't heard it leave."

"No," Keechie said.

Bowie moved toward her.

"Sit down if you want to," Keechie said.

He lowered himself to the bottom of the doorway. There was a car under the shed of the brightly lighted filling station up the highway. Two men were standing beside it and watching the attendant fill the tank. "I don't know what could be holding that Daddy of yours," he said.

"I have an idea. If it had to be done I should have done it."

Bowie shook his head. "We don't have any business around here anyway."

The lights of a car popped around the curve from town, sprayed the highway with luminous foam. Bowie strained back against the door screen. The car passed.

"I read it in the paper about you," Keechie said.

Bowie's head went up and down.

"I guess you thought you had to leave?"

"I didn't see any use of doing any more Time. It wasn't getting me anywhere. All that was keeping me in there was money."

Keechie shook her head. "You won't get anywhere like this. Not with company like that back yonder."

"I don't know," Bowie said. "What will be, will be."

"That Chicamaw wouldn't be anything else if he could."

"I think you got them boys down wrong now. You take old T-Dub. He's got him a little farm picked out already up in Kentucky. He wants to settle down."

"That Chicamaw Mobley has never liked anything but trouble all his life."

Bowie grinned. "He's a little wild all right."

The car under the shed of the other filling station drove away. The attendant went back and sat on the bench.

"If I wasn't so hot I'd like to have me a filling station," Bowie said. "Now what I would like to have is a tourist camp."

"That would be too slow for you," Keechie said. "You want to live your life fast."

"You got me down wrong, Keechie. You'd see me following a one-eyed mule and a Georgia walking stock if I had to
and what's more, like it. If I could."

Keechie took a pack of cigarettes from her polo shirt
pocket, pushed up one and offered it to Bowie. When he
touched her hand, the velvety glow stiffened his blood. The
lighted cigarette trembled between his fingers.

"How come you to ever get in trouble?" Keechie said.

"I never was in but one."

"That one."

"You mean the Chair?"

"Yes."

"Just some fellows on the carnival I was traveling with said
they knew how to make some money and I just sort of went
along to see how it was done. I wanted to get some money
so I could go up to Colorado and join another show. Them
boys had a safe picked out and I just went along."

"You were on a carnival?"

"I went on it when I was fourteen. Just roustaboutin'."

"Did you run away from home?"

"I just left. Year after Dad died."

"Your Dad is dead?"

"Killed. Man killed him."

Shoes crunched at the side of the station and Bowie's head
jerked. It was Chicamaw. "I wondered what had become of
you?"

"Just talking," Bowie said.

"Don't let me bother you." Chicamaw went on back.

Keechie flipped the cigarette toward the pick-up and Bowie
watched its glow on the dark ground.

"Did you shoot that man in Selpa?" Keechie said.

"It was me or him," Bowie said. "He was coming around
the car after me with a gun."

The chair under Keechie creaked a little as she moved.

"If I had run like the others I wouldn't be this way now.
The guy that knew all about robbing safes was the first one
to run. The Big Shot."

Keechie took another cigarette.

"You smoke a lot," he said.

"I don't want it." She broke it in her hand.

"I know a man can't last Out Here long. But I'm not going to try and last. I'm going to back off and it isn't going to be long. I can still square myself up."

"No," Keechie said. "You can't beat it this way."

"Deep down in me I know I can't, but I myself says I can."

Another car was coming around the curve. Suddenly, its lights were flooding the shed under which they sat. Neither moved.

It was a coupe and Dee. He got out of the car awkwardly. He was drunk all right. "Hadtufftime," he said.

Bowie went back and told Chicamaw and T-Dub. "You think it's too late to start tonight?" he said.

"Hell, no," Chicamaw said. He and T-Dub went in the Bunk.

The motor of the Model-T around in front fired and Bowie started moving fast toward the shed. When he got around there, the pick-up was already on the highway. He watched it go, listening to the sound of the motor perishing in the darkness.

T-Dub and Chicamaw were piling things in the car. "Where's them cotton-picking sacks?" T-Dub said.

"I got them," Bowie said. He went over to the chair where she had been sitting and picked up the sacks.

"Hadtufftime," Dee said. "Tufftime."

They drove off. Shortly the wind was whipping the sacks on the fenders and insects swirled in the lamp beams and splattered on the windshield.

Chapter IV

THE two five-gallon cans rattled emptily in the coupe's rear and the red level of the gasoline gauge was below the half mark, but Fort Worth and Dallas were behind now, given the run-around without a rumble. One hundred and forty miles

out this straight stretch and they would be in MacMasters.
Bowie was driving.

On this side of MacMasters, at an old, abandoned wildcat
well that T-Dub had described, Bowie and Chicamaw were
getting out and T-Dub was going on in to contact his sister-
in-law. Just as soon as he got a house, he would come back
and get them.

They talked about houses now. When they had about five
places, T-Dub said, and all had good hotel-lobby fronts, he
would say they had a real set-up. He wanted a house in Zelton
and another one in Gusherton. Then one in that resort town,
Clear Waters, and one in Lothian and Twin Montes. These
towns were within a radius of two hundred miles and not
more than an hour's driving apart. A house in each of them
would give you a Hole that you could be cooling off in within
an hour after a bank was sacked.

Always get places with double garages, T-Dub said, and
keep the cars out of sight. And never let the neighbors see
more than one man at a time. And don't let anybody ever do
any questioning. If there was any questioning, you do it yourself. Now up here in Zelton and Gusherton, they could be
lease buyers or promoters as soon as they got good fronts.

"We're cotton pickers tonight and look it," Chicamaw said.
"How much cotton can you pick a day, Country Boy?"

"Oh, a pound if I worked real hard," Bowie said. He
looked at the fuel mark. It was getting damned low.

"And another thing," T-Dub said. "Always give the landlady the best of the deal. Keep her satisfied."

"I had me a landlady down in Florida," Chicamaw said,
"and I want you to know that there was one woman that
could drink me under the table. There wasn't anything that
woman wouldn't do. And just when everything was going
smooth with us, they got me."

T-Dub started telling about a house he had in Colorado.
The damnedest, smallest thing got him in a rank there, this
right arm almost shot off and a big Law with a double-barreled shotgun jamming it in his eyes and him standing there
and not even able to lift his arms. The thing he had done
though was going off and staying a couple of weeks and not
telling the milkman. That bastard got scared over a couple of

dollars and he went to the woman that owned the house. She went over to the house and saw it all locked up and she just went in. She got an eyeful. He had that damned machine gun in that house and a bunch of shells. She goes to the Law and they show her a bunch of pictures and sure enough she picks him out. The Laws sit around that house and here he comes back. They would have killed him if it hadn't been for a woman on the porch of a house across the street. She got to shouting and screaming and telling the Laws to stop or they would have killed him. He had them black eyes where that big yellow bastard poked him with that shotgun for a month and a half.

"We sure got to stop and gas up pretty soon," Bowie said.

"That state of Colorado though," T-Dub said. "You ain't never going to get me back in it. They were going to try and put the Chair on me up there. I was praying for Oklahoma to come and get me. They had me positively identified in that state anyway. This Colorado 'cuter was after me right now and I just figured that I had been unlucky enough to draw him and I wasn't going to be lucky enough to beat that Chair. There was a little old auditor that used to come around to us boys in them death cells and talk. Kind of wanted to write pieces for the magazines or something. I got to feeling him out and finally I just showed him a *five-hundred* dollar bill. I had carried that in the sole of my shoe for six months. He tumbles and brings me a .25 automatic and some tape too just like I asked. I taped that right between my legs and Man, I was set. I had made up my mind that if they went ahead and started putting that Chair on me I was going to kill everybody around me that was man enough to die."

"They didn't even try you up there though, did they?" Chicamaw said.

"Naw. That's how come me to be back in Alky. Oklahoma finally come and got me. A little old jailer up here in the Panhandle took that gun off of me. I'd been trying to get rid of it for two weeks."

The highway turned in a banking curve and then down the highway they could see the scattered lights of a small, sleeping town. "We got to gas up here," Bowie said.

Everything was closed in the town. Small globes burned in

the rears of the stores, over the sacks of grain, the cans of oil and tire tubes in the filling stations and the show-cases in the hardware store.

"Looks like we going to have to wake somebody up," T-Dub said.

"We can just unlatch one ourselves," Chicamaw said.

Bowie drove under the shed of the filling station across the street from the Hardware Store. It was dark under the shed, but in the office a light burned. He got out and went up to the door. On the desk lay a man, suspenders down and his head on a rolled coat. There was an empty scabbard on his left hip.

"Hell, wake him up," Chicamaw said.

Bowie rattled the door and the man stirred, raised up and began to work his mouth like his jaws were sore. That old boy is a Law all right, Bowie thought.

Old Boy came out. He had a pistol in the scabbard now. "What do you boys want?" he said.

"Little gasoline, Pardner," T-Dub said.

Old Boy scratched his head. The hair looked like rope frazzle. "How much?"

"Fill it up," T-Dub said.

Old Boy moved toward the coupe; looked inside of it. T-Dub stepped toward him, brought the barrel of the revolver up into Old Boy's back like he was driving an uppercut. "Unlatch that pump, you nosy old belch before I beat your ears down good and proper."

Old Boy looked like he was trying to spit acid off the end of his tongue. Chicamaw snatched the six-shooter out of his scabbard. "And do it right now," T-Dub said.

"For God's sakes, boys," Old Boy said. "Take it easy now. I got a wife and four kids, boys. For God's sakes now. I'm an old man."

"You going to unlatch that pump?"

"For God's sakes, boys." Old Boy brought out the rattling ring of keys.

The car was serviced now and T-Dub told Old Boy to get in the car.

"We might just as well unlatch that hardware store over there while we're here and got him," Chicamaw said.

T-Dub drove with Old Boy sitting beside him; Chicamaw and Bowie stood on the running boards. They stopped in front of the Hardware Store.

Chicamaw pried at the door with the tire tool and when the lock burst, it sounded like all four tires on the coupe had blown out.

Bowie pushed back the glass door of the gun-case and began piling the weapons in his arms like sticks of wood. Chicamaw was filling the cotton sack with shells and cartridges.

The town was still undisturbed as they left it.

Behind the high signboard, twenty miles from the town, Chicamaw bound Old Boy, pulling his arms behind a post and twisting wire around the thumbs.

"You can holler somebody down in the morning," Bowie said.

"That's all right, boys. Perfectly all right. You boys are all right."

The white center line of the black asphalt was running under them again like a spout of gray water.

"I'll swear," Chicamaw said. He was looking at the six-shooter he had taken off Old Boy. It was an old frontier model, a .38 on a .45 frame. "I wish you could see this."

"What is it?" T-Dub said. "Hell, I'm driving."

There were six notches on the cedar butt of the revolver.

"I didn't know we were doing business with a bad man," T-Dub said.

"Nigger killer," Chicamaw said. "That's how he got these on here. That town was full of niggers back there."

"I ought to have stuffed it down his throat," T-Dub said. "I got fed up on him right now. Started big-eyeing this car."

"He was trying to pull a smartie all right," Bowie said.

"That back there might heat us up a little," T-Dub said. "This car here now, but I believe these cotton sacks cover it pretty well. He never saw no license on this car you can tell the world. We got to get some duplicate plates though pretty soon. You can buy all them you want for a dollar apiece. We ought to get a dozen sets."

"Naw, that old boy back there couldn't tell you whether this was a truck or a Packard," Bowie said. "Squawking the way he was."

Day began to break with a haze like cigarette smoke in a closed room and the barbed wire and cedar posts of the fences and the low, twisted mesquite trees began to take form. Bowie rubbed the bristle on his chin. "You know I haven't washed my teeth since we left Alky," he said.

The wildcat-well spot was a good place to hole up for a day or so all right. It was three miles from the Zelton Highway, a gully-scarred mesquite-clumped distance. The weed-grown road beside it was as rough as a cog wheel. It went on North, T-Dub said, beyond those cedar-timbered hills yonder and connected with a lateral road that tied up with the Gusherton Highway.

The mesquites were thick and made a fence for the clearing on which the old derrick rose. Its timbers were as gray as an old mop; away from it a little piece lay a huge wooden bull-wheel with rusty bolts.

Not even possum hunters ever came to this spot, T-Dub had said. He had holed up here three days once after he sacked a bank.

This afternoon, the second that T-Dub had been away from them, Bowie sat on a spread cotton-picking sack, trying the action again of his 12-gauge pump gun. He and Chicamaw had drawn straws for this Baby. It had a pistol grip and a ventilated rib. But the rib was coming off and about four inches of the barrel just as soon as Bowie got hold of a hack saw.

Near the edge of the sack lay more of the guns they had gotten in the Hardware Store, the polished stocks and barrels glittering in the afternoon sun. There were two 12-gauge shotguns, a .30-30 rifle and a .30-06. There was a .22 pump rifle.

Chicamaw patted the scarred stock of the shotgun he had sawed off at Dee's. "I'll still take old Betsy," he said. "All you have to do with her is point her in a general direction." He was drinking. He had found a half-gallon of whisky in the back of the coupe that Dee Mobley must have left.

"This baby here has got a trigger pull and action like a watch," Bowie said. He brought the gun to his shoulder and drew bead on the pulley at the top of the derrick. "Boy, oh boy," he said. "What I could do to a covey of quail."

Chicamaw picked up the fruit jar and started unscrewing the cap. He extended it toward Bowie.

"I'll pass this time."

Chicamaw drank and then shuddered and clenched his teeth.

"Now when I get a pistol on me I'll be willing to call it a deal," Bowie said. "There's an army store in Gusherton, T-Dub said, and I might be able to pick me up one there."

"We got us enough guns now to start us a little war all right," Chicamaw said.

Bowie squinted down the sights of the gun.

"I'll take a .30-30 myself," Chicamaw said. "I can cut capers with them little gentlemen. I know one thing though you can shoot a man through the pratt with one and it won't bring him down. I saw it happen. I did it. Me and a couple of boys were running out of Wichita and a carload of Laws jumped us. That old wreck we were in wouldn't do forty. So I just told these boys to let me out at that bridge and I'd stop them gentlemen.

"I got out and here they come. I cracked down and them Laws started flushing out of that car like it was going to explode. One of them weighed around two hundred pounds easy and I popped him while he was running across a field. He just kept going. He didn't drop until he got in the timber."

"He finally dropped though, uh?"

"He told me about it himself later. He come up to Alky. He knew who did it. Laughed about it. Thanked me for not killing him. I could have killed him all right."

"I don't care about being jumped myself," Bowie said. "I'd just as soon they stay away from me."

"The Laws never got me in a rank but twice in my life. The first time was in this State and I was just a snotty-nose punk. I'd been unlatching so many safes that I'll swear I begin to think it was on the level."

Bowie laughed.

"They got me all right in this State once. Four years I done down here on one of these prison farms, boy."

"Man, I hear they're tough. These prison farms?"

"You heard right." Chicamaw started taking the cap off the jar again. "It's not everybody that beats them farms."

Bowie placed the shotgun on the ground and picked up the .22 rifle. "I always wanted one of these little guns when I was a kid," he said.

"That time they got me in Florida," Chicamaw said, "and sent me back to Oklahoma was just my fault. That landlady I was going with and me just got a little reckless. I wish I knew where that woman was. She wasn't no spring chicken, but I'll take her to anything you could ever show me."

"How come them to ever get you down there?"

"I had a run-in with a Jew down there in a gambling place. I was drunk. I don't mind telling you. This Jew didn't want to play stud poker. He had to play draw or nothing. I called him a Christ-killer and a few other things and he said he wasn't going to take it. I told him he'd take it or else. He started out of that place and I decided I'd better frisk him. I caught him and throwed down on him. He didn't have a gun on though. I was smart enough to get out myself because you know they're hard on you in that State for showing a gun, but I got too smart and went back there the next Sunday and there was more Laws on me than I thought there was in Miami."

"A man sure ought to stay sober Out Here," Bowie said.

"What are you trying to do, preach to me?"

" 'Course not, Chicamaw."

Chicamaw took another drink.

"There I was down there in Florida with twelve thousand dollars and a woman that was the stuff. That woman just wouldn't leave that town with me. Where I wanted to go with that stake was Mexico. Hole up down there like I did after beating them here in this State. If she had just gone with me."

"How is that Mexico business?" Bowie said.

"I done a year down there. It's just like any place else though. If you haven't got no money it's no good."

"I don't imagine I'd like it down there. Some of them greasers might try to kick you around like fellows do them up here and I wouldn't stand for that."

"If you got the pesos to throw, you can get by down there. But you can't make no money down there and when my four hundred dollars went I had to get out."

"I don't savvy their lingo either and gettin' across that bor-der would bother me."

"I never had to show a passport all the time I was down there and besides, you can buy one. Fifty pesos will get you anything you want in that Chili country. Them Laws down there are all hoss thieves."

"You savvy that lingo of theirs?"

"Seguro."

"Rattle me off something."

"En Mexico hay muchas señoritas con culas muy bonitas," Chicamaw said.

"You're another one. What did you say?"

"I said there was a lot of pretty gals in that country with prettier behinds."

"You look kind of like a Spick anyway. That's why you got by so good and then rattling off that stuff that way."

Chicamaw drank again. "I stayed on an old hacienda down there that was run by an old boy that used to be a thief himself. One of them revolution thieves. There was three more white guys on the place, all of us cooling off for something up here. I told you about Old Windy Hawkins."

"Who were the other two?"

"Banker from New Mexico and then the one we called Tangle Eyes. He was a deputy sheriff right out this line here close to El Paso."

"What did he do?"

"Killed a couple of farm boys. He just wasn't smart enough to make it. You remember when they had them big placards plastered up all over this state offering five thousand dollars reward for dead bank bandits?"

"Man, I was in Alky so long that I never knew nothing 'bout Out Here."

"They were doing it all right. This Tangle Eyes just planted a couple of old boys in front of a bank and let them have it. He just wasn't foxy enough."

"They don't still have that five-thousand dollar stuff in this State, do they?"

"Christ, no. The bankers had to stop it before they got everybody killed. The Laws were planting more people than there was bank robbers."

Spilled liquor wet the lines in Chicamaw's face, ran over his Adam's apple and down his neck. He put the bottle down and wiped his face on his shoulder. "You're in a good tough state, Boy. You didn't see that in the paper the other day. 'Bout five men dropping dead from heat prostration on that Bingham Prison farm. Heat, my hind foot. I know what killed them."

"I'm backing out of this just as soon as I get a little salted away," Bowie said. "I been intending to tell you boys."

Chicamaw lifted his left arm demonstratively and held his right hand up. "It's pretty tough when a man will take a hatchet and whack his arm off like this!"

"Goddamn, do they do that?"

"I saw four boys chop themselves in one week. One would whack the other and then that one would come down on the other one."

Bowie felt like his eyes were wired together.

"Them boys wanted to get off that farm pretty bad to do that, didn't they? And they just didn't want to get out of work. That's what they tell you in the Capital and them prison bosses say. There ain't a man in this State prison system that couldn't do the work they got. It's the way they work you and what they do to you."

"It don't sound good to me."

"Say it's cotton-picking time. All right. Maybe the cotton is five miles from the bunk house. Well, the building tenders rout you out at daybreak. Them are the little snitches that are doing a couple of years for busting a two-bit grocery and they give them saps and dirks and let them run over you. Anyway, they get you out and then the next thing you are going out in that field. Don't think you walk that five miles. You run it. Just as fast as that farm boss wants to lope his horse. And you do that back and forth three times a day. And if you fall out, it's spurs then and the bat or a barrel that night."

"That sure don't sound good to me."

"I've had them drop by me and they were as dead as door-nails. And one of them Bosses sitting up there on a horse with a double-barreled shotgun and he can't even read or write and saying: 'Old Thing, ain't you going to get up?' "

"Man," Bowie said.

"Yeah, they call you Old Thing. And if they get it in for you, you're not going to last. They'll say 'Reach down there, Old Thing, and pick up that piece of grass.' If you're not foxy and don't see that shotgun laying there in that grass, your pratt is mud because they want to go back and say you were trying to get to a gun."

"That sure don't sound worth a damn to me."

"I've heard that farm sound like a slaughter pen. Men squealing and begging like hogs. You don't last on that farm if you're any man at all. Unless you beat it. Then you either come off there a whining rat or still a man."

"I couldn't stand them doing me that way," Bowie said.

The dreggy contents of the fruit jar jostled as Chicamaw shook it around. He drank.

"No, I couldn't take that kind of stuff at all," Bowie said.

"Boy, I'm going up this road a long ways," Chicamaw said. "Plenty of people are going to know it. I ain't going to kill nobody. They're just going to kill themselves."

Bowie watched Chicamaw drain the jar. Now I know why he ain't got no toes on that right foot, he thought.

Chapter V

THEY had a furnished house in Zelton now all right, but they were as broke as bums. In MacMasters yesterday too, T-Dub had almost had a rumble and then he came over here and almost the same thing happened. While he was getting the coupe gassed up in MacMasters, a car of Laws drove right up alongside of him with guns sticking out all over. It just turned out that the Laws were looking for a couple of fellows that had made a Hole in the jail in the next town. Then in this town he draws up at a *Stop* sign and right there, looking him straight in the face, is a Law he has known since he was a kid. But that Law must not have recognized him.

"Naw, he didn't recognize you," Bowie said. He was lying on the cretonne-covered iron cot of the living-room. "You could have told it the way he acted right there."

"It's not anything to feel good about anyway," T-Dub said.

"We got a good Hole-up in this joint though," Bowie said.

"Seventy-five dollars is a lot of money for a dump like this,"

Chicamaw said. He sat slumped in the rocking-chair by the empty fireplace. His eyes were red-veined from yesterday's drinking.

"Things are always high in these oil towns," Bowie said. "This is a pretty good place when you take everything into consideration."

It was a five-room corner house, three blocks off Main Street. On the corner back of them was a machine shop, grinding day and night. Across the street was a fenced-in lot piled with drilling materials. On the opposite corner was a church tabernacle and across from it a two-story, barn-looking building that was a lodging house for oil-field workers. Moving cars kept sand and dust sifting through the window screens all the time and there was nearly always somebody walking on the street.

Right now, the three of them were waiting on Mattie, T-Dub's sister-in-law. She had gone up to the hamburger stand on the corner to get sandwiches and a milk bottle full of hot coffee. She was using her own money to feed them.

"I'm fed up on running around in these overalls like a damned Hoosier too," T-Dub said. "Now, Bowie, you look more like an oil-field guy in them khaki pants."

"I feel more like a hungry man than anything else," Bowie said.

"Quit crying, T-Dub," Chicamaw said. "I can get us some eatin' money from Old Windy over in MacMasters. I can give Mattie a note and it will be good for fifty bucks."

"Fifty dollars won't do us no good," T-Dub said. "It's going to take a couple of thousand. I'll be doggoned if I'm going to charge this bank here half-cocked. We need cars and a bunch of stuff."

"It takes money to make money all right," Bowie said.

"You know that little town we come through this morning," T-Dub said. "Morehead? The one that's got the bandstand in the middle of the street?"

"Yeah," Bowie said.

"There's a bank there that I robbed when I was a kid. Sawed me off a bar and crawled through and got fourteen dollars in pennies. I used to live in that little town."

Bowie grinned.

"What are you grinning about?" T-Dub said.

"You crawling through them bars and sacking up them pennies."

"I was a cutter then. I was getting me some bicycle money. It was the day after Christmas."

"What were you saying about Morehead?" Chicamaw said.

"I've got half a mind to charge that bank there. I just got a hunch. That bank will go for four or five thousand."

"And it might go for five hundred," Chicamaw said. "I swore one time that I never would fool with them two-bit banks again."

"Beggars can't be choosers. What do you think about it, Bowie?"

"Anything suits me. Whatever you-all say."

"Don't get me wrong, T-Dub," Chicamaw said. "If you boys want to charge a filling station I'm with you."

"When you hear me talking about banks you're not listening to me talk about my first one," T-Dub said.

The footsteps on the porch were like a man's and they listened. It was Mattie though. T-Dub went to the door and she came in. She was a big woman with hips like sacks of oats; the lines in her face were like the veins in dried corn-blades. She had a grease-slotted sack in her hand. "I thought they never were going to get these damned things cooked," she said.

"What's the matter, Mattie?" T-Dub said.

"Nothing." She put the sack on the fireplace shelf. Her toes knotted the leather of the loose black pumps. "I'm going to be checking it to you boys though in just a few minutes. I got to get back to my job."

"I sure hate to see you having to work as hard as you do, Mattie," T-Dub said. "I sure don't know what we would have done without you."

Bowie nodded.

"This is a cash on the barrel-head proposition to me," Mattie said. "I need some money."

"You're going to get it, girl," T-Dub said.

After Mattie left they started eating the hamburgers and T-Dub told them about her. She worked in a sandwich shop for a dollar a day. Showed you what a woman would do when she liked a man. His brother had been in two years and she had never missed a week without sending him money. One woman in ten thousand. He was going to see to it that she got hold of a good piece of money so she could buy a lawyer and spring that bud of his. He was going to stake them to a tourist camp too. Wasn't going to be any more need of that brother of his having to be a thief.

"This is not getting that Morehead business settled," Chicamaw said.

"I'm just waiting on you two," T-Dub said. "We can sack them gentlemen up right tomorrow. Rabbit that seven miles through MacMasters and then cool off at that wildcat. When it gets dark, come right back through that town, right on over here and tomorrow night I don't think we'll be setting here quite as busted."

"Call your shot, Bowie," Chicamaw said.

"I'm in," Bowie said. "I'm ready."

"It's settled," T-Dub said.

Chicamaw said some boys liked to rob a bank before it opened and others around ten-thirty in the morning and two o'clock, but any old time suited him.

T-Dub said that the bank in Morehead didn't have more than three or four working in it and they wouldn't have to count on handling more than the same number of customers if any at all. This bank here in this town though would be a man-sized job. Four men would be the best number to charge a bank like it. One man holding the car down outside and seeing to it that nobody came out; one holding down the lobby and keeping everybody in and the other two working the vault and cages and seeing to it that nobody kicked off any switches.

Bowie was lying on the cot again. I can rib myself up to do anything, he thought.

"Time you split money four ways though you haven't got enough to go around," Chicamaw said. "Three is plenty."

"I'm just telling you," T-Dub said. "These won't be the first banks I ever charged."

"I didn't mean anything," Chicamaw said.

"He didn't mean nothing," Bowie said. He sat up and

looked at the hearth, but the cigarette stubs on it were too short to snipe.

"The Outside man has the hardest job," T-Dub said. "Some of these ding-bats think the guy in the car has the snap. But he's the man that gets the rumbles first. The Inside is a snap. I never saw a banker yet that wouldn't fork over as soon as you throwed down on him. You can always figure that a man that's got sense enough to work in a bank has sense enough to act like a little man when you throw down on him."

"I've had to high-pressure a few of them," Chicamaw said.

"Only Hoosiers kill," T-Dub said.

"I don't believe you have to kill them," Bowie said.

"Them bankers will tell you to help yourself. It's insured. It's them billionaires up in New York that lose it. Them capitalists."

"I hope that Morehead bank will go for a nice piece," Bowie said.

"We'll get cigarette money anyway," Chicamaw said.

"Nossir, I've never robbed anybody in my life that couldn't afford to lose it," T-Dub said. "You couldn't hire me to rob a filling station or hamburger joint."

"I don't believe in that either," Bowie said. "Them boys in them filling stations don't make but two or three dollars a day and if they're robbed, they got to make it up. I'd just as soon beg as do that."

"I know one thing," Chicamaw said. "I'm going to be wearing me a fifteen-dollar Stetson and a sixty-dollar suit here pretty soon or it might be a black suit with some silk plush around me, but I'm sure not going to be wearing no overalls."

T-Dub went back to the kitchen and returned with three broom-straws. "The short man works the Outside," he said.

Bowie drew the short straw.

The others slept now. Bowie lay in the living-room's darkness, his elbow on the window-sill, his fingers scratching the screen. Five thousand, gentlemen, and I'm backing off.

The bed in the middle room creaked and Bowie listened. He smiled. That Indian, he thought.

Voices sounded in the yard outside and Bowie sat up, his hand extended toward the pump gun beside the cot. It was two men with dinner-pails cutting across the yard; going back to the machine-shop. Bowie lay back.

The next time I see that Little Soldier, he thought, I'll be driving a brand-new auto job and looking pretty good in a gray suit and red polka-dot tie and a flannel shirt with pearl buttons. I'll say to her: "I'm looking for that little girl that gave me a big lecture here a couple of years ago." She would look plenty surprised. He'd get a smile out of her though.

Who was that snoring? That old soldier. I got to be doing a little of that myself. One . . . two . . . three . . . four . . . five . . . six. . . .

Chapter VI

WITH its four blocks of filling stations and lunchrooms on the north side of the widened highway and then the intersecting, one-block main street, the town of Morehead had a business district shaped like a funnel. The funnel's mouth was corroded with low buildings of stone and wooden fronts. With Bowie driving the coupe, the three moved up it now toward the frame band-stand at the end of the block. It was ten-thirty o'clock.

The Farmers State Bank stood on the left corner near the band-stand. It was a one-story structure with two cement columns and barred windows. "There's our meat," Chicamaw said. T-Dub touched his forehead in a mock salute. "We'll be in to see you in a few minutes, gentlemen. Don't be impatient."

Bowie made a U turn around the band-stand and then drove, motor idling, past the bank, the Pressing Shop with its window display of bolted goods, the patent-medicine display of the Drug Store and then cut in to park diagonally in front of the Variety Store. In the Variety Store windows were women's underwear. To the left of it was a Meat Market and then a Grocery. Two farmer-looking men sat on cakes of salt lick in front of the Grocery. A youth in a red sweater with an M on it came out of the Pressing Shop and got in a truck.

T-Dub and then Chicamaw got out of the coupe. Chicamaw turned around, winked. "Ten dollars, the Sox beat the Giants this afternoon?" he said.

Bowie grinned. "Called."

The two moved up the street, the bagging seat of T-Dub's overalls wrinkling and Chicamaw's head bobbing on his long neck. They turned and entered the bank.

The bubble in Bowie's stomach broke and sprayed; he put the car in reverse, backed out and then moved down the street toward the highway.

The woman in the sedan ahead stopped parallel in front of the Post Office and Bowie turned out and passed her. That's the way I'll be parking in front of that bank in a minute, he thought. There were two men in broad-brimmed hats and boots standing on the corner in front of the Dry Goods Store. They did not look up. A dog, its ribs bulging, trotted across the street in front of Bowie toward the depot. There was a crated plow on the station's loading platform.

Bowie turned the second corner, passing the Lumber Yard. One block this way now and then another turn and he would be at the Bank again. That dream again last night? His Dad. He could hardly remember what his Dad looked like and yet he was as clear as himself in these dreams. Always the same thing happening. Him in that pool hall with his Dad and that other man getting ready to hit his Dad with the cue; him hollering and his Dad not hearing; him trying to shoot the gun and kill the man and the pistol breaking into pieces in his hand.

Bowie turned the last corner. Maybe that dream meant bad luck coming? If he counted to *thirteen* now with his fingers crossed, it would break the bad luck. *One . . . two . . . three . . . four. . . .*

Bowie stopped in front of the bank . . . *twelve . . . thirteen . . .* pulled the sawed-off shotgun up a little higher between his knees. Come on, Pals. Come on, you Old Soldier. Come on, you Indian. We got tall tracks to make. . . .

There were two more men standing now in front of the Grocery, one smoking a pipe with a curved stem. The pipe-smoker turned and looked up the street toward the Bank. All right, Square-John, that's a good way to get your eyes full and get in trouble. The man turned back.

T-Dub came out of the bank, the front of his overalls bulging! Chicamaw following, two cigar-boxes under his left arm. Bowie looked up and down the street, across to the other side. Nobody big-eyeing or smelling anything yet.

They got in the car and Bowie gunned the motor; Chicamaw slammed the door. The two men sitting on the salt cakes stood up and the others turned and looked.

Bowie swerved onto the highway, the left wheels groaning; the approaching oil truck stopped with a jerk. The driver shouted. Bowie pressed the accelerator harder; the *City Limits* dropped behind. The boy driving a cow with a stick turned his head and watched them go by.

"Anything behind us yet?" Bowie said.

"Naw," Chicamaw said. "Them guys are not going to get out of that Vault for a half-hour. They don't know the Civil War is over yet back there in that town."

T-Dub looked back. "Clear as a whistle."

"You-all do any good?" Bowie said.

"I think so," T-Dub said. He pulled a revolver from inside his overalls. "I picked me up a brand new Colt .45 here anyway. I'll will you that pearl-handled job, Bowie. Did you see me get it out of that till, Chicamaw?"

"Yeah, I saw you."

"Sacked up something else though, didn't you?" Bowie said.

"It went for three or four thousand, I think," T-Dub said.

Chicamaw turned back. "Naw, they don't know yet what it's all about back there."

A car zoomed over the rise ahead, hurtled toward them. It had a California license.

"Four thousand isn't bad, is it?" Bowie said.

"I don't say we got that much," T-Dub said.

"Man, you didn't expect us to stop and count it before we come out of there, did you?" Chicamaw said.

Bowie laughed.

The skyline of Zelton showed now: the fourteen-story hotel, the standpipe, the college buildings on the hill. "We're

going to be holed up before they get out of that vault,"
T-Dub said. "Makes me half decide to go on to the house,
but I want to save that place. We'll just go on to that wildcat."

Bowie turned the coupe off the highway and onto a dirt
road this side of Zelton. They passed the Filteration Plant, the
City Mule Barns, and then Bowie turned back East and presently they were on a paved, residential street. They crossed
the town and cut back onto the highway by the Airport.

As they neared the turn-in to the old oil derrick, a car ahead
of them approached and Bowie slowed. It was a big sedan
with a negro driving and a man in the back seat smoking a
cigar. After it was out of sight, Bowie turned the coupe onto
the derrick road.

Chicamaw climbed the ladder of the derrick and started a
lookout toward the highway. Bowie spread the big cotton-
picking sack on the ground and T-Dub dumped the contents
of the small canvas bag on it. The pile of currency, in rubber-
banded packs of hundreds and twenties and tens and fives and
ones, was as big as the crown of a cowboy Stetson. The two
cigar boxes were spilling silver.

Chicamaw whistled and they looked up. "What's that stuff
you boys are playing with down there?" he said.

"For Christ's sake," T-Dub said.

"Nose-wipin' paper, you damned Indian," Bowie said.
"And there's ten bucks of it you'll never see. Them Giants
have the Sox in a hole by now."

"Another ten says you're a liar."

"Accepted."

"Voices carry out here," T-Dub said. "You guys do your
talking after while."

"Let's pipe down, Chicamaw," Bowie said.

T-Dub took four hundred and twenty-five dollars from the
pile and snapped a rubber band around it. This represented
the amount he had started out with and he put it in his shirt
pocket. Bowie took a ten-dollar bill. "I'll take out six for
Chicamaw," he said. "That's what he had."

Three piles of currency grew as T-Dub dealt out the bills
like playing cards. Finally, it was divided and there was one
thousand and twenty-five dollars apiece. The silver, it was decided, would just be left in the boxes and they would use it

for general expenses like gasoline and beer and cigarettes. There were three or four hundred dollars of it.

Chicamaw descended the ladder and joined them.

"I just started telling Bowie here about that old banker back there," T-Dub said. "That old boy like to have never got it in his head that it was a stick-up."

"Never did put up his hands, did he?" Chicamaw said.

T-Dub laughed. "He never did. He was sitting at a desk there, Bowie, when we went in, just pecking away at an old Oliver typewriter and I had to almost kick the chair out from under him. 'Whatthehell?' he says. 'Whatdoyouthinkthisis?' I had to yank him up and knee him back into the Vault. I think we had the place half sacked before he ever caught on."

"All them others acted like little men," Chicamaw said. "They couldn't get in that Vault quick enough."

"No customers?" Bowie said.

"One," T-Dub said. "Didn't you take a sack off him, Chicamaw?"

"Yeah," said Chicamaw. "I got thirty or forty dollars here I think." He pulled a small money sack out of his hip pocket. "Naw, I don't have no kick coming about that little Bank, but we could have sacked up that Bank in Zelton just as easy. And had ten or twelve apiece. Isn't that right, T-Dub?"

"We'll get to them gentlemen," T-Dub said.

Long ranges of clouds, thick as beaten egg-whites, moved in the afternoon sky. Through the rifts, the dome was as clear as bluing water. The only sounds were the thrumming cars over on the highway and they would stop and listen to them pass. When they talked now, it was in quiet voices.

As soon as it got dark, it was decided, they would return to Zelton and then Bowie could take the coupe out to the edge of the town and burn it. Chicamaw would get a bus and go to El Paso and come back in a couple of days with two fast, light cars and some extra license plates. T-Dub would go over to MacMasters, get Mattie to rent a car and they would get at least two more houses. One in Gusherton and one in Clear Waters.

"We ought to have a sure-enough set-up here in two or three more days," Bowie said.

"Might be that kid sister of Mattie's will go along with me

and her to get them houses," T-Dub said. "You know, boys, I hadn't seen that little old girl since she was in diapers. Cute as a bug now. I want you two to meet her."

"What I'd like to have right now is something to eat," Chicamaw said. "You guys realize we haven't eaten nothing since them hamburgers last night."

"Funny, I'm not hungry," Bowie said. "What I could take on is a good tailor-made cigarette."

"I remember the last time I was cooling off in the country like this we had us a radio and we were gettin' a ball game," T-Dub said. "Chicamaw, maybe you'd better get radios put on them cars. Sure help to pass away the time when you're out like this."

Chapter VII

BUNDLE-LADEN Zelton people jostled and tripped and cut around Bowie in this Saturday-night shopping spree. He was downtown tonight just to stay away from that furnished house. Three nights now he had stayed in it alone and it was getting on his nerves. He had stayed in all morning and afternoon thinking that surely the boys would show up today, but Chicamaw was still somewhere out toward El Paso and T-Dub was rustling houses.

Tonight, Bowie had planned on going to a picture show, but there was nothing on at the two theaters except shoot-em-up cowboy stuff. Rain on that kind of show, he thought.

In front of the Drug Store with the window display of ko-daks and photographs he paused now. There was a picture of a young couple with a baby; a hunter standing beside a car on the running board of which was an antlered deer; a bath-ing-suit girl in a canoe. Bowie peered closer. The gun in the hunter's hand was a .415 Winchester and the deer had six points.

Bowie went on. That Keechie Mobley would make a good picture, I'll bet.

Shaded lights behind the plate glass flushed the colors of

the women's things; the silk blouses, dresses, hose, under-things. Now in a little town like she had to live in, Keechie never saw a bunch of pretty things like this.

In the panel mirror of the Department Store entryway, Bowie looked at his reflection: the iron-gray suit, the broad-brimmed hat, the white handkerchief in his breast pocket. His right hip pocket bulged a little with the .38 T-Dub had given him. Just as soon as I get around to it, I'm going to get a holster and strap and wear it under my arm. Then I won't notice it any more than my hat. I look pretty good though. What was it old T-Dub said about him: "That Bowie looks more like a Law than he does a thief." And Chicamaw: "Like a country boy come to town." That Indian.

Bowie turned and went back up the street, past the 5 & 10, J. C. Penny's, and on the corner, The Guaranty State Bank. He turned it and then was on Front Street, a dim-lighted thoroughfare of small cafés and dollar-hotels. On the other side of the street was the Texas & Pacific Railroad lawn with its mulberry trees, the depot and the freight offices and plat-forms.

A negro in a porter's cap and white jacket sat on a stool in front of the hotel doorway. On the white globe above his head were the lighted letters: *Okeh Rooms.*

"Looking for a nice lady friend tonight, Boss?" the porter said.

"Hell no, you black bastard," Bowie said.

In front of the *New York Café*, on the corner, a policeman stood talking to a bareheaded man who had one foot on the bumper of an automobile at the curb. Bowie walked past them. You got the advantage of Laws all right. You can tell them, but they can't tell you. And the detectives and deputy sheriffs out here might just as well have uniforms, you can tell them so easy. All of them in cowboy boots and white hats and black suits and shoe-string ties. And say that flatfoot back there recognized him when he went past? All right, all that Law had was a pistol. And didn't he have one on too? One thing though, he had to get out in the country pretty soon and practise up with this .38. Get used to it.

Bowie turned toward the railroad lawn, going to the fur-nished house.

There were two new-looking automobiles in the driveway of the house and Bowie checked the impulse to break into a lope. That Indian is back just as sure as the dickens, he thought. The cars were Ford V-8's. One a black job with a trunk and the other was gun-metal colored, both sedans.

It was T-Dub who let Bowie in. He had on a new blue-serge suit and tan shoes.

"Chicamaw come in?" Bowie said.

T-Dub thumbed toward the sound of rushing water in the bathroom. "Taking a bath and gettin' drunk as a Lord. I think he bought up all the tequilla in Juarez."

"I begin to think you two had fell in somewhere," Bowie said. "How long you been here?"

"I got here a little after dark and he was here then." T-Dub went over and lay down on the cot. There was a pile of scattered newspapers beside it.

"I guess you read about Morehead," Bowie said. "Wasn't that a joke? Got one number right in that license. *Three*. And calling it a green coupe and the only thing green about that old Chevvy was the stripe around it."

"Them newspapers never get nothing right. You been casing this bank here any?"

"Every morning since you-all been gone. I went down yesterday morning before daybreak and I been inside of it three times. That Vault kicks off either at nine or maybe before because it's open when the doors open."

"Who goes in first?"

"Nigger. The porter. Around six o'clock. It's a bird's-nest on the ground to go in with him. And the nearest Law is up at the Depot right at that time watching that passenger come in."

"Don't sound half bad."

"How you been doing, T-Dub?"

"We got them houses all right. She went with us on both trips. Lula. That's Mattie's kid sister. I told you about her though."

"Gusherton and Clear Waters?"

"Yep. That Clear Waters place looks like a millionaire's dump. Lula sure liked it."

"Them cars out there look like old Chicamaw has been

doing his stuff. That was a job to tow that gun-metal job all the way in here."

T-Dub sat up. "You know I'd just as soon charge this bank here Monday as not. What do you say?"

"Tomorrow would suit me if it wasn't Sunday."

"I'm going to see the girls tomorrow," T-Dub said.

Chicamaw came out of the bathroom and into the living-room. He had on silk shorts and undershirt and his hair dripped water. The big veins of his biceps and forearms looked like pale earthworms.

"If it's not the old Country Boy himself?" he said.

"Hi, Chicamaw."

"Been teaching Sunday-school over in that tabernacle while we were gone?"

"I been asking for a job down at this nice little bank they got in this town."

"Old Bowie," Chicamaw said. "Believe anything anybody tells him." He looked at T-Dub and winked.

"Anybody except you," Bowie said.

Chicamaw laughed and his bare feet slapped the floor back toward the bedroom.

T-Dub picked up the newspaper again and Bowie went over and sat down in the rocker and lit a cigarette.

The flung newspaper rattled on the pile. "Every time I pick up a paper I see that damned little Squirt's name," T-Dub said. "If I ever run across him you going to see a guy get the damnedest behind-kicking a man ever got."

"Who's that, T-Dub?"

"Newspaper guy. He gave me the dirty end of the stick one time. I tried to make a Hole in this prison in this State one time and it went haywire and this Squirt comes to me and wants me to tell him all about it so he can write a big story for the magazine. Couple of the boys had gotten killed and I was shot right through the fleshy part here of my hip and it was all a mess. Everybody knew all about it anyway and this Squirt said if I would tell him the straight of it he would get it printed and split the money with me. I didn't even have cigarette money so I told him. You should have seen the way it come out in that magazine. I was the Big Shot, see. And I sent them two boys over that got killed first because I figured the guards would use up all their ammunition and then me and the other boy still down at the bottom of the ladder would have a clear way. Anybody knows that the Chair boys get the first break and that's why they went over first. Hell, I didn't go on up because the damned ladder had broke. One of them joint ladders you know. Then that Squirt getting it put in the magazine like that."

"Don't guess he ever sent you any money?"

T-Dub looked up and sneered.

Chicamaw came back in with a bottle of tequilla in his hand. He had on brown tweed trousers with pleats, a blue shirt and yellow tie. He offered the bottle and Bowie shook his head.

"For Christ's sake, come on and be human," he said.

Bowie took a drink.

"I ran into a pooloo in a sandwich stand close to Pecos that we knew up in Alky," Chicamaw said. "You guys remember that kid we called Satchel Pratt?"

Bowie and T-Dub nodded.

"He knew me right off and crawled all over that car and got to telling me how he knew where there was a good piece of money."

"Tin safe somewhere with thirty dollars in it," T-Dub said.

"I played him along. Told him I'd shove on and be back to the number he gave me right after dark and we would go and get together on that job he had."

"I remember that kid," Bowie said. "He played a banjo pretty good."

"I brought you something, boy, from the city," Chicamaw said. "I run into some good Colt .45's out there and you can throw that .38 job of yours away."

"Man, I'm glad to hear that."

"You got to promise me that you won't sleep with it under your pillow though."

"Now what's the joke?" Bowie said.

Chicamaw looked at T-Dub and winked. "All right," he said and pointed his finger at Bowie. "I'll bet that's the way you been sleeping at nights?"

"Yes."

Chicamaw looked at T-Dub and then back at Bowie. "That's just what I thought. Look here, man. Always sleep with your gun under the cover by your side. Then if anybody walks in on you, you got as much of a throw-down on them as they got on you. Just let 'em have it. But you sure can't do any reaching up and behind you . . . like *this*."

"I never thought of that before," Bowie said. "I'm sure glad you told me, Chicamaw."

T-Dub stood up. "What do you say we start talking about this bank here? Bowie is ready to go Monday, Chicamaw."

"You don't have to ask me if I'm ready. I'm always ready." He lifted the bottle and there was a gurgling sound.

"Boys, it's going to be my thirtieth," T-Dub said.

Chapter VIII

LAST night, T-Dub had drawn the short straw, but because he knew more about the Inside of a bank, it was decided Chicamaw would drive the black V-8 and Bowie would go Inside with T-Dub. They had gotten out of bed at four o'clock this morning, driven out to the Derrick Hole and left the gun-metal sedan. Now it was six o'clock and they sat parked in front of the Sears, Roebuck Company store next to the Guaranty State Bank. The empty street looked as wide as a river.

"If Bowie and me are not out of there by nine o'clock," T-Dub said, "you better be coming in after us, Chicamaw."

Chicamaw lifted his head in a laughing gesture.

Somewhere the sound of a street-sweeping machine whirred and threshed. Away down the street, in front of the Café, a man came out and got in a car. The slamming door echoed in the canyon of buildings. The car vanished.

"Here it comes, Boys," Bowie said. He pointed up the street. A negro in a gray rope sweater was approaching. Bowie and T-Dub got out of the car and stood beside it.

The negro was a middle-aged man with sideburns like steel wool. He stood there at the bank door, selecting a key on the ring. He inserted the key and grasped the knob.

"We're going in with you, Shine," T-Dub said. Bowie

pressed the gun's barrel firmly against the rope sweater and
they went into the bank's clean, early-morning gloom. Bowie
squatted down and looked under the slit of the drawn blind.
Chicamaw was driving off.

The negro breathed like he had been running, his wrists
sticking rigidly out of the frayed sweater cuffs. "I doesn't
quite understand this," he said.

"Don't bother yourself, Shine," T-Dub said. "You're liable
to wake up with somebody patting you in the face with a
spade if you do."

Bowie started tying the negro's thumbs behind him with
copper wire. "Mistah, I been porterin' heah fawh twenty
yeahs. You can ask anybody in Zelton. Everybody heah knows
old Ted. Right heah in this bank fawh twenty yeahs. When
they had the old building. Yassah, I been . . ."

"That's enough, Shine," T-Dub said. "Now you'd like to
be able to go to church again next Sunday, wouldn't you?"

"Yassah."

"Then you just answer the questions I'm going to ask you."

"Yassah. I never lied to nobody in mah life. You can ask
anybody in Zelton about me."

The clock over the front door indicated *6:30*. On both sides
of the gray tile floor at the front of the bank were brown
railings and inside of these were clean desks with lettered
stands: *President . . . Vice-President . . . Vice-President. . . .*
The bronze cages fenced the passageway of glass-topped
tables back to the Vault. It was a big, broad door of aluminum
and black colors. To the right was a passageway that led to
the side-entrance door.

"What time does that big vault back there unlatch, Shine?"
T-Dub said.

"Cap'n, that something I doesn't know about. Some of the
big bosses don't even know that. Mistah Berger knows about
it."

"What time does he come down?"

"He's the fust one. Li'l' before eight."

Bowie moved around. Through the slits of the Venetian
blind at the side-entrance door he saw the closed, steel doors
of the freight depot. An oil truck went past.

The clock clicked: *7:00*.

More automobiles were sounding on the streets outside
now. A switch engine whistled and then the intersection railroad signal began to dong. The exhaust of a bus popped,
fluttered. Bowie read the hand-lettered football schedule on
the wire stand by the front door.

The knob of the front door turned and the man smelling
of hair tonic and shaving lotion came in. He was short and
had a belly as round as the sides of a mare in foal.

"Mister Berger?" T-Dub said. He had an open pocket knife
in his left hand.

The man stood there, his left hand extended in a paralyzed,
door-closing movement. His head went up and down.

"Mister Berger, this is a stick-up, and if you want to stay a
healthy man, and I think you do, you'll just co-operate."

"I see," Mister Berger said.

It was 7:15.

The heavy doors of the freight depot creaked and groaned
in opening. Box-cars bumped in the railroad yards. Automobile horns sounded.

7:45.

Through the blind slots of the side door, Bowie saw the
black flannel coat, the silk-clad ankles of a woman. He turned
and T-Dub, standing in front of the Vault with Mister Berger
and Shine, nodded. Bowie opened the door.

The woman gasped like she had been pricked with a pin
and Bowie put his hand over her mouth. She became limp in
his arms. "Take it easy now, Lady," Bowie said. "Nobody is
going to hurt you."

"Be calm, Miss Biggerstaff," Mister Berger said, "these
men are not desperadoes."

"I never kill anybody," T-Dub said, "if they just do what I
tell them to."

8:30.

Bowie peered through the blind slots. The black V-8 was
parked there now, Chicamaw's head down over a spread newspaper on the steering wheel. A match worked in his mouth.
That Indian.

Mister Berger and T-Dub were inside the Vault now. A cage
door clicked and rattled. Bowie's toes squirmed in his shoes.
Sack it, T-Dub. Dump it in. Just a minute, Chicamaw. . . .

Mister Berger came out; then T-Dub with the bulging laundry sack slung across his back.

"Ready?" T-Dub said.

"Ready," Bowie said.

"We're going to take you folks with us," T-Dub said. "There's a Ford just out that door there and you go out there and get in it and don't let me see any of you looking at anybody 'cause if you do you're liable to get somebody killed."

There were two men in striped overalls working on the loading platform across the street, but they did not stop. Mister Berger and Miss Biggerstaff and Shine got in the back; then Bowie. He told Shine to lay on the floor. T-Dub got in front with Chicamaw.

They moved off. The young fellow parking the coupe stared. He had on a tan suit and horn-rimmed glasses.

T-Dub turned around. "You know him?"

"One of the boys in the bank," Mister Berger said.

The speed indicator rose: past the Candy Factory . . . Produce Company . . . Cotton Compress . . . Nigger Town. . . . A farmer, high up on the cotton wagon, saluted. Chicamaw waved back.

They crossed the railroad tracks and then sped up the straight, dirt road toward the picket of telephone poles that marked the highway.

Miss Biggerstaff looked at Bowie. "What are you going to do with us?"

"Don't worry, Lady."

"I have done everything in the world I could, Men," Mister Berger said.

T-Dub turned around. "You folks just sit steady now. You have done all right and everything is okeh now."

Bowie could see the grinning lines on Chicamaw's cheek. He smiled too. The speedometer needle vibrated on *80*. Miss Biggerstaff shivered as if she were cold.

Holding to the top rung of the derrick ladder, Bowie saw the car leave the highway, its aluminum glittering like signal mirrors, and come onto this road. He whistled and below, T-Dub and Chicamaw picked up the corners of the spread cotton-picking sack with its piles of currency.

But the car was only turning around. Bowie whistled again and shook his head violently. The canvas was spread again.

Over in the black sedan, Mister Berger, Miss Biggerstaff and Shine sat, the feet of the men bound in copper wire. For three hours now, T-Dub had been dealing the bills and still he was wetting his fingers and going on. That's the prettiest sight I ever saw, Bowie thought. Bar none. He shifted his arm through the rung and grasped his belt. Bar none.

Chicamaw relieved Bowie on the lookout.

T-Dub grinned as Bowie approached. "Nossir, Bowie, that wasn't my first bank, but I never saw one go sweeter."

"I never saw a prettier sight then looking down here from up there," Bowie said.

Over in the black car, the glass rattled and Bowie saw Miss Biggerstaff rapping. "Go see what they want," T-Dub said.

Bowie came back. "It's the Lady. I think she wants to go to the bathroom. I think that's what she wants."

"She won't rabbit. Let her out."

"That Berger over there told me we got ten thousand dollars in securities here that's not worth anything to us and mean a lot to him."

"He's a damned liar. There's sixty thousand dollars' worth here, but he can have them back. They're no good to us."

At last the money was counted and divided. There was twenty-two thousand six hundred and seventy-five dollars apiece.

In the dusk, Chicamaw and Bowie tied Mister Berger and Shine to mesquites. Then Chicamaw went on up the road, out of sight, and presently they heard the motor of the gunmetal firing. It moved toward the hills and the Gusherton Highway.

Bowie drove the black car and T-Dub sat in the back with Miss Biggerstaff. "We're just going to take you up here a couple of miles, Lady," T-Dub said, "and then you can walk back and untie that gentleman friend of yours."

On the Gusherton Highway, Bowie and T-Dub got in the gun-metal with Chicamaw and left the flaming black car behind.

The house in the resort town of Clear Waters was an eight-room Spanish stucco with a patio, a three-car garage and big, sparrow-filled poplar trees in the parkways. It was a corner place and across from it was a four-story apartment house.

Bowie sat in the living-room now, soaking in its richness. There was a radio and a secretary and brocaded coverings on the divan and chairs. The lights on the rough plaster of the walls were shaped like candlesticks. Confession and Movie magazines littered the floor and the ashtrays were full of cigarette butts stained with lipstick. From the kitchen, where Mattie and Lula and T-Dub were cooking, came the smell of ham and eggs.

Chicamaw came in, his hair plastered and smelling of perfumed oil and indicated the room with a roll of his head. "Pretty good for some old boys that didn't have a pot or a window to throw it out three weeks ago, eh, Big Boy?"

"Pretty nice," Bowie said.

"You tied up with some fast company, didn't you, Boy?"

"I'll say."

Lula came in with T-Dub following. She was tall and had on a cotton house-dress and blue anklets. Her shaved legs had scratches on them and there was the tattoo of a red heart on the back of her left hand.

"Don't you think Lula and me would make a team," T-Dub said. They sat on the divan and T-Dub put his arm around her waist and began fingering the cloth over her stomach. "Last time I saw this little outfit she was just about up to my knees and now look at her."

"He's nuts," Lula said.

"I think you got him going, Lula," Bowie said.

Lula slapped T-Dub's hand away and reached in his coat pocket and brought out a package of cigarettes. She extended them toward Bowie and then Chicamaw. They shook their heads.

T-Dub held a match for her. "Yessir, this little girl is going to put a tattoo on her for me pretty soon." He winked at Bowie and then Chicamaw. "And it ain't going to be on her hand."

The smoke gushed from Lula's nostrils and she flecked the cigarette toward the ashtray. "I wouldn't be so sure about that now, Mister," she said. "And if I'm going up to that drug

store before our midnight supper, you better be giving me a
few nickels and let me get started."

Mattie came in. She had a dish towel tied over the black
silk dress like an apron. "You boys come and get it. Was that
Lula leaving, T-Dub?"

"We ought to wait until she gets back 'fore we eat," T-Dub
said.

"Come on," Mattie said.

Their knives and forks scraped and slashed the eggs and
ham. "I don't wonder that bud of mine isn't working his head
off to get out with cooking like this, Mattie," T-Dub said.

"It's not cooking that's going to get him out," Mattie said.

Lula thrust the newspaper toward T-Dub. "It's all over the
front page," she said. "All over it."

T-Dub pushed plates aside and spread the newspaper, and
Chicamaw and Bowie bent over him.

ZELTON, Sept. 28—In one of the boldest bank hold-ups in West
Texas history, three armed bandits this morning robbed the Guaranty
State Bank here, kidnaped A. T. Berger, vice-president, his secretary,
Miss Alma Biggerstaff, and escaped with what bank officials estimated
at more than $100,000 in cash and securities.

Berger and Miss Biggerstaff with Ted Phillips, negro bank porter,
also kidnaped by the trio, were picked up by passing motorists, 21
miles east of here at 8 o'clock tonight. Miss Biggerstaff was in a
hysterical condition from the day of terror and imprisonment.

Working with the precision of master criminals, the robbers entered
the bank before the doors opened this morning. Arriving bank employees, unable to get into the bank at 8 o'clock, sounded the alarm.
William Pleasant, bank bookkeeper, saw a black, crowded sedan leave
the bank's side entrance as he was getting ready to park, but did not
realize its full significance until later.

Today's holdup followed within less than a week the $3,000 rob-
bery of the Farmers State Bank at Morehead, adjoining community.
Local authorities believe both crimes were committed by the same
band.

One of the bandits, Police Chief Robert Blakely announced here
tonight, has been positively identified as an escaped Oklahoma
convict.

"Oh, oh," T-Dub said. "They got me identified."

"I don't care which one they got identified," Chicamaw

said, "they ain't going to have to guess long to know who was with you."

The food in Bowie's stomach felt like it was expanding.

A posse of more than two hundred police officers and citizens combed the country around here throughout the day in a fruitless search. At a called meeting this morning of the Chamber of Commerce, directors authorized the posting of a $100 reward for the capture, dead or alive, of any member of the gang.

"Now what did we do, boys?" Chicamaw said.

L. E. Sellers, a farmer living four miles east of town, reported that a loaded car passed him shortly after 8 o'clock this morning, traveling East at a high rate of speed.

The bandits were described as being well-dressed men around 30 years of age.

"If it had not been for the bravery of Mr. Berger," Miss Biggerstaff declared, "I am afraid we would not be alive to tell our stories. They threatened our lives almost every minute. Mister Berger talked to them coolly."

The two bank robberies in this vicinity this past week mark the first time in four years that a bank has been robbed in this section. The last one was at Stocton, 40 miles southwest of here, by the famous Trawler gang. Trawler was hanged by an enraged mob at Stocton last December after he killed a jailer in a desperate attempt to escape.

T-Dub pushed the newspaper aside. "Well, boys, that's the situation."

"They sure did put it all over the front page, didn't they?" Lula said.

"The next time, Sweetheart," T-Dub said, "you bring us some good news."

"Christ, let's finish eating," Chicamaw said.

Bowie lay on the ivory-inlaid bed, under the smooth sheet and silken comfort, in the feminine, mirror-paneled room where the perfume of powders and toilet waters still lingered. That blows me up, he thought. Yessir, that sure blows me up on going back to Alky.

Up in the living-room, Lula giggled and then there was T-Dub's rumbling laugh. The Mexican orchestra of the

Border radio station was playing *La Golondrina*, a background of guitars strumming plaintively.

Bowie moved and the .45 was cold against his naked thigh. Yessir, that sure blows me up. But what are you gripin' about, Man? You got twenty-two thousand dollars right under this bed.

Chapter IX

ON the afternoon of their third day in the Clear Waters Stucco, Chicamaw became staggering drunk and bumped around the house, his shirt tail hanging, and demanding who in the hell had hid his tequilla. Mattie and Lula threatened to leave and T-Dub became white-faced. Bowie finally got Chicamaw into the back bedroom. "Come on now, Chicamaw," he said, "and sleep a while. It'll be good for you."

"I'm not sleepy," Chicamaw said. "I'm drunk. I don't mind telling you I'm drunk. They ain't but two things I like to do and that's love and drink and there ain't enough women here to go around so I'm drinking. What do you think I left Alky for?"

"Don't talk so loud, Chicamaw."

"What do you think I left Alky for? To drink chicory coffee and look at art magazines?"

"Take it easy now, Pal."

"All right, old boy, old boy, old boy."

"You're scaring them girls."

"Let old Battle Axe leave."

"Snap out of it, Chicamaw."

"Old Country Boy is telling me what to do. You're just a big old farm boy, Bowie, but goddamit, you got something and I don't mind telling you, I can't figure it out. Let's you and me shell out of this place, Bowie. Go up to Oklahoma. Let's get us a bus and go to Dallas and get us a Packard and throw us a good one. You're going to Oklahoma with me, aren't you, Pal?"

"We ought to cool off here a few more days. There's still some heat out there."

"You going to Oklahoma with me, aren't you, Pal?"

"We'll talk about that later. What you want to do now is get yourself some sleep. You got to snap out of it, man. That real estate man was in here this morning taking an inventory and he big-eyed around plenty and that man that come up to the front door and said he was a census taker might just be nosying. There might be a little war around this place before you know it."

"You going to Oklahoma with me, aren't you, Pal?"

"We'll talk about that after you sleep a while. That and going to Mexico."

"Come on now, Bowie, wouldn't you like to go up to Oklahoma and see that little cousin of mine?"

"She's not interested in seeing me."

"That home town of mine is just forty miles from there and I want to see my folks, Bowie. I got to see them."

"I'd like to see Dee get three or four hundred dollars."

Chicamaw compressed his lips and closed his eyes and there was a whistling in his nostrils as he breathed. Bowie watched him for a little while and then bent down to unlace his shoe. Chicamaw's eyes opened. "You know why I want to go to Oklahoma?"

"Sure, boy. See your Old Man and Old Lady. And you want me to go along and stand on the corner with that pump gun of mine and see to it that nobody comes nosying around."

"That ain't all."

"You want to say hello to your folks."

"My folks know what I want and I got to take them the money to do it with. Them folks of mine haven't got a pot or a window to throw it out and I got to get them some money. Bowie, they ain't going to catch me floating around in no tank in them doctor schools if they ever get me. That's what they do to you if you can't pay the undertaker. They'll throw you in one of them tanks and carve on you."

"You must be drunk, boy, to talk that way."

"I want to be planted right. Goddamit, I'll give them every cent of it and I want to be planted right."

"I'll go get you a cold towel."

"Don't you leave me, boy."

T-Dub came in. His shaven face had a pink flush now and his hair was as white and soft as a baby's brush from the vinegar washing Lula had given it. He touched his forehead in a salute. "Feeling better, Chicamaw?"

"Who hid that tequilla, T-Dub?"

"Man, I don't know where it is."

"Tell that Battle Axe to rout it up."

"You're drunk, man, but you better start quieting down," T-Dub said.

"Old Foxy T-Dub," Chicamaw said. "Old Foxy."

Mattie came in, holding out a magazine. "Maybe this will sober him up some," she said.

It was a True Detective magazine and on the opened page were all their pictures: *Oklahoma Fugitives. $100 Reward.*

Bowie brushed it back. "He don't care about seeing that thing. Go burn that damned thing up."

T-Dub and Mattie left.

"Bowie, you going to Oklahoma with me?"

"If you'll go to sleep now I'll go. I don't mean that, boy. I'll go with you anyway."

"Then I'll go to Mexico with you, Bowie."

"That sure suits me."

Bowie lowered himself to the edge of the bed and after a little while, Chicamaw slept.

Bowie went up to the living-room and there were Mattie and Lula standing at the door, dressed up and bags around them. T-Dub was pale again. "The girls are going down to the Penitentiary to see my bud," he said. "I'm going to take them to the depot."

Bowie nodded.

"Your friend decided to quiet down?" Mattie said. The short fur jacket looked like she had another bag under it.

"He's all right," Bowie said.

"I was telling them that there's not a finer boy when he's sober," T-Dub said.

"He's all right," Bowie said.

"I hope we see you again soon, Bowie," Lula said. There was lipstick salve on her chin.

"Goodbye," Bowie said.

After T-Dub and the girls left, Bowie went back to the bedroom and looked at Chicamaw. He was snoring and had his mouth open. It was growing dark and Bowie stepped over and raised the blind a little. Then he sat down on the bench in front of the vanity.

I'll go on up there with him, he thought. There's nothing else for me to do and there's gettin' to be too many women around this joint. I'm ready to go to Mexico right now myself. If these boys want to rob that bank at Gusherton I'll help them, but I'm ready to clear out of this myself.

The breathing sounds in Chicamaw's throat sounded like air escaping from a flabby tire.

Mexico? Deer and wild turkey and cougars and bears even. A .414 Winchester would be the best for deer. A bear? Now that's something I'll have to do some figuring on when I get down there. Christ. If I was in Mexico with a .22 I would be satisfied. And just rabbits to hunt. Let me down there, man, and I'll run them rabbits down on foot.

The front door sounded and Bowie went up to the living-room. It was T-Dub. He went over and sat down on the divan and began flecking at bits of cigarette ash on the blue serge of his broad thighs. "I hated to see that little girl go," he said.

"You'll see her again," Bowie said.

"That Chicamaw back there has got it down all wrong," T-Dub said. "You can't make women a money-on-the-barrel-head proposition. Love 'em and leave 'em. It don't work when you meet somebody decent. He's nuts though."

"This business is no good for a girl," Bowie said. "That's what he means."

"Where would we have been if it hadn't been for Mattie?"

"I know it. It's a proposition."

T-Dub said that if Bowie and Chicamaw went to Oklahoma, he might go down to Houston and try and get Lula to go off with him on a little trip to Galveston or New Orleans. Mattie would come back and keep their houses held down. He had given her two thousand dollars to buy a car and have something to run around on.

Bowie said he and Chicamaw would come in and do their part on that two thousand.

In the distance, a siren sounded and they looked at each

other and listened. The sound grew nearer and then they heard the bells of the fire engine clanging and they relaxed.

"But I been thinking, Bowie, and you're not going to get three together like us again nor a set-up like we got now. In a couple of months if we just stay foxy we can have fifty thousand apiece and then will be the time to back off for keeps."

"If we're going to charge that bank at Gusherton I'm in favor of doing it and gettin' it over with."

T-Dub shook his head. "These banks out here are looking for trouble now. Look at what happened to those two kids day before yesterday. Trying to work right in our heat."

"You kill somebody though like they did and your heat really gets hot."

"They were Hoosiers."

Bowie began cleaning his finger-nails with a split match.

"What I want to do," T-Dub said, "is get me about fifty thousand salted away and invest it in one of the Big Syndicates and get it paid back to me two or three hundred dollars a month. I'd like to find me a doctor that's a thief like us and get him to saw off these finger-prints and I'd grow a beard about a foot long and rear back up in them Kentucky hills on that little farm and let the mistletoe hang on my coat tail for the rest of the world."

"I hate to stay cooped up like this in a house," Bowie said. "I'm like a mule though, I never know what I do want."

"You got to put up with things I don't care how you make your money. And you take a chance in anything. Take them aviators. I got a cousin that's in the army and he was writing my bud and telling him how he was soloing around up there. I'll bet that kid don't last as long as I do."

"I know I'm in this a lot deeper than I planned to be. I'm going to be like that Indian back there I guess. Go up this road as long as I can. Win, lose or draw."

"I made my mistake when I was a kid," T-Dub said. He lifted his leg and looked at the polished toe of the shoe critically. "But a kid can't see things. I should have made a lawyer or run a store or run for office and robbed people with my brain instead of a gun. But I never was cut out to work for any two or three dollars a day and have to kiss somebody's behind to get that."

"I don't guess I could have done anything else except what I have," Bowie said. "What will be, will be."

A little after midnight, Chicamaw's feet padded in the hallway and then he came into the lighted room, rubbing his nose and twisting his face. "Got a cigarette, anybody?" he said.

Bowie gave him a cigarette. Chicamaw went over and sat on the divan by T-Dub. The cigarette trembled in his hand and he began rubbing his ankles together and finally he reached down and scratched the left one. "What time is it gettin' to be?" he said.

"After twelve," Bowie said.

"What have I been doing around here?" Chicamaw said. "I feel like hell."

"You just been guzzling a little," T-Dub said. "The girls left."

"Did they?"

"They went down to see my bud."

Chicamaw scratched his other ankle and then his elbow.

"Bowie and me have been talking business," T-Dub said. "If you boys are going to Oklahoma, what do you say we let things rock for about a month and all of us meet up again in that house in Gusherton, say, November fifteenth?"

The cigarette fell out of Chicamaw's hand and he grunted as he picked it up. "Suits me."

"I'm in," Bowie said.

"November fifteenth in Gusherton then," T-Dub said. "Boys, if we sack them up over there it will be my thirty-first."

Chapter X

IT was cold this morning and the fallen leaves of the poplar-trees rustled and clattered on the sidewalk in the wind. Bowie carried Chicamaw's black Gladstone and his own brown strapped bag out to the gun-metal and put them in the back seat. In Dallas I'm going to buy myself an overcoat. Pretty good to know you got the old mazuma in your pockets to buy yourself a coat and anything else you might need. And I sure got it on me. Seven thousand in that bag; ten thousand in this coat pocket and these two pants pockets. And three thousand in silver in the trunk of this car.

Chicamaw came out with the guns in a blanket and then T-Dub with a black Gladstone. T-Dub's collar was turned up around his throat and he moved like his bones were on hinges. He said it was rheumatism.

"All you need is a good dose of Lula," Chicamaw said.

At the Sante Fe depot downtown, T-Dub got out, saluted and grinned and went on in. He was going to Houston.

On the road to Dallas, Bowie and Chicamaw talked about how they were going to do things there. They would register in at the biggest hotel, Bowie as *A. J. Peabody* and Chicamaw as *Frank Masters*, baseball players from Denver, Colorado. They would stay there all day, Chicamaw getting his car, and right after dark take out for Oklahoma.

"You better not go too strong on one of those big cars," Bowie said. "Get one of them big jobs and everybody will be big-eyeing you."

"That shows you what you know about it, boy. If I could get me a green Packard with red wheels and a calliope whistle I'd do it. Then they big-eye the car instead of you."

"After we give this car to Dee I think I'll get me another V-8," Bowie said.

The quiet of the thick-carpeted hotel room—*814*—was that of a bathroom and Bowie, alone now, soaked in it. A hotel is just about the safest place for a man, he thought. Say one of these hotel clerks thought he saw something? Well, he wouldn't be in any too big a hurry to call a bunch of Laws in. People staying in hotels wouldn't appreciate a little war busting in their faces. Then it was pretty hard for a man to get in a rank as long as he was throwing money. People taking your money just didn't run off and squawk. Men just weren't made that way. He took a sheaf of currency from his inside coat pocket and dropped it on the blue counterpane. "And, Brother, I got it to throw."

After bathing and shaving, Bowie went down and sat in the lobby. Everybody around him had on pressed suits and shined shoes and watch chains across their vests. They're not the kind of fellows that big-eye you, Bowie thought. It's these Hoosiers in these little filling stations that don't have anything else to do but chew tobacco and look in them damned detective magazines.

After a little while, he went to the street and started looking in the shop windows. In a mirror he studied his hat and decided that the brim was too broad. Too much like a cowboy. He went in the Department Store on the corner, and besides the new hat he bought a double-breasted blue overcoat, two handbags and a powder-blue suit with a belted back. I'll show that Indian a fancy thing or two in duds myself.

In the Jewelry Store, he bought an open-faced watch and chain and then a ladies' wrist watch with six diamonds on the band. That Little Soldier will open her eyes when I hand her this.

It was noon when he returned to 814 and Chicamaw had not showed up.

He tried on the powder-blue, but it was just too much of a go-to-hell suit for him. That Little Soldier would give him the laugh if he turned up in it. What am I ribbing myself up about that girl for? I'm just going to fool around here and make a donkey out of myself. That girl has other things to think about besides a damned thief like you, Man.

Now was the time, he decided, to send some money to Mama. Five of these one-hundred dollar bills with one of these pieces of hotel stationery around them and one of them envelopes. I wouldn't mind sending her five thousand if it wasn't for that no-good husband she's got. He'll get every damned bit of it. Now if it was that second husband she had it would be okeh. He was a pretty good fellow. Dumb, but I wouldn't mind helping him.

Old Jim and Red up there in Alky could sure stand a few bucks. Jim sure liked his sweet milk and them charging twenty cents a quart up there in that Prison when you could buy it in town for a nickel. And old Red wouldn't smoke nothing but tailor-mades. I'll get to you boys. I'll stop in one of these post-offices pretty soon and send you boys a hundred apiece. I've got to do some stopping in some of these towns pretty soon and get some of these dollar bills changed into twenties. Got enough of them things to pack a washtub. I'll just start shoving them through these bank windows, twenty and thirty at a time, and pretty soon I'll get rid of them.

Bowie pulled off his shoes and lay on the bed. *814*. Oh, oh. *Eight* plus *one* plus *four* equals *thirteen*. Aw, there's nothing to that. That's carrying it too far.

Mexico? Man, money will go a long ways down there. Three of them pesos for a dollar. Twenty thousand? Jesus Christ. That would be forty-five thousand pesos even after he took out for a car and the other expenses he would have while he stayed up here. Now if I go on through with it at Gusherton? Jesus Christ. I'll be a damned rich man. . . .

Bowie woke up with Chicamaw standing above him. "I thought I was going to have to pop my pistol to get you up. Man, you'd be a pushover." He smelled of liquor.

"What time is it?"

"If we're going to get out of here right after dark we better be gettin' in the saddle."

Bowie had the delicate, spraying feeling in his belly.

When Chicamaw, up there ahead of him in the new Auburn, held out his hand, Bowie slowed and then turned in to park alongside of him at the sandwich stand. It was a neon-lighted place with beer signs and a lettered board of sandwich prices. When the uniformed girl came out, Chicamaw said he wanted twelve bottles of beer to carry.

After the girl went back into the stand, Chicamaw pointed up the street toward the filling station on the left corner with the *Gas . . . 13¢* sign. "I run in that very station up there once and there was an old boy in there that sure big-eyed me. He had a wooden leg, I remember. I noticed him, see, out of the corner of my eye and finally he says to me: 'Boy, it ain't none of my business, but I know you.' I says to him: 'Brother, you just think you know me.' He says: 'You're Elmo Mobley as sure as hell, but after you leave here, I never have seen nobody that even looked like you.'"

"He really knew you, did he?"

"Sure he did. But I never did let on, see. He says to me: 'Boy, I just wish you had got this bank here 'fore it went busted and took my wad. I'd rather for a poor boy like you to have it than them goddamned bankers. Both of them bankers are out of prison now and still living swell on what they stole from me and about four or five hundred more folks here.' "

"I'll be doggoned. He was Real People."

"I gave him a ten and told him to keep the change."

"You run into Real People once in a while all right."

The girl returned with the bottles of beer in a sack and Chicamaw put them in his car. He said to Bowie: "If you're in such a big hurry, I'll just let you set the pace out of this town and I'm telling you, boy, you better stomp it or I'm liable to run over you."

"Okeh," Bowie said.

Bowie moved out the boulevard toward the Oklahoma Highway, the rear-vision mirror of his car reflecting the following lights of Chicamaw's automobile. *I'm going to be in Keota in an hour and a half.* This buggy is going to get stomped. He felt of the small hard bulge in his left vest pocket. Yes, the watch was still there. He pressed the accelerator harder.

The one-lamped car approached on the intersecting street ahead from the right, but there was a Stop Sign there and Bowie stepped back on the gas. The other car lunged right on across the Stop Sign and Bowie stomped brake and clutch, swerved, but the One-Lamp hit and then a bucket was shoved down over Bowie's head and tons of shattering glass were burying him. He thought: *This is liable to get me in trouble. . . .*

Thrown from the sprung door of his car, Bowie rose from the parquet grass, feeling like the figure in a slow-motion picture. He was on his feet now, a terrific weight on his back. Yonder was his car, the radiator caved in against a broken lamp-post and behind it was an old coupe, somebody inside of it groaning, its one lamp still burning.

Human forms moved like shadows about Bowie now. "Are you hurt, Friend?" a Shadow said. "No," Bowie said. He moved toward his car, dragging the weight that was like a plow. *I got to get that stuff. . . . I got to get that stuff. . . .*

It was a woman in the wrecked coupe: "Oh, my God. Oh, my God. Oh, my God. . . ."

Bowie reached his car, grasped at the handle with hands that felt like they had gone to sleep. He staggered with the push. "Get on over in my car, you damned boob," Chicamaw said.

Somewhere now there was a sound like a thousand trucks straining up a high hill in first gear. Them's not trucks, Man, Bowie thought. Sirens. His fingers groped at the emptiness of his right hip. Gun gone. That's the kind of luck I have, gentlemen. He moved across the street, through the working Shadows, dragging the Plow, toward Chicamaw's car.

He climbed into the front seat and then thrown bags were thumping in the rear. To hell with the rest, Chicamaw, boy. Come on. Everybody and his dog is coming. . . .

The flashlight was like a blow-torch in Bowie's face. The Voice behind it said: "What's your hurry, Buddy?"

"I'm in no hurry," Bowie said.

"I'm taking him to a doctor, Officer," Chicamaw said. Another bag thumped in the back. "He's bunged up pretty bad."

"I'm pretty bad bunged up," Bowie said. The flashlight clicked off and then he saw Officer, the bulging chin that was like a licked hog's knuckles. Another form in a black hat was with him.

"Where you from?" Officer said.

"Denver," Chicamaw said. "You fellows come on to the hospital, by God, if you want to ask questions."

"There's a woman over there hurt and from what I can hear you were traveling too fast," Officer said. "You get out of that car and come on with me. And you too, Buddy."

"Not this time, Friend," Chicamaw said.

Second Officer said: "Listen here, Bub, you going to get in jail yourself here 'fore you know it."

"Not this time, Friend. . . ." Shoes scraped and then the hoofs of a thousand horses were thundering on a tin roof above Bowie's head. Guns! Bowie reached toward the panel pocket: *This is liable to get me killed.*

Like a cut radio, the noise ended. Then Chicamaw was getting under the wheel; the motor roared like an airplane taking off and Shadows scattered in the street ahead of them like cotton-tail rabbits.

The car sliced the highway wind with the sound of simmering water. Chicamaw pressed the panel button and the illuminated speedometer, to Bowie, glowed through a mist. Chicamaw tapped and the instrument board was dark again. "You're bleeding like a stuck pig," he said.

"I'm all right."

"You better snap out of it."

"It was a Little War."

"They were men enough to start it. Let 'em be men enough to take it."

"It was an old one-light Jalope that got me. Come right out and got me good."

"I'm going to dump you at Dee's. There's plenty of heat behind us and I'm going to let you out and get on up the road and burn this car."

"It was a Little War. That old Jalope."

"You're not hurt bad, are you? You're bleeding like a stuck pig."

"I'm all right."

They whipped around the red tail-light of another car; then the twin glow of another.

I'm just sick at my stomach, Bowie thought. That's all. Why I used to get sick just from standing up when Mama was cuttin' my hair. Her name was Peabody then. No, that was the first man. It was Vines, the carpenter one, then. See, Chicamaw, that shows you I have snapped and my mind is clear. Vines was his name. Pain seized Bowie's back with the grip of a twisted monkey-wrench and his belly muscles became as rigid as a washboard.

"What the hell?" Chicamaw said.

"I'm all right."

Chicamaw ran the car under the darkened shed of Dee Mobley's filling station, got out and vanished behind it. Just let me lay down for an hour, Bowie thought, and then I'll feel just as good as ever.

Chicamaw came back with Dee and when Bowie got out, his legs felt like cooked macaroni and he sunk to his knees. "Ain't that funny?" he said. They carried him back to the Bunk.

"I put everything under the bed here," Chicamaw said.

"Thanks, Chicamaw," Bowie said.

The motor of Chicamaw's car roared and he was gone and then Dee Mobley gave Bowie a drink of whisky. It clawed his mouth and throat like fingernails.

Dee kept sitting down and getting up and moving around the room. Finally, he said: "You're not hurt bad, are you?"

"No," Bowie said.

"You see any use of me staying here?"

Bowie shook his head. "Not a bit, Dee."

"I don't know what kind of trouble you boys got in," Dee said, "but I don't see any use of me hanging around your heat. You're welcome to this place though, and if it wasn't for the fact that I'd be losing money I'd just as soon close it up and put a sign out there on the front door and go up to Tulsy. I could put plenty of grub in here and water and you could stay here as long as you wanted."

"Don't worry about the money."

"I got to worry about it, Bowie."

Bowie gave Dee ten fifty-dollar bills. "You better let your folks know to stay away from here."

"Nobody comes around here except Keechie and I'll give her some of this money and she can visit up in Muskogee or somewhere."

"You better do that."

The scraping branches of the pecan-tree against the Bunk's tin roof sounded like cat claws on a screen. I could be a lot worse off, Bowie, old boy, and don't you think different. I could be laying back yonder. You doggone whistling. I still got the money. The silver is gone, but to hell with that. That old Jalope. *814*. That was it. *Eight* plus *one* plus *four* equals *thirteen*. There you are; that was it. And if it hadn't been for that Chicamaw?

Chapter XI

DAWN oozed through the cracks of the closed Bunk door, the veins of the drawn window-blind, and pressed with leaden heaviness on Bowie's frozen soreness. The suit of winter underwear, Dee Mobley's, hung on the post of the bed like a scab. I will get up in a minute, Bowie thought, and light that stove. I'm chilled and that's what is wrong with me.

He touched his loosened front teeth with his tongue and heard them creak in their sockets. A car droned around the curve, thundered past the filling station and faded with the sound of a covey of quail in flight.

I'm going to get up. *One for the money, two for the show.* Now when I say *four to go,* I will get up. But what's the use of gettin' up? I've got all day. *One for the money . . .* Chicamaw won't be gone more than two days. He might show up right tonight. *One for the money . . .*

This might not really be happening, him lying here in this place and getting ready to get up. This was just his Spirit? His Real Self was back up that road. No, that was his Spirit too. His Real Self had got the Chair. I'm like a cat with nine lives. That's it. One of them in the Chair and one of them back yonder. Seven left. I'm going to go ding-batty if I keep lying here. *One for the money!* . . . A car was coming under the shed of this filling station. Bowie sat up, his right hand reaching for the floor. Man, you don't even have a gun. . . .

The knob turned and then the unarmed figure in the red sweater was standing there. It was Keechie. Bowie's face felt like it was encased in a cellophane mask and if he breathed his skin would crackle.

She closed the door and came toward him. "What's the matter with you?"

He breathed. "Accident."

She stood beside the bed. "What's the matter?"

He touched his mouth. "I guess you see my lips now. They're busted up pretty bad."

"Anything broke?"

He shook his head.

"Shot?"

"Just sprung my back a little."

She went over to the kerosene stove and then a match popped and the igniting wick sputtered. Bowie lowered himself back to the pillow. The pan of water rattled on top of the heater.

Two lines creased Keechie's face from her cheekbones to

the corners of her thin, dry lips. Her eyes were the color of powdered burnt sugar. "Hungry?" she said.

He shook his head. "Your Dad said you were going up to Muskogee or some place."

"Uh huh."

"I guess he left all right."

"Yes."

"I guess you better be careful about staying here, Keechie. I've been in a little trouble."

"You look like it."

The hot, wet towel melted the brittle casing on his face, softened his lips. Her fingers touched his face and he wanted to lick them. Just let her stay a little while. Just a little while. . . .

"I got money," he said. "On me and in that brown bag under this bed. Nineteen thousand dollars."

She straightened, cupping the towel in her hands, looked at him.

"I don't know why I said that."

"I'm glad you have it if that's what you want."

"That wasn't what I wanted to say. What I wanted to say was I don't guess it's best for you to be here."

"You need help."

"I just thought that I had this money and maybe you would like to take a trip or go some place. All girls like to go places."

"I don't know what other girls like to do."

"Now I didn't mean anything by that, Keechie. Now don't get me down wrong."

"I would do this for a dog," Keechie said. "If you will turn over and pull your shirt up I will put some liniment on your back."

She left at noon, but she was coming back. It would be after dark and she would bring plasters and cigarettes and something for him to gargle. She would leave the model-T and walk back out, telling her Aunt Mara that she was leaving town. She would sleep in the filling station at nights.

Bowie rested on the bed, his back and head propped against a quilt and pillow. It's all right, he thought. I've had more than my share of bad luck and I know it's going to be all right for two or three days.

The cotton underwear on the bed looked like the skin of a dead rabbit. Bowie got up, picked the rusty file from the window sill and scraped the garment to the floor. Then he kicked it under the bed.

Chapter XII

THEIR spoons tinkled in the peanut-butter glasses of soft-boiled eggs and crumbled crackers. Keechie sat on the edge at the foot of the bed, the golden glow of the oil heater's jagged crown caressing her face.

"It's about time you started eatin' something," Bowie said. "I never heard of anybody not eatin' any more than you do and not gettin' any more sleep. Just two or three hours a night. I never heard of it."

"I've gone three nights without sleeping and it doesn't bother me at all. I've done it all my life."

"You've fallen off some too since I saw you last and you better start sleepin' and eatin' more, young lady. Now me, I've got to have my eight and nine and ten hours at night or I'm just blowed up."

Their spoons scraped in the emptied glasses and they laughed.

"Don't you ever want to leave this town, Keechie?" Bowie said.

"Yes." She got up and took the glass out of his hand; placed it with her own on the table. Then she came back and sat down. She talked. Her voice was as soft as the reflection on the heater's dull brass.

Once, she said, an old couple drove into the filling station and she got acquainted with them. The man was paralyzed and they were touring the country for his health. They dropped her post-cards and talked about her coming to live with them and she would like to have gone, but then the cards stopped and finally one day she got a card from the woman saying the old man was dead.

"It makes it pretty hard on a girl when she doesn't have . . ."

"Have what?"

"A Mama."

Keechie shook her head. "It depends on the mother."

"I don't know what I would have done without mine. Never has bawled me out for a thing."

"My Aunt says my Mother is the reason why my Father drinks and goes on like he does, but that doesn't have a thing to do with it. He is no good and perhaps she was, but I can't see that she is any better."

Outside, there was a sound like the sirens in Texaco City and Bowie stiffened and the skin on his chin and throat stretched.

"What's the matter?" Keechie said. She got up.

It was only wind in the telephone wires over on the highway. "Nothing," Bowie said.

"Your back?"

He shook his head. "This old world is some old world, ain't it, Keechie?"

"Yes."

"Who's your fellow, Keechie?"

"Why do you ask that?"

"I just thought I would ask."

"Why?"

"It isn't any of my business. Most girls have fellows and I was just asking."

"I don't know what most girls have."

"I don't believe you like men folks, do you, Keechie?"

"They are as good as the women I have seen."

"I believe you are kinda down on people."

"I don't know."

"And you never have had a fellow?"

"No."

"Even just to go to church with or something like that?"

"No. Why, do you think I should have?"

"Why, no. I was just asking. That's your own business."

"I never did see any use of it." Keechie reached over him and picked up the pack of cigarettes on the window-sill. The breasts under the polo shirt stirred.

"I'll take one too," Bowie said. "You know I don't know what could have happened to that Chicamaw. I guess he is seeing his folks."

"You will get along a lot better if he stays away from you."

"Aw, Keechie, you just got that cousin of yours down wrong."

"I'm not kin to anybody."

"You're a Little Soldier, that's what you are."

"Why do you call me that?"

"Because you are. Isn't it all right?"

"Yes."

She went over to the table and picked up the granite coffee pot and looked inside of it. She put it down and then picked it back up.

"Keechie."

She turned, the coffee pot in her hand.

"You know I have been wanting to give you something ever since I been here and I'd like to give it to you now."

"What is it?"

"A little old watch."

She returned the pot to the table.

"Do you want it?"

"Do you want to give it to me?"

"Yes."

"Yes, I want it."

Chapter XIII

On the fourth night, Chicamaw came, his eyes like a dog sick with distemper, his face the color of ham rind. Bowie's head quivered on his neck and he called, but Keechie left the Bunk without speaking to Chicamaw.

"You look like you been making it all right," Chicamaw said.

"I been all right."

"Well, I haven't been doing so well. I've throwed every cent I got."

"I'll swear, Chicamaw. What's been the trouble?"

Chicamaw said he had throwed it in a Tulsa hotel gambling. He did have a new car though and some guns. A tommy gun too. By god, he had a Big Papa out there now and he was as ready as anybody to start a Little War.

"You didn't see your folks?"

Chicamaw shook his head and began plucking at a hair in his nostril. "I didn't want to go around them as hot as I was, Bowie."

"Well, you're not broke, Chicamaw. I still got it, see, and you're welcome to what you need."

"Sure makes me anxious to get back with T-Dub in Gusherton and get me another piece of money. You going to feel like getting up in a few days and running these roads again?"

"I guess I could go right now."

"No, I wouldn't ask you to go now. If you'll let me have five thousand I'll go on over and see the folks. Make it six thousand. Will you do that?"

"Christ, yes, man."

"Can you beat me throwing that much though, Bowie? You know I'm a damned good poker player. They just took me to a cleaning. When I get to thinking about it, damned if I don't believe there was something crooked about it."

"Them big gamblers are thieves. You better stay away from them, boy."

"I guess you been reading the papers all right?"

"I haven't seen anything."

"Is that so?"

"I been just laying right here. You mean Texaco City?"

"Man, we're hot."

"Them Laws?"

"We're hotter than gun barrels, boy."

There was a scratching sound and Bowie looked toward the closed door expectantly, but it did not open. It was the pecan-tree touching the Bunk.

Chicamaw left the Bunk and returned quickly. Bowie had the brown bag on the bed and was taking money from it. Chicamaw put the two .45's on the bed.

"Sure glad to see them guns," Bowie said.

"Thanks for this loan," Chicamaw said. "You know I been

thinking about you, Bowie. You don't throw your money away and you don't get drunk. You're just a big old country boy, Bowie, but by God, I believe you're going to make it. You got something and I just can't figure it out."

"It didn't do me no good in Texaco City."

"Well, I guess I'll be shoving off, Bowie. Now if I get jumped and can't get back here in a couple of days or you have to rabbit from here, I'll see you in Gusherton. We sure can't let old T-Dub down."

"You be careful, Chicamaw. Go a little easier on the whiss, boy."

"Then if I don't see you here in a couple of days I'll see you in Gusherton?"

"What is it them Mexicans say when it's okeh?" Bowie said.

"'*Sta bien,*" Chicamaw said.

"'*Sta bien,*" Bowie said. "Man, I sure do want to get down there in that chili country some of these days. A man can't live like this always, Chicamaw. You know that."

"We'll make it down there, boy. Don't you worry."

Chapter XIV

IN the early mornings, when shadows crawled in a gray gloom and Bowie lay alone in the Bunk, he thought of First Officer, his hog-knuckle chin; the smothering bucket and shattering glass; the Chair, Spirits, Cats. The branches of the pecan-tree scratched the roof a hundred times and Keechie was never coming, he thought. For God's sake, man, *snap.* But at last she did come and then all that screwy Spirit stuff got out of his damned head.

In this evening's twilight, the polished peanut-butter glasses glowed with the delicacy of a blue flame. Bowie watched Keechie: the flipping cloth in her hands was like a blowing skirt and he seized her bare, strong fingers with his gaze. She had paint on her mouth tonight, but looking at her lips was like spying on her unclad through a keyhole.

She straightened the drying cloth on the back of the chair

and then picked up the kerosene can. "I'd better fill up your heater for tonight," she said.

"You ought to put a coat on," he said.

While she was gone, he planned what he would do in the morning when he woke up. He would not read the Sunday newspaper she had gotten him until in the morning. And then he would only look at the funny pages and the comics.

Keechie returned and filling the stove, she came to the bed. "I hope you get a good night's rest."

He played with the point of his shirt collar. "I hate to see you go."

"Do you?"

"I guess I've kinda got the blues tonight."

"I have done about everything I could around here, but I'm in no hurry. If you want me to stay——"

"Just a little while if you ain't in no hurry."

She lowered herself to the edge of the bed and crossed her legs. The sound of the tree now was like a gentle rain.

"I don't like to look behind," he said. "I try to just think of maybe the good things that will happen ahead. But I guess I know what is going to happen."

"No, you don't, Bowie. The things that you are afraid of most never happen. I'm a lot older than you in a lot of ways."

"I never have seen nothing like you before, Keechie. I know now what makes a fellow get him a little missus and swing a dinner pail."

"You mean that?"

"Yes."

She moved and he reached out and said: "Don't go."

"I'm not."

"My ears are ringing," he said.

She bent toward him and touched his face. He seized her then, brought her toward him. "Don't you go. Don't you go."

"I'm not, Bowie."

Strength swelled within him. I can snap her little body in my hands. I can break her little body in my grip. Her tight lips yielded until there was only softness and then her breath became as naked as her body. . . .

*

Frying bacon spluttered in the skillet on top of the oil heater and then it popped and Keechie jerked back and turned and smiled at Bowie.

"You better be careful, Little Girl," he said. She sure did look different. Where did he ever get the idea that she wasn't pretty? Those lines in her face. Where were they? And that little mouth was as soft and pretty.

"Wonder if you could take time out and come over here and give your Daddy a kiss?" he said.

She came over, the fork in her hand and bent down. "There's nothing sick about you," she said.

He kissed her. "I feel like a million bucks. I been thinking about getting up and running a half-mile before I eat."

"You just stay there. How do you want your eggs?"

"Any old way."

"How do you want them?"

"Any old way, honey. Over easy I guess. And hand me that newspaper over there while you don't have anything else to do."

She handed him the newspaper and he pointed at the three pale prongs of sunlight that lay on the splintered floor near the window. "Look, I believe the sun is going to shine today."

"I noticed the stars last night and I thought then that it might be clear today."

He began turning the pages and then he saw the thing that seized his eyes like a fish-hook:

TEXACO CITY, Texas, Oct. 6—Fingerprints found on the steering wheel of the wrecked, new automobile which the fugitive slayers of Plainclothesmen Vic Redford and Jake Hadman abandoned here last week, may lead to the identity of the killers, Chief of Detectives Musser revealed here today. The chief said his department was basing its hopes on this and also a revolver found nearby.

Redford and Hadman, veteran peace officers, were ruthlessly slain in a gun battle on Ector Boulevard while investigating an automobile crash. A woman received minor injuries in the collision.

"Are you very hungry this morning?" Keechie said.

The white of the paper glimmered like heat on the highway and Bowie jerked his eyes away. "I didn't understand what you said?"

"What's the matter, Bowie?"

"Nothing. Not a thing. I was just reading here."

"What are you reading?"

"Just something here."

Six suspects arrested here in connection with the case have been released. Two are still being questioned.

The abandoned automobile of the killers was purchased in El Paso, Texas, it was reported. Witnesses of the battle say that three and possibly four men were in the car that sped away after the shooting. One witness declared he saw a woman in the outlaw machine.

A police benefit here last night for the widows of the two slain officers netted $320.

Bowie took the warm plate with its eggs and bacon from Keechie's hand and put it on his lap. After a little while, he stuck the fork into the egg's yellow.

"What's the matter, Bowie?" She sat on the bed's edge with a plate on her knees.

"I don't want to hold nothing back from you, Keechie. I'm pretty deep in this business. I'm a lot deeper in it than I was when I was here before. I want you to know that."

"What is it?"

"I had some trouble back up the road. Two Laws killed."

Keechie placed her plate on the floor.

"You can see that I'm in it pretty deep now."

"Did you do it?"

"Them Laws?"

"Yes."

Bowie's head went up and down.

"You did not. You can't tell me that. I know who did it. Chicamaw. You can't conceal anything from me." She clutched his trouser cuff. "He did it."

"It don't make any difference who did it. And you got Chicamaw down all wrong. I wouldn't be sittin' here now if it wasn't for him."

"You did not do it, Bowie."

"I wouldn't tell you nothing but the straight. I got it on my back and there's no gettin' around it."

Keechie got up and the plate on the floor rattled and broke.

She looked down at it and for a moment her mouth twisted as if she were going to cry.

Bowie held up his plate. "Don't mind that. We can split this."

Keechie picked up the plate fragments and the spilled food. On the table was Bowie's untouched food.

"I'll just tell you the straight of it, Keechie. I'm not sorry. I'm not sorry for anything I ever did in this world. That when I was just a punk kid and they put the Chair on me don't count. But I'm not sorry for a one of these banks. The only regret I got is that I didn't get one hundred thousand instead of ten. I'm just a black sheep and there's no gettin' around it."

"The only thing black about you is your hair," Keechie said.

"You're a Little Soldier, Keechie. You're a Little Soldier from them toe-nails of yours up to your hair, but you can't get mixed up with me."

Keechie's face twisted like he had driven his fist into it. He grasped her arm. "Keechie, what's the matter?"

She shook her head.

He pulled her to him. "What's the matter, honey?"

"Didn't you mean that last night?"

"Mean what?"

"Bowie. You know what you said."

"Honey, I can't think of everything right now. What was it, honey? You come on now and tell me."

"You said you wished you had me."

"Sure I do. Godamighty, honey."

"What do you mean then? Getting too mixed up with you?"

"Don't you see how it is? When a man has them Laws after him and it's all in the papers they'll shoot you and ask questions afterwards. They'd just as soon shoot a woman down with him as not."

"Is that what you mean?"

"You see now, don't you, honey?"

"Does anybody else have any strings on you, Bowie? Anybody else?" She pulled away from his grasp.

"What do you mean?"

"Is there anybody else? A woman?"

"Oh, no, honey. Lord, no."

"I just wanted to know."

"How come you to ask a thing like that?"

"I'm in this pretty deep and I just wanted to know."

Bowie lay back against the pillow. "Keechie, come and lie down beside me a little while."

She got on the bed beside him.

"You like me, Keechie?"

"Yes."

"A whole lot?"

"Yes."

"Hundred bushels full?"

"Yes."

"Thousand bushels full?"

"Yes."

"A hundred thousand million trillion gillion bushels full?"

"Yes."

"Keechie, I love you." Her finger nails dug into the flesh of his throat.

There were sounds in the filling station and Keechie got out of bed and went across the darkened room to the door; Bowie following, in his underwear, a .45 in his right hand. Keechie peered through the cautiously opened crack of the door. After a long time she closed the door easily and Bowie stepped back. "It's my Aunt. Stealing some groceries."

Neither was sleepy now. They lay in bed, both their heads on the one pillow. "You know I been thinking, Keechie. This business of me staying here can't go on. I been here eight days now and Dee is going to be coming back pretty soon and this just can't go on now."

"Do you have anything in mind?"

"How would you like to go somewhere with me?"

"You want me to go?"

"You know doggone well I want you to go."

"What do you have in mind?"

"I'd like to get in a big city, Keechie. I mean like New Orleans or Louisville. Old T-Dub was always talking about them towns. In them big cities, people don't big-eye you so much and if you keep your nose clean, you can last as long as you want to."

"I guess so."

"I just don't know what's happened to that Chicamaw. That Indian can take care of himself though. He's probably gettin' everything fixed up at his folks'."

"We don't have to go around any of them, do we? Mister Masefeld and them?"

"No sir, honey. Not you. I should say not."

"I've been thinking some too, Bowie, and what I have had on my mind is what some people that used to live next door to my Aunt told me. Mister Carpenter and his wife and they had a girl my age named Agnes. Mister Carpenter had tuberculosis and they moved away down in Texas almost to the border in the Guadaloupe Hills. Agnes wrote and told me about it. They lived away out in the hills and wouldn't go to town for two months at a time and Agnes said that the only people they ever saw were some Mexican sheepherders and then a few sick people like Mister Carpenter. People chasing the cure, Agnes said they were."

"Close to Mexico, uh?"

"Bowie, I don't see why we couldn't go to a place like that and just live to ourselves and pretty soon people would forget all about Bowie Bowers and then finally there would just be the real Bowie Bowers."

"You know I hadn't thought of that. Them little towns though, Keechie, are bad. Everybody wants to know your business."

"We won't be in a town. We'll be away out and don't have to see anybody."

"You know I sure hadn't thought of that."

"That's where I would like to go."

"Man, we got the money to do it. Right here under this bed and in my breeches and coat yonder."

"I think that would be the best and just stay away from everybody you ever knew."

"How you and me going to get out of this place, Keechie? No car or nothing?"

"We can manage."

"Any trains stop here at night?"

"Two o'clock to Tulsy."

"We could get that train, by golly. You could walk about a half-block ahead of me and get a couple of tickets and I'll be hanging around and every once in a while we'll give each other a wink and then we'll sit in separate seats on the train and . . ."

"We'll sit together on the train."

"Sure, we can sit together on the train and then we'll get in Tulsy and I'll buy us a new V-8 and then we'll scat down to this Guadaloupe Hills country. Where is that place, Keechie?"

"I've looked at it on the map a hundred times. When Agnes was writing me I wanted to go down there. There's deer and wild turkey and squirrels and everything else, Agnes said."

"Man, I could knock me off a deer. I'll get me a .30-30 or a .415 Winchester and you and me will eat venison, kiddo. You just let me down there, Keechie, and I won't even need no gun. Just give me a rock."

"If we go down there, either you or me will suppose to be a lunger, you know, with t.b. Maybe both of us had better be. Now in renting a cabin or something we'll have to let on."

"I'll look like the best t.b. in the world."

"That's the thing for us to do. And you just forget everybody you ever knew."

"You'll have to get you some clothes in Tulsy, honey. How about a fur coat? To set that watch off I gave you?"

"We'll think about that later."

"I'll buy you a whole windowful of clothes. You can get anything you want. All you got to do is name it."

"We can't look like no millionaires. We're going to be sick people."

"Ah, you can get a few things. How you like them riding boots and pants, Keechie? Aw, I don't know though whether I'd like to see you in pants or not. You just get dresses. And plenty of them silk doodads. We'll get a couple of thermos jugs and keep them filled with soda pop and get some blankets and sun glasses and an extra can or two of gasoline and we'll split the breeze."

"When do you think we should go?"

"What time is it now?"

"It must be twelve."

"We can make it. Two hours. Let's get in the saddle, honey."

"Tonight, Bowie?"

"You doggone whistling. And honey we got the money to do it on too. Twenty thousand good old bucks. I mean fourteen. That's a lot of money, Keechie. You can say what you want to about money, Keechie, but by god, it talks."

"I guess so," Keechie said. "Well, let's start dressing."

Chapter XV

MESQUITE trees persisted even into this foothills country, but the Plains were far behind now. There were Spanish oaks and cedars and in the late afternoon this way the sage grass had a lavender flush. Away ahead, in the distance, a long range of sharp hills embroidered the horizon. Above the range, the sky was streaked with white, rigid panels as if the rain had crystallized and awaited a crack of lightning to unleash.

Keechie was driving and Bowie sat low in the seat, his hands deep in his pockets. She drove like Chicamaw, her left hand on the cross-bar and the other on the wheel; took the curves like they weren't there. In the holster under Bowie's left arm was a .45 and in the panel pocket another. There were four blankets in the back, a thermos jug of coffee, a sack of sandwiches, four cartons of tailor-made cigarettes. And Keechie had on hose that cost two dollars and shoes that cost ten and that military cravenette coat. It was her own fault that she didn't get the fur, but she looked like a Little Soldier in that coat and he had to hand it to her. And the way she had that little brown hat cocked over her eye. . . .

Down the road, beyond the Curve sign, the cement disappeared around the stone-studded bank; straight ahead, low, white barriers and space and blue sky. What if they just kept going straight and into that space and sky? They would keep going like a plane right over that valley. But cars don't fly.

What if they did go off? It would just mean that he and Kee-chie had drawn the poor cards. But what if they made it? It would mean Luck was riding with them for a long time to come. . . .

The wheels of the machine hung tenaciously on the curve and now they were on a long straight-away again. They ain't nothing going to stop us, Little Soldier.

"Light me a cigarette, Bowie."

"Yes, ma'am."

The dairy barn was white with green trimming and over its roof, white and black pigeons circled. On the porch of the house lay a big dog, its paws dangling over the edge. They passed an old sedan, its slender wheels wobbling, the top tattered and in pennants.

"Them old Jalopes," Bowie said. "They cause more accidents than anything else on the road. It's no crime to be poor, Keechie, but there ought to be a law against letting cars like that out on the highways."

They passed a Schoolhouse, two filling stations and on the porch of the General Store sat two men bent over a checker board. The black lettering on the highway board read: *San Antonio . . . 186.*

Down this highway, thirty miles more and then they would turn west on a dirt road. Out that road one hundred miles and they would be in them little hill towns, Antelope Center, Arbuckle. There they would start house hunting.

On the left was a cemetery with a half-dozen low tombstones and then an unpainted, box house. Farther down, at the wooden gate, two cows with swollen bags waited.

"You know anything about cows, Bowie? Do they ever have twins?"

"You got me there."

"I was just wondering."

"It looks like to me they could though. With that woman up in Canada doing what she did, it looks like to me a cow could do it."

"Those cows back there made me think of it."

"That woman up there in Canada, Keechie. That shows you nothing is impossible in this old world, doesn't it?"

"It sure does."

"And I was thinking back there. What is it you say we are doing? *Chasing the cure*. Well, what if we really did have t.b.? Well, I don't know but what I'd rather be a lot hotter than I am now than have something like that riding me. Don't you kind of feel that way about it?"

"I should say I do."

Bowie chose the big filling station with its stucco front and Keechie turned the car up the curving driveway. There was another car under the shed, a woman at the wheel, but it drove off as they stopped. The next time we gas up, Bowie thought, we'll be having us a home to go to. Just fifty miles more now and they would be in that town of Arbuckle.

The filling station attendant in the leather jacket said: "Yessir?"

"Fill 'er up and I got a couple of cans."

Keechie entered the Rest Room door and Bowie went over to the Coca Cola box and lifted the lid. The exhausts of stopping motorcycles popped and he turned. The two cops were coming right in here.

The Cops came toward the Coca Cola box and Bowie moved over. The tall cop was as brown as saddle leather and the short one had chapped, scaling lips. They had on gray uniforms and black Sam Browne belts. Their pistols were pearl-handled.

"What kind you want?" Tall Cop said.

"Coke," Short Cop said.

Their lips made drinking sounds on the mouths of the bottles.

"Got you a new one there, haven't you?" Tall Cop said.

"Yeah," Bowie said. "Them jobs over there can outrun it in reverse though, can't they?"

"They'll outrun that car all right."

"I guess them motorcycles there will outrun just about anything that gets on these roads, won't they?"

"Don't you think it, Mister," Short Cop said. "There's plenty of them out there I don't go after."

"You can tie them up in traffic sometimes," Tall Cop said.

"Ninety is about all I want to push that 'cycle over there of mine," Short Cop said, "and if anybody has anything that will do better than that I just check it to them."

Keechie came around the corner, stopped and then started smoothing the dress about her hips. Bowie winked and she went on to the car and got under the wheel.

"That all, Sir?" the Attendant said.

Bowie paid him.

They drove off and Bowie turned and reached toward the back seat. Tall Cop and Short Cop were sitting on top of the Coca Cola box.

"You didn't bat an eye, you doggone little dickens. Not an eye."

"What were you talking to them about?"

"Damned if I know."

"It looked like to me you were trying to make friends."

"They didn't know me from Adam's off ox, Keechie. Why, they're that way all over the country. How they going to know you? Look at a picture. Well, what's that?"

"I would stay away from them."

"Man, when they drove in that station though, I says to myself: 'Here's where a Little War starts.' "

"You better look behind."

Bowie looked back. The ribbon was clean. "Not a thing, honey. Nossir, you didn't bat an eye."

"I think maybe I had better start carrying that pistol in the pocket there, Bowie."

"Not that big gun, honey. That thing would jump clean out of your hands. I'll get you a little gun one of these days pretty soon though. Every woman ought to have a gun. I'm going to get you one. There's always some sonofabitch ready to get smart with a woman."

"I'm not afraid of that gun."

"Did you ever shoot a .45?"

"No, but I have a real strong grip. I could out-crack any of the girls in school on pecans. You remember that game. I won all the time."

"Yeah, I remember that game. What did we call it?"

"Hully gull."

"That's it. Yessir, Keechie, it just goes to show you how a

man don't have to jump from his shadow. I'll bet I could go right up to the Law over here in this town of Arbuckle and ask him if he knew of a furnished house and I'll bet he wouldn't know me from Adam's off ox."

"I will do the asking about the houses. I will go to the real estate office and do the asking."

"You going to tell them we're lungers, sure enough?"

"That is what we are down here for now, Bowie, and you want to remember it."

Bowie made a coughing sound and slapped his chest. "The bug is gettin' me down. How's it doing you, Little Lunger?"

"You'll make it, old Foot-in-the-Grave."

There were no furnished houses in the little town of Arbuckle or near it, the Real Estate Woman told Keechie, but over at Antelope Center, she said, forty miles farther West, the cottages of an old Sanitarium were being remodeled for tourists and sick people and deer hunters. Bowie and Keechie went to Antelope Center.

It was almost noon when they left the graveled highway, two miles west of Antelope Center, turned through an arched gate and started climbing the narrow, high-centered road. Through the cedars and frost-browned oaks, on the side of the Hill, stood a big gray building.

"Looks like a jail," Bowie said.

"It won't hurt to look," Keechie said.

The closed building was the old hospital, its cement the color of dead broomweed. Through the dust-filmed windows there were stacks of bare beds and piles of mattresses. Back of it and east, rows of small stucco cottages fenced it like a carpenter's tri-square. The cottages had glassed-in rooms and stone chimneys and there were lettered boards over the entrances: *Come Inn . . . Suits Us . . . Journey's Inn . . . Bella Vista.*

The man raking the weeds in front of the corner cottage in the V of the Square stopped, leaned on the handle and looked at their car. When Keechie got out, he dropped the rake and came toward them.

The man had on a khaki army shirt and a white cloth belt held his slick, blue serge trousers. He was middle-aged and his teeth were broken and tobacco-stained. Yes, he had some cottages. He was the caretaker out here. He had just fixed up another cottage and it was twelve dollars and fifty cents a month and that included water and electricity. It was the last house at that end. Now he lived in that house on the corner, and below him a School Teacher batched and next to him an Auto Salesman with his wife and two children. They were the only ones that lived out here now, but he hadn't got around to fixing up any more cottages. They were fine people, the folks that lived out here.

"You want to look at it, honey?" Keechie said.

"Yeah, I'd just as soon."

"You take that School Teacher feller yonder," the Caretaker said, "he got him a hot plate from Sears, Roebuck and he's just batching fine."

Bowie got out of the car.

The Caretaker thrust out his hand. "Lambert is my name, young man. Old Bill Lambert. Traveled out of San Antonio for thirty-five years, leather goods, saddles, grips and harness. Had a lung collapse on me here a year ago and this air up here, Son, is fine. What's your business, Son?"

Bowie removed his hand from the other's grip. "I'm a sick man right now. Used to play ball."

"Son, you come to the right place. Not a healthier place in the United States than right in here. Ball Player, uh? Well, we got a School Teacher and two Salesmen and now we got a Ball Player. Now that Salesman feller over yonder used to be worth a right smart of money. Owned his own business right yonder in Antelope and just went busted like any of us can do. His wife didn't like it much out here at first, her being used to gas and fancy things, but now she just likes it fine. Your missus will like it too."

"Pretty quiet out here, I guess?" Bowie said.

"You won't get lonesome. Now that Salesman has got him a radio and everybody out here is fine people."

"Used to be a lot of people out here, I guess?"

"I don't know all the history of this place. Now all this was built right after the War, I think, and then it petered out and then for a while it was a sort of tourist camp and I might just as well tell you folks because I'm not the kind to hold nothing back. This place got a pretty bad reputation with the folks in Antelope because here a couple of years back some bootleggers got out and people come out here and throwed wild parties. But that's not any more, son. Your wife will be just as safe here as any place in the world now."

"He has to stay awful quiet," Keechie said. "Let's go look at the place."

Bill Lambert walked ahead on the narrow sidewalk in front of the closed cottages, talking, spitting. "Now it's nothing swell, you know, but I'll fix it up just like you want it. There's one thing, I want to put you in some linoleum in the kitchen and if you ever have company and need an extra cot, why just let me know."

He stopped in front of the last cottage—*Welcome Inn*—and opened the scraping screen and inserted the key in the lock. The wooden floors inside creaked under their feet. In this front room there were a blackened, empty stone fireplace and an iron army cot covered with a yellowed counterpane. There were two hide-bottomed rocking-chairs and a rickety breakfast table. In the windowed sleeping-room there was a broad iron bed, a huge dresser with a smoky mirror and two straight dining-room chairs. The kitchen had a three-burner, grease-caked oil stove, a sink and an enamel-topped table. The bath had a shower and the toilet seat was split and part of it lay on the cement floor.

"Some strong lye soap and a mop and whitewash would help a lot around here," Keechie said. "Don't you think so, honey?"

Bowie grinned. "Don't you think the price though will about keep us busted?"

"Now I tell you, Mister . . ." Bill Lambert said. "What did you say your name was, Son?"

"Vines. V-i-n-e-s."

"Well, I tell you now, Mister Vines. It's just the best I can do. A bunch of millionaires own this out here and you know how they are. I been trying my best to fix these places up here and get some money to do it with because people just want things a little nicer for the money, but I tell you, it's just like gettin' blood out of a turnip to get something from one of these millionaires. Now you take Mister Philpott over there, he's the Salesman, they've fixed that place up over there just as pretty as a picture."

"There is a lot to do around here all right," Keechie said.

"I'll tell you what I'll do," Bill Lambert said. "I don't want to rush you folks, but if you decide to take it I'll throw in a half-cord of wood for nothing and tack that linoleum down the first thing this afternoon right after dinner."

"We must stay awfully quiet," Keechie said.

"Don't you worry about that, Mizzis Vines. Now you take here last month, it was the night of September fifteenth, there was a couple come out here and I thought I smelled liquor, but I didn't want to cause no trouble and I let them have the place although they just wanted it for two or three days. Well, before the night was over she was running around right in this house here, without anything on and kicking up as high as them trees and the blinds up to the ceiling and so I just politely told them we didn't want that going on around here. Now, Son, you want your wife protected and that is just the way I do out here. This is a place for respectable people and any time anybody runs around here kicking . . ."

"That's all right, Mister Lambert," Bowie said.

"Just one more thing now, Mister Vines, and then I'll let you go. Now you take Mizzis Philpott over there. One day she goes off and while she's gone her oil stove burns over and I busts in there and saves the whole place. They were mighty appreciative of that."

"I'm very satisfied," Bowie said.

"If we ever catch you in this house, you had better be putting out a fire," Keechie said.

Lambert laughed. "All right, Lady. All right. Now then I'll just leave you two together and let you decide."

Alone, Bowie and Keechie walked in the rooms. "Think it will do, Keechie?"

"I'm crazy about it."

"If I ever catch old Filthy MacNasty peepin' around here, I'll kick his hind-end clear off," Bowie said.

"He's harmless. Bowie, this is just the thing."

Bowie walked in the sleeping-room, Keechie following. "Some of them big, red Indian blankets would sure look pretty in here," he said. "And we'll get us a big radio to sit in yonder."

"I can go to town this afternoon and I'll buy enough groceries to last us three months," Keechie said.

"I forgot to ask old Filthy if there was really some deer around here," Bowie said.

Keechie sat on the edge of the bed and moved up and down on it experimentally. "Good springs and mattress, Bowie."

"I'm sold on it myself," Bowie said. "Go on out and pay Filthy a couple of months' rent and tell him I'll tack the damned linoleum down."

Chapter XVI

THERE was one hundred dollars' worth of bright-colored blankets on the big bed and the cot now, a radio that was as big as the fireplace in the living-room, two automatic shotguns and a rifle on the mantel and Keechie had a cigarette-case with a diamond in it. They had done a lot in four weeks. Old Filthy never did snoop around any more and just once had somebody come, Mrs. Philpott, the Salesman's wife, to borrow some sugar. Out here they never did see anybody except that little Philpott boy, Alvin, and then he was away down in the woods back of their place with a .22 rifle and that Spitz dog of his, Spots.

Bowie sat in front of the radio this evening, smoking the curved-stem pipe that Keechie liked, and thought how everything was looking pretty good. In that food-packed kitchen, Keechie was frying Irish potatoes the way he liked them, crisp and brown.

I don't care nothing about it myself, Bowie thought, but we can start taking in some picture shows down there in that town pretty soon. Girls like to get out and go places. And that Law down there? I got him spotted and he ain't never going to get close to me.

In the darkened living-room, the flames of the fireplace logs splashed on the ceiling and walls. Had he brought in the wood tonight? Yes. What time was it? *Seven-thirty.* Christ, that Mexican orchestra Keechie liked was on. Bowie switched the dial. This was the station all right, but now they were talking about them damned constipation crystals.

If they were jumped now and had to rabbit, this radio and everything would have to be left behind. Well, I'm no damned soda skeet making ten dollars a week. I'll buy another one. Five hundred-dollar one and two hundred dollars' worth of blankets and if we go busted I know where I can get plenty more.

He placed another log on the fire and sat back down. The prongs of light shadow-boxed now on the walls, hooking and jabbing frenziedly. The orchestra was playing and Bowie got up and went back to the kitchen. Keechie was standing in front of the oven with a cloth in her hand.

"Hear that piece?"

Keechie nodded. *"La Golondrina."*

"Always makes me kind of sad somehow. Makes me think of them boys."

"Why?"

"I don't know. I been thinking about Chicamaw though, Keechie. I don't know whether I did that boy right or not up there in Keota, Keechie. He might have been expecting me to wait for him there and I didn't leave him no note or nothing."

"How were you going to leave him a note?"

"I don't know."

"Well, quit worrying about it then."

"I was just thinking about them."

"You have somebody else to worry about now."

"We just all started out together and you can't keep from thinking about things like that."

Bowie went back to the living-room and sat down. The fire had lowered and its glow filtered the darkness like a luminous screen. A cowboy singer was yodeling now about the prairie.

I do have to meet them boys in Gusherton, Bowie thought. They never did let me down and I sure can't go back on them. Why, they would just wait and wait and wait on me and I wouldn't let them do that. She will understand. You will understand, won't you, honey?

The cowboy was singing *Nobody's Darling but Mine:*

> *Goodbye, Goodbye, Little Darling,*
> *I'm leaving this Old World behind.*
> *Oh promise me that you will never*
> *Be Nobody's Darling, but Mine. . . .*

Bowie cut the Voice off. I wish we could get more newspaper news over this and not that Mussolini and Africa and Congress and stuff like that. No news is good news though. If anything had happened to them boys, we would have heard about it.

Keechie called him. On the enameled table there were black-eyed peas, corn bread, fried potatoes, pineapple preserves and black coffee.

After supper, Bowie took the galvanized-iron tub of hot water off the stove and carried it into the living-room and lowered it to the floor in the hearth's glow. Keechie was going to take a bath.

He spread the bath mat and towels on the hearth around the tub and then looked around the room. The blinds were pulled close all right.

Standing, her naked thighs and legs glinted through the tub's rising vapors. She's sure filling out, Bowie thought. Now she raised her left arm and the soaped, dripping cloth in her right hand moved toward the shadowed pit. "I didn't know you were such a hairy little thing," he said.

Her arm came down. "Do you think I should shave?"

"I should say not. I like it. Don't you ever do it."

"I won't then. As long as I have you."

The whipping, drying towel covered and revealed and Bowie felt the heat of her burnished body glow in his eyes. He got up and picked up the white flannel pajamas off the radio. They smelled of clean soap. He handed them to her.

"Are you going to wash your feet tonight?" she said.

"Not tonight, honey. I washed them last night."

They lay under the warm, soft blankets now and Keechie's fingers played in the flannel over his chest. Outside, on the narrow cement walk, wind-kicked leaves scraped and scurried. In the daytime, he had watched the leaves leave the oak and they had twisted and spiraled to the ground like birds shot with an airgun.

She lay quietly now and he said softly: "Keechie?"

She half raised. "What is it, Bowie? Did you call me?"

"I thought you were asleep."

She peered at him hard. "What is it?"

"Nothing, honey. I didn't go to wake you up."

"What is it, Bowie?"

Distant, tiny, taut wires trilled in Bowie's ears. "I just been thinking."

"About what?"

"Just about things in general. Got to thinking about some of the boys up there in Alky. They come in there, Keechie, bragging about the women they got Outside waiting for them and after a little while they hush up and there's nothing more heard about it."

"I don't know anything about that."

"It doesn't make any difference, I don't suppose. I don't care what kind of a man you take. A doctor or a big college professor or any kind of a man and let him die and pretty soon his wife will be out running around with somebody else. These widows are just about as bad as any kind of a woman."

"I don't know about women like that."

"Some of these women bury a man and in no time at all pick right up with another. There's women, Keechie, that will take up with a dozen men in their lives. Just one right in after another."

"Those women didn't love."

"Well, I don't know about that now, Keechie. They are bound to have been pretty crazy about them and maybe they didn't love all of them, but they loved some of them."

"A woman just loves once."

"What makes a woman live with one man a while and then with another one and then just run around with four or five more?"

"They just don't love."

"They must like it, Keechie, or they wouldn't do it."

"I don't know why other women do things. Maybe they

are just looking and can't find anybody and then I guess some of them marry for a living."

"It just looks like to me that every woman will do it."

"I don't know what other women do."

"Now what would you do, Keechie, if I got in a little trouble somewhere and you and me might not be able to see each other again?"

Keechie did not say anything. The tiny wires were as loud as crickets now and they swarmed in Bowie's ears. "Didn't you hear me?"

"There wouldn't be anything for me after you were gone. There is no use to think about that."

"Keechie, look at all these other women. Maybe they don't the first year and maybe they go two or three or four years, but pretty soon you see them lettin' some man slobber all over them."

Keechie was quiet.

"Now what do you have to say to that, Keechie?"

"I guess a woman is kind of like a dog, Bowie. You take a good dog now and if his master dies that dog won't take food from anybody and he'll bite anybody that tries to pet him and if he goes on, he'll rustle his own food and a lot of times he will just die too."

"You know that's right?"

"A bad dog will eat out of anybody's hands and take things from anybody."

"That's those big thoroughbred dogs that cost a pile of money that do that I guess. Them are real dogs."

"Maybe they do. I never did see, I don't guess, a real thoroughbred. The dog I am thinking about was there in Keota. I don't know what he was. Nobody else I don't guess. Old Man Humphrey owned him and after he died I felt so sorry for that dog. But he wouldn't have anything to do with anybody and he wouldn't eat or drink and then he just died too."

"I'll be doggone, Keechie. You know that's right. It just goes to show you. You know, honey, you are the smartest little old thing I ever did see."

"I'm not smart."

"You're a Little Soldier that's what you are."

"You go to sleep now."

The ringing in Bowie's ears faded far, far away and his eyes grew heavy and he closed them. . . .

Chapter XVII

THE back yard of *Welcome Inn* had the width of an alley and then a fence of barbed wire and beyond that was ranch land, sage-grass and broomweed; far-reaching woods of green, pollen-blowing cedars and gray-trunked scrub-oaks. In it, long-horned, white-faced cattle grazed and sometimes one would come to their fence and nose in the rusty iron drum of burned cans and garbage. Once, Keechie had seen a doe and she called Bowie, but when he got to the back door, it was gone. Away to the south, beyond the woods, the Hills embossed the sky in a great, crawling circle. This evening, the sinking sun had flushed the horizon to a pretty pink like Keechie's underthings.

They sat now on the back steps of the cottage, Keechie in the coat of Bowie's gray suit. She was funny that way, always wearing something of his and even sleeping at nights in one of his shirts and he had paid fifteen dollars for that negligee and boudoir slippers.

Keechie pointed now and in the woods they saw the Philpott boy, Alvin, and the dog.

"I been kind of wanting to get out there with that kid some evening," Bowie said. "I never have seen him bringing back anything."

"He's having a good time though," Keechie said.

"Guess I just got too much else to think about." He tapped the bowl of his pipe on his palm and then slung the charred tobacco with a finger-spreading movement and wiped his hand across his thigh. The lining of his mouth felt thin and his tongue needle-pointed. I'll tell her after we go in, he thought. Only four days now and I got to be in Gusherton. That's all there is to it.

"Alvin yonder made me think of the little girl who used to live down on the corner from my Aunt. She died."

"Huh," Bowie said.

"She was awfully pretty. She used to say pieces in the church and her Mama fixed her up so pretty. It liked to have killed her Mama and I guess it was the reason that her Father went crazy. He was crazy before that, I would say though. He was a printer and he saved gold pieces. Every bit of money he saved he would go to the bank and get gold pieces. Go up in the front room at nights and sit at a table and count it and look at it. His wife told him that it was going to bring bad luck."

"And then the kid died?"

"And it took every bit of the gold he had saved to pay for the funeral."

Bowie started filling his pipe. "Chicamaw was telling me about that lawyer friend of his he knew down in Mexico. Hawkins. That lawyer didn't believe in this heaven or hell stuff and said that the only way a man lived on was through his children. That was as far as this After-Life business went."

"Is that why you would like to have children?"

He looked at her. "Why, I never said nothing about having children."

"I know it."

"Why, would you like to have a baby?"

"Some day, maybe."

"Some day is right."

She stood up on the step and pulled the coat about her throat. "I'm satisfied now."

The match snapped and he flipped it and felt in his pocket for another. "No, a baby wouldn't have very much business with us."

"Well, if it couldn't be with us, I'd rather for it to be just you and me."

It was getting dark. The storm-broken limb yonder on the big oak-tree was twisted about the trunk like a petrified snake.

Bowie got up, knocking the unlighted tobacco out on the heel of his shoe. "I been thinking about the boys, Keechie. I guess I'll have to see them in a few days."

"Why?"

"A little business. I promised them I would meet them on the fifteenth of this month."

"Why?"

"Just business. I'll just be gone a couple of days and be back here before you know it."

"What are you planning on?"

"I just promised them, Keechie. That's all."

"What are you planning on doing?"

"Now I want you to understand, Keechie, that I'm not looking for trouble any more. I'm going up there, but I don't have anything in mind except just not let them boys wait and depend on me. We got a bank picked there all right, but I'm not planning on robbing it."

Keechie turned and grasped the door-knob. "I'm going with you," she said. Then she went in the house.

He stood there alone. Up at the end of the row of cottages there was the sound of ax splitting wood. After a little while, he went in the house.

She lay on the bed in the darkness of the sleeping-room and he went over and sat on its edge. "No, you are not, Keechie," he said.

She did not say anything. She got up and went to the kitchen and he listened to the sound of water running in a glass. Presently, she came back.

"I said you weren't going," he said.

"I heard you."

"Well, quit running around when I'm talking to you."

She sat down on the bed beside him.

"Being in my heat is bad enough and you're certainly not going to get around three of us. I made up my mind about that a long time ago."

"All right, Bowie."

"Now let's get this straight. What do you mean all right?"

"I mean it will be all right."

"How are you going to be feeling when I come back?"

"All right."

"You are going to be here, aren't you?"

"Yes."

"And it is all right?"

Keechie got up and took her coat off, folded it and laid it

on the bed rail. "You are keeping your promise and when you get up there you are going to let them know you are through with all that kind of business?"

"After Gusherton, I'm through."

"You know that I expect that, Bowie?"

"I sure do."

"All right then."

Keechie went into the kitchen and Bowie heard the wick of the oil stove sputter and then the rattle of the kettle on the flames. He lay down on the bed. After a little while the water in the kettle began to simmer. It sounded like a whimpering baby.

Chapter XVIII

THE front door of the Gusherton house parted and there was the smell of cold bacon and raw onion and then in the crack of light was Lula's water-color face. The door opened farther and Bowie went in and now he was shaking T-Dub's rocklike hand.

"Where's Chicamaw?" Bowie said.

T-Dub nodded toward the rear of the house. "Sleeping one off."

"For God's sake don't wake him up," Lula said. She had on a green velvet dinner gown that reached her ankles, and was adjusting a gold earring in her lobe. "I will absolutely leave."

"He sure has been guzzlin' it, Bowie," T-Dub said. "I don't know what's going to become of that boy."

"He's sleeping, is he?" Bowie said.

"Don't you wake him up now," Lula said.

Bowie lowered himself to the studio couch, balancing his hat on his close-pressed knees. T-Dub looked tired: like the morning they had walked the railroad ties all night. "Take his hat, Lula," he said. "Boy, you act like you just dropped in to say hello."

"I've been traveling pretty long and fast today," Bowie said.

He watched Lula carry the hat and place it on the table by the door under the mirror.

"Where you been keeping yourself, Bowie?"

"Down south of here. Say, Chicamaw has been drinking a whole lot?"

"Oh, Christ, man. He brought an old bat in here last night that I'll swear to God he must have picked up in Nigger Town. Right in this house with Lula here."

"She was as drunk as he was and of all the goings-on," Lula said. "I told T. W. there that if you weren't here by nine o'clock tonight I was packing up and going to the hotel."

"She was too drunk to notice anything," T-Dub said. "That was one thing and as soon as he passed out I took her out and dumped her."

Lula had the other earring adjusted now and she smiled at Bowie. "We have something to show you and if you will just sit there I'll bring it right back."

"Okeh," Bowie said.

Lula disappeared in the back. "She has been prettying up for two hours just because you were coming, I think," T-Dub said.

"How you been gettin' along, T-Dub?"

"Just gettin' by. Chicamaw had to go over day before yesterday to MacMasters and get fifty dollars off that lawyer friend of his to buy us gasoline and something to eat."

"You don't mean you have throwed all that, do you?"

"I got a family on my back, Bowie. I sunk twelve thousand dollars in a tourist camp over in MacMasters for that bud of mine and Mattie."

"How is he?"

"We've had hard luck about him. The parole board turned him down. I think that next year, though, he'll make it."

"That's too bad. I guess poor old Mattie is still up in the air."

"Me and Lula have been having a pretty good time too. In that New Orleans. Money will just naturally get away from you fast down there."

"Chicamaw been with you?"

T-Dub shook his head. "I thought he was with you all the time and then I figured too that he wasn't. But I haven't seen him. He showed up here three nights ago it was. Drinking jake."

"I'll swear. I wish he would ease up on that drinking a little."

Lula came in. She had a roll of parchment-looking paper tied in a red ribbon and she looked at T-Dub now. "Do you want me to show it to him?"

T-Dub was grinning and his head went up and down.

Lula, smelling of fresh perfume, bent toward Bowie, unrolling the parchment and then spread it on his knees. It was a Marriage License.

"Did you two go and get hitched?"

T-Dub's head was still going up and down.

"Why, you got your right name on here, T-Dub," Bowie said.

"Just turned the initials around. W. T. Masefeld."

"That sure floors me," Bowie said. He handed the license back up to Lula.

"How are you and that little Oklahoma girl getting along?" T-Dub said.

Bowie's eyes quivered. "Who is that?"

"What's her name? Keechie. Keechie Mobley?"

"What do you know about her?"

"You remember, Bowie. I met her when we were all up there at Dee's place. I didn't know though that you two had teamed up until I begin to see that stuff in the papers."

Bowie's Adam's apple ached like it had been hit and he could not swallow. "What stuff is that?"

"Haven't you been seeing any of it?"

Bowie shook his head.

"I read something just last Sunday I think it was," Lula said. "Had her picture."

"Picture?" Bowie said.

"Why, hell, Bowie, I thought you knew all about that. That Dee Mobley up there claims you kidnaped her and I told Lula here that all that guy had done was yellowed up. Some Law got to pumping him and he just about let out that kind of a squawk. I told Lula here that that was the way it was. I knew damned well you wouldn't kidnap anybody. I mean a girl like that."

"And it's in the papers?" Bowie said.

"The last one was just last Sunday," Lula said. "It was a picture of her, I know, that she had taken when she was going to high school."

"Huh," Bowie said.

"It will die down, Bowie. I wouldn't let it worry me."

"It don't worry me."

Lula went over and sat crosswise on T-Dub's legs; he spread them and she lay against him and put her arm around his neck, the Marriage License roll in her left hand.

That means you and me have come to the parting of the ways, Little Soldier, Bowie thought. You can't be running with me no more.

T-Dub and Lula made a smacking sound as they kissed.

You can go on back up to Oklahoma and get everything squared up, Bowie thought. Let them think what they want. You have some money now, Little Soldier, and you can tell that old man of yours to go straight to Burning Hell.

"You go on back and pretty up some more, Sugar," T-Dub said. "Bowie and me want to talk a little business."

"Don't you go and get a headache now," Lula said.

I'd like to see some Law bother you while I'm gone, Bowie thought. Lay just one finger on you. I'll take care of myself, Brother Law, but you lay one finger on that girl and goddamn you, I'll get a machine gun and hunt *you* down!

Lula disappeared in the back of the house.

"This bank here is a bird's-nest on the ground," T-Dub said. "And it will go for fifty thousand or not a dime."

"I can use money," Bowie said. "A man never knows when he's going to need money and plenty of it in this business."

"You're not going to get three boys like us together every day," T-Dub said. "That is the way I look at it."

"And Chicamaw has been feeling pretty low?"

"Bowie, I think he would charge that bank tomorrow by himself if you and me both backed out."

"Well, he won't have to do it by himself."

They robbed the First National Bank of Gusherton at *10:01*

o'clock the following morning, Chicamaw looking like a man with galloping consumption and driving Bowie's car; T-Dub complaining of rheumatism. There were no rumbles and at *10:15* they were switching cars, setting a match to Bowie's machine, and at *10:30* Chicamaw drove T-Dub's car, T-Dub and Bowie crouched in the back, into the garage of their house at the edge of the city. Chicamaw went on in the house and fifteen minutes later T-Dub and then, after another interval, Bowie.

The bank went for only seventeen thousand dollars.

At noon, T-Dub fried bacon and eggs and made toast, but only Chicamaw ate. Bowie drank coffee.

That afternoon there was a football game on the radio and Bowie lost ten dollars to Chicamaw.

"You guys give me the jitters," Chicamaw said. "Why don't you say something?"

"You need a drink," T-Dub said.

"I need something to taper off on and just as soon as it gets dark I'm going to town and get it."

A little before dusk a car entered the driveway and they picked up guns, but it was only some damned bastard turning around to go back to town.

At dusk, T-Dub said he was going up to the first Drug Store and give Lula a ring at the Red Bonnet Hotel. "I might just go on down and pick her up and we'll shell out for New Orleans right tonight. You want to go down with me, either one of you?"

"I do," Chicamaw said.

"If you boys are going, I think I'll just go with you too," Bowie said. "You can just drop me off at the bus station. I got some business to attend to and I want to get it over with."

Chicamaw had his hat on his head. "Why don't you hang around with us some, Bowie? I believe you're getting stuck up or something."

"I'll see you boys pretty soon."

"You want to watch yourself on these busses," T-Dub said.

"When I get down the line a couple of hundred miles I'll hop off and get me a car," Bowie said.

T-Dub named the night club on Bourbon Street in New

Orleans and said he and Lula would be in it the night of
December first.

"Okeh," Bowie said. "I guess you'll be there too, Chicamaw?"

"If I don't stump my toe," Chicamaw said.

The child in the shrunken coat slid off the Waiting Room
bench, stood there, the drawers leg hanging, her hands behind
her, looking at Bowie. He winked again. The child approached and when she got close, she thrust out her hand,
palm up, fingers stretched.

"Oh, you want a nickel?" Bowie said.

The mother got up, a woman in a faded red coat with a
cheap fur collar, and came toward them with her hands outstretched. "Is she bothering you?" she said.

"I should say not. Where are you going, Little Lady?"

"Grandpa's," Little Lady said. She extended the other hand
now. "Why of all things, honey," the woman said.

Bowie placed the quarter on the child's palm and the fingers
closed about it. "How about you sittin' up here by me a little
while?" Bowie said. He patted the bench. The child looked
at the coin and then up at her mother. The woman helped
her up on the bench.

The hard heels of the Policeman scraped on the tile floor
toward the ticket window and he talked for a moment with
the clerk there and then turned and moved back toward the
door. At the door, he stepped back and then aside and two
girls in fur coats, carrying week-end bags entered, a man in a
tweed topcoat following. The Policeman went on out and the
girls and the tweed-coated man stood at the ticket window
now.

Bowie carried Little Lady in his arms, and inside the
crowded bus a bald-headed man in the third seat got up and
gave Bowie and the Mother his seat.

The woman talked. The skin in the hollows of her eyes had
the coloring of tobacco-stained cigarette paper. She said her
husband was a barber and couldn't find work and she was
going now to her father until things got better. The child was
just getting over a bad cold.

Little Lady slept on Bowie's lap and now he shifted her a little so her head would not touch the hardness of the gun under his arm. The mother said she was hoping her husband had work by Christmas.

The finger-nails of Little Lady's limp fingers were black-rimmed and looked like paper. Keechie's nails were always clean and rounded short and pretty; not long and sharp like Lula's. The night before he left she had trimmed his toe-nails. All right now, Big Boy, don't start that stuff. . . . Now this woman here was having a tough time. She could stand a little piece of money and here he was with almost six thousand dollars on him.

The Mother was silent now, her head pressed back against the seat, eyes closed. Pasteboard showed through the paint of the purse on her lap.

What if he slipped a twenty in that purse? If he picked up that purse and she grabbed out and started yelling? It would win the fur-lined bathtub. It would bring him luck to get some money in that purse though. If he got five twenty-dollar bills in that purse and she didn't wake up it would break any jinx that was waiting up this road here. If he counted to thirteen and got five twenties in that purse there wouldn't anything stop him on this trip.

The woman was snoring now, the money in her purse.

A little after daybreak, Little Lady and her Mother left the bus and at eight o'clock, in San Angelo, Bowie got off and at ten o'clock he was driving south in the new automobile.

The clouds above the lowering sun looked like a picture of sea waves in the moonlight. A tiny flame was burning in Bowie's stomach. I've got to eat something. I haven't had anything to eat since. . . . Jesus Christ . . . I haven't eaten since day before yesterday. I'll be doggoned. I'm going to fool around and starve myself to death. Thinking about other things and here I am starving myself to death.

The sign read: *EATS*. Bowie drove into the broad parkway and stopped close to the screened door of the roadside lunch stand, a low, frame structure plastered with tin beer signs.

Bowie went in. There were a counter and five stools and a playing electric gramophone by a slot machine. A man in a white apron came from the back through the arched door and moved up inside the counter. The face of a woman peered through the kitchen slot.

"Soft boil me two and coffee," Bowie said. He straddled the first stool.

The man had a double chin, lumpy and soft-looking like the belly of a frog.

The gramophone was playing *El Rancho Grande*. Next to the cash register, held by the bottle of catsup and white mustard jar, was a folded newspaper. Bowie reached toward the newspaper and then brought his hand back. To hell with them damned newspapers.

The music ended and the machine made a clicking sound and was still. Frog Chin moved around the cash register and presently the coin slot jingled and then the machine was playing again: *El Rancho Grande*.

Bowie stirred the soft-boiled eggs and then broke crackers and dropped the crumbs into the glass. He got the salt and pepper and then picked up the newspaper. It was a San Antonio paper. He took a bite and then spread the front page:

GUSHERTON, Texas, Nov. 16—One bandit was dead here tonight, another wounded and the wife-accomplice of the slain desperado was in jail as a vengeful aftermath of the bold, $17,000 holdup of the First National Bank here this morning.

The dead bandit is T. W. (Tommy Gun) Masefeld, escaped Oklahoma convict and sought for two months in connection with a half-dozen bank robberies in West Texas. He was shot to death by officers as he sat in a car parked in front of the Red Bonnet Hotel. His companion, Elmo (Three-Toed) Mobley, badly wounded, was in the hospital here under heavy guard.

Bowie A. Bowers, fast-triggered killer and leader of the bank bandit gang, had still eluded late tonight the combing search of a posse that numbered more than 300 peace officers and outraged citizens.

Mrs. Lula Masefeld, reputed wife of the slain bandit, was captured a few minutes after the shooting and lodged in jail.

The downtown gun battle terrorized scores of pedestrians and sent motorists scurrying for safety. The officers beat their quarry to the draw and neither bandit was able to fire.

Ten thousand dollars of the First National Bank loot was recovered in the bullet-riddled automobile. Credit for the heavy blow against the gang was being given tonight to Hotel Detective Chris Lawton.

It was he who secured the tip that resulted in the laying of a trap for the bandit gang.

"What's the matter," Frog Chin said, "aren't them eggs all right?"

"Sure," Bowie said. He dipped the spoon into the glass.

At least three men and possibly two women participated in the sensational robbery here. Two bandits, identified as Bowie Bowers and Masefeld, entered the bank at 10 o'clock, forced a half-dozen bank workers and officials and a dozen customers into the vault at the points of six-shooters, rifled the safe and tills and escaped in the waiting car of confederates. Witnesses who saw the bandit machine speed away declared there was a woman in it.

Bowers, who escaped from the Oklahoma Penitentiary while serving a life term for murder, is wanted in connection with the murders of two Texaco City peace officers and a half-dozen bank robberies in Oklahoma, Kansas and Texas. Phantom-like, he has been seen traveling about the country in high-speed motor cars with a woman companion, said by Oklahoma authorities to be Keechie Mobley, cousin of the bandit wounded and captured here tonight.

"Those eggs done enough for you?"

"Fine," Bowie said. He took a bite and the food was like the man's phlegm in his mouth.

A woman is believed to have figured in Bowers' escape in Texaco City just as authorities here believe his disappearance here was abetted by a woman.

Mobley was suffering from wounds in the head and chest, but attending physicians declared he had a fighting chance to live. If he survives, however, he faces the electric chair. District Attorney Herbert Morton announced here tonight that he would ask the supreme penalty in the event Mobley went to trial.

"I loved Tommy more than anything in the world," pretty 19-year-old Lula Masefeld sobbed in her jail cell tonight. "He was the best thing in the world to . . ."

Bowie folded the newspaper and placed it back behind the bottle and jar. Then he got up and reached in his pocket before the cash register.

"It is getting so that you can't please anybody these days," Frog Chin said.

"I just wasn't hungry," Bowie said.

As he walked toward the car, his feet felt like clumps of prickly pear.

Chapter XIX

THE green-shaded lamp in the kitchen of *Welcome Inn* was burning, their signal that there had been no rumbles while he was gone, and now he closed the car door quietly and the leaves on the walk crackled under his moving shoes. He lifted on the knob so the door would not scrape and went in. Pale coals studded the mound of dark ashes in the fireplace and then he saw Keechie sitting on the end of the cot by the shadowy radio.

"I'm back," he said and he had the feeling that no sound had left his mouth and the words were melting in his hollow stomach. He strained: "I saw the light burning. You remembered all right."

"I did not know whether you were coming back or not," Keechie said.

He went over and stood on the hearth, clasping his hands behind him. Water dripped in the kitchen sink. "How has everything been?"

"All right."

The motor of a speeding car away over on the highway beat like a tom-tom.

"You want me to turn that light off in the kitchen?" Bowie said.

"If you want to."

"It doesn't matter. It really doesn't make any difference to me."

"I don't see that it makes any difference whether you came back here or not."

The heat at the base of his skull ignited and a film, like smoke, burned his eyes. "Oh, you mean about me, I guess?"

"Yes."

"Everything has happened pretty fast," he said. "Before you could say Jack Robinson, everything happened. You know about it?"

"Yes."

"About you?"

"Yes."

He moved toward her. "Doggone it, Keechie. I didn't mean for you to get mixed up in a business like this."

"Don't you worry about me."

He stopped.

"I will have to learn to take care of myself."

"All that old money is yours, Keechie. It will take care of you. Just don't go back around that . . . that old man of yours."

"I am not going back there. Don't worry about that."

"You will have to go back there, I guess. But don't you worry about that business. Them goddamned dingbats can't put nothing on you, nothing in this God's world."

"When did you start thinking about me?"

"Thinking about you?"

"You surely didn't think about me when you were gone?"

"Didn't think about you while I was gone?"

Keechie stood up. "You lied to me. *Lied.*"

"Why, Keechie." He moved toward her. "Why, you don't understand, Keechie."

"Don't you touch me." Her fists were clenched. "You took them. It was me or them and you knew it and you took them."

He lowered his hands. "I don't like to talk about them boys."

"They don't mean anything to me. They never did. You knew that. All right, you and me are through."

She was going toward the door now and he saw that she had on the cravenette coat and there was her two bags on the floor. "Where are you going?" he said.

"What does it matter to you?"

He reached her, bent and grasped the wrist of the hand reaching for the bag. She wrenched from him. "I told you not to touch me."

"You wait a minute," he said.

She stood there, making breathing sounds like her nostrils were stopped.

"You want to leave this way?" he said.

"Absolutely."

"Sore like this?"

"Whatever you want to call it."

His groin felt like it was emptying.

"Is that all?" Keechie said.

"You wait a minute."

"You won't stop me."

"No, I won't stop you, but you just wait a minute."

She stood there and now he turned and went over to the fireplace and looked at the smothering coals. He went into the kitchen and came back with crumpled papers and kindling and he scattered the ashes and placed them on the coals. The papers blazed and then he arranged sticks of wood on the flames.

"You don't have any business leaving this time of night," he said. "If anybody is going to leave this house, it's me."

"I'm not staying here."

"All right. Now I'm going to get it straight after a while. If you just have to go, all right. Now I'm going out this door here and I'm going to be gone on a long walk and if nothing will do you, but you have to go, there's a car out there and the keys are in it and you know where the money is."

"I don't want anything of yours."

"Don't be a damned fool." The knob grated with his wrench and he went out the door.

A bulbous crescent hung heavily in the bottom of the moon's slate-colored disk. Wind gushed in the trees with the sound of a distant river and the tops of the cedars, silhouetted against the cobalt and starlit heavens, whipped and threshed like tiny Christmas trees in a storm. He walked now on the gray woodcutters' road that twisted and slashed deep into the woods.

This is what you wanted, isn't it, Big Boy? It had to stop some time and what's the difference how it happened? You just keep going down this road and walk, by God, until these damned legs of yours come off. *Keechie in front of the oil heater in the Bunk, floor dust tatting the hem of her skirt.* All right now, don't start that stuff.

The wind's chill crawled under his trouser cuffs and down the neck of his collar and he turned up his lapels. I have plenty

of things to do. Nothing in this old world will do you any
more good, T-Dub, but, Chicamaw, you got a friend. Don't
you think different for a minute, boy. You're just as liable as
not to be running these roads again with me pretty soon and
it's not going to be any year from now.

His shadow glided on the road beside him, stubby and slender. *Keechie picking cigarette butts off the floor to make him a
smoke with a cigarette paper she had found.* Now lay off that
stuff, goddamit. What difference does it make how it happened, just so it happened? Okeh. Okeh. Okeh. *Okeh!*

The broken tree stump yonder with its two short, outflung
limbs looked like a man. Bowie pressed his hand against the
gun's butt in the holster under his arm. Hell, I don't need a
gun with one Law. Brave men. Heroes. Fifty of them to get
one Thief, hundred, two hundred, three hundred. Big Shots.
Heroes.

A plummeting meteor fragment streaked the heavens like
the spark of a shaken log, vanished. That means you're gone,
Little Soldier. That means you have left.

He left the woods now, moved across the clearing toward
Welcome Inn, in a dawning mist that blew like sifted ashes.
The car stood where he had left it. Christ, girl, you didn't
leave this place walking? Now you didn't do *that.* Why, girl,
you're liable to get in trouble. . . . Smoke was coming from
the chimney.

She sat in front of the burning logs, smoking a cigarette,
her coat off. "I couldn't leave," she said.

His neck was rigid, fixed; he could not move it.

"I couldn't leave," she repeated.

"I noticed the car out there," he said.

"There wasn't anything for me Out There," she said.
"Nothing. *Nothing!*"

Bowie placed his hand on her shoulder, patted. "You ought
to turn in."

"I guess so."

"That is what I would do."

After a little while, Keechie got up and moved toward the
sleeping-room and he followed; stood in the doorway and
watched her lie down on the bed. Then he went over and sat
on the edge.

"I didn't want to leave you," Keechie said.

His head went up and down.

"You wouldn't have let me go, would you, Bowie?"

"No."

"Even if I had wanted to?"

"No."

"You would have made me stay?"

"Yes."

"I help you, don't I, Bowie?"

"Yes."

"A whole, whole lot?"

"Yes."

Keechie closed her eyes and presently she sucked in a deep breath through her mouth and nose, jerked convulsively and he placed his hands on her. She jerked again, easier though, and now her mouth was closed and she slept. Bowie took the gun out of his holster and placed it just under the edge of the bed, loosened his tie, unbuttoned his collar. Then he lay down beside her.

Chapter XX

KEECHIE said it looked like Santa Claus would have to come this year in a boat instead of a sleigh. It had rained for six days. In the daytime, the rain-shrouded woods and hills were merged with the sky and their cottage stood on a tiny island. They went to bed at night with the rain caressing their roof and awoke in the morning with it still beating a gentle, broken rhythm.

It was getting close to five o'clock this afternoon and any time now Alvin Philpott, the little boy, would be showing up with the San Antonio newspaper. Bowie had made a deal with him four weeks before, fifty cents a week, and every afternoon now, as Alvin came home from school, he brought a paper. They were going to get the boy something for Christmas. That was only four days off now.

"How would you like to have a little egg nogg for Christmas?" Keechie said. She stood there in the kitchen doorway, a sweet potato in one hand, a peeling knife in the other.

Bowie placed Keechie's polished oxford on the floor and picked up the other one. "Did you ever drink any of that?"

Keechie shook her head. "Maybe I did when I was little, I don't know. I just saw a recipe in the paper and I think nearly everybody drinks it around Christmas time. The eggs in it are good for you."

"If it's just the same to you," Bowie said, "we'll just get a quart of whisky and drink it straight. But no egg noggs for me. I got sick as a horse on it once and I swore to God in heaven that if I ever got over it, I would never drink no more egg nogg no more."

Keechie laughed and went back into the kitchen. They were going to have pork chops and candied sweet potatoes with marshmallows for supper.

Bowie rubbed the brown polish into Keechie's shoe. We'll do something Christmas all right, he thought. It won't be just like any other day. He had that Christmas present to his Mama off his mind now. One thousand dollars. He and Keechie had driven yesterday to San Antonio and mailed the envelope. There was one thing, though, he had to do pretty soon and that was get some money to that lawyer friend of Chicamaw's in MacMasters. Archibald J. Hawkins. He and Keechie would have to go back to San Antonio and attend to that. Two thousand dollars in an envelope to a lawyer? The guy might be dead and somebody else would get it? The thing to do was go in some bank in San Antonio and get a draft and send it to Hawkins. Lawyers knew better than to go south with a thief's money. That one in Tulsa had found that out. Now he could send Chicamaw a postal order for one hundred dollars. In the Christmas rush in them banks and post-offices in San Antonio, nobody would big-eye Keechie or him.

The screen rattled and Bowie got up and went to the door. It was Alvin. Water dripped from the boy's nose and he pulled the dry newspaper from underneath his soggy coat.

"You going to get wet, boy, if you ain't careful," Bowie said.

"It don't bother me," Alvin said.

After Alvin left, Bowie went back to the kitchen. "I know now what we will get that kid," he said. "A raincoat."

"That will be better than a shotgun," Keechie said.

There was nothing in the newspapers. There was enough in there day before yesterday, Bowie thought. Chicamaw was going to trial February fourth. That lawyer Hawkins sure had to have some money pretty soon because they would sure put the Chair on Chicamaw if he didn't get some money.

After supper, Keechie and Bowie played checkers. It was raining harder now, wind whistling in the window-screens and water splashing in the puddles under the eaves.

Bowie stacked the checkers in the box with the sliding top. "You know I been thinking, Keechie, about what you said the other day about it being easier for a woman to disguise than a man. I believe it's easier for a man when you get to thinking about it. A man can grow a beard and wear glasses and get his hair cut different."

"He can't use powder and paint though."

"He sure can. He can dress up like a woman and get by with it."

"I'd like to see you dressed up like a woman."

"Not me."

"And I'm not going to dress up like a man."

"I know it," Bowie said. "But you know, Keechie, there's men in this world though that go around all the time dressed up like women. They're no good."

"There was a woman in Keota that smoked cigars and acted just like a man," Keechie said.

"Them people are no good, Keechie. Absolutely. They're no good."

"There are more no-good people in this world than there are good ones," Keechie said. "A blind man can see that."

"Up there in Alky, Keechie, you never saw the like. You would never have thought so many no-good people could be gotten up all together at one time. That was one of the reasons why I just couldn't stand it there any longer. I don't know though, but what it's just about the same Out Here."

The window-screens whined and Bowie listened. Then he

put his finger in his ear and jiggled it. "Yessir, Keechie, I think
you hit the nail on the head when you said that the only way
to beat this game was just go off and pull the Hole in after
you. Not have a single friend."

"You can't trust anybody, Bowie."

"I've always said that, honey. I wouldn't trust Jesus Christ
if he come right in this door right this minute."

"You just have to depend on yourself in this world and
nobody else," Keechie said.

Bowie got up and placed the box of checkers and the board
on the mantel. He turned, placed his elbows on the mantel's
edge and pushed his stomach out away from the heat. "But
you know, Keechie, you never will see three boys like us together again. I think about that Chicamaw up there in that
jail pulling through by himself and I'll bet he doesn't even
have cigarette money."

"Nobody but a lawyer can help him now."

"I know it. That's what I have been thinking about. I'll bet
that boy is beginning to think that he doesn't have a friend
in this world."

"There is nothing you can do about it. Unless you want to
get him some money."

"That will do it, Keechie. It will do it nine times out of ten
in this world. That's what I have to do. Get him a lawyer
lined up. And a good one."

"You don't have to go anywhere around him though?"

"What are you talking about? I should say not. No, all I
have to do is to get some mazuma to a good lawyer and that
will be all there is to it."

Keechie got up and went over to the wood box. She carried the stick to the fireplace and said: "Move over a little,
Bowie."

Sparks popped under the dropped wood and Keechie stood
there watching the flames lengthen. "Don't that rain sound
good, Bowie?"

"What did you say, Keechie?"

"I said don't you like to hear that rain on the house?"

"Uh huh. I sure do. You bet I do."

"I like it," Keechie said.

The floor planks creaked as Bowie began moving about. "I

should have brought in more wood today," he said. "I guess this rain is just going to keep on forever."

On Christmas Eve morning, icicles hung from the eaves, but the day was breaking clear. The sun was going to shine. Bowie and Keechie lay in bed, talking now about how Alvin was going to act when they gave him the rain-coat this afternoon. They had bought the raincoat in Ante-lope Center yesterday and also a half-dozen handkerchiefs that they were going to give Alvin to give to Filthy MacNasty.

"If we're going to go to San Antonio this morning and get back here by four o'clock, we got to be gettin' up and going," Bowie said. "We're not going to get any business done much less seeing a show at this rate."

"Well, I don't see nothing holding you down in this bed, Booie-Wooie," Keechie said.

"You usually get up before I do, don't you? What's got hold of your legs this morning? Can't you take them icicles this morning?"

"Sure. I was just waiting to see you show what a he-man you are. Why don't you get up and start the fire this morn-ing?"

"Who, me?"

"I hope it's you and not somebody else I'm talking to."

"By God, I hope so too. Now let me see. All I got to do is just get up and sort of walk in there to that fireplace. All right, you win, Keechie-Weechie." Bowie swept back the covers, got out, tucked the blankets back under Keechie and trotted, barefooted, into the cold living-room.

In the kitchen, Bowie saw the flooded floor and then the burst pipe of the shower in the bathroom.

"I will go and get Filthy and tell him to phone a plumber," Keechie said.

"No, you just stay here," Bowie said. "I'll go."

It was ten o'clock when the rattling, banging Ford pick-up with the vise stopped in front of the cottage. Bowie, the mop in his hand, stood at the window and watched the plumber get out. The man had a head shaped like an Irish potato and an unlit cigar stub in the corner of his mouth.

"You the folks that are having a little trouble out here?" Plumber said.

Bowie thumbed toward the back. "Bathroom."

Plumber looked at Keechie standing by the bed.

"In the bathroom," Bowie said.

Plumber's smile was soggy. The cigar stub darkened against his draining face. "We been swamped," he said. "Freeze. Bathroom?"

Bowie pointed.

Plumber moved across the living-room and into the hallway toward the bath.

Bowie turned and looked at Keechie.

Keechie framed the question with soundless lips: What do you think?

Bowie's head went up and down.

Plumber came out of the hallway walking briskly toward the door. "Tools," he said.

They watched him through the window. He got in the pick-up, started the motor and then the machine moved off with a violent jerk.

Bowie pointed at Keechie's coat. "Get on out and start our car."

Mud-thickened water geysered from the puddles at the Gate and splattered on their windshield. Bowie pressed the wiper button and then turned onto the highway. The road extended ahead, gray and slick as phlegm; gravel rattled under the fenders.

"Light me a cigarette," Bowie said.

Keechie looked in the panel pocket. "We don't have a one, Bowie, not a one."

"Can you beat that?"

"We will get some."

"Can you beat that. Now that's what I call luck for you. You mean to say there's not a one there?"

"We will get some, Bowie."

"Now that's what I call luck."

Thunder rolled. It was like the hills around them had been undermined and were bumping around.

"I'm sure fed up on rain," Bowie said. "I'm sure fed up on it."

"Where are we going, Bowie?"

"MacMasters."

"MacMasters?"

"I'm going to see a lawyer there."

"MacMasters," Keechie repeated.

The highway stretched on like a long ribbon of wet funeral cloth; the rain-drunk weeds of the right-of-way rushing behind.

"Alvin won't get his raincoat," Keechie said. "It was laying there on the radio."

Bowie cleared his throat. "I been thinking. It's a good thing we gassed up yesterday and got them cans filled. What if we were just starting out with a couple of gallons like we had yesterday morning? By golly, we sure got some gas in this buggy."

"We're lucky," Keechie said.

Chapter XXI

THE house of J. Archibald Hawkins, the lawyer, was a straight, two-story house with a porch of warped planks and next to the First Christian Church. In the furniture-stuffed Front Room, there was a roll-desk, its top stacked with law books of tan and red cloth; a piano with two hymn-books on the rack and framed portraits on the shawl-scarfed top. The worn places in the carpet looked like burlap sacking and on the square of cracked linoleum by the broad, sliding door a gas-stove ejected long, curling flames.

When Hawkins smiled, his eyes became wrinkled pockets and his cheeks looked like balls wrapped in cellophane. His Sister, who lived with him, had gone to Amarillo to see her son and it had looked like he was going to spend Christmas night alone. "It appears though," he said, "that I have some pretty distinguished company."

Bowie, sitting there on the claw-carved, leather divan grinned, and Keechie looked down and covered the strip of house dress over her legs with the coat's skirt.

"Now about Chicamaw again, Judge?" Bowie said.

"We will get him fixed up," Hawkins said. He did not practice criminal law himself, he added, but he knew personally the members of the Law Firm in Gusherton who could do something with the case. It would take money though.

"How much?" Bowie said.

Hawkins smiled. "Just about all they decide a man has."

"Around how much?"

"I know this firm will not take a case for less than two thousand."

"Say three thousand?" Bowie said.

Hawkins nodded. "It is a pretty good newspaper case too."

"I'd like to see Chicamaw get some money too. Think you can manage it?"

"I can see him very easily."

"And I'll leave you five hundred for all this trouble."

"I can certainly use it."

Bowie crossed his leg and leaned forward with his elbow on his knee and chin in hand. "You know anything how that happened in Gusherton? Them boys gettin' in trouble, I mean?"

Hawkins nodded. "Yes, I know. That girl. What is her name? Masefeld's wife."

"Good lord," Bowie said. "Sure enough?"

"It was pure simple-mindedness. That hotel detective over there made some advances that were unwelcome to her and, instead of ignoring them, she made a scene. Complained to the Manager and said she had a husband and plenty of money. It seems this hotel detective got suspicious then sure enough and plugged in on her telephone. He got the tip that way."

"I'll swear," Bowie said.

"She is going to testify for the State in Chicamaw's trial."

"I'll swear."

Keechie said they had better be going.

Hawkins said that he had a big chicken back there in the oven and it would only take a half-hour for it to warm. Wouldn't they keep an old man company a little on Christmas night?

Bowie looked at Keechie. She consented.

The lawyer talked. There are more millionaires in this

country than in any other, he said, and at the same time more robbers and killers. Therein lay significance. Extremes in riches make extremes in crime. As long as a Social System permitted the acquisition of extreme riches, there would be equalizing crime and the Government and all law-enforcement organizations might as well fold their hands and accept it.

"The Rich," Hawkins said, "can't drive their big automobiles and flaunt bediamonded wives and expect every man just to simply look on admiringly. The sheep will do it and the sheep will even laud it and support it, but at the same time these sheep will feel something that they do not understand and demonstrate it and that is known as so-called glorification of the big criminal."

"I'm not proud of nothing I ever done," Bowie said.

Money interests fix the punishment for crime in this country, Hawkins said, and consequently there is no moral justice. A bum steals a pair of shoes from another and that is a great crime, but what will happen to the complaining bum at the police station? If that same thief pilfers fifteen cents from the telephone box of a big utility company, he can receive fifteen years, but if he snatches that amount from the cup of a blind beggar, he may get a twenty-dollar fine. . . .

Hawkins' stomach gurgled and Bowie looked down, saw the dried mud on the toe of his shoe and then looked at Keechie's shoes. There was mud on them too.

"Now you take the Stupid Sheep I was talking about a moment ago," Hawkins said, "just like this young fellow that lives right down here in a little two-room apartment across the corner from me. He drives a milk truck for a millionaire creamery man here and he works ten and twelve hours a day and he goes home at night and there is a baby that he has to help his wife with. His wife is sick. Still weak and unable to work from bearing that child. Now you take that boy. Is it strange that he doesn't feel what these newspapers yap about glorification of the criminal?"

"These newspapers never get nothing straight," Bowie said. "They got me working in towns that I have never even been inside of."

"There is nothing like a man hunt and trust the newspapers

to make an arena and ballyhoo the Kill. The Romans were
not cruel. At least no more cruel than these newspapers that
get their readers' tongues hanging out for the Kill. And just
here last week the Chamber of Commerce gave the Creamery
Millionaire a silver loving-trophy as being MacMasters' most
useful citizen of the year. And the irony of it all is that you
take that fourteen-dollar-a-week boy that is working for him
and put him on a jury and some Prosecutor who wants his
name in the newspapers more than anything else will have that
boy thinking that red-hot spikes are too mild for a bank
robber."

"I get a kick out of robbing banks," Bowie said. "I don't
mind admittin' it."

Keechie touched the back of Bowie's hand. "It's getting
pretty late."

"We'll go in a minute, honey."

"We have some chicken coming up," Hawkins said. "I bet
you young folks think I am a long-winded old cuss."

"Go on," Bowie said. "I like to hear you."

"Speaking of crime," Hawkins said. His stomach gurgled.
"There was a Consumptive that come down here from
Detroit in an old rattletrap here a couple of months ago and
he had two little dogs. That is all that man had and he
moved in a little shack on the river down here close to town
and then that ranchman, who lived across the river and is
worth, I guess, fifty thousand dollars, killed those two dogs
with a shotgun and there is not a law in this state that
will punish that cold-blooded, low-down, degenerate murderer."

" 'Fraid he would get a cow bit, I guess?" Bowie said.

"That. But that man shoots dogs down like he would rat-
tlesnakes."

"They caught a fellow in the town I used to live in," Keechie said, "throwing weenies with poison in them out to dogs.
He was just driving around town doing it."

Bowie looked at her. "You never did tell me about that,"
he said.

"Prisons are simply pimples on a corrupt world," Hawkins
said. "The great criminals, I mean the real enemies of man's
welfare and peace and happiness, never go near a prison and

the dead ones, out in these cemeteries, have the highest tomb-stones over their heads. Normal men with abnormal tendencies. Abnormal men with normal tendencies. My God. It is a wonder people do not smell, their minds are so rotten. Excuse me, young lady."

"Them capitalist fellows are thieves like us," Bowie said. "They rob widows and orphans."

"I do not fool myself one minute," Hawkins said. "I possess that. You take me, Bowers, and that five hundred you have given me. I am going to run for Justice of the Peace this spring. When an old broken-down lawyer gets old, Son, he runs for Justice of the Peace."

"You don't look old," Bowie said.

"Anyway I am going into this next election and I rather think I am going to have that Office. I will get a couple of constables, gun-toters, and these boys will go out and break up Negro dice games, raid petty little home-brew joints in Mexican town and take in some of these tourists that are exceeding the speed limit by a few miles. We will make good fees. Vultures are all we are."

"I guess a man has to make a living," Bowie said.

"In this system he is forced to be a criminal."

"I never robbed nobody that couldn't stand to lose it," Bowie said.

Hawkins looked at Keechie. "And whatever road a man takes there is always a woman that will follow him."

"If this man here will just get up and start," Keechie said, "I will follow him right now."

"Don't pay no attention to her, Judge," Bowie said.

The gurgling sounded in Hawkins' stomach again.

The strung, colored lights of this town's Main Street illuminated an empty, quiet thoroughfare. On the Court House lawn, a big, lighted Christmas tree glowed greens and reds and yellows. The sign at the edge of the town read: *New Orleans . . . 590 mi.*

"You think we will be there this time tomorrow night?" Keechie said.

"Uh huh. Keechie, I can just see that Indian's face when

them big lawyers start coming in his cell. He's sure going to know he's got a friend Out Here."

"You have done everything you could now."

Bowie turned his head toward her and grinned. "Say, did you hear Old Windy's guts growling?"

"I thought he was never going to stop talking."

"I never heard anything like it," Bowie said. "You could have heard it out in the street."

Chapter XXII

BOWIE and Keechie had the renting of a furnished house on their minds when they entered New Orleans, but it was late and they were so tired that they looked at an apartment and there were so many nice things about the very first one that they took it. The place—*The Colonial Apartments*—was a remodeled home and as big as an old West Texas court house. On an avenue of palm-fenced homes and big churches, this house was shadowed and darkened by spreading cotton-woods and hackberries, and crêpe myrtles screened the windows.

Mrs. Lufkin was the owner of *The Colonial Apartments*. She was a stout-bosomed woman with dyed black hair and smelled like a brewery. Mrs. Lufkin did not have much to do with the running of the apartments, leaving this to Rebecca, the little Negro woman with gold teeth. From Rebecca, Bowie and Keechie learned about the other occupants of the place: the Professor who taught in the University up the avenue; the Interne and his Nurse-Wife who were at the hospital most of the time; the four girls who lived in the two apartments upstairs and were students in the University. Rebecca said Mrs. Lufkin bought whisky five gallons at a time and she prayed for her every night.

The ceiling of their living-room was so high that Keechie could not touch the plastered dome even when Bowie lifted her. There was a wide, high fireplace of polished granite and a log gas-heater. In a few days, when they made that one big shopping tour downtown, they would get a radio to put beside the library table and beaded parlor lamp. And a red-checkered cloth for the kitchen table, Keechie said.

The sleeping-room had a tiled floor and in it were wedged a bed and a clear-mirrored vanity. The kitchen was small too, but it would look a lot better, Bowie said, when that big pantry was filled with stuff to eat. The bathroom was as big as the kitchen and steaming water gushed from the *hot* tap. Now you can get all the baths you want, Bowie said, and when Keechie said she had been thinking about that, Bowie said he did not see how they had put up with it back in those Texas hills.

They would get a telephone put in, they decided, and any time there was drug-store buying or anything like that to do, they would have delivery boys bring it to their door. Rebecca had said that she went to the Grocery every morning and would be glad to get their things too. They would give her a few dollars a week, Bowie said, and that old black gal would break her neck for them. There would not be anybody to see except Rebecca and delivery boys and at nights they could duck in suburban picture shows.

The best thing about it all, Keechie said, was that no one in the world knew where they were. She lettered the slip that Bowie inserted in the slot of the mailbox in the lobby: *Mr. & Mrs. F. T. Haviland.*

When the trial of Chicamaw started back in Gusherton, Bowie waited in the kitchen every afternoon listening for the thump of the thrown newspaper on the back steps. There were three days of the trial and then on the fourth day, Bowie read in the Sunday-morning paper of its outcome. Chicamaw had beaten the Chair. He had drawn a pair of nines—ninety-nine years.

Bowie carried the newspaper back to Keechie who was still in bed this Sunday morning. "That boy beat them," Bowie said. "They're not going to kick any Switch off on him. It's right here in the paper, Keechie."

"I'm glad," Keechie said.

"Go ahead and read it, Keechie. Here it is, right here."

"Now you will feel a lot better," Keechie said.

"And don't think he is just sittin' up there in that jail with his brains sittin' too. And he won't have to kill anybody to beat that Pen either. Any day you want to kill somebody, Keechie, you can beat a Pen easy."

"That is none of your worry now."

"Go ahead and read it. I'll stir us up some breakfast. How about me cooking it up this morning? How about it?"

"All right."

By ten o'clock, sunlight was knifing through the crêpe myrtle and the raised windows, cutting bright squares on the living-room carpet and blue linoleum of the kitchen. This is one day I'm not going to stay cooped up, Bowie thought. We're going to get out. Keechie sat on the vanity bench with a curling iron in her hand. She had on the Chinese wrapper with the yellow and red dragon designs.

"Let's get out of this place today, Keechie. What do you say?"

"Where?"

"Don't make one bit of difference to me. Just so we go."

"Would you like to go walking in that Park up the avenue?"

"You're doggone whistling."

Keechie put the curling iron on the vanity and stood up. "I've always wanted to go through it in the daytime. I'll wear my gray flannel suit."

"I'll strut out in that double-breasted. Say, Little Soldier, you're getting as broad as I don't know what."

Keechie looked down her body, at her hips.

"You're puttin' on plenty," Bowie said.

"Don't you like it?"

"I should say I do. You could get as big as the side of a barn and I'd like it."

"Well, there's no danger of that."

The lower limbs of the big oak in the Park grew on the ground as if the task of going up was too much. The gray Spanish moss that fringed the boughs, Keechie said, was whiskers and showed how old the trees were. They circled the tree now and moved across the smooth fairway of the golf course, pausing near the fluttering pennant on the green, and then went on toward the lagoon. A couple passed ahead of them, a wire-haired terrier straining on a leash held by the woman. The man bent down now to tie a shoe-lace and then trotted to catch up.

"If I had a dog I would want one of them big police babies," Bowie said. "They're mean as hell."

Swans glided on the lagoon, the traced water smoothing behind them. Around the bend of water-dipping willows, a rowboat came, the oars splashing; three girls in it. The swans moved closer to the shore. On the boat were the letters *Nellie*. The girl rowing had on brown slacks and a white sweater. Bowie and Keechie lowered themselves to the grass of the bank's edge and watched the girls and the boat disappear around the bend below.

"What are you thinking about?" Keechie said.

"I had an aunt named Nell," Bowie said. "I was thinking about her."

"Your Daddy's sister?"

Bowie shook his head. "Mama's. We lived with her a while, I mean Grandma's, after my Dad got killed. It's funny that I got to thinking about her."

"What about her?"

"Oh, I don't know. She used to come on Sunday afternoons and bring a big old sack of red-hots and licorice drops and candy like that. You remember that kind of candy, don't you?"

Keechie nodded. She reached out and plucked a bit of grass from the silk of Bowie's socks.

"Makes me think of that boy I was running around with too then," Bowie said. "You know that kid, the last time I heard of him, was a big football player in Oklahoma University and he was just a cutter and a half. We were a pair now. His Dad was the County Treasurer in that town and why he was running around up back alleys and gettin' junk and sellin' it, I don't know. That boy had more devilment in him than anybody I ever did know. We got to going in vacant houses and tearing the plumbing out and selling the brass and lead. I remember one day we made eighty cents. We bought four of them nickel pies apiece. That kid always had money in his pockets. He would steal it out of his Dad's pants at nights."

Keechie plucked a blade of Bermuda grass and began chewing the white root.

"I don't know how come me to ever think of him, but he just knew about everything that was going on in that town. That's how come me to go out to them houses at the edge of town one day. The Red Light district. He said there was women out there who would give kids nickels and dimes if they just went out there and hung around the back door."

The hoofs of running horses sounded and then on the bridle path, on the other side of the lagoon and through the trees, they saw the bright jackets of the women riders.

"I saw her, but I don't think that she knows to this day that it was me. When the old woman in the House started hollering at us to get away, she come to the back door and I saw her."

"Saw who?" Keechie said.

Bowie looked at her. "My Aunt. I thought I told you."

"Oh," Keechie said.

"She didn't recognize me though."

Keechie leaned against Bowie's leg, picked another bit of dead grass and smoothed the silk.

The horsewomen were passing yonder again, posting.

"Ain't that a helluva way to ride?" Bowie said. "Bobbing your bottom up and down like that?"

"Uh huh."

Bowie indicated that golf green behind them with a twist of his head. "That's something else I never figured why anybody could get interested in. Batting that little old ball around and puttin' it in holes."

"Some people don't have anything else to do," Keechie said. "It wouldn't bother me though if they stood on their heads if they were having a good time."

"Me neither."

They walked now along the lagoon's bank toward the white dome of the Memorial Band-stand. Bowie stopped and pointed at the rat swimming in the water toward the little island of weeping willows. "I'll bet that rat has him a Hole over there," he said.

"I didn't know rats could swim," Keechie said.

"Them kind can. I know one kind that can't do anything but snitch. Them are yellow and have two legs."

"Oh," Keechie said. "Now I get you."

"I can tell you something else about some of these boys that are gettin' in trouble every day," Bowie said. "They like to see their names in the newspapers. Why, Keechie, there's guys that will put on acts and do anything just to get their names big in the newspapers."

"I had just as soon talk about something else," Keechie said.

"Just one more thing, Keechie. Have you been thinking about us not gettin' our names in the paper no more? There hasn't been hardly one thing since that damned plumber flushed us back yonder in them damned old rainy hills."

"Just don't do anything to get your name in the paper," Keechie said. "That is the thing."

"Say we got jumped here, Keechie. Now I know. There isn't a chance just as long as we keep our noses clean like we're doing. But just say we were. Where would you like to go?"

"I don't know."

"You know where I would like to go? Mexico. It takes somebody, though, that knows the ropes to get you across that border and situated good down there. Now you take Chicamaw, he knew the ropes down there from A to Z."

"Well, Chicamaw isn't here and he isn't going to be here."

"I know it. I was just telling you, honey."

The couple coming across the narrow rustic bridge were holding hands, and Bowie and Keechie stepped aside and gave them passageway. The girl had on a white silk dress and the black hair of the fellow grew long and curling down his neck. As they stepped off the bridge, the fellow put his arm around the girl supportingly.

Bowie and Keechie went on. "You can tell by looking at them they're not married," Bowie said.

"How can you tell?"

"I don't know. Just the way he was holding her hand as if she was going to fall off that bridge or something, I guess."

"Clever, aren't you?"

"I notice little things like that."

"Maybe she would have fallen off if he hadn't been helping her. Married or not married. A girl likes that anyway."

Bowie looked at her. "Say, do you want me to hold your hand like that?" He reached toward her. Keechie swept his hand down. "Just keep that to yourself," she said.

"Gollee, honey. What's come over you? What did I do?"

Keechie turned around. "Let's go home."

"Gollee, can you beat that. What have I done?"

Keechie started back and he caught up and walked alongside her again. Near the broad stone arch of the Park's exit, a bunch of boys, their shirt tails flapping, were playing with an indoor ball. Bowie asked Keechie to wait a minute and they stood there and watched the players a little while.

The sunshine was gone now and the air touched their bodies like cold feathers. The avenue would be quiet and then, with the spreading green of the green signal light down the thoroughfare, the gears of the waiting automobiles would grate and crash, and then they came, passing in rushing trains.

"I've been thinking about old T-Dub," Bowie said. "I guess that girl was just dumb. But you know they were like a couple of kids showing me that Marriage License."

"First I had heard about it," Keechie said.

"Didn't I ever tell you about that? Well, they were just like a couple of kids, dragging that License out and showing it all around."

"I guess it mattered to them."

Bowie looked at Keechie, a loosened curl moved on her upturned coat collar. "I guess it did," he said. "They were like a couple of kids."

A street-car crashed past, its trolley popping, a glued mass of humanity through its closed windows. At the intersection, Bowie touched Keechie's arm as they stepped down off the curb.

"Would you marry me, Keechie?"

She looked up at him, then ahead again. "I don't know whether I would or not."

"Now just what do you mean by that?"

"I can't see what difference some writing on a scrap of paper makes if that's what you are thinking about."

"I don't either. That's what I have been thinking. What

difference does a piece of red ribbon around some paper make? Besides, you're married to me already if you didn't know it."

Keechie looked up at him again. "Where do you get that?"

"It's the law, Keechie. Honest. If you introduce a woman three times in public as your wife, you're just as much married as if you had a Justice of the Peace and nine preachers to do it. Honest. That's the law and you can't get around it."

"I didn't know that."

"You take you and me now. All right, didn't Filthy MacNasty get it that way and Mrs. Lufkin up here and Rebecca and anybody that looks at that mail box? You can't get around it."

"I didn't know that."

"You can't get around it," Bowie said. "That's the law."

At the next crossing, he took her arm and held it the rest of the way home.

Chapter XXIII

FOR several days now Keechie had not been feeling well and this morning, after she smoked a cigarette, she felt sick at her stomach and had to lie down. Bowie rinsed towels under the cold tap in the kitchen and put them on her forehead.

It was only May, but the damp heat was like a jail cell in July. It clogged the nostrils and sweat streaked Bowie's cheeks from his sideburns. He said it was the heat that was making Keechie feel this way; that and the change of climate. The thing they had better do was go to town and duck in and see a doctor. Keechie said no, she had just been smoking too many cigarettes and everything would be all right in a day or so.

A little before noon, Keechie said sherbert appealed to her, pints and pints of it, orange or pineapple. Bowie said he would walk to the Drug Store and get it because it might take the delivery boy an hour to get here and he wanted her to have it while she was hungry.

On the newspaper rack in front of the Drug Store, there was a Noon Edition and Bowie picked it up and went on in. The Soda Clerk was at the table of two women and Bowie went on to the fountain, spread the newspaper and began to read the headlines.

Soda Clerk placed his hands, palms down, on the surface at the edge of the spread newspaper and Bowie looked up. "Dollar's worth of orange and pineapple sherbert," he said.

In this headline, the words *Prison Farm* swelled and Bowie began reading underneath it:

BINGHAM, Texas, May 29—Deputy Sheriff Oscar Dunning of Winkford County arrived here yesterday afternoon after a 650-mile trip with a bench warrant for the custody of Amos Ackerman, inmate of the Bingham Prison Farm, near here, but he was a half-hour too late to get his man alive. Ackerman, serving five years for assault with intent to kill, was shot to death by prison guards at 2:30 o'clock yesterday afternoon when he made a bold dash for freedom.

Deputy Dunning was planning on returning Ackerman to Winkford County to testify in a scheduled murder trial there.

Ackerman, a trusty and member of a chopping-cotton squad working two miles from the prison buildings, was sent back to get some tools and on the way made his ill-fated break. When he did not show up, a search was instituted and prison dogs led guards to a pile of brush just off the farm property. Ignoring the commands to halt, he was slain, prison officials stated.

The effort of Ackerman to escape, farm officials declared, was a lone attempt and not participated in by any other inmates. Extra precautions to prevent escapes were ordered by Farm Captain Fred Stammers today. There are several desperate criminals on the Farm now, including Elmo (Three-Toed) Mobley, bank robber, who arrived here last week from the State Penitentiary.

Outside, the sun stung Bowie's face like a shaving lotion and his knee-bones felt like dry sponges. He walked rapidly.

Water was gushing in the bathroom and Bowie went in there. In the filling tub, Keechie sat, her hair in a knot, water lapping the under-swell of her breasts.

"Feeling better, honey?" Bowie said.

"I'll say," Keechie said. There was the clean smell of soap and Keechie's body. Her long eyelashes clung to the wet skin. "What have you there in your hand?" she said.

"Paper."

The lathering soap in the washrag slowed. "What's the matter?"

"Nothing. Except they got him on a goddamned farm."

"Chicamaw?"

"Yes."

Keechie turned and looked at the gushing tap and then she bent and twisted it shut.

"You can't imagine what it is to be on one of those farms," Bowie said. "He won't last six months. They don't send you out to them farms unless they want to get rid of you. If you're any kind of a man you won't last, and by God, he's a man."

Keechie placed the soap and cloth on the rack and then pulled the stopper. The draining water began to swish and gurgle.

Bowie took the bath-mat off the basin and straightened it on the tile at the side of the tub. "It's cotton-chopping time now and you know what they do to them boys? Run 'em out there like horses and kick 'em with spurs and hit 'em with saps. They drop dead out in them fields, Keechie. Five of them in one day. It was in the papers."

"Well, you can't do anything about it."

Bowie helped her over the tub's rim, put the towel about her shoulders.

"Something could be done about it all right!" he said.

"For instance?"

"I mean if a man wanted to. I could go down there with one man to drive a car and take a machine gun and clean out that whole goddamned farm. Them dirty Laws and newspapers. Calling me a Number One this and a Number One that. I could set them sonsofbitches a real pace. If I wanted to hurt somebody, I wouldn't be sittin' here twiddling my thumbs."

Keechie spread the house dress about her waist and thighs. "You call this twiddling your thumbs?"

"Aw, honey, I don't mean you and me. I do tell you, though, one thing about you and me. We got to start getting out of this place here more. Get out and enjoy ourselves for a change. Go down to some of these night clubs in that French Quarter that we're all the time hearing over the radio and do a little drinking and have a good time."

"I think we can go out a little," Keechie said.

"That's what makes you feel bad in the mornings," Bowie said. "Staying cooped up like this all the time. It's not good for anybody."

"I think we can start going out some, but I don't see any use of drinking."

"We can drink beer."

"Beer, I guess, will be all right."

"You have to drink in those places. You couldn't go in one of those places and just sit there. You'd look like a I-don't-know-what."

"I'm going to get my feet dirty if you don't go in there and get my bedroom slippers," Keechie said. "In the bottom left-hand drawer."

Bowie came back with the slippers. They were red felt with black fur. "I just happened to think. I went out of that Drug Store without paying for that newspaper. I just paid for the sherbert. I'll bet them people over there think I tried to beat them out of it."

Bowie waited in their paralleled parked car under the shade of the French-balconied Second-Hand Store on Chartres Street. Keechie was up yonder in that big Department Store on Canal getting a dinner gown and sandals and a wrap. They were going to do this stepping out tonight in the right way.

Bowie turned now and looked at the wrapped boxes on the back seat. There was a white linen suit in the long box and a panama hat in the round one; white oxfords and baby-blue socks in the other. He was going to look like something himself tonight. He had a blue shirt and yellow tie like the combination Chicamaw had had.

The street on which he waited was the narrowest, craziest one he had ever seen. There were old chairs and stands and vases in front of the Antique Shop that didn't look worth ten cents a dozen and the window yonder was a crazy-quilt of oil paintings. On the corner was a bar: *Vieux Carre Haven.* A man stumbled out of the swinging doors and stood there, swaying uncertainly. He had on a white cotton shirt and faded blue-denim trousers.

If she stays much longer, Bowie thought, I'm going to duck

in that bar and get a beer. It takes a woman a lot longer to do things than a man. But he had fooled around and let that girl get down to where she didn't have a thing to wear. She might as well have had a shoe clerk or a flatfoot Law for a man. Not a fellow that had got himself almost thirty thousand dollars over in Texas in a couple of months.

The drunk was coming toward Bowie's car. His shirt was grass-stained and a tattoo showed through the torn sleeve. He grinned loosely: "You got a dime, Mack, for an old boy that sure needs a drink?"

"I'll give you a quarter to get that stinking breath out of my face," Bowie said. He put a half-dollar in the cupped hand. "I just got out Stir this morning," Stink Breath said. "Thirty days I done."

"I don't give a damn," Bowie said. "Get on."

Stink Breath moved toward the bar, his hands spread like an exhausted wrestler, disappeared inside. Toward the water-front, the whistle of a tugboat groaned.

Why couldn't a man get hold of some thief lawyer, Bowie thought, and get him to write out a Bench Warrant? Then get a Sheriff's badge and a big hat. He could go on one of them prison farms, show that and take any man off he wanted to. Them Farm Captains and Bosses couldn't see nothing but that Warrant.

A man in a beret and golf knickers stopped now in front of the window of oil paintings, shaded his forehead and pressed against the glass. He scratched his thigh.

It could be done all right, Bowie thought. Just go on that Farm like you owned it and flash your badge and be from one of those far western counties out by El Paso. Deputies and sheriffs were going on them farms every day and gettin' men.

Keechie was coming, stepping around other pedestrians, headed for the car. Bowie pushed out the door. "I begin to think you had fell in somewhere," he said.

"They are going to get the things out by five o'clock," Keechie said. "Sure good to be back here. All those women crowding around give me the creeps."

"Lady, could you spare a dime to a man that hasn't had a bite to eat?" It was Stink Breath, his face framed in the lowered window of the car.

"Get to hell away from here," Bowie said.

"Lady, if you can't spare anything but a nickel."

Bowie pushed the door on his side out with his foot. "Bowie," Keechie called. "Bowie!"

Bowie grasped Stink Breath's collar, kicked him in the seat. The collar ripped in his hands. He kicked again. "If you don't want to get your head stomped in this sidewalk, you get up this street, you bastard."

Stink Breath loped up the sidewalk. The man in the beret, the two men that stood now in the Second-Hand Store doorway, were laughing. Bowie grinned. "Bowie, get in here," Keechie said.

Bowie got in the car. "Something ought to be done about stew bums like that," he said.

"You ought to quit making a fool out of yourself," Keechie said.

They moved from the curb. "I'll bet he takes his next drink standing up," Bowie said.

Fastened couples churned to the beating music in a center of foaming light, but here among the tables and under the low ceiling, Bowie and Keechie sat in lavender darkness. The Mexican musicians on the palm-screened platform were playing *La Paloma*. Bowie beat on the gray tablecloth with his index finger. Now Keechie pressed a cigarette in the clay ashtray that was shaped like a sombrero. "You sure like Spanish music, don't you?" she said.

"That's one thing them Chilis can do."

"I like it too."

"I don't see anything to that dancing out there though, do you?"

"I never did care about dancing."

Bowie touched the frosted glass of beer. "Looks silly to me. Switching your tail around. Look at that gink out there, that four-eyed one, the one with the girl in the blue dress? . . . Don't he think he's a card now?"

Keechie lifted her glass, took a sip of the foamless beer and put it down. "You didn't think that when that Mexican girl was dancing," she said.

"What did I do?"

"You couldn't even find time to light my cigarette."

"I don't remember that. I'm talking about that kind of dancing out there now, honey."

The waiter came and picked up Bowie's emptied glass. His shirt front was a slick gray and the knuckles of his hand looked like a row of English walnuts. "Beer?" he said.

Bowie looked at Keechie. "Want to try something a little stronger? Whisky?"

Keechie shook her head.

"Two more beers," Bowie said. The knuckles moved away.

The orchestra was playing *La Cucaracha* now and the legs of the dancing couples were working faster and more heavily. Bowie beat on the beer glass with the ashtray. "You know, Keechie, I sure wouldn't mind going down to that country. Plenty of fellows have gone down there and liked it swell and you couldn't drag them back to this country."

"I don't know whether I would like living among a bunch of foreigners or not," Keechie said.

"I tell you a man that knows the ropes of that country. That Judge Hawkins. What that man doesn't know about that country isn't on the books."

"That man."

"I've heard you could live down there for a little or nothing. You and me could live like a couple of I-don't-know-whats down there on what we got salted away. In two or three years I'll bet I could get lined up with one of those big mining companies and where would we be then? I don't know but what that is a doggone good idea, Keechie?"

Keechie put her fingers around the glass, but did not pick it up. "It might be all right."

"Now I tell you an old boy that really knows it. Chicamaw. If he was here with us I'd be ready to start out tonight. Put that boy in the back seat of our car with a .30-30 and that Mexican army couldn't stop us from crossing that border. But if anybody knows the ropes, you can make it as easy as falling off a log."

Keechie got up and pulled her wrap off the back of the chair. "Let's go home," she said.

Bowie looked up at her. "Goodness me, honey. Why, I didn't think we was gettin' started good."

"I've had enough of this," Keechie said.

The music stopped. Bowie rose slowly. "Are you feeling bad again?"

"Yes," Keechie said.

Chairs scraped around them as the returning dancers started seating themselves. Bowie beckoned Knuckles.

Chapter XXIV

BOWIE picked up another ink-crusted pen off the table of crumbling blotters and tried the point. This one would write. A revolving door down the darkening corridor of the Post Office made a swishing, jolting sound and Bowie watched. It was a Negro in a porter's uniform, a bundle of papers and letters in his arms. The Negro's shoes crackled on the tile and echoed hollowly in the empty building. Bowie wrote:

Dear Mr. Hawkins:

Enclosed here is $200. I want you to get hold for me a Bench Warrant and get a seal and everything on it. Make it out for Elmo T. Mobley on the Bingham Prison Farm. Make it from Becas County and fix it up real proper and everything. Also I want a Sheriff badge.

A door swished again. The man in the straw hat and seersucker suit dropped the letter in the slot and presently the door bumped and Bowie was alone again.

I want you to please have these things ready and I may come in on you any time. So have them ready. Do it as soon as possible. Remember Xmas night. I am the same fellow.

Yours very truly,
Xmas Nite.

P. S. There will be another hundred for you when the goods are delivered. X. N.

Bowie sealed the envelope, pounded the flap with his closed hand and went over and dropped the letter in the slot.

On the sidewalk outside, he stopped and looked at the fresh, gold-painted lettering on the door of his car:

Sunshine Co. Products
F. T. Haviland, Agent

Around Lee Circle and then out St. Charles Avenue, Bowie drove. Chances are I never will see that Judge, he thought, but that letter will be just in case. I thought of it and I would just keep thinking about it if I didn't get the thing off my chest. This is just kind of like insurance, just looking ahead.

There was somebody in his apartment and Bowie brought his hand back from the knob and listened. Feet approached the door and then it opened. It was Mrs. Lufkin. Smelling of liquor and perfume. "Oh, how do you do, Mister Haviland?"

"All right." Through the doorway he saw Keechie sitting on the couch. She looked all right.

"Pretty warm weather we are having?" Mrs. Lufkin said.

"Too warm," Bowie said. He squeezed past Mrs. Lufkin and went inside.

"Well, goodbye," Mrs. Lufkin said.

"Goodbye," Keechie said.

Bowie closed the door. "What was that old souse doing in here?"

Keechie got up. "She wants us to move."

"Why?"

"It's nothing. She has a chance to rent it to some professor that wants it for a year and she said she knew we weren't permanent."

"You don't think she's smelled something?"

Keechie shook her head. "Oh, no."

"Well, what are we going to do?"

"There isn't anything to do, unless you want to pay her a lot of rent."

"I'll be damned if I do that. I'm ready to get out of this hot dump anyway. I can't see why anybody else would want it."

"There's plenty of places here."

"Sure. It don't worry me."

Keechie lowered herself back to the divan and lay down. "Did you get the sign on the car?"

"You ought to see it, honey. I got that fellow to do it that we saw that afternoon hanging around that Square, the one with the Jesus Christ beard. On both sides. We ought to have thought of that a long time ago."

"I thought you were never coming back."

He went over and sat down on the divan and jiggled the toe of her shoe. "It took him a pretty good while."

"Anything happen?"

"Not a thing."

After the supper of canned soup and crackers, Bowie and Keechie looked at road maps. This one here covered the whole United States and the regions were illustrated with bright-colored sketches: cattle in Texas, oil-wells in Oklahoma, shocks of wheat in Kansas.

"Doggoned if I know where to go," Bowie said.

"Looks like it would be easy with all this to pick from."

"Well, we don't have to leave New Orleans, you know."

"Oh, I'm fed up on this town, honey. It's just too doggone hot."

Keechie pointed at the Southwest Texas region. "Right in there somewhere is the place we lived."

"That's another place you couldn't drag me," Bowie said.

"Or any place else in Texas," Keechie said.

Bowie tapped the Gulf of Mexico. "You ever seen the ocean, Keechie?"

She shook her head.

"Me neither. I'm almost thirty years old and you know I never have seen the ocean. Can you beat that? Say, how would you like to live on the ocean?"

"Sounds pretty good to me."

Bowie folded the map. "We got plenty of time. It never pays to decide a thing too quick. We got a couple of weeks and by then we'll know exactly where we want to light out for."

"Sure," Keechie said.

Keechie whimpered in her sleep again and this time Bowie sat up and looked at her. In the moonlight that filtered through the crêpe myrtle and screen, he saw her mouth pucker like a child and she whimpered again. A mosquito sang with needle-like vibration in Bowie's ear and he waved his hand over Keechie's head. She was quiet now and he eased back, moving his hand over her head from time to time.

It's malaria, he thought. That's what it is. These goddamned mosquitoes.

Keechie sobbed out. It was a dry, throat-lodging cry. She turned over, her face toward the window and lay quiet. The mosquito sang, and he raised up and fanned furiously.

Back in the kitchen, the clock ticked, smothered now by the rush of a speeding car on the avenue; ticked again. She had bought that clock in Antelope Center and of all things to bring. She bought it the same day she got that big gunny sack of Irish potatoes. They had left it and there wasn't a fourth of them used.

Keechie made sounds now like she was losing her breath and he placed his hand on her shoulder and shook gently: "Keechie, Keechie. What's the matter, honey?"

She raised, her eyes wide open. "What is it?" she said. "Bowie?"

"You ain't feeling well, honey."

"What is it?"

"Are you hurtin'? Hurtin' any place, honey?"

Keechie let her head back on the pillow. "I'm all right."

"You must have been dreaming. Nightmare or something."

She did not say anything. An automobile horn sounded on the avenue, a street-car was coming.

"You been crying in your sleep, Keechie."

"I had a dream. I guess that was it."

"What was it?"

"Forget it. I'm all right."

The street-car grated in a stop in front of the house; ground and clicked on.

"Did you think you were falling off something? I've dreamed that. Gun breaking in my hand. I dreamed I couldn't make my Dad hear me a hundred times."

"I dreamed you had gone away," Keechie said.

"Me?"

"It's all right now. Go on and go to sleep. You're going to be worn out in the morning."

"Where did I go?"

"I don't know. You had just gone and I thought I was trying to find you. I couldn't find you."

"Well, there's no danger of me going any place without you."

"You went to town yesterday."

"That's different. I mean off any place. No, honey, it looks like you and me are going up the same road together."

"Up the same road?"

"It sure looks that way."

"Is that the way you want it, Bowie?"

"That's the way I want it, honey, but sometimes I think about you."

"That's the way I want it, Bowie, and you remember it."

Bowie slapped his hands together. "That damned mosquito been bothering you?"

"I hadn't noticed it," Keechie said.

"You sleepy?"

"No, I'm wide awake now."

This street-car rumbled on past and soon was a distant, fading hum.

"I been trying to figure out some place for us to go," Bowie said. "It's got me worried."

"There's plenty of places."

"You know, I have just about decided that we got to make Mexico. If only I knew the ins and outs of that damned country. I could kick myself for not pumping some fellows that had been down there. But there's nothing to this, Keechie. I'm not going to really feel good about us until we're plumb out of this country."

"We can go to Mexico."

"If I just knew the ropes about all that border down there and just knew one of them Thief officials down there that Chicamaw was telling me about. Now you take old Hawkins. I don't know but what it would be a good idea to go and see him."

"Not him," Keechie said.

"Why not?"

"There's plenty of other men that know about Mexico."

"Who?"

"I don't know, but there's plenty."

"But who?"

"There's plenty of men that know."

"But who, Keechie? That don't do no good. Just name me somebody that we could go to and he would give us all the lowdown that we got to have? I'm not any plain tourist, you know. I'm not the governor of this state, you know."

"Now don't get smart. What I am telling you is that you don't have any business back there in Texas. Or around anybody that knows you."

Bowie clutched at the air. "I'm going to get up and brain this mosquito in just about two seconds."

There was a little wind and stirred leaves of the crêpe myrtle sighed on the screen.

"Do you really want to go to Mexico, Bowie?"

"It's about all I know to do."

"Do you think Hawkins can really help?"

"I don't know of anybody else. I was just as sure you would take me up when I mentioned him about that. I even dropped him a line."

"When?"

"When I was getting that sign put on. That day."

"Yesterday, you mean?"

"Yes."

"Why didn't you tell me?"

"I just didn't. I'm telling you now."

"Did you write about Chicamaw?"

"Yes."

Keechie sat up.

"Now look here, Keechie. Now don't start that. Honey, I'm just worried to death." He sat up.

Keechie got off the bed. "You needn't say any more. That's all I want to know."

"Now look here, Keechie. Where you going?"

"What difference does that make?"

"Now look here, Keechie. Now come on, honey."

"Which is it, Bowie? Make up your mind right now. Once and forever. Which is it, Chicamaw or me?"

"It's you. If it wasn't you, I'd been down on that farm long before now and cleaning it from one end to the other gettin' him off. I know now how you feel about it, Keechie. I'm just learning. You been a Little Soldier to me and I'm going to play square with you."

Keechie shivered.

"As long, honey, as I'm any good to you, I'm going to stay with you. I'm telling you straight now, Keechie. I've had things on my mind and I don't mind admitting it to you, but they're all over. That's it, Keechie. The best I know how to tell you."

Keechie lowered herself to the edge of the bed. "Did you really want to see that lawyer about Mexico?"

"When we were talking while ago? . . . Yes, I did. I meant it."

Keechie picked up the edge of the twisted sheet and shook it with a flapping sound out over Bowie. Then she folded it back on her side of the bed and got under it.

"And you think the lawyer is the only one to see?" Keechie said.

"I leave it up to you, Keechie. It's all up to you."

"When do you want to go?"

"I leave that up to you."

"Tomorrow?"

"It suits me."

The clock was ticking again now in the kitchen. A truck passed on the narrow street by their window and presently there was the sound of milk bottles clattering in a tin rack. The moonlight was gone now and the sleeping-room was dark. Bowie raised up and listened to Keechie's even breathing. She was sleeping sound. He eased back, lay there a moment and then cautiously pulled up his foot and scratched the mosquito bite again.

Chapter XXV

THE moon had an eye-squinching brightness, radiating six splintered beams, broad as planks. It deepened the dark hollows of Keechie's eyes, shadowed the lines that slashed her face from cheek bones to tight lips. She sat there in their car, parked on the by-road just off the highway, her eyes closed, head resting on the back of the seat.

Bowie, standing on the ground with one foot on the running board, looked again toward the lights of MacMasters, as golden as oil lamps in the clear air. They had stopped here a little after sundown, deciding it was best to wait until ten o'clock or so and be sure that Hawkins would be at home.

"You feel any better, honey?" Bowie said.

"I want something ice-cold to drink," Keechie said. "I know I would feel a lot better if I had a cold soda pop."

"We'll get it when we gas up. The very first thing. I wish now we had stopped back up the road, but there was just so many Square Johns hanging around then."

"I can get along without it."

Bowie moved around the front of the car, got under the wheel. "We can go now," he said. "To hell with this waiting."

The neon sign on the left, at the city's edge, read: *Alamo Plaza Courts.* It burned in front of a filling station and behind that was a court of white frame cottages. On a bench under the shed of the station sat a man, an old fellow, licking a cone of ice cream. Bowie turned in and the old man rose.

"Fill it up," Bowie said. He went on to the big wooden ice-box.

The spring of the screen door whined and Bowie looked up. The woman coming out was Mattie. She was heavier; gold on her teeth. "Hi you do," she said.

"Okeh," Bowie said. He brought a bottle out of the icy water.

"Passing through?" Mattie said.

Bowie moved his head, indicating the old man holding the hose by the clicking pump.

"Papa," Mattie said.

"Just passing through," Bowie said.

Mattie looked at Keechie in the car, and Bowie jerked the bottle's cap and started back.

"Who is that?" Keechie said.

"T-Dub's sister-in-law." She took the bottle from his hand. "It's cold. She's Real People."

"I'll drink this when we get started."

"Go ahead and drink it, honey. I'll get plenty to carry."

Mattie lifted the ice-box top for Bowie. "How is everything around here?" he said.

"Okeh," Mattie said.

"How's the husband?"

"Still In There."

Bowie ran his hands over the bottles. "That's too bad."

"The cokes are at that end if that's what you are looking for," Mattie said.

"How's my heat around here?" Bowie said.

"You can find better places to run around in."

Papa hung the hose on the rack. "How's your oil?" he said. His voice squeaked like the broken note of a clarinet. "All right," Bowie said. He paid Mattie.

"Take care of yourself," Mattie said.

"Same to you," Bowie said.

The air on the boulevard was cool and clean. Out at its end was Hawkins' house.

"Aren't you going to drink that, honey?" Bowie said.

"Not now."

"What's the matter?"

"I'm afraid it might come up."

"Doggone, sugar."

"I think I had better lie down in the back. If I lie down a little while I think I will feel better."

Bowie drew alongside the curbing, stopped, got out and helped Keechie into the back. He took her coat, spread it over her feet, got back under the wheel and drove on.

There were four unoccupied automobiles parked in front of Hawkins' house. The church was dark.

"What are those cars, Bowie?" Keechie said.

"You just lay back down now, honey."

"I feel better. You think it's all right to go up there?"

"I'll be right back now before you can turn around. You just take it easy now."

The porch planks creaked and gave under Bowie's steps and then he knocked on the door. Under the half-raised blind he could see the trousered legs of men seated at a card table.

The door parted and there was a middle-aged woman in a black dress and white-lace collar.

"Judge in?"

"Why, yes. Won't you come in?"

"I'll just wait here."

The woman hesitated. "Who can I tell him?"

"Mister Knight. Mister Knight."

Bowie watched the legs through the window. The card table moved and then feet were coming to the door.

The porch globe showered light. Hawkins was in shirt sleeves and had a pipe in his right hand. He switched it quickly, reached and then the porch was dark again. "Wait a minute," he said. The door closed and Bowie backed down off the porch steps, his fingers grasping the butt of the gun under his arm.

The door opened again and Bowie went back up on the porch and took the extended envelope. It was heavy and he felt the badge's pin. "You busy?" he said.

Hawkins nodded toward the window. "Company," he whispered.

"I want to get some low down on Mexico."

Hawkins shook his head. "Can't help you there, son. That's the Sheriff in there."

"Okeh," Bowie said.

His heels clicked on the sidewalk toward the car. *I promised him another hundred, but to hell with him. He's just a little too busy. I don't need this damned stuff anyway. Where's Keechie?*

She lay face down in the bottom of the car, her left arm crooked like it was broken. "Keechie," he said. "Keechie." She was limp and heavy. "Keechie, honey. Baby. Keechie." Her teeth were clenched and he couldn't hear her breathing. He straightened her on the seat, got up in front and his hand shook on the knob above the grinding gears.

Papa pushed off the bench and approached. "Where's a vacant cabin?" Bowie said.

"Just about what kind of a price do you have in mind, Mister?"

"Any of 'em."

"We got some for a dollar and a half and some for . . ."

"Where's that woman that was around here?"

"You mean my darter? The girl that was . . ."

"Where is she?" Bowie started getting out of the car.

The screen's spring rasped and then Mattie came. "I got to have a place," Bowie said.

Mattie went around into the Court and Bowie followed her in the car. At the far, low end she pointed at the corner cabin and Bowie parked in front of it. Mattie went on in and turned on the light.

Bowie lowered Keechie to the bed, straightened the skirt down over her knees. Her face was drained, the lines deep. Mattie stood in the half-opened screen.

"I can't figure it out," Bowie said. He picked up a towel off the foot of the bed and went to the sink and turned on the water. "I can't figure it out. Go get a doctor, Mattie. Go on and get a doctor out here."

He started bathing Keechie's face. "Go on, Mattie. For Christ's sake." Mattie left.

He held the sopping towel under the running water again, went back and rubbed the back of her neck, pressed it under her collar on her chest. "Come on, Little Soldier. Show your old man you got it in you. You bet you got it in you. You bet you have . . ."

Her body quivered and then she sucked in with parted lips. "That's a girl. That's a girl." Her eyes opened and she moved her head from side to side and then suddenly looked at him. "Did you see him?" she said.

"Everything's swell, kiddo. Don't you worry about it one minute. Everything's swell."

"I'm glad." Her mouth twisted and she reached and clutched Bowie's hand. "Something is wrong with me, Bowie. I hate to tell you. I know it."

"Don't worry, honey. The doctor is coming. Don't you worry."

Keechie closed her eyes and Bowie took the dry towel and wiped her face. Then he took off her shoes. "I'm glad," she said. It was toneless, like she was talking in her sleep.

Bowie sat on the stone edge of the fish pond in the Court's center, watching the Doctor, a little man in a tan suit, through

the half-raised blind of the cabin. I ought to have stayed in
there. That Doctor's got sick people on his mind and not
criminals. That Mattie.

The lights of a car brightened the yard. Papa came around
and the car followed him, an old machine with packed running boards. It went on around to the row on the other side.

"I just can't get over it," Bowie said out loud.

The door of the cabin opened, laying a slab of light on the
grass, and then Mattie was coming out. Bowie went to her.
"What does he say?" he said.

"There's nothing wrong with her except she's pregnant,"
Mattie said. "I could have told you that."

"Who said it?"

"He did. Anybody could tell."

Bowie looked at the light from the half-raised blind. "I
don't want to get mixed up any farther in this," Mattie said.
"You're going to have to go on." Bowie did not answer. He
moved toward the cabin; into the smell of licorice and pare-
goric.

The Doctor had a splotch of moustache over his mouth and
sagging eyerims. "That is the only thing to do," he said. "Just
keep her quiet and lying on her back and I think she will come
out of it fine. But she cannot keep this up. I have given her
something and that is going to keep her asleep quite a while.
Rest is the thing."

Keechie's breasts were rising and falling in even breathing.
"She sure is sleeping like she is awfully tired," Bowie said.

"That is the best thing," Doctor said. "Now I have put
some medicine there on the table there and tomorrow, if she
is still in pain, you can give it to her. She is likely to sleep a
good while, and if she does awaken she more than likely will
go right back to sleep again."

"She sure is sleeping."

"If you need me, call me," Doctor said.

"Sure, Doctor. Don't worry about that."

Bowie sat now on the chair by the sink in the cabin's darkness, watching Keechie's form, listening to her breathing. He
got up now and touched her straightened arm, picked it up
and put it on her breast; placed it back by her side. Then he
left the cabin.

Mattie came out and walked around with him into the deep shadow of the station's side. "That girl can't be moved," Bowie said.

"I don't want anything happening around here," Mattie said. "I've done all I'm going to in this."

"If it's money that's holding you, don't worry about that."

"I don't want any of your money. All I want you to do is get off this place." The screen sounded and Mattie turned her head and started off.

"Hold it," Bowie said. Mattie stopped. "Now you listen to me," Bowie said. "You're a thief just like me and you ain't going to yellow on me when I'm asking you to lay off. She's not going to be moved, see, and if you or anybody else don't like it, it's just too goddamned bad."

Mattie walked on away.

Keechie had not moved. He lifted the blind, a square of moonlight baring her feet. He pulled the blind back down, took off her hose and placed the sheet over her legs.

The Court was quiet. In Bowie's ears, the cricket-ringing sounds were growing. That yellow Hawkins, he thought. The two-faced sonofabitch.

If only that Indian was here. Them white teeth. Little Soldier, it can't be got around. They got me in a rank now. The whole, lousy, yellow bunch.

Water dripped in the sink and he got up and tightened the tap.

We got to hole-up right pretty soon, girl. There ain't no *ifs* and *ands* about it. I have fooled around long enough.

You got Something Else to think about now, Little Soldier. Old Bowie is not so big in this picture now. But they can't put nothing on you, Keechie. They just can't do it. Don't you let them make you think it for a minute. Don't you let 'em.

The dropped match from his fingers rattled on the floor and he watched her. She did not move and he breathed again. But you're plumb out, honey. You're not going to be waking up until away in tomorrow.

If that Chicamaw was here, Keechie, we could beat them easy. He's the only friend we got in this world. You don't know it, Keechie, but I do, honey. He's the only one in this world that would help us. You and me are going up this road together and we got to find us a Hole and pull it in after us. 'Specially now. You can't run these roads much longer. That Mexico, Keechie. They ain't but one person in this world that can get us down there. Just one.

Somewhere in the night a dog bayed.

Say it worked, Keechie. Say I run that hundred and twenty miles over to that Farm from here, get there by seven o'clock this morning and spring that boy? You would be asleep, honey, and never know a thing about it. I would be back and you'd wake up and that Chicamaw would be with us and then I'd like to see somebody stop us. Honey, we'd be holed up in Mexico two days from now. Deep, Keechie. Pulled in after us.

The dog bayed again.

Well, say it didn't work, Keechie? Say it flopped? All right, Little Soldier, you got Somebody Else to think about now. Old Bowie stepped out don't mean so much. You don't have nobody to beat, Keechie. They can't hang a thing in this world on you. All you have ever done is just kind of run around with me. Say it flopped all right, Keechie? Well, there you are.

Bowie got up and buttoned his coat.

The high, net-wire fence was broken here by a wooden Arch: *Bingham Prison Camp*—and Bowie left the highway and turned his machine through it. Stone-bordered beds of flowers colored the sides of the gray road that led up there to the Buildings. There was the smell of sweet-peas.

There was the Office, a squat, brick building with an empty flagpole and behind it, long, barrack-looking buildings, stone foundations whitewashed, and barns.

A figure in the white sacking of a convict, on his knees and breaking clods around the rose bush with his hands, looked up as Bowie got out of his car. He lowered his head as Bowie passed on toward the Office porch, the two men in khaki uniforms sitting on a bench, cartridge belts around their waists, shotguns beside them.

"How do you do?" Bowie said.

The heads of the Guards moved. "Howdy . . . Hidy."

Bowie indicated the porch-shadowed door. "Captain Stammers in?"

The two nodded.

Bowie entered the smell of disinfectant, looked at the face framed in the top of the high, bookkeeper's desk, a Convict's; moved down the desk's length and stopped before the two men on the bench. The big one was dressed like the men on the porch, the other in blue serge trousers and white shirt. He got up.

"Captain Stammers?" Bowie said.

"That's me," the man said. He had thin black hair, parted in the middle, and held his left arm crooked as if it were in pain. He did not have a gun on. Bowie extended his hand. "I'm Sheriff Haviland, Becos County."

Captain Stammers pumped Bowie's hand. "Glad to know you, Sheriff. What can I do for you?"

The Guard on the bench got up and moved toward the door. "See you after while, Captain," he said.

"I want to see a boy you got on your place here," Bowie said. "Elmo Mobley."

"Yeah, we got him. Let me see now. He's in Boss Hebert's squad today I think. Now what is it we can do for you there?"

"I have a Bench Warrant, but I don't intend to take him." Bowie pulled the paper from his inside coat pocket and handed it to Stammers. "I just wanted to talk to him a little on this trip." The paper crackled as Stammers opened the Warrant:

THE STATE OF TEXAS

To the Honorable *Sheriff A. T. Haviland, Sheriff of Becos County*, Texas, GREETING;

On this *12 day of May A.D. 1935*, it appearing to the Court that there is now pending on the docket of this Court, a certain case entitled the STATE of Texas VS. *Elmo T. Mobley*, being our case *No. 754*, wherein said defendant is charged with the offense of murder,

Whereas, said case . . .

"You don't want to take him?" Stammers said. He started folding the paper.

"No, I just want to talk to him."

Stammers went over and picked the gray hat off the hook and turned and touched his left arm. "Neuritis, bad," he said.

"I've heard that it's bad," Bowie said.

On the porch, Stammers said to the three guards: "Watch that telephone, boys."

Bowie moved toward his car and Stammers followed. "We can just go in my car," Bowie said.

"Did you ever hear of anybody that found out anything to help it?" Stammers said.

"It just has to wear off, I hear," Bowie said.

Stammers pointed at the dirt road that twisted back of the building and toward the cotton-fields. Bowie moved onto it.

The cotton was fresh and green, the earth around it freshly hoed. "Mighty nice stand you got out here, Captain."

"Rain last week," Stammers said. He picked up his left hand and placed the elbow on his stomach. "Nice rain last week."

Puffs of dust rose from the chopping hoes of the working convicts yonder, fifteen or twenty men; two men on horses, shotguns in the cradles of their arms, watching. Faces of working men lifted and looked at the car, bent back again.

The horseman with the boots and jagged Spanish spurs approached. He was a heavy man with a billowing waist. There was a pistol on his belt; a rifle in the saddle scabbard.

"Mobley is in that bunch, isn't he?" Stammers said.

Spanish Spurs nodded. "Yessir."

"Bring him over here."

At the head of the squad, a figure raised, listened and then stepped out. He was coming now, the hoe in hand. Spanish Spurs spoke and Chicamaw threw the hoe down.

Chicamaw looked hard and well. He studied Bowie and then Stammers and then Bowie again.

"Get in this car, Mobley," Bowie said. "I want to talk to you a little while, boy. We'll go back up to your office, Captain."

"Sure."

Chicamaw sat in the front alongside Bowie; Stammers in the back. They were going now back up the road toward the Buildings. "You didn't stop by State and see the Warden, did you?" Stammers said.

"No, I went to Houston a different way. I'm stopping there on my way back though."

"Well, give the Warden my regards. You didn't go to the Convention this year, did you, Sheriff?"

"No, I didn't," Bowie said.

"You know I was a Sheriff for fourteen years. I'd like to have gone to that Convention this year."

Bowie nudged Chicamaw's thigh, indicated the panel pocket. Chicamaw pulled the ivory knob, grasped the pistol and turned on Stammers. "It's a break, Captain," he said. "Sit there."

"We're going right out through this gate up here, Captain," Bowie said. "Don't you let on to nobody in no way. You understand, don't you?"

"I understand."

The porch was empty. The Convict, working around the rose bush, looked up and then stood. Bowie passed the Office and the chaff of the road began peppering the fenders. He swerved up and onto the highway; opened the throttle wide.

"Well, boys, this is going to cost me," Stammers said.

"Don't let it get you down, Cap," Chicamaw said.

"It seems to me now that I had seen you before, Sheriff, but by God, I still don't know."

"Just forget it, Captain," Bowie said. "I guess you'll find out soon enough. How long do you think it will be before your boys back there figure something is wrong?"

"I wish I knew."

Chicamaw looked deeper in the car pocket, reached in it and explored with his hand.

"What you looking for?" Bowie said.

"Nothing," Chicamaw said.

"This is going to cost me, boys," Stammers said.

"Tell that to the Warden, Cap, " Chicamaw said.

"You been treated pretty good on that Farm, boy," Stammers said.

"Pipe down, Chicamaw," Bowie said. "For Christ's sake."

The highway sign read: *MacMasters . . . 68 mi.* At the off-road, Bowie turned and they drove along through the timber. After a half-mile, Bowie stopped and they all got out and crawled through the fence, and in the woods Bowie tied Stammers to a tree.

Heat glimmered from the highway's cement slabs. "Say they been pretty good to you back there?" Bowie asked.

"They don't use a bat or barrel any more," Chicamaw said. "Them big political boys stopped all that. They'd still do it, but they're afraid they'll lose them sixty-dollar jobs."

"That's something though."

Chicamaw turned and looked in the back of the car. "You're not going to tell me you didn't bring no pint along, are you?"

Bowie shook his head. "No liquor in this party, Chicamaw. I got some business that needs attending and it takes a clear head."

"I don't believe you're ever going to be human," Chicamaw said. "I tell you, man, I don't see how you do it. You get out here and run these roads and pull a thing like that back yonder and beat these Laws right and left, and, by God, Bowie, I don't see how in the hell you do it. You're just a big country boy and just chumpy as hell at times and yet you do it."

"What did you want to do, stay back yonder?"

"Me? Don't kid yourself. Not with that Texaco City trouble still up in the air. Man, I been thinking any day here they would come. You're the boy they want on that. Them fingerprints of yours sure played hell there. I was pretty foxy in that though. They got you tagged on that, but what they got on me for sure?"

"It's raised a lot of heat all right," Bowie said. "That trouble."

"You seem to beat it all right," Chicamaw said. "You just keep going right on."

"Just luck," Bowie said.

"That's it. Call it that. You're no more a criminal than that damned radiator cap there. And yet you do it. It rips my guts out. You're just a big Sunday-school chump and yet you can pull a thing like that back yonder and run these roads and make me look like thirty cents."

Bowie's head jerked. "You going crazy? What the hell is gettin' the matter with you?"

"It rips my guts out. Take you and on top of that a damned

little old girl that was never outside of a filling station and, by God, the papers don't do nothing but print about you all the time. Why, it makes me look like a damned penny slot machine . . ."

Bowie stopped at the side of the highway.

"What's the matter?" Chicamaw said. "What's this idea?"

Bowie got out of the car and walked around and pulled out Chicamaw's door. "Come on," he said. "You sonofabitch, come on."

"Good God, Bowie. What's got into you?"

"Get out."

Chicamaw got out.

"The only reason I'm not letting you have it right here," Bowie said, "is because there might be some dogs that will do it."

"Listen, Bowie. I want to go see my folks. I ain't never seen 'em, Bowie. Let me get that gun in the car."

"Get."

Chicamaw started running up the road.

A car with a blaring loudspeaker and bannered with lettering about a picture show was the only moving machine on the heat-stilled Square of MacMasters. The music was *Stars and Stripes Forever*. Bowie turned off the Square and moved out the highway that led to the Courts. Nossir, God, I never asked nothing from you before. Not a thing in this world. But just let me get up there the rest of the way now. And if it ain't asking too much, keep her still asleep. Just let her wake up and I'll be sittin' there. . . .

The driveway and yard of *Alamo Plaza Courts* were deserted. Bowie drove on down and parked parallel in front of the closed door and lowered blind.

She lay there on the bed, her eyes closed, still breathing, just as he had left her. He looked around. Nothing had been moved. Nothing. Thanks, God.

The afternoon heat pressed against the cabin, making the walls as hot as a dying stove. The roof's tar melted and smelled. Bowie stood above Keechie, flapping the wet towel. The little curls on her forehead trembled under the cooling air. Honey, you got to be waking up pretty soon and eating something. I mean real wide awake.

Dusk seeped into the room now, drying the sweat on Bowie's forehead, stiffening the hairs on his arms. Keechie stirred greater now, and he bent over. Her eyes opened. They were like petals submerged in tiny bowls of unchanged water.

"Bowie?" she said.

"Hello, sleepyhead."

"Bowie?"

"It's about time you were waking up."

"You wouldn't leave me, would you?"

"Me? You don't mean me. I should say not. Don't be silly now waking up."

"Bowie?"

"What, Keechie?"

"I mean it."

"God knows now too, Keechie. I mean it."

Keechie closed her eyes. He touched her. "Listen, Little Soldier, you got to get something inside that stomach of yours. How about a soda pop? Ice-cold to start things off?"

Keechie's head moved up and down on the pillow.

"Now let's see." Bowie stood erect and began rubbing his hands. "Just about what kind of flavor now would the little lady crave? Strawberry?"

Keechie nodded.

Bowie moved through the gloom to the door, pulled it back. *"Don't let a move out of you,"* the Voice said. It was like the swish of a missing blade. Cat with seven lives, Bowie thought. He whipped out his gun. Steampipes burst in his ears. *Seven.* He swirled in the bell of the roaring loudspeaker on the Square: *Stars and Stripes Forever.* Cat . . . *seven.* Things were wrinkling, folding gently, like paper dolls in a puff of cigarette smoke. *Strawberry . . .*

MacMasters, Texas, June 21—The crime-blazed trail of the Southwest's phantom desperado, Bowie Bowers, and his gun-packing girl companion, Keechie Mobley, was ended here early tonight in a battle with a sharp-shooting band of Rangers and peace officers who beat their covered quarry to the draw. The escaped convict, bank robber and quick-triggered killer, and his woman aide were trapped in the cabin of a tourist camp, one mile east of this city, and killed instantly in one burst of machine and rifle fire.

Stirred to a vengeful heat after Bowers' sensational liberation of his old pal, Elmo (Three-Toed) Mobley, from the Bingham Prison Farm early this morning, grim-faced officers swooped down on the camp. After the battle, Bowers lay sprawled in the doorway of the cabin, the girl inside on the floor. A gun was clutched in Bowers' hand, another near the hand of Keechie Mobley. Both were bullet-riddled, their deaths instantaneous.

A bag containing almost $10,000 in currency was recovered in the splintered cabin, also a quantity of what officers declared was narcotics.

The killings brought to a dramatic climax a search of more than a year for the desperado and his companion. Wanted in at least four states for murders, bank robberies, filling-station holdups, kidnapings of peace officers, Bowers had become one of the Southwest's most feared criminals.

This peaceful, thriving little city was stunned tonight by the news that it had harbored in its environs this pair. Knots of excited people thronged the streets tonight and crowds were viewing the bodies in a local undertaking parlor.

Tall, steel-eyed Ranger Captain Leflett refused to comment at length on the case, declaring that the owners of the tourist camp where the pair was slain, were unaware of the identity of their notorious guests. When he reported to his Chief in the State Capital, he declared simply: "Chief, we have got them."

Elmo Mobley, freed by Bowers earlier in the day when Captain Stammers was kidnaped, was captured by a farmer who became suspicious when he saw Mobley running in the road and then recognized the prison clothing.

Rewards totaling more than $1,000 will be distributed among the twenty picked officers who took part in the slayings.

Supplied a tip before daybreak this morning, local officers began acting quickly. Telephone and telegraph wires hummed to the State Capital and Penitentiary. An airplane brought Ranger Captain Leflett and four men.

At the State Penitentiary, according to news dispatches received here, Warden Joel Howard admitted to reporters, it is said, that the tip was furnished after a "deal" had been made for the liberation of an inmate in the prison there. "Bowers was a ruthless, cunning criminal," Warden Howard declared, "and we had to exert every resource to bring him down."

THE BIG CLOCK

by Kenneth Fearing

For Nan

Contents

George Stroud I

I FIRST met Pauline Delos at one of those substantial parties Earl Janoth liked to give every two or three months, attended by members of the staff, his personal friends, private moguls, and public nobodies, all in haphazard rotation. It was at his home in the East Sixties. Although it was not exactly public, well over a hundred people came and went in the course of two or three hours.

Georgette was with me, and we were introduced at once to Edward Orlin of *Futureways*, and to others in the group who had the familiar mark upon them. Of Pauline Delos, I knew only the name. But although there could not have been anyone in the organization who hadn't heard a great deal about the lady, there were few who had actually seen her, and fewer still who had ever seen her on any occasion when Janoth was also present. She was tall, ice-blonde, and splendid. The eye saw nothing but innocence, to the instincts she was undiluted sex, the brain said here was a perfect hell.

"Earl was asking about you a moment ago," Orlin told me. "Wanted you to meet somebody."

"I was delayed. As a matter of fact, I've just finished a twenty-minute conversation with President McKinley."

Miss Delos looked mildly interested. "Who did you say?" she asked.

"William McKinley. Our twenty-fourth President."

"I know," she said, and smiled. A little. "You probably heard a lot of complaints."

A man I recognized as Emory Mafferson, a tiny little dark fellow who haunted one of the lower floors, *Futureways*, also, I think, spoke up.

"There's a guy with an iron face like McKinley's in the auditing department. If that's who you mean, you bet there were complaints."

"No. I was truly and literally detained in a conversation with Mr. McKinley. At the bar of the Silver Lining."

"He was," said Georgette. "I was, too."

"Yes. And there were no complaints at all. Quite the con-

trary. He's making out quite well, it seems." I had myself
another Manhattan from a passing tray. "He's not under a
contract, of course. But working steadily. In addition to being
McKinley he's sometimes Justice Holmes, Thomas Edison,
Andrew Carnegie, Henry Ward Beecher, or anyone important
but dignified. He's been Washington, Lincoln, and Christopher Columbus more times than he can remember."

"I call him a very convenient friend to have," said Delos.
"Who is he?"

"His earthly alias is Clyde Norbert Polhemus. For business
purposes. I've known him for years, and he's promised to let
me be his understudy."

"What's he done?" Orlin asked, with reluctance. "Sounds
like he materialized a bunch of ghosts, and can't put them
back."

"Radio," I said. "And he can put anyone anywhere."

And that was about all, the first time I met Pauline Delos.
The rest of the late afternoon and early evening passed as
always in this comfortable little palace, surrounded as it was
by the big and little palaces of greater and lesser kingdoms
than Janoth Enterprises. Old conversation in new faces. Georgette and I met and talked to the niece of a department store.
Of course the niece wanted to conquer new territory. She
would inherit several acres of the old territory, anyway. I met
a titan in the world of mathematics; he had connected a
number of adding machines into a single unit, and this
super-calculator was the biggest in the world. It could solve
equations unknown to and beyond the grasp of its inventor.
I said: "That makes you better than Einstein. When you have
your equipment with you."

He looked at me uneasily, and it occurred to me I was a
little drunk.

"I'm afraid not. It was a purely mechanical problem, developed for special purposes only."

I told him he might not be the best mathematician on earth
but he was certainly the fastest, and then I met a small legal
cog in a major political engine. And next Janoth's latest in-
vention in the way of social commentators. And others, all of
them pretty damned important people, had they only known

it. Some of them unaware they were gentlemen and scholars. Some of them tomorrow's famous fugitives from justice. A sizable sprinkling of lunatics, so plausible they had never been suspected and never would be. Memorable bankrupts of the future, the obscure suicides of ten or twenty years from now. Potentially fabulous murderers. The mothers or fathers of truly great people I would never know.

In short, the big clock was running as usual, and it was time to go home. Sometimes the hands of the clock actually raced, and at other times they hardly moved at all. But that made no difference to the big clock. The hands could move backward, and the time it told would be right just the same. It would still be running as usual, because all other watches have to be set by the big one, which is even more powerful than the calendar, and to which one automatically adjusts his entire life. Compared to this hook-up, the man with the adding machines was still counting on his fingers.

Anyway, it was time I collected Georgette and went home. I always go home. Always. I may sometimes detour, but eventually I get there. Home was 37.4 miles, according to the railroad timetable, but it could be 3,740 miles, and I would still make it. Earl Janoth had emerged from somewhere, and we said good-bye.

There was one thing I always saw, or thought I saw, in Janoth's big, pink, disorderly face, permanently fixed in a faint smile he had forgotten about long ago, his straight and innocent stare that didn't, any more, see the person in front of him at all. He wasn't adjusting himself to the big clock. He didn't even know there was a big clock. The large, gray, convoluted muscle in back of that childlike gaze was digesting something unknown to the ordinary world. That muscle with its long tendons had nearly fastened itself about a conclusion, a conclusion startlingly different from the hearty expression once forged upon the outward face, and left there, abandoned. Some day that conclusion would be reached, the muscle would strike. Probably it had, before. Surely it would, again.

He said how nice Georgette was looking, which was true, how she always reminded him of carnivals and Hallowe'en, the wildest baseball ever pitched in history, and there was as usual a real and extraordinary warmth in the voice, as though this were another, still a third personality.

"I'm sorry an old friend of mine, Major Conklin, had to leave early," he said to me. "He likes what we've been doing recently with *Crimeways*. I told him you were the psychic bloodhound leading us on to new interpretations, and he was interested."

"I'm sorry I missed him."

"Well, Larry recently took over a string of graveyard magazines, and he wants to do something with them. But I don't think a man with your practical experience and precision mentality could advise him. He needs a geomancer."

"It's been a pleasant evening, Earl."

"Hasn't it? Good night."

"Good night."

"Good night."

We made our way down the long room, past an atmospheric disturbance highly political, straight through a group of early settlers whom God would not help tomorrow morning, cautiously around a couple abruptly silent but smiling in helpless rage.

"Where now?" Georgette asked.

"A slight detour. Just for dinner. Then home, of course."

As we got our things, and I waited for Georgette, I saw Pauline Delos, with a party of four, disappearing into the night. Abandoning this planet. As casually as that. But my thought-waves told her to drop in again. Any time.

In the taxi, Georgette said: "George, what's a geomancer?"

"I don't know, George. Earl got it out of the fattest dictionary ever printed, wrote it on his cuff, and now the rest of us know why he's the boss. Remind me to look it up."

George Stroud II

ABOUT five weeks later I woke up on a January morning, with my head full of a letter Bob Aspenwell had written me from Haiti. I don't know why this letter came back to me the instant sleep began to go. I had received it days and days before. It was all about the warmth down there, the ease, and above all, the simplicity.

He said it was a Black Republic, and I was grinning in my sleep as I saw Bob and myself plotting a revolt of the whites determined not to be sold down the river into *Crimeways*. Then I really woke up.

Monday morning. On Marble Road. An important Monday.

Roy Cordette and I had scheduled a full staff conference for the April issue, one of those surprise packages good for everyone's ego and imagination. The big clock was running at a leisurely pace, and I was well abreast of it.

But that morning, in front of the mirror in the bathroom, I was certain a tuft of gray on the right temple had stolen at least another quarter-inch march. This renewed a familiar vision, beginning with mortality at one end of the scale, and ending in senile helplessness at the other.

Who's that pathetic, white-haired old guy clipping papers at the desk over there? asked a brisk young voice. But I quickly tuned it out and picked another one: *Who's that distinguished, white-haired, scholarly gentleman going into the directors' room?*

Don't you know who he is? That's George Stroud.

Who's he?

Well, it's a long story. He used to be general manager of this whole railroad. Railroad? Why not something with a farther future? *Airline. He saw this line through its first, pioneer stages. He might have been one of the biggest men in aviation today, only something went wrong. I don't know just what, except that it was a hell of a scandal. Stroud had to go before a Grand Jury, but it was so big it had to be hushed up, and he got off. After that, though, he was through. Now they let him put out the*

*papers and cigars in the board room when there's a meeting.
The rest of the time he fills the office inkwells and rearranges the
travel leaflets.*

Why do they keep him on at all?

*Well, some of the directors feel sentimental about the old fel-
low, and besides, he has a wife and daughter dependent on him.*
Hold that copy, boy. This is years and years from now. *Three
children, no, I think it's four. Brilliant youngsters, and awfully
brave about Stroud. Won't hear a word against him. They think
he still runs the whole works around here. And did you ever see
the wife? They're the most devoted old couple I ever saw.*

Drying my face, I stared into the glass. I made the dark,
bland, somewhat inquisitive features go suddenly hard and
still. I said:

"Look here, Roy, we've really got to do something." *About
what?* "About getting ourselves some more money." I saw
the vague wave of Roy Cordette's thin, long-fingered hand,
and discerned his instant retreat into the land of elves, hob-
goblins, and double-talk.

*I thought, George, you went all over this with Hagen three
months ago. There's no doubt about it, you and I are both crowding the limit. And then some.*

"What is the limit, do you happen to know?"

*The general level throughout the whole organization, I should
say, wouldn't you?*

"Not for me. I don't exactly crave my job, my contract, or
this gilded cage full of gelded birds. I think it's high time we
really had a showdown."

Go right ahead. My prayers go with you.

"I said *we.* In a way it involves your own contract as well
as mine."

*I know. Tell you what, George, why don't the three of us talk
this over informally? You and Hagen and myself?*

"A good idea." I reached for the phone. "When would be
convenient?"

You mean today?

"Why not?"

*Well, I'll be pretty busy this afternoon. But all right. If Steve
isn't too busy around five.*

"A quarter to six in the Silver Lining. After the third round.

You know, Jennett-Donohue are planning to add five or six new books. We'll just keep that in mind."

So I heard, but they're on a pretty low level, if you ask me. Besides, it's a year since that rumor went around.

A real voice shattered this imaginary scene.

"George, are you ever coming down? George has to take the school bus, you know."

I called back to Georgette that I was on my way and went back to the bedroom. And when we went into conference with Steve Hagen, then what? A vein began to beat in my forehead. For business purposes he and Janoth were one and the same person, except that in Hagen's slim and sultry form, restlessly through his veins, there flowed some new, freakish, molten virulence.

I combed my hair before the bedroom dresser, and that sprout of gray resumed its ordinary proportions. To hell with Hagen. Why not go to Janoth? Of course.

I laid the comb and brush down on the dresser top, leaned forward on an elbow, and breathed into the mirror: "Cut you the cards, Earl. Low man leaves town in twenty-four hours. High man takes the works."

I put on my tie, my coat, and went downstairs. Georgia looked up thoughtfully from the usual drift of cornflakes surrounding her place at the table. From beneath it came the soft, steady, thump, thump, thump of her feet marking time on a crossbar. A broad beam of sunlight poured in upon the table, drawn close to the window, highlighting the silverware, the percolator, the faces of Georgia and Georgette. Plates reflected more light from a sideboard against one wall, and above it my second favorite painting by Louise Patterson, framed in a strip of walnut, seemed to hang away up in the clouds over the sideboard, the room, and somehow over the house. Another picture by Patterson hung on the opposite wall, and there were two more upstairs.

Georgette's large, glowing, untamed features turned, and her sea-blue eyes swept me with surgical but kindly interest. I said good morning and kissed them both. Georgette called to Nellie that she could bring the eggs and waffles.

"Orange juice," I said, drinking mine. "These oranges just told me they came from Florida."

My daughter gave me a glance of startled faith. "I didn't hear anything," she said.

"You didn't? One of them said they all came from a big ranch near Jacksonville."

Georgia considered this and then waved her spoon, flatly discarding the whole idea. After a full twenty seconds of silence she seemed to remember something, and asked: "What man were you talking to?"

"Me? Man? When? Where?"

"Now. Upstairs. George said you were talking to a man. We heard."

"Oh."

Georgette's voice was neutral, but under the neutrality lay the zest of an innocent bystander waiting to see the first blood in a barroom debate.

"I thought you'd better do your own explaining," she said.

"Well, that man, George. That was me, practicing. Musicians have to do a lot of practicing before they play. Athletes have to train before they race, and actors rehearse before they act." I hurried past Georgette's pointed, unspoken agreement. "And I always run over a few words in the morning before I start talking. May I have the biscuits. Please?"

Georgia weighed this, and forgot about it. She said: "George said you'd tell me a story, George."

"I'll tell you a story, all right. It's about the lonely cornflake." I had her attention now, to the maximum. "It seems that once there was a little girl."

"How old?"

"About five, I think. Or maybe it was seven."

"No, six."

"Six she was. So there was this package of cornflakes—"

"What was her name?"

"Cynthia. So these cornflakes, hundreds of them, they'd all grown up together in the same package, they'd played games and gone to school together, they were all fast friends. Then one day the package was opened and the whole lot were emptied into Cynthia's bowl. And she poured milk and cream and sugar in the bowl, and then she ate one of the flakes. And after a while, this cornflake down in Cynthia's stomach began to wonder when the rest of his friends were going to arrive.

But they never did. And the longer he waited, the lonelier he grew. You see, the rest of the cornflakes got only as far as the tablecloth, a lot of them landed on the floor, a few of them on Cynthia's forehead, and some behind her ears."

"And then what?"

"Well, that's all. After a while this cornflake got so lonely he just sat down and cried."

"Then what'd he do?"

"What could he do? Cynthia didn't know how to eat her cornflakes properly, or maybe she wasn't trying, so morning after morning the same thing happened. One cornflake found himself left all alone in Cynthia's stomach."

"Then what?"

"Well, he cried and carried on so bad that every morning she got a bellyache. And she couldn't think why because, after all, she really hadn't eaten anything."

"Then what'd she do?"

"She didn't like it, that's what she did."

Georgia started in on her soft-boiled eggs, which promised to go the way of the cereal. Presently she lowered the handle of the spoon to the table and rested her chin on the tip, brooding and thumping her feet on the crossbar. The coffee in my cup gently rippled, rippled with every thud.

"You always tell that story," she remembered. "Tell me another."

"There's one about the little girl—Cynthia, aged six—the same one—who also had a habit of kicking her feet against the table whenever she ate. Day after day, week in and week out, year after year, she kicked it and kicked it. Then one fine day the table said, 'I'm getting pretty tired of this,' and with that it pulled back its leg and whango, it booted Cynthia clear out of the window. Was she surprised."

This one was a complete success. Georgia's feet pounded in double time, and she upset what was left of her milk.

"Pull your punches, wonder boy," said Georgette, mopping up. A car honked outside the house and she polished Georgia's face with one expert wipe of the bib. "There's the bus, darling. Get your things on."

For about a minute a small meteor ran up and down and around the downstairs rooms, then disappeared, piping. Georgette came back, after a while, for her first cigarette and her second cup of coffee. She said, presently, looking at me through a thin band of smoke: "Would you like to go back to newspaper work, George?"

"God forbid. I never want to see another fire engine as long as I live. Not unless I'm riding on it, steering the back end of a hook-and-ladder truck. The fellow on the back end always steers just the opposite to the guy in the driver's seat. I think."

"That's what I mean."

"What do you mean?"

"You don't like *Crimeways*. You don't really like Janoth Enterprises at all. You'd like to steer in just the opposite direction to all of that."

"You're wrong. Quite wrong. I love that old merry-go-round."

Georgette hesitated, unsure of herself. I could feel the laborious steps her reasoning took before she reached a tentative, spoken conclusion: "I don't believe in square pegs in round holes. The price is too great. Don't you think so, George?" I tried to look puzzled. "I mean, well, really, it seems to me, when I think about it, sometimes, you were much happier, and so was I, when we had the roadhouse. Weren't we? For that matter, it was a lot more fun when you were a race-track detective. Heavens, even the all-night broadcasting job. It was crazy, but I liked it."

I finished my waffle, tracing the same circuit of memories I knew that she, too, was following. Timekeeper on a construction gang, race-track operative, tavern proprietor, newspaper legman, and then rewrite, advertising consultant, and finally—what? Now?

Of all these experiences I didn't know which filled me, in retrospect, with the greater pleasure or the more annoyance. And I knew it was a waste of time to raise such a question even in passing.

Time.

One runs like a mouse up the old, slow pendulum of the big clock, time, scurries around and across its huge hands, strays inside through the intricate wheels and balances and springs of the inner mechanism, searching among the cobwebbed mazes of this machine with all its false exits and dangerous blind alleys and steep runways, natural traps and artificial baits, hunting for the true opening and the real prize.

Then the clock strikes one and it is time to go, to run down the pendulum, to become again a prisoner making once more the same escape.

For of course the clock that measures out the seasons, all gain and loss, the air Georgia breathes, Georgette's strength, the figures shivering on the dials of my own inner instrument board, this gigantic watch that fixes order and establishes the pattern for chaos itself, it has never changed, it will never change, or be changed.

I found I had been looking at nothing. I said: "No. I'm the roundest peg you ever saw."

Georgette pinched out her cigarette, and asked: "Are you driving in?"

I thought of Roy and Hagen and the Silver Lining.

"No. And I may be home late. I'll call you."

"All right, I'll take you to the station. I may go in for a while myself, after lunch."

Finishing my coffee I sped through the headlines of the first three pages of the morning paper and found nothing new. A record-breaking bank robbery in St. Paul, but not for us. While Georgette gave instructions to Nellie I got into my coat and hat, took the car out of the garage, and honked. When Georgette came out I moved over and she took the wheel.

This morning, Marble Road was crisp but not cold, and very bright. Patches of snow from a recent storm still showed on the brown lawns and on the distant hills seen through the crooked black lace of the trees. Away from Marble Road, our community of rising executives, falling promoters, and immovable salesmen, we passed through the venerable but slightly weatherbeaten, huge square boxes of the original citizens. On the edge of the town behind Marble Road lay the bigger estates, scattered through the hills. Lots of gold in them, too. In about three more years, we would stake a claim of several acres there, ourselves.

"I hope I can find the right drapes this afternoon," said Georgette, casually. "Last week I didn't have time. I was in Doctor Dolson's office two solid hours."

"Yes?" Then I understood she had something to say. "How are you and Doc Dolson coming along?"

She spoke without taking her eyes from the road. "He says he thinks it would be all right."

"He thinks? What does that mean?"

"He's sure. As sure can be. Next time I should be all right."

"That's swell." I covered her hand on the wheel. "What have you been keeping it secret for?"

"Well. Do you feel the same?"

"Say, why do you think I've been paying Dolson? Yes. I do."

"I just wondered."

"Well, don't. When, did he say?"

"Any time."

We had reached the station and the 9:08 was just pulling in. I kissed her, one arm across her shoulders, the other arm groping for the handle of the door.

"Any time it is. Get ready not to slip on lots of icy sidewalks."

"Call me," she said, before I closed the door.

I nodded and made for the station. At the stand inside I took another paper and went straight on through. There was plenty of time. I could see an athlete still running, a block away.

The train ride, for me, always began with Business Opportunities, my favorite department in any newspaper, continued with the auction room news and a glance at the sports pages, insurance statistics, and then amusements. Finally, as the train burrowed underground, I prepared myself for the day by turning to the index and reading the gist of the news. If there was something there, I had it by the time the hundreds and thousands of us were intently journeying across the floor of the station's great ant heap, each of us knowing, in spite of the intricate patterns we wove, just where to go, just what to do.

And five minutes later, two blocks away, I arrived at the Janoth Building, looming like an eternal stone deity among a forest of its fellows. It seemed to prefer human sacrifices, of the flesh and of the spirit, over any other token of devotion. Daily, we freely made them.

I turned into the echoing lobby, making mine.

George Stroud III

J ANOTH ENTERPRISES, filling the top nine floors of the Janoth Building, was by no means the largest of its kind in the United States. Jennett-Donohue formed a larger magazine syndicate; so did Beacon Publications, and Devers & Blair. Yet our organization had its special place, and was far from being the smallest among the many firms publishing fiction and news, covering political, business, and technical affairs.

Newsways was the largest and best-known magazine of our group, a weekly publication of general interest, with a circulation of not quite two million. That was on floor thirty-one. Above it, on the top floor of the building, were the business offices—the advertising, auditing, and circulation departments, with Earl's and Steve Hagen's private headquarters.

Commerce was a business weekly with a circulation of about a quarter of a million, far less than the actual reading public and the influence it had. Associated with it were the four-page daily bulletin, *Trade*, and the hourly wire service, *Commerce Index*. These occupied floor thirty.

The twenty-ninth floor housed a wide assortment of technical newspapers and magazines, most of them published monthly, ranging from *Sportland* to *The Frozen Age* (food products), *The Actuary* (vital statistics), *Frequency* (radio and television), and *Plastic Tomorrow*. There were eleven or twelve of these what's-coming-next and how-to-do-it publications on this floor, none with a large circulation, some of them holdovers from an inspired moment of Earl Janoth's, and possibly now forgotten by him.

The next two floors in descending order held the morgue, the library and general reference rooms, art and photo departments, a small but adequate first-aid room in frequent use, a rest room, the switchboards, and a reception room for general inquiries.

The brains of the organization were to be found, however, on floor twenty-six. It held *Crimeways*, with Roy Cordette as Associate Editor (Room 2618), myself as Executive Editor (2619), Sydney Kislak and Henry Wyckoff, Assistant Editors

(2617), and six staff writers in adjoining compartments. In theory we were the nation's police blotter, watchdogs of its purse and conscience, sometimes its morals, its table manners, or anything else that came into our heads. We were diagnosticians of crime; if the FBI had to go to press once a month, that would be us. If the constable of Twin Oaks, Nebraska, had to be a discerning social critic, if the National Council of Protestant Episcopal Bishops had to do a certain amount of legwork, that would be us, too. In short, we were the weather bureau of the national health, recorders of its past and present crimes, forecasters of those in the future. Or so, at one time or another, we had collectively said.

With us on the twenty-sixth floor, also, were four other magazines having similar set-ups: *Homeways* (more than just a journal of housekeeping), *Personalities* (not merely the outstanding success stories of the month), *Fashions* (human, not dress), and *The Sexes* (love affairs, marriages, divorces).

Finally, on the two floors below us, were the long-range research bureaus, the legal department, the organization's public relations staff, office supplies, personnel, and a new phenomena called *Futureways*, dedicated to planned social evolution, an undertaking that might emerge as a single volume, a new magazine, an after-dinner speech somewhere, or simply disappear suddenly leaving no trace at all. Edward Orlin and Emory Mafferson were both on its staff.

Such was the headquarters of Janoth Enterprises. Bureaus in twenty-one large cities at home and twenty-five abroad fed this nerve-center daily and hourly. It was served by roving correspondents and by master scientists, scholars, technicians in every quarter of the world. It was an empire of intelligence.

Any magazine of the organization could, if necessary, command the help and advice of any channel in it. Or of all of them. *Crimeways* very often did.

We had gone after the missing financier, Paul Isleman, and found him. That one could be credited to me. And we had exercised the legal department, the auditing bureau, and a dozen legmen from our own and other units to disentangle Isleman's involved frauds, while one of our best writers, Bert Finch, had taken a month to make the whole complicated business plain to the general public.

We had found the man who killed Mrs. Frank Sandler, beating the cops by three-tenths of a second. This one, also, could be credited to George Stroud. I had located the guy through our own morgue—with the aid of a staff thrown together for the job.

I went straight through my room into Roy's, stopping only to shed my hat and coat. They were all there in 2618, looking tired but dogged, and vaguely thoughtful. Nat Sperling, a huge, dark, awkward man, went on speaking in a monotonous voice, referring to his notes.

". . . On a farm about thirty miles outside Reading. The fellow used a shotgun, a revolver, and an ax."

Roy's remote, inquiring gaze flickered away from me back to Sperling. Patiently, he asked: "And?"

"And it was one of those gory, unbelievable massacres that just seem to happen every so often in those out-of-the-way places."

"We have a man in Reading," Roy meditated, out loud. "But what's the point?"

"The score this fellow made," said Nat. "Four people, an entire family. That's really big-scale homicide, no matter where it happens."

Roy sighed and offered a wisp of a comment. "Mere numbers mean nothing. Dozens of people are murdered every day."

"Not four at a clip, by the same man."

Sydney Kislak, perched on a broad window ledge in back of Elliot, sounded a brisk footnote: "Choice of weapons. Three different kinds."

"Well, what was it all about?" Roy equably pursued.

"Jealousy. The woman had promised to run away with the killer, at least he thought she had, and when she brushed him off instead, he shot her, her husband, then he took a gun and an ax to their two—"

Roy murmured absently: "In a thing like that, the big point to consider is the motive. Is it relevant to our book? Is it criminal? And it seems to me this bird just fell in love. It's true that something went wrong, but basically he was driven to his act by love. Now, unless you can show there is something inherently criminal or even anti-social in the mating instinct—" Roy slowly opened and closed the fingers of the hand on the desk before him. "But I think we ought to suggest it to Wheeler for *Sexes.* Or perhaps *Personalities.*"

"*Fashions,*" murmured Sydney.

Roy continued to look expectantly at Nat, across whose candid features had struggled a certain amount of reluctant admiration. He concentrated again on his notes, apparently decided to pass over two or three items, then resumed.

"There's a terrific bank robbery in St. Paul. Over half a million dollars, the biggest bag in history."

"The biggest without benefit of law," Henry Wyckoff amended. "That was last night, wasn't it?"

"Yesterday afternoon. I got the Minneapolis bureau on it, and we already know there was a gang of at least three people, maybe more, working on this single job for more than three years. The thing about this job is that the gang regularly incorporated themselves three years ago, paid income taxes, and paid themselves salaries amounting to $175,000 while they were laying their plans and making preparations for the hold-up. Their funds went through the bank they had in mind, and it's believed they had several full-dress rehearsals before yesterday, right on the spot. A couple of the guards had even been trained, innocently it's believed, to act as their extras. One of them got paid off with a bullet in the leg."

Nat stopped and Roy appeared to gaze through him, a pinch of a frown balancing itself delicately against the curiosity in his blue, tolerant eyes.

"Figures again," he delicately judged. "What is the difference whether it is a half million, half a thousand, or just half a dollar? Three years, three months, or three minutes? Three criminals, or three hundred? What makes it so significant that it must be featured by us?"

"The technical angle, don't you think?" suggested Wyckoff. "Staying within the law while they laid the groundwork. Those rehearsals. Working all that time right through the bank. When you think of it, Roy, why, no bank or business in the world is immune to a gang with sufficient patience, resources, and brains. Here's the last word in criminal technique, matching business methods against business methods.

Hell, give enough people enough time and enough money and brains, and eventually they could take Fort Knox."

"Exactly," said Roy. "And is that new? Attack catching up with defense, defense overtaking attack, that is the whole history of crime. We have covered the essential characteristics of this very story, in its various guises, many times before—too many. I can't see much in that for us. We'll give it two or three paragraphs in *Crime Wavelets.* 'Sober, hard-working thugs invest $175,000, three years of toil, to stage a bank robbery. Earn themselves a profit of $325,000, net.' At three men working for three years," he calculated, "that amounts to something over thirty-six thousand a year each. Yes. 'This modest wage, incommensurate with the daring and skill exercised, proves again that crime does not pay—enough.' About like that. Now, can't we get something on a little higher level? We still need three leading articles."

Nat Sperling had no further suggestions to make. I saw it was already 10:45, and with little or nothing done, an early lunch seemed an idle dream. Also, I would have to write off any hope for a conference today with Roy and Hagen. Tony Watson took the ball, speaking in abrupt, nervous rushes and occasionally halting altogether for a moment of pronounced anguish. It seemed to me his neurasthenia could have shown more improvement, if not a complete cure, for the four or five thousand dollars he had spent on psychoanalysis. Still, considering the hazards of our occupation, it could be that without those treatments Tony would today be speechless altogether.

"There's a bulletin by the Welfare Commission," he said, and after we waited for a while he went on, "to be published next month. But we can get copies. I've read it. It's about the criminal abortion racket. Pretty thorough. The commission spent three years investigating. They covered everything, from the small operators to the big, expensive, private s-sanatoriums. Who protects them, why and how. Total estimated number every year, amount of money the industry represents, figures on deaths and prosecutions. Medical effects, pro and con. Causes, results. It's a straight, exhaustive study of the subject. First of its kind. Official, I mean."

Long before Tony had finished, Roy's chin was down upon his chest, and at the close he was making swift notes.

"Do they reach any conclusions? Make any recommendations?" he asked.

"Well, the report gives a complex of causes. Economic reasons are the chief cause of interrupted pregnancies among married women, and among—"

"Never mind that. We'll have to reach our own conclusions. What do they say about old-age assistance?"

"What? Why, nothing, as I recall."

"Never mind, I think we have something. We'll take that bulletin and show what it really means. We'll start by giving the figures for social security survivor benefits. Funeral allowances, in particular, and make the obvious contrasts. Here, on the one hand, is what our government spends every year to bury the dead, while here, at the other end of the scale of life, is what the people spend to prevent birth. Get in touch with the Academy of Medicine and the College of Physicians and Surgeons for a short history of the practice of abortion, and take along a photographer. Maybe they have a collection of primitive and modern instruments. A few pictures ought to be very effective. A short discussion of ancient methods ought to be even more effective."

"Magic was one of them," Bert Finch told Tony.

"Fine," said Roy. "Don't fail to get that in, too. And you might get in touch with the Society of American Morticians for additional figures on what we spend for death, as contrasted with what is spent to prevent life. Call up a half a dozen department stores, ask for figures on what the average expectant mother spends on clothes and equipment up to the date of birth. And don't forget to bring in a good quotation or two from Jonathan Swift on Irish babies."

He looked at Tony, whose meager, freckled features seemed charged with reserve.

"That isn't exactly what I had in mind, Roy. I thought we'd simply dramatize the findings. The commission's findings."

Roy drew a line under the notes on his pad.

"That's what we will be doing, a take-out on the abortion racket. A round-up of the whole subject of inheritance and illegitimacy. But we will be examining it on a higher level, that's all. Just go ahead with the story now, and when the bulletin comes out we'll check through it and draw attention to the real implications of the general picture, at the same time pointing out the survey's omissions. But don't wait for the survey to be released. Can you have a rough draft in, say, two or three weeks?"

Tony Watson's strangled silence indicated that about two thousand dollars' worth of treatments had been shot to hell. Presently, though, he announced: "I can try."

The conference went on, like all those that had gone before, and, unless some tremendous miracle intervened, like many hundreds sure to follow.

Next month Nat Sperling's quadruple-slaying on a lonely farm would become a penthouse shooting in Chicago, Tony's bent for sociological research would produce new parole-board reports, novel insurance statistics, a far-reaching decision of the Supreme Court. Whatever the subject, it scarcely mattered. What did matter was our private and collective virtuosity.

Down the hall, in Sydney's office, there was a window out of which an almost forgotten associate editor had long ago jumped. I occasionally wondered whether he had done so after some conference such as this. Just picked up his notes and walked down the corridor to his own room, opened the window, and then stepped out.

But we were not insane.

We were not children exchanging solemn fantasies in some progressive nursery. Nor were the things we were doing here completely useless.

What we decided in this room, more than a million of our fellow-citizens would read three months from now, and what they read they would accept as final. They might not know they were doing so, they might even briefly dispute our decisions, but still they would follow the reasoning we presented, remember the phrases, the tone of authority, and in the end their crystallized judgments would be ours.

Where our own logic came from, of course, was still another matter. The moving impulse simply arrived, and we, on the face that the giant clock turned to the public, merely registered the correct hour of the standard time.

But being the measure by which so many lives were shaped and guided gave us, sometimes, strange delusions.

At five minutes to twelve, even the tentative schedule lined up for the April book was far too meager. Leon Temple and Roy were engaged in a rather aimless cross-discussion about a radio program that Leon construed as a profound conspiracy against reason, and therefore a cardinal crime, with Roy protesting the program was only a minor nuisance.

"It's on a pretty low level, and why should we give it free advertising?" he demanded. "Like inferior movies and books and plays, it's simply not on our map."

"And like confidence games, and counterfeit money," Leon jibed.

"I know, Leon, but after all—"

"But after all," I intervened, "it's noon, and we've come around to ultimate values, right on the dot."

Roy looked around, smiling. "Well, if you have something, don't let it spoil."

"I think maybe I have," I said. "A little idea that might do everyone a certain amount of good, ourselves included. It's about *Futureways.* We all know something of what they're doing downstairs."

"Those alchemists," said Roy. "Do they know, themselves?"

"I have a strong feeling they've lost their way with Funded Individuals," I began. "We could do a double service by featuring it ourselves, at the same time sending up a trial balloon for them."

I elaborated. In theory, Funded Individuals was something big. The substance of it was the capitalization of gifted people in their younger years for an amount sufficient to rear them under controlled conditions, educate them, and then provide for a substantial investment in some profitable enterprise through which the original indebtedness would be repaid. The original loan, floated as ordinary stocks or bonds, also paid life-insurance premiums guaranteeing the full amount of the issue, and a normal yearly dividend.

Not every one of these incorporated people—Funded Individuals was our registered name for the undertaking—would be uniformly successful, of course, however fortunate and talented he might originally be. But the Funded Individuals were operated as a pool, with a single directorship, and our figures had demonstrated that such a venture would ultimately show a tremendous overall profit.

It went without saying that the scheme would mean a great deal to those persons chosen for the pool. Each would be capitalized at something like one million dollars, from the age of seventeen.

I told the staff that the social implications of such a project, carried to its logical conclusions, meant the end of not only poverty, ignorance, disease, and maladjustment, but also inevitably of crime.

"We can suggest a new approach to the whole problem of crime," I concluded. "Crime is no more inherent in society than diphtheria, horse-cars, or black magic. We are accustomed to thinking that crime will cease only in some far-off Utopia. But the conditions for abolishing it are at hand—right now."

The idea was tailored for *Crimeways*, and the staff knew it. Roy said, cautiously: "Well, it does show a perspective of diminishing crime." His thin face was filled with a whole train of afterthoughts. "I see where it could be ours. But what about those people downstairs? And what about the thirty-second floor? It's their material, and they have their own ideas about what to do with it, haven't they?"

I said I didn't think so. Mafferson, Orlin, and half a dozen others downstairs in the research bureau known as *Futureways* had been working on Funded Individuals off and on for nearly a year, with no visible results as yet, and with slight probability there ever would be. I said: "The point is, they don't know whether they want to drop Funded Individuals, or what to do with it if they don't. I think Hagen would welcome any sort of a move. We can give the idea an abbreviated prevue."

" 'Crimeless Tomorrow,' " Roy improvised. " 'Research Shows Why. Finance Shows How.' " He thought for a moment. "But I don't see any pictures, George."

"Graphs."

We let it go at that. That afternoon I cleared the article with Hagen, in a three-minute phone call. Then I had a talk with Ed Orlin, who agreed that Emory Mafferson would be the right man to work with us, and presently Emory put in his appearance.

I knew him only casually. He was not much more than five feet high, and gave the illusion he was taller sitting than standing. He radiated a slight, steady aura of confusion.

After we checked over his new assignment he brought forward a personal matter.

"Say, George."

"Yes?"

"How are you fixed on the staff of *Crimeways*? After we line up Funded Individuals?"

"Why, do you want to join us?"

"Well, I damn near have to. Ed Orlin looked almost happy when he found I was being borrowed up here."

"Don't you get along with Ed?"

"We get along all right, sometimes. But I begin to think he's beginning to think I'm not the *Futureways* type. I know the signs. It's happened before, see."

"You write short stories, don't you?"

Emory appeared to grope for the truth. "Well."

"I understand. It's all right with me, Emory, if you want to come on here. What in hell, by the way, is the *Futureways* type?"

Emory's brown eyes swam around behind thick spectacles like two lost and lonely goldfish. The inner concentration was terrific. "First place, you've got to believe you're shaping something. Destiny, for example. And then you'd better not do anything to attract attention to yourself. It's fatal to come up with a new idea, for instance, and it's also fatal not to have any at all. See what I mean? And above all, it's dangerous to turn in a piece of finished copy. Everything has to be serious, and pending. Understand?"

"No. Just don't try to be the *Crimeways* type, that's all I ask."

We got Emory and Bert Finch teamed for the "Crimeless Tomorrow" feature, and at five o'clock I phoned Georgette to say I'd be home, after all, but Nellie told me Georgette had gone to her sister's in some emergency involving one of Ann's children. She would be home late, might not be home at all. I told Nellie I'd have supper in town.

It was five-thirty when I walked into the Silver Lining, alone. I had a drink and reviewed what I would have said to Roy and Steve Hagen, had they been present to listen. It did not sound as convincing as I had made it sound this morning. Yet there must be a way. I could do something, I had to, and I would.

The bar of the Silver Lining is only twenty feet from the nearest tables. Behind me, at one of them, I heard a woman's voice saying that she really must leave, and then another voice saying they would have to meet again soon. Half turning, I saw the first speaker depart, and then I saw the other woman. It was Pauline Delos. The face, the voice, and the figure registered all at once.

We looked at each other across half the width of the room, and before I had quite placed her I had smiled and nodded. So did she, and in much the same manner.

I picked up my drink and went to her table. Why not?

I said of course she didn't remember me, and she said of course she did.

I said could I buy her a drink. I could.

She was blonde as hell, wearing a lot of black.

"You're the friend of President McKinley," she told me. I admitted it. "And this was where you were talking to him. Is he here tonight?"

I looked all around the room.

I guess she meant Clyde Polhemus, but he wasn't here.

"Not tonight," I said. "How would you like to have dinner with me, instead?"

"I'd love it."

I think we had an apple-brandy sidecar to begin with. It did not seem this was only the second time we had met. All at once a whole lot of things were moving and mixing, as though they had always been there.

George Stroud IV

W E WERE in the Silver Lining for about an hour. We had dinner there, after Pauline made a phone call rearranging some previous plans.

Then we made the studio broadcast of *Rangers of the Sky*; the program itself was one of my favorites, but that was not the main attraction. We could have heard it anywhere, on any set. Quite aside from the appeal of the program, I was fascinated by the work of a new sound-effects man who, I believed, was laying the foundation for a whole new radio technique. This chap could run a sequence of dramatic sound, without voice or music, for as much as five minutes. Sustaining the suspense, and giving it a clear meaning, too. I explained to Pauline, who seemed puzzled but interested, that some day this fellow would do a whole fifteen- or thirty-minute program of sound and nothing but sound, without voice or music of course, a drama with no words, and then radio would have grown up.

After that Pauline made some more phone calls, rearranging some other plans, and I remembered Gil's bar on Third Avenue. It wasn't exactly a bar and it wasn't exactly a night club; perhaps it might have been called a small Coney Island, or just a dive. Or maybe Gil had the right name and description when he called it a museum.

I hadn't been there for a year or two, but when I had been, there was a game Gil played with his friends and customers, and to me it had always seemed completely worth while.

Although most of Gil's was an ordinary greased postage stamp for dancing to any kind of a band, with any kind of entertainment, there was one thing about it that was different. There was a thirty-foot bar, and on a deep shelf in back of it Gil had accumulated and laid out an inexhaustible quantity of junk—there is no other word for it—which he called his "personal museum." It was Gil's claim that everything in the world was there, somewhere, and that the article, whatever it was, had a history closely connected with his own life and doings. The game was to stump him, on one point or the other.

I never had, though all told I certainly had spent many happy hours trying to do so, and lots of money. At the same time, Gil's logic was sometimes strained and his tales not deeply imaginative. There was a recurrent rumor that every time Gil got stuck for something not in stock, he made it a point to go out and get its equivalent, thus keeping abreast of alert students of the game. Furthermore, his ripostes in the forenoon and early afternoon of the day were not on a par with the results achieved later on, when he was drunk.

"Anything?" Pauline asked, surveying the collection.

"Anything at all," I assured her.

We were seated at the bar, which was not very crowded, and Pauline was looking in mild astonishment at the deceptive forest of bric-a-brac facing us. There was even a regular bar mirror behind all that mountain of gadgets, as I knew from personal experience. Shrunken heads, franc notes, mark notes, confederate money, bayonets, flags, a piece of a totem pole, an airplane propeller, some mounted birds and butterflies, rocks and seashells, surgical instruments, postage stamps, ancient newspapers—wherever the eye wandered it saw some other incongruity and slipped rather dazedly on to still more.

Gil came up, beaming, and I saw he was in form. He knew me by sight only. He nodded, and I said: "Gil, the lady wants to play the game."

"Surely," he said. Gil was an affable fifty, I would have guessed, or maybe fifty-five. "What can I show you, Miss?"

I said, "Can you show us a couple of highballs, while she makes up her mind?"

He took our orders and turned to set them up.

"Anything at all?" Pauline asked me. "No matter how ridiculous?"

"Lady, those are Gil's personal memoirs. You wouldn't call a man's life ridiculous, would you?"

"What did he have to do with the assassination of Abraham Lincoln?"

She was looking at the headline of a yellowed, glass-encased newspaper announcing same. Of course, I had once wondered the same thing, and I told her: The paper was a family heirloom; Gil's grandfather had written the headline, when he worked for Horace Greeley.

"Simple," I pointed out. "And don't ask for lady's hats. He's got Cleopatra's turban back there, and half a dozen other moth-eaten relics that could pass for anything at all."

Gil slid our drinks before us, and gave Pauline his most professional smile.

"I want to see a steamroller," she said.

Gil's beam deepened and he went down the bar, returned with a black and jagged metal cylinder that had once served, if I properly remembered a wild evening, as Christopher Columbus' telescope—a relic certified by the Caribbean natives from whom Gil had personally secured it.

"I can't show you the whole steamroller, ma'am," Gil told Pauline. "Naturally, I haven't room here. Someday I'll have a bigger place, and then I can enlarge my personal museum. But this here is the safety valve from off a steamroller, this is. Go on," he pushed it at her. "It's a very clever arrangement. Look it over."

Pauline accepted the article, without bothering to look at it.

"And this is part of your personal museum?"

"The last time they paved Third Avenue," Gil assured her, "this here steamroller exploded right out in front there. The safety valve, which you have ahold of right there in your hand, came through the window like a bullet. Creased me. As a matter of fact, it left a scar. Look, I'll show you." I knew that scar, and he showed it again. That scar was Gil's biggest asset. "The valve off that steamroller was defective, as you can tell by looking at it. But, as long as it was right here anyway, why, I just left it up in back of the bar where it hit. It was one of the narrowest escapes I ever had."

"Me too," I said. "I was right here when it happened. What'll you have, Gil?"

"Why, I don't mind."

Gil turned and earnestly poured himself a drink, his honest reward for scoring. We lifted our glasses, and Gil jerked his gray, massive head just once. Then he went down the bar to an amateur customer who loudly demanded to see a pink elephant.

Gil patiently showed him the pink elephant, and courteously explained its role in his life.

"I like the museum," said Pauline. "But it must be terrible, sometimes, for Gil. He's seen everything, done everything, gone everywhere, known everyone. What's left for him?"

I muttered that history would be in the making tomorrow, the same as today, and we had another drink on that thought. And then Gil came back and Pauline had another experiment with his memories, and the three of us had another round. And then another.

At one o'clock we were both tired of Gil's life, and I began to think of my own.

I could always create a few more memories, myself. Why not?

There were many reasons why I should not. I weighed them all again, and I tried once more to explain somehow the thing that I knew I was about to do. But they all slipped away from me.

I conjured all sorts of very fancy explanations, besides the simple one, but either the plain or the fancy reasons were good enough; I was not particular on what grounds I behaved foolishly, and even dangerously.

Perhaps I was tired of doing, always, what I ought to do, wearier still of not doing the things that should not be done.

The attractions of the Delos woman multiplied themselves by ten, and then presently they were multiplying by the hundreds. We looked at each other, and that instant was like the white flash of a thrown switch when a new circuit is formed and then the current flows invisibly through another channel.

Why not? I knew the risks and the cost. And still, why not? Maybe the risks and the price were themselves at least some of the reasons why. The cost would be high; it would take some magnificent lying and acting; yet if I were willing to pay that price, why not? And the dangers would be greater still. Of them, I couldn't even begin to guess.

But it would be a very rousing thing to spend an evening with this blonde mystery that certainly ought to be solved. And if I didn't solve it now, I never would. Nobody ever would. It would be something lost forever.

"Well?" she said.

She was smiling, and I realized I had been having an imaginary argument with a shadow of George Stroud standing just
in back of the blazing nimbus she had become. It was amazing. All that other Stroud seemed to be saying was: *Why not?*
Whatever he meant, I couldn't imagine. Why not what?

I finished a drink I seemed to have in my hand, and said:
"I'll have to make a phone call."

"Yes. So will I."

My own phone call was to a nearby semi-residential hotel.
The manager had never failed me—I was putting his sons and
daughters through school, wasn't I?—and he didn't fail me
now. When I returned from the booth, I said: "Shall we go?"

"Let's. Is it far?"

"Not far," I said. "But it's nothing extravagant."

I had no idea, of course, where in that rather sad and partially respectable apartment-hotel we would find ourselves.
Pauline took all this for granted, apparently. It gave me a second thought; and the second thought whisked itself away the
moment it occurred. Then I hoped she wouldn't say anything
about anyone or anything except ourselves.

I needn't have worried. She didn't.

These moments move fast, if they are going to move at all,
and with no superfluous nonsense. If they don't move, they
die.

Bert Sanders, the manager of the Lexington-Plaza, handed
me a note when he gave me the key to a room on the fifth
floor. The note said he positively must have the room by noon
tomorrow, reservations had been made for it. The room itself,
where I found my in-town valise, was all right, a sizable family
vault I believed I had lived in once or twice before.

I was a little bit surprised and dismayed to see it was already
three o'clock, as I brought out the half bottle of Scotch, the
one dressing gown and single pair of slippers, the back number of *Crimeways*—how did that get here?—the three volumes
of stories and poetry, the stack of handkerchiefs, pajamas, aspirin tablets comprising most of the contents of the valise. I
said: "How would you like some Scotch?"

We both would. Service in the Lexington-Plaza perished at
about ten o'clock, so we had our drinks with straight tap

water. It was all right. The life we were now living seemed to quicken perceptibly.

I remembered to tell Pauline, lying on the floor with a pillow under her head and looking more magnificent than ever in my pajamas, that our home would no longer be ours after noon. She dreamily told me I needn't worry, it would be all right, and why didn't I go right on explaining about Louise Patterson and the more important trends in modern painting. I saw with some surprise I had a book open in my lap, but I had been talking about something else entirely. And now I couldn't remember what. I dropped the book, and lay down on the floor beside her.

"No more pictures," I said. "Let's solve the mystery."

"What mystery?"

"You."

"I'm a very average person, George. No riddle at all."

I believe I said, "You're the last, final, beautiful, beautiful, ultimate enigma. Maybe you can't be solved."

And I think I looked at our great big gorgeous bed, soft and deep and wide. But it seemed a thousand miles away. I decided it was just too far. But that was all right. It was better than all right. It was perfect. It was just plain perfect.

I found out again why we are on this earth. I think.

And then I woke up and saw myself in that big, wide bed, alone, with a great ringing and hammering and buzzing going on. The phone was closest, so I answered it, and a voice said: "I'm sorry, sir, but Mr. Sanders says you have no reservation for today."

I looked at my watch; 1:30.

"All right."

I believe I moaned and lay back and ate an aspirin tablet that somebody had thoughtfully laid on the table beside the bed, and then after a while I went to the door that was still pounding and buzzing. It was Bert Sanders.

"You all right?" he asked, looking more than a little worried. "You know, I told you I've reserved this suite."

"My God."

"Well, I hate to wake you up, but we have to—"

"All right."

"I don't know exactly when—"

"My God."

"If I'd thought—"

"All right. Where is she?"

"Who? Oh, well, about six o'clock this morning—"

"My God, never mind."

"I thought you'd want to sleep for a few hours, but—"

"All right." I found my trousers and my wallet and I somehow paid off Bert. "I'll be out of here in three minutes. Was there anything, by the way—?"

"Nothing, Mr. Stroud. It's just that this room—"

"Sure. Get my bag out of here, will you?"

He said he would, and after that I got dressed in a hurry, looking around the room for possible notes as I found a clean shirt, washed but did not attempt to shave, poured myself a fraction of an inch that seemed to be left in a bottle of Scotch somehow on hand.

Who was she?

Pauline Delos. Janoth's girl friend. Oh, God. What next?

Where did Georgette think I was? In town, on a job, but coming home a little late. All right. And then?

What was I supposed to be doing at the office today?

I couldn't remember anything important, and that was not so bad.

But about the major problems? Well, there was nothing I could do about them now, if I had been as stupid as all this. Nothing. Well, all right.

I combed my hair, brushed my teeth, put on my tie.

I could tell Georgette, at her sister's in Trenton, that I had to work until three in the morning and didn't want to phone. It would have awakened the whole household. Simple. It had always worked before. It would work this time. Had to.

I closed my valise, left it for Bert in the middle of the room, went downstairs to the barber shop in the lobby. There I got a quick shave, and after that I had a quicker breakfast, and then a split-second drink.

It was three o'clock in the afternoon when I got back to my desk, and there was no one around except Lucille, Roy's and my secretary, listlessly typing in the small room connecting our two offices. She did not appear curious, and I couldn't find any messages on my desk, either, just a lot of inter-office memos and names.

"Anyone phone me, Lucille?" I asked.

"Just those on your pad."

"My home didn't call? Nothing from my wife?"

"No."

So it was all right. So far. Thank God.

I went back to my desk and sat down and took three more aspirin tablets. It was an afternoon like any other afternoon, except for those nerves. But there should be nothing really the matter with them, either. I began to go through the routine items listed by Lucille. Everything was the same as it had always been. Everything was all right. I hadn't done anything. No one had.

George Stroud V

AND ALL of that went off all right. And two months passed. And during those two months, Mafferson and I worked up the data and the groundwork for Funded Individuals, and we also worked up a take-out of bankruptcy for the May issue, and a detailed story about bought-and-sold orphans for the June book.

Then one evening, early in March, I had one of those moods. I reached for the phone, and from our confidential telephone service got the number I wanted. When the number answered I said: "Hello, Pauline. This is your attorney."

"Oh, yes," she said, after a second. "That one."

It was a spring day, I told her, as it was: the first. We fixed it to have cocktails at the Van Barth.

Georgette and Georgia were in Florida, returning in two days. Earl Janoth was in Washington, for at least a couple of hours, and possibly for a week. It was a Friday.

Before leaving that night I stepped into Roy's office and found him conferring with Emory Mafferson and Bert Finch. I gathered that Emory was filled with doubts regarding "Crimeless Tomorrow, Science Shows Why, Finance Shows How."

Emory said: "I can see, on paper, how Funded Individuals works out fine. I can see from the insurance rates and the business statistics that it works out for a few people who happen to be funded, but what I don't see is, what's going to happen if everyone belongs to the corporation pool? See what I'm driving at?"

Roy was being at his confident, patient, understanding best. "That's what it's supposed to lead to," he said. "And I think it's rather nice. Don't you?"

"Let me put it this way, Roy. If a person capitalized at a million dollars actually returns the original investment, plus a profit, then there's going to be a tremendous rush to incorporate still more individuals, for still more profit. And pretty soon, everyone will be in clover except the stockholders. What do they get out of the arrangement?"

Roy's patience took on palpable weight and shape. "Profit," he said.

"Sure, but what can they do with it? What have they got? Just some monetary gain. They don't, themselves, lead perfectly conditioned lives, with a big sum left over to invest in some new, paying enterprise. Seems to me the only people that get it in the neck with this scheme are the subscribers who make the whole thing possible."

Roy said: "You forget that after this has been in operation a few years, funded people will themselves be the first to reinvest their capital in the original pool, so that both groups are always interested parties of the same process."

I decided they were doing well enough without interference from me, and left.

In the bar of the Van Barth I met a beautiful stranger in a rather austere gray and black ensemble that looked like a tailored suit, but wasn't. I hadn't been waiting for more than ten minutes. After we settled on the drink she would have, Pauline said, rather seriously: "I shouldn't be here at all, you know. I have a feeling it's dangerous to know you."

"Me? Dangerous? Kittens a month old get belligerent when they see me coming. Open their eyes for the first time and sharpen up their claws, meowing in anticipation."

She smiled, without humor, and soberly repeated: "You're a dangerous person, George."

I didn't think this was the right note to strike, and so I struck another one. And pretty soon it was all right, and we had another drink, and then after a while we went to Lemoyne's for supper.

I had been living pretty much alone for the last three weeks, since Georgette and Georgia had gone to Florida, and I felt talkative. So I talked. I told her the one about what the whale said to the submarine, why the silents had been the Golden Age of the movies, why Lonny Trout was a fighter's fighter, and then I suggested that we drive up to Albany.

That is what we finally did. I experienced again the pleasure of driving up the heights of the only perfect river in the world, the river that never floods, never dries up, and yet never seems to be the same twice. Albany we reached, by stages, in about three hours.

I had always liked the city, too, which is not as common-place as it may look to the casual traveler, particularly when the legislature is in session. If there is anything Manhattan has overlooked, it settled here.

After registering under a name I dreamed up with some care and imagination, Mr. and Mrs. Andrew Phelps-Guyon, we went out and spent a couple of hours over food and drink, some entertainment and a few dances on a good, not crowded floor, at a damnably expensive night club. But it was an evening with a definite touch of spring, snatched from the very teeth of the inner works, and exceedingly worth while.

We had breakfast at about noon, and shortly afterwards started a slow drive back to the city, by a different route. It was a different river we followed again, of course, and of course, I fell in love with it all over again; and of course, Pauline helped.

It was late Saturday afternoon when we reached the neighborhood of 58 East, Pauline's apartment building, so early she admitted she had time and lots of it. We went to Gil's. Pauline played the game for about three rounds. I thought Gil was stuck when she asked to see Poe's Raven, but he brought out a stuffed bluebird or something, well advanced in its last molting, and explained it was Poe's original inspiration, personally presented his close friend, Gil's great-grandfather. And then I remembered it was a long time, all of three months, since I'd explored Antique Row.

That is Third Avenue from about Sixtieth Street all the way down to Forty-second, or thereabouts; there may be bigger, better, more expensive and more authentic shops scattered elsewhere about the city, but the spirit of adventure and re-discovery is not in them, somehow. I once asked, on a tall evening in a Third Avenue shop, for the Pied Piper of Hamlin's pipe. They happened to have it, too. I forget what I did with it, after I bought it for about ten dollars and took it first to the office, where it seemed to have lost its potency, and then home, where somebody broke it and then it disappeared. But it wasn't Third Avenue's fault if I hadn't known how to take care of it properly.

This afternoon Pauline and I dawdled over some not very interesting early New England bedwarmers, spinning wheels converted to floor and table lamps, and the usual commodes disguised as playchairs, bookshelves, and tea carts. All very sound and substantial stuff, reflecting more credit to the ingenuity of the twentieth century than to the imagination of the original craftsmen. It was interesting, some of it, but not exciting.

Then at about half-past seven, with some of the shops closing, we reached a little but simply jam-packed place on Fiftieth Street. Maybe I had been in here before, but I couldn't remember it and neither, seemingly, did the proprietor remember me.

I rummaged about for several minutes without his help, not seeing anything I may have missed before, but I had a fine time answering Pauline's questions. Then after a while somebody else came in and I became increasingly aware of the dialogue going forward at the front of the shop.

"Yes, I have," I heard the dealer say, with some surprise. "But I don't know if they're exactly the type you'd want. Hardly anyone asks for pictures in here, of course. I just put that picture in the window because it happened to be framed. Is that the one you wanted?"

"No. But you have some others, haven't you? Unframed. A friend of mine was in here a couple of weeks ago and said you had."

The customer was a big, monolithic brunette, sloppily dressed and with a face like an arrested cyclone.

"Yes, I have. They're not exactly in perfect condition."

"I don't care," she said. "May I see them?"

The dealer located a roll of canvases on an overhead shelf, and tugged them down. I had drifted down to the front of the shop by now, constituting myself a silent partner in the proceedings. The dealer handed the woman the entire roll, and I practically rested my chin on his left shoulder.

"Look them over," he told the woman.

He turned his head, frowning, and for a fraction of a moment one of his eyes loomed enormously, gazing into one of mine. Mine expressed polite curiosity.

"Where did you get these?" the customer asked.

She unrolled the sheaf of canvases, which were about four by five, some more and some less, and studied the one on top from her reverse viewpoint. It showed a Gloucester clipper under full sail, and it was just like all pictures of clippers, unusual only for a ring of dirt, like an enlarged coffee ring, that wreathed the vessel and several miles of the ocean. To say it was not exactly in perfect condition was plain perjury. The ring, I thought, was about the size of a barrelhead, and that would be about where it came from.

"They were part of a lot," the dealer guardedly told her. The big woman cut loose with a loud, ragged laugh. "Part of a lot of what?" she asked. "Material for an arson? Or is this some of that old WPA stuff they used to wrap up ten-cent store crockery?"

"I don't know where it came from. I told you it wasn't in the best of shape."

She thrust the one on top to the rear, exposing a large bowl of daisies. Nobody said anything at all, this time; I just closed my eyes for a couple of seconds and it went away.

The third canvas was an honest piece of work of the tenement-and-junkyard school; I placed it as of about fifteen years ago; I didn't recognize the signature, but it could have been painted by one of five or six hundred good, professional artists who had done the same scene a little better or a little worse.

"Pretty good," said the shop proprietor. "Colorful. It's real."

The tall, square brunette intently went on to the next one. It was another Gloucester clipper, this one going the other way. It had the same magnificent coffee ring that they all did. And the next one was a basket of kittens. "My Pets," I am sure the nice old lady who painted it had called this one. Anyway, the show was diversified. Clipper artists stuck to clippers, backyard painters did them by the miles, and the nice old lady had certainly done simply hundreds and hundreds of cats. Our gallery had them all.

"I'm afraid you haven't got anything here that would interest me," said the woman.

The man tacitly admitted it, and she resumed the show. Two more pictures passed without comment, and I saw there were only two or three more.

Then she turned up another one, methodically, and I suddenly stopped breathing. It was a Louise Patterson. There was no mistaking the subject, the treatment, the effect. The brothers and sisters of that picture hung on my walls in Marble Road. I had once paid nine hundred dollars for one of them, not much less for the others, all of which I had picked up at regular Patterson shows on Fifty-seventh Street.

The customer had already slipped a tentative finger in back of it to separate it from the next canvas and take it away, when I cleared my throat and casually remarked: "I rather like that."

She looked at me, not very amiably, swung the picture around and held it up before her, at arm's length; it curled at the edges where it wasn't frayed, and it had a few spots of something on it in addition to the trademark of the outsized coffee ring. It was in a frightful condition, no less.

"So do I," she flatly declared. "But it's in one hell of a shape. How much do you want for it?"

The question, ignoring me entirely, was fired at the dealer. "Why—"

"God, what a mess."

With her second shot she doubtless cut the dealer's intended price in half.

"I wouldn't know how to value it, exactly," he admitted. "But you can have it for ten dollars?"

It was the literal truth that I did not myself know what a Patterson would be worth, today, on the regular market. Nothing fabulous, I knew; but on the other hand, although Patterson hadn't exhibited for years, and for all I knew was dead, it did not seem possible her work had passed into complete eclipse. The things I had picked up for a few hundred had been bargains when I bought them, and later still the artist's canvases had brought much more, though only for a time.

I beamed at the woman. "I spoke first," I said to her, and then to the dealer: "I'll give you fifty for it."

The dealer, who should have stuck to refinished porch furniture, was clearly dazzled and also puzzled. I could tell the exact moment the great electric light went on in his soul: he had something, probably a Rembrandt.

"Well, I don't know," he said. "It's obviously a clever pic-

ture. Extremely sound. I was intending to have this lot ap-
praised, when I had the time. This is the first time I've really
looked at the lot, myself. I think—"

"It is not a Raphael, Rubens, or Corot," I assured him.

He leaned forward and looked more closely at the picture.
The canvas showed two hands, one giving and the other receiving a coin. That was all. It conveyed the whole feeling,
meaning, and drama of money. But the proprietor was un-
wrinkling the bottom right-hand corner of the canvas, where
the signature would be rather legibly scrawled. I began to
perspire.

"Pat something," he announced, studying it carefully, and
the next moment he sounded disappointed. "Oh. Patterson,
'32. I ought to know that name, but it's slipped my mind."

I let this transparent perjury die a natural death. The large
brunette, built like an old-fashioned kitchen cabinet, didn't
say anything either. But she didn't need to. She obviously
didn't have fifty dollars. And I had to have that picture.

"It's a very superior work," the dealer began again. "When
it's cleaned up, it'll be beautiful."

"I like it," I said. "For fifty bucks."

He said, stalling: "I imagine the fellow who painted it called
the picture *Toil*. Something like that."

"I'd call it *Judas*," Pauline spoke up. "No, *The Temptation
of Judas*."

"There's only one coin," said the dealer, seriously. "There
would have to be thirty." Still stalling, he took the canvases
and began to go through those we had not seen. A silo, with
a cow in front of it. A nice thing with some children playing
in the street. The beach at Coney Island. Depressed at stirring
no further interest, he declared, "And that's all I have."

To the brunette, and smiling glassily, I said: "Why don't
you take the *Grand Street Children*, for about five dollars? I'll
take the *Judas*."

She unchained a whoop of laughter that was not, as far as
I could make out, either friendly or hostile. It was just loud.

"No, thanks, I have enough children of my own."

"I'll buy you a frame, we'll fix it here, and you can take it
home."

This produced another shriek, followed by a roar.

"Save it for your fifty-dollar masterpiece." This sounded derisive. I asked her, with a bite in it: "Don't you believe it's worth that?"

"A picture that is worth anything at all is certainly worth a lot more than that," she suddenly blazed. "Don't you think so? It is either worth ten dollars or a million times that much." Mentally I agreed with this perfectly reasonable attitude, but the shop proprietor looked as though he did, too. And I had to have that picture. It wasn't my fault I had only sixty odd dollars left after one of the most expensive week ends in history, instead of ten million. "But what do I know about paintings? Nothing. Don't let me interfere. Maybe sometime," there was another bloodcurdling laugh, "I'll have the right kind of wallpaper, and just the right space to match the *Grand Street Children*. Save it for me."

She went away, then, and in the quiet that came back to the little shop I firmly proved I would pay what I said I would and no more, and eventually we went away, too, and I had my prize.

Pauline still had some time, and we stopped in at the cocktail lounge of the Van Barth. I left the canvas in the car, but when we'd ordered our drinks Pauline asked me why on earth I'd bought it, and I described it again, trying to explain. She finally said she liked it well enough, but could not see there was anything extraordinarily powerful about it.

It became evident she was picture-blind. It wasn't her fault; many people are born that way; it is the same as being color-blind or tone-deaf. But I tried to explain what the work of Louise Patterson meant in terms of simplified abstractionism and fresh intensifications of color. Then I argued that the picture must have some feeling for her since she'd surely picked the right title for it.

"How do you know it's right?" she asked.

"I know it. I feel it. It's just what I saw in the picture myself."

On the spur of the moment I decided, and told her, that Judas must have been a born conformist, a naturally common-sense, rubber-stamp sort of fellow who rose far above himself when he became involved with a group of people who were hardly in society, let alone a profitable business.

"Heavens, you make him sound like a saint," Pauline said, smiling and frowning.

I told her very likely he was.

"A man like that, built to fall into line but finding himself always out of step, must have suffered twice the torments of the others. And eventually, the temptation was too much for him. Like many another saint, when he was tempted, he fell. But only briefly."

"Isn't that a little involved?"

"Anyway, it's the name of my picture," I said. "Thanks for your help."

We drank to that, but Pauline upset her cocktail.

I rescued her with my handkerchief for a hectic moment, then left her to finish the job while I called the waiter for more drinks, and he cleared the wet tabletop. After a while we had something to eat, and still more drinks, and a lot more talk.

It was quite dark when we came out of the lounge, and I drove the few blocks to 58 East. Pauline's apartment, which I had never been in, was in one of those austere and permanent pueblos of the Sixties. She asked me to stop away from the entrance, cool as she explained: "I don't think it would be wise for me to go in with a strange overnight bag. Accompanied."

The remark didn't say anything, but it gave me a momentarily uncomfortable measure of the small but nevertheless real risks we were running. I erased that idea and said nothing, but I ran past the building and parked half a block from the lighted, canopied entrance.

There I got out to hand her the light valise she had brought with her to Albany, and for a moment we paused.

"May I phone?" I asked.

"Of course. Please do. But we have to be—well—"

"Of course. It's been wonderful, Pauline. Just about altogether supreme."

She smiled and turned away.

Looking beyond her retreating shoulders I vaguely noticed a limousine pull in at the curb opposite the building's entrance. There was something familiar about the figure and carriage of the man who got out of it. He put his head back into the car to issue instructions to a chauffeur, then turned for a moment in my direction. I saw that it was Earl Janoth.

He noticed Pauline approaching, and I am certain that he looked past her and saw me. But I did not think he could have recognized me; the nearest street lamp was at my back.

And what if he had? He didn't own the woman.

He didn't own me, either.

I stepped into my car and started the motor, and I saw them disappearing together into the lighted entrance.

I didn't feel very happy about this unlucky circumstance, as I drove off, but on the other hand, I didn't see how any irreparable damage could have been done.

I drove back to Gil's. There, it was the usual raucous Saturday night. I had a whole lot of drinks, without much conversation, then I took the car around to my garage and caught the 1:45 for home. It was early, but I wanted to be clear-eyed when Georgette and Georgia got back from Florida in the afternoon. I would return by train, pick them up in the car, and drive them home.

I brought in my own bag, at Marble Road, and of course I didn't forget *The Temptation of St. Judas*. The picture I simply laid down on the dining room table. It would have to be cleaned, repaired, and framed.

I glanced at the Pattersons in the downstairs rooms and at the one upstairs in my study, before I went to bed. The *Temptation* was better than any of them.

It occurred to me that maybe I was becoming one of the outstanding Patterson collectors in the United States. Or anywhere.

But before I went to bed I unpacked my grip, put away the belongings it had contained, then put the grip away, too.

Earl Janoth I

B
Y GOD, I never had such an evening. I flatter myself that I am never inurbane by impulse only, but these people, supposedly friends of mine, were the limit, and I could have strangled them one by one.

Ralph Beeman, my attorney for fifteen years, showed damned little interest and less sympathy when the question of the wire renewal for *Commerce Index* came up, or was deliberately brought up. The whole bunch of them quite openly discussed the matter, as though I myself were some sort of immaterial pneuma, not quite present at all, and as though I might actually lose the franchise. Really, they weighed alternatives, when I did lose it.

"Ralph and I have something to say about that," I said, heartily, but the mousey bastard didn't turn a hair. He was just plain neutral.

"Oh, certainly. We'll renew no matter whom we have to fight."

To me, it sounded as though he thought the fight was already lost. I gave him a sharp look, but he chose not to understand. It would have been well, had Steve been present. He is immensely alert to such winds and undercurrents as I felt, but could not measure, everywhere around me.

Ten of us were having dinner at John Wayne's, and since he is a smooth but capable political leader, if we were discussing anything at all it should have been politics. But by God, since I came into his home, a festering old incubus dating back at least a hundred years, we hadn't talked about anything except Janoth Enterprises, and what difficulties we were having. But I wasn't having any difficulties. And I wasn't having any of this, either.

Then there was an awkward moment when Hamilton Carr asked me how I had made out in Washington. I had just returned, and I had an uncomfortable feeling that he knew exactly everyone I had seen there and what I was about. Yet it was really nothing. I had thought of broadening the corporate basis of Janoth Enterprises, and my trip to Washington was

simply to obtain quick and reliable information on what procedure I might follow to achieve that end and fully observe
all SEC regulations.

Ralph Beeman had gone down with me, had not said much
while we were there, and I gave him another emphatic
thought. But it couldn't be. Or were they all, in fact, in some
kind of a conspiracy against me? Voyagers to new continents
of reason have been caught offguard before.

But Hamilton Carr was no enemy; at least, I had never
thought he was; he was simply my banking adviser. He had
always known, to the last dime, what the paper issued by
Janoth Enterprises was worth, and who held it. Tonight, he
said: "You know, Jennett-Donohue still want either to buy or
merge."

I gave him a huge laugh.

"Yes," I said. "So do I. What will they sell for?"

Carr smiled; it was icy dissent. God damn you, I thought,
what's up?

There was a blasted foreign person present with a fearful
English accent who went by the name of Lady Pearsall, or
something equally insignificant, and she told me at great
length what was wrong with my magazines. Everything was
wrong with them, according to her. But it hadn't crossed her
mind that I had gone far out of my way to obtain the very
best writers and editors, the broadest and richest minds to be
had. I had combed the newspapers, the magazines, the finest
universities, and paid the highest salaries in the field, to hire
what I knew were the finest bunch of journalists ever gathered
together under one roof. She gobbled away extensively, her
Adam's apple moving exactly like a scrawny turkey's, but to
hear her tell it, I had found my writers in the hospitals, insane
asylums, and penitentiaries.

I could smile at everything she had to say, but I didn't feel
like smiling at what Carr and Beeman and finally a man by
the name of Samuel Lydon had to say.

"You know," he told me, "there may not always be the
same demand for superior presentation there has been in the
past. I've been getting reports from the distributors." Anyone
could. It was public knowledge. "I think you would like me
to be quite candid with you, Mr. Janoth."

"Certainly."

"Well, the returns on some of your key magazines have shown strange fluctuations. Out of proportion to those of other publications, I mean." I placed him now. He was executive vice-president of a local distributing organization. "I wondered if there was any definitely known reason?"

This was either colossal ignorance or outrageous effrontery. *If I knew of definite reasons.* I looked at him, but didn't bother to reply.

"Maybe it's that astrology magazine of yours," said Geoffrey Balack, ineffectual, vicious, crude, and thoroughly counterfeit. He was some kind of a columnist. I had hired him once, but his work had not seemed too satisfactory, and when he left to take another job I had thought it was a fortunate change all round. Looking at him now, I couldn't remember whether he'd quit, or whether Steve had fired him. Or possibly I had. Offensively, now, he brushed a hand back over the rather thin hair on his head. "That's one I never understood at all. Why?"

I was still smiling, but it cost me an effort.

"I bought that little book, *Stars*, for its title alone. Today it has nothing to do with astrology. It is almost the sole authority in astrophysics."

"Popular?"

That didn't deserve a reply, either. This was what we had once considered a writer with insight and integrity. And good writers cost money, which I was more than glad to pay.

But they were growing more expensive all the time. Other publishing organizations, even though they were not in the same field at all, were always happy to raid our staff, though they rarely tampered with each others'. The advertising agencies, the motion pictures, radio, we were always losing our really good men elsewhere, at prices that were simply fantastic. A man we had found ourselves, and nursed along until we found just the right way to bring out the best and soundest that was in him, might then casually leave us to write trash for some perfume program, or speeches for a political amplifier. Contract or no contract, and at a figure it would be almost ruinous to the rest of the organization if we thought of meeting it.

Either that or they wanted to write books. Or went crazy. Although, God knows, most of them were born that way, and their association with us merely slowed up and postponed the inevitable process for a time.

Well. We still had the finest writers to be had, and the competition only kept us on our toes.

When it came to the point where Jennett-Donohue or Devers & Blair offered twenty-five thousand for a fifteen-thousand-dollar editor, we would go thirty thousand. If radio offered fifty thousand for a man we really had to keep, we'd go to sixty. And when Hollywood began raiding our copy boys and legmen for a million—well, all right. No use being morbid. But sometimes it's impossible not to be.

It was ten o'clock—the earliest moment possible—before I was able to leave. I had enough to worry about, without taking on any extra nonsense from this particular crowd.

It is all a matter of one's inherited nerves and glands. No matter how much one rationalizes, one has either a joyless, negative attitude toward everyone and everything, like these people, and it is purely a matter of the way in which the glands function, or one has a positive and constructive attitude. It is no great credit to me. But neither is it any credit to them.

In the car, I told Bill to drive me home, but halfway there I changed my mind. I told him to drive to Pauline's. Hell, she might even be there. Home was no place to go after an evening squandered among a bunch of imitation cynics, disappointed sentimentalists, and frustrated conspirators.

Without a word Bill spun the wheel and we turned the corner. It reminded me of the way he had always taken my orders, thirty years ago during the hottest part of a circulation war out West, then in the printer's strike upstate. That was why he was with me now. If he wouldn't talk even to me, after thirty odd years, he would never talk to anyone.

When we drew up in front of the place and I got out, I put my head in the window next to him and said: "Go on home, Bill. I'll take a taxi. I don't think I'll need you until tomorrow evening."

He looked at me but said nothing, and eased the car away from the curb.

Earl Janoth II

O N THE SIDEWALK I turned to go in, but as I turned, I caught sight of Pauline. She was leaving someone at the next corner. I couldn't see her face, but I recognized her profile, the way she stood and carried herself, and I recognized the hat she had recently helped to design, and the beige coat. As I stood there she started to walk toward me. The man with her I did not recognize at all, though I stared until he turned and stepped into a car, his face still in the shadows.

When Pauline reached me she was smiling and serene, a little warm and a little remote, deliberate as always. I said: "Hello, dear. This is fortunate."

She brushed away an invisible strand of hair, stopped beside me.

"I expected you'd be back yesterday," she said. "Did you have a nice trip, Earl?"

"Fine. Have a pleasant week end?"

"Marvelous. I went riding, swimming, read a grand book, and met some of the most interesting brand-new people."

We had moved into the building by now. I glanced down and saw that she carried an overnight bag.

I could hear though not see somebody moving behind the high screen that partitioned off the apartment switchboard and, as usual, there was no sign of anyone else. Perhaps this isolation was one of the reasons she had liked such a place in the beginning.

There was an automatic elevator, and now it was on the main floor. As I opened the door, then followed her in and pushed the button for five, I nodded toward the street.

"Was he one of them?"

"One of who? Oh, you mean the brand-new people. Yes."

The elevator stopped at five. The inner door slid noiselessly open, and Pauline herself pushed open the outer door. I followed her the dozen or so carpeted steps to 5A. Inside the small four-room apartment there was such silence and so much dead air it did not seem it could have been entered for days.

"What were you doing?" I asked.

"Well, first we went to a terrible place on Third Avenue by the name of Gil's. You'd love it. Personally, I thought it was a bore. But it's some kind of a combination between an old archeology foundation, and a saloon. The weirdest mixture. Then after that we went up and down the street shopping for antiques."

"What kind of antiques?"

"Any kind that we thought might be interesting. Finally, we bought a picture, that is, he did, in a shop about three blocks from here. An awful old thing that just came out of a dust-bin, it looked like, and he practically kidnapped it from another customer, some woman who bid for it, too. Nothing but a couple of hands, by an artist named Patterson."

"A couple of what?"

"Hands, darling. Just hands. It was a picture about Judas, as I understand it. Then after that we went to the Van Barth and had a few drinks, and he brought me home. That's where you came in. Satisfied?"

I watched her open the door of the small closet in the lobby and drop her bag inside of it, then close the door and turn to me again with her shining hair, deep eyes, and perfect, renaissance face.

"Sounds like an interesting afternoon," I said. "Who was this brand-new person?"

"Oh. Just a man. You don't know him. His name is George Chester, in advertising."

Maybe. And my name is George Agropolus. But I'd been around a lot longer than she had, or, for that matter, than her boy friend. I looked at her for a moment, without speaking, and she returned the look, a little too intently. I almost felt sorry for the new satellite she'd just left, whoever he was.

She poured us some brandy from a decanter beside the lounge, and across the top of her glass she crinkled her eyes in the intimate way supposed to fit the texture of any moment. I sipped my own, knowing again that everything in the world was ashes. Cold, and spent, and not quite worth the effort. It was a mood that Steve never had, a mood peculiarly my own. The question crossed my mind whether possibly others, too, experienced the same feeling, at least occasionally, but that could hardly be. I said: "At least, this time it's a man."

Sharply, she said: "Just what do you mean by that?"

"You know what I mean."

"Are you bringing up that thing again? Throwing Alice in my face?" Her voice had the sound of a wasp. Avenue Z was never far beneath the surface, with Pauline. "You never forget Alice, do you?"

I finished the brandy and reached for the decanter, poured myself another drink. Speaking with deliberate slowness, and politely, I said: "No. Do you?"

"Why, you goddamn imitation Napoleon, what in hell do you mean?"

I finished the brandy in one satisfying swallow.

"And you don't forget Joanna, do you?" I said, softly. "And that Berleth woman, and Jane, and that female refugee from Austria. And God knows who else. You can't forget any of them, can you, including the next one."

She seemed to choke, for a speechless moment, then she moved like a springing animal. Something, I believe it was an ashtray, went past my head and smashed against the wall, showering me with fine glass.

"You son of a bitch," she exploded. "You talk. You, of all people. *You*. That's priceless."

Mechanically, I reached for the decanter, splashed brandy into my glass. I fumbled for the stopper, trying to replace it. But I couldn't seem to connect.

"Yes?" I said.

She was on her feet, on the other side of the low table, her face a tangle of rage.

"What about you and Steve Hagen?"

I forgot about the stopper, and simply stared.

"What? What about me? And Steve?"

"Do you think I'm blind? Did I ever see you two together when you weren't camping?"

I felt sick and stunned, with something big and black gathering inside of me. Mechanically, I echoed her: "Camping? With Steve?"

"As if you weren't married to that guy, all your life. And as if I didn't know. Go on, you son of a bitch, try to act surprised."

It wasn't me, any more. It was some giant a hundred feet tall, moving me around, manipulating my hands and arms and even my voice. He straightened my legs, and I found myself standing. I could hardly speak. My voice was a sawtoothed whisper.

"You say this about Steve? The finest man that ever lived? And me?"

"Why, you poor, old carbon copy of that fairy gorilla. Are you so dumb you've lived this long without even knowing it?" Then she suddenly screamed: "Don't. Earl, don't."

I hit her over the head with the decanter and she stumbled back across the room. My voice said: "You can't talk like that. Not about us."

"Don't. Oh, God, Earl, don't. Earl. Earl. Earl."

I had kicked over the table between us, and I moved after her. I hit her again, and she kept talking with that awful voice of hers, and then I hit her twice more.

Then she was lying on the floor, quiet and a little twisted. I said: "There's a limit to this. A man can take just so much."

She didn't reply. She didn't move.

I stood above her for a long, long time. There was no sound at all, except the remote, muffled hum of traffic from the street below. The decanter was still in my hand, and I lifted it, looked at the bottom edge of it faintly smeared, and with a few strands of hair.

"Pauline."

She lay on her back, watching something far away that didn't move. She was pretending to be unconscious.

A fear struck deeper and deeper and deeper, as I stared at her beautiful, bright, slowly bleeding head. Her face had an expression like nothing on earth.

"Oh, God, Pauline. Get up."

I dropped the decanter and placed my hand inside her blouse, over the heart. Nothing. Her face did not change. There was no breath, no pulse, nothing. Only her warmth and faint perfume. I slowly stood up. She was gone.

So all of my life had led to this strange dream.

A darkness and a nausea flooded in upon me, in waves I had never known before. This, this carrion by-product had suddenly become the total of everything. Of everything there had been between us. Of everything I had ever done. This accident.

For it was an accident. God knows. A mad one.

I saw there were stains on my hands, and my shirt front. There were splotches on my trousers, my shoes, and as my eyes roved around the room I saw that there were even spots high on the wall near the lounge where I had first been sitting.

I needed something. Badly. Help and advice.

I moved into the bathroom and washed my hands, sponged my shirt. It came to me that I must be careful. Careful of everything. I closed the taps with my handkerchief. If her boy friend had been here, and left his own fingerprints. If others had. Anyone else. And many others had.

Back in the other room, where Pauline still lay on the carpet, unchanging, I remembered the decanter and the stopper to it. These I both wiped carefully, and the glass. Then I reached for the phone, and at the same time remembered the switchboard downstairs, and drew away.

I let myself out of the apartment, again using my handkerchief as a glove. Pauline had let us in. The final image of her own fingers would be on the knob, the key, the frame.

I listened for a long moment outside the door of 5A. There was no sound throughout the halls, and none from behind that closed door. I knew, with a renewed vertigo of grief and dread, there would never again be life within that apartment. Not for me.

Yet there had been, once, lots of it. All collapsed to the size of a few single moments that were now a deadly, unreal threat.

I moved quietly down the carpeted hall, and down the stairs. From the top of the first floor landing I could just see the partly bald, gray head of the man at the switchboard. He hadn't moved, and if he behaved as usual, he wouldn't.

I went quietly down the last flight of stairs and moved across the lobby carpet to the door. At the door, when I opened it, I looked back. No one was watching, there was no one in sight.

On the street, I walked for several blocks, then at a stand

on some corner I took a taxi. I gave the driver an address two blocks from the address I automatically knew I wanted. It was about a mile uptown.

When I got out and presently reached the building it was as quiet as it had been at Pauline's.

There was no automatic elevator, as there was at Pauline's, and I did not want to be seen, not in this condition. I walked up the four flights to the apartment. I rang, suddenly sure there would be no answer.

But there was.

Steve's kindly, wise, compact, slightly leathery face confronted me when the door swung open. He was in slippers and a dressing gown. When he saw me, he held the door wider, and I came in.

He said: "You look like hell. What is it?"

I walked past him and into his living room and sat down in a wide chair.

"I have no right to come here. But I didn't know where else to go."

He had followed me into his living room, and he asked, impassively: "What's the matter?"

"God. I don't know. Give me a drink."

Steve gave me a drink. When he said he would ring for some ice, I stopped him.

"Don't bring anyone else in on this," I said. "I've just killed someone."

"Yes?" He waited. "Who?"

"Pauline."

Steve looked at me hard, poured himself a drink, briefly sipped it, still watching me.

"Are you sure?"

This was insane. I suppressed a wild laugh. Instead, I told him, curtly: "I'm sure."

"All right," he said, slowly. "She had it coming to her. You should have killed her three years ago."

I gave him the longest look and the most thought I had ever given him. There was an edge of iron amusement in his locked face. I knew what was going on in his mind: *She was a tramp, why did you bother with her?* And I know what went on in my mind: *I am about the loneliest person in the world.*

"I came here, Steve," I said, "because this is just about my last stop. I face, well, everything. But I thought—hell, I don't know what I thought. But if there is anything I should do, well. I thought maybe you'd know what that would be."

"She deserved it," Steve quietly repeated. "She was a regular little comic."

"Steve, don't talk like that about Pauline. One of the warmest, most generous women who ever lived."

He finished his drink and casually put down the glass.

"Was she? Why did you kill her?"

"I don't know, I just don't know. From here I go to Ralph Beeman, and then to the cops, and then I guess to prison or even the chair." I finished my drink and put down the glass. "I'm sorry I disturbed you."

Steve gestured. "Don't be a fool," he said. "Forget that prison stuff. What about the organization? Do you know what will happen to it the second you get into serious trouble?"

I looked at my hands. They were clean, but they had undone me. And I knew what would happen to the organization the minute I wasn't there, or became involved in this kind of trouble.

"Yes," I said. "I know. But what can I do?"

"Do you want to fight, or do you want to quit? You aren't the first guy in the world that ever got into a jam. What are you going to do about it? Are you going to put up a battle, or are you going to fold up?"

"If there's any chance at all, I'll take it."

"I wouldn't even know you, if I thought you'd do anything else."

"And of course, it's not only the organization, big as that is. There's my own neck, besides. Naturally, I'd like to save it."

Steve was matter of fact. "Of course. Now, what happened?"

"I can't describe it. I hardly know."

"Try."

"That bitch. Oh, God, Pauline."

"Yes?"

"She said that I, she actually accused both of us, but it's

utterly fantastic. I had a few drinks and she must have had several. She said something about us. Can you take it?"

Steve was unmoved. "I know what she said. She would. And then?"

"That's all. I hit her over the head with something. A decanter. Maybe two or three times, maybe ten times. Yes, a decanter. I wiped my fingerprints off of it. She must have been insane, don't you think? To say a thing like that? She's a part-time Liz, Steve, did I ever tell you that?"

"You didn't have to."

"So I killed her. Before I even thought about it. God, I didn't intend anything like it, thirty seconds before. I don't understand it. And the organization is in trouble, real trouble. Did I tell you that?"

"You told me."

"I don't mean about this. I mean Carr and Wayne and—"

"You told me."

"Well, at dinner tonight I was sure of it. And now this. Oh, God."

"If you want to save the whole works you'll have to keep your head. And your nerve. Especially your nerve."

All at once, and for the first time in fifty years, my eyes were filled with tears. It was disgraceful. I could hardly see him. I said: "Don't worry about my nerve."

"That's talking," Steve said, evenly. "And now I want to hear the details. Who saw you go into this place, Pauline's apartment? Where was the doorman, the switchboard man? Who brought you there? Who took you away? I want to know every goddamn thing that happened, what she said to you and what you said to her. What she did and what you did. Where you were this evening, before you went to Pauline's. In the meantime, I'm going to lay out some clean clothes. You have bloodstains on your shirt and your trousers. I'll get rid of them. Meanwhile, go ahead."

"All right," I said, "I was having dinner at the Waynes'. And they couldn't seem to talk about anything else except what a hell of a mess Janoth Enterprises was getting into. God, how they loved my difficulties. They couldn't think or talk about anything else."

"Skip that," said Steve. "Come to the point."

I told him about leaving the Waynes', how Bill had driven me to Pauline's.

"We don't have to worry about Bill," said Steve.

"God," I interrupted. "Do you really think I can get away with this?"

"You told me you wiped your fingerprints off the decanter, didn't you? What else were you thinking of when you did it?"

"That was automatic."

Steve waved the argument away.

"Talk."

I told him the rest of it. How I saw this stranger, leaving Pauline, and how we got into a quarrel in her apartment, and what she had said to me, and what I had said to her, and then what happened, as well as I remembered it.

Finally, Steve said to me: "Well, it looks all right except for one thing."

"What?"

"The fellow who saw you go into the building with Pauline. Nobody else saw you go in. But he did. Who was he?"

"I tell you, I don't know."

"Did he recognize you?"

"I don't know."

"The one guy in the world who saw you go into Pauline's apartment, and you don't know who he was? You don't know whether he knew you, or recognized you?"

"No, no, no. Why, is that important?"

Steve gave me a fathomless glance. He slowly found a cigarette, slowly reached for a match, lit the cigarette. When he blew out the second drag of smoke, still slowly, and thoughtfully blew out the match, and then put the burned match away and exhaled his third lungful, deliberately, he turned and said: "You're damned right it is. I want to hear everything there is to know about that guy." He flicked some ashes into a tray. "Everything. You may not know it, but he's the key to our whole set-up. In fact, Earl, he spells the difference. Just about the whole difference."

Steve Hagen

W E WENT over that evening forward and backward. We put every second of it under a high-powered microscope. Before we finished I knew as much about what happened as though I had been there myself, and that was a lot more than Earl did. This jam was so typical of him that, after the first blow, nothing about it really surprised me.

It was also typical that his simple mind could not wholly grasp how much was at stake and how much he had jeopardized it. Typical, too, that he had no idea how to control the situation. Nor how fast we had to work. Nor how.

Pauline's maid would not return to the apartment until tomorrow evening. There was a good chance the body would not be discovered until then. Then, Earl would be the first person seriously investigated by the police, since his connection with her was common knowledge.

I would have to claim he was with me throughout the dangerous period, and it would have to stick. But Billy would back that.

After leaving the Waynes', Earl had come straight here. Driven by Billy. Then Billy was given the rest of the night off. That was all right, quite safe.

There would be every evidence of Earl's frequent, former visits to Pauline's apartment, but nothing to prove the last one. Even I had gone there once or twice. She had lots of visitors running in and out, both men and women. But I knew, from Earl's squeamish description, the injuries would rule out a woman.

The cover I had to provide for Earl would be given one hell of a going over. So would I. That couldn't be helped. It was my business, not only Earl's, and since he couldn't be trusted to protect our interests, I would have to do it myself.

Apparently it meant nothing to him, the prospect of going back to a string of garbage-can magazines edited from a due-bill office and paid for with promises, threats, rubber checks, or luck. He didn't even think about it. But I did. Earl's flair for capturing the mind of the reading public was far more valuable than the stuff they cram into banks. Along with this vision, though, he had a lot of whims, scruples, philosophical foibles, a sense of humor that he sometimes used even with me. These served some purpose at business conferences or social gatherings, but not now.

If necessary, if the situation got too hot, if Earl just couldn't take it, I might draw some of the fire myself. I could afford to. One of our men, Emory Mafferson, had phoned me here about the same time Earl was having his damned expensive tantrum. And that alibi was real.

The immediate problem, no matter how I turned it over, always came down to the big question mark of the stranger. No other living person had seen Earl, knowing him to be Earl, after he left that dinner party. For the tenth time, I asked: "There was nothing at all familiar about that person you saw?"

"Nothing. He was in a shadowy part of the street. With the light behind him."

"And you have no idea whether he recognized you?"

"No. But I was standing in the light of the entranceway. If he knew me, he recognized me."

Again I thought this over from every angle. "Or he may sometime recognize you," I concluded. "When he sees your face in the papers, as one of those being questioned. Maybe. And maybe we can take care they aren't good pictures. But I wish I had a line on that headache right now. Something to go on when the story breaks. So that we can always be a jump ahead of everyone, including the cops."

All I knew was that Pauline said the man's name was George Chester. This might even be his true name, though knowing Pauline, that seemed improbable, and the name was not listed in any of the phone books of the five boroughs, nor in any of the books of nearby suburbs. She said he was in advertising. That could mean anything. Nearly everyone was.

They had gone to a place on Third Avenue called Gil's, and for some reason it had seemed like an archeological foundation. This sounded authentic. The place could be located with no difficulty.

They had stopped in at a Third Avenue antique shop, and there the man had bought a picture, bidding for it against some woman who apparently just walked in from the street, as they did. It would not be hard to locate the shop and get more out of the proprietor. The picture was of a couple of hands. Its title, or subject matter, was something about Judas. The artist's name was Patterson. The canvas looked as though it came out of a dustbin. Then they had gone to the cocktail lounge of the Van Barth. It should not be hard to get another line on our character there. He certainly had the picture with him. He may even have checked it.

But the antique shop seemed a surefire bet. There would have been the usual long, pointless talk about the picture. Even if the proprietor did not know either the man or the woman customer, he must have heard enough to offer new leads regarding the clown we wanted. The very fact he had gone into the place, then bought nothing except this thing, something that looked like it belonged in an incinerator, this already gave our bystander an individual profile. I said: "What kind of a person would do that, buy a mess like that in some hole-in-the-wall?"

"I don't know. Hell, I'd do it myself, if I felt like it."

"Well, I wouldn't feel like it. But there's another line. We can surely get a lead on the artist. We'll probably find a few clips in our own morgue. It's possible the man we are looking for is a great admirer of this artist, whoever he is. We can locate Patterson and get the history of this particular picture. Two hands. A cinch. There may be thousands, millions of these canvases around the city, but when you come right down to it, each of them has been seen by somebody besides the genius who painted it, and somebody would be certain to recognize it from a good description. After that, we can trace it along to the present owner."

Earl had by now come out of his first shock. He looked, acted, sounded, and thought more like his natural self. "How are we going to find this man, ahead of the police?" he asked.

"What have we got two thousand people for?"

"Yes, of course. But doesn't that mean—after all—isn't that spreading suspicion just that much farther?"

I had already thought of a way to put the organization in motion without connecting it at all with the death of Pauline.

"No. I know how to avoid that."

He thought that over for a while. Then he said: "Why should you do this? Why do you stick your neck out? This is serious."

I knew him so well I had known, almost to the word, he would say that.

"I've done it before, haven't I? And more."

"Yes. I know. But I have a hell of a way of rewarding friendship like that. I merely seem to exact more of it. More risks. More sacrifices."

"Don't worry about me. You're the one who's in danger."

"I hope you're not. But I think you will be, giving me an alibi, and leading the search for this unknown party."

"I won't be leading the search. We want somebody else to do that. I stay in the background." I knew that Earl himself would go right on being our biggest headache. I thought it would be better to take the first hurdle now. "In the first place, I want to disassociate you from this business as far as possible. Don't you agree that's wise?" He nodded, and I slowly added, as an afterthought, "Then, when our comedian is located, we want an entirely different set of people to deal with him."

Earl looked up from the thick, hairy knuckles of the fingers he seemed to be studying. His face had never, even when he was most shaken, lost its jovial appearance. I wondered whether he had seemed to be smiling when he killed the woman, but of course he had been.

The question forming in that slow, unearthly mind of his at last boiled up. "By the way. What happens when we do locate this person?"

"That all depends. When the story breaks, he may go straight to the police. In that case our alibi stands, and our line is this: He says he saw you on the scene. What was he doing there, himself? That makes him as hot as you are. We'll make him even warmer. We already know, for instance, that he spent a large part of the evening with Pauline."

Earl's round, large, staring eyes showed no understanding for a moment, then they came to life. "By God, Steve. I wonder—no. Of course you mean that only to threaten him off."

I said: "Put it this way. If the case goes to trial, and he persists in being a witness, that's the line we'll raise. Your own movements are accounted for, you were with me. But what was he doing there? What about this and that?—all the things we are going to find out about him long in advance. The case against you won't stand up."

Earl knew I had omitted something big, and in his mind he laboriously set out to find what it was. I waited while he thought it over, knowing he couldn't miss. Presently, he said: "All right. But if he doesn't go to the police the minute this breaks? Then what?"

I didn't want him to become even more hysterical, and if that were possible, I didn't want him to be even upset. I said, dispassionately: "If we find him first, we must play it safe."

"Well. What does that mean?"

Elaborately, I explained: "We could have him watched, of course. But we'd never know how much he actually did or did not realize, would we? And we certainly wouldn't know what he'd do next."

"Well? I can see that."

"Well. What is there to do with a man like that? He's a constant threat to your safety, your position in life, your place in the world. He's a ceaseless menace to your very life. Can you put up with an intolerable situation like that?"

Earl gave me a long, wondering, sick, almost frightened regard.

"I don't like that," he said, harshly. "There has already been one accident. I don't want another one. No. Not if I know what you mean."

"You know what I mean."

"No. I'm still a man."

"Are you? There are millions of dollars involved, all because of your uncontrollable temper and your God-forsaken stupidity. Yours, yours, not mine. Besides being an idiot, are you a coward, too?"

He floundered around for a cigar, got one, and with my help, finally got it going. Then, finally, he sounded a raw croak: "I won't see a man killed in cold blood." And as though he'd read my thoughts he added, "Nor take any part in it, either."

I said, reasonably: "I don't understand you. You know what kind of a world this is. You have always been a solid part of it. You know what anyone in Devers & Blair, Jennett-Donohue, Beacon, anyone above an M.E. in any of those houses would certainly do to you if he could reach out at night and safely push a button—"

"No. I wouldn't, myself. And I don't think they would, either."

He was wrong, of course, but there was no use arguing with a middle-aged child prodigy. I knew that by tomorrow he would see this thing in its true light.

"Well, it needn't come to that. That was just a suggestion. But why are you so worried? You and I have already seen these things happen, and we have helped to commit just about everything else for a lot less money. Why are you so sensitive now?"

He seemed to gag.

"Did we ever before go as far as this?"

"You were never in this spot before. Were you?" Now he looked really ghastly. He couldn't even speak. By God, he would have to be watched like a hawk and nursed every minute. "Let me ask you, Earl, are you ready to retire to a penitentiary and write your memoirs, for the sake of your morals? Or are you ready to grow up and be a man in a man's world, take your full responsibilities along with the rewards?" I liked Earl more than I had ever liked any person on earth except my mother, I really liked him, and I had to get both of us out of this at any cost. "No, we never went this far before. And we will never, if we use our heads, ever have to go this far again."

Earl absently drew at his cigar. "Death by poverty, famine, plague, war, I suppose that is on such a big scale the responsibility rests nowhere, although I personally have always fought against all of these things, in a number of magazines dedicated to wiping out each one of them, separately, and in some cases, in vehicles combating all of them together. But a personal death, the death of a definite individual. That is quite different."

He had reduced himself to the intellectual status of our own writers, a curious thing I had seen happen before. I risked it, and said: "We could take a chance on some simpler way, maybe. But there is more at stake than your private morals,

personal philosophy, or individual life. The whole damned organization is at stake. If you're wiped out, so is that. When
you go, the entire outfit goes. A flood of factory-manufac-
tured nonsense swamps the market."

Earl stood up and paced slowly across the room. It was a
long time before he answered me.

"I can be replaced, Steve. I'm just a cog. A good one, I
know, but still only a cog."

This was better. This was more like it. I said, knowing him:
"Yes, but when you break, a lot of others break, too. Whenever a big thing like this goes to pieces—and that is what
could happen—a hell of a lot of innocent people, their plans,
their homes, their dreams and aspirations, the future of their
children, all of that can go to pieces with it. Myself, for instance."

He gave me one quick glance. But I had gambled that he
was a sucker for the greatest good to the most people. And
after a long, long while he spoke, and I knew that at heart he
was really sound.

"Well, all right," he said. "I understand, Steve. I guess what
has to be, has to be."

George Stroud VI

T HE AWFULNESS of Monday morning is the world's great common denominator. To the millionaire and the coolie it is the same, because there can be nothing worse.

But I was only fifteen minutes behind the big clock when I sat down to breakfast, commenting that this morning's prunes had grown up very fast from the baby raisins in last night's cake. The table rhythmically shook and vibrated under Georgia's steadily drumming feet. It came to me again that a child drinking milk has the same vacant, contented expression of the well-fed cow who originally gave it. There is a real spiritual kinship there.

It was a fine sunny morning, like real spring, spring for keeps. I was beginning my second cup of coffee, and planning this year's gardening, when Georgette said: "George, have you looked at the paper? There's a dreadful story about a woman we met, I think. At Janoth's."

She waited while I picked up the paper. I didn't have to search. Pauline Delos had been found murdered. It was the leading story on page one.

Not understanding it, and not believing it, I read the headlines twice. But the picture was of Pauline.

The story said her body had been discovered at about noon on Sunday, and her death had been fixed at around ten o'clock on the night before. Saturday. I had left her at about that hour.

"Isn't that the same one?" Georgette asked.

"Yes," I said. "Yes."

She had been beaten to death with a heavy glass decanter. No arrest had been made. Her immediate friends were being questioned; Earl Janoth was one of them, the story went, but the publisher had not seen her for a number of days. He himself had spent the evening dining with acquaintances, and after dinner had spent several hours discussing business matters with an associate.

"A horrible story, isn't it?" said Georgette.

"Yes."

"Aren't you going to finish your coffee? George?"

"Yes?"

"You'd better finish your coffee, and then I'll drive you to the station."

"Yes. All right."

"Is something the matter?"

"No, of course not."

"Well, heavens. Don't look so grim."

I smiled.

"By the way," she went on. "I didn't tell you I liked that new picture you brought home. The one of the two hands. But it's in terrible condition, isn't it?"

"Yes, it is."

"It's another Patterson, isn't it?"

A hundred alarm bells were steadily ringing inside of me.

"Well, perhaps."

"Pity's sake, George, you don't have to be so monosyllabic, do you? Can't you say anything but 'yes,' 'no,' 'perhaps'? Is something the matter?"

"No. Nothing's the matter."

"Where did you get this new canvas?"

"Why, I just picked it up."

I knew quite well I had seen Earl entering that building at ten o'clock on Saturday evening. She was alive when they passed into it. He now claimed he had not seen her for several days. Why? There could be only one answer.

But had he recognized me?

Whether he had or not, where did I stand? To become involved would bring me at once into the fullest and fiercest kind of spotlight. And that meant, to begin with, wrecking Georgette, Georgia, my home, my life.

It would also place me on the scene of the murder. That I did not like at all. Nothing would cover Janoth better.

Yet he almost surely knew someone had at least seen him there. Or did he imagine no one had?

"George?"

"Yes?"

"I asked you if you knew much about this Pauline Delos?"

"Very little."

"Goodness. You certainly aren't very talkative this morning."

I smiled again, swallowed the rest of my coffee, and said: "It is a ghastly business, isn't it?"

Somehow Georgia got packed off to school, and somehow I got down to the station. On the train going into town I read every newspaper, virtually memorizing what was known of the death, but gathering no real additional information.

At the office I went straight to my own room, and the moment I got there my secretary told me Steve Hagen had called and asked that I see him as soon as I got in.

I went at once to the thirty-second floor.

Hagen was a hard, dark little man whose soul had been hit by lightning, which he'd liked. His mother was a bank vault, and his father an International Business Machine. I knew he was almost as loyal to Janoth as to himself.

After we said hello and made about one casual remark, he said he would like me to undertake a special assignment.

"Anything you have on the fire downstairs at the moment," he said, "let it go. This is more important. Have you anything special, at this moment?"

"Nothing." Then because it could not be avoided, plausibly, I said: "By the way, I've just read about the Pauline Delos business. It's pretty damn awful. Have you any idea—?"

Steve's confirmation was short and cold. "Yes, it's bad. I have no idea about it."

"I suppose Earl is, well—"

"He is. But I don't really know any more about it than you do."

He looked around the top of his desk and located some notes. He raked them together, looked them over, and then turned again to me. He paused, in a way that indicated we were now about to go to work.

"We have a job on our hands, not hard but delicate, and it seems you are about the very best man on the staff to direct it." I looked at him, waiting, and he went on. "In essence, the job is this: We want to locate somebody unknown to us. Really, it's a missing person job." He waited again, and when I said nothing, he asked: "Would that be all right with you?"

"Of course. Who is it?"

"We don't know."

"Well?"

He ruffled his notes.

"The person we want went into some Third Avenue bar and grill by the name of Gil's last Saturday afternoon. He was accompanied by a rather striking blonde, also unidentified. They later went to a Third Avenue antique shop. In fact, several of them. But in one of them he bought a picture called *Judas*, or something to that effect. He bought the picture from the dealer, overbidding another customer, a woman who also wanted to buy it. The picture was by an artist named Patterson. According to the morgue," Steve Hagen pushed across a thin heavy-paper envelope from our own files, "this Louise Patterson was fairly well known ten or twelve years ago. You can read up on all that for yourself. But the picture bought by the man we want depicted two hands, I believe, and was in rather bad condition. I don't know what he paid for it. Later, he and the woman with him went to the cocktail lounge of the Van Barth for a few drinks. It is possible he checked the picture there, or he may have had it right with him."

No, I hadn't. I'd left it in the car. Steve stopped, and looked at me. My tongue felt like sandpaper. I asked: "Why do you want this man?"

Steve clasped his hands in back of his neck and gazed off into space, through the wide blank windows of the thirty-second floor. From where we sat, we could see about a hundred miles of New York and New Jersey countryside.

When he again turned to me he was a good self-portrait of candor. Even his voice was a good phonographic reproduction of the slightly confidential friend.

"Frankly, we don't know ourselves."

This went over me like a cold wind.

"You must have some idea. Otherwise, why bother?"

"Yes, we have an idea. But it's nothing definite. We think our party is an important figure, in fact a vital one, in a business and political conspiracy that has reached simply colossal proportions. Our subject is not necessarily a big fellow in his own right, but we have reason to believe he's the payoff man between an industrial syndicate and a political machine, the one man who really knows the entire set-up. We believe we can crack the whole situation, when we find him."

So Earl had gone straight to Hagen. Hagen would then be the business associate who provided the alibi. But what did they want with George Stroud?

It was plain Earl knew he had been seen, and afraid he had been recognized. I could imagine how he would feel.

"Pretty vague, Steve," I said. "Can't you give me more?"

"No. You're right, it is vague. Our information is based entirely on rumors and tips and certain, well, striking coincidences. When we locate our man, then we'll have something definite for the first time."

"What's in it? A story for *Crimeways*?"

Hagen appeared to give that question a good deal of thought. He said, finally, and with apparent reluctance: "I don't think so. I don't know right now what our angle will be when we have it. We might want to give it a big play in one of our books, eventually. Or we might decide to use it in some entirely different way. That's up in the air."

I began to have the shadowy outline of a theory. I tested it.

"Who else is in on this? Should we co-operate with anyone? The cops, for instance?"

Cautiously, and with regret, Steve told me: "Absolutely not. This is our story, exclusively. It must stay that way. You will have to go to other agencies for information, naturally. But you get it only, you don't give it. Is that perfectly clear?"

It was beginning to be. "Quite clear."

"Now, do you think you can knock together a staff, just as large as you want, and locate this person? The only additional information I have is that his name may be George Chester, and he's of average build and height, weight one-forty to one-eighty. It's possible he's in advertising. But your best lead is this place called Gil's, the shop where he bought the picture, and the bar of the Van Barth. And that picture, perhaps the artist. I have a feeling the picture alone might give us the break."

"It shouldn't be impossible," I said.

"We want this guy in a hurry. Can you do it?"

If I didn't, someone else would. It would have to be me. "I've done it before."

"Yes. That's why you're elected."

"What do I do when I find this person?"

"Nothing." Steve's voice was pleasant, but emphatic. "Just let me know his name, and where he can be found. That's all."

It was like leaning over the ledge of one of these thirty-second floor windows and looking down into the street below. I always had to take just one more look.

"What happens when we locate him? What's the next step?"

"Just leave that to me." Hagen stared at me, coldly and levelly, and I stared back. I saw, in those eyes, there was no room for doubt at all. Janoth knew the danger he was in, Hagen knew it, and for Hagen there was literally no limit. None. Furthermore, this little stick of dynamite was intelligent, and he had his own ways, his private means.

"Now, this assignment has the right-of-way over everything, George. You can raid any magazine, use any bureau, any editor or correspondent, all the resources we have. And you're in charge."

I stood up and scooped together the notes I had taken. The squeeze felt tangible as a vise. My personal life would be destroyed if I ran to the cops. Death if Hagen and his special friends caught up with me.

"All right, Steve," I said. "I take it I have absolute carte blanche."

"You have. Expense, personnel, everything." He waved toward the windows overlooking about ten million people. "Our man is somewhere out there. It's a simple job. Get him."

I looked out of the windows myself. There was a lot of territory out there. A nation within a nation. If I picked the right kind of a staff, twisted the investigation where I could, jammed it where I had to, pushed it hard where it was safe, it might be a very, very, very long time before they found George Stroud.

George Stroud VII

I HATED to interrupt work on the coming issues of our own book, and so I decided to draw upon all the others, when needed, as evenly as possible.

But I determined to work Roy into it. Bert Finch, Tony, Nat, Sydney, and the rest of them would never miss either of us. And although I liked Roy personally, I could also count upon him to throw a most complicated monkey-wrench into the simplest mechanism. Leon Temple, too, seemed safe enough. And Edward Orlin of *Futureways*, a plodding, rather wooden esthete, precisely unfitted for the present job. He would be working for George Stroud, in the finest sense.

I told Roy about the new assignment, explained its urgency, and then I put it up to him. I simply had to have someone in charge at the office, constantly. This might be, very likely would be, a round-the-clock job. That meant there would have to be another man to share the responsibility.

Roy was distantly interested, and even impressed. "This takes precedence over everything?"

I nodded.

"All right. I'm in. Where do we start?"

"Let me line up the legmen first. Then we'll see."

Fifteen minutes later I had the nucleus of the staff gathered in my office. In addition to Roy and Leon, there were seven men and two women drawn from other magazines and departments. Edward Orlin, rather huge and dark and fat; Phillip Best of *Newsways*, a small, acrid, wire-haired encyclopedia. The two women, Louella Metcalf and Janet Clark, were included if we needed feminine reserves. Louella, drawn from *The Sexes*, was a tiny, earnest, appealing creature, the most persistent and transparent liar I have ever known. Janet was a very simple, eager, large-boned brunette whose last assignment had been with *Homeways*; she did every job about four times over, eventually doing it very well. Don Klausmeyer of *Personalities* and Mike Felch of *Fashions* had also been conscripted, and one man each from *Commerce*, *Sportland*, and the auditing department. They would do for a convincing start.

From now on, everything would have to look good. Better than good. Perfect. I gave them a crisp, businesslike explanation.

"You are being asked to take on a unique and rather strange job," I said. "It has to be done quickly, and as quietly as possible. I know you can do it.

"We have been given a blank check as far as the resources of the organization are concerned. If you need help on your particular assignment, help of any sort, you can have it. If it's a routine matter, simply go to the department that can give it. If it's something special, come either to me, or to Roy, here, who will be in charge of the work whenever for some reason I have to be elsewhere myself.

"We are looking for somebody. We don't know much about this person, who he is, where he lives. We don't even know his name. His name may be George Chester, but that is doubtful. It is possible he is in the advertising business, and that will be your job, Harry." I said this to Harry Slater, the fellow from *Commerce*. "You will comb the advertising agencies, clubs, if necessary the advertising departments of first the metropolitan newspapers and magazines, then those farther out. If you have to go that far, you will need a dozen or so more men to help you. You are in complete charge of that line of investigation." Harry's inquiries were safe, and they could also be impressive. I added: "Take as many people as you need. Cross-check with us regularly, for the additional information about our man that will be steadily coming in from all the other avenues we will be exploring at the same time. And that applies to all of you.

"We not only don't know this man's right name or where he lives—and that will be your job, Alvin." This was Alvin Dealey, from the auditing department. "Check all real estate registers in this area, all tax records, public utilities, and all phone books of cities within, say, three or four hundred miles, for George Chester, and any other names we give you. Take as many researchers as you need.

"Now, as I said, we not only don't know this man's name or whereabouts, but we haven't even got any kind of a phys-

ical description of him. Just that he is of average height, say
five nine to eleven, and average build. Probably between one-
forty and one-eighty.

"But there are a few facts we have to go upon. He is an
habitué of a place on Third Avenue called Gil's. Here is a
description of the place." I gave it, but stayed strictly within
the memo as given by Steve Hagen. "This man was in that
place, wherever it is, last Saturday afternoon. At that time he
was there with a woman we know to be a good-looking
blonde. Probably he goes there regularly. That will be your
job, Ed. You will find this restaurant, night club, saloon, or
whatever it is, and when you do you will stay there until our
man comes into it." Ed Orlin's swarthy and rather flabby face
betrayed, just for an instant, amazement and incipient distaste.

"On the same evening our subject went into an antique
shop, also on Third Avenue. He went into several, but there
is one in particular we want, which shouldn't be hard to find.
You will find it, Phil. Because the fellow we are looking for
bought a picture, unframed, while he was in the place, and he
bought it after outbidding another customer, a woman." I
did not elaborate by a hairsbreadth beyond Steve's written
memo. "The canvas was by an artist named Louise Patterson,
it depicted two hands, was in bad condition, and the name of
it, or the subject matter, had something to do with Judas. The
dealer is certain to remember the incident. You can get an
accurate description of our man from him. Perhaps he knows
him, and can give us his actual identity.

"Don, here is our file on this Louise Patterson. There is a
possibility that this picture can be traced from the artist to the
dealer and from him to our unknown. Look up Patterson, or
if she's dead, look up her friends. Somebody will remember
that canvas, what became of it, may even know who has it
now. Find out." I had suddenly the sick and horrid realization
I would have to destroy that picture. "Perhaps the man we
are looking for is an art collector, even a Patterson enthusiast.

"Leon, I want you and Janet to go to the bar of the Van
Barth, where this same blonde went with this same person,
on the same evening. At that time he had the picture, and
perhaps he checked it. Find out. Question the bartenders, the
checkroom attendants for all they can give you regarding the

man, and then I guess you'd better stay right there and wait for him to turn up, since he's probably a regular there, as well as Gil's. You may have to be around for several days and if so you will have to be relieved by Louella and Dick Englund."

Leon and Janet looked as though they might not care to be relieved, while Louella and Dick perceptibly brightened. It was almost a pleasure to dispense such largesse. I wished them many a pleasant hour while they awaited my arrival.

"That is about all I have to give you now," I concluded. "Do you all understand your immediate assignments?" Apparently, the lieutenants in charge of the hunt for George Stroud all did, for none of them said anything. "Well, are there any questions?"

Edward Orlin had one. "Why are we looking for this man?"

"All I know about that," I said, "is the fact that he is the intermediary figure in one of the biggest political-industrial steals in history. That is, he is the connecting link, and we need him to establish the fact of this conspiracy. Our man is the payoff man."

Ed Orlin took this information and seemed to retire behind a wall of thought to eat and digest it. Alvin Dealey earnestly asked: "How far can we go in drawing upon the police for information?"

"You can draw upon them, but you are not to tell them anything at all," I said, flatly. "This is our story, in the first place, and we intend to keep it ours. In the second place, I told you there is a political tie-up here. The police machinery we go to may be all right at one end, ours, but we don't know and we have no control over the other end of that machine. Is that clear?"

Alvin nodded. And then the shrewd, rather womanish voice of Phillip Best cut in. "All of these circumstances you have given us concern last Saturday," he said. "That was the night Pauline Delos was killed. Everyone knows what that means. Is there any connection?"

"Not as far as I know, Phil," I said. "This is purely a big-time business scandal that Hagen himself and a few others have been digging into for some time past. Now, it's due to break." I paused for a moment, to let this very thin logic take what hold it could. "As far as I understand it, Earl intends to go through with this story, regardless of the ghastly business last Saturday night."

Phil's small gray eyes bored through his rimless glasses. "I just thought, it's quite a coincidence," he said. I let that pass without even looking at it, and he added: "Am I to make inquiries about the woman who was with the man?"

"You will all have to do that." I had no doubt of what they would discover. Yet even delay seemed in my favor, and I strongly reminded them, "But we are not looking for the woman, or any other outside person. It is the man we want, and only the man."

I let my eyes move slowly over them, estimating their reactions. As far as I could see, they accepted the story. More important, they seemed to give credit to my counterfeit assurance and determination.

"All right," I said. "If there are no more questions, suppose you intellectual tramps get the hell out of here and go to work." As they got up, reviewing the notes they had taken, and stuffed them into their pockets, I added, "And don't fail to report back, either in person or by phone. Soon, and often. Either to Roy or myself."

When they had all gone, except Roy, he got up from his chair beside me at the desk. He walked around in front of it, then crossed to the wall facing it, hands thrust into his pockets. He leaned against the wall, staring at the carpet. Presently, he said: "This is a crazy affair. I can't help feeling that Phil somehow hit the nail on the head. There is a curious connection there, I'm certain, the fact that all of this happened last Saturday."

I waited, with a face made perfectly blank.

"I don't mean it has any connection with that frightful business about Pauline Delos," he went on, thoughtfully. "Of course it hasn't. That would be a little too obvious. But I can't help thinking that something, I don't know what, something happened last week on Friday or Saturday, perhaps while Janoth was in Washington, or certainly a few days before, or even last night, Sunday, that would really explain why we are looking for this mysterious, art-collecting stranger at this moment, and in such a hurry. Don't you think so?"

"Sounds logical," I said.

"Damn right it's logical. It seems to me, we would do well to comb the outstanding news items of the last two weeks, particularly the last five or six days, and see what there is that might concern Janoth. This Jennett-Donohue proposition, for instance. Perhaps they are actually planning to add those new books in our field. That would seriously bother Earl, don't you think?"

Roy was all right. He was doing his level best.

"You may be right. And again it may be something else, far deeper, not quite so apparent. Suppose you follow up that general line? But at the same time, I can't do anything except work from the facts supplied to me."

Actually, I was at work upon a hazy plan that seemed a second line of defense, should it come to that. It amounted to a counterattack. The problem, if the situation got really bad, was this: How to place Janoth at the scene of the killing, through some third, independent witness, or through evidence not related to myself. Somewhere in that fatal detour his car had been noted, he himself had been seen and marked. If I had to fight fire with fire, somehow, surely he could be connected.

But it would never come to that. The gears being shifted, the wheels beginning to move in this hunt for me were big and smooth and infinitely powered, but they were also blind. Blind, clumsy, and unreasoning. "No, you have to work with the data you've been given," Roy admitted. "But I think it would be a good idea if I did follow up my hunch. I'll see if we haven't missed something in recent political developments."

At the same time that I gave him silent encouragement, I became aware of the picture above his head on the wall against which he leaned. It was as though it had suddenly screamed.

Of course. I had forgotten I had placed that Patterson there, two years ago. I had bought it at the Lewis Galleries, the profiles of two faces, showing only the brow, eyes, nose, lips, and chin of each. They confronted each other, distinctly Pattersonian. One of them showed an avaricious, the other a skeptical leer. I believe she had called it *Study in Fury*.

It was such a familiar landmark in my office that to take it away, now, would be fatal. But as I looked at it and then looked away I really began to understand the danger in which I stood. It would have to stay there, though at any moment someone might make a connection. And there must be none, none at all, however slight.

"Yes," I told Roy, automatically, feeling the after-shock in fine points of perspiration all over me. "Why not do that? We may have missed something significant in business changes, as well as politics."

"I think it might simplify matters," he said, and moved away from the wall on which the picture hung. "Janoth was in Washington this week end, remember. Personally, I think there's a tie-up between that and this rush order we've been given."

Thoughtfully, Roy moved away from the wall, crossed the thickly carpeted floor, disappeared through the door leading to his own office.

When he had gone I sat for a long moment, staring at that thing on the wall. I had always liked it before.

But no. It had to stay there.

Edward Orlin

GIL'S TAVERN looked like just a dive on the outside, and also on the inside. Too bad I couldn't have been assigned to the Van Barth. Well, it couldn't be helped.

It was in the phone book, and not far off, so that part of it was all right. I walked there in twenty minutes.

I took along a copy of *War and Peace*, which I was rereading, and on the way I saw a new issue of *The Creative Quarterly*, which I bought.

It was a little after one o'clock when I got there, time for lunch, so I had it. The food was awful. But it would go on the expense account, and after I'd eaten I got out my notebook and put it down. Lunch, $1.50. Taxi, $1.00. I thought for a minute, wondering what Stroud would do if he ever came to a dive like this, then I added: Four highballs, $2.00.

After I'd finished my coffee and a slab of pie at least three days old I looked around. It was something dug up by an archeological expedition, all right. There was sawdust in the corners, and a big wreath on the wall in back of me, celebrating a recent banquet, I suppose: CONGRATULATIONS TO OUR PAL.

Then I saw the bar at the end of the long room. It was incredible. It looked as though a whole junkyard had been scooped up and dumped there. I saw wheels, swords, shovels, tin cans, bits of paper, flags, pictures, literally hundreds upon hundreds of things, just things.

After I paid for the 85¢ lunch, a gyp, and already I had indigestion, I picked up my Tolstoy and *The Creative Quarterly* and walked down to the bar.

The nearer I came to it the more things I saw, simply thousands of them. I sat down and noticed there was a big fellow about fifty years old, with staring, preoccupied eyes, in back of it. He came down the bar, and I saw that his eyes were looking at me but didn't quite focus. They were like dim electric lights in an empty room. His voice was a wordless grunt.

"A beer," I said. I noticed that he spilled some of it when

he put the glass down in front of me. His face really seemed almost ferocious. It was very strange, but none of my business. I had work to do. "Say, what've you got in back of the bar there? Looks like an explosion in a five-and-ten-cent store."

He didn't say anything for a couple of seconds, just looked me over, and now he seemed really sore about something.

"My personal museum," he said, shortly.

So that was what the memo meant. I was in the right place, no doubt about it.

"Quite a collection," I said. "Buy you a drink?"

He had a bottle on the bar by the time I finished speaking. Scotch, and one of the best brands, too. Well, it was a necessary part of the assignment. Made no difference to me; it went on the expense account.

He dropped the first jigger he picked up, left it where it fell, and only finally managed to fill the second one. But he didn't seem drunk. Just nervous.

"Luck," he said. He lifted the glass and the whisky was all gone, in five seconds, less than five seconds, almost in a flash. When he put down the jigger and picked up the bill I laid on the bar he noisily smacked his lips. "First of the day," he said. "That's always the best. Except for the last."

I sipped my beer, and when he laid down the change, he was charging 75¢ for his own Scotch, I said: "So that's your personal museum. What's in it?"

He turned and looked at it and he sounded much better. "Everything. You name it and I've got it. What's more, it's an experience what happened to me or my family."

"Sort of a petrified autobiography, is that it?"

"No, just my personal museum. I been around the world six times, and my folks before me been all over it. Farther than that. Name me one thing I haven't got in that museum, and the drinks are on me."

It was fantastic. I didn't see how I'd ever get any information out of this fellow. He was an idiot.

"All right," I said, humoring him. "Show me a locomotive."

He muttered something that sounded like, "Locomotive? Now, where did that locomotive get to." Then he reached away over in back of a football helmet, a stuffed bird, a bowl heaped to the brim with foreign coins, and a lot of odds and ends I couldn't even see, and when he turned around he laid a toy railroad engine on the bar. "This here locomotive," he confided, slapping it affectionately and leaning toward me, "was the only toy of mine what got saved out of the famous Third Avenue fire next to the carbarns fifty years ago. Saved it myself. I was six years old. They had nine roasts."

I finished my beer and stared at him, not sure whether he was trying to kid me or whether he was not only half drunk but completely out of his mind besides. If it was supposed to be humor, it was certainly corny, the incredibly childish slap-stick stuff that leaves me cold. Why couldn't I have gotten the Van Barth, where I could at least read in peace and comfort, without having to interview a schizophrenic, probably homicidal.

"That's fine," I said.

"Still runs, too," he assured me, and gave the key a twist, put the toy down on the bar, and let it run a few feet. It stopped when it bumped into *The Creative Review*. He actually sounded proud. "See? Still runs."

God, this was simply unbelievable. I might as well be back in the office.

The lunatic gravely put the toy back behind the bar, where I heard its spring motor expend itself, and when he turned around he wordlessly filled up our glasses again, mine with beer and his with Scotch. I was still more surprised when he tossed off his drink, then returned and absently paused in front of me, appearing to wait. For God's sake, did this fellow expect a free drink with every round? Not that it mattered. He had to be humored, I suppose. After I'd paid, and by now he seemed actually friendly, he asked: "Yes, sir. That's one of the best private museums in New York. Anything else you'd care to see?"

"You haven't got a crystal ball, have you?"

"Well, now, as it happens, I have." He brought out a big glass marble from a pile of rubbish surmounted by a crucifix and a shrunken head. "Funny how everybody wants to see that locomotive, or sometimes it's the airplane or the steamroller, and usually they ask to see the crystal ball. Now this here little globe I picked up in Calcutta. I went to a Hindu gypsy what told fortunes, and he seen in the glass that I was in danger of drowning. So I jumped the ship I was on and went on the beach awhile, and not two days passed before that boat went down with all hands. So I says to myself, Holy Smoke, how long's this been going on? I never put much stock in that stuff before, see? So I went back to this fellow, and I says, I'd like to have that there gadget. And he says, in his own language of course, this been in his family for generations after generations and he can't part with it."

This juvenile nonsense went on and on. My God, I thought it would never stop. And I had to look as though I were interested. Finally it got so boring I couldn't stand any more of it. I said: "Well, I wish you'd look into that globe and see if you can locate a friend of mine for me."

"That's a funny thing. When I finally paid the two thousand rupees he wanted, and I took it back to my hotel, I couldn't make the damn thing work. And never could since."

"Never mind," I said. "Have another drink." He put the marble away and drew another beer and poured himself another Scotch. I couldn't see how a fellow like this stayed in business for more than a week.

Before he could put his drink away I went on: "A friend of mine I haven't seen for years comes in here sometimes, and I wonder if you know him. I'd like to see him again. Maybe you know what would be a good time to find him here."

The man's eyes went absolutely blank.

"What's his name?"

"George Chester."

"George Chester." He stared at the far end of the room, apparently thinking, and a little of the mask fell away from him. "That name I don't know. Mostly, I don't know their names, anyway. What's he look like?"

"Oh, medium height and build," I said. "A mutual acquaintance told me he saw him in here late last Saturday afternoon. With a good-looking blonde."

He threw the shot of whisky into his mouth and I don't believe the glass even touched his lips. Didn't this fellow ever take a chaser? He frowned and paused.

"I think I know who you mean. Clean-cut, brown-haired fellow?"

"I guess you could call him that."

"I remember that blonde. She was something for the books. She wanted to see the raven that fellow wrote about, nevermore quoth he. So I let her have a look at it. Yes, they were in here a couple of nights ago, but he don't come around here very often. Four or five years ago he was in here lots, almost every night. Smart, too. Many's the time I used to show him my museum, until me and some hacker had to pick him up and carry him out. One night he wouldn't go home at all, he wanted to sleep right inside the museum. 'Book me the royal suite on your ocean liner, Gil,' he kept saying. We got him home all right. But that was several years ago." He looked at me with sharp interest. "Friend of yours?"

I nodded. "We used to work for the same advertising agency."

He puzzled some more. "I don't think he did then," he decided. "He worked for some newspaper, and before that he and his wife used to run a joint upstate, the same as mine. No museum, of course. Seems to me his name might have been George Chester, at that. I had to garage his car once or twice when he had too much. But he gradually stopped coming in. I don't think he was here more than twice in the last three or four months. But he might come in any time, you never can tell. Very intelligent fellow. What they call eccentric."

"Maybe I could reach him through the blonde."

"Maybe."

"Who is she, do you know?"

This time his whole face went blank. "No idea, sir."

He moved up the bar to serve some customers who had just entered, and I opened *The Creative Review*. There was a promising revaluation of Henry James I would have to read, though I knew the inevitable shortcomings of the man who wrote it. A long article on Tibetan dance ritual that looked quite good.

I finished my beer and went to a phone booth. I called the office and asked for Stroud, but got Cordette instead.

"Where's Stroud?" I asked.

"Out. Who's this?"

"Ed Orlin. I'm at Gil's Tavern."

"Found it, did you? Get the right one?"

"It's the right one, no question. And what a dive."

"Pick up anything?"

"Our man was here last Saturday, all right, and with the blonde."

"Fine. Let's have it."

"There isn't much. The bartender isn't sure of his name, because the guy doesn't come in here any more." I let that sink in, for a moment. I certainly hoped to get called off this drab saloon and that boring imbecile behind the bar. "But he thinks his name may actually be George Chester. He has been described by the bartender, who is either a half-wit or an out-right lunatic himself, as very intelligent and eccentric. Believe me, Chester is probably just the opposite."

"Why?"

"It's that kind of a place. Eccentric, yes, but only a moron would come into a dump like this and spend hours talking to the fellow that runs this menagerie."

"Go on."

"The physical description we have does not seem far wrong, but there's nothing to add to it, except that he's brown-haired and clean-cut."

"All right. What else? Any line on the blonde?"

"Nothing."

"That certainly isn't much, is it?"

"Well, wait. Our man is unquestionably a dipsomaniac. Four or five years ago he was in here every night and had to be sent home in a taxi. At that time he was a newspaperman, the bartender believes, and he never heard of him as working for an advertising concern. And before he was a newspaper-man he ran a tavern somewhere upstate, with his wife."

"A drunk. Formerly, with his wife, a tavern proprietor. Probably a newspaperman, eccentric, clean-cut in appearance. It isn't much, but it's something. Is that all?"

"That's all. And our baby hasn't been in here more than twice in the last eight or ten months. So what should I do? Come back to the office?"

There was a pause, and I had a moment of hope.

"I think not, Ed. He was in there two days ago, he might not wait so long before he returns. And you can work on the bartender some more. Psychoanalyze him for more details. Have a few drinks with him."

Oh, my God.

"Listen, this fellow is a human blotter."

"All right, get drunk with him, if you have to. But not too drunk. Try some of the other customers. Anyway, stick around until we call you back, or send a relief. What's the address and the phone number?"

I gave them to him.

"All right, Ed. And if you get anything more, call us at once. Remember, this is a hurry-up job."

I hoped so. I went back to the bar, already a little dizzy on the beers. It would be impossible to concentrate on the magazine, which demanded an absolutely clear head. One of the customers was roaring at the bartender, "All right, admit you ain't got it. I ask you, show me a *mot de passe* out of that famous museum, so-called."

"No double-talk allowed. You want to see something, you got to ask for it in plain language."

"That is plain language. Plain, ordinary French. Admit it, and give us a beer. You just ain't got one."

"All right, all right, I'll give you a beer. But what is this here thing? How do you spell it? Only don't ask for nothing in French again. Not in here, see?"

Well, there was a newspaper at the end of the bar, thank God. This morning's, but it could kill a couple of hours.

George Stroud VIII

W HEN they all cleared out of my office on their various assignments, I called in Emory Mafferson. His plump face was in perpetual mourning, his brain was a seething chaos, his brown eyes seemed always trying to escape from behind those heavy glasses, and I don't believe he could see more than ten feet in front of him, but somewhere in Emory I felt there was a solid newspaperman and a lyric investigator.

"How are you coming along with Funded Individuals?" I asked him.

"All right. I've explained it all to Bert, and we're finishing the article together."

"Sure Bert understands it?"

Emory's face took a turn for the worse.

"As well as I do," he finally said. "Maybe better. You know, I can't help feeling there's something sound in back of that idea. It's a new, revolutionary vision in the field of social security."

"Well, what's troubling you?"

"How can you have a revolution without a revolution?"

"Just leave that to Bert Finch. He has your *Futureways* notes, and he can interpret the data as far as you've gone with it. Suppose you let Bert carry on alone from here?"

Emory sighed.

If I understood him, many an afternoon supposedly spent in scholarly research at the library or interviewing some insurance expert had found him instead at Belmont, the Yankee Stadium, possibly home in bed.

"All good things have to come to an end sometime, Emory."

"I suppose so."

I came abruptly to the point. "Right now I have got to work on a special, outside job. At the same time, one of the most sensational murders of the year has occurred, and beyond a doubt it will assume even greater proportions and sometime *Crimeways* will want a big story about it."

"Delos?"

I nodded.

"And I don't want *Crimeways* left at the post. You wanted to go on our regular staff. This can start you off. Suppose you go down to Center Street, Homicide Bureau, and pick up everything you can, as and when it happens. The minute you've got it, phone it to me. I'll be busy with this other assignment, but I want to be up-to-date on the Delos story, every phase of it."

Emory looked more stunned and haggard than ever. Those brown goldfish eyes swam three times around the bowl of his glasses.

"God, you don't expect me to break this thing alone, do you?"

"Of course not. If we wanted to break it, we'd give it a big play, thirty or forty legmen. I just want all the facts ready when the case is broken, by the cops. All you have to do is keep in close touch with developments. And report back to me, and only me, regularly. Got it?"

Emory looked relieved, and said he understood. He got up to go. My private detective force wasn't much bigger standing than sitting, and looked even less impressive.

"What have you got for me to go on?" he asked.

"Nothing. Just what you have, no more."

"Will this be all right with Bert?"

I said I'd arrange that, and sent him on his way. After he'd gone I sat and looked at that Patterson *Study in Fury* on the opposite wall, facing me, and did nothing but think.

The signature was quite visible, and even moving the canvas downward into the lower part of the frame would not obscure it. I did not believe it possible, but there might, also, be others in the Janoth organization who would recognize a Patterson simply from the style.

I could not remove that picture. Even if I changed it for another, the change would be noticed by someone. Maybe not by Roy, the writers, or the reporters, but by someone. Lucille or one of the other girls, somebody else's secretary, some research worker.

If only that picture weren't there. And above all, if only I had never brought home *The Temptation of St. Judas.*

Because Georgette had seen the new picture.

Hagen was certain whoever had bought it could be traced through it. If he thought it necessary, he would insist upon a far more intensive search for it than the one I had, as a safe-guard, assigned Don Klausmeyer to undertake. I knew Don would never trace it clear through from the artist to the dealer, let alone to me. But Hagen might at any moment take independent steps; I could think of some, myself, that would be dangerous.

I had better destroy the *Temptation*.

If somebody did his job too well, if Hagen went to work on his own, if some real information got to him before I could short-circuit it, that thing would nail me cold. I must get rid of it.

I put on my hat and went into Roy's office, with two half-formed ideas, to destroy that picture now and to find a means of locating Earl Janoth at 58 East through other witnesses. I could trust no one but myself with either of these jobs.

"I'm going out on a lead, Roy," I told him. "Take over for a while. And by the way, I've assigned somebody to follow the Delos murder. We'll want to handle it in an early issue, don't you think?" He nodded thoughtfully. "I've assigned Mafferson."

He nodded again, dryly and remotely. "I believe Janoth will want it followed, at least," he said. "By the way, I'm having the usual missing-person index prepared."

This was a crisscross of the data that came in, as rapidly as it came, simplified for easy reference. I had myself, at one time or another, helped to simplify it.

Over my shoulder I said, briskly: "That's the stuff."

I went out to the elevators, rode down and crossed the street to the garage. I decided to get the car, drive out to Marble Road and burn up that business right now.

In the garage, I met Earl Janoth's chauffeur, Billy, coming out of it. He had just brought in Janoth's car. I had ridden in it perhaps a dozen times, and now he nodded, impassively pleasant.

"Hello, Mr. Stroud."

"Hello, Billy."

We passed each other, and I felt suddenly cold and aware. There were two people Janoth trusted without limit, Steve

Hagen and Billy, his physical shadow. When and if the missing unknown was located, Billy would be the errand boy sent to execute the final decision. He would be the man. He didn't know it, but I knew it.

Inside the garage an attendant was polishing Janoth's already shining Cadillac. I walked up to him, memorizing the car's license. Somebody else, somewhere, had seen it that night, and Earl, I hoped, and seen them where they were not supposed to be.

"Want your car, Mr. Stroud?"

I said hello and told him I did. I had often stopped for a minute or two with this particular attendant, talking about baseball, horses, whisky, or women.

"Got a little errand to do this afternoon," I said, and then gave him a narrow smile. "I'll bet this bus is giving you plenty of trouble."

I got a knowing grin in return.

"Not exactly trouble," he confided. "But the cops have been giving it a going over. Us too. Was it cleaned since Saturday night? How long was it out Saturday night? Did I notice the gas, the mileage, anything peculiar? Hell, we guys never pay any attention to things like that. Except, of course, we know it wasn't washed, and it wasn't even gassed."

He called to another attendant to bring down my car, and while I waited for it, I asked: "I suppose the cops third degree'd the chauffeur?"

"Sure. A couple of them tackled him again a few minutes ago. But the driver's got nothing to worry about. Neither has Mr. Janoth. They drove to a dinner somewhere and then they drove straight to some other place. Your friend Mr. Hagen's. It checks okay with us. They never garage this car here nights or week ends, so what would we know about it? But I don't mind cops. Only, I don't like that driver. Nothing I could say, exactly. Just, well."

He looked at me and I gave him an invisible signal in return and then my car was brought down.

I got into it and drove off, toward Marble Road. But I hadn't gone more than three blocks before I began to think it all over again, and this time in a different mood.

Why should I destroy that picture? I liked it. It was mine.

Who was the better man, Janoth or myself? I voted for myself. Why should I sacrifice my own property just because of
him? Who was he? Only another medium-sized wheel in the
big clock.

The big clock didn't like pictures, much. I did. This particular picture it had tossed into the dustbin. I had saved it from
oblivion, myself. Why should I throw it back?

There were lots of good pictures that were prevented from
being painted at all. If they couldn't be aborted, or lost, then
somebody like me was despatched to destroy them.

Just as Billy would be sent to destroy me. And why should
I play ball in a deadly set-up like that?

What would it get me to conform?

*Newsways, Commerce, Crimeways, Personalities, The Sexes,
Fashions, Futureways,* the whole organization was full and
overrunning with frustrated ex-artists, scientists, farmers, writers, explorers, poets, lawyers, doctors, musicians, all of whom
spent their lives conforming, instead. And conforming to
what? To a sort of overgrown, aimless, haphazard stenciling
apparatus that kept them running to psychoanalysts, sent
them to insane asylums, gave them high blood pressure, stomach ulcers, killed them off with cerebral hemorrhages and
heart failure, sometimes suicide. Why should I pay still more
tribute to this fatal machine? It would be easier and simpler
to get squashed stripping its gears than to be crushed helping
it along.

To hell with the big gadget. I was a dilettante by profession.
A pretty good one, I had always thought. I decided to stay in
that business.

I turned down a side street and drove toward 58 East. I
could make a compromise. That picture could be put out of
circulation, for the present. But it would really be a waste of
time to destroy it. That would mean only a brief reprieve, at
best. Its destruction was simply not worth the effort.

And I could beat the machine. The super-clock would go
on forever, it was too massive to be stopped. But it had no
brains, and I did. I could escape from it. Let Janoth, Hagen,
and Billy perish in its wheels. They loved it. They liked to
suffer. I didn't.

I drove past 58 East, and began to follow the course the

other car must have taken going away. Either Janoth had dismissed Billy when he arrived, and returned by taxi, or he had ordered Billy to come back later. In any case, Janoth had dined at the Waynes', according to all accounts, and then, as I knew, he had come to 58 East, and then of course he must have gone directly to Hagen's.

I followed the logical route to Hagen's. I saw two nearby cabstands. Janoth must have used one of them if he had returned by taxi, unless he had found a cruising cab somewhere between the two. He certainly would not have been so stupid as to pick one up near 58 East.

The farthest cabstand was the likeliest. I could begin there, with a photograph of Janoth, then try the nearer, and if necessary I could even check the bigger operators for cruisers picking up fares in the neighborhood on that evening. But that was a tall order for one man to cover.

From Hagen's, timing the drive, I went to the Waynes', then turned around and drove slowly back to 58 East. The route Earl must have followed took about thirty minutes. Allowing another thirty minutes for the fight to develop, that meant Earl was covering up about one hour. This checked with the facts known to me.

Perhaps he had stopped somewhere along the way, but if so, no likely place presented itself.

That gave me only two possible leads, a cab by which Earl may have made his getaway, or possibly some attendant at Pauline's or Hagen's.

It was pretty slim. But something.

I drove back to the office, garaged the car again, and went up to 2619. There was no one there, and no memos. I went straight on into 2618.

Roy, Leon Temple, and Janet Clark were there.

"Any luck?" Roy asked me.

"I don't know," I said.

"Well, we're starting to get some reports." Roy nodded with interest toward the cross-reference chart laid out on a big blackboard covering half of one wall. "Ed Orlin phoned a while ago. He located Gil's with no trouble and definitely placed the man and the woman there. Interesting stuff. I think we're getting somewhere."

"Fine," I said.

I went over to the board, topped with the caption: *X.*

In the column headed: "Names, Aliases," I read: *George Chester?*

Under "Appearance" it said: *Brown-haired, clean-cut, average height and build.*

I thought, thank you, Ed.

"Frequents": *Antique shops, Van Barth, Gil's. At one time frequented Gil's almost nightly.*

It was true, I had.

"Background": *Advertising? Newspapers? Formerly operated an upstate tavern-resort.*

Too close.

"Habits": *Collects pictures.*

"Character": *Eccentric, impractical. A pronounced drunk.*

This last heading was something that had been added by Roy in the Isleman and Sandler jobs. He imagined he had invented it, and valued it accordingly.

I said, standing beside the word-portrait of myself: "We seem to be getting somewhere."

"That isn't all," Roy told me. "Leon and Janet have just returned from the Van Barth with more. We were discussing it, before putting it on the board."

He looked at Leon, and Leon gave his information in neat, precise, third-person language.

"That's right," he said. "First of all it was established that Chester was in the lounge on Saturday night. He did not check the Judas picture he bought, but he was overheard talking about it with the woman accompanying him. And the woman with him was Pauline Delos."

I registered surprise.

"Are you sure?"

"No doubt about it, George. She was recognized by the waiter, the bartender, and the checkroom girl, from the pictures of her published in today's papers. Delos was in there Saturday night, with a man answering to the description on the board, and they were talking about a picture called *Judas* something-or-other. There can be no doubt about it." He looked at me for a long moment, in which I said nothing, then he finally asked: "I feel that's significant, don't you?

Doesn't this alter the whole character of the assignment we are on? Personally, I think it does. Somebody raised the very same question this morning, and now it looks as though he had been right."

I said: "That's logical. Do the police know Delos was in there Saturday night?"

"Of course. Everyone in the place promptly told them."

"Do the police know we are looking for the man with her?"

"No. But they are certainly looking for him, now. We didn't say anything, because we thought this was exclusive with us. But what should we do about it? We're looking for George Chester, and yet this Delos tie-up is terrific, seems to me."

I nodded, and lifted Roy's phone.

"Right," I said. When I had Steve Hagen I barked into the receiver: "Steve? Listen. The woman with our man was Pauline Delos."

The other end of the wire went dead for five, ten, fifteen, twenty seconds.

"Hello, Steve? Are you there? This is George Stroud. We have discovered that the woman who was with the person we want was Pauline Delos. Does this mean something?"

I looked at Roy, Janet, and Leon. They seemed merely expectant, with no second thoughts apparent in their faces. At the other end of the wire I heard what I thought was a faint sigh from Steve Hagen.

"Nothing in particular," he said, carefully. "I knew that she saw this go-between. Perhaps I should have told you. But the fact that she was with him that night does not concern the matter we have in hand. What we want, and what we've got to have, is the name and whereabouts of the man himself. Delos is a blind alley, as far as our investigation is concerned. The murder is one story. This is a different, unrelated one. Is that plain?"

I said I understood him perfectly, and after I broke the connection I repeated the explanation almost verbatim to the three people in the room.

Roy was complacent.

"Yes," he said. "But I said all along this was an issue related to some recent crisis, and now we know damn well it is."

He rose and went over to the blackboard, picked up some

chalk. I watched him as he wrote under "Associates": *Pauline Delos*. Where the line crossed "Antique shops," "Gil's," "Van Barth" he repeated the name. Then he began to add a new column.

"At the same time, Leon and Janet brought in something more tangible," he went on. "Tell George about it."

Leon's small and measured voice resumed the report. "When they left the cocktail lounge of the Van Barth, our subject forgot something and left it behind him."

Nothing about me moved except my lips.

"Yes?"

Leon nodded toward Roy's desk and his eyes indicated an envelope. I seemed to float toward it, wondering whether this had all been an extravagant, cold-blooded farce they had put together with Hagen, whether I had actually mislaid or forgotten something that gave me away altogether. But the envelope was blank.

"A handkerchief," I heard Leon say, as from a great distance. "It can probably be traced, because it's obviously expensive, and it has what I believe is an old laundry mark."

Of course. She had borrowed it. When she spilled her cocktail I had used it, then given it to her. And it had been left there.

I turned the envelope over and shook the handkerchief from the unsealed flap. Yes. I could even see, faintly, the old stain.

"I wouldn't touch it, George," said Leon. "We may be able to raise a few fingerprints. It's a very fine, smooth fabric."

So I had to do that. I picked up the handkerchief and unfolded it. And laid it down and spread it out, very carefully and cautiously.

"I imagine it already has plenty," I said. "The waitress's, the cashier's, yours, one more set won't matter." I inspected the familiar square of linen with grave attention. It was one of a lot I had bought at Blanton's & Dent's, about a year ago. And there was the faint, blurred, but recoverable laundry mark on a bit of the hem, several months old, for it must have been put there when I last spent a week in the city and sent some of my things to a midtown laundry. "Yes, I imagine this can be traced."

I refolded the handkerchief, stuffed it back into the envelope. I could now account for the presence of my own fingerprints, but I knew I could not save the handkerchief itself from the mill.

I handed the envelope to Leon.

"Do you want to take this to Sacher & Roberts?" That was the big commercial laboratory we used for such work. "Whatever they find, we'll put another team on it. I suppose Dick and Louella relieved you at the Van Barth?"

"Oh, sure. Our man comes in there once or twice a week, they said."

"We've got the fellow covered at this place called Gil's, and at the Van Barth," Roy pointed out. "He'll come back, and then we've got him."

I nodded, rather thoughtfully. I said: "Certainly. He'll return to one place or the other. Then that will be that."

I don't know how that conference broke up. I think Leon went on to Sacher & Roberts. I believe I left Roy making additional entries on the big progress-board. I told him to eat and get some rest when he'd finished, I would be leaving around seven.

If they actually brought out prints on that handkerchief, we would all have to volunteer our own, mine with the rest. That in itself I had taken care of. But for a long, long time in my own office I sat trying to remember whether my fingerprints could be found anywhere on Pauline's overnight bag. Such a duplication could not be explained away. Hardly.

I forced myself to relive that last day with Pauline. No. I had not touched that grip anywhere except on the handle, and Pauline's final touches had certainly smudged them all out.

Sometime in the afternoon I took a call from Don Klausmeyer.

"Oh, yes, Don," I said. "Any luck with Patterson?"

Don's slow, malicious, pedantic voice told me: "I had a little trouble, but I found her. I've been talking to her for about an hour, going over old catalogues of her shows, looking at her fifth-rate pictures, and trying to keep her four kids out of my hair."

"Okay. Shoot."

"I have turned up one very significant fact. Louise Patterson was the customer who bid, unsuccessfully, for her own picture in the dealer's shop that night. A friend saw her canvas there, told her about it, and it was Patterson's hope that she could buy it back for herself. God knows why."

"I see. Anything else?"

"Do you understand? It was Patterson herself, in the shop that night."

"I get it. And?"

"And she described the man who bought the picture, at great length. Are you ready to take it?"

"Let's have it."

"This is Patterson speaking. Quote. He was a smug, self-satisfied, smart-alecky bastard just like ten million other rubber-stamp sub-executives. He had brown hair, brown eyes, high cheekbones, symmetrical and lean features. His face looked as though he scrubbed and shaved it five times a day. He weighed between one sixty and one sixty-five. Gray tweed suit, dark blue hat and necktie. He knows pictures, says she, and is certainly familiar with the works of L. Patterson, which he doubtless collects, but only for their snob-appeal. Personally, I think the dame overestimates herself. She admits she's been forgotten for the last ten years. But to go on. Our man is a good deal of an exhibitionist. He imagines he is Superman and that is what he plays at being. The woman with him was beautiful if you like Lesbians in standard, Park Avenue models. Unquote. Got it?"

"Yes."

"Does it help?"

"Some," I said.

"I've been poking around the studio-loft she lives in—God what a paradise for rats and termites—looking at acres and acres of pictures. Artistically she's impossible." How would Don know? "But they reminded me of something I'm sure I've seen somewhere very recently. If I can only remember what it is, maybe I'll have another lead."

He laughed and I echoed him, but I was staring straight at *Study in Fury* on the wall opposite me.

"Maybe you will, but don't worry about it. I'll see you tomorrow."

When he hung up I stared at that picture, without really seeing it, for a long five minutes. Then I took my scribbled notes and went into Roy's empty office and duly entered Don's report on the chart. By now it was crystallizing into a very unpleasant definition of myself indeed. And after that, I took three good, recent photographs of Earl Janoth out of the morgue.

A little past seven o'clock Roy returned. We arranged about relieving each other on the following day and then I went out, feeling I'd had about all I could stand for the time being. But I still had work to do.

At the cabstand I had that afternoon selected as the likeliest, I got my first real break. A good one. A driver identified Janoth as a passenger he'd ridden a little after ten o'clock last Saturday night. The driver was positive. He knew when he'd picked him up, and where, and where he'd put him down. A block from Hagen's.

I knew this might save my neck, as a last desperate resort. But it would not necessarily save my home.

It was around midnight when I reached Marble Road. Georgia and Georgette were asleep.

I found *The Temptation of St. Judas* where I had left it, in a closet downstairs, and in twenty minutes I had it concealed in back of another canvas.

It could be discovered, and easily, if they ever really caught up with me. But if anyone ever got this far, I was finished anyway.

Earl Janoth III

FIVE DAYS after Steve first organized the search we had enough material concerning that damned phantom to write a long biography of him. We had dates, addresses, his background, a complete verbal description of him, X-rays of every last thought, emotion, and impulse he'd ever had. I knew that blundering weak fool better than his own mother. If I shut my eyes I could actually see him standing in front of me, an imbecilic wisp of a smile on his too good-looking face, I could hear his smooth, studied, disarming voice uttering those round, banal whimsicalities he apparently loved, I could almost reach out and touch him, this horrid wraith who had stumbled into my life from nowhere to bring about Pauline's death and my possible ruin.

Yet we didn't have the man himself. We had nothing.

"Candidly, I think you are holding something back," said George Stroud. He was talking to Steve. I had insisted on being present, though not directly participating, when we re-examined the paralysis that seemed to grip our plans. "And I think that thing, whatever it may be, is the one solid fact we need to wrap up the whole business."

"Stick to the facts," said Steve. "Your imagination is running away with you."

"I think not."

We were in Steve's office, Steve behind his desk, myself a little to one side of it, Stroud facing Steve. The room was filled with sunlight, but to me it looked dim, like the bottom of a pool of water. I don't believe I'd slept more than two hours a night in the last week.

The damned wolves were closing in on me. I'd been questioned by dozens of detectives and members of the district attorney's staff three, four, and sometimes five times a day, every day. At first they'd been polite. Now they weren't bothering much with that any more.

And Wayne knew it. Carr knew it. They all knew it. It was a secret only to the general public. In the downtown district and on Forty-second Street it was open knowledge. Nobody, conspicuously, had phoned or come near me for days. The more tightly the official gang closed in on me, the farther my own crowd drew away. The more they isolated me, the easier it became for the police. I could handle one pack of wolves, but not two.

There was no real evidence against me. Not yet. But neither was there any prospect that the pressure to get it would be relaxed.

I could stand that. But we had to find that damned will-o'-the-wisp, and find him before anyone else did. He was the one serious threat I faced. If the police got to him first, as at any moment they might, and eventually would, I knew exactly what he would say, and what would happen.

It didn't make sense. We had this mountain of data, and yet we were, for all practical purposes, right where we had started.

"All right, let's stick to the facts," Stroud told Steve. "You say this man is the key figure in a political-industrial deal. But we haven't turned up one single political connection, and no business connections worth mentioning. Why not? I say, because there aren't any."

Steve told him sharply: "There are. You simply haven't dug deeply enough to get them. I'm holding nothing back except rumors and suspicions. They'd do you no good at all. In fact, they'd simply throw you off."

Stroud's voice was soft and rather pleasant, but it carried a lot of emphasis.

"I couldn't be thrown off more than I was, when you knew Delos was right in the middle of the situation, but you somehow forgot to tell me so."

This senseless bickering would get us nowhere. I had to intervene.

"What is your own opinion, George?" I asked him. "How do you account for the fact we seem to be going around in circles? It isn't like you to be held up so long on a simple thing like this. What is your honest theory about this business?"

Stroud turned and gave me a long, keen regard. He was what I had always classified as one of those hyper-perceptive people, not good at action but fine at pure logic and theory.

He was the sort who could solve a bridge-hand at a glance, down to the last play, but in a simple business deal he would be helpless. The cold fighter's and gambler's nerve that Steve had was completely lacking in him, and he would consider it something foreign or inhuman, if indeed he understood it at all.

After five days of the present job Stroud showed the strain. That was a good thing, because he had to understand this was not merely a routine story.

"Yes, I have a theory," he told me. "I believe the Delos murder and the man we want are so closely connected they are identical. I am forced to reject Steve's idea that one is only accidentally related to the other."

I nodded. It was inevitable, of course. We hadn't selected Stroud to lead the investigation because of his good looks, fancy imagination, or vanity, which was colossal.

I glanced at Steve, trusting he would go on from there more sensibly.

"I follow your reasoning, George," he said. "And I think you are right. But here is something you've overlooked, and we now have to consider. We know that Pauline had knowledge of this big combination. She helped to fill in the background, fragmentary as it is, of the whole thing. She would naturally follow it up if she could. Suppose she did just that? Suppose somebody caught her doing it? And got to her first. Have you thought of that?"

Stroud paused, remote and deliberate. He was just a little too keen for this.

"If this deal is for such high stakes, and if the other parties have already gone the limit," he said, and stopped for an even longer pause, "then we're in rough company. Our man is either in Mexico and still going south, or he has already been disposed of altogether, in such a way he will never again be found."

"That can't be," Steve told him, sharply. "Here's why. A man like this, eccentric, with a wide and varied circle of acquaintances, married and with at least one child, a responsible position somewhere, would leave a pretty big hole if he suddenly dropped out of circulation. Yet you've been in close touch with the Missing Persons Bureau—since when?"

"Tuesday morning."

"Tuesday. And no one like our man has been reported. His disappearance would certainly leak out somewhere, somehow. It hasn't, and that means he's still around." Stroud nodded, cautiously, and Steve went swiftly to another point. "Now let's look at some of these other leads a little more closely. You're still checking the list of upstate liquor licenses suspended or not renewed with the Board?"

Stroud passed a handkerchief across his perspiring face.

"Yes, but that's a tall order. There are hundreds." Stroud looked down for a moment of abstraction at the handkerchief, then he folded the cloth with great deliberation and thrust it slowly and carefully away. "The list is being fed straight to me. If I get anything, you'll know at once."

It was a strange thing to say. Of course we would.

"You've seen the story *Newsways* ran about this Patterson woman?" Steve asked, and Stroud said he had. "It's too early for results. But our spread is going to put that woman on the map. Somebody is certain to recognize and remember that *Judas* picture from our description of it. Our evaluation of it as 'priceless' is sure to locate it. It's my hunch the picture alone will nail our man to the wall."

Stroud smiled faintly, but said nothing, and then they went on to other lines of investigation involving tax lists, advertising agencies, newspapers, fingerprints on a handkerchief, all of them ending in so much fog and vapor. At length, I heard Steve saying: "Now those bars, art galleries, and so on."

"All covered."

"Exactly. And why hasn't our man shown, by now? To me, that's fantastic. No one suddenly abandons his habitual routine of life. Not without some good reason."

"I've already suggested he has either left the country, or been killed," said Stroud. "Here are some more versions of the same general theory. He may have killed Delos, himself, and in that case he's naturally not making himself conspicuous. Or he knows that he's in fast company, knows the score, and he's gone to ground, right where he is, so that the same thing won't happen to him."

I carefully looked away from Steve, and also away from

Stroud. In a curious way Stroud's conclusion was almost perfect. The room was momentarily too quiet.

"You think he may believe himself to be in danger?" Steve presently asked.

"He knows somebody is playing for keeps. Why wouldn't he be worried?"

"And he's keeping pretty well under cover." Steve appeared to be groping toward something. He stared absently at Stroud. "At least, he stays away from all the places where he always went before." Steve was silent for a moment, then he asked: "How many people in the organization, George, know about this particular job?"

Stroud seemed not to understand him.

"Our own?"

"Right here at Janoth Enterprises. How many, at a guess?"

Stroud displayed a thin smile. "Well, with fifty-three people now working on this assignment, I'd say everyone knows about it. The entire two thousand."

"Yes," Steve admitted. "I guess so."

"Why?"

"Nothing. For a second I thought I had something." Steve came back into himself, leaned aggressively forward. "All right, I guess that reports on everything. And it's still nothing."

"Do you think I've missed a bet anywhere?" Stroud demanded.

"Just bear down on it, that's all."

"I shall. Now that we've decided the killing and our particular baby are identical twins, there are a lot more lines we can follow."

"What lines?"

Stroud got up to go. He put a cigarette in his mouth, reflected before lighting it.

"For one thing, I'll have some men cover all the cabstands in the neighborhood of Pauline Delos' apartment. On the night of her death, and a few minutes after it, somebody took a taxi away from that vicinity, and he couldn't help being rather noticeable." He lit his cigarette, drew deeply, casually exhaled. "The driver will remember, and tell us all about him."

My eyes went to Steve, and stayed there. I knew he understood, because he did not, even for a second, glance in my direction.

"I don't follow that, George," he said, in a dead-level voice.

"It's quite simple. Our subject took Pauline to Gil's, to a number of antique shops, and to the Van Barth. Why wouldn't he take her home? Of course he did. Our timing checks with the police timing. He took her home and then he had to leave. No matter what happened there, no matter who killed her, no matter what he saw or what he knew, he had to leave. The first and most obvious line to follow is that he left in a taxi."

I was forced to say, "Perhaps he had his own car."

"Perhaps he did."

"He may have walked," said Steve. "Or taken a bus."

"That's true. But we can't afford to pass up the fact he may have done none of those things. He may have taken a cab. We'll just put a bet on that and hope for the best." Stroud had never lacked confidence in himself, and now it was engraved all over him. He moved toward the door. Standing there, he added, finally: "It's my hunch we'll discover he did take a cab, we'll locate the driver, find out where he went, and that will close our whole assignment."

There was a long and complete silence after he had gone, with Steve intently staring at the door that closed behind him. I thought I was reading his mind. "Yes. You're right."

"About what?"

"We'll close the assignment, all right. We're going to call the whole job off."

"No, we're not. Why should we? I was thinking of something else. About Stroud. I don't like that bastard."

"It's the same thing. I don't want Stroud looking for that taxi."

There was a smoldering anger in Steve that seemed to feed itself, perceptibly mounting.

"That's nothing. You'll never be tied to that. Our staff is good, but not that good. What worries me is what's holding us up? Why is it the only smart idea Stroud can dream up is one we don't like? He's cutting corners somewhere—but where?"

"Pull him off the job. Right now. Before he sends another

team out looking for that driver. I hate the way his mind works."

Steve's eyes were shining like an animal's, and as insensate. "We can't drop the inquiry, and there's no point in replacing Stroud. We have to go through with it, and Stroud has to deliver the goods. He has to do it a damn sight quicker, that's all. We started with an inside track, but that advantage we're losing, now, every hour."

I thought of hunters stalking big game, and while they did so, the game closed in on its own prey, and with the circle eventually completing itself, unknown disaster drew near to the hunters. It was a thing ordained. I said: "You don't know the whole situation. There have been a number of informal, really secret board meetings recently, and that dinner last Saturday—"

Steve interrupted, still watching me. "Yes. You told me."

"Well, if this business goes the wrong way, or even drags itself out, that's all they'll need to take some kind of overt action. I'm certain they've been discussing it these last four or five days. If that should happen—well, that's even worse than this."

Steve seemed not to hear. He looked out at me, and upon the whole of life, deeply and steadily as a bronze, inhumanized idol. Surprisingly, he asked: "You haven't been sleeping much, have you?"

"Not since it happened."

He nodded, spoke with persuasive but impersonal finality. "You're going to a hospital. You've got a strep throat. Forget about everything. Doc Reiner is sending you to bed for a couple of days. With no visitors. Except me."

Georgette Stroud

I HADN'T seen George when he came home last night. He had worked late, even though it had been Sunday. For that matter, I hadn't seen him any evening during the past week. It was nothing unusual for him to work late, either here or at the office. Some evenings he did not return at all.

But this Monday morning I knew something was different. It was not just another long and tough assignment, though that is what he said it was.

When he came down to breakfast I saw what I had only been feeling, but without knowing it. Now I knew something was altogether unusual, and I forced myself to search for it.

He kissed Georgia and myself and sat down. Always, when he started breakfast, he said something about the first dish he happened to see. Now he began with his grapefruit, and said nothing.

"Tell me a story, George," Georgia presently demanded, as though a perfectly novel idea had just occurred to her.

"Story? Story? What's a story, anyway? Never heard of it."

That was all right, though a little mechanical.

"Go on. George said you would. She promised."

"All right, I'll tell you a story. It's about a little girl named Sophia."

"How old?"

"Six."

Again there was that wrong note. She always had to coax him before he gave her right age.

"So what did she do?"

"Well, this is really about Sophia and her very best friend, another little girl."

"And what was her name?"

"Sonia, as it happens."

"How old?"

"Six."

"So what did they do?"

I saw, for the first time, he must have lost a lot of weight. And when he talked to me, he was not there at all. Normally,

483

he wrapped himself in clouds of confetti, but anyone who knew him at all understood exactly what he meant and just where he could be found. But now he really, really wasn't there. His light evasions weren't light. They were actual evasions. The clouds of confetti were steel doors.

It crossed my mind he had been like this two years ago, during the affair I knew he had with Elizabeth Stoltz. That one I was certain about. And there had been others before that, I had believed then, and more than ever believed now.

A wave of utter unreality swept over me. And I recognized the mood, too well, like the first twinges of a recurrent ailment. It was too hideous to be real. That, that was what made it finally so hideous.

"Well, Sophia never saw her friend Sonia except at certain times. Only when Sophia climbed up on a chair and looked into the mirror to wash her face or comb her hair. Whenever she did that she always found Sonia, of all people, there ahead of her."

"So what did they do then?"

"So then they had long, long talks. 'What's the idea, always getting in my way?' Sophia would ask. 'You go away from here, Sonia, and leave me alone.'"

"So what did Sonia say?"

"Well, that's the strangest thing of all. Sonia never said a word. Not one word. But whatever Sophia did in front of the looking glass, Sonia copied her. Even when Sophia stuck out her tongue and called Sonia an old copycat."

"Then what happened?"

"This went on for a long time, and Sophia was pretty mad, believe me." Yes, George, Sophia was pretty damn mad. Just how many years, George, did it go on? "But she thought it over, and one day she told Sonia, 'If you don't stop getting in my way every time I come to the mirror, Sonia, why, I'll never get out of your way, either.'"

"So then what?"

"That's just what Sophia did. Every time Sonia, the little girl who never talked, came to the mirror to comb her hair, so did Sophia. And everything Sonia did, Sophia copied her right back."

No. I don't think so. I think they both did something else. They simply went away from each other.

It can't be. I can't go through that horror again.

What is the matter with him? Is he insane? I can't fall over that terrible cliff again.

Can he ever change and grow up? He's been all right since the Stoltz girl. I thought that would be the last, because she had to be the last. There is a limit beyond which nerves cannot be bruised and torn, and still live. If that is what it is, I cannot endure it again.

Is he quite sane? He can't be, to be so blind.

"I have a best friend," Georgia announced.

"I should hope so."

"A new one."

"What do you and your best friend do?"

"We play games. But sometimes she steals my crayons. Her name's Pauline."

"I see. And then what happens?"

It was too pat, like something rehearsed and coming out of a machine, a radio or a phonograph.

The horn of the school bus sounded and Georgia jumped up. I dabbed at her face with my napkin, then followed her into the hall where she rushed for her school bag, contents one drawing pad, one picture book, and the last time I looked into it, a handful of loose beads, some forgotten peanuts, the broken top of a fountain pen.

I stood there for a moment after I kissed her good-bye and she ran down the walk. Perhaps I was wrong.

I had to be wrong. I would be wrong. Until I was forced to be otherwise.

On my way back to the breakfast room I saw the last issue of *Newsways*, and remembered something. I brought it with me.

"George," I said, "you forgot to bring home a *Newsways*."

He went on with his eggs and coffee and said, absently: "It slipped my mind. I'll bring one home tonight without fail. And *Personalities*, just off."

"Never mind the *Newsways*, I bought one yesterday." He looked at me and saw the magazine, and for just an instant there was something strange and drawn in his face I had never seen before, then it was gone so quickly I wasn't sure it had been there at all. "There's something in it I meant to ask you about. Did you read the article about Louise Patterson?"

"Yes, I read it."

"It's grand, isn't it? It's just what you've been saying for years." I quoted a sentence from the article. " 'Homunculus grows to monstrous size, with all the force of a major explosion, by grace of a new talent suddenly shooting meteorlike across the otherwise turgid skies of the contemporary art world. Louise Patterson may view her models through a microscope, but the brush she wields is Gargantuan.' "

"Yes, it's grand. But it is not what I've been saying for years."

"Anyway, they recognize her talent. Don't be so critical, just because they use different words than you would. At least they admit she's a great painter, don't they?"

"That they do."

Something was away off key. The words were meant to be lightly skeptical, but the tone of his voice was simply flat.

"For heaven's sake, George, don't pretend you aren't pleased. You must have seven or eight Pattersons, and now they're all terribly valuable."

"Priceless. I believe that's the *Newsways* term for them." He dropped his napkin and stood up. "I'll have to run. I think I'll drive in as usual, unless you need the car."

"No, of course not. But wait, George. Here's one thing more." I found another paragraph in the same article, and read from it. " 'This week interest of the art world centered in the whereabouts of Patterson's lost masterpiece, her famed *Judas*, admittedly the most highly prized canvas of all among the priceless works that have come from the studio of this artist. Depicting two huge hands exchanging a coin, a consummate study in flaming yellow, red, and tawny brown, this composition was widely known some years ago, then it quietly dropped from view.' And so on."

I looked up from the magazine. George said: "Neat but not gaudy. They make it sound like a rainbow at midnight."

"That's not what I'm driving at. Would you know anything about that picture?"

"Why should I?"

"Didn't I see an unframed picture you brought home, about a week ago, something like that?"

"You sure did, Georgie-porgie. A copy of it."

"Oh, well. What became of it?"

George winked at me, but there was nothing warm in back of it. There was nothing at all. Just something blank.

"Took it to the office, of course. Where do you think those plumbers got such an accurate description of the original?" He patted my shoulder and gave me a quick kiss. "I'll have to step on it. I'll call you this afternoon."

When he'd gone, and I heard the car go down the driveway, I put down the magazine and slowly got up. I went out to Nellie in the kitchen, knowing how it feels to be old, really old.

Emory Mafferson

I'D NEVER known Stroud very well until recently, and for that matter I didn't know him now. Consequently, I couldn't guess how, or whether, he fitted the Janoth pattern.

When he told me not to be the *Crimeways* type, that meant nothing. This was standard counsel on all of our publications, and for all I knew, Stroud was merely another of the many keen, self-centered, ambitious people in the organization who moved from office to office, from alliance to alliance, from one ethical or political fashion to another, never with any real interest in life except to get more money next year than this, and always more than his colleagues did.

Yet I had a feeling Stroud was not that simple. All I knew about him, in fact, was that he considered himself pretty smooth, seemed to value his own wit, and never bought anything we manufactured here.

Neither did I. Until now.

Leon Temple was in Stroud's office when I came in late that Monday morning, asking Stroud to O.K. an order for some money he swore he had to have for this new, hysterical assignment nearly everyone except myself seemed to be working on. From what I gathered, Temple did nothing but loaf around the cocktail lounge of the Van Barth with a nice little wisp of a thing by the name of Janet Clark. Roaming around the office and trying to figure the best approach to Stroud, I felt like an outsider. They were having one long, happy party, while I spent my days in the ancient Homicide Bureau or the crumbling ruins of the District Attorney's office.

When Stroud signed the order for cash and Leon Temple had gone, I went over and lifted myself to the window ledge in back of his desk. He swung his chair around and in the cross-light I saw what I had not noticed before, that the man's face was lined and hard.

"Anything new, Emory?" he asked.

"Well. Yes. Largely routine stuff. But I wanted to talk about something else."

"Shoot."

"Do you know about the strange thing that happened a week ago last Saturday night?"

"The night of the murder?"

"Yes. But this is about Funded Individuals. I met Fred Steichel, M.E. of Jennett-Donohue, that night. Do you know him?"

"I've met him. But I don't know what you are referring to."

"Well, I know Fred pretty well. His wife and mine were classmates, and still see a lot of each other. We met at a dinner, and there was quite a party afterwards. Fred got drunk, and he began to tell me all about Funded Individuals. In fact, he knew as much about it as I did."

Stroud showed no great concern. "No reason why he shouldn't. It isn't a profound secret. Anything like that gets around."

"Sure, in a general way. But this was different. Fred's all right when he's sober, but he's obnoxious when he's drunk, and that night he was deliberately trying to make himself about as unpleasant as possible. It amused him to recite our computations, quote the conclusions we'd reached, and even repeat some of the angles we'd tried out for a while and then abandoned. The point is, he had the exact figures, the precise steps we'd taken, and he had, for instance, a lot of the phrases I'd personally used in my reports. Not just generally correct, but absolutely verbatim. In other words, there was a leak somewhere, and he'd seen the actual research, the reports, and the findings."

"And then?"

"Well, I got pretty sore. It's one thing that Jennett-Donohue hears rumors about what we're doing, but it's another thing if they have access to supposedly confidential records. I mean, what the hell? I just didn't like the way Fred talked about Funded Individuals. As though it's a dead pigeon. According to him, I was wasting my time. It was only a matter of weeks or days before the whole scheme would be shelved. So the more I thought it over, the less I liked it. He didn't get that data just by accident, and his cockiness wasn't based entirely on a few drinks."

Stroud nodded.

"I see. And you thought it's something we ought to know about."

"I did, and I do. I don't pretend to understand it, but it's my baby, I invested a lot of work in it, and it's something more than the run-of-the-mill mirages we put together around here. It fascinates me. There's something about it almost real." Stroud was at least listening with interest, if not agreement, and I pressed the argument. "It's not just another inspirational arrow shot into the air. This is a cash-and-carry business. And the minute you know there can be a society in which every individual has an actual monetary value of one million dollars, and he's returning dividends on himself, you also know that nobody is going to shoot, starve, or ruin that perfectly sound investment."

Stroud gave me a faint, understanding, but wintry smile.

"I know," he said. "All right, I'll tell Hagen or Earl about this peculiar seepage of our confidential material."

"But that's the point, I already did. That was the strange thing about that Saturday night. I phoned you first, and I couldn't reach you, then I phoned Hagen. He was in, and he agreed with me that it was damn important. He said he would take it up with Earl, and he wanted to see me the first thing Monday morning. Then I didn't hear another word from him."

Stroud leaned back in his chair, studying me, and plainly puzzled. "You called Hagen that night?"

"I had to let somebody know."

"Of course. What time did you call?"

"Almost immediately. I told Steichel I would, and the bastard just laughed."

"Yes, but what time?"

"Well, about ten-thirty. Why?"

"And you talked only to Hagen? You didn't talk to Earl, did you?"

"I didn't talk to him, no. But he must have been there at the time I called. That's where he was that night, you know."

Stroud looked away from me, frowning.

"Yes, I know," he said, in a very tired, distant voice. "But exactly what did Hagen say, do you recall?"

"Not exactly. He told me he would take it up with Earl.

That's a double-check on Earl's whereabouts, isn't it? And Hagen said he would see me Monday morning. But on Monday morning I didn't hear from him, I haven't heard from him since, and I began to wonder what happened. I thought maybe he'd relayed the whole matter to you."

"No, I'm sorry, he didn't. But I'll follow it up, of course. I quite agree with you, it's important. And with Hagen." I saw again that wintry smile, this time subzero. "A human life valued at a million paper dollars would make something of a story, wouldn't it? Don't worry, Emory, your dreamchild will not be lost."

He was one of those magnetic bastards I have always admired and liked, and of course envied and hated, and I found myself, stupidly, believing him. I knew it couldn't be true, but I actually believed he was genuinely interested in protecting Funded Individuals, and would find a way, somehow, to give it a full hearing and then, in the end, contrive for it a big, actual trial. I smiled, digging some notes out of my pocket, and said: "Well, that's all I wanted to talk about. Now, here's the latest dope the cops have on the Delos murder. I already told you they know she was out of town from late Friday until the following Saturday afternoon." Stroud gave a half nod, and concentrated his attention. I went on: "Yesterday they found out where she was. She was in Albany, with a man. There was a book of matches found in her apartment, from a night club in Albany that doesn't circulate its matches from coast to coast, only there on the spot, and in the course of a routine check-up with Albany hotels, they found that's where she actually was. Got it?"

He nodded, briefly, waiting and remote and again hard. I said: "The cops know all about this job you're doing here, by the way, and they're convinced the man you are looking for and the man who was with Delos last Friday and Saturday in Albany is one and the same person. Does that help or hinder you any?"

He said: "Go on."

"That's about all. They are sending a man up there this afternoon or tomorrow morning, with a lot of photographs which he will check with the night club, the hotel, and elsewhere. I told you they had the Delos woman's address book.

Well, this morning they let me look at it. They've been rounding up pictures of every man mentioned on this extensive list
of hers, and most likely the guy that was with her in Albany
is one of them. Do you follow me?"

"I follow you."

"They know from the general description of this man, as
they got it over the phone from the personnel of the hotel
and the club up there, that he most definitely was not Janoth.
At the hotel, they were registered as Mr. and Mrs. Andrew
Phelps-Guyon, a phoney if there ever was one. Does the name
mean anything to you?"

"No."

"Your name was in the woman's address book, by the way."

"Yes," he said. "I knew Pauline Delos."

"Well, that's all."

Stroud seemed to be considering the information I had
given him.

"That's fine, Emory," he said, and flashed me a quick, heat-
less smile. "By the way, is the department looking for a photograph of me?"

"No. They've already got one. Something you once turned
in for a license or a passport. The man they are sending upstate has quite a collection. He has fifty or sixty photographs."

"I see."

"I can go along to Albany with this fellow, if you like," I
said. "If he doesn't accomplish anything else, I imagine he'll
be able to identify the man you've been hunting for, yourself."

"I'm sure he will," he said. "But don't bother. I think that
can be done better right here."

George Stroud IX

T HE TWO LINES of investigation, the organization's and the official one, drew steadily together like invisible pincers. I could feel them closing.

I told myself it was just a tool, a vast machine, and the machine was blind. But I had not fully realized its crushing weight and power. That was insane. The machine cannot be challenged. It both creates and blots out, doing each with glacial impersonality. It measures people in the same way that it measures money, and the growth of trees, the life-span of mosquitoes and morals, the advance of time. And when the hour strikes, on the big clock, that is indeed the hour, the day, the correct time. When it says a man is right, he is right, and when it finds him wrong, he is through, with no appeal. It is as deaf as it is blind.

Of course, I had asked for this.

I returned to the office from a lunch I could not remember having tasted. It had been intended as an interlude to plan for new eventualities and new avenues of escape.

The Janoth Building, covering half of a block, looked into space with five hundred sightless eyes as I turned again, of my own free will, and delivered myself once more to its stone intestines. The interior of this giant God was spick-and-span, restfully lighted, filled with the continuous echo of many feet. A visitor would have thought it nice.

Waiting for me, on my desk, I found the list of nonrenewed licenses for out-of-town taverns, for six years ago. I knew this was the one that would have my own name. That would have to be taken care of later. Right now, I could do nothing but stuff it into the bottom drawer of my desk.

I went into Roy's room and asked him: "Starved?"

"Considerably, considerably."

"The St. Bernards have arrived." He slowly stood up, rolled down the sleeves of his shirt. "Sorry if I kept you waiting. Any developments?"

"Not that I know of, but Hagen wants to see you. Maybe I'd better postpone lunch until you've talked with him."

"All right. But I don't think I'll keep you waiting."

I went upstairs. These conferences had daily become longer, more frequent, and more bitter. It was cold comfort to have a clear understanding of the abyss that Hagen and Janoth, particularly Janoth, saw before them.

For the hundredth time I asked myself why Earl had done this thing. What could possibly have happened on that night, in that apartment? God, what a price to pay. But it had happened. And I recognized that I wasn't really thinking of Janoth, at all, but of myself.

When I stepped into Hagen's office he handed me a note, an envelope, and a photograph.

"This just came in," he said. "We're giving the picture a half-page cut in *Newsways*, with a follow-up story."

The note and the envelope were on the stationery of a Fifty-seventh Street gallery. The photograph, a good, clear 4 × 6, displayed one wall of a Louise Patterson exhibition, with five of her canvases clearly reproduced. The note, from the dealer, simply declared the photograph had been taken at a show nine years ago, and was, as far as known, the only authentic facsimile of the picture mentioned by *Newsways* as lost.

There could be no mistaking the two hands of my *Judas*. It was right in the middle. The dealer duly pointed out, however, that its original proper title was simply: *Study in Fundamentals.*

The canvas at the extreme right, though I recognized none of the others, was the *Study in Fury* that hung on my wall downstairs.

"This seems to answer the description," I said.

"Beyond any doubt. When we run that, quoting the dealer, I'm certain we'll uncover the actual picture." Maybe. It was still concealed behind another canvas on Marble Road. But I knew that if Georgette saw the follow-up, and she would, my story of finding a copy of it would not hold. For the photograph would be reproduced as the only known authentic facsimile. "But I hope to God we have the whole thing cleaned up long before then." I tensed as he looked at the photograph again, certain he would recognize the *Fury*. But he didn't. He laid it down, regarded me with a stare made out of acid. "George, what in hell's wrong? This has drifted along more than a week."

"It took us three weeks to find Isleman," I said.

"We're not looking for a man missing several months. We're looking for somebody that vanished a week ago, leaving a trail a mile wide. Something's the matter. What is it?" But, without waiting for an answer, he discarded the question, and began to check off our current leads. "How about those lapsed licenses?"

I said they were still coming in, and I was cross-checking them as fast as they were received. Methodically, then, we went over all the ground we had covered before. By now it was hash. I'd done a good job making it so.

Before leaving I asked about Earl, and learned he was out of the hospital, after two days. And that was all I learned.

I returned to my office about an hour after I had come upstairs. When I walked in I found Roy, Leon Temple, and Phil Best. It was apparent, the second I stepped into the room, there had been a break.

"We've got him," said Leon.

His small and usually colorless face was all lit up. I knew I would never breathe again.

"Where is he?"

"Right here. He came into this building just a little while ago."

"Who is he?"

"We don't know yet. But we've got him." I waited, watching him, and he explained: "I slipped some cash to the staff of the Van Barth, let them know there'd be some more, and they've all been looking around this district in their free hours. One of the porters picked him up and followed him here."

I nodded, feeling as though I'd been kicked in the stomach.

"Nice work," I said. "Where is this porter now?"

"Downstairs. When he phoned me, I told him to watch the elevators and follow the guy if he came out. He hasn't. Now Phil's bringing over the antique dealer, Eddy is bringing a waitress from Gil's, and then we'll have all six banks of elevators completely covered. I've told the special cops what to do when our man tries to leave. They'll grab him and make him identify himself from his first birthday up to now."

"Yes," I said. "I guess that's that." It was as though they had treed an animal, and that, in fact, was just the case. I was the animal. I said: "That's smart stuff, Leon. You used your head."

"Dick and Mike are down on the main floor, helping the fellow from the Van Barth. In about two minutes we'll have every door and exit covered, too."

I suddenly reached for my coat, but didn't go through with it. I couldn't, now, it was too late. Instead, I pulled out some cigarettes, moved around in back of my desk and sat down.

"You're certain it's the right man?" I asked.

But of course there was no question. I had been seen on my way back from lunch. And followed.

"The porter is positive."

"All right," I said. The phone rang and mechanically I answered it. It was Dick, reporting that they now had the elevators fully covered. In addition to the porter, a night bartender at the Van Barth, Gil's waitress, and the dealer had all arrived. "All right," I said again. "Stay with it. You know what to do."

Methodically, Phil Best explained, in his shrewish voice, what was unmistakably plain.

"If he doesn't come out during the afternoon, we're sure to pick him up at five-thirty, when the building empties." I nodded, but my stunned and scattered thoughts were beginning to pull themselves together. "It'll be jammed, as usual, but we can have every inch of the main floor covered."

"He's in the bag," I said. "We can't miss. I'm going to stay right here until we get him. I'll send out for supper, and if necessary I'll sleep upstairs in the restroom on the twenty-seventh floor. Personally, I'm not going to leave this office until we've got it all sewed up. How about the rest of you?"

I wasn't listening to what they replied.

Even Roy would know that if a man came into a building, and didn't go out, he must logically still be inside of it. And this inescapable conclusion must eventually be followed by one and only one logical course of action.

Sooner or later my staff must go through the building, floor by floor and office by office, looking for the only man in it who never went home.

It wouldn't take long, when they did that. The only question was, who would be the first to make the suggestion.

Louise Patterson

T HIS TIME when I answered the doorbell, which had been ringing steadily for the last four days, I found that tall, thin, romantic squirt, Mr. Klausmeyer, from that awful magazine. It was his third visit, but I didn't mind. He was such a polite, dignified worm, much stuffier than anyone I'd ever met before, he gave my apartment a crazy atmosphere of respectability or something.

"I hope I'm not disturbing you, Mrs. Patterson," he said, making the same mistake he'd made before.

"MISS Patterson," I shrieked, laughing. "You are, but come in. Haven't you caught your murderer yet?"

"We aren't looking for any murderer, Miss Patterson. I have told you the—"

"Save that for *Hokum Fact's* regular subscribers," I said. "Sit down."

He carefully circled around the four children, where the two younger ones, Pete's and Mike's, were helping the older pair, Ralph's, as they sawed and hammered away at some boards and boxes and wheels, building a wagon, or maybe it was some new kind of scooter. Mr. Klausmeyer carefully hitched up his pants, he would, before sitting down in the big leather chair that had once been a rocker.

"You have us confused with *True Facts*," he firmly corrected me. "That's another outfit altogether, not in the same field with any of our publications. I'm with Janoth Enterprises. Until recently I was on the staff of *Personalities*." With wonderful irony he added, "I'm sure you've heard of it. Perhaps you've even read it. But right now I'm working on a special—"

"I know, Mr. Klausmeyer. You wrote that article about me in *Newsways Bunk*." He looked so mad that if he hadn't come because of his job I'm sure he would have gotten up and gone like a bat out of hell. "Never mind," I said, simply whooping. "I enjoyed it, Mr. Klausmeyer. Really I did. And I appreciated it, too, even if you did get it all cockeyed, and I know you didn't really mean any of those nice things you tried to say about me. I know you're just looking for that murderer. Would you like some muscatel? It's all I have."

I dragged out what was left of a gallon of muscatel and found one of my few remaining good tumblers. It was almost clean.

"No, thank you," he said. "About that article, Miss Patterson—"

"Not even a little?"

"No, really. But regarding the article—"

"It isn't very good," I admitted. "I mean the wine," I explained, then I realized I was simply bellowing, and felt aghast. Mr. Klausmeyer hadn't done anything to me, he looked like the sensitive type who takes everything personally, and the least I could do was to refrain from insulting him. I made up my mind to act exactly like an artist should. I poured myself a glass of the muscatel and urged him, quite gently, "I do wish you'd join me."

"No, thanks. Miss Patterson, I didn't write that article in *Newsways*."

"Oh, you didn't?"

"No."

"Well, I thought it was a perfectly wonderful story." It came to me that I'd said the wrong thing again, and I simply howled. "I mean, within limits. Please, Mr. Klausmeyer, don't mind me. I'm not used to having my pictures labeled 'costly.' Or was it 'invaluable'? The one the murderer bought for fifty bucks."

Mr. Klausmeyer was mad, I could see, and probably I was boring him besides. I swore I would keep my mouth shut and act reasonably for at least fifteen minutes, no matter what he said, and no matter how I felt. Fifteen minutes. That's not so long.

"I merely supplied some of the information," Mr. Klausmeyer carefully explained. "For instance, I supplied the *Newsways* writer with the description of the *Judas* picture, exactly as you gave it to me."

The son of a bitch.

"God damn it all," I screamed, "where do you get that *Judas* stuff? I told you the name of the picture was *Study in Fundamentals*. What in hell do you mean by giving my own picture some fancy title I never thought of at all? How do you dare, you horrible little worm, how do you dare to throw your idiocy all over my work?"

I looked at him through a haze of rage. He was another picture burner. I could tell it just by looking at his white, stuffy face. Another one of those decent, respectable maniacs who'd like nothing better than to take a butcher knife and slash canvases, slop them with paint, burn them. By God, he looked exactly like Pete. No, Pete's way had been to use them to cover up broken window panes, plug up draughts, and stop leaks in the ceiling. He was more the official type. His method would be to bury them in an authorized warehouse somewhere, destroy the records, and let them stay there forever.

I drank off the muscatel, poured myself some more, and tried to listen to him.

"I did use your own title, I assure you, but there must have been a slip somewhere in the writing and editing. That will be corrected in a story *Newsways* is now running, with a photograph of the *Study in Fundamentals.*"

"I know you, you damned arsonist." His large gray eyes bugged out just the way Ralph's had when he showed me the pile of scraps and ashes and charred fragments, all that was left of five years' work, heaped up in the fireplace. How proud he'd been. You really amount to something, I guess, if you know how to destroy something new and creative. "What do you want now?" I demanded. "Why do you come here?"

I saw that Mr. Klausmeyer was quite pale. I guess if he hadn't been a tame caterpillar doing an errand for *Anything But the News* he would have picked up Elroy's scout hatchet and taken a swing at me.

"We've located the man who bought your picture, Miss Patterson," he said, with great control. "We believe we know where he is, and he'll be found at any moment. We wish you'd come to the office, so that you can identify him. Of course, we'll pay you for your time and trouble. We'll give you a hundred dollars if you can help us. Will you?"

"So you've found the murderer," I said.

With emphatic weariness, Mr. Klausmeyer repeated: "We are not looking for a murderer, Miss Patterson. I assure you, we want this man in some altogether different connection."

"Crap," I said.

"I beg your pardon?"

"Nonsense. Detectives have been around here, asking me the same questions you have. You are both looking for the same man, the one who bought my picture, and murdered that Delos woman. What do you think I am? Apparently you think I'm a complete dope."

"No," Mr. Klausmeyer told me, strongly. "Anything but that. Will you come back to the office with me?"

A hundred dollars was a hundred dollars.

"I don't know why I should help to catch a man with brains enough to like my *Study in Fundamentals*. I haven't got so many admirers I can afford to let any of them go to the electric chair."

Mr. Klausmeyer's face showed that he fully agreed, and it pained him that he couldn't say so.

"But perhaps we can help you reclaim your picture. You wanted to buy it back, didn't you?"

"No. I didn't want to buy it back, I just didn't want it to rot in that black hole of Calcutta."

And I knew no one would ever see that picture again. It was already at the bottom of the East River. The murderer would have to do away with it to save his own hide. He would get rid of anything that connected him with the dead woman.

Yet one more noble little angel of destruction.

I realized this, feeling mad and yet somehow cold. It was no use telling myself that I didn't care. The canvas was not one of my best. And yet I did care. It was hard enough to paint the things, without trying to defend them afterwards from self-appointed censors and jealous lovers and microscopic deities. Like Mr. Klausmeyer.

"All right," I said. "I'll go. But only for the hundred dollars."

Mr. Klausmeyer rose like something popping out of a box. God, he was elegant. When he died they wouldn't have to embalm him. The fluid already ran in his veins.

"Certainly," he said, warmly.

I looked around and found my best hat on the top shelf of the bookcases. Edith, who was four—she was Mike's—scolded me for taking away her bird's nest. I explained the nest would be back in place before nightfall. Leaving, I put the whole trading-post in charge of Ralph junior until further notice. He looked up, and I think he even heard me. Anyway, he understood.

In a taxi, on the way to his office, Mr. Klausmeyer tried to be friendly.

"Splendid children," he told me. "Very bright and healthy. I don't believe you told me much about your husband?"

"I've never been married," I said, again shrieking with laughter, against my will. God, I would learn how to act refined, beginning tomorrow, if it was the last thing I ever did. "They're all LOVE children, Mr. Klausmeyer." He sat so straight and earnest and looking so sophisticated I had to postpone my graduation from kindergarten for at least another minute. And then I had that awful sinking sensation, knowing I'd behaved like a perfect fool. As of course I was. Nobody knew that better than I did. But Mr. Klausmeyer was so perfect, I wondered if he could possibly know it. Probably not. Perfect people never understand much about anything.

"Excuse me, Mr. Klausmeyer, if I confide in you. I've never done it before. There's something about you *Factways* people that seems to invite all kinds of confidences."

I suppose this lie was just too transparent, for he said nothing at all, and a moment later we were getting out of the cab, Mr. Klausmeyer looking just too pleased and preoccupied for words because he would soon be rid of me. God damn him. If I'd been dressed when he arrived, if I'd really wanted to make an impression, I could have had him under my thumb in five seconds. But who wanted to have an angleworm under her thumb?

I was drunk and sedate for the whole three minutes it took us to enter the building and ride up in the elevator. Dignity was a game two could play at. But after I'd used up mine, and we got out of the elevator, I asked: "Just what am I supposed to do, Mr. Klausmeyer? Besides collect a hundred dollars?"

Of course, without meaning to, I'd cut loose with another raucous laugh.

"Don't worry about your hundred dollars," he said, shortly. "The man who bought your picture is somewhere in this building. It is just a question of time, until we locate him. All you have to do is identify him when we do locate him."

I was suddenly awfully sick of Mr. Klausmeyer, the detectives who'd been questioning me, and the whole insane affair. What business was it of mine, all of this? I had just one business in life, to paint pictures. If other people got pleasure out of destroying them, let them; perhaps that was the way they expressed their own creative instincts. They probably referred to the best ones they suppressed or ruined as their outstanding masterpieces.

It was a black thought, and I knew it was not in the right perspective. As Mr. Klausmeyer put his hand on the knob of an office door, and pushed it open, I said: "You must be a dreadfully cynical and sophisticated person, Mr. Klausmeyer. Don't you ever long for a breath of good, clean, wholesome, natural fresh air?"

He gave me a polite, but emotional glare.

"I've always avoided being cynical," he said. "Up until now."

We entered a room filled with a lot of other office angleworms.

"How many children have you got, Mr. Klausmeyer?" I asked, intending to speak in a low voice, but evidently I was yelling, because a lot of people turned around and looked at us.

"Two," he whispered, but it sounded like he was swearing. Then he put on a smile and brought me forward. But as I crossed the room, and looked around it, my attention was abruptly centered upon a picture on the wall. It was one of mine. *Study in Fury*. It was amazing. I could hardly believe it. "George," Mr. Klausmeyer was saying, "this is Miss Patterson, the artist." It was beautifully framed, too. "Miss Patterson, this is George Stroud, who has charge of our investigation. She's agreed to stay here until we have the man we want. She can give us some help, I believe."

A good-looking angleworm got up in back of a desk and came forward and shook hands with me.

"Miss Patterson," he said. "This is an unexpected pleasure."

I looked at him, and started to bellow, but lost my breath. Something was quite mad. It was the murderer, the very same man who bought the picture in the Third Avenue junkshop.

"How d'you do?" I said. I turned to Mr. Klausmeyer, but Mr. Klausmeyer just looked tired and relieved. I stared back at Mr. Stroud. "Well," I said, uncertainly, "what can I do for you?"

For the fraction of a second we looked at each other with complete realization. I knew who he was, and he knew that I knew. But I couldn't understand it, and I hesitated.

This ordinary, bland, rather debonair and inconsequential person had killed that Delos woman? It didn't seem possible. Where would he get the nerve? What would he know about the terrible, intense moments of life? I must be mistaken. I must have misunderstood the whole situation. But it was the same man. There was no doubt about it.

His eyes were like craters, and I saw that their sockets were hard and drawn and icy cold, in spite of the easy smile he showed. I knew this, and at the same time I knew no one else in the room was capable of knowing it, because they were all like poor Mr. Klausmeyer, perfect.

"It's very kind of you to help us," he said. "I imagine Don explained what we're doing."

"Yes." My knees were suddenly trembling. This was away over my head, all of it. "I know everything, Mr. Stroud. I really do."

"I don't doubt it," he said. "I'm sure you do."

Why didn't somebody do something to break this afternoon nightmare? Of course it was a nightmare. Why didn't somebody admit it was all a stupid joke? What fantastic lie would this Stroud person invent, plausible as all hell, if I chose to identify him here and now?

I gave an automatic, raucous laugh, yanked my hand away from his, and said: "Anyway, I'm glad somebody likes my *Study in Fury*."

"Yes, I like it very much," said the murderer.

"It's yours?" I squeaked.

"Of course. I like all of your work."

There were about five people in the office, though it

seemed more like fifty, and now they all turned to look at the *Fury*. Mr. Klausmeyer said: "I'll be damned. It really is Miss Patterson's picture. Why didn't you tell us, George?"

He shrugged.

"Tell you what? What is there to tell? I liked it, bought it, and there it is. It's been there for a couple of years."

Mr. Klausmeyer looked at the Stroud person with renewed interest, while the rest of them gaped at me as though for the first time convinced I was an artist.

"Would you care for a drink, Miss Patterson?" the murderer invited me. He was actually smiling. But I saw it was not a smile, only the desperate imitation of one.

I swallowed once, with a mouth that was harsh and dry, then I couldn't help the feeble, half-measure of a roar that came out of me. Even as I laughed, I knew I wasn't laughing. It was plain hysteria.

"Where in hell's my *Study in Fundamentals*?" I demanded. "The one your lousy magazine calls *Judas*."

Stroud was very still and white. The others were only blank. Mr. Klausmeyer said, to Stroud: "I told her we'd try to get the picture back for her." To me, he patiently explained, "I didn't say we had it, Miss Patterson. I meant that we'd automatically find the picture when we found the man."

"Will you?" I said, looking hard at Stroud. "I think more likely it's been destroyed."

Something moved in that rigid face of his, fixed in its casual, counterfeit smile.

"No," he said, at last. "I don't think so, Miss Patterson. I have reason to believe your picture is quite safe." He turned back to his desk and lifted the phone. Holding it, he gave me a hard, uncompromising stare it was impossible for me to misconstrue. "It will be recovered," he told me. "Provided everything else goes off all right. Do you fully understand?"

"Yes," I said. God damn him. He was actually blackmailing me. It was me who should be blackmailing him. In fact, I would. "It damn well better be safe. I understand it's worth thousands and thousands of dollars."

He nodded.

"We think so. Now, what would you like to drink?"

"She likes muscatel," said Mr. Klausmeyer.

"Rye," I yelled. What did I care why he killed her? If the *Fury* was safe, probably the *Fundamentals* was safe, too, and it actually was worth a lot of money—now. And if it wasn't safe, I could always talk up later. Besides, he really did collect my pictures. "Not just one. A whole lot. Order a dozen."

It would take something to stay in the same room with a murderer. And at the same time remember that dignity paid, at least in public.

George Stroud X

SOMETIME very early I woke on a couch I'd had moved into my office, put on my shoes and necktie, the only clothing I'd removed, and in a mental cloud moved over to my desk.

My watch said a few minutes after eight. Today was the day. I still didn't know how I would meet it. But I knew it was the day. The police would finish the check-up in Albany. Somebody would think of combing the building.

Yesterday should have been the day, and why it wasn't, I would never really know. When that Patterson woman walked in here I should have been through. I knew why she hadn't identified me, the fact that I had not destroyed her picture, and my threat that I still would, if she opened her mouth. Artists are curious. I shuddered when I thought how close I'd come, actually, to getting rid of that canvas. She could still make trouble, any time she felt like it, and maybe she would. She was erratic enough. At about eight in the evening she'd packed herself off. But she might be back. At any moment, for any reason, she might change her mind.

Nobody answered when I pressed the button for a copy boy, and at last I phoned the drugstore downstairs. Eventually I got my sandwich and my quart of black coffee. In Roy's office, Harry Slater and Alvin Dealey were keeping the death watch.

Shortly before nine the rest of the staff began to come in. Leon Temple arrived, and then Roy, Englund, and Don and Eddy reached the office almost simultaneously.

"Why don't you go home?" Roy asked me. "There's nothing you can do now, is there?"

I shook my head. "I'm staying."

"You want to be in at the finish?"

"Right. How's everything downstairs?"

Leon Temple said: "Tighter than a drum. Phil Best has just spelled Mike. We've got the whole night side of the Van Barth down there, and some more special cops. I don't understand it."

This was it. I felt it coming. "What don't you understand?" I asked.

"Why that guy hasn't come out. What the hell. He's here, but where is he?"

"Maybe he left before we threw a line around the place," I said.

"Not a chance."

"He may have simply walked in one door and out the other," I argued. "Perhaps he knew he was being followed."

"No," said Leon. "That porter followed him right to the elevator. He took an express. He could be anywhere above the eighteenth floor. For all we know, he's somewhere up here in our own organization."

"What can we do about it?" Englund asked.

"He'll show," I said.

"I thought time was essential, George," Roy reminded me.

"It is."

"It occurs to me," said Leon, "if he doesn't show—" So it was going to be Leon Temple. I looked at him and waited. "We could take those eyewitnesses, with the building police, and some of our own men, and go through the whole place from top to bottom. We could cover every office. That would settle it. It would take a couple of hours, but we'd know."

I had to appear to consider the idea. It already looked bad that I hadn't suggested it myself. I nodded, and said: "You have something."

"Well, shall we do it?"

If I knew where those eyewitnesses were, if I could be informed of their progress from floor to floor and from suite to suite, there might still be a way. No game is over until the whistle blows.

"Get started," I said. "You handle this, Leon. And I want you to keep me informed of every move. Let me know what floor you start on, which direction you're working, and where you're going next."

"O.K.," he said. "First, we'll get witnesses and cops on every floor above eighteen. They'll cover the stairs, the elevators, and I'll have them be careful to watch people moving from office to office, the mail-chutes, johns, closets—everything." I nodded, but didn't speak. "I think that would be right, don't you?"

God, what a price. Here was the bill, and it had to be paid. Of course this was whining, but I knew no man on earth ever watched his whole life go to bits and pieces, carrying with it the lives of those close to him also down into ashes, without a silent protest. The man who really accepts his fate, really bows without a quiver to the big gamble he has made and lost, that is a lie, a myth. There is no such man, there never has been, never will be.

"All right," I said. "Keep me informed."

"I'd like to take Dick and Eddy and Don. And some more, as soon as they come in."

"Take them."

"And I think those witnesses should be encouraged."

"Pay them. I'll give you a voucher." I signed my name to a cashier's form, leaving the amount blank, and tossed it to Leon. "Good hunting," I said, and I think I created a brief smile.

Pretty soon the office was empty, and then Leon called to say they were going through the eighteenth floor, with all exits closed and all down-elevators being stopped for inspection. There was just one way to go. Up.

I had a half-formed idea that there might be some safety in the very heart of the enemy's territory, Steve's or Earl's offices on the thirty-second floor, and I was trying to hit upon a way to work it when the phone rang and it was Steve himself. His voice was blurred and strained, and somehow bewildered, as he asked me to come up there at once.

In Hagen's office I found, besides Steve, Earl Janoth and our chief attorney, Ralph Beeman, with John Wayne, the organization's biggest stockholder, and four other editors. And then I saw Fred Steichel, M.E. of Jennett-Donohue. All of them looked stunned and slightly embarrassed. Except Steichel, who seemed apologetic, and Earl, who radiated more than his customary assurance. He came forward and heartily shook my hand, and I saw that the self-confidence was, instead, nervous tension mounting to near hysteria.

"George," he said. "This makes me very glad." I don't

think he really saw me, though, and I don't believe he saw, actually saw, anyone else in the room as he turned and went on, "I see no reason why we should wait. What I have to say now can be drawn up and issued to the entire staff later, expressing my regret that I could not have the pleasure of speaking to each and every one of them personally." I sat down and looked at the fascinated faces around me. They sensed, as I did, the one and only thing that could be impending. "As you may know, there have been certain differences on our controlling board, as to the editorial policies of Janoth publications. I have consistently worked and fought for free, flexible, creative journalism, not only as I saw it, but as every last member of the staff saw it. I want to say now I think this policy was correct, and I am proud of our record, proud that I have enlisted the services of so much talent." He paused to look at Hagen, who looked at no one as he stonily concentrated upon a scramble of lines and circles on the pad before him. "But the controlling board does not agree that my policies have been for the best interests of the organization. And the recent tragedy, of which you are all aware, has increased the opposition's mistrust of my leadership. Under the circumstances, I cannot blame them. Rather than jeopardize the future of the entire venture, I have consented to step aside, and to permit a merger with the firm of Jennett-Donohue. I hope you will all keep alive the spirit of the old organization in the new one. I hope you will give to Mr. Steichel, your new managing editor, the same loyalty you gave to Steve and myself."

Then the attorney, Beeman, took up the same theme and elaborated upon it, and then Wayne began to talk about Earl's step as being temporary, and that everyone looked to his early return. He was still speaking when the door opened and Leon Temple stepped inside. I went over to him.

"We've drawn a blank so far," he told me. "But just to be sure, I think we should go through both Janoth's and Hagen's offices."

In the second that the door opened and shut, I saw a knot of people in the corridor, a porter from Gil's and a waiter from the Van Barth among them.

"Drop it," I said. "The assignment is killed."

Leon's gaze went slowly around the room, absorbing a scene that might have been posed in some historical museum. His eyes came back to me, and I nodded.

"You mean, send them all away?"

"Send them away. We are having a big change. It is the same as Pompeii."

Back in the room I heard Wayne say to Hagen: "—either the Paris bureau, or the Vienna bureau. I imagine you can have either one, if you want it."

"I'll think it over," Hagen told him.

"The organization comes ahead of everything," Earl was too jovially and confidently reiterating. It was both ghastly and yet heroic. "Whatever happens, that must go on. It is bigger than I am, bigger than any one of us. I won't see it injured or even endangered."

Our new managing editor, Steichel, was the only person who seemed to be on the sidelines. I went over to him.

"Well?" I said.

"I know you want more money," he told me. "But what else do you want?"

I could see he would be no improvement at all. I said: "Emory Mafferson."

I thought that would catch him off balance, and it did.

"What? You actually want Mafferson?"

"We want to bring out Funded Individuals. In cartoon strips. We'll dramatize it in pictures." Doubt and suspicion were still there, in Steichel's eyes, but interest began to kindle. "Nobody reads, any more," I went on. "Pictorial presentation, that's the whole future. Let Emory go ahead with Funded Individuals in a new five-color book on slick paper."

Grudgingly, he said: "I'll have to think that one over. We'll see."

T HE REST of that day went by like a motion picture running wild, sometimes too fast, and again too slow.

I called up Georgette, and made a date to meet her for
dinner that evening at the Van Barth. She sounded extra gay,
though I couldn't imagine why. I was the only member of the
family who knew what it meant to go all the way through life
and come out of it alive.

I explained that the last assignment was over, and then she
put Georgia on the wire. The conversation proceeded like
this:

"Hello? Hello? Is that you, George? This is George."

"Hello, George. This is George."

"Hello."

"Hello."

"Hello? Hello?"

"All right, now we've said hello."

"Hello, George, you have to tell me a story. What's her
name?"

"Claudia. And she's at least fifteen years old."

"Six."

"Sixteen."

"Six. Hello? Hello?"

"Hello. Yes, she's six. And here's what she did. One day
she started to pick at a loose thread in her handkerchief, and
it began to come away, and pretty soon she'd picked her handkerchief until all of it disappeared and before she knew it she
was pulling away at some yarn in her sweater, and then her
dress, and she kept pulling and pulling and before long she
got tangled up with some hair on her head and after that she
still kept pulling and pretty soon poor Claudia was just a heap
of yarn lying on the floor."

"So then what did she do? Hello?"

"So then she just lay there on the floor and looked up at
the chair where she'd been sitting, only of course it was empty
by now. And she said, 'Where am I?' "

Success. I got an unbelieving spray of laughter.

"So then what did I do? Hello? Hello?"

"Then you did nothing," I said. "Except you were always careful after that not to pull out any loose threads. Not too far."

"Hello? Is that all?"

"That's all for now."

"Good-bye. Hello?"

"We said hello. Now we're saying good-bye."

"Good-bye, good-bye, good-bye, good-bye."

After that I phoned an agency and got a couple of tickets for a show that evening. And then, on an impulse, I phoned the art dealer who had sent us the photograph of the Louise Patterson exhibit. I told him who I was, and asked: "How much are Pattersons actually worth?"

"That all depends," he said. "Do you want to buy, or have you got one you want to sell?"

"Both. I want a rough evaluation."

"Well. Frankly, nobody knows. I suppose you're referring to that recent article in your *Newsways*?"

"More or less."

"Well. That was an exaggeration, of course. And the market on somebody like Patterson is always fluctuating. But I'd say anything of hers would average two or three thousand. I happen to have a number of canvases of hers, exceptional things, you could buy for around that figure."

"What would the *Judas* bring? I mean the one with the hands. You sent us a photograph of it."

"Well, that's different. It's received a lot of publicity, and I suppose that would be worth a little more. But, unfortunately, I haven't got the picture itself. It is really lost, apparently."

"It isn't lost," I said. "I have it. How much is it worth?"

There was a perceptible wait.

"You actually have it?"

"I have."

"You understand, Mr.—"

"Stroud. George Stroud."

"You understand, Mr. Stroud, I don't buy pictures myself. I simply exhibit pictures, and take a commission from the sales made through my gallery. But if you really have that *Judas* I believe it can be sold for anywhere between five and ten thousand dollars."

I thanked him and dropped the phone.

The big clock ran everywhere, overlooked no one, omitted no one, forgot nothing, remembered nothing, knew nothing. Was nothing, I would have liked to add, but I knew better. It was just about everything. Everything there is.

That afternoon Louise Patterson came roaring into the office, more than a little drunk. I had been expecting her. She wanted to talk to me, and I packed us both off to Gil's.

When we were lined up at the bar at Gil's she said: "What about that picture of mine. What have you done with it?"

"Nothing. I have it at my home. Why should I have done anything with it?"

"You know why," she thundered. "Because it proves you killed Pauline Delos."

Three customers looked around with some interest. So then I had to explain to her that I hadn't, and in guarded language, suppressing most of the details, I outlined the police theory of the case. When I had finished, she said, disappointedly: "So you're really not a murderer, after all?"

"No. I'm sorry."

A cyclone of laughter issued from her. For a moment she couldn't catch her breath. I thought she'd fall off her chair.

"I'm sorry, too, Mr. Stroud. I was being so brave yesterday afternoon in your office, you have no idea. God, what I won't do to save those pictures of mine. The more I saw you the more sinister you looked. Come to think of it, you really are sinister. Aren't you?"

She was quite a woman. I liked her more and more. Yesterday she'd looked like something out of an album, but today she'd evidently taken some pains to put herself together. She was big, and dark, and alive.

Gil ranged down the bar in front of us.

"Evening," he said to both of us, then to me, "Say, a friend of yours was hanging around here for the last week or so, looking for you. He sure wanted to see you. Bad. But he ain't here now. A whole lot of people been looking for you."

"I know," I said. "I've seen them all. Give us a couple of rye highballs, and let the lady play the game."

Then for a while Gil and the Patterson woman worked away
at it. She started by asking for a balloon, which was easy, the
only toy Gil had saved from the old fire next to the carbarns,
and ended by asking for a Raphael, also quite simple, a postcard he'd mailed to his wife from Italy, on a long voyage.

Something like eight drinks later Patterson remembered
something, as I'd known she sooner or later would.

"George, there's something I don't understand. Why did
they want me to identify you? What was the idea?"

She was more than a little drunk, and I gravely told her:
"They wanted to find out who had that picture of yours. It
was believed lost. Remember? And it's priceless. Remember
that? And naturally, our organization wanted to trace it
down."

She stared for a moment of semi-belief, then exploded into
another storm of laughter.

"Double-talk. I want the truth. Where's my picture? I want
it back. I could have it back the minute you were found, according to Mr. Klausmeyer." The memory of Don seemed to
touch off another wave of deafening hilarity. "That angleworm. To hell with him. Well, where is it?"

"Louise," I said.

"It's worth a lot of money, it belongs to me, and I want
it. When are you going to give it to me?"

"Louise."

"You're a double-talker. I can spot a guy like you a hundred
miles away. You've got a wife, no children, and a house you
haven't paid for. Tonight you're slumming, and tomorrow
you'll be bragging all over the commuter's special that you
know a real artist, the famous Louise Patterson." She
slammed a fist on the bar. Gil came back to us and phleg-
matically assembled two more drinks. "But to hell with all
that. I want my *Study in Fundamentals*. It was promised to
me, and it's worth a lot of money. Where is it?"

"You can't have it," I said, bluntly. "It's mine."

She glared, and snarled.

"You bastard, I think you mean it."

"Certainly I mean it. After all, it is mine. I paid for it, didn't
I? And it means something to me. That picture is a part of
my life. I like it. I want it. I need it."

She was, all at once, moderately amiable.

"Why?"

"Because that particular picture gave me an education. It is continuing to give me an education. Maybe, sometime, it will put me through college." I looked at my watch. If I could get to the Van Barth in ten minutes, I would be approximately on time. "But I'll make a deal with you. I've got that *Fury* in the office, and four other things of yours at home. You can have them all, instead of the *Temptation of St. Judas*, which is not for sale at any price. Not to anyone."

She asked me, wistfully: "Do you really like it so much?"

I didn't have time to explain, and so I simply said: "Yes."

This shut her up, and I somehow got her out of the place. In front of Gil's I put her into a cab, and paid the driver, and gave him her address.

I caught the next taxi that passed. I knew I'd be a few minutes late at the Van Barth. But it didn't seem to matter so much.

The big, silent, invisible clock was moving along as usual. But it had forgotten all about me. Tonight it was looking for someone else. Its arms and levers and steel springs were wound up and poised in search of some other person in the same blind, impersonal way it had been reaching for me on the night before. And it had missed me, somehow. That time. But I had no doubt it would get around to me again. Inevitably. Soon.

I made sure that my notebook was stowed away in an inside pocket. It had Louise's address, and her phone number. I would never call her, of course. It was enough, to be scorched by one serious, near-disaster. All the same, it was a nice, interesting number to have.

My taxi slowed and stopped for a red light. I looked out of the window and saw a newspaper headline on a corner stand.

EARL JANOTH, OUSTED PUBLISHER,
PLUNGES TO DEATH.

NIGHTMARE ALLEY

by William Lindsay Gresham

Contents

Madame Sosostris, famous clairvoyante,
Had a bad cold, nevertheless
Is known to be the wisest woman in Europe,
With a wicked pack of cards. Here, said she,
Is your card, the drowned Phoenician Sailor,
(Those are pearls that were his eyes. Look!)
Here is Belladonna, the Lady of the Rocks,
The lady of situations.
Here is the man with three staves, and here the Wheel,
And here is the one-eyed merchant, and this card,
Which is blank, is something he carries on his back,
Which I am forbidden to see. I do not find
The Hanged Man. Fear death by water . . .

—*The Waste Land*

For at Cumae I saw with my own eyes the Sibyl hanging in a bottle.
And when the boys asked her, "What do you want, Sibyl?" she answered, "I want to die."

—*The Satyricon*

The Fool

*who walks in motley, with his eyes closed,
over a precipice at the end of the world.*

STAN CARLISLE stood well back from the entrance of the canvas enclosure, under the blaze of a naked light bulb, and watched the geek.

This geek was a thin man who wore a suit of long underwear dyed chocolate brown. The wig was black and looked like a mop, and the brown greasepaint on the emaciated face was streaked and smeared with the heat and rubbed off around the mouth.

At present the geek was leaning against the wall of the pen, while around him a few—pathetically few—snakes lay in loose coils, feeling the hot summer night and sullenly uneasy in the glare. One slim little king snake was trying to climb up the wall of the enclosure and was falling back.

Stan liked snakes; the disgust he felt was for them, at their having to be penned up with such a specimen of man. Outside the talker was working up to his climax. Stan turned his neat blond head toward the entrance.

". . . where did he come from? God only knows. He was found on an uninhabited island five hundred miles off the coast of Florida. My friends, in this enclosure you will see one of the unexplained mysteries of the universe. Is he man or is he beast? You will see him living in his natural habitat among the most venomous rep-tiles that the world provides. Why, he fondles those serpents as a mother would fondle her babes. He neither eats nor drinks but lives entirely on the atmosphere. And we're going to feed him one more time! There will be a slight additional charge for this attraction but it's not a dollar, it's not a quarter—it's a cold, thin dime, ten pennies, two nickels, the tenth part of a dollar. Hurry, hurry, hurry!"

Stan shifted over to the rear of the canvas pen.

The geek scrabbled under a burlap bag and found something. There was the wheet of a cork being drawn and a couple of rattling swallows and a gasp.

The "marks" surged in—young fellows in straw hats with their coats over their arms, here and there a fat woman with beady eyes. Why does that kind always have beady eyes, Stan wondered. The gaunt woman with the anemic little girl who had been promised she would see everything in the show. The drunk. It was like a kaleidoscope—the design always changing, the particles always the same.

Clem Hoately, owner of the Ten-in-One show and its lecturer, made his way through the crowd. He fished a flask of water from his pocket, took a swig to rinse his throat, and spat it on the ground. Then he mounted the step. His voice was suddenly low and conversational, and it seemed to sober the audience.

"Folks, I must ask ya to remember that this exhibit is being presented solely in the interests of science and education. This creature which you see before ya . . ."

A woman looked down and for the first time spied the little king snake, still frantically trying to climb out of the pit. She drew in her breath shrilly between her teeth.

". . . this creature has been examined by the foremost scientists of Europe and America and pronounced a man. That is to say: he has two arms, two legs, a head and a body, like a man. But under that head of hair there is the brain of a beast. See how he feels more at home with the rep-tiles of the jungle than with humankind."

The geek had picked up a black snake, holding it close behind the head so it couldn't snap at him, and was rocking it in his arms like a baby, muttering sounds.

The talker waited while the crowd rubbered.

"You may well ask how he associates with poisonous serpents without harm. Why, my friends, their poison has no effect whatsoever upon him. But if he were to sink his teeth in my hand nothing on God's green earth could save me."

The geek gave a growl, blinking stupidly up into the light from the bare bulb. Stan noticed that at one corner of his mouth there was a glint from a gold tooth.

"But now, ladies and gentlemen, when I told you that this creature was more beast than man I was not asking you to take my word for it. Stan—" He turned to the young man, whose brilliant blue eyes had not a trace of revelation in them. "Stan, we're going to feed him one more time for this audience alone. Hand me the basket."

Stanton Carlisle reached down, gripped a small covered market basket by the handle, and boosted it over the heads of the crowd. They fell back, jamming and pushing. Clem Hoately, the talker, laughed with a touch of weariness. "It's all right, folks; nothing you haven't seen before. No, I reckon you all know what this is." From the basket he drew a half-grown leghorn pullet, complaining. Then he held it up so they could see it. With one hand he motioned for silence.

The necks craned down.

The geek had leaned forward on all fours, his mouth hanging open vacantly. Suddenly the talker threw the pullet into the pit with a whirl of feathers.

The geek moved toward it, shaking his black cotton mop of wig. He grabbed for the chicken, but it spread its stumpy wings in a frenzy of self-preservation and dodged. He crawled after it.

For the first time the paint-smeared face of the geek showed some life. His bloodshot eyes were nearly closed. Stan saw his lips shape words without sound. The words were, "You son of a bitch."

Gently the youth eased himself out of the crowd, which was

straining, looking down. He walked stiffly around to the entrance, his hands in his pockets.

From the pit came a panicky clucking and cackling and the crowd drew its breath. The drunk beat his grimy straw hat on the rail. "Get 'at ole shicken, boy! Go get 'at ole shicken!"

Then a woman screamed and began to leap up and down jerkily; the crowd moaned in an old language, pressing their bodies tighter against the board walls of the pit and stretching. The cackling had been cut off short, and there was a click of teeth and a grunt of someone working hard.

Stan shoved his hands deeper in his pockets. He moved through the flap entrance back into the main ring of the Ten-in-One show, crossed it to the gate and stood looking out on the carnival midway. When his hands came from his pockets one of them held a shiny half-dollar. He reached for it with his other hand and it vanished. Then with a secret, inner smile of contempt and triumph, he felt along the edge of his white flannel trousers and produced the coin.

Against the summer night the ferris wheel lights winked with the gaiety of rhinestones, the calliope's blast sounded as if the very steam pipes were tired.

"Christ a-mighty, it's hot, huh, kid?"

Clem Hoately, the talker, stood beside Stan, wiping the sweat from the band of his panama with a handkerchief. "Say, Stan, run over and get me a bottle of lemon soda from the juice joint. Here's a dime; get yourself one too."

When Stan came back with the cold bottles, Hoately tilted his gratefully. "Jesus, my throat's sore as a bull's ass in fly time."

Stan drank the pop slowly. "Mr. Hoately?"

"Yeah, what?"

"How do you ever get a guy to geek? Or is this the only one? I mean, is a guy born that way—liking to bite the heads off chickens?"

Clem slowly closed one eye. "Let me tell you something, kid. In the carny you don't ask nothing. And you'll get told no lies."

"Okay. But did you just happen to find this fellow—doing—doing this somewhere behind a barn, and work up the act?"

Clem pushed back his hat. "I like you, kid. I like you a lot. And just for that I'm going to give you a treat. I'm *not* going to give you a boot in the ass, get it? That's the treat."

Stan grinned, his cool, bright blue eyes never leaving the older man's face. Suddenly Hoately dropped his voice.

"Just because I'm your pal I ain't going to crap you up. You want to know where geeks came from. Well, listen—you don't find 'em. You *make* 'em."

He let this sink in, but Stanton Carlisle never moved a muscle. "Okay. But how?"

Hoately grabbed the youth by the shirt front and drew him nearer. "Listen, kid. Do I have to draw you a damn blueprint? You pick up a guy and he ain't a geek—he's a drunk. A bottle-a-day booze fool. So you tell him like this: 'I got a little job for you. It's a temporary job. We got to get a new geek. So until we do you'll put on the geek outfit and fake it.' You tell him, 'You don't have to do nothing. You'll have a razor blade in your hand and when you pick up the chicken you give it a nick with the blade and then make like you're drinking the blood. Same with rats. The marks don't know no different.' "

Hoately ran his eye up and down the midway, sizing up the crowd. He turned back to Stan. "Well, he does this for a week and you see to it that he gets his bottle regular and a place to sleep it off in. He likes this fine. This is what he thinks is heaven. So after a week you say to him like this, you say, 'Well, I got to get me a real geek. You're through.' He scares up at this because nothing scares a real rummy like the chance of a dry spell and getting the horrors. He says, 'What's the matter? Ain't I doing okay?' So you say, 'Like crap you're doing okay. You can't draw no crowd faking a geek. Turn in your outfit. You're through.' Then you walk away. He comes following you, begging for another chance and you say, 'Okay. But after tonight out you go.' But you give him his bottle.

"That night you drag out the lecture and lay it on thick. All the while you're talking he's thinking about sobering up and getting the crawling shakes. You give him time to think it over, while you're talking. Then throw in the chicken. He'll geek."

The crowd was coming out of the geek show, gray and

listless and silent except for the drunk. Stan watched them with a strange, sweet, faraway smile on his face. It was the smile of a prisoner who has found a file in a pie.

The Magician

*who holds toward heaven the wand of fire
and points with his other hand toward earth.*

IF YOU'LL step right over this way, folks, I want to call your attention to the attraction now appearing on the first platform. Ladies and gentlemen, you are about to witness one of the most spectacular performances of physical strenth the world has ever seen. Now some of you young fellows in the crowd look pretty husky but I want to tell you, gents, the man you are about to see makes the ordinary blacksmith or athalete look like a babe in arms. The power of an African gorilla in the body of a Greek god. Ladies and gents, Herculo, the world's most perfect man."

Bruno Hertz: If only once she would over here look while I have the robe off I would be glad to drop dead that minute. *Um Gotteswillen*, I would cut my heart out and hand it to her on a plate. Cannot she ever see that? I cannot get up courage to hold her hand in the kinema. Why has a man always to feel over some woman like this? I cannot even tell Zeena how crazy I am for her because then Zeena would try to put us together and then I would feel a *dummkopf* from not knowing how to say to her. Molly—a beautiful *Amerikanische* name. She will never love me. I know it in my heart. But I can tear to pieces any of the wolves in the show such as would hurt that girl. If one of them would try, then maybe Molly could see it. Perhaps then she could guess the way I feel and would give me one word for me to remember always. To remember, back in Wien.

". . . right over here, folks. Will you step in a little closer? On account of this exhibit ain't the biggest thing you ever seen; how about it, Major? Ladies and gentlemen, I now present for your edification and amusement Major Mosquito, the tiniest human being on record. Twenty inches, twenty pounds, and twenty years—and he's got plenty of big ideas for his age. Any of you girls would like to date him after the show, see me and I'll fix ya up. The Major will now entertain you with a little specialty number of his own, singing and tap-dancing to that grand old number, 'Sweet Rosie O'Grady.' Take it away, Major."

Kenneth Horsefield: If I lit a match and held it right close under that big ape's nose I wonder if I'd see the hairs in his nose-holes catch fire. Christ, what an ape! I'd like to have him tied up with his mouth propped open and then I'd sit back smoking my cigar and shoot his teeth out one after another. Apes. They're all apes. Especially the women with their big moon faces. I'd like to sink a hammer in 'em and watch 'em splash like pumpkins. Their great, greasy red mouths open like tunnels. Grease and filth, all of them.

Christ, there it goes. That same crack. The one woman makes it to the other behind her hand. If I see that same hand come up and that same routine once more I'll yell the goddamned place down. A million dames and always the same goddamned crack behind the same goddamned hand and the other one always champing on gum. Some day I'll blast 'em. I don't keep that equalizer in my trunk to play Boy Scout with. And that's the dame I'll blast. I'd of done it before now. Only they'd laugh at seeing me hold the butt with one hand and work the trigger with the other.

*

Joe Plasky: "Thank you, professor. Ladies and gents, I am known as the Half-man Acrobat. As you can see, my legs are both here but they're not much good to me. Infantile paralysis when I was a kid—they just naturally never growed. So I just made up my mind to tie 'em in a knot like this and forget about 'em and go on about my business. This is the way I get upstairs. Up on the hands. Steady. Here we go with a hop, skip, and a jump. Turn around and down we go, easy as pie. Thank you, folks.

"Now here's another little number I worked out by myself. Sometimes in a crowded trolley car I don't have room enough to stand on both hands. So up we go. Steady. And I stand on one! Thank you very much.

"Now then, for my next number I'm going to do something that no other acrobat in the world has ever attempted. A full somersault from a handstand back onto the hands. Are we all set? Let's go. It's a good trick—if I do it. Maybe some of you folks in the front row had better move back a couple steps. Don't bother. I'm just kidding. I've never missed yet, as you can see, for I'm still in the land of the living. All right, here we go—up—and *over!* Thank you very much, folks.

"And now if you'll just step right in close I'm going to give away a few little souvenirs. Naturally, I can't get rich giving away merchandise, but I'll do my best. I have here a little booklet full of old songs, recitations, jokes, wheezes, and parlor games. And I'm not going to charge you a dollar for it, nor even a half, but a cold, thin dime. That's all it costs, folks, a dime for a full evening of fun and fancy. And with it I'm going to give away, as a special inducement at this performance only, this little paper shimmy-dancer. Hold a match behind the paper: you see her shadow; and this is how you make her shake.

"You want one? Thank you, bud. Here you are, folks—brimful of assorted poems, dramatic readings, and witty sayings by the world's wisest men. And only a dime. . . ."

Sis wrote me the kids are both down with whooping cough. I'll send them a box of paints to help keep them quiet. Kids love paints. I'll send them some crayons, too.

*

"Sailor Martin, the living picture gallery. Ladies and gents, this young man that you see before you went to sea at an early age. He was shipwrecked on a tropical island which had only one other inhabitant—an old seafaring man, who had been there most of his life—a castaway. All he had managed to save from the wreck of his ship was a tattoo outfit. To pass the time he taught Sailor Martin the art and he practiced on himself. Most of the patterns you see are his own work. Turn around, Sailor. On his back, a replica of that world-famous painting, the Rock of Ages. On his chest—turn around, Sailor—the Battleship *Maine*, blowing up in Havana Harbor. Now if any of you young fellows in the audience would like an anchor, American flag, or sweetheart's initials worked on your arm in three beautiful colors, step right up to the platform and see the Sailor. No sissies need apply."

Francis Xavier Martin: Boy, that brunette working the electric-chair act is a beaut. Have I got what would make her happy and moan for more! Only Bruno would land on me like a ton of tomcats. I wonder if I'll hear from that redhead in Waterville. God, I can get one on thinking about her yet. What a shape—and knowing right where to put it, too. But this brunette kid, Molly, is the nuts. What a pair of bubbies! High and pointed—and that ain't no cupform either, brother; that's God.

I wish to Christ that kraut Bruno would bust a blood vessel some day, bending them horseshoes. Goddamn, that Molly kid's got legs like a racehorse. Maybe I could give her one jump and then blow the show. Jesus, it would be worth it, to get into that.

"Over here, folks, right over here. On this platform you see one of the most amazing little ladies the wide world has ever known. And right beside her we have an exact replica of the electric chair at Sing Sing prison. . . ."

Mary Margaret Cahill: Don't forget to smile; Dad always said that. Golly, I wish Dad was here. If I could only look out there and see him grinning up at me everything would be

hunky dory. Time to drop the robe and give them an eyeful.
Dad, honey, watch over me. . . .

Dad taught Molly all kinds of wonderful things while she
was growing up and they were fun, too. For instance, how to
walk out of a hotel in a dignified manner with two of your
best dresses wrapped around you under the dress you had on.
They had to do that once in Los Angeles and Molly got all
of her clothes out. Only they nearly caught Dad and he had
to talk fast. Dad was wonderful at talking fast and whenever
he got in a tight place Molly would go all squirmy inside with
thrill and fun because she knew her dad could always wiggle
out just when the others thought he was cornered. Dad was
wonderful.

Dad always knew nice people. The men were sometimes
soused a little but the ladies that Dad knew were always beautiful and they usually had red hair. They were always wonderful to Molly and they taught her to put on lipstick when she
was eleven. The first time she put it on by herself she got
on too much and Dad burst out laughing loud and said
she looked like something from a crib house—and jail bait at
that.

The lady that Dad was friendly with at the time—her name
was Alyse—shushed Dad and said, "Come over here, darling.
Alyse'll show you. Let's take this off and start over. The idea
is to keep people from knowing that you have any makeup on
at all—especially at your age. Now watch." She looked at
Molly's face carefully and said, "This is where you start. And
don't let anybody talk you into putting rouge on anywhere
else. You have a square face and the idea is to soften it and
make it look round." She showed Molly just how to do it and
then took it all off and made her do it herself.

Molly wanted Dad to help her but he said it wasn't his
business—getting it off was more in his line, especially on the
collars of shirts. Molly felt awful, having to do it all by herself
because she was afraid she wouldn't do it right and finally she
cried a little and then Dad took her on his lap and Alyse
showed her again and after that it was all right and she always
used makeup, only people didn't know about it. "My, Mr.
Cahill—what a lovely child! Isn't she the picture of health!

Such lovely rosy cheeks!" Then Dad would say, "Indeed, ma'am, lots of milk and early to bed." Then he would wink at Molly because she didn't like milk and Dad said beer was just as good for you and she didn't like beer very much but it was always nice and cold and besides you got pretzels with it and everything. Also Dad said it was a shame to go to bed early and miss everything when you could sleep late the next day and catch up—unless you had to be at the track for an early workout, to hold the clock on a horse, and then it was better to stay up and go to bed later.

Only, when Dad had made a real killing at the track he always got lit and when he got lit he always tried to send her off to bed just when everything was going swell and because other people in the crowd were always trying to get her to take some, Molly never cared for liquor. Once, in a hotel where they were stopping, there was a girl got terribly drunk and began to take her clothes off and they had to put her to bed in the room next to Molly's. There were a lot of men going in and coming out all night and the next day the cops came and arrested the girl, and Molly heard people talking about it and somebody said later that they let the girl go but she had to go to the hospital because she had been hurt inside someway. Molly couldn't bear the thought of getting drunk after that because anything might happen to you and you shouldn't let anything happen to you with a man unless you were in love with him. That was what everybody said and people who made love but weren't really in love were called tramps. Molly knew several ladies who were tramps and she asked Dad one time why they were tramps and that's what he said: that they'd let anybody hug and kiss them either for presents or money. You shouldn't do that unless the guy was a swell guy and not likely to cross you up or take a powder on you if you were going to have a baby. Dad said you should never let anybody make love to you if you couldn't use his toothbrush, too. He said that was a safe rule and if you followed that you couldn't go wrong.

Molly could use Dad's toothbrush and often did, because one of their brushes was always getting left behind in the hotel or sometimes Dad needed one to clean his white shoes with.

Molly used to wake up before Dad and sometimes she

would run in and hop into his bed and then he would grunt and make funny snorey noises—only they sounded all funny and horrible—and then he would make believe he thought there was a woodchuck in the bed and he would blame the hotel people for letting woodchucks run around in their joint and then he would find out it was Molly and no wood-chuck and he would kiss her and tell her to hurry up and get dressed and then go down and get him a racing form at the cigar stand.

One morning Molly ran in and there was a lady in bed with Dad. She was a very pretty lady and she had no nightie on and neither did Dad. Molly knew what had happened: Dad had been lit the night before and had forgotten to put on his pajamas and the girl had been lit and he had brought her up to their rooms to sleep on account of she was too tight to go home and he had intended to have her sleep with Molly but they had just fallen asleep first. Molly lifted the sheet up real, real careful and then she found out how she would look when she got big.

Then Molly got dressed and went down and got the racing form on the cuff and came back and they were still asleep, only the lady had snuggled in closer to Dad. Molly stood quiet in a corner a long time and kept still, hoping they would wake up and find her and she would run at them and go "Woo!" and scare them. Only the lady made a low noise like a moan and Daddy opened one eye and then put his arms around her. She opened her eyes and said, "Hello, sugar," all slow and sleepy, and then Dad started kissing her and she woke up after a while and started to kiss back. Finally Dad got on top of the lady and began to bounce up and down in the bed and Molly thought that was so funny that she burst out laughing and the lady screamed and said, "Get that kid out of here."

Dad was wonderful. He looked over his shoulder in one of his funny ways and said, "Molly, how would you like to sit in the lobby for about half an hour and pick me a couple of winners out of that racing form? I have to give Queenie here her exercise. You don't want to startle her and make her sprain a tendon." Dad kept still until Molly had gone but when she was outside the door she could hear the bed moving and she wondered if this lady could use Dad's toothbrush and she hoped she wouldn't because Molly wouldn't want to use it afterwards. It would make her sick to use it.

When Molly was fifteen one of the exercise boys at the stable asked her to come up in the hay loft and she went and he grabbed her and started kissing her and she didn't like him enough to kiss him and besides it was all of a sudden and she started wrestling with him and then she called, "Dad! Dad!" because the boy was touching her and Dad came bouncing up into the loft and he hit the boy so hard he fell down on the hay as if he was dead, only he wasn't. Dad put his arm around Molly and said, "You all right, baby?" And Dad kissed her and held her close to him for a minute and then he said, "You got to watch yourself, kidlet. This world's full of wolves. This punk won't bother you no more. Only watch yourself." And Molly smiled and said:

"I couldn't have used his toothbrush anyhow." Then Dad grinned and rapped her easy under the chin with his fist. Molly wasn't scared any more only she never strayed very far from Dad or from other girls. It was awful that had to happen because she could never feel right around the stables any more, and couldn't talk to the exercise boys and the jockeys any more in the old way and even when she did they were always looking at her breasts and that made her feel all weak and scarey inside somehow even when they were polite enough.

She was glad she was beginning to have breasts, though, and she got used to boys looking at them. She used to pull the neck of her nightie down and make like the ladies in evening dresses and once Dad bought her an evening dress. It was beautiful and one way you looked at it it was light rose and the other way it was gold and it came down off the shoulders and was cut low and it was wonderful. Only that was the year Centerboard ran out of the money and Dad had the bankroll on him to show and they had to sell everything they had to get a grubstake. That was when they went back to Louisville. That was the last year.

Dad got a job with an old friend who ran a gambling place down by the river, and Dad was his manager and wore a tuxedo all the time.

Things were going fine after a while and as soon as Dad

squared up some of his tabs he registered Molly at a dancing school and she started to learn acrobatic and tap. She had a wonderful time, showing him the steps as she learned them. Dad could dance a lot of softshoe himself and he never had a lesson. He said he just had Irish feet. Also he wanted her to take music lessons and sing, only she never could sing—she took after Mother that way. When the school gave a recital Molly did a Hawaiian number with a real hula skirt somebody had sent Dad from Honolulu and her hair falling over her shoulders like a black cloud and flowers in her hair and dark makeup and everybody applauded and some of the boys whistled and that made Dad mad because he thought they were getting fresh but Molly loved it because Dad was out there and as long as he was there she didn't care what happened.

She was sixteen and all grown up when things went to smash. Some fellows from Chicago had come down and there was trouble at the place where Dad worked. Molly never did find out what it was, only a couple of big men came to the house one night about two o'clock and Molly knew they were cops and she went all weak, thinking Dad had done something and they wanted him but he had always told her that the way to deal with cops was to smile at them, act dumb, and give them an Irish name.

One said, "You Denny Cahill's daughter?" Molly said yes. He said, "I got some mighty tough news for you, kid. It's about your dad." That was when Molly felt her feet slip on glass, like the world had suddenly tilted and it was slippery glass and she was falling off it into the dark and would fall and fall forever because there was no end to the place where she was falling.

She just stood there and she said, "Tell me."

The cop said, "Your dad's been hurt, girlie. He's hurt real bad." He wasn't like a shamus now; he was more like the sort of man who might have a daughter himself. She went up close to him because she was afraid of falling.

She said, "Is Dad dead?" and he nodded and put his arm around her and she didn't remember anything more for a while, only she was in the hospital when she came to and somehow she was all groggy and sleepy and she thought she had been hurt and kept asking for Dad and a cross nurse said she had better keep quiet and then she remembered and Dad was dead and she started to scream and it was like laughing, only it felt horrible and she couldn't stop and then they came and stuck her arm with a hype gun and she went out again and it was that way for a couple of times and finally she could stop crying and they told her she would have to get out because other people needed the bed.

Molly's grandfather, "Judge" Kincaid, said she could live with him and her aunt if she would take a business course and get a job in a year and Molly tried but she couldn't ever get it into her head somehow, although she could remember past performances of horses swell. The Judge had a funny way of looking at her and several times he seemed about to get friendly and then he would chill up. Molly tried being nice to him and calling him Granddad but he didn't like that and once, just to see what would happen, she ran up to him when he came in and threw her arms around his neck. He got terribly mad that time and told her aunt to get her out of the house, he wouldn't stand having her around.

It was terrible without Dad to tell her things and talk to and Molly wished she had died along with Dad. Finally she got a scholarship to the dancing school and she worked part time there with the young kids and Miss La Verne, who ran the school, let her stay with her. Miss La Verne was very nice at first and so was her boy friend, Charlie, who was a funny-looking man, kind of fat, who used to sit and look at Molly and he reminded her of a frog, the way he used to spread his fingers out on his knees, pointing in, and pop his eyes.

Then Miss La Verne got cross and said Molly better get a job, but Molly didn't quite know how to begin and finally Miss La Verne said, "If I get you a job will you stick with it?" Molly promised.

It was a job with a carny. There was a Hawaiian dance show, what they called a kooch show—two other girls and Molly. The fellow who ran it and did the talking was called Doc Abernathy. Molly didn't like him a bit and he was always trying to make the girls. Only Jeannette, one of the dancers, and Doc were steady and Jeannette was crazy-mad jealous of the other two. Doc used to devil her by horsing around with them.

Molly always liked Zeena, who ran the mental act in the Ten-in-One show across the midway. Zeena was awfully nice and she knew more about life and people than anybody Molly had ever met except Dad. Zeena had Molly bunk in with her, when she stayed in hotels, for company, because Zeena's husband slept in the tent to watch the props, he said. Really it was because he was a souse and he couldn't make love to Zeena any more. Zeena and Molly got to be real good friends and Molly didn't wish she was dead any more.

Then Jeannette got nastier and nastier about Doc's paying so much attention to Molly and she wouldn't believe that Molly didn't encourage him. The other girl told her, "With a chassis like that Cahill kid's got you don't have to do no encouraging." But Jeannette thought Molly was a stinker. One day Doc whispered something to her about Molly and Jeannette started for her looking like a wild animal with her lips pulled back over her teeth. She smacked Molly in the face and before Molly knew what was going on she had pulled off her shoe and was swinging at her, beating her in the face with it. Doc came rushing over and he and Jeannette had a terrible battle. She was cursing and screaming and Doc told her to shut up or he would smash her in the tits. Molly ran out and went over to the Ten-in-One and the boss fired Doc out of the carny and the kooch show went back to New York.

"Fifteen thousand volts of electricity pass through her body without hurting a hair of the little lady's head. Ladies and gentlemen, Mamzelle Electra, the girl who, like Ajax of Holy Writ, defies the lightning. . . ."

Glory be to God, I hope nothing happens to that wiring. I want Dad. God, how I want him here. I've got to remember to smile. . . .

"Stand over here, Teddy, and hold onto Ma's hand. So's you won't git tromped on and kin see. That there's a 'lectric chair, same's they got in the penitentiary. No, they ain't going to hurt the lady none, leastways I hope not. See? They strap her in that chair—only there's something about her body that don't take 'lectricity. Same's rain rolls right off the old gander's back. Don't be scared, Teddy. Ain't nothing going to happen to her. See how the 'lectricity makes her hair stand out stiff? Lightning'll do the same thing I heard tell. There. See? She's holding a 'lectric bulb in one hand and grabbing the wire with the other. See the bulb light? That means the 'lectricity is passing right through her 'thout hurting her none. I wisht your pa was that way with 'lectricity. He got a powerful bad burn last winter, time the wires blowed down and he was helping Jim Harness get his road cleared. Come along, Teddy. That's all they're going to do over here."

Now I can get up. Sailor Martin's looking at me again. I can't keep saying no to him every time he asks me to go out with him. But he can always think faster than I can. Only I mustn't let him, ever. I mustn't be a tramp; I don't want it this way, the first time. Dad . . .

Stanton Carlisle: The great Stanton stood up and smiled, running his glance over the field of upturned faces. He took a deep breath. "Well, folks, first of all I'm going to show you how to make money. Is there anybody in the crowd who's willing to trust me with the loan of a dollar bill? You'll get it back—if you can run fast. Thanks, bud. Now then—nothing in either hand, nothing up the sleeves."

Showing his hands empty, save for the borrowed bill, Stan gave a hitch to his sleeves. In the folds of his left sleeve was a roll of bills which he acquired deftly. "Now then, one dollar— Wait a minute, bud. Are you sure you gave me only one? You're sure. Maybe that's all you got with you, eh? But here are two—one and two. Count 'em. It's a good trick, especially along toward the end of the week."

Which one will smile at the oldest gag? One out of every five. Remember that. One in five is a born chump.

He produced the bills one after another, until he had a green fan of them. He returned the bill to the lad. In doing so he turned his left side from the crowd, got a metal cup in his hand. It hung by an elastic from his left hip.

"Now then, out of nowhere they came. Let's see what happens to them when we roll them up. One, two, three, four, five, six. All present and accounted for. Into a roll—" He

placed the bills in his left hand, slipping them into the vanisher. "Blow on the hand—" The vanisher, released, thudded
softly against his hip under his coat. "Lo and behold! Gone!"

There was a scattering of applause, as if they were a little
ashamed of it. The chumps.

"Where did they go? You know, day after day I stand here—
wondering just where they do go!" That's Thurston's gag. By
God, I'm going to use it until I see one face—just one—in
this bunch of rubes that gets the point. They never do. But
that dollar bill production goes over. Poverty-struck bastards—they all wish they could do it. Make money out of the
air. Only that's not the way I make mine. But it's better than
real estate. My old man and his deals. Church vestryman on
Sundays, con man the rest of the week. Frig him, the Bible-
spouting bastard.

"Now then, if I can have your attention for a moment. I
have here a bunch of steel rings. Each and every one of them
a separate, solid hoop of steel. I have one, two, three-four,
five, sixseveneight. Right? Now I take two. Tap 'em. Joined
together! Would you take these, madam, and tell me if you
can find any joints or signs of an opening? No? Thank you.
All solid. And again, two separate rings. Go! Joined!"

Better speed it up, they're getting restless. This is the life,
though. Everyone looking at you. How does he do it? Gosh,
that's slick. Trying to figure it out. It's magic to them, all
right. This is the life. While they're watching and listening
you can tell 'em anything. They believe you. You're a magician. Pass solid rings through each other. Pull dollars out of
the air. Magic. You're top man—while you keep talking.

"And now, folks, eight separate and distinct rings; yet by a
magic word they fly together and are joined inextricably into
a solid mass. There you are! I thank you for your kind attention. Now I have here a little booklet that's worth its weight
in gold. Here is a collection of magic tricks that you can do—
an hour's performance before your club, lodge, or church
gathering or in your own parlor. An hour's practice—a lifetime of fun, magic, and mystery. This book formerly sold for
a dollar, but for today I'm going to let you have it for two
bits—a quarter of a dollar. Let's hurry it up, folks, because I
know you all want to see and hear Madam Zeena, the seeress,

and her act does not go on until everyone who wants one of these great books gets one. Thank you, sir. And you. Any more? Right.

"Now then, folks, don't go 'way. The next complete show will not start for twenty minutes. I call your attention to the next platform. Madam Zeena—miracle woman of the ages. She sees, she knows, she tells you the innermost secrets of your past, your present, and your future. Madam Zeena!"

Stan jumped down lightly from his own small platform and pushed through the crowd to a miniature stage draped in maroon velvet. A woman had stepped out from between the curtains. The crowd flowed over and stood waiting, looking up at her, some of the faces absently chewing, hands cupping popcorn into mouths.

The woman was tall, dressed in flowing white with astrological symbols embroidered on the hem of her robe. A cascade of brassy blond hair fell down her back and a band of gilt leather studded with glass jewels was around her forehead. When she raised her arms the loose sleeves fell back. She had large bones, but her arms were white and capable-looking, with a spattering of freckles. Her eyes were blue, her face round, and her mouth a shade too small, so that she looked a trifle like an elaborate doll. Her voice was low-pitched with a hearty ring to it.

"Step right up, folks, and don't be bashful. If there's any of you that want to ask me a question Mr. Stanton is now passing among you with little cards and envelopes. Write your question on the card; be careful not to let anybody else see what you write, because that's your business. I don't want anybody asking me about somebody else's business. Just let's all mind our own and we'll stay out of trouble. When you've written your question, sign your initials to the card or write your name as a token of good faith. Then give the sealed envelope to Mr. Stanton. You'll see what I'm going to do next.

"Meantime, while we're waiting for you to write your questions, I'm going to start right in. It isn't necessary for you to write anything, but that helps you to fix it firmly in mind and keeps your mind from wandering off it, same as if you want to remember somebody's name you just met it helps to jot it down. Isn't that so?"

One out of every five heads nodded, entranced, and the rest looked on, some with dull eyes, but most of them with questions written on their faces.

Questions? They've all got questions, Stan thought, passing out cards and envelopes. Who hasn't? Answer their questions and you can have them, body and soul. Or just about. "Yes, madam, you can ask her anything. The questions are held in strictest confidence. No one will know but yourself."

"First of all," Zeena began, "there's a lady worried about her mother. She's asking me mentally, 'Is mother going to get better?' Isn't that so? Where is that lady?"

Timidly a hand went up. Zeena pounced on it. "Well, madam, I'd say your mother has had a lot of hard work in her life and she's had a lot of trouble, mostly about money. But there's something else in there that I don't see quite clear yet." Stan looked at the woman who had raised her hand. Farmer's wife. Sunday best, ten years out of style. Zeena could go to town on this one—a natural.

"I'd say, ma'am, that what your mother needs is a good long rest. Mind, I'm not saying how she's going to get it—what with taxes and sickness in the family and doctor's bills piling up. I know how it is because I've had my share of troubles, same as all of us, until I learned how to govern my life by the stars. But I think if you and your brothers—no, you have a couple of sisters, though, haven't you? One sister? Well, if you and your sister can work out some way to let her get a couple weeks' rest I think her health ought to improve mighty quick. But you just keep following a doctor's orders. That is, you better get her to a doctor. I don't think them patent medicines will do her much good. You got to get her to a doctor. Maybe he'll take a few bushels of potatoes or a shoat as part of the bill. Anyhow, I think she'll be all right if you have plenty of faith. If you'll see me right after the demonstration, maybe I can tell you more. And you want to watch the stars and make sure you don't do anything at the wrong time of the month.

"I see now that Mr. Stanton has got a good handful of questions, so if he'll bring them right up here on the stage we'll continue with the readings."

Stan pushed through the crowd to a curtained door on one

side of the little proscenium. He passed through. Inside there
was a flight of rough board steps leading to the stage. It was
dark and smelled of cheap whisky. Under the steps there was
a square window opening into the low, boxlike compartment
beneath the stage. At the window a bleary, unshaven face
blinked out over a spotlessly clean white shirt. One hand held
out a bunch of envelopes. Without a word Stan handed the
man the envelopes he had collected, received the dummy
batch, and in a second was onstage with them. Zeena moved
forward a little table containing a metal bowl and a dark
bottle.

"We'll ask the gentleman to drop all the questions into this
bowl. Now then, people ask me if I have spirit aid in doing
what I do. I always tell them that the only spirits I control
are the ones in this bottle—spirits of alcohol. I'm going to
pour a little on your questions and drop a match into the
bowl. Now you can see them burning, and that's the last of
them. So anybody who was afraid someone would find out
what he wrote or that I was going to handle his question can
just forget it. I've never touched them. I don't have to because I get an impression right away."

Stan had backed to one corner of the stage and stood
watching the audience quietly as they strained their necks upward, hanging on every word of the seeress. In the floor,
which was a few inches above their eye level, was a square
hole. Zeena stroked her forehead, covering her eyes with her
hand. At the opening appeared a pad of paper, a grimy thumb
holding it, on which was scrawled in crayon, "What to do
with wagon? J. E. Giles."

Zeena looked up, folding her arms with decision. "I get an
impression— It's a little cloudy still but it's getting clearer. I
get the initials *J* . . . *E* . . . *G.* I believe it's a gentleman. Is
that right? Will the person who has those initials raise his
hand, please?"

An old farmer lifted a finger as gnarled as a grapevine.
"Here, ma'am."

"Ah, there you are. Thank you, Mr. *Giles.* The name *is*
Giles, isn't it?"

The crowd sucked in its breath. "I thought so. Now then,
Mr. Giles, you have a problem, isn't that right?" The old

man's head wagged solemnly. Stan noted the deep creases in his red neck. Old sodbuster. Sunday clothes. White shirt, black tie. What he wears at funerals. Tie already tied—he hooks it onto his collar button. Blue serge suit—Sears, Roebuck or a clothing store in town.

"Let me see," Zeena went on, her hand straying to her forehead again. "I see— Wait. I see green trees and rolling land. It's plowed land. Fenced in."

The old man's jaw hung open, his eyes frowning with concentration, trying not to miss a single word.

"Yes, green trees. Probably willow trees near a crick. And I see something under those trees. A— It's a wagon."

Watching, Stan saw him nod, rapt.

"An old, blue-bodied wagon under those trees."

"By God, ma'am, it's right there this minute."

"I thought so. Now you have a problem on your mind. You are thinking of some decision you have to make connected with that wagon, isn't that so? You are thinking about what to do with the wagon. Now, Mr. Giles, I would like to give you a piece of advice: don't sell that old blue-bodied wagon."

The old man shook his head sternly. "No, ma'am, I won't. Don't belong to me!"

There was a snicker in the crowd. One young fellow laughed out loud. Zeena drowned him out with a full-throated laugh of her own. She rallied, "Just what I wanted to find out, my friend. Folks, here we have an honest man and that's the only sort I want to do any business with. Sure, he wouldn't think of selling what wasn't his, and I'm mighty glad to hear it. But let me ask you just one question, Mr. Giles. Is there anything the matter with that wagon?"

"Spring's broke under the seat," he muttered, frowning.

"Well, I get an impression that you are wondering whether to get that spring fixed before you return the wagon or whether to return it with the spring broken and say nothing about it. Is that it?"

"That's it, ma'am!" The old farmer looked around him triumphantly. He was vindicated.

"Well, I'd say you had just better let your conscience be your guide in that matter. I would be inclined to talk it over with the man you borrowed it from and find out if the spring was weak when he loaned it to you. You ought to be able to work it out all right."

Stan quietly left the stage and crept down the steps behind the draperies. He squeezed under the steps and came out beneath the stage. Dead grass and the light coming through chinks in the box walls, with the floor over his head. It was hot, and the reek of whisky made the air sweetly sick.

Pete sat at a card table under the stage trap. Before him were envelopes Stan had passed him on his way up to the seeress; he was snipping the ends off with scissors, his hands shaking. When he saw Stan he grinned shamefacedly.

Above them Zeena had wound up the "readings" and gone into her pitch: "Now then, folks, if you really want to know how the stars affect your life, you don't have to pay a dollar, nor even a half; I have here a set of astrological readings, all worked out for each and every one of you. Let me know your date of birth and you get a forecast of future events complete with character reading, vocational guidance, lucky numbers, lucky days of the week, and the phases of the moon most conducive to your prosperity and success. I've only a limited amount of time, folks, so let's not delay. They're only a quarter, first come, first served and while they last, because I'm getting low."

Stan slipped out of the sweatbox, quietly parted the curtains, stepped into the comparatively cooler air of the main tent, and sauntered over toward the soft drink stand.

Magic is all right, but if only I knew human nature like Zeena. She has the kind of magic that ought to take anybody right to the top. It's a convincer—that act of hers. Yet nobody can do it, cold. It takes years to get that kind of smooth talk, and she's never stumped. I'll have to try and pump her and get wised up. She's a smart dame, all right. Too bad she's tied to a rumdum like Pete who can't even get his rhubarb up any more; so everybody says. She isn't a bad-looking dame, even if she is a little old.

Wait a minute, wait a minute. Maybe here's where we start to climb. . . .

CARD III

The High Priestess

*Queen of borrowed light who guards
a shrine between the pillars Night and Day.*

Beyond the flowing windshield the taillight of the truck
ahead wavered ruby-red in the darkness. The windshield
wiper's tock-tock-tock was hypnotic. Sitting between the two
women, Stan remembered the attic at home on a rainy day—
private, shut off from prying eyes, close, steamy, intimate.

Molly sat next to the door on his right, leaning her head
against the glass. Her raincoat rustled when she crossed her
legs. In the driver's seat Zeena bent forward, peering between
the swipes of the wiper, following blindly the truck that held
the snake box and the gear for the geek show, Bruno's
weights, and Martin's baggage with the tattoo outfit. The
geek, with his bottle, had crawled into a little cavern made by
the piled gear and folded canvas.

In her own headlights, when the procession stopped at a
crossing, Zeena could see Bruno's chunky form in a slicker
swing from the cab and plod around to the back to look at
the gear and make sure the weights were fast. Then he came

over and stepped on the running board. Zeena cranked down the window on her side. "Hi, Dutchy—wet enough for you?"

"Joost about," he said softly. "How is things back here? How is Pete?"

"Right in back of us here having a snooze on the drapes. You reckon we'll try putting up in this weather?"

Bruno shook his head. His attention crept past Zeena and Stan, and for a moment his eyes lingered sadly on Molly, who had not turned her head.

"I joost want to make sure everything is okay." He turned back into the rain, crossing the streaming beam of the headlights and vanishing in the dark. The truck ahead began to move; Zeena shifted gears.

"He's a fine boy," she said at last. "Molly, you ought to give Bruno a chance."

Molly said, "No, thanks. I'm doing okay. No, thanks."

"Go on—you're a big girl now. Time you was having some fun in this world. Bruno could treat you right, by the looks of him. When I was a kid I had a beau that was a lumberjack— he was built along the lines of Bruno. And oh, boy!"

As if suddenly aware that her thigh was pressed close to Stan's, Molly squeezed farther into the corner. "No, thanks. I'm having fun now."

Zeena sighed gustily. "Take your time, kid. Maybe you just ain't met the right fella. And Stan here ought to be ashamed of himself. Why, me and Pete was married when I was seventeen. Pete wasn't much older'n Stan. How old are you, Stan?"

"Twenty-one," Stan said, keeping his voice low.

Approaching a curve, Zeena braced herself. Stan could feel the muscles of her thigh tighten as she worked the wheel. "Them was the days. Pete was working a crystal act in vaudeville. God, he was handsome. In a soup and fish he looked about two feet taller than in his street clothes. He wore a little black beard and a turban. I was working in the hotel when he checked in and I was that green I asked him when I brought in the towels if he'd tell my fortune. I'd never had my fortune told. He looked in my hand and told me something very exciting was going to happen to me involving a tall, dark man. I got the giggles. It was only because he was so good-looking.

I wasn't bashful around men. Never was. I couldn't have kept that hotel job a minute if I had been. But the best I'd been hoping for was to hook some gambler or race-track man—hoping he would help me get on the stage."

Suddenly Molly spoke. "My dad was a race-track man. He knew a lot about horses. He didn't die broke."

"Well, now," Zeena said, taking her eyes from the point of ruby light ahead long enough to send Molly a warm look in the darkness. "What d'you know. Oh, the gamblers was the great sheiks in my day. Any gal who could knock herself off a gambling man was doing something. We started when we were fourteen or fifteen. Lordy, that was fifteen years ago! Seems like yesterday some ways and like a million years in others. But the gamblers were the heartbreakers. Say, honey—I'll bet your dad was handsome, eh? Girls generally take after their fathers."

"You bet he was handsome. Daddy was the best-looking man I ever saw. I always said I'd never get married until I found a man as good-looking as Daddy—and as sweet. He was grand."

"Umm. Tall, dark, and handsome. Guess that lets you out, Stan. I don't mean about being tall. You're tall enough. But Molly likes 'em dark."

"I could get some hair dye," Stan said.

"Nope. Nope, never do. That might fool the public, Goldy Locks, but it would never fool a wife. Less'n you wanted to dye all over." She threw back her head and laughed. Stan found himself laughing too, and even Molly joined in.

"Nope," Zeena went on, "Pete was a real brunette all over; and, boy, could he love. We got married second season I traveled with him. He had me doing the back-of-the-house steal with the envelopes at first, in an usherette's uniform. Then we worked out a two-person act. He worked the stage, with his crystal, and I worked the audience. We used a word code at first and he used to ring in that part of the act as a stall while another girl was copying out the questions backstage. I'd go out and have people give me articles and Pete would look into his crystal and describe them. When we started we only used about ten different things and it was simple, but half the time I would get mixed up and then Pete would do some tall ad-libbing. But I learned. You should of seen our act when we were working the Keith time. By God, we could practically send a telegram word by word, and nobody could tumble, it was that natural, what we said."

"Why didn't you stay in vaudeville?" Stan asked intently. Suddenly he knew he had said the wrong thing; but there was no way to recall it, so he kept quiet.

Zeena paid close attention to her driving for a moment and then she rallied. "Pete's nerve began to go back on him." She turned and looked back into the rear of the van at the curled, sleeping figure, covered with a raincoat. Then she went on, dropping her voice. "He began muffing the code and he always needed a few shots before going on. Booze and mentalism don't mix. But we do as well in the carny, figuring up the net at the end of the year. And we don't have to cut no dash—living in swell hotels and all that. Horoscopes are easy to pitch and cost you about twenty-five a thousand. And we can take it easy in the winter. Pete don't drink much then. We got a shack down in Florida and he likes it down there. I do a little tea-leaf reading and one winter I worked a mitt camp in Miami. Palmistry always goes good in a town like Miami."

"I like Miami," Molly said softly. "Dad and I used to go there for the races at Hialeah and Tropical Park. It's a grand place."

"Any place is grand, long as you got the old do-re-mi in the grouch bag," Zeena said. "Say, this must be it. They're turning. I can tell you I ain't going to sleep in the truck tonight. Little Zeena's going to get her a room with a bathtub if they got any in this town. What say, kid?"

"Anything suits me," Molly said. "I'd love to have a hot bath."

Stan had a vision of what Molly would look like in the bathtub. Her body would be milk-white and long-limbed there in the water and a black triangle of shadow and her breasts with rosy tips. He would stand looking down at her and then bend over and she would reach soapy arms up but she would have to be someone else and he would have to be someone else, he thought savagely, because he had never managed to do it yet and always something held him back or the girl seemed to freeze up or suddenly he didn't want her any more once it was within reach and besides there was never the time or the place was wrong and besides it took a lot of dough and a car and all kinds of stuff and then they would expect you to marry them right away and they would probably get a kid the first thing. . . .

"Here we are, chillun," Zeena said.

The rain had slackened to a drizzle. In the lights of head-lamps the roughnecks were busy tearing canvas from the trucks. Stan threw his slicker over his shoulders, went around to open the rear doors of the truck. He crawled in and gently shook Pete by the ankle. "Pete, wake up. We're here. We've got to put up."

"Oh, lemme sleep five minutes more."

"Come on, Pete. Zeena says to give us a hand putting up."

He suddenly threw off the raincoat which covered him and sat up shivering. "Just a minute, kid. Be right with you." He crawled stiffly from the truck and stood shaking, tall and stooped, in the cool night air. From one pocket he drew a bottle, offering it to Stan, who shook his head. Pete took a pull, then another, and corked the bottle. Then he drew the cork out, finished it, and heaved it into the night. "Dead soldier."

The floodlights were up and the carny boss had laid out the midway with his marking stakes. Stan shouldered planks that fitted together to make Zeena's stage and drew one bundle of them from the van.

The top of the Ten-in-One was going up. Stan gave a hand on the hoist, while watery dawn showed over the trees and in houses on the edge of the fair grounds lights began to snap on in bedrooms, then in kitchens.

In the growing lavender of daybreak the carny took shape. Booths sprang up, the cookhouse sent the perfume of coffee along the dripping air. Stan paused, his shirt stuck to him with sweat, a comfortable glow in the muscles of his arms and back. And his old man had wanted him to go into real estate!

Inside the Ten-in-One tent Stan and Pete set up the stage for the mental act. They got the curtains hung, moved the bridge table and a chair under the stage, and stowed away the cartons of horoscopes.

Zeena returned. In the watery gold light of morning lines showed around her eyes, but she held herself as straight as a tent pole. "Got me a whole damn bridal suite—two rooms and bawth. C'mon over, both of you, and have a good soak."

Pete needed a shave, and his gaunt, angular face seemed stretched tighter over his bones. "I'd like to, sugar. Only I got to do a few little chores first in town. I'll see you later on."

"It's 28 Locust Lane. You got enough dough?"

"You might let me have a couple of dollars from the treasury."

"Okay, honey. But get some coffee into you first. Promise Zeena you'll have breakfast."

Pete took the money and put it carefully away in a billfold. "I shall probably have a small glass of iced orange juice, two three-minute eggs, melba toast and coffee," he said, his voice suddenly vibrant. Then he seemed to fade. He took out the billfold and looked in it. "Must make sure I got my money safe," he said in an off-key, strangely childish tone. He started off across the lot toward a shack at the edge of the village. Zeena watched him go.

"I'll bet that joint is a blind pig," she said to Stan. "Pete's sure a real clairvoyant when it comes to locating hidden treasure—long as it gurgles when you shake it. Well, you coming back and clean up? Look at you! Your shirt's sticking to you with sweat!"

As they walked, Stan breathed in the morning. Mist hung over the hills beyond the town, and from a slope rising from the other side of the road came the gentle tonk of a cowbell. Stan stopped and stretched his arms.

Zeena stopped too. "Never get nothing like this working the two-a-day. Honest, you know, Stan, I'd get homesick just to hear a cow moo."

The sun, breaking through, sparkled in wagon ruts still deep with rain. Stan took her arm to help her across the puddles. Under the warm, smooth rubber of the raincoat he pressed the soft bulge of her breast. He could feel the heat steaming up over his face where the cool wind struck it.

"You're awful nice to have around, Stan. You know that?"

He stopped walking. They were out of sight of the carnival grounds. Zeena was smiling at something inside herself. Awkwardly his arm went around her and he kissed her. It was lots different from kissing high-school girls. The warm, intimate searching of her mouth left him weak and dizzy. They broke apart and Stan said, "Wow."

Zeena let her hand stay for an instant pressed against his cheek; then she turned and they walked on, hand in hand.

"Where's Molly?" he asked after a while.

"Pounding her ear. I talked the old gal that has the house into giving us the two rooms for the price of one. While I was waiting for her to put up her husband's lunch I took a quick peek in the family Bible and got all their birth dates down pat. I told her right off that she was Aries—March 29th. Then I gave her a reading that just set her back on her heels. We got a real nice room. Always pays to keep your eyes open, I always say. The kid had her a good soak and hit the hay. She'll be pounding her ear. She's a fine kid, if she could only grow up some and stop yelping for her daddy every time she has a hangnail. But she'll get over it, I reckon. Wait till you see the size of these rooms."

The room reminded Stan of home. The old house on Linden Street and the big brass bedstead in his parents' room, where it was all tumbled and smelling of perfume on Mother's pillow and of hair restorer on his father's side.

Zeena threw off her raincoat, rolled a newspaper into a tight bar, tied it with string in the middle and hung the coat up on a hook in the closet. She pulled off her shoes and stretched out on the bed, reaching her arms wide. Then she drew out her hairpins and the brassy hair which had been in a neat double roll around her head fell in pigtails. Swiftly she unbraided them and let the hair flow around her on the pillow.

Stan said, "I guess I'd better get that bath. I'll see if there's any hot water left." He hung his coat and vest on a chairback. When he looked up he saw that Zeena had her eyes on him. Her lids were partly closed. One arm was bent under her head and she was smiling, a sweet, possessive smile.

He came over to her and sat beside her on the edge of the bed. Zeena covered his hand with hers and suddenly he bent and kissed her. This time there was no need for them to stop and they didn't. Her hand slid inside his shirt and felt the smooth warmth of his back tenderly.

"Wait, honey. Not yet. Kiss me some more."

"What if Molly should wake up?"

"She won't. She's young. You couldn't wake that kid up. Don't worry about things, honey. Just take it easy and slow."

All the things Stan had imagined himself saying and doing at such a time did not fit. It was thrilling and dangerous and his heart beat so hard he felt it would choke him.

"Take all your things off, honey, and hang 'em on the chair, neat."

Stan wondered that he didn't feel in the least ashamed now that this was it. Zeena stripped off her stockings, unhooked her dress and drew it leisurely over her head. Her slip followed.

At last she lay back, her bent arm under her head, and beckoned him to come to her. "Now then, Stan honey, you can let yourself go."

"It's getting late."

"Sure is. You got to get your bath and get back. Folks'll think Zeena's gone and seduced you."

"They'd be right."

"Damned if they wouldn't." She raised herself on her elbows and let her hair fall down on each side of his face and kissed him lightly. "Get along with you. Skat, now."

"Can't. You're holding me pinned down."

"Try'n get away."

"Can't. Too heavy."

"See'f you can wiggle loose."

There was a knock at the door, a gentle, timid tapping. Zeena threw her hair out of her eyes. Stan started but she laid one finger on his lips. She swung off the bed gracefully and pulled Stan up by one hand. Then she handed him his trousers, underwear, and socks and pushed him into the bathroom.

Behind the bathroom door Stan crouched, his ear to the panel, his heart hammering with alarm. He heard Zeena get her robe out of a bag and take her time about answering the tap. Then the hall door opened. Pete's voice.

"Sorry t'wake you, sugar. Only—" His voice sounded thicker. "Only, had little shopping to do. I sorta forgot 'bout getting breakfast."

There was the snap of a pocketbook opening. "Here's a buck, honey. Now make sure it's breakfast."

"Cross my heart, hope die."

Stan heard Zeena's bare feet approach the bathroom. "Stan," she called, "hurry up in there. I want to get some sleep. Get out of that tub and fall into your pants." To Pete she said, "The kid's had a hard night, tearing down and putting up in all that rain. I expect he's fallen asleep in the tub. Maybe you better not wait for him."

The door closed. Stan straightened up. She had never turned a hair, lying to Pete about him being in the bathtub. It comes natural in women, he thought. That's the way they all do when they have guts enough. That's the way they would all like to do. He found himself trembling. Quietly he drew a tub of hot water.

When it was half full he lay in it and closed his eyes. Well, now he knew. This was what all the love-nest murderers killed over and what people got married to get. This was why men left home and why women got themselves dirty reputations. This was the big secret. Now I know. But there's nothing disappointing about the feeling. It's okay.

He let his hands trail in the hot water and splashed little ripples over his chest. He opened his eyes. Drawing his hand out of the steamy warmth he gazed at it a moment and then carefully took from the back of it a hair that gleamed brassy-gold, like a tiny, crinkled wire. Zeena was a natural blonde.

The weeks went by. The Ackerman-Zorbaugh Monster Shows crawled from town to town, the outline of the sky's edge around the fair grounds changing but the sea of up-turned faces always the same.

The first season is always the best and the worst for a carny. Stan's muscles hardened and his fingers developed great sure-ty, his voice greater volume. He put a couple of coin sleights in the act that he would never have had the nerve to try in public before.

Zeena taught him many things, some of them about magic.

"Misdirection is the whole works, honey. You don't need no fancy production boxes and trap doors and trick tables. I've always let on that a man that will spend his time learning misdirection can just reach in his pocket and put something in a hat and then go ahead and take it out again and everybody will sit back and gasp, wondering where it came from."

"Did you ever do magic?" he asked her.

Zeena laughed. "Not on your sweet life. There's very few girls goes in for magic. And that's the reason. A gal spends all her time learning how to attract attention to herself. Then in magic she has to unlearn all that and learn how to get the audience to look at something else. Strain's too great. The dolls can never make it. I couldn't. I've always stuck to the mental business. It don't hurt anybody—makes plenty of friends for you wherever you go. Folks are always crazy to have their fortunes told, and what the hell— You cheer 'em up, give 'em something to wish and hope for. That's all the preacher does every Sunday. Not much different, being a fortuneteller and a preacher, way I look at it. Everybody hopes for the best and fears the worst and the worst is generally what happens but that don't stop us from hoping. When you stop hoping you're in a bad way."

Stan nodded. "Has Pete stopped hoping?"

Zeena was silent and her childish blue eyes were bright. "Sometimes I think he has. Pete's scared of something—I think he got good and scared of himself a long time ago. That's what made him such a wiz as a crystal-reader—for a few years. He wished like all get out that he really could read the future in the ball. And when he was up there in front of them he really believed he was doing it. And then all of a sudden he began to see that there wasn't no magic anywhere to lean on and he had nobody to lean on in the end but himself—not me, not his friends, not Lady Luck—just himself. And he was scared he would let himself down."

"So he did?"

"Yeah. He did."

"What's going to happen to him?"

Zeena bristled. "Nothing's going to happen to him. He is a sweet man, down deep. Long as he lasts I'll stick to him. If it hadn't been for Pete I'd of probably ended up in a crib house. Now I got a nice trade that'll always be in demand as long as there's a soul in the world worried about where next month's rent is coming from. I can always get along. And take Pete right along with me."

Across the tent the talker, Clem Hoately, had mounted the platform of Major Mosquito and started his lecture. The Major drew back one tiny foot and aimed a kick with deadly accuracy at Hoately's shin. It made the talker stammer for a moment. The midget was snarling like an angry kitten.

"The Major is a nasty little guy," Stan said.

"Sure he is. How'd you like to be shut up in a kid's body that way? With the marks all yawping at you. It's different in our racket. We're up head and shoulders above the marks. We're better'n they are and they know it. But the Major's a freak born."

"How about Sailor Martin? He's a made freak."

Zeena snorted. "He's just a pecker carrying a man around with it. He started by having a lot of anchors and nude women tattooed on his arms to show the girls how tough he was or something. Then he got that battleship put on his chest and he was off. He was like a funny paper, with his shirt off, and he figured he might as well make his skin work for him. If he was ever in the Navy, I was born in a convent."

"He doesn't seem to be making much time with your Electric Chair pal."

Zeena's eyes flashed. "He better not. That kid's not going to get it until she runs into some guy that'll treat her right. I'll see to that. I'd beat the be-Jesus out of any snot-nose that went monkeying around Molly."

"You and who else?"

"Me and Bruno."

Evansburg, Morristown, Linklater, Cooley Mills, Ocheke-tawney, Bale City, Boeotia, Sanders Falls, Newbridge.

Coming: Ackerman-Zorbaugh Monster Shows. Auspices Tall Cedars of Zion, Caldwell Community Chest, Pioneer Daughters of Clay County, Kallakie Volunteer Fire Department, Loyal Order of Bison.

Dust when it was dry. Mud when it was rainy. Swearing, steaming, sweating, scheming, bribing, bellowing, cheating, the carny went its way. It came like a pillar of fire by night, bringing excitement and new things into the drowsy towns— lights and noise and the chance to win an Indian blanket, to ride on the ferris wheel, to see the wild man who fondles those rep-tiles as a mother would fondle her babes. Then it vanished in the night, leaving the trodden grass of the field and the debris of popcorn boxes and rusting tin ice-cream spoons to show where it had been.

Stan was surprised, and gnawed by frustration. He had had Zeena—but how few chances ever came his way for him to have her again. She was the wise one, who knew all the ropes of the carny and everywhere else. She knew. And yet, in the tight world of the carnival, she could find very few opportunities to do what her eyes told Stan a dozen times a day that she would take pleasure in doing.

Pete was always there, always hanging around, apologetic, crestfallen, hands trembling, perfumed with bootleg, always a reminder of what he had been.

Zeena would beg off from a rendezvous with Stan to sew a button on Pete's shirt. Stan couldn't understand it; the more he thought about it the more confused and bitter he got. Zeena was using him to satisfy herself, he kept repeating. Then the thought struck him that maybe Zeena played a game of make-believe with him, and actually saw over his shoulder a shadow of Pete as he had been—handsome and straight and wearing his little black beard.

The thought would strike him right in the middle of his act and his patter would turn into a snarl.

One day Clem Hoately was waiting beside the platform when he came down after the last show. "Whatever's eating you, kid, you better turn it off while you're on the box. If you can't be a trouper, pack up your junk and beat it. Magicians come two for a nickel."

Stan had acquired enough carny to reach over, take a half dollar from Hoately's lapel, and vanish it in his other hand before walking away. But the call-down by the older man burnt into him. No woman or man his own age could drive the gall into his system like that. It took an old bastard, particularly when the stubble on his face looked silvery like fungus growing on a corpse. The bastard.

Stan went to sleep that night on his cot in the Ten-in-One tent with fantasies of slowly roasting Hoately over a fire, inquisition fashion.

Next day, just as they were about to open, Hoately stopped by his platform while Stan was opening a carton of pitch books.

"Keep them half-dollar tricks in the act, son. They got a nice flash. The marks love it."

Stan grinned and said, "You bet." When the first tip came wandering in he gave them all he had. His sale of the magic books almost doubled. He was on top of the world all day. But then came night.

By night Zeena's body plagued his dreams and he lay under the blanket, worn out and with his eyes burning for sleep, thinking back and having her over and over in memory.

Then he waited until closing one night. He stepped back of the curtains on her miniature stage. Zeena had taken off the white silk robe and was putting her hair up, her shoulders white and round and tantalizing over her slip. He took her roughly in his arms and kissed her and she pushed him away. "You beat it out of here. I got to get dressed."

"All right. You mean we're washed up?" he said.

Her face softened and she laid her palm gently against his cheek. "Got to learn to call your shots, honey. We ain't married folks. We got to be careful. Only one person I'm married to and that's Pete. You're a sweet boy and I'm fond as all hell of you. Maybe a little too fond of you. But we got to have some sense. Now you be good. We'll get together one of these days—or nights. And we'll have fun. That's a promise. I'll lay it on the line just as soon as ever we can."

"I wish I could believe it."

She slid her cool arms around his neck and gave him the promise between his lips, warm, sweet, and searching. His heart began to pound.

"Tonight?"

"We'll see."

"Make it tonight."

She shook her head. "I got to make Pete write some letters. He can't if he gets too loaded and he's got some that need answering. You can't let your friends down in show business. You find that out when you get on your uppers and have to hit 'em for a loan. Maybe tomorrow night."

Stan turned away, rebellious and savage, feeling as if the whole surface of his mind had been rubbed the wrong way. He hated Zeena and her Pete.

On his way over to the cookhouse for his supper he passed Pete. Pete was sober and shaky and profane. Zeena would have hidden his bottle in view of the letter-writing session. His eyes had begun to pop.

"Got a spare dollar on you, kid?" Pete whispered.

Zeena came up behind them. "You two boys stay right here and have your supper," she said, pushing them toward the cookhouse. "I've got to find a drugstore in this burg that keeps open late. Nothing like a girl's being careful of her beauty, huh? I'll be right back, honey," she said to Pete, fastening a loose button of his shirt. "We got to catch up on our correspondence."

Stan ate quickly, but Pete pushed the food around, wiped his mouth on the back of his hand, and wiped his hand carefully with his napkin.

He crushed the napkin into a hard, paper wad and aimed it at the cook's back with a curse.

"You got a spare fin, kid?"

"No. Let's get on back to the tent. You got the new Billboard to read. Zeena left it under the stage."

They walked back in silence.

Stan put up his cot and watched the Ten-in-One settle down for the night. Under the astrology stage a single light burned, winking through the cracks of the boards. Inside Pete was sitting at the table, trying to read the Billboard and going over and over the same paragraph.

Why couldn't Zeena have let him accompany her to the store, Stan asked himself. Then, on the way, maybe they could have warmed up and she would have forgotten about Pete and writing letters.

Zeena had slipped the bottle under the seat of Major Mosquito's chair. Stan jumped down from his own platform and crossed the tent softly. The Major's tiny cot was just above his head; he could hear above him the quick breathing which sounded soprano. His hand found the bottle, drew it out.

There was only an inch or two left in it. Stan turned back and crept up the steps of Zeena's theater. A few moments later he came down and squeezed into the understage compartment. The bottle, more than half full now, was in his hand.

"How about a drink, Pete?"

"Glory be to God!" The flask was nearly snatched from his hand. Pete jerked the cork, holding it out to Stan automatically. The next instant he had it in his mouth and his Adam's apple was working. He drained it and handed it back. "God almighty. A friend in need as the saying goes. I'm afraid I didn't leave much for you, Stan."

"That's all right. I don't care for any right now."

Pete shook his head and seemed to pull himself together. "You're a good kid, Stan. You got a fine act. Don't let anything ever keep you out of the big time. You can go places, Stan, if you don't get bogged down. You should have seen us when we were on top. Used to pack 'em in. They'd sit through four other acts just to see us. Boy, I can remember all the times we had our names on the marquee in letters a foot high—top billing—everywhere we went. We had plenty fun, too.

"But you— Why, kid, the greatest names in the business started right where you are now. You're the luckiest kid in the world. You got a good front—you're a damn good-looking kid and I wouldn't crap you up. You can talk. You can do sleights. You got everything. Great magician someday. Only don't let the carny . . ." His eyes were glazing over. He stopped speaking and sat rigid.

"Why don't you turn out the light and take it easy until Zeena gets back?" Stan suggested.

A grunt was his only answer. Then the man stood up and threw back his shoulders. "Kid, you should have seen us when we played the Keith time!"

Good God, is this idiot never going to pass out, Stan thought. Beyond the wooden walls of the understage compartment and the canvas of the tent was the sound of a car's engine starting, the whirr of the starter rising through the night as the nameless driver pressed it. The motor caught and Stan heard the gears.

"You know, kid—" Pete drew himself up until his head nearly touched the boards of the ceiling. The alcohol seemed to stiffen his back. His chin came up commandingly. "Stan, lad like you could be a great mentalist. Study human nature!" He took a long, last pull at the bottle and finished it. Barely swaying, he opened his eyes wide and swallowed.

"Here—chord from the orchestra, amber spot—and I'm on. Make my spiel, give 'em one laugh, plenty mystery. Then I jump right into the reading. Here's m'crystal." He focused his eyes on the empty whisky bottle and Stan watched him with an uneasy twinge. Pete seemed to be coming alive. His eyes became hot and intent.

Then his voice altered and took on depth and power. He passed his left hand slowly over the bottle's surface. "Since the dawn of history," he began, his words booming in the wooden box-room, "mankind has sought to see behind the veil which hides him from tomorrow. And through the ages certain men have gazed into the polished crystal and seen. Is it some property of the crystal itself? Or does the gazer use it merely to turn his eyes inward? Who can tell? But visions come. Slowly, shifting their form, visions come . . ."

Stan found himself watching the empty bottle in which a single pale drop slanted across the bottom. He could not take his eyes away, so contagious was the other's absorption.

"Wait! The shifting shapes begin to clear. I see fields of grass and rolling hills. And a boy—a boy is running on bare feet through the fields. A dog is with him."

Too swiftly for his wary mind to check him, Stan whispered the words, "Yes. Gyp."

Pete's eyes burned down into the glass. "Happiness then . . . but for a little while. Now dark mists . . . sorrow. I see people moving . . . one man stands out . . . evil . . . the boy hates him. Death and the wish of death . . ."

Stan moved like an explosion. He snatched for the bottle; it slipped and fell to the ground. He kicked it into a corner, his breath coming quick and rapid.

Pete stood for a moment, gazing at his empty hand, then dropped his arm. His shoulders sagged. He crumpled into the folding chair, resting his elbows on the card table. When he raised his face to Stan the eyes were glazed, the mouth slack. "I didn't mean nothing, boy. You ain't mad at me, are ya? Just fooling around. Stock reading—fits everybody. Only you got to dress it up." His tongue had thickened and he paused, his head drooping, then snapping up again. "Everybody had some trouble. Somebody they wanted to kill. Usually for a boy it's the old man. What's childhood? Happy one minute, heartbroke the next. Every boy had a dog. Or neighbor's dog—"

His head fell forward on his forearms. "Just old drunk. Just lush. Lord . . . Zeena be mad. Don't you let on, son, you gimme that little drink. She be mad at you, too." He began to cry softly.

Stan felt his stomach heave with disgust. He turned without a word and left the steaming compartment. In comparison, the air of the Ten-in-One tent, darkened now and still, felt cool.

It seemed as if half the night had worn away before Zeena did come back. Stan met her, talking in whispers so as not to disturb the others in the tent, now snoring heavily in their bunks.

"Where's Pete?"

"Passed out."

"Where'd he get it?"

"I—I don't know. He was over by the geek's layout."

"God damn it, Stan, I told you to watch him. Oh, well, I'm tuckered out myself. Might as well let him sleep it off. Tomorrow's another day."

"Zeena."

"What is it, honey?"

"Let me walk you home."

"It ain't far and I don't want you getting ideas. The landlady of this dump has a face like a snapping turtle. We don't want to start no trouble in this burg. We've had enough trouble with the wheels pretty near getting shut down for gambling. This is bluenose."

They had left the tent and the darkened midway stretched out ahead of them, light still streaming from the cookhouse. "I'll walk you over," Stan said. There was a leaden feeling in his chest and he fought to throw it off. He laced his fingers in hers and she did not draw her hand away.

In the shadow of the first trees on the edge of the lot they stopped and kissed and Zeena clung to him. "Gosh, honey, I've missed you something awful. I guess I need more loving than I thought. But not in the room. That old battle-ax is on the prowl."

Stan took her arm and started along the road. The moon had set. They passed a field on a little rise and then the road dipped between clay banks with fields above road level. "Let's go up there," Stan whispered.

They climbed the bank and spread their coats out on the grass.

Stan reached the Ten-in-One tent just before light. He crept into his bunk and was out like a shot. Then something was chirping in his ear and tugging at his shoulder. A voice like a fiddle's E string was cutting through the layers of fatigue and the void which was in him from having emptied his nerves.

"Kid, wake up! Wake up, you big lump!" The shrill piping got louder.

Stan growled and opened his eyes. The tent was tawny gold with sun on the outside of it above him. The pestiferous force at his shoulder was Major Mosquito, his blond hair carefully dampened and brushed over his bulging baby forehead.

"Stan, get up! Pete's dead!"

"What?"

Stan shot off the bunk and felt for his shoes. "What happened to him?"

"Just croaked—the stinking old rum-pot. Got into that bottle of wood alcohol Zeena keeps to burn the phoney questions. It was all gone or pretty near. And Pete's dead as a herring. His mouth's hanging open like the Mammoth Cave. Come on, take a look. I kicked him in the ribs a dozen times and he never moved. Come and look at him."

Without speaking Stan laced up his shoes, carefully, correctly, taking great pains with them. He kept fighting back the thought that wouldn't stay out of his mind. Then it broke over him like a thunder storm: "They'll hang me. They'll hang me. They'll hang me. Only I didn't mean it. I only wanted to pass him out. I didn't know it was wood— They'll hang me. I didn't mean it. They'll—"

He leaped from the platform and pressed through the knot of show people around the seeress's stage. Zeena stepped out and stood facing them, tall and straight and dry-eyed.

"He's gone all right. He was a good guy and a swell trouper. I told him that alky was bad. Only last night I hid his bottle on him—" She stopped and suddenly ducked back through the curtains.

Stan turned and pushed through the crowd. He walked out of the tent into the early sun and kept on to the edge of the grounds where the telephone poles beside the road carried their looping strands off into the distance.

His foot clinked against something bright and he picked up a burned-out electric bulb which lay in the ashes of a long-dead fire. It was iridescent and smoky inside, dark as a crystal ball on a piece of black velvet. Stan kept it in his hand, looking for a rock or a fence post. His diaphragm seemed to be pressing up around his lungs and keeping him from drawing his breath. On one of the telephone poles was a streaked election poster, carrying the gaunt face of the candidate, white hair falling dankly over one eyebrow, lines of craft and rapacity around the mouth that the photographer couldn't quite hide.

"Elect MACKINSEN for SHERIFF. HONEST—INCORRUPTIBLE—FEARLESS."

Stan drew back his arm and let the bulb fly. "You son-of-a-bitch whoremonger!" Slowly, as if by the very intensity of his attention he had slowed down time itself, the bulb struck the printed face and shattered, the sparkling fragments sailing high in the air and glittering as they fell.

As if an abscess inside him had broken, Stan could breathe again and the knot of fear loosened. He could never fear again with the same agony. He knew it. It would never come again as bad as that. His mind, clear as the bright air around him, took over, and he began to think.

CARD IV

The World

Within a circling garland a girl dances;
the beasts of the Apocalypse look on.

SINCE MORNING, Stan's brain had been full of whirring wheels, grinding away at every possible answer. Where were you when he was over by the geek? On my platform, setting up my cot. What did you do then? Practiced a new move with cards. What move? Front-and-back-hand palm. Where did he go? Under the stage, I guess. You were watching him? Only that he didn't go outside. Where were you when Zeena came back? At the entrance waiting for her. . . .

Now the crowd was thinning out. Outside the stars had misted over and there was a flash of lightning behind the trees. At eleven Hoately stopped the bally. The last marks left and the inhabitants of the Ten-in-One smoked while they dressed. At last they gathered with sober faces around Hoately. Only Major Mosquito seemed unaffected. He started to whistle gaily, someone told him to pipe down.

When the last one was ready they filed out and got into cars. Stan rode with Hoately, the Major, Bruno, and Sailor

Martin toward the center of town where the undertaker's parlor was located.

"Lucky break the funeral happened on a slow night," the Sailor said. No one answered him.

Then Major Mosquito chirruped, "O death, where is thy sting? O grave, where is thy victory?" He spat. "Why do they have to crap it up with all that stuff? Why can't they just shovel 'em under and let 'em start falling apart?"

"You shut up!" Bruno said thickly. "You talk too much for little fellow."

"Go frig a rubber duck."

"Tough on Zeena," Bruno said to the others. "She is fine woman."

Clem Hoately, driving with one hand carelessly on the wheel, said, "That rum-pot ain't going to be missed by nobody. Not even Zeena after a while. But it makes you take a good think for yourself. I remember that guy when he was big stuff. I ain't touched a drop in over a year now and I ain't going to, either. Seen too much of it."

"Who's going to work the act with Zeena?" Stan asked after a time. "She going to change her act? She could handle the questions herself and work one ahead."

Hoately scratched his head with his free hand. "That ain't too good nowadays. She don't have to change the act. You could work the undercover part. I'll take the house collection. We'll throw the Electric Girl between your spot and Zeena's, give you time to slip in and get set."

"Suits me."

He said it, Stan kept repeating. It wasn't my idea. The Major and Bruno heard him. He said it.

The street was empty and the light from the funeral parlor made a golden wedge on the sidewalk. Behind them the other car drew up. Old Maguire, the Ten-in-One's ticket seller and grinder, got out, then Molly; then Joe Plasky swung himself out on his hands and crossed the sidewalk. He reminded Stan of a frog, moving deliberately.

Zeena met them at the door. She was wearing a new black outfit, a dress with enormous flowers worked on it in jet. "Come on in, folks. I—I got Pete all laid out handsome. I just phoned a reverend and he's coming over. I thought it was nicer to get a reverend if we could, even if Pete wasn't no church man."

They went inside. Joe Plasky fumbled in his pocket and held an envelope up to Zeena. "The boys chipped in for a stone, Zeena. They knew you didn't need the dough but they wanted to do something. I wrote the Billboard this afternoon. They'll carry a box. I just said, 'Mourned by his many friends in show business.'"

She bent down and kissed him. "That's—that's damn sweet of you all. I guess we better get into the chapel. This looks like the reverend coming."

They took their places on folding chairs. The clergyman was a meek, dull little old man, looking sleepy. Embarrassed, too, Stan figured. As if carny folks were not quite human—like they had all left their pants off only he was too polite to let on he noticed.

He put on his glasses. ". . . we brought nothing into this world and it is certain we can carry nothing out. The Lord gave, and the Lord hath taken . . ."

Stan, sitting beside Zeena, tried to concentrate on the words and guess what the reverend was going to say next. Anything to keep from thinking. It's not my fault he's dead. I didn't mean to kill him. I killed him. There it starts again and all day I wasn't feeling anything and I thought I'd lost it.

"Lord, let me know my end, and the number of my days; that I may be certified how long I have to live . . ."

Pete never knew his end. Pete died happy. I did him a favor. He had been dying for years. He was afraid of living and he was trying to ease himself out only I had to go and kill him. I didn't kill him. He killed himself. Sooner or later he would have taken a chance on that wood alky. I only helped him a little. Christ, will I have to think about this damn thing the rest of my life?

Stan slowly turned his head and looked at the others. Molly was sitting with the Major between her and Bruno. In the back row Clem Hoately had his eyes shut. Joe Plasky's face held the shadow of a smile that was too deeply cut into it ever to vanish completely. It was the sort of smile Lazarus must have had afterwards, Stan thought. Sailor Martin had one eye closed.

The sight of the Sailor rushed Stan back to normal. He had done that a hundred times himself, sitting beside his father on the hard pew, watching his mother in a white surplice there in the choir stall with the other ladies. There's a blind spot in your eye and if you shut one eye and then let the gaze of the other travel in a straight line to one side of the preacher's head there will be a point where his head seems to disappear and he seems to be standing there preaching without any head.

Stan looked at Zeena beside him. Her mind was far away somewhere. The reverend speeded up.

"Man that is born of woman hath but a short time to live, and is full of misery. He cometh up and is cut down, like a flower; he fleeth as it were a shadow, and never continueth in one stay. In the midst of life we are in death . . ."

Behind them Major Mosquito heaved a sharp sigh and wriggled, the chair creaking. Bruno said, "Shoosh!"

When they got to the Lord's Prayer Stan found his voice with relief. Zeena must hear it. If she heard it she couldn't suspect him of having anything to do with— Stan lowered his voice and the words came automatically. She mustn't ever think—and yet she had looked at him sharp when he had said Pete was hanging around the geek. She mustn't think. Only he mustn't overplay it. God damn it, this was the time for misdirection if ever there was one. ". . . *for thine is the kingdom, the power and the glory for ever and ever.*"

"Amen."

The undertaker was silently brisk. He removed the coffin lid and set it noiselessly behind the casket. Zeena brought her handkerchief up to her face and turned away. They formed a line and passed by.

Clem Hoately came first, his furrowed face showing nothing. Then Bruno, holding Major Mosquito on his forearm so he could look down and see. Molly came next and Sailor Martin fell in behind her, moving close. Then old Maguire, his cap crushed in his hand. Joe Plasky hopped across the floor, pushing one of the folding chairs. When it came his turn to view the remains he moved the chair into place by the head of the coffin and swung himself up on the seat. He looked down and the smile was still around the corners of his eyes although his mouth was sober. Without thinking he made the sign of the cross.

Stan swallowed hard. It was his turn and there was no way of getting out of it. Joe had hopped to the floor and pushed the chair against the wall; Stan shoved both hands deep into his pockets and approached the casket. He had never seen a corpse; the skin of his scalp prickled at the thought.

He drew his breath and forced himself to look.

It seemed at first like a wax figure in a dress suit. One hand rested easily on the white waistcoat, the other was by the side. It held a round, clear glass ball. The face was rosy—the undertaker had filled out the drawn cheeks and painted the skin until it glowed with a waxen counterfeit of life. But there was something else that hit Stan like a blow between the ribs. Carefully fashioned of crêpe hair and stuck to the chin was a lifelike, neatly trimmed, little black beard.

"For the last demonstration Mamzelle Electra will perform a feat never attempted since Ben Franklin harnessed the lightning with his kite string. Holding the two filaments of a carbon arc light, she will allow the death-dealing current to pass through her body. . . ."

Stan quietly slipped into the compartment below the stage of Zeena, the Woman Who Knows. It no longer smelled of whisky. Stan had installed a piece of canvas as a ground sheet and had cut ventilation scrolls in the sides of the boxlike little room. Over the bridge table and on three sides of it he had erected a cardboard shield so he could open the envelopes and copy the questions on the pad by the light of a flashlight.

The rustle of feet surging around the stage outside, then Zeena's voice in her opening spiel. Stan took a bundle of dummy questions—blank cards in small envelopes—and stood by the window where Hoately would pass behind the curtains.

They parted at the side of the stage; Hoately's hand appeared. Quickly Stan took the collected questions and placed the dummy batch in the hand which vanished upward. Stan heard the creak of feet on the boards above him. He sat down at the table, switched on the shaded flashlight bulb, squared up the pack of envelopes and cut the ends from them with one snip of the scissors. Moving quickly, he shook out the cards and arranged them before him on the table.

Question: "Where is my son?" Handwriting old-fashioned. Woman over sixty, he judged. A good one to open with—the signature was clear and spelled out in full—Mrs. Anna Briggs Sharpley. Stan looked for two more complete names. One was signed to a wiseacre question which he put aside. He reached for the black crayon and the pad, wrote, "Where son?" printed the name swiftly but plainly, and held the pad up to the hole in the stage at Zeena's feet.

"I get the impression of the initial *S*. Is there a Mrs. Sharpley?"

Stan found himself listening to the answers as if they held a revelation.

"You think of your boy as still a little fellow, the way you knew him when he used to come asking you for a piece of bread with sugar on it. . . ."

Where the hell did Zeena get all that stuff from? She was no more telepathic than that kid, Molly, was electricity proof. The Electric Chair act was gaffed like everything in the carny. But Zeena—

"My dear lady, you must remember that he's a man grown now and probably has children of his own to worry about. You want him to write to you. Isn't that so?"

It was uncanny how Zeena could fish out things just by watching the person's face. Stan got a sudden thrust of cold fear. Of all the people in the world for him to hide anything from, it had to be a mind reader. He laughed a little in spite of his anxiety. But there was something which pulled him toward Zeena more strongly than his fear that she would find out and make him a murderer. How do you get to know so much that you can tell people what they are thinking about just by looking at them? Maybe you had to be born with the gift.

"Is Clarissa here? Clarissa, hold up your hand. That's a good girl. Now Clarissa wants to know if the young fellow she's been going around with is the right one for her to marry. Well, Clarissa, I may disappoint you but I have to speak the truth. You wouldn't want me to tell you no fibs. I don't think this boy is the one for you to marry. Mind, he may be and I don't doubt that he's a mighty fine young man. But something tells me that when the right young fellow comes along you won't ask me, you won't ask anybody—you'll just up and marry him."

That question had come up before and Zeena nearly always answered it the same way. The thought struck Stan that it was not genius after all. Zeena knew people. But people were a lot alike. What you told one you could tell nine out of ten. And there was one out of five that would believe everything you told them and would say yes to anything when you asked them if it was correct because they were the kind of marks that can't say no. Good God, Zeena is working for peanuts! Somewhere in this racket there is a gold mine!

Stan picked up another card and wrote on the pad: "Advise important domestic step, Emma." By God, if she can answer that one she must be a mind reader. He held it up to the trap and listened.

Zeena pattered on for a moment, thinking to herself and then her voice lifted and her heel knocked gently. Stan took down the pad and knew that this would be the blow-off question and he could relax. After this one she would go into the pitch.

"I have time for just one more question. And this is a question that I'm not going to ask anybody to acknowledge. There's a lady here whose first name begins with E. I'm not going to tell her full name because it's a very personal question. But I'm going to ask Emma to think about what she is trying to tell me mentally."

Stan switched off the flashlight, crept out of the understage compartment and tiptoed up the stairs behind the side curtains. Parting them carefully with his fingers he placed his eye to the crack. The marks' faces were a mass of pale circles below him. But at the mention of the name "Emma" he saw one face—a pale, haggard woman who looked forty but might be thirty. The lips parted and the eyes answered for an instant. Then the lips were pressed tight in resignation.

Zeena lowered her voice. "Emma, you have a serious problem. And it concerns somebody very near and dear to you. Or somebody who used to be very near and dear, isn't that right?" Stan saw the woman's head nod involuntarily.

"You are contemplating a serious step—whether to leave this person. And I think he's your husband." The woman bit her under lip. Her eyes grew moist quickly. That kind cries at the drop of a hat, Stan thought. If only she had a million bucks instead of a greasy quarter.

"Now there are two lines of vibration working about this problem. One of them concerns another woman." The tension left the woman's face and a sullen frown of disappointment drew over it. Zeena changed her tack. "But now the impressions get stronger and I can see that while there may have been some woman in the past, right now the problem is something else. I see cards . . . playing cards falling on a table . . . but no, it isn't your husband who's playing. It's the place . . . I get it now, clear as daylight. It's the back room of a saloon."

A sob came from the woman, and people twisted their heads this way and that; but Emma was watching the seeress, unmindful of the others.

"My dear friend, you have a mighty heavy cross to bear. I know all about it and don't you think I don't. But the step that confronts you now is a problem with a good many sides. If your husband was running around with other women and didn't love you that would be one thing. But I get a very strong impression that he does love you—in spite of everything. Oh, I know he acts nasty-mean sometimes but you just ask yourself if any of the blame is yours. Because here's one thing you must never forget: a man drinks because he's unhappy. Isn't anything about liquor that makes a man bad. A man that's happy can take a drink with the boys on Saturday night and come home with his pay safe in his pocket. But when a man's miserable about something he takes a drink to forget it and one isn't enough and he takes another snort and pretty soon the week's pay is all gone and he gets home and sobers up and then his wife starts in on him and he's more miserable than he was before and then his first thought is to go get drunk again and it runs around and around in a circle."

Zeena had forgotten the other customers, she had forgotten the pitch. She was talking out of herself. The marks knew it and were hanging on every word, fascinated.

"Before you take that step," she went on, suddenly coming back to the show, "you want to be sure that you've done all you can to make that man happy. Maybe you can't learn what's bothering him. Maybe he don't quite know himself. But try to find it. Because if you leave him you'll have to find some way to take care of yourself and the kids anyhow. Well, why not start in tonight? If he comes home drunk put him to bed. Try talking to him friendly. When a man's drunk he's a lot like a kid. Well, treat him like a son and don't go jumping on him. Tomorrow morning let him know that you understand and mother him up a little. Because if that man loves you—" Zeena paused for breath and then rushed on. "If that man loves you it don't matter whether he makes a living or not. It don't matter if he stays sober or not. If you've got a man that really loves you, you hang on to him like grim death for better or worse." There was a catch in her voice and for a long moment silence hung in the air over the waiting crowd. "Hang on—because you'll never regret it as much as you'll regret sending him away and now folks if you really want to know how the stars affect your life you don't have to pay five dollars or even one dollar I have here a set of astrological readings all worked out for each and every one of you let me know your date of birth and you get a forecast of future events complete with character reading, vocational guidance, lucky numbers. . . ."

For the long haul the Ackerman-Zorbaugh Monster Shows took to the railroad. Trucks loaded on flatcars, the carnies themselves loaded into old coaches, the train boomed on through darkness—tearing past solitary jerk towns, past sidings of dark freight empties, over trestles, over bridges where the rivers lay coiling their luminous way through the star-shadowed countryside.

In the baggage car, among piles of canvas and gear, a light burned high up on the wall. A large packing case with auger holes bored in its sides to admit air, stood in the middle of a cleared space. From inside it came intermittent scrapings. At one end of the car the geek lay on a pile of canvas, his ragged, overalled knees drawn up to his chin.

Around the snake box men made the air gray with smoke.

"I'm staying." Major Mosquito's voice had the insistence of a cricket's.

Sailor Martin screwed up the left side of his face against the smoke of his cigarette and dealt.

"I'm in," Stan said. He had a Jack in the hole. The highest card showing was a ten in the Sailor's hand.

"I'm with you," Joe Plasky said, the Lazarus smile never changing.

Behind Joe sat the hulk of Bruno, his shoulders rounding under his coat. He watched intently, his mouth dropping open as he concentrated on Joe's hand.

"I'm in, too," Martin said. He dealt. Stan got another Jack and pushed in three blues.

"Going to cost you to string along," he said casually.

Martin had dealt himself another ten. "I'll string along."

Major Mosquito, his baby head close to the boxtop, stole another glance at his hole card. "Nuts!"

"Guess it's between you gents," Joe said placidly. Bruno, from behind him, said, "Ja. Let them fight it out. We take it easy this time."

Martin dealt. Two little ones fell between them. Stan threw more blues in. Martin met him and raised him two more.

"I'll see you."

The Sailor threw over his hole card. A ten. He reached for the pot.

Stan smiled and counted his chips. At a sound from the Major all of them jumped. "Hey!" It was like a long-drawn fiddle scrape.

"What's eating you, Big Noise?" Martin asked, grinning.

"Lemme see them tens!" The Major reached toward the center of the snake box with his infant's hand and drew the cards toward him. He examined the backs.

Bruno got up and moved over behind the midget. He picked up one of the cards and held it at an angle toward the light.

"What's eating you guys?" Martin said.

"Daub!" Major Mosquito wailed, taking his cigarette from

the edge of the box and puffing it rapidly. "The cards are marked with daub. They're smeared to act like readers. You can see it if you know where to look."

Martin took one and examined it. "Damn! You're right."

"They're your cards," the Major went on in his accusing falsetto.

Martin bristled. "What d'ya mean, my cards? Somebody left 'em around the cookhouse. If I hadn't thought to bring 'em we wouldn't have had no game."

Stan took the deck and riffled them under his thumb. Then he riffled again, throwing cards face down on the table. When he reversed them they were all high ones, picture cards and tens. "That's daub, all right," he said. "Let's get a new deck."

"You're the card worker," Martin said aggressively. "What do you know about this? Daub is stuff you smear on the other fellow's cards during the game."

"I know enough not to use it," Stan said easily. "I don't deal. I never deal. And if I wanted to work any angles I'd stack them on the pick up until I got the pair I wanted on top the deck, undercut and injog the top card of the top half, shuffle off eight, outjog and shuffle off. Then I'd undercut to the outjog—"

"Let's get a new deck," Joe Plasky said. "We won't any of us get rich arguing about how the cards got marked. Who's got a deck?"

They sat silent, the expansion joints of the rails clicking by beneath them. Then Stan said, "Zeena has a deck of fortune-telling cards we can play with. I'll get them."

Martin took the marked deck, stepped to the partly open door and sent the cards flying into the wind. "Maybe a new deck will change my luck," he said. "I been going bust every hand except the last one."

The car shook and pounded on through the dark. Behind the open door they could see the dark hills and a sliver of moon setting behind them with a scattering of stars.

Stan returned and with him came Zeena. Her black dress was relieved by a corsage of imitation gardenias, her hair caught up on top of her head with a random collection of blond hairpins.

"Howdy, gents. Thought I'd take a hand myself if I wouldn't be intruding. Sure gets deadly back in that coach. I reckon I've read every movie magazine in the outfit by this time." She opened her purse and placed a deck of cards on the box. "Now you boys let me see your hands. All clean? 'Cause I don't want you smooching up these cards and getting 'em dirty. They're hard enough to get hold of."

Stan took the deck carefully and fanned them. The faces were an odd conglomeration of pictures. One showed a dead man, his back skewered with ten swords. Another had a picture of three women in ancient robes, each holding a cup. A hand reaching out of a cloud, on another, held a club from which green leaves sprouted.

"What do you call these things, Zeena?" he asked.

"That's the Tarot," she said impressively. "Oldest kind of cards in the world. They go all the way back to Egypt, some say. And they're sure a wonder for giving private readings. Every time I have something to decide or don't know which way to turn I run them over for myself. I always get some kind of an answer that makes sense. But you can play poker with 'em. They got four suits: wands are diamonds, cups are hearts, swords are clubs, and coins are spades. This bunch of pictures here—that's the Great Arcana. They're just for fortunetelling. But there's one of 'em—if I can find it—we can use for a joker. Here it is." She threw it out and placed the others back in her purse.

Stan picked up the joker. At first he couldn't figure out which end was the top. It showed a young man suspended head down by one foot from a T-shaped cross, but the cross was of living wood, putting out green shoots. The youth's hands were tied behind his back. A halo of golden light shone about his head and on reversing the card Stan saw that his expression was one of peace—like that of a man raised from the dead. Like Joe Plasky's smile. The name of the card was printed in old-fashioned script at the bottom. *The Hanged Man.*

"Holy Christ, if these damn things don't change my luck, nothing will," the Sailor said.

Zeena took a pile of chips from Joe Plasky, ante'd, then

shuffled and dealt the hole cards face down. She lifted hers a trifle and frowned. The game picked up. Stan had an eight of cups in the hole and dropped out. Never stay in unless you have a Jack or better in the hole and drop out when better than a Jack shows on the board. Unless you've got the difference.

Zeena's frown deepened. The battle was between her, Sailor Martin, and the Major. Then the Sailor dropped out. The Major's hand showed three Knights. He called. Zeena held a flush in coins.

"Ain't you the bluffer," the Major piped savagely. "Frowning like you had nothing and you sitting on top a flush."

Zeena shook her head. "I wasn't meaning to bluff, even. It was the hole card I was frowning at—the ace of coins, what they call pentacles. I always read that 'Injury by a trusted friend.'"

Stan uncrossed his legs and said, "Maybe the snakes have something to do with it. They're scraping around under the lid here like they were uncomfortable."

Major Mosquito spat on the floor, then poked his finger in one of the auger holes. He withdrew it, chirruping. From the hole flicked a forked thread of pink. The Major drew his lips back from his tiny teeth and quickly touched the lighted ember of his cigarette to the tongue. It flashed back into the box and there was the frenzied scraping of coils twisting and whipping inside.

"Jesus!" Martin said. "You shouldn't of done that, you little stinker. Them damn things'll get mad."

The Major threw back his head. "Ho, ho, ho, ho! Next time I'll do it to you—I'll make a hit on the Battleship *Maine*."

Stan stood up. "I've had enough, gents. Don't let me break up the game, though."

Balancing against the rock of the train, he pushed through the piled canvas to the platform of the next coach. His left hand slid under the edge of his vest and unpinned a tiny metal box the size and shape of a five-cent piece. He let his hand drop and the container fell between the cars. It had left a dark smudge on his finger. Why do I have to frig around with all this chickenshit stuff? I didn't want their dimes. I wanted to see if I could take them. Jesus, the only thing you can depend on is your brains!

In the coach, under the dimmed lights, the crowd of carnival performers and concessioners sprawled, huddled, heads on each others' shoulders; some had stretched themselves on newspapers in the aisles. In the corner of a seat Molly slept, her lips slightly parted, her head against the glass of the black window.

How helpless they all looked in the ugliness of sleep. A third of life spent unconscious and corpselike. And some, the great majority, stumbled through their waking hours scarcely more awake, helpless in the face of destiny. They stumbled down a dark alley toward their deaths. They sent exploring feelers into the light and met fire and writhed back again into the darkness of their blind groping.

At the touch of a hand on his shoulder Stan jerked around. It was Zeena. She stood with her feet apart, braced easily against the train's rhythm. "Stan, honey, we don't want to let what's happened get us down. God knows, I felt bad about Pete. And I guess you did too. Everybody did. But this don't stop us from living. And I been wondering . . . you still like me, don't you, Stan?"

"Sure—sure I do, Zeena. Only I thought—"

"That's right, honey. The funeral and all. But I can't keep up mourning for Pete forever. My mother, now—she'd of been grieving around for a year but what I say is, it's soon enough we'll all be pushing 'em up. We got to get some fun. Tell you what. When we land at the next burg, let's us ditch the others and have a party."

Stan slid his arm around her and kissed her. In the swaying, plunging gait of the train their teeth clicked and they broke apart, laughing a little. Her hand smoothed his cheek. "I've missed you like all hell, honey." She buried her face in the hollow of his throat.

Over her shoulder Stan looked into the car of sleepers. Their faces had changed, had lost their hideousness. The girl Molly had waked up and was eating a chocolate bar. There was a smudge of chocolate over her chin. Zeena suspected nothing.

Stan raised his left hand and examined it. On the ball of the

ring finger was a dark streak. Daub. He touched his tongue
to it and then gripped Zeena's shoulder, wiping the stain on
the black dress.

They broke apart and pushed down the aisle to a pile of
suitcases where they managed to sit. In her ear Stan said,
"Zeena, how does a two-person code work? I mean a good
one—the kind you and Pete used to work." Audiences in evening clothes. Top billing. The Big Time.

Zeena leaned close, her voice suddenly husky. "Wait till we
get to the burg. I can't think about nothing except you right
now, honey. I'll tell you some time. Anything you want to
know. But now I want to think about what's coming between
the sheets." She caught one of his fingers and gave it a
squeeze.

In the baggage coach Major Mosquito turned over his hole
card. "Three deuces of swords showing and one wild one in
the hole makes four of a kind. Ha, ha, ha, ha. *The Hanged
Man!*"

When Stan woke up it was still dark. The electric sign which
had been flaring on and off with blinding regularity, spelling
out the name of Ayres' Department Store, was quiet at last
and the smeared windowpane was dark. Something had wak-
ened him. The mattress was hard and sagging; against his back
he felt the warmth of Zeena's body.

Silently the bed shook and Stan's throat tightened with
a reflex of fear at the unknown and the darkness until he
felt the shake again and then a muffled gasp. Zeena was
crying.

Stan turned over and slid his arm around her and cupped
her breast with his hand. She had to be babied when she got
this way.

"Stan, honey—"

"What's the matter, baby?"

Zeena turned heavily and pressed a damp cheek against his
bare chest. "Just got to thinking about Pete."

There was nothing to say to this so Stan tightened his arms
around her and kept quiet.

"You know, today I was going through some of the stuff
in the little tin trunk—Pete's stuff. His old press books and

old letters and all kinds of stuff. And I found the notebook he used to keep. The one he had the start of our code in. Pete invented that code himself and we were the only people that ever knew it. Pete was offered a thousand dollars for it by Allah Kismet—that was Syl Rappolo. He was one of the biggest crystal-workers in the country. But Pete just laughed at him. That old book was just like a part of Pete. He had such nice handwriting in them days . . .''

Stan said nothing but turned her face up and began kissing her. He was fully awake now and could feel the pulse jumping in his throat. He mustn't seem too eager. Better love her up first, all the way if he could do it again.

He found that he could.

It was Zeena's turn to keep quiet. Finally Stan said, ''What are we going to do about your act?''

Her voice was suddenly crisp. ''What about the act?''

''I thought maybe you were thinking of changing it.''

''What for? Ain't we taking in more on the pitch than ever? Look, honey, if you feel you ought to be cut in for a bigger percentage don't be bashful—''

''I'm not talking about that,'' he interrupted her. ''In this damn state nobody can write. Every time I stick a card and a pencil under the nose of some mark he says, 'You write it for me.' If I could remember all that stuff I could let 'em keep the cards in their pockets.''

Zeena stretched leisurely, the bed creaking under her. ''Don't you worry about Zeena, honey. When they can't write their names they're even more receptive to the answers. Why, I could quit the question-answering part of the act and just get up there and spiel away and then go into the pitch and still turn 'em.''

A thrill of alarm raced along Stan's nerves at the thought of Zeena's being able to do without him before he could do without her. ''But I mean, couldn't we work a code act? You could still do it, couldn't you?''

She chuckled. ''Listen, schniggle-fritz, I can do it in my sleep. But it takes a hell of a lot of work to get all them lists and things learned. And the season's more than half over.''

''I could learn it.''

She thought for a while and then she said, ''It's all right

with me, honey. It's all down in Pete's book. Only don't you lose that book or Zeena'll cut your ears off."

"You have it here?"

"Wait a minute. Where's the fire? Sure I've got it here. You'll see it. Don't go getting sizzle-britches."

More silence. At last Stan sat up and swung his feet to the floor. "I better get back to that pantry they rented me for a room. We don't want the townies here to get any more ideas than they've got already." He snapped on the light and began to put on his clothes. In the garish light overhead Zeena looked haggard and battered like a worn wax doll. She had the sheet pulled over her middle but her breasts sagged over it. Her hair was in two brassy braids and the ends were uneven and spiky. Stan put on his shirt and knotted his tie. He slipped on his jacket.

"You're a funny fella."

"Why?"

"Getting all dressed up to walk thirty feet down the hall of a fleabag like this at four in the morning."

Somehow Stan felt this to be a reflection on his courage. His face grew warm. "Nothing like doing things right."

Zeena yawned cavernously. "Guess you're right, kiddo. See you in the morning. And thanks for the party."

He made no move to turn out the light. "Zeena, that note-book— Could I see it?"

She threw off the sheet, got up and squatted to snap open the suitcase. Does a woman always look more naked after you've had her, Stan wondered. Zeena rummaged in the bag and drew out a canvas-covered book marked "Ledger."

"Now run along, honey. Or come back to bed. Make up your mind."

Stan tucked the book under his arm and switched off the light. He felt his way to the door and with caution turned back the bolt. Yellow light from the hall sliced over the patchy wallpaper as he opened the door.

There was a whisper from the bed. "Stan—"

"What is it?"

"Come kiss your old pal good night."

He stepped over, kissed her cheek and left without another word, closing the door softly behind him.

The lock of his own door sounded like a rifle shot.

He looked each way along the hall but nothing stirred.

Inside, he tore off his clothes, went to the washbowl and washed and then threw himself down on the bed, propping the book on his bare stomach.

The first pages were taken up with figures and notations:

"Evansport. July 20th. Books—$33.00 taken in. Paid—Plants at $2—$6.00. Plants: Mrs. Jerome Hotchkiss. Leonard Keely, Josiah Boos. All okay. Old spook workers. Boos looks like deacon. Can act a little. Worked the found ring in the coat lining . . ."

"Spook workers" must refer to the local confederates employed by traveling mediums. Swiftly Stan flipped the pages. More expenses: "F. T. rap squared. Chief Pellett. $50." That would be an arrest on a charge of fortune telling.

Stan felt like Ali Baba in the cavern of riches left by the Forty Thieves.

Impatiently he turned to the back of the book. On the last page was a heading: "Common Questions." Beneath it was a list, with figures:

"Is my husband true to me? 56, 29, 18, 42.

"Will mother get well? 18, 3, 7, 12.

"Who poisoned our dog? 3, 2, 3, 0, 3." Beside this was the notation, "Not a big item but a steady. Every audience. Can pull as cold reading during stall part of act."

The figures, then, were a record of the number of similar questions collected from the same audience. The question "Is my wife faithful?" had only about a third the number of entries as the one about the husband.

"The chumps," Stan whispered. "Either too bashful to ask or too dumb to suspect." But they were anxious to find out, all of them. As if jazzing wasn't what they all want, the goddamned hypocrites. They all want it. Only nobody else must have it. He turned the page.

"There is a recurring pattern followed by the questions asked. For every unusual question there will be fifty that you have had before. Human nature is the same everywhere. All have the same troubles. They are worried. Can control anybody by finding out what he's afraid of. Works with question-answering act. Think out things most people are afraid of and hit them right where they live. Health, Wealth, Love. And Travel and Success. They're all afraid of ill health, of poverty, of boredom, of failure. Fear is the key to human nature. They're afraid. . . ."

Stan looked past the pages to the garish wallpaper and through it into the world. The geek was made by fear. He was afraid of sobering up and getting the horrors. But what made him a drunk? Fear. Find out what they are afraid of and sell it back to them. That's the key. The key! He had known it when Clem Hoately had told him how geeks are made. But here was Pete saying the same thing:

Health. Wealth. Love. Travel. Success. "A few have to do with domestic troubles, in-laws, kids, pets. And so on. A few wisenheimers but you can ditch them easily enough. Idea: combine question-answering act with code act. Make list of questions, hook up with code numbers. Answer vague at first, working toward definite. If can see face of spectator and tell when hitting."

On the following pages was a neatly numbered list of questions. There were exactly a hundred. Number One was "Is my husband true to me?" Number Two was "Will I get a job soon?"

Outside the front of Ayres' Department Store had turned rosy-red with the coming sun. Stan paid it no heed. The sun slid up, the sound of wagon tires on concrete told of the awakening city. At ten o'clock there was a tap on the door. Stan shook himself. "Yes?"

Zeena's voice. "Wake up, sleepy head. Rise and shine."

He unlocked the door and let her in.

"What you got the light on for?" She turned it out, then saw the book. "Lord's sake, kid, ain't you been to bed at all?"

Stan rubbed his eyes and stood up. "Ask me a number. Any number up to a hundred."

"Fifty-five."

"Will my mother-in-law always live with us?"

Zeena sat down beside him and ran her fingers through his hair. "You know what I think, kid? I think you're a mind reader."

The carny turned south and the pines began to line sandy

roads. Cicadas drummed the late summer air and the crowds of white people were gaunter, their faces filled with desolation, their lips often stained with snuff.

Everywhere the shining, dark faces of the South's other nation caught the highlights from the sun. They stood in quiet wonder, watching the carny put up in the smoky morning light. In the Ten-in-One they stood always on the fringe of the crowd, an invisible cordon holding them in place. When one of the whites turned away sharply and jostled them the words "Scuse me," fell from them like pennies balanced on their shoulders.

Stan had never been this far south and something in the air made him uneasy. This was dark and bloody land where hidden war traveled like a million earthworms under the sod.

The speech fascinated him. His ear caught the rhythm of it and he noted their idioms and worked some of them into his patter. He had found the reason behind the peculiar, drawling language of the old carny hands—it was a composite of all the sprawling regions of the country. A language which sounded Southern to Southerners, Western to Westerners. It was the talk of the soil and its drawl covered the agility of the brains that poured it out. It was a soothing, illiterate, earthy language.

The carny changed its tempo. The outside talkers spoke more slowly.

Zeena cut the price of her horoscopes to a dime each but sold "John the Conqueror Root" along with them for fifteen cents. This was a dried mass of twisting roots which was supposed to attract good fortune when carried in a bag around the neck. Zeena got them by the gross from an occult mail-order house in Chicago.

Stan's pitch of the magic books took a sudden drop and Zeena knew the answer. "These folks down here don't know nothing about sleight-of-hand, honey. Half of 'em figure you're doing real magic. Well, you got to have something superstitious to pitch."

Stan ordered a gross of paper-backed books, "One Thousand and One Dreams Interpreted." He threw in as a free gift a brass lucky coin stamped with the Seal of Love from the Seventh Book of Moses, said to attract the love of others and lead to the confusion of enemies. His pitch picked up in fine style. He learned to roll three of the lucky coins over his fingers at once. The tumbling, glittering cascade of metal seemed to fascinate the marks, and the dream books went fast.

He had learned the verbal code for questions not a day too soon, for the people couldn't write or were too shy to try.

"*Will* you *kindly* answer this lady's question *at once*?" Stan had cued the question, "Is my daughter all right?"

Zeena's voice had taken on a deeper southern twang. "Well, now, I get the impression that the lady is worried about someone near and dear to her, someone she hasn't heard from in a long time, am I right? Strikes me it's a young lady— It's your daughter you're thinking of, isn't it? Of course. And you want to know if she's well and happy and if you'll see her again soon. Well, I believe you will get some news of her through a third person before the month is out. . . ."

There was one question that came up so often that Stan worked out a silent signal for it. He would simply jerk his head in Zeena's direction. The first time he used it the question had come to him from a man—massive and loose-jointed with clear eyes smoldering in a handsome ebony face. "Am I ever going to make a trip?"

Zeena picked it up. "Man over there is wondering about something that's going to happen to him and I want to say right here and now that I believe you're going to get your wish. And I think it has something to do with travel. You want to make a trip somewheres. Isn't that so? Well, I see some troubles on the road and I see a crowd of people—men, they are, asking a lot of questions. But I see the journey completed after a while, not as soon as you want to make it but after a while. And there's a job waiting for you at the end of it. Job with good pay. It's somewhere to the north of here; I'm positive of that."

It was sure-fire. All of 'em want North, Stan thought. It was the dark alley, all over again. With a light at the end of it. Ever since he was a kid Stan had had the dream. He was running down a dark alley, the buildings vacant and black and menacing on either side. Far down at the end of it a light burned; but there was something behind him, close behind him, getting closer until he woke up trembling and never reached the light. They have it too—a nightmare alley. The North isn't the end. The light will only move further on. And the fear close behind them. White and black, it made no difference. The geek and his bottle, staving off the clutch of the thing that came following after.

In the hot sun of noon the cold breath could strike your neck. In having a woman her arms were a barrier. But after she had fallen asleep the walls of the alley closed in on your own sleep and the footsteps followed.

Now the very country simmered with violence, and Stan looked enviously at the sculptured muscles of Bruno Hertz. It wasn't worth the time and backbreaking effort it took to get that way. There must be an easier way. Some sort of jujitsu system where a man could use his brains and his agility. The Ackerman-Zorbaugh Monster Shows had never had a "Hey-rube" since Stan had been with them, but the thought of one ate at his peace of mind like a maggot. What would he do in a mob fight? What would they do to him?

Then Sailor Martin nearly precipitated one.

It was a steaming day of late summer. The South had turned out: hollow-eyed women with children in their arms and clinging to their skirts, lantern-jawed men, deadly quiet.

Clem Hoately had mounted the platform where Bruno sat quietly fanning himself with a palm-leaf fan. "If you'll step right this way, folks, I want to call your attention to one of the miracle men of all time—Herculo, the strongest man alive."

Stan looked back to the rear of the tent. In the corner by the geek's enclosure Sailor Martin had a couple of local youths engrossed in the strap on the barrelhead. He took a leather strap, folded it in the middle, then coiled it on the top of a nail keg. He placed his own finger in one of the two loops in the center and pulled the strap. His finger had picked the real loop in the strap. Then he bet one of the marks he couldn't pick the real loop. The mark bet and won and the Sailor handed him a silver dollar.

Zeena drew the curtains of the little stage and came out at the side. She drew a handkerchief from her bosom and touched her temples with it. "Whew, ain't it a scorcher to-

day?" She followed Stan's glance to the rear of the tent. "The
Sailor better go easy. Hoately don't like anybody to case the
marks on the side this far south. Can't blame him. Too likely
to start a rumpus. I say, if you can't make a living with your
pitch you don't belong in no decent Ten-in-One. I could pick
up plenty of honest dollars if I wanted to give special private
readings and remove evil influences and all that stuff. But that
just leads to trouble."

She stopped speaking and her hand tightened on Stan's
arm. "Stan, honey, you better take a walk over there and see
what's going on."

Stan made no move to go. On the platform he was king;
the marks in their anonymous mass were below him and his
voice held them, but down on their level, jammed in among
their milling, collective weight, he felt smothered.

Suddenly one of the youths drew back his foot and kicked
over the nail keg on which Martin had wound the strap with
the elusive loop. The Sailor's voice was raised just a fraction
above conversational level and he seemed to be speaking to
the mark when he said, clearly and coolly, "Hey, rube!"

"Go on, Stan. Hurry. Don't let 'em get started."

As if he had a pistol pointed at his back, Stan marched
across the tent to the spot where trouble was simmering.
From the corner of his eye he saw Joe Plasky hop on his hands
down the steps behind his own platform and swing his way
toward the corner. He would not be alone, at least.

Plasky got there first. "Hello, gents. I'm one of the owners
of the show. Everything all right?"

"Like hell it is," blustered one of the marks. A young
farmer, Stan judged. "This here tattooed son-of-a-bitch got
five dollars of my money by faking. I seen this here strap swindle afore. I aims to get my money back."

"If there's any doubt in your mind about the fairness of
any game of chance in the show I'm sure the Sailor here will
return your original bet. We're all here to have a good time,
mister, and we don't want any hard feelings."

The other mark spoke up. He was a tall, raw-boned sodbuster with a mouth which chronically hung open, showing
long yellow teeth. "I seen this here trick afore, too, mister.
Cain't fool me. Cain't nobody pick out that loop, way this

feller unwinds it. A feller showed me how it works one time. It's a gahdamned swindle."

Joe Plasky's smile was broader than ever. He reached in the pocket of his shirt and drew out a roll of bills and took off a five. He held it up to the farmer. "Here's the money out of my own pocket, son. If you can't afford to lose you can't afford to bet. I'm just returning your bet because we want everybody to have a good time and no hard feelings. Now you boys better mosey along."

The youth shoved the five into the pocket of his pants and the two of them slouched out. Plasky turned to the Sailor. His smile was still there, but a hard, steady light shone in his eyes. "You dumb bastard! This is a tough town. The whole damn state is tough. And you haven't any more sense than to start a Hey-rube. For Christ's sake watch your step! Now give me the five."

Sailor Martin spat between his teeth into the dust. "I won that fin and I could of handled them two jakes. Who elected you Little Tin Jesus around here?"

Plasky put his fingers in his mouth and whistled a single blast. The tip around the last platform was on its way out and Hoately turned back. Joe waved his hand in an arc and Hoately signaled back and let the canvas drop to close the front entrance. Outside old Maguire began to grind, trying to gather a tip and hold them until the show was opened again.

Bruno dropped lightly from his platform and strode over. Stan felt Zeena beside him. Major Mosquito was running back on his infant's legs, shrilling something incoherent.

Joe Plasky said evenly, "Sailor, you been leaving a trail of busted hearts and busted cherries all along the route. Now you're going to hand me that fin and pack up your gear. You're quitting the show. Hoately will back me up."

Stan's knees were weak. Zeena's hand was on his arm, her fingers gripping it. Would he be expected to take on the Sailor? Joe was a cripple, Bruno a superman. Stan was broader and heavier than the Sailor but the thought of a fight sickened him. He never felt that fists were good enough. He would have carried a gun except that it was a lot of trouble and he was afraid of killing with it.

Martin eyed the group. Bruno stood quietly in the background. "I don't fight no cripples, polack. And I don't owe you no five." The Sailor's lips were pale, his eyes hot.

The half-man acrobat reached up and took him by the hand, gripping the fingers together and bending them so that the tattooed man quickly sank to his knees. "Hey, leggo, you bastard!"

Silently and with his face a blank, Plasky crossed his fore-arms. He let go of Martin's hand and seized the collar of his robe in both fists. Then he levered his wrists together, forcing the backs of his hands into the Sailor's throat. Martin was caught in a human vise. His mouth dropped. He clawed fran-tically at the crossed arms of the half-man but the more he tugged, the tighter they crushed him. His eyes began to bulge and his hair fell over them.

Major Mosquito was leaping up and down, making fighting motions and shadowboxing. "Kill him! Kill him! Kill him! Choke him till he's dead! Kill the big ape!" He rushed in and began hammering the Sailor's staring face with tiny fists. Bruno picked him up, wriggling, and held him at arm's length by the collar of his jacket.

Joe began to shake the tattoo artist, gently at first and then harder. The calm deadliness of that ingenious and unbreakable hold filled Stan with terror and wild joy.

Clem Hoately came running up. "Okay, Joe. Guess he's educated. Let's break it up. We got a good tip waiting."

Joe smiled his smile of one raised from the dead. He re-leased Sailor, who sat up rubbing his throat and breathing hard. Plasky reached into the pocket of the robe and found a wad of bills, took out a five and put the rest back.

Hoately picked the Sailor up and stood him on his feet. "You knock off, Martin. I'll pay you up to the end of the month. Pack up your stuff and leave whenever you want to."

When Martin was able to speak his voice was a hoarse whis-per. "Okay. I'm on my way. I can take my needles into any barber shop and make more dough than in this crummy lay-out. But watch out, all of you."

Middle evening and a good crowd. Beyond the canvas and the gaudily painted banners Hoately's voice was raspy.

"Hi, look! Hi, look! Hi, look! Right this way for the monster aggregation of nature's mistakes, novelty entertainments, and the world-renowned museum of freaks, marvels, and curiosities. Featuring Mamzelle Electra, the little lady who defies the lightning."

Stan looked across at Molly Cahill. When she held the sputtering arc points together she always flinched; the last day or two, whenever he saw it, a little thrill leaped up his spine. Now she bent over and placed her compact behind the electric chair. Bending stretched her sequinned trunks tight over her buttocks.

It's funny how you can see a girl every day for months and yet not see her, Stan thought. Then something will happen—like the way Molly's mouth presses together when she holds the arc points and the fire starts to fly. Then you see her all different.

He dragged his glance away from the girl. Across the tent the massive chest of Bruno Hertz shone pink with sweat as he flexed the muscles of his upper arms, rippling under the pink skin, and the crowd rubbered.

Molly was sitting demurely in a bentwood chair beside the heavy, square menace with its coiled wires, its straps and its chilling suggestion of death which was as phoney as everything else in the carny. She was studying a green racing form. Absorbed, she reached down and scratched one ankle and Stan felt the ripple go up his back again.

Molly's eyes were on the racing sheet but she had stopped looking at it and was looking through it, her mind in the dream she always dreamed.

There was a man in it and his face was always in shadow. He was taller than she and his voice was low and intense and his hands were brown and powerful. They walked slowly, drinking in the summer reflected from every grass blade, shining from every pebble in fields singing with summer. An old rail fence and beyond it a field rising like a wave, a pasture where the eyes of daisies looked up at a sky so blue it made you ache.

His face was shadowy still, as his arms stole about her. She pressed her hands against the hardness of his chest, but his mouth found hers. She tried to turn her head away; but then his fingers were caressing her hair, his kisses falling upon the hollow of her throat while his other hand found her breast . . .

"Over here, folks, right over here. On this platform we have a little lady who is one of the marvels and mysteries of the age—Mamzelle Electra!"

Stan came up the steps behind Joe Plasky's platform and sat on the edge of it. "How they going?"

Joe smiled and went on assembling the novelties in his joke books, slipping the free gifts between the pages. "Can't complain. Good crowd tonight, ain't it?"

Stan shifted his seat. "I wonder if the Sailor will try to do us any dirt?"

Joe swung himself closer on his calloused knuckles and said, "Can't tell. But I don't think so. After all, he is carny. He's a louse, too. But we just want to keep our eyes open. I don't think he'll try to call me in spades—not after he's felt the *nami juji.*"

Stan frowned. "Felt what?"

"*Nami juji.* That's the Jap name for it—that crosshanded choke I slipped on him. That takes some of the starch out of 'em."

The blond head was alert. "Joe, that was terrific, what you did. How in hell did you ever learn that?"

"Jap showed me. We had a Jap juggler when I was with the Keyhoe Shows. It's easy enough to do. He taught me a lot of ju-jit stuff only that's one of the best."

Stan moved closer. "Show me how you do it."

Plasky reached over and slid his right hand up Stan's right coat lapel until he was grasping the collar at the side of Stan's throat. He crossed his left arm over his right and gripped the left side of the collar. Suddenly Stan felt his throat caught in an iron wedge. It loosened immediately; Plasky dropped his hands and smiled. Stan's knees were trembling.

"Let me see if I can do it." He gripped Plasky's black turtle-neck sweater with one hand.

"Higher up, Stan. You got to grab it right opposite the big artery in the neck—here." He shifted the younger man's hand slightly. "Now cross your forearms and grab the other side. Right. Now then, bend your wrists and force the backs of your hands into my neck. That cuts off the blood from the brain."

Stan felt a surge of power along his arms. He did not know that his lips had drawn back over his teeth. Plasky slapped his arm quickly and he let go.

"Christ a-mighty, kid, you want to be careful with that! If you leave it on just a mite too long you'll have a corpse on your hands. And you got to practice getting it quick. It's a little hard to slip on but once you've got it the other fella can't break it—unless he knows the real Jap stuff."

Both men looked up as Maguire, the ticket seller, hurried toward them.

"She-ess-oo flee-ess-eyes!" He ducked past them to where Hoately stood on the Electric Girl's platform.

Plasky's smile widened as it always did in the face of trouble. "Shoo flies, kid. Cops. Just take it easy and you'll be all right. Here's where Hoately will have to do some real talking. And the fixer will have to earn his pay. I been expecting they'd slough the whole joint one of these days."

"What happens to us?" Stan's mouth had gone dry.

"Nothing, kid, if everybody keeps his head. Never argue with a cop. That's what you pay a mouthpiece for. Treat 'em polite and yes 'em to death and send for a mouthpiece. Hell, Stan, you got a lot to learn yet about the carny."

A whistle sounded from the entrance. Stan's head spun toward it.

A big, white-haired man with a badge pinned to his denim shirt stood there. His hat was pushed back and he had his thumbs hooked in his belt. A holster containing a heavy revolver hung from a looser belt on a slant. Hoately raised his voice, grinning down at the marks below Molly's platform.

"That will conclude our performance for the time being, folks. Now I guess you're all kind of dry and could stand a nice cold drink so I call your attention to the stand directly across the midway where you can get all the nice cold soda pop you can drink. That's all for now, folks. Come back to-morrow night and we'll have a few surprises for you—things you didn't see tonight."

The marks obediently began to drift out of the tent and

Hoately approached the law. "What can I do for you, Chief? My name's Hoately and I'm owner of this attraction. You're welcome to inspect every inch of it and I'll give you all the cooperation you want. We've got no girl shows and no games of skill or chance."

The old man's hard little colorless eyes rested on Hoately as they would on a spider in the corner of a backhouse. "Stand here."

"You're the boss."

The old man's gaze flickered over the Ten-in-One tent. He pointed to the geek's enclosure. "What you got in there?"

"Snake charmer," Hoately said casually. "Want to see him?"

"That ain't what I heard. I heard you got an obscene and illegal performance going on here with cruelty to dumb animals. I got a complaint registered this evening."

The showman pulled out a bag of tobacco and papers and began to build a cigarette. His left hand made a quick twist, and the cigarette took form. He licked the paper with his tongue and struck a match. "Why don't you stay as my guest and view the entire performance, Chief? We'd be glad—"

The wide mouth tightened. "I got orders from the marshal to close down the show. And arrest anybody I see fit. I'm arresting you and—" He slid his eyes over the performers: Bruno placid in his blue robe, Joe Plasky smilingly assembling his pitch items, Stan making a half dollar vanish and reappear, Molly still sitting in the Electric Chair, the sequins of her skimpy bodice winking as her breasts rose and fell. She was smiling tautly. "And I'm taking that woman there—indecent exposure. We got decent women in this town. And we got daughters; growin' girls. We don't allow no naked women paradin' around and makin' exposes of 'emselves. The rest of you stay right here in case we need you. All right, you two, come along. Put a coat on that girl first. She ain't decent enough to come down to the lockup thataway."

Stan noticed that the stubble on the deputy marshal's chin was white—like a white fungus on a dead man, he thought savagely. Molly's eyes were enormous.

Hoately cleared his throat and took a deep breath. "Looky

here, Chief, that girl's never had no complaints. She's got to wear a costume like that on account of she handles electric wires and ordinary cloth might catch fire and . . ."

The deputy reached out one hand and gripped Hoately by the shirt. "Shut up. And don't try offering me any bribes, neither. I ain't none o' your thievin' northern police, kissin' the priest's toe on Sundays and raking in the graft hell-bent for election six days a week. I'm a church deacon and I aim to keep this a clean town if I have to run every Jezebel out of it on a fence rail."

His tiny eyes were fastened on Molly's bare thighs. He raised his glance ever so slightly to take in her shoulders and the crease between her breasts. The eyes grew hot and the slack mouth raised at the corners. Beside the Electric Girl's platform he noticed a neat young man with corn-yellow hair saying something to the girl who nodded and then darted her attention back to the deputy.

The law lumbered over, dragging Hoately with him. "Young lady, git off that contraption." He reached up a red-knuckled hand toward Molly. Stan was on the other side of the platform feeling for the switch. There was an ominous buzzing and crackling: Molly's black hair stood straight up like a halo around her head. She brought her finger tips together. Blue fire flowed between them. The deputy stopped, stony. The girl reached out, and sparks jumped in a flashing stream from her fingers to the deputy's. With a shout he drew back, releasing Hoately. The buzz of the static generator stopped and a voice drew his attention; it was the blond youth.

"You can see the reason, Marshal, for the metal costume the young lady is forced to wear. The electricity would ignite any ordinary fabric and only by wearing the briefest of covering can she avoid bursting into flame. Thousands of volts of electricity cover her body like a sheath. Pardon me, Marshal, but there seem to be several dollar bills coming out of your pocket."

In spite of himself, the deputy followed Stan's pointing finger. He saw nothing. Stan reached out and one after another five folded dollar bills appeared from the pocket of the denim shirt. He made them into a little roll and pressed them into the old man's hand. "Another minute and you'd have lost your money, Marshal."

The deputy's eyes were half shut with disbelief and hostile suspicion; but he shoved the cash into his shirt pocket.

Stan went on, "And I see that you have bought your wife a little present of a few silk handkerchiefs." From the cartridge belt Stan slowly drew out a bright green silk, then another of purple. "These are very pretty. I'm sure your wife will like them. And here's a pure white one—for your daughter. She's about nineteen now, isn't she, Marshal?"

"How'd you know I got a daughter?"

Stan rolled the silks into a ball and they vanished. His face was serious, the blue eyes grave. "I know many things, Marshal. I don't know exactly how I know them but there's nothing supernatural about it, I am sure. My family was Scotch and the Scotch are often gifted with powers that the old folks used to call 'second sight.'"

The white head with its coarse, red face, nodded involuntarily.

"For instance," Stan went on, "I can see that you have carried a pocket piece or curio of some kind for nearly twenty years. Probably a foreign coin."

One great hand made a motion toward the pants pocket. Stan felt his own pulse racing with triumph. Two more hits and he'd have him.

"Several times you have lost that luck-piece but you've found it again every time; and it means a lot to you, you don't exactly know why. I'd say that you should always carry it."

The deputy's eyes had lost some of their flint.

From the tail of his eye Stan saw that the Electric Chair above them was empty; Molly had disappeared. So had everyone else except Hoately who stood slightly to the rear of the deputy, nodding his head wisely at every word of the magician's.

"Now this isn't any of my business, Marshal, because I know you are a man who is fully capable of handling his own affairs and just about anything else that is liable to come along. But my Scotch blood is working right this minute and it tells me that there is one thing in your life that is worrying you and it's something you find it difficult to handle. Because all your strength and your courage and your authority in the town seem to be of no avail. It seems to slip through your grasp like water—"

"Wait a minute, young fella. What are you talkin' 'bout?"

"As I said, it's absolutely none of my business. And you are a man in the prime of life and old enough to be my father and by rights you should be the one to give me good advice and not the other way round. But in this case I may be able to do you a good turn. I sense that there are antagonistic influences surrounding you. Someone near to you is jealous of you and your ability. And while part of this extends to your work as a peace officer and your duties in upholding the law, there is another part of it that has to do with your church . . ."

The face had changed. The savage lines had ironed out and now it was simply the face of an old man, weary and bewildered. Stan hurried on, panicky for fear the tenuous spell would break, but excited at his own power. If I can't read a Bible-spouting, whoremongering, big-knuckled hypocrite of a church deacon, he told himself, I'm a feeblo. The old son-of-a-bitch.

Stan's eyes misted over as if they had turned inward. His voice grew intimate. "There is someone you love very dearly. Yet there is an obstacle in the way of your love. You feel hemmed-in and trapped by it. And through it all I seem to hear a woman's voice, a sweet voice, singing. It's singing a beautiful old hymn. Wait a moment. It's 'Jesus, Savior, Pilot Me.' "

The deputy's mouth was open, his big chest was lifting and falling with his breath.

"I see a Sunday morning in a peaceful, beautiful little church. A church into which you have put your energy and your labor. You have labored hard in the Lord's vineyard and your labor has borne fruit in the love of a woman. But I see her eyes filled with tears and somehow your own heart is touched by them . . ."

Christ, how far do I dare go with this? Stan thought behind the running patter of his words.

"But I feel that all will come out well for you. Because you have strength. And you'll get more. The Lord will give you strength. And there are malicious tongues about you, ready to do you an injury. And to do this fine woman an injury if they can. Because they are like whited sepulchers which appear beautiful outward but are full of dead men's bones and all uncleanness and . . ."

The deacon's eyes were hot again but this time not at Stan. There was a hunted look in them too as the youth bore down:

"And the spirit of our Lord and Savior, Jesus Christ, has shined upon them but in vain, because they see as through a glass, darkly, and the darkness is nothing but a reflection of their own blackness and sin and hypocrisy and envy. But deep inside yourself you will find the power to combat them. And defeat them. And you will do it with the help of the God you believe in and worship.

"And while I feel the spirit talking to me straight out, like a father to his son, I must tell you that there's a matter of some money coming to you that will cause you some disappointment and delay but you will get it. I can see that the people in this town have been pretty blind in the past but something in the near future will occur which will wake them up and make them realize that you are a more valuable man than they ever would admit. There's a surprise for you—about this time next year or a little later, say around November. Something you've had your heart set on for a long time but it will come true if you follow the hunches you get and don't let anybody talk you out of obeying your own good judgment which has never let you down yet—whenever you've given it a free rein."

Hoately had evaporated. Stan turned and began to move slowly toward the gate. The midway outside was buzzing with little groups of talk. The entire carny had been sloughed and the deputies had chased the townies off the lot. Stan walked slowly, talking still in a soft, inward voice. The old man followed beside him, his eyes staring straight ahead.

"I'm very glad to have met you, Marshal. Because I expect to be back here again some day and I'd like to see if my Scotch blood had been telling me true, as I'm sure it has. I'm sure you don't mind a young fellow like myself presuming to tell you these things, because, after all, I'm not pretending to advise you. I know you've lived a lot longer than I and have more knowledge of the ways of the world than I could ever have. But when I first set eyes on you I thought to myself, 'Here's a man and a servant of the law who is troubled deep in his mind,' and then I saw that you had no reason to be because things are going to turn out just the way you want them to, only there will be a little delay . . .''

How the hell shall I finish this off, Stan wondered. I can talk myself right back into the soup if I don't quit.

They reached the entrance and Stan paused. The deputy's red, hard face turned toward him; the silence seemed to pour over Stan and smother him. This was the pay-off, and his heart sank. There was nothing more to be said now. This was where action started. Stan felt out of his depth. Then he suddenly knew the business that would work, if anything would. He turned away from the old man. Making his face look as spiritual as possible, he raised one hand and rested it easily in a gesture of peace and confidence against the looped canvas. It was a period at the end of the sentence.

The deputy let out a long, whistling breath, hooked his thumbs in his belt, and stood looking out on the darkening midway. Then he turned back to Stan and his voice was just an ordinary old man's voice. "Young fella, I wisht I'd met you a long time ago. Tell the others to go easy in this town because we aim to keep it clean. But, by God, when—if I'm ever elected marshal you ain't got nothing to worry about, long as you have a good, clean show. Good night, son."

He plodded away slowly, his shoulders squared against the dark, authority slapping his thigh on a belt heavy with cartridges.

Stan's collar was tight with the blood pounding beneath it. His head was as light as if he had a fever.

The world is mine, God damn it! The world is mine! I've got 'em across the barrel and I can shake them loose from whatever I want. The geek has his whisky. The rest of them drink something else: they drink promises. They drink hope. And I've got it to hand them. I'm running over with it. I can get anything I want. If I could hand this old fart a cold reading and get away with it I could do it to a senator! I could do it to a governor!

Then he remembered where he had told her to hide.

In the black space where the trucks were parked, Zeena's van was behind the others, dark and silent. He opened the cab door softly and crept in, his blood hammering.

"Molly!"

"Yes, Stan." The whisper came from the black cavern behind the seat.

"It's okay, kid. I stalled him. He's gone."

"Oh, Stan, gee, you're great. You're great."

Stan crawled back over the seat and his hand touched a soft, hot shoulder. It was trembling. His arm went about it. "Molly!"

Lips found his. He crushed her back on a pile of blankets.

"Stan, you won't let anything happen to me—will you?"

"Certainly not. Nothing's ever going to happen to you while I'm around."

"Oh, Stan, you're so much like my dad."

The hooks which held the sequinned bodice came open in his shaking fingers. The girl's high, pointed breasts were smooth under his hands, and his tongue entered her lips.

"Don't hurt me, Stan, honey. Don't." His collar choked him, the blood hammering in his throat. "Oh. Stan—hurt me, hurt me, hurt me—"

The Empress

who sits on Venus' couch amid the
ripening grain and rivers of the earth.

T HE NIGHT was quiet at last, with only the katydids. The ferris wheel stood as gaunt as a skeleton against the stars; the cookhouse lights were lonely in the dark.

Stan stepped down into the grass beside the van and held his hand up to help Molly. Her palm was hot and damp. When she stood beside him she clung to him for a moment and pressed her forehead against his cheek. They were almost the same height. Her hair smelled sweet and tickled his lips. He shook his head impatiently.

"Stan, honey, you do love me—don't you?"

"Sure I do, baby."

"And you won't tell a soul. Promise me you won't tell. Because I never let any man do it to me before, honest."

"Are you sure?" Stan thrilled at his power over her. He wanted to hear her voice with fear in it.

"Yes, honey. Yes. Honest. You hurt me something terrible at first. You know—"

"Yes."

"Darling, if I'd ever done it before you wouldn't have hurt me. Only I'm glad you hurt me, honey, I'm glad. Because you were the first."

The air was chilly; she began to shiver. Stan slipped off his jacket and put it around her shoulders. "Gee, you're good to me, Stan."

"I'll always be."

"Always?" Molly stopped and turned to face him, resting both hands on his forearm. "What do you mean, Stan?"

"Just always."

"You mean until the season's over and we all split up?" Her voice held a deeper question.

Stan had decided. In his mind he saw the blaze of the foots, with himself standing there straight. In command. Molly was in the audience in an evening gown, walking slowly down the aisle. The marks—the audience—craned their necks to look at her. She was an eyeful. The placards at each side of the stage said simply, STANTON. The big time.

"Molly, you like show business, don't you?"

"Why, sure, Stan. Daddy always wanted to see me in show business."

"Well, what I mean is— Well, let's head for the big time. Together."

Her arm slid around his waist and they walked on again, slowly. "Darling, that's wonderful. I was hoping you'd say that to me."

"I mean it. Together we can get right to the top. You've got the class and the shape. I mean, you're beautiful and we can work up a two-person code act that'll knock 'em dead."

Molly's arm tightened around him. "Stan, that's what I always wanted. Daddy would be awful proud of us. I know he would. He'd be crazy about you, Stan. The way you can talk your way out of a tight place. That's what he admired most in anybody. That and not double-crossing a pal, ever. Daddy said he wanted on his tombstone, 'Here lies Denny Cahill. He never crossed up a pal.' "

"Did he get it?"

"No. My grandfather wouldn't hear of it. The stone just says, 'Dennis Cahill' and under it the dates when he was born and when he passed away. Only one night, just before I left Louisville, I went out and wrote it below the dates with chalk. I'll bet some of the chalk is still there.''

They had reached the Ten-in-One. Inside a single bulb glowed. Stan peered in. "All clear, kid. Get into your things. I wonder where the others are?"

While Molly was dressing behind the curtains of Zeena's stage Stan walked over to the cookhouse and found the cook cleaning coffee urns. "Where's the bunch?"

"Scattered. The bulls run in a couple of fellows on the wheels and games. They even sloughed the cat rack. The fixer'll get 'em sprung tomorrow. And I'll have to put on a tub of water so they can boil up and get the crumbs out of their clothes. Want a cup o' java?"

"No, thanks. I want to find my bunch. Got any idea where they went?"

The cook wiped his hands and lit a cigarette. "Hoately's gone up the road to a lunch wagon or something. Roadside joint. You can't miss it. He said he didn't want to hang around the lot tonight. Can't blame him. Seems somebody put in a beef to the cops about the geek show you fellows got. And about the wheels. Way I heard it, that tattooed guy used to be in the Ten-in-One and had the run-in with Plasky was in town shooting off his mouth."

"Sailor Martin?"

"That's the son-of-a-bitch. What I heard, he worked on the townies and got them to beef to the cops. Can you imagine a carny doing that? Somebody ought to stick a butcher knife up his rear end and kick the handle off."

Stan heard a low whistle from outside and said good night to the cook. Molly was standing in the shadow of the Ten-in-One, looking prim and neat in a dark suit and a white silk blouse. He took her arm and they set off down the road.

It was a chicken-dinner shack; from inside came voices and laughs. He pushed open the screen door.

At a table with a red-checkered tablecloth the bunch was gathered. Pints of whisky stood among plates of chicken bones. Hoately was talking:

". . . and the minute I heard the kid go into that jerk-'em-to-Jesus routine I knowed we was all set. I want to tell you, it was something to watch. That old buzzard's trap was hanging open a mile—lapping up every word the kid handed him."

He paused and let out a whoop at the sight of Stan and Molly.

The others helloed; Zeena bustled up and put her arms around Molly and kissed her. "Sakes alive, honey, I'm glad to see you. You come over and sit down right by Zeena. Where on earth did you skedaddle to? We knew they didn't pinch you or Stan because Clem hung around and watched. But I was looking all over for you."

"I hid in the van," Molly said. She looked down at her purse and ran her finger over the clasp.

"And Stan!" Zeena enveloped him in a hug and kissed him warmly on the mouth. "Stan, boy, you sure done noble. I always knew you were a mentalist. Imagine that—giving a cold reading to a cop and getting away with it! Oh, I just love you."

The rasping, fiddle voice of Major Mosquito cut through. "Come on over and have a drink. Hoately's treat. Come on over. I'm getting stinko."

They took their seats, and a gangling youth with spiky hair brought in two more plates of chicken. "Watch them bottles, folks. Town's hell on enforcement."

Stan and Molly sat together. Suddenly they were ravenous and dug into the chicken.

Joe Plasky said, "Nice going, kid. You kept your head. You're real carny, and no mistake."

Bruno said nothing. He had been about to start on his fourth plate of chicken but now it lay in front of him, neglected. Molly caught Stan's hand and squeezed it under the tablecloth. They exchanged a quick look.

Zeena poured herself a drink and took it in two swallows. "Liquor's terrible, Clem. It's that bad, I nearly left some—as the Scotch fella says."

Clem Hoately was picking his teeth with a sharpened match. "Short notice. I asked one of the deputies—young fellow who looked okay—where I could pick up a pint. He sent me to his brother-in-law. Town's all right if you case it careful. We won't have no trouble after tonight. That old son-of-a-bitch that sloughed us was the toughest they got. We'll open tomorrow night and pack 'em in. Best advertising in the world."

Molly looked startled. "I—I shouldn't think it would be safe."

Hoately grinned. "You can wear riding boots and breeches. That'll be all right. You got the shape to look good in 'em. Don't worry about it."

Zeena took a chicken bone from her mouth and said, "I think we all ought to give Stan a great big hand. We might have got into a peck of trouble if it hadn't been for him. I always say, there's nothing like the second sight. Anybody who can give a good reading'll never starve. Only, gosh"— she turned to face Stan—"I never knew you could spout the Bible, the way Clem's been telling us." She paused, chewing, and then went on, "Stan, 'fess up. Were you ever really a preacher?"

He shook his head, hard lines at the corners of his mouth. "That was my old man's idea once—to make me one. Only I couldn't see it. Then he wanted me to go into real estate. But that's too slow a turn. I wanted magic. But the old gent was a great hand at quoting scripture. I guess a lot of it rubbed off onto me."

Major Mosquito, holding a tumbler in both hands, lifted it. "Here's to the Great Stanton, purveyor of fun, magic, mystery and bullshit! He's a jolly good fellow, he's a jolly good . . ."

Bruno Hertz said, "You shut up. You talk too much for little fellow." His sad steer's eyes were on Molly. Suddenly he blurted out, "Molly, you and Stan going to get married?"

The room got as quiet as if a needle had been lifted off a record. Molly choked and Zeena slapped her on the back. Her face was red when she answered, "Why—what makes you think—"

Bruno, bold and desperate, stumbled on. "You and Stan been together! You going to get married?"

Stan looked up and met the strongman's gaze levelly. "As a matter of fact, Molly and I are going to head for vaudeville. We've got it all figured out. In the two-a-day nobody's going to run her in for wearing skimpies."

Zeena set down her glass. "Why—why, I think that's just splendid. Clem, did you hear? They're going to try the two-a-day. I think it's perfectly fine. I think it's great." She crushed Molly in another hug. Then she reached out and rumpled Stan's hair. "Stan,—ain't—ain't you the foxy one! And you all the time—making out like you never—never knew the child was on the face of the earth." She dumped more whisky in her glass and said, "All right, folks, here's a toast to the bride and groom. Long life and may all your troubles be little ones—eh, Molly?"

Hoately lifted his coffee cup. Major Mosquito said, "Hooray! Let me hide under the bed, the first night. I'll be quiet. Just let me—"

Bruno Hertz poured a small drink for himself and gazed at Molly over the glass. *"Prosit, Liebchen."* Under his breath he muttered, "Better wish luck. You going to need luck. Maybe some day you going to need—"

Joe Plasky's Lazarus smile was like a lamp. "All the best, kids. Glad to see it. I'll give you a letter to a couple of booking agents in New York."

Zeena cleared the plates and glasses from before her with an unsteady sweep. She reached into her purse and drew out a pack of cards. "Here you are, kids. Now's a good time to see what the Tarot has for you. The Tarot's always got an answer." She shuffled. "Go ahead, honey. Cut 'em. Let's see what you cut."

Molly cut the cards and Zeena grabbed them and turned them over. "Well, what d'you know—The Empress! That's her, honey. See, she's sitting on a couch and it's got the sign of Venus on it. That's for love. And she's got stars in her hair. That's for all the good things your husband's going to give you."

Major Mosquito squeaked with laughter, and Bruno hissed at him to keep quiet.

"The Empress is a good fortune card in love, honey. Couldn't be better 'cause it means you'll get what you want most." She shuffled again and held them up to Stan, who had stood up and moved in behind Molly's chair. Molly had taken his hand and was holding it near her cheek.

"Go on, Stan. You cut 'em, see what comes out."

Stan released Molly's hand. In the stacked cards, the edge of one showed darker than the others from handling and Stan cut to it without thinking, turning his half of the deck face up.

Major Mosquito let out a squall. Zeena knocked over the bottle and Hoately caught it before it had gurgled away. Bruno's stolid face was alight with something like triumph. Molly looked puzzled and Stan laughed. The midget across the table was beating the cloth with a spoon and crying out in an ecstasy of drunken glee:

"Ha! Ha! Ha! Ha! *The Hanged Man!*"

Resurrection of the Dead

*At the call of an angel with fiery wings, graves
open, coffins burst, and the dead are naked.*

". . . I CAN SEE, madam, that there are many persons surrounding you who are envious of your happiness, your culture, your good fortune and—yes, I must be frank—your good looks. I would advise you, madam, to go your own way, doing those things which you know down deep in your heart of hearts is right. And I am sure your husband, who sits beside you in the theater now, will agree with me. There is no weapon you can use against malicious envy except the confidence in your way of life as the moral and righteous one, no matter what the envious say. And it is one of these, madam, and I believe you know of whom I am speaking, who has poisoned your dog."

The applause was slow in starting. They were baffled; they were awe-struck. Then it began from the back of the theater and traveled forward, the people whose questions had been whispered to Molly and whose questions he had answered, clapping last. It was a storm of sound. And Stan, hearing it through the heavy drop curtain, breathed it in like mountain air.

The curtains parted for his second bow. He took it, bowing slowly from the waist and then he extended his hand and Molly swept from the wings where she had arrived by the door backstage behind the boxes. They bowed together, hand in hand, and then the curtains cut down again and they moved off through the wings and up the concrete stairs that led to the dressing rooms.

Stan opened the dressing-room door, stood aside for Molly to go in, then followed and shut the door. He sat for a moment on the wicker couch, then whipped off his white tie and unbuttoned the neckband of his stiff shirt and lit a cigarette.

Molly had stepped out of the skin-tight evening gown she wore and hung it on a hanger. She stood for a moment without a stitch on, scratching her ribs under the arms. Then she slipped on a robe, caught up her hair in a knot and began to dab cold cream on her face.

Finally Stan spoke. "Two nights running is too much."

Her hand stopped, pressed against her chin. Her head was turned away from him. "I'm sorry, Stan. I guess I was tired."

He got up and moved over, looking down at her. "After five years you still fluff it. My God, what do you use for brains anyway? What's eighty-eight?"

Her wide, smoky-gray eyes were brilliant with tears. "Stan, I—I'll have to think about it. When you come at me all of a sudden that way I have to think. I—just have to think," she finished lamely.

He went on, his voice cool. "Eighty-eight!"

"Organization!" she said, smiling quickly. "Shall I join some club, fraternity, or organization? Of course. I hadn't forgotten it, Stan. Honest, honey."

He went over to the couch and lay back on it. "You'll say it backwards and forwards a hundred times before you go to sleep tonight. Right?"

"Sure, Stan."

She brightened, relieved that the tension had passed. The towel came away from her face pink from the makeup. Molly patted powder on her forehead, started to put on her street lipstick. Stan took off his shirt and threw a robe around his shoulders. With a few practiced swipes he cold-creamed his face, frowning at his reflection. The blue eyes had grown frosty. There were lines, faint ones, at the corners of his mouth. They had always been there when he smiled but now he noticed for the first time that they stayed there when his face was relaxed. Time was passing over his head.

Molly was fastening the snaps of her skirt. "Glory be, but I'm tired. I don't want to go anywhere tonight but to bed. I could sleep for a week."

Stan sat gazing at his image in the mirror, made hard by the lights blazing around the edge. He was like a stranger to himself. He wondered what went on behind that familiar face, the square jaw, the corn-yellow hair. It was a mystery, even to himself. For the first time in months he thought of Gyp and could see him clearly through the mist of years, bounding through fields grown lush with neglected weeds of late summer.

"Good boy," he muttered. "Good old boy."

"What was it, honey?" Molly was sitting on the wicker couch reading a movie magazine while she waited for him to dress.

"Nothing, kid," he said over his shoulder. "Just mumbling in my beard."

Who poisoned our dog? People around you who envy you. Number fourteen. One: Will. Four: Tell. *Will* you *tell* this lady what she is thinking about?

Stan shook his head and rubbed his face evenly with the towel. He hung up his suit of tails and stepped into his tweed trousers. He ran a comb through his hair and knotted his tie.

Outside the snow was falling lightly, lingering on the dark surface of the dirty window of the dressing room.

At the stage door the winter met them with an icy breath. They found a cab and got in and Molly slipped her arm through his and rested her cheek against his shoulder and stayed that way.

"Here y'are, buddy. Hotel Plymouth."

Stan handed the driver a dollar and helped Molly out.

They passed through the revolving door into the drowsy heat of the lobby and Stan stopped by the cigar counter for cigarettes. He lifted his eyes to the desk and then he stopped and Molly, turning back to see if he was coming, hurried up. She put her hand on his arm. "Stan, darling—what's the matter with you? God, you look terrible. Are you sick, honey? Answer me. Are you sick? You're not mad at me, are you, Stan?"

Abruptly he turned away and strode out of the lobby into the wind and the winter night. The cold air felt good and his face and neck needed the cold. He turned to the girl. "Molly, don't ask any questions. I just saw somebody I'm trying to duck. Go upstairs and pack our stuff. We're checking out. Got any dough? Well, square up the bill and have the bellhop bring the stuff out."

Without asking any more questions she nodded and went in.

When she came down the woman at the desk, the night clerk, smiled up at her from a detective story. "Will you make up my bill, please? Mr. and Mrs. Stanton Carlisle."

The woman smiled again. She was white-haired and Molly wondered why so many white-haired women insist on bright lipstick. It makes them look like such crows, she thought. If I ever get white-haired I'll never wear anything darker than Passion Flower. Yet this woman had been quite a chick in her day, Molly decided. And she had lived. There was something about her that made you think she had been in show business. But then lots of good-looking people had when they were young and that really didn't mean a thing. It was managing to stay in show business and stay at the top that counted. Never getting to be a has-been and washed-up. That was the worst thing, to be washed-up. Only you had to save a pile of money while you were in the chips. And what with staying at the best places and buying dinners and drinks for managers and newspapermen and people they never seemed to get much ahead at the end of a season on the road. That is, the more the act was worth, the more it seemed to take to sell it.

"That will be eighteen dollars and eighty-five cents," the woman said. She looked searchingly at Molly. "Is—is your husband coming back to the hotel?"

Molly thought fast. "No. As a matter of fact, he's already waiting for me further downtown. We have to make a train."

The woman's face was not smiling any more. It had a

hunted, hopeful look which was, at the same time, strangely hungry. Molly didn't like it a blessed bit. She paid and went out.

Stan was pacing up and down savagely. A cab was standing by the curb with its meter ticking. They put the bags in and rode off.

All hotels are the same place, Molly thought later, lying beside Stan in the partial darkness. Why do they always have street lights outside the windows and car lines in the street and elevators in the wall right beside your head and people upstairs who bang things? But anyhow it was better than never getting around or seeing anything.

Watching Stan undress had stirred her and made her remember so many good times and she had hoped he would feel like it even if they were both as tired as dogs. He had been so cross lately and they always seemed to be tired when they went to bed. With a little flare of panic she wondered if she were losing her looks or something. Stan could be so wonderful. It made her go all wriggly and scarey inside to think about it. God, it was worth waiting for—when he really wanted a party. But then she remembered something else and she began saying to herself, "Eighty-eight—organization. Shall I join some club, union, fraternity, or organization? Shall I join some club, union, fraternity, or organization?" She repeated it three times before she fell asleep with her lips slightly open and her cheek on one palm, her black hair tumbled over the pillow.

Stan reached out and felt around on the bedside table for the cigarettes. He found one and his match flared. Below them a late car whined into hearing from the distance, the steel rails carrying the sound. But he let it slip from his mind.

A memory was coming back. A day when he was eleven years old.

It was like other days of early summer. It began with a rattle of locusts in the trees outside the bedroom window. Stan Carlisle opened his eyes, and the sun was shining hotly.

Gyp sat on the chair beside the bed, whining gently deep in his throat and touching the boy's arm with one paw.

Stan reached out lazily and rubbed the mongrel's head

while the dog writhed in delight. In a moment he had leaped onto the bed joyfully wagging all over. Then Stan was fully awake and remembered. He pushed Gyp off and began brushing violently at the streaks of dried clay left on the sheets by the dog's paws. Mother always got mad when Gyp Jumped Up.

Stan stole to the door, but the door to his parents' room across the hall was still closed. He tiptoed back and idly pulled on his underwear and the corduroy knickers. He stuffed a paper-backed book inside his shirt and laced up his shoes.

Down in the yard he could see the garage doors open. Dad had left for the office.

Stan went downstairs. Being careful not to make any noise he got a bottle of milk from the ice box, a loaf of bread and a jar of jelly. Gyp got bread and milk in a saucer on the floor.

While Stan sat in the early morning stillness of the empty kitchen, cutting off slices of bread and loading them with jelly, he read the catalog:

". . . a real professional outfit, suitable for theater, club, or social gathering. An hour's performance complete. With beautiful cloth-bound instruction book. Direct from us or at your toy or novelty dealer's. $15.00."

After his eighth slice of bread and jelly he put the remains of his breakfast away and went out on the back porch with the catalog. The sun was growing hotter. The brightness of the summer morning filled him with a pleasant sadness, as if at the thought of something noble and magic which had happened long ago in the days of knights and lonely towers.

Upstairs he heard the sharp rap of small heels on the floor and then the roar of water in the bathtub. Mother had gotten up early.

Stan hurried upstairs. Above the rush of the water he could make out his mother's voice, singing in a hard, glittering soprano, "Oh, my laddie, my laddie, I luve the kent you carry. I luve your very bonnet with the silver buckle on it . . ."

He was disturbed and resentful of the song. Usually she sang it after he had been sent up to bed, when the parlor was full of people and Mark Humphries, the big dark man who taught singing, was playing the accompaniment while Dad sat in the dining room, smoking a cigar and talking in low tones about deals with one of his own friends. It was part of the grown-up world with its secrets, its baffling changes from good temper to bad without warning. Stan hated it.

He stepped into the bedroom that always smelled of perfume. The shining brass bedstead was glittering big and important in the bar of sunlight through the blind. The bed was rumpled.

Stan went over and buried his face in the pillow that smelled faintly of perfume, drawing in his breath through it again and again. The other pillow smelled of hair tonic.

He knelt beside the bed, thinking of Elaine and Lancelot— how she came floating down on a boat and Lancelot stood by the bank looking at her and being sorry she was dead.

The rush of water in the bathroom had given way to splashing and snatches of singing. Then the chung of the stopper and the water gurgling out.

Beyond the window, with its shades making the room cool and dark, a cicada's note sounded, starting easy and getting loud and dying away, sign of hot weather coming.

Stan took one more breath of the pillow, pushing it around his face to shut out sound and everything except its yielding softness and its sweetness.

There was a sharp click from the latch of the bathroom door. The boy frantically smoothed out the pillow; he tore around the big brass bed and out into the hall and across to his own room.

Downstairs he heard Jennie's slow step on the back porch and the creak of the kitchen chair as she slumped her weight into it to rest before she took off her hat and her good dress. It was the day for Jennie to do the wash.

Stan heard his mother come out of the bathroom; then he heard the bedroom door close. He crept out into the hall and paused beside it.

Inside there was a pat of bare feet on the floor and the catch of the bedroom door quietly slipped on. Grownups were always locking themselves in places. Stan got a sudden shiver of mystery and elation. It started in his lower back and rippled up between his shoulder blades.

Through the closed door came the soft clink of a perfume

bottle being set down on the dressing table and then there was the scrape of chair legs. The chair creaked ever so little; it scraped the floor again; the bottle clinked as the stopper was put in.

When she came out she would be dressed up and ready to go downtown and she would have a lot of jobs for him to do while she was gone—like cleaning up the closet in his room or cutting the grass on the terrace.

He moved stealthily along the hall and eased open the door to the attic stairs, closed it behind him gently and went up. He knew the creaky steps and skipped them. The attic was hot and heavy with the smell of wood and old silk.

Stan stretched out on an iron bed covered with a silk patch-work quilt. It was made of strips of silk sewn in squares, different colors on each side and a single square of black silk in the center of each. Grandma Stanton made it the winter be-fore she died.

The boy lay face down. The sounds of the house filtered up to him from far away. The whining scrape of Gyp, banished to the back porch. Jennie in the cellar and the chug of the new washing machine. The brisk clatter of Mother's door opening and the tap of her high heels on the stairs. She called his name once sharply and then called something down to Jennie.

Jennie's voice came out the cellar window, mournful and rich. "Yes, Mis' Carlisle. If I see him I tell him."

For a moment Stan was afraid Mother would go out the back door and that Gyp would Jump Up and make her cross and then she would start talking about getting rid of him. But she went out the front door instead. Stan heard the mail box rattle. Then she went down the steps.

He leaped up and ran over to the attic window where he could see the front lawn through the maple tops below him.

Mother was walking quickly away toward the car line.

She would be going downtown to Mr. Humphries for her singing lesson. And she would not be back for a long time. Once she paused before the glass signboard on the lawn of the church. It told what Dr. Parkman would preach about next Sunday, but it was so black, and with the glass in front of it, it was like looking into a mirror. Mother stopped, as if reading about next Sunday's sermon; turning her head first one way and then another, she pulled her hat a little more forward and touched her hair.

She went on then, walking slower. The boy watched her until she was out of sight.

On every hilltop and rise Stan turned and gazed back across the fields. He could spy the roof of his own house rising among the bright green of the maples.

The sun beat down.

The air was sweet with the smell of summer grasses. Gyp bounded through the hummocks, chasing away almost out of sight and bouncing back again.

Stan climbed a fence, crossed a pasture, and then mounted a stone wall, boosting Gyp over. On the other side of the wall the fields were thicker with brush and little oak bushes and pines and beyond it the woods began.

When he stepped into their dark coolness he felt again that involuntary shudder, which was part pleasure and part apprehension, rise between his shoulder blades. The woods were a place to kill enemies in. You fought them with a battle-ax and you were naked and nobody dared say anything about it because you had the ax always hanging from your wrist by a piece of leather. Then there was an old castle deep in the forest. It had green moss in the cracks between the stones and there was a moat around it full of water and it stood there deep and still as death and from the castle there was never a sound or a sign of life.

Stan trod softly now and held his breath, listening to the green silence. The leaves were tender under his feet. He stepped over a fallen tree and then looked up through the branches to where the sun made them bright.

He began to dream. He and Lady Cynthia rode through the forest. Cynthia was Mother's name, only Lady Cynthia was not like Mother except that she looked like her. She was just a beautiful lady on a white palfrey and the bridle was set with gems and jewels that winked in the dappled light through the branches. Stan was in armor and his hair was long and cut straight across and his face was tanned dark and with no freckles. His horse was a powerful charger as black as midnight. That was its name—Midnight. He and Lady Cynthia had

come to the forest to seek an adventure, for in the forest was
a powerful old magician.

Stan came out on a long-disused timber road where he
slipped out of the dream, for he remembered that they had
been here on the picnic. That was the time they had come
out with Mr. and Mrs. Morris and Mark Humphries had
driven Mother and Dad and Stan in his car with the top down.
They brought the food in baskets.

Sudden anger rose up in him when he thought how his dad
had had to spoil the day by having a fuss with Mother about
something. He had spoken in low tones but then Mother had
said, "Stan and I are going for a walk all by ourselves, aren't
we, Stan?" She was smiling at the others the way she did when
something was wrong. Stan had felt that delicious shudder go
up between his shoulders.

That was the time they found the Glade.

It was a deep cleft in a ridge and you would never know it
was there unless you stumbled on it. He had been back since
but on that day Mother had been there and all of a sudden,
as if she had felt the magic of the place, she had knelt and
kissed him. He remembered the perfume she had on. She had
held him off at arm's length and she was really smiling this
time, as if at something deep inside herself, and she said,
"Don't tell anybody. This place is a secret just between us."

He had been happy all the way back to the others.

That night when they were back home and he was in bed,
the sound of his father's voice, rasping and rumbling through
the walls, had made him sick with rebellion. What did he have
to always be fussing with Mother for? Then the thought of
the Glade, and of how she looked when she kissed him, made
him wriggle with delight.

But the next day it was all gone and she spoke sharp to him
about everything and kept finding jobs for him to do.

Stan started down the loggers' road. In a damp spot he
stooped and then knelt like a tracker examining a spoor. The
spot was fed by a trickle of spring. Across it were the tracks
of auto tires, their clear and sacrilegious imprints just beginning to fill with water.

Stan hated them—the grownups were everywhere. He
hated their voices most of all.

Cautiously he crossed the road, calling Gyp to him to keep him from rustling through the brush. He held the dog's collar and went on, taking care not to tread on any dead twigs. The Glade had to be approached with the reverence of silence. He climbed the last bank on his hands and knees and then on looking over the crest he froze.

Voices were coming from the Glade.

He peered further over. Two people were lying on an Indian blanket and with a hot rush Stan knew that one was a man and the other was a woman and this was what men and women did secretly together that everybody stopped talking about when he came around, only some grownups never talked about it at all. Curiosity leaped inside of him at the thought of spying on them when they didn't know he was there. He was seeing it all—all of it—the thing that made babies grow inside of women. He could hardly breathe.

The woman's face was hidden by the man's shoulder, and only her hands could be seen pressing against his back. After a while they were still. Stan wondered if they were dead—if they ever died doing it and if it hurt them but they had to do it even so.

At last they stirred and the man rolled over on his back. The woman sat up, holding her hands to her hair. Her laughter rang up the side of the Glade, a little harsh but still silvery.

Stan's fingers tightened on the grass hummock under his hand. Then he spun around, dragging Gyp by the collar, and stumbled, sliding and bumping, down the slope to the road. He ran with his breath scorching his throat, his eyes burning with tears. He ran all the way back and then went up in the attic and lay on the iron bed and tried to cry, but then he couldn't.

He heard Mother come in after a while. The light outside began to darken and shadows got longer.

Then he heard the car drive up. Dad got out. Stan could tell by the way he slammed the car door that he was mad. Downstairs he heard his father's voice, rasping through the floors, and his mother's raised, the way she spoke when she was exasperated.

Stan came downstairs, one step at a time, listening.

His father's voice came from the living room. ". . . I don't care for any more of your lies. I tell you, Mrs. Carpenter saw the two of you turning up the road into Mills' Woods. She recognized you and she saw Mark and she recognized the car."

Mother's tone was brittle. "Charles, I should think you would have a little more—*pride*, shall we say?—than to take the word of anyone as malicious and as common as your *friend*, Mrs. Carpenter."

Dad was hammering on the mantelpiece with his fist; Stan could hear the metal thing that covered the fireplace rattle. "New York hats! A nigger to clean up the house! Washing machines! Music lessons! After all I've given you, you turn around and hand me something like this. You! I ought to horsewhip that snake-in-the-grass within an inch of his life!"

Mother spoke slowly. "I rather think Mark Humphries can take care of himself. In fact, I should dearly love to see you walk right up to him on the street and tell him the things you've been saying to me. Because he would tell you that you are a liar. And you would get just what you're asking for; just what you're asking for. Besides that, Charles, you have a filthy mind. You mustn't judge others by yourself, dear. After all, it is quite possible for a person with some breeding to enjoy an hour's motoring in friendship and nothing more. But I realize that if you and—Clara Carpenter, shall we say? . . ."

Dad let out a noise that was something like a roar and something like a sob. "By the Eternal, I've sworn never to take the Lord's name in vain, but you're enough to try the patience of a saint. God *damn* you! D'you hear? *God damn you and all*—"

Stan had reached the ground floor and stood with his fingers running up and down the newel post of the stairs, looking in through the wide double doors of the living room. Mother was sitting very straight on the sofa without leaning back. Dad was standing by the mantel, one hand in his pocket and the other beating against the wood. When he looked up and saw Stan he stopped short.

Stan wanted to turn and run out the front door but his father's eyes kept him fastened to the floor. Mother turned her head and saw him and smiled.

The telephone rang then.

Dad started and plunged down the hall to answer it, his savage "Hello!" bursting like a firecracker in the narrow hallway.

Stan moved painfully, like walking through molasses. He crossed the room and came near his mother whose smile had hardened and grown sick-looking. She whispered, "Stan, Dad is upset because I went riding with Mr. Humphries. We wanted to take you riding with us but Jennie said you weren't here. But—Stan—let's make believe you did go with us. You'll go next time. I think it would make Dad feel better if he thought you were along."

From the hall his father's voice thundered, "By the Eternal, why did the fool have to be told in the first place? I was against telling him. It's the Council's business to vote on the committee's recommendation. We had it in the bag, sewed up tight. Now every idiot in town will know just where the streets will be cut and that property will shoot sky-high by tomorrow morning. . . ."

As Mother leaned close to Stan he smelled the perfume she had on her hair. She always put it on when she went downtown to take her singing lesson. Stan felt cold inside and empty. Even when she kissed him. "Whose boy are you, Stan? You're Mother's boy, aren't you, dear?"

He nodded and walked clumsily to the double doors. Dad was coming back. He took Stan roughly by the shoulder and shoved him toward the front door. "Run along, now. Your mother and I are talking."

Mother was beside them. "Let him stay, Charles. Why don't you ask Stanton what—what he did this afternoon?"

Dad stood looking at her with his mouth shut tight. He still had Stan by the shoulder. Slowly he turned his head. "Stan, what's your mother talking about?"

Stan swallowed. He hated that slack mouth and the stubble of pale yellow on the chin that came out when Dad hadn't shaved for several hours. Mark Humphries did a trick with four little wads of newspaper and a hat and had showed Stan how to do it. And he used to ask riddles.

Stan said, "We went riding with Mr. Humphries in his automobile." Over his father's arm, still holding him, Stan saw

Mother's face make a little motion at him as if she were kissing the air.

Dad went on, his voice quiet and dangerous. "Where did you go with Mr. Humphries, son?"

Stan's tongue felt thick. Mother's face had gotten white, even her mouth. "We—we went out where we had the picnic that time."

Dad's fingers loosened and Stan turned and ran out into the falling dusk. He heard the front door close behind him.

Someone switched on the living-room lamp. After a while Dad came out, got in his car and went downtown. Mother had left some cold meat and bread and butter on the kitchen table and Stan ate it alone, reading the catalog. Only it had lost its flavor and there seemed to be something terribly sad about the blue willow-pattern plate and the old knife and fork. Gyp whined under the table. Stan handed him all his own meat and got some jelly and ate it on the bread. Mother was upstairs in the spare bedroom with the door locked.

The next day Mother got breakfast for him. He said nothing and neither did she. But she wasn't a grownup any more. Or he wasn't a kid any more. There were no more grownups. They lied when they got scared, just like anybody. Everybody was alike only some were bigger. He ate very little and wiped his mouth and said, "Excuse me," politely. Mother didn't ask him to do any jobs. She didn't say anything at all.

He tied Gyp up to the kennel and set out for the woods where the old loggers' road cut into them. He moved in a dream and the shine of the sun seemed to hold back its warmth. At the top of the Glade he paused and then slid doggedly down its slope. Around him the trees rose straight and innocent in the sun and the sound of a woodpecker came whirring through them. The grass was crushed in one place; close by Stan found a handkerchief with "C" embroidered in a corner.

He looked at it with a crawling kind of fascination and then scooped out a hole in the earth and buried it.

When he got back he kept catching himself thinking about things as if nothing had happened, then stopping and the wave of desolation would sweep over him.

Mother was in her room when he came upstairs.

But something was lying big and square on his bed. He raced in.

There it was. The "Number 3" set—Marvello Magic. A full hour's entertainment, suitable for stage, club, or social gathering, $15.00. Its cover was gay with a picture of Mephistopheles making cards rise from a glass goblet. On the side of the box was a paper sticker which read, "Myers' Toy and Novelty Mart" and the address downtown. The corners of the box were shiny with imitation metal bindings, printed on the paper.

Stan knelt beside the bed, gazing at it. Then he threw his arms around it and beat his forehead against one of the sharp corners until the blood came.

Outside the trolley had approached and slid under the hotel window, groaning its lonely way through the night. Stan was trembling. He threw back the covers, switched on the bed light and stumbled into the bathroom. From his fitted case he took a vial and shook a white tablet into his hand. He found the tooth glass, swallowed the tablet with a gulp of tepid water.

When he got back in bed it was several minutes before the sedative began to work and he felt the peaceful grogginess stealing up to his brain.

"Christ, why did I have to go thinking of that?" he said aloud. "After all these years, why did I have to see her? And Christmas only a week off."

The Emperor

*carved on his throne the name of power
and on his scepter the sign of power.*

"STAN, honey, I'm scared."

He slowed the car and bent to look at the road signs. Sherwood Park—8 miles. "We're nearly there. What are you scared of? Because these people have a lot of jack? Whistle the eight bars of our opener and you'll snap out of it."

"I've tried that, Stan. Only—gosh, it's silly. But how'll I know which fork to grab? The way they lay out these fancy dinners looks like Tiffany's window."

The Great Stanton turned off the highway. Late light of summer evening lay over the sky; his headlights threw back the pale undersides of leaves as the roadster sped up the lane. On either side elms stood in columns of dignity.

"Nothing to it. Watch the old dame at the head of the table. Just stall until she dives in and she'll cue you on the hardware. My mother's folks had barrels of jack once. The old lady knew her way around. That's what she used to tell my old man whenever they went anywhere."

The house rose out of the dusk behind a sweep of lawn as big as a golf course. At the door a Negro butler with tiny brass buttons said, "Let me rest your coat and hat, sir."

"My name is Stanton. Stanton the Mentalist."

"Oh. Mis' Harrington say to show you right upstairs. She say you be wanting to have dinner upstairs, sir."

Stan and Molly followed him. Through an archway they could see women in evening dresses. A man in a dinner jacket stood with his back to a dark, enormous fireplace. He held a cocktail glass, gripping it by the foot instead of the stem.

The room was on the top floor, rear; the ceiling slanted.

"Dinner'll be served right soon, sir. Anything you want, just pick up that phone and push button eight on the box. That's butler's pantry."

When he had closed the door Stan locked it. "Relax, kid," he said wryly, "we're eating private. Let's get loaded first and try out the batteries."

He opened their traveling bags; Molly drew her dress over her head and hung it in a closet. From one of the bags she shook out a black net evening gown laden with sequins. "Hold the wires, honey, so they won't catch in my hair."

Expertly Stan eased the dress over her head. It was high-cut in the back with a ruff. He took a curved metal band attached to a flat earphone and slipped it over her head while the girl held her hair forward. When she threw it back the hair covered her ears so that the compact headset was completely hidden. Stan reached into the low V of the neck, found a miniature plug, and connected the headset. From his own suitcase he took his tails and began to stud a dress shirt.

"Go slow on that makeup, kid. Remember—you're not working behind foots now. And don't do any bumps or grinds while you're supposed to be hypnotized."

Standing in his underwear, he put on a linen vest with pockets like a hunting jacket's. They bulged with flat flashlight batteries. A wire dangled; strapping it to his leg in three places, he carried it down and drew on a black silk sock, feeding the wire through a tiny hole. His shoe followed, then the wire plugged into a socket at the side of the shoe. Finally he put on his shirt. Moistening his fingers, he rubbed them on a handkerchief, took from a wax paper envelope a spotless white tie, and tied it, frowning in the mirror of the dresser. In his coat a spider web of fine wire was sewed into the lining as an aerial; another plug connected it with the hidden vest which held the transmitter.

The Great Stanton adjusted his suspenders, then buttoned his waistcoat; he gave his hair a touch with the brushes and handed Molly a whiskbroom so that she could dust his shoulders for him.

"Gee, honey, you look handsome."

"Consider yourself kissed good and hard. I don't want to get smeared up. For God's sake take some of that lipstick off."

Under the toes of his left foot was the reassuring bulge of the contact key. Stan reached under his white vest and threw an invisible switch. He walked across the floor. "Get any buzz?"

"Not yet."

"Now." He pressed hard with his toes inside his shoe; but Molly made no sign. "God damn! If I'd been able to get a line on who was going to be at this shindig I'd have worked a straight crystal routine. There's too many things to come loose in this damn wireless gimmick." He ran his hands over the girl's dress, checking. Then he said, "Hold up your hair." The headset plug had slipped out. Stan spread its minute prongs with the point of a nail file and rasped them bright with irritable strokes. He connected it and Molly rearranged her hair.

On the other side of the room he again pressed with his left toes.

"I've got it, honey. Nice and clear. Now walk and see if it buzzes when you don't want it to."

Stan paced back and forth, keeping his weight off his toes, and Molly said she couldn't hear a thing, only when he wiggled his toes and made the contact.

"Okay. Now I'm in another room. What are the tests?"

"A card, a color, and a state."

"Right. What's this?"

Molly closed her eyes. From the earphone came a faint buzz three times—spades. Then a long buzz and three short ones—five plus three is eight. "Eight of spades."

"Right."

A tap from the door made Stan hiss for her to keep quiet.

"Dinner is served, sir. Mis' Harrington send her respects. She'll let you know on the phone when it's time for you all to come down. Better let me open up this bottle now, sir; we's powerful busy downstairs." He eased the cork out, his polished fingers dark against the napkin.

Stan felt in his pocket for a quarter and caught himself just in time. The butler bowed out.

"Gee, lookit, Stan! Champagne!"

"One glass for you, Cahill. We're working. If you load up on that stuff you'll be calling the old girl 'dearie.'"

"Aw, Stan."

He poured, put a few drops in his own glass, then carried the bottle into the bathroom and emptied the rest, bubbling gaily, down the drain of the washbowl.

From the rear Mrs. Bradburn Harrington looked like a little girl, but, Christ, what a crow when you see her head-on, Stan thought. She tapped a brass gong until the babble died. "Now I have a real treat for us. Mr. Stanton, whom I'm sure many of us have seen in the theater, will show us some wonderful things. I don't know just what they're going to do so I'll let Mr. Stanton tell you all about it himself."

Stan stood in the hall beside Molly. He took a deep breath and smoothed down his hair with both hands. The butler suddenly appeared beside him, holding a silver plate. On it was a slip of paper, folded. "Mis' Harrington tell me to give you this, sir."

Stan took it, unfolded it deftly with one hand, and read it at a single glance. He crushed it and swept it into his pocket, his face darkening. Molly whispered, "What's the matter, hon? What's happened?"

"Nothing!" he spat out savagely. "It's in the bag."

From the drawing room Mrs. Harrington's voice continued, ". . . and it will all be very exciting, I'm sure. May I present Mr. Stanton."

Stan drew a breath and walked in. He bowed to the hostess, again to the guests. "Ladies and gentlemen, what we are about to do may have many explanations. I shall offer none. In the realm of the human mind science has hardly scratched the surface. Most of its mysteries lie hidden from us yet. But down through the years certain people have had unusual gifts. I take no credit for mine." This time his bow was hardly more than a lowering of the eyes. This audience was the top. This was class. With a momentary shock Stan recognized a famous novelist, tall, slightly stooped, half bald. One of the season's debutantes, who had already made the papers with an affair involving a titled émigré, sat primly holding a highball on her knee, her white dress so low-cut that Stan fancied he could see the aureoles of her nipples.

"My family was Scotch originally, and the Scotch are said to possess strange faculties." The gray head of a stern-faced old judge nodded. "My ancestors used to call it 'second sight.' I shall call it simply—mentalism. It is a well-known fact that the minds of two people can establish a closer communication than words. A *rapport*. I discovered such a person several years ago. Ladies and gentlemen, allow me to present my assistant, Miss Cahill."

Molly swept in smiling, with her long stride, and rested her hand lightly on Stan's bent forearm. The debutante turned to a young man sitting on the arm of her chair. "Friend of yours, Diggie?" He closed her lips with his hand, staring fascinated at Molly.

Her eyes were half closed, her lips slightly parted. The old judge quietly took off his reading glasses.

"If I may trouble you, I should like to have Miss Cahill recline on that sofa."

There was a scurry of people finding other seats and a man snickered. Stan led Molly to the sofa and arranged a pillow behind her. She lifted her feet and he tucked the folds of the sequinned gown up from the floor. Reaching into his waistcoat pocket he drew out a ball of rock crystal the size of a marble and held it above the level of her eyes. "Concentrate."

The room was still at last.

"Your eyelids are growing heavy. Heavy. Heavy. You cannot lift them. You are falling asleep. Sleep. Sleep . . ."

Molly let her breath out in a long sigh and the lines about her mouth relaxed. Stan picked up her hand and laid it in her lap. She was limp. He turned to the company: "I have placed her in deep hypnosis. It is the only way I know by which telepathy can be made sure. I shall now pass among you, and I shall ask you to show me a number of objects, such as jewels, theater tickets, anything you wish."

He turned back to the reclining girl. "Miss Cahill, I shall touch a number of objects in this room. As I touch them you are to describe them. Is that clear?"

Dreamily she nodded. Her voice was a whisper. "Yes. Objects. Describe . . ."

Stan crossed the room and the old judge held out a gold fountain pen. Stan took it, focused his attention on it, his eyes widening. His back was to Molly and her head was turned toward the back of the sofa. She could see nothing. But her voice came as from a distance, just clear enough for them to hear if they listened hard. "A pen. A fountain pen. Gold. And something's . . . engraved. *A . . . G . . . K.*"

There was a ripple of applause, which Stan stopped with a lifted hand.

The hostess pointed to the spray of little brown orchids she wore as a corsage. Molly's voice went on, far away. "Flowers . . . beautiful flowers . . . they're . . . they're . . . or . . . orchids, I think."

The crowd sucked in its breath.

The debutante with the scarlet lips and the low-cut dress beckoned to Stan. When he drew near she reached into the pocket of the young man beside her and took out a gold mesh vanity case. Throwing open the cover, she held it so that only Stan could see what it contained. He frowned and she giggled up at him. "Go on, Mister Mindreader. Read my mind."

Stan stood motionless. He took a deep breath and by straining it against his throat forced the color to rise in his face.

"Look. He blushes too," said the girl.

The Great Stanton never moved but Molly's voice went on. "Something . . . something . . . do I have to tell what it is?"

Over his shoulder Stan said softly, "No, never mind it."

The girl snapped the bag shut and replaced it in the man's pocket. "You win, brother. You win." She gulped down the rest of her drink.

The Great Stanton bowed. "Lest I be accused of using trickery and signaling Miss Cahill, I should like a committee to follow me from the room for a few moments. Five or six persons will do nicely. And I shall ask someone here to take a slip of paper and record what Miss Cahill says while I am out of the room."

The hostess volunteered, and three couples followed Stan across the hall and into the library. When they were inside he closed the door. Something touched his hand; it was cold and made him jump. The guests laughed. Beside him stood a harlequin Great Dane, gazing up with eyes that held mastery in their steadiness and an odd loneliness too. The dog nudged Stan's leg with his paw and the mentalist began to scratch him idly behind the ears while he spoke to the others.

"I should like one of you now to choose some card in a pack of fifty-two."

"Deuce of clubs."

"Fine. Remember it. Now will someone select a color?"

"Chartreuse."

"That's a little difficult to visualize, but we'll try. Now will one of the ladies think of a state—any state in the union."

"That's easy," the girl spoke with a drawl. "There's only one state worth thinking about—Alabama."

"Alabama. Excellent. But would you care to change your mind?"

"No, indeedy. It's Alabama for sure."

Stanton bowed. "Shall we join the others?"

He held the door for them and they filed out. Stan knelt and laid his cheek against that of the Great Dane. "Hello, beautiful. Bet you wish you were my dog, don't you?"

The Dane whined softly.

"Don't let 'em get you down, boy. Bite 'em in their fat asses."

He rose, brushed his lapel, and strolled back to the lights and the voices.

Molly still lay on the couch, looking like a sleeping princess waiting for the kiss of a deliverer. The room was in a hubbub.

"The deuce of clubs! And the color—they picked chartreuse and she couldn't decide whether it was yellow or green! Isn't it amazing! And Alabama!"

"How would you like to have him for a husband, darling? Someone I know would have to scoot back to Cannes."

"Miraculous. Nothing short of miraculous."

Stan sat beside Molly, took one of her hands in his and said, "Wake up! Come now, wake up!"

She sat up, passing the back of her hand over her eyes. "Why—what's happened? Oh! Was I all right?"

"You were splendid," he said, looking into her eyes. "Every test was perfect."

"Oh, I'm so glad."

Still holding her hand, he drew her to her feet. They walked to the door, turned and bowed slightly and passed through it, applause clattering behind them.

"Stan, don't we stay for the party? I mean, the rest of it?"

"Shut up!"

"But—Stan—"

"I said shut up! I'll tell you later. Beat it upstairs. I'll be up in a little while and we'll get to hell out of here."

Obediently she went, pressing her lips together, fighting back an impulse to cry. This was nothing more than any other show; she had hoped there would be a party afterwards and dancing and more champagne.

Stan crossed over to the library, and the dog met him, jumping up. Heedless of his starched shirt bosom, Stan let him. "You know a pal, don't you, boy."

"Mr. Stanton—"

It was the old man who looked like a judge.

"I couldn't let you go without telling you how miraculous your work is."

"Thank you."

"I mean it, my boy. I'm afraid you don't realize what you've stumbled onto here. This goes deeper than you realize."

"I have no explanation for it," Stan said abruptly, still scratching the dog behind the ears.

"But I think I know your secret."

Silence. Stan could feel the blood surging up over his face. Good Christ, another amateur magician, he thought, raging. I've got to ditch him. But I've got to get him on my side, first. At last he said, smiling, "Perhaps you have the solution. A few persons of unusual intelligence and scientific knowledge might be able to guess at the main principle."

The old man nodded sagely. "I've guessed it, my boy. I've guessed it. This is no code act."

Stan's smile was intimate and his eyes danced with fellow-ship. God, here it comes. But I'll handle him somehow.

"Yes, my boy. I know. And I don't blame you for keeping your secret. It's the young lady."

"Yes?"

The judge lowered his voice. "I know it isn't telepathy. You have *spirit aid*!"

Stan felt like shouting. Instead he closed his eyes, the shadow of a smile passing over his mouth.

"They don't understand, my boy. I know why you have to present it as second sight. They're not ready to receive the glorious truth of survival. But our day will come, my boy. It will come. Develop your gift—the young lady's mediumship. Cherish it, for it is a fragile blossom. But what a soul-stirring thing it is! Oh, to think of it—this precious gift of medium-ship, this golden bridge between us and those who have joined the ranks of the liberated, there to dwell on ever-ascending planes of spiritual life—"

The door opened and both men turned. It was Molly. "Oh. I'm sorry. I didn't know you were busy. Say, Stan—"

"Miss Cahill, I should like you to meet Judge Kimball. It *is* Judge Kimball, I am certain of it, although I do not recall ever having seen your photograph."

The old man nodded, smiling as if he and Stan shared a secret. He patted Molly's hand. "A great gift, my dear child, a great gift."

"Yeah, it's a gift all right, Judge. Well, I guess I'll be going back upstairs."

Stan took both her hands in his and shook them. "You were splendid tonight, my dear. Splendid. Now run along and I'll join you shortly. You had better lie down and rest for a few minutes."

When he released her Molly said, "Oops," and looked at her left hand; but Stan urged her toward the door, closing it gently behind her. He turned back to the judge.

"I'll confess, Judge. But"—he tilted his head toward the room across the hall—"they wouldn't understand. That is why I dropped in here for a moment. Someone here does understand." He looked down at the dog. "Don't you, boy?"

The Dane whined softly and crept closer.

"You know, Judge, they can sense things that are beyond all human perception. They can see and hear presences about us which we can never detect." Stan had moved toward a reading lamp beside an armchair. "For instance, I received a very faint but clear impression just now that someone from the Other Side is in the room. I am sure it is a young girl, that she is trying to get through to us. But I can tell nothing more about her; I cannot see her. If only our handsome friend here could talk he might be able to tell us."

The dog was staring into a dark corner of the book-lined room. He growled questioningly. Then, while the old man watched, fascinated, the Dane leaped up and shot into the corner, standing there alert and quiet, looking upward.

The mentalist slid his hand unobtrusively into his trousers pocket. "They know, sir. They can see. And now—I bid you good evening."

The house had grown full of unseen presences for the old judge; in thinking of some who might be near him now, his eyes grew wet. Slowly, elegantly, his shoulders straight, the Great Stanton ascended the stairs with the tread of an emperor, and the judge watched him go. A wonderful young man.

In the room with the tilted ceiling Molly was lying on the bed in her brassière and panties, smoking a cigarette. She sat up, hugging her knees. "Stan, for crying out loud, tell me why you got so mad at me when I wanted to stay for the party! Other private bookings we always stay and have fun and I don't get lit on three champagnes, honest I don't, honey. You think I don't know how to behave!"

He shoved his hands into his pockets, pulled out a slip of paper and crushed it, then flung it into a corner of the room. He spoke in a savage whisper. "For Christ's sake, don't go turning on the tears until we get out of here. I said *no* because it wasn't the spot for it. We gave 'em just enough. Always leave 'em wanting more. We built ourselves up and I didn't see any sense in knocking it all down again. For Christ's sake, we gave 'em a goddamned miracle! They'll be talking about it the rest of their lives. And they'll make it better every time they tell it. And what do we get for it? Three hundred lousy bucks and get treated like an extra darky they hired to pass the booze around. This is the big time, all right. Get your name in lights a foot high and then come out to one of these joints and what do they hand you—a dinner on a plate like a hobo at a back door."

He was breathing heavily, his face red and his throat working. "I'll sweat it out of them. By Christ, that old guy downstairs gave me the angle. I'll shake 'em loose from a pile of dough before I'm done. I'll have 'em begging me to stay a week. I'll have 'em wondering why I take my meals in my room. And it'll be because they're not fit to eat with—the bastards. I've been crazy not to think of this angle before, but from now on I know the racket. I've given 'em mentalism and they treat it like a dog walking on his hind legs. Okay. They're asking for it. Here it comes."

He stopped and looked down at the staring girl, whose face was chalky around the lips. "You did okay, kid." He smiled with one corner of his mouth. "Here's your ring, baby. I needed it for a gag."

Frowning still, Molly slipped the diamond back on her finger and watched the tiny specks of light from it spatter the dark corner of the sloping ceiling.

Stan carefully unhooked the wires and got out of his clothes. He went into the bathroom and Molly heard the bolt slammed shut.

You never could tell why Stan did anything. Here he was, madder than a wet hen, and he wouldn't say why and besides she wouldn't have pulled any boners; she'd just have smiled and kept her voice low and made believe she was tired from being hypnotized. She hadn't muffled any signals. What was eating him?

She got up and retrieved the crumpled slip from the corner. That was when it all started, when the colored waiter handed it to Stan just before they went on. Her fingers shook as she opened it.

"Kindly do not mingle with the guests."

The Sun

*On a white horse the sun child, with flame
for hair, carries the banner of life.*

I'M NOT going to put on the light. Because we're not going
to argue all night again. I tell you, there's not a goddamned bit of difference between it and mentalism. It's nothing but our old act dressed up so it will lay 'em in the aisles.
And for real."

"Honey, I don't like it."

"In God's name, what's the matter with it?"

"Well, what if there are—what if people do come back? I
mean, well, they mightn't like it. I can't explain it. I'm
scared."

"Listen, baby. I been over this a hundred times. If anybody's
going to come back they're not going to get steamed up
because we fake a little. We'll be doing the marks a favor; we'll
make 'em plenty happy. After all, suppose you thought you
could really speak to your dad, now. Wouldn't that make you
happy?"

"Oh, God, I wish I could. Maybe it's because I've wished
so hard for just that and hoped that maybe someday I could."

"I know, kid. I know how it is. Maybe there's something in it after all. I don't know. But I've met half a dozen spook workers in the past year and they're hustlers, every one of them. I tell you, it's just show business. The crowd believes we can read minds. All right. They believe it when I tell them that 'the lawsuit's going to come out okay.' Isn't it better to give them something to hope for? What does a regular preacher do every Sunday? Only all he does is promise. We'll do more than promise. We'll give 'em proof!"

"I—honey, I just can't."

"But you don't have to *do* anything! I'll handle all the effects. All you have to do is get into a cabinet and go to sleep if you want to. Leave everything else to me."

"But s'pose we got caught? I can't help it; I think it's mean. Remember how I told you once, the night you—you asked me to team up with you—about how I chalked on Daddy's tombstone 'He never crossed up a pal?' I was scared to death out there in that cemetery, and I was scared every minute until I touched Daddy's headstone, and then I started to cry and I said his name over and over, just as if he could hear me, and then somehow I felt like he really could. I was certain he could."

"All right. I thought you were his daughter. I thought you had guts enough to turn a trick that would get you the kind of life he'd want you to have. Give us a few years in this dodge and just one big job and then we can knock off. Stop jackassing all around the country and settle down. We'll—we'll get married. And have a house. And a couple of dogs. We'll—have a kid."

"Don't fib, honey."

"I mean it. Don't you think I want a kid? But it takes dough. A wad of dough. Then it'll be Florida in the winter and the kid sitting between us in the grandstand when the barrier goes up and they streak out, fighting for the rail. That's the kind of life I want and I've got my angles worked out, every one of them. Got my ordination certificate today. Baby, you're in bed with a full-blown preacher. I bet you never thought you'd bed down with a reverend! Last week I had a tailor make me an outfit—black broadcloth. I got a turnaround collar and everything. I can put on a pair of black gloves and a black hood and work in a red light like a dark-room lamp—and nobody can see a thing. I've even got cloth buttons so they won't reflect light. I tell you, it's a perfect setup. Don't you know a spook worker never takes a real rap? If anybody grabs, the chumps rally around him and start alibi-ing their heads off. Do you think I'm a feeblo to go mon-keying around with scientific committees or any other wise guys that are likely to upset the works? Pick your crowd and you can sell 'em anything. And all *you* have to do is sit there with the old ladies admiring you and thanking you afterward for all the comfort you've brought 'em. But if you are yellow I can do it alone. You can go back to the carny and find yourself another kooch show and start all over."

"No, honey. I didn't mean—"

"Well, I do mean. I mean just that. One way is the big dough and plenty of class and a kid and clothes that will make you look like a million bucks. The other way is the carny, doing bumps and grinds and waggling your fanny for a bunch of rubes for a few more years. And then what? You know what. Make up your mind."

"Just let me think about it. Please, honey."

"You've thought about it. Don't make me do anything I don't want to do. Look, baby, I love you. You know that. No, don't pull away. Keep quiet. I said I love you. I want a kid by you. Get it? Put your other arm around me. It's like old times, eh, kid? There. Like it? Sure you do. This is heaven, kid. Don't break it up."

"Oh, honey, honey, honey."

"That's better. And you will do it? Say you will. Say yes, baby."

"Yes. Yes—I'll do anything."

In the old gray stone house near Riverside Drive, Addie Peabody (Mrs. Chisholm W.) answered the door herself. She had given Pearl the evening off and Pearl had gone willingly enough, in view of what was coming.

The first to arrive were Mr. and Mrs. Simmons, and Mrs. Peabody shooed them into the parlor. "Honestly, I was just dying for somebody to talk to, I thought the afternoon would never go by, I'd have gone to the matinee but I just knew I couldn't sit through one, I'd be so excited about tonight, they say this new medium is simply grand—and so young, too. They say she hasn't a speck of background, she's so spontaneous and natural, she used to be a show girl I hear but it really doesn't matter, it's one of the strangest things how the gift strikes people in all walks of life and it's so often among humble people. I'm sure none of us will ever develop full power although they do say the Reverend Carlisle is simply wonderful at developmental sittings. I have a friend who's been developing with him for nearly a year now and she has noticed some amazing phenomena in her own home when not a soul was there but herself. She's simply mad about Mr. Carlisle, he's so sincere and sympathetic."

In twos and threes the rest of the company gathered. Mr. Simmons made one or two little jokes just to liven things up, but they were all in good taste and not offensive, because, after all, you should approach a séance with joy in your heart and all the people have to be attuned or the phenomena are likely to be scarce and very disappointing.

The bell rang a steady, insistent note, full of command. Mrs. Peabody hurried out, taking a quick look in the hall mirror and straightening her girdle before she opened the door. Outside, the light above the door fell on the heads of two people, the first a tall, dramatic-looking woman in her late twenties, rather flashily dressed. But Mrs. Peabody's glance slid over her and came to rest on the man.

The Rev. Stanton Carlisle was about thirty-five. He was holding his black hat and the lamplight made his hair glisten golden—just like the sun, she thought. He made her think of Apollo.

Mrs. Peabody noticed in her first swift glance that he was dressed in street clericals with a black vest and a turn-about collar. He was the first spiritualist minister she had ever seen who wore clericals but he was so distinguished-looking that it didn't seem a bit ostentatious; anybody would have taken him for an Episcopalian.

"Oh, Mr. Carlisle, I just knew it was you. I got a distinct impression the minute you rang the bell."

"I am sure we shall establish an excellent vibrational harmony, Mrs. Peabody. May I present our medium, Mary Margaret Cahill."

Inside, Mrs. Peabody introduced them to the others. She served tea and it was so English—just like having the vicar over, she thought. Miss Cahill was a sweet-looking girl, and after all some people can't help being born on the wrong side of the tracks. She probably did the best she could with what she had to start with. Even if she did look a little cheap she was beautiful and had an odd, haggard expression about her mouth that touched Mrs. Peabody's heart. Mediumship takes so much out of them—we owe them such a tremendous debt.

Mr. Carlisle was charming and there was something about his voice that stirred you, as if he were speaking just to you even when he addressed the others. He was so understanding.

Finally Mrs. Peabody stood up. "Shall I play something? I always say there's nothing like having an old-fashioned family organ. They're so sweet-toned and so much nicer than a piano." She sat at the console and struck a gentle chord. She would have to get the pedal levers oiled; the left one squeaked a little. The first piece she turned to was "The Old Rugged Cross" and one by one the company picked it up, Mr. Simmons coming in with a really fine baritone.

The Rev. Carlisle cleared his throat. "Mrs. Peabody, I wonder if you recall that splendid old hymn, 'On the Other Side of Jordan.' It was a favorite of my sainted mother's, and I should dearly love to hear it now."

"Indeed I do. At least, it's in the hymnal."

Mr. Simmons volunteered to lead, standing by the organ, with the others humming:

> On the other side of Jordan
> In the sweet fields of Eden
> Where the Tree of Life is blooming
> There is rest for me.
> > There is rest for the weary,
> > There is rest for the weary,
> > On the other side of Jordan
> > There is rest for me.

Mrs. Peabody's eyes were wet when the hymn was finished,

and she knew that this was the psychological moment. She sat silently on the bench and then closed her eyes and let her fingers find the chords. Everyone sang it softly.

> *Shall we gather by the river,*
> *The beautiful, the beautiful river.*
> *Yes, we shall gather by the river*
> *That flows by the throne of God.*

She played the "Amen" chords softly, drawing them out, and then turned to the Rev. Carlisle. His eyes were closed; he sat upright and austere with his hands resting on the knees of his black broadcloth trousers. When he spoke he kept his eyes closed.

"Our hostess has provided us with a fine cabinet. The niche between the organ and the wall will serve beautifully. And, I believe, there are hangings which can be lowered. Let us all compose ourselves with humble hearts, silently, and in the presence of God who hath hid these things from the wise and prudent and hast revealed them unto babes.

"I call upon the Spirit of Eternal Light, whom some call God the Father and some call the Holy Ghost; who, some believe, came among the earth-bound as our Lord and Savior, Jesus the Christ; who spoke to Gautama under the Bo tree and gave him enlightenment, whose praise was taught by the last of India's great saints, Sri Ramakrishna. Marvel not at what we shall attempt, for the hour is coming in which all that are in the graves shall hear his voice and shall come forth. Many of them that sleep in the dust of the earth shall awake, but some who did evil in their days upon the earth shall be reborn and remain among the earth-bound for yet another existence. No spirit who has ever returned speaks to us of hell fire but rather of rebirth and another chance. And when a man has done much evil he does not descend into a pit of eternal torment but wanders between the worlds, neither earth-bound nor liberated; for the Lord, being full of compassion, forgives their iniquity. He remembers that they were but flesh, a wind that passeth away and cometh not again until the prayers and faith of liberated and earth-bound alike cause their absorption into the Universal Soul of God, who is in all things and from which everything is made that was made. We ask that the Great Giver of Love enter our hearts and make us to become as little children, for without innocence we cannot admit those presences who draw near about us now, anxious to speak to us and make their nearness known. For it is written: 'He bowed the heavens also, and came down: and darkness was under his feet. And he rode upon a cherub, and did fly: yea, he did fly upon the wings of the wind.' Amen."

He opened his eyes and Mrs. Peabody thought she had never seen eyes as blue or with a glance so resembling an eagle's. Spiritual power flowed out of him; you could just feel it.

The spiritualist continued, "Let Mrs. Simmons sit nearest to the cabinet on the far side. Mrs. Peabody on the other side, before the organ which she plays so beautifully. I shall sit here, next to her. Mr. Simmons next to his wife."

An armchair was carried into the niche for Miss Cahill who sat tautly, her knees close together, her hands clenched. The Rev. Carlisle stepped into the niche.

"Are you sure you feel equal to it this evening, my dear?"

Miss Cahill smiled bravely up at him and nodded.

"Very well. You are among friends. No one here will break the circle. There are no skeptics to endanger your life by suddenly flooding you with light. No one will move from his chair when it is dangerous to the vibration lines. Any ectoplasmic emanations from your body will be carefully observed but not touched so you have nothing to fear. Are you perfectly comfortable?"

"Yes. Comfortable. Fine."

"Very well. Do you want music?"

Miss Cahill shook her head. "No. I feel so—so sleepy."

"Relax, my dear friend."

She closed her eyes.

Mrs. Peabody tiptoed about and extinguished all the lamps except one. "Shall I close the cabinet curtains?"

Carlisle shook his head. "Let us first have her with us. Without anything between us. Let us form the circle."

Silently they took their places. Minutes crept by; a chair creaked and outside a car passed. Behind the velvet drapes which shut off the street light it sounded out of key and impertinent. The Rev. Carlisle seemed in a trance himself.

Knock!

Everyone gasped and then smiled and nodded.

Knock!

Carlisle spoke. "Ramakrishna?"

Three sharp raps answered him.

"Our dear teacher—our loving *guru* who has never left us in spirit—we greet you in the love of God, which you imparted so divinely while you were earth-bound. Will you speak to us now through the lips of our dear medium, Mary Cahill?"

Miss Cahill stirred in her chair and her head drew back. Her lips opened and her voice came softly, as from a great distance:

"The body of man is a soul-city containing the palace of the heart which contains, in turn, the lotus of the soul. Within its blossom are heaven and earth contained, are fire and water, sun and moon, and lightning and stars."

Her voice came, monotonous, as if it were a transmitter of the words of another. "He, whose vision is clouded by the veils of maya, will ask of that city, 'What is left of it when old age covers it and scatters it; when it falls to pieces?' To which the enlightened one replies, 'In the old age of the body the soul ages not; by the death of the body it is not slain.' There is a wind that blows between the worlds, strewing the lotus petals to the stars."

She stopped and let out her breath in a long sigh, pressing her hands against the chair arms and then letting them drop into her lap.

"Our guide has spoken," Carlisle said gently. "We may expect a great deal tonight, I am sure."

Miss Cahill opened her eyes, then jumped from the chair and began to walk about the room, touching the furniture and the walls with the tips of her fingers. She turned to the Rev. Carlisle. "D'you mind if I get into something more comfortable?"

The reverend nodded. "My friends, it has always been my aim to present tests of mediumship under such conditions that the slightest suspicion of fraud is impossible. We must face it: there are fraudulent mediums who prey on the noblest and purest emotions known to man. And I insist that the gifts of Mary Cahill be removed from the category of ordinary mediumship. She is able, at an expense to her strength it is true, to work in a faint light. I should like a number of the ladies here tonight to accompany her when she changes her clothes and make sure that there is no chance of fraud or trickery, that nothing is concealed. I know that you do not for one moment harbor such thoughts, but to spread the gospel of Spiritualism we must be able to say to the world—and to our most hostile critics—I *saw*. And under test conditions."

Mrs. Peabody and Mrs. Simmons rose and Miss Cahill smiled to them and waited. Carlisle opened a small valise, drawing out a robe of white watered silk and a pair of white slippers. He handed these to the medium and the ladies filed out.

Mrs. Peabody led the way up to her own bedroom. "Here you are, dear. Just change your things in here. We'll be waiting downstairs."

Miss Cahill shook her head. "Mr. Carlisle wants you to stay. I don't mind a bit." The ladies sat down, tongue-tied with embarrassment. The medium slowly drew off her dress and slip. She rolled down her stockings neatly and placed them beside her shoes. When she stood completely stripped before them, leisurely shaking out the robe, a sadness gripped Mrs. Peabody, deep and nameless. She saw the naked woman, unashamed there in the frilly celibacy of her own bedroom, and a lump rose in her throat. Miss Cahill was so beautiful and it was all so innocent, her standing there with her mind, or certainly part of her mind, far away still in that mysterious land where it went voyaging. It was with regret and a feeling she had had as a little girl when the last curtain descended on a play, that she watched Miss Cahill finally draw the robe about her and tie the cord loosely. She stepped into the slippers and smiled at them; and Mrs. Peabody got up, straightening her dress.

"My dear, it is so good of you to come to us. We appreciate it so."

She led the way downstairs.

In the living room all the lights were extinguished, save for a single oil lamp with a shade of ruby-red glass which the clergyman had brought with him. It gave just enough light for each person to see the faces of the others.

The Rev. Carlisle took the medium by the hand and led her to the armchair in the niche. "Let us try first without closing the curtains."

They formed the circle, waiting patiently, devoutly. Mary Cahill's eyes were closed. She moaned and slumped lower in the chair, twisting so that her head rested against its back. A low whimper came from deep within her, and she twisted again and began to breathe heavily. The cord of the white robe loosened, the fringed ends fell to the carpet. Then her body suddenly arched itself and the robe fell open.

With a swift intake of breath the sitters leaned forward.

"Mrs. Peabody, do you mind?" The reverend's voice was like a benediction.

She hurried over, feeling the warmth in her face, and closed the robe, tying the cord firmly. She couldn't resist giving the girl's hand an affectionate little pat, but the medium seemed unconscious.

When she had regained her chair she looked over at the Rev. Carlisle. He sat upright, eyes closed, his hands motionless on his knees. In the dim red glow of the lamp his face, above the severe collar, seemed to hang in mid-air; his hands to float as motionless as if they were made of papier-mâché. Save for the indistinct circle of faces the only other thing visible in the room was the medium in her white robe. Her hair was part of the darkness.

Slowly and gently spirit sounds began. Gentle raps, then louder knocks. Something set the glass prisms of the chandelier tinkling, and their musical voices continued for several minutes, as if a ghostly hand were playing with them—as a child might play with them if it could float to the ceiling.

Mrs. Simmons spoke first, in a hushed, awed voice. "I see a light."

It was there. A soft, greenish spark hovered near the floor beside Mrs. Peabody and then vanished. Mrs. Peabody felt a breeze—the psychic breeze of which Sir Oliver Lodge had written. Then, moving high in the air across the room, was another light. She tilted her eyeglasses a trifle to bring it into sharper focus. It was a hand with the forefinger raised as if toward heaven. It vanished.

The shadows now seemed to flit with lights but some, she

knew, were in her own eyes. The next time, however, they all
saw it. Floating near the floor, in front of the medium, was a
glowing mass which seemed to unwind from nowhere. It took
form and rose before her and for a moment obscured her face.

It grew brighter and Mrs. Peabody made out the features
of a young girl. "Caroline! *Carol*, darling—is it you?"

The whisper was gentle and caressing. "Mother. Mother.
Mother."

It was gone. Mrs. Peabody took off her glasses and wiped
her eyes. At last Caroline had come through to her. The perfect image of the child! They seem to stay the age when they
pass over. That would make Caroline still sixteen, bless her
heart. "Carol—don't leave! Don't go, darling! Come back!"

Darkness. The oil lamp sputtered, the flame died down and
pitch black enfolded them. But Mrs. Peabody did not notice
it. Her eyes were tight shut against the tears.

The Rev. Carlisle spoke. "Will someone turn on the lights?"

Orange glow leaped out brilliantly, showing the reverend
still sitting with his hands on his knees. He rose now and went
to the medium; with a handkerchief he wiped the corners of
her eyes and her lips. She opened her eyes and got to her feet
swaying, saying nothing.

The spiritualist steadied her arm and then she smiled once
at the company. "Let me go upstairs," she said breathlessly.

When she was gone they crowded around the Rev. Stanton
Carlisle, pressing his hand and all talking at once from the
release of the tension.

"My dear friends, this is not our last evening. I see many
more in the future. We shall indeed explore the Other Side
together. Now I must go as soon as Miss Cahill is ready. We
must look after our medium, you know. I will go up to her
now and I shall ask all of you to remain here and not to say
good-bye. She has been under tremendous strain. Let us leave
quietly."

He smiled his blessing on them and closed the door softly
behind him. On the hall table was a blue envelope, "To our
dear medium as a token of our appreciation." Inside was Mrs.
Peabody's check for seventy dollars.

"Ten bucks apiece," Stan said under his breath and crushed

the envelope in his fingers. "Hang on to your hat, lady; you ain't seen nothing yet."

Upstairs he entered Mrs. Peabody's room and shut the door. Molly was dressed and combing her hair.

"Well, kid, we laid 'em in the aisles. And with the light on every minute and the medium visible. The robe business was terrific. Jesus, what misdirection! They couldn't have pried their eyes away even if they'd known what I was doing."

From under his clerical vest he drew two papier-mâché replicas of a man's hands and two black mittens. From a large flat pocket inside his coat came a piece of black cardboard on which was pasted a picture of a movie actress cut from a magazine cover and touched up with luminous paint. From his sleeve he took a telescopic reaching-rod made of blue steel. Bundling all the props into the white robe he stuffed them into the valise which he had brought upstairs. Then he lifted his shoe, pulled a luminous-headed thumbtack from the instep, tossed it in, and shut the bag.

"You all set, kid? You better endorse this before I forget it. It's only seventy skins, but, baby, we're just starting. I got it fixed so we can slip downstairs and out without a lot of congratulations and crap. Baby, next time we really turn the heat on the old gal."

Molly's lip was trembling. "Stan, Mrs. Peabody's awful sweet. I—I can't go on with this sort of stuff. I just can't. She wants to speak to her daughter so bad and all you could do was whisper at her a little."

The Rev. Stanton Carlisle was an ordained spiritualist minister. He had started by sending two dollars and an affidavit, saying that he had produced spirit messages, to the United Spiritual League, and had received a medium's certificate. To get his Minister's certificate he had sent five dollars and had been interviewed by an ordained minister who turned his rostrum over to Candidate Carlisle for a few minutes one Thursday night. Messages were forthcoming and the new minister of the spiritualist gospel was sworn in. He was now entitled to perform marriages, conduct services, and bury the dead. He threw back his head and laughed silently.

"Don't worry, kid. She'll hear from her daughter. And in

something louder than a whisper. And she'll see her too. This routine with the lights on and the medium in view all the time was just the convincer. The next time we work with this bunch we'll work in a regular dark séance or a curtain over the cabinet. And do you know who's going to give Mrs. Peabody the big thrill of talking to her daughter? See if you can guess."

"No. Not me, Stan. I couldn't."

He was suddenly steely. "You don't want me to let on to all those nice old folks down there that I have been deceived by a fraudulent medium, do you, sugar? You've got 'em eating out of your hand, my little kooch dancer. And when the time comes—you're going to be one ghost that talks. Come on, kid. Let's beat it out of here. The sooner I ditch this bag of props the rosier life will get. You think you're the only one in this show that ever gets the shakes?"

The guests stayed late for a buffet supper. Mrs. Peabody had rallied from the shock of recognizing her daughter and was fully launched in praise of the new medium and her mentor, the Rev. Stanton Carlisle. "You know, I got a definite psychic flash the moment that man touched the doorbell, the very moment. And when I opened the door there he was with the light shining on his hair—just like a halo in the sun, it was a perfect halo effect. He's like Apollo, I said to myself. Those were the very words."

When the other sitters had gone Addie Peabody was too excited to sleep. At last she drew on a housecoat and came downstairs, feeling constantly the unseen presence of Caroline beside her. At the organ she let her hands fall on the keyboard in chords, and they sounded so spiritual and inspired. There was certainly a new quality about her playing. Then from beneath her fingers a melody took shape and she played with her eyes closed, from memory:

> *On the other side of Jordan*
> *In the sweet fields of Eden,*
> *Where the Tree of Life is blooming*
> *There is rest for me.*

The Hierophant

They kneel before the high priest,
wearer of the triple crown and bearer of the keys.

THE FACE floated in air, unearthly in its greenish radiance, but it was the face of a girl and when it spoke Addie could see the lips move. Once the eyes opened, heartbreakingly dark and empty. Then the glowing lids closed again; the voice came:

"Mother . . . I love you. I want you to know."

Addie swallowed hard and tried to control her throat. "I know, darling. Carol, baby—"

"You may call me Caroline . . . now. It was the name you gave me. You must have loved it once. I was so foolish to want a different name. I understand so many things now."

The voice grew fainter as the face receded in the darkness. Then its glow changed and diminished until it was a pool of light near the floor. It vanished.

The voice whispered again, this time amplified by the metal trumpet which had been placed in the cabinet with the medium. "Mother . . . I have to go back. Be careful. . . . There are bad forces here, too. All of us are not good. Some are evil. I feel them all around me. Evil forces . . . Mother . . . good-bye."

The trumpet clanged against the music rack of the organ and tumbled to the floor. It rolled against the leg of Addie's chair and stopped. Groping for it, she picked it up eagerly but it was silent and chill except at the narrow end where it was warm as if from Caroline's lips.

The raps which had disturbed them on the last two evenings now began and jumped from the walls, the organ, her own chair back, the floor, everywhere. They rapped in the mocking cadences and ridiculous rhythms that spiteful children use to torment a teacher.

A vase crashed from the mantelpiece and shattered on the tiles of the hearth. Addie screamed.

The tones of the Rev. Carlisle came from the darkness near her. "Let us have patience. I call upon the presence which has come here unbidden to listen to me. We are not hostile to you. We wish you no harm. We are here to help you attain liberation by prayer, if you can only listen."

A mocking rap on the back of his own chair answered him.

Mrs. Peabody felt the trumpet snatched from her hands. It clanged on the ceiling above her head and then a voice came from it and the rappings and rustlings stopped. The voice was low and vibrant and deeply accented.

"The way to God lies through the Yoga of Love." It was the control spirit, Ramakrishna. "You little, mischievous ones of the baser planes, listen to our words of love and grow in spirit. Do not plague us nor our medium nor the sweet spirit of the girl who has visited her mother and was driven away by you. Listen to the love in our hearts which are as mountain streams pouring out their love to the distant sea which is the great heart of God. *Hari Aum!*"

With the fall of the trumpet to the floor the room became still.

At the door, while he was saying good night, the Rev. Carlisle took Addie's hand firmly between his own. "We must have faith, Mrs. Peabody. Poltergeist disturbances are not infrequent phenomena. Sometimes it is possible for us, and our liberated dear ones, to overcome them by prayer. I shall pray. Your little girl, Caroline, may not be able to aid us very much but I am sure she will try—from her side of the River. And now, take courage. I will be near you even after I have gone. Remember that."

Addie closed the front door with dread of the vast, empty house behind and above her. If only she could get a girl to live in. But Pearl had left and then the Norwegian couple and after them old Mrs. Riordan. It was impossible. And Mr. Carlisle had said it would do no good to go to a hotel; the elementals attached themselves to people and not to houses and that would be horrible. In a hotel before the maids and the bellboys and everybody.

Besides, this had been Caroline's home when they all had been alive—*in earth life*, she corrected herself. They had bought this house when Caroline was three. Just before Christmas it was. And she had had her Christmas tree in the niche where Miss Cahill always sat at the séances. Addie took a chiffon handkerchief from her belt and blew her nose. It was awful that all this had to start just when Caroline had begun to come through so wonderfully.

The armchair was still in the niche and Addie sat down in it gingerly. That corner was really Miss Cahill's now; she had sanctified it by her sacrifices and her suffering just to enable Caroline to speak to them and appear in full form. Addie sank deeper into the chair, trying to reason away the feeling that somehow this wasn't *her* home any more. She tried thinking back to Caroline's third Christmas and the gifts. There was a little wooden telephone, she remembered, and Caroline had spent all Christmas Day "calling up" people.

Now the house wasn't like home any longer—it belonged to a terrifying stranger. A stupid, jealous boor of a spirit that broke things and rapped on windowpanes until Addie thought she would lose her mind. It was everywhere; there was no escaping it. Even when she went shopping or took in a movie she seemed to feel things crawling under her skin. She had tried to tell herself it was just nerves but Mr. Carlisle had once mentioned a case he had helped to exorcise—where the poltergeist actually haunted a man's skin. And now she was positive of it. She broke into a fit of sobbing which made her sides ache. But it was a relief. You just couldn't feel any more miserable and that was a relief in a way.

The house was silent but on the long journey upstairs she felt herself watched. It was not by anything that had eyes, just an evil intelligence that *saw* without any eyes.

Addie Peabody braided her hair hastily and threw some water on her face, rubbing it a couple of times with a towel.

In bed, she tried to read one of the books the Rev. Carlisle had given her on Ramakrishna and the Yoga of Love but the words jumbled up and she found herself reading the same sentence over and over, hoping that the raps would not start again. They were only taps on her windowpane and the first time they came she had run to the window and opened it, thinking boys were throwing pebbles. But no one was there; the rooming houses across the street were all dark and asleep with their windows as black as caverns and the dingy lace curtains of one or two blowing out on the night wind. That was nearly a week ago.

Tap!

Addie jumped and looked at the bed-table clock. Ten minutes after one. She turned off the reading light and left on the night lamp in its opaque shade with the light glowing through the delicate cut-out letters: "God is Love."

Tap!

Addie switched on the light and looked at the clock. One-twenty. She gripped the leather traveling clock in her hands, straining her eyes until she could see the minute hand actually moving, slowly and inevitably, like life itself going by. She put the clock down and clutched the spread tightly with both hands and waited. It was one-thirty. Maybe it wouldn't come again. Oh, please, God, I have faith; indeed I do. Don't let it—

Tap!

She threw on her robe and hurried downstairs, snapping on the lights as she went. Then the emptiness of the illumined house made her flesh creep. She put out the upstairs lights by the hall switch and the blackness up the staircase seemed to smother her.

In the kitchen Addie filled a kettle, spilling water down her sleeve, and set it on the stove for tea. A crash from the pantry made her grab the robe together at her throat.

"Dear—" She addressed the air, hoping, willing to make it hear her. "I don't know who you are, dear, but you must be a little boy. A mischievous little boy. I—I wouldn't want to punish you, dear. God—God is love."

A crash from the cellar shook the floor under her feet. She was too frightened to go down to see but she knew that the big shovel by the furnace had fallen over. Then, through the still house, standing with its lights on in the midst of the sleeping city, she heard another sound from below, a sound which made her cover her ears and run back upstairs leaving the kettle humming on the stove.

From the cellar had come the metallic rasp of the coal shovel, creeping over the concrete in little jumps as if it had sprouted legs like a crab. An inch at a time. Scrape. Scrape.

This time she picked up the telephone and managed to dial a number. The voice which answered was muffled and indistinct but it was like a warm shawl thrown over her shoulders.

"I am sorry to hear it, Mrs. Peabody. I shall start an intensive meditation at once, spending the night in mental prayer, holding the thought. I don't believe that the phenomena will trouble you further. Or, at least, not tonight."

Addie fell asleep as soon as she got back in bed. She had made herself a cup of tea, and once she fancied she heard a sound from the cellar but even if she had she would not have been afraid, for the Rev. Carlisle was with her now, in spirit. If only she could persuade him to stay over for a few days at the house. She must ask him again.

The old gray stone house was dark and as silent as its neighbors. A milkman, driving on his lonely route, saw a man in a dark overcoat pulling what looked like a length of heavy fish-line out of a cellar window. He wondered if he oughtn't to tell the cops but the guy was probably a wack. There were a lot of 'em in this territory.

Light was beginning to show at the window when Molly Cahill turned over and found Stan slipping into bed beside her. She buried her face in the hollow of his throat for a moment and then turned back and fell asleep. You can always smell perfume on them if they've been with another woman. That was what people said.

Addie Peabody got up late and called the Rev. Carlisle but there was no answer. She had the oddest feeling that the ringing she heard in her own telephone also came from one of the rooming houses across the street but she put it down to her nerves. Anyhow, nobody answered.

A little later when she opened the medicine cabinet to get the toothpaste one of those big brown roaches, about three inches long, was in there and flew out at her. She was sure the poltergeist had put it in there just to devil her.

And at breakfast the milk tasted like garlic and that she knew was the poltergeist because they always sour milk or make the cows' milk taste of garlic. And it was certified milk from the best company. She dressed hurriedly and went out. In the beauty parlor the chatter of Miss Greenspan and the heat of the dryer were restful and reassuring. Addie treated herself to a facial and a manicure, and felt better. She did some shopping and saw part of a movie before she got so restless she had to leave.

It was late afternoon when she returned. She had hardly taken off her things when she smelled smoke. For a moment she was paralyzed, not knowing whether to go and find out what was burning or call the fire department and she stood between the two ideas for several seconds while the smell got stronger. Then she saw that something was burning in the umbrella stand in the hall—evil-smelling and smoky. It wasn't doing any damage, just smoking and Addie carried the brass stand out in the back yard. The odor was like old-fashioned phosphorous matches. That was why the ancients always said the Evil One appeared in a burst of fire and brimstone—poltergeist fires smelled like phosphorus.

Minute by minute the evening drew on. The fire had set all her nerves on edge again; she had always been deathly afraid of fires. And then the raps started at the windows and even on the fanlight above the front door.

What a relief it was when she heard the doorbell ring and knew it was Mr. Carlisle and Miss Cahill. The Simmonses were not coming tonight, and with a little guilty pang Addie thought of it with elation—she would have Mr. Carlisle all to herself. That always seemed to get the best results. It was hard to get good results with so many different sets of vibrations even though the Simmonses were just as dear and devoted as any spiritualists she had ever known.

Miss Cahill seemed even more tired and run-down-looking than ever and Addie insisted on giving her a hot Ovaltine before the séance but it didn't seem to strengthen her any. The lines about her mouth grew deeper if anything.

After she had played "On the Other Side of Jordan" Mr. Carlisle asked her if Caroline had a favorite hymn. She had to answer truthfully that Caroline was not a religious child. She sang hymns in Sunday school, of course, but she never sang any around the house.

"Mrs. Peabody, what *did* she sing about the house? That is, what songs of a serious nature? An old love song perhaps?"

Addie thought back. It was amazing what she could remember when Mr. Carlisle was there; it was like being nearer to Caroline just to talk with him. And now she remembered. "Hark, hark, the lark at heaven's gate sings!" She turned and played it, gently at first and then more strongly until it filled the room and a metal dish vibrated in sympathy. She played it over and over, hearing Caroline's thin but true-pitched young voice through the blast of the organ. Her legs ached with pumping before she stopped.

Mr. Carlisle had already extinguished all the lights and drawn the curtain before the cabinet. She took her place in the straight-backed chair beside him and he turned out the last light and let the dark flow around them.

Addie started when she heard the trumpet clink as it was levitated. Then from a great distance came a shrill, sweet piping—like a shepherd playing on reeds. ". . . And Phoebus 'gins arise, His steeds to water at those springs . . ."

A cool breeze fanned her face and then a touch of something material stroked her hair. From the dark, where she knew the cabinet to be, came a speck of greenish light. It trembled and leaped like a ball on a fountain, growing in size until it stopped and unfolded like an opening flower. Then it grew larger and took shape, seeming to draw a veil from before its face. It was Caroline, standing in the air a few inches above the floor.

The green light that was her face grew brighter until Addie could see her eyebrows, her mouth and her eyelids. The eyes opened, their dark, cavernous blankness wrenched her heart.

"Caroline—baby, speak to me. Are you happy? Are you all right, baby?"

The lips parted. "Mother . . . I . . . must confess something."

"Darling, there isn't anything to confess. Sometimes I did scold you, but I didn't— Please forgive me."

"No . . . I must confess. I am not . . . not altogether liberated. I had selfish thoughts. I had mean thoughts. About you. About other people. They keep me on a low plane . . . where the lower influences can reach me and make trouble for me. Mother . . . help me."

Addie had risen from her chair. She stumbled toward the materialized form but the hand of the Rev. Carlisle caught her wrist quickly. She hardly noticed. "Caroline, baby! Anything—tell me what to do!"

"This house . . . evil things have entered it. They have taken it away from us. Take me away."

"Darling—but how?"

"Go far away. Go where it is warm. To California."

"Yes. Yes, darling. Tell Mother."

"This house . . . ask Mr. Carlisle to take it for his church. Let us never live here any more. Take me to California. For if you go I will go with you. I will come to you there. And we will be happy. Only when this house is a church can I be happy. Please, Mother."

"Oh, baby, of course. Anything. Why didn't you ask me before?"

The form was growing dim. It sank, wavering, and the light went out.

The pair in the cab was the usual stuff: gab, gab, gab. Jesus, what a laugh!—"they lived happy ever afterwards." The hackie slid between a bus and a sedan, grazing the car and making the driver mutter in alarm.

"G'wan, ya dumb son-of-a-bitch," he yelled back.

The couple were at it again and he listened in, for laughs.

"I tell you, we've got our foot in the door. Don't you see, baby, this is where it starts? With this house, I can gimmick it up from cellar to attic. I can give 'em the second coming of Christ if I want to. And you were swell, baby, just swell."

"Stan, take your hands off me."

"What's eating you? Get hold of yourself, kid. How about a drink before you hit the hay?"

"I said take your hands off me! I can't stand it! I can't stand it! Let me out of this cab! I'll walk. Do you hear? Let me out!"

"Baby, you better calm down."

"I won't. I won't go up there with you. Don't touch me."

"Hey, driver, let us out. Right here at the corner. Anywhere."

The cabbie took a quick look in his rear vision mirror. Before he got control of the wheel he had nearly piled the boat up against a light pole. Holy gees, the dame's face was glowing bright green right inside his own cab!

From Ed Wolfehope's column, "The Hardened Artery":

". . . She is a widow who owned a fine old mansion in the Seventies near the Drive. Her only child died years ago and she lived on in the house because of memories. Recently a pair of spook workers 'materialized' the daughter and she told her mother to give them the house and move to the West Coast. No one knows how much they took the widow for in cash first. But she left on her journey beaming and rosy—kissed both crooks at the train gate. And they put guys in jail for welching on alimony! . . ."

From "The Trumpet Voice":

"To the Editor:

"A friend of mine recently sent me a piece from a Broadway columnist, which is one lie from beginning to end about me and the Reverend Stanton Carlisle. I want to say it could not have been a practical joker with an air pistol who made the raps on my window. I kept my eyes open the whole time. And anybody who knows anything about Psychic Phenomena knows all about poltergeist fires.

"Miss Cahill and the Reverend Carlisle are two of the dearest people I have ever been privileged to meet and I can testify that all the séances they conducted were under the strictest test conditions and no decent person could even have dreamed of fraud. At the very first séance I recognized my dear daughter Caroline who 'died' when she was sixteen, just a few days before her high school commencement. She came back again and again in the other sittings and I could almost have touched her dear golden hair, worn in the very style she wore it when she passed over. I have a photograph of her taken for her high school yearbook which shows her hair worn this way and it was something no one but I could have possibly known of.

"The Reverend Carlisle never said one word asking for my house. It was Caroline who told me to give it to him and in fact I had a hard time to persuade him to take it and Caroline had to come back and beg him before he would give in. And I am happy to say that here in California, under the guidance of the Rev. Hallie Gwynne, Caroline is with me almost daily. She is not as young as she was in New York and I know that means she is reflecting my own spiritual growth. . . ."

Sun beat on the striped awnings while six floors below them Manhattan's streets wriggled in the rising heat from the pavement. Molly came out of the kitchenette with three fresh cans of cold beer and Joe Plasky, sitting on the overstuffed sofa with his legs tied in a knot before him, reached up his calloused hand for the beer and smiled. "Sure seems funny—us loafing in midseason. But that's Hobart for you—too many mitts in the till. Show gets attached right in the middle of the season."

Zeena filled an armchair beside the window, fanning herself gently with a copy of *Variety*. She had slipped off her girdle and was wearing an old kimono of Molly's, which hardly met in the middle. "Whew! Ain't it a scorcher? You know, this is the first summer I've ever been in New York. I don't envy you all here. It ain't quite this bad in Indiana. Say, Molly"— she finished the last swallow of beer and wiped her mouth with the back of her hand—"if they ever get this mess straightened out, why don't you come out with us and finish the season? You say Stan is working this new act of his solo."

Molly sat down next to Joe and stretched out her long legs; then she curled them under her and lit a cigarette, the match shaking just a little. She was wearing an old pair of rehearsal rompers; she still looked like a kid in them, Zeena noticed a little sadly.

Molly said, "Stan's awfully busy at the church. The folks are crazy about him. He gives reading services every night. I used to help him with those but he says a straight one-ahead routine is good enough. Then he has development classes every afternoon. I—I just take it easy."

Zeena set down the empty can on the floor and took the full one which Molly had put on the window sill. "Lambie-pie, you need a good time. Why don't you get yourself slicked up and come out with us? We'll get you a date. Say, I know a swell boy with Hobart Shows this season—an inside talker. Let's hire a car and get him and have dinner up the line some-wheres. He's a swell dancer and Joe don't mind sitting out a couple, do you, snooks?"

Joe Plasky's smile, turned on Zeena, deepened; his eyes grew softer. "Swell idea. I'll call him now."

Molly said quickly, "No, please don't bother. I'm really fine. I don't feel like going anywhere in this heat. Really, I'm okay." She looked at the little leather traveling clock on the mantel, which Addie Peabody had given her. Then she switched on the radio. As the tubes warmed, the voice came through clearer. It was a familiar voice but richer and deeper than Zeena had ever heard it before.

". . . therefore, my beloved friends, you can see that our claims for evidence of survival are attested to and are based on proof. Men of the caliber of Sir Oliver Lodge, Sir Arthur Conan Doyle, Camille Flammarion, and Sir William Crookes did not give their lives to a dream, to a chimera, to a delusion. No, my unseen friends of the radio audience, the glorious proofs of survival lie about us on every hand.

"We at the Church of the Heavenly Message rest content and secure in our faith. And it is with the deepest gratitude that I thank them, the splendid men and women of our con-gregation, for their generosity, which has enabled me to bring you this Sunday afternoon message for so many weeks.

"Some persons think of the 'new religion of Spiritualism' as a closed sect. They ask me, 'Can I believe in the power of our dear ones to return and still not be untrue to the faith of my fathers?' My dearly beloved, the doors of Spiritual Truth are open to all—it is something to cherish close to your heart *within* the church of your own faith. Whatever your creed it will serve simply to strengthen it, whether you are accustomed to worship God in meeting house, cathedral, or synagogue. Or whether you are one of the many who say 'I do not know' and then proceed to worship unconsciously under the leafy arches of the Creator's great Church of the Out of Doors, with, for your choir, only the clear, sweet notes of the song sparrow, the whirr of the locust among the boughs.

"No, my dear friends, the truth of survival is open to all. It is cool, pure water which will gush from the forbidding rock of reality at the touch of a staff—your own willingness to believe the evidence of your own eyes, of your own God-given senses. It is we, of the faith of survival, who can say with joy and *certainty* in our heart of hearts, 'O death, where is thy sting? O grave, where is thy victory?' "

Joe Plasky's smile was now a faint, muscular imprint on his face; nothing more. He leaned across Molly and gently switched off the radio. "Got a deck of cards, kid?" he asked her, his face lighting up again. "I mean a deck of your own cards—the kind your dad would have played with. The kind that read from only one side."

The Moon

Beneath her cold light howl the dog and the wolf.
And creeping things crawl out of slime.

IN THE black alley with a light at the end, the footsteps followed, drawing closer; they followed, and then the heart-stopping panic as something gripped his shoulder.

". . . in about another fifteen minutes. You asked me to wake you, sir." It was the porter shaking him.

Stan sat up as though a rope had jerked him, his pulse still hammering. In the early light he sat watching the fields whip by, trying to catch his breath, to shake off the nightmare.

The town looked smaller, the streets narrower and cheaper, the buildings dingier. There were new electric signs, dark now in the growing dawn, but the horse chestnuts in the square looked just the same. The earth doesn't age as fast as the things man makes. The courthouse cupola was greener with time and the walls were darker gray.

Stanton Carlisle walked slowly across the square and into the Mansion House, where Old Man Woods was asleep on the leather couch behind the key rack. Knocking on the counter brought him out, blinking. He didn't recognize the man with the arrogant shoulders, the cold blue eyes; as the Rev. Carlisle signed the register he wondered if anyone at all would recognize him. It was nearly seventeen years.

From the best room, looking out on Courthouse Square, Stan watched the town wake up. He had the bellboy bring up a tray of bacon and eggs, and he ate slowly, looking out on the square.

Marston's Drug Store was open; a boy came out and emptied a pail of gray water into the gutter. Stan wondered if it was the same pail after all these years—his first job, during high school vacation. This kid hadn't been born then.

He had come back, after all. He could spend the day loafing around town, looking at the old places, and catch the night train out and never go near the old man at all.

Pouring himself a second cup of coffee, the Rev. Carlisle looked at his face in the polished surface of the silver pot. Hair thinner at the temples, giving him a "widow's peak" that everyone said made him look distinguished. Face fuller around the jaw. Broader shoulders, with imported tweed to cover them. Pink shirt, with cuff links made from old opal earrings. Black knitted tie. All they could remember would be a kid in khaki pants and leather jacket who had waited behind the water tank for an open freight-car door.

Seventeen years. Stan had come a long way without looking back.

What difference did it make to him whether the old man lived or died, married or suffered or burst a blood vessel? Why was he here at all?

"I'll give it the once over and then highball out of here tonight," he said, drawing on his topcoat. Picking up his hat and gloves he took the stairs, ancient black woodwork with hollows worn in the marble steps. On the porch of the Mansion House he paused to take a cigarette from his case, cupping the flame of his lighter against the October wind.

Horse-chestnut leaves were a golden rain in the early sun, falling on the turf of the park where the fountain had been turned off for the winter. In its center a stained bronze boy smiled up under his bronze umbrella at the shower which wasn't falling.

Stan followed the south side of the park and turned up Main Street. Myers' Toy and Novelty Mart had taken in the shop next to it and expanded. In the window were construction kits for airplanes with rubber-band motors. Mechanical tractors. A playsuit of what looked like long red underwear, with a toy rocket-pistol. A new generation of toys.

Leffert's Kandy Kitchen was closed but the taffy still lay golden in metal trays in the window with almonds pressed in it to form flower-petal designs. Christmas was the time for Leffert's taffy, not autumn. Except the autumn when they had beaten Childers Prep; he had taken a bag of it to the game.

The wind whirled down the street, making store signs creak above him. The autumns were colder than they used to be, but the snow of winter wasn't as deep.

On the edge of town Stan looked out across rolling country. A farmhouse had stood on the ridge once. Must have burned down or been pulled down. Dark against the sky Mills' Woods lay over the rise, too far to walk; and what was the use of going through all that again. She was probably dead by now. It didn't matter. And the old man was dying.

Stan wondered if he could get a bus out of town before the night train left. Or he might load up with magazines and go to the hotel and read. It was well past noon but there was a lot of the day left.

Then a side street led him down familiar ways; here and there a lot stood empty, with a gaping cellar where a house had been.

He didn't realize he had walked so far when the sight of the school brought him up short. In a country of square, brick boxes some long-dead genius on a school board had made them build this high school differently: gray stone with casement windows, like a prep school or an English college. The lawn was still green, the ivy over the archway scarlet with the old year.

It was a cool June evening and Stan wore a blue coat with white pants; a white carnation in his lapel. Sitting on the platform he watched the audience while the speaker droned on.

His father was out there, about ten rows back. And alone. Couples everywhere else, only his father, it seemed, was alone.

". . . and to Stanton Carlisle, the Edwin Booth Memorial medal for excellence in dramatic reading."

He was before them now but applause didn't register; he couldn't hear it. The excitement under his ribs was pleasant. The power of the eyes upon him lifted him out of the black emptiness in which he had been sunk all evening. Then, as he turned, he suddenly heard the applause and saw his father, beaming, smashing his palms together, shooting quick looks left and right, enjoying the applause of the others.

"Taxi!" Stan saw the old limousine lumbering toward him and flagged it. The driver was Abe Younghusband, who didn't recognize him until he gave the address.

"Oh, say, you must be Charlie Carlisle's boy, ain't you? Ain't seen you around for some time."

"Sixteen—nearly seventeen years."

"That a fact? Well, guess there's lots of improvements since you left. Say, I heard you're a preacher now. That ain't true, is it?"

"Sort of half and half. More of a lecturer."

They turned off the car tracks, down the familiar street with the maples scarlet in the rays of the afternoon sun.

"I always figured you'd go on the stage. I still remember that show you put on at the Odd Fellows' Hall, time you borrowed Chief Donegan's watch and made believe you was smashing the hell out of it. His face was sure something to see. But I guess you got kind of tired of that stuff after a while. My boy's a great one on tricks. Always sending away for stuff. Well, here we are. I hear Charlie's pretty shaky these days. I hear he's turned worse during the last week."

The house looked tiny and run to seed. A wooden staircase had been built up one side of it, and a door cut into the attic floor. The yard was scuffed, with bare patches; the maples that used to shelter the house had been cut down. Where Gyp's kennel had stood there was still a rectangle in the ground. The earth forgets slowly.

The woman who answered the door was white-haired and stout, the lines about her mouth petulant. It was Clara Carpenter; but what a tub she had turned into!

"How do you do. Mrs. Carpenter?"

"Mrs. *Carlisle*. Oh." Her face lost some of its caution. "You must be Stan Carlisle. Come right in. Your dad's been asking me a dozen times an hour when you were coming." She lowered her voice. "He's not a bit well, and I can't make him stay in bed. Maybe you can persuade him to take it easy, a little. It's his heart, you know." She called upstairs, "Charlie, somebody to see you." To Stan she said, "I guess you know your way upstairs. The big bedroom. I'll be up directly."

The stairs, the newel post, the two ridiculous spouted urns on the mantelpiece, seen through the double doors. The metal fireplace covering. The wallpaper was different, and the upper hall looked different some way, but he didn't stop to find out why.

The old man was seated in a chair by the window, with a knitted afghan over his knees; seamed face, scrawny neck. His eyes looked frightened and sullen.

"Stanton?" Charlie Carlisle moved with difficulty, hands gripping the chair arms. "Stanton, come over here and let me take a good look. Gosh, you—you don't look so very different, son. Only you've filled out a lot. You're—you're looking all right, son."

Stan tried to throw his shoulders back. But a weight was pressing them, a deadly weight that made his knees tremble. The life seemed to be leaking out of him, flowing into the carpet under his feet. He took a chair on the other side of the window and leaned back in it, drawing his breath, trying to fight off the crushing weariness.

"I didn't know you'd married Clara," Stan said at last, getting a cigarette out and lighting it. He offered one to his father, who shook his head.

"Doctor's got me cut down to one cigar a day. Yes, I kept bachelor's hall for quite a spell after you left. I—I always figured I'd hear from you, boy, and then I'd tell you. Clara's a fine girl. Ever hear from your mother?"

The words had a hard time coming out, his lips were so tired. "No. Never did."

"I'm not surprised. Guess she didn't find us exciting enough. What do they call it now—glamour? That's what Cynthia wanted. Glamour. Well, if she found it I don't reckon she's got much of it now." The mouth came down in creases of bitterness. "But tell me what you been doing, Stan. I said to Clara, sure he'll come. I said, we had our differences, and I guess he's been busy, making his own way. I said, I know he'll come if I tell him I'm in bad shape. Feel a lot better today, though. I told the doctor I'd be back at the office in a month. Feel a lot better. What's this I hear you're a minister of the gospel, Stan? Clara heard you on the radio one day, she said. That's how we knew where to send that telegram."

The Rev. Carlisle uncrossed his legs and knocked the ashes from his cigarette into a jardiniere holding a fern. "I'm more of a lecturer. But I do have a Minister's certificate."

The elder Carlisle's face brightened. "Son, I'm gladder to hear that from you, and believe it, than any other news I've heard in a month of Sundays. You work your way through seminary? Why, son, I wanted you to go. I was willing to lay out cold cash to pay your way. You know that. Only you couldn't see it at the time. Always fooling with that magic nonsense. I'm glad you finally got that out of your system. It was your mother put those ideas in your head, Stan, buying you that box of tricks. I haven't forgotten it. But I don't even know your denomination."

The Rev. Carlisle closed his eyes. His voice sounded flat and toneless in his own ears. "It's not a big or a rich church, Dad. The United Spiritual League. It's devoted to preaching the gospel that the soul survives earthly death, and that those of us who still are earth-bound can receive intelligence—from those who have passed over to the higher spheres."

"You mean you're a spiritualist? You believe the dead come back?"

Stan forced a smile, his eyes wandering up to the ceiling where cracks made the outline of an old man's face. The sun was slanting through the window now and night was coming but not fast enough. He came back with a start.

"I'm not going to try converting you, Dad. I am secure in my faith. Many others share my views, but I am no prose-lytizer."

His father was silent for a time, swallowing uneasily. His head seemed to nod back and forth a fraction of an inch as he sat, a quick, rhythmic, involuntary nod of weakness. "Well, everybody to his own faith. I don't hold with spiritualism much. But if you're convinced, that's all that matters. Real estate is all shot, here in this town, son. If I was younger I'd pull out. Town's dying. I been trying to get the Civic Betterment Committee to put on a little campaign—make it a good, open-shop town and no nonsense. Attract industry. But they don't listen. Property values way down— Oh, here's Clara. Reckon it's most suppertime. We been talking so much."

"I'll wash up and be right down," Stan said. The load of weariness— There was a place where he might leave it, where it might slip from him like a weight cut from his neck.

In the hall he turned left and his hand was reaching for the knob when, with a cold flash, he realized that he was facing a smooth, papered wall. The attic door was not there! Looking down, he saw a single step at the bottom of the wall. So that was it—the stairs outside. It was an apartment now, cut off from the rest of the house. Strangers living in it, under the slope of the roof, around the brick chimney. The iron bed, the silk patchwork, smell of camphor and silk and lumber and the tight mesh of maple leaves below, seen through the narrow windows where you could make out the signboard on the lawn of the church. The house was dying, too.

Stan closed the bathroom door and locked it. The same taps on the washbowl anyhow, even though the walls were painted a different color. And the odd mix-up of tiles in the floor, where he used to find half-tiles and try to count them. The old-fashioned tub on its high legs; marble-topped commode with its old-fashioned mahogany drawers; shaving stand with its circular cabinet and a mirror on a swivel, where Dad kept his shaving brush, his mug and his soap, his hones.

Stan wondered if the water still made the sharp sucking gurgle in the tub when the stopper was pulled out—as it did when his mother had finished splashing and singing to herself. He recalled the day when he had fallen out of the tree, and Mother had picked him up in her arms and carried him upstairs, bleeding all down the front of her dress. She hadn't minded the dress getting messed up. He had made leggings of corrugated cardboard, like explorers wear in the jungle. One of them had been bloody; after the doctor had sewed up the cut in his forehead Mother undressed him, taking the cardboard leggings off carefully. She had put them on the marble top of the commode. They stayed there for a long time, until the blood stains became black. Jennie finally threw them out—said they gave her the jimjams.

If only they could all have stayed together a few more years. If Mother had not minded the town. If Dad had always been as weak and as friendly as he was now that he was dying. If only he could have been dying for twenty years, Stan might have loved him. Now there was nothing but the old things, and they were going past him and would soon be gone.

He drew his breath and tried again to strain his shoulders back. I mustn't forget to ask the old man about the church and how to go about selling it when it's time to pull out. But the Church of the Heavenly Message seemed too far away to matter, now. The old man was slipping into that dark hole where you fall and fall forever because there's no bottom to it. We are all creeping to its edge, some slowly, some, like the old man, balanced on the brink. And then what? Like the rush of wind past a bullet, probably, forever and ever. Gyp was dead all these years. Even the memories of him were dead and forgotten except in one mind. And when that was gone Gyp would be forgotten entirely. When the old man was dead and under ground Stan could forgive it.

Gyp never knew what hit him. They said the vet just put chloroform on a rag and dropped it in the box.

But that end of rope, tied to the leg of the workbench in the garage—it had been cut when Stan came home from school. Why did they tie Gyp up in there if they wanted to get rid of him? There was no they. Only he. Gyp had a chain on his kennel. Why the rope?

Oh, Christ, let me get to hell out of here. But the voice that had said "son" held him. The house was swallowing him. And they had sealed up the attic door; there was no way. All the years had dropped off, tearing with them his poise, so carefully built up tone by tone. They had taken his cleverness, his smile, his hypnotic glance, leaving him powerless and trapped inside the walls of old familiarity.

He had come back because Dad was dying and Mother was gone and the maples were cut down, the square still visible where Gyp's kennel had stood, and the shaving stand on its smooth pillar of wood, still in the same place and still smooth under his hand, smelling sweetly of shaving soap.

The strop.

It hung from the brass hook where it had always hung. It was smooth, black with handling and with oil, shining.

The garage at night with the moonlight making bars of silver across the floor, silvering the workbench, sparkling on the bar of the vise and on the lidless coffee cans of nails and bolts. Shining blue and cold on the concrete floor. And the shadows hiding dread and shame.

"Take down your pants."

That was to add to the shame: nakedness.

Stan fumbled with the belt of his knickers, stalling for split seconds.

"Hurry up. I said drop 'em."

His knickers bound his feet about the ankles. He couldn't run. He had to take it. "Now bend over." A hand on his shoulder pushed him into the patch of moonlight, where his nakedness could show. Stan saw the shadow of the strop rise and braced himself. The pain split its way up to his brain in waves and he bit his lip, his breath catching at the bottom of his lungs. He pushed his knuckles in his mouth so they wouldn't hear him next door. The moonlight was a fuzzy blur of tears; and the strop, when it struck the roundness of his bare flesh, made a sound that got to his brain before the stab of pain—and the rope's end, tied to the leg of the workbench there in the smell of oil and gasoline on the day when the sun went out.

Downstairs Charlie Carlisle fidgeted with his napkin, pushing himself back in the chair by bracing his hands against its polished arms. "Confound it, Clara, what d'you s'pose the boy's doing up there? Oh, there you are, son. Sit right down."

When Charlie raised his glance to the man who entered the dining room he caught his old, quick breath at something he saw. It was Stan, much as he had appeared a few minutes before. Maybe with his face fresh-washed and his hair damped down a little. But in the set of the shoulders was something strange. And when old Charlie met his son's eyes they were a sharper blue than any he had ever seen before; as hard as a frozen pond.

The Great Stanton pulled back a chair and sat down swiftly and gracefully, opening his napkin with a single snap. Mrs. Carlisle brought in a platter of chicken. When rice and gravy arrived Charlie said, "Sit down, Clara. Quit running in and out. Stan'll pronounce the blessing."

The Rev. Carlisle ran his hands once over his hair and took a deep breath. His voice came resonantly:

"Almighty God, our heavenly father, we thank Thee from the bottom of our hearts for what we are about to receive. We come to Thee steeped in sin and corruption, our hearts black with guilt, knowing that in the river of Thy forgiveness they will be washed as white as snow."

His father had slid one heavily veined hand over his eyes.

"He who watches the sparrow's fall will hold us in the hollow of his hand to the end of our days, on earth and beyond."

Clara was frowning in bewilderment or worrying about the chicken getting cold.

". . . in the name of thy son, our Lord and Savior, Jesus Christ, we ask it. Amen."

The old man said "Amen" and then grinned weakly at his wife. "No matter what denomination, Clara, it's a proud day when we can have a son saying grace and him a preacher. Pass Stan the rice."

Clara was not one to eat in silence. She began a brief history of the community during the past sixteen years, full of hot summers, hard winters, deaths, births, weddings, and disasters.

Stan ate quickly and took a second helping of everything. At last he slid his plate away from him and lit a cigarette. He looked at Clara Carpenter Carlisle for a long minute; the penetrating blue glance made her conscious of the old apron over her good dress.

"My dear friend, have you ever thought that these persons whom you have mourned as dead will never die?"

Under that brilliant stare she began to simper and found it difficult to control her hands. "Why, Stan, I—I've always *believed*. But I think it's one of those things you just have to feel. I never paid much attention. I took it for granted, about. heaven."

The Rev. Carlisle wiped his lips with his napkin and took a swallow of water. "I have seen magnificent proofs that the spirit does not lie fallow until the Day of Judgment. The spirits of the liberated are around us every moment. How often have we said, in anguish, 'If only I could speak to him again. And feel the touch of his hand.' "

Both the older Carlisles looked embarrassed, eyed one another and then each took a sip of coffee.

Stan's mellow voice rolled on. "Yes. And the glorious truth is that it can be done. The spirits of the liberated are around us even now, as we speak." His eyes were still on Clara; he dropped his voice. "I feel one presence beside me now, distinctly. Insistently. Trying to get through."

On his father's face was the suggestion of a sly grin.

"It is one who loved me in its earth existence. But it is not human."

They stared at him.

"A small spirit, a humble presence. But brimming with devotion and loyalty. I believe it is the spirit of my old dog, Gyp." Charles Carlisle had slumped forward, his arms before him on the tablecloth, but now he sat up straighter, the bitter lines around his mouth deeper and more biting.

"Son, you don't believe that! That's blasphemous! You can't mean it—about a dog having a soul same as a man."

Stan smiled. "As I said before, I shall not try to convert you, Dad. Only the ones who have passed over into spirit life can do that. But I have communicated with Gyp—not in words, naturally, since Gyp did not speak in words. Yet this house is full of his presence. He has spoken to me, trying to tell me something." Watching his father keenly, Stan noticed a little flash of alarm on the wrecked face. He covered his eyes with his hand, watching his father's hands on the cloth before him, and bore in:

"Something about his last day on earth. I remember you told me, when I came home from school, that you had had a veterinary chloroform Gyp. But there's some contradiction, here. I get another impression . . ."

A pulse was beginning to pound in the shrunken wrist.

"Gyp has been trying to tell me something . . . wait a minute . . . the garage!'"

His father's hands clenched into fists and then released the tablecloth, which they had seized.

"That's it . . . I see it clearly before me. Gyp is tied to the leg of the workbench in the garage. I see something rising and falling . . . in anger . . . faster and faster."

The clatter of a fork on the floor made Stan look up. The old man's face was ashy; he kept shaking his head, trying to speak. "No. No, son. Don't."

"That was the day—the day Mother left. With Mark Humphries. You came home and found her note. Gyp got in your way—you had to vent your temper on something. If I'd been home you'd have licked me. But Gyp got it. He died."

Old Carlisle had heaved to his feet, one hand clawing at his shirt collar. Stan turned, swaying a little, and walked stiffly through the doors into the living room, across it to the hall. When he took down his hat and coat his arms felt numb and heavy. One last glimpse of Clara shaking capsules from a bottle and holding a glass of water; the old man swallowing painfully.

The moon brightened concrete steps leading down the terrace where the grass was ragged. Stan's legs felt stiff as he descended to the street where the arching maples closed over him, moonlight showering through their leaves now black with night. A sound came from the house he had left, an old man weakly crying.

In a patch of silver the Rev. Carlisle stopped and raised his face to the full moon, where it hung desolately, agonizingly bright—a dead thing, watching the dying earth.

CARD XI

The Lovers

They stand between the Eden trees; winged Love hovers over-head while Knowledge lies in serpent coils upon the ground.

W HEN Molly woke up the third time, Stan was dressing. She looked at the clock: four-thirty. "Where you
going?"

"Out."

She didn't question him, but lay awake watching. His
movements were so jumpy lately you didn't dare speak to him
for fear he would bite your head off. Lately he had been sleeping worse and worse, and Molly worried about him taking so
many sleeping pills all the time. They didn't have any more
effect on him, it seemed, and his temper got worse and he
looked like hell. She began to cry softly and Stan stopped in
the middle of buttoning his shirt and came over.

"Now what?"

"Nothing. Nothing. I'm all right."

"What's eating you, kid?"

"Stan—" Molly sat up, holding the covers in front of her
for warmth. "Stan, let's quit and go back to the old act."

671

He went on buttoning. "Where we going to book it? On street corners? Vaudeville's a dead pigeon. I know what I'm doing. One live John and we're set."

She drew the covers up tighter. "Honey, you look like hell. Why don't you go see a doctor? I—I mean give you something for your nerves or something. Honest, I'm worried sick you're going to have a nervous breakdown or something."

He rubbed his eyes. "I'm going out for a walk."

"It's snowing."

"I've got to get out, do you hear? I'm going down to the church and look over the props. I've got an idea I want to try out. Go back to sleep."

It was no use. He would just keep going until he dropped and Molly prayed it wouldn't happen some time in the middle of a reading—or of a séance, where it would blow up the whole works. If anybody made trouble the cops would nail her along with Stan and in the shape Stan was in he couldn't talk his way out of a jam no matter how bad it was. Molly was worried sick and took half a sleeping pill herself when he had gone.

It was too early to go out and get a racing form, and all the magazines were old, and nothing was on the radio except platter programs, and they made her feel so lonesome— records being dedicated to the boys in Ed's Diner out on the turnpike. She wished she was in the diner with the truck drivers having a few laughs.

Stan let himself into the old Peabody house. He was glad he had banked the furnace the night before; down in the cellar he threw in more coal. Soon the fire was roaring and he stood with the heat on his face, watching blue flames feel their way up through the black coal.

After a moment he sighed, shook himself, and unlocked an old metal cabinet which had once held paint and varnish. Inside was a phonograph turntable which he switched on, placing a pickup arm into position above the aluminum record. Then he went upstairs.

The vast room which had been a parlor and a dining room before he knocked the partition out, was still chilly. Stan turned on the lamps. The bridge chairs sat in empty rows, waiting for something to happen to him—something to go wrong. Walking over to a lamp with a dead bulb, he snapped the switch, gave the amplifying tubes a minute to warm up, then crossed to the desk, where the trumpet usually lay at the developmental classes and trumpet séances.

Near the organ his foot, from long habit, found the loosened board beneath the carpet, and he put his weight on it. Ghostly, with the sound of a voice through a metal tube, came the deep tones of Ramakrishna, his spirit guide. "*Hari Aum.* Greetings, my beloved *chelas*, my disciples of earth life. You who have gathered here tonight." The voice stopped; Stan felt a crawling fear flowing over his scalp. The wiring must have broken again. And there was no time to rip it out. Or was it the loudspeaker? Or the motor? He ran down to the cellar; but the disc was still revolving. It must be in the amplifying unit. There was no time to fix it. The séance was scheduled for that evening. He could always blame it on conditions; a séance without phenomena was common enough for all mediums. But Mrs. Prescott was bringing two trusted friends, both social register. He had looked up all the dope on them and the recording was ready. They might not come back. They might be the ones who would bring in the live John he was waiting for.

Stan took off his coat and put on an old smock; he checked the tubes, the wiring. Then he went back upstairs and began to pry the panel loose. The loudspeaker connections were tight enough. Where was the break? And there was no time, no time, no time. He thought of a dozen stalls to tell a radio repairman, and threw them all out. Once he let anyone know the house was wired he was sunk. He thought of getting a repairman from Newark or somewhere. But there was no one he could trust.

Loneliness came over him, like an avalanche of snow. He was alone. Where he had always wanted to be. You can only trust yourself. There's a rat buried deep in everybody and they'll rat on you if they get pushed far enough. Every new face that showed up at the séances now seemed charged with suspicion and malice and sly knowledge. Could there be a cabal forming against him in the church?

Frantically he switched on the phonograph again and

stepped on the board. "*Hari Aum.* Greetings, my beloved *chelas*, my disciples of earth life . . ." It wasn't broken! The last time he must have shifted his weight unconsciously off the loose board that closed the circuit. He stopped it now with a chilling fear that the next words the voice, his own voice, would say would not be words he had recorded on aluminum—the record would turn on him with a malevolent life of its own.

In the silence the house was closing in. The walls had not moved, nor the ceiling; not when he looked straight at them. He ran his hands over his hair once and took a deep breath. Hum the first eight bars of our opener. But it was no use.

Outside, across backyards, a dog barked.

"Gyp!"

His own voice startled him. Then he began to laugh.

He laughed as he walked into the hall, laughing up the stairs and in and out of bedrooms, now chastely bare. In the dark-séance room he snapped on the light. Blank white walls. Still laughing and chuckling he snapped the light off and felt for the panel in the baseboard where he kept the projector.

He aimed it at the wall; and there it was, jumping up and down crazily as his hand shook with laughing—the hazy image of an old woman. He twisted a knob and she vanished. Another twist and a baby appeared in a halo of golden mist, jumping crazily as his hand shook with laughing. "Dance, you little bastard," his voice thundered against the close walls.

He twisted the hand projector until the baby floated upside down, and he roared with laughter. He fell to the floor, laughing, and aimed the beam at the ceiling, watching the baby fly up the angle of the wall and come to rest overhead, still smiling mistily. Laughing and strangling, Stan began to beat the projector against the floor; something snapped, and the light went out.

He crawled to his feet and couldn't find the door and stopped laughing then, feeling his way around and around. He counted nine corners. He began to shout and then he found it and let himself out, dripping with sweat.

In his office the day was breaking gray through the Venetian blinds. The desk light wouldn't come on and he seized it and

jerked it out of the wall plug and tossed it into a corner.
The blinds got tangled with the cord; he gathered them in
his arms and wrenched; the whole business came down on top
of him and he fought his way free of them. At last the card
index.

R. R. R. God damn it. Who had stolen the R's? Raphaelson,
Randolph, Regan—here it was. *Woman psychologist, mentioned
by Mrs. Tallentyre. Said to be interested in the occult. Has recommended that her patients take yoga exercises.* But the phone
number, Jesus God, it wasn't there. Only her name—Dr.
Lilith Ritter. Try the phone book. R. R. R.

The voice that answered the telephone was cool, low-
pitched, and competent. "Yes?"

"My name is Carlisle. I've been having trouble sleeping—"

The voice interrupted. "Why not consult your physician? I
am not a doctor of medicine, Mr. Carlisle."

"I've been taking pills, but they don't seem to help. I've
been working too hard, they tell me. I want to see you."

There was silence for a long moment; then the cool voice
said, "I can see you the day after tomorrow at eleven in the
morning."

"Not before then?"

"Not before then."

Stan beat his fist once against the desk top, squeezing his
eyes shut. Then he said, "Very well, Dr. Ritter. At eleven
o'clock—Tuesday."

Whatever she might look like, the dame had a wonderful
voice. And he must have pulled her out of a sound sleep. But
Tuesday— What was he supposed to do until then, chew the
rug?

The house grew warmer. Stan went over and pressed his
forehead against the chill of the windowpane. Down in the
street a girl in a fur coat and no stockings was walking an Irish
setter. Stan's eyes followed the curve of the bare legs, wondering if she had on anything under the fur coat. Some of
them run out that way—naked under their furs—to buy cigarettes or club soda or a douche bag.

Back in the flat Molly would be lying sprawled across the
bed with her hair caught up on top of her head with a single

pin. She would be wearing the black chiffon negligee but she might as well have on a calico wrapper. There was no one to look at her.

The Irish-setter girl turned, tugging at the leash, and the fur coat swung open, showing a pink slip. With a growl of frustration Stan twisted away from the window. He sat down at the desk and pulled out his appointment book. Message service that evening at eight-thirty. Monday morning, developmental class in trance mediumship and the Science of Cosmic Breath. God, what a herd of hippos. The Science of Cosmic Breath: in through the left nostril, on a count of four. Retain breath for count of sixteen. Exhale through the right nostril to count of eight. Measure the counts by repeating *Hari Aum, Hari Aum.*

Monday afternoon, lecture on the Esoteric Significance of the Tarot Symbols.

Stan took the Tarot deck from the side drawer and slowly his fingers began remembering; the front-and-back-hand palm, making the cards vanish in the air and drawing them out from under his knee. He paused at one card and laid it before him, holding his head in his hands, studying it. The Lovers. They were naked, standing in Eden with the snake down on the ground all ready to wise them up. Over their heads was the angel-form, its wings extended above the trees of Life and Knowledge. *Where the Tree of Life is blooming, there is rest for me.*

The lovers were naked. A wave of prickling crawled up over his scalp out of nowhere and, as he watched, the rounded hips and belly of the woman seemed to rotate. Jesus, if this is what I wanted I could have stayed with the Ten-in-One and been talker for the kooch show! There's a guy that always gets plenty.

He swept the cards to the floor and drew the telephone toward him, dialing. This time the voice said, "Yes, sir. I'll see if Mrs. Tallentyre's in."

She was in to the Rev. Carlisle.

"Mrs. Tallentyre, I spent most of last night in meditation. And from my meditation I drew a thought. I shall have to seek three days of silence. Unfortunately I cannot go to the Himalayas, but I think the Catskills will serve. You understand, I'm sure. I would appreciate it if you will take charge of the service tonight and notify class members that I have been called away. Just say that I have gone in search of the Silence. I shall return, without fail, on the third day."

That was that. Now lock up. Lock the office door—time to clean up all the havoc later. Leave the appointment book downstairs on the hall table. Mrs. Tallentyre had a key to the outside door. Leave the inner door unlocked.

He put on his coat and a few minutes later was hurrying through the soft snow.

"Gee, honey, I'm glad you come back! Are you okay?"

"Yeah. Sure. How many times do I have to tell you I can take care of myself?"

"Want a couple of eggs? I'm starved. Let me fix you a couple. The coffee's all ready."

Stan stood in the kitchen door watching her. She was wearing the black chiffon negligee; against the early winter light from the window she might as well not have had on a stitch. Whoever figured out dames' clothes knew his onions. What made her seem so far away and long ago? The one dame who wouldn't cross him up. And the shape was still something you usually see behind footlights or in magazines.

Stan ran his hands once over his hair and said, "Come here." They stood watching each other for a moment, and he saw her take a deep breath. Then she turned off the gas under the skillet and ran over and threw her arms around his neck.

It was like kissing the back of your own hand but he picked her up in his arms and carried her into the bedroom. She clung to him and slid her hand under his shirt and he drew the chiffon open and started to kiss her shoulder but it was no use.

And now she was crying, looking up at him reproachfully as he threw on his jacket.

"Sorry, kid. I've got to get away. I'll be back Tuesday. I've—I've got to breathe."

When he had thrown some stuff in a keyster and locked it and hurried out Molly pulled the covers over her, still crying, and drew up her knees. After a while she got up and put on a robe and fried herself an egg. She didn't seem to be able to get enough salt on it, and in the middle of breakfast she suddenly took the plate and slammed it on the floor of the kitchen.

"Oh, God damn it, what's eating him? How can I know how to give him a party if I don't know what's the matter?"

After a while she got dressed and went out to have her hair washed and set. First she went around to the barber shop and saw Mickey, and he handed her sixteen dollars. The horse had paid off at seven to one.

With the wheels clicking past under him, Stan felt a little better. The Palisades had fingers of snow pointing up their slopes, and the river was rough with broken ice, where gulls sailed and settled. He read, sketchily, in Ouspensky's *A New Model of the Universe*, looking for tag lines he could pull out and use, jotting notes in the margin for a possible class in fourth dimensional immortality. Immortality was what they wanted. If they thought they could find it in the fourth dimension he would show them how. Who the hell knew what the fourth dimension was, anyway? Chumps. Johns.

A girl was having trouble getting her valise down from the rack and Stan leaped up to help her. Getting off at Poughkeepsie. His hand touched hers on the valise handle and he felt blood rising over his face. The kid was luscious; his eyes followed her as she walked primly down the car, carrying the bag before her. He crossed the train and watched her, out on the platform.

When he got to Albany he took a cab to the hotel, stopping off to buy a fifth of Scotch undercover from a saloon.

The room was good-sized and cleaner than most.

"You ain't been through lately, Mr. Charles. Territory been changed?"

Stan nodded, throwing his hat on the bed and getting out of his overcoat. "Bring some club soda. And plenty of ice."

The boy took a five and winked. "Like some company? We got swell gals in town—new since you was here last. I know a little blonde that's got everything. And I mean everything."

Stan lay down on the other bed and lit a cigarette, folding his hands behind his head. "Brunette."

"You're the boss."

He smoked when the boy had gone. In the ceiling cracks he could make out the profile of an old man. Then there was a tap on the door—the soda and ice. The boy scraped the collodion seal from the Scotch bottle.

Quiet again. In the empty, impersonal wilderness of the hotel Stan listened to noises coming up from the street. The whir of the elevator, stopping at his floor; footsteps soft in the corridor. He swung off the bed.

The girl was short and dark. She had on a tan polo coat and no hat, but there was an artificial gardenia pinned in her hair over one ear.

She came in, her nose and cheeks rosy from the cold, and said, "Howdy, sport! Annie sent me. Say—how'd ya know I drink Scotch?"

"I read minds."

"Gee, you musta." She poured two fingers' into a glass and offered it to Stan, who shook his head.

"On the wagon. But don't let that stop you."

"Okay, sport. Here's lead in your pencil." When she finished it she poured herself another and then said, "You better give me the fin now before I forget it."

Stan handed her a ten-dollar bill and she said, "Gee, thanks. Say, would you happen to have two fives?"

Silence. She broke it. "Lookit—radio in every room! That's something new for this dump. Say, let's listen to Charlie McCarthy. D'you mind?"

Stan was looking at her spindly legs. As she hung the polo coat carefully in the closet he saw that her breasts were tiny. She was wearing a Sloppy Joe sweater and a skirt. They used to look like whores. Now they look like college girls. They all want to look like college girls. Why don't they go to college, then? They wouldn't be any different from the others. You'd never notice them. Christ, what a crazy way to run a world.

She was having a good time listening to the radio gags, and the whisky had warmed her. Taking off her shoes, she curled her feet under her. Then motioning Stan to throw her a cigarette, she stripped off her stockings and warmed her feet with her hands, giving him a flash at the same time.

When the program was over she turned the radio down a little and stood up, stretching. She drew off her sweater carefully, so as not to disturb the gardenia, and spread it over the chair back. She was thin, with sharp shoulder blades; her collar bones stood out starkly. When she dropped her skirt it was a little better but not too good. On one thigh, evenly spaced, were four bruises, the size of a big man's fingers.

She stood smoking, wearing nothing but the imitation gardenia and Stan let his eyes go back to the old man's face in the ceiling.

Tear-ass out of town, ride for hours, hotel, buy liquor, and for this. He sighed, stood up and slipped off his jacket and vest.

The girl was humming a tune to herself and now she did a soft-shoe dance step, her hands held up by her face, and spun around, then sang the chorus of the song that was coming over the loudspeaker. Her voice was husky and pleasant with power under control.

"You sing, too?" Stan asked dryly.

"Oh, sure. I only party to fill in. I sing with a band sometimes. I'm studying the voice." She threw back her head and vocalized five notes. "Ah . . . ah . . . AH . . . ah . . . ah."

The Great Stanton stopped with his shirt half off, staring. Then he seized the girl and threw her on the bed.

"Hey, look out, honey, not so fast! Hey, for Christ's sake, be careful!"

He twisted his hand in her hair. The girl's white, waxy face stared up at him, fearful and stretched tight. "Take it easy, honey. Don't. Listen, Ed McLaren, the house dick, is a pal of mine. Now go easy—Ed'll beat the hell out of any guy that did that."

The radio kept on. ". . . bringing you the music of Phil Requete and his Swingstars direct from the Zodiac Room of the Hotel Teneriffe. And now our charming vocalist, Jessyca Fortune, steps up to the mike with an old-fashioned look in her eye, as she sings—and swings—that lovely old number of the ever popular Bobbie Burns, 'Oh, Whistle and I'll Come to You, My Lad.'"

Ice in the river, piled against the piers of boat clubs, a dark channel in the middle. And always the click of the rail joints underneath. North south east west—cold spring heat fall—

love lust tire leave—wed fight leave hate—sleep wake eat sleep
—child boy man corpse—touch kiss tongue breast—strip grip
press jet—wash dress pay leave—north south east west . . .

Stan felt the prickle crawl up over his scalp again. The old
house was waiting for him and the fat ones with pince-nez
and false teeth; this woman doc probably was one of them,
for all the music of voice and cool, slow speech. What could
she do for him? What could anybody do for him? For anybody? They were all trapped, all running down the alley toward the light.

The nameplate said, "Dr. Lilith Ritter, Consulting Psychologist. Walk In."

The waiting room was small, decorated in pale gray and
rose. Beyond the casement window snow was falling softly in
huge flakes. On the window sill was a cactus in a rose-colored
dish, a cactus with long white hair like an old man. The sight
of it ran along Stan's nerves like a thousand ants. He put
down his coat and hat and then quickly looked behind a picture of sea shells drawn in pastel. No dictaphone. What was
he afraid of? But that would have been a beautiful place to
plant a bug if you wanted to work the waiting room gab angle
when the doc's secretary came in.

Did she have a secretary? If he could make the dame he
might get a line on this woman doc or whatever she was, find
out how much overboard she was on occult stuff. He might
swap developmental lessons for whatever she gave her patients—some kind of advice. Or did she interpret dreams or
something? He lit a cigarette and it burned his finger as he
knocked the ashes off. In reaching down to pick it up he
knocked down an ashtray. He got on his hands and knees to
pick up the butts and that was where he was when the cool
voice said, "Come in."

Stan looked up. This dame wasn't fat, she wasn't tall, she
wasn't old. Her pale hair was straight and she wore it drawn
into a smooth roll on the nape of her neck. It glinted like
green gold. A slight woman, no age except young, with enormous gray eyes that slanted a little.

Stan picked up the ashtray and put it on the edge of a table.

It fell off again but he didn't notice. He was staring at the woman who stood holding the door open into another room. He weaved to his feet, lurching as he came near her. Then he caught a whiff of perfume. The gray eyes seemed as big as saucers, like the eyes of a kitten when you hold its nose touching yours. He looked at the small mouth, the full lower lip, carefully tinted but not painted. She said nothing. As he started to push past her he seemed to fall; he found his arm around her and held on knowing that he was a fool, knowing something terrible would strike him dead, knowing he wanted to cry, to empty his bladder, to scream, to go to sleep, wondering as he tightened his arms around her. . . .

Stan lay sprawling on the floor. She had twisted his shoulders, turning him until his back was toward her, and then planted one neat foot at the back of his knee. Now she knelt beside him on the carpet, gripping his right hand in both of hers, forcing it in toward the wrist and keeping him flat by the threatened pain of the taut tendons. Her expression had not changed.

She said, "The Rev. Stanton Carlisle, I believe. Pastor of the Church of the Heavenly Message, lecturer on Tarot symbolism and yogic breathing, a producer of ghosts with cheesecloth—or maybe you use a little magic lantern. Now if I let you up will you promise to be co-operative?"

Stan had thrown one arm over his eyes and he felt the tears slipping down his face into his ears. He managed to say, "Promise."

The deft hands released his and he sat up, hiding his face with his palms, thinking of a pillow that had been slept on and perfumed, with shame washing back and forth over him, the light too strong for his eyes, and the tears that wouldn't stop running. Something in his throat seemed to be strangling him from inside.

"Here—drink this."

"What—what is it?"

"Just a little brandy."

"Never drink it."

"I'm telling you to drink it. Quickly."

He felt blindly for the glass, held his breath and drank, coughing as it burned his throat.

"Now get up and sit over here in this chair. Open your eyes and look at me."

Dr. Lilith Ritter was regarding him from across a wide mahogany desk. She went on, "I thought I'd be hearing from you, Carlisle. You were never cut out to run a spook racket solo."

The Star

*shines down upon a naked girl who, between land
and sea, pours mysterious waters from her urns.*

"LIE BACK on the couch."

"I don't know what to talk about."

"You say that every time. What are you thinking about?"

"You."

"What about me?"

"Wishing you sat where I could see you. I want to look at you."

"When you lie down on the couch, just before you lean back, you run your hands over your hair. Why do you do that?"

"That's my get-set."

"Explain."

"Every vaudeville actor has some business: something he does in the wings just before he goes on."

"Why do you do that?"

"I've always done it. I used to have a cowlick when I was

a kid and my mother would always be telling me to slick it down."

"Is that the only reason?"

"What difference does it make?"

"Think about it. Did you ever know anybody who did that—anybody else in vaudeville?"

"No. Let's talk about something else."

"What are you thinking about now?"

"Pianos."

"Go on."

"Pianos. People playing pianos. For other people to sing. My mother singing. When she sang my old man would go in the dining room and whisper all the time to one of his pals. The rest would be in the living room listening to my mother."

"She played the piano herself?"

"No. Mark played. Mark Humphries. He'd sit down and look up at her as if he was seeing right through her clothes. He'd run his hands once over his hair—"

"Yes?"

"But it's crazy! Why would I want to swipe a piece of business from that guy? After she'd run off with him I used to lie awake nights thinking up ways to kill him."

"I think you admired him."

"It was the dames that admired him. He was a great big guy with a rumbling voice. The dames were crazy over him."

"Did this Humphries drink?"

"Sure. Now and then."

"Did your father drink?"

"Hell, no. He was White Ribbon."

"The first day you were here I offered you a glass of brandy to help you get hold of yourself. You said you never drank it."

"God damn it, don't twist everything around to making it look as if I wanted to be like my old man. Or Humphries either. I hated them—both of 'em."

"But you wouldn't take a drink."

"That was something else."

"What?"

"None of your—I—it's something I can't tell you."

"I'm being paid to listen. Take your time. You'll tell me."

"The stuff smelled like wood alcohol to me. Not any more but the first time."

"Did you ever drink wood alcohol?"

"Christ, no, it was Pete."

"Pete who?"

"I never knew his last name. It was in Burleigh, Mississippi. We had a guy in the carny named Pete. A lush. One night he tanked up on wood alky and kicked off."

"Did he have a deep voice?"

"Yes. How did you know?"

"Never mind. What was he to you?"

"Nothing. That is—"

"What are you thinking about?"

"Damn it, quit deviling me."

"Take your time."

"He—he was married to Zeena, who ran the horoscope pitch. I was—I was—I was screwing her on the side I wanted to find out how she and Pete had done their vaude mental act and I wanted a woman and I made up to her and Pete was always hanging around I gave him the alky to pass him out I didn't know it was wood or I'd forgotten it he died I was afraid they'd pin it on me but it blew over. That's all. Are you satisfied?"

"Go on."

"That's all. I was scared of that murder rap for a long time but then it blew over. Zeena never suspected anything. And then Molly and I teamed up and quit the carny and it all seemed like a bad dream. Only I never forgot it."

"But you felt so guilty that you would never drink."

"For God's sake—you can't do mentalism and drink! You've got to be on your toes every minute."

"Let's get back to Humphries. Before he ran away with your mother you preferred him to your father?"

"Do we have to go over that again? Sure. Who wouldn't? But not after—"

"Go on."

"I caught him—"

"You caught him making love to your mother? Is that it?"

"In the Glade. We'd found it, together. Then I went there.

And I saw it. I tell you, I saw it. All of it. Everything they did. I wanted to kill my old man. He drove her to Humphries, I thought. I wanted—I wanted—"

"Yes."

"I wanted them to take me with them! But she didn't, God damn her, she left me with the old son-of-a-bitch to rot in his goddamned hick town. I wanted to go away with her and see something and maybe get into show business. Humphries had been in show business. But I was left there to rot with that Bible-spouting old bastard."

"So you became a Spiritualist minister."

"I'm a hustler, God damn it. Do you understand that, you frozen-faced bitch? I'm on the make. Nothing matters in this goddamned lunatic asylum of a world but dough. When you get that you're the boss. If you don't have it you're the end man on the daisy chain. I'm going to get it if I have to bust every bone in my head doing it. I'm going to milk it out of those chumps and take them for the gold in their teeth before I'm through. You don't dare yell copper on me because if you spilled anything about me all your other Johns would get the wind up their necks and you wouldn't have any more at twenty-five bucks a crack. You've got enough stuff in that bastard tin file cabinet to blow 'em all up. I know what you've got in there—society dames with the clap, bankers that take it up the ass, actresses that live on hop, people with idiot kids. You've got it all down. If I had that stuff I'd give 'em cold readings that would have 'em crawling on their knees to me. And you sit there out of this world with that dead-pan face and listen to the chumps puking their guts out day after day for peanuts. If I knew that much I'd stop when I'd made a million bucks and not a minute sooner. You're a chump too, blondie. They're all Johns. They're asking for it. Well, I'm here to give it out. And if anybody was to get the big mouth and sing to the cops about me I'd tell a couple of guys I know. They wouldn't fall for your jujit stuff."

"I've been shouted at before, Mr. Carlisle. But you don't really know any gangsters. You'd be afraid of them. Just as you're afraid of me. You're full of rage, aren't you? You feel you hate me, don't you? You'd like to come off that couch and strike me, wouldn't you?—but you can't. You're quite

688   WILLIAM LINDSAY GRESHAM

helpless with me. I'm one person you can't outguess. You can't fool me with cheesecloth ghosts; you can't impress me with fake yoga. You're just as helpless with me as you felt seeing your mother run away with another man when you wanted to go with her. I think you went with her. You ran away, didn't you? You went into show business, didn't you? And when you start your act you run your hands over your hair, just like Humphries. He was a big, strong, attractive man, Humphries. I think you have become Humphries—in your mind."

"But he—he—"

"Just so. I think you wanted your mother in the same way."

"God damn your soul, that's—"

"Lie back on the couch."

"I could kill you—"

"Lie back on the couch."

"I could— Mother. Mother. Mother."

He was on his knees, one hand beating at his eyes. He crawled to her and threw his head in her lap, burrowing in. Dr. Lilith Ritter, gazing down at the disheveled corn-colored hair, smiled slightly. She let one hand rest on his head, running her fingers gently over his hair, patting his head reassuringly as he sobbed and gasped, rooting in her lap with his lips. Then, with her other hand, she reached for the pad on the desk and wrote in shorthand: "Burleigh, Mississippi."

In the spring darkness the obelisk stood black against the sky. There were no clouds and only a single star. No, a planet; Venus, winking as if signaling Earth in a cosmic code that the worlds used among themselves. He moved his head a fraction, until the cold, brilliant planet seemed to rest on the bronze tip of the stone shaft. The lights of a car, winding through the park, sprayed for a moment across the stone and the hieroglyphics leaped out in shadow. Cartouches with their names, the boasts of the dead, invocations to dead gods, prayers to the shining, fateful river which rose in mystery and found the sea through many mouths, flowing north through the ancient land. Was it mysterious when it still lived? he wondered. Before the Arabs took it over and the chumps started measuring the tunnel of the Great Pyramid in inches to see what would happen in the world.

The spring wind stirred her hair and trailed a loose wisp of it across his face. He pressed her cheek against his and with his other hand pointed to the planet, flashing at the stone needle's point. She nodded, keeping silence; and he felt the helpless wonder sweep over him again, the impotence at touching her, the supplication. Twice she had given it to him. She had given it as she might give him a glass of brandy, watching his reactions. Beyond that elfin face, the steady eyes, there was something breathing, something that was fed blood from a tiny heart beating under pointed breasts. But it was cobweb under the fingers. Cobweb in the woods that touches the face and disappears under the fingers.

The hot taste of need rose in his mouth and turned sour with inner turmoil and the jar of forbidding recollection. Then he drew away from her and turned to look at her face. As the wind quickened he saw her perfectly molded nostrils quiver, scenting spring as an animal tastes the wind. Was she an animal? Was all the mystery nothing more than that? Was she merely a sleek, golden kitten that unsheathed its claws when it had played enough and wanted solitude? But the brain that was always at work, always clicking away behind the eyes—no animal had such an organ; or was it the mark of a superanimal, a new species, something to be seen on earth in a few more centuries? Had nature sent out a feeling tentacle from the past, groping blindly into the present with a single specimen of what mankind was to be a thousand years hence?

The brain held him; it dosed him with grains of wild joy, measured out in milligrams of words, the turn of her mouth corner, one single, lustful flash from the gray eyes before the scales of secrecy came over them again. The brain seemed always present, always hooked to his own by an invisible gold wire, thinner than spider's silk. It sent its charges into his mind and punished him with a chilling wave of cold reproof. It would let him writhe in helpless misery and then, just before the breaking point, would send the warm current through to jerk him back to life and drag him, tumbling over and over through space, to the height of a snow mountain where he could see all the plains of the earth spread out before him, and all the power of the cities and the ways of men. All were his, could be his, would be his, unless the golden thread broke and sent him roaring into the dark chasm of fear again.

The wind had grown colder; they stood up. He lit cigarettes and gave her one and they passed on, circling the obelisk, walking slowly past the blank, unfinished wall of the Museum's back, along the edge of the park where the busses trailed their lonely lights away uptown.

He took her hand in his and slid it into the pocket of his topcoat, and for a moment, as they walked, it was warm and a little moist, almost yielding, almost, to the mind's tongue, sweet-salty, yielding, musky; then in an instant it changed, it chilled, it became the hand of a dead woman in his pocket, as cold as the hand he once molded of rubber and stretched on the end of his reaching rod, icy from a rubber sack of cracked ice in his pocket, straight into the face of a believer's skeptical husband.

Now the loneliness grew inside him, like a cancer, like a worm of a thousand branches, running down his nerves, creeping under his scalp, tying two arms together and squeezing his brain in a noose, pushing into his loins and twisting them until they ached with need and not-having, with wanting and not-daring, with thrust into air, with hand-gripping futility—orgasm and swift-flooding shame, hostile in its own right, ashamed of shame.

They stopped walking and he moved toward a backless bench under the trees which were putting out the first shoots of green in the street lamp's glow, delicate, heartbreakingly new, the old spring which would bring the green softly, gently, like a young girl, into the earth's air long after they and the fatal, coursing city, were gone. They would be gone forever, he thought, looking down into her face which was now as empty as a ball of crystal reflecting only the window light.

The rush, the rocketing plunge of the years to death, seized hold of him and he gripped her, pressing her to him in a fierce clutch after life. She let him hold her and he heard himself moaning a little under his breath as he rubbed his cheek against the smooth hair. Then she broke away, reached up and brushed his lips with hers and began to walk again. He fell in

behind her for a few steps, then came abreast of her and took
her hand once more. This time it was firm, muscular, determined. It closed on his own fingers for a single reassuring
instant, then broke away and she thrust her hands into the
pockets of her coat and strode on, the smoke of her cigarette
whirling back over her shoulder like a sweet-smelling scarf in
the wind.

When she walked she placed her feet parallel, as if she were
walking a crack in the sidewalk. In spite of high heels the
ankles above them never wavered. She wore gunmetal stockings, and her shoes had buckles of cut steel.

Two ragged little boys, gleeful at being out after midnight,
came bounding toward them, chasing each other back and
forth across the walk by the wall where the trees leaned over.
One of them pushed the other, screaming dirty words, and
the one pushed caromed toward Lilith. Turning like a cat released in mid-air, she spun out of his path and the boy
sprawled to the cinders, his hands slipping along, grinding
cinders into the palms. He sat up and as Stan turned to watch,
he suddenly sprang at his companion with his fists. Kids always
play alike. Roughhouse around until one gets hurt and then
the fight starts. A couple of socks and they quit and the next
minute are friends again. Oh, Christ, why do you have to
grow up into a life like this one? Why do you ever have to
want women, want power, make money, make love, keep up
a front, sell the act, suck around some booking agent, get
gypped on the check—?

It was late and the lights were fewer. Around them the
town's roar had softened to a hum. And spring was coming
with poplar trees standing slim and innocent around a glade
with the grass hummocks under one's hands—can't I ever forget it? His eyes blurred and he felt his mouth tighten.

The next moment Lilith's hand was through his arm, pressing it, turning him across the avenue to the apartment house
where she lived, where she worked her own special brand of
magic, where she had her locked files full of stuff. Where she
told people what they had to do during the next day when
they wanted a drink, when they wanted to break something,
when they wanted to kill themselves with sleeping tablets,
when they wanted to bugger the parlor maid or whatever they

wanted to do that they had become so afraid of doing that
they would pay her twenty-five dollars an hour to tell them
either why it was all right to do it or go on doing it or think
about doing it or how they could stop doing it or stop wanting to do it or stop thinking about doing it or do something
else that was almost as good or something which was bad but
would make you feel better or just something to do to be able
to do something.

At her door they stopped and she turned to him, smiling
serenely, telling him in that smile that he wasn't coming in
tonight, that she didn't need him, didn't want him tonight,
didn't want his mouth on her, didn't want him to kneel beside
her, kissing her, didn't want anything of him except the
knowledge that when she wanted him in the night and wanted
his mouth on her and wanted him kneeling beside her, kissing
her, she would have him doing all those things to her as she
wanted them done and just when she wanted them done and
just how she wanted them done to her because she had only
what she wanted from anybody and she had let him do those
things to her because she had wanted them done to her not
because he could do them better than anyone else although
he didn't know if there was anybody else and didn't want to
know and it didn't matter and she could have him any time
she wanted those things done to her because that was the way
she was and she was to be obeyed in all things because she
held in her hand the golden thread which carried the current
of life into him and she held behind her eyes the rheostat that
fixed the current and she could starve him and dry him up
and kill him by freezing if she wanted to and this was where
he had gotten himself only it didn't matter because as long as
one end of the golden wire was embedded in his brain he
could breathe and live and move and become as great as she
wanted since she sent the current along the wire for him to
become great with and live with and even make love to Molly
with when Molly begged him to tell her if he didn't want her
any more so she might get some man before she looked like
an old hay-burner and her insides were too tight for her ever
to have a kid.

All these things he saw in the full lower lip, the sharp cheekbones and chin, the enormous eyes of gray that looked like

ink now in the dark of the vestibule. He was about to ask her something else and he wet his lips with his tongue. She caught his thought, nodded, and he stood there, three steps below her with his hand holding his hat, looking up at her and needing and then she gave him what he was begging for, her lips for a full, warm, soft, sweet, moist moment and her little tongue between his like the words, "Good night" formed of soft moisture. Then she had gone and there he was for another day, another week, another month, willing to do anything she said, as long as she would not break the golden wire and now he had her permission, which she had pulled out of his mind, and he hurried off to take advantage of it before she changed her mind and sent him refusal, chilling along the invisible wire embedded in his brain, that would stop his hand six inches from his lips.

Three doors down was a little cocktail bar with a glass sign over it that was illumined some way from inside and said "BAR." Stan hurried in. The murals jagged crazily this way and that up the three-toned wall and a radio was playing softly where the bar man nodded on a stool at one end of the bar. Stan laid a dollar on the polished wood.

"Hennessy, Three Star."

" 'Inside, above the din and fray, We heard the loud musicians play The "Treues Liebes Herz" of Strauss—' "

"What's that?"

"It's from *The Harlot's House*. Shall we go in?"

They were walking down a side street in the early summer twilight; ahead of them Lexington Avenue was gaudy with neon. In the basement of an old brownstone was a window painted in primary blues and reds; above it a sign, "Double Eagle Kretchma." Gypsy music was filtering out on the heated air.

"It looks like a joint to me."

"I like joints—when I'm in the mood for dirt. Let's go in."

It was dark with a few couples sliding around on the little dance floor. A sad fat man with blue jowls, wearing a Russian blouse of dark green silk, greasy at the cuffs, came toward them and took them to a booth. "You wish drinks, good Manhattan? Good Martini?"

"Do you have any real vodka?" Lilith was tapping a cigarette.

"Good vodka. You, sir?"

Stan said, "Hennessy, Three Star, and plain water."

When the drinks came he offered the waiter a bill but it was waved away. "Later. Later. Have good time first. Then comes the payment—the bad news, huh? Have good time—always have to pay for everything in the end." He leaned across the table, whispering, "This vodka—it's not worth what you pay for it. Why you want to come here anyhow? You want card reading?"

Lilith looked at Stan and laughed. "Let's."

From the shadows in the back of the room a woman stepped out and waddled toward them, her bright red skirt swishing as her hips rolled. She had a green scarf around her head, a curved nose, loose thin lips and a deep, greasy crease between her breasts which seemed ready to burst from her soiled white blouse at any moment. When she wedged herself into the booth beside Stan her round hip was hot and burning against his thigh.

"You cut the cards, lady; we see what you cut, please. Ah, see! Good sign! This card called The Star. You see this girl—she got one foot on land, one foot on water; she pour wine out on land and water. That is good sign, lucky in love, lady. I see man with light hair going to ask you to marry him. Some trouble at first but it come out all right."

She turned up a card. "This one here—Hermit card. Old man with star in lantern. You search for something, no? Something you lose, no? Ring? Paper with writing on it?"

Against Lilith's blank, cold face the gypsy's questions bounded back. She turned another card. "Here is Wheel of Life. You going to live long time with not much sickness. Maybe some stomach trouble later on and some trouble with nervous sickness but everything pass off all right."

Lilith took a puff of her cigarette and looked at Stan. He pulled two bills from his wallet and held them to the gypsy. "That'll do, sister. Scram."

"Thank you, mister. But lots more fortune in cards. Tell lots of thing about what going to happen. Bad luck, maybe; you see how to keep it away."

"Go on, sister. Beat it."

She shoved the bills into her pocket along with the Tarot deck and heaved out of the booth without looking back.

"She'll probably put the hex on us now," Stan said. "Christ, what corn. Why the hell did I ever leave the carny? I could be top man in the mitt camp right now and tucking ten grand in the sock at the end of every season."

"You don't want to, darling." Lilith sipped her vodka. "Do you think I'd be sitting here with you if your only ambition was to be top man in a—what did you call it?"

"Mitt camp." He grinned weakly. "You're right, doctor. Besides I'd probably have pulled the switch once too often and gotten jugged." He answered her frown. "The switch is what the gypsies call *okana borra*—the great trick. You have the chump tie a buck up in his hanky. He sleeps on it and in the morning he has two bucks and comes running back with all his savings out of the teapot. Then when he wakes up next time he has nothing in the hank but a stack of paper and he comes back looking for the gypsy."

"You know such fascinating bits of folklore, Mr. Carlisle. And you think you could ever be happy using those very keen, crafty brains of yours to cheat some ignorant farmer? Even if you did make ten thousand a year and loaf all winter?"

He finished the brandy and signaled the waiter for a refill. "And when it rains you read mitts with your feet in a puddle and a river down the back of your neck. I'll stick to Mrs. Peabody's house—it's got a better roof on it."

Lilith's eyes had narrowed. "I meant to speak to you, Stan, when we got a chance. There are two women who will be introduced to your congregation, not directly through me, naturally, but they'll get there. One of them is a Mrs. Barker. She's interested in yoga; she wants to go to India but I told her not to uproot her life at this stage. She needs something to occupy her time. I think your Cosmic Breath would be just about right."

Stan had taken a slip of paper from his pocket and was writing. "What's her first name?"

"Give me that paper." She put it in the ashtray and touched her lighter to it. "Stan, I've told you not to write down anything. I don't want to have to remind you again. You talk very glibly about making a million with your brains and yet you continue to act as naïve as a carnival grifter."

He downed the drink desperately and found another in its place and finished that one as quickly.

Lilith went on. "The name is Lucinda Barker. There's nothing else you need to know."

There was silence for a minute, Stan sullenly rattling the ice in the chaser glass.

"The other woman is named Grace McCandless. She's single, forty-five years old. Kept house for her father until he died three years ago. She's gone through Theosophy and come out the other side. She wants proof of survival."

"Give—can you tell me something about the old man?"

"He was Culbert McCandless, an artist. You can look him up with the art dealers probably."

"Look, Lilith, give me just one 'test.' I know you're afraid I'll louse it up and they'll think back to you. But you've got to trust me. After all, lady, I've been in this racket all my life."

"Well, stop apologizing and listen. McCandless went to bed with his daughter—once. She was sixteen. They never did it again but they were never separated. Now that's all you'll get. I'm the only person in the world who knows this, Stan. And if your foot slips I shall have to protect myself. You know what I mean."

"Yeah. Yeah, pal. Let's get out of here. I can't stand the bum air."

Above them the summer leaves cut off the glow of the city in the night sky. By the obelisk they paused for a moment and then Lilith took the lead and they passed it. The back of the Museum seemed to leer at him, full of unspoken threats with doom straining at its leash in the shadows.

When she came out of the bathroom her hands gleamed white against the black silk robe as she tied the cord. On her feet were tiny black slippers. Lilith sat at the desk by the bedroom window and from its side compartment took a case containing several flat drawers, labeled "Sapphires," "Cat's Eyes," "Opals," "Moss Agates."

She said, without looking at him, "The notes wouldn't do

you the slightest bit of good, Stan. They're all in my own shorthand."

"What do you mean?"

Her glance, raised to his for the first time, was calm and benevolent. "While I was in the bathroom you went into my office and tried out the key you had made for my file cabinet. I saw it on the dressing table after you had taken off your clothes. Now it's not there. You've hidden it. But I recognized the notches. You took the impression from my key the last time you went to bed with me, didn't you?"

He said nothing but smoked quickly; the ember of his cigarette became long and pointed and angry red.

"I was going to send you home, Stan, but I think you need a little lesson in manners. And I need my toenails fixed. You can help me with the polish. It's in the drawer of the bed table. Bring it over here."

Dully he stamped out his cigarette, spilling some of the embers and quickly sweeping them back into the tray. He took the kit of nail polish and went over to her, feeling the air against his naked flesh cold and hostile. He threw his shirt over his shoulders and sat down on the carpet at her feet.

Lilith had taken the drawer marked sapphires from its little cabinet and was lifting the stones with a pair of jeweler's forceps, holding them in the light of the desk lamp. Without looking at him she shook one foot free of its slipper and placed it on his bare knee. "This is very good for you, darling. Occupational therapy."

The Great Stanton twisted cotton on the end of an orangewood stick and dipped it into the bottle of polish remover. It smelled acrid and sharply chemical as he swabbed one tiny toenail with it, taking off the chipped polish evenly. Once he paused to kiss the slender foot at the instep but Lilith was absorbed in her tray of gems. Growing bolder, he drew aside the black silk and kissed her thigh. This time she turned and pulled the robe primly over her knees, giving him a glance of amused tolerance. "You've had enough sinfulness for one evening, Mr. Carlisle. Be careful not to spill polish on the rug. You wouldn't want me to rub your nose in it and then throw you out the back door by the scruff of your neck, would you, darling?"

Bracing his hand against the curved instep he began to paint her nails. The rose-colored enamel spread evenly and he thought of the workbench out in the garage and its paint cans. Painting a scooter he had made out of boxes and old baby-carriage wheels. Mother said, "That's beautiful, Stanton. I have several kitchen chairs you can paint for me." The old man had been saving that paint for something. That meant another licking.

"Stan, for heaven's sake, be more careful! You hurt me with the orange stick."

He had finished the first foot and started on the other without knowing it.

"What would you do for a shoeshine if you didn't have me around?" He was startled at the amount of hostility in his own voice.

Lilith laid down a sapphire, narrowing her eyes. "I might have another friend of mine do them. Possibly someone who could take me to the theater, who didn't have to be so afraid of being seen with me. Someone who wouldn't have to sneak in and out."

He set down the bottle of polish remover. "Lilith, wait until we make a killing. One big-time believer—" But he didn't sound convinced himself; his voice died. "I—I want to be seen with you, Lilith. I—I didn't think up this setup. You were the one who told me to hang on to Molly. If I went back to the carny—"

"Stanton Carlisle. Pastor of the Church of the Heavenly Message. I didn't think you could be jealous. I didn't think you had that much of a heart, Stan. I thought all you cared about was money. And power. And more money."

He stood up, throwing off the shirt, his hands clenched. "Go on, pal. You can tell me about as many other guys as you want. This is fifty-fifty. I'm not jealous if another guy shakes hands with you. How's that so different from—the other thing?"

She watched him through eyes almost closed. "Not so very different. No. Not different at all. I shook hands regularly with the old judge—the one who set me up in practice when I was a court psychiatrist on a city salary. All cats have gray paws in the dark, you know, Stan. And I can vaguely recall, when I was sixteen, how five boys in our neighborhood waited for me one evening as I was coming home from night school. They took me into a vacant lot and shook hands with me one after the other. I think each came back twice."

He had turned as she spoke, his mouth hanging open idiotically, his hair falling over his face. He lurched over to the dressing table with its wing mirrors, gaped at his image, his eyes ravaged. Then in a spatter of desperate groping he seized the nail scissors and gouged at his forehead with them.

The stab of pain was followed instantly by a tearing sensation in his right wrist and he saw that Lilith stood beside him, levering his hand behind his shoulder until he dropped the scissors. She had not forgotten to pull up her robe and held it bunched under one arm to keep it from brushing her toes with their wet enamel.

"Put a drop of iodine on it, Stan," she said crisply. "And don't try drinking the bottle. There's not enough in it to do more than make you sick."

He let the cold water roar past his face and then tore at his hair with the rich, soft towel. His forehead wasn't bleeding any more.

"Stan, darling—"

"Yeah. Coming."

"You never do anything by halves, do you, lover? So few men have the courage to do what they really want to do. If you'll come in here and fuss over me a little more—I love to be fussed over, darling—I'll tell you a bedtime story, strictly for adults."

He was putting on his clothes. When he was dressed he pulled up a hassock and said, "Give me your foot."

Smiling, Lilith put the gems away and leaned back, stretching her arms luxuriously, watching him with the sweetest of proprietary smiles.

"That's lovely, darling. Much more accurately than I could do it. Now about the bedtime story—for I've decided to risk it and ask you to stay over with me. You can, darling. Just this once. Well, I know a man—don't be silly, darling, he's a patient. Well, he started as a patient and later became a friend—

but not like you, darling. He's a very shrewd, capable man and he might do us both a lot of good. He's interested in psychic phenomena."

Stan looked up at her, holding her foot in both his hands. "How's he fixed for dough?"

"Very well-heeled as you would put it, darling. He lost a sweetheart when he was in college and he has been weighed down with guilt from it ever since. She died from an abortion. Well, at first I thought I'd have to pass him along to one of my tame Freudians—he seemed likely to get out of hand with me. But then he became interested in the psychic. His company makes electric motors. You'll recognize the name—Ezra Grindle."

The Chariot

holds a conqueror. Sphinxes draw him.
They turn in opposite directions to rend him apart.

GRINDLE, EZRA, industrialist, b. Bright's Falls, N. Y. Jan. 3, 1878, s. Matthias Z. and Charlotte (Banks). Brewster Academy and Columbia U. grad. 1900 engineering. m. Eileen Ernst 1918, d. 1927. Joined sales staff, Hobbes Chem. and Dye, 1901, head of Chi. office 1905; installed plants Rio de Janeiro, Manila, Melbourne 1908–10; export mgr. 1912. Dollar-a-year man, Washington, D. C. 1917–18. Amer. Utilities, gen. mgr. 1919, v.p. 1921. Founded Grindle Refrigeration 1924, Manitou Casting and Die 1926 (subsidiary), in 1928 merged five companies to form Grindle Sheet Metal and Stamping. Founded Grindle Electric Motor Corp. 1929, pres. and chairman of board. Author: The Challenge of Organized Labor, 1921; Expediting Production: a Scientific Guide, 1928; Psychology in Factory Management (with R. W. Gilchrist) 1934. Clubs: Iroquois, Gotham Athletic, Engineering Club of Westchester County. Hobbies: billiards, fishing.

From *The Roll Call*—1896, Brewster Academy:

EZRA GRINDLE ("Spunk") Major: Math. Activities: chess club, math club, manager of baseball 3 years, business manager of *The Roll Call* 2 years. College: Columbia. Ambition: to own a yacht. Quotation: "By magic numbers and persuasive sound"—Congreve.

   When the red-haired kid looked up he saw a man standing by the counter. The clerical collar, the dead-black suit, the panama with a black band, snapped him to life.

   "My son, I wonder if you would be so kind as to help me on a little matter?" He slipped a breviary back into his pocket.

   "Sure, Father. What can I do for you, Father?"

   "My son, I am preparing a sermon on the sin of destroying life before birth. I wonder if you could find me some of the clippings which have appeared in your newspaper, recounting the deaths of unfortunate young women who have been led to take the lives of their unborn infants. Not the most recent accounts, you understand—of these there are so many. I want to see some of the older accounts. Proving that this sin was rampant even in our parents' time."

   The kid's forehead was pulled up with the pain of thought. "Gee, Father, I'm afraid I don't getcha."

   The smooth voice lowered a little. "Abortions, my son. Look under A-B."

   The kid blushed and pounded away importantly. He came back with an old envelope. ABORTION, DEATHS—1900–10.

   The man in the clerical collar riffled through them quickly. 1900: MOTHER OF TWO DIES FROM ILLEGAL OPERATION. SO-CIETY GIRL . . . HUSBAND ADMITS . . . DEATH PACT . . .

DEATH OF A WORKING GIRL
By ELIZABETH McCORD

   Last night in Morningside Hospital a slender young girl with raven tresses covering her pillow turned her face to the wall when a youth fought his way into the ward where she lay on the brink of death. She would not look upon him, would not speak to him although he begged and implored her forgiveness. And in the end he slunk away, eluding Officer Mulcahy who had been stationed in the hospital to watch for just such an appearance of the man responsible for the girl's condition and untimely death. He did not escape, however, before a keen-eyed little probationer nurse had noted the initials E.G. on his watch fob.

Somewhere in our great city tonight a coward crouches and trembles, expecting at any moment the heavy hand of the law to descend on his shoulder, his soul seared (let us hope) by the unforgiving gesture of the innocent girl whose life he destroyed by his callous self-interest and criminal insistence.

This girl—tall, brunette and lovely in the first bloom of youth—is but one of many. . . .

The man in black clucked his tongue. "Yes—even in our parents' time. Just as I thought. The sin of destroying a little life before it has been born or received Holy Baptism."

He stuffed the clippings back into the envelope and beamed his thanks on the kid with red hair.

In Grand Central the good father picked up a suitcase from the check room. In a dressing cubicle he changed into a linen suit, a white shirt, and a striped blue tie.

Out on Madison Avenue he stopped, grinning, as he turned the pages of a worn breviary. The edges were crinkled from rain; and on the fly leaf was written in faded, Spencerian script, "Fr. Nikola Tosti" and a date. The blond man tossed it into a trash can. In his pocket was a clipping, the work of a sob sister thirty years ago. *May 29, 1900.*

The morgue office of Morningside Hospital was a room in the basement inhabited by Jerry, the night attendant, a shelf of ancient ledgers, and a scarred wreck of a desk. There were two kitchen chairs for visitors, a radio, an electric fan for hot nights and an electric heater for cold ones. The fan was going now.

A visitor in soiled gray slacks and a sport shirt looked up as Jerry came back into the room.

"I borrowed a couple of shot glasses from the night nurse on West One—the little number with the gams. These glasses got markings on 'em but don't let that stop us. Fill 'em up.

Say, brother, it's a break we got together over in Julio's and you had this bottle. I hadn't had a chance to wet the whistle all evening. I was dying for a few shots."

His new friend pushed a straw skimmer further back on his head and filled the medicine glasses with applejack.

"Here's lead in the old pencil, huh?" Jerry killed his drink and held out the glass.

Blondy filled it again and sipped his brandy. "Gets kind of dull, nights, eh?"

"Not so bad. I listen to the platter programs. You get some good records on them programs. And I do lots of crossword puzzles. Say, some nights they don't give you a minute's peace around here—stiffs coming down every ten minutes. That's mostly in the winter and in the very hot spells—old folks. We try not to get 'em in here when they're ready to put their checks back in the rack but you can't keep 'em out when a doctor says 'In she goes.' Then we got the death entered on our books and the city's books. It don't look good. Thanks, don't care if I do."

"And you got to keep 'em entered in all these books? That would drive me nuts." The blond man put his feet on the desk and looked up at the shelf full of ledgers.

"Naa. Only in the current book—here, on the desk. Them books go all the way back to when the hospital started. I don't know why they keep 'em out here. Only once in a while the Medical Examiner's office comes nosing around, wanting to look up something away back, and I dust 'em off. This ain't a bad job at all. Plenty of time on your hands. Say—I better not have any more right now. We got an old battle-ax, the night supervisor. She might come down and give me hell. Claim I was showing up drunk. I never showed up drunk on the job yet. And she never comes down after three o'clock. It ain't bad."

Cool blue eyes had picked out a volume marked *1900*.

Jerry rattled on. "Say, y'know that actress, Doree Evarts—the one that did the Dutch night before last in the hotel across the way? They couldn't save her. This evening, 'bout eight o'clock, I got a call to collect one from West Five—that's private. It was her. I got her in the icebox now. Wanna see her?"

The stranger set down his glass. His face was white but he said, "Sure thing. I ain't never seen a dead stripper. Boy, oh, boy, but I seen her when she was alive. She used to flash 'em."

The morgue man said, "Come on. I'll introduce you."

In the corridor were icebox doors in three tiers. Jerry went down the line, unlatched one and pulled out a tray. On it lay a form covered by a cheap cotton sheet which he drew back with a flourish.

Doree Evarts had cut her wrists. What lay on the galvanized tray was like a dummy, eyes half open, golden hair damp and matted. The nostrils and mouth were plugged with cotton.

There were the breasts Doree had snapped by their nipples under the amber spotlight, the belly which rotated for the crowd of smoke-packed old men and pimply kids, the long legs which spread in the final bump as she made her exit. Her nail polish was chipped and broken off; a tag with her name on it was tied to one thumb; her wrists were bandaged.

"Good-looking tomato—once." Jerry pulled up the sheet, slid in the drawer and slammed the door. They went back to the office and the visitor knocked off two quick brandies.

Doree had found the end of the alley. What had she been running from that made her slice at her veins? Nightmare coming closer. What force inside her head, under the taffy-colored hair, pushed her into this?

The dank office swam in the heat of the brandy as Jerry's voice clattered on. "You get lotsa laughs some nights. One time—last winter it was—we had a real heavy night. I mean a real night. They was conking out like flies, I'm telling you. Lotsa old folks. Every five, ten minutes the phone'd ring: 'Jerry, come on up, we got another one.' I'm telling you, I didn't get a minute's peace all night. Finally I got the bottom row of boxes filled and then the second row. Now, I didn't want to go sticking 'em up in that top row—I'd have to get two ladders and two other guys to help me lift 'em. Well, what would you do? Sure. I doubled 'em up. Well, along about four o'clock the old battle-ax phones down and asks me where such-and-such a stiff is and I tell her—it was a dame. Then she asks about a guy and I look up the book and I tell her. Well, I'd shoved 'em into the same box. What the hell—they was dead people! She blows up and you shoulda heard her."

Good Christ, was this guy never going to shut up and get out for a minute? Just one minute would be enough. On the shelf over Jerry's head. *1900.*

"She was raising hell. She says, 'Jerry'—you shoulda heard her; you wouldn't believe it—'Jerry, I think you might have the decency'—those was her very words—'I think you might have the decency not to put men and women together in the same refrigerator compartment!' Can you beat that? I says to her, I says, 'Miss Leary, do you mean to insinuate that I should go encouraging homo-sex-uality amongst these corpses?'" Jerry leaned back in his swivel chair, slapping his thigh, and his companion laughed until tears came, getting the tightness worked out of his nerves.

"Oh, you shoulda heard her rave then! Wait a minute—there's the phone." He listened, then said, "Right away, keed," and pushed back his chair. "Got a customer. Be right back. Gimme a shot before I go."

His hard heels rang off down the corridor. The elevator stopped, opened, closed, and hummed as it went up.

1900. May 28th. Age: 95, 80, 73, 19 . . . 19 . . . Doris Mae Cadle. Diagnosis: septicemia. Admitted—hell, where was she from? No origin. Name, age, diagnosis. The only young one on the 28th and on the page before and after it. The elevator was coming down and he shoved the ledger back in its place.

Jerry stood in the doorway, swaying slightly, his face glistening. "Wanna give me a hand? A fat one! Jesus!"

"No. She ain't lived here in my time. 'Course, I only took over the house eight years ago. Mis' Meriwether had the house before me. She's been in the Home for the Blind ever since. Cataracts, you know."

A soft, cultured voice said: "Mrs. Meriwether, I hate to bother you with what is, after all, only a hobby of mine. I am a genealogist, you see. I am looking up the branches of my mother's family—the Cadles. And in an old city directory I noted that someone by that name lived at the house which you ran as a rooming house about thirty-five years ago. Of course, I don't expect you to remember."

"Young man, I certainly do remember. A fine girl she was,

Doris Cadle. Remember it like it was yesterday. Some kind of blood poisoning. Took her to the hospital. Too late. Died. Buried in Potter's Field. I didn't know where her folks was. I would have put up the money to get her a plot only I didn't have it. I tried to get up a purse but none of my roomers could make it up."

"She was one of the Cadles of New Jersey?"

"Might a been. Only, as I recall, she come from Tewkesbury, Pennsylvania."

"Tell me, Mrs. Meriwether, are you related to the Meriwethers of Massachusetts?"

"Well, now, young man, that's right interesting. I had a grandmother come from Massachusetts. On my father's side she was. Now, if you're interested in the Meriwethers—"

"Mrs. Cadle, I thought I had all the data I needed but there are a couple of other questions I'd like to ask for the government records." The dark suit, the brief case, the horn-rimmed glasses over a polka-dot bow tie, all spoke of the servant of government.

"Come in. I been tryin' to find Dorrie's pitcher. Ain't seen it sence I showed it to you a while ago."

"Doris Mae. That was your second child, I believe. But you put the picture back in the Bible, Mrs. Cadle."

His voice sounded dry and bored. He must get awful tired, pestering folks this way all day and every day.

"Let's look again. Here—here it is. You just didn't look far enough. Did I ask you the date of your daughter's graduation from high school?"

"Never graddiated. She took a business course and run off to New York City and we never seen her no more."

"Thank you. You said your husband worked in the mines from the age of thirteen. How many accidents did he have in that time? That is, accidents that caused him to lose one or more days from work?"

"Oh, Lord, I can sure tell you about them! I mind one time just after we was married . . ."

The collector of vital statistics walked slowly toward the town's single trolley line. In his brief case was a roll of film recording both sides of a postcard. One was a cheap photograph of a young girl, taken at Coney Island. She was sitting in a prop rowboat named *Sea Breeze*, and holding an oar. Behind her was a painted lighthouse. On the message side was written in precise, characterless handwriting:

Dear Mom and all,

I am sending this from Coney Island. It's like the biggest fair you ever saw. A boy named Spunk took me. Isn't that a silly nickname? I had my picture taken as you can see. Tell Pop and all I wish I was with you and hug little Jennie for me. Will write soon.

Fondly,

DORRIE

Conversation flattened out to an eager rustle as the Rev. Carlisle entered the room and walked to the lectern in the glass alcove, where ferns and palms caught the summer sun in a tumult of green. The rest of the room was cool and dark, with drawn hangings before the street windows.

He opened the Bible with the gold-plated clasps, ran his hands once over his hair, then gazed straight out above the heads of the congregation which had assembled in the Church of the Heavenly Message.

"My text this morning is from Ephesians Five, verses eight and nine: *'For ye were sometimes darkness, but now are ye light in the Lord: walk as children of light: for the fruit of the Spirit is in all goodness and righteousness and truth . . .'*"

Mrs. Prescott was late, damn her. Or was it the mark who was holding up the works? He must be the kind of bastard that always comes late—thinks the world will hold the curtain waiting for him.

Blue eyes lifted from the page and smiled their blessing on the faces before them. About twenty in the house with a few odd husbands dragged along; and a couple of male believers.

"Dearly beloved, on this day of summer, with God's glorious sunlight illuminating the world, we find an object lesson in its brilliance . . ."

Where was Tallentyre? She was supposed to ride herd on Prescott and the mark.

". . . for we, who once walked in darkness of fear and ignorance and doubt, find our path through the earth-plane made bright and shining by the surety of our faith."

At the other end of the shadowy room the front door opened and closed. In the dim light two stout women in flowered print dresses came in—Tallentyre and Prescott. Son-of-a-bitch! Did the chump back out at the last minute? With a flash of anxiety Stan wondered if somebody might have wised him up.

Then in the doorway a man appeared, big, in a light gray flannel suit, holding a panama in his hand. A black silhouette in the gentle glow cast by the fanlight. The spread of shoulder spoke of arrogant ownership. The man was an owner—land, buildings, acres, machines. And men. Two round, owl-like saucers of light winked from the dark head—the light of the conservatory reflected from rimless glasses as he turned his head, whispering to Prescott. Then he sat down in the back row, pulling out one of the bridge chairs to make room for his legs.

The Rev. Carlisle drew breath and fixed his eyes on the gold-embossed Bible before him.

"My dear friends, let me tell you a story. There was a man who had been in the Great War. One dark night he was sent scouting into No Man's Land with one of his buddies—a star shell rose from the enemy trenches and illuminated the field. Well might he have prayed at that moment with David, *'Hide me from my deadly enemies who compass me about.'* The man of whom I speak dashed for the security of a shell hole, pushing his companion aside, while the machine guns of the Germans began to fill the field with death."

Ezra Grindle was fanning himself idly with his panama.

"The soldier who was left without cover fell, mortally wounded. And before the baleful glare of the star shell died, the other soldier, crouching in the shell crater, saw his companion's eyes fixed on him in a mute look of scorn and accusation.

"My dear friends, years passed. The survivor became a pillar of society—married, a father, respected in his community. But always, deep in his soul, was the memory of that dying boy's face—the eyes—accusing him!"

The panama was motionless.

"This man recently became interested in Spiritual Truth. He began to attend the church of a medium who is a dear friend of mine in a city out west. He unburdened his heart to the medium. And when they finally established contact with the 'buddy' whose earth life was lost through his cowardice, what do you suppose were the first words the friend in spirit uttered to that guilt-ridden man? They were, 'You are forgiven.'

"Picture to yourselves, my friends, the unutterable joy which rose in that man's tortured heart when the crushing weight of guilt was lifted from him and for the first time in all those years he was a free man—drinking in the sun and the soft wind and the bird song of dawn and eventide."

Grindle was leaning forward, one hand on the back of the chair in front of him. Mrs. Prescott whispered something in his ear; but he was deaf to it. He seemed caught and held by the voice of the man behind the lectern, a man in white linen with a black clerical vest, whose hair, in the shaft of summer sun, was as golden as his voice.

"My dear friends, there is no need for *God* to forgive us. How can we sin against the wind which blows across the fields of ripening grain, how can we injure the soft scent of lilacs in the spring twilight, the deep blue of an autumn sky or the eternal glory of the stars on a winter's night? No, no, my friends. We can sin only against mankind. And man, in his next mansion of the soul, says to us tenderly, lovingly, 'You are forgiven, beloved. When you join us you will know. Until then, go with our love, rejoice in our forgiveness, take strength from us who live forever in the shadow of his hand.'"

The tears had mounted to the clergyman's eyes and now, in the light of the alcove, they glistened faintly on his cheeks as he stopped speaking, standing erect with the bearing of an emperor in his chariot.

"Let us pray."

At the back of the room a man who had spent his life ruining competitors, bribing congressmen, breaking strikes, arming vigilantes, cheating stockholders, and endowing homes for unwed mothers, covered his eyes with his hand.

"Reverend, they tell me you bring voices out of trumpets."

"I have *heard* voices from trumpets. I don't bring them.

They come. Mediumship is either a natural gift or it is acquired by devotion, by study, and by patience."

The cigars had cost Stan twenty dollars; but he pushed the box across the desk easily and took one himself, holding his lighter for the tycoon. The Venetian blinds were drawn, the windows open, and the fan whirring comfortably.

Grindle inhaled the cigar twice, let the smoke trickle from his nostrils, approved it, and settled farther back in his chair.

As if suddenly remembering an appointment, the spiritualist said, "Excuse me," and jotted notes on a calendar pad. He let Grindle smoke on while he made a telephone call, then turned back to him, smiling, waiting.

"I don't care about trumpet phenomena in *your* house. I want to see it in *my* house."

The clergyman's face was stern. "Mr. Grindle, spirit phenomena are not a performance. They are a religious experience. We cannot say where and when they will appear. They are no respecters of houses. Those who have passed over may reveal themselves in the humble cottage of the laborer and ignore completely the homes of wealth, of culture, and of education."

The big man nodded. "I follow you there, Carlisle. In one of your sermons you said something about Spiritualism being the only faith that offers *proof* of survival. I remember you said that the command 'Show me' is the watchword of American business. Well, you hit the nail right on the head that time. I'm just asking to be shown, that's all. That's fair enough."

The minister's smile was unworldly and benign. "I am at your service if I can strengthen your resolve to find out more for yourself."

They smoked, Grindle eyeing the spiritualist, Carlisle seemingly deep in meditation.

At the left of Grindle's chair stood a teakwood coffee table, a relic of the Peabody furnishings. On it sat a small Chinese gong of brass. The silence grew heavy and the industrialist seemed to be trying to force the other man to break it first; but neither broke it. The little gong suddenly spoke—a clear, challenging note.

Grindle snatched it from the table, turning it upside down

and examining it. Then he picked up the table and knocked the top with his knuckles. When he looked up again he found the Rev. Carlisle smiling at him.

"You may have the gong—and the table, Mr. Grindle. It never before has rung by an exudation of psychic power— what we call the odylic force—as it did just now. Someone must be trying to get through to you. But it is difficult—your innate skepticism is the barrier."

On the big man's face Stan could read the conflict—the fear of being deceived against the desire to see marvels and be forgiven by Doris Mae Cadle, 19, septicemia, May 28, 1900: *But I tell you, Dorrie, if we get married now it will smash everything, everything.*

Grindle leaned forward, poking the air with the two fingers which gripped his cigar. "Reverend, out in my Jersey plant I've got an apothecary's scale delicate enough to weigh a human hair—just one human hair! It's in a glass case. You make that scale move and I'll give your church ten thousand dollars!"

The Rev. Carlisle shook his head. "I'm not interested in money, Mr. Grindle. You may be rich. Perhaps I am too—in a different way." He stood up but Grindle stayed where he was. "If you wish to arrange a séance in your own home or anywhere else, I can try to help you. But I should warn you— the place does not matter. *What matters is the spiritual environment.*" He had been speaking slowly, as if weighing something in his mind, but the last sentence was snapped out as if he had come to a decision.

"But God damn it—pardon me, Reverened—but I know all this! You'll get full co-operation from me. I've got an open mind, Carlisle. An open mind. And the men I'll pick for our committee will have open minds too—or they'll hear from me later. When can you come?"

"In three weeks I shall have a free evening."

"No good. In three weeks I'll have to be up in Quebec. And I've got this bee in my bonnet. I want to find out once and for all, Carlisle. Show me one tiny speck of incontrovertible evidence and I'll listen to anything else you have to say. Can't you consider this an emergency and come out to the plant tonight?" Stan had moved toward the door and Grindle followed him. "Mr. Grindle, I believe you are a sincere seeker."

They descended the carpeted stairs and stood for a moment at the front door. "Then you'll come, Reverend? Tonight?"

Carlisle bowed.

"That's splendid. I'll send the car for you at six. Will that be all right? Or how about coming out earlier and having dinner at the plant? We all eat in the same cafeteria, right with the men. Democratic. But the food's good."

"I shall not want anything very heavy, thank you. I'll have a bite before six."

"Right. The car will pick you up here at the church." Grindle smiled for the first time. It was a chilly smile, tight around the eyes, but was probably his best attempt. Stan looked at the big man closely.

Hair thin and sandy. Forehead domed and spattered with freckles. A large rectangle of a face with unobtrusive, petulant features set in the center of it. Habitual lines about the mouth as if etched there by gas pains, or by constantly smelling a faintly foul odor. Voice peevish and high-pitched, bluster on the surface, fear underneath. Afraid somebody will get a dime away from him or a dime's worth of power. Waistline kept in by golf and a rowing machine. Maybe with shoulder braces to lean against when troubles try to make him stoop like one of his bookkeepers. Hands large, fingers covered with reddish fur. A big, irritable, unsatisfied, guilt-driven, purse-proud, publicity-inflamed dummy—stuffed with thousand dollar bills.

The hand which the Rev. Carlisle raised as a parting gesture was like a benediction—in the best possible taste.

When Stan got back to the apartment it was two o'clock in the afternoon. Molly was still asleep. He jerked the sheet off her and began tickling her in the ribs. She woke up cross and laughing. "Stan, stop it! Oh—oh, honey, it must be good news! What is it?"

"It's the live One, kid. He's nibbling at last. Séance tonight out at his joint in Jersey. If it goes over we're set! If not, we're in the soup. Now go out and get me a kitten."

"A what? Stan, you feeling okay?"

"Sure, sure, sure. Fall into some clothes and go out and

find me a delicatessen store that has a kitten. Bring it back with you. Never mind if you have to swipe it."

When she had gone he eased the eraser from the end of a pencil, wedged the pencil in the jamb of a door and bored into the shaft with a hand drill. Then he pushed the eraser back and put the pencil in his pocket.

The kitten was a little tiger tom about three months old.

"Damn, it couldn't be a white one!"

"But, honey, I didn't know what you wanted with it."

"Never mind, kid. You did okay." He shut himself and the kitten up in the bathroom for half an hour. Then he came out and said to Molly, "Here. Now you can take him back."

"Take him back? But I promised the man I'd give him a good home. Aw, Stan, I thought we could keep him." She was winking back tears.

"Okay, okay, kid. Keep him. Do anything you want with him. If this deal goes over I'll buy you a pedigreed panther."

He hurried back to the church, and Molly set a saucer of milk on the floor and watched the kitten lap it up. She decided to call him Buster.

"Here's where the Grindle property starts, sir," said the chauffeur. They had rolled through Manhattan, under the river with the tunnel walls gleaming, past the smoke of North Jersey and across a desolation of salt marshes. Ahead of them, over a flat waste of cinders and struggling marsh grass, the smokestack and long, glass-roofed buildings of the Grindle Electric Motor Corporation rose glittering in the last sunlight.

The car slowed down at a gate in a barbed fence around the top of which ran wire held by insulators.

The private cop on duty at the gate nodded to the chauffeur and said, "Go right in, Mr. Carlisle. Report at Gatehouse Number Five."

They drove down a gravel road and came to another wire fence and Gatehouse Number Five. "Have to go in and register, sir," said the chauffeur.

Inside the concrete shack a man in a gray military shirt, a Sam Browne belt and a dark blue cap, was sitting at a desk. He was reading a tabloid; when he looked up Stan read his life history from the face: Thrown off some small city police force for excessive brutality; or caught in a shakedown and sent up—the face bore the marks of the squad room and the prison, one on top of the other.

"Carlisle? Waiting for you. Sign this card." It projected from a machine like a cash register. Stan signed. Then the cop said, "Pull the card out." Stan grasped its waxed surface and pulled. "Watch out—don't tear it. Better use both hands."

The Rev. Carlisle used both hands. But what was it all about? He handed the card to Thickneck, then realized that he had left them a record of his fingerprints on its waxed surface.

"Now step inside here and I'll go through the regulations."

It was a small dressing room.

"Take off your coat and hand it to me."

"May I ask what this is for?"

"Orders of Mr. Anderson, Head of Plant Security."

"Does Mr. Grindle know about this?"

"Search me, Reverend; you can ask him. Now give me your coat. Anderson is tightening up on regulations lately."

"But what are you searching for?"

Stumpy fingers felt in pockets and along seams. "Sabotage, Reverend. Nothing personal. The next guy might be a senator, but we'd have to frisk him." The examination included the Rev. Carlisle's shoes, his hatband and the contents of his wallet. As the cop was returning the vest a pencil fell out; he picked it up and handed it to the clergyman who stuck it in his pocket. On his way out Stan gave the cop a cigar. It was immediately locked up in the green metal desk, and the Great Stanton wondered if it was later tagged, "Bribe offered by the Rev. Stanton Carlisle. Exhibit A."

At the door of the plant a thin, quick-moving man of thirty-odd with black patent-leather hair stepped out and introduced himself. "My name's Anderson, Mr. Carlisle. Head of Plant Security." The left lapel of his blue serge suit bulged ever so slightly. "The committee is waiting for you."

Elevators. Corridors. Plaster walls pale green. A white spot painted on the floor in all the corners. "They'll never spit in a corner painted white." The hum of machines and the clank of yard engines outside. Then one glass-paneled door opening on a passage walled with oak. Carpets on the floor. The re-

ception room belonged in an advertising agency; it was a
sudden burst of smooth, tawny leather and chrome.

"This way, Mr. Carlisle."

Anderson went ahead, holding open doors. The directors'
room was a long one with a glass roof but no windows. The
table down its center must have been built there; certainly it
could never be taken out now.

Grindle was shaking his hand and presenting him to the
others: Dr. Downes, plant physician; Mr. Elrood of the legal
staff; Dr. Gilchrist, the industrial psychologist, also on the
plant staff; Professor Dennison, who taught philosophy at
Grindle College; Mr. Prescott ("You know Mrs. Prescott, I
believe, through the church.") and Mr. Roy, both directors
of the company. With Anderson and Grindle they made
eight—Daniel Douglas Home's traditional number for a séance. Grindle knew more than he let on. But didn't his kind
always?

At the far end of the table—it seemed a city block away—
stood a rectangular glass case a foot high; inside it was an
apothecary's precision balance, a cross arm with two circular
pans suspended from it by chains.

Grindle was saying, "Would you care to freshen up a little?
I have an apartment right off this room where I stay when
I'm working late."

It was furnished much like Lilith's waiting room. Stan shut
the bathroom door and washed sweat from his palms. "If I
get away with it this time," he whispered to the mirror, "it's
the Great Stanton and no mistake. Talk about your Princeton
audiences . . ."

One last look around the drawing room revealed a flowing
cloud of blue fur, out of which shone eyes of bright yellow as
the cat streamed down from a chair and floated along the floor
toward him. Stan's forehead smoothed out. "Come to papa,
baby. Now it's in the bag."

When he joined the committee he was carrying the cat in
his arms and Grindle smiled his tight, unpracticed smile. "I
see you've made friends with Beauty. But won't she disturb
you?"

"On the contrary. I'd like to have her stay. And now, perhaps you gentlemen will tell me what this interesting appa-

ratus is and how it works." He dropped the cat gently to the carpet, where she tapped his leg once with her paw, demanding to be taken up again, then crawled under the table to sulk.

The head of Plant Security stood with his hand resting on top of the glass. "This is a precision balance, Mr. Carlisle. An apothecary's scale. The indicator in the center of the bar registers the slightest pressure on either of the two pans. I had one of our boys rig up a set of electrical contacts under the pans so that if either one is depressed—by so much as the weight of a hair—this electric bulb in the corner of the case flashes on. The thing is self-contained; flashlight batteries in the case supply current. The balance has been set level and in this room there are no vibrations to disturb it. I watched it for an hour this afternoon and the light never flashed. To turn on that light some force must depress one of the pans of the balance. Is that clear?"

The Rev. Carlisle smiled spiritually. "May I inspect it?"

Anderson glanced at Grindle, who nodded. The private police chief opened the doors of the case and hovered close. "Don't touch anything, Reverend."

"I'm afraid I don't understand much about electricity. But you're sure that this lighting device hasn't interfered with the free movement of the scale? What are these copper strips?" He pointed to them with the end of a pencil from which the eraser was missing, indicating two narrow metal strips leading from under the pans of the balance to insulated connections behind it.

"They're contact points. Two on each side. If either pan moves it touches these points, closes the circuit and the light goes on." Anderson swiftly shut the glass doors and latched them.

The Rev. Carlisle was not listening. His face had grown blank. Moving as if in a dream, he returned to the far end of the room and slipped down into the chair at the end of the table, thirty feet from the mechanism in its glass house.

Without speaking, Grindle motioned the others to their places—Anderson on Stan's left, Grindle taking a chair on his right, the rest on either side. The precision balance had half the long table to itself.

The Rev. Carlisle closed his eyes, folded his arms, and

placed his head upon them as if trying to catch a nap. His breathing deepened, jerky and rasping. Once he stirred and muttered something incoherent.

"He's gone into a trance?"

The boss must have shut the speaker up with a look.

Silence grew. Then Grindle scratched a match to light a cigar and several others took courage and smoked. The room was in semi-darkness and the tension of the waiting men piled up.

The medium had been searched at the gate. Their eyes had been on him every second since he arrived. He had never touched the instrument—Anderson had been watching him for the slightest move. They had all been warned to look out for threads, or for attempts to tilt the massive table. Mr. Roy had quietly slipped from his chair and was sitting on the floor, watching the medium's feet beneath the table even though they were thirty feet from the balance. The scale was enclosed in glass; Anderson had latched the doors. And this medium claimed to be able to move solids without touching them! They waited.

On his right Stan could feel the great man, his attention frozen on the rectangular glass frame. They waited. Time was with the spiritualist. This was a better break than he had ever dreamed of. First the cat showing up, then this magnificent nerve-racking stall for the committee. Would it work after all?

He heard Grindle whisper, "Beauty—Beauty, come here!"

Stan raised his head, moaning a little, and from under one eyelid saw that the cat had wriggled from Grindle's lap and now stood gazing into the balance case.

A gasp ran around the waiting circle. The light had snapped on, burning clear and ruby-red, a tiny bulb, Christmas-tree size, in an upright socket in one corner.

Stan moaned again, his hands closing into fists. The light went out; his fists relaxed.

Grindle cut short the buzzing whispers by a snap of his fingers.

Another wait. Stan's breath came heavier. He felt the saliva in his mouth thickening; his tongue was dry, the saliva like cotton; he forced it out over his lower lip. This was one time when he didn't have to fake the foam.

The light flared again and the medium's breathing became a whistling, agonizing battle.

Off again. Stan let out a sigh.

Silence. Time ticking by on someone's wrist watch. At the foot of the table the Persian looked back, frowning, at Grindle, saying in cat talk, "Let me get into that glass box."

The light again. This time it stayed on. Anderson slid from his seat while Stan's heart pounded but Grindle motioned him back and he compromised by standing in his place. From under folded arms Stan could see Anderson's lean hand, the nails softly polished, braced against the mahogany as he bent forward. The light went out.

This time the medium trembled and threw himself back in his chair, his head lolling. Thickly he said, "Open the case. Let the air into it! Take the cover off and examine the apparatus. Hurry!"

Anderson was already there. The Rev. Carlisle crumpled down in his chair, eyes closed, the foam thick on his lower lip and chin.

Through slit lids he could see Anderson and the psychologist taking the balance from its box. Beauty had stood close by and now was tapping with her paw at the metal contacts on the floor of the case. Grindle picked her up, squirming, and shut her up in the apartment.

Then Stan felt something touch his lips; he let his eyelids flick open. The doctor was standing over him, holding a bit of sterile gauze which he dropped into a flat glass culture dish, putting it back in his pocket. Go ahead, you goddamned wisenheimer townie, analyze it for soap! I could give you a good specimen right in the eye.

Now Grindle had Stan by the arm and was leading him toward the apartment. Over his shoulder he said, "Good evening, gentlemen. You may go."

With Grindle alone Stan began to recover. The industrialist offered him brandy and he drank it slowly. Beauty stared at him from hot, yellow eyes.

"I'll have the car take you back to New York, Mr. Carlisle, as soon as you feel up to traveling."

"Oh, thank you so much. I—I feel a little shaky. Did any phenomena occur?"

"The light in the cabinet went on three times." Behind the
rimless glasses Grindle's gray, small eyes almost flashed.
"That's proof enough for me, Mr. Carlisle. I shan't drag you
all the way out here again. I told you I'm a hard-headed man.
I needed proof. Well—" His voice broke with a tiny shading
of emotion which habitual restraint could not hide. "I've seen
something tonight that cannot possibly be explained by fraud
or trickery. The conditions were absolutely air-tight. Some
force inside the case depressed the pans of that balance and if
anybody ever talks to me about magnets I'll laugh right in
his face. The instrument is made of brass. This plant is miles
from city vibrations—it's rooted in concrete. There were
no threads. You never came near the thing; never touched
it. . . ."

Grindle was pacing the carpet, smoking furiously, his face
flushed.

The Rev. Carlisle finished his brandy and stretched out an
affectionate hand to the Persian cat. Safe! This was the money-
bags mountain and he stood, not on the top of it, but in sight
of the top. He rose at last, rubbing his eyes wearily. The great
man had been talking.

". . . ten thousand dollars. I told you I'd do it and I mean
what I say. The check will reach you."

"Please, Mr. Grindle, let's not talk about money. If I have
given you proof—"

"Well, you have. You have, man! Let me—"

"The church can always use donations, Mr. Grindle. You
can take care of that through Mrs. Prescott. I know she will
be pleased. A fine, devoted woman. But for me it is enough
to know that some little corner of the glorious truth has been
revealed."

Beauty, lolling in the most comfortable chair in the room,
suddenly started up and began to scratch her chin with her
hind foot. Stan eased Grindle away toward the door. As it
closed behind them he saw Beauty biting industriously at the
fur over her ribs.

On the steps of the plant its owner paused. From his pocket
he took out two envelopes, held them to the light and handed
one to Stan. "Here—might as well give you this now, Carlisle.

I was going to send it to Mrs. Prescott as you suggested, but you can save me the trouble. This other we won't need." He tore the envelope and its contents to bits.

"I don't understand, Mr. Grindle."

The smile broke out again with a glitter of white teeth. "It was a warrant for your arrest—in case you tried any fraudulent methods of producing phenomena. It wasn't my idea, Mr. Carlisle. I have to take advice once in a while, you know, from some of the boys who look after my interests."

Stan was erect and the blue eyes were hard. "That warrant was signed by a judge?"

"I presume so."

"And on what grounds was I supposed to be arrested—if you or one of your employees thought he detected trickery?"

"Why, with conspiracy with intent to defraud."

"And how would I have defrauded you, Mr. Grindle? Out of taxi fare from New York?"

The big man frowned. "You understand, I had nothing to do with it. Mr. Anderson—"

"You may tell Mr. Anderson," said the Rev. Carlisle tautly, "that I would be quite capable of suing for false arrest. I have never taken a penny for exercising gifts of mediumship. I never shall. Good night, sir."

He got into the waiting car and said coldly to the driver, "Just to the railroad station—don't drive me all the way in to New York."

Grindle stood gaping after him, then turned and went back to the plant.

Anderson was a good lad, devoted, devoted. Couldn't ask for more loyalty. But God damn it, he didn't understand. He just didn't understand the deeper, the spiritual things of life. Well, from now on Andy would be told to keep his nose out of psychic research.

The others had left the directors' room but Anderson was still there. He was attacking the end of the conference table with mighty heaves, trying to make the light flash.

"Give it up, Andy," the Chief said acidly. "On home. Go on."

"I'll find out how he did it! He did something."

"Andy, you can't find it in your soul anywhere to admit that it might have been an odylic force that you can't see or feel or measure?"

"Nuts, Chief. I know a hustler when I see one."

"I said go home, Andy."

"You're the boss."

As he was leaving Grindle called to him: "And fire the woman you had taking care of Beauty's coat. It's a disgrace—she's been neglected."

Anderson's voice was smoldering but weary. "What is it now, Chief?"

"It's disgusting—Beauty's coat is swarming with fleas."

"Okay, Chief. She gets the gate tomorrow." He walked quickly from the plant, found his car in the parking lot and rammed in the ignition key irritably. That goddamned phoney reverend. He would be just the one to weasel inside the Chief. And the Chief would protect him. But how in the jumping blue blazes of merry hell did he ever turn that light on and off inside the case? Odylic force, balls!

"Is that your odylic force, Reverend?"

"Yeah. That's it, babe. Like it?"

She chuckled, warm and enfolding, beneath him in the dark of the bedroom.

"Wait, lover. Let's rest."

They rested. Stan said, "He's going overboard, all right. He's not so tough—just another chump."

"Go easy with him, Stan."

"I'm easy. Every test a little stronger until he's fattened up for the full-form stuff. There's only one thing—"

"Molly?"

"Yeah, Molly. That dame's going to give us a lot of trouble."

"She can be handled."

"Yeah. But it wears you out, handling. Lilith, I'm sick of the dame. She's like a rock around my neck."

"Patience, darling. There's no one else."

They lay silent for a time, seeing each other with their finger tips and with their mouths.

"Lilith—"

"What, lover?"

"What does that guy really want? I've beaten him over the head with 'forgiveness' but I get only half a response. He doesn't gobble it. There's something else. Okay. We bring back the dead dame. She tells him he's forgiven and everything's jake. But where do we go from there?"

Dr. Lilith Ritter, at the moment in a very unethical but satisfying position in relation to one of her patients, laughed deep in her throat.

"What does he want to *do*? With his first love? Don't be so naïve, lover. He wants to do this . . . and this . . ."

"But—no; that's no good. Not with Molly. She'll never—"

"Oh, yes, she will."

"Lilith, I know that dame. She never stepped out of line once in all the years we been teamed up. I can't sell her on jazzing the chump."

"Yes, you can, darling."

"Christ's sake, *how?*"

The warm mouth closed his and he forgot Molly and the con game which kept him in a torment of scheming. Through their pressed lips Lilith murmured, "I'll tell you when the time comes."

The psychic lamp, provided by the Rev. Carlisle, shed no light except through a single dark-red disc in the center of its tin slide. The medium, dressed in a black silk robe, black silk pajamas and slippers, lay back in an armchair on one side of the billiard-room doorway. Grindle, in his shirtsleeves, sat opposite him, the lamp on a coffee table at his side. Dark curtains covered the door and a faint breeze tugged at them. Carlisle had raised one window in the inner room a few inches for ventilation. It was not open far enough for a man to stick his head through and it had been sealed. Grindle had pressed his signet ring into the hot wax. The other windows were sealed shut. There was a fifteen foot drop to the lawn outside, which sloped down to the river.

Beyond the darkened billiard room the two men waited. The medium's head was thrown back. His left wrist was fastened to Grindle's right by a long strand of copper wire, and he had poured salt water on their wrists.

The heel of the reverend's slipper was pressed tight against the leg of his chair.

Rap!

It seemed to come from the table bearing the red lantern.

Rap!

"Is there one in spirit life speaking?" The medium's words were a hoarse whisper.

Rap! Rap! Rap!

"We greet you. Are conditions favorable? May we turn up the lamp a little?"

Three more raps answered him. Grindle leaned over and raised the lamp's wick until a warning rap commanded him to stop. His big face was intent and ill at ease, but Stan detected no craft or outright skepticism. He was interested, moving in the right direction.

They waited. More silence. Then from beyond the dark draperies of the doorway came another knock—a hollow, musical sound, as if something had struck the window. Grindle started from his chair but the warning, upraised hand of the spiritualist stopped him. Carlisle's breathing came fast now, and heavy, and he seemed to lose consciousness.

The "sitter" began to sweat. Did he imagine a tingling discharge of current at his wrist where the wire was bound?

Another sound, a distinct click, from the billiard room. Then a whole chorus of clicks which he made out to be billiard balls, knocking against one another, sometimes in rhythm, as if they were dancing.

Sweat began to roll from the industrialist's forehead. It was a hot night, but not that hot. His shirt was sticking to his chest and his hands were dripping.

The ghostly billiard game went on; then a white ivory ball rolled out from under the curtains and hit the table-leg between him and the medium.

Carlisle stirred uneasily and a voice came from his stiff lips: "*Hari Aum!* Greetings, newcomer to the Life of Spiritual Truth. Greetings, our new *chela*. Believe not blindly. Believe the proof of the mind given you by the senses. They cannot give you the Truth but they point the Path. Trust my disciple, Stanton Carlisle. He is an instrument on which spiritual forces play as a lover plays his *sitar* beneath the window of his beloved. Greetings, Ezra. A friend has come to you from Spirit Life. *Hari Aum!*"

The resonant, accented chanting broke off. Grindle snapped his attention from the lips of the medium to the curtains before the darkened room. The clicks of billiard balls now sounded closer, as if they were rolling and knocking on the floor just beyond the curtains. He stared, his lips drawn back from his dentures, his breath whistling. A white ball rolled slowly from under the curtains and stopped six inches inside the room where they sat. The red cue ball followed it. Click!

While he watched, the hairs on the back of the big man's neck raised, the skin drew tight over his temples. For in the dim, ruby light a tiny hand felt its way out from under the curtains, groped delicately for the red ball, found it, and rolled it after the white one. Click! And the hand was gone.

With an unconscious shout Grindle leaped up and threw himself after the vanishing hand, only to spin around and claw at the curtains of the doorway to keep himself from falling. For his right wrist was firmly secured by copper wire to the wrist of the medium who was now groaning and gasping, his eyes half open and rolled up, until the whites looked as stark as the eyes of a blind beggar.

Then Grindle felt the room beyond them to be empty and still. He stood, fighting for breath, making no further attempt to enter.

The medium drew a long breath and opened his eyes. "We can remove the wire now. Were there any phenomena of note?"

Grindle nodded, still watching the doorway. "Get me out of this harness, Reverend! I want a look in there."

Stan helped unwind the wire and said, "One favor, Mr. Grindle—I wonder if you could get me a glass of brandy?"

His host poured him one and knocked off two straight ones himself. "All set?"

He drew the curtains and snapped the wall switch.

A reassuring glow fell from the hanging lamp above the billiard table. Stan's hand on his arm restrained him from entering.

"Careful, Mr. Grindle. Remember our test precautions."

The floor had been thickly sprinkled with talcum powder. Now it bore traces, and as Grindle knelt to examine them he saw with a chill that they were the unmistakable bare footprints of a small child.

He rose, wiping his face with a wad of handkerchief. The room had been the scene of grotesque activity. Cues had been taken from their racks and thrust into the open mouths of stuffed sailfish on the wall. The cue chalk had been thrown down and smashed. And everywhere were the tiny footprints.

Carlisle stood in the doorway for a moment, then turned back and sank into his chair and covered his eyes with his hand as if he were very tired.

At last the light in the billiard room snapped off and Grindle stood beside him, pale, breathing heavily. He poured himself another brandy and gave one to the medium.

Ezra Grindle was shaken as no stock-market crash or sudden South American peace treaty could have shaken him. For with a crumb of cue chalk a message had been written on the green felt of the billiard table. It held the answer to a vast, secret, shameful ache inside him—a canker which had festered all these years. Not a soul in the world could know of its existence but himself—a name he had not spoken in thirty-five years. It held the key to an old wrong which he would willingly give a million hard-earned dollars to square with his conscience. A million? Every cent he owned!

The message was in a characterless, copybook hand:

Spunk darling,
    We tried to come to you but the force was not strong enough. Maybe next time. I so wanted you to see our boy.

DORRIE

He drew the doors together and locked them. He raised his hand for the bell rope, then dropped it, and poured himself another brandy.

At his side stood the tall, silken figure in black, his face compassionate.

"Let us pray together—not for them, Ezra, but for the living, that the scales may fall from their eyes. . . ."

The train to New York was not due for half an hour and

Mrs. Oakes, who had been visiting her daughter-in-law, had read the time table all wrong; now she would have to wait.

On the station platform she walked up and down to relieve her impatience. Then, on a bench, she saw a little figure stretched out, its head pillowed on its arms. Her heart was touched. She shook him gently by the shoulder. "What's the matter, little man? Are you lost? Were you supposed to meet mamma or papa here at the station?"

The sleeper sat up with a snarl. He was the size of a child; but was dressed in a striped suit and a pink shirt with a miniature necktie. And under his button nose was a mustache!

The mustachioed baby pulled a cigarette from his pocket and raked a kitchen match on the seat of his trousers. He lit the cigarette and was about to snap away the match when he grinned up at her from his evil, old baby face, thrust one hand into his coat and drew out a postcard, holding the match so she could see it.

Mrs. Oakes thought she would have a stroke. She tried to run away, but she couldn't. Then the train came and the horrible little creature swung aboard, winking at her.

The Tower

*rises from earth to heaven but
avenging lightning finds its walls.*

BEYOND the garden wall a row of poplars rustled in the
night wind. The moon had not risen; in the gentle darkness the voice was a monotonous, musical ripple, as soothing
as the splash of a fountain.

"Your mind is quiet . . . a lamp in a sheltered corner where
the flame does not flicker. Your body is relaxed. Your heart is
at peace. Your mind is perfectly clear but at ease. Nothing
troubles you. Your mind is a still, calm pool without a ripple . . ."

The big man had a white scarf knotted around his neck and
tucked into his tweed jacket. He let his hands lie easily on the
arms of the deck chair; his legs in tawny flannel trousers were
propped on the footrest.

Beside him the spiritualist in black was all but invisible
under the starlight.

"Close your eyes. When you open them again, stare straight
at the garden wall and tell me what you see."

"It's faint—" Grindle's voice was flaccid and dreamy. All the bite had gone out of it.

"Yes?"

"It's growing clearer. It's a city. A golden city. Towers. Domes. A beautiful city—and now it's gone."

The Rev. Carlisle slipped back into his pocket a "Patent Ghost Thrower, complete with batteries and lenses, to hold 16 millimeter film, $7.98" from a spiritualists' supply house in Chicago.

"You have seen it—the City of Spiritual Light. My control spirit, Ramakrishna, has directed us to build it. It will be patterned after a similar city—which few outsiders have ever seen—in the mountains of Nepal. I myself was permitted to see it under Ramakrishna's guidance. I was teleported physically to the spot. I was leaving the church one snowy night last winter when I felt Ramakrishna near me."

The tycoon's head was nodding belief.

"I was walking through the snow when suddenly the street vanished; it became a stony mountain path. I felt light as air but my feet seemed heavy. That was the altitude. Then, stretching below me in a little valley, I saw the City—just as you have described your vision of it a few moments ago. And I knew that it had been revealed to me for a purpose. Once this realization dawned on me the mountains, the rugged outline of bare peaks and glaciers, softened. They seemed to close in and I was back on the doorstep of the Church of the Heavenly Message. But there, stretching away up the sidewalk, were my own tracks of a few minutes before! A few yards farther on they *stopped. I had dematerialized when I reached that spot.*"

Grindle said, "A wonderful experience. I've heard of such experiences. The holy men of Tibet claim to have them. But I never thought I'd ever meet a man who had reached such psychic heights." His voice was humble and old and a little foolish. Then he started up from his chair.

A vague light had drifted past on the garden wall. It had the shape of a young girl.

The medium said, "You must relax. No tension. All receptivity—all love."

Grindle settled back.

The sky clouded over; the darkness deepened. This time he did not stir but said hopefully, "I—I think I see something, out there by the sundial. Something moving—a spot of light."

It was true. By the shadows at the base of the sundial was a spot of greenish light. Expanding slowly, it moved toward them, a cloud of glowing vapor taking form.

This time the industrialist sat up in spite of Stan's reproving hand on his wrist.

The apparition drifted closer until they could see that it was a girl, dressed in shining garments which floated about her like a mist. Her dark hair was bound by a tiara in which seven bright jewels shone by their own cold light. She seemed to move a few inches above the ground, drifting toward them down a breath of night wind.

The believer's voice had become a feeble, despairing whisper. "Dorrie— Could it be Dorrie?"

"My dear . . ." The materialized form spoke in a voice which seemed part of the garden and the night. "It's Dorrie. But only for a moment. I can't stay . . . it's hard . . . hard to come back, darling."

The Rev. Carlisle's hand tightened on the older man's arm; but the clergyman himself seemed to have passed into a deep trance.

The ghostly figure was fading. It receded, lost outline, sank into a single dot of green glow and then vanished.

"Dorrie—Dorrie—come back. Please come back. Please—" He was on his knees now by the sundial, where the light had disappeared. His broad stern in the tawny slacks was toward Stan, who could have planted a kick right in the middle of it.

Grindle knelt for several seconds, then got to his feet heavily and dropped back into the deck chair, covering his face with his hands.

Beside him the Rev. Carlisle stirred and sat up. "Was there a full materialization? I 'went under' very rapidly. I could feel the force leaving me as the light grew. What happened?"

"I—I saw an old friend."

Molly was so happy she could cry. It had been a long time since they'd had anything like a holiday together. Stan had been acting so screwy she was afraid he was living on Queer Street. And then, all of a sudden, these three days—just driving anywhere, stopping at chicken-dinner shacks and road-houses. Dancing and, in the daytime, going for a swim wherever a lake looked good. It was heaven; she got sad thinking about going back to the flat and starting all over again, doing nothing, just waiting for Stan to come home or something.

Stan was still awfully jumpy and sometimes you'd talk to him and he'd seem to be listening and then he'd say, "What was that, kid?" and you'd have to go through it all over again. But it was great to be getting around like this.

Stan looked nice in a bathing suit. That was something to be thankful for. Some guys were sweet guys but too skinny or with a pot. Stan was just right. She guessed they were both just right by the way other fellows ran their eyes over her chassis when she stepped out on a diving board. What hippos some girls her own age turned out to be!

The Great Stanton pulled himself out of the water and lay beside her on the float. They had the lake all to themselves except for some kids at the other end. He sat looking down at her and then leaned over and kissed her. Molly threw her arms around him. "Oh, honey, don't ever let anything bust us up, honey! All I want is you, Stan."

He slid his arm under her head. "Baby, how'd you like to do this every day in the year? Huh? Well, if this deal goes over we're set. And every day is Christmas."

Molly had a cold, sinking feeling inside her. He had said that so many times. Once it was "Get the house away from old Mrs. Peabody." Always something. She didn't really believe it any more.

He felt her go limp. "Molly! Molly! look at me! Honest to God, this is the thing I've been building toward ever since I started in this racket. I've run myself almost into the nut college building the guy. My foot's never slipped yet. And if you think that guy is easy to handle—"

She pressed her face against his chest and began to cry. "Stan, why do we have to be this way? He seemed like a nice sort of old guy—from what I could tell in the dark up there. I felt like an awful heel, honest. I don't mind taking some guy that thinks he's wise and is trying to be a cheater himself—"

He held her tighter. "Molly, we're in this deeper than you have any idea. That guy has millions. He has a whole private army. You ought to see that joint in Jersey. It's like a fort. If we step on the flypaper from now on they'll turn that bunch of private cops loose on us like a pack of bloodhounds. They'll find us no matter where we scram to. We've got to go into it all the way. I've put him in touch with his girl that died when he was a kid in college. He wants to make it up to her somehow. Money doesn't mean anything to that guy. He's willing to give anything—just to get square with his conscience. He's overboard on the spook dodge. He's letting his business run itself. He's living on Dream Street."

Stan had straightened the girl until she sat on the edge of the float, her feet in the cool water. He took both her hands. "Baby, from now on it depends on you. Whether every day is Christmas and I can get my nerves back in shape and act like a human being—or whether the wolves start howling for our blood."

Molly's eyes were big now and Stan bored in.

"Now, look. This is what we've got to do."

When she had heard it she sat for a moment with her hair falling over her face, looking down at her bare thighs and the bright yellow of the bathing suit. She ran her hands slowly from her crotch down to her knees. They felt cold and the water was cold around her feet; she raised them and drew them up, leaning her head on her knees, not looking at the man beside her.

"That's how it is, kid. I'll make it up to you. Honest to God, baby. Don't you see—this is the only thing that can put us back together again?"

Suddenly she stood up, throwing her hair back. Her fingers trembled as she drew on her cap. Then, without looking at him, she dived from the float and set out for the dock. Stan was churning the water with his legs, trying to overtake her. She reached the dock and raced up the ladder with him close behind. When they got to the cabin he bolted the door.

Molly whipped off her cap and shook out her hair. Then she slipped the bathing suit down and left it on the floor in a sodden pile, stepping out of it. Stan watched her, his heart thumping with anxiety. Now.

She said, "Stan, take a good look. Make believe you never saw me undressed before. I mean it. Now then, tell me, if I— if I—do it—will I look any different? To you?"

He kissed her so hard that her lip began to bleed.

Lilith opened the door for him and they went into her office. She sat behind the desk, where the contents of a tray of star sapphires lay spread out on a square of black velvet. She tumbled them back into the tray and swung out the false drawer fronts on the right-hand side of the desk, revealing the steel door of a safe. She put the gems away and spun the dial twice, then closed the panel and took a cigarette from the box on her desk.

Stan held his lighter. "She's hooked."

"The virtuous Molly?"

"Sure. It took some selling but she'll play ball. Now let's lay out the moves from here on in. I planted the City of Spiritual Light with him just before the first full-form job in the garden up at his place. Next séance, we'll start warming him up to the idea of kicking in some dough."

Stan had brought with him a portfolio. He drew the tapes and opened it, laying an architect's drawing before the woman who claimed to be a psychiatrist.

A bird's-eye view of a dream city, clustered about a central tower which rose from the desert amid a circling park of palms.

"Very pretty, Reverend."

"There's more." He lifted out the drawing. Beneath it was a Geodetic Survey map of an Arizona county. Drawn in red ink and carefully lettered was the location of the City.

Lilith nodded. "And this is the spot where you are going to take off into thin air? That's very well thought out, darling." She frowned, looking at the map. "Where are you going to hide the second car?"

"I'm going to leave it somewhere in this jerk town, marked over here."

"No good, darling. It must be hidden out of town—somewhere in the desert. Let's go through it again. You go out by train; you buy a car in Texas and drive into this town of Peñas, where you put it in a garage. Then you hire a car in Peñas. You drive your new car outside the town and park it. You walk back, pick up the hired car, go to your own car, tow it to the spot near the site of the City and hide it well and drive back to Peñas in the hired car. You come back here by train. Correct?"

"Right. Then when we get ready to blow I drive out there, telling him to follow me in a day or two. I drive my car out to the site of the City and just off the highway. I get out, walk a hundred yards straight into the sand, then backtrack to the car, and from there follow the rock to the highway; hike on up the highway and pull out the new car. And drive like hell back east. And I've disappeared in the middle of the desert. He'll come along, following this map, and find the car. He'll follow the footprints—and blam! Gone! And me carrying all that dough. Ain't it a shame?"

She laughed softly at him over her cigarette. "It's complicated, Stan. But you'll probably be able to get away with it. I believe you could make a living selling spiritualism to other mediums."

"Say!" He leaned forward, his eyes narrow, thinking quickly; then he relaxed and shook his head. "No go. It's peanuts—they never have any real dough. Industry is the only place where dough is any more."

She looked back at the idealized drawing of the City of Spiritual Light. "There's one thing, Stan, that I wish you'd tell me."

"Sure, baby."

"How *did* you move that precision balance out at his factory?"

The Rev. Carlisle laughed. It was something he very seldom did; but now he laughed in a high key and was still bubbling when he spoke. "I'll tell you, doctor, as soon as we've got the chump cleaned. It's a promise."

"Very well. It was probably something ridiculous."

Stan changed the subject. "I'll get busy this week and rent a shack jammed right up next to his estate."

Dr. Lilith was filing a thumbnail. "Don't be so dramatic, darling. Yonkers is good enough. I agree that it should be in

Westchester. The City of Light location will spread any hue and cry out in the southwest. But I don't think there will be any hue and cry. However, he may take the matter up with this Mr. Anderson. Don't forget that he has some very shrewd men working for him. Mr. Anderson would try to outthink you. He knows he is dealing with an ingenious man. He would start his hunt for you on his own hook, and it would begin at the country place and fan out from there. No. Yonkers is neither here nor there." She dropped the nail file back into the drawer. "How are you going to brush off the faithful Penelope?"

"Molly?" Stan was pacing the room, his hands in his pockets. "I'll give her a couple of grand and tell her to meet me some place in Florida. All she needs is a few bucks and a race track to keep her happy. She'll be in a daze as long as the dough holds out. If she wins a little she'll forget the day of the month and everything else. When she's broke she can go back to the carny and work the Ten-in-One. Or get a job as a hat check somewhere. She won't starve."

Lilith stood up and came over to him, stretching tailored gray arms up around his neck and giving him her mouth.

They swayed for a moment and Stan rubbed his cheek against the smooth hair. Then she pushed him away. "Run along, Reverend. I've a patient due in five minutes."

When Grindle got to the church he found the Rev. Carlisle in his study upstairs. On the desk, spread out under the lamp, were letters with currency clipped to them. Stan picked up one which held a ten-dollar bill and read aloud: " 'I know the wonderful future which the City holds for us all in the line of a pooling of our spiritual forces. What a joy it will be when our friends and loved ones in spirit life can be with us as often as we wish. God bless you, Stanton Carlisle.' Well, the rest of it is of no consequence." He smiled at the ten-spot. "It's very touching, Ezra, some of the letters. Many of them are from uneducated people—yet their faith is so pure and unselfish. The City will be a dream come true. They should thank Ramakrishna, though, for everything I do is done with the hand of that great spiritual leader on my shoulder."

Grindle sat staring at the ember of his cigar. "I'll do my

share, Stanton. I'm pretty well fixed. I'll do what I can. This idea of pooling all the spiritual power in one spot makes sense to me. Same as any business merger. But my part isn't easy: I've built such a wall around myself that I can't get out any more. They're all devoted, loyal people. None better. But they won't understand. I'll have to think of some way . . ."

While the turntable revolved Stan leaned over the machine with a clothesbrush, keeping the blank record clear of acetate threads cut by the recording needle. Suddenly he raised the needle arm, tore the record from the turntable and slung it into a corner. "God damn it, kid, you've got to sound *wistful*. The dame and the old guy can be together forever, frigging like rabbits, only he's got to help the church build this City. Now take it again. And get in there and *sell* it."

Molly was almost crying. She turned back the pages of her script and leaned closer to the mike, watching Stan put on a new record blank.

I can't *act*. Oh, golly, I've got to try!

She started to cry, forcing the words out between catches of her breath, struggling through it and winking so she could still read the script. Toward the end she was crying so hard she couldn't see it at all and ad-libbed the rest. She was waiting any minute for Stan to blow up and bawl her out, but he let it ride.

When she was through he raised the recording arm. "That's the stuff, kid—plenty of emotion. Let's listen to it."

The playback sounded awful, Molly thought. All full of weepy noises and gasps. But Stan was grinning. He nodded to her and when he had heard it all he said, "That's the stuff, kid. That'll shake him loose. You wait and see. You think that sounds corny? Forget it. The chump's overboard. I could roll up my pants legs, throw a sheet over me, and he'd take me for his long lost love. But we're going to need one circus to nail him to the cross."

Moonlight struck through fern leaves in the conservatory; the rest of the church was in darkness. The minutes slid by— twenty of them by Stan's luminous-dial watch. He shifted his feet and found the floor board by the organ.

A tinkle came from the trumpet lying on the lectern, across the Bible. Grindle leaned forward, clenching his fists.

The trumpet stirred, then floated in air, moonlight winking from its aluminum surface. The chump moaned, cupping one hand behind his ear so as not to miss a single syllable. But the voice came thin and clear, a little metallic.

"Spunk darling . . . this is Dorrie. I know you haven't forgotten us, Spunk. I hope to materialize enough for you to touch me soon. It's wonderful . . . that you are with us in building the City. We can be together there, darling. Really together. We will be. Believe that. I'm so glad that you are working with us at last. And don't worry about Andy and the rest. Many of them will come to accept the truth of survival in time. Don't try to convince them now. And don't alarm them: you have some securities—some bonds—that they don't know about. That is the way out, dear. And let no one know how much you give, for all must feel that the City is their very own. Give your part to Stanton, bless him. And don't forget, darling . . . next time I come to you . . . I shall come as a bride."

It was late when Stan pressed the buzzer outside the apartment. Lilith opened the door, frowning. "I don't like your coming here so much, Stan. Somebody might see you."

He said nothing but hurried in and threw his brief case on her desk, tugging at the straps. Lilith closed the Venetian blinds a little tighter.

From the case he dug a helter-skelter of papers, the faked letters with currency still attached, which Lilith gathered up, pulling off the cash. She emptied them into the fireplace and put a match to them.

Stan was feverishly smoothing out bills and arranging them in stacks. "The convincer boodle did the trick, babe. I took every cent I had in the sock—eleven grand." He patted the piles of bills. "Jesus, what blood I've sweat to get it in this goddamned racket! But here's the payoff."

In two legal-sized brown envelopes were thick oblong packets. He drew them out and broke confining strips of paper. "There it is, baby. How many people ever see that much cash in all their lives? *One hundred and fifty thousand!* Look at it!

Look at it! And the McCoy. I never saw *one* five-yard note before. God almighty, we're lousy with 'em!"

The doctor was amused. "We'd better put them away, darling. That's a lot of money for one person to carry in his pocket. You might spend it foolishly."

While Stan gathered the crumpled bills of the convincer into a wad and slipped a rubber band around them Lilith assembled the "take" and placed it carefully back in the brown envelopes, sealing them. She swung open the dummy drawers of the desk and when she dialed the combination Stan automatically tried to get a peek but her shoulder was in the way. Lilith put the money away and spun the dial.

When she stood up the Rev. Carlisle was staring into the polished mahogany of the desktop, his face flushed. "Wounds of God! A hundred and fifty grand!"

She handed him a double brandy and poured one for herself. He took the glass from her hand and set it on the bookcase. Then he slid his arms around her roughly. "Baby, baby— God, this high class layout had me dizzy but I get it good and clear now. Baby, you're nothing but a *gonif* and I love you. We're a couple of hustlers, a pair of big-time thieves. How does it feel?"

He was grinning down at her, squeezing her ribs until they hurt. She took his wrists and loosened them a little, closing her eyes and raising her face to him. "You're wonderful, darling, the way you read my mind."

Dr. Lilith Ritter did not go to bed right away. After Carlisle had gone she sat smoking and drawing careful parallel lines on a scratch pad. Once she turned back to the file cabinet behind her and took out a folder identified only by a number. It contained a chart on graph paper, an idea with which she often played, an emotional barometric chart, marked with dates, showing a jagged rise and fall. It was an emotional diagram of Stanton Carlisle. She did not trust it entirely; but the curve had reached a high point, and on four other occasions such peaks had been followed by sudden drops into depression, instability, and black despair. Finally she put the folder away, undressed, and drew a tub of hot water into which she threw pine bath salts.

She lay in the water reading the financial section of the evening paper. Grindle Motors was off two points; it would go still lower before it started to rise again. Lilith's smile, as she tossed the paper to the floor and snuggled deeper in the comforting, scented warmth, was the smile of a well-fed kitten.

With a twist of triumphant glee her mind drew pictures of her two sisters as she had seen them last: Mina, spare and virginal, still proud of a Phi Beta key after all these years of beating Latin into the heads of brats. And Gretel—still looking like a wax angel off a *Tannenbaum*, with half a lung left to breathe with and a positive Wassermann.

Old Fritz Ritter had kept a State Street saloon called "The Dutchman's." His daughter Lille smiled. "I must be part Swedish," she said softly to a bar of pink soap, molded in the form of a lotus. "The middle way."

For two days Ezra Grindle had dropped from sight. His legal staff, his chauffeur-bodyguard, and his private chief of police, Melvin Anderson, had conferred again and again as to where the boss might be, without getting anywhere. Anderson knew little about the Old Man's activities lately and was afraid to stick a tail on him for fear he would find out about it. The Chief was cagy as hell. The lawyers learned that Grindle had not touched his checking accounts. Nothing, at least, had cleared. But he had been into one of his safe-deposit boxes. It was difficult to find out what securities the Chief had liquidated or how much. And where was he? He had left word: "I shall be away on business."

The lawyers went over the will. If he had made a new one they would have drawn it. All his faithful employees were remembered, and the rest was distributed to his pet colleges, medical foundations, and homes for unwed mothers. They would just have to wait.

In a tiny bedroom, lit only by a skylight, on the top floor of the Church of the Heavenly Message, the great man sat with his glasses off and his dentures in a glass of water beside him. He was wearing the yellow robe of a Tibetan lama. On the pale green wall of his cell was painted in Sanskrit the word *Aum*, symbol of man's eternal quest for spiritual At-One-ness with the All Soul of the Universe.

At intervals Grindle meditated on spiritual things but often he simply daydreamed in the cool quiet. The dreams took him back to the campus, and her lips when he kissed her for the first time. She wanted to see his college and he was showing her the buildings which stood there in the night, illumined, important. Afterward they strolled in Morningside Park, and he kissed her again. That was the first time she let him touch her breast . . .

He went over every detail. It was amazing what meditation could do. He remembered things he had forgotten for years. Only Dorrie's face eluded him; he could not bring it back. He could recall the pattern of her skirt, that day at Coney Island, but not her face.

With the pleasure of pressing a sore tooth, he brought back the evening, walking on the Drive, when she told him what she had been afraid of; and now it was true. It seemed that no time had passed at all. His frantic inquiries for a doctor. He had exams the very time she was supposed to go; she went by herself. Afterwards, up in the room, she seemed all right, only shaky and depressed. What a hellish week that was! He had to put her out of his mind until exams were through. Then the next night—they told him she was in the hospital and he ran all the way over there and they wouldn't let him in. And when he did get in Dorrie wouldn't speak to him. It went around and around in his head—like a Tibetan prayer wheel. But it was slowing down. Soon it would stop and they would be Joined in Spirit.

The skylight had grown a darker blue. The Rev. Carlisle brought him a light supper and gave him further Spiritual Instruction. When the night had come there was a tap at the door and Carlisle entered, carrying with both hands a votive candle in a cup of ruby-red glass. "Let us go to the chapel."

Grindle had never seen that room before. A large divan was piled with silk cushions and in an alcove was a couch covered with black velvet for the medium. The entire room was hung in folds of dark drapery. If there were any windows they were covered.

The clergyman led his disciple to the divan; taking his hand he pressed him back against the cushions. "You are at peace. Rest, rest."

Grindle felt foggy and vague. The bowl of jasmine tea which he had been given for supper had seemed bitter. Now his head was swimming lightly and reality retreated to arm's length.

The medium placed the votive candle in a sconce on the far wall; its flickering light deepened the shadows of that dead-black room and, on looking down, the bridegroom could barely make out the form of his own hands. His eyesight blurred.

Carlisle was chanting something which sounded like Sanskrit, then a brief prayer in English which reminded Grindle of the marriage service; but somehow the words refused to fit together in his mind.

In the alcove the medium lay back on the couch and the black curtains flowed together by their own power. Or was it the medium's odylic force?

They waited.

From far away, from hundreds of miles it seemed, came the sound of wind, a great rushing of wind or the beating of giant wings. Then it died and there arose the soft, tinkling notes of a *sitar*.

Suddenly from the alcove which served as a cabinet came the trumpet voice of the control spirit, Ramakrishna, last of India's saints, greatest of *bhakti* yogis, preacher of the love of God.

"*Hari Aum!* Greetings, my beloved new disciple. Prepare your mind for its juncture with the Spirit. On the seashore of endless worlds, as children meet, you will join for an instant the Life of Spirit. Love has made smooth your path—for all Love is but the Love of God. *Aum.*"

Ghostly music began again. From the curtains before the alcove a light flashed, then a sinuous coil of glowing vapor poured from between them, lying in a pool of mist close to the floor. It swelled and seemed to foam from the cabinet in a cascade. Its brilliance grew, until on looking down Grindle could see his own figure illumined by the cold flaming brilliance of the light. It rose now and pulsated, glowing bright and then dimming slightly. The air was filled with a mighty rhythm, like the heart of a titan, roaring and rushing.

742742742

742742742

742742742742

The pool of luminous matter began to take form. It swayed as a cocoon might sway from a moth's emerging. It became a cocoon, holding something dark in its center. Then it split and drew back toward the cabinet, revealing the form of a girl, lying on a bed of light, but illumined only by the stuff around her. She was naked, her head resting on one bent arm.

Grindle sank to his knees. "Dorrie—Dorrie—"

She opened her eyes, sat up and then rose, modestly drawing a film of glowing mist over her body. The old man groped forward awkwardly on his knees, reaching up to her. As he drew near, the luminous cloud fell back and vanished. The girl stood, white and tall, in the flicker of the votive candle across the room; and as she gazed down at him her hair fell over her face.

"Dorrie—my pet—my honey love—my bride . . ."

He picked her up in his arms, overjoyed at the complete materialization, at the lifelike smoothness of her body—she was so heartbreakingly earthly.

Inside the cabinet the Rev. Carlisle was busy packing yards of luminous-painted China silk back into the hem of the curtains. Once he put his eye to the opening and his lips drew back over his teeth. Why did people look so filthy and ridiculous to anyone watching? Christ!

The second time in his life he had seen it. Filth.

The bride and bridegroom were motionless now.

It was up to Molly to break away and get back to the cabinet. Stan turned the switch and the rhythmic, pounding heartbeat filled the room, growing louder. He tossed one end of the luminous silk through the curtains.

The quiet forms on the divan stirred, and Stan could see the big man burrowing his face between Molly's breasts. "No—Dorrie—my own, my precious—I can't let you go! Take me with you, Dorrie—I don't want earth life without you . . ."

She struggled out of his arms; but the bridegroom seized her around the waist, rubbing his forehead against her belly.

Stan grabbed the aluminum trumpet. "Ezra—my beloved disciple—have courage. She must return to us. The force is growing weaker. In the City—"

"No! Dorrie—I must—I—once more . . ."

This time another voice answered him. It was not a spiritual voice. It was the voice of a panicky showgirl who has more than she can handle. "Hey, quit it, for God's sake! Stan! Stan! *Stan!*"

Oh, bleeding wounds of Christ, the dumb, stupid bitch!

The Rev. Carlisle tore the curtains apart. Molly was twisting and kicking; the old man was like one possessed. In his pent-up soul the dam had broken, and the sedative Stan had loaded into his tea had worn off.

Grindle clutched the squirming girl until she was jerked from his hands.

"Stan! For God's sake *get me out of here! Get me out!*"

Grindle stood paralyzed. For in the dim, red, flickering light he saw the face of his spiritual mentor, the Rev. Stanton Carlisle; it was snarling. Then a fist came up and landed on the chin of the spirit bride. She dropped to the floor, knees gaping obscenely.

Now the hideous face was shouting at Grindle himself. "You goddamned hypocrite! Forgiveness? All you wanted was a piece of ass!" Knuckles smashed his cheekbone and Grindle bounced back on the divan.

His brain had stopped working. He lay looking stupidly at the red, jumping light. A door opened somewhere and somebody ran out. He stared at the leaping red flame, not thinking, not living, just watching. He heard something stir near him but couldn't turn his head. He heard sounds of crying and somebody say "Oh, good God," and then the faltering slap of bare feet and a girl's voice sobbing and a fumbling for a door and a door opening and staying open against a hallway where there was a dim yellow light but it all made no sense to Ezra Grindle and he preferred to watch the little flame in its ruby-red glass cup flickering and dancing up and down. He lay there a long time.

Below him the front door slammed once. But it didn't seem to matter what happened. He groaned and turned his head.

One arm—his left one—numb. And all one side of his face frozen. He sat up and stared about him. This dark room—there had been a girl's body. Dorrie's. She was a bride. It was his wedding. The Rev. Carlisle—

Slowly he remembered things in little snatches. But was it the Rev. Carlisle who hit Dorrie? Or was it an evil spirit impersonating him?

Grindle stood up, having trouble balancing. Then he shuffled over to the door. One leg was numb. He was in the hallway of a house. There was a room upstairs.

He held onto the banister and took a step but he fell against the wall and sank to his knees. He crawled, step by step, dragging his left leg, which felt wooden and dead. He had to get upstairs for some reason—his clothes were upstairs—but everybody had gone—dematerialized.

He found the cell with the green walls and hauled himself to his feet, his breath whistling. What had happened? His clothes were still in the closet. Have to put them on. There was a wedding. There was a bride. Dorrie. They had been together, just as Stan had foretold. Stanton— Where was he? Why had Stanton left him this way?

Grindle was annoyed with Stanton. He struggled to get his trousers on and his shirt. Have to sit down and rest. Dorrie was there in spirit. Who else could it be but Dorrie, his Dorrie, come back again? Had she lived after all? And come back to him? A dream—?

But they had gone.

Glasses. Wallet. Keys. Cigar case.

He limped back into the hall. Stairs again, a mile of them going steeply down. Hold on. Have to hold on tight. Andy! Where was Andy and why had he let him get caught this way in a house with so many stairs and what had hurt his leg? With a sudden surge of anger Grindle wondered if he had been kidnapped. Shot? Slugged over the head? There were desperate men who might—*the mob rule grows ever more menacing, even as we sit here tonight, gentlemen, enjoying our cigars and our* . . . That was from a speech.

And the door to that black room open.

Grindle felt as if twenty years had fallen over him like a blanket. Twenty more years. He stood looking into the dark. There was a cabinet over there, and a single splash of green light still lay on the floor.

"Stanton! Dorrie! Stanton, where are you!"

Halfway across the room he stumbled and crawled the rest

of the way to the pool of light. But it wasn't moist and musky, like Dorrie. It felt like fabric.

"Stanton!"

Grindle struck a match and found a wall switch. The light revealed that the patch of luminous vapor was a piece of white silk sticking out from the bottom hem of the black curtains in the alcove.

But Stanton had struck Dorrie!

He drew aside the curtains. There was the couch, all right. Maybe Stanton had fallen behind it when the evil presence— this was Thursday? I've missed the board meeting. They would hold it without me; too important. I should have been there, to act as a sea anchor on Graingerford. But Russell would be there. Dependable man. But could Russell convince them by himself of the soundness of the colored-labor policy? The competition was doing it—it was a natural. Graingerford be damned.

On the floor by the couch lay a control box with several switches on its bakelite panel. Grindle turned one.

Above him began the faint, ghostly music of a *sitar*. Another turn of the switch and it stopped.

He sat on the medium's couch for a moment, holding the box on his knees, the wire trailing from it underneath the black velvet cover toward the wall. A second switch produced the cosmic heartbeat and the rushing wind. Another—*"Hari Aum!"*

At the sound of Ramakrishna's voice he snapped it off. The click of the switch seemed to turn on his own reason. In one jagged, searing flash he saw everything. The long build-up, the psychic aura, the barrage of suggestion, the manufactured miracles.

Dorrie— But how, in heaven's name, did that sanctimonious devil find out about Dorrie? I've never spoken her name all these years—not even to Dr. Ritter. Even the doctor doesn't know about Dorrie or how she died.

The villain must be genuinely psychic. Or some debased telepathic power. A fearful thought—such a black heart and such uncanny powers. Maybe Dr. Ritter can explain it.

Downstairs. Got to get downstairs. Telephone. In that devil's office—

He made it.

"Andy? I'm perfectly all right—just can't talk very plain. Something's the matter with one side of my face. Probably neuralgia. Andy, for the Lord's sake, stop fussing. I tell you I'm all right. It doesn't matter where I am. Now keep quiet and listen. Get Dr. Samuels. Get him out of bed and have him up home when I get there. I'll be there in two hours. I want a checkup. Yes, this evening. What time is it? Get Russell up there too. I've got to find out what happened at the meeting this morning."

The voice at the other end of the wire was frantic. Grindle listened for a time and then said, "Never mind, Andy. I've just been—away."

"One question, Chief. Are you with that spirit preacher?"

The Chief's voice grew clearer. "Andy—I forbid you ever to mention that man's name to me again! That's an order. You and everyone else in the organization. Is that clear? And I forbid anyone to ask me where I've been. I know what I'm doing. This is final."

"Okay, Chief. The curtain is down."

He made two more calls. One was for a cab and the other was to Dr. Lilith Ritter. There was one chamber in his brain that wasn't functioning yet. He didn't dare open it until he was safely in Dr. Ritter's office.

Molly had not stopped for clothes. She pulled on her shoes, threw a coat around her, grabbed her purse, and ran from that awful house. She ran all the way home.

In the flat Buster miaowed to her, but she gave him a quick pat. "Not now, sugar. Mamma has to scram. Oh, my God!"

She heaved a suitcase onto the bed and threw into it everything small and valuable she could see. Still crying in little bubbling starts, she drew on the first panties and bra that came out of a drawer; she got into the first dress she touched in the closet, shut the keyster, and put Buster in a big paper bag.

"Oh, my God, I've got to hurry." Play dumb and give them an Irish name. "I've got to hurry, somewhere. Stan—oh, damn you, damn you, damn you, I *don't* feel dirty! He was just as clean as you, you damn cheap hustler. Oh—Daddy—"

The hotel people were nice about Buster. She expected cops any minute but nothing happened. And the address she found in the *Billboard* was the right one. A reply to her telegram got back early the next morning:

SENDING DOUGH NEED GIRL SWORD CABINET ACT COME HOME SWEETHEART

ZEENA

Justice

holds in one hand a balance, in the other a sword.

LILITH opened the door; she said nothing until they were in the office and she had seated herself behind the desk, asking softly, "Did she?"

Stan had discarded clerical bib and collar. He was sweating, his mouth cottony. "She went all the way. Then she blew up. I—I knocked out the pair of them and left them there."

Lilith's eyes half closed. "Was that necessary?"

"Necessary? Wounds of God! Don't you think I tried to weasel out of it? The old bastard was like a stallion kicking down a stall to get into a mare. I dropped both of them and beat it."

Lilith was drawing on her gloves. She took a cigarette from her purse. "Stan, it may be some time before I can meet you." She swung open the panel and dialed the safe combination. "He may come to me—I'll try to persuade him not to hunt for you." She laid the convincer wad and the two brown envelopes on the desk. "I don't want to keep this any longer, Stan."

When he had stuffed the money into his pockets Lilith smiled. "Don't get panicky. He won't be able to start any action against you for several hours. How hard did you hit him?"

"I just pushed him. I don't think he was all the way out."

"How badly is the girl hurt?"

"For God's sake, she isn't *hurt*! I just dropped her; she'll come out of it quick. If she stays groggy it will give the chump something to worry about: what to do with her. If she gets clear she'll head straight back to the flat and wait for me. She'll have a good long wait. I've got the keyster parked uptown in a check room. The phoney credentials and everything. If Molly had any brains she could put the con on that mark for hush money: claim he attacked her in the dark séance room. Christ, why didn't I think of that angle sooner? But it's sour now. I'm on my way."

He lifted Lilith's face and kissed her, but the lips were cool and placid. Stan was staring down into her eyes. "It's going to be a long time, baby, before we get together."

She stood up and moved closer to him. "Don't write to me, Stan. And don't get drunk. Take sedative pills if you have to, but don't get drunk. Promise me."

"Sure. Where you going to write to me?"

"Charles Beveridge, General Delivery, Yonkers."

"Kiss me."

This time her mouth was warm.

At the door he slid his arm around her, cupping her breast with his hand, and kissed her again. Suddenly he drew up, his face sharp with alarm. "Wait a minute, baby. He's going to start thinking back on who tipped me to that abortion. And he's going to think straight to you! Come on, sweetheart, we've both got to scram."

Lilith laughed: two sharp notes like the bark of a fox. "He doesn't know that I know that. I worked it out from things he *wouldn't* say." Her eyes were still laughing. "Don't tell me how to look out for myself, lover. Tell me—" A black-gloved hand pressed his arm. "Tell me how you made that precision balance move!"

He grinned and said over his shoulder, "Yonkers," as he walked swiftly out of the door.

Mustn't use the car. Cab drivers remember people. Subway to Grand Central. Walk, do not run, to the nearest exit. One hundred and fifty grand. Christ, I could hire a flock of private cops myself.

In a dressing room under the station he opened the traveling bag and pulled out a shirt and a light suit. There was a fifth of Hennessy; he uncapped the bottle for a short one.

A hundred and fifty grand. Standing in his underwear he fastened on a money vest with twelve pockets. Then he took up the roll of currency—one handful—his profits from the church racket. Take a fifty and a few twenties and stash the rest away.

Snapping off the rubber band from the fat roll he peeled off the fifty. The next bill was a single. And the one after it. But he hadn't cluttered up the convincer boodle with singles! Had he added any money to the pile that night in Lilith's office? Singles!

He spread out the wad, passing the bills from one hand to the other. Then he turned so that the light above the wash bowl would fall on them and riffled through them again. Except for the outside fifty the whole works was nothing but ones!

Stan's eyebrows began to itch and he dug at them with his knuckles. His hands smelled of money and faint perfume from bills carried by women.

The Great Stanton took another pull of brandy and sat down carefully on the white dressing stool. What the hell had gone sour now? Counting over showed three hundred and eighty-three dollars in the boodle. There had been eleven thousand—and the "take"? Good Christ!

He let the dollars fall to the floor and snatched at one of the brown envelopes, cutting his thumb as he tore it open.

There was a shuffle of feet outside and the attendant's white duck trousers appeared beneath the door. "You all right in there, sir?"

"Yeah, yeah, sure."

This pile ought to be all five-century notes—

"You ain't feeling faint, is you, mister?"

Oh, good God, leave me alone. "No. I'm okay, I tell you."

"Well, that's fine, sir. I just thought I heard noise like some gentleman having a fit. Gentleman have a fit in here last week and I had to crawl under the door and hold him down. Had to get the porter, mop up all the blood where he cut his self."

"For God's sake, man, *let me get dressed!*" Stan grabbed a dollar from the scattered bills at his feet and held it under the door.

"Oh—oh! Thank *you*, sir. Thank *you*."

Stan tore off the brown paper. Singles!

The other envelope was tough; he ripped into it with his teeth. Again—the thick packet contained nothing but one-dollar bills!

The pastor of the Church of the Heavenly Message crushed a handful of them in his fist, his eyes traveling along the black lines between the tiles of the floor. He let out an explosive sound like a cough; lifting his fist he beat the crumpled paper against his forehead twice. Then he fired the money into a corner and turned on both faucets of the washbowl. In the roaring water he let himself go; he sank his face in the basin and screamed, the sound bubbling up past his ears through the rush of water. He screamed until his diaphragm was sore and he had to stop and sit down on the floor, stuffing a towel in his mouth and tearing it with his teeth.

At last he hoisted himself up and reached for the brandy, swallowing until he had to stop and gasp for breath. In the mirror's merciless light he saw himself: hair streaming, eyes bloodshot, mouth twisted. Bleeding wounds of Christ!

The gypsy switch.

He stood, swaying, his hair falling damply over his eyes.

Dr. Lilith Ritter said, "Sit down, Mr. Carlisle."

Her voice was cold, kind, and sad—and as professional as the click of a typewriter.

His head began to shake as if he were saying no to a long series of questions. It went on shaking.

"I've done everything I can," said the sad voice through cigarette smoke. "When you first came to me you were in bad shape. I had hoped that by getting at the roots of your anxiety I could avert a serious upset. Well—" The hand gestured briefly with its star sapphire. "I failed."

He began rubbing his fingers along the top of the desk,

listening to the small whimpering noise of sweat against mahogany.

"Listen to me, Mr. Carlisle." The doctor leaned forward
earnestly. "Try to understand that these delusions are part of
your condition. When you first came to me you were tortured
by guilt connected with your father—and your mother. All of
these things you think you have done—or that have been
done to you lately—are merely the guilt of your childhood
projected. Do I make myself clear?"

The room was rocking, the lamps were double rings of
light, sliding back and forth through each other while the
walls billowed. His head shook: no.

"The symbolism is quite obvious, Mr. Carlisle. You were
filled with the unconscious desire to kill your father. You
picked up somewhere—I don't know where—the name of
Grindle, an industrialist, a man of power, and identified him
with your father. You have a very peculiar reaction to older
men with a stubble of white beard. It makes you think of
fungus on the face of a corpse—the corpse you wanted your
father to be."

The doctor's voice was very soft now; soothing, kind, un-
answerable.

"When you were a child you saw your mother having
intercourse. Therefore tonight in hallucination you thought
you saw Grindle, the father-image, in intercourse with your
mistress—who has come to represent your mother. And that's
not all, Mr. Carlisle. Since I have been your counselor you
have made a transference to me—you see me also as your
mother. That explains your sexual delusions with regard to
me."

He slid his hands over his face, mashing the palms into his
eyes, gripping strands of hair between his fingers and wrench-
ing until pain freed his frozen lungs and let him draw a breath.
His thoughts ran over and over, playing the same words until
they became meaningless: grindle grindle grindle grindle
mother mother mother stop stop stop. The voice didn't stop.

"There is one thing more you must face, Mr. Carlisle: the
thing that is destroying you. Ask yourself why you wanted to
kill your father. Why was there so much guilt connected with
that wish? Why did you see me—me, the mother-image—in

hallucinations both as your mistress and as a thief who had cheated you?"

She was standing up now and leaning across the desk, her face quite near him. She spoke gently.

"You wanted intercourse with your mother, didn't you?"

His hand went up to cover his eyes again, his mouth opened to make a wordless noise that could have been anything, a yes, a no, or both. He said, "Uh—uh—uh—uh." Then it seemed that all the pain in him was concentrated in the back of his right hand in a sudden, furious stab like a snake bite. He dropped it and stared at the doctor, momentarily in focus again. She was smiling.

"One other thing, Mr. Carlisle." She blew cigarette smoke. "The man you claimed to have killed in Mississippi—I thought at first that was merely another delusion involving the father-image. On investigation, however, I discovered there really was such a death—Peter Krumbein, Burleigh, Mississippi. I know you'll be glad to know *that*, at least, really did happen. It was quite easy to trace. Not so many years ago, was it, Mr. Carlisle?"

She turned away suddenly and picked up the telephone, the smooth voice brisker now. "Mr. Carlisle, I've done all I can for you, but you *must* have hospital care. These hallucinations— We can't have you wandering about and getting into trouble. Just put yourself in my hands; you can trust me absolutely.

"Bellevue Hospital? Psychiatric Division, please."

The buzzer hummed; a latch clicked in the foyer. Then the door into the waiting room opened and closed. Someone coming.

He backed away, looking at her, his mouth hanging open, his eyes bulging. Door. Have to get out. People. Danger.

"Psychiatric Division? This is Dr. Lilith Ritter. Please send an ambulance . . ."

The door, rushing behind him, shut off her voice.

Get out. Street. Hide. He clung to the knob, holding the door shut so she couldn't follow him.

Dream. Nightmare. Delusion. Nothing . . . nothing real. Tongue . . . naked . . . talk . . . money . . . dream . . . nightmare.

Dimly, through wood, he heard the telephone click into its cradle. Snap of a latch . . . waiting room. Then her voice. "Will you come in, please?"

Silence.

He sucked without thinking at the back of his right hand, where there was a red, smarting mark like a cigarette burn.

Safe? People coming! Got to get—

Another voice beyond the panels, high-pitched. Man. "Doctor—a ghastly mess . . ."

"Lie straight on the couch, please. Let me take your glasses, Mr. Grindle."

The Devil

Beneath his bat-wings the lovers stand in chains.

T HERE was a plate of glass shaped like a star in the floor
where the dancers swayed and shuffled. When the band
went into a sweet one the house lights dimmed out and the
star glowed, shining up the girls' skirts, leaving their faces in
darkness, but X-raying their clothes from the hips down. They
screamed and giggled as their partners pushed them across
the star and back into obscurity.

In one corner of the room the mentalist rose from his chair,
steadying himself by a hand on its back. "Thank you, sir, and
your charming girl friend, for your interest and for the drink.
You understand, folks, I've got other people waiting . . ."

The drunk slid a silver dollar along the table and the mind
reader took it in his finger tips. It vanished in a quick movement. He bowed and turned away.

The girl snickered, the noise bubbling in her glass as she
drank. "Daddy, isn't he spooky?" She kept on chuckling.
"Now, then, sweetheart, you heard what he said! He said, 'A
man who has a good head for business will give you the thing

nearest to your heart, something which once lived in a wire cage.' You heard him, daddy. What d'you s'pose he meant?"

The man said thickly, "Anything you say, kid, goes. You know that. Anything. Gee, honey, you got the prettiest lil pair of—" He remembered the slip of paper that the mind reader had told him to tuck under the strap of his wrist watch and he pulled it out, unfolding it and trying to focus on it. The girl struck a match.

In her affected scrawl, using small circles for dots, was written, "Will Daddy buy me that red-fox jacket?" He stared at the slip and then grinned. "Sure, kid. Anything for you, kid. You know that. Le's get outa here—go up t'your place. C'mon, honey, 'fore I'm too lit—too lit t'enjoy"—he broke wind but never noticed it—"anything."

At the bar Stan knocked off another quick one on the house. Even through the curtain of alky the maggot in his mind kept burrowing. How long will this joint last? They get crummier and crummier. That shiny-haired bastard—private. Private. Private information. Private investigations. Private reports, private shellackings. Private executions?

The thought turned and twisted in his mind, burning the alcohol out of it. Jesus, why did I ever have to tangle with that old crumb? How was I to know that Molly— Oh, God, here we go again.

A waiter stepped close and said, "Table eighteen, bud. The gal's named Ethel. Had three husbands and the clap. The guy with her is a drummer. Plumbers' supplies."

Stanton finished his drink and dropped a quarter in the waiter's vest pocket as he brushed past him.

On his way to the table Stan saw the boss, his navy-blue shirt sleeves rolled up and canary yellow tie pulled down, talking to two men in rumpled suits. They had not removed their hats. Both necks were thick.

A cold ripple slipped down his back. Wind seemed to whistle inside his undershirt. Cold. Oh, Jesus, here they come. Grindle. Grindle. Grindle. The old man's power covered the country like a pair of bat-wings, flapping cold and black.

Stan walked slowly to the back of the room, ducked behind a partition and squeezed his way through the kitchen and out into the alley at the rear of the Pelican Club, breaking into a run when he was clear of the building. He didn't dare go back for his hat. Christ, I ought to hang it on a nail right by the back door. But they'll block that the next time.

Always different faces, different guys. They must hire private dicks in every state, all of them different. Anderson sits inside that barbed-wire fort and spins it out like a spider, millions of bucks to smash one guy. Mexico. I've got to jump the border if I'm ever going to shake them. Three thousand miles of this damn country and no hole to duck into. How do those goons do it so quick? Mind readers—they must chase after every guy doing a mental act and take a sample of his hair, see if it's blond.

Across the dark rooftops a train whistled, long and mournfully. Stan ducked down another alley and leaned against the wall, listening to the roaring jolt of his own heart, fighting to get his breath. Lilith, Lilith. Across two thousand miles stretched the invisible golden wire still, and one end was buried in his brain.

Back in the Pelican Club the boss said, "Now you fellas run along. You tell McIntyre I'm not putting in no cig or novelty girls and I'm holding on to the hat check myself. It ain't for sale."

The Hermit

An old man follows a star that burns in his lantern.

IN THE LIGHT of the fire the cards fell, forming the pattern of a cross. Stan dealt them slowly, watching them fall.

The gully was shielded from wind, the fire hidden from the tracks a quarter of a mile away across fields standing high with brittle weed-stalks. Weeds grew to the edge of the gully, the fire turning them yellow against the sky where stars hung, icy and remote.

The Empress. She smirked at him from beneath her crown of stars, holding a scepter with a golden ball on its end. The pomegranates embroidered on her robe looked like strawberries. Beyond her, trees stood stiffly—like the trees on a theater backdrop in a tank town. At her feet the ripening wheat-heads. Smell of ripening wheat. Venus sign on the couch where she sat. Smell of ripening wheat.

What did they think, the wriggling bugs of the scum, jetting into the world to meet acids, whirling douches, rubber scum bags, upholstery of cars, silk drawers, clotted handkerchief . . . two hundred million at a shot . . .

Across the fire the fat man lifted a steaming can from the embers with a pair of pliers. "Got yourself a can, bud? Java's done."

Stan knocked tobacco crumbs from a tin and twisted a rag around it. "In there, pal."

The coffee set his stomach churning again. Christ, I need a drink. But how to snake out the bottle without that bastard cutting himself in?

He eased the bottle neck from his coat and pretended to be studying the cards while the white mule trickled into the steaming can.

The squat hobo raised his face. "My, *my!* What is this that gives off so heavenly an aroma?" His voice was like sandpaper. "Could it be *Odeur de Barleycorn*? Or is it a few drops—just the merest suggestion behind the ears—of that rare and subtle essence, 'Parfum Pourriture d'Intestin— You never know she wears it until it's . . . too late'? *Come on, blondy, gimme the bottle!*"

Through his smile Stan said, "Sure. Sure, pal. I was going to break it out later. I'm waiting for another pal of mine. He's out trying to get a lump."

The fat man took the bottle of rotgut, measured it by eye, and very accurately drank half of it, handing it back and returning to his coffee. "Thanks, bud. The only pal you got is right in there. You better soak it up before some other bo muscles in on us." He shifted his weight, crossed his legs, and took a long drink of coffee, which trickled down the shiny blue surface of his jowls. A two days' growth of beard made him look like a pirate.

He rested the can on his knee and wiped his chin, running his tongue around between his lips and gums. Then he said, "That's right, bud—kill the bottle. How would you like it if we had an unexpected guest?" His voice took on a reedy, mincing tone and he held his head coyly on one side, lifting bushy eyebrows. "He'd find us in a dither—it being the maid's day off. All we'd have to offer him would be a drink of that fine, mellow, wood-aged polecat piss." The jowls swayed as he shook his head in mock concern. Then the dark face brightened. "Or perhaps he would be that priceless gem—the guest-who-always-fits-in—ready at a moment's notice to don an apron (one of your frilly best, naturally, kept just for those special people) and join you in the kitchen, improvising a snack."

Stan brought the bottle to his mouth again and tilted it; the raw whisky found holes in his teeth and punished him, but he finished it and heaved the bottle into the weeds.

The fat man threw another branch on the fire and squatted beside Stan. "What kind of cards are those, bud?"

The man's shirt was almost clean, pants cuffs scarcely frayed. Probably rode the plush a lot. In his lapel was a tiny steering-wheel emblem of a boat club.

Stan gazed up into his face. "My friend, you are a man who has seen life. I get the impression that somewhere in your life has been an office with a broad carpet. I see a window in an office building with something growing in it. Could it be little cedar trees—in a window box?"

The fat hobo stood up, swishing the coffee in his can. "Everybody had cedars. I had a better idea—an inspiration. Grass hummocks—just plain grass tufts. But this will show you the *genius*. What do you think I put in them? *Katydids!* I'd bring up a client late at night—town all dark there below us. Tell him to step back from the window and listen. You couldn't believe you were in the city." He looked down and his face tightened. "Wait a minute, bud. How'd you know about them grass tufts?"

The Great Stanton smiled thinly, pointing to the cards before him. "This is the Tarot of the Romany cartomancers. A set of symbols handed down from remote antiquity, preserving in their enigmatic form the ancient wisdom through the ages."

"What d'you do with 'em? Tell fortunes?" The gravel voice had lost its hostility.

"I receive impressions. You have two children. Is that correct?"

The fat man nodded. "Christ knows, I had once. If that bitch hasn't let 'em kill themselves while she was out whoring around."

"Your third wife?"

"Yeah, that's right. Wait a minute. How'd you know I was a three-time loser?"

"I drew the impressions from your mind, my friend, using the cards of the Tarot as a concentrative. Now, if you wish me to continue, I shall be glad to. The fee will be twenty-five cents, or its equivalent in merchandise."

The hobo scratched his scalp. "Okay, bud. Go ahead." He threw a quarter beside the cards and Stan picked it up. Five shots. Gathering the cards he shuffled them, having the fat man cut them with his left hand.

"You see, the first to appear is the *Hermit*. An old man, leaning on a staff, follows a star that burns in his lantern. That is your quest—your journey through life, always seeking something just out of your reach. Once it was wealth. It became the love of women. Next, you sought security—for yourself and others. But misfortune descended on you. Things inside you began to tear in opposite directions. And you would have five or six drinks before you took the train home at night. Isn't that right?"

The glowering, dark face nodded.

"The *Hermit* is the card of the Search. The Search for the Answer."

"Come again, bud." The fat man's tone was subdued and hopeless. "What brains I ever had was knocked loose by yard dicks years ago."

Stan closed his eyes. "Man comes into the world a blind, groping mite. He knows hunger and the fear of noise and of falling. His life is spent in flight—flight from hunger and from the thunderbolt of destiny. From his moment of birth he begins to fall through the whistling air of Time: down, down into a chasm of darkness . . ."

The hobo stood up cautiously and edged around the fire. He watched the cartomancer warily. Nuts can blow their tops easy—and this one still held a can of hot coffee.

The Great Stanton spoke aloud to himself. The jolt of whisky had loosened his stomach and drawn it out from his backbone. Now he rambled; with a foolish, drunken joy he let his tongue ride, saying whatever it wanted to say. He could sit back and rest and let his tongue do the work. Why beat my brains out reading for a bum that was probably too crooked and phoney even for the advertising racket? The tongue does the work. Good old tongue, man's best friend—and woman's second best. What the hell am I talking about?

". . . we come like a breath of wind over the fields of morning. We go like a lamp flame caught by a blast from a darkened window. In between we journey from table to table, from bottle to bottle, from bed to bed. We suck, we chew, we swallow, we lick, we try to mash life into us like an am-am-*amoeba* God damn it! Somebody lets us loose like a toad out of a matchbox and we jump and jump and jump and the guy always behind us, and when he gets tired he stomps us to death and our guts squirt out on each side of the boot of All Merciful Providence. The son-of-a-bitch!"

The world began to spin and he opened his eyes to keep his balance. The fat man wasn't listening. He was standing with his back to the fire, throwing pebbles at something beyond the circle of light.

When he turned around he said, "A goddamned, mangy, fleabitten abortion of a *dog* was trying to horn in on our fire. The stinking abomination. I hate 'em! They come up to you, smelling, groveling, please-kick-my-ass-mister. I *hate* 'em! They slaver all over you. You rub 'em behind the ears and they practically come in your face out of gratitude."

Stanton Carlisle said, "My friend, at some time a dog did you an injury. I think the dog was not yours but that it belonged to another—to a woman."

The bo, moving agilely with the grace of an athlete gone fat, was standing beside him now, fists working, the knuckles rippling as he spoke. "Sure it was a dog—a toadying, cringing, vomit-eating, goddamned abortion of a dog! Sure he belonged to a woman, you crazy bastard! And the dog was *me*!"

They held the pose like figures in a tableau. Only the firelight moved, jumping and flickering on the weeds and on the two faces, the pudgy one dark and tormented, the gaunt face of the blond hobo a blank.

There was a whining scuffle from the bank overhead and both men turned. An emaciated dog slid down and tremblingly approached the warmth, tail flattened between his haunches, eyes rolling.

Stan chirped between his teeth. "Come here, boy. Here. Over here by me."

The dog bounded toward him, yelping with delight at the sound of a friendly voice. He had almost reached Stan when the squat hobo drew back his foot. The kick lifted the animal, squirming and squealing, into the air; it fell, legs spraddled, in the middle of the fire, screamed, and shot away into the dark, trailing sparks from singed fur.

Stan swept the coffee in a curve; it glistened in the firelight, a muddy arc, and caught the fat man in the eyes. He stumbled back, wiping his sleeve across them. Then he lowered his head, resting his jowl on his left shoulder and stepping in with a rocking motion, left fist forward, right hand half open, ready to defend his face. In a soft, cultured voice he said, "Get your hands up, brother. You are in for a very unpleasant three minutes. I'll play with you that long and then send you off to dreamland."

The Rev. Carlisle had doubled in the middle, as if taken by a violent stomach cramp. He moaned, bending over, and the fat man dropped his guard an inch. It was low enough.

When Stan sprang he carried a thick faggot from the fire and with one lunge caught the hobo with its burning point just below the breast bone. The man went down limply and heavily, like a dummy stuffed with sand.

Stan watched him gape, fighting for breath. Then he smashed the torch into the open mouth, feeling the teeth crush under it.

The alcohol was draining out of his mind. He was alone and cold, under an immensity of sky—naked as a slug, as a tadpole. And the shadow of the crushing foot seemed to move closer. Stan began to run.

Far away, up on the drag, he heard the hoot of a whistle and he ran faster, staggering, a stitch in his side. Oh, Jesus— the Tarot. I left it by the fire. One more signpost pointing to the Rev. Carlisle.

A freight was slowing. He ran, his breath scorching, looking ahead, through the dark, for obstructions on the line. An iron step came whipping by him and he reached for it, but it tore from his fingers. The job was picking up speed.

A wide-open boxcar door slid up to him and he leaped.

Then, with the scalding panic rushing over him, he knew that he had missed and was swinging under.

A hand from the car gripped his shoulder and held him, half inside the car and half out, while under his feet the earth flew past.

The freight high-balled along.

Time

One foot on earth and one on water,
an angel pours eternity from cup to cup.

IN THE parking lot the Maryland sun beat down, flashing from rows of windshields, from chromium handles and the smooth curves of enameled mudguards.

Cincinnati Burns eased the battered convertible into line while Molly, standing out on the gravel, shouted, "Cut her left, honey. More left."

He drew out the ignition key and it was suddenly snatched from his hand and hurled out between the cars. Cincy said, "You little devil! You're mighty sassy. Ain't you? Ain't you?" He boosted the child high in the air while it screamed with joy.

Molly came running up. "Let me hold him, Cincy, while you get the key." He passed the baby to her and it grabbed a damp handkerchief from the gambler's coat pocket and waved it triumphantly.

"Come on, precious. Let's let Daddy get the key. Hey, quit kicking me in the tummy."

The big man set the boy on his shoulder, handing Molly his hat for safekeeping, and they headed for the grandstand. The gambler shifted the baby and looked at the stop watch on his wrist. "Plenty of time, kitten. The third race is our spot."

They stopped to buy paper cups of raspberry sherbet and Cincinnati whispered suddenly, "You hold the bambino, Molly. There's Dewey from St. Louis."

Treading softly, he approached from the rear and squatted down behind a glum, lantern-jawed man in a seersucker suit. Cincy took a pack of matches and holding his thick fingers, knuckles covered with red hair, as delicately as if he were threading a needle, he stuck a match between Dewey's shoe sole and the upper. Lighting the match, he sneaked back a few steps and then strolled over to where his wife and son were watching from behind the refreshment stand.

When the match burned down the long-faced horse player shot into the air as if hoisted by a rope and began smacking at his foot.

Molly, Cincy, and young Dennis, peeking around the corner of the stand, began to shout in unison. Molly dropped her cup of sherbet, and Dennis Burns, seeing it fall, threw his after it gleefully.

"Hey, what goes on?" Cincy rattled change in his pocket and said, "You go on. I'll catch up to ye's."

When he joined them he held four cups of sherbet. "Here, kids—one to suck on and one to drop. Dewey is sure a sucker for the hotfoot. This must be a thousand times somebody gives him the hotfoot. It's a dozen times, at least, that I give him the hotfoot myself. Let's get up in the stand, kitten. I'll get you organized and then I've got to get the roll down on that hay-burner in the third; he shouldn't drop dead, *kenna-hurra*. You wouldn't know that, that's Gaelic. If he breaks a leg we're going to have to talk fast back at that fleabag. What the hell, it's time we was pulling out of that trap anyhow. Every time I wake up in the morning and get a glim full of that wallpaper I feel like I ought to slip you five bucks."

The Wheel of Fortune

spins past Angel, Eagle, Lion, and Bull.

STAN lay on the splintery boards, feeling the vibration against his elbows, smelling the acrid odor of machine oil rising from the planks. The freight thundered along, gaining speed.

The hands drew him further in and then slid under his armpits and helped him to sit up. "You all right, son? You sure come near swinging yourself into Kingdom Come." The voice was soft and friendly.

Now they were passing the outskirts of a town, lonely street lamps sending bars of light winking through the door. The man who had dragged him in was a Negro, dressed in denim overalls and a denim work coat. Above the bib of the overalls a white shirt was visible in the shadows. His smile was the only part of his face Stan could see.

Getting to his feet he braced himself against the sway of the car under him and worked his fingers and arms, easing the strain out of them. "Thanks, pal. It was too dark for me to put on any speed myself—couldn't see what was ahead of me on the drag."

"It's tough, dark night like this. You can't see the grab-irons. You can't hardly see *nothing*. How about a smoke?"

Stan felt a bag of tobacco pressed into his hand. He twisted himself a cigarette and they shared the match. The Negro was a young fellow, slim, with smooth, handsome features and close-cropped hair.

Stan drew in smoke and let it dribble from his nose. Then he began to shake, for the steady pound of the wheels under him brought back the stab of that hopeless, desperate fear, "This is it," and he trembled harder.

"You cold, mister? Or you got a fever?"

"Just shaken up. I thought I was going to hand in my checks."

Their cigarettes perfumed the darkness. Outside the rising moon rode with them, dipping beyond treetops.

"You a working stiff, mister, or just on the road?"

"On the road."

"Plenty fellows likes it that way. Seem like I'd rather work than knock myself out hustling."

"What kind of work do you do?"

"Any kind. Porter work, handyman. I run a freight elevator once. I can drive pretty good. Biggest old truck you can find, I'll drive her. I've shipped out: cook's helper and dishwasher. I can chop cotton. Reckon there ain't anything you can't do, you set your mind on it."

"Bound north?"

"New Jersey. Going to try and get me a job at Grindle's. What I hear, they taking on men. Taking on colored."

Stan braced his back against the closed door on the other side of the car and drew a final puff from the cigarette, sending the butt flipping through the open door, trailing sparks.

Grindle. Grindle. Grindle. To drown out the chatter of the wheels he said, "Why are they hiring guys all of a sudden? Business must be picking up."

The youth laughed a little. "Business staying right where she is. They hiring because they done a whole mess of firing a while back. They hiring all colored, this new bunch, what I hear."

"What's the idea of that?" Tame lawyers, tame psychologists, tame muscle-men. Bastards.

"What you s'pose? They get all the colored boys in there, and then they stir up the white boys, and pretty soon they all messing around with each other and forget all about long hours and short pay."

Stan was only half listening. He crawled into the corner next to the Negro and sat down, stretching his legs out in front of him. "Hey, bud, you wouldn't happen to have a drink in your pocket, would you?"

"Hell, no. All I got is four bits and this bag of makings. Traveling fast and light."

Four bits. Ten shots of nickel whisky.

The Great Stanton ran his hands over his hair.

"My friend, I owe you a great debt for saving my life."

"You don't owe me nothing, mister. What you expect me to do? Let you slide under and make hamburg steak out of yourself? You forget all about it."

Stan swallowed the cottony saliva in his mouth and tried again. "My friend, my ancestors were Scotch, and the Scotch are known to possess a strange faculty. It used to be called second sight. Out of gratitude, I want to tell you what I see in the future about your life. I may be able to save you many trials and misfortunes."

His companion chuckled. "You better save that second sight. Get it to tell you when you going to miss nailing a freight."

"Ah, but you see, my friend, it led me to the very car where I would find assistance. I *knew* you were in this car and would help me."

"Mister, you ought to play the races and get rich."

"Tell me this—I get a decided impression that you have a scar on one knee. Isn't that so?"

The boy laughed again. "Sure, I got scars on *both* my knees. I got scars on my ass, too. Anybody got scars all over him, he ever done any work. I been working since I could walk. I was pulling bugs off potato plants, time I quit messing my britches."

Stan took a deep breath. He couldn't let this wisenheimer townie crawl all over him.

"My dear friend, how often in your life, when things looked bad, have you thought of committing suicide?"

"Man, you sure got it bad. Everybody think they like to die sometime—only they always wants to be hanging around afterwards, watching all the moaning and grieving they folks going to do, seeing them laid out dead. They don't want to die. They just want folks to do a little crying and hollering over 'em. I was working on a road gang once and the captain like to knock me clean out of my skin. He keep busting me alongside the head whether I raise any hell or not—just for fun. But I didn't want to kill myself. I wanted to get loose. And I *got* loose, and here I am—sitting here. But that captain get his brains mashed out with a shovel a couple months later by a big crazy fellow, worked right next to me on the chain. Now that captain's dead and I ain't mourning."

A fear without a form or a name was squirming inside Stanton Carlisle. Death and stories of death or brutality burrowed under his skin like ticks and set up an infection that worked through him to his brain and festered in it.

He forced his mind back to the reading. "Let me tell you this, friend: I see your future unrolling like thread from a spool. The pattern of your days ahead. I see men—a crowd of men—threatening you, asking questions. But I see another man, older than yourself, who will do you a good turn."

The Negro stood up and then squatted on his haunches to absorb the vibration of the car. "Mister, you must of been a fortuneteller sometime. You talk just like 'em. Why don't you relax yourself? You last a lot longer, I'm telling you."

The white hobo jumped to his feet and lurched over to the open door, bracing his hand against the wall of the car and staring out across the countryside. They roared over a concrete bridge; a river flashed golden in the moonlight and was gone.

"You better stand back a little, son. You go grabbing scenery that way and somebody spot you if we pass a jerk stop. They phone on ahead, and when she slow down you got the bulls standing there with oak towels in their hands, all ready to rub you down."

Stan turned savagely. "Listen, kid, you got everything figured out so close. What sense does it all make? What sort of

God would put us here in this goddamned, stinking slaugh-
terhouse of a world? Some guy that likes to tear the wings off
flies? What use is there in living and starving and fighting the
next guy for a full belly? It's a nut house. And the biggest
loonies are at the top."

The Negro's voice was softer. "Now you talking, brother.
You let all that crap alone and come over here and talk. We
got a long run ahead of us and ain't no use trying to crap
each other up."

Dully Stan left the doorway and crumpled into the corner.
He wanted to shout out, to cry, to feel Lilith's mouth again,
her breasts against him. Oh, Jesus, there I go. God damn her,
the lying, double-crossing bitch. They're all alike. But Molly,
the dumb little tomato. Quickly he wanted her. Then disgust
mounted—she would leech on to him and drain the life out
of him. Dull, oh, Christ, and stupid. Oh, Jesus . . . Mother.
Mark Humphries, God damn his soul to hell, the thieving
bastard. Mother . . . the picnic . . .

The Negro was speaking again and the words filtered
through. ". . . take on like that. Why don't you tell me what
you moaning about? You never going to see me again. Don't
make no difference to me what you done. I mind my own
business. But you'll feel better a hundred per cent, get it off
your mind."

The prying bastard. Let me alone . . . He heard his own
voice say, "Stars. Millions of them. Space, reaching out into
nothing. No end to it. The rotten, senseless, useless life we
get jerked into and jerked out of, and it's nothing but whoring
and filth from start to finish."

"What's the matter with having a little poontang? Nothing
dirty about that, 'cept in a crib you likely get crabs or a dose.
Ain't anything dirty about it unless you feels dirty in your
mind. Gal start whoring so as to get loose from cotton-chopping or standing on their feet ten, eleven hours. You can't
blame no gal for laying it on the line for money. On her back
she can rest."

Stan's torrent of despair had dried up. For a second he
could draw breath—the weight seemed to have been lifted
from his chest.

"But the purpose back of it all—why are we put here?"

"Way I look at it, we ain't put. We growed."

"But what started the whole stinking mess?"

"Didn't have to start. It's always been doing business. People ask me: how this world get made without God make it? I ask 'em right back: who make God? They say he don't need making; he always been there. I say: well then, why you got to go bringing him in at all? Old world's always been there, too. That's good enough for me. They ask me: how about sin? Who put all the sin and wickedness and cussedness in the world? I say: who put the boll weevil? He growed. Well, mean people grow where the growing's good for 'em—same as the boll weevil."

Stan was trying to listen. When he spoke his voice was thick and flat. "It's a hell of a world. A few at the top got all the dough. To get yours you got to pry 'em loose from some of it. And then they turn around and knock your teeth out for doing just what they did."

The Negro sighed and offered Stan the tobacco, then made himself another cigarette. "You said it, brother. You said it. Only they ain't going have it forever. Someday people going to get smart *and* mad, same time. You can't get nothing in this world by yourself."

Stan smoked, watching the gray thread sail toward the door and whip off into the night. "You sound like a labor agitator."

This time the Negro laughed aloud. "God's sake, man, labor don't need agitation. You can't agitate people when they's treated right. Labor don't need stirring up. It need squeezing together."

"You think they've got sense enough to do it?"

"They *got* to do it. I *know*."

"Oh. You *know*."

The lad in denims was silent for a moment, thinking. "Looky here—you plant four grains of corn to a hill. How you *know* one going to come up? Well, the working people, black *and* white—their brains growing just like corn in the hill."

The freight was slowing.

God, let me get out of here . . . this damn, slap-happy darkie, whistling in the lion's den. And Grindle . . . every second, moving closer to the fort . . .

"Hey, watch yourself, son. She's still traveling."

The train lost speed quickly. It was stopping. Stan jumped to the ground and the Negro followed, looking left and right. "This ain't good. Got no business stopping here. Oh—oh—it's a frisk."

At either end of the train, lights appeared, brakemen walking the tops carrying lanterns; flashlights of railroad bulls playing along the body rods and into open boxcars.

The young hobo said, "Something funny—this division ain't never been hostile before. And they frisking from both ends at once . . ."

On the other side of the freight a train whistled in, hissing, glowing, the red blaze of the engine shining under the boxcar and throwing the hoboes' shadows across the cinders ahead of them.

"Hey, son, let's try and jump that passenger job. You a fast rambler?"

The Rev. Carlisle shook his head. The furies were drawing close, Anderson's web was tangling him. This was the end of it. Dully he clambered back into the boxcar and sank down into a corner, burying his face in his bent elbow, while with hoarse voices and a stamp of feet the furies moved in . . .

"Hey, bo—" The whisper through the door barely penetrated. "Come on—let's nail that rattler. We make better time too."

Silence.

"So long, boy. Take it easy."

Doom had stepped onto the roof; then a light stabbed into the car, searching the corners. Oh, Jesus, this is it—this is it.

"Come on, you bastard, unload. And get your hands up."

He stood, blinking in the glare of the flashlight, and raised his arms.

"Come on, hit the grit!"

Stan stumbled to the door and sat down, sliding his feet into darkness. A big hand gripped his arm and jerked him out.

From the top of the car the head-end shack peered over, holding his brake club under one arm. "You got him?"

A voice behind the flashlight said, "I got one. But he ain't no coon. Way we got the tip, the guy was a coon."

The brakeman above them signaled with his lantern and

from the dark came the chug of a gasoline-driven handcar. It sped up and Stan could see that it was crowded with men—dark clothes—it was no track gang. When it stopped the men piled off and hurried across the rails.

"Where is he? On the freight? Who's shaking down the rattler?"

"We got boys frisking the rattler, don't worry."

"But we got it from Anderson . . ."

This is it. This is it. This is it.

". . . that the guy was colored." One of the newcomers came closer and brought out a flashlight of his own. "What's that in your pocket, bud?"

Stanton Carlisle tried to speak but his mouth was gritty.

"Keep your hands up. Wait a minute. This isn't a weapon. It's a Bible."

His lungs loosened; he could draw half a breath. "Brother, you hold in your hand the most powerful weapon in the world—"

"Drop it!" Big Hand shouted. "Maybe it's a pineapple made to look like a Bible."

The other voice was cool. "It's just a Bible." He turned to the white hobo. "We're looking for a colored lad. We know he boarded this train. If you can give us information which might lead to his arrest, you would be serving the forces of justice. And there might be something in it for you."

Justice. *Something in it* could mean folding money. Justice. A buck—ten cans of alky . . . justice. White-stubble justice . . . a buck—twenty shots . . . oh, frig them with their razorstrops, their *brake clubs* . . .

He opened his eyes wide, staring straight ahead in the light-beam. "Brother, I met a colored brother-in-God when I was waiting to nail this job. I tried to bring him to Jesus, but he wouldn't listen to the Word. I gave him my last tract—"

"Come on, parson, where did he go? Was he riding here in the car with you?"

"Brother, this colored brother-in-God nailed her some-where up at the head-end. I was hoping we could ride to-gether so I could tell him about our Lord and Savior Jesus Christ who died for our sins. I've rode from coast-to-coast a dozen times, bringing men to Christ. I've brought only a couple thousand so far . . ."

"Okay, parson, give Jesus a rest. We're looking for a goddamned nigger Red. You saw him grab her up front? Come on, guys, let's spread out. He's here someplace . . ."

The man with big hands stayed with Stanton while the others swarmed over the freight, swung between the cars and moved off into the darkness. The Rev. Carlisle had slipped into a low mutter which the yard dick made out to be a sermon, addressed either to an invisible congregation or to the air. The goddamned Holy Joe had thrown them off; now the coon had a chance of getting clear.

At last the freight whistled, couplings started and clanked, and it groaned off. Beyond it the passenger train, sleek and dark, waited while flashlights sprayed into the blinds, the side boxes of the diner, and along the tops.

Then it too began to move. As the club car slid past, Stan glimpsed through long windows a waiter in a white coat. He was uncapping a bottle while an arm in a tweed coat held a glass of ice.

A drink. Good Christ, a drink. Could I put the bite on this bull? Better not try it, no time to build it.

The railroad detective spat between his teeth. "Look here, parson, I'm going to give you a break. I ought to send you over. But you'd probably have the whole damn jail yelling hymns. Come on, crumb, take the breeze."

The big hands turned Stan around and pushed; he stumbled over tracks and up an embankment. In the distance the light of a farmhouse glowed. A drink. Oh, Jesus—

The passenger flyer picked up speed. In the club car a wrist shot from a tweed sleeve, revealing a wrist watch. Ten minutes' delay! Confound it, the only way to travel was by plane.

Under the club car, squeezed into a forest of steel springs, axles, brake rods and wheels, a man lay hidden. As the rattler gained speed, Frederick Douglass Scott, son of a Baptist minister, grandson of a slave, shifted his position to get a better purchase as he rolled on toward the North and the fort with its double fence of charged wire.

Shoulders braced against the truck frame, feet against the opposite side, he balanced his body on an inch-thick brake rod which bent under him. Inches below, the roadbed raced by, switches clawing up at him as the car pounded past them. The truck hammered and bucked. A stream of glowing coals, thrown down by the engine, blew over him and he fought them with his free hand, beating at the smoldering denim, while the train thundered on; north, north, north.

A specter was haunting Grindle. It was a specter in overalls.

Death

wears dark armor; beside his horse
kneel priests and children and kings.

THE PITCHMAN rounded a corner, looking both ways down the main street for the cop, and then slid into the darkened vestibule of the bank building. If the rain held off he might get a break at that. The movie theater was about to let out; fellows would be coming out with their girls.

As the first of the crowd drifted past him he drew a handful of gaudy envelopes from a large pocket inside his coat and fanned them in his left hand so that the brightly printed zodiac circle and the symbols stood out, a different color for each sign.

He ran his free hand once over his hair and took a breath. His voice was hoarse; he couldn't get it much above a whisper. "My friends if you'll just step this way for a single moment you may find that you have taken a step which will add to your health happiness and prosperity for the rest of your lives . . ."

One couple stopped and he spoke directly to them. "I

wonder if the young lady would mind telling me her birth date it costs you nothing folks because the first astrological chart this evening will be given away absolutely free of charge . . ."

The young fellow said, "Come on." They walked on past. The goddamned townies.

Need a drink. Jesus, I've got to pitch. I got to unload five of them.

"Here you are folks everybody wants to know what the future holds in store come in a little closer folks and I'll tell you what I'm going to do I'm going to give each and every one of you a personal reading get your astronomical forecast which shows your lucky numbers, days of the month and tells you how to determine the right person for you to marry whether you've got anybody in mind or not . . ."

They moved by him, some staring, some laughing, none stopping.

Hideous. Their faces suddenly became distorted, like caricatures of human faces. They seemed to be pushed out of shape. Some of them looked like animals, some like embryo chicks when you break an egg that is half incubated. Their heads bobbed on necks like stalks and he waited for their eyes to drop out and bounce on the sidewalk.

The pitchman started to laugh. It was a chuckle, bubbling up inside of him at first, and then it split open and he laughed, screaming and stamping his foot.

A crowd began to knot around him. He stopped laughing and forced out the words. "Here you are folks while they last." The laugh was fighting inside of him, tearing at his throat. "A complete astrological reading giving your birthstones, lucky numbers." The laugh was hammering to get out. It was like a dog tied to the leg of a workbench, fighting to get free of a rope. Here it came. "Whah, whah, whah, whah! Hoooooooooooooooo!"

He beat the handful of horoscopes against his thigh, leaning his other hand against the stone lintel of the vestibule. The crowd was giggling at him or with him, some wondering when he was going to stop suddenly and try to sell them something.

One woman said, "Isn't it disgusting! And right in the doorway of the bank! It's indecent."

The pitchman heard her and this time he sat down limply on the marble steps, letting the horoscopes scatter around him, holding his belly as he laughed.

Something hit the crowd at its edge and mashed it forward and to each side. Then the blue legs moved in.

"I told you to beat it out of town."

The face of the cop seemed a mile above him, as if it were looking over the rim of a well.

Same cop. Two-dollar fine and get out of town.

"Wheeeeeeee! Ho—ho. Hah. Officer . . . officer . . . whah-hoooooooo!"

The hand that jerked him to his feet seemed to plunge out of the sky. "I told you to scram, bum. Now you going to walk down to the lockup or you going on a stretcher?"

A quick thrust and his hand was twisted halfway up his back; he was walking bent over to keep from getting his wrist broken. Through waves of laughter the world seeped in, coming in slices, as if the laughter split at the seams and showed a little raw and bloody reality before it closed up again.

"Where we going, officer? No, no, don't tell me. Let me guess. Down cellar?"

"Shut up, bum. Keep walking or you'll get your arm broke. I've got a good mind to work you over before we get down there."

"But, officer, they've seen me once down there. They'll get awfully tired of seeing me. They'll think it ridiculous, me showing up there so often. Won't they? Won't they? Won't they? You've got no rope around my neck. How can you be sure I won't run? Wait for the moon—it's coming out from under the rain pretty soon; any minute now. But you don't understand that. Officer, wait . . ."

They had left the crowd and cut down a side street. To the left was an alley, dark, but with a light at the other end of it. The cop shifted his grip on the prisoner's hand, letting go for a fraction of a second, and the pitchman spun free and began to run. He was sailing through air; he couldn't feel his feet touching the stones. And behind him the heavy splat of shoes on cobbles. He raced toward the light at the end of the alley, but there was nothing to be afraid of. He had always been here, running down the alley and it didn't matter; this was all there was any time, anywhere, just an alley and a light and the footsteps spanging on the cobbles but they never catch you, they never catch you, they never catch— A blow between his shoulders knocked him forward and he saw the stones, in the faint light ahead, coming up toward him, his own hands spread out, fingers bent a little on the left hand, thumbs at an eager angle, all spraddled out as if he were making shadows on a wall, of two roosters' heads, the thumbs forming the beaks and the spread fingers the notches of the combs.

The nightstick had struck him, whirling through the space between the two men. It bounded off, hitting a brick wall with a clear, wooden ping as the cobbles met his hands and the jar of the fall snapped his neck back. He was on his hands and knees when the foot caught him in the ribs and sent him sprawling on his side.

The great oval face ducked out of sight. The cop had bent to pick up the nightstick and the top of his cap cut off the sight of the face, above its V of shirt and black tie. That was all you could see.

He heard the shattering crack of the nightstick across his shoulders before the pain fought its way down the clogged nerves and went off, spraying around inside his brain like a hose jet of hot steel. He heard his own breath pop out between his teeth and he drew his feet under him. He was half-way erect when the stick knocked the rest of the breath out of him, smashing against his ribs.

It was somebody else's voice. "Officer . . . oh, Jesus . . . I ain't done nothing . . . gimme a break . . . oh, Jesus . . ."

"I'll give ye a break. I'll break every bone in your head, you stinking crumb. You as'd for it. Now you're gonna get it."

The stick landed again and the pain was white and incandescent this time as it slowly slid up his spine toward the brain on top.

The world came back and Stanton Carlisle, his mind sharpened to a point, saw where he was. He saw the lift of the cop's upper lip, revealing a gold crown. And in the faint light, behind him now, he noticed that the cop needed a shave. He was not over forty; but his hair and the beard beginning to sprout over the jowls were pearly. Like fungus on a corpse. At that instant pain from the blow across his buttocks reached his mind and a thousand tumblers fell into place; a door swung open.

Stan closed in, clamping one hand on the cop's lapel. His other hand crossed it, under the jowls, seizing the opposite lapel in its fist. Then, twisting sideways to protect his groin, Stanton began to squeeze. He heard the nightstick drop and felt the big hands tearing at his forearms, but the harder they pulled the tighter his fists dug into the throat. The day-old beard was like sandpaper on the backs of his hands.

Stan felt the wall of the alley jar against his shoulder, felt his feet leave the ground and the dark weight fall on him; but the only life in him now was pouring out through his hands and wrists.

The mountain on him wasn't moving. It was resting. Stan got one foot free and rolled both of them over so he was on top. The massive body was perfectly still. He tightened the choke still more, until his knuckles felt as if they would burst, and he began to tap the cop's head against the cobbles. Rap. Rap. Rap. He liked the sound. Faster.

Then his hands let go of themselves and he stood up, the hands falling to his sides. They wouldn't work any more, wouldn't obey him.

A bundle of astro-readings had fallen out and lay scattered on the stones, but he couldn't pick them up. He walked, very straight and precise, toward the light at the other end of the alley. Everything was sharp and clear now and he didn't even need a drink any more.

The freights would be risky. He might try the baggage rack of a long-haul bus, under the tarpaulin. He had traveled there once before.

Nothing more to bother about. For the cop was dead.

I can kill him again. I can kill him again. Any time he starts after me I can keep killing him. He's mine. My own personal corpse.

They'll bury him, just like you bury a stiff, clotted handkerchief.

I can kill him again.

But he won't come again. He's a dead pigeon.
I can kill him again.
But he's dead from a bum ticker.
I can kill him.

Strength

A rose-crowned woman closes
a lion's jaws with her bare hands.

I
N THE EVENING light a tall figure, gaunt, with matted yellow hair, leaned over the top fence rail, watching a man
and woman planting corn. The woman thrust a hoe handle
into the earth and the man, who seemed to have no legs,
hopped along on his hands, dropping grains of corn into the
hills and smoothing the earth over them.

"Wait a minute, Joe. There's somebody wants us."

The big woman strode over plowed ground, pulling off her
gloves. "I'm sorry, bud, but we ain't got nothing in the ice-
box to give you for a lump. And I ain't got time now to fix
you a sit-down. You wait till I get my pocketbook from the
house and I'll let you have four bits. There's a lunch wagon
down the road." She stopped and caught her breath, then
said hoarsely, "Glory be, it's Stan Carlisle!" Over her shoulder
she called, "Joe! Joe! Come here this minute!"

The hobo was leaning on the fence, letting it carry his
weight. "Hi, Zeena. Saw your ad—magazine."

The man drew near them, hopping along on his hands. His legs, twisted into a knot out of the way, were hidden by a burlap sack which he had drawn over them and tied around his waist. He swung up and sat looking at Stan silently, smiling as Lazarus must have smiled, newly risen. But his eyes were wary.

Zeena pushed back her straw hat and recovered her voice. "Stanton Carlisle, I swore if I ever set eyes on you again I'd sure give you a piece of my mind. Why, that child was pretty near out of her head, time she got to the carny. Everybody there thought she was touched, way she'd stumble around. I had her working the sword-box layout and she could just about step in and out of it, she was that bad. You sure done yourself proud by that girl, I must say. Oh, you was going to be mighty biggety—make a star out of her and everything. Well, you got there. But what good did it ever do her? Don't think I've ever forgot it." Her voice faltered and she sniffed, rubbing the back of a work-glove across her nose. "And what do you do but end up putting that kid, that sweet kid, on the turf—same as any two-bit pimp. It ain't any fault of yours that the kid pulled out of it so good. Oh, no. I hope she's forgot every idea she ever had about you. It ain't your fault she's married now to a grand guy and's got the cutest little kid of her own you ever laid eyes on. Oh, no, you done your best to land that girl in a crib house."

She stopped for breath, then went on in a different tone, "Oh, for God's sake, Stan, come in the house and let me fry you a slice of ham. You look like you ain't had a meal in a week."

The hobo wasn't listening. His knees had sagged; his chin scraped the fence rail and then he sank in a heap, like a scarecrow lifted from its pole.

Zeena dropped her gloves and began to climb the fence. "Joe, go down and hold the gate open. Stan's passed out. We got to get him in the house."

She lifted the emaciated body easily in her arms and carried it, legs dangling, toward the cottage.

Morning sun struck through the dotted curtains of the kitchen, falling on the golden hair of a man at the table, busy shoveling ham and eggs into his mouth. He stopped chewing and took a swallow of coffee.

". . . that skull buster was known all the way up and down the line. He beat two old stiffs to death in the basement of the jug last year. I knew when he got me up that alley that the curtain was going down."

Zeena turned from the stove with a skillet in one hand and a cake turner in the other. "Take it easy, Stan. Here's some more eggs. I reckon you got room for 'em." She filled his plate again.

Near the door Joe Plasky sat on a cushion, sorting mail into piles by states. It came in bundles; the mailman left it in a small barrel out on the road. On the barrel was painted: "ZEENA—PLASKY." They had outgrown an R.F.D. box long ago.

"He started working me over with the club." Stan paused with a forkful of egg in the air, looking at Joe. "So I let him have it. I clamped the *nami juji* on him and hung on. He went out for good."

Zeena stopped, holding the cake turner. She said, "Oh, my God." Then her eyes moved to Joe Plasky, who went on calmly sorting mail.

Joe said, "If it happened the way you tell it, kid, it was him or you. That Jap choke is a killer, all right. But you're a hot man, Stan. You've got to move quiet. And fast."

Zeena shook herself. "Well, he ain't moving till we get him fed up some. The boy was starved. Have some more coffee, Stan. But, Joe, what's he going to do? We can't—"

Joe smiled a little wider but his eyes were dark and turned inward, thinking. Finally he said, "They got your prints up there?"

Stan swallowed. "No. They don't print you on vag and peddling falls. Not in that town, anyway. But they know it was a blond pitchman working horoscopes."

Joe thought some more. "They didn't mug you?"

"No. Just a fine and a boot in the tail."

The half-man acrobat pushed aside the piles of letters and hopped over to the stairway, which led to the attic bedrooms. He swung up the stairs and out of sight; overhead they could hear a scrape as he crossed the floor.

Stan pushed back his plate and took a cigarette from the pack on the window sill. "Zeena, I've been living in a god-damned nightmare—a dream. I don't know what ever got into me. When vaudeville conked out we could have worked the night clubs. I don't know yet how I ever got tangled up with the spook racket."

The big woman was piling dishes in the sink. She was silent.

Stanton Carlisle's voice went on, getting back something of the old resonance. "I don't know what ever got into me. I don't expect Molly ever to forgive me. But I'm glad the kid got herself a good spot. I hope he's a swell guy. She deserves it. Don't tell her you ever saw me. I want her to forget me. I had my chance and I fluffed, when it came to Molly. I've fluffed everything."

Zeena turned back to him, her hands shining from the soapy water. "What you going to do, Stan, when you leave here?"

He was staring at the ember of his cigarette. "Search me, pal. Keep on bumming, I guess. The pitch is out. Everything's out. Good God, I don't know—"

On the stairs Joe Plasky made a scraping noise, coming down slowly. When he entered the kitchen he held a large roll of canvas under his arm. He spread it on the linoleum and unrolled it in two sections—gaudily painted banners showing enormous hands, the mounts and lines in different colors with the characteristics ascribed to each.

"Sophie Eidelson left these with us last season," he said. "Thought maybe you could use 'em. McGraw and Kauff-man's is playing a town down the line from here—be there all this week. There's worse places to hole up in than a carny."

Zeena dried her hands hastily and said, "Stan, give me a cigarette, quick. I've got it! Joe's got the answer. You could work it in a Hindu makeup. I've got an old blue silk kimono I can fix over for a robe. I reckon you know how to tie a turban."

The Great Stanton ran his hands over his hair. Then he knelt on the floor beside the half-man, pulling the palmistry banners further open and examining them. In his face Zeena could see the reflection of the brain working behind it. It seemed to have come alive out of a long sleep.

"Jesus God, this is manna from heaven, Joe. All I'll need is a bridge table and a canvas fly. I can hang the banners from the fly. They're looking for a pitchman, not a mitt reader. Oh, Jesus, here we go."

Joe Plasky moved away and picked up a burlap sack containing outgoing mail. He slung it over his shoulder and held the top of it in his teeth, setting off for the door on his hands. "Got to leave this for the pickup," he said, around the burlap. "You folks stay here—I've got it."

When he had gone Zeena poured herself a cup of coffee and offered one to Stan, who shook his head. He was still examining the banners.

"Stan—" She began to talk as if there was something which had to be said, something which was just for the two of them to hear. She spoke quickly, before Joe could return. "Stan, I want you to tell me something. It's about Pete. It don't hurt me to talk about him now. That was so long ago it seems like Pete never hit the skids at all. Seems like he died while we were still at the top of the heap. But I got to thinking—a kid will do an awful lot to lay some gal he's all steamed up about. And you were a kid, Stan, and hadn't ever had it before. I expect old Zeena looked pretty good to you in them days, too. Pete wouldn't ever have drank that bad alky. And you didn't know it was poison. Now come clean."

The Great Stanton stood up and thrust his hands into his pockets. He moved until the sun, shining through the window of the kitchen door, struck his hair. Soap and hot water had turned it from mud to gold again. His voice this time filled the kitchen; subtly, without increasing in power, it vibrated.

"Zeena, before you say another word, do me one favor. You remember Pete's last name?"

"Well— Well, he never used it. He wrote it on our marriage license. Only I ain't thought of it for years. Yes, I can remember it."

"And it's something I could never guess. Am I right? Will you concentrate on that name?"

"Stan— What—"

"Concentrate. Does it begin with *K*?"

She nodded, frowning, her lips parted.

"Concentrate. *K* . . . *R* . . . *U* . . . *M*—"

"Oh, my God!"

"The name was *Krumbein*!"

Joe Plasky pushed at the door and Stan moved aside. Zeena buried her mouth in the coffee cup and then set it down and hurried out of the room.

Joe raised his eyebrows.

"We were cutting up old times."

"Oh. Well, in that outfit I know McGraw a little—only you better not use my name, Stan. A guy as hot as you."

"What's calluses on the ends of the fingers, left hand?"

"Plays a stringed instrument."

"What's a callus here, on the right thumb?"

"A stonecutter."

"How about a callus in the bend of the first finger, right hand?"

"A barber—from stropping the razor."

"You're getting it, Stan. There's lots more that I forget— I ain't read mitts steady in many a year. If Sophie was here she could give you hundreds of things like that. She's got a whole notebook full of stuff. It locks with a key. But you'll make out all right. You always could read."

Zeena and Joe were sitting in the shade of the porch, opening letters and shaking out dimes. The woman said, "Hand me some more Scorpios, hon. I'm fresh out."

Joe ripped open a carton. The astrological booklets came in stamped-and-sealed envelopes. They addressed them quickly with fountain pens and threw them in a wire basket to be bundled up later for the postman.

Zeena said, "Beats all, Stan, how this mail-order business snowballs up. We put in one little ad and plowed back the dimes into the business. Now we got five chains of magazines covered and we can't hardly stop shaking out dimes to tend to the place here."

The Great Stanton reached into a saucepan by the side of the steamer chair where he lay in the sun. Taking a handful of dimes he counted out five batches of ten and rolled them into a red paper wrapper—five dollars' worth. The little red cylinders piled up in a china bowl on the other side of the chair, but he had carelessly allowed several to fall beside him. They were hidden between his thigh and the canvas chair-seat.

Joe hopped off the porch and over toward Stan, holding a basket of dimes in his teeth. He emptied them into the saucepan, smiling. "Little more and we're going to buy another place—farm next to this one. We've pretty near got this place mortgage-free. Long as people want horoscopes, I mean, astro-readings—you can't call 'em horoscopes through the mail unless they're drawn to the hour and minute of birth— long as they keep going like this we're set. And if they slack off, we've still got the farm."

Stan leaned back and let the sun strike through his eyelids. He was gaining. A week had filled him out. Almost back to his old weight. His eyes had cleared and his hands hardly shook at all. He hadn't had anything but beer in a week. A guy who's good at the cold reading will never starve. When Joe turned back to the porch Stanton slid the red cylinders from the chair to his pants pocket.

The truck bounced off the side road in a cloud of dust, white under the full moon, and turned into a state highway. Zeena drove carefully to spare the truck and Joe sat next to her, one arm on her shoulders to steady himself when they stopped suddenly or slowed down. Stan was next to the door of the cab, his palmistry banners in a roll between his knees.

Town lights glittered ahead as they topped a gradual rise. They coasted down it.

"Almost there, Stan."

"You'll make it, kid," Joe said. "McGraw's a hard cookie, but he ain't a nickel-nurser once you got him sold."

Stan was quiet, watching the bare streets they were rolling through. The bus station was a drugstore which kept open all night. Zeena stopped down the block and Stan opened the door and slid out, lifting out the banners.

"So long, Zeena—Joe. This—this was the first break I've had in a hell of a while. I don't know how—"

"Forget it, Stan. Joe and me was glad to do what we could. A carny's a carny and when one of us is jammed up we got to stick together."

"I'll try riding the baggage rack on this bus, I guess."

Zeena let out a snort. "I knew I'd forgot something. Here, Stan." From the pocket of her overalls she took a folded bill and, leaning over Joe, pressed it into the mentalist's hand. "You can send it back at the end of the season. No hurry."

"Thanks a million." The Great Stanton turned, with the rolled canvas under his arm, and walked away toward the drugstore. Halfway down the block he paused, straightened, threw back his shoulders and then went on, holding himself like an emperor.

Zeena started the truck and turned it around. They drove out of town in a different direction and then took a side road which cut into the highway further south, turning off it to mount a bluff overlooking the main drag. "Let's wait here, snooks, and try to get a peek into the bus when it goes by. I feel kind of funny, not being able to see him to the station and wait until it came along. Don't seem hospitable."

"Only smart thing to do, Zee. A fellow as hot as him."

She got out of the cab and her husband hopped after her; they crossed a field and sat on the bank. Above them the sky had clouded over, the moon was hidden by a thick ceiling.

"You reckon he'll make it, Joe?"

Plasky shifted his body on his hands and leaned forward. Far down the pale concrete strip the lights of a bus rose over the grade. It picked up speed, tires singing on the roadbed, as it bore down toward them. Through its windows they could make out the passengers—a boy and a girl, in a tight clinch on the back seat. One old man already asleep. It roared below the bank.

Stanton Carlisle was sharing a seat with a stout woman in a gay flowered-print dress and a white sailor straw hat. He was holding her right hand, palm up, and was pointing to the lines.

Joe Plasky sighed as the bus tore past them into darkness with a fading gleam of ruby taillights. "I don't know what'll happen to him," he said softly, "but that guy was never born to hang."

The Hanged Man

hangs head downward from the living wood.

IT WAS a cheap straw hat, but it added class. He was the type of guy who could wear a hat. The tie chain came from the five-and-ten, but with the suit and the white shirt it looked like the real thing. The amber mirror behind the bar always makes you look tanned and healthy. But he was tanned. The mustache was blackened to match the hair-dyeing job Zeena had done.

"Make mine a beer, pal."

He took it to a table, put his hat on an empty chair and unfolded a newspaper, pretending to read it. Forty-five minutes before the local bus left. They don't know who they're looking for up there—no prints, no photo. Stay out of that state and they'll look for you till Kingdom Come.

The beer was bitter and he began to feel a little edge from it. This was all right. Keep it at beer for a while. Get a stake, working the mitt camp. Get a good wad in the grouchbag and then try working Mexico. They say the language is a cinch to learn. And the damn country's wide open for ragheads.

They advertise in all the papers down there. Give that mess
with the cop time to cool and I can come back in a few years
and start working California. Take a Spanish name maybe.
There's a million chances.

A guy who's good at the cold reading will never starve.

He opened the newspaper, scanning the pictures, thinking
his way along through the days ahead. I'll have to hustle the
readings and put my back into it. In a carny mitt camp you
got to spot them quick, size 'em up and unload it in a hurry.
Well, I can do it. I should have stayed right with the carny.

Two pages of the paper stuck and he went back and pried
them apart, not caring what was on them, just so as not to
skip any. In Mexico . . .

The picture was alone on the page, up near the top. He
looked at it, concentrating on the woman's face, his glance
merging the screen of black dots that composed it, filling in
from memory its texture, contour, color. The scent of the
sleek gold hair came back to him, the sly twist of her little
tongue. The man looked twenty years older; he looked like a
death's head—scrawny neck, flabby cheeks . . .

They were together. They were together. Read it. Read
what they're doing.

PSYCHOLOGIST WEDS MAGNATE
In a simple ceremony. The bride wore a tailored . . . Best man
was Melvin Anderson, long-time friend and advisor . . . Honeymoon
cruise along the coast of Norway . . .

Somebody was shaking him, talking at him. Only it wasn't
any grass tuft—it was a beer glass. "Jees, take it easy, bud.
How'd ya bust it? Ya musta set it down too hard. We ain't
responsible, you go slinging glasses around and get cut. Why
don't ya go over to the drugstore. We ain't responsible . . ."

Darkness of street darkness with the night's eyes up above
the roof cornices oh Jesus he was bleeding suitable for a full
evening's performance gimme a rye and plain water, yeah, a
rye make it a double.

It's nothing, I caught it on a nail, doc. No charge? Fine,
doc. Gimme a rye—yeah, and plain water better make it a
double rye and plain water seeping into the tire tracks where
the grownups were everywhere.

I ain't pushing, bud, let's have no hard feelings, I'm your friend, my friend I get the impression that when you were a lad there was some line of work or profession you wanted to follow and furthermore you carry in your pocket a foreign coin or lucky piece you can see Sheriff that the young lady cannot wear ordinary clothes because thousands of volts of electricity cover her body like a sheath and the sequins rough against his fingers as he unhooked the smoothness of her breasts trembling pressing victory into we'll make a team right to the top and they give you a handout like a tramp at a back door but the doors have been closed, gentlemen, let them look for threads till Kingdom Come and the old idiot gaping there in the red light of the votive candle oh Jesus you frozen-faced bitch give me that dough yeah make it a rye, water on the side . . .

You could hardly see the platform for the smoke and the waiter wore a butcher's apron his sleeves were rolled up and his arms had muscles like Bruno's only they were covered with black hair you had to pay him every time and the drinks were small get out of this crummy joint and find another one but the dame was singing while the guy in a purple silk shirt rattled on the runt piano the old bag had on a black evening dress and a tiara of rhinestones

> *Put your arms around me, honey, hold me tight!*

She drew the mike toward her and her tits bulged on each side of the rod Christ what an old bag . . .

> *Cuddle up and cuddle up with all your might!*

She rubbed her belly against the microphone . . .

> *Oh! Oh! I never knew*
> > *any boy*
> > > *like*
> > > > *you!*

"Waiter—waiter, tell the singer to let me buy her a drink . . ."

When you look at me my heart . . . begins to float,
Then it starts a-rocking like a . . . a motor boat!
Oh! Oh! I never knew
Any boy . . . like . . . you!

"Whew, I'm all winded. Ya like that number? The old ones always the best, ain't they? Thanks, sport—same as ever for me, Mike. Ain't I seen you in here before, honey? Gee, you been missin' a good time . . ."

All hallways look alike and the lights burning black dressers and yellow bedspreads kiss me "Yeah, sure, honey, keep your pants on long enough for me to catch my breath. Them stairs—whew!"

Smell of face powder sweat perfume "Yeah, honey, I'll peel. Wait a minute, can't you? Never mind a chaser, just lean on the bottle, sport. Boy, this ain't bad. C'mon over and get friendly, honey, mamma's going to treat you right. Gee, ain't you the handsome one! Hey, honey, how about giving me my present now, huh? Where'd you get all them dimes? Holy gee, you musta stuck up a streetcar company. No more jumpsteady for me, honey, let's 'make a baby'—I got to get back."

Groping in the dark he found it, lying on its side there was still a drink in it oh Jesus I got to get out of here before they see this room . . .

The sun blinding him, feel in the lining, maybe some of them slipped down . . . one more roll of dimes . . . tie them in the tail of the undershirt this damn fleabag's a fleabag but the bottle don't need any corkscrew and to hell with water I fixed 'em all, the bastards, they'll never find me . . . covered my tracks too smart for 'em the bastards I bashed him right in the face and he fell back on the divan with his mouth hanging open the old bastard never knew what hit him but I'll slip them yet and work it in a Hindu outfit with dark makeup but there was one more drink the damn thieves somebody sneak in here and lap it up let me out of here got to get air oh Jesus the goddamned chairs are sliding back and forth back and forth and if I hold on tight to the carpet I won't slide and hit the wall with his fist beating away on the mantelpiece she sits straight up on the edge of the sofa looking at herself in the glass sign in front of the church when they boarded up the attic door and his hands bunching up the tablecloth as I rammed it into him, Gyp. That fat bastard I hope I blinded him following the star that burns in his lantern head down from the living wood.

In the office trailer McGraw was typing out a letter when he heard a tap on the screen door. He shaded his eyes against the desk lamp and said out of the side of his mouth, "Yeah, what?"

"Mis'er McGraw?"

"Yeah, yeah. What d'ya want? I'm busy."

"Wanna talk t'you, 'bout a 'traction. Added 'traction."

McGraw said, "Come on in. What you got to sell?"

The bum was hatless, shirt filthy. Under his arm he carried a roll of canvas. "Allow me t'introduce myself—Allah Rahged, top-money mitt reader. Got m'banners all ready t'go t'work. Best cold reader in the country. Lemme give you demonstration."

McGraw took the cigar out of his mouth. "Sorry, brother, I'm full up. And I'm busy. Why don't you rent a vacant store and work it solo?" He leaned forward, rolling up the paper in the typewriter. "I mean it, bud. We don't hire no boozers! Jesus! You smell like you pissed your pants. Go on, beat it!"

"Jus' give me chance make a demonstration. Real, old-time, A-number-one mitt reader. Take one look at the mark, read past, present—"

McGraw was letting his cold little eyes slide over the man whose head came within an inch of the trailer roof. The hair was dirty black, but at the temples and over the forehead was a thin line of yellow. Dyed. A lammister.

The carny boss suddenly smiled up at his visitor. "Take a seat, bud." From a cupboard behind him he lifted a bottle and two shot glasses. "Have a snort?"

"I thank you, sir. Very refreshing. I'll need only a fly and a bridge table—hang my banners on the edges of the fly."

McGraw shook his head. "I don't like a mitt camp. Too much trouble with the law."

The bum was eyeing the bottle, his red eyes fastened on it.

"Have another? No, I don't like mitt camps. Old stuff. Always got to have something new. Sensational."

The other nodded absently, watching the bottle. McGraw put it back in the cupboard and stood up. "Sorry, bud. Some other outfit, maybe. But not us. Good night."

The rum-dum pushed himself up, hands on the chair arms, and stood, swaying, blinking down at McGraw. Then he ran the back of his hand across his mouth and said, "Yeah. Sure." He stumbled, reached the screen door, and pulled it open, gripping it with his hand to keep his balance. He had forgotten the soiled canvas banners with their gaudily painted hands. "Well, so long, mister."

"Hey, wait a minute."

The lush was already back in the chair, leaning forward, his hands spread against his chest, elbows on the chair arms, head lolling. "Hey, mister, how 'bout 'nother li'l shot 'fore I go?"

"Yeah, sure. But I just happened to think of something. I got one job you might take a crack at. It ain't much, and I ain't begging you to take it; but it's a job. Keep you in coffee and cakes and a shot now and then. What do you say? Of course, it's only temporary—just until we get a real geek."

I MARRIED A DEAD MAN

by Cornell Woolrich

THE SUMMER NIGHTS are so pleasant in Caulfield. They smell of heliotrope and jasmine, honeysuckle and clover. The stars are warm and friendly here, not cold and distant, as where I came from; they seem to hang lower over us, be closer to us. The breeze that stirs the curtains at the open windows is soft and gentle as a baby's kiss. And on it, if you listen, you can hear the rustling sound of the leafy trees turning over and going back to sleep again. The lamplight from within the houses falls upon the lawns outside and copperplates them in long swaths. There's the hush, the stillness of perfect peace and security. Oh, yes, the summer nights are pleasant in Caulfield.

But not for us.

The winter nights are too. The nights of fall, the nights of spring. Not for us, not for us.

The house we live in is so pleasant in Caulfield. The blue-green tint of its lawn, that always seems so freshly watered no matter what the time of day. The sparkling, aerated pinwheels of the sprinklers always turning, steadily turning; if you look at them closely enough they form rainbows before your eyes. The clean, sharp curve of the driveway. The dazzling whiteness of the porch-supports in the sun. Indoors, the curving white symmetry of the bannister, as gracious as the dark and glossy stair it accompanies down from above. The satin finish of the rich old floors, bearing a telltale scent of wax and of lemon-oil if you stop to sniff. The lushness of pile carpeting. In almost every room, some favorite chair waiting to greet you like an old friend when you come back to spend a little time with it. People who come and see it say, "What more can there be? This is a home, as a home should be." Yes, the house we live in is so pleasant in Caulfield.

But not for us.

Our little boy, our Hugh, his and mine, it's such a joy to watch him growing up in Caulfield. In the house that will some day be his, in the town that will some day be his. To watch him take the first tottering steps that mean—now he can walk. To catch and cherish each newly minted word that fumblingly issues from his lips—that means, now he's added another, now he can talk.

But even that is not for us, somehow. Even that seems thefted, stolen, in some vague way I cannot say. Something we're not entitled to, something that isn't rightfully ours.

I love him so. It's Bill I mean now, the man. And he loves me. I know I do, I know he does, I cannot doubt it. And yet I know just as surely that on some day to come, maybe this year, maybe next, suddenly he'll pack his things and go away and leave me. Though he won't want to. Though he'll love me still, as much as he does on the day that I say this.

Or if he doesn't, it will be I who will. I'll take up my valise and walk out through the door, never to come back. Though I won't want to. Though I'll love him still, as much as I do on the day that I say this. I'll leave my house behind. I'll leave my baby behind, in the house that will some day be his, and I'll leave my heart behind, with the man it belongs to (How could I take it with me?), but I'll go and I'll never come back.

We've fought this thing. How bitterly we've fought it, in every way that we know how. In every way there is. We've driven it away, a thousand times we've driven it away, and it comes back again in a look, a word, a thought. It's there.

No good for me to say to him, "You didn't do it. You've told me so once. Once was enough. No need to repeat it now again, this late. I *know* you didn't. Oh, my darling, my Bill, you don't lie. You don't lie, in money, or in honor, or in love—"

(But this isn't money, or honor, or love. This is a thing apart. This is murder.)

No good, when I don't believe him. At the moment that he speaks, I may. But a moment later, or an hour, or a day or week, again I don't. No good, for we don't live just within a single moment, we can't. The other moments come, the hours, weeks, and, oh God, the years.

For each time, as he speaks, I know it wasn't I. That's all I know. So well, too well, I know. And that leaves only—

And each time, as I speak, perhaps he knows that it wasn't he (but I cannot know that, I cannot; there is no way for him to reach me). So well he knows, so well. And that leaves only—

No good, no good at all.

One night six months ago I dropped upon my knees before him, with the boy there between us. Upon my bended knees. I put my hand on the little boy's head, and I swore it to him then and there. Speaking low, so the child wouldn't understand.

"By my child. Bill, I swear to you on the head of my child, that I didn't. Oh Bill, I didn't do it—"

He raised me up, and held me in his arms, and pressed me to him.

"I know you didn't. I know. What more can I say? In what other way can I tell you? Here, lie against my heart, Patrice. Perhaps that can tell you better than I— Listen to it, can't you tell that it believes you?"

And for a moment it does, that one moment of our love. But then the other moment comes, that one that always comes after. And he has already thought, "But I know it wasn't I. I know so well it wasn't I. And that leaves only—"

And even while his arms go tighter than ever about me, and his lips kiss the wetness from my eyes, he already doesn't again. He already doesn't.

There's no way out. We're caught, we're trapped. The circle viciously completes itself each time, and we're on the inside, can't break through. For if he's innocent, then it has to be me. And if I am, it has to be he. But I *know* I'm innocent. (Yet he may know he is too.) There's no way out.

Or, tired with trying to drive it away, we've rushed toward it with desperate abandon, tried to embrace it, to be done with it once and for all in that way.

One time, unable to endure its long-drawn, unseen, ghostly vigil over our shoulders any longer, he suddenly flung himself out of the chair he'd been in, though nothing had been said between us for an hour past. Flung the book he hadn't been reading, only pretending to, far from him like a brickbat. Flung himself up as wildly as though he were going to rush forward to grapple with something he saw there before him. And my heart flung itself wildly up with him.

He surged to the far end of the room and stopped there—
at bay. And made a fist, and raised his arm, and swung it with
a thundering crash against the door, so that only the panel's
thickness kept it from shattering. Then turned in his helpless
defiance and cried out:

"I don't care! It doesn't matter! Do you hear me? It doesn't
matter! People have done it before. Lots of times. And lived
out their happiness afterward. Why shouldn't we? He was no
good. It was what he deserved. He wasn't worth a second
thought. The whole world said so then, and they'd still say so
now. He isn't worth a single minute of this hell we've gone
through—"

And then he poured a drink for each of us, lavish, reckless,
and came back toward me with them. And I, understanding,
agreeing, one with him, rose and went to meet him halfway.

"Here, take this. Drink on it. Drown it. Drown it until it's
gone. One of us *did* do it. It doesn't matter. It's done with.
Now let's get on with living."

And striking himself on the chest, "All right, *I* did it. There.
I was the one. Now it's settled. Now it's over at last—"

And then suddenly our eyes looked deep into one another's, our glasses faltered in mid-air, went down, and it was
back again.

"But you don't believe that," I whispered, dismayed.

"And you do," he breathed, stricken.

Oh, it's everything, it's everywhere.

We've gone away, and it's where we go. It's in the blue
depths of Lake Louise, and high up in the fleecy cloud for-
mations above Biscayne Bay. It rolls restlessly in with the surf
at Santa Barbara, and lurks amid the coral rocks of Bermuda,
a darker flower than the rest.

We've come back, and it's where we've come back to.

It's between the printed lines on the pages of the books we
read. But it peers forth dark, and they fade off to illegibility.
"Is he thinking of it now, as I read? As I am? I will not look
up at him, I will keep my eyes to this, but—is he thinking of
it now?"

It's the hand that holds out its coffee-cup across the break-
fast-table in the mornings, to have the urn tipped over it.
Bloody-red for a moment in fancy, then back again to pale as

it should be. Or maybe, to the other, it's that other hand opposite one, that does the tipping of the urn; depending upon which side of the table the beholder is sitting.

I saw his eyes rest on my hand one day, and I knew what he was thinking at that instant. Because I had looked at his hand much the same way on a previous day, and I had been thinking then what he was thinking now.

I saw him close his eyes briefly, to efface the sickly illusion; and I closed mine to dispel the knowledge of it that his had conveyed to me. Then we both opened them, and smiled at one another, to tell one another nothing had happened just then.

It's in the pictures that we see on the theatre-screen. "Let's get out of here, I'm—tired of it, aren't you?" (Somebody is going to kill somebody, up there, soon, and he knows it's coming.) But even though we do get up and leave, it's already too late, because he knows why we're leaving, and I know too. And even if I didn't know until then, this—the very fact of our leaving—has told me. So the precaution is wasted after all. *It's* back in our minds again.

Still, it's wiser to go than to stay.

I remember one night it came too quickly, more suddenly than we could have foretold, there was less warning given. We were not able to get all the way out in time. We were still only making our way up the aisle, our backs to the screen, when suddenly a shot rang out, and then a voice groaned in accusation, "You've—you've killed me."

It seemed to me it was *his* voice, and that he was speaking to us, to one of us. It seemed to me, in that moment, that every head in the audience turned, to look our way, to stare at us, with that detached curiosity of a great crowd when someone has been pointed out to them.

My legs for a moment seemed to refuse to carry me any further. I floundered there for a minute as though I were going to fall down helpless upon the carpeted aisle. I turned to look at him and I saw, unmistakably, that his head had cringed for a moment, was down defensively between his shoulders. And he always carried it so straight and erect. A moment later it *was* straight again, but just for that instant it hadn't been, it had been hunched.

Then, as though sensing that I needed him just then, because, perhaps, he needed me, he put his arm around my
waist, and helped me the rest of the way up the aisle that way,
steadying me, promising me support rather than actually
giving it to me.

In the lobby, both our faces were like chalk. We didn't look
at one another, it was the mirrors on the side told us that.

We never drink. We know enough not to. I think we sense
that, rather than close the door on awareness, that would only
open it all the wider and let full horror in. But that particular
night, I remember, as we came out, he said, "Do you want
something?"

He didn't say a drink; just "something." But I understood
what that "something" meant. "Yes," I shuddered quietly.

We didn't even wait until we got home; it would have taken
us too long. We went in to a place next door to the theatre,
and stood up to the bar for a moment, the two of us alike,
and gulped down something on the run. In three minutes we
were out of there again. Then we got in the car and drove
home. And we never said a word the whole way.

It's in the very kiss we give each other. Somehow we trap
it right between our lips, each time. (Did I kiss him too
strongly? Will he think by that I forgave him, again, just then?
Did I kiss him too weakly? Will he think by that I was thinking
of it, again, just then?)

It's everywhere, it's all the time, it's *us*.

I don't know what the game was. I only know its name;
they call it life.

I'm not sure how it should be played. No one ever told
me. No one ever tells anybody. I only know we must have
played it wrong. We broke some rule or other along the way,
and never knew it at the time.

I don't know what the stakes are. I only know we've forfeited them, they're not for us.

We've lost. That's all I know. We've lost, we've lost.

One

T HE DOOR was closed. It had a look of pitiless finality about it, as though it would always be closed like this from now on. As though nothing in the world could ever make it open again. Doors can express things. This one did. It was inert, it was lifeless; it didn't lead anywhere. It was not the beginning of anything, as a door should be. It was the ending of something.

Above the push-button there was a small oblong rack, of metal, affixed to the woodwork, intended to frame a name-card. It was empty. The card was gone.

The girl was standing still in front of the door. Perfectly still. The way you stand when you've been standing for a long time; so long, you've forgotten about moving, have grown used to not moving. Her finger was to the push-button, but it wasn't pushing any more. No pressure was being exerted; no sound came from the battery behind the door-frame. It was as though she had been holding it that way so long, she had forgotten to take that, too, away.

She was about nineteen. A dreary, hopeless nineteen, not a bright, shiny one. Her features were small and well turned, but there was something too pinched about her face, too wan about her coloring, too thin about her cheeks. Beauty was there, implicit, ready to reclaim her face if it was given the chance, but something had beaten it back, was keeping it hovering at a distance, unable to alight in its intended realization.

Her hair was hazel-colored, and limp and listless, as though no great heed had been paid to it for some time past. The heels of her shoes were a little run-down. A puckered darn in the heel of her stocking peered just over the top of one. Her clothing was functional, as though it were worn for the sake of covering, and not for the sake of fashion, or even of appeal. She was a good height for a girl, about five-six or seven. But she was too thin, except in one place.

Her head was down a little, as though she were tired of carrying it up straight. Or as though invisible blows had lowered it, one by one.

She moved at last. At long last. Her hand dropped from the push-button, as if of its own weight. It fell to her side, hung there, forlorn. One foot turned, as if to go away. There was a wait. Then the other turned too. Her back was to the door now. The door that wouldn't open. The door that was an epitaph, the door that was finality.

She took a slow step away. Then another. Her head was down now more than ever. She moved slowly away from there, and left the door behind. Her shadow was the last part of her to go. It trailed slowly after her, upright against the wall. Its head was down a little, too; it too was too thin, it too was unwanted. It stayed on a moment, after she herself was already gone. Then it slipped off the wall after her, and *it* was gone too.

Nothing was left there but the door. That remained silent, obdurate, closed.

Two

IN the telephone-booth she was motionless again. As motionless as before. A telephone pay-station, the door left shunted back in order to obtain air enough to breathe. When you are in one for more than just a few moments, they become stifling. And she had been in this one for more than just a few moments.

She was like a doll propped upright in its gift-box, and with one side of the box left off, to allow the contents to be seen. A worn doll. A leftover, marked-down doll, with no bright ribbons or tissue wrappings. A doll with no donor and no recipient. A doll no one bothered to claim.

She was silent there, though this was meant to be a place for talking. She was waiting to hear something, something that never came. She was holding the receiver pointed toward her ear, and it must have started out by being close to it, at right angles to it, as receivers should be. But that was a long time before. With the passage of long, disappointing minutes it had drooped lower and lower, until now it was all the way down at her shoulder, clinging there wilted, defeated, like some sort of ugly, black, hard-rubber orchid worn for corsage.

The anonymous silence became a voice at last. But not the one she wanted, not the one she was waiting for.

"I am sorry, but I have already told you. There is no use waiting on the line. That number has been discontinued, and there is no further information I can give you."

Her hand dropped off her shoulder, carrying the receiver with it, and fell into her lap, dead. As if to match something else within her that was dead, by the final way it fell and stirred no more.

But life won't grant a decent dignity even to its epitaphs, sometimes.

"May I have my nickel back?" she whispered. "*Please*. I didn't get my party, and it's—it's the last one I've got."

Three

SHE climbed the rooming-house stairs like a puppet dangling from slack strings. A light bracketed against the wall, drooping upside-down like a withered tulip in its bell-shaped shade of scalloped glass, cast a smoky yellow glow. A carpet-strip ground to the semblance of decayed vegetable-matter, all pattern, all color, long erased, adhered to the middle of the stairs, like a form of pollen or fungus encrustation. The odor matched the visual imagery. She climbed three flights of them, and then turned off toward the back.

She stopped, at the last door there was, and took out a long-shanked iron key. Then she looked down at the bottom of the door. There was a triangle of white down by her foot, protruding from under the seam. It expanded into an envelope as the door swept back above it.

She reached into the darkness, and traced her hand along the wall beside the door, and a light went on. It had very little shine. It had very little to shine on.

She closed the door and then she picked up the envelope. It had been lying on its face. She turned it over. Her hand shook a little. Her heart did too.

It had on it, in hasty, heedless pencil, only this:

"Helen Georgesson."

No Miss, no Mrs., no other salutation whatever.

She seemed to come alive more fully. Some of the blank hopelessness left her eyes. Some of the pinched strain left her face. She grasped the envelope tight, until it pleated a little in her hold. She moved more briskly than she had until now. She took it over with her to the middle of the room, beside the bed, where the light shone more fully.

She stood still there and looked at it again, as though she were a little afraid of it. There was a sort of burning eagerness in her face; not joyous, but rather of desperate urgency.

She ripped hastily at the flap of it, with upward swoops of her hand, as though she were taking long stitches in it with invisible needle and thread.

Her hand plunged in, to pull out what it said, to read what it told her. For envelopes carry words that tell you things; that's what envelopes are for.

Her hand came out again empty, frustrated. She turned the envelope over and shook it out, to free what it must hold, what must have stubbornly resisted her fingers the first time.

No words came, no writing.

Two things fell out, onto the bed. Only two things.

One was a five-dollar bill. Just an impersonal, anonymous five-dollar bill, with Lincoln's picture on it. And over to the side of that, the neat little cachet they all bear, in small-size capitals: "This certificate is legal tender for all debts public and private." For all debts, public and *private*. How could the engraver guess that that might break somebody's heart, some day, somewhere?

And the second thing was a strip of railroad-tickets, running consecutively from starting-point to terminus, as railroad tickets do. Each coupon to be detached progressively en route. The first coupon was inscribed "New York"; here, where she was now. And the last was inscribed "San Francisco"; where she'd come from, a hundred years ago—last spring.

There was no return-ticket. It was for a one-way trip. There and—to stay.

So the envelope *had* spoken to her after all, though it had no words in it. Five dollars legal tender, for *all* debts, public and private. San Francisco—and no return.

The envelope plummeted to the floor.

She couldn't seem to understand for a long time. It was as though she'd never seen a five-dollar bill before. It was as though she'd never seen an accordion-pleated strip of rail-road-tickets like that before. She kept staring down at them.

Then she started to shake a little. At first without sound. Her face kept twitching intermittently, up alongside the eyes and down around the corners of the mouth, as if her expression were struggling to burst forth into some kind of fulminating emotion. For a moment or two it seemed that when it did, it would be weeping. But it wasn't.

It was laughter.

Her eyes wreathed into oblique slits, and her lips slashed back, and harsh broken sounds came through. Like rusty laughter. Like laughter left in the rain too long, that has got all mildewed and spoiled.

She was still laughing when she brought out the battered valise, and placed it atop the bed, and threw the lid back. She was still laughing when she'd filled it and closed it again.

She never seemed to get through laughing. Her laughter never stopped. As at some long-drawn joke, that goes on and on, and is never done with in its telling.

But laughter should be merry, vibrant and alive.

This wasn't.

Four

THE train had already ticked off fifteen minutes' solid, steady headway, and she hadn't yet found a seat. The seats were full with holiday crowds and the aisles were full and the very vestibules were full; she'd never seen a train like this before. She'd been too far behind at the dammed-up barrier, and too slow and awkward with her cumbersome valise, and too late getting on. Her ticket only allowed her to get aboard, it gave her no priority on any place to sit.

Flagging, wilting, exhausted, she struggled down car-aisle after car-aisle, walking backward against the train-pull, eddying, teetering from side to side, leaden valise pulling her down.

They were all packed with standees, and this was the last one now. No more cars after this. She'd been through them all. No one offered her a seat. This was a through train, no stops for whole States at a time, and an act of courtesy now would have come too high. This was no trolley or bus with a few moments' running time. Once you were gallant and stood, you stood for hundreds and hundreds of miles.

She stopped at last, and stayed where she'd stopped, for sheer inability to turn and go back again to where she'd come from. No use going any further. She could see to the end of the car, and there weren't any left.

She let her valise down parallel to the aisle, and tried to seat herself upon its upturned edge as she saw so many others doing. But she floundered badly for a moment, out of her own topheaviness, and almost tumbled in lowering herself. Then when she'd succeeded, she let her head settle back against the sideward edge of the seat she was adjacent to, and stayed that way. Too tired to know, too tired to care, too tired even to close her eyes.

What makes you stop, when you have stopped, just where you have stopped? What is it, what? Is it something, or is it nothing? Why not a yard short, why not a yard more? Why just there where you are, and nowhere else?

Some say: It's just blind chance, and if you hadn't stopped there, you would have stopped at the next place. Your story would have been different then. You weave your own story as you go along.

But others say: You could not have stopped any place else but this even if you had wanted to. It was decreed, it was ordered, you were meant to stop at this spot and no other. Your story is there waiting for you, it has been waiting for you there a hundred years, long before you were born, and you cannot change a comma of it. Everything you do, you have to do. You are the twig, and the water you float on swept you here. You are the leaf and the breeze you were borne on blew you here. This is your story, and you cannot escape it; you are only the player, not the stage manager. Or so some say.

On the floor before her downcast eyes, just over the rim of the seat-arm, she could see two pairs of shoes uptilted, side by side. On the inside, toward the window, a diminutive pair of pumps, pert, saucy, without backs, without sides, without toes, in fact with scarcely anything but dagger-like heels and a couple of straps. And on the outside, the nearer side to her, a pair of man's brogues, looking by comparison squat, bulky, and tremendously heavy. These hung one above the other, from legs coupled at the knee.

She did not see their faces and she did not want to. She did not want to see anyone's face. She did not want to see anything.

Nothing happened for a moment. Then one of the pumps edged slyly over toward one of the brogues, nudged gently into it, as if in a deft little effort to communicate something. The brogue remained oblivious; it didn't get the message. It got the feeling, but not the intent. A large hand came down, and scratched tentatively at the sock just above the brogue, then went up again.

The pump, as if impatient at such obtuseness, repeated the effort. Only this time it delivered a good sharp dig, with a bite to it, and on the unprotected ankle, above the armor-like brogue.

That got results. A newspaper rattled somewhere above, as if it had been lowered out of the way, to see what all this unpleasant nipping was about.

A whispered remark was voiced above, spoken too low to be distinguishable by any but the ear for which it was intended.

An interrogative grunt, in masculine timbre, answered it.

Both brogues came down even on the floor, as the legs above uncoupled. Then they swivelled slightly toward the aisle, as if their owner had turned his upper body to glance that way.

The girl on the valise closed her eyes wearily, to avoid the gaze that she knew must be on her.

When she opened them again, the brogues had come out through the seat-gap, and the wearer was standing full-height in the aisle, on the other side of her. A good height too, a six-foot height.

"Take my seat, miss," he invited. "Go ahead, take my place for awhile."

She tried to demur with a faint smile and a halfhearted shake of the head. But the velour back looked awfully good.

The girl who had remained in it added her insistence to his. "Go ahead, honey, take it," she urged. "He wants you to. We want you to. You can't stay out there like that, where you are."

The velour back looked awfully good. She couldn't take her eyes off it. But she was almost too tired to stand up and effect the change. He had to reach down and take her by the arm and help her rise from the valise and shift over.

Her eyes closed again for a moment, in ineffable bliss, as she sank back.

"There you are," he said heartily. "Isn't that better?"

And the girl beside her, her new seat-mate, said: "Why, you *are* tired. I never saw anyone so all-in."

She smiled her thanks, and still tried to protest a little, though the act had already been completed, but they both overrode her remonstrances.

She looked at the two of them. Now she at least wanted to see their two faces, if no others, though only a few moments ago she hadn't wanted to see any faces, anywhere, ever again. But kindness is a form of restorative.

They were both young. Well, she was too. But they were both happy, gay, basking in the world's blessings, that was the difference between them and her. It stood out all over them. There was some sort of gilded incandescence alight within both of them alike, something that was more than mere good spirits, more than mere good fortune, and for the first few moments she couldn't tell what it was. Then in no time at all, their eyes, and every turn of their heads, and every move they made, gave it away: they were supremely, brimmingly in love with one another. It glowed out all over them, almost like phosphorus.

Young love. New untarnished love. That first love that comes just once to everyone and never comes back again.

But, conversationally, it expressed itself inversely, at least on her part if not his; almost every remark she addressed to him was a friendly insult, a gentle slur, an amiable depreciation. Not so much as a word of tenderness, or even ordinary human consideration, did she seem to have for him. Though her eyes belied her. And he understood. He had that smile for all her outrageous insolences, that worshipped, that adored, that understood so well.

"Well, go on," she said with a peremptory flick of her hand. "Don't stand there like a dope, breathing down the backs of our necks. Go and find something to do."

"Oh, pardon me," he said, and pretended to turn the back of his collar up, as if frozen out. He looked vaguely up and down the aisle. "Guess I'll go out on the platform and smoke a cigarette."

"Smoke two," she said airily. "See if I care."

He turned and began to pick his way down the thronged aisle.

"That was nice of him," the newcomer said appreciatively, glancing after him.

"Oh, he's tolerable," her companion said. "He has his good points." She gave a shrug. But her eyes made a liar out of her.

She glanced around to make sure he'd gone out of earshot. Then she leaned slightly toward the other, dropped her voice confidentially. "I could tell right away," she said. "That's why I made him get up. About you, I mean."

The girl who'd been on the valise dropped her eyes for an instant, confused, deprecating. She didn't say anything.

"I am too. You're not the only one," her companion rushed on, with just a trace of vainglory, as if she couldn't wait to tell it quickly enough.

The girl said, "Oh." She didn't know what else to say. It sounded flat, superficial; the way you say "Is that so?" or "You don't say?" She tried to force a smile of sympathetic interest, but she wasn't very good at it. Out of practice at smiling, maybe.

"Seven months," the other added gratuitously.

The girl could feel her eyes on her, as though she expected some return in kind to be made, if only for the record.

"Eight," she said, half-audibly. She didn't want to, but she did.

"Wonderful," was her companion's praise for this arithmetical information. "Marvelous." As though there were some sort of a caste system involved in this, and she unexpectedly found herself speaking to one of the upper brackets of nobility: a duchess or a marquise, who outranked her by thirty days. And all around them, snobbishly ignored, the commonality of the female gender.

"Wonderful, marvelous," echoed the girl inwardly, and her heart gave a frightened, unheard sob.

"And your husband?" the other rushed on. "You going to meet him?"

"No," the girl said, looking steadily at the green velour of the seat-back in front of them. "No."

"Oh. D'dyou leave him back in New York?"

"No," the girl said. "No." She seemed to see it written on the seat-back in transitory lettering, that faded again as soon as it was once read. "I've lost him."

"Oh, I'm sor—" Her vivacious companion seemed to know grief for the first time, other than just grief over a broken doll or a school-girl crush betrayed. It was like a new experience passing over her radiant face. And it was, even now, bound to be someone else's grief, not her own; that was the impression you had. That she'd never had any grief of her own, had none now, and never would have. One of those star-blessed rarities, glittering its way through the world's dark vale.

She bit off the rest of the ejaculation of sympathy, gnawed at her upper lip; reached out impulsively and placed her hand upon her companion's for a moment, then withdrew it again.

Then, tactfully, they didn't speak any more about such things. Such basic things as birth and death, that can give such joy and can give such pain.

She had corn-gold hair, this sun-kissed being. She wore it in a hazy aureole that fluffed out all over her head. She had freckles that were like little flecks of gold paint, spattered from some careless painter's brush all over her apricot cheeks, with a saddle across the bridge of her tiny, pert nose. It was her mouth that was the beautiful part of her. And if the rest of her face was not quite up to its matchless beauty, that mouth alone was sufficient to make her lovely-looking, unaided, drawing all notice to itself as it did. Just as a single light is enough to make a plain room bright; you don't have to have a whole chandelier. When it smiled, everything else smiled with it. Her nose crinkled, and her eyebrows arched, and her eyes creased, and dimples showed up where there hadn't been any a minute before. She looked as though she smiled a lot. She looked as though she had a lot to smile about.

She continually toyed with a wedding-band on her third finger. Caressed it, so to speak, fondled it. She was probably unconscious of doing so by this time; it must have become a fixed habit by now. But originally, months ago, when it was first there, when it was new there, she must have taken such a fierce pride in it that she'd felt the need for continually displaying it to all the world—as if to say, "Look at *me*! Look what I've got!"—must have held such an affection for it that she couldn't keep her hands off it for very long. And now, though pride and affection were in nowise less, this had formed itself into a winning little habit that persisted. No matter what move her hands made, no matter what gesture they expressed, it always managed to come uppermost, to be foremost in the beholder's eye.

It had a row of diamonds, and then a sapphire at each end for a stop. She caught her new seat-mate's glance resting upon it, so then she turned it around her way a little more, so she could see it all the better, gave it a pert little brush-off with her fingers, as if to dispel the last, lingering, hypothetical grain of dust. A brush-off that pretended she didn't care any more about it just then. Just as her attitude toward him pretended she didn't care anything about him either. A brush-off that lied like the very devil.

They were both chatting away absorbedly, as new-found friends do, by the time he reappeared some ten minutes later. He came up to them acting secretive and mysterious in a rather conspicuous way. He looked cautiously left and right first, as if bearing tidings of highest secrecy. Then screened the side of his mouth with the edge of one hand. Then leaned down and whispered, "Pat, one of the porters just tipped me off. They're going to open up the dining-car in a couple of minutes. Special, inside, advance information. You know what that'll mean in this mob. I think we better start moving up that way if we want to get in under the rope on the first shift. There'll be a stampede under way as soon as word gets around."

She jumped to her feet with alacrity.

He immediately soft-pedalled her with the flats of both hands, in comic intensity. "Sh! Don't give it away! What are you trying to do? Act indifferent. Act as if you weren't going anywhere in particular, were just getting up to stretch your legs."

She smothered an impish chuckle. "When I'm going to the dining-car, I just *can't* act as if I weren't going anywhere in particular. It stands out all over me. You're lucky if you hold me down to a twenty-yard dash." But to oblige his ideas of Machiavellian duplicity, she exaggeratedly arched her feet and tiptoed out into the aisle, as though the amount of noise she made had any relation to what they were trying to do.

In passing, she pulled persuasively at the sleeve of the girl beside her. "Come on. You're coming with us, aren't you?" she whispered conspiratorially.

"What about the seats? We'll lose them, won't we?"

"Not if we put our baggage on them. Here, like this." She raised the other girl's valise, which had been standing there in the aisle until now, and between them they planked it lengthwise across the seat, effectively blocking it.

The girl was on her feet now, dislodged by the valise, but she still hung back, hesitant about going with them.

The young wife seemed to understand; she was quick that way. She sent him on ahead, out of earshot, to break trail for them. Then turned to her recent seat-mate in tactful reassurance. "Don't worry about—anything; *he*'ll look after everything." And then, making confidantes of the two of them about this, to minimize the other's embarrassment, she promised her: "I'll see that he does. That's what they're for, anyway.

The girl tried to falter an insincere denial, that only proved the surmise had been right. "No, it isn't that—I don't like to—"

But her new friend had already taken her acceptance for an accomplished fact, had no more time to waste on it. "Hurry up, we'll lose him," she urged. "They're closing in again behind him."

She urged her forward ahead of herself, a friendly hand lightly placed just over her outside hip.

"You can't neglect yourself now, of all times," she cautioned her in an undertone. "I *know*. They told me that my-self."

The pioneering husband, meanwhile, was cutting a wide swath for them down the center of the clogged aisle, causing people to lean acutely in over the seats to give clearance. And yet with never a resentful look. He seemed to have that way about him; genial but firm.

"It's useful to have a husband who used to be on the football team," his bride commented complacently. "He can run your interference for you. Just look at the width of that back, would you?"

When they had overtaken him, she complained petulantly, "Wait for me, can't you? I have two to feed."

"So have I," was the totally unchivalrous remark over his shoulder. "And they're both me."

They were, by dint of his foresight, the first ones in the dining-car, which was inundated within moments after the doors had been thrown open. They secured a choice table for three, diagonal to a window. The unlucky ones had to wait on line in the aisle outside, the door inhospitably closed in their faces.

"Just so we won't sit down to the table still not knowing each other's names," the young wife said, cheerfully unfolding her napkin, "he's Hazzard, Hugh, and I'm Hazzard, Patrice." Her dimples showed up in depreciation. "Funny name, isn't it?"

"Be more respectful," her young spouse growled, without lifting his forehead from the bill of fare. "I'm just trying you out for it. I haven't decided yet whether I'll let you keep it or not."

"It's mine now," was the feminine logic he got. "I haven't decided whether I'll let *you* keep it or not."

"What's your name?" she asked their guest.

"Georgesson," the girl said. "Helen Georgesson."

She smiled hesitantly at the two of them. Gave him the outside edge of her smile, gave her the center of it. It wasn't a very broad smile, but it had depth and gratitude, the little there was of it.

"You've both been awfully friendly to me," she said.

She looked down at the menu card she held spread between

her hands, so they wouldn't detect the flicker of emotion that made her lips tremble for a moment.

"It must be an awful lot of fun to be—you," she murmured wistfully.

Five

BY the time the overhead lights in their car had been put out, around ten, so that those who wanted to sleep could do so, they were already old and fast friends. They were already "Patrice" and "Helen" to one another; this, as might have been surmised, at Patrice's instigation. Friendship blooms quickly in the hothouse atmosphere of travel; within the space of hours, sometimes, it's already full-blown. Then just as suddenly is snapped off short, by the inevitable separation of the travelers. It seldom if ever survives that separation for long. That is why, on ships and trains, people have fewer reticences with one another, they exchange confidences more quickly, tell all about themselves; they will never have to see these same people again, and worry about what opinion they may have formed, whether good or bad.

The small, shaded, individual sidelights provided for each seat, that could be turned on or off at will, were still on for the most part, but the car was restfully dimmer and quieter, some of its occupants already dozing. Patrice's husband was in an inert, hat-shrouded state on the valise that again stood alongside his original seat, his crossed legs precariously slung upward to the top of the seat ahead. However, he seemed comfortable enough, judging by the sonorous sounds that escaped from inside his hat now and then. He had dropped out of their conversation fully an hour before, and, an unkind commentary this on the importance of men to women's conversations, to all appearances hadn't even been missed.

Patrice was acting the part of a look-out, her eyes watchfully and jealously fastened on a certain door, far down the aisle behind them, in the dim distance. To do this, she was kneeling erect on the seat, in reverse, staring vigilantly over the back of it. This somewhat unconventional position, however, did nothing whatever to inhibit her conversational flow, which proceeded as freely and blithely as ever. Only, owing to her elevated stance, the next seat back now shared the benefit of most of it, along with her own. Fortunately, however, its occupants were disqualified from any great amount of interest in it by two facts; they were both men, and they were both asleep.

A ripple of reflected light suddenly ran down the sleek chromium of the door that had her attention.

"She just came out," she hissed with an explosive sibilance, and executed an agitated series of twists, turns, and drops on the seat, as though this were something vital that had to be acted upon immediately. "Hurry up! *Now!* Now's our chance. Get a move on. Before somebody else gets there ahead of us. There's a fat woman three seats down been taking her things out little by little. If she ever gets in first, we're sunk!" Carried away by her own excitement (and everything in life, to her, seemed to be deliciously, titillatingly exciting), she even went so far as to give her seat-mate a little push and urge her: "Run! Hold the door for us. Maybe if she sees you there already, she'll change her mind."

She prodded her relaxed spouse cruelly and heartlessly in a great many places at once, to bring him back to awareness.

"Quick! Hugh! The overnight-case! We'll lose our chance. Up there, stupid. Up there on the rack—"

"All right, take it easy," the somnolent Hugh grunted, eyes still completely buried under his obliterating hat-brim. "Talk, talk, talk, Yattatta, yattatta, yattatta. Woman is born to exercise her jaw."

"Man is born to get a poke on his, if he doesn't get a move on."

He finally pushed his hat back out of the way. "What do you want from me now? You got it down yourself."

"Well, get your big legs out of the way and let us by! You're blocking the way—"

He executed a sort of drawbridge maneuver, folding his legs back to himself, hugging them, then stretching them out again after the passage had been accomplished.

"Where y'going, in such a hurry?" he asked innocently.

"Now, isn't that stupid?" commented Patrice to her companion.

The two of them went almost running down the aisle, without bothering to enlighten him further.

"He takes a thirty-six sleeve, and it doesn't do me a bit of good in an emergency," she complained en route, swinging the kit.

He had turned his head to watch them curiously, and in perfectly sincere incomprehension. Then he went, "Oh." Understanding their destination now, if not the turmoil attendant on it. Then he pulled his hat down to his nose again, to resume his fractured slumbers where they had been broken off by this feminine logistical upheaval.

Patrice had closed the chromium door after the two of them, meanwhile, and given its inside lock-control a little twist of defiant exclusion. Then she let out a deep breath. "There. We're in. And possession is nine-tenths of the law. I'm going to take as long as I want," she announced determinedly, setting down the overnight-case and unlatching its lid. "If anybody else wants to get in, they'll just have to wait. There's only room enough for two anyway. And even so, they have to be awfully good friends."

"We're nearly the last ones still up, anyway," Helen said.

"Here, have some?" Patrice was bringing up a fleecy fistful of facial tissues from the case; she divided them with her friend.

"I missed these an awful lot on the Other Side. Couldn't get them for love nor money. I used to ask and ask, and they didn't know what I meant—"

She stopped and eyed her companion. "Oh, you have nothing to rub off, have you? Well, here, rub some of this on; then you'll have that to rub off."

Helen laughed. "You make me feel so giddy," she said with a wistful sort of admiration.

Patrice hunched her shoulders and grimaced impishly. "It's my last fling, sort of. From tomorrow night on I may have to be on my best behavior. Sober and sedate." She made a long face, and steepled her hands against her stomach, in mimicry of a bluenosed clergyman.

"Oh, on account of meeting your in-laws," Helen remembered.

"Hugh says they're not like that at all; I have absolutely nothing to worry about. But of course he just may be slightly prejudiced in their favor. I wouldn't think much of him if he wasn't."

She was scouring a mystic white circle on each cheek, and then spreading them around, mouth open the whole while, though it played no part in the rite itself.

"Go ahead, help yourself," she invited. "Stick your finger in and dig out a gob. I'm not sure what it does for you, but it smells nice, so there's nothing to lose."

"Is that really true, what you told me?" Helen said, following suit. "That they've never even seen you until now? I can't believe it."

"Cross my heart and hope to die, they've never laid eyes on me in their lives. I met Hugh on the Other Side, like I told you this afternoon, and we were married over there, and we went on living over there until just now. My folks were dead, and I was on a scholarship, studying music, and he had a job with one of these government agencies; you know, one of these initialed outfits. They don't even know what I *look* like!"

"Didn't you even send them a picture of yourself? Not even after you were married?"

"We never even had a wedding-picture taken; you know how us kids are nowadays. Biff, bing, bang! and we're married. I started to send them one of myself several times, but I was never quite satisfied with the ones I had. Self-conscious, you know; I wanted to make *such* a good first impression. One time Hugh even arranged a sitting for me at a photographer, and when I saw the proofs I said, 'Over my dead body you'll send these!' Those French photographers! I knew I was going to meet them eventually, and snapshots are so—so— Anyway the ones *I* take. So finally I said to him, 'I've waited this long, I'm not going to send any to them at all now. I'll save it up for a surprise, let them see me in the flesh instead, when they finally do. That way, they won't build up any false hopes and then be disappointed.' I used to censor all his letters too, wouldn't let him describe me. You can imagine how he would have done it. 'Mona Lisa,' Venus on the half-shell. I'd say, 'No you don't!' when I'd catch him at it, and scratch it out. We'd have more tussles that way, chase each other around the room, trying to get the letter back or trying to get it away from me."

She became serious for a moment. Or at least, approached as closely to it as she seemed capable of.

"Y'know, now I wish I hadn't done that, sort of. Played hide and seek with them like this, I mean. Now I *have* got cold feet. Do you think they'll really like me? Suppose they don't? Suppose they have me built up in their expectations as someone entirely different, and—"

Like the little boy in the radio skit who prattles about a self-invented bugaboo until he ends up by frightening himself with it.

"How on earth do you make the water stay in this thing?" she interrupted herself. She pounded lightly on the plunger set into the washbasin. "Every time I get it to fill, it runs right out again."

"Twist it a little, and then push down on it, I think."

Patrice stripped off her wedding-band before plunging her hands in. "Hold this for me, I want to wash my hands. I have a horror of losing it. It slipped down a drain on the Other Side, once, and they had to take out a whole section of pipe before they could get it out for me."

"It's beautiful," Helen said wistfully.

"Isn't it, though?" Patrice agreed. "See? It has our names, together, around it on the inside. Isn't that a cute idea? Keep it on your finger for me a minute, that's the safest."

"Isn't it supposed to be bad luck to do that? I mean, for you to take it off, and for me to put it on?"

Patrice tossed her head vaingloriously. "I *couldn't* have bad luck," she proclaimed. It was almost a challenge.

"And I," thought Helen sombrely, "couldn't have good."

She watched it curiously as it slowly descended the length of her finger, easily, without forcing. There was a curiously familiar feeling to it, as of something that should have been there long ago, that belonged there and had been strangely lacking until now.

"So this is what it feels like," she said to herself poignantly.

The train pounded on, its headlong roar deadened, in here where they were, to a muted jittering.

Patrice stepped back, her toilette at last completed. "Well, this is my last night," she sighed. "By this time tomorrow night we'll already be there, the worst'll be over." She clasped her own arms, in a sort of half-shiver of fright. "I hope they like what they're getting." She nervously stole a sidelong look at herself in the glass, primped at her hair.

"You'll be all right, Patrice," Helen reassured her quietly. "Nobody could help but like you."

Patrice crossed her fingers and held them up to show her. "Hugh says they're very well-off," she rambled on. "That makes it all the worse sometimes." She tittered in recollection. "I guess they must be. I know they even had to send us the money for the trip home. We were always on a shoestring, the whole time we were over there. We had an awful lot of fun, though. I think that's the only time you have fun, when you're on a shoestring, don't you?"

"Sometimes—you don't," remembered Helen, but she didn't answer.

"Anyway," her confidante babbled on, "as soon as they found out I was Expecting, that did it! They wouldn't hear of my having my baby over there. I didn't much want to myself, as a matter of fact, and Hugh didn't want me to either. They should be born in the good old U.S.A., don't you think so? That's the least you can do for them."

"Sometimes that's *all* you can do for them," Helen thought wryly. "That—and seventeen cents."

She had finished now in turn.

Patrice urged, "Let's stay in here long enough to have a puff, now that we're here. We don't seem to be keeping anybody else out. And if we try to talk out there, they might shush us down; they're all trying to sleep." The little lighter-flame winked in coppery reflection against the mirrors and glistening chrome on all sides of them. She gave a sigh of heartfelt satisfaction. "I love these before-retiring talks with another girl. It's been ages since I last had one. Back in school, I guess. Hugh says I'm a woman's woman at heart." She stopped short and thought about it with a quizzical quirk of her head. "Is that good or bad? I must ask him."

Helen couldn't repress a smile. "Good, I guess. I wouldn't want to be a man's woman."

"I wouldn't either!" Patrice hastily concurred. "It always makes me think of someone who uses foul language and spits out of the corner of her mouth."

They both chuckled for a moment in unison. But Patrice's butterfly-mind had already fluttered on to the next topic, as she dropped ash into the waste-receptacle. "Wonder if I'll be able to smoke openly, once I'm home?" She shrugged. "Oh well, there's always the back of the barn."

And then suddenly she had reverted to their mutual condition again.

"Are you frightened? About *it*, you know?"

Helen made the admission with her eyes.

"I am too." She took a reflective puff. "I think everyone is, a little, don't you? Men don't think we are. All I have to do is look at Hugh—" she deepened the dimple-pits humorously—"and I can see he's frightened enough for the two of us, so then I don't let on that I'm frightened too. And *I* reassure *him*."

Helen wondered what it was like to have someone to talk to about it.

"Are *they* pleased about it?"

"Oh sure. They're tickled silly. First grandchild, you know. They didn't even ask us if we *wanted* to come back. 'You're coming back,' and that was that."

She pointed the remnant of her cigarette down toward one of the taps, quenched it with a sharp little jet of water.

"Ready? Shall we go back to our seats now?"

They were both doing little things. All life is that, the continuous doing of little things, all life long. And then suddenly a big thing strikes into their midst—and where are the little things, what became of them, what were they?

Her hand was to the door, reversing the little hand-latch that Patrice had locked before, when they first came in. Patrice was somewhere behind her, replacing something in the uplidded dressing-kit, about to close it and bring it with her. She could see her vaguely in the chromium sheeting lining the wall before her. Little things. Little things that life is made up of. Little things that stop—

Her senses played a trick on her. There was no time for them to synchronize with the thing that happened. They played her false. She had a fleeting impression, at first, of having done something wrong to the door, dislodged it in its entirety. Simply by touching that little hand-latch. It was as though she were bringing the whole door-slab down inward on herself. As though it were falling bodily out of its frame, hinges and all. And yet it never did, it never detached itself, it never came apart from the entire wall-section it was imbedded in. So the second fleeting impression, equally false and equally a matter of seconds only, was that the entire wall of the compartment, door and all, was toppling, threatening to come down on her. And yet that never did either. Instead, the whole alcove seemed to upend, shift on a crazy axis, so that what had been the wall before her until now, had shifted to become the ceiling over her; so that what had been the floor she was standing on until now, had shifted to become the wall upright before her. The door was gone hopelessly out of reach; was a sealed trap overhead, impossible to attain.

The lights went. All light was gone, and yet so vividly explosive were the sensory images whirling through her mind that they glowed on of their own incandescence in the dark; it took her a comparatively long time to realize she was steeped in pitch-blackness, could no longer see physically. Only in afterglow of imaginative terror.

There was a nauseating sensation as if the tracks, instead of being rigid steel rods, had softened into rippling ribbons, with the train still trying to follow their buckling curvature. The car seemed to go up and down, like a scenic railway performing foreshortened dips and rises that followed one another quicker and quicker and quicker. There was a distant rending, grinding, coming nearer, swelling as it came. It reminded her of a coffee-mill they had had at home, when she was a little girl. But that one didn't draw you into its maw, crunching everything in sight, as this one was doing.

"Hugh!" the disembodied floor itself seemed to scream out behind her. Just once.

Then after that the floor fell silent.

There were minor impressions. Of seams opening, and of heavy metal partitions being bent together over her head,

until the opening that held her was no longer foursquare, but
tent-shaped. The darkness blanched momentarily in sudden
ghostly pallor that was hot and puckery to breathe. Escaping
steam. Then it thinned out again, and the darkness came back
full-pitch. A little orange light flickered up somewhere, far off.
Then that ebbed and dimmed again, and was gone, too.

There wasn't any sound now, there wasn't any motion.
Everything was still, and dreamy, and forgotten. What was
this? Sleep? Death? She didn't think so. But it wasn't life either. She remembered life; life had been only a few minutes
ago. Life had had lots of light in it, and people, and motion,
and sound.

This must be something else. Some transitional stage, some
other condition she hadn't been told about until now. Neither
life, nor death, but something in-between.

Whatever it was, it held pain in it; it was *all* pain, only pain.
Pain that started small, and grew, and grew, and grew. She
tried to move, and couldn't. A slim rounded thing, cold and
sweating, down by her feet, was holding her down. It lay
across her straight, like a water pipe sprung out of joint.

Pain that grew and grew. If she could have screamed, it
might have eased it. But she couldn't seem to.

She put her hand to her mouth. On her third finger she
encountered a little metal circlet, a ring that had been drawn
over it. She bit on it. That helped, that eased it a little. The
more the pain grew, the harder she bit.

She heard herself moan a little, and she shut her eyes. The
pain went away. But it took everything else with it; thought,
knowledge, awareness.

She opened her eyes again, reluctantly. Minutes? Hours?
She didn't know. She only wanted to sleep, to sleep some
more. Thought, knowledge, awareness, came back. But the
pain didn't come back; that seemed to be gone for good.
Instead there was just this lassitude. She heard herself whimpering softly, like a small kitten. Or was it she?

She only wanted to sleep, to sleep some more. And they
were making so much noise they wouldn't let her. Clanging,
and pounding on sheets of loose tin, and prying things away.
She rolled her head aside a little, in protest.

An attenuated shaft of light peered through, from somewhere up over her head. It was like a long thin finger, a spoke, prodding for her, pointing at her, trying to find her in the dark.

It didn't actually hit her, but it kept probing for her in all the wrong places, all around her.

She only wanted to sleep. She mewed a little in protest—or was it she?—and there was a sudden frightened flurry of activity, the pounding became faster, the prying became more hectic.

Then all of it stopped at once, there was a complete cessation, and a man's voice sounded directly over her, strangely hollow and blurred as when you talk through a tube.

"Steady. We're coming to you. Just a minute longer, honey. Can you hold out? Are you hurt? Are you bad? Are you alone under there?"

"No," she said feebly. "I've—I've just had a baby down here."

Six

RECOVERY was like a progressive equalization of badly unbalanced solstices. At first time was all nights, unbroken polar nights, with tiny fractional days lasting a minute or two at a time. Nights were sleep and days were wakefulness. Then little by little the days expanded and the nights contracted. Presently, instead of many little days during the space of each twenty-four hours, there was just one long one in the middle of it each time, the way there should be. Soon this had even begun to overlap at one end, to continue beyond the setting of the sun and impinge into the first hour or two of evening. Now, instead of many little fragmentary days in the space of one night, there were many little fragmentary nights in the space of one day. Dozes or naps. The solstices had reversed themselves.

Recovery was on a second, concurrent plane as well. Dimension entered into it as well as duration. The physical size of her surroundings expanded along with the extension of her days. First there was just a small area around her that entered into awareness each time; the pillows behind her head, the upper third of the bed, a dim face just offside to her, bending down toward her, going away, coming back again. And over and above everything else, a small form allowed to nestle in her arms for a few moments at a time. Something that was alive and warm and hers. She came more alive then than at any other time. It was food and drink and sunlight; it was her lifeline back to life. The rest remained unfocussed, lost in misty gray distances stretching out and around her.

But this core of visibility, this too expanded. Presently it had reached the foot of the bed. Then it had jumped over that, to the wide moat of the room beyond, its bottom hidden from sight. Then it had reached the walls of the room, on all three sides, and could go no further for the present; they stopped it. But that wasn't a limitation of inadequate awareness any more, that was a limitation of physical equipment. Even well eyes were not made to go through walls.

It was a pleasant room. An infinitely pleasant room. This could not have been a haphazard effect achieved at random. It was too immediate, too all-pervading; every chord it struck was the right one: whether of color, proportion, acoustics, bodily tranquility and well-being, and above all, of personal security and sanctuary, of belonging somewhere at last, of having found a haven, a harbor, of being let be. The height of scientific skill and knowledge, therefore, must have entered into it, to achieve that cumulative effect that her mind could only label pleasant.

The over-all effect was a warm glowing ivory shade, not a chill, clinical white. There was a window over to her right, with a Venetian blind. And when this was furled, the sun came through in a solid slab-like shaft, like a chunk of copper-gold ore. And when it was unfurled, the dismembered beams blurred and formed a hazy mist flecked with copper-gold motes that clung to the whole window like a halo. And still at other times they brought the slats sharply together, and formed a cool blue dusk in the room, and even that was grateful, made you close your eyes without effort and take a nap.

There were always flowers standing there, too, over to her right near the head of the bed. Never the same color twice. They must have been changed each day. They repeated themselves, but never in immediate succession. Yellow, and then the next day pink, and then the next day violet and white, and then the next day back to yellow again. She got so she looked for them. It made her want to open her eyes and see what color they would be this time. Maybe that was why they were there. The Face would bring them over and hold them closer for her to see, and then put them back again.

The first words she spoke each day were: "Let me see my little boy." But the second, or not far behind, were always: "Let me see my flowers."

And after awhile there was fruit. Not right at first, but a little later on when she first began to enjoy appetite again. That was in a different place, not quite so close, over by the window. In a basket, with a big-eared satin bow standing up straight above its handle. Never the same fruit twice, that is to say, never the same arrangement or ratio of the various species, and never any slightest mark of spoilage, so she knew it must be new fruit each day. The satin bow was never the same twice, either, so presumably the basket was a different one too. A new basketful of fresh fruit each day.

And if it could never mean quite as much to her as the flowers that is because flowers are flowers and fruit is fruit. It was still good to look at in its way. Blue grapes and green, and purple ones, with the sunlight shining through them and giving them a cathedral-window lustre; bartlett pears, with a rosy flush that almost belonged to apples on their yellow cheeks; plushy yellow peaches; pert little tangerines; apples that were almost purple in their apoplectic full-bloodedness.

Every day, nestled in cool, crisp, dark-green tissue.

She hadn't known that hospitals were so attentive. She hadn't known they provided such things for their patients; even patients who only had seventeen cents in their purses— or would have, had they had purses—when they were admitted.

She thought about the past sometimes, remembered it, reviewed it, the little there was of it. But it brought shadows into the room, dimmed its bright corners, it thinned even the thick girder-like shafts of sunlight coming through the window, it made her want the covers closer up around her shoulders, so she learned to avoid thinking of it, summoning it up.

She thought:

I was on a train. I was closeted in the washroom with another girl. She could remember the metallic sheen of the fixtures and the mirrors. She could see the other girl's face; three dimples in triangular arrangement, one on each cheek, one at the chin. She could even feel the shaking and vibration, the slight unsteadiness of footing, again, if she tried hard enough. But it made her slightly nauseated to do so, because she knew what was coming next, in a very few seconds. She knew now, but she hadn't known then. She usually snapped off the sensory image, as if it were a light-switch, in a hurry at this point, to forestall what was surely coming next.

She remembered New York. She remembered the door that wouldn't open. She remembered the strip of one-way tickets falling out of an envelope. That was when the shadows really formed around, good and heavy. That was when the temperature of the room really went down. When she went back behind the train-trip, to remember New York, on the other side of it.

She quickly shut her eyes and turned her head aside on the pillow, and shut the past out.

The present was kinder by far. And you could have it so easy, any given moment of the day. You could have it without trying at all. Stay in the present, let the present do. The present was safe. Don't stray out of it—not in either direction, forward or backward. Because there was only darkness, way out there all around it, and you didn't know what you'd find. Sit tight; lie tight, right where you were.

She opened her eyes and warmed to it again. The sunlight coming in, thick and warm and strong enough to carry the weight of a toboggan from the window-sill to the floor. The technicolored burst of flowers, the beribboned basket of fruit. The soothing quiet all around. They'd bring the little form in pretty soon, and let it nestle against her, and she'd know that happiness that was something new, that made you want to circle your arms and never let go.

Let the present do. Let the present last. Don't ask, don't seek, don't question, don't quarrel with it. Hang onto it for all you were worth.

Seven

IT was really the flowers that were her undoing, that brought the present to an end.

She wanted one of them one day. Wanted to separate one from the rest, and hold it in her hand, and smell its sweetness directly under her nose; it wasn't enough any longer just to enjoy them visually, to look at them in the abstract, in group-formation.

They'd been moved nearer by this time. And she herself could move now more freely. She'd been lying quietly on her side admiring them for some time when the impulse formed.

There was a small one, dangling low, arching over in her direction, and she thought she'd get that. She turned more fully, so that she was completely sideward, and reached out toward it.

Her hand closed on its stalk, and it quivered delicately with the pressure. She knew she wouldn't have been able to break the stalk off short just with one hand alone, and she didn't want to do that anyway; didn't want to damage the flower, just borrow it for awhile. So she started to withdraw the stalk vertically from the receptacle, and as it paid off and seemed never to come to an end, this swept her hand high upward and at last back over her own head.

It struck the bed-back, that part that was so close to her that she could never have seen it without making a complete head-turn, and something up there jiggled and quivered a little, as if threatening to detach itself and come down.

She made the complete head-turn, and even withdrew out from it a little, into a half-sitting position, something she had never attempted before, to bring it into focus.

It was a featherweight metal frame, a rectangle, clasped to the top bar of the bed, loose on its other three sides. Within was held a smooth mat of paper, with fine neat writing on it that blurred until it had stopped the slight swaying that her impact had set in motion.

It had been inches from her head, just over her head, all this time, but she'd never seen it until now.

Her chart.

She peered at it intently.

Suddenly the present and all its safety exploded into fragments, and the flower fell from her extended hand onto the floor.

There were three lines at the top, in neat symmetry. The first part of each was printed and left incomplete; the rest was finished out in typescript.

It said at the top: "Section—"

And then it said: "Maternity."

It said below that: "Room—"

And then it said: "25."

It said at the bottom: "Patient's Name—"

And then it said: "Hazzard, Patrice (Mrs.)."

Eight

THE nurse opened the door, and her face changed. The smile died off on it. You could detect the change in her face from all the way over there, even before she'd come any closer to the bed.

She came over and took her patient's temperature. Then she straightened the chart.

Neither of them said anything.

There was fear in the room. There was shadow in the room. The present was no longer in the room. The future had taken its place. Bringing fear, bringing shadow, bringing strangeness; worse than even the past could have brought.

The nurse held the thermometer toward the light and scanned it. Then her brows deepened. She put the thermometer down.

She asked the question carefully, as though she had gauged its tone and its tempo before allowing herself to ask it. She said, "What happened? Has something upset you? You're running a slight temperature."

The girl in the bed answered with a question of her own. Frightenedly, tautly. "What's that doing on my bed? Why is it there?"

"Everyone who's ill has to have one," the nurse answered soothingly. "It's nothing, just a—"

"But look—the name. It says—"

"Does the sight of your own name frighten you? You mustn't look at it. You're really not supposed to see it there. Sh, don't talk now any more."

"But there's something I— But you have to tell me, I don't understand—"

The nurse took her pulse.

And as she did so, the patient was suddenly looking at her own hand, in frozen, arrested horror. At the little circlet with diamonds, enfolding the third finger. At the wedding-band. As though she'd never seen it before, as though she wondered what it was doing there.

The nurse saw her trying to take it off, with flurried little tugs. It wouldn't move easily.

The nurse's face changed. "Just a moment, I'll be right back," she said uneasily.

She brought the doctor in with her. Her whispering stopped as they crossed the threshold.

He came over to the bed, put his hand to her forehead.

He nodded to the nurse and said, "Slight."

He said, "Drink this."

It tasted salty.

They put the hand under the covers, out of sight. The hand with the ring on it.

They took the glass from her lips. She didn't want to ask any questions, any more. She did, but some other time, not right now. There was something they had to be told. She'd had it a minute ago, but now it had escaped her again.

She sighed. Some other time, but not right now. She didn't want to do anything right now but sleep.

She turned her face toward the pillow and slept.

Nine

IT came right back again. The first thing. With the first glimpse of the flowers, the first glimpse of the fruit, right as her eyelids first went up and the room came into being. It came right back again.

Something said to her: Tread softly, speak slow. Take care, take care. She didn't know what or why, but she knew it must be heeded.

The nurse said to her, "Drink your orange juice."

The nurse said to her, "You can have a little coffee in your milk, starting from today on. Each day a little more. Won't that be a pleasant change?"

Tread softly, speak with care.

She said, "What happened to—?"

She took another sip of beige-colored milk. Tread warily, speak slow.

"To whom?" the nurse finally completed it for her.

Oh, careful now, careful. "There was another girl in the train washroom with me. Is she all right?" She took another sip of milk for punctuation. Hold the glass steady, now; that's right. Don't let it shake. Down to the tray again, even and slow; that's it.

The nurse shook her head reticently. She said, "No."

"She's dead?"

The nurse wouldn't answer. She too was treading softly. She too felt her way, she too wouldn't rush in. She said, "Did you know her very well?"

"No."

"You'd only met her on the train?"

"Only on the train."

The nurse had paved her own way now. It was safe to proceed. The nurse nodded. She was answering the question two sentences before, by delayed action. "She's gone," she said quietly.

The nurse watched her face expectantly. The pavement held; there was no cave-in.

The nurse ventured a step farther.

"Isn't there anyone else you want to ask about?"

"What happened to—?"

The nurse took the tray away, as if stripping the scene for a crisis.

"To *him*?"

Those were the words. She adopted them. "What happened to him?"

The nurse said, "Just a moment." She went to the door, opened it, and motioned to someone unseen.

The doctor came in, and a second nurse. They stood waiting, as if prepared to meet an emergency.

The first nurse said, "Temperature normal." She said, "Pulse normal."

The second nurse was mixing something in a glass.

The first nurse, her own, stood close to the bed. She took her by the hand and held it tightly. Just held it like that, tight and unyielding.

The doctor nodded.

The first nurse moistened her lips. She said, "Your husband wasn't saved either, Mrs. Hazzard."

She could feel her face pale with shock. The skin pulled as though it were a size too small.

She said, "No, there's something wrong— No, you're making a mistake—"

The doctor motioned unobtrusively. He and the second nurse closed in on her swiftly.

Somebody put a cool hand on her forehead, held her pressed downward, kindly but firmly; she couldn't tell whose it was.

She said, "No, please let me tell you!"

The second nurse was holding something to her lips. The first one was holding her hand, tight and warm, as if to say, "I am here. Don't be frightened, I am here." The hand on her forehead was cool but competent. It was heavy, but not too heavy; just persuasive enough to make her head lie still.

"Please—" she said listlessly.

She didn't say anything more after that. They didn't either.

Finally she overheard the doctor murmur, as if in punctuation: "She stood that very well."

Ten

IT came back again. How could it fail to now? You cannot sleep at all times, only at small times. And with it came: Tread softly, speak with care.

The nurse's name was Miss Allmeyer, the one she knew best.

"Miss Allmeyer, does the hospital give everyone those flowers every day?"

"We'd like to, but we couldn't afford it. Those flowers cost five dollars each time you see them. They're just for you."

"Is it the hospital that supplies that fruit every day?"

The nurse smiled gently. "We'd like to do that too. We only wish we could. That fruit cost ten dollars a basket each time you see it. It's a standing order, just for you."

"Well, who—?" Speak softly.

The nurse smiled winningly. "Can't you guess, honey? That shouldn't be very hard."

"There's something I want to tell you. Something you must let me tell you." She turned her head restlessly on the pillows, first to one side, then the other, then back to the first.

"Now, honey, are we going to have a bad day? I thought we were going to have such a good day."

"Could you find out something for me?"

"I'll try."

"The handbag; the handbag that was in the train-washroom with me. How much was in it?"

"*Your* handbag?"

"The handbag. The one that was there when I was in there."

The nurse came back later and said, "It's safe; it's being held for you. About fifty dollars or so."

That wasn't hers, that was the other one.

"There were two."

"There is another," the nurse admitted. "It doesn't belong to anyone now." She looked down commiseratingly. "There was just seventeen cents in it," she breathed almost inaudibly.

She didn't have to be told that. She knew by heart. She remembered from before boarding the train. She remembered from the train itself. Seventeen cents. Two pennies, a nickel, a dime.

"Could you bring the seventeen cents here? Could I have it just to look at it? Could I have it here next to the bed?"

The nurse said, "I'm not sure it's good for you, to brood like that. I'll see what they say."

She brought it, though, inside a small envelope.

She was alone with it. She dumped the four little coins from the envelope into the palm of her hand. She closed her hand upon them tightly, held them gripped like that, fiercely, in a knot of dilemma.

Fifty dollars, symbolically. Symbol of an untold amount more.

Seventeen cents, literally. Symbol of nothing, for there wasn't any more. Seventeen cents and nothing else.

The nurse came back again and smiled at her. "Now, what was it you said you wanted to tell me?"

She returned the smile, wanly. "It can keep for awhile longer. I'll tell you some other time. Tomorrow, maybe, or the next day. Not—not right today."

Eleven

THERE was a letter on the breakfast-tray.

The nurse said, "See? Now you're beginning to get mail, just like the well people do."

It was slanted toward her, leaning against the milk glass. On the envelope it said:

"Mrs. Patrice Hazzard"

She was frightened of it. She couldn't take her eyes off it. The glass of orange juice shook in her hand. The writing on it seemed to get bigger, and bigger, and bigger, as it stood there.

"MRS. PATRICE HAZZARD"

"Open it," the nurse encouraged her. "Don't just look at it like that. It won't bite you."

She tried to twice, and twice it fell. The third time she managed to rip one seam along its entire length.

"Patrice, dear:
"Though we've never seen you, you're our daughter now, dear. You're Hugh's legacy to us. You're all we

have now, you and the little fellow. I can't come to you, where you are; doctor's orders. The shock was too much for me and he forbids my making the trip. You'll have to come to us, instead. Come soon, dear. Come home to us, in our loneliness and loss. It will make it that much easier to bear. It won't be long now, dear. We've been in constant touch with Dr. Brett, and he sends very encouraging reports of your progress—"

The rest didn't matter so much; she let it fade from her attention.

It was like train-wheels going through her head.

Though we've never seen you.

Though we've never seen you.

Though we've never seen you.

The nurse eased it from her forgetful fingers after awhile, and put it back in its envelope. She watched the nurse fearfully as she moved about the room.

"If I weren't Mrs. Hazzard, would I be allowed to stay in this room?"

The nurse laughed cheerfully. "We'd put you out, we'd throw you right outside into one of the wards," she said, bending close toward her in mock threat.

The nurse said, "Here, take your young son."

She held him tightly, in fierce, almost convulsive protectiveness.

Seventeen cents. Seventeen cents lasts such a short time, goes such a short way.

The nurse felt in good humor. She tried to prolong their little joke of a moment ago. "Why? Are you trying to tell me you're not Mrs. Hazzard?" she asked banteringly.

She held him fiercely, protectively close.

Seventeen cents, seventeen cents.

"No," she said in a smothered voice, burying her face against him, "I'm not trying to tell you that. I'm not trying."

Twelve

SHE was in a dressing-robe, sitting by the window in the sun. It was quilted blue silk. She wore it every day when she got up out of bed. On the breast-pocket it had a monogram embroidered in white silk; the letters "PH" intertwined. There were slippers to match.

She was reading a book. On the flyleaf, though she was long past it, it was inscribed "To Patrice, with love from Mother H." There was a row of other books on the stand beside the bed. Ten or twelve of them; books with vivacious jackets, turquoise, magenta, vermilion, cobalt, and with vivacious, light-hearted contents to match. Not a shadow between their covers.

There was a scattering of orange peel, and two or three seeds, in a dish on a low stand beside her easy chair. There was a cigarette burning in another, smaller dish beside that one. It was custom-made, it had a straw tip, and the initials "PH" on it had not yet been consumed.

The sunlight, falling from behind and over her, made her hair seem hazily translucent, made it almost seem like golden foam about her head. It skipped the front of her, from there on down, due to the turn of the chair-back, and struck again in a little golden pool across one outthrust bare instep, lying on it like a warm, luminous kiss.

There was a light tap at the door and the doctor came in.

He drew out a chair and sat down facing her, leaving its straight back in front of him as an added note of genial informality.

"I hear you're leaving us soon."

The book fell and he had to pick it up for her. He offered it back to her, but when she seemed incapable of taking it, he put it aside on the stand.

"Don't look so frightened. Everything's arranged—"

She had a little difficulty with her breathing. "Where—? Where to?"

"Why, home, of course."

She put her hand to her hair and flattened it a little, but then it sprang up again, gaseous as before, in the sun.

"Here are your tickets." He took an envelope out of his

pocket, tried to offer it to her. Her hands withdrew a little, each one around a side of the chair toward the back. He put the envelope between the pages of the discarded book finally, leaving it outthrust like a place-mark.

Her eyes were very large. Larger than they had seemed before he came into the room. "When?" she said with scarcely any breath at all.

"Wednesday, the early afternoon train."

Suddenly panic was licking all over her, like a shriveling, congealing, frigid flame.

"No, I can't! No! Doctor, you've got to listen—!" She tried to grab his hand with both of hers and hold onto it.

He spoke to her playfully, as if she were a child. "Now, now, here. What's all this? What *is* all this?"

"No, doctor, no—!" She shook her head insistently.

He sandwiched her hand between both of his, and held it that way, consolingly. "I understand," he said soothingly. "We're a little shaky yet, we've just finished getting used to things as they are— We're a little timid about giving up familiar surroundings for those that are strange to us. We all have it; it's a typical nervous reaction. Why, you'll be over it in no time."

"But I can't *do* it, doctor," she whispered passionately. "I can't *do* it."

He chucked her under the chin, to instill courage in her. "We'll put you on the train, and all you have to do is ride. Your family will be waiting to take you off at the other end."

"My family."

"Don't make such a face about it," he coaxed whimsically.

He glanced around at the crib.

"What about the young man here?"

He went over to it, and lifted the child out; brought him to her and put him in her arms.

"You want to take him home, don't you? You don't want him to grow up in a hospital?" He laughed at her teasingly. "You want him to *have* a home, don't you?"

She held him to her, lowered her head to him.

"Yes," she said at last, submissively. "Yes, I want him to have a home."

Thirteen

A TRAIN again. But how different it was now. No crowded aisles, no jostling figures, no flux of patient, swaying humanity. A compartment, a roomette all to herself. A little table on braces, that could go up, that could go down. A closet with a full-length mirrored door, just as in any ground-fast little dwelling. On the rack the neat luggage in recessive tiers, brand-new, in use now for the first time, glossy patent finish, hardware glistening, "PH" trimly stencilled in vermilion on the rounded corners. A little shaded lamp to read by when the countryside grew dark. Flowers in a holder, going-away flowers—no, coming-homeward flowers—presented by proxy at the point of departure; glazed fruit-candies in a box; a magazine or two.

And outside the two wide windows, that formed almost a single panel from wall to wall, trees sailing peacefully by, off a way in a single line, dappled with sunshine; dark green on one side, light apple-green on the other. Clouds sailing peacefully by, only a little more slowly than the trees, as if the two things worked on separate, yet almost-synchronized, belts of continuous motion. Meadows and fields, and the little ripples that hillocks made off in the distance every once in awhile. Going up a little, coming down again. The wavy line of the future.

And on the seat opposite her own, and more important by far than all this, snug in a little blue blanket, small face still, small eyes closed—something to cherish, something to love. All there was in the world to love. All there was to go on for, along that wavy line outside.

Yes, how different it was now. And—how infinitely preferable the first time had been to this one. Fear rode with her now.

There hadn't been fear then. There hadn't been a seat, there hadn't been a bite to eat, there had only been seventeen cents. And just ahead, unguessed, rushing ever nearer with the miles, there had been calamity, horror, the beating of the wings of death.

But there hadn't been fear. There hadn't been this gnawing

inside. There hadn't been this strain and counterstrain, this pulling one way and pulling the other. There had been the calm, the certainty, of going along the right way, the only way there was to go.

The wheels chattered, as they always chatter, on every train that has ever run. But saying now, to her ear alone:

> "You'd better go back, you'd better go back,
>   Clicketty-clack, clicketty-clack,
>   Stop while you can, you still can go back."

A very small part of her moved, the least part of her moved. Her thumb unbracketed, and her four fingers opened slowly, and the tight white knot they'd made for hours past dissolved. There in its center, exposed now—

An Indian-head penny.

A Lincoln-head penny.

A buffalo nickel.

A Liberty-head dime.

Seventeen cents. She even knew the dates on them by heart, by now.

> "Clicketty-clack,
>   Stop and go back,
>   You still have the time,
>   Turn and go back."

Slowly the fingers folded up and over again, the thumb crossed over and locked them in place.

Then she took the whole fist and struck it distractedly against her forehead and held it there for a moment where it had struck.

She stood up suddenly, and tugged at one of the pieces of luggage, and swivelled it around, so that its outermost corner was now inward. The "PH" disappeared. Then she did it to the piece below. The second "PH" disappeared.

The fear wouldn't disappear. It wasn't just stencilled on a corner of her, it was all over her.

There was a light knock outside the door, and she started as violently as though it had been a resounding crash.

"Who's there?" she gasped.

A porter's voice answered, "Five mo' minutes fo' Caul-field."

She reared from the seat, and ran to the door, flung it open. He was already going down the passage. "No, wait! It can't be—"

"It sho' enough is, though, ma'm."

"So quickly, though. I didn't think—"

He smiled back at her indulgently. "It always comes between Clarendon and Hastings. That's the right place fo' it. And we've had Clarendon already, and Hastings's comin' right after it. Ain't never change since I been on this railroad."

She closed the door, and swung around, and leaned her whole back against it, as if trying to keep out some catastrophic intrusion.

> "Too late to go back,
> Too late to go back—"

"I can still ride straight through, I can ride past without getting off," she thought. She ran to the windows and peered out ahead, at an acute angle, as if the oncoming sight of it in itself would resolve her difficulty in some way.

Nothing yet. It was coming on very gradually. A house, all by itself. Then another house, still all by itself. Then a third. They were beginning to come thicker now.

"Ride straight through, don't get off at all. They can't make you. Nobody can. Do this one last thing, that's all there's time for now."

She ran back to the door and hurriedly turned the little finger-latch under the knob, locking it on the inside.

The houses were coming in more profusion, but they were coming slower too. They didn't sail any more, they dawdled. A school-building drifted by; you could tell what it was even from afar. Spotless, modern, brand-new looking, its concrete functionalism gleaming spic-and-span in the sun; copiously glassed. She could even make out small swings in motion, in the playground beside it. She glanced aside at the small blanketed bundle on the seat. That would be the kind of school she'd want—

She didn't speak, but her own voice was loud in her ears. "Help me, somebody; I don't know what to do!"

The wheels were dying, as though they'd run out of lubrication. Or like a phonograph record that runs down.

"Cli-ck, cla-ck,
Cli-i-ck, cla-a-a-ck."

Each revolution seemed about to be the last.

Suddenly a long shed started up, just outside the windows, running along parallel to them, and then a white sign suspended from it started to go by, letter by letter in reverse.

"D-L-E-I-"

It got to the F and it stuck. It wouldn't budge. She all but screamed. The train had stopped.

A knock sounded right behind her back, the vibration of it seeming to go through her chest.

"Caulfield, ma'm."

Then someone tried the knob.

"Help you with yo' things?"

Her clenched fist tightened around the seventeen cents, until the knuckles showed white and livid with the pressure.

She ran to the seat and picked up the blue blanket and what it held.

There were people out there, just on the other side of the window. Their heads were low, but she could see them, and they could see her. There was a woman looking right at her.

Their eyes met; their eyes locked, held fast. She couldn't turn her head away, she couldn't withdraw deeper into the compartment. It was as though those eyes riveted her where she stood.

The woman pointed to her. She called out in jubilation, for the benefit of someone else, unseen. "There she is! I've found her! Here, this car up here!"

She raised her hand and she waved. She waved to the little somnolent, blinking head coifed in the blue blanket, looking solemnly out the window. Made her fingers flutter in that special wave you give to very small babies.

The look on her face couldn't have been described. It was as when life begins all over again, after an interruption, a hiatus. It was as when the sun peers through again at the end, at the end of a bleak wintry day.

The girl holding the baby put her head down close to his, almost as if averting it from the window. Or as if they were communing together, exchanging some confidence in secret, to the exclusion of everyone else.

She was.

"For you," she breathed. "For you. And God forgive me."

Then she carried him over to the door with her, and turned the latch to let the harassed porter in.

Fourteen

SOMETIMES there is a dividing-line running across life. Sharp, almost actual, like the black stroke of a paintbrush or the white gash of a chalk-mark. Sometimes, but not often.

For her there was. It lay somewhere along those few yards of car-passage, between the compartment-window and the car-steps, where for a moment or two she was out of sight of those standing waiting outside. One girl left the window. Another girl came down the steps. A world ended, and another world began.

She wasn't the girl who had been holding her baby by the compartment-window just now.

Patrice Hazzard came down those car-steps.

Frightened, tremulous, very white in the face, but Patrice Hazzard.

She was aware of things, but only indirectly; she only had eyes for those other eyes looking into hers from a distance of a few inches away. All else was background. Behind her back the train glided on. Bearing with it its hundreds of living passengers. And, all unknown, in an empty compartment, a ghost. Two ghosts, a large one and a very small one.

Forever homeless now, never to be retrieved.

The hazel eyes came in even closer to hers. They were kind; they smiled around the edges; they were gentle, tender. They hurt a little. *They were trustful.*

She was in her fifties, their owner. Her hair was softly graying, and only underneath had the process been delayed. She was as tall as Patrice, and as slim; and she shouldn't have been, for it wasn't the slimness of fashionable effort or artifice, and something about her clothes revealed it to be recent, only the past few months.

But even these details about her were background, and the man of her own age standing just past her shoulder was background too. It was only her face that was immediate, and the eyes in her face, so close now. Saying so much without a sound.

She placed her hands lightly upon Patrice's cheeks, one on each, framing her face between them in a sort of accolade, a sacramental benison.

Then she kissed her on the lips, in silence, and there was a lifetime in the kiss, the girl could sense it. The lifetime of a man. The many years it takes to raise a man, from childhood, through boyhood, into a grown son. There was bitter loss in the kiss, the loss of all that at a single blow. The end for a time of all hope, and weeks of cruel grief. But then too there was the reparation of loss, the finding of a daughter, the starting over with another, a smaller son. No, with the same son; the same blood, the same flesh. Only going back and starting again from the beginning, in sweeter sadder sponsorship this time, forewarned by loss. And there was the burgeoning of hope anew.

There were all those things in it. They were spoken in it, they were felt in it; and they were meant to be felt in it, they had been put into it for that purpose.

This was not a kiss under a railroad-station shed; it was a sacrament of adoption.

Then she kissed the child. And smiled as you do at your own. And a little crystal drop that hadn't been there before was resting on its small pink cheek.

The man came forward and kissed her on the forehead.

"I'm Father, Patrice."

He stooped and straightened, and said, "I'll take your things over to the car." A little glad to escape from an emotional moment, as men are apt to be.

The woman hadn't said a word. In all the moments she'd been standing before her, not a word had passed her lips. She saw, perhaps, the pallor in her face; could read the shrinking, the uncertainty, in her eyes.

She put her arms about her and drew her to her now, in a warmer, more mundane, more everyday greeting than the one that had passed before. Drew the girl's head to rest upon her own shoulder for a moment. And as she did so, she spoke for the first time, low in her ear, to give her courage, to give her peace.

"You're home, Patrice. Welcome home, dear."

And in those few words, so simply said, so inalterably meant, Patrice Hazzard knew she had found at last all the goodness there is or ever can be in this world.

Fifteen

AND so this was what it was like to be home; to be in a home of your own, in a room of your own.

She had another dress on now, ready to go down to table. She sat there in a wing chair waiting, very straight, looking a little small against its outspread back. Her back was up against it very straight, her legs dropped down to the floor very straight and meticulously side by side. She had her hand out resting on the crib, the crib they'd bought for him and that she'd found already here waiting when she first entered the room. He was in it now. They'd even thought of that.

They'd left her alone; she would have had to be alone to savor it as fully as she was doing. Still drinking it in, hours after; basking in it, inhaling the essence of it; there was no word for what it did to her. Hours after; and her head every now and then would still give that slow, comprehensive, mar-velling sweep around from side to side, taking in all four walls of it. And even up overhead, not forgetting the ceiling. A roof over your head. A roof to keep out rain and cold and loneli-ness— Not just the anonymous roof of a rented building, no; the roof of home. Guarding you, sheltering you, keeping you, watching over you.

And somewhere downstairs, dimly perceptible to her acutely attuned ears, the soothing bustle of an evening meal in preparation. Carried to her in faint snatches now and then at the opening of a door, stilled again at its closing. Footsteps busily crossing an uncarpeted strip of wooden floor, then coming back again. An occasional faint clash of crockery or china. Once even the voice of the colored housekeeper, for an instant of bugle-like clarity. "No, it ain't ready yet, Miz' Hazzard; need five mo' minutes."

And the laughingly protesting admonition that followed, miraculously audible as well: "Sh, Aunt Josie. We have a baby in the house now; he may be napping."

Someone was coming up the stairs now. They were coming up the stairs now to tell her. She shrank back a little in the chair. Now she was a little frightened, a little nervous again. Now there would be no quick escape from the moment's confrontation, as at the railroad station. Now came the real meeting, the real blending, the real taking into the fold. Now was the real test.

"Patrice dear, supper's ready whenever you are."

You take *supper* in the evening, when you're home, in your own home. When you go out in public or to someone else's home, you may take *dinner*. But in the evening, in your own home, it's *supper* you take, and never anything else. Her heart was as fiercely glad as though the trifling word were a talisman. She remembered when she was a little girl, those few brief years that had ended so quickly— The call to *supper*, only *supper*, never anything else.

She jumped from the chair and ran over and opened the door. "Shall I—shall I bring him down with me, or leave him up here in the crib till I come back?" she asked, half-eagerly, half-uncertainly. "I fed him already at five, you know."

Mother Hazzard slanted her head coaxingly. "Ah, why don't you bring him down with you just tonight, anyway? It's the first night. Don't hurry, dear, take your time."

When she came out of the room holding him in her arms moments later, she stopped a moment, fingered the edge of the door lingeringly. Not where the knob was, but up and down the unbroken surface where there was no knob.

Watch over my room for me, she breathed unheard. I'm coming right back. Take care of it. Don't let anyone— Will you?

She would come down these same stairs many hundreds of times to come, she knew, as she started down them now. She would come down them fast, she would come down them slowly. She would come down them blithely, in gayety. And perhaps she might come down them in fear, in trouble. But now, tonight, this was the very first time of all that she was coming down them.

She held him close to her and felt her way, for they were new to her, she hadn't got the measure of them, the feel of them, yet, and she didn't want to miss her step.

They were standing about in the dining-room waiting for her. Not rigidly, formally, like drill-sergeants, but in unself-conscious ease, as if unaware of the small tribute of consideration they were giving her. Mother Hazzard was leaning forward, giving a last-minute touch to the table, shifting something a little. Father Hazzard was looking up toward the lights through the spectacles with which he'd just been reading, and polishing them off before returning them to their case. And there was a third person in the room, somebody with his back half to her at the moment of entrance, surreptitiously pilfering a salted peanut from a dish on the buffet.

He turned forward again and threw it away when he heard her come in. He was young and tall and friendly-looking, and his hair was— A camera-shutter clicked in her mind and the film rolled on.

"There's the young man!" Mother Hazzard revelled. "There's the young man himself! Here, give him to me. You know who this is, of course." And then she added, as though it were wholly unnecessary even to qualify it by so much, "Bill."

But who—? she wondered. They hadn't said anything until now.

He came forward, and she didn't know what to do, he was so close to her own age. She half-offered her hand, hoping that if it was too formal the gesture would remain unnoticed.

He took it, but he didn't shake it. Instead he pressed it between both of his, held it warmly buried like that for a moment or two.

"Welcome home, Patrice," he said quietly. And there was something about the straight, unwavering look in his eyes as he said it that made her think she'd never heard anything said so sincerely, so simply, so loyally, before.

And that was all. Mother Hazzard said, "You sit here, from now on."

Father Hazzard said unassumingly, "We're very happy, Patrice," and sat down at the head of the table.

Whoever Bill was, he sat down opposite her.

The colored housekeeper peeked through the door for a minute and beamed. "Now this look right! This what that table been needing. This just finish off that empty si—"

Then she quickly checked herself, clapping a catastrophic hand to her mouth, and whisked from sight again.

Mother Hazzard glanced down at her plate for a second, then immediately looked up again smiling, and the hurt was gone, had not been allowed to linger.

They didn't say anything memorable. You don't say anything memorable across the tables of home. Your heart speaks, and not your brain, to the other hearts around you. She forgot after awhile to notice what she was saying, to weigh, to reckon it. That's what home is, what home should be. It flowed from her as easily as it did from them. She knew that was what they were trying to do for her. And they were succeeding. Strangeness was already gone with the soup, never to return. Nothing could ever bring it back again. Other things could come—she hoped they wouldn't. But never strangeness, the unease of unfamiliarity, again. They had succeeded.

"I hope you don't mind the white collar on that dress, Patrice. I purposely saw to it there was a touch of color on everything I picked out; I didn't want you to be too—"

"Oh, some of those things are so lovely. I really hadn't seen half of them myself until I unpacked just now."

"The only thing that I was afraid of was the sizes, but that nurse of yours sent me a complete—"

"She took a tapemeasure all over me one day, I remember that now, but she wouldn't tell me what it was for—"

"Which kind for you, Patrice? Light or dark?"

"It really doesn't—"

"No, tell him just this once, dear; then after that he won't have to ask you."

"Dark, then, I guess."

"You and me both."

He spoke a little less frequently than the remaining three

of them. Just a touch of shyness, she sensed. Not that he was
strained or tonguetied or anything. Perhaps it was just his way;
he had a quiet, unobtrusive way.

The thing was, who exactly was he? She couldn't ask outright now any longer. She'd omitted to at the first moment,
and now it was twenty minutes too late for that. No last name
had been given, so he must be—

I'll find out soon, she reassured herself. I'm bound to. She
was no longer afraid.

Once she found he'd just been looking at her when her
eyes went to him, and she wondered what he'd been thinking
while doing so. And yet not to have admitted that she knew,
that she could tell by the lingering traces of his expression,
would have been to lie to herself. He'd been thinking that
her face was pleasant, that he liked it.

And then after a little while he said, "Dad, pass the bread
over this way, will you?"

And then she knew who he was.

Sixteen

EPISCOPAL CHURCH OF ST. BARTHOLOMEW, social kingpin
among all the churches of Caulfield, on a golden April Sunday
morning.

She stood there by the font, child in her arms, immediate
family and their close friends gathered beside her.

They had insisted upon this. She hadn't wanted it. Twice
she had postponed it, for two Sundays in succession now, after
all the arrangements had been made. First, by pleading a cold
that she did not really have. Secondly, by pleading a slight one
that the child actually did have. Today she hadn't been able
to postpone it any longer. They would have finally sensed the
deliberation underlying her excuses.

She kept her head down, hearing the ceremony rather than
seeing it. As though afraid to look on openly at it. As though
afraid of being struck down momentarily at the feet of all of
them for her blasphemy.

She had on a broad-brimmed hat of semi-transparent horsehair and that helped her, veiling her eyes and the upper part of her face when she cast it down like that.

Mournful memories, they probably thought. Grief-stricken.

Guilty, in reality. Scandalized. Not brazen enough to gaze at this mockery unabashed.

Arms reached out toward her, to take the child from her. The godmother's arms. She gave him over, trailing the long lace ceremonial gown that—she had almost said "his father"—that a stranger named Hugh Hazzard had worn before him, and that *his* father, Donald, had worn before *him*.

Her arms felt strangely empty after that. She wanted to cross them protectively over her breast, as though she were unclad. She forced herself not to with an effort. It was not her form that was unclad, it was her conscience. She dropped them quietly, clasped them before her, looked down.

"Hugh Donald Hazzard, I baptize thee—"

They had gone through the parody of consulting her preferences in this. To her it was a parody; not to them. She wanted him named after Hugh, of course? Yes, she had said demurely, after Hugh. Then how about the middle name? After her own father? Or perhaps two middle names, one for each grandfather? (She actually hadn't been able to recall her own father's name at the moment; it came back to her some time after, not without difficulty. Mike: a scarcely remembered figure of a looming longshoreman, killed in a drunken brawl on the Embarcadero when she was ten.)

One middle name would do. After Hugh's father, she had said demurely.

She could feel her face burning now, knew it must be flushed with shame. They mustn't see that. She kept it steadily down.

"—in the name of the Father, and of the Son, and of the Holy Ghost. Amen."

The minister sprinkled water on the child's head. She could see a stray drop or two fall upon the floor, darken into coin dots. A dime, a nickel, two pennies. Seventeen cents.

The infant began to wail in protest, as numberless infants before it since time immemorial. The infant from a New York furnished rooming house who had become heir to the first, the wealthiest family in Caulfield, in all the county, maybe even in all that State.

"You have nothing to cry about," she thought morosely.

Seventeen

THERE was a cake for him, on his first birthday, with a single candle standing defiantly in the middle of it, its flame like a yellow butterfly hovering atop a fluted white column. They made great to-do and ceremony about the little immemorial rites that went with it. The first grandson. The first milestone.

"But if he can't make the wish," she demanded animatedly, "is it all right if I make it for him? Or doesn't that count?"

Aunt Josie, the cake's creator, instinctively deferred to in all such matters of lore, nodded pontifically from the kitchen-doorway. "You make it for him, honey; he git it just the same," she promised.

Patrice dropped her eyes and her face sobered for a moment.

Peace, all your life, Safety, such as this. Your own around you always, such as now. And for myself—from you, someday—forgiveness.

"You got it? Now blow."

"Him or me?"

"It count just like for him."

She leaned down, pressed her cheek close to his, and blew softly. The yellow butterfly fluttered agitatedly, shrivelled into nothingness.

"Now cut," coached the self-imposed mistress of ceremonies.

She closed his chubby little hand around the knife-handle, enfolded it with her own, and tenderly guided it. The mystic incision made, she touched her finger to the sugary icing, scraped off a tiny crumb, and then placed it to his lips.

A great crowing and cooing went up, as though they had all just been witnesses to a prodigy of precocity.

A lot of people had come in, they hadn't had so many

people all in the house at one time since she'd first been there. And long after the small honor-guest had been withdrawn from the scene and taken upstairs to bed, the festivities continued under their own momentum, even accelerated somewhat. In that way grown-ups have of appropriating a child's party, given the slightest encouragement.

She came down again, afterward, to the lighted, bustling rooms, and moved about among them, chatting, smiling, happier tonight than she ever remembered being before. A cup of punch in one hand, in the other a sandwich with one bite gone, that she never seemed to get around to taking a second bite out of. Every time she raised it toward her mouth somebody said something to her, or she said something to somebody. It didn't matter, it was more fun that way.

Bill brushed by her once, grinning. "How does it feel to be an *old* mother?"

"How does it feel to be an *old* uncle?" she rejoined pertly over her shoulder.

A year ago seemed a long time away; just a year ago tonight, with its horror and its darkness and its fright. That hadn't happened to her; it *couldn't* have. That had happened to a girl named— No, she didn't want to remember that name, she didn't even want to summon it back for a fleeting instant. It had nothing to do with her.

"Aunt Josie's sitting up there with him. No, he'll be all right; he's a very *good* baby about going to sleep."

"Coming from a detached observer."

"Well, I *am* detached at this minute, so I'm entitled to say so. He's all the way upstairs and I'm down here."

She was in the brightly lighted living-room of her home, here, with her friends, her family's friends, all gathered about her, laughing and chatting. A year ago was more than a long time away. It had never happened. No, it had never happened. Not to her, anyway.

A great many of the introductions were blurred. There were so many firsts, on an occasion like this. She looked about, dutifully recapitulating the key-people, as befitted her role of assistant hostess. Edna Harding and Marilyn Bryant, they were those two girls sitting one on each side of Bill, and vying with one another for his attention. She suppressed a mischievous grin. Look at him, sober-faced as a totem pole. Why, it was enough to turn his head—if he hadn't happened to have a head that was unturnable by girls, as far as she'd been able to observe. Guy Ennis was that dark-haired young man over there getting someone a punch-cup; he was easy to memorize because he'd come in alone. Some old friend of Bill's, evidently. Funny that the honeybees didn't buzz around him more thickly, instead of unresponsive Bill. He looked far more the type.

Grace Henson, she was that stoutish, flaxen-haired girl over there, waiting for the punch-cup. Or was she? No, she was the less stout but still flaxen-haired one at the piano, softly playing for her own entertainment, no one near her. One wore glasses and one didn't. They must be sisters, there was too close a resemblance. It was the first time either one of them had been to the house.

She moved over to the piano and stood beside her. She might actually be enjoying doing that, for all Patrice knew, but she should at least have somebody taking an appreciative interest.

The girl at the keyboard smiled at her. "Now this." She was an accomplished player, keeping the music subdued, like an undertone to the conversations going on all over the room.

But suddenly all the near-by ones had stopped. The music went on alone for a note or two, sounding that much clearer than it had before.

The second flaxen-haired girl quitted her companion for a moment, stepped up behind the player's back, touched her just once on the shoulder, as if in some kind of esoteric remonstrance or reminder. That was all she did. Then she went right back to where she'd been sitting. The whole little pantomime had been so deft and quick it was hardly noticeable at all.

The player had broken off, uncertainly. She apparently had understood the message of the tap, but not its meaning. The slightly bewildered shrug she gave Patrice was evidence of that.

"Oh, finish it," Patrice protested unguardedly. "It was lovely. What's it called? I don't think I've ever heard it before."

"It's the Barcarolle, from *Tales of Hoffman*," the other girl answered unassumingly.

The answer itself was in anticlimax. Standing there beside the player, she became conscious of the congealing silence immediately about her, and knew it wasn't due to that, but to something that must have been said just before. It had already ended as she detected it, but awareness of it lingered on—in her. Something had happened just then.

I've said something wrong. I said something that was wrong just now. But I don't know what it was, and I don't know what to do about it.

She touched her punch-cup to her lips, there was nothing else to do at the moment.

They only heard it near me. The music left my voice stranded, and that only made it all the more conspicuous. But who else in the room heard? Who else noticed? Maybe their faces will tell—

She turned slowly and glanced at them one by one, as if at random. Mother Hazzard was deep in conversation at the far end of the room, looking up over her chair at someone. She hadn't heard. The flaxen-haired girl who had delivered the cautioning tap had her back to her; she might have heard and she might not. But if she had, it had made no impression; she was not aware of her. Guy Ennis was holding a lighter to a cigarette. He had to click it twice to make it spark, and it had all his attention. He didn't look up at her when her glance strayed lightly past his face. The two girls with Bill, they hadn't heard, it was easy to see that. They were oblivious of everything else but the bone of contention between them.

No one was looking at her. No one's eyes met hers.

Only Bill. His head was slightly down, and his forehead was querulously ridged, and he was gazing up from under his brows at her with a strange sort of inscrutability. Everything they were saying to him seemed to be going over his head. She couldn't tell if his thoughts were on her, or a thousand miles away. But his eyes, at least, were.

She dropped her own.

And even after she did, she knew that his were still on her none the less.

Eighteen

As they climbed the stairs together, after, when everyone had gone, Mother Hazzard suddenly tightened an arm about her waist, protectively.

"You were so brave about it," she said. "You did just the right thing; to pretend not to know what it was she was playing. Oh, but my dear, my heart went out to you, for a moment, when I saw you standing there. That look on your face. I wanted to run to you and put my arms around you. But I took my cue from you, I pretended not to notice anything either. She didn't mean anything by it, she's just a thoughtless little fool."

Patrice moved slowly up the stairs at her side, didn't answer.

"But at the sound of the very first notes," Mother Hazzard went on ruefully, "he seemed to be right back there in the room with all of us again. So *present*, you could almost see him in front of your eyes. The Barcarolle. His favorite song. He never sat down to a piano but what he played it. Whenever and wherever you heard that being played, you knew Hugh was about someplace."

"The Barcarolle," Patrice murmured almost inaudibly, as if speaking to herself. "His favorite song."

Nineteen

"—DIFFERENT now," Mother Hazzard was musing comfortably. "I was there once, as a girl, you know. Oh, many years ago. Tell me, has it changed much since those days?"

Suddenly she was looking directly at Patrice, in innocent exclusive inquiry.

"How can she answer that, Mother?" Father Hazzard cut in drily. "She wasn't there when you were, so how would she know what it was like then?"

"Oh, you know what I mean," Mother Hazzard retorted indulgently. "Don't be so hanged precise."

"I suppose it has," Patrice answered feebly, turning the

handle of her cup a little further toward her, as if about to lift it, and then not lifting it after all.

"You and Hugh were married there, weren't you, dear?" was the next desultory remark.

Again Father Hazzard interrupted before she could answer, this time with catastrophic rebuttal. "They were married in London, I thought. Don't you remember that letter he sent us at the time? I can still recall it: 'married here yesterday.' London letterhead."

"Paris," said Mother Hazzard firmly. "Wasn't it, dear? I still have it upstairs, I can get it and show you. It has a Paris postmark." Then she tossed her head at him arbitrarily. "Anyway, this is one question Patrice *can* answer for herself."

There was suddenly a sickening chasm yawning at her feet, where a moment before all had been security of footing, and she couldn't turn back, yet she didn't know how to get across.

She could feel their three pairs of eyes on her, Bill's were raised now too, waiting in trustful expectancy that in a moment, with the wrong answer, would change to something else.

"London," she said softly, touching the handle of her cup as if deriving some sort of mystic clairvoyance from it. "But then we left immediately for Paris, on our honeymoon. I think what happened was, he began the letter in London, didn't have time to finish it, and then posted it from Paris."

"You see," said Mother Hazzard pertly, "I was partly right, anyhow."

"Now isn't that just like a woman," Father Hazzard marvelled to his son.

Bill's eyes had remained on Patrice. There was something almost akin to grudging admiration in them; or did she imagine that?

"Excuse me," she said stifledly, thrusting her chair back. "I think I hear the baby crying."

Twenty

AND then, a few weeks later, another pitfall. Or rather the same one, ever-present, ever lurking treacherously underfoot as she walked this path of her own choosing.

It had been raining, and it grew heavily misted out. A rare occurrence for Caulfield. They were all there in the room with her and she stopped by the window a moment in passing to glance out.

"Heavens," she exclaimed incautiously, "I haven't seen everything look so blurry since I was a child in San Fran. We used to get those fogs th—"

In the reflection on the lighted pane she saw Mother Hazzard's head go up, and knew before she had even turned back to face them she had said the wrong thing. Trodden incautiously again, where there was no support.

"In San Francisco, dear?" Mother Hazzard's voice was guilelessly puzzled. "But I thought you were raised in— Hugh wrote us you were originally from—" And then she didn't finish it, withholding the clue; no helpful second choice was forthcoming this time. Instead a flat question followed. "Is that where you were born, dear?"

"No," Patrice said distinctly, and knew what the next question was sure to be. A question she could not have answered at the moment.

Bill raised his head suddenly, turned it inquiringly toward the stairs. "I think I hear the youngster crying, Patrice."

"I'll go up and take a look," she said gratefully, and left the room.

He was in a soundless sleep when she got to him. He wasn't making a whimper that anyone could possibly have heard. She stood there by him with a look of thoughtful scrutiny on her face.

Had he really thought he heard the baby crying?

Twenty-One

THEN there was the day she was slowly sauntering along Congress Avenue, window-shopping. Congress Avenue was the main retail thoroughfare. Looking at this window-display, looking at that, not intending to buy anything, not needing to. But enjoying herself all the more in this untrammelled state. Enjoying the crowd of well-dressed shoppers thronging the sunlit sidewalk all about her, the great majority of them women at that forenoon hour of the day. Enjoying the bustle, the spruce activity, they conveyed. Enjoying this carefree moment, this brief respite (an errand for Mother Hazzard, a promise to pick something up for her, was what had brought her downtown), all the more for knowing that it was a legitimate absence, not a dereliction, and that the baby was safe, well taken care of while she was gone. And that she'd enjoy returning to it all the more, after this short diversion.

It was simply a matter of taking the bus at the next stop ahead, instead of at the nearer one behind her, and strolling the difference between the two.

And then from somewhere behind her she heard her name called. She recognized the voice at the first syllable. Cheerful, sunny. Bill. She had her smile of greeting ready before she had even turned her head.

Two of his long, energetic strides and he was beside her.

"Hello there. I thought I recognized you."

They stopped for a minute, face to face.

"What are you doing out of the office?"

"I was on my way back just now. Had to go over and see a man. And you?"

"I came down to get Mother some imported English yarn she had waiting for her at Bloom's. Before they send it out, I can be there and back with it."

"I'll walk with you," he offered. "Good excuse to loaf. As far as the next corner anyhow."

"That's where I'm taking my bus anyway," she told him.

They turned and resumed their course, but at the snail's pace she had been maintaining by herself before now.

He crinkled his nose and squinted upward appreciatively. "It does a fellow good to get out in the sun once in awhile."

"Poor abused man. I'd like to have a penny for every time you're out of that office during hours."

He chuckled unabashedly. "Can I help it if Dad sends me?

Of course, I always happen to get right in front of him when he's looking around for someone to do the leg-work."

They stopped.

"Those're nice," she said appraisingly.

"Yes," he agreed. "But what are they?"

"You know darned well they're hats. Don't try to be so superior."

They went on, stopped again.

"Is this what they call window-shopping?"

"This is what they call window-shopping. As if you didn't know."

"It's fun. You don't get anywhere. But you see a lot."

"You may like it now, because it's a novelty. Wait'll you're married and get a lot of it. You won't like it then."

The next window-display was an offering of fountain pens, a narrow little show-case not more than two or three yards in width.

She didn't offer to stop there. It was now he who did, halting her with him as a result.

"Wait a minute. That reminds me. I need a new pen. Will you come in with me a minute and help me pick one out?"

"I ought to be getting back," she said halfheartedly.

"It'll only take a minute. I'm a quick buyer."

"I don't know anything about pens," she demurred.

"I don't myself. That's just it. Two heads are better than one." He'd taken her lightly by the arm by now, to try to induce her. "Ah, come on. I'm the sort they sell anything to when I'm alone."

"I don't believe a word of it. You just want company," she laughed, but she went inside with him nevertheless.

He offered her a chair facing the counter. A case of pens was brought out and opened. They were discussed between him and the salesman, she taking no active part. Several were uncapped, filled at a waiting bottle of ink at hand on the counter, and tried out on a pad of scratch-paper, also at hand for that purpose.

She looked on, trying to show an interest she did not really feel.

Suddenly he said to her, "How do you like the way this

writes?" and thrust one of them between her fingers and the block of paper under her hand, before she quite knew what had happened.

Incautiously, her mind on the proportions and weight of the barrel in her grasp, her attention fixed on what sort of a track the nib would leave, whether a broad bold one or a thin wiry one, she put it to the pad. Suddenly "Helen" stood there on the topmost leaf, almost as if produced by automatic writing. Or rather, in the fullest sense of the word, it was just that. She checked herself just in time to prevent the second name from flowing out of the pen. It was already on the preliminary upward stroke of a capital G, when she jerked it clear.

"Here, let me try it a minute myself." Without warning he'd taken both pen and pad back again, before she could do anything to obliterate or alter what was on it.

Whether he saw it or not she couldn't tell. He gave no indication. Yet it was right there under his eyes, he must have, how could he have failed to?

He drew a cursory line or two, desisted.

"No," he said to the salesman. "Let me see that one."

While he was reaching into the case, she managed to deftly peel off the topmost leaf with that damaging "Helen" on it. Crumpled it surreptitiously in her hand, dropped it to the floor.

And then, belatedly, realized that perhaps this was even worse than had she left it on there where it was. For surely he'd seen it anyway, and now she'd only pointed up the fact that she did not want him to. In other words, she'd doubly damned herself; first by the error, then by taking such pains to try to efface it.

Meanwhile, his interest in the matter of pens had all at once flagged. He looked at the clerk, about to speak, and she could have almost predicted what he was about to say—had he said it—his expression conveyed it so well. "Never mind. I'll stop in again some other time." But then instead he gave her a look, and as though recalled to the necessity for maintaining some sort of plausibility, said hurriedly, almost indifferently, "All right, here, make it this one. Send it over to my office later on."

He scarcely looked at it. It didn't seem to matter to him which one he took.

And, she reminded herself, after making such to-do about her coming in with him to help him select one.

"Shall we go?" he said, a trifle reticently.

Their parting was strained. She didn't know whether it was due to him or due to herself. Or just due to her own imagining. But it seemed to her to lack the jaunty spontaneity of their meeting just a few minutes ago.

He didn't thank her for helping him select a pen, and she was grateful for that at least. But his eyes were suddenly remote, abstracted, where until now they had been wholly on her at every turn of speech. They seemed to be looking up this way toward the top of a building, looking down that way toward the far end of the street, looking everywhere but at her any more, even while he was saying "Here's your bus," and arming her into it, and reaching in from where he stood to pay the driver her fare. "Goodbye. Get home all right. See you tonight." And tipped his hat, and seemed to have already forgotten her even before he had completed the act of turning away and going about his business. And yet somehow she knew that just the reverse was true. That he was more conscious of her than ever, now that he seemed least so. Distance had intervened between them, that was all.

She looked down at her lap, while the bus swept her along past the crowded sidewalks. Funny how quickly a scene could change, the same scene; the sunlit pavements and the bustling shoppers weren't fun any more to watch.

If it had been a premeditated test, a trap— But no, it couldn't have been that. That much at least she was sure of, though it was no satisfaction. He *couldn't* have known that he was going to run into her just where he had, that they were going to walk along just as they had, toward that pen emporium. At the time he'd left the house this morning, she hadn't even known herself that she was coming downtown like this; that had come up later. So he couldn't have lain in wait for her there, to accost her. That much at least had been spontaneous, purely accidental.

But maybe as they were strolling along, and he first looked

up and saw the store sign, that was when it had occurred to him, and he'd improvised it, on the spur of the moment. What was commonly said must have occurred to him then, as it only occurred to her now. That when people try out a new pen, they invariably write their real names. It's almost compulsory.

And yet, even for such an undeliberated, on-the-spot test as that, there must have been some formless suspicion of her already latent in his mind, in one way or another, or it wouldn't have suggested itself to him.

Little fool, she said to herself bitterly as she tugged at the overhead cord and prepared to alight, why didn't you think of that before you went in there with him? What good was hindsight now?

A night or two later his discarded coat was slung over a chair and he wasn't in the room with it at the moment. She needed a pencil for something for a moment anyhow, that was her excuse for it. She sought the pocket and took out the fountain pen she found clasped to it. It was gold and had his initials engraved on it; some valued, long-used birthday or Christmas present from one of his parents probably. More-over, it was in perfect writing order, couldn't have been im-proved on, left a clear, deep, rich trace. And he wasn't the sort of man who went around displaying two fountain pens at a time.

It had been a test, all right. And she had given a positive reaction, as positive as he could have hoped for.

Twenty-Two

SHE'D heard the doorbell ring some time before, and dim sounds of conglomerate greeting follow it in the hall below, and knew by that some visitor must have arrived, and must still be down there. She didn't think any more about it. She'd had Hughie in his little portable tub at the moment, and that, while it was going on, was a full-time job for anyone's atten-tion. By the time she'd finished drying and talcuming and dressing him, putting him to bed for the night, and then lin-gering treacherously by him awhile longer, to watch her opportunity and worm the last celluloid bath-duck out of his tightly closed little fist, the better part of an hour had gone by. She felt sure the caller, whoever he was, must already be long gone by that time. That it had been a masculine visitor was something she could take for granted; anyone feminine from six to sixty would automatically have been ushered upstairs by the idolatrous Mother Hazzard to look in on the festive rite of her grandson's bath. In fact it was the first time she herself had missed attending one in weeks, if only to hold the towel, prattle in an unintelligible gibberish with the small person in the tub, and generally get in the uncomplaining mother's way. Only something of importance could have kept her away.

She thought they were being unusually quiet below, when she finally came out of her room and started down the stairs. There was a single, droning, low-pitched voice going on, as if somebody were reading aloud, and no one else was audible.

They were all in the library, she discovered a moment later; a room that was never used much in the evenings. And when it was, never by all of them together, at one time. She could see them in there twice over, the first time from the stairs themselves, as she came down them, and then in an afterglimpse, through the open doorway at nearer range, as she doubled back around the foot of the stairs and passed by in the hall just outside.

The three of them were in there, and there was a man with them whom she didn't know, although she realized she must have seen him at least one or more times before, as she had everyone who came to this house. He was at the table, the reading-lamp lit, droning aloud in a monotonous, singsong voice. It wasn't a book; it seemed more like a typed report. Every few moments a brittly crackling sheet would sweep back in reverse and go under the others.

No one else was saying a word. They were sitting at varying distances and at varying degrees of attention. Father Hazzard was drawn up to the table with the monologist, following every word closely, and nodding in benign accord from time to time. Mother Hazzard was in an easy chair, a basket on her lap, darning something and only occasionally looking up in sketchy aural participation. And Bill, strangely present, was off on the very outskirts of the conclave, a leg dangling over the arm of his chair, head tilted all the way back with a protruding pipe thrust ceilingward, and giving very little indication of listening at all. His eyes had a look of vacancy, as though his mind were elsewhere while his body was dutifully and filially in the room with them.

She tried to get by without being seen, but Mother Hazzard looked up at just the wrong time and caught the flicker of her figure past the door-gap. "There she is now," she said. A moment later her retarding call had overtaken and halted her. "Patrice, come in here a moment, dear. We want you."

She turned and went back, with a sudden constriction in her throat.

The droning voice had interrupted itself to wait. A private investigator? No, no, he couldn't be. She'd met him here in the house on a friendly basis, she was sure of it. But those voluminous briefs littered in front of him—

"Patrice, you know Ty Winthrop."

"Yes, I know we've met before." She went over and shook hands with him. She kept her eyes carefully off the table. And it wasn't easy.

"Ty is Father's lawyer," Mother Hazzard said indulgently. As though that were really no way to describe an old friend, but it was the shortest one for present purposes.

"And golf rival," supplied the man at the table.

"Rival?" Father Hazzard snorted disgustedly. "I don't call that rivalry, what you put up. A rival has to come up somewhere near you. Charity-tournament is more what I'd call it."

Bill's head and pipe had come down to the horizontal again. "Lick him with one hand tied behind your back, eh Dad?" he egged him on.

"Yeah, *my* hand," snapped the lawyer, with a private wink for the son. "Especially last Sunday."

"Now, you three," reproved Mother Hazzard beamingly. "I have things to do. And so has Patrice. I can't sit in here all night."

They became serious again. Bill had risen and drawn up a chair beside the table for her. "Sit down, Patrice, and join the party," he invited.

"Yes, we want you to hear this, Patrice," Father Hazzard urged, as she hesitated. "It concerns you."

Her hand tried to stray betrayingly toward her throat. She kept it down by sheer will-power. She seated herself, a little uneasily.

The lawyer cleared his throat. "Well, I think that about takes care of it, Donald. The rest of it remains as it was before."

Father Hazzard hitched his chair nearer. "All right. Ready for me to sign now?"

Mother Hazzard bit off a thread with her teeth, having come to the end of something or other. She began to put things away in her basket, preparatory to departure. "You'd better tell Patrice what it is first, dear. Don't you want her to know?"

"I'll tell her for you," Winthrop offered. "I can put it in fewer words than you." He turned toward her and gazed friendlily over the tops of his reading-glasses. "Donald's changing the provisions of his will, by adding a codicil. You see, in the original, after Grace here was provided for, there was an equal division of the residue made between Bill and Hugh. Well now we're altering that to make it one-quarter of the residue to Bill and the remainder to you."

She could feel her face beginning to flame, as though a burning crimson light were focussed on it, and it alone, that they could all see. An agonizing sensation of wanting to push away from the table and make her escape, and of being held trapped there in her chair, came over her.

She tried to speak quietly, quelling her voice by moistening her lips twice over. "I don't want you to do that. I don't want to be included."

"Don't look that way about it," Bill said with a genial laugh. "You're not doing anybody out of anything. I have Dad's business—"

"It was Bill's own suggestion," Mother Hazzard let her know.

"I gave both the boys a lump sum in cash, to start them off, on the day they each reached their twenty-first—"

She was on her feet now, facing all of them in turn, almost

panic-stricken. "No, please! Don't put my name down on it at all! I don't want my name to go down on it!" She all but wrung her clasped hands toward Father Hazzard. "Dad! Won't you listen to me?"

"It's on account of Hugh, dear," Mother Hazzard let him know in a tactful aside. "Can't you understand?"

"Well, I know; we all feel bad about Hugh. But she has to go on living just the same. She has a child to think of. And these things shouldn't be postponed on account of sentiment; they have to be taken care of at the right time."

She turned and fled from the room. They made no attempt to follow her.

She closed the door after her. She stormed back and forth, two, three times, holding her head locked in her upended arms. "Swindler!" burst from her muffledly. "Thief! It's just like someone climbing in through a window and—"

There was a low knock at the door about half an hour later. She went over and opened it, and Bill was standing there.

"Hello," he said diffidently.

"Hello," she said with equal diffidence.

It was as though they hadn't seen one another for two or three days past, instead of just half an hour before.

"He signed it," he said. "After you went up. Winthrop took it back with him. Witnessed and all. It's done now, whether you wanted it or not."

She didn't answer. The battle had been lost, downstairs, before, and this was just the final communiqué.

He was looking at her in a way she couldn't identify. It seemed to have equal parts of shrewd appraisal and blank in-comprehension in it, and there was just a dash of admiration added.

"You know," he said, "I don't know why you acted like that about it. And I don't agree with you, I think you were wrong in acting like that about it." He lowered his voice a little in confidence. "But somehow or other I'm glad you acted like that about it. I like you better for acting like that about it." He shoved his hand out to her suddenly. "Want to shake goodnight?"

Twenty-Three

SHE was alone in the house. That is, alone just with Hughie, in his crib upstairs, and Aunt Josie, in her room all the way at the back. They'd gone out to visit the Michaelsons, old friends.

It was nice to be alone in the house once in awhile. Not too often, not all the time, that would have run over into loneliness. And she'd known what that was once, only too well, and didn't want to ever again.

But it was nice to be alone like this, alone *without* loneliness, just for an hour or two, just from nine until eleven, with the sure knowledge that they were coming back soon. With the whole house her own to roam about in; upstairs, down, into this room, into that. Not that she couldn't at other times—but this had a special feeling to it, doing it when no one else was about. It did something to her. It nourished her feeling of *belonging*, replenished it.

They'd asked her if she didn't want to come with them, but she'd begged off. Perhaps because she knew that if she stayed home alone she'd get this very feeling from it.

They didn't importune her. They never importuned, never repeated any invitation to the point of weariness. They respected you as an individual, she reflected, that was one of the nice things about them. Only one of the nice, there were so many others.

"Then next time, maybe," Mother had smiled in parting, from the door.

"Next time without fail," she promised. "They're very nice people."

She roamed about for awhile first, getting her "feel" of the place, saturating herself in that blessed sensation of "belonging." Touching a chair-back here, fingering the texture of a window-drape there.

Mine. My house. My parents' house and mine. Mine. Mine. My *home*. My chair. My window-drape. No, hang back like that, that's the way I want you to.

Silly? Childish? Fanciful? No doubt. But who is without childishness, fancies? What is life without them? Or, *is* there life without them?

She went into Aunt Josie's pantry, took the lid off the cookie-jar, took one out, took a big bite out of it.

She wasn't hungry. They'd all finished a big dinner only a couple of hours ago. But—

My house. I can do this. I'm entitled to them. They're waiting there for me, to help myself whenever I feel like it.

She put the lid on the jar, started to put the light out.

She changed her mind suddenly, went back, took out a second one.

My house. I can even take two if I want to. Well, I *will* take two.

And one in each hand, each with a big defiant bite taken out of it, she came out of there. They weren't food for the mouth, actually, they were food for the soul.

The last crumbs brushed off her fingers, she decided to read a book finally. Utter repose had come to her now, a sense of peace and well-being that was almost therapeutic in its depth. It was a sensation of *healing*, of becoming one, becoming whole again. As though the last vestiges of an old ache, from an old split in her personality (as indeed there was one in the fullest sense), had been effaced. A psychiatrist could have written a learned paper on this; that just roaming about a house, in utter security, in utter relaxation, for half an hour or so, could achieve such a result for her, beyond all capacity of cold-blooded science, in the clinic, to have done likewise. But, human beings are human beings, and science isn't what they need; it's a home, a house of their own, that no one can take away from them.

It was the right time, almost the only time, for reading a book. You could give it your full attention, you could lose yourself in it. You became one with it for awhile, selfless.

In the library, it took her some time to make a definitive selection. She did a considerable amount of leaf-fluttering along the shelves, made two false starts back to the chair for an opening paragraph or two, before she'd finally settled on something that gave an indication of suiting her.

Marie Antoinette, by Katharine Anthony.

She'd never cared much for fiction, somehow. Something about it made her slightly uncomfortable, perhaps a reminder of the drama in her own life. She liked things (her mind expressed it) *that had really happened.* Really happened, but long ago and far away, to someone entirely else, someone that never could be confused with herself. In the case of a fictional character, you soon, involuntarily, began identifying yourself with him or her. In the case of a character who had once been an actual living personage, you did not. You sympathized objectively, but it ended there. It was always, from first to last, someone else. Because it had once, in reality, *been* someone else. (Escape, they would have called this, though in her case it was the reverse of what it was for others. They escaped from humdrum reality into fictional drama. She escaped from too much personal drama into a reality of the past.)

For an hour, maybe more, she was one with a woman dead a hundred and fifty years; she lost track of time.

Dimly, with only a marginal part of her faculties, she heard brakes go on somewhere outside in the quiet night.

". . . Axel Fersen drove swiftly through the dark streets." (They're back. I'll finish this chapter first.) "An hour and a half later, the coach passed through the gate of Saint-Martin. . . ."

A key turned in the front door. It opened, then it closed. But no murmur of homecoming voices eddied in. Vocal silence, if not the total kind. Firm, energetic footsteps, a single pair, struck across the preliminary gap of bare flooring adjacent to the door, then blurred off along the hall carpeting.

". . . A little way beyond, they saw a large travelling-carriage drawn up at the side of the road." (No, that's Bill, not they. He's the one just came in. I forgot, they didn't take the car with them, the Michaelsons live just around the corner) "a large travelling-carriage drawn up at the side of the road. . . ."

The tread went to the back. Aunt Josie's pantry-light flashed on again. She couldn't have seen it from where she was, but she knew it by the click of its switch. She knew all the lights by the clicks of their switches. The direction from which the click came, and its sharpness or faintness of tone. You can learn those things about a house.

She heard water surge from a tap, and then an emptied glass go down. Then the lid of the cookie-jar went down, with its heavy, hollowed, ringing, porcelain thud. It stayed down for some time, too, was in no hurry to go back on again.

". . . drawn up at the side of the road." (Aunt Josie'll have a fit. She always scolds him. She never scolds me, for doing the very same thing. I guess she used to when he was a boy, and can't get over the habit) "The pseudo Madame Korff and her party entered the carriage. . . ."

The lid went back on again at long last. The footsteps started forward again, emerged into the back of the hall. They stopped short, backed up a step, the floor creaked slightly with doubled weight in one place.

". . ." (He dropped a chunk on the floor, stopped to pick it up. Doesn't want her to see it lying there in the morning, and know what he's been up to. I bet he's still afraid of Aunt Josie in his heart, in a little-boy way.) ". . ."

But her thoughts were not consciously of him or on him. They were on her book. It was the perimeter of her mind, the unused residue, that kept up a running commentary to itself, and which the center of her attention paid no heed to.

He subsided for awhile, was lost to awareness. Must have been slumped somewhere, finishing his cookies. Probably with a leg thrown over a chair-arm, if he was in a chair at all.

He had known they were going over to the Michaelsons, and must have thought she had gone with them, that he was alone in the house. The library was to the right of the stairs, and he had taken the left channel, to the pantry and returned, hadn't come near here as yet, so he couldn't have known that she was in here. The shaded lamp she was beside had a limited radius of reflection that did not reach past the room-doorway.

Suddenly his lithe footfalls were underway again, had re-commenced, the nibbling interlude at an end. They struck out into the hall again, clarifying as they emerged from wherever it was he had been, rounded the bottom of the stairs, and turned in on this side. They were coming straight toward here, toward this room she was unsuspectedly in.

She went ahead steadily reading, trapped by the mounting interest of the passage she had just entered upon, held fast. Didn't even raise her eyes.

His tread reached the threshold. Then it stopped short there, almost with a recoil.

For perhaps a moment he stood stock-still, looking at her.

Then, abruptly, he took an awkward step in retreat, a full step to the rear, turned, went away again.

It was almost subconsciously that she knew all this; not in full consciousness, at least not as yet. It was there, clinging to her awareness, but it hadn't penetrated it as yet.

". . ." (Why did he turn and go away like that, when he saw me in here alone?) ". . . and disposed themselves upon the comfortable cushions. . . ." (He intended coming in here. He did come as far as the door. Then when he saw that I was in here, and didn't seem to have seen him yet, he backed away. Why? Why was that?) "Axel Fersen took the reins. . . ."

Slowly the spell of the book unravelled, disintegrated. Her eyes left its pages for the first time. She raised her head questioningly, still holding the book open before her.

Why? Why did he do that?

It isn't that he was afraid of disturbing me. We're all one family, we don't stand on ceremony like that with one another. We all go from room to room as we like without a by-your-leave, except in the upstairs-rooms, and this isn't upstairs, this is down here. He didn't even say hello. When he saw that I didn't see him, he wanted it left that way, did his best to keep it that way, tried not to attract my attention. Withdrew *backward* the first step, and only then turned around.

The front door had reopened, but without closing behind him. He'd gone out front for a moment, to put the car away. She heard the thump of its door as he shut it on himself, heard its gears mesh into motion.

Doesn't he like me? Is that why he doesn't want to find himself alone in a room with me, when no one else is here? Is he holding something against me? I thought—it seemed—as if his full confidence had been given to me long ago, but—To balk like that, curb himself, almost swerve away, at the very threshold.

And then suddenly, quite simply, almost matter-of-factly, she knew. It came to her. Some indefinable something had told her. Something that no word could explain. Something too tenuous to bear the weight of *any* words.

No, it's not because he doesn't like me. It's because he does like me, *does* like me, that he backed away like that, doesn't want to be in the room alone with me if he can avoid it. Likes me too well. Is already beginning to fall in love with me. And—and thinks he shouldn't. Is fighting it. That hopeless, last-ditch fight that's never won.

Determinedly, but quite unhurriedly, she closed her book, carried it over to the gap from which she'd extracted it, pushed it in. She left the lamp on for him (since he had seemed to want to come in here), but quitted the room herself, left it to him, went out into the hall, went up the stairs and into her own room, closed the door of that for the night.

She undid her hair, brushed it for retiring.

She heard the rumble of the garage-doors, heard the padlock strike against them as he let it fall back to rest, heard him come into the house again. He went straight back toward the library, and went in, this time unhesitatingly (to accost her now, to face it, to bring it out, his decision taken during those few minutes' breathing spell?)—to find it empty. The lamp on, the reader gone.

Seconds later she remembered that she'd left her cigarette burning there, on the table, under the lamp, beside where she'd been sitting. Had forgotten to pick it up when she came out. It must be burning still, she'd only just lit it before she'd first heard the car drive up outside.

It wasn't that she was alarmed about possible damage. He'd see it at a glance, and put it out for her.

But it would tell him. For, just as he had intended coming in when he hadn't, it would reveal to him that she *hadn't* intended getting up and leaving when she had.

She not only knew, now, that he was beginning to love her, but, by token of that telltale cigarette, he knew that she knew.

Twenty-Four

IN the light of the full-bodied moon the flower-garden at the back of the house was as bright as noon when she stepped out into it. The sanded paths that ran around it foursquare, and through it like an X, gleamed like snow, and her shadow glided along them azure against their whiteness. The little rock-pool in the center was polka-dotted with silver disks, and the wafers coalesced and separated again as if in motion, though they weren't, as her point of perspective continually shifted with her rotary stroll.

The perfume of the rose-bushes was heavy on the June night, and sleepy little insects made a somnolent humming noise, as though they were talking in their sleep.

She hadn't wanted to sleep yet, and she hadn't wanted to read, it was too close in the library with the lamp on. She hadn't wanted to sit alone on the front porch any longer, once Mother and Father Hazzard had left her and gone up to their room. She'd gone up a moment and looked in at Hughie, to see if he was all right, and then she'd come out here. To the flower-garden in the back, safely secluded behind its tall surrounding hedge.

Eleven struck melodiously from the little Reformed church over on Beechwood Drive, and the echoes lingered in the still air, filling her with a sense of peace and well-being.

A quiet voice, seeming to come from just over her shoulder, said: "Hello; I thought that was you down there, Patrice."

She turned, startled, and couldn't locate him for a minute. He was above her, perched edgewise on the sill of his open window.

"Mind if I come down and join you for a cigarette?"

"I'm going in now," she said hastily, but he'd already disappeared.

He stepped down from the back porch and the moonlight sifted over his head and shoulders like talcum as he came toward her. She turned in company with him, and they walked slowly on together side by side. Once all around the outside path, and then once through a bisecting middle one.

She reached out and touched a flower once in passing; bent it a little toward her, then let it sway back again undamaged.

A full-blown white rose; the perfume was almost like a bomb-shell in their faces for a moment.

He didn't even do that much; didn't do anything. Didn't say anything. Just walked beside her. One hand slung in his pocket. Looking steadily down, as though the sight of the path fascinated him.

"I hate to tear myself away, it's so lovely down here," she said at last.

"I don't give a hang about gardens," he answered almost gruffly. "Nor walking in them. Nor the flowers in them. You know why I came down here. Do I have to tell you?"

He flung his cigarette down violently, backhand, with the same gesture as if something had angered him.

Suddenly she was acutely frightened. She'd stopped short.

"No, wait, Bill. Bill, wait— Don't—"

"Don't what? I haven't said anything yet. But you know already, don't you? I'm sorry, Patrice, I've got to tell you. You've got to listen. It's got to come out."

She was holding out her hand protestingly toward him, as if trying to ward off something. She took a backward step away, broke their proximity.

"*I* don't like it," he said rebelliously. "It does things to me that are new. I was never bothered before. I never even had the sweetheart-crushes that they all do. I guess that was my way to be. But this is it, Patrice. This is it now, all right."

"No, wait— Not now. Not yet. This isn't the time—"

"This is the time, and this is the night, and this is the place. There'll never be another night like this, not if we both live to be a hundred. Patrice, I love you, and I want you to ma—"

"Bill!" she pleaded, terrified.

"Now you've heard it, and now you're running away. Patrice," he asked forlornly, "what's so terrible about it?"

She'd gained the lower-porch step, was poised on it for a moment in arrested flight. He came after her slowly, in a sort of acquiescent frustration, rather than in importunate haste.

"I'm no lover," he said. "I can't say it right—"

"Bill," she said again, almost grief-strickenly.

"Patrice, I see you every day and—" He flung his arms

apart helplessly. "What am I to do? I didn't ask for it. I think it's something good. I think it's something that should be."

She leaned her head for a moment against the porch-post, as if in distress. "Why did you have to say it yet? Why couldn't you have— Give me more time. Please, give me more time. Just a few months—"

"Do you want me to take it back, Patrice?" he asked ruefully. "How can I now? How could I, even if I hadn't spoken? Patrice, it's so long since, now. Is it Hugh, is it still Hugh?"

"I've never been in love bef—" she started to say, penitently. She stopped suddenly.

He looked at her strangely.

I've said too much, flashed through her mind. Too much, or not enough. And then in sorrowful confirmation: Not enough by far.

"I'm going in now." The shadow of the porch dropped between them like an indigo curtain.

He didn't try to follow. He stood there where she'd left him.

"You're afraid I'll kiss you."

"No, that isn't what I'm afraid of," she murmured almost inaudibly. "I'm afraid I'll want you to."

The door closed after her.

He stood out there in the full bleach of the moonlight, motionless, looking sadly downward.

Twenty-Five

IN the morning the world was sweet just to look at from her window. The sense of peace, of safety, of belonging, was being woven about her stronger all the time. Soon nothing could tear its fabric apart again. To wake up in your own room, in your own home, your own roof over your head. To find your little son awake before you and peering expectantly out through his crib, and giving you that crowing smile of delight that was already something special he gave to no one but you. To lift him up and hold him to you, and have to curb yourself, you wanted to squeeze so tightly. Then to carry him over to the window with you, and hold the curtain back, and look out at the world. Show him the world you'd found for him, the world you'd made for him.

The early sunlight like goldenrod pollen lightly dusting the sidewalks and the roadway out front. The azure shadows under the trees and at the lee sides of all the houses. A man sprinkling a lawn a few doors down, the water fraying from the nozzle of his hose twinkling like diamonds. He looked up and saw you, and he gave you a neighborly wave of the hand, though you didn't know him very well. And you took Hughie's little hand at the wrist, and waved it back to him in answering greeting.

Yes, in the mornings the world was sweet all right.

Then to dress, to dress for two, and to go downstairs to the pleasant room waiting for you below; to Mother Hazzard, and her fresh-picked flowers, and her affectionate, sunny greeting, and the mirror-like reflection of the coffee-percolator (that always delighted him so) showing squat, pudgy images seated around it on its various facets: an elderly lady, and a much younger lady, and a very young young-man, the center of attraction in his high chair.

To be safe, to be at home, to be among your own.

Even mail for you, a letter of your own, waiting for you at your place. She felt a pleased little sense of completion at sight of it. There was no greater token of permanency, of belonging, than that. Mail of your own, sent to your home.

"Mrs. Patrice Hazzard," and the address. Once that name had frightened her. It didn't now. In a little while she would no longer even remember that there had been another name, once, before it. A lonely, frightened name, drifting ownerless, unclaimed, about the world now—

"Now Hughie, not so fast, finish what you've got first."

She opened it, and there was nothing in it. Or rather, nothing written on it. For a moment she thought there must have been a mistake. Just blank paper. No, wait, the other way around—

Three small words, almost buried in the seam that folded

the sheet in two, almost overlooked in the snowy expanse that surrounded them.

"Who are you?"

Twenty-Six

IN the mornings the world was bitter-sweet to look at from her window. To wake up in a room that wasn't rightfully yours. That you knew—and you knew somebody else knew— you had no right to be in. The early sunlight was pale and bleak upon the ground, and under all the trees and on the lee side of all the houses, tatters of night lingered, diluted to blue but still gloomy and forbidding. A man sprinkling the lawn a few doors down was a stranger; a stranger you knew by sight. He looked up, and you hurriedly shrank back from the window, child and all, lest he see you. Then a moment later, you already wished you hadn't done that, but it was too late, it was done.

Was he the one? Was he?

It isn't as much fun any more to dress for two. And when you start down the stairs with Hughie, those stairs you've come down so many hundreds of times, now at last you've learned what it's like to come down them heavyhearted and troubled, as you said you might some day have to, that very first night of all. For that's how you're coming down them now.

Mother Hazzard at the table, beaming; and the flowers; and the gargoyle-like reflections on the percolator-panels. But you only have eyes for one thing, furtive, straining eyes, from as far back as the threshold of the doorway. From farther back than that, even; from the first moment the table has come into sight. Is there any white on it, over on your side of it? Is there any rectangular white patch showing there, by or near your place? It's easy to tell, for the cloth has a printed pattern, with dabs of red and green.

"Patrice, didn't you sleep well, dear?" Mother Hazzard asked solicitously. "You look a little peaked."

She hadn't looked peaked out on the stairs a moment ago. She'd only been heavyhearted and troubled then.

She settled Hughie in his chair, and took a little longer than was necessary. Keep your eyes away from it. Don't look at it. Don't think about it. Don't try to find out what's in it, you don't want to know what's in it; let it stay there until after the meal, then tear it up un—

"Patrice, you're spilling it on his chin. Here, let me."

She had nothing to do with her own hands, from that point on. And she felt as though she had so many of them; four or five at least. She reached for the coffee-pot, and a corner of it was in the way. She reached for the sugar-bowl, and another corner of it was in the way. She drew her napkin toward her, and it sidled two or three inches nearer her, riding on that. It was all about her, it was everywhere at once!

She wanted to scream, and she clenched her hand tightly, down beside her chair. I mustn't do that, I mustn't. Hughie's right here next to me, and Mother's just across the table—

Open it, open it fast. Quick, while you still have the courage.

The paper made a shredding sound, her finger was so thick and maladroit.

One word more this time.

"Where are you from?"

She clenched her hand again, down low beside her chair. White dissolved into it, disappearing through the finger-crevices.

Twenty-Seven

IN the mornings the world was bitter to look at from the window. To wake up in a strange room, in a strange house. To pick up your baby—that was the only thing that was rightfully yours—and edge toward the window with him, creeping up slantwise and peering from the far side of it, barely lifting the curtain; not stepping forward to the middle of it and throwing the curtain widely back. That was for people in their own homes, not for you. And out there, nothing. Nothing that belonged to you or was for you. The hostile houses of a hostile town. An icy wash of sun upon a stony ground. Dark shadows like frowns under each tree and leeward of each house. The man watering the lawn didn't turn around to greet you today. He was more than a stranger now, he was a potential enemy.

She carried her boy with her downstairs, and every step was like a knell. She was holding her eyes closed when she first went into the dining-room. She couldn't help it; she couldn't bring herself to open them for a moment.

"Patrice, you don't look right to me at all. You ought to see your color against that child's."

She opened her eyes.

Nothing there.

But it would come. It would come again. It had come once, twice; it would come again. Tomorrow maybe. The day after. Or the day after that. It would surely come again. There was nothing to do but wait. To sit there, stricken, helpless, waiting. It was like holding your head bowed under a leaky faucet, waiting for the next icy drop to detach itself and fall.

In the mornings the world was bitter, and in the evenings it was full of shadows creeping formlessly about her, threatening from one moment to the next to close in and engulf her.

Twenty-Eight

SHE hadn't slept well. That was the first thing she was conscious of on awakening. The cause, the reason for it, that came right with it. That was what really mattered; not the fact that she hadn't slept well, but knowing the cause, the reason for it. Only too well.

It wasn't new. It was occurring all the time lately, this not sleeping well. It was the rule rather than the exception.

The strain was beginning to tell on her. Her resistance was wearing away. Her nerves were slowly being drawn taut, a little more so each day. She was nearing a danger-point, she knew. She couldn't stand very much more of it. It wasn't when they came; it was in-between, waiting for the next one to come. The longer it took to come, the greater her tension, instead of the less. It was like that well-known simile of the second dropped shoe, prolonged ad infinitum.

She couldn't stand much more of it. "If there's another one," she told herself, "something will snap. Don't let there be another one. Don't."

She looked at herself in the glass. Not through vanity, conceit, to see whether damage had been done her looks. To confirm, objectively, the toll that was being taken. Her face was pale and worn. It was growing thinner again, losing its roundness, growing back toward that gauntness of cheek it had had in New York. Her eyes were a little too shadowed underneath, and just a little too bright. She looked tired and frightened. Not acutely so, but chronically. And that was what was being done to her by this.

She dressed herself, and then Hughie, and carried him down with her. It was so pleasant in the dining-room, in the early morning like this. The new-minted sun pouring in, the color of champagne; the crisp chintz curtains; the cheery colored ware on the table; the fragrant aroma of the coffee-pot; the savory odor of fresh-made toast seeping through the napkin thrown over it to keep it warm. Mother Hazzard's flowers in the center of the table, always less than an hour old, picked from her garden at the back. Mother Hazzard herself, spruce and gay in her printed morning-dress, beaming at her. Home. Peace.

"Leave me in peace," she pleaded inwardly. "Let me be. Let me have all this. Let me enjoy it, as it's meant to be enjoyed, as it's waiting around to be enjoyed. Don't take it from me, let me keep it."

She went around the table to her and kissed her, and held Hughie out to her to be kissed. Then she settled him in his highchair, between the two of them, and sat down herself.

Then she saw them, waiting for her.

The one on top was a department-store sales brochure, sealed in an envelope. She could identify it by the letterhead in the upper corner. But there was something under it, another one. Its corners stuck out a little past the top one.

She was afraid to bring it into fuller view, she postponed it.

She spooned Hughie's cereal to his mouth, took alternating sips of her own fruit juice. It was poisoning the meal, it was tightening up her nerves.

It mightn't be one of those, it might be something else. Her hand moved with a jerk, and the department-store folder was out of the way.

"Mrs. Patrice Hazzard."

It was addressed in pen and ink, a personal letter. She never got letters like that from anyone; who wrote to her, whom did she know? It must be, it was, one of those again. She felt a sick, cold feeling in her stomach. She took in everything about it, with a sort of hypnotic fascination. The three-cent purple stamp, with wavy cancellation-lines running through it. Then the circular postmark itself, off to the side. It had been posted late, after twelve last night. Where? She wondered. By whom? She could see in her mind's eye an indistinct, furtive figure slinking up to a street mail-box in the dark, a hand hastily thrusting something into the chute, the clang as the slot fell closed again.

She wanted to get it out of here, take it upstairs with her, close the door. But if she carried it away with her unopened, wouldn't that look secretive, wouldn't that call undue attention to it? It was safe enough to open it here in the very room; they never pried in this house, they never asked questions. She knew she could even have left it lying around open after having read it herself, and it would have been safe, nobody would have put a hand to it.

She ran her knife through the flap, slit it.

Mother Hazzard had taken over Hughie's feeding, she had eyes for no one but him. Every mouthful brought forth a paean of praise.

She'd opened the once-folded inner sheet now. The flowers were in the way, they screened the shaking of her hand. So blank it was, so much waste space, so little writing. Just a line across the middle of the paper, where the crease ran.

"What are you doing there?"

She could feel her chest constricting. She tried to quell the sudden inordinate quickness of her breathing, lest it betray itself.

Mother Hazzard was showing Hughie his plate. "All gone. Hughie ate it all up! Where *is* it?"

She'd lowered it into her lap now. She managed to get it back into its envelope, and fold that over, singly and then doubly, until it fitted into the span of her hand.

"One more and something will snap." And here it was, the one more.

She could feel her self-control ebbing away, and didn't know what catastrophic form its loss might take. "I've got to get out of this room," she warned herself. "I've got to get away from this table—now—quickly!"

She stood up suddenly, stumbling a little over her chair. She turned and left the table without a word.

"Patrice, aren't you going to have your coffee?"

"I'll be right down," she said smotheredly, from the other side of the doorway. "I forgot something."

She got up there, into her room, and got the door closed.

It was like the bursting of a dam. She hadn't known what form it would take. Tears, she'd thought, or high-pitched hysterical laughter. It was neither. It was anger, a paroxysm of rage, blinded and baffled and helpless.

She went over to the wall and flailed with upraised fists against it, held high over her head. And then around to the next wall and the next and the next, like somebody seeking an outlet, crying out distractedly: "Who are you yourself? Where are you sending them from? Why don't you come out? Why don't you come out in the open? Why don't you come out where I can see you? Why don't you come out and give me a chance to fight back?"

Until at last she'd stopped, wilted and breathing fast with spent emotion. In its wake came sudden determination. There was only one way to fight back, only one way she had to rob the attacks of their power to harm—

She flung the door open. She started down the stairs again. Still as tearless as she'd gone up. She was going fast, she was rippling down them in a quick-step. She was still holding it in her hand. She opened it up, back to its full size, and started smoothing it out as she went.

She came back into the dining-room still at the same gait she'd used on the stairs.

"—drank all his milk like a good boy," Mother Hazzard was crooning.

Patrice moved swiftly around the table toward her, stopped short beside her.

"I want to show you something," she said tersely. "I want you to see this."

She put it down on the table squarely in front of her and stood there waiting.

"Just a moment, dear; let me find my glasses," Mother Hazzard purred acquiescently. She probed here and there among the breakfast things. "I know I had them with me when Father was here at the table; we were both reading the paper." She looked over toward the buffet on the other side of her.

Patrice stood there waiting. She looked over at Hughie. He was still holding his spoon, entire fist folded possessively around it. He flapped it at her joyously. Home. Peace.

Suddenly she'd reached over to her own place at the table, picked up the department-store circular still lying there, re-placed the first letter with that.

"Here they are, under my napkin. Right in front of me the whole time." Mother Hazzard adjusted them, turned back to her. "Now what was it, dear?" She opened the folder and looked at it.

Patrice pointed. "This pattern, right here. The first one. Isn't it—attractive?"

Behind her back, held in one hand, the abducted missive slowly crumpled, deflated, was sucked between her fingers into compressed invisibility.

Twenty-Nine

QUIETLY and deftly she moved about the dimly lighted room, passing back and forth, and forth and back, with armfuls of belongings from the drawers. Hughie lay sleeping in his crib, and the clock said almost one.

The valise stood open on a chair. Even that wasn't hers. It was the one she'd first used on the train-ride here, new-looking as ever, the one with "PH" on its rounded corner. She'd have to borrow it. Just as she was borrowing the articles she picked at random, to throw into it. Just as she was borrowing the very clothes she stood in. There were only two things in this whole room with her now that were rightfully hers. That little bundle sleeping quietly there in the crib. And that seventeen cents lying spread out on a scrap of paper on the dresser-top.

She took things for him, mostly. Things he needed, things to keep him warm. They wouldn't mind, they wouldn't begrudge that; they loved him almost as much as she did, she reasoned ruefully. She quickened her movements, as if the danger of faltering in purpose lay somewhere along this train of thought if she lingered on it too long.

For herself she took very little, only what was of absolute necessity. Underthings, an extra pair or two of stockings—

Things, things. What did things matter, when your whole world was breaking up and crumbling about you? *Your* world? It wasn't *your* world, it was a world you had no right to be in.

She dropped the lid of the valise, latched it impatiently on what it held, indifferent to whether it held enough, or too much, or too little. A little tongue of white stuff was trapped, left protruding through the seam, and she let it be.

She put on the hat and coat she'd left in readiness across the foot of the bed. The hat without consulting a mirror, though there was one right at her shoulder. She picked up her handbag, and probed into it with questing hand. She brought out a key, the key to this house, and put it down on the dresser. Then she brought out a small change-purse and shook it out. A cabbagy cluster of interfolded currency fell out soundlessly, and a sprinkling of coins, these last with a tinkling sound and some rolling about. She swept them all closer together, and then left them there on top of the dresser. Then she picked up the seventeen cents and dropped that into the change-purse instead, and replaced it in the handbag, and thrust that under her arm.

She went over beside the crib, then, and lowered its side. She crouched down on a level with the small sleeping face.

She kissed it lightly on each eyelid. "I'll be back for you in a minute," she whispered. "I have to take the bag down first and stand it at the door. I can't manage you both on those stairs, I'm afraid." She straightened up, lingered a moment, looking down at him. "We're going for a ride, you and I; we don't know where, and we don't care. Straight out, along the way the trains go. We'll find someone along the road who'll let us in next to him—"

The clock said a little after one now.

She went over to the door, softly opened it, and carried the valise outside with her. She eased it closed behind her, and then she started down the stairs valise in hand, with infinite slowness, as though it weighed a lot. Yet it couldn't have been the valise alone that seemed to pull her arm down so, it must have been the leadenness of her heart.

Suddenly she'd stopped, and allowed the valise to come to rest on the step beside her. They were standing there without a sound, down below her by the front door, the two of them. Father Hazzard and Doctor Parker. She hadn't heard them until now, for they hadn't been saying anything. They must have been standing there in a sort of momentary mournful silence, just preceding leavetaking.

They broke it now, as she stood there unseen, above the bend of the stairs.

"Well, goodnight, Donald," the doctor said at last, and she saw him put his hand to Father Hazzard's shoulder in an attempt at consolation, then let it trail heavily off again. "Get some sleep. She'll be all right." He opened the door, then he added: "But no excitement, no stress of any kind from now on, you understand that, Donald? That'll be your job, to keep all that away from her. Can I count on you?"

"You can count on me," Father Hazzard said forlornly.

The door closed, and he turned away and started up the stairs, to where she stood riveted. She moved down a step or two around the turn to meet him, leaving the valise behind her, doffed hat and coat flung atop it now.

He looked up and he saw her, without much surprise, without much of anything except a sort of stony sadness.

"Oh, it's you, Patrice," he said dully. "Did you hear him? Did you hear what he just said?"

"Who is it—Mother?"

"She had another of those spells soon after we retired. He's been in there with her for over an hour and a half. It was touch and go, for a few minutes, at first—"

"But Father! Why didn't you—?"

He sat down heavily on the stair-step. She sat down beside him, slung one arm about his shoulders.

"Why should I bother you, dear? There wouldn't have been anything you could have— You have the baby on your hands all day long, you need your rest. Besides, this isn't anything new. Her heart's always been weak. Way back before the boys were born—"

"I never knew. You never told me— But is it getting worse?"

"Things like that don't improve as you get on in years," he said gently.

She let her head slant to rest against his shoulder, in compunction.

He patted her hand consolingly. "She'll be all right. We'll see that she is, you and I, between us, won't we?"

She shivered a little, involuntarily, at that.

"It's just that we've got to cushion her against all shocks and upsets," he said. "You and the young fellow, you're about the best medicine for her there is. Just having you around—"

And if in the morning she had asked for Patrice, asked for her grandchild, and he'd had to tell her— She fell strangely silent, looking down at the steps under their feet, but no longer seeing them. And if she'd come out of her room five minutes later, just missing the doctor as he left, she might have brought death into this house, in repayment for all the love that had been lavished on her. Killed the only mother she'd ever known.

He misunderstood her abstraction, pressed her chin with the cleft of his hand. "Now don't take it like that; she wouldn't want you to, you know. And Pat, don't let her know you've found out about it. Let her keep on thinking it's her secret and mine. I know she'll be happier that way."

She sighed deeply. It was a sigh of decision, of capitulation to the inevitable. She turned and kissed him briefly on the side of the head and stroked his hair a couple of times. Then she stood up.

"I'm going up," she said quietly. "Go down and put out the hall-light after us, a minute."

He retraced his steps momentarily. She picked up the valise, the coat, the hat, and quietly reopened the door of her own room.

"Goodnight, Patrice."

"Goodnight, Father; I'll see you in the morning."

She carried them in with her, and closed the door, and in the darkness on the other side she stood still a minute. A silent, choking prayer welled up in her.

"Give me strength, for there's no running away, I see that now. The battle must be fought out here where I stand, and I dare not even cry out."

Thirty

THEN they stopped suddenly. There were no more. No more came. The days became a week, the week became a month. The month lengthened toward two. And no more came.

It was as though the battle had been won without striking a blow. No, she knew that wasn't so; it was as though the battle had been broken off, held in abeyance, at the whim of the crafty, shadowy adversary.

She clutched at straws—straws of attempted comprehension—and they all failed her.

Mother Hazzard said: "Edna Harding got back today; she's been visiting their folks in Philadelphia the past several weeks."

But no more came.

Bill remarked: "I ran into Tom Bryant today; he tells me his older sister Marilyn's been laid up with pleurisy; she only got out of bed for the first time today."

"I *thought* I hadn't seen her."

But no more came.

Caulfield: Population 203,000, she thought. That was what the atlas in the library said. And a pair of hands to each living soul of them. One to hold down the flap of a letter-box, on some secret shadowy corner; the other to quickly, furtively slip an envelope through the slot.

No more came. Yet the enigma remained. What was it? Who was it? Or rather, what had it been? Who had it been?

Yet deep in her innermost heart she knew somehow the present tense still fitted it, none other would do. Things like that didn't just happen and then stop. They either never began at all, or else they ran on to their shattering, destructive conclusion.

But in spite of that, security crept back a little; frightened off once and not so bold now as before, but crept tentatively back toward her a little.

In the mornings the world was bitter-sweet to look at, seeming to hold its breath, waiting to see—

Thirty-One

MOTHER HAZZARD knocked on her door just as she'd finished tucking Hughie in. There wasn't anything exceptional about this, it was a nightly event, the filching of a last grandmotherly kiss just before the light went out. Tonight, however, she seemed to want to talk to Patrice herself. And not to know how to go about it.

She lingered on after she'd kissed him, and the side of the crib had been lifted into place. She stood there somewhat uncertainly, her continued presence preventing Patrice from switching out the light.

There was a moment's awkwardness.

"Patrice."

"Yes, Mother?"

Suddenly she'd blurted it out. "Bill wants to take you to the Country Club dance with him tonight. He's waiting down there now."

Patrice was so completely taken back she didn't answer for a moment, just stood there looking at her.

"He told me to come up and ask you if you'd go with him." Then she rushed on, as if trying to talk her into it by sheer profusion of wordage, "They have one about once each month, you know, and he's going himself, he usually does, and—why don't you get dressed and go with him?" she ended up on a coaxing note.

"But I—I—" Patrice stammered.

"Patrice, you've got to begin sooner or later. It isn't good for you not to. You haven't been looking as well as you might lately. We're a little worried about you. If there's something troubling you— You do what Mother says, dear."

It was apparently an order. Or as close to an order as Mother Hazzard could ever have brought herself to come. She had opened Patrice's closet-door, meanwhile, and was peering helpfully inside. "How about this?" She took something down, held it up against herself to show her.

"I haven't very much—"

"It'll do nicely." It landed on the bed. "They're not very formal there. I'll have Bill buy you an orchid or gardenia on the way, that'll dress it up enough. You just go and get the *feel* of it tonight. It'll begin coming back to you little by little." She smiled reassuringly at her. "You'll be in good hands." She patted her on the shoulder as she turned to go outside. "Now that's a good girl. I'll tell Bill you're getting ready."

Patrice overheard her call down to him from above-stairs, a moment later, without any attempt at modulating her voice: "The answer is yes. I talked her into it. And you be very nice to her, young man, or you'll hear from me."

He was standing waiting for her just inside the door when she came downstairs.

"Am I all right?" she asked uncertainly.

He was suddenly overcome with some sort of awkwardness. "Gee, I—I didn't know how you could look in the evening," he said haltingly.

For the first few moments of the drive, there was a sort of shyness between them, almost as though they'd only just met tonight for the first time. It was very impalpable, but it rode with them. He turned on the radio in the car. Dance music rippled back into their faces. "To get you into the mood," he said.

He stopped, and got out, and came back with an orchid.

"The biggest one north of Venezuela," he said. "Or wherever they come from."

"Here, pin it on for me." She selected a place. "Right about here."

Abruptly, he balked at that, for some strange reason. All but shied away bodily. "Oh no, that you do yourself," he said, more forcefully than she could see any reason for.

"I might stick myself," he added lamely as an afterthought. A little too long after.

"Why, you great big coward."

The hand that would have held the pin was a trifle unsteady, she noticed, when he first put it back to the wheel. Then it quieted.

They drove the rest of the way. The rest of the way lay mostly through open country. There were stars overhead.

"I've never *seen* so many!" she marvelled.

"Maybe you haven't been looking up enough," he said gently.

Toward the end, just before they got there, a peculiar sort of tenderness seemed to overcome him for a minute. He even slowed the car a little, as he turned to her.

"I want you to be happy tonight, Patrice," he said earnestly. "I want you to be *very* happy."

There was a moment's silence between them, then they picked up speed again.

Thirty-Two

AND for the next one, right after that, the tune they played was "Three Little Words." She remembered that afterward. That least of all things about it, the tune they had been playing at the time. She was dancing it with Bill. For that matter she'd been dancing them all with him, steadily, ever since they'd arrived. She wasn't watching, she wasn't looking around her, she wasn't thinking of anything but the two of them.

Smiling dreamily, she danced. Her thoughts were like a little brook running swiftly but smoothly over harmless pebbles, keeping time with the tinkling music.

I like dancing with him. He dances well, you don't have to keep thinking about your feet. He's turned his face toward me and is looking down at me; I can feel it. Well, I'll look up at him, and then he'll smile at me; but I won't smile back at him. Watch. There, I knew that was coming. I will *not* smile back. Oh, well, what if I did? It slipped out before I could stop it. Why shouldn't I smile at him, anyway? That's the way I feel about him; smilingly fond.

A hand touched Bill's shoulder from behind. She could see the fingers slanted downward for a second, on her side of it, without seeing the hand or arm or person it belonged to.

A voice said: "May I cut in on this one?"

And suddenly they'd stopped. Bill had stopped, so she had to, too.

His arms left her. A shuffling motion took place, Bill stepped aside, and there was someone else there in his place. It was like a double exposure, where one person dissolves into another.

Their eyes met, hers and the new pair. His had been waiting for hers, and hers had foolishly run into his. They couldn't move again.

The rest was horror, sheer and unadulterated. Horror such as she'd never known she could experience. Horror under the electric lights. Death on the dance floor. Her body stayed upright, but otherwise she had every feeling of death coursing through it.

"Georgesson's the name," he murmured unobtrusively to Bill. His lips hardly seemed to stir at all. His eyes didn't leave hers.

Bill completed the ghastly parody of an introduction. "Mrs. Hazzard, Mr. Georgesson."

"How do you do?" he said to her.

Somehow there was even worse horror in the trite phrase than there had been in the original confrontation. She was screaming in silent inward panic, her lips locked tight, unable even to speak Bill's name and prevent the transfer.

"May I?" Georgesson said, and Bill nodded, and the transfer had been completed; it was too late.

Then for a moment, blessed reprieve. She felt his arms close about her, and her face sank into the sheltering shadow of his shoulder, and she was dancing again. She no longer had to stand upright, unsupported. There, that was better. A minute to think in. A minute to get your breath in.

The music went on, their dancing went on. Bill's face faded away in the background.

"We've met before, haven't we?"

Keep me from fainting, she prayed, keep me from falling.

He was waiting for his answer.

Don't speak; don't answer him.

"*Who'd* he say you were?"

Her feet faltered, missed.

"Don't make me keep on doing this, I can't. Help me— outside someplace—or I'm—"

"Too warm for you?" he said politely.

She didn't answer. The music was dying. She was dying.

He said, "You went out of step, just then. My fault, I'm afraid."

"Don't—" she whimpered. "Don't—"

The music stopped. They stopped.

His arm left her back, but his hand stayed tight about her wrist, holding her there beside him for a moment.

He said, "There's a veranda outside. Over there, out that way. I'll go out there and wait for you, and we can—go ahead talking."

She hardly knew what she was saying. "I can't— You don't understand—" Her neck wouldn't hold firm; her head kept trying to lob over limply.

"I think I do. I think I understand perfectly. I understand you, and you understand me." Then he added with a grisly sort of emphasis that froze her to the marrow: "I bet we two understand one another better than any other two people in this whole ballroom at the moment."

Bill was coming back toward them from the sidelines.

"I'll be out there where I said. Don't keep me waiting too long, or—I'll simply have to come in and look you up again." His face didn't change. His voice didn't change. "Thanks for the dance," he said, as Bill arrived.

He didn't let go her wrist; he transferred it to Bill's keeping, as though she were something inanimate, a doll, and bowed, and turned, and left them.

"Seen him around a few times. Came here stag, I guess."
Bill shrugged in dismissal. "Come on."

"Not this one. The one after."

"Are you all right? You look pale."

"It's the lights. I'm going in and powder. You go and dance
with someone else."

He grinned at her. "I don't want to dance with someone
else."

"Then you go and—and come back for me. The one after."

"The one after."

She watched him from just outside the doorway. He went
out front toward the bar. She watched him go in there. She
watched him sit down on one of the tall stools. Then she
turned and went the other way.

She walked slowly over to the doors leading outside onto
the veranda, and stood in one of them, looking out into the
fountain-pen-ink blueness of the night. There were wicker
chairs, in groups of twos and threes, spaced every few yards,
encircling small tables.

The red sequin of a cigarette-coal had risen perpendicularly
above one, all the way down at the end, imperiously summoning her. Then it shot over the balustrade laterally, cast
away in impatient expectancy.

She walked slowly down that way, with the strange feeling
of making a journey from which there was to be no return,
ever. Her feet seemed to want to take root, hold her back of
their own volition.

She came to a halt before him. He slung his hip onto the
balustrade, and sat there askew, in insolent informality. He
repeated what he'd said inside. "*Who*'d he say you were?"

The stars were moving. They were making peculiar eddying
swirls like blurred pinwheels all over the sky.

"You abandoned me," she said with leashed fury. "You
abandoned me, with five dollars. Now what do you want?"

"Oh, then we have met before. I *thought* we had. Glad you
agree with me."

"Stop it. What do you want?"

"What do I want? I don't want anything. I'm a little confused, that's all. I'd like to be straightened out. The man introduced you under a mistaken name in there."

"What do you want? What are you doing down here?"

"Well, for that matter," he said with insolent urbanity, "what are you doing yourself down here?"

She repeated it a third time. "What do you want?"

"Can't a man show interest in his ex-protégée and child? There's no way of making children ex, you know."

"You're either insane or—"

"You know that isn't so. You wish it were," he said brutally.

She turned on her heel. His hand found her wrist again, flicked around it like a whip. Cutting just as deeply.

"Don't go inside yet. We haven't finished."

She stopped, her back to him now. "I think we have."

"The decision is mine."

He let go of her, but she stayed there where she was. She heard him light another cigarette, saw the momentary reflection from behind her own shoulder.

He spoke at last, voice thick with expelled smoke. "You still haven't cleared things up," he purred. "I'm as mixed-up as ever. This Hugh Hazzard married—er—let's say you, his wife, in Paris, a year ago last June fifteenth. I went to considerable expense and trouble to have the exact date on the records there verified. But a year ago last June fifteenth you and I were living in our little furnished room in New York. I have the receipted rent-bills to show for this. How could you have been in two such far-apart places at once?" He sighed philosophically. "Somebody's got their dates mixed. Either he had. Or I have." And then very slowly, "Or *you* have."

She winced unavoidably at that. Slowly her head came around, her body still remaining turned from him. Like one who listens hypnotized, against her will.

"It was you who's been sending those—?"

He nodded with mock affability, as if on being complimented on something praiseworthy. "I thought it would be kinder to break it to you gently."

She drew in her breath with an icy shudder of repugnance.

"I first happened on your name among the train-casualties, when I was up in New York," he said. He paused. "I went down there and 'identified' you, you know," he went on matter-of-factly. "You have that much to thank me for, at any rate."

He puffed thoughtfully on his cigarette.

"Then I heard one thing and another, and put two and two together. I went back for awhile first—got the rent-receipts together and one thing and another—and then finally I came on the rest of the way down here, out of curiosity. I became quite confused," he said ironically, "when I learned the rest of the story."

He waited. She didn't say anything. He seemed to take pity on her finally. "I know," he said indulgently, "this isn't the time nor place to—talk over old times. This is a party, and you're anxious to get back and enjoy yourself."

She shivered.

"Is there anywhere I can reach you?"

He took out a notebook, clicked a lighter. She mistakenly thought he was waiting to write at her dictate. Her lips remained frozen.

"Seneca 382," he read from the notebook. He put it away again. His hand made a lazy curve between them. In the stricken silence that followed he suggested after awhile, casually: "Lean up against that chair so you don't fall; you don't seem very steady on your feet, and I don't want to have to carry you bodily inside in front of all those people."

She put her hands to the top of the chair-back and stood quiet, head inclined.

The rose-amber haze in the open doorway down at the center of the terrace blotted out for a moment, and Bill was standing there looking for her.

"Patrice, this is our dance."

Georgesson rose for a second from the balustrade in sketchy etiquette, immediately sank back against it.

She made her way toward him, the blue pall of the terrace covering her uncertainty of step, and went inside with him. His arms took charge of her from that point on, so that she no longer had to be on her own.

"You were both standing there like statues," he said. "He can't be very good company."

She lurched against him in the tendril-like twists of the rumba, her head dropped to rest on his shoulder.

"He isn't very good company," she agreed sickly.

Thirty-Three

THE phone-call came at a fiendishly unpropitious moment.

He'd timed it well. He couldn't have timed it better if he'd been able to look through the walls of the house and watch their movements on the inside. The two men in the family were out. She'd just finished putting Hughie to sleep. She and Mother Hazzard were both up on the second floor, separately. Which meant that she was the only one fully eligible to answer.

She knew at the first instant of hearing it who it was, what it was. She knew too, that she'd been expecting it all day, that she'd known it was coming, it was surely coming.

She stood there rooted, unable to move. Maybe it would stop if she didn't go near it, maybe he would tire. But then it would ring again some other time.

Mother Hazzard opened the door of her room and looked out.

Patrice had swiftly opened her own door, was at the head of the stairs, before she'd fully emerged.

"I'll get it on this phone, dear, if you're busy."

"No, never mind, Mother, I was just going downstairs, anyway, so I'll answer it there."

She knew his voice right away. She hadn't heard it for over two years, until just last night, and yet it was again as familiar to her as if she'd been hearing it steadily for months past. Fear quickens the memory.

He was as pleasantly aloof at first as any casual caller on the telephone. "Is this the younger Mrs. Hazzard? Is this Patrice Hazzard?"

"This is she."

"I suppose you know, this is Georgesson."

She did know, but she didn't answer that.

"Are you—where you can be heard?"

"I'm not in the habit of answering questions like that. I'll hang up the receiver."

Nothing could seem to make him lose his equanimity. "Don't do that, Patrice," he said urbanely. "I'll ring back again. That'll make it worse. They'll begin wondering who it is keeps on calling so repeatedly. Or, eventually, someone else

will answer—you can't stay there by the phone all evening—
and I'll give my name if I have to and ask for you." He waited
a minute for this to sink in. "Don't you see, it's better for
you this way."

She sighed a little, in suppressed fury.

"We can't talk very much over the phone. I think it's better
not to, anyway. I'm talking from McClellan's Drugstore, a few
blocks from you. My car's just around the corner from there,
where it can't be seen. On the left side of Pomeroy Street,
just down from the crossing. Can you walk down that far for
five or ten minutes? I won't keep you long."

She tried to match the brittle formality of his voice with
her own. "I most certainly can not."

"Of course you can. You need cod-liver-oil capsules for
your baby, from McClellan's. Or you feel like a soda, for yourself. I've seen you stop in there more than once, in the evening."

He waited.

"Shall I call back? Would you rather think it over awhile?"

He waited again.

"Don't do that," she said reluctantly, at last.

She could tell he understood: her meaning had been a positive and not a negative one.

She hung up.

She went upstairs again.

Mother Hazzard didn't ask her. They weren't inquisitive
that way, in this house. But the door of her room was open.
Patrice couldn't bring herself to reenter her own without at
least a passing reference. Guilty conscience, this soon? she
wondered bitingly.

"That was a Steve Georgesson, Mother," she called in. "Bill
and I ran into him there last night. He wanted to know how
we'd enjoyed ourselves."

"Well, that was real thoughtful of him, wasn't it?" Then
she added, "He must be a decent sort, to do that."

Decent, Patrice thought dismally, easing the door closed
after her.

She came out of her room again in about ten minutes' time.
Mother Hazzard's door was closed now. She could have gone
on down the stairs unquestioned. Again she couldn't do it.

She went over and knocked lightly, to attract attention.

"Mother, I'm going to take a walk down to the drugstore and back. Hughie's out of his talc. And I'd like a breath of air. I'll be back in five minutes."

"Go ahead, dear. I'll say goodnight to you now, in case I'm asleep by the time you're in again."

She rested her outstretched hand helplessly against the door for a minute. She felt like saying, Mother, don't let me go. Forbid me. Keep me here.

She turned away and went down the stairs. It was her own battle, and no proxies were allowed.

She stopped beside the car, on darkened Pomeroy Street.

"Sit in here, Patrice," he said amiably. He unlatched the door for her, from where he sat, and even palmed the leather cushion patronizingly.

She settled herself on the far side of the seat. Her eyes snapped refusal of the cigarette he was trying to offer her.

"We can be seen."

"Turn this way, toward me. No one'll notice you. Keep your back to the street."

"This can't go on. Now once and for all, for the first time and the last, what is it you want of me, what is this about?"

"Look, Patrice, there doesn't have to be anything unpleasant about this. You seem to be building it up to yourself that way, in your own mind. I have no such— It's all in the way you look at it. I don't see that there has to be any change in the way things were going along—before last night. You were the only one knew before. Now you and I are the only ones know. It ends there. That is, if you want it to."

"You didn't bring me out here to tell me that."

He went off at a tangent. Or what seemed to be a tangent. "I've never amounted to—as much as I'd hoped, I suppose. I mean, I've never gotten as far as I should. As I once expected to. There are lots of us like that. Every once in awhile I find myself in difficulties, every now and then I get into a tight squeeze. Little card-games with the boys. This and that. You know how it is." He laughed deprecatingly. "It's been going on for years. It's nothing new. But I was wondering if you'd care to do me a favor—this time."

"You're asking me for money."

She almost felt nauseated. She turned her face away.

"I didn't think there were people like you outside of—outside of penitentiaries."

He laughed in good-natured tolerance. "You're in unusual circumstances. That attracts 'people like me.' If you weren't, you *still* wouldn't think there were any, you wouldn't know any different."

"Suppose I go to them now and tell them of this conversation we've just been having, of my own accord. My brother-in-law would go looking for you and beat you within an inch of your life."

"We'll let the relationship stand unchallenged. I wonder why women put such undue faith in a beating-up? Maybe because they're not used to violence themselves. A beating doesn't mean much to a man. Half an hour after it's over, he's as good as he was before."

"You should know," she murmured.

He tapped a finger to the points of three others. "There are three alternatives. You go to them and tell them. Or I go to them and tell them. Or we remain in status quo. By which I mean, you do me a favor, and then we drop the whole thing, nothing further is said. But there isn't any fourth alternative."

He shook his head slightly, in patient disapproval. "You overdramatize everything so, Patrice. That's the unfailing hallmark of cheapness. You're a cheap girl. That's the basic difference between us. I may be, according to your lights, a rotter, but I have a certain tone. As you visualize it, I'd stride in there, throw my arms out wide in declamation, and blare, 'This girl is not your daughter-in-law!' Not at all. That wouldn't work with people like that. It would overreach itself. All I'd have to do would be to let you accuse yourself out of your own mouth. In their presence. You couldn't refuse the house to me. 'When you were in Paris with Hugh, Patrice, which bank did you live on, Left or Right?' 'What was the name of the boat you made the trip back on, again?' 'Well, when I ran into you over there that day with him—oh, you forgot to mention that we'd already met before, Pat?—why is it you looked so different from what you do today? You don't look like the same girl at all.' Until you crumpled and caved in."

He was capable of it. He was too cold about the whole thing, that was the dangerous feature. No heat, no impulse, no emotion to cloud the issue. Everything planned, plotted, graphed, ahead of time. Drafted. Charted. Every step. Even the notes. She knew their purpose now. Not poison-pen letters at all. They had been important to the long-term scheme of the thing. Psychological warfare, nerve warfare, breaking her down ahead of time, toppling her resistance before the main attack had even been made. The research-trip to New York in-between, to make sure of his own ground, to make sure there was no flaw, to leave her no loophole.

He skipped the edge of his hand off the wheel-rim, as if brushing off a particle of dust. "There's no villain in this. Let's get rid of the Victorian trappings. It's just a business transaction. It's no different from taking out insurance, really." He turned to her with an assumption of candor that was almost charming for a moment. "Don't you want to be practical about it?"

"I suppose so. I suppose I should meet you on your own ground." She didn't try to project her contempt; it would have failed to reach him, she knew.

"If you get rid of these stuffy fetishes of virtue and villainy, of black and white, the whole thing becomes so simple it's not even worth the quarter of an hour we're giving it here in the car."

"I have no money of my own, Georgesson." Capitulation. Submission.

"They're one of the wealthiest families in town, that's common knowledge. Why be technical about it? Get them to open an account for you. You're not a child."

"I couldn't *ask* them outright to do such a—"

"You don't *ask*. There are ways. You're a woman, aren't you? It's easy enough; a woman knows how to go about those things—"

"I'd like to go now," she said, reaching blindly for the door-handle.

"Do we understand one another?" He opened it for her. "I'll give you another ring after awhile."

He paused a moment. The threat was so impalpable there was not even a change of inflection in the lazy drawl.

"Don't neglect it, Patrice."

She got out. The crack of the door was the unfelt slap-in-the-face of loathing she gave him.

"Goodnight, Patrice," he drawled after her amiably.

Thirty-Four

"—PERFECTLY plain," she was saying animatedly. "It had a belt of the same material, and then a row of buttons down to about here."

She was purposely addressing herself to Mother Hazzard, to the exclusion of the two men members of the family. Well, the topic in itself was excuse enough for that.

"Heaven sakes, why didn't you take it?" Mother Hazzard wanted to know.

"I couldn't do that," she said reluctantly. She stopped a moment, then she added: "Not right—then and there." And played a lot with her fork. And felt low.

They must have thought the expression on her face was wistful disappointment. It wasn't. It was self-disgust.

You don't have to ask openly. There are ways; it's easy enough. A woman knows how to go about those things.

This was one of them now.

How defenseless those who love you are against you, she thought bitterly. How vicious and how criminal it is to trade on that self-imposed defenselessness. As I am doing now. Tricks and traps and wiles, those are for strangers. Those should be used against such only. Not against those who love you; with their guard down, with their eyes trustfully closed. It made her skin crawl in revulsion. She felt indecent, unclean, obscene.

Father Hazzard cut into the conversation. "Why didn't you just charge it up and have it sent? You could have used Mother's account. She deals there a lot."

She let her eyes drop. "I wouldn't have wanted to do that," she said reticently.

"Nonsense—" He stopped suddenly. Almost as though someone had trodden briefly on his foot under the table.

She caught Bill glancing at her. He seemed to be holding

the glance a moment longer than was necessary. But before she could verify this, it had stopped, and he resumed bringing the suspended forkful of pie-fill up to his mouth.

"I think I hear Hughie crying," she said, and flung her napkin down and ran out to the stairs to listen.

But in the act of listening upward, she couldn't avoid overhearing Mother Hazzard's guarded voice in the dining-room behind her, spacing each word with strictural severity.

"Donald Hazzard, you ought to be ashamed of yourself. Do you men-folk have to be told *every*thing? Haven't you got a grain of tact in your heads?"

Thirty-Five

IN the morning Father Hazzard had lingered on at the table, she noticed when she came down, instead of leaving early with Bill. He sat quietly reading his newspaper while she finished her coffee. And there was just a touch of secretive self-satisfaction in his attitude, she thought.

He rose in company with her when she got up. "Get your hat and coat, Pat, I want you to come with me in the car. This young lady and I have business downtown," he announced to Mother Hazzard. The latter tried, not altogether successfully, to look blankly bewildered.

"But what about Hughie's feeding?"

"I'll give him his feeding," Mother Hazzard said serenely.

"You'll be back in time for that. I'm just borrowing you."

She got in next to him a moment later and they started off.

"Did poor Bill have to walk to the office this morning?" she asked.

"Poor Bill indeed!" he scoffed. "Do him good, the big lug. If I had those long legs of his, I'd walk it myself, every morning."

"Where are you taking me?"

"Now just never you mind. No questions. Just wait'll we get there, and you'll see."

They stopped in front of the bank. He motioned her out and led her inside with him. He said something to one of the guards in an aside, and he and she sat down to wait for a moment on a bench.

For the briefest moment only. Then the guard had come back with a noticeable deference. He led them toward a door marked "Manager, Private." Before they could reach it it had already opened and a pleasant-faced, slightly stout man wearing horn-rimmed spectacles was waiting to greet them.

"Come in and meet my old friend Harve Wheelock," Father Hazzard said to her.

They seated themselves in comfortable leather chairs in the private office, and the two men shared cigars.

"Harve, I've got a new customer for you. This is my boy Hugh's wife. Not that I think your mangy old bank is any good, but—well, you know how it is. Just habit, I reckon."

The manager shook appreciatively all over, as if this were some joke between them that had been going on for years. He winked for Patrice's benefit. "I agree with you there. Sell it to you real cheap."

"How cheap?"

"Quarter of a million." Meanwhile he was penning required entries on a filing-form, as though he had all the information called for at his fingers' tips, didn't need to ask anything about it.

Father Hazzard shook his head. "Too cheap. Can't be any good." He offhandedly palmed an oblong of light blue paper onto the desk, left it there face down.

"You think it over and let me know," the manager said drily. And to her, reversing his pen, "Sign here, honey."

Forger, she thought scathingly. She handed it back, her eyes downcast. The strip of light blue was clipped to it and it was sent out. A midget black book came back in its stead.

"Here you are, honey." The manager tendered it to her across his desk.

She opened it and looked at it, unnoticed, while the two resumed their friendly bickering hammer and tongs. It was so spotless, so unused yet. At the top it said "Mrs. Hugh Hazzard." And there was just one entry, under today's date. A deposit.

"5000.00"

Thirty-Six

SHE stood there holding the small round canister, staring frozenly at it as though she couldn't make out what was in it. She'd been holding it like that for long moments, without actually seeing it. She tilted it at last and dumped its contents into the washbowl. It had been better than half-full.

She went out, and closed the door, and went across the hall and knocked softly.

"I'm stepping out for just a moment, Mother. Hughie upset his whole can of talc in the bath just now, and I want to get another before I forget."

"All right, dear. The walk'll do you good. Oh—bring me back a bottle of that shampoo while you're in there, dear. I'm on the last of it now."

She got that slightly sickened feeling she was beginning to know so well. It was so easy to fool those who loved you. But who were you really fooling—them or yourself?

His arm was draped negligently atop the car-door, elbow out. The door fell open. He made way for her by shifting leisurely over on the seat, without offering to rise. His indolent taking of her for granted was more scathingly insulting than any overt rudeness would have been.

"I'm sorry I had to call. I thought you'd forgotten about our talk. It's been more than a week now."

"Forgotten?" she said drily. "I wish it were that easy."

"I see you've become a depositor of the Standard Trust since our last meeting."

She shot him an involuntary look of shock, without answering.

"Five thousand dollars."

She drew a quick breath.

"Tellers will chat for a quarter cigar." He smiled. "Well?"

"I haven't any money with me. I haven't used the account yet. I'll have to cash a check in the morning and—"

"They give a checkbook with each account, don't they? And you have that with you, most likely—"

She gave him a look of unfeigned surprise.

"I have a fountain pen right here in my pocket. I'll turn on the dashboard-lights a minute. Let's get it over and done with; the quickest way's the best. Now; I'll tell you what to write. To Stephen Georgesson. Not to Cash or Bearer. Five hundred."

"Five hundred?"

"That's academic."

She didn't understand what he meant, and was incautious enough to let him go on past that point without stopping him.

"That's all. And then your signature. The date, if you want."

She stopped short. "I can't do this."

"I'm sorry, you'll have to. I don't want it any other way. I won't accept cash."

"But this passes through the bank with both our names on it, mine as payer, yours as payee."

"There's such a flood of checks passing through the bank every month, it's not even likely to be noticed. It could be a debt of Hugh's, you know, that you're settling up for him."

"Why are you so anxious to have a check?" she asked irresolutely.

A crooked smile looped one corner of his mouth. "Why should you object, if I don't? It's to your advantage, isn't it? I'm playing right into your hands. It comes back into your possession after it clears the bank. After that you're holding tangible evidence of this—of blackmail—against me if you should ever care to prosecute. Which is something you haven't got so far. Remember, up to this point, it's just your word against mine, I can deny this whole thing happened. Once this check goes through, you've got living proof."

He said, a little more tartly than he'd yet spoken to her, "Shall we get through? You're anxious to get back. And I'm anxious to pull out of here."

She handed him the completed check and pen.

He was smiling again now. He waited until she'd stepped out and he'd turned on the ignition. He said above the low throb of the motor, "Your thinking isn't very clear, nor very quick, is it? This check is evidence against *me*, that *you're* holding, if it clears the bank and returns to you. But if it doesn't—if it's kept out, and never comes up for payment at all—then it's evidence against *you*, that *I'm* holding."

The car glided off and left her standing behind looking after it in her shattered consternation.

Thirty-Seven

SHE all but ran toward the car along the night-shaded street, as if fearful it might suddenly glide into motion and escape her, instead of directing her steps toward it grudgingly as she had the two previous times. She clung to the top of the door with both hands when she'd reached it, as if in quest of support.

"I can't stand this! What are you trying to do to me?"

He was smugly facetious. His brows went up. "Do? I haven't done anything to you. I haven't been near you. I haven't seen you in the last three weeks."

"The check wasn't debited."

"Oh, you've had your bank statement. That's right, yesterday was the first of the month. I imagine you've had a bad twenty-four hours. I must have overlooked it—"

"No," she said with fierce rancor, "you're not the kind would overlook anything like that, you vicious leech! Haven't you done enough to me? What are you trying to do, drive me completely out of my mind—"

His manner changed abruptly, tightened. "Get in," he said crisply. "I want to talk to you. I'll drive you around for a quarter of an hour or so."

"I can't *ride* with you. How can you ask me to do that?"

"We can't just stand still in this one place, talking it over. That's far worse. We've done that twice already. We can circle the lake drive once or twice; there's no one on it at this hour and no stops. Turn your collar up across your mouth."

"Why are you holding the check? What are you meaning to do?"

"Wait until we get there," he said. Then when they had, he answered her, coldly, dispassionately, as though there had been no interruption.

"I'm not interested in five hundred dollars."

She was beginning to lose her head. Her inability to fathom

his motives was kindling her to panic. "Give it back to me, then, and I'll give you more. I'll give you a thousand. Only, give it back to me."

"I don't want to be *given* more. I don't want to be *given* any amount. Don't you understand? I want the money to belong to *me*, in my own right."

Her face was suddenly stricken white. "I don't understand. What are you trying to say to me?"

"I think you're beginning to, by the look on your face." He fumbled in his pocket, took something out. An envelope, already sealed and stamped for mailing. "You asked me where the check was. It's in here. Here, read what it says on it. No, don't take it out of my hand. Just read it from where you are."

> "Mr. Donald Hazzard
> Hazzard and Loring
> Empire Building
> Caulfield."

"No—" She couldn't articulate, could only shake her head convulsively.

"I'm mailing it to him at his office, where you can't intercept it." He returned it to his pocket. "The last mail-collection, here in Caulfield, is at nine each night. You may not know that, but I've been making a study of those things recently. There's a mail-box on Pomeroy Street, just a few feet from where I've been parking the last few times I've met you. It's dark and inconspicuous around there, and I'll use that one. It takes the carrier until nine-fifteen to reach it, however; I've timed him several nights in a row and taken the average."

He silenced her with his hand, went on: "Now, if you reach there before the carrier does, this envelope stays out of the chute. If you're not there yet when he arrives, I drop it in. You have a day's grace, until nine-fifteen tomorrow night."

"But what do you want me to be there for—? You said you didn't want more—"

"We're going to take a ride out to Hastings, that's the next town over. I'm taking you to a justice of the peace there, and he's going to make us man and wife."

He slowed the car as her head lurched soddenly back over the top of the seat for a moment.

"I didn't think they swooned any more—" he began. Then as he saw her straighten again with an effort and pass the back of her hand blurredly before her eyes, he added: "Oh, I see they don't; they just get a little dizzy, is that it?"

"Why are you doing this to me?" she said smotheredly.

"There are several good reasons I can think of. It's a good deal safer, from my point of view, than the basis we've been going on so far. There's no chance of anything backfiring. A wife, the law-books say, cannot testify against her husband. That means that any lawyer worth his fee can whisk you off the stand before you can so much as open your mouth. And then there are more practical considerations. The old couple aren't going to be around forever, you know. The old lady's life is hanging by a thread. And the old man won't last any time without her. Old Faithful, I know the type. When they go, you and Bill share unequally between you— Don't look so horrified; that lawyer of theirs hasn't exactly talked, but this is a small town, those things sort of seep around without even benefit of word-of-mouth. I can wait that year, or even two or three if I have to. The law gives a husband one-third of his wife's property. Three-quarters of—I may be underestimating, but roughly I'd say four hundred thousand, that's three hundred thousand. And then a third of that again— Don't cover your ears like that, Patrice; you look like someone out of a Marie Corelli novel."

He braked. "You can get out here, Patrice. This is close enough." And then he chuckled a little, watching her flounder to the pavement. "Are you sure you're able to walk steady? I wouldn't want to have them think I'd plied you with—"

The last thing he said was, "Make sure your clock isn't slow, Patrice. Because the United States Mail is always on time."

Thirty-Eight

THE headlight-beams of his car kept slashing up the road ahead of them like ploughshares, seeming to cast aside its topsoil of darkness, reveal its borax-like white fill, and spill that out all over the roadway. Then behind them the livid furrows would heal again into immediate darkness.

It seemed hours they'd been driving like this, in silence yet acutely aware of one another. Trees went by, dimly lit up from below, along their trunks, by the passing reflection of their headlight-wash, into a sort of ghostly incandescence. Then at times there weren't any trees, they fell back, and a plushy black evenness took their place—fields or meadows, she supposed— that smelled sweeter. Clover. It was beautiful country around here; too beautiful for anyone to be in such a hell of suffering in the midst of it.

Roads branched off at times, too, but they never took them. They kept to this wide, straight one they were on.

They passed an indirectly lighted white sign, placed at right angles to the road so that it could be read as you came up to it. It said "Welcome to Hastings," and then underneath, "Population—" and some figures too small to catch before they had already gone by.

She glanced briefly after it, in a sort of fascinated horror.

He'd apparently seen her do it, without looking directly at her. "That's across the State line," he remarked drily. "Travel broadens one, they say." It was nine forty-five now according to her wristwatch. It had taken them only half an hour's drive to get here.

They passed through the town's nuclear main square. A drugstore was still open, two of the old-fashioned jars of colored water that all drugstore-windows featured once upon a time flashing emerald and mauve at them as they went by. A motion-picture theatre was still alive inside, but dying fast externally, its marquee already dark, its lobby dim.

He turned up one of the side streets, a tunnel under leafy shade trees, its houses all set back a lawn-spaced distance so that they were almost invisible in the night-shade from the roadway. A dim light peering through from under the recesses of an ivy-covered porch seemed to attract him. He shunted over to the walk suddenly, and back a little, and stopped opposite it.

They sat for awhile.

Then he got out on his side, came around to hers, and opened the door beside her.

"Come in," he said briefly.

She didn't move, she didn't answer.

"Come on in with me. They're waiting."

She didn't answer, didn't move.

"Don't just sit there like that. We had this all out before, back at Caulfield. Move. Say something, will you?"

"What do you want me to say?"

He gave the door an impatient slap-to again, as if in momentary reprieve. "Get yourself together. I'll go over and let them know we got here."

She watched him go, in a sort of stupor, as though this were happening to someone else; heard his tread go up the wooden plank-walk that led up to the house. She could even hear the ring of the bell, from within the house, all the way out here where she was. It was no wonder, it was so quiet. Just little winged things buzzing and humming in a tree overhead.

She wondered: How does he know I won't suddenly start the car and drive off? She answered that herself: He knows I won't. He knows it's too late for that. As I know it. The time for stopping, for drawing back, for dashing off, that was long ago. So long ago. Long before tonight. That was in the compartment on the train coming here, when the wheels tried to warn me. That was when the first note came. That was when the first phone-call came, the first walk down to the drugstore. I am as safely held fast here as though I were manacled to him.

She could hear their voices now. A woman saying, "No, not at all; you made very good time. Come right in."

The doorway remained open, lighted. Whoever had been standing in it had withdrawn into the house. He was coming back toward her now. The sound of his tread along the wooden walk. She gripped the edge of the car-seat with her hands, dug them in under the leather cushions.

He was up to her now, standing there.

"Come on, Patrice," he said casually.

That was the full horror of it, his casualness, his matter-of-factness. He wasn't acting the part.

She spoke quietly too, as quietly as he, but her voice was as thin and blurred as a thrumming wire.

"I can't do it. Georgesson, don't ask me to do this."

"Patrice, we've been all over this. I told you the other night, and it was all settled then."

She covered her face with cupped hands, quickly uncovered it again. She kept using the same four words; they were the only ones she could think of. "But I can't do it. Don't you understand? I can't *do* it."

"There's no impediment. You're not married to anyone. Even in your assumed character, you're not married to anyone, much less as yourself. I investigated all that in New York."

"Steve. Listen, I'm calling you Steve."

"That doesn't melt me," he assured her jocosely. "That's my name, I'm supposed to be called that." He lidded his eyes at her. "It's my *given* name, not one that I took for myself—*Patrice.*"

"Steve, I've never pleaded with you before. In all these months, I've taken it like a woman. Steve, if there's anything human in you at all I can appeal to—"

"I'm only too human. That's why I like money as much as I do. But your wires are crossed. It's my very humanness, for that reason, that makes your appeal useless. Come on, Patrice. You're wasting time."

She cowered away edgewise along the seat. He drummed his fingers on the top of the door and laughed a little.

"Why this horror of marriage? Let me get to the bottom of your aversion. Maybe I can reassure you. There is no personal appeal involved; you haven't any for me. I've got only contempt for you, for being the cheap, tricky little fool you are. I'm leaving you on the doorstep of your ever-loving family again, just as soon as we get back to Caulfield. This is going to be a paper marriage, in every sense of the word. But it's going to stick, it's going to stick to the bitter end. Now does that take care of your mid-Victorian qualms?"

She cast the back of her hand across her eyes as though a blow had just blinded her.

He wrenched the door open.

"They're waiting for us in there. Come on, you're only making it worse."

He was beginning to harden against her. Her opposition was commencing to inflame him against her. It showed inversely, in a sort of lethal coldness.

"Look, my friend, I'm not going to drag you in there by the hair. The thing isn't worth it. I'm going inside a minute and call the Hazzard house from here, and tell them the whole story right now. Then I'll drive you back where I got you from. They can have you—if they want you any more." He leaned toward her slightly across the door. "Take a good look at me. Do I look like I was kidding?"

He meant it. It wasn't an empty bluff, with nothing behind it. It might be a threat that he would prefer not to have to carry out, but it wasn't an idle threat. She could see that in his eyes, in the cold sullenness in them, the dislike of herself she read in them.

He turned and left the car-side and went up the plank-walk again, more forcefully, more swiftly, than he'd trod it before.

"Excuse me, could I trouble you for a minute—" she heard him start to say as he entered the open doorway, then the rest was blurred as he went deeper within.

She struggled out, clinging to the flexing door like somebody walking in his sleep. Then she wavered up the plank-walk and onto the porch, and the ivy rustled for a minute as she teetered soddenly against it. Then she went on toward the oblong of light projected by the open doorway, and inside. It was like struggling through knee-deep water.

A middle-aged woman met her in the hallway.

"Good evening. Are you Mrs. Hazzard? He's in here."

She took her to a room on the left, parted an old-fashioned pair of sliding doors. He was standing in there, with his back to them, beside an old-fashioned telephone-box bracketed to the wall.

"Here's the young lady. You can both come into the study when you're ready."

Patrice drew the doors together behind her again. "Steve," she said.

He turned around and looked at her, then turned back again.

"Don't—you'll kill her," she pleaded.

"The old all die sooner or later."

"Has it gone through yet?"

"They're ringing Caulfield for me now."

It wasn't any sleight-of-hand trick. His finger wasn't anywhere near the receiver-hook, holding it shut down. He was in the act of carrying it out.

A choking sound broke in her throat.

He looked around again, less fully than before. "Have you decided once and for all?"

She didn't nod, she simply let her eyelids drop closed for a minute.

"Operator," he said, "cancel that call. It was a mistake." He replaced the receiver.

She felt a little sick and dizzy, as when you've just looked down from some great height and then drawn back again.

He went over to the sliding-doors and swung them vigorously back.

"We're ready," he called into the study across the hall.

He crooked his arm toward her, backhand, contemptuously tilting up his elbow for her to take, without even looking around at her as he did so.

She came forward and they went toward the study together, her arm linked in his. Into where the man was waiting to marry them.

Thirty-Nine

IT was on the way back that she knew she was going to kill him. Knew she must, knew it was the only thing left to be done now. She should have done it sooner, she told herself. Long before this; that first night as she sat with him in his car. It would have been that much better. Then this, tonight's ultimate horror and degradation, would at least have been avoided. She hadn't thought of it then; that was the one thing that had never occurred to her. It had always been flight, escape from him in some other way; never safety in this way—his removal.

But she knew she was going to do it, now. Tonight.

Not a word had passed between them, all this way, ever since leaving the justice's house. Why should one? What was there to say? What was there to do, now—except this one final thing, that came to her opposite a white-stockinged telegraph-pole, about four miles out of Hastings. Just like that it came: click, snap, and it was there. As though she had passed through some electric-eye beam stretched across the road, there from that particular telegraph-pole. On the one side of it, still, just passive despair, fatalism. On the other, full-grown decision, remorseless, irrevocable: I'm going to kill him. To-night. Before this night ends, before the light comes again.

Neither of them said anything. He didn't, because he was content. He'd done what he'd set out to do. He did whistle lightly, once, for a short while, but then he stopped that again. She didn't say anything, because she was undone. Destroyed, in the fullest sense of the word. She'd never felt like this before. She didn't even feel pain of mind any more. Struggle was ended. She was numb now. She'd even had more feeling left in her after the train-crash than now.

She rode all the way with her eyes held shut. Like a woman returning from a funeral, at which everything worth keeping has been interred, and to whom nothing left above ground is worth looking at any longer.

She heard him speak at last. "There, was that so bad?" he said.

She answered him mechanically, without opening her eyes. "Where are you—? What do you want me to do now?"

"Exactly nothing. You go on just as you were before. This is something between the two of us. And I want it to stay that way, understand? Not a word to the Family. Not until I'm ready. It'll be Our Little Secret, yours and mine."

He was afraid if he took her with him openly, they'd change the will, she supposed. And afraid if he left her with them, and they learned of it, they'd have it annulled for her.

How did you kill a man? There was nothing here, no way. The country was flat, the road level, straight. If she snatched at the wheel, tried to throw the car out of control, nothing much would happen. You needed steep places, hairbreadth turns. And the car was only trundling along, not going fast.

It would only roll off into the dirt maybe, strike a telegraph-pole, shake them up a little.

Besides, even if that had been the feasible way, she didn't want to die with him. She only wanted him to die. She had a child she was devoted to, a man she loved. She wanted to live. She'd always had an unquenchable will to live, all her life; she still had it now. Numbed as she was, it was still flickering stubbornly inside her. Nothing could put it out, or—she would already have contemplated another alternative, proba-bly, before now.

Oh God, she cried out in her mind, if I only had a—

And in that instant, she knew how to do it. Knew how she was going to do it. For the next word-symbol flashing before her senses was "gun," and as it appeared it brought its own answer to the plea.

In the library, at home. There was one in there, somewhere.

A brief scene came back to mind, from many months ago. Buried until now, to suddenly reappear, as clear as if it had just taken place a moment ago. The reading-lamp, comfort-ably lit and casting its cheerful glow. Father Hazzard, sitting there by it, lingering late over a book. The others gone to bed, all but herself. She the last one to leave him. A brief kiss on his forehead.

"Shall I lock up for you?"

"No, you run along. I will, in a moment."

"You won't forget, though?"

"No, I won't forget." And then he'd chuckled, in that dry way of his: "Don't be nervous, I'm well-protected down here. There's a revolver in one of the drawers right by me here. We keep it specially for burglars. That was Mother's idea, once, years ago—and there hasn't been hide nor hair of one in all the time since."

She'd laughed at this melodramatic drollery, and told him quite truthfully: "It wasn't prowlers I was thinking of, but a sudden rainstorm in the middle of the night and Mother's best drapes."

She'd laughed. But now she didn't.

Now she knew where there was a gun.

You crooked your finger through. You pulled. And you had peace, you had safety.

They stopped, and she heard the car-door beside her clack open. She raised her eyes. They were in a leafy tunnel of the street trees. She recognized the symmetrical formation of the trees, the lawn-slopes on either side of them, the dim contours of the private homes in the background. They were on her own street, but further over, about a block away from the house. He was being tactful, letting her out at a great enough distance from her own door to be inconspicuous.

He was sitting there, waiting for her to take the hint and get out. She looked at her watch, mechanically. Not even eleven yet. It must have been around ten when it happened. It had taken them forty minutes coming back; they'd driven slower than going out.

He'd seen her do it. He smiled satirically. "Doesn't take long to marry, does it?"

It doesn't take long to die, either, she thought smoulderingly.

"Don't you—don't you want me to come with you?" she whispered.

"What for?" he said insolently. "I don't want you. I just want what eventually—comes with you. You go upstairs to your unsullied little bed. (I trust it is, anyway. With this Bill in the house.)"

She could feel heat in her face. But nothing much mattered, nothing counted. Except that the gun was a block away, and he was here. And the two of them had to meet.

"Just stay put," he advised her. "No unexpected little trips out of town, now, Patrice. Unless you want me to suddenly step forward and claim paternity of the child. I have the law on my side, now, you know. I'll go straight to the police."

"Well—will you wait here a minute? I'll—I'll be right out. I'll get you some money. You'll need some—until—until we get together again."

"Your dowry?" he said ironically. "So soon? Well, as a matter of fact, I don't. Some of the men in this town play very poor cards. Anyway, why give me what's already mine? Piecemeal. I can wait. Don't do me any favors."

She stepped down, reluctantly.

"Where can I reach you, in case I have to?"

"I'll be around. You'll hear from me, every now and then. Don't be afraid of losing me."

No, it had to be tonight, tonight, she kept telling herself grimly. Before the darkness ended and the daybreak came. If she waited, she'd lose her courage. This surgery had to be performed at once, this cancer on her future removed.

No matter where he goes in this city tonight, she vowed, I'll track him down, I'll find him, and I'll put an end to him. Even if I have to destroy my own self doing it. Even if I have to do it in sight of a hundred people.

The car-door swung closed. He tipped his hat satirically.

"Good night, Mrs. Georgesson. Pleasant dreams to you. Try sleeping on a piece of wedding-cake. If you haven't wedding-cake, try a hunk of stale bread. You'll be just as crummy either way."

The car sidled past her. Her eyes fastened on the rear license-plate, clove to it, memorized it, even as it went skimming past. It dwindled. The red tail-light coursed around the next corner and disappeared. But it seemed to hang there before her eyes, like a ghost-plaque, suspended against the night, for long minutes after.

NYo9231

Then that, too, dimmed and went out.

Somebody was walking along the quiet night sidewalk, very close by. She could hear the chip-chipping of the high heels. That was she. The trees were moving by her, slowly rearward. Somebody was climbing terraced flagstone steps. She could hear the gritty sound of the ascending tread. That was she. Somebody was standing before the door of the house now. She could see the darkling reflection in the glass opposite her. It moved as she moved. That was she.

She opened her handbag and felt inside it for her doorkey. Hers, was good. The key they'd given her. It was still there. For some reason this surprised her. Funny to come home like this, just as though nothing had happened to you, and feel for your key, and put it into the door, and—and go into the house. To *still* come home like this, and *still* go into the house.

I have to go in here, she defended herself. My baby's asleep in this house. He's asleep upstairs in it, right now. This is where I have to go; there isn't any other place for me to go.

She remembered how she'd had to lie, earlier tonight, asking Mother Hazzard to mind Hughie for her while she visited a new friend. Father had been at a business meeting and Bill had been out.

She put on the lights in the lower hall. She closed the door. Then she stood there a minute, her breath rising and falling, her back supine against the door. It was so quiet, so quiet in this house. People sleeping, people who trusted you. People who didn't expect you to bring home scandal and murder to them, in return for all their goodness to you.

She stood there immobile. So quiet, so still, there was no guessing what she had come back here for, what she had come back here to do.

Nothing left. Nothing. No home, no love, even no child any more. She'd even forfeited that prospective love, tarnished it for a later day. She'd lose him too, he'd turn against her, when he was old enough to know this about her.

He'd done all this to her, one man. It wasn't enough that he'd done it once, he'd done it twice now. He'd wrecked two lives for her. He'd smashed up the poor inoffensive seventeen-year-old simpleton from San Francisco who had had the bad luck to stray his way. Smashed her up, and wiped his feet all over her five-and-ten-cent-store dreams, and spit on them. And now he'd smashed up the cardboard lady they called Patrice.

He wouldn't smash up anybody more!

A tortured grimace disfigured her face for a moment. The back of her wrist went to her forehead, clung there. An inhalation of terrible softness, yet terrible resolve, shook her entire frame. Then she tottered on the bias toward the library entrance, like a comic drunk lacking in sufficient coordination to face squarely in the direction in which he is hastening.

She put on the big reading-lamp in there, center-table.

She went deliberately to the cellarette, and opened that, and poured some brandy and downed it. It seemed to blast its way down into her, but she quelled it with a resolute effort.

Ah, yes, you needed that when you were going to kill a man.

She went looking for the gun. She tried the table-drawers first, and it was not in there. Only papers and things, in the way. But he'd said there was one in here, that night, and there must be, somewhere in this room. They never told you anything that was untrue, even lightly; he, nor Mother, nor—nor Bill either for that matter. That was the big difference between them and her. That was why they had peace—and she had none.

She tried Father Hazzard's desk next. The number of drawers and cubicles was greater, but she sought them all out one by one. Something glinted, as she moved a heavy business-ledger aside, in the bottommost under-drawer, and there it lay, thrust in at the back.

She took it out. Its inoffensive look, at first, was almost a disappointment. So small, to do so great a thing. To take away a life. Burnished nickel, and bone. And that fluted bulge in the middle, she supposed, was where its hidden powers of death lay. In her unfamiliarity, she pounded at its back with the heel of her hand, and strained at it, trying to get it open, risking a premature discharge, hoping only that if she kept fingers clear of the trigger she would avert one. Suddenly, with astonishing ease at the accidental right touch, it had broken downward, it slanted open. Round black chambers, empty.

She rummaged in the drawer some more. She found the same small cardboard box, half-noted in her previous search, that she had hastily cast aside. Inside, cotton-wool, as if to hold some very perishable medicinal capsule. But instead, steel-jacketed, snub-nosed, the cartridges. Only five of them.

She pressed them home, one by one, into the pits they were meant for. One chamber remained empty.

She closed the gun.

She wondered if it would fit into her handbag. She tried it spadewise, the flat side up, and it went in.

She closed the handbag, and took it with her, and went out of the room, went out to the back of the hall.

She took out the classified directory, looked under "Garages."

He might leave it out in the streets overnight. But she didn't think he would. He was the kind who prized his cars and his hats and his watches. He was the kind of man prized everything but his women.

The garages were alphabetized, and she began calling them alphabetically.

"Have you a New York car there for the night, license 09231?"

At the third place the night attendant came back and said: "Yes, we have. It was just brought in a few minutes ago."

"Mr. Georgesson?"

"Yeah, that's right. What about it, lady? Whaddya want from us?"

"I—I was out in it just now. The young man just brought me home in it. And I find I left something with him. I have to get hold of him. Please, it's important. Will you tell me where I can reach him?"

"We ain't supposed to do that, lady."

"But I can't get in. He has my doorkey, don't you understand?"

"Whyn'tcha ring your doorbell?" the gruff voice answered.

"You fool!" she exploded, her fury lending her plausible eloquence. "I wasn't supposed to be out with him in the first place! I don't want to attract any attention. I *can't* ring the doorbell!"

"I getcha, lady," the voice jeered, with that particular degree of greasiness she'd known it would have, "I getcha." And a double tongue-click was given for punctuation. "Wait'll I check up."

He left. He got on again, said: "He's been keeping his car with us for some time now. The address on our records is 110 Decatur Road. I don't know if that's still—"

But she'd hung up.

Forty

SHE used her own key to unlock the garage-door. The little roadster that Bill habitually used was out, but the big car, the sedan, was in there. She backed it out. Then she got out a moment, went back to refasten the garage-door.

There was the same feeling of unreality about this as before; a sort of dream-fantasy, a state of somnambulism, yet with over-all awareness. The chip-chip of footsteps along the cement garage-driveway that were someone else's, yet were her own—sounding from under her. It was as though she had experienced a violent personality split, and one of her selves, aghast and helpless, watched a phantom murderess issue from the cleavage and start out upon her deadly quest. She could only pace this dark thing, this other self, could not recapture nor reabsorb it, once loosed. Hence (perhaps) the detached objectivity of the footsteps, the mirror-like reproduction of her own movements.

Reentering the car, she backed it into the street, reversed it, and let it flow forward. Not violently, but with the suave pick-up of a perfectly possessed driver. Some other hand, not hers—so firm, so steady, so pure—remembered to reach for the door-latch and draw the door securely closed with a smart little clout.

Outside, the street-lights went spinning by like glowing bowls coming toward her down a bowling-alley. But each shot was a miss, they went alternately too far out to this side, too far out to that. With herself and the car, the kingpin in the middle that they never knocked down.

She thought: That must be Fate, bowling against me. But I don't care, let them come.

Then the car had stopped again. So easy it was to go forth to kill a man.

She didn't study it closely, to see what it was like. It didn't matter what it was like; she was going in there, it was going to happen there.

She pedalled the accelerator again, went on past the door and around the corner. There she made a turn, for the right-of-way was against her, pointed the car forward to the way from which she had just come, brought it over against the sidewalk, stopped it there, just out of sight.

She took up her bag from beside her on the seat, as a woman does who is about to leave a car, secured it under her arm.

She shut off the ignition and got out. She walked back around the corner, to where she'd just come from, with the quick, preoccupied gait of a woman returning home late at night, who hastens to get off the street. One has seen them that way many times; minding their own business with an added intentness, for they know they run a greater risk of being accosted then than during the daylight hours.

She found herself alone on a gloomy nocturnal strip of sidewalk in front of a long rambling two-story structure, hybrid, half commercial and half living quarters. The ground floor was a succession of unlighted store-fronts, the upper a long row of windows. The white shape of a milk bottle stood on the sill of one of these. One was lighted, but with the shade drawn. Not the one with the milk bottle.

Between two of the store-fronts, recessed, almost secretive in its inconspicuousness, there was a single-panel door, with a waffle-pattern of multiple small panes set into it. They could be detected because there was a dim hall-light somewhere beyond them, doing its best to overcome the darkness.

She went over to it and tried it, and it swung out without any demur, it had no lock, was simply a closure for appearances' sake. Inside there was a rusted radiator, and a cement stair going up, and at the side of this, just as it began, a row of letter boxes and push-buttons. His name was on the third she scanned, but not in its own right, superimposed on the card of the previous tenant, left behind. He had pencil-scratched the name off, and then put in his own underneath. "S. Georgesson." He didn't print very well.

He didn't do anything very well, except smash up people's lives. He did that very well, he was an expert.

She went on up the stairs and followed the hall. It was a jerry-built, makeshift sort of a place. During the war shortage they must have taken the attic or storage-space part of the stores below and rigged it up into these flats.

What a place to live, she thought dimly.

What a place to die, she thought remorselessly.

She could see the thin line the light made under his door. She knocked, and then she knocked again, softly like the first time. He had his radio on in there. She could hear that quite distinctly through the door.

She raised her hand and smoothed back her hair, while waiting. You smoothed your hair—if it needed it—just before you
were going to see anyone, or anyone was going to see you.
That was why she did it now.

They said you were frightened at a time like this. They said
you were keyed-up to an ungovernable pitch. They said you
were blinded by fuming emotion.

They said. What did they know? She felt nothing. Neither
fear nor excitement nor blind anger. Only a dull, aching determination all over.

He didn't hear, or he wasn't coming to open. She tried the
knob, and this door too, like the one below, was unlocked, it
gave inward. Why shouldn't it be, she reasoned, what did he
have to fear from others? They didn't take from him, he took
from them.

She closed it behind her, to keep this just between the two
of them.

He didn't meet her eyes. The room was reeking with his
presence, but it was a double arrangement, bed- and living-
quarters, and he must be in the one just beyond, must have
just stepped in as she arrived outside. She could see offside
light coming through the opening.

The coat and hat he'd worn in the car with her tonight
were slung over a chair, the coat broadside across its seat, the
hat atop that. A cigarette that he'd incompletely extinguished
a few short moments ago was in a glass tray, stubbornly
smouldering away. The drink that he'd started, then left, and
was coming back to finish any second now—the drink with
which he was celebrating tonight's successful enterprise—
stood there on the edge of the table. The white block of its
still-unmelted ice cube peered through the side of the glass,
through the straw-colored whiskey it floated in.

The sight of it brought back a furnished room in New York.
He took his drinks weak; he liked them strong, but he took
them weak when it was his own whiskey he was using. "There's
always another one coming up," he used to say to her.

There wasn't now. This was his last drink. (You should have
made it stronger, she thought to herself wryly.)

Some sort of gritty noise was bothering her. A pulsation, a
discord of some sort. It was meant for music, but no music

could have reached her as music, as she was now. The hyper-
tension of her senses filtered it into a sound somewhat like a
scrubbing-brush being passed over a sheet of ribbed tin. Or
maybe, it occurred to her, it was on the inside of her, and not
outside anywhere.

No, there it was. He had a small battery-portable standing
against the side wall. She went over to it.

"Che gelida mannina—" some far-off voice was singing;
she didn't know what that meant. She only knew that this was
no love-scene, this was a death-scene.

Her hand gave a brutal little wrench, like wringing the neck
of a chicken, and there was a stupor of silence in his two
shoddy rooms. This one out here, and that one in there.

Now he'd step out to see who had done that.

She turned to face the opening. She raised her handbag
frontally to her chest. She undid it, and took out the gun,
and fitted her hand around it, the way her hand was supposed
to go. Without flurry, without a tremor, every move in perfect
coordination.

She sighted the gun toward the opening.

"Steve," she said to him, at no more than room-to-room
conversational pitch in the utter stillness. "Come out here a
second. I want to see you."

No fear, no love, no hate, no anything at all.

He didn't come. Had he seen her in a mirror? Had he
guessed? Was he that much of a coward, cringing away even
from a woman?

The fractured cigarette continued to unravel into smoke-
skeins. The ice cube continued to peer through the highball
glass, foursquare and uneroded.

She went toward the opening.

"Steve," she rasped. "Your wife is here. Here to see you."

He didn't stir, he didn't answer.

She made the turn of the doorway, gun wheeling before
her like some sort of foreshortened steering-gear. The second
room was not parallel to the first, it was over at a right angle
to it. It was very small, just an alcove for sleeping in. It had
a bulb up above, as though a luminous blister had formed on
the calcimined surface of the ceiling. There was also a lamp
beside the iron cot, and that was lit as well, but it was upside-

down. It was standing on its head on the floor, its extension-wire grotesquely looped in air.

She'd caught him in the act of getting ready for bed. His shirt was lying over the foot of the cot. That was all he'd taken off. And now he was trying to hide from her, down on the floor somewhere, below cot-level, on the far side of it. His hand peered over it—he'd forgotten that it showed—clutching at the bedding, pulling it into long, puckered lines. And the top of his head showed, burrowed against the cot—just a glimpse of it—bowed in attempt at concealment, but not inclined deeply enough. And then, just on the other side of that, though his second hand *didn't* show, more of those puckered wrinkles ran over the edge of the bedding at one place, as though it were down below there somewhere out of sight, but hanging on for dear life.

And when she looked at the floor, out beyond the far side of the cot, she could glimpse the lower part of one leg, extended out behind him in a long, lazy sprawl. The other one didn't show, must have been drawn up closer under his body.

"Get up," she sneered. "At least I thought I hated a man. Now I don't know what you are." She passed around the foot of the cot, and his back came into view. He didn't move, but every line of his body expressed the arrested impulse to get away.

Her handbag sprang open and she pulled something out, pitched it at him. "Here's the five dollars you gave me. Remember?" It fell between his shoulderblades, and lay there lengthwise across his spine, caught in the sharp up-curve his back made, oddly like a label or tag loosely pasted across him.

"You love money so," she said scathingly. "Now here's the interest. Turn around and get it."

She'd fired before she'd known she was going to. As though there were some cue in the words for the gun to take of its own accord, without waiting for her. The crash surprised her, she could feel it go up her whole arm, as though someone had stingingly slapped her wristbone, and the fiery spittle that gleamed for a moment at the muzzle made her blink her eyes and swerve her head aside involuntarily.

He didn't move. Even the five-dollar bill didn't flutter off him. There was a curious low moaning sound from the tubular rod forming the head of the cot, as when a vibration is slowly dimming, and there was a black pockmark in the plaster of the wall, sharply off to one side of it, that seemed to leap up into being for the first time only as her eyes discovered it.

Her hand was at his shoulder now, while her mind was trying to say "I didn't—I didn't—" He turned over lazily, and ebbed down to the floor, in a way that was almost playful, as if she had been threatening to tickle him and he was trying to avoid it.

Indolent dalliance, his attitude seemed to express. There was even a sort of gashed grin across his mouth.

His eyes seemed to be fixed on her, watching her, with that same detached mockery they'd always shown toward her. As if to say, "What are you going to do now?"

You could hardly tell anything was the matter. There was only a little dark streak by the outside corner of one eye, like a patch of patent leather used instead of court plaster; as though he'd hurt himself there and then covered it over. And where that side of his head had come to rest against the lateral thickness of the bedding, there was a peculiar sworled stain, its outer layers of a lighter discoloration than its core.

Somebody screamed in the confined little room. Not shrilly, but with a guttural wrench, almost like the bark of a terrified dog. It must have been she, for there was no one in there to scream but her. Her vocal chords hurt, as though they had been strained asunder.

"Oh, God!" she sobbed in an undertone. "I didn't need to come—"

She cowered away from him, step by faltering step. It wasn't that little glistening streak, that daub of tar, nor yet the way he lay there, relaxed and languid, as if they had had such fun he was exhausted, and it was too much trouble to get up off his back and see her out. It was his eyes that knifed her with fear, over and over, until panic had welled up in her, as though gushing through a sieve. The way they seemed fixed on her, the way they seemed to follow her backward, step by step. She went over a little to one side, and that didn't get her away from them. She went over a little to the other, and that didn't get her away from them either. Contemptuous, patronizing, mocking, to the end; with no real tenderness in them for her, ever. He looked on her in death as he'd looked on her in life.

She could almost hear the drawled words that went with that look. "Where d'you think you're going now? What's your hurry? Come back here, you!"

Her mind screamed back: "Away from here—! Out of here—! Before somebody comes—! Before anybody sees me!"

She turned and fled through the opening, and beat her way through the outside room, flailing with her arms, as though it were an endless treadmill going the other way, trying to carry her back in to him, instead of a space of a brief few yards.

She got to the door and collided against it. But then, after the first impact, after her body was stopped against it, instead of stilling, it kept on thumping, and kept on thumping, as though there were dozens of her hurling themselves against it in an endless succession.

Wood shouldn't knock so, wood shouldn't bang so— Her hands flew up to her ears and clutched them. She was going mad.

The blows didn't space themselves and wait between. They were aggressive, demanding, continuous. They were already angered, and they were feeding on their own anger with every second's added delay. They drowned out, in her own ears, her second, smothered scream of anguish. A scream that held more real fear in it than even the first one had, in the other room just now. Fear, not of the supernatural now, but of the personal; a fear more immediate, a fear more strong. Agonizing fear, trapped fear such as she'd never known existed before. *The fear of losing the thing you love.* The greatest fear there is.

For the voice that riddled the door, that welled through, bated but flinty with stern impatience, was Bill's.

Her heart knew it before the sound came, and then her ears knew it right as it came, and then its words told her after they had come.

"Patrice! Open. Open this door. Patrice! Do you hear me? I knew I'd find you here. Open this door and let me in, or I'll break it down!"

A moment too late she thought of the lock, and just a moment in time he thought of it too. That it had been unlocked
the whole while, just as she had found it to be earlier. She
crushed herself flat against it, with a whimper of despair, just
too late, just as the knob gave its turn and the door-seam
started to widen.

"No!" she ordered breathlessly. "No!" She tried to hold it
closed with the full weight of her whole palpitating body.

She could almost feel the currents of his straining breath
beating into her face. "Patrice, you've—got—to—let—me—
in—there!"

And between each word she lost ground, her heels scraped
futilely backward over the surface of the floor.

He could see her now, and she could see him, through the
fluctuating gap their opposing pressures made, widening a
little, then narrowing again, then widening more than ever.
His eyes, so close to her own, were a terrible accusation, far
worse than that dead man's had been inside. Don't look at
me, don't look at me! she implored them despairingly in her
mind. Oh, turn away from me, for I can't bear you!

Back she went, steadily and irresistibly, and still she tried to
bar him, to the last, after his arm was in and his shoulder,
straining her whole body insensately against him, flattening
her hands till they showed bloodless against the door.

Then he gave one final heave to end the unequal contest,
and she was swept back along the whole curved arc of the
door's path, like a leaf or a piece of limp rag that got caught
in the way. And he was in, and he was standing there next to
her, his chest rising and falling a little with quickened breath.

"No, Bill, no!" she kept pleading mechanically, even after
the cause of her plea was lost. "Don't come in. Not if you
love me. Stay out."

"What're you doing here?" he said tersely. "What brought
you?"

"I want you to love me," was all she could whimper, like
a distracted child. "Don't come in. I want you to love me."

He took her suddenly, and shook her fiercely by the shoulder for a moment. "I saw you. What did you come here to
do? What did you come here for, at this hour?" He released
her again. "What's this?" He picked up the gun, which she

had completely lost track of until now in her turmoil. It must have fallen, or she must have flung it to the floor, in her flight from the inner room.

"Did you bring it with you?" He came back toward her again. "Patrice, *answer* me!" he said with a flinty ferocity she hadn't known he possessed. "What did you come here for?"

Her voice kept backing and filling in her throat, as if unable to rise to the top. At last it overflowed. "To—to—to kill him." She toppled soddenly against him, and his arm had to go around her, tight and firm, to keep her up.

Her hands tried to crawl up his lapels, up his shirt-front, toward his face, like wriggling white beggars pleading for alms.

A swipe of his hand and they were down again.

"And did you?"

"Somebody—did. Somebody—has already. In there. He's dead." She shuddered and hid her face against him. There is a point beyond which you can't be alone any more. You have to have someone to cling to. You have to have someone to hold you, even if he is to reject you again in a moment or two and you know it.

Suddenly his arm dropped and he'd left her. It was terrible to be alone, even just for that minute. She wondered how she'd stood it all these months, all these years.

Life was such a crazy thing, life was such a freak. A man was dead. A love was blasted into nothingness. But a cigarette still sent up smoke in a dish. And an ice cube still hovered unmelted in a highball glass. The things you wanted to last, they didn't; the things it didn't matter about, they hung on forever.

Then he reappeared from the other room, stood in the opening looking at her again. Looking at her in such a funny way. A little too long, a little too silent—she couldn't quite make out what it was she didn't like about it, but she didn't like him to look at her that way. Others, it didn't matter. But not him.

Then he raised the gun, which he was still holding, and put it near his nose.

She saw his head give a grim nod.

"No. No. I didn't. Oh, please believe me—"

"It's just been fired," he said quietly.

There was something rueful about the expression of his eyes now, as if they were trying to say to her: Why don't you want to tell me? Why don't you get it out of the way by telling me, and then I'll understand. He didn't say that, but his eyes seemed to.

"No, I didn't. I fired it at him, but I didn't hit him."

"All right," he said quietly, with just that trace of weariness you show when you don't believe a thing, but try to gloss it over to spare someone.

Suddenly he'd thrust it into the side-pocket of his coat, as though it were no longer important, as though it were a past detail, as though there were things of far greater moment to be attended to now. He buttoned his coat determinedly, strode back to her; his movements had a sort of lithe intensity to them now that they'd lacked before.

An impetus, a drive.

He swept a sheltering arm around her again. (That sanctuary that she'd been trying to find all her life long. And only had now, too late.) But this time in hurried propulsion toward the door, and not just in support. "Get out of here, quick," he ordered grimly. "Get down to the street again fast as you can."

He was pulling her along, hurrying her with him, within the curve of his protective arm. "Come on. You can't be found here. You must have been out of your mind to come here like this!"

"I was," she sobbed. "I am."

She was struggling against him a little now, trying to keep herself from the door. She pried herself away from him suddenly, and stood back, facing him. Her hands kept rebuffing his arms each time they tried to reclaim her.

"No, wait. There's something you've got to hear first. Something you've got to know. I tried to keep you out, but now you're in here with me. I've come this far; I won't go any further." And then she added, "The way I was."

He reached out and shook her violently, in his exasperation. As if to get some sense into her. "Not now! Can't you understand? There's a man dead in the next room. Don't you

know what it means if you're found here? Any minute somebody's apt to stick his head into this place—"

"Oh, you fool," she cried out to him piteously. "You're the
one who doesn't understand. The damage has been done already. Can't *you* see that? I *have* been found here!" And she
murmured half-audibly, "By the only one who matters to me.
What's there to run away and hide from now?" She brushed
the back of her hand wearily across her eyes. "Let them come.
Bring them on now."

"If you won't think of yourself," he urged her savagely,
"think of Mother. I thought you loved her, I thought she
meant something to you. Don't you know what a thing like
this will do to her? What are you trying to do, kill her?"

"Somebody used that argument before," she told him
vaguely. "I can't remember who it was, or where it was."

He'd opened the door cautiously and looked out. Narrowed it again, came back to her. "No sign of anyone. I can't
understand how that shot wasn't heard. I don't think these
adjoining rooms are occupied."

She wouldn't budge. "No, this is the time, and this is the
place. I've waited too long to tell you. I won't go a step further, I won't cross that door-sill—"

He clenched his jaw. "I'll pick you up and carry you out of
here bodily, if I have to! Are you going to listen to me? Are
you going to come to your senses?"

"Bill, I'm not entitled to your protection. I'm not—"

His hand suddenly clamped itself to her mouth, sealing it.
He heaved her clear of the floor, held her cradled in his arms.
Her eyes strained upward at him in muted helplessness, above
his restraining hand.

Then they dropped closed. She didn't struggle against him.

He carried her that way out the door, and along the hall,
and down those stairs she'd climbed so differently a little while
ago. Just within the street-entrance he set her down upon her
feet again.

"Stand here a minute, while I look out." He could tell by
her passiveness now that her recalcitrance had ended.

He withdrew his head. "No one out there. You left the car
around the corner, didn't you?" She didn't have time to

wonder how he knew that. "Walk along close to me, I'm going to take you back to it."

She took his arm within a doublecoil of her own two, and clinging to him like that, they came out unobtrusively and hurried along together close in beside the building-front, where the shadow was deepest.

It seemed a long distance. No one saw them; better still, no one was there to see them. Once a cat scurried out of a basement-vent up ahead of them. She crushed herself tighter against him for a moment, but no sound escaped her. They went on, after the brief recoil.

They rounded the corner, and the car was there, only its own length back away from the corner.

They crossed on a swift diagonal to it, and he unlatched the door for her and armed her in. Then suddenly the door was closed again, between them, and he'd stayed on the outside.

"Here are the keys. Now take it home and—"

"No," she whispered fiercely. "No! Not without you! Where are you going? What are you going to do?"

"Don't you understand? I'm trying to keep you out of it. I'm going back up there again. I have to. To make sure there's nothing there linking you. You've got to help me. Patrice, what was he doing to you? I don't want to know why, there isn't time for that now, I only want to know *what*."

"Money," she said laconically.

She saw his clenched hand tighten on the rim of the door, until it seemed to be trying to cave it in. "How'd you give it to him, cash or check?"

"A check," she said fearfully. "Only once, about a month ago."

He was speaking more tautly now. "You destroyed it when it came back, of c—?"

"I never got it back. He purposely kept it out. He must still have it someplace."

She could tell by the way he stiffened and slowly breathed in, he was more frightened by that than he had been by anything else she had told him so far. "My God," he said batedly. "I've got to get that back, if it takes all night." He lowered

his head again, leaned it in toward her. "What else? Any letters?"

"None. I never wrote him a line in my life. There's a five-
dollar bill lying in there, by him, but I don't want it."

"I'd better pick it up anyway. Nothing else? You're sure?
Now, think, Patrice. Think hard."

"Wait; that night at the dance—he seemed to have my telephone number. Ours. Jotted down in a little black notebook
he carries around with him." She hesitated. "And one other
thing."

"What? Don't be afraid; tell me. What?"

"Bill—he made me marry him tonight. Out at Hastings."

This time he brought his hand up, let it pound back on the
door-rim like a mallet. "I'm glad he's—" he said balefully. He
didn't finish it. "Did you sign your own name?"

"The family's. I had to. That was the whole purpose of it.
The justice is mailing the certificate in to him, here at this
address, in a day or two."

"There's still time enough to take care of that, then. I can
drive out tomorrow and scotch it out there, at that end.
Money works wonders."

Suddenly he seemed to have made up his mind what he
intended doing. "Go home, Patrice," he ordered. "Go back
to the house, Patrice."

She clung fearfully to his arm. "No— What are you going
to do?"

"I'm going back up there. I have to."

She tried to hold him back. "No! Bill, no! Someone may
come along. They'll find *you* there. Bill," she pleaded, "for
me—don't go back up there again."

"Don't you understand, Patrice? Your name has to stay out
of it. There's a man lying dead upstairs in that room. They
mustn't find anything linking you to him. You never knew
him, you never saw him. I have to get hold of those things—
that check, that notebook. I have to get rid of them. Better
still, if I could only move him out of there, leave him somewhere else, at a distance from here, he mightn't be identified
so readily. He might never be identified at all. He's not from
town here, there isn't anybody likely to inquire in case of his
sudden disappearance. He came and he went again; bird of

passage. If he's found in the room there, it'll be at once established who he is, and then that'll bring out of lot of other
things."

She saw him glance speculatively along the length of the
car, as if measuring its possibilities as a casket.

"I'll help you, Bill," she said with sudden decision. "I'll
help you—do whatever you want to do." And then, as he
looked at her dubiously, "Let me, Bill. Let me. It's a small
way of—making amends for being the cause of the whole
problem."

"All right," he said. "I can't do it without the car, anyway.
I need that." He crowded in beside her. "Give me the wheel
a minute. I'll show you what I want you to do."

He drove the car only a yard or two forward, stopped it
again. It now stood so that only the hood projected beyond
the corner building-line, the rest of it still remained sheltered
behind that. The driver's seat was exactly aligned with the row
of store-fronts around the turn.

"Look down that way, from where you sit," he instructed
her. "Can you see that particular doorway from here?"

"No. I can see about where it is, though."

"That's what I mean. I'll stand in it, light up a cigarette.
When you see that, bring the car on around in front of it.
Until then, stay back here where you are. If you see anything
else, if you see something go wrong, don't stay here. Drive
straight out and away, without making the turn. Drive for
home."

"No," she thought stubbornly, "no, I won't. I won't run
off and leave you here." But she didn't tell him so.

He'd gotten out again, was standing there facing her, looking cautiously around on all sides of them, without turning
his head too much, just holding his body still, glancing over
his shoulders, first on this side, then on that.

"All right," he said finally. "It's all right now. I guess I can
go now."

He touched the back of her hand consolingly for a
minute.

"Don't be frightened, Patrice. Maybe we'll be lucky, at that.
We're such novices at anything like this."

"Maybe we'll be lucky," she echoed, abysmally frightened.

She watched him turn and walk away from the car.

He walked as he always walked, that was one nice thing about him. He didn't slink or cringe. She wondered why that should have mattered to her, at such a time as this. But it made what he, what they, were about to attempt to do a little less horrible, somehow.

He'd turned and he'd gone inside the building where the man was lying dead.

Forty-One

IT seemed like an eternity that he'd been up there. She'd never known time could be so long.

That cat came back again, the one that had frightened her before, and she watched its slow, cautious circuitous return to the place from which they had routed it. She could see it while it was still out in the roadway, but then as it closed in toward the building-line, the deeper shading swallowed it.

You can kill a rat, she found herself addressing it enviously in her mind, and they praise you for it. And your kind of rat only bites, they don't suck blood.

Something glinted there, then was gone again.

It was surprising how clearly she could see the match-flame. She hadn't expected to be able to. It was small, but extremely vivid for a moment. Like a luminous yellow butterfly held pinned for a second at full wing-spread against a black velvet backdrop, then allowed to escape again.

She promptly bore down on the starter, trundled around the corner, and brought the car down to him with facile stealth. No more than a soft whirr and sibilance of its tires.

He'd turned and gone in again before she'd reached him. The cigarette that he'd used to attract her lay there already cast down.

She didn't know where he wanted to—wanted to put what he was bringing out. Front or back. She reached out and opened the rear door on his side, left it that way, ready and waiting for him.

Then she stared straight ahead through the windshield, with

a curious sort of rigidity, as though she were unable to move her neck.

She heard the building-door open, and still couldn't turn her neck. She strained, tugged at it, but it was locked in some sort of rigor of mortal terror, wouldn't carry her head around that way.

She heard a slow, weighted tread on the gritty sidewalk—his—and accompanying it a softer sound, a sort of scrape, as when two shoes are turned over on their softer topsides, or simply on their sides, and trail along that way, without full weight to press them down.

Suddenly his voice breathed urgently (almost in her ear, it seemed), "The front door. The front."

She couldn't turn her head. But she could move her arms at least. She extended them without looking, broke the latch open for him. She could hear her own breath singing in her throat, like the sound a teakettle-spout makes when it is simmering toward a catastrophic overflow.

Someone settled on the seat beside her. Just the way anyone does, with the same crunchy strain on the leather. He touched her side, he nudged her here and there.

The muscular block shattered, and her head swung around.

She was looking into his face. Not Bill's, not Bill's. The mocking eyes wide open in the dark. *His* head had had to swing toward her, just as hers had toward him—it couldn't have remained inert!—to make the grisly face-to-face confrontation complete. Even in death he wouldn't let her alone.

A strangled scream wrenched at her windpipe.

"Now, none of that," the voice of Bill said, from just on the other side of him. "Get in back. I want the wheel. I want him next to me."

The sound of his voice had a steadying effect on her. "I didn't mean it," she murmured blurredly. She got out, got in again, holding onto the car for support in the brief transit between the two places. She didn't know how she did it, but she did.

He must have known what she was going through, though he didn't look at her.

"I told you to go home," he reminded her quietly.

"I'm all right," she said. "I'm all right. Go ahead." It came

out tinny, like something on a worn-out disk played by a
feathered needle.

The door cracked shut, and they were in motion.

Bill kept the car down to a laggard crawl the first few moments, using only one hand to the wheel. She saw him reach
over with the other and tilt down the hat-brim low over the
face beside him.

He found time for a word of encouragement to her, conscious of her there behind him, though still he didn't turn to
glance at her.

"Can you hear me?"

"Yes."

"Try not to be frightened. Try not to think of it. We've
been lucky so far. The check and the notebook were on him.
Either we make it or we don't. Look at it that way. It's the
only way. You're helping me, too, that way. See, if you're too
tense, then I'm too tense too. You react on me."

"I'm all right," she said with that same mechanical bleat as
before. "I'll be quiet. I'll be controlled. Go ahead."

After that, they didn't talk. How could you, on such a ride?

She kept her eyes away. She'd look out the side as long as
she could; then when that became a strain, she'd look up at
the car ceiling for a moment to rest. Or down at the floor
directly before her. Anywhere but straight ahead, to where
those two heads (she knew) must be lightly quivering in syn-
chronization to the same vibration.

She tried to do what he'd told her. She tried not to think
of it. "We're coming home from a dance," she said to herself.
"He's bringing me home from the Country Club, that's all.
I'm wearing that black net with the gold disks. Look, see? I'm
wearing that black dress with the gold disks. We had words,
so I'm—I'm sitting in the back, and he's sitting alone up
front."

Her forehead was a little cold and damp. She wiped it off.

"He's bringing me home from the movies," she said to
herself. "We saw—we saw—we saw—" Another of those
blocks, this time of the imagination, occurred; it wouldn't
come. "We saw—we saw—we saw—"

Suddenly she'd said to him, aloud, "What was the name of
that picture we just now came away from?"

"Good," he answered instantly. "That's it. That's a good idea. I'll give you one. Keep going over it." It took him a moment to get one himself. "Mark Stevens in *I Wonder Who's Kissing Her Now*," he said suddenly. They'd seen that together back in the sunlight, a thousand years ago (last Thursday). "Start in at the beginning, and run through it. If you get stuck, I'll help you out."

She was breathing laboredly, and her forehead kept getting damp again all the time. "He wrote songs," she said to herself, "and he took his foster-sister to a—to a variety-show, and he heard one of them sung from the stage—"

The car made a turn, and the two heads up front swung together, one almost landed on the other's shoulder. Somebody pried them apart.

She hurriedly squeezed her eyes shut. "When—when did the title-song come into it?" she faltered. "Was that the opening number, they heard from the gallery?"

He'd halted for a light, and a taxicab had halted beside him, wheel-cap to wheel-cap. "No, that was—" He looked at the taxicab. "That was—" He looked at the taxicab again, the way you look vaguely at some external object when you're trying to remember something that has nothing to do with it. "That was 'Hello, Ma Baby.' Cakewalk number, don't you remember? The title-song didn't come until the end. He couldn't get words for it, don't you remember?"

The light had changed. The taxicab had slipped on ahead, quicker to resume motion. She crushed the back of her hand against her mouth, sank her teeth into it. "I can't," she sighed to herself. "I can't." She wanted to scream to him, "Oh, open the door! Let me out! I'm not brave! I thought I could, but I can't— I don't care, only let me get out of here, now, right where we are!"

Panic, they called this panic.

She bit deeper into her own skin, and the hot frenzied gush subsided.

He was going a little faster now. But not too fast, not fast enough to attract suspicion or catch any roving eye. They were in the outskirts now, running along the turnpike that breasted the sunken railroad right-of-way. You were supposed to go a little faster along there.

It took her several moments to realize that the chief hazard was over. That they were already out of Caulfield, clear of it; or at least clear of its built-up heart. Nothing had happened. No untoward event. They hadn't grazed any other car. No policeman had come near them, to question them over some infraction, to look into the car. All those things that she had dreaded so, had failed to materialize. It had been a ride completely without incident. The two of them might have been alone in the car, for all the risk they'd run—outwardly. But inwardly—

She felt all shrivelled-up inside, and old; as though there were permanent wrinkles on her heart.

"He wasn't the only one that died tonight," she thought. "I died too, somewhere along the way, in this car. So it didn't work, it was all for nothing. Better to have stayed back there, still alive, and taken the blame and the punishment."

They were out in open country now. The last cardboard-box factory, kept at a civic-minded distance away from the city limits, the last disused-brewery stack, even those had long slipped by. The embankment that carried the turnpike had started a very gradual rise, the broad swath of railroad-tracks, by illusory contrast, seemed to depress still further. The neat, clean-cut concrete-facing that had been given the embankment further in toward town didn't extend this far out; here there was just a natural slope, extremely steep, but with weeds and bushes clinging to it.

He'd stopped all of a sudden, for no apparent reason. Run the two outside wheels off the road on the railroad's side, and stopped there. That was all the space that was allowed, just two wheels of the car; even that was an extremely precarious position to take. The downslope began almost outside the car door.

"Why here?" she whispered.

He pointed. "Listen. Hear it?" It was a sound like the cracking of nuts. Like a vast layer of nuts, all rolling around and being cracked and shelled.

"I'd like to get him out of town," he said. He got out, and scrambled down the slope a way, until she could only see him from the waist up, and stood looking down. Then he picked up something—a stone, maybe, or something—and she saw him throw. Then he turned his head a little, and seemed to be listening.

Finally he fought his way back up to her again, digging his feet in sideways to gain leverage.

"It's a slow freight," he said. "Outbound. It's on the inside track, I mean the one right under us here. I could see a lantern go by on the roof of one of the cars. It's unearthly long—I think they're empties—and it's going very slow, almost at a crawl. I threw a stone, and I heard it hit one of the roofs."

She had already guessed, and could feel her skin crawling.

He was bending over the form on the front seat, going through its pockets. He ripped something out of the inside coat-pocket. A label or something.

"They don't always get right of way like the fast passengers do. It may have to stop for that big turnpike crossing not far up, you know the one I mean. The locomotive must be just about reaching it by now—"

She'd fought down her repulsion; she'd made up her mind once more, though this was going to be even worse than back there at the doorway. "Shall I— Do you want me to—?" And she got ready to get out with him.

"No," he said, "no. Just stay in it and watch the road. The slope is so steep, that when you get down below a certain point with—anything—it will plunge down the rest of the way by itself. It's been sheared off at the bottom, it's a sheer drop."

He'd swung the front door out as far as it would go, now. "How's the road?" he asked.

She looked back first, all along it. Then forward. The way it rose ahead made it even easier to sight along.

"Empty," she said. "There's not a moving light on it any-where."

He dipped down, did something with his arm, and then the two heads and the two pairs of shoulders rose together. A minute later the front seat was empty.

She turned away and looked at the road, looked at the road for all she was worth.

"I'll never be able to sit on the front seat of this car again," it occurred to her. "They'll wonder why, but I'll always balk, I'll always think of what was there tonight."

He had a hard time getting him down the slope, he had to be a brake on the two of them at once, and the weight was double. Once the two of them went down momentarily, in a stumble, and her heart shot up into her throat, as though there were a pulley, a counterweight, working between them and it.

Then he regained his balance again.

Then when she could only see him from the waist up, he bent over, as if laying something down before him, and when he'd straightened up again, he was alone, she could only see him by himself.

Then he just stood there waiting.

It was a gamble, a wild guess. A last car, a caboose, could have suddenly come along, and—no more train to carry their freight away. Just trackbed left below, to reveal what lay on it as soon as it got light.

But he'd guessed right. The sound of cracking nuts thinned, began to die out. A sort of rippling wooden shudder, starting way up ahead, ran past them and to the rear. Then a second one. Then silence.

He dipped again.

Her hands flew up to her ears, but she was too late. The sound beat her to it.

It was a sick, hollow thud. Like when a heavy sack is dropped. Only, a sack bursts from such a drop. This didn't.

She put her head down low over her lap, and held her hands pressed to her eyes.

When she looked up again, he was standing there beside her. He looked like a man who has himself in hand, but isn't sure that he isn't going to be sick before long.

"Stayed on," he said. "Caught on that catwalk, or whatever it is, that runs down the middle of each roof. I could see him even in the dark. But his hat didn't. That came off and went over."

She wanted to scream: "Don't! Don't *tell* me! Let me not know! I know too much already!" But she didn't. And by that time it was over with, anyway.

He got in again and took the wheel, without waiting for the train to recommence its run.

"It'll go on again," he said. "It has to. It was already

on its way once. It won't just stand there the rest of the night."

He ran the car back onto the rim of the road again, and then he brought it around in a U-turn, facing back to Caulfield. And still nothing came along, nothing passed them. On no other night could this road have been so empty.

He let their headlight beams shoot out ahead of them now.

"Do you want to come up here and sit with me?" he asked her quietly.

"No!" she said in a choked voice. "I couldn't! Not on *that* seat."

He seemed to understand. "I just didn't want you to be all alone," he said compassionately.

"I'll be all alone from now on, anyway, no matter where I sit," she murmured. "And so will you. We'll both be all alone, even together."

Forty-Two

SHE heard the brakes go on, and felt the motion of the car stop. He got out and got into the back next to her. They stayed just the way they were for several long moments. She with her face pressed against the bosom of his shirt, buried against him as if trying to hide it from the night and all that had happened in the night. He with one hand to the back of her head, holding it there, supporting it.

They didn't move nor speak at first.

Now I have to tell him, she kept thinking with dread. Now the time is here. And how shall I be able to?

She raised her head at last, and opened her eyes. He'd stopped around the corner from their own house. (*His* own. How could it ever be hers again? How could she ever go in there, after what had happened tonight?) He'd stopped around the corner, out of sight of it, and not right at the door. He was giving her the chance to tell him; that must be why he had done it.

He took out a cigarette, and lit it for her in his mouth, and offered it to her inquiringly. She shook her head. So then he threw it out the side of the car.

His mouth was so close to hers, she could smell the aroma of the tobacco freshly on his breath. It'll never be this close again, she thought, never; not after I'm done with what I have to tell him now.

"Bill," she whispered.

It was too weak, too pleading. That feeble a voice would never carry her through. And it had such rocky words ahead of it.

"Yes, Patrice?" he answered quietly.

"Don't call me that." She turned toward him with desperate urgency, forcing her voice to be steady. "Bill there's something you've got to know. I don't know where to begin it, I don't know how— But, oh, you've got to listen, if you've never listened to me before!"

"Sh, Patrice," he said soothingly. "Sh, Patrice." As though she were a fretful child. And his hand gently stroked her hair; downward, and then downward again, and still downward.

She moaned, almost as though she were in pain. "No—don't—don't—don't."

"I know," he said almost absently. "I know what you're trying so hard, so brokenheartedly, to tell me. That you're not Patrice. That you're not Hugh's wife. Isn't that it?"

She sought his eyes, and he was gazing into the distance, through the windshield and out ahead of the car. There was something almost abstract about his look.

"I know that already. I've always known it. I think I've known it ever since the first few weeks you got here."

The side of his face came gently to rest against her head, and stayed there, in a sort of implicit caress.

"So you don't have to try so hard, Patrice. Don't break your heart over it. There isn't anything to tell."

She gave an exhausted sob. Shuddered a little with her own frustration. "Even the one last chance to redeem myself, you've taken away from me," she murmured hopelessly. "Even that little."

"You don't have to redeem yourself, Patrice."

"Every time you call me that, it's a lie. I can't go back to that house with you. I can't go in there ever again. It's too late now—two years too late, two years—but at least let me tell it to you. Oh God, let me get it out! Patrice Hazzard was

killed on the train, right along with your brother. I was deserted by a man named—"

Again he placed his hand over her mouth, as he had at
Georgesson's place. But more gently than he had then.

"I don't want to know," he told her. "I don't want to hear.
Can't you understand, Patrice?" Then took his hand away, but
now she was silent, for that was the way he wanted her to be.
And that was the easier way to be. "*Won't* you understand
how I feel?" He glanced about for an instant, this way and
that, as if helplessly in search of some means of convincing
her. Some means that wasn't there at hand. Then back to her
again, to try once more; speaking low and from the heart.

"What difference does it make if there once was another
Patrice, another Patrice than you, a girl I never knew, some
other place and some other time? Suppose there *were* two?
There are a thousand Marys, a thousand Janes; but each man
that loves Mary, he loves only his Mary, and for him there are
no others in the whole wide world. And that's with me too.
A girl named Patrice came into my life one day. And that's
the only Patrice there is for me in the world. I don't love the
name, I love the girl. What kind of love do you think I have,
anyway? That if she got the name from a clergyman, it's on;
but if she helped herself to it, it's off?"

"But she *stole* the name, took it away from the dead. And
she lay in someone else's arms first, and then came into your
house with her child—"

"No, she didn't; no," he contradicted her with tender stubbornness. "You still don't see, you still won't see; because
you're not the man who loves you. She couldn't have; because
she *wasn't*, until I met her. She only began then, she only
starts from then. She only came into existence, as my eyes first
took her in, as my love first started in to start. Before then
there wasn't any she. My love began her, and when my love
ends, she ends with it. She has to, because she *is* my love.
Before then, there was a blank. A vacant space. That's the way
with any love. It can't go back before itself.

"And it's you I love. The you I made for myself. The you
I hold in my arms right now in this car. The you I kiss like
this, right now . . . right now . . . and now.

"Not a name on a birth-certificate. Not a name on a Paris

wedding-license. Not a bunch of dead bones taken out of a railroad-car and buried somewhere by the tracks.

"The name of my love is Patrice to me. My love doesn't know any other name, my love doesn't want any."

He swept her close to him, this time with such quivering violence that she was almost stunned. And as his lips found hers, between each pledge he told her:

"You are Patrice. You'll always be Patrice. You'll *only* be Patrice. I give you that name. Keep it for me, forever."

They lay that way for a long while; one now, wholly one. Made one by love; made one by blood and violence.

Presently she murmured, "And you knew, and you never—?"

"Not right away, not all in a flash. Life never goes that way. It was a slow thing, gradual. I think I first suspected inside of a week or two after you got here. I don't know when I was first sure. I think that day I bought the fountain pen."

"You must have hated me that day."

"I didn't hate you that day. I hated myself, for stooping to such a trick. (And yet I couldn't have kept from doing it, I couldn't have, no matter how I tried!) And do you know what I got from it? Only fear. Instead of *you* being the frightened one, I was. I was afraid that you'd take fright from it, and that I'd lose you. I knew *I'd* never be the one to expose you; I was too afraid I'd lose you that way. A thousand times I wanted to tell you, 'I know; I know all about it,' and I was afraid you'd take flight and I'd lose you. The secret wasn't heavy on you; it was me it weighted down."

"But in the beginning. How is it you didn't say anything in the very beginning? Surely you didn't condone it from the very start?"

"No; no, I didn't. My first reaction was resentment, enmity; about what you'd expect. But for one thing, I wasn't sure enough. And the lives of too many others were involved. Mainly there was Mother. I couldn't risk doing that to her. Right after she'd lost Hugh. For all I knew it might have killed her. And even just to implant seeds of suspicion, that would have been just as bad, that would have wrecked her happiness. Then too, I wanted to see what the object was, the game. I thought if I gave you enough rope— Well, I gave you rope and rope, and there was no game. You were just you. Every day it became a little harder to be on guard against you. Every day it became a little easier to look at you, and think of you, and like you. Then that night of the will—"

"You knew what you did, and yet you let them go ahead and—"

"There was no real danger. Patrice Hazzard was the name they put down in black and white. If it became necessary, it would have been easy enough to break it; or rather restrict it to its literal application, I should say. Prove that you and Patrice Hazzard were not identically one and the same and, therefore, that you were not the one intended. The law isn't like a man in love; the law values names. I pumped our lawyer a little on the q.t., without of course letting on what I had on my mind, and what he told me reassured me. But what that incident did for me once and for all, was to show me there was no game, no ulterior motive. I mean, that it wasn't the money that was at the bottom of it. Patrice, the fright and honest aversion I read on your face that night, when I came to your door to tell you about it, couldn't have been faked by the most expert actress in creation. Your face got as white as a sheet, your eyes darted around as though you wanted to run out of the house for dear life then and there; I touched your hand, and it was icy-cold. There is a point at which acting stops, and the heart begins.

"And that gave me the answer. I knew from that night on what it was you really wanted, what it was that had made you do it: safety, security. It was on your face a hundred times a day, once I had the clue. I've seen it over and over. Every time you looked at your baby. Every time you said, 'I'm going up to my room.' The way you said '*my* room.' I've seen it in your eyes even when you were only looking at a pair of curtains on the window, straightening them out, caressing them. I could almost hear you say, 'They're mine, I belong here.' And every time I saw it, it did something to me. I loved you a little more than I had the time before. And I wanted you to have all that rightfully, permanently, beyond the power of anyone or anything to ever take it away from you again—"

He lowered his voice still further, till she could barely hear the message it breathed.

"At my side. As my wife. And I still do. Tonight more than ever, a hundred times more than before. Will you answer me now? Will you tell me if you'll let me?"

His face swam fluidly before her upturned eyes.

"Take me home, Bill," she said brokenly, happily. "Take Patrice home to your house with you, Bill."

Forty-Three

FOR a moment, as he braked and as she turned her face toward it, her overtired senses received a terrifying impression that it was on fire, that the whole interior was going up in flame. And then as she recoiled against him, she saw that bright as the light coming from it was, brazier-bright against the early-morning pall, it was a steady brightness, it did not quiver. It poured from every window, above and below, and spilled in gradations of intensity across the lawn, and even as far as the frontal walk and the roadway beyond, but it was the static brightness of lighted-up rooms. Rooms lighted up in emergency.

He nudged and pointed wordlessly, and on the rear plate of the car already there, that they had just drawn up behind, stood out the ominous "MD." Spotlighted, menacing, beetling, within the circular focus of their own headlights. Prominent as the skull and crossbones on a bottle label. And just as fear-inspiring.

"Doctor Parker," flashed through her mind.

He flung open the door and jumped down, and she was right behind him.

"And we sat talking back there all this time," she heard him exclaim.

They chased up the flagstone walk, she at his heels, outdistanced by his longer legs. He didn't have time to use his key. By the time he'd got it out and put it to where the keyhole had last been, the keyhole was already back out of reach and Aunt Josie was there instead, frightened in an old flowered bathrobe, face as gray as her hair.

They didn't ask her who it was; there was no need to.

"Ever since happass eleven," she said elliptically. "*He's* been with her from midnight straight on through."

She closed the door after them.

"If you'd only phoned up," she said accusingly. "If you'd only leff word where I could reach you." And then she added, but more to him than to Patrice, "Daybreak. I hope the party was wuth it. It sure must have been a good one. I know one thing, it sure coss more than any party you ever went to in your life. Or ever likely to go to."

Patrice screamed out within herself, wincing: How right you are! It wasn't good, no, it wasn't—but oh, how costly!

Dr. Parker accosted them in the upper hall. There was a nurse there with him. They had thought he'd be in with her.

"Is she asleep?" Patrice breathed, more frightened than reassured at this.

"Ty Winthrop's been in there alone with her for the past half-hour. She insisted. And when people are quite ill, you overrule them; but when they're even more ill than that, you don't. I've been checking her pulse and respiration at ten-minute intervals."

"That bad?" she whispered in dismay. She caught the stricken look on Bill's face, and found time to feel parenthetically sorry for him even while she asked it.

"There's no immediate danger," Parker answered. "But I can't make you any promises beyond the next hour or two." And then he looked the two of them square in the eyes and said, "It's a bad one this time. It's the daddy of them all."

It's the last one, Patrice knew then with certainty.

She crumpled for a moment, and a scattered sob or two escaped from her, while he and Bill led her over to a hall-chair, there beside the sickroom-door, and sat her down.

"Don't do that," the doctor admonished her, with just a trace of detachment—perhaps professional, perhaps personal— "There's no call for it at this stage."

"It's just that I'm so worn-out," she explained blurredly.

She could almost read his answering thought. Then you should have come home a little earlier.

The nurse traced a whiff of ammonia past her nose, eased her hat from her head, smoothed her hair soothingly.

"Is my baby all right?" she asked in a moment, calmer.

It was Aunt Josie who answered that. "I know how to look after him," she said a trifle shortly. Patrice was out of favor right then.

The door opened and Ty Winthrop came out. He was putting away his glasses.

"They back yet—?" he started to say. Then he saw them. "She wants to see you."

They both started up at once.

"Not you," he said to Bill, warding him off. "Just Patrice. She wants to see her alone, without anyone else in the room. She repeated that several times."

Parker motioned her to wait. "Let me check her pulse first."

She looked over at Bill while they were standing there waiting, to see how he was taking it. He smiled untroubledly. "I understand," he murmured. "That's her way of seeing *me*. And a good way it is, too. Just about the best."

Parker had come out again.

"Not more than a minute or two," he said disapprovingly, with a side look at Winthrop. "And then maybe we'll all get together to see that she gets a little rest."

She went in there. Somebody closed the door after her.

"Patrice, dear," a quiet voice said.

She went over to the bed.

The face was still in shadow, because of the way they'd left the lamp.

"You can raise that a little, dear. I'm not in my coffin yet."

Her eyes looked up at Patrice in the same way they had that first day at the railroad station. They were kind. They smiled around the edges. They hurt a little, they were so *trustful*.

"I didn't dream—" she heard herself saying. "We drove out further than we'd intended to— It was such a beautiful night—"

Two hands were feebly extended for her to clasp.

She dropped suddenly to her knees and smothered them with kisses.

"I love you," she pleaded. "That much is true; oh, that much is true! If I could only make you believe it. My mother. You're my mother."

"You don't have to, dear. I know it already. I love you too, and my love has always known that you do. That's why you're my little girl. Remember that I told you this: *you're my little girl.*"

And then she said, very softly, "I forgive you, dear. I forgive my little girl."

She stroked Patrice's hand consolingly.

"Marry Bill. I give you both my blessing. Here—" She gestured feebly in the direction of her own shoulder. "Under my pillow. I had Ty put something there for you."

Patrice reached under, drew out a long envelope, sealed, unaddressed.

"Keep this," Mother Hazzard said, touching the edge for a moment. "Don't show it to anyone. It's just for you. Do not open until—after I'm not here. It's in case you need it. When you're in greatest need, remember I gave it to you— open it then."

She sighed deeply, as though the effort had tired her unendurably.

"Kiss me. It's late. So very late. I can feel it in every inch of my poor old body. *You* can't feel how late it is, Patrice, but *I* can."

Patrice bent low above her, touched her own lips to hers.

"Goodbye, my daughter," she whispered.

"Goodnight," Patrice amended.

"Goodbye," she insisted gently. There was a faint, prideful smile on her face, a smile of superior knowledge, as of one who knows herself to be the better informed of the two.

Forty-Four

LONELY vigil by the window, until long after it had grown light. Sitting there, staring, waiting, hoping, despairing, dying a little. Seeing the stars go out, and the dawn creep slowly toward her from the east, like an ugly gray pallor. She'd never wanted to see daybreak less, for at least the dark had covered her sorrows like a cloak but every moment of increasing light diluted it, until it had reached the vanishing-point, it was gone, there wasn't any more left.

Motionless as a statue in the blue-tinged window, forehead pressed forward against the glass, making a little white ripple of adhesion across it where it touched. Eyes staring at nothing, for nothing was all there was out there to see.

I've found my love at last, only to lose him; only to throw him away. Why did I find out tonight I loved him, why did I have to know? Couldn't I have been spared that at least?

The day wasn't just bitter now. The day was ashes, lying all around her, cold and crumbled and consumed. No use for pinks and blues and yellows to try to tint it, like watercolors lightly applied from some celestial palette; no use. It was dead. And she was sitting there beside its bier.

And if there was such a thing as penance, absolution, for mistakes that, once made, can never be wholly undone again, can only be regretted, she should have earned it on that long vigil. But maybe there is none.

Her chances were dead and her hopes were dead, and she couldn't atone any further.

She turned and slowly looked behind her. Her baby was awake, and smiling at her, and for once she had no answering smile ready to give him. She couldn't smile, it would have been too strange a thing to fit upon her mouth.

She turned her face away again, so that she wouldn't have to look at him too long. Because, what good did crying do? Crying to a little baby. Babies cried to their mothers, but mothers shouldn't cry to their babies.

Outside, the man came out on that lawn down there, pulling his garden-hose after him. Then when he had it all stretched out, he let it lie, and went back to the other end of it, and turned the spigot. The grass began to sparkle, up where the nozzle lay inert, even before he could return to it and take it up. You couldn't see the water actually coming out, because the nozzle was down too flat against the ground, but you could see a sort of iridescent rippling of the grass right there, that told there was something in motion under it.

Then he saw her at her window, and he raised his arm and waved to her, the way he had in the beginning, that first day. Not because she was she, but because his own world was all in order, and it was a beautiful morning, and he wanted to wave to someone to show them how he felt.

She turned her head away. Not to avoid his friendly little salutation, but because there was a knocking at her door. Someone was knocking at her door.

She got up stiffly and walked over toward it, and opened it.

A lonely, lost old man was standing out there, quietly, unassumingly. Bill's father was standing out there, very wilted, very spent. A stranger, mistaking her for a daughter.

"She just died," he whispered helplessly. "Your mother just died, dear. I didn't know whom to go to, to tell about it—so I came to your door." He seemed unable to do anything but just stand there, limp, baffled.

She stood there without moving either. That was all she was able to do too. That was all the help she could give him.

Forty-Five

THE leaves were dying, as she had died. The season was dying. The old life was dying, was dead. They had buried it back there just now.

"How strange," Patrice thought. "To go on, before one can go on to something new, there has to be death first. Always, there has to be a kind of death, of one sort or another, first. Just as there has been with me."

The leaves were brightly dying. The misty black of her veil dimmed their apoplectic spasms of scarlet and orange and ochre, tempered them to a more bearable hue in the fiery sunset, as the funeral limousine coursed at stately speed homeward through the countryside.

She sat between Bill and his father.

"I am the Woman of the Family now," she thought. "The only woman of their house and in their house. That is why I sit between them like this, in place of prominence, and not to the outside."

And though she would not have known how to phrase it, even to herself, her own instincts told her that the country and the society she was a part of were basically matriarchal, that it was the woman who was essentially the focus of each home, the head of each little individual family-group. Not brazenly, aggressively so, not on the outside; but within the walls, where the home really was. She had succeeded to this primacy now. The gangling adolescent who had once stood outside a door that wouldn't open.

One she would marry and be his wife. One she would look after in filial devotion, and ease his loneliness and cushion his decline as best she could. There was no treachery, no deceit, in her plans; all that was over with and past.

She held Father Hazzard's hand gently clasped in her own, on the one side. And on the other, her hand curved gracefully up and around the turn of Bill's stalwart arm. To indicate: You are mine. And I am yours.

The limousine had halted. Bill got out and armed her down. Then they both helped his father and, one on each side of him, walked slowly with him up the familiar terraced flagstones to the familiar door.

Bill sounded the knocker, and Aunt Josie's deputy opened the door for them with all the alacrity of the novice. Aunt Josie herself, of course, a titular member of the family, had attended the services with them, was on her way back now in the lesser of the two limousines.

She closed the door in respectful silence, and they were home.

It was she who first saw them, Patrice. They were in the library.

Bill and his father, going on ahead, supporting arm about waist, had passed the open doorway obliviously. She had lingered behind for a moment, to give some muted necessary orders.

"Yes, Mrs. Hazzard," Aunt Josie's deputy said docilely.

Yes, Mrs. Hazzard. That was the first time she had heard it (Aunt Josie always called her "Miss Pat"), but she would have that now all her life, as her due. Her mind rolled it around on its tongue, savoring it. Yes, Mrs. Hazzard. Position. Security. Impregnability. The end of a journey.

Then she moved forward and, passing the doorway, saw them.

They were sitting in there, both facing it. Two men. The very way they held their heads—they were not apologetic, they were not disclaiming enough, for such a time and such a place and such a visit. Their faces, as she met them, did not say: "Whenever you are ready." Their faces said: "*We* are ready for you now. Come in to us."

Fear put out a long finger and touched her heart. She had stopped.

"Who are those two men?" she breathed to the girl who had let her in. "What are they doing in there?"

"Oh, I forgot. They came here about twenty minutes ago, asking to see Mr. Hazzard. I explained about the funeral, and suggested maybe they'd better come back later. But they said no, they said they'd wait. I couldn't do anything with them. So I just let them be."

She went on past the opening. "He's in no condition to speak to anyone now. You'll have to go in there and—"

"Oh, not old Mr. Hazzard. It's Mr. Hazzard his son they want."

She knew then. Their faces had already told her, the grim way they had both sized her up that fleeting second or two she had stood in the doorway. People didn't stare at you like that, just ordinary people. Punitive agents did. Those empowered by law to seek out, and identify, and question.

The finger had become a whole icy hand now, twisting and crushing her heart in its grip.

Detectives. Already. So soon, so relentlessly, so fatally soon. And today of all days, on this very day.

The copybooks were right, the texts that said the police were infallible.

She turned and hurried up the stairs, to overtake Bill and his father, nearing the top now, still linked in considerate, toiling ascent.

Bill turned his head inquiringly at sound of her hasty step behind them. Father Hazzard didn't. What was any step to him any more? The only one he wanted to hear would never sound again.

She made a little sign to Bill behind his father's back. A quick little quirk of the finger to show that this was something to be kept between the two of them alone. Then said, trying to keep her voice casual, "Bill, as soon as you take Father to his room, I want to see you for a minute. Will you come out?"

He came upon her in her own room, in the act of lowering an emptied brandy-jigger from her lips. He looked at her curiously.

"What'd you do, get a chill out there?"

"I did," she said. "But not out there. Here. Just now."

"You seem to be shaking."

"I am. Close the door." And when he had, "Is he sleeping?"

"He will be in another minute or two. Aunt Josie's giving him a little more of that sedative the doctor left."

She kneaded her hands together, as though she were trying to break each bone separately. "They're here, Bill. About the other night. They're here already."

He didn't have to ask, he knew what she meant by "the other night." There was only one other night for them, there would always be only one, from now on. As the nights multiplied, it would become "that night," perhaps; that was the only alteration.

"How do you know? Did they tell you?"

"They don't have to. I know." She snatched at his coat-lapels, as though she were trying to rip them off him. "What are we going to do?"

"*We* are not going to do anything," he said with meaning. "*I*'ll do whatever is to be done about it."

"Who's that?" she shuddered, and crushed herself close to him. Her teeth were almost chattering with nervous tension.

"Who is it?" he asked at full voice.

"Aunt Josie," came through the door.

"Let go of me," he cautioned in an undertone. "All right, Aunt Josie."

She put her head in and said, "Those two men that're down there, they said they can't wait for Mr. Hazzard any more."

For a moment a little hope wormed its way through her stricken heart.

"They said if he don't come down, they'll have to come up here."

"What do they want? Did they tell you?" he said to Aunt Josie.

"I asked 'em twice, and each time they said the same thing.

'Mr. Hazzard.' What kind of an answer is that? They're bold
ones."

"All right," he said curtly. "You've told us."

She closed the door again.

He stood for awhile irresolute, his hand curled around the
back of his neck. Then straightened with reluctant decision,
squared off his shoulders, hitched down his cuffs, and turned
to face the door. "Well," he said, "let's get it over with."

She ran to join him. "I'll go with you."

"You won't!" He took her hand and put it off his arm, in
rough rejection. "Let's get that straight right now. You're
staying up here, and you're staying out of it. Do you hear me?
No matter what happens, you're staying out of it."

He'd never spoken to her like that before.

"Are you taking me to be your husband?" he demanded.

"Yes," she murmured. "I've already told you that."

"Then that's an order. The first and the last, I hope, that
I'll ever have to give you. Now look, we can't tell two stories
about this. We're only telling one: mine. And it's one that
you're not supposed to know anything about. So you can't
help me, you can only harm me."

She seized his hand and put her lips to it, as a sort of god-
speed.

"What are you going to tell them?"

"The truth." The look he gave her was a little odd. "What
did you expect me to tell them? *I* have nothing to lie about,
as far as it involves me alone."

He closed the door and he went out.

Forty-Six

As she found her hands leading the way down for her, one
over the other, along the bannister-rail, while her feet followed them more slowly, a step behind all the way, she realized how impossible it would have been to follow his
injunction, remain immured up there, without knowing, without listening; how futile of him to expect it of her. She
couldn't have been involved as she was, she couldn't have

been a woman at all, and obeyed him. This wasn't prying; you didn't pry into something that concerned you as closely as this did her. It was your right to know.

Hand over hand down the bannister, the rest of her creeping after, body held at a broken crouch. Like a cripple struggling down a staircase.

A quarter of the way down, the murmur became separate voices. Halfway down, the voices became words. She didn't go beyond there.

Their voices weren't raised. There was no blustering or angry contradiction. They were just men talking quietly, politely together. Somehow, it struck more fear into her that way.

They were repeating after him something he must have just now said.

"Then you do know someone named Harry Carter, Mr. Hazzard."

She didn't hear him say anything. As though he considered one affirmation on that point enough.

"Would you care to tell us what relationship—what connection—there is between you and this man Carter?"

He sounded slightly ironical, when he answered that. She had never heard him that way toward herself, but she caught a new inflection to his voice, and recognized it for irony. "Look, gentlemen, you already know. You must, or why would you be here? You want me to repeat it for you, is that it?"

"What we want is to hear it from you yourself, Mr. Hazzard."

"Very well, then. He is a private detective. As you already know. I selected and hired him. As you already know. And he was being paid a fee, he was being retained, to watch, to keep his eye on, this man Georgesson whom you're concerned with. As you already know."

"Very well, we do already know, Mr. Hazzard. But what we don't already know, what he couldn't tell us, because he didn't know himself, was what was the nature of your interest in Georgesson, why you were having him watched."

And the other one took up where the first had left off: "Would *you* care to tell us that, Mr. Hazzard? Why were you having him watched? What was your reason for doing that?"

Out on the stairs, her heart seemed to turn over and lie down flat on its face. "My God," went echoing sickly through her mind. "Now I come into it!"

"That's an extremely private matter," he said sturdily.

"I see; you don't care to tell us."

"I didn't say that."

"But still, you'd rather not tell us."

"You're putting words into my mouth."

"Because you don't seem to supply us with any of your own."

"It's essential for you to know this?"

"We wouldn't be here if it weren't, I can assure you. This man of yours, Carter, was the one who reported Georgesson's death to us."

"I see." She heard him take a deep breath. And she took one with him. Two breaths, one and the same fear.

"Georgesson was a gambler," he said.

"We know that."

"A crook, a confidence man, an all-around shady operator."

"We know that."

"Then here's the part you don't. Back about—it must be four years ago—three, anyway—my older brother Hugh was a senior at Dartmouth College. He started down here to spend the Christmas holidays at home, with us. He got as far as New York, and then he never got any further. He never showed up. He wasn't on the train that was to have brought him in the next day. We got a long-distance phone-call from him, and he was in trouble. He was practically being held there against his will. He'd gotten into a card-game, it seems, the night before with this Georgesson and a few of his friends—set-up, of course—and they'd taken him for I don't know how many thousands, which he didn't have, and they wanted a settlement before they'd let him go. They had him good, it had the makings of a first-class mess in it. Hugh was just a high-spirited kid, used to associating with decent people, gentlemen, not that kind of vermin, and he hadn't known how to handle himself. They'd built him up for it all evening long, liquored him up, thrown a couple of mangy chorus-girls at him in the various spots they'd dragged him around to first—well, anyway, because of my mother's health and the family's good name, there could be no question of calling the police into it, it would have been altogether too smelly. So my father went up there in person—I went along with him, incidentally—and squared the thing off for him. At about fifty cents to the dollar, or something like that. Got back the I.O.U.'s they'd extorted from the kid. And brought him home with us.

"That's about all there was to it. Not a very new story, it's happened over and over. But naturally, I wasn't likely to forget this Georgesson in a hurry. Well, when I learned he was down here in Caulfield a few weeks ago, showing his face around, I didn't know if it was a coincidence or not, but I wasn't taking any chances. I got in touch with a detective agency in New York and had them send Carter down here, just to try to find out what he was up to.

"And there you have it. Now does that answer your question? Is that satisfactory?"

They didn't say it was, she noticed. She waited, but she didn't hear them say it was.

"He didn't approach you or your family in any way? He didn't molest you?"

"He didn't come near us."

(Which was technically correct, she agreed wryly; she'd had to go to him each time.)

"You would have heard about it before now, if he had," he assured them. "I wouldn't have waited for you to look me up, I would have looked you up."

With catastrophic casualness a non-sequitur followed. She suddenly heard one of them ask him, "Do you want to bring along a hat, Mr. Hazzard?"

"It's right outside in the hall," he answered drily. "I'll pick it up as we go by."

They were coming out of the room. With an infantile whimper, that was almost like that of a little girl running away from goblins in the dark, she turned and fled up the stairs again, back to her room.

"No—! No—! No—!" she kept moaning with feverish reiteration.

They were arresting him, they were accusing him, they were taking him with them.

Forty-Seven

DISTRACTED, she flung herself down on the bench before her dressing-table. Her head rolled soddenly about on her shoulders, as though she were drunk. Her hair was displaced, burying one eye.

"No—! No—!" she kept insisting. "They can't— It isn't fair—"

They wouldn't let him go— They'd never let him go again— He wouldn't come back— He'd never come back to her—

"Oh, for the love of God, help me! I can't take any more of this!"

And then, as in the fairy tales, as in the story-books of old, where everything always comes out all right, where good is good and bad is bad, and the magic spell is always broken just in time for the happy ending, there it was—right under her eyes—

Lying there, waiting. Only asking to be picked up. A white oblong, a sealed envelope. A letter from the dead.

A voice trapped in it seemed to whisper through the seams to her, faint, far away: "When you're in the most need, and I'm not here, open this. When your need is the greatest, and you're all alone. Goodbye, my daughter; my daughter, goodbye . . ."

"I, Grace Parmentier Hazzard, wife of Donald Sedgwick Hazzard, being on my death-bed, and in the presence of my attorney and lifelong counsellor Tyrus Winthrop, who will duly notarize my signature to this and bear witness to it if called upon to do so by the legally constituted authorities, hereby make the following statement, of my own free will and volition, and declare it to be the truth:

"That at approximately 10.30 P.M. on the evening of 24th September, being alone in the house with just my devoted friend and housekeeper, Josephine Walker, and my grandchild, I received a long-distance telephone-call from Hastings, in the neighboring State. That the caller was a certain Harry Carter, known to me as a private investigator and employed by my family and myself as such. That he informed me that just a few moments earlier my beloved daughter-in-law, Patrice, the widow of my late son, Hugh, had been driven against her will to Hastings by a man using the name of Stephen Georgesson, and had there been compelled to enter into a marriage-ceremony with him under duress. And that at that time, while he spoke to me, they were on their way back here, to this city, together.

"Upon receipt of this information, and having obtained from this Mr. Carter the address of the aforementioned Stephen Georgesson, I dressed myself, called Josephine Walker to me, and told her I was going out, and would be away for only a short time. She tried to dissuade me, and to prevail upon me to reveal my purpose and where I was going, but I would not. I instructed her to wait for me close beside the front door, in order to admit me at once upon my return, and under no circumstances, then or at any later time, to reveal to anyone that I had left the house at that time or under those circumstances. I caused her to take an oath upon the Bible, and knowing the nature of her religious beliefs and early upbringing knew she would not break it afterward no matter what befell.

"I removed and carried with me a gun which habitually was kept in a desk in the library of my home, having first inserted into it the cartridges. In order to lessen recognition as much as possible, I put on the heavy veil of mourning which I had worn at the time of the death of my elder son.

"I walked a short distance from my own door, entirely alone and unaccompanied, and at the first opportunity engaged a public taxicab. In it I went to the quarters of Stephen Georgesson, to seek him out. I found he had not yet returned when I first arrived, and I therefore waited, sitting in the taxi a short distance from his door, until I saw him return and enter. As soon as he had, I immediately entered in turn, right after him, and was admitted by him. I raised my veil in order to let him see my face, and I could see that he guessed who I was, although he'd never seen me before.

"I asked him if it was true that he had just now forced my dead son's wife to enter a marriage-pact with him, as had been reported to me.

"He readily admitted it, naming the place and time.

"Those were the only words that passed between us. Nothing further was said. Nothing further needed to be.

"I immediately took out the gun, held it close toward him, and fired it at him as he stood there before me.

"I fired it only once. I would have fired it more than once, if necessary, in order to kill him; it was my full intention to kill him. But having waited to see if he would move again, and seeing that he did not, but lay as he had fallen, then and only then I refrained from firing it any more and left the place.

"I had myself returned to my own home in the same taxi that had brought me. Within a short time after, I became extremely ill from the excitement and strain I had undergone. And now, knowing that I am dying, and being in full possession of my faculties and with full re- alization of what I am doing, I wish to make this state- ment before I pass away and have it, in the case of wrongful accusation of others, should that occur, brought to the attention of those duly constituted to deal with the matter. But only in such case, not other- wise.

      (*Signed*)   Grace Parmentier Hazzard.
(*Witnessed and attested*)
Tyrus Winthrop, Att'y at Law."

She reached the downstairs doorway with it too late. The doorway was empty by the time she swayed that far, and clung there, all dazed and disheveled. They'd gone, and he'd gone with them.

She just stood there in the doorway. Empty in an empty doorway.

Forty-Eight

AND then, there he was at last.

He was so very real, so photographically real down there, that paradoxically, she couldn't quite believe she was seeing him. The very herringbone weave of his coat stood out, as if a magnifying glass were being held to the pattern, for her special inspection. The haggardness of his face, the faint trace of shadow where he needed a shave, she could see everything about him so clearly, as if he were much nearer than he was. Fatigue, maybe, did that, by some reverse process of concentration. Or eyes dilated from long straining to see him, so that now they saw him with abnormal clarity.

Anyway, there he was.

He turned, and came in toward the house. And just before he took the final step that would have carried him too far in under her to be in sight any more, his eyes went up to the window and he saw her.

"Bill," she said silently through the glass, and her two hands flattened to the pane, as if framing the unheard word into a benediction.

"Patrice," he said silently, from down below; and though she didn't hear him, didn't even see his lips move, she knew that was what he said. Just her name. So little, so much.

Suddenly she'd fled from the room as madly as though she'd just been scalded. The upflung curtain settled down again to true, and the backflung door ricocheted back again toward closure, and she was already gone. The baby's wondering head turned after her far too slowly to catch her in her flight.

Then she stopped short again, below the turn of the stairs, and waited for him there, unable to move any further. Stood waiting for him to come to her.

He left his hat, just as though this were any other time he was returning home, and came on up to where she was standing. And somehow her head, as if it were tired of being all alone, went down upon his shoulder and stayed there against his own.

They didn't speak at first. Just stood there pressed together, heads close. There was no message; there was only—being together.

"I'm back, Patrice," was all he said at last.

She shuddered a little and nestled closer. "Bill, now what will they—?"

"Nothing. It's over. It's already through. At least, as far as I'm concerned. That was just for purposes of identification. I had to go with them and look at him, that was all."

"Bill, I opened this. She says—"

She gave it to him. He read it.

"Did you show it to anyone else?"

"No."

"Don't." He tore it once across, and stuffed the remnants into his pocket.

"But suppose—?"

"It's not needed. His gambler-friends are already down on the books for it, by this time. They told me they found evidence to indicate that a big card-game had taken place up there earlier that night."

"I didn't see any."

He gave her an eloquent look. "They did. By the time they got there."

She widened her eyes a little at him.

"They're willing to let it go at that. So let us let it go at that too, Patrice." He sighed heavily. "I'm all-in. Feel like I've been on my feet for a week straight. I'd like to sleep forever."

"Not forever, Bill, not forever. Because I'll be waiting around, and that would be so long—"

His lips sought the side of her face, and he kissed her with a sort of blind stupefaction.

"Walk me up as far as the door of my room, Patrice. Like to take a look at the youngster, before I turn in."

His arm slipped wearily around her waist.

"*Our* youngster from now on," he added softly.

Forty-Nine

"MR. WILLIAM HAZZARD was married yesterday to Mrs. Patrice Hazzard, widow of the late Hugh Hazzard, at a quiet ceremony at St. Bartholomew's Episcopal Church, in this city, performed by the Reverend Francis Allgood. There were no attendants. Following their marriage Mr. and Mrs. Hazzard left immediately for a honeymoon trip through the Canadian Rockies."—*All Caulfield morning and evening newspapers.*

Fifty

WHEN the reading of the will had been concluded—that was on a Monday following their return, about a month later—Winthrop asked the two of them to remain behind a moment after the room had been cleared. He went over and closed the door after the others present had left. Then he went to the wall, opened a built-in safe, and took out an envelope. He sat down at his desk.

"Bill and Patrice," he said, "this is meant for you alone."

They exchanged a look.

"It is not part of the estate, so it concerns no one else but the two of you.

"It is from her, of course. It was transcribed on her deathbed, less than an hour before she died."

"But we already—" Bill tried to say.

Winthrop silenced him with upturned hand. "There were two of them. This is the second. Both dictated to me during the hours of that same night, or I should say, early morning. This follows the other. The first she gave you herself that same night, as you know. The other she turned over to me. I was to hold it until today, as I have done. Her instructions to me were: It is for the two of you alike. It is not to be delivered to the one without the other. When delivered, it is not to be opened by the one without the other. And finally, it is only to be delivered in the case of your marriage. If you were not married at this time, as she wanted you to be—and you know she did, very much—then it was to be destroyed by me, unopened. Singly, it is not for either one of you. United in marriage, it is a last gift to the two of you, from her.

"However. You need not read it if you do not want to. You can destroy it unopened. I am under pledge not to reveal what is in it, even though I naturally know, for I took her words down at the bedside, and witnessed and notarized her signature in my capacity as her attorney. You must, therefore, either read it or not read it for yourselves. And if you do read it, then when you have read it, you are to destroy it just the same."

He waited a moment.

"Now, do you want me to deliver it to you, or do you prefer that I destroy it?"

"We want it, of course," Patrice whispered.

"We want it," Bill echoed.

He extended it to them lengthwise. "You kindly place your fingers on this corner. You on this." He withdrew his own fingers, and they were left holding it.

"I hope it brings you the extra added happiness she wanted you both to have. I know that that is why she did it. She asked me to bless you both, for her, as I gave it to you. Which I do now. That concludes my stewardship in the matter."

They waited several hours, until they were alone together in their room that night. Then when he'd finished putting on his robe, and saw that she had donned a silken bridal something over her nightdress, he took it out of his coat-pocket and said:

"Now. Shall we? You do want to, don't you?"

"Of course. It's from her. We want to read it. I've been counting the minutes all evening long."

"I knew you'd want to. Come on over here. We'll read it together."

He sat down in an easy chair, adjusted the hood of the lamp over one shoulder. She perched beside him on the arm of the chair, slipped an arm about his shoulders.

The sealing-wax wafers crumbled and the flap shot upright, under his fingers.

In silent intensity, heads close together, they read:

"My beloved children:

"You are married by now, by the time this reaches you. (For if you are not, it will not reach you; Mr. Winthrop will tell you all about that.) You are happy. I hope I have given you that happiness. I want to give you even a little more. And trust and pray that out of your plenty, you will spare a little of it for me, even though I am gone and no longer there with you. I do not want a shadow to cross your minds every time you recall me. I cannot bear to have you think ill of me.

"I did not do that thing, of course. I did not take that young man's life. Perhaps you have already guessed it. Perhaps you both know me well enough to know I could not have done such a thing.

"I knew that he was doing something to threaten Patrice's happiness, that was all. That was why we were having Mr. Carter investigate him. But I never actually set eyes on him, I never saw him.

"I was alone in the house last night (for as Mr. Winthrop writes this for me, it is still last night, though you will not read it for a long time to come). Even Father, who never goes out without me, had to attend an important emergency meeting at the plant. It meant settling the strike that much sooner, and I pleaded with him to go, though he did not want to. I was alone, just Aunt Josie and the child and I.

"Mr. Carter phoned around ten-thirty o'clock and told me he had bad news; that a marriage-service had just been performed joining the two of them at Hastings. I had taken the call on the downstairs phone. The shock brought on an attack. Not wishing to alarm Aunt Josie, I tried to get up the stairs to my room unaided. By the time I had reached the top, I became exhausted and could only lie there, unable to move any further or to call out.

"While I was lying there helpless like that, I heard the outside door open and recognized Bill's step below. I tried to attract his attention, but my voice was too weak, I couldn't reach him with it. I heard him go into the library, stay there several moments, then come out again. Afterward I remembered hearing something click between his hands right then, as he stood there by the door. And I knew he never uses a cigarette-lighter. Then he left the house.

"When Aunt Josie had come out some time later,

found me there, and carried me to my bed, and while we were waiting for the doctor, I sent her to the library to see if that gun that belonged there was still there. She did not understand why I wanted her to do this, and I did not tell her. But when she came back and told me that the gun was missing, I was afraid what that might mean.

"I knew by then that I was dying. One does. I had time to think, lying there during those next long hours. I could think so clearly. I knew that there was a way in which either my Bill or my Patrice might need my protection, once I was no longer there to give it. I knew I had to give it none the less, as best I could. I wanted them to have their happiness. I wanted above all my little grandchild to have his security, his start in life without anything to mar it. I knew what the way was in which I could give this to them.

"So as soon as Dr. Parker would allow it, I had Ty Winthrop called to my bedside. To him, in privacy, I dictated the sworn statement which you have had by now.

"I hope, my dear ones, you have not had to use it. I pray you have not, and never will have to.

"But this is its retraction. This is the truth, just meant for you two alone. One tells the truth to one's loved ones, one does not have to swear to and notarize it. There is no guilt upon me. This is my wedding gift to you. To make your happiness even more complete than it is already.

"Burn it after you have read it. This is a dying woman's last wish. Bless you both.

Your devoted Mother."

The match made a tiny snap. Stripes of black crept up the paper, then ran together, before any flame could be seen. Then there was a little soundless puff, and suddenly yellow light glowed all around it.

And as it burned, over this yellow light, they turned their heads and looked at one another. With a strange, new sort of fright they'd never felt before. As when the world drops away, and there is nothing left underfoot to stand on.

"*She* didn't do it," he whispered, stricken.

"*She* didn't," she breathed, appalled.

"Then—?"

"Then—?"

And each pair of eyes answered, "You."

THE SUMMER NIGHTS are so pleasant in Caulfield. They smell of heliotrope, of jasmine, and of clover. The stars are warm and close above us. The breeze is gentle as a baby's kiss. The soothing whisper of the leafy trees, the lamplight falling on the lawns, the hush of perfect peace and security.

But not for us.

The house we live in is so pleasant here in Caulfield. Its blue-green lawn, always freshly watered; the dazzling whiteness of the porch-supports in the sun; the gracious symmetry of the bannister that curves down from above; the gloss of rich old floors; the lushness of pile carpeting; in every room some favorite chair that's an old friend. People come and say, "What more can there be? This is a home."

But not for us.

I love him so. More than ever before, not less. So bitterly I love him. And he loves me. And yet I know that on some day to come, maybe this year, maybe next, but surely to come, suddenly he'll pack and go away and leave me. Though he'll love me still, and never stop even after he's gone.

Or if he doesn't, I will. I'll take up my valise, and walk out through the door, and never return. I'll leave my heart behind, and leave my child behind, and leave my life behind, but I'll never come back.

It's certain, it's assured. The only uncertainty is: which one of us will be the first to break.

We've fought this thing. In every way we know, in every way there is. No good, no good at all. There's no way out. We're caught, we're trapped. For if he's innocent, then it has to be me. And if I am, it has to be he. But I *know* I'm innocent. (Yet he may know he is too.) We can't break through, there's no way out.

It's in the very kiss we give each other. Somehow we trap it right between our lips, each time. It's everywhere, it's all the time, it's *us*.

I don't know what the game was. I'm not sure how it should be played. No one ever tells you. I only know we must have played it wrong, somewhere along the way. I don't even know what the stakes are. I only know they're not for us.

We've lost. That's all I know. We've lost. And now the game is through.

The End.

BIOGRAPHICAL NOTES

NOTE ON THE TEXTS

NOTES

Biographical Notes

JAMES M. CAIN   Born July 1, 1892, in Annapolis, Maryland. Moved with family in 1903 to Chestertown, Maryland, where father served as president of Washington College. Graduated from Washington College 1910. Studied singing, but eventually abandoned musical career. Taught English and mathematics at Washington College, 1914–17. Worked as reporter for Baltimore *American* and then Baltimore *Sun* before enlisting in army; served in France with headquarters of 79th Division and edited the weekly divisional newspaper, *The Lorraine Cross*. Resumed work with Baltimore *Sun* after the war. Married Mary Rebekah Clough in 1920. Published articles in *Atlantic Monthly* and *Nation*; worked briefly as coal miner in 1922. Marriage ended in divorce in 1923. Taught journalism at St. John's College, Annapolis, 1923–24. Moved to New York in 1924 and wrote for New York *World* and other publications. Married Elina Sjosted Tyszecka in 1927. Published fiction and articles in *The American Mercury*, including satirical political dialogues collected in 1930 as *Our Government*. Worked for ten months in 1931 as managing editor of *The New Yorker*. Moved to Hollywood, where he worked for 17 years as screenwriter for most of the major studios (credits include *Hot Saturday*, 1932; *Dr. Socrates*, 1935; *Algiers*, 1938; *Stand Up and Fight*, 1939; *Money and the Woman*, 1940; *The Bridge of San Luis Rey*, 1943; *The Great Gatsby*, 1945; *The Glass Heart*, 1946). First novel, *The Postman Always Rings Twice*, published 1934 (a stage version written by Cain ran on Broadway in 1936). *Double Indemnity* serialized in *Liberty* magazine in 1938. Published novels *Serenade* (1937), *Mildred Pierce* (1941), *Love's Lovely Counterfeit* (1942). Second marriage ended in divorce in 1942. *Double Indemnity* successfully filmed in 1943, directed by Billy Wilder and starring Barbara Stanwyck and Fred MacMurray; magazine serials *Double Indemnity*, *Career in C Major* (1938), and *The Embezzler* (1940) collected in *Three of a Kind* (1943). Married movie actress Aileen Pringle in 1944; divorced the following year. Movie versions of *Mildred Pierce*, directed by Michael Curtiz and starring Joan Crawford, and *The Postman Always Rings Twice*, directed by Tay Garnett and starring Lana Turner and John Garfield, appeared, 1945–46. Civil War novel *Past All Dishonor* published 1946. Campaign organized by Cain in 1946 to establish American Authors Authority, organization intended to protect and administer authors' copyrights, met with intense opposition from studios, publishers, and other writers, some of whom accused Cain of being a pawn of Communists;

978   BIOGRAPHICAL NOTES

he abandoned plan the following year. Married opera singer Florence MacBeth in 1947 and moved with her to Hyattsville, Maryland. Published novels *Sinful Woman* (1947), *The Moth* (1948), *Jealous Woman* (1950), *The Root of His Evil* (1951, revision of 1938 magazine serial), *Galatea* (1953), *Mignon* (1963), *The Magician's Wife* (1965). Wife died in 1966. Reputation revived by publication of *Cain × 3* (1969), omnibus of early novels with introduction by Tom Wolfe. Published novels *Rainbow's End* (1975) and *The Institute* (1976); other late novels rejected for publication, *Cloud Nine* and *The Enchanted Isle*, were published posthumously (1984–85). Died October 27, 1977.

HORACE MCCOY Born April 14, 1897, in Pegram, Tennessee. Moved with family to Nashville at age two. Worked as auto mechanic and traveling salesman after dropping out of high school. Moved with family to Dallas in 1915. Enlisted in Texas National Guard in 1917; received training as aerial observer, and served in France in 1918 as bombardier and aerial photographer. Returned to Dallas, worked as reporter for *Dallas Dispatch*, and then joined *Dallas Journal* as sports editor. Married Loline Scherer in 1921; son Stanley born 1924. Active as actor in acclaimed Dallas Little Theatre, 1925–31. Began contributing stories to *Black Mask* in 1927; published 16 stories, 1927–34, most concerning the adventures of Texas Ranger Jerry Frost and his Air Border Patrol; also published in other pulps including *Battle Aces, Action Stories, Western Trails,* and *Man Stories.* Marriage broke up; lost newspaper job in 1929. Became editor in 1930 of recently launched magazine *The Dallasite,* which soon failed. Eloped with a Dallas socialite, but marriage was quickly annulled. Went to Hollywood in 1931 to pursue an acting career; was cast only in a few minor roles. Became contract screenwriter with RKO in 1932. Married Helen Vinmont, daughter of wealthy oilman, in 1933 (they had a daughter, Amanda, born 1940, and a son, Peter, born 1945). First novel, *They Shoot Horses, Don't They?,* published 1935. Second novel, *No Pockets in a Shroud,* based on Dallas experiences as actor and reporter, was rejected by American publishers but appeared in England in 1937 with substantial changes demanded by English publisher; third novel, *I Should Have Stayed Home,* published 1938. Worked steadily as screenwriter for RKO, Paramount, and Warner Brothers for the next two decades; credits include *Postal Inspector,* 1936; *The Trail of the Lonesome Pine,* 1936; *The Texans,* 1938; *Gentleman Jim,* 1942; *Appointment in Berlin,* 1943; *Montana Belle,* 1952; *The Turning Point,* 1952 (his screen treatment was posthumously published in 1956 as novel *Corruption City*); *The Lusty Men,* 1952; *The World in His Arms,* 1952; *Rage at Dawn,* 1955. Became aware in the late 1940s that his work was highly appreciated in Europe, particularly France. Published novel *Kiss Tomorrow Good-bye* in 1948; it received weak reviews but sold well (film version, starring James Cagney, released 1950); issued in paperback by New American Library along with three earlier novels (most in abridged versions). Visited France in 1951. Final novel *Scalpel* (1952), based on screen treatment about a doctor's career, became bestseller. Worked on novel *The Hard-Rock Man*, never completed. Died of a heart attack on December 15, 1955.

EDWARD ANDERSON   Born June 19, 1905, in Weatherford, Texas. Moved with family through many small towns in Texas and Oklahoma before his father, an itinerant printer, settled in Ardmore, Oklahoma. Worked as freelance newspaperman during 1920s. Traveled to Europe in 1930, working on freighter; visited Belgium, France, and Germany. On return to U.S. settled in Abilene, Texas, where his family was living. Formed close friendship with writer John Knox, who introduced him to writings of Knut Hamsun, Maxim Gorky, Karl Marx, and others. Left Abilene to live hobo life, traveling around U.S. and spending time in San Francisco, Boston, and New York; returned to Abilene in late 1933. Sold short stories based on hobo experiences to *Story*. Married Polly Anne Bates in 1934 and moved to New Orleans; wrote articles for *True Detective* and other magazines, and subsequently took newspaper job at the *New Orleans States*. Novel *Hungry Men* won *Story* prize for best first novel and was published by Doubleday in 1935. Daughter Helen Ann born 1935; son Dick Edward born 1936. Returned to Texas and wrote second novel, *Thieves Like Us*, based partly on interviews with cousin Roy Johnson, who was serving life sentence for armed robbery. Went to Denver to work for *Rocky Mountain News*; also wrote for local radio shows. *Thieves Like Us* published by Frederick A. Stokes in 1937. At suggestion of agent Adeline Schulberg, went to Los Angeles to write for movies; worked briefly at Paramount and Warner Brothers before joining staff of *Los Angeles Examiner*. Sold movie rights to *Thieves Like Us* for $500. Subsequent fiction remained unpublished. Son Ross born 1941. Marriage broke up in 1946. After losing job with *Examiner* worked successively for *Sacramento Bee* and *Fort Worth Star-Telegram*. Remarried Polly Anne in 1949. Film version of *Thieves Like Us*, titled *They Live By Night* (directed by Nicholas Ray), opened in 1950 after two-year delay; the novel was reissued in paperback. Marriage broke up again in 1950 as a result of Anderson's heavy drinking; he resumed a drifting life, working sporadically at newspapers in different parts of the U.S., marrying twice more. With third wife, Lupe, settled again in Texas; daughter Sarita born 1956. Espoused extreme right-wing political views along with religious beliefs based on Swedenborgianism. Died from heart attack September 5, 1969.

KENNETH FEARING   Born July 28, 1902, in Oak Park, Illinois; father, Harry Fearing was successful Chicago attorney; mother, Olive Flexner, a newspaper reporter, was member of Jewish family originally from Bohemia. Parents' marriage broke up a year after Fearing's birth and he was raised mostly by father's sister. Attended University of Illinois for two years, then transferred to University of Wisconsin, where he met writers Carl Rakosi and Margery Latimer, and was editor of the college literary magazine; graduated in 1924. Settled in New York City; maintained close relationship with Latimer until 1928. Worked sporadically at odd jobs but mostly devoted himself to writing; wrote prolifically for pulp magazines under pseudonyms; contributed poetry and reviews to periodicals including *New Masses, Poetry,* and *The New Yorker.* First book of poems, *Angel Arms,* published 1929. Married medical social worker Rachel Meltzer in 1933; son Bruce born 1935. Published *Poems* (1935) and *Dead Reckoning* (1938); wrote a number of unpublished novels before *The Hospital* appeared in 1939. Awarded Guggenheim fellowship (1937–38) and prize from American Academy of Arts and Letters (1944); stayed in Europe (mostly in London) with Rachel for nine months, 1936–37. In addition to other volumes of poetry—*Collected Poems of Kenneth Fearing* (1940), *Afternoon of a Pawnbroker* (1943), *Stranger at Coney Island* (1948)—published novels *Dagger of the Mind* (1941), *Clark Gifford's Body* (1942), *The Big Clock* (1946). Marriage broke up in 1942; married artist Nan Lurie in 1945. Film version of *The Big Clock,* directed by John Farrow and starring Ray Milland and Charles Laughton, released 1948 (Fearing had negotiated disadvantageous contract signing away future rights). Interviewed by FBI on his political associations in 1950, said he was "not yet" a member of the Communist Party. Second marriage broke up in 1952; in later years suffered from effects of poverty and long-term heavy drinking. Later novels were *Loneliest Girl in the World* (1951), *The Generous Heart* (1954), and *The Crozart Story* (1960); final poetry collection, *New and Selected Poems,* appeared in 1956. Worked on staff of *Newsweek,* 1952–54, and as publicist for Muscular Dystrophy Association of America, 1955–58. Died of cancer on June 26, 1961.

WILLIAM LINDSAY GRESHAM   Born August 20, 1909, in Baltimore, Maryland. Moved with family to Fall River, Massachusetts, and then to New York City in 1917; graduated Erasmus Hall High School in Brooklyn, 1926. Worked at odd jobs and as folk singer in Greenwich Village cafés; joined Civilian Conservation Corps in 1933. Married after leaving the CCC. After brief stint as reviewer for New York *Evening Post*, worked as advertising copy writer; contributed stories to pulp magazines. Joined Communist Party in 1936; went to Spain the following year and served for 15 months as medic with the Abraham Lincoln Brigade. Returning to U.S. in January 1939, spent time in tuberculosis ward, attempted suicide, underwent lengthy psychoanalysis, and worked as editor for true crime magazine. After divorcing first wife, married poet Joy Davidman in 1942; they had two sons, David and Douglas, born in 1944 and 1945, and lived successively in Ossining and Staatsburg, New York. Gresham's first novel, *Nightmare Alley*, published in 1946; it was a bestseller and was filmed the following year, directed by Edmund Goulding and starring Tyrone Power. His second novel, *Limbo Tower*, appeared in 1949. Gresham and his wife were deeply influenced by ideas of C. S. Lewis, and announced their joint conversion in articles published in 1951 anthology *These Found the Way: Thirteen Converts to Protestant Christianity*. Struggled with alcoholism, was occasionally violent, and engaged frequently in extramarital affairs; stopped attending Presbyterian church and pursued interests in Zen Buddhism, occult traditions, and L. Ron Hubbard's Dianetics. Divorced Joy Davidman in 1954 and married her cousin Renee Pierce (Davidman resettled with children in England, married C. S. Lewis in 1956, and died in 1960). Gresham's later books included *Monster Midway: An Uninhibited Look at the Glittering World of the Carny* (1953), *Houdini: The Man Who Walked Through Walls* (1959), and *The Book of Strength*. Lived in New Rochelle; became partially blind and was diagnosed with cancer in 1962. Committed suicide with overdose of sleeping pills in Dixie Hotel in New York City, where he had registered under a false name, on September 14, 1962.

CORNELL WOOLRICH Born Cornell George Hopley-Woolrich on December 4, 1903, in New York City. Moved with parents to Mexico in 1907, where father worked as engineer; marriage soon broke up, and Woolrich remained with father while mother returned to New York. After several years rejoined mother, living with her and her family in luxurious house on Manhattan's Upper West Side. First novel, *Cover Charge*, written while an undergraduate at Columbia and published 1926, followed by *Children of the Ritz* (1927), *Times Square* (1929), *A Young Man's Heart* (1930), *The Time of Her Life* (1931), and *Manhattan Love Song* (1932). Went to Hollywood in 1928 to work on movie version of *Children of the Ritz*. Married Gloria Blackton, daughter of pioneering filmmaker J. Stuart Blackton, in December 1930; marriage ended three months later (break-up may have been precipitated by wife's discovery of Woolrich's homosexual activities). Woolrich returned to New York to rejoin his mother; traveled with her to Europe in April 1931, staying mostly in France, and returned to U.S. in 1933. Moved with mother into apartment in Hotel Marseilles in New York City, where they lived for the next 25 years. Began to write crime stories for pulp magazines, contributing prolifically to *Detective Fiction Weekly*, *Dime Detective*, *Argosy*, *Black Mask*, and others. First crime novel, *The Bride Wore Black*, published 1940. Published series of crime novels, sometimes under names William Irish and George Hopley: *The Black Curtain* (1941), *Black Alibi* (1942), *Phantom Lady* (1942, as William Irish), *The Black Angel* (1943), *Deadline at Dawn* (1944, as William Irish), *The Black Path of Fear* (1944), *Night Has a Thousand Eyes* (1945, as George Hopley), *Waltz into Darkness* (1947, as William Irish), *Rendezvous in Black* (1948), *I Married a Dead Man* (1948, as William Irish), *Fright* (1950, as George Hopley), *Savage Bride* (1951), *Strangler's Serenade* (1951, as William Irish). Many of his novels and stories were adapted into movies, including *The Leopard Man*, *Phantom Lady*, *Deadline at Dawn*, *Black Angel*, *The Chase*, *Fear in the Night*, *Night Has a Thousand Eyes*, *The Window*, *No Man of Her Own* (based on *I Married a Dead Man*), and *Rear Window*, and for radio and television. Productivity diminished drastically in final two decades of life; suffered from alcoholism and became even more reclusive. Mother died in October 1957. *Hotel Room*, collection of stories without a crime theme, published 1958. Final completed novel, *Death Is My Dancing Partner*, published 1959; *The Doom Stone* (1960), reprint of a 1939 pulp novella, was last book to appear in his lifetime. (An unfinished novel, *Into the Night*, was completed by Lawrence Block and published in 1987.) Changed name legally to William Irish in 1961. Untreated infection became gangrenous, necessitating amputation of right leg in January 1968. Died September 25, 1968, six days after suffering a stroke.

Note on the Texts

This volume collects six American novels of the 1930s and 1940s that have come to be identified with the "noir" genre of crime fiction: *The Postman Always Rings Twice* by James M. Cain (1934); *They Shoot Horses, Don't They?* by Horace McCoy (1935); *Thieves Like Us* by Edward Anderson (1937); *The Big Clock* by Kenneth Fearing (1946); *Nightmare Alley* by William Lindsay Gresham (1946); and *I Married a Dead Man* by Cornell Woolrich (1948).

James M. Cain began work on his first novel in the late autumn of 1932, writing the narrative in the third person until early in 1933, when he decided to use a first-person narration. Cain showed an early version of the novel to screenwriter Vincent Lawrence, who persuaded him to rewrite and shorten the section of the book dealing with the court proceedings against Cora. In the summer of 1933 Cain submitted a 159-page typescript to Alfred A. Knopf under the title *Bar-B-Q*. Knopf asked for significant revisions, which Cain refused to make; after H. L. Mencken and Blanche Knopf recommended publication of the novel, Knopf reversed himself and accepted the version Cain had submitted. Cain did agree to change the title and chose *The Postman Always Rings Twice* after considering *Black Puma* and *The Devil's Checkbook*. *The Postman Always Rings Twice* was published by Alfred A. Knopf on February 19, 1934. Cain did not revise the novel after its initial publication. The text printed here is that of the first edition.

Horace McCoy began writing a short story titled "Marathon Dance" sometime after he moved to southern California in early 1931. He later retitled the story "They Shoot Horses, Don't They?" and wrote at least three different manuscript versions that varied in length from 3,500 to 6,000 words. In 1932 and 1933 McCoy submitted the story to magazines, but it was rejected for reasons of length and profanity. (He also submitted a proposal for a film titled "Marathon Dancers" to Universal in the summer of 1932; the relationship between the film proposal and "They Shoot Horses, Don't They?" is not known.) McCoy then expanded the story into a novel and apparently completed an initial draft by November 1933. He continued to work on the novel until early in 1935, when he sent the manuscript to Harold Matson, his New York literary agent. Simon and Schuster accepted the novel for publication, and McCoy corresponded with the book's designer, Philip Van Doren Stern, about the typographical presentation of the judge's sentencing speech. *They Shoot Horses,*

Don't They?, Horace McCoy's first novel, was published by Simon and Schuster on July 25, 1935. McCoy did not make any revisions in the novel after its publication. This volume prints the text of the first edition and follows its typographical presentation of the courtroom scenes.

Edward Anderson began writing *Thieves Like Us*, his second novel, in 1935. After interviewing a cousin who was imprisoned for armed robbery in the Texas state penitentiary in Huntsville, Anderson worked on the book, then titled *They're Thieves Like Us*, in a rented cabin near Kerrville, Texas. In 1936 he sent a manuscript to Bernice Baumgarten, his New York literary agent, who suggested that the book be submitted to *True Detective* magazine for serialization. Anderson rejected this suggestion and, after revising the manuscript, had Baumgarten submit the novel to hardcover book publishers. *Thieves Like Us* was published by Frederick A. Stokes Company in 1937. Anderson made no changes in the novel after its publication. This volume prints the text of the first edition.

Kenneth Fearing wrote *The Big Clock*, his fourth published novel, between August 1944 and October 1945. A condensed version of the book appeared in *The American Magazine* in October 1946 under the title "The Judas Picture." *The Big Clock* was published by Harcourt, Brace, and Company in the fall of 1946. Fearing did not make changes in the novel after its publication. This volume prints the text of the first edition.

William Lindsay Gresham attributed the origin of *Nightmare Alley* to conversations he had with a former carnival worker while they were both serving as volunteers with the Loyalist forces in the Spanish Civil War. Gresham wrote the novel, his first, while working as an editor for a "true crime" pulp magazine in New York City during the 1940s. He outlined the plot and wrote the first six chapters over a period of two years, then finished the book in four months. *Nightmare Alley* was published by Rinehart and Company, Inc., in 1946. Gresham did not revise the novel after its initial publication. This volume prints the text of the first edition.

Cornell Woolrich began publishing crime stories in pulp magazines in 1934 and became a prolific writer of suspense novels during the 1940s. Between 1940 and 1948 Woolrich published six novels under his own name, four novels under the name William Irish, and one novel as George Hopley, while continuing to write short stories for magazines. *I Married a Dead Man* is an expanded and rewritten version of "They Call Me Patrice," a novella that appeared in *Today's Woman* in April 1946. Woolrich used the characters and basic plot of the novella but made significant revisions, including adding passages of first-person narration and writing a new ending (in the novella a character introduced at the end of the story confesses to the murder). *I Married a Dead Man* was published as a Story Press Book by J. B. Lippincott Company in July 1948; it appeared, as had all three of the Woolrich novels previously published by Lippincott, under the name William Irish. Woolrich made no changes in the novel after its publication. The text presented in this volume is that of the first edition.

This volume presents the texts of the original printings chosen for inclusion here, but it does not attempt to reproduce features of their typographic design, such as display capitalization of chapter openings. The texts are printed without change, except for the correction of typographical errors. Spelling, punctuation, and capitalization are often expressive features, and they are not altered, even when inconsistent or irregular. The following is a list of typographical errors corrected, cited by page and line number: 6.32, potatoes.; 46.3, around?; 53.24, Sackett.; 75.30, that?; 87.6, dowstairs; 185.9, Mother's; 233.35, .12-gauge; 245.36, a two; 248.22, .12-gauge; 248.28, .12-gauge; 259.35, twelve; 267.28, boy; 275.21, Stoctor; 304.5, sung; 304.30, Bowie.; 309.31, said,; 313.27, a such; 318.40, his coat; 320.4, Chickamaw; 349.33, curb."; 354.31, everyday; 356.15, gone done; 356.23, of; 494.24, it's; 495.20, breath; 718.11, very; 743.26, heards; 762.26, agily; 803.3, it; 803.36, unmisakably; 838.26, last; 845.28, passengers,; 859.17, guilessly; 872.26, return; 877.1, helplessly,; 878.36, in it,; 881.16, had came; 891.5, I"; 892.1, where-/ever; 902.37, if; 931.20, of two; 943.13, carboose; 951.31, saying,; 953.34, irridescent; 968.21, doned; 968.36, You. Errors corrected second printing: 553.34, He; 564.39, They.

Notes

In the notes below, the reference numbers denote page and line of this volume (the line count includes headings). No note is made for material included in standard desk-reference books such as Webster's *Collegiate*, *Biographical*, and *Geographical* dictionaries. For references to other studies and further biographical background than is contained in the Biographical Notes, see Roy Hoopes, *Cain* (New York: Holt, Rinehart and Winston, 1982); John Thomas Sturak, "The Life and Writings of Horace McCoy, 1897–1955" (unpublished dissertation, The University of California Los Angeles, 1966); Mark Roydan Winchell, *Horace McCoy* (Boise: Boise State University, 1982); Patrick Bennett, *Rough and Rowdy Ways: The Life and Hard Times of Edward Anderson* (College Station: Texas A&M University Press, 1988); Kenneth Fearing, *Complete Poems* (Orono, Maine: The National Poetry Foundation, 1994), edited by Robert M. Ryley; Patricia B. Santora, "The Life of Kenneth Flexner Fearing (1902–1961)," *CLA Journal 32* (1989); William Lindsay Gresham, "From Communist to Christian," *Presbyterian Life*, February 18, 1950; Francis M. Nevins, Jr., *Cornell Woolrich: First You Dream, Then You Die* (New York, London, Tokyo: The Mysterious Press, 1988); *Blues of a Lifetime: The Autobiography of Cornell Woolrich* (Bowling Green: Bowling Green State University Press, 1991), edited by Mark T. Bassett; *Tough Guy Writers of the Thirties* (Carbondale and Edwardsville: Southern Illinois University Press, 1968), edited by David Madden; and Geoffrey O'Brien, *Hardboiled America: Lurid Paperbacks and the Masters of Noir* (revised edition, New York: Da Capo Press, 1997).

THE POSTMAN ALWAYS RINGS TWICE

2.2   *Vincent Lawrence*]   Playwright and screenwriter (1890–1946) known in Hollywood for his mastery of plot construction; he was a close friend of Cain and advised him during the writing of *The Postman Always Rings Twice*.

4.34   wind wing]   A small panel in a car window that can be adjusted for ventilation.

11.14   the Chief]   The Super Chief, a luxury train running between Los Angeles and Chicago.

14.36   Mother Machree]   Song (1910) by Rida Johnson Young, Ernest R. Ball, and Chauncey Olcott; it was the theme song of the popular Irish tenor John McCormack.

25.33   Hoppe] William F. Hoppe (1887–1959), American billiards champion.

25.36–37   Blind Tom the Sightless Piano Player] Thomas Greene Bethune (1849–1908), pianist and composer born in slavery in Columbus, Georgia. He was a child prodigy and amazed audiences with his total musical and verbal recall and his ability to mimic natural and instrumental sounds; he could perform more than 700 pieces from memory.

31.12–19   "There's a long . . . long trail with you."] Song (1913) by Stoddard King and Zo Elliott, popular with troops in World War I.

54.5   Cadona] Mexican trapeze artist Alfredo Codona (1893–1937) became famous for doing the triple aerial somersault.

61.28–29   Dempsey-Firpo fight] Heavyweight boxing champion Jack Dempsey defeated challenger Luis Angel Firpo ("The Wild Bull of the Pampas") at the Polo Grounds in New York City on September 14, 1923. The fight ended in the second round after three minutes and 57 seconds of fighting time.

THEY SHOOT HORSES, DON'T THEY?

98.2–4   *Michael Fessier . . . Harry Clay Wither*] Michael Fessier (1907–88), novelist (*Fully Clothed and in His Right Mind*, 1935) and Hollywood screenwriter whose credits included *Women Are Trouble*, *Song of the City*, and *Wings of the Navy*; Harry Clay Wither, managing editor of the *Dallas Journal*, was a close friend and mentor of McCoy.

109.28   von Sternberg . . . a Russian picture] Josef von Sternberg's *The Scarlet Empress*, starring Marlene Dietrich as Catherine the Great, was released in 1934.

109.30–31   Mamoulian . . . Boleslawsky] Rouben Mamoulian (1898–1987) and Richard Boleslawsky (1889–1937) were prestigious Hollywood directors of the early sound period.

112.40–113.1   Margaret Sullavan . . . Josephine Hutchinson] Margaret Sullavan (1911–60), movie actress whose films included *Only Yesterday* (1933) and *Little Man, What Now?* (1934); Josephine Hutchinson (b. 1904), movie actress whose films included *Happiness Ahead* (1934) and *Oil for the Lamps of China* (1935).

128.8   Alice Faye] Movie star (b. 1912) who appeared in a long series of musicals beginning with *George White's Scandals* (1934).

THIEVES LIKE US

216.4–5   ROY . . . ANNE] Anderson's cousin, Roy Johnson, was serving a life sentence for armed robbery when Anderson interviewed him as background for *Thieves Like Us*; Polly Anne Bates was Anderson's first wife.

217.1–3   "Men do not . . . of his house."]   Proverbs 6:30–31.

249.14   pratt]   Buttocks.

276.1   *La Golondrina*]   Mexican song written in 1883 by Narciso Serradell.

304.34–35   that woman up in Canada]   Elzire Dionne, mother of quintuplets, born in Ontario in 1934, who became the object of intense public interest.

326.8   *El Rancho Grande*]   Song (1934) by Silvano Ramos.

355.23   *La Paloma*]   Traditional Mexican song.

356.11   *La Cucaracha*]   Traditional Mexican song which became a popular hit in 1934.

THE BIG CLOCK

380.1   *Nan*]   Fearing's second wife, Nan Lurie.

418.11   WPA stuff]   Art commissioned by the Works Projects Administration.

442.2   M.E.]   Managing Editor.

463.16   *mot de passe*]   French: password.

NIGHTMARE ALLEY

518.2   *Joy Davidman*]   Gresham's second wife (1915–60), a poet who won the Yale Series of Younger Poets award in 1938 for *Letter to a Comrade.*

521.1–13   Madame Sosostris . . . death by water]   T. S. Eliot, *The Waste Land*, lines 43–55.

521.15–17   For at Cumae . . . "I want to die."]   The anecdote is recounted, in Petronius' novel, by the wealthy freedman Trimalchio during his banquet.

548.33   soup and fish]   Tuxedo.

606.15   *Prosit, Liebchen*]   German: Cheers, darling.

639.4–7   *Shall we gather . . . throne of God.*]   Cf. Robert Lowry, "Beautiful River."

653.21–34   "Hark, hark the lark . . . at those springs . . ."]   Shakespeare, *Cymbeline*, Act II, scene iii, lines 20–22.

657.27–28   Sir Oliver Lodge, Sir Arthur Conan Doyle, Camille Flammarion, Sir William Crookes]   Sir Oliver Lodge (1851–1940), English physicist; Sir Arthur Conan Doyle (1859–1930), English novelist; Camille Flammarion (1842–1925), French astronomer; Sir William Crookes (1832–1919), English physicist and chemist.

716.15   Daniel Douglas Home]   Daniel Dunglas Home (1833–86), Scottish spiritualist medium.

793.24–32   *"Put your arms around me . . . you!"*]   *Put Your Arms Around Me Honey*, 1910 song by Junie McCree and Albert Von Tilzer.

I MARRIED A DEAD MAN

856.1   *Tales of Hoffman*]   *Les Contes d'Hoffmann*, opera by Jacques Offenbach (1819–80); never completed by the composer, it had its first performance in Paris in 1881.

870.37   *Marie Antoinette* by Katharine Anthony]   Anthony (1877–1965) published her biography in 1932; she also wrote biographies of Margaret Fuller, Catherine the Great, and Louisa May Alcott.

871.17   Axel Fersen]   Count Hans Axel von Fersen (1755–1810), Swedish officer resident at Versailles who aided the royal family in their unsuccessful attempt to flee France in 1791.

872.6   Madame Korff]   Name assumed by Mme. de Tourzel, the governess of the French royal family, during their attempted flight.

892.28   "Three Little Words."]   Song (1930) by Harry Ruby and Bert Kalmar.

926.8   *"Che gelida mannina—"*]   Aria sung by Rodolfo to Mimi in Puccini's *La Bohème* (Italian: "What a frozen little hand").

940.3–4   Mark Stevens in *I Wonder Who's Kissing Her Now*]   Stevens played the songwriter Joseph E. Howard in the 1947 Warner Brothers musical directed by Lloyd Bacon.

Library of Congress Cataloging-in-Publication Data

Crime novels : American noir of the thirties and forties.
      p.   cm. — (The Library of America ; 94)
    Contents: The postman always rings twice / James M.
Cain — They shoot horses, don't they / Horace McCoy —
Thieves like us / Edward Anderson — The big clock /
Kenneth Fearing — Nightmare alley / William Lindsay
Gresham — I married a dead man / Cornell Woolrich.
    ISBN 1–883011–46–9
    1. Detective and mystery stories, American.   2. American
fiction—20th century. 3. Crime—Fiction. I. Cain,
James M. (James Mallahan), 1892–1977. Postman always
rings twice. II. McCoy, Horace, 1897–1955. They shoot
horses, don't they?   III. Anderson, Edward, 1905–1969.
Thieves like us. IV. Fearing, Kenneth, 1902–1961.
Big clock. V. Gresham, William Lindsay, 1909–1962.
Nightmare alley. VI. Woolrich, Cornell, 1903–1968. I
married a dead man. VII. Series.
PS648.D4C695   1997
813'.087208052—dc21   97–2485
                                           CIP

THE LIBRARY OF AMERICA SERIES

The Library of America fosters appreciation of America's literary heritage by publishing, and keeping permanently in print, authoritative editions of America's best and most significant writing. An independent nonprofit organization, it was founded in 1979 with seed funding from the National Endowment for the Humanities and the Ford Foundation.

This book is set in 10 point Linotron Galliard,
a face designed for photocomposition by Matthew Carter
and based on the sixteenth-century face Granjon. The paper
is acid-free lightweight opaque and meets the requirements
for permanence of the American National Standards Institute.
The binding material is Brillianta, a woven rayon cloth made
by Van Heek–Scholco Textielfabrieken, Holland. Composition
by The Clarinda Company. Printing and binding
by Edwards Brothers Malloy, Ann Arbor.
Designed by Bruce Campbell.